MW00849650

'Why?'

'Because it's too small. "Five feet high is the door, and three abreast may enter it" say the runes. But the dragon could not creep into a hole that size, not even when he was a young dragon, certainly not after he had devoured so many of the maidens of the valley.'

'It seems a great big hole' piped up Bilbo. He loved maps, and in his hall there was a large one of the Country Round (where he lived), with all his favourite walks marked on it in red ink. He was so interested he forgot to be shy and keep his mouth shut. 'How could such an enormous door (he was a hobbit, remember) be secret?'

'Lots of ways' said Bl. 'Which one of them we don't know without looking.'

WITHERED HEATH.

WILD WOOD

MOUNTAIN

Ruins of Dale Town

R. Running

Five feet high the door and three may walk abreast. [Stand by the grey stone when the thrush knocks and the rising sun with the last light of Durin's Day shine upon the keyhole.]

Stand by the grey stone when the thrush knocks. Then the setting sun with the last light of Durin's Day will shine upon the key-hole.

Lake Town

Mirkwood

marshes

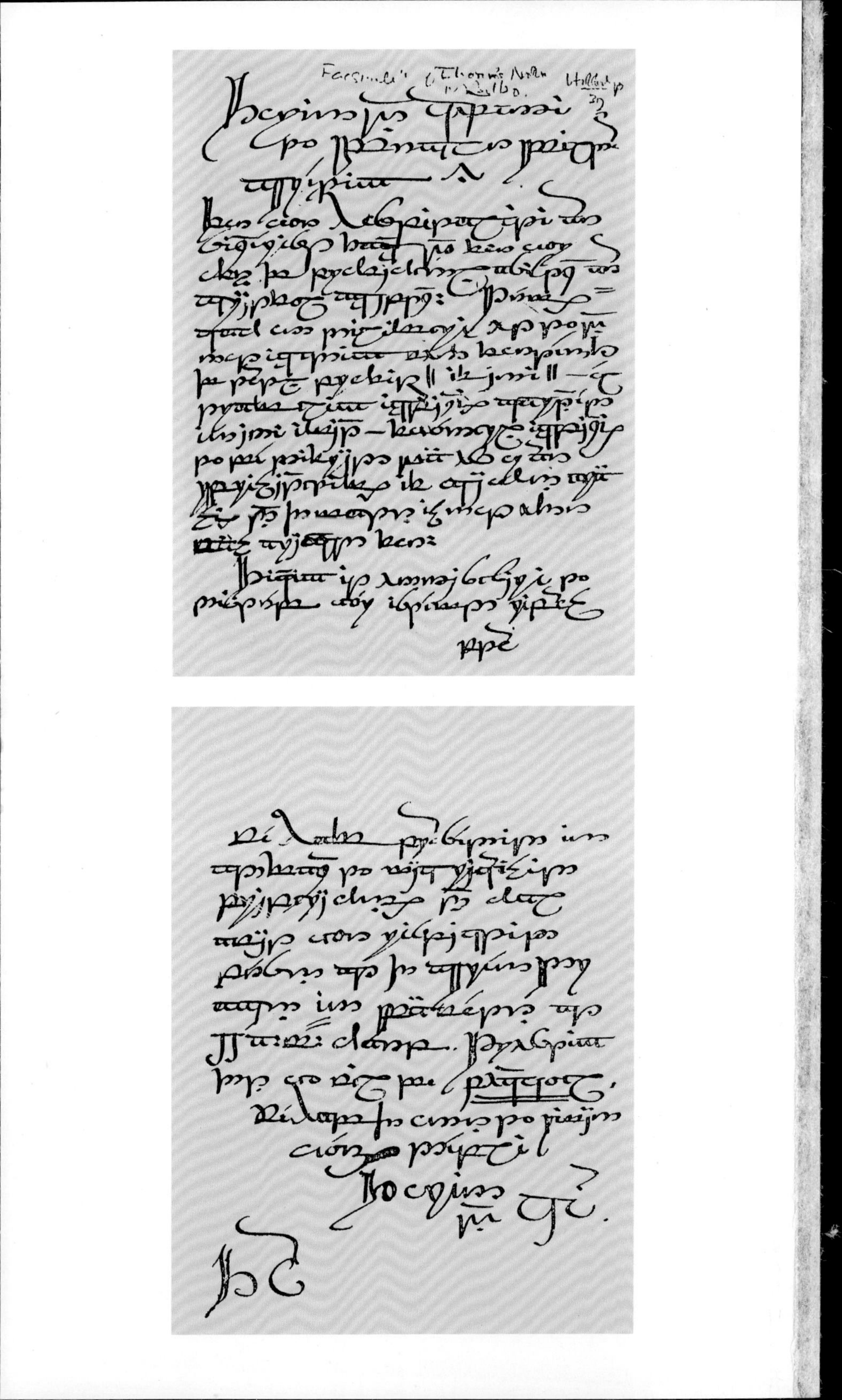

Facsimile [illegible] Thomas Nelson [illegible] Hallerup p 3[illegible]

THE HISTORY OF THE HOBBIT

The History of The Hobbit

John D. Rateliff

WILLIAM MORROW

An Imprint of HarperCollins*Publishers*

to
Charles B. Elston
&
Janice K. Coulter

THE HISTORY OF THE HOBBIT.

This revised and expanded one-volume edition published by HarperCollins*Publishers* 2011

First published in Great Britain as *The History of The Hobbit: Mr Baggins* and *The History of The Hobbit: Return to Bag-End* by HarperCollins*Publishers* 2007

The illustrations in this book are reproduced courtesy of the Bodleian Library, University of Oxford, from their holdings labelled MS. Tolkien Drawings 1, 2, 4, 8, 15, 20, 22, 30, 31, 33; 83 fol. 29r; 87 fol. 39; 89 fols. 17, 19, 21, 23-6, 36, 45, 48, 48v & 49; that on plate XII (bottom left) is reproduced with the permission of the Department of Special Collections and University Archives, Raynor Memorial Libraries, Marquette University, Milwaukee, Wisconsin, from their collection labelled Ad.Ms.H.2.

Set in PostScript Monotype Plantin by
Palimpsest Book Production Limited, Falkirk, Stirlingshire

Printed and bound in Italy by Rotolito S.p.A.

Library of Congress Cataloging-in-Publication Data has been applied for.

ISBN 978-0-063-33078-8

22 23 24 25 26 10 9 8 7 6 5 4 3 2 1

This book is produced from independently certified FSC™ paper to ensure responsible forest management.

For more information visit: www.harpercollins.co.uk/green

CONTENTS

INTRODUCTION

This book offers for the first time a complete edition of the manuscript of J. R. R. Tolkien's *The Hobbit*, now in the Special Collections and University Archives of Marquette University. Unlike most previous editions of Tolkien's manuscripts, which incorporate all changes in order to present a text that represents Tolkien's final thought on all points whenever possible, this edition tries rather to capture the first form in which the story flowed from his pen, with all the hesitations over wording and constant recasting of sentences that entailed. Even though the original draft strongly resembles the published story in its general outlines and indeed much of its expression, nevertheless the differences between the two are significant, and I have made it my task to record them as accurately as possible.

Since the published story is so familiar, it has taken on an air of inevitability, and it may come as something of a shock to see how differently Tolkien first conceived of some elements, and how differently they were sometimes expressed. Thus, to mention a few of the more striking examples, in this original version of the story Gollum does not try to kill Bilbo but instead faithfully shows him the way out of the goblin-tunnels after losing the riddle-contest.[1] The entire scene in which Bilbo and the dwarves encounter the Enchanted Stream in Mirkwood did not exist in the original draft and was interpolated into the story later, at the typescript stage, while their encounter with the Spiders was rewritten to eliminate all mention of a great ball of spider-thread by means of which Bilbo navigated his way, Theseus-like, through the labyrinth of Mirkwood to find his missing companions. No such character as Dain existed until a very late stage in the drafting, while Bard is introduced abruptly only to be killed off almost at once. In his various outlines for the story, Tolkien went even further afield, sketching out how Bilbo would kill the dragon himself, with the Gem of Girion (better known by its later name, as 'the Arkenstone') to be his promised reward from the dwarves for the deed. The great battle that forms the story's climax was to take place on Bilbo's return journey, not at the Lonely Mountain; nor were any of the dwarves to take part in it, nor would Thorin and his admirable (great-) nephews die.

Tolkien was of course superbly skilled at nomenclature, and it can be disconcerting to discover that the names of some of the major characters were different when those characters were created. For much of the original story the wizard who rousts the hobbit from his comfortable hobbit-hole is *Bladorthin*, not 'Gandalf', with the name *Gandalf* belonging instead to the dwarven leader known in the published story as 'Thorin Oakenshield'; the great werebear Gandalf & Company encounter east of the Misty Mountains is *Medwed*, not 'Beorn'. Other names were more ephemeral, such as *Pryftan* for the dragon better known as Smaug, *Fimbulfambi* for the last King under the Mountain, and *Fingolfin* for the goblin-king so dramatically beheaded by Bullroarer Took. On a verbal level, the chilling cry of *Thief, thief, thief! We hates it, we hates it, we hates it for ever!* was not drafted until more than a decade after the Gollum chapter had originally been written, and did not make its way into print until seven years after that; the wizard's advice to Bilbo and the dwarves on the eaves of Mirkwood was 'keep your peckers up' (rather than the more familiar 'keep your spirits up' that replaced it), and even the final line in the book is slightly different.

Yet, for all these departures, much of the story will still be familiar to those who have read the published version – for example, all the riddles in the contest with Gollum are present from the earliest draft of that chapter, all the other dwarves' names remain the same (even if their roles are sometimes somewhat different), and Bilbo still undergoes the same slow transformation from stay-at-home-hobbit to resourceful adventuring burglar. In synopsis, the draft and the published book would appear virtually identical, but then Tolkien explicitly warned us against judging stories from summaries ('On Fairy-Stories', page 21). With as careful and meticulous an author as Tolkien, details matter, and it is here that the two versions of the story diverge. Think of this original draft as like the unaired pilot episode of a classic television series, the previously unissued demo recordings for a famous album, or the draft score of a beloved symphony. Or, to use a more literary analogy, the relationship between this draft and the published book is rather like that between Caxton's incunabulum *Le Morte D'Arthur* and the manuscript of the same work, discovered in 1934, known as the Winchester Malory. In both cases, it is the professionally published, more structured form of the book which established itself as a classic, while the eventual publication of something closer to what the author first wrote reveals a great deal about how the book was originally put together, what its author's intentions were, and more about its affinities with its sources, particularly when (in the case of *The Hobbit*) those sources are Tolkien's own earlier unpublished works. That Tolkien himself in this case was responsible for establishing the polished final text does not obscure the fact that here we have two different versions of the same story, and rediscovering the earlier form casts new light on the familiar one. In the words of Tolkien's classic essay 'On Fairy-Stories',

> Recovery . . . is a re-gaining . . . of a clear view . . . We need . . . to clean our windows; so that the things seen clearly may be freed from the drab blur of . . . familiarity . . . Of all faces those of our *familiares* [intimates, familiars] are the ones . . . most difficult really to see with fresh attention, perceiving their likeness and unlikeness . . . [T]he things that are . . . (in a bad sense) familiar are the things that we have appropriated . . . We say we know them. They have become like the things which once attracted us . . . and we laid hands on them, and then locked them in our hoard, acquired them, and acquiring ceased to look at them.
>
> —OFS.53–4.

This need for 'Recovery' is particularly apt in the case of *The Hobbit*, which in recent years has come to be seen more and more as a mere 'prelude' to *The Lord of the Rings*, a lesser first act that sets up the story and prepares the reader to encounter the masterpiece that follows. Such a view does not do justice to either book, and ignores the fact that the story of Bilbo's adventure was meant to be read as a stand-alone work, and indeed existed as an independent work for a full seventeen years before being joined by its even more impressive sequel. I hope that this edition may serve as a means by which readers can see the familiar book anew and appreciate its power, its own unique charm, and its considerable artistry afresh.

(i)
Chronology of Composition

'In a Hole in the Ground'

The story is now well known of how, one day while grading student exams, Tolkien came across a blank page in one exam book and on the spur of the moment wrote on it 'in a hole in the ground there lived a hobbit'. This scrap of paper is now lost and what survives of the earliest draft is undated, but Tolkien recounted the momentous event several times in interviews and letters; by assembling all the clues from these recollections into a composite account, we can establish the chronology of composition with relative certainty.

Auden

All I remember about the start of *The Hobbit* is sitting correcting School Certificate papers in the everlasting weariness of that annual task forced on impecunious academics with children. On a blank leaf I scrawled: 'In a hole in the ground there lived a hobbit.' I did not and do not know why. I did nothing about it, for a long time, and for some years I got no further than the production of Thror's Map. But it became *The Hobbit* in the early 1930s . . .

—letter of 7th June 1955 to W. H. Auden;
Letters of J. R. R. Tolkien, p. 215.

Harshaw

Two . . . English boys . . . asked Mr Tolkien how he happened to write *The Hobbit*. He replied that he was in the midst of correcting 286 examination papers one day when he suddenly turned over one of the papers and wrote: 'At the edge of his hole stood the Hobbit.' As he later tried to think just who and what this Hobbit was, his amazing story developed.

—circa September 1956; Ruth Harshaw,
'When *Carnival of Books* Went to Europe',
ALA Bulletin, February 1957, p. 120.

BBC TV

The actual beginning – though it's not really the beginning, but the actual flashpoint I remember very clearly. I can still see the corner of my house in 20 Northmoor Road where it happened. I had an enormous pile of exam papers there. Marking school examinations in the summertime is very laborious and unfortunately also *boring*. And I remember picking up a paper and actually finding – I nearly gave an extra mark for it; an extra five marks, actually – there was one page of this particular paper that was left blank. Glorious! Nothing to read. So I scribbled on it, I can't think why, In a hole in the ground there lived a hobbit.

—*Tolkien in Oxford*, BBC Television, 1968.

Plimmers

It all began when I was reading exam papers to earn a bit of extra money. That was agony. One of the tragedies of the underpaid professor is that he has to do menial jobs. He is expected to maintain a certain position and to send his children to good schools. Well, one day I came to a blank page in an exam book and I scribbled on it. 'In a hole in the ground there lived a hobbit'.

I knew no more about the creatures <sic> than that, and it was years before his story grew. I don't know where the word came from. You can't catch your mind out. It might have been associated with Sinclair Lewis's Babbitt.[2] Certainly not rabbit, as some people think. Babbitt has the same bourgeois smugness that hobbits do. His world is the same limited place.

—'The Man Who Understands Hobbits',
Charlotte and Denis Plimmer, early 1967;
Daily Telegraph Magazine, 22nd March 1968, pages 31–32.

Carpenter

I am not sure but I think the Unexpected Party (the first chapter) was hastily written before 1935 but certainly after 1930 when I moved to 20 Northmoor Road.

—undated; quoted in Humphrey Carpenter,
Tolkien: A Biography, p. 177.

It is clear from these accounts that Tolkien did not remember the exact date, but he did retain a strong visual image of the scene. Two specific facts emerge: it was summertime, and the place was his study at 20 Northmoor Road. From this we can determine that the event took place no earlier than the summer of 1930, since it was early that year when the Tolkien family moved into the house from their former residence next door at 22 Northmoor Road (Carpenter, p. 113; Christopher Tolkien, Foreword to the fiftieth anniversary edition of *The Hobbit* [1987], p. vi).[3]

This dating was challenged by Michael Tolkien, the author's second son (1920–1983), who stated in his unpublished memoirs that he clearly recalled his father standing with his back to the fire in his study at 22 Northmoor Road and saying that he was going to start telling his sons 'a long story about a small being with furry feet, and asked us what he should be called – then, answering himself, said "I think we'll call him a 'Hobbit'."' (quoted in Christopher Tolkien's

Foreword, p. vi). Father John Tolkien, the eldest son (1917–2003), was equally definite that the story began before the move from 22 to number 20 Northmoor Road: 'The first beginnings of the Hobbit were at 22 Northmoor Road; in my father's study, the room to the left of the front door as one looks at the house. I remember clearly the wood block floor, mats etc . . . [T]here were no family readings for us all in 20 Northmoor Road, where we moved early in 1930. I was 12+ & I think could read for myself! The room with its many bookshelves was not conducive to that sort of thing. As far as I remember the readings were always in the study . . . The Hobbit started with a couple or so chapters, to which if we were lucky a couple or more would be added at the next Christmas . . . I went to boarding school in September 1931 and so although very close to the family, all sorts of stories may have been told which I cannot date.'[4] Carpenter, writing in 1976, notes that Michael and John Tolkien 'are not certain that what they were listening to at that time was necessarily a *written* story: they believe that it may well have been a number of impromptu tales which were later absorbed into *The Hobbit* proper' (Carpenter, p. 177).

In support of his claim for an earlier origin of the book, in his guest-of-honor speech to the Tolkien Society's Annual Dinner in May 1977 Michael described the stories he and his brothers and sister had written in imitation of *The Hobbit*.[5] Michael recounts that these stories were populated by characters like Philpot Buggins, Ollum the giant frog, blokes (hobbits), smellers (wolves), the dwarves Roary, Borey, Gorey, Biffer, Trasher, Gasher, Beater, Bomber, Lammer, Throw-in (the chief dwarf), and young Blow-in and Go-in; Albert Bolger the troll, joshers, snargs, and the wizards Kimpu, Mandegar, and Scandalf the Beanpiper. Michael Tolkien dated his own contributions to this family apocrypha to 1929, when he was nine years old (Michael Tolkien, May 1977 speech; see also Christopher Tolkien, Foreword, p. vi), and thus argued that *The Hobbit* must have been begun by that date.

While it is quite likely that many elements incorporated into *The Hobbit* came from family lore predating the book (see for example my commentary following Chapter VII), and *The Hobbit* was undoubtedly influenced by the other stories Tolkien read his children in the 'Winter Reads' (which, despite Fr. John's comment, continued to at least 1937[6] and probably beyond), Michael's own account provides evidence that the stories he describes could not have preceded the actual writing of the book; too many of the names are parodies of forms that only emerged at a later stage, well into the composition of the manuscript. For example, Scandalf the wizard and Throw-in the head dwarf are clearly modelled on *Gandalf* and *Thorin* – but for the first two-thirds of the story the wizard was named Bladorthin and for more than half of it the chief dwarf is named Gandalf, not Thorin; these two characters seem not to have received their now-familiar names until around 1932. Furthermore, Tolkien himself is quite clear on the point that he made up the name 'hobbit' spontaneously at the moment of writing it down – that is, that the word itself emerged in a written text.

The most specific proof may be found in a commentary Tolkien wrote on the text for the dust-jacket for *The Hobbit* and sent to his publisher accompanying a letter dated 31st August 1937, in which he remarked 'My eldest boy was thirteen when he heard the serial. It did not appeal to the younger ones who had to grow up to it successively' (cf. *Letters* p. 21). Since John Tolkien was born on 16th November 1917, the events Tolkien is recalling here could not have taken place before the end of 1930; furthermore, Tolkien notes that 'the younger ones' (Michael was born 22nd October 1920 and Christopher 21st November 1924 and were thus respectively about nine and five in the summer of 1930, while Priscilla was still an infant, having been born in 1929) showed little interest at the time. Michael's account not only contains inconsistencies but directly contradicts both the evidence of the manuscript and the accounts set down by his father, both at the time of the book's publication and many years later. Given these facts, we should feel fully justified in accepting the word of the author recorded closer to the event over the childhood memories of a member of the original audience set down some 45 to 50 years after the fact.

If we grant a starting date of no earlier than the summer of 1930, is there any other evidence to help us narrow the field? In fact there is, in the form of letters and memoranda set down by C. S. Lewis, Stanley Unwin, Christopher Tolkien, and Tolkien himself. Early in 1933, Lewis wrote the following to his old friend Arthur Greeves:

> Since term began I have had a delightful time reading a children's story which Tolkien has just written. I have told of him before: the one man absolutely fitted, if fate had allowed, to be a third in our friendship in the old days, for he also grew up on W. Morris and George Macdonald. Reading his fairy tale has been uncanny – it is so exactly like what we [i.e., Lewis and Greeves] wd. both have longed to write (or read) in 1916: so that one feels he is not making it up but merely describing the same world into which all three of us have the entry. Whether it is really *good* (I think it is until the end) is of course another question: still more, whether it will succeed with modern children.

—letter of 4th February 1933 from C. S. Lewis to Arthur Greeves; *They Stand Together: The Letters of C. S. Lewis to Arthur Greeves*, ed. Walter Hooper [1979], p. 449.

The 'term' Lewis refers to is the spring, or Hilary, semester at Oxford, which traditionally starts on or near St Hilary's Day (13th January). Two points in Lewis's letter that particularly stand out are that he refers to Tolkien's story as having just been written, and that he criticizes the ending of the tale as not being as good as the rest of the story. From this we can conclude that Tolkien probably finished writing the Ms. over the 1932 Christmas break (that is, December 1932–January 1933) and, as was his habit, loaned it to his friend for criticism and critique right away. Furthermore, what Lewis read was a complete story, not a large fragment of one lacking the final chapters – not only would he have surely commented on being handed a tale that broke off at the most dramatic moment, but he specifically singles out that portion of the tale for criticism.

This interpretation of events wins additional support from another contemporary document, the Father Christmas letters. Every year, Tolkien's children received a personal letter from Father Christmas (the English Santa Claus) describing all the adventures Father Christmas and his companion, the North Polar Bear, had had since the last letter. Most of these adventures deal with various disasters which have prevented Father Christmas from sending all the presents the children had asked for (North Polar Bear's falling down stairs on top of packages, mixing up labels, and the like), but the letters for 1932 and 1933 represent a dramatic shift in tone. In them, the world of Father Christmas and his friends suddenly becomes very like that of *The Hobbit* with the introduction of goblins to the series, right down to details such as characters becoming lost in goblin-caves, being rescued by an ancient and magical bear, and finding themselves besieged by hordes of goblins – whom they defeat with a combination of Father Christmas's magic, the combat prowess of a great bear, and the aid of their elven allies the Red Gnomes. What's more, in the striking picture of Father Christmas, Cave Bear, and a leanish North Polar Bear exploring the goblin-caves that accompanied the 1932 letter (Plate VI [top left]), we can even see both Gollum and Smaug make a cameo appearance: Smaug appears on the wall of the first passageway to the right, while Gollum can be seen peeking around a corner of the same passage, near the picture of the mammoth (see Plate VI [detail]). At least four goblins lurk in the passages to the left, while the middle column depicts goblins on drasils, the *Father Christmas Letters*' equivalent of the goblin wolf-riders encountered in the Battle of Five Armies.

The presence of the Cave-Bear, Elves, and a magician[7] at the battle with the goblins argues that the final chapters were in progress at the time this letter was written and not, as Carpenter suggests, only set down shortly before the submission of the book to Allen & Unwin. Carpenter believed that

> . . . shortly after he had described the death of the dragon, Tolkien abandoned the story.
>
> Or to be more accurate, he did not write any more of it down. For the benefit of his children he had narrated an impromptu conclusion to the story, but, as Christopher Tolkien expressed it, 'the ending chapters were rather roughly done, and not typed out at all'. Indeed they were not even written in manuscript. The typescript of the nearly finished story . . . was occasionally shown to favoured friends, together with its accompanying maps (and perhaps already a few illustrations). But it did not often leave Tolkien's study, where it sat, incomplete and now likely to remain so. The boys were growing up and no longer asked for 'Winter Reads', so there was no reason why *The Hobbit* should ever be finished.
>
> —Carpenter, pp. 179–80.

Unfortunately, this will not do. Certainly there was a pause in the writing – in fact, several pauses; see 'A Note on the Text', below. But there is no evidence that the story was abandoned in an unfinished state, and a good deal of evidence that it was not. One is the notable fact that none of the people to whom the manuscript was lent before its publication[8] made any comment on the story's having been incomplete – remarkable in itself if we believe with Carpenter that the final quarter of the book was missing. Carpenter's account confuses the issue further by stating that 'there was a completed typescript in existence (lacking only the final chapters) in time for it to be shown to C. S. Lewis late in 1932' (Carpenter, p. 177); in fact, as we have seen, Lewis not only read but specifically criticizes the ending. Furthermore, Lewis's letter to Greeves makes it clear that Lewis was not reading Tolkien's story over the Christmas break – in the paragraph preceding the one already cited, he tells his friend 'In the way of reading [,] Lockhart [i.e., John G. Lockhart's *Life of Sir Walter Scott*] kept me going through the whole vac. [vacation] and I am still only at Vol. 8' (*They Stand Together*, p. 448); the next paragraph introduces the new topic of what he had been reading 'Since term began' – i.e., *The Hobbit*.

More evidence appears in the letter thirteen-year-old Christopher Tolkien wrote to Father Christmas in December 1937, shortly after the book's publication, where he says

> He [JRRT] wrote it ages ago, and read it to John, Michael, and me in our winter 'reads' after tea in the evening; but the ending chapters were rather roughly done, and not typed out at all; he finished it about a year ago . . .
>
> —quoted in Christopher Tolkien,
> Foreword, p. vii.

While Carpenter evidently interpreted this to mean that the final chapters had not been written at all but existed only in a hasty outline (what I have dubbed Plot Notes B and C), I suggest that we take young Christopher's remarks literally and that by 'roughly done' he meant that the conclusion of the book existed only in his father's handwritten manuscript, not typescript; then 'about a year ago' (in fact, in the autumn of 1936) Tolkien had returned to the text and at last typed out the final section in order to submit it to the publisher.

Two additional pieces of evidence from the period immediately following upon the book's publication help us complete our chronology. In a memorandum made by Stanley Unwin after a meeting with Tolkien on Wednesday 27th October 1937 to discuss a possible follow-up to the success of *The Hobbit*,[9] Unwin notes in passing that 'He mentioned that THE HOBBIT took him two or three years to write because he works very slowly.' This detail coincides perfectly with the dates from our other evidence – i.e., that the story was begun in the summer of 1930 and finished in early January 1933, a period of two and a half years from first inspiration to final chapter. Finally, in a letter Tolkien wrote to the English newspaper *The Observer* in response to a letter of inquiry which had appeared in the 16th January 1938 issue asking about the sources for his book, he concluded with the following tease:

> Finally, I present the future researcher with a little problem. The tale halted in the telling for about a year at two separate points: where are they? But probably that would have been discovered anyway.
>
> —J. R. R. Tolkien, letter to *The Observer*, printed Sunday, 20th February 1938; see Appendix II.

If, as Tolkien told Unwin, the story took 'two or three years' to write but, as he noted to *The Observer*, that period was punctuated by two hiatuses of approximately a year each, then the actual writing of the book took place in several short, intense bursts – in fact, during the vacations between term-time – which I in this book refer to as the First Phase, Second Phase, and Third Phase. Such was, indeed, Tolkien's regular habit of composition, as careful perusal of *Letters* and the *History of Middle-earth* volumes dealing with *The Lord of the Rings* manuscripts will reveal; see 'A Note on the Text' below for more information on the actual writing of the book.

There still remains one unresolved crux: why did Tolkien tell Auden (in 1955) and the Plimmers (in 1967) that a gap of several years intervened between the writing of the first chapter (The First Phase) and the rest of the book, when his earlier testimony to Unwin and the letter to *The Observer* make it clear that in fact the hiatus could have lasted no more than a single year? The answer I think lies in Tolkien's tendency to exaggerate the passage of time and date events *before* they actually occurred; as an event recedes into the distance, he will often assign an earlier and earlier date for it.

A prime and unusually well documented example is the short tale 'Leaf by Niggle'. In March of 1945, Tolkien had written to Stanley Unwin '. . . I woke up one morning (more than 2 years ago) with that odd thing virtually complete in my head. It took only a few hours to get down, and then copy out . . .' (JRRT to Stanley Unwin, letter of circa 18th March 1945; *Letters* p. 113). The story was, therefore, written sometime in early 1943 or late 1942; Tolkien submitted it to the *Dublin Review* on 12 October 1944 (*Letters* p. 97; Hammond's *Descriptive Bibliography* p. 348 notes that the editor had written to Tolkien soliciting submissions on 6th September), and it appeared in the January 1945 issue. Twelve years later, in his letter of 24th June 1957 to Caroline Whitman Everett (*Letters* p. 257), Tolkien tells much the same story:

> I have not published any other short story but *Leaf by Niggle*. They do not arise in my mind. *Leaf by Niggle* arose suddenly and almost complete. It was written down almost at a sitting, and very nearly in the form in which it now appears. Looking at it myself now from a distance I should say that, in addition to my tree-love (it was originally called *The Tree*), it arose from my own preoccupation with *The Lord of the Rings*, the knowledge that it would be finished in great detail or not at all, and the fear (near certainty) that it would be 'not at all'. The war had arisen to darken all horizons. But no such analyses are a complete explanation even of a short story.

By 1962, however, Tolkien had began to shift the origin of the story to an earlier date; he told his aunt Jane Neave that the story 'was written (I think) just before the War began, though I first read it aloud to my friends early in 1940' (JRRT to Jane Neave, letter of 8th-9th September 1962; *Letters* p. 320). Thus, whereas the 1957 letter makes it clear that the war was already underway at the time the story was written, the 1962 letter moves it back to 'just before' the war. By the time Tolkien wrote the introduction to the 1964 collection *Tree & Leaf* in October 1963 (Hammond, *Descriptive Bibliography* pp. 183–4), he believed that 'Leaf by Niggle' and the essay 'On Fairy-Stories' had been 'written in the same period (1938–9) when *The Lord of the Rings* was beginning to unroll itself . . .' and that 'The story was not published until 1947' (*Tree & Leaf*, p. [5]), thus exaggerating the period between composition and publication from about two years to almost nine while pushing the date of actual composition back by some 4 to 5 years.[10]

Like Michael Tolkien's attempt to push the starting date of work on *The Hobbit* back into the 1920s, we must reject Tolkien's later assertion of a gap of several years between the writing of the first line and resumption of work on the story – not just because it directly contradicts remarks he made much earlier, at the time of the book's publication (when we might reasonably expect his recollection to be more accurate), but because it creates unresolvable paradoxes in the evidence. The simple fact is that if Tolkien began the story after the move to 20 Northmoor Road in 1930, then stopped for several years before proceeding further, *and* paused twice for a year or so during the actual composition (these pauses being attested by changes in paper in the manuscript itself), he could not possibly have loaned the completed tale to Lewis in January 1933 – yet we know he did. The external evidence of the date of the move and the weight of the contemporary documentary evidence (especially Lewis's letter to Arthur Greeves and the 1932 Father Christmas letter) between them establish a consistent body of evidence which agrees with all the facts of Tolkien's other recollections. Accordingly, we may state with some confidence that the story was indeed begun in the summer of 1930 and completed in January 1933.

(ii)

A Note on the Text

> Edith has gone to bed and the house is in darkness when [Tolkien] gets home. He builds up the fire in the study stove and fills his pipe. He ought, he knows, to do some more work on his lecture notes for the next morning, but he cannot resist taking from a drawer the half-finished manuscript of a story that he is writing to amuse himself and his children. It is probably, he suspects, a waste of time; certainly if he is going to devote any attention to this sort of thing it ought to be to *The Silmarillion*. But something draws him back night after night to this amusing little tale – at least it seems to amuse the boys. He sits down at the desk, fits a new relief nib to his dip pen (which he prefers to a fountain pen), unscrews the ink bottle, takes a sheet of old examination paper (which still has a candidate's essay on the Battle of Maldon on the back of it), and begins to write: 'When Bilbo opened his eyes, he wondered if he had; for it was just as dark as with them shut. No one was anywhere near him. Just imagine his fright! . . .'

> We will leave him now. He will be at his desk until half past one, or two o'clock, or perhaps even later, with only the scratching of his pen to disturb the silence, while around him Northmoor Road sleeps.
>
> —Humphrey Carpenter, *Tolkien: A Biography*, pp. 120–21.

The preceding passage from the chapter 'Oxford Life' in Carpenter's biography concludes his fictional recreation of a typical 'day in the life' of J. R. R. Tolkien. While entertaining, it is by no means accurate as an account of *The Hobbit*'s composition. For one thing, the text Carpenter quotes is not that of the Ms. (see p. 153) but the published book (cf. *The Annotated Hobbit* p. [115]). Nor is the manuscript of *The Hobbit* written on the back of student exams, with the exception of a single page;[11] I suspect Carpenter has gone astray here by confusing the manuscript of *The Lord of the Rings*, parts of which were drafted on any scraps of paper its author could lay his hands on during the wartime paper shortage, including many from students' exams, with that of *The Hobbit*, which contains very little extraneous material. Finally, the idea that the book was written by burning the midnight oil, faithfully added to night after night after a long day's academic chores, has no evidence to support it and a good deal against it. For one thing, Tolkien's letters are full of references that make it clear that almost all his creative writing was done not in term-time but during his too-brief vacations between academic semesters, and indeed his son Christopher confirms (private communication) that this was his father's usual pattern of composition.

The physical appearance of the manuscript also argues for periodic bursts of rapid writing rather than the nightly diligence Carpenter projects. As Carpenter himself notes elsewhere,

> The manuscript of *The Hobbit* suggests that the actual writing of the main part of the story was done over a comparatively short period of time: the ink, paper, and handwriting style are consistent, the pages are numbered consecutively, and there are almost no chapter divisions. It would also appear that Tolkien wrote the story fluently and with little hesitation, for there are comparatively few erasures or revisions.
>
> —Carpenter, pp. 177–8.

In fact, as we shall see, there are a great many changes made to the rough draft in the process of writing, and many more afterwards. Parts of the manuscript show signs of having been written in great haste, while other sections are careful fair copy. Nor does Carpenter's suggestion account for the several sharp breaks that occur in the Ms. where the handwriting, names of characters, and paper all change. Large sections are consistent in writing style and the paper used, only to have no less than three sudden and marked changes in writing paper and handwriting, the first and last of which almost certainly mark the long hiatuses Tolkien describes in his letter to *The Observer*. In short, the situation is far more complicated, and also much more interesting, than Carpenter indicates.

The present text is organized around the major breaks in the Ms., which occur midway through the first chapter (between typescript page 12 & manuscript page 13), just after what is now the beginning of Chapter IX (between manuscript pages 118 & 119), and about a third of the way through what is now Chapter XV (following manuscript page 167). The very first stage of writing that grew out of the scribbled line 'In a hole in the ground . . .', which I call the First Phase, is now represented by six surviving pages of manuscript (an incomplete draft corresponding roughly to pages 25–32 of the first edition or pages 45–54 of *The Annotated Hobbit*) and by the twelve-page typescript that replaced this earliest draft before the missing pages were lost. These I refer to as 'The Pryftan Fragment' and 'The Bladorthin Typescript', respectively, after the names of the dragon and wizard used in each.

The Second Phase begins with manuscript page 13, which picks up exactly where page 12 of the Bladorthin Typescript had left off, completing its final sentence. Written on good-quality 'foolscap' paper, this comprises the main stage of Tolkien's work on the book. Tolkien once admitted that 'They say it is the first step that costs the effort. I do not find it so. I am sure I could write unlimited "first chapters". I have indeed written many' (JRRT to Charles Furth, 17th February 1938; *Letters* p. 29). The Second Phase marks the stage at which an intriguing opening developed into a nearly complete story. Given its length (over one hundred and fifty manuscript pages), it's not surprising that this phase was interrupted several times, these points being marked by Tolkien's pausing to draw up outlines or sketch out 'plot notes' of upcoming sections. These various interruptions are described in detail in the main text that follows; for now, we need only note the major break that occurred in the middle of the Second Phase, just at the point when Bilbo and the twelve remaining dwarves are ambushed and captured by the wood-elves, in what is now early in Chapter IX. Here Tolkien clearly paused for some months, because when he resumed he changed to a completely different type of writing paper, these being the unlined backs of lined sheets of writing paper probably extracted from the unused portion of students' exam booklets. Thus, the Second Phase falls into two distinct parts: manuscript pages 13–118 on the good-quality 'foolscap' paper Tolkien favored (it also recurs as his paper of choice when writing *The Lord of the Rings*) and manuscript pages 119–67 on slightly poorer quality paper.

The Third Phase, which saw the completion of the initial draft, can be divided into several stages like the phase that preceded it. First Tolkien returned to the beginning of the story and created the First Typescript, covering what is now Chapters I through XII and part of Chapter XIV. He then made a handwritten fair copy manuscript of Chapter XIII and inserted this into the typescript. Finally, and most importantly, he completed the story by the addition of another forty-five pages of very hastily written manuscript, again on the same good-quality paper as the bulk of the Second Phase. This final section, which starts in Chapter XIV (again completing a sentence left unfinished on the last page of the typescript as it then existed) and covers Chapters XV through the end of the book (i.e., Chapter XIX), was almost certainly written in December 1932 and January 1933. The resulting composite typescript/fair copy/manuscript, sometimes referred to by Tolkien as the 'home manuscript' (cf. JRRT to Susan Dagnall, letter of 4th January 1937; *Letters* p. 14), was then circulated among Tolkien's friends over the next several years. Sometime in the summer of 1936[12] Tolkien was asked to submit *The Hobbit* to Allen & Unwin, so he at this time extended the First Typescript to include Chapter XIII, the rest of Chapter XIV, and Chapters XV through XIX to the end of the book.

In addition to the First Typescript, there is also another copy of the completed story. For many years the processors at Marquette and also scholars consulting the original manuscripts were puzzled by the presence of a second typescript that in some ways seemed earlier than what I have called the First Typescript but in others was demonstrably later.[13] Taum Santoski solved this problem by demonstrating that this text, which I call the Second Typescript, was made *after* the First Typescript and derives from it, but that it was rejected by Tolkien who then made the final layer of pre-submission revisions on the First Typescript instead, which thus became the 'Typescript for Printers' (i.e., the text from which the printers set the book). A clue within Carpenter's biography makes it possible for us to reconstruct the story behind this second typescript's creation, establish its relationship with the first typescript, and see the reason why it was ultimately rejected in favor of its predecessor.

Since Tolkien had, characteristically, made many revisions to his typescript while he had been re-reading the entire story and preparing it for submission to the publisher, the desirability of a cleaner typescript would have become obvious, especially given Tolkien's difficult handwriting. Tolkien himself had no time to undertake this onerous task, and so he set his son Michael to create a second typescript that would incorporate all the changes (mostly handwritten in black ink) on the original. According to Carpenter, Michael (then sixteen), had badly injured his right hand on broken glass and so did all his typing for the book one-handed (Carpenter, p. 180).[14] Although Carpenter does not distinguish between the two typescripts, it is clear that the Second Typescript was not made by Tolkien himself but by an inexpert typist who often skipped or misread words, occasionally dropped lines, sometimes had difficulty in reading Tolkien's handwriting, and generally produced a poor-quality text. As a daunting task undertaken by a dutiful son and apparently completed within a very short space of time, the Second Typescript speaks well of Michael's filial piety, but as an accurate text of *The Hobbit* it is sadly lacking. Even when carefully corrected by Tolkien, it is still inferior to the by now rather battered First Typescript, which therefore became the copy Tolkien ultimately sent off to Allen & Unwin (on 3rd October 1936 according to Carpenter; see *Letters* p.14) and which thence went to the printers, Unwin Brothers.

In the end, however, it is fortunate that the Second Typescript exists, because it enables us to date some of the changes Tolkien made to the work. Just as he revised the manuscript in two distinct stages (in ink at or soon after the time of composition, and in pencil later when preparing it to be superseded by the typescript), so too he revised the First Typescript in layers, and it is often not self-evident whether a given reading dates from the time when he was completing the tale (that is, corrections made in the course of typing or not long after) or several years later when he was preparing the text for submission to the publisher. However, comparison with the corresponding section of the Second Typescript often resolves the question: if a revision made in ink on the First Typescript is incorporated into the Second Typescript as first typed, then it belongs to the earlier layer of changes; if on the other hand it is written onto both typescripts then it is generally part of the later set of revisions. The issue is confused by two factors. First, Tolkien inked in corrections to set right Michael's accidental omissions and errors. This led early processors at Marquette, seeing that these sections appeared as ink additions to one typescript (Michael's) but as first typed in the other (Tolkien's), to mistake these corrections for new additions to the text taken up in the other typescript and thus assume that Michael's Typescript predated the 'Typescript for Printer'. Second, even after he had rejected the Second Typescript as the current text, Tolkien continued to scrupulously enter corrections he made to the First Typescript onto the other rejected typescript as well. Thus, very late changes appear added to both. In effect, the Second Typescript became Tolkien's safe copy, from which he could reconstruct the work if the final 'Typescript for Printer' were to become lost in the mail, be destroyed by an accident at the printer, or suffer some other misfortune.

For the most part, while including all revisions to the manuscript page itself I have not recorded changes between the manuscript and the typescript(s), since these invariably move the story closer to its familiar published form, although I have, on occasion, noted just when some significant line or event entered into the tale between draft and publication (e.g., a rider, first typescript, second typescript, or page proofs). Similarly, I have only rarely noted changes made between the typescripts and page proofs, or on the page proofs themselves; anyone examining the three sets of page proofs[15] now at Marquette will be deeply impressed by Tolkien's close attention to detail, his ability to spot potential contradictions, and his gift (no doubt developed through years of practice with academic publications) of replacing a problematic passage with new text that takes up exactly the same amount of space, but to address every change made at every stage would call for a variorum edition – a worthy goal, but one beyond the scope of this book.

With the material I have labelled the Fourth Phase, we enter into the post-publication history of *The Hobbit*. While the book was so successful that a sequel was called for almost at once, at several times in later years Tolkien returned to the original story and re-wrote parts of it to better suit his evolving conception of Middle-earth and the role which the story of Bilbo's adventure played in it. The first and most important of these re-visionings is what I here call the Fourth Phase: his recasting of the encounter with Gollum in Chapter V to bring that character's actions into line with what he had written about him in *The Lord of the Rings* (then unpublished and indeed still unfinished). This *tour-de-force*, perhaps the most famous scene Tolkien ever wrote, was drafted in 1944, sent to Allen & Unwin in 1947, and published as the 'second edition' of *The Hobbit* in 1951.

Another significant piece of writing relating to *The Hobbit* is 'The Quest of Erebor', originally written as part of Appendix A of *The Lord of the Rings* in the early 1950s but in the event omitted from that work for reasons of space. This presents Bilbo's story, particularly the opening chapter of the book, from Gandalf's point of view and sets it firmly within the larger context of the war against Sauron. While a fascinating and relevant piece, I have not included it here because it is readily available elsewhere: different drafts or excerpts of it have been published in *Unfinished Tales* (pp. 321–36), *The Annotated Hobbit* (revised edition, pp. [367]–77), *The War of the Ring* (HME VIII, pp. 357–8), and *The Peoples of Middle-earth* (HME XII, pp. 281ff).

This brings us to our final text, the 1960 Hobbit, representing the Fifth Phase of Tolkien's work on the book. In this previously unpublished material, Tolkien returned to the concerns of 'The Quest of Erebor' and set out to re-write the entire *Hobbit* in the style of *The Lord of the Rings*. Although he wisely abandoned this new draft at the start of Chapter III, this fascinating glimpse into a radically different approach to the story helps us appreciate the story as it stands all the more, besides providing some interesting and hitherto unknown details about Bilbo's itinerary. A few years later, when Tolkien was asked by his American publisher to revise both *The Lord of the Rings* and *The Hobbit* in order to assert the American copyright against the unauthorized edition of the former that had just been issued by Ace Books, he used a few of the changes he had contemplated in the 1960 Hobbit but for the most part refrained from any but minor changes to the established text. It might be argued that these constitute a 'Sixth Phase' of work on the book, but if so it would be the only one that was imposed on Tolkien from without rather than arose from within. Since the 1966 'third edition' changes are both minor and very well documented by Douglas Anderson in *The Annotated Hobbit* I have not listed them all here and instead refer readers either to his excellent book or to Hammond's definitive *Descriptive Bibliography*, pages 28–39.

More information on each of these stages is contained in the head-note to each section of the text.

(iii)
The Plan of This Edition

My presentation of the text is intended to distinguish as much as possible what Tolkien wrote from my own commentary and notes upon it. The format for each chapter is thus a brief headnote by me, followed by Tolkien's text, often followed by a brief tailnote. Next come Text Notes (TN) discussing difficult readings, highlighting various changes or sequences of changes, and the like. After this comes my Commentary in the form of mini-essays on topics arising out of that chapter, followed by Notes upon the commentary. Wherever possible, I have kept my own commentary and Tolkien's texts typographically distinct.

It must be stressed that there are no chapter divisions in the original manuscript, which flows as one continuous text with no more than the occasional skipped line to mark a change in scene or passage of time. My decision after much internal debate to follow Marquette's lead, and also Christopher Tolkien's practice at various points in *The History of Middle-earth* – that is, to insert chapter breaks where Tolkien himself later chose to make chapter divisions – comes as a result of my conviction that doing so greatly improves ease of reference, making it possible for those familiar with the published book to find any corresponding manuscript passage with relative ease. Nevertheless, these chapter breaks are an editorial contrivance and some readers may wish to ignore them, moving directly from the end of one 'Chapter' to the continuation of the text at the beginning of the next.

Formatting

It had been my original intent to record every brushstroke, cancellation, and addition to each manuscript page, so that in lieu of a facsimile reproduction this book could serve as a means by which scholars of Tolkien's work could follow every step, letter by letter and line by line, of the process by which Tolkien created his work. However, over the long course of working with the manuscript for this edition I have been persuaded that such mechanical fidelity would produce only confusion and slowly come to the conclusion that an edition of a manuscript should be, well, edited. Accordingly, I have silently omitted minor changes (such as Tolkien's own correction of miswritten or misspelled words) and sometimes slightly re-arranged material for clarity. I have also provided punctuation where necessary (mainly quotation marks and periods at the end of sentences), although I have kept this to a minimum in order to preserve the lightly-punctuated flow of the original. Changes in the manuscript by Tolkien himself are indicated by brackets; brackets have also been used in a few instances to mark missing words necessary for the sense that have been provided editorially. An arrow coming at the end of the bracketed passage [thus >] indicates that the material within the brackets was replaced by what follows. By contrast, an arrow coming at the beginning of a bracketed passage [> thus] indicates that the material within the brackets replaced what came before. My reason for this flexibility in their application has been the goal of producing a coherent sentence where possible in each case. Occasionally I have supplied rubrics such as [*added*:] or [*cancelled*:] within the brackets where this improves the clarity of the sequence of changes or makes a sentence easier to read.

Any transcription of Tolkien's manuscripts will inevitably encounter difficulties with accurately reading his handwriting, which can vary from the most beautiful calligraphy worthy of an illuminated medieval manuscript to mere wavy lines rather like the print-out from an oscilloscope. Familiarity with his characteristic ligatures, a good grasp of Tolkienian phraseology, and comparison with the published versions of such passages have often enabled me to read them, but I confess that sometimes his scrawl has defeated me. Unfortunately, it is those very passages that were most hastily written down and which vary the most from the final text which are of course the most interesting to us, such as the First Outline (see pp. 229–30). In any case it is important to approach this or any other Tolkien manuscript with a fresh eye and remain wary of reading into the earliest draft the familiar wording of a published text. In the edition which follows, doubtful readings of nearly illegible words are presented within French brackets: <thus>, while wholly illegible words are either replaced by <illegible> or ellipses (. . .), with possible readings often suggested in an associated Text Note. For the use of future scholars who might wish to examine the manuscript readings for themselves, I have deposited at Marquette a copy of my complete line-by-line and page-by-page transcript of all the manuscript material for *The Hobbit* in the Archives. I have also deposited a copy of Taum Santoski's unfinished edition [circa 1989] for those who wish to compare his readings with my own. Finally, my website (www.sacnothscriptorium.com) hosts a list of errata for this book, while my blog (www.sacnoths.blogspot.com) features updates on all things Tolkienian, among other topics.

Manuscript Citations

This book is filled with references to specific manuscript and typescript pages. Of these, 'Ms. p. XX' means that Tolkien himself gave that manuscript page this number; similarly 'Ts. p. XX' indicates that Tolkien gave that page that number in the First Typescript. By contrast, the processors at Marquette broke up the two-hundred-odd pages of the manuscript (plus the two typescripts and miscellaneous outlines and rejected sheets) into manageable smaller chunks, placing each section that corresponded to a chapter in the published book into its own folder. Thus, a citation such as 'Ms. page 13; Marq. 1/1/1:3' indicates that this text comes from the page of handwritten manuscript that Tolkien numbered '13' (in fact, the first page of the Second Phase), and that in the Marquette Tolkien Collection the page in question may be found in series 1 (*The Hobbit*), box 1 (manuscripts and typescripts), folder 1 (Chapter 1), page 3 (the first two sheets in this folder being unnumbered title pages). Similarly, the first page of text of the First Typescript (Ts. page 1; Marq.

1/1/51:2) appears in series 1, box 1, folder 51, page 2 (the first page in this folder being another unnumbered handwritten title page, this one including for the first time the subtitle *or There and Back Again*); the corresponding page in the Second Typescript is 1/1/32:2 (preceded by yet another title page). Since Tolkien wrote the bulk of the manuscript on two-sided sheets (e.g., Ms. page 14 is on the back of Ms. page 13), this means that no neat division between chapters is possible; sometimes the opening paragraphs of one chapter appear on the last sheet in the folder for the previous chapter, while the closing paragraphs of another chapter might appear on the first sheet in the folder holding the next chapter.

In addition to the main body of manuscripts at Marquette purchased from Tolkien himself in the late 1950s, some additional material was generously donated to the collection by Christopher Tolkien in four installments: in 1987, 1988, 1990, and 1997. While most of this additional material was from *The Lord of the Rings*, it included the all-important stray sheet from the First Phase of *The Hobbit* bearing the earliest draft of the Lonely Mountain map, reproduced by Christopher in his Foreword to the fiftieth anniversary *Hobbit* and serving as my book's Frontispiece. Pending an eventual reprocessing of the entire collection to incorporate this material into its proper sequence with the other manuscripts already at Marquette, these manuscripts and typescripts have their own designators: the page serving as my book's Frontispiece being MSS-1 Tolkien, Mss 1/1/1.

Finally, a small amount of manuscript material pertaining to *The Hobbit* but not part of the original draft, some of which did not even exist at the time Tolkien sold the bulk of his *Hobbit* papers to Marquette, remains in the hands of the Estate. These have been assigned page numbers by Christopher Tolkien for ease of reference when he generously made them available to Taum Santoski and myself, and to distinguish them from the two sets of Marquette material I refer to these as Ad.Ms.H.xx (= Additional Manuscript Hobbit p. xx). For example, the Fourth Phase handwritten draft revision of the Gollum chapter occupies Ad.Ms.H.34–52, while the Fifth Phase day-by-day itinerary of Bilbo's trip from Hobbiton to Rivendell appears on Ad.Ms.H.21–24.

Where I have had occasion to cite materials in other collections, such as the Bodleian Library's Department of Western Manuscripts in Oxford, I have used the citation system used by those libraries at the time I consulted the materials in question.

(iv)
Abbreviations and Acknowledgments

A great many works are cited, some repeatedly, over the course of this work. In order to save space and reduce redundancy, I use abbreviations in the place of some oft-cited titles. The most important of these is Douglas A. Anderson's *The Annotated Hobbit*, which I have taken for my base text of the published book. The reasons for this are twofold: not only is Anderson's the best text in print, incorporating all authorial changes, but his book and mine are complementary. He takes as a starting point the first printing of 1937 and scrupulously records every change and correction to the text by Tolkien from that point onward, while I look backwards from the moment of the first printing to tell the story of how the book was written.

I also make frequent reference to such essential works as *The Lord of the Rings*, *Letters of J. R. R. Tolkien*, *J. R. R. Tolkien: Artist & Illustrator*, and of course the *History of Middle-earth* series.

Finally, I draw throughout on the work of my friend Taum Santoski. This book began as a collaboration between us, and while in the event all the text and commentary are my own, I have relied upon Taum's pioneering work at establishing the correct manuscript sequence. Taum's particular fields of expertise were Tolkien's invented languages and his artwork, and it is to be deeply regretted that he set down so little of this in writing; accordingly, I draw on my memory of our many conversations about the book at various points.

DAA: Douglas A. Anderson, *The Annotated Hobbit* [1988; revised edition, 2002]. All references here are to the revised and expanded second edition of Anderson's superlative work unless otherwise stated. Where I have needed to refer to the first [1937] or second [1951] or third [1966] editions of Tolkien's original book, I have used the copies most readily available to me, these being the 3rd (1942), 13th (1961), and 31st (?1974) printings, respectively.

'Foreword': Christopher Tolkien, Foreword to the fiftieth anniversary edition of *The Hobbit* [1987].

HME: The *History of Middle-earth* series (twelve volumes), ed. Christopher Tolkien. The twelve volumes of this series are individually cited as follows:

BLT I: *The Book of Lost Tales*, Part I [1983]
BLT II: *The Book of Lost Tales*, Part II [1984]
HME III: *The Lays of Beleriand* [1985]
HME IV: *The Shaping of Middle-earth* [1986]

HME V: *The Lost Road* [1987]
HME VI: *The Return of the Shadow* [1988]
HME VII: *The Treason of Isengard* [1989]
HME VIII: *The War of the Ring* [1990]
HME IX: *Sauron Defeated* [1992]
HME X: *Morgoth's Ring* [1993]
HME XI: *The War of the Jewels* [1994]
HME XII: *The Peoples of Middle-earth* [1996]

Of these, volumes I & II contain a two-part presentation of 'The Book of Lost Tales', volumes VI, VII, VIII, & IXa form the subseries 'The History of *The Lord of the Rings*' (to which the first half of volume XII forms an unofficial appendage), and volumes X & XI comprise 'The Later Silmarillion'. In addition, one should not neglect *The History of Middle-earth Index* [2002], a compilation of the indexes of all twelve volumes, which is extremely useful in tracking changes in names and the reappearance of specific names and characters from volume to volume. In this edition, I have drawn heavily on the first five volumes, these being the materials that either preceded (I–III) or are contemporary with the writing (IV) or publication (V) of *The Hobbit*. The most important individual works within these volumes for my study of *The Hobbit*, and the ones most frequently cited, have been the component tales of *The Book of Lost Tales* (particularly 'Turambar and the Foalókë' and 'The Nauglafring', both in BLT II), the long epic poem 'The Lay of Leithian' (HME III), the synoptic 1926 'Sketch of the Mythology' (HME IV), and the 1930 *Quenta* (HME IV).

LotR: *The Lord of the Rings* by J. R. R. Tolkien. One volume edition, illustrated by Alan Lee [1991]. Among the many, many editions of *The Lord of the Rings* I have chosen this one as my base text, because it is widely available, because its one-volume format makes it easy to use, and because it predates certain post-authorial changes. However, any reference to a specific point in *The Hobbit*'s sequel should be easy to find by anyone even moderately familiar with the story. Where reference to the first edition text seemed desirable, I have used my copy of the first Allen & Unwin edition, which consists of a first printing of volume I [1954] and a second printing of volumes II [1955] and III [1955].

Letters: *The Letters of J. R. R. Tolkien*, ed. by Humphrey Carpenter with the assistance of Christopher Tolkien [1981; revised edition with expanded index, 2000].

A&U: Allen & Unwin correspondence with JRRT, October 1936 through December 1937. Although not quite complete, this file of letters between Tolkien and various members of the firm of George Allen & Unwin – primarily Stanley Unwin, Susan Dagnall, and

Charles Furth – along with a few internal memos provides a wealth of information about the publication of the book, as well as a few details about its presubmission history. I am grateful to Mary Butler, formerly of HarperCollins, for making this file available to me in the early stages of this project.

Hammond Scull: *J. R. R. Tolkien: Artist & Illustrator* by Wayne G. Hammond & Christina Scull [1995]. Individual paintings and drawings within this book are cited by the number Hammond & Scull assign them. Thus H-S#134 refers to figure 134 in their book, 'Untitled (Smaug Flies around the Lonely Mountain)' reproduced on page 142 of *Artist & Illustrator*.

Hammond: *J. R. R. Tolkien: A Descriptive Bibliography* by Wayne G. Hammond with Douglas A. Anderson [1993]. This is the definitive record of publishing information about each of Tolkien's works, including misprints and variations between editions, and a brief but detailed account of each book's genesis.

Carpenter: *Tolkien: A Biography* by Humphrey Carpenter [1977]. The authorized biography; inaccurate in some details but after thirty years still unsurpassed as an overview of Tolkien's life.

OED: *The Oxford English Dictionary*. Specific citations come from the two-volume set more properly known as *The Compact Edition of the Oxford English Dictionary* [1971].

OFS: 'On Fairy-Stories' by J. R. R. Tolkien, in *Tree and Leaf* [1964; expanded edition 1988]. An earlier version of this essay had appeared in the memorial festschrift *Essays Presented to Charles Williams* [1947], but unless stated otherwise all my citations come from the slightly revised 1964 form of this seminal work.

FGH: *Farmer Giles of Ham* by J. R. R. Tolkien [1949; expanded edition 1999].

FCL: *The Father Christmas Letters* by J. R. R. Tolkien, ed. Baillie Tolkien [1976]. Most citations have been taken from the expanded edition (as *Letters from Father Christmas* [1999]).

ATB: *The Adventures of Tom Bombadil* by J. R. R. Tolkien [1962]. Individual poems are cited by number – e.g., the fourteenth poem, 'The Hoard', is referred to as ATB poem #14.

Beowulf Essay: 'Beowulf: The Monsters and the Critics' [1936]. I have used the 1978 facsimile reproduction (by the Arden Library) of the original 1936 publication but the essay is also readily available in *The Monsters & the Critics and Other Essays* [1983; trade paperback 1997].

Silm: *The Silmarillion*, ed. Christopher Tolkien [1977; revised edition 1999].

UT: *Unfinished Tales of Númenor and Middle-earth*, ed. Christopher Tolkien [1979].

Acknowledgments

This project has been in the works for many years, and a great many people have helped, both those I consulted on specific points and those who offered more general support and encouragement.

In addition to those acknowledged in my notes, I would like to thank the following for their contributions.

- to Christopher Tolkien, for allowing me to undertake this project, for his patience with many questions over the course of it, and for his exceptional example through his many editions of his father's work, particularly the *History of Middle-earth* series.
- to my friend the late Taum Santoski, for entrusting me to take over this project and see it through to fruition.
- to the late Rayner Unwin, for his encouragement and good advice in the early stages of this project.
- to Charles Elston, who as archivist of the Marquette Tolkien collection made the materials under his protection available to all Tolkien scholars. Also to those at the Marquette Archives, particularly Terry Margherita, Tracy Muench, and Phil Runkel, who patiently sat for many hours while I transcribed manuscripts or checked and re-checked transcriptions, sometimes with a magnifying glass or light table. And also to Matt Blessing, the current archivist, for his patience with many follow-up questions in the project's final stages.
- to the late Terry Tuttle, who despite his own worsening health gave me free access to Taum Santoski's papers, without which my work as Taum's literary executor would have been much more difficult.
- to all the participants in the Tolkien Symposiums over the last sixteen years, including Verlyn Flieger, Richard West, Wayne Hammond, Christina Scull, Marjorie Burns, Paul Thomas, Doug Anderson, the late Richard Blackwelder, Matt Fisher, Carolyn Kiel, Taum Santoski, Chris Mitchell, Gary Hunnewell, Vaughn Howland, Janice Coulter, David Bratman, Arden Smith, Carl Hostetter, and others.
- to Jessica Yates, whose Seeing-Stone project first put me in touch with Tolkien scholars in other parts of the world.
- to Richard West, Gwendolyn Kestrel, and especially Jim Pietrusz for their generosity in loaning me material or aid in helping me locate obscure works inaccessible to an independent scholar without access to Interlibrary Loan.
- to Judith Priestman and others of the Bodleian's Department of Western Manuscripts for their help during my four research trips to the Bodleian in 1981, 1985, 1992, and especially 1987.
- to the Marion E. Wade collection at Wheaton College, in gratitude for their having awarded me a Clyde S. Kilby Research Grant in 1997 to help fund the ongoing research for this project, and to

Lyle Dorsett, Marjorie Mead, Chris Mitchell, and others at the Wade Center for their courtesy during my many visits to the Wade researching this and other projects over the years.

- to the Tolkien Society, for featuring me as a guest speaker at their Hobbit Workshop in May 1987; to Nancy Martsch and *Beyond Bree* for asking me to talk about this project as Guest of Honor at BreeMoot 3 in Minneapolis in 1997; and to the Mythopoeic Society, at whose 1993 and 1997 conferences I presented earlier versions of two chapters.
- to Doug Anderson, for his generosity in sharing his knowledge about Tolkien chronology and of all things *Hobbit*.
- to David Salo, for having patiently answered many questions about Tolkien's invented languages and Old English studies.
- to Wayne Hammond & Christina Scull, for helping with many points regarding Tolkien's publication history.
- to Steve Brown, Wolf & Shelly Baur, Mark Sehestedt, and Jeff Grubb, for continually encouraging me to 'get it done'; and to the Burrahobbits and Mithlonders, participants in two Tolkien-centric fantasy book discussion groups, who have heard much of this material piecemeal over the years.
- to Kate Latham, Chris Smith, David Brawn, and Mary Butler, for their patience.
- to Doug Anderson, Paul Thomas, and Richard West, for reading through the complete book and offering advice and corrections, and to Charles Noad for meticulously proofing the whole.
- to my mother, for her faith and support.
- to my wife, Janice Coulter, whose help and patience made it possible for me to complete this project despite many interruptions over a long period. In addition to helping me with the initial transcription and the proofing thereof, she has served as my sounding board, sometimes pointing out connections that had eluded me and offering insights that enabled me to work my way through some of the tangles that confronted me.
- to Mrs. Henry, my junior high librarian who, when I returned *The Hobbit* to the library in September of 1973 (having read it twice back-to-back) and lamented that there weren't any more like it anywhere, told me about *The Lord of the Rings* . . .
- And to Susan Dagnall, for asking.

NOTES

1 This version of the Gollum story made it into print in the first edition, not being replaced until the second edition of 1951; contrast Chapter V: Gollum beginning on p. 153 with The Fourth Phase, beginning on page 729.

2 *Babbitt* [1922], by American author Sinclair Lewis, depicts the world and outlook of a small-town businessman who wishes to escape from the stifling conformity of his world and fails, although the end of the story holds out hope that his son might be more fortunate (one might perhaps draw an analogy between Bungo Baggins, who was strictly respectable and never had any adventures, and his more fortunate son Bilbo). It might be thought that Lewis's becoming the first American to win a Nobel Prize for literature in 1930 might have drawn Tolkien's attention at the opportune moment to have helped inspire the word 'hobbit', but this is unlikely since the prize was not announced until November 1930 and the evidence suggests that Tolkien had invented the name several months earlier during the summer of that year.

For more on the origin of the word 'hobbit', see Appendix I: *The Denham Tracts*.

3 An additional piece of information regarding the starting date of *The Hobbit* comes from a note Tolkien wrote to accompany his desk when he donated it to be sold for the benefit of the charity Help the Aged. Entitled 'This Desk' and dated July 27th, 1972, the handwritten note states that

This Desk

Was bought for me by my wife in 1927. It was my first desk, and has remained the one that I chiefly used for literary work until her death in 1971.

On it The Hobbit was entirely produced: written, typed, and illustrated.

The Lord of the Rings was written and revised in many places in Oxford and elsewhere; but on this desk were also written, at various times, the manuscript drafts of Books III, IV, V, and VI, until the last words of the Tale were reached in 1949.

I have presented this desk to HELP THE AGED in memory of my wife, Edith Mary, in the hope that its sale may help this Charity to house some old people of Britain in peace and comfort.

J. R. R. Tolkien

Merton College,
Oxford
July 27th,
1972.

Therefore, even if we do not accept Tolkien's statement that the first impulse came after the 1930 move to the new house, the book could not have been started before 1927.

Both the note and the desk are now on display at the Wade Center at Wheaton College.

4 Personal communication, Fr. John Tolkien to John D. Rateliff, 6th February 1997.

5 I am grateful to the late Lester Simons, long-time Membership Secretary of the Tolkien Society, for providing me with an audiocassette recording of this event.

6 See pp. 634 & 545.

7 Lest the description of Father Christmas as a 'magician' give us pause, we should remember that Michael Tolkien recounts that the wizard 'Kimpu' in the family apocrypha derived his name from young Priscilla's best attempt to say 'Father Christmas' – another argument, by the way, for a slightly later date than the one Michael suggests. Also, in the 1933 Father Christmas Letter the North Polar Bear interrupts the letter to say 'You have no idea what the old man can doo! Litening and Fierworks and Thunder of Guns!' (*Letters from Father Christmas*, p. 88) – a description which sounds very much like Gandalf at work: cf. Bilbo's memory of the wizard's fireworks at his grandfather's parties (Chapter I) and the bolts of lightning that strike dead the goblins in the mountain-pass (Chapter IV).

8 For example, Elaine Griffiths' comments in her interview with Ann Bonsor (BBC Radio Oxford [1974]) are so specific that we can tell that the version of the story she read was the First Typescript, yet she makes no mention of the story's being incomplete. Accordingly, we must reject Carpenter's theory that Tolkien abandoned the story at the point where the Second Phase manuscript breaks off (see p. 633); the overwhelming probability is that the 'home manuscript' Tolkien lent out was a composite typescript/manuscript consisting of the first typescript up to the death of Smaug, including a fair-copy handwritten insertion of the revised text of what is now Chapter XIII, and followed by forty-five pages of handwritten manuscript completing the story (see pp. 637–8). For more examples of composite typescript/manuscript texts by Tolkien, see the discussion below of the Bladorthin Typescript and the Second Phase manuscript and also see Verlyn Flieger's discussion of the earliest surviving draft of SWM, itself a typescript/manuscript composite, reproduced in facsimile in the Extended Edition of *Smith of Wootton Major* [2005], pages 102–29.

We do not know how many people read the story outside of the Tolkien family before its submission to Allen & Unwin, but they include C. S. Lewis (see above), a 12–13 year old girl (*Letters* p. 21), the Rev. Mother of Cherwell Edge (*Letters* pp. 215, 346, 374), Elaine Griffiths, and lastly Griffiths' friend Susan Dagnall, whose positive response encouraged Tolkien to formally submit the story in early October 1936. Quite possibly there were others; cf. Tolkien's comment that 'The MS. certainly wandered about' (JRRT to C. A. Furth at Allen & Unwin, 31st August 1937; *Letters* p. 21). The composite typescript/manuscript was apparently read to the Inklings (see *Letters* p. 36), probably at about the time Tolkien submitted it to the publisher, since the group seems not to have existed when the manuscript was first written.†

† The Inklings seem to have coalesced as a group during 1933–4; Dr. 'Humphrey' Havard, who along with Tolkien, Lewis, and Warnie Lewis formed one of the four core members, told me he was invited to join upon his moving to Oxford and making Lewis's acquaintance in 1934. It was certainly in existence by 1936, when Lewis mentions the group by name in his first letter to Charles Williams.

9 This meeting took place on 27th October, not 15th November as Carpenter states in *Letters* p. 25. They met again on Monday 15th November, when Tolkien turned over copies of 'The Lay of Leithian', the 1937 *Quenta Silmarillion*, and *The Lost Road*, and perhaps also Lewis's *Out of the Silent Planet* as well. Unwin had already requested, as a result of their earlier meeting, that Tolkien go ahead and 'put together the volume of short fairy stories' (SU to JRRT, 28th October 1937; A&U archives) of which *Farmer Giles*, which had already been read and approved but felt to be too short for publication by itself (e.g., A&U to JRRT 16th November 1937; A&U archives), would have been one, but in the brief time between their meetings Tolkien had not yet done so (having no doubt been kept busy preparing the other submissions). *Mr Bliss* had also already been read and provisionally accepted, provided that Tolkien could re-draw its many illustrations into a simpler style that would be easier (and cheaper) to reproduce. In the event, discouraging reader reports of *The Lost Road* (by Susan Dagnall, who admired the work but thought it unlikely to be a commercial success) and 'The Lay of Leithian' (by outside reader Edward Crankshaw, who much preferred the prose *Quenta Silmarillion*) led Unwin to urge Tolkien to attempt 'another book about THE HOBBIT' or, failing that, assemble 'a volume of stories like FARMER GILES' (SU to JRRT, 15th December 1937). At some point between the 16th and 19th, Tolkien wrote the first chapter of what would become *The Lord of the Rings* (or 'The New Hobbit', as he and his friends long referred to it), as Unwin was 'thrilled to learn' (SU to JRRT, 20th December 1937; A&U archives), stating that 'another book . . . on the lines of THE HOBBIT is now assured of success'. How right he was.

Unwin's memo, drawn up immediately following the 27th October meeting, is itself of great interest, and I therefore quote it here in full:

Professor Tolkien.

1. He has a volume of short fairy stories in various styles practically ready for publication.
2. He has the typescript of a History of the Gnomes, and stories arising from it.
3. MR. BLISS.
4. THE LOST ROAD, a partly written novel of which we could see the opening chapters.
5. A great deal of verse of one kind and another which would probably be worth looking at.
6. BEOWOLF <sic> upon which he has as yet done very little.†

He spoke enthusoastically <sic> of a children's book called MARVELLOUS LAND OF SNERGS illustrated by George Morrow and published by Benn some few years ago. He mentioned that THE HOBBIT took him two or three years to write because he works very slowly.

S.U. October, 1937

– unpublished memo; Allen & Unwin archives.

† This is a reference to the revision of the Clark Hall prose translation upon which Tolkien and Elaine Griffiths had been working the year before; it was eventually published in 1940 after Griffiths had been replaced by Tolkien's fellow Inkling Charles Wrenn. See pp. 693–4 for more on how this project seems to have first sparked contact between JRRT and Allen & Unwin and initiated the relationship that proved so beneficial to both.

10 For another example, in his Introductory Note to *Tree and Leaf* [1964]† Tolkien stated that his essay 'On Fairy-Stories' had been delivered as a lecture in 1938, and footnoted this 'Not 1940 as incorrectly stated in 1947' (e.g., by Tolkien himself in the first sentence of the version of the essay printed in *Essays Presented to Charles Williams*, p. 38). However, as Christopher Tolkien notes in his Preface to the revised edition of *Tree and Leaf* [1988], the lecture actually took place on 8th March 1939. Although the error is minor, once again we see Tolkien, on later consideration, characteristically pushes back a date.

For a final and perhaps extreme example, Clyde Kilby stated, in his memoir of Tolkien included in his book *Tolkien and The Silmarillion* [1976], that during the summer of 1966 Tolkien told him that 'he was writing some of *The Silmarillion* . . . about 1910' and also claims that '[Tolkien] told one of his closest friends that he had the whole of his mythic world in his mind as early as 1906'; unfortunately he does not identify his source for his statement. In fact, we know through Christopher Tolkien's work in the *History of Middle-earth* series that the earliest prose tales date to about 1916–17, while the earliest Middle-earth poetry, the Eärendel poems, date to 1914. In addition, Kilby says that 'Tolkien told me that some of the poems in *Tom Bombadil* [e.g., *The Adventures of Tom Bombadil*] had been written by him "as a boy"' (*Tolkien and The Silmarillion*, pp. 47–8). Even if we assume that by 'as a boy' Tolkien meant not childhood but undergraduate days, none of the Bombadil poems are known to predate the 1920s, when Tolkien was in his thirties, and most of the rest were written in the 1930s.

† This Introductory Note was written in October 1963 according to Hammond, *Descriptive Bibliography*, pages 183–4.

11 This solitary exception is manuscript page 155, near the end of the Second Phase. The front of this sheet bears the scene from Chapter XIII describing the death of Smaug, while the back has several lines from a student's attempt at Old English describing a meeting in Winchester between King Edward the Confessor and Godwin of Wessex, the father of Harold Godwinson.

A small amount of other extraneous material (*not* student essays) can be found on the versos of some pages. One of the outlines (Plot Notes F) is written on the back of a fragment from an unsent letter, but these were after all merely notes to himself and never part of the main manuscript. Similarly, some *Lord of the Rings*-era drafting for changes to the Gollum chapter (1/1/21:1–2) are on a page with the letterhead of The Catenian Association, the Oxford chapter of which Tolkien was the Vice-President at the time, while most of Tolkien's 1944 draft for the replacement Gollum chapter (The Fourth Phase) was written on the back of old handouts Tolkien had prepared for classes; see p. 740 (Text Note 1).

12 A snippet from an otherwise unpublished letter quoted by Carpenter reveals that Tolkien was already hard at work preparing the text for submission to the publisher before 10th August 1936: '*The Hobbit* is now nearly finished, and the publishers clamouring for it' (*Tolkien: A Biography*, p. 180).

13 Thus, in the sequence of *Hobbit* manuscripts at Marquette, this second typescript appears before the First Typescript in the filing system. For example, the manuscript of Chapter V is 1/1/5, the First Typescript of Chapter V is 1/1/55, and the Second Typescript of Chapter V is 1/1/36.

14 Presumably it was this injury, which would have kept young Michael from normal summer activities, that caused his father to ask him to undertake this task at all.

15 These consist of two copies of the First Page Proofs (Marq. 1/2/1 and 1/2/2) and one copy of the Second Page Proofs (Marq. 1/2/3). Of these, Marq. 1/2/1 represents the copy that Tolkien originally read through and marked up, while Marq. 1/2/2 is an exact duplicate from the printer onto which he then carefully wrote all those corrections as neatly as possible and returned to the publisher, keeping 1/2/1 for his own reference. The Second Proofs, Marq. 1/2/3, incorporate those changes and give Tolkien a last chance to correct mistakes made by the printer, fix hereto undetected errors surviving from the Typescript for Printers, and make any last-minute changes he felt absolutely necessary.

THE FIRST PHASE

Chapter I (a)

THE PRYFTAN FRAGMENT

The original page from a student essay upon which Tolkien scribbled down the words 'In a hole in the ground there lived a hobbit' does not survive, but a substantial fragment of six pages (three sheets) from the original manuscript has been preserved. This I have dubbed 'The Pryftan Fragment', after the name given the dragon at this earliest stage of the story. The fragment lacks both a beginning and an end, but it does form a continuous text which is given below.

It is not clear now how far this initial stage of composition carried the story. According to Tolkien's later recollections, the story halted before the end of the first chapter and may indeed have stopped at the point where the fragment ends.[1] Nor is it clear what happened to the missing pages. They may have been given to some friend, as Tolkien gave away other bits of *Hobbit* material – specifically, the original of the Mirkwood picture (Christopher Tolkien, Foreword to the 50th Anniversary *Hobbit*, p. x; *Pictures by Tolkien*, plate 37) and a very fine unused picture of Smaug flying around the Lonely Mountain (Foreword, p. xiii). Nor was *The Hobbit* the only one of his works he treated in this way: he gave an elaborate illuminated manuscript of his still-unpublished poem 'Doworst' to his friend R. W. Chambers[2] and similarly gave away both the manuscript of and copyright to the then-unpublished poem 'Bilbo's Last Song' to his secretary Joy Hill in gratitude for her years of service.[3] Inherently unlikely as it may seem from our historical perspective that Tolkien would give away the single most famous page of manuscript he ever produced,[4] his generosity in other cases on record makes it a distinct possibility.

Or the missing pages may have been deliberately destroyed by Tolkien after being translated into typescript. Contrary to legend, Tolkien did occasionally destroy manuscript material when, as in this case, it was rough draft workings that had definitely been superseded by a later fair copy or typescript. For example, in both *The Book of Lost Tales* (cf. BLT I.45, 64, 130, 174, 203; BLT II.3, 69, 138, 146, 221) and in sections of the *Lord of the Rings* material, Tolkien would often draft a passage in pencil, then write a revised form of the text over it in ink, typically afterwards erasing whatever pencilled jottings remained, completely obliterating the initial version. While it may be argued that such extraordinary measures were forced upon him by paper shortages in wartime, no such explanation will suffice in the case of *Mr. Bliss*. The little hand-made booklet reproduced in facsimile in 1982 is a carefully made fair copy that clearly required extensive preliminary drafting for both the art and the text, yet only a stray leaf or two bearing sketches for some of the illustrations survived to accompany the hand-painted manuscript book when it arrived at Marquette in the late 1950s; it seems clear, in this case at least, that Tolkien himself discarded the missing rough draft material. Furthermore, Christopher Tolkien notes an analogous case of missing rough draft for the 1937 *Quenta Silmarillion*, where only a small portion of the pages upon which Tolkien worked out the revisions incorporated in this text survive (HME V.199). Then, too, the *Hobbit* manuscript itself shows one clear, unambiguous case where Tolkien ripped a page of Ms. in half; the piece which survives does so only because its back was re-used for some outline notes.[5] Tolkien kept a great deal of his own manuscript, probably so he could reconstruct the text should the final version be lost or mislaid[6] (and of course because this would enable him to re-use elsewhere ideas and elements that had dropped out of this particular story), but even he did not keep everything.

Finally, and most probably, the missing manuscript pages may simply have been lost by accident. According to Tolkien, C. S. Lewis on two separate occasions accidentally destroyed the only copy of a story Tolkien had loaned to him to read (Carpenter, *The Inklings* [1978], p. 48), and other mishaps doubtless occurred. Perhaps it would be better not to speculate on how the missing pages were lost, but to ask how the surviving pages happened to be preserved. Two of the sheets (four pages of text) from this first stage of composition (Marq. 1/1/22:1–4) came to Marquette in June 1957, mixed in with the rest of the *Hobbit* manuscript and typescripts but very distinct from them in the style of Tolkien's handwriting and the type of paper used. The third sheet was retained by Tolkien, either inadvertently or because it bore the first sketch of what came to be known as Thror's Map.[7] Reproduced in facsimile in Christopher Tolkien's Foreword to the 50th anniversary edition of *The Hobbit* (Unwin Hyman 1987, pp. ii–iii),[8] it did not join its fellows at Marquette until July 1987 (MSS–1 Tolkien, Mss. 1/1/1).

While the Marquette processors made no record of how the papers were arranged upon arrival, we are unusually fortunate in that some surviving correspondence relating to the sale casts valuable light upon both Tolkien's own recollections concerning the papers and on how he had them stored before they came to Marquette.[9] Tolkien initially told Bertram Rota, the London bookseller who acted as Marquette's agent in the sale of the manuscripts, that there was no actual manuscript, only the 'original typescript' sent to the printer, the corrected proofs, and his illustrations for the book (Rota to Ready, 10th January 1957). After 'looking through his cupboards' he turned up the original *Farmer Giles* typescript ('There is no hand-written version of this work, which was composed on the type-writer') and asked for 'a bit longer to dig around and see if he finds any more bits and pieces concerning "The Hobbit" and "The Lord of the Rings"' (Rota to Ready, 5th May 1957). By 13th May, he had discovered the manuscript of *Farmer Giles*, the very existence of which he had forgotten so completely as to deny a week before that there ever had been one (Rota to Ready, 13th May 1957); a month later when Rota arrived in Oxford to collect the first installment of the papers for shipment to Marquette, he discovered that 'Tolkien has found . . . more than we expected . . . When I wrote on May 5th I reported that Tolkien said there was no hand-written manuscript of "The Hobbit". Now he has found it . . .' (Rota to Ready, 13th June 1957).

Even allowing for mistakes or misunderstandings on Rota's part (evidenced elsewhere in his letters to Ready), it is quite clear from this account that Tolkien's memory of the *Hobbit* manuscript, superseded as it had been by the typescript some quarter-century before, was understandably vague. It is also clear that the material was not all kept in one file, but scattered among his papers,[10] and that Tolkien had some difficulty in locating and pulling all the pieces together. In fact, as we shall see, some pieces evaded his search and are still retained by the family to this day.[11]

The following is the complete text of the surviving fragment; comments and observations follow the transcription. I have provided punctuation as necessary and corrected a few obvious slips (e.g., replaced 'the the' with simply 'the') but otherwise have edited this first draft as lightly as possible.

NOTES

1 Long afterwards, Tolkien scribbled the following note in pencil in the left margin on the front of the third sheet of this fragment:

> Only page preserved
> of the first scrawled copy of
> The <u>Hobbit</u> which did not
> reach beyond the first chapter

In a letter to W. H. Auden written in 1955 recounting the origins of the book, Tolkien recalled that '. . . for some years I got no further than the production of Thror's Map' (JRRT to WHA, 7th June 1955; *Letters* p. 215). Tolkien might well have meant this quite literally, since the earliest draft of the map takes up slightly more than half of this same page (the next to last of the fragment).

2 For the full story of this manuscript, whose present whereabouts are unknown, see Douglas A. Anderson's article 'R. W. Chambers and *The Hobbit*', in *Tolkien Studies*, vol. III [2006], pp. 139 & 144.

3 Interview with the late Joy Hill; Battersea, London, May 1987.

4 Douglas A. Anderson notes in *The Annotated Hobbit* (1988; revised

edition 2002, page [29]; hereafter DAA) that the opening passage of the book has become so much a part of our cultural heritage that it has even found its way into *Bartlett's Familiar Quotations* [1980 & ff].

5 This fragment of draft, and the associated outline (Plot Notes E: 'Little Bird'), are reproduced below on pp. 620–621 & 626 of Part 2 of this book.

6 This would account for his habit of going back and transcribing later changes onto earlier copies of texts, thus ensuring that the revisions would survive if the latest fair copy or final typescript were accidentally destroyed or lost in the post – a serious and all-too-real concern in those days before the advent of easy access to photocopiers.

7 Tolkien's agreement with Marquette specified that he should retain any illustrative material among the manuscripts (with the obvious exception of *Mr. Bliss*), although due to the intermingling of the two in the event some illustrations came to Marquette and some text was retained by Tolkien. Tolkien kept no clear tally of exactly what he had sent to Marquette; when he was revising the text of *The Lord of the Rings* for the second edition, he wrote to the Archivist asking if Marquette had a particular piece of Ms. to which he needed to refer – a piece which we now know Tolkien had in fact retained (letter, JRRT to 'The Librarian' [Wm A. Fitzgerald], Marquette University, 3rd August 1965). And clearly when he came across this solitary sheet with Thror's Map, probably sometime in the mid-1960s, he had forgotten about the existence of the other two sheets (see Note 1 above).

8 It was this facsimile publication in the 50th anniversary edition that enabled the late Taum Santoski to recognize that the solitary leaf retained by Tolkien and marked by him as the sole surviving sheet was in fact cognate with the two sheets that had come to Marquette thirty years before. As a result of his insight, we can now reunite all three, thus re-creating roughly half of the original opening chapter of *The Hobbit* as it stood in the First Phase manuscript (see below).

9 This correspondence is now at Marquette.

10 Adding to the confusion was the fact that at the time of the transfer some of Tolkien's papers were at his house on Sandfield Road (into which he had only moved a few years before) and some were at his office at Merton College (Tolkien to [Fitzgerald], 3rd August 1965), which he was at that time beginning to clean out in anticipation of his upcoming retirement.

11 Along with several miscellaneous items, these include the 1947 Hobbit (see 'The Fourth Phase', beginning on p. 729) and the 1960 Hobbit (the 'Fifth Phase'), the latter of which was of course not yet in existence at the time of Tolkien's sale of the original draft, typescripts, and galleys to Marquette. I have given all these items the designator 'Ad.Ms.H.' [Additional Manuscript Hobbit] to distinguish them from the materials at Marquette ('Marq.') – e.g., Ad.Ms.H.6–7, Marq. 1/1/22:1–4, &c.

As they sang the hobbit felt the love of beautiful things made by hands and by cunning and by magic moving through him; [*added*: A fierce and jealous love, the desire of the hearts of dwarves. Then] something Tookish awoke within [>inside] him, and he wished to go and see the great mountains and the seas, the pine trees and the waterfalls, and explore the caves [of<] and wear a sword instead of a walking stick.[TN1] He looked out of the window. The stars were out in a dark sky[TN2] above the trees. He thought of the jewels of the dwarves shining in dark caves. Then in the wood beyond the Water a flame leapt up – somebody lighting a wood fire probably – and he thought of plundering dragons lighting on his quiet hill and setting it all in flames. Then he shuddered, and quite suddenly he was plain Mr Baggins of Bag-end Under-Hill again.

He got up trembling, he had [*added*: less than] half a mind to fetch the lamp, and more than half a mind to go out to fetch it[TN3]. and hide in the cellar behind the beer-barrel and not come out again till all the dwarves had gone away.

Suddenly he found them all looking at him with eyes shining in the dark.[TN4] 'Where are you going?' said Gandalf in a tone that seemed to show he guessed both halves of the hobbit's mind.[TN5]

'What about a little light?' said Bilbo.

'We like the dark' said all the dwarves: 'Dark for dark business. There are many hours before dawn'.

'Oh' said Bilbo and sat down again in a hurry – he sat on the fender and knocked the poker and the shovel over with a crash.

'Hush' said Bladorthin. '[Silence in the>] Let Gandalf speak.'

[This is some part of what Gandalf said, > And this is how he began >]

'Bladorthin, Dwarves, and Mr Baggins.[TN6] We are met together in the house of our friend and fellow-conspirator, this most excellent and audacious Hobbit – praised be his wine, and ale –' (but this praise was lost on Bilbo Baggins who was wagging his mouth in protest against being a fellow-conspirator and audacious, but no noise would come he was so upsettled). 'We are met to discuss our plans. [Before we go forth>] We shall start soon before the break of day on our long journey – a journey from which some of us [*cancelled*: may] (or all of us with the probable exception of Bladorthin) may never return. The object of our journey is [all>] well-known to all of you. To Mr Baggins, and to one or two of the younger dwarves (Kili and Fili at any rate – if I am not mistaken) the exact situation [may be unknown>] at the moment may [be >] require explanation.'

This was Gandalf's style. In the end he would probably have said all he wanted to, and left a little time over for some of the others to have a word. But on this occasion he was rudely interrupted.

Poor Bilbo could not bear it any longer. At 'may never return' he began to feel a shriek coming up inside, and very soon after it burst out like a whistling engine coming out of a tunnel.

All the dwarves sprang up knocking over the table. Bladorthin struck a blue light on the end of his magic staff and [by the >] in its glare they saw the poor little hobbit kneeling on the hearthrug shaking like a jelly (a jelly that is melting). Then he fell flat and kept on calling out 'struck by lightning, struck by lightning' over and over again. And that was all they could get out of him for a long while. So they took him and laid him on the drawing room sofa with a lamp [*added*: and a drink] beside him, and went back to their dark business.

'Excitable little man' said Bladorthin as they sat down again. 'Gets funny queer fits, but one of the best, one of the best – as brave [> fierce] as a dragon in a pinch –' (if you have ever seen a dragon in a pinch you would realize that this was only poetical exaggeration applied to any hobbit, even the Old Took's great uncle Bullroarer who <was> so large he could sit on a Shetland pony; and charged the ranks of the goblins of the Gram Hill [> Mount Gram] in the battle of the Green Fields of Fellin[TN7] and knocked their king [> King Fingolfin]'s[TN8] head clean off with a wooden club. It sailed two hundred yards and went down a rabbit hole, and in this way the battle was won [*added*: by checkmate] and the game [> games] of Golf [*added*: & chess] invented simultaneously).[TN9]

In the meanwhile the dwarves had forgotten about Bullroarer's gentler descendant, and he was recovering in the drawing room.[TN10]

After a while (and a drink) he crept nervously to the door of the parlour. This is what he heard – Dwalin speaking.

'Humph, will he do it, d'you think. It is all very well for Bladorthin to talk about his hobbit being fierce, but one shriek like that in a moment of excitement when we really get to work [> to close quarters] will [> would] be enough to kill the lot of us. Personally I think there was more fright in it than excitement, and if it hadn't been for the secret sign on the door, I should have been sure I had come to the wrong house, as soon as [*added*: I] clapped eyes on the [*added*: fat] little fellow bobbing on the mat. He looks more like a grocer than a burglar!'

Then Mr Baggins turned the handle & walked in. Took had won. He would [*cancelled*: <rather>] go without bed and breakfast to be thought fierce, and never be called 'a fat little fellow bobbing on the mat' again. Many a time afterwards the Baggins part regretted his decision and his strange behaviour at that moment; but [*added*: now] he went right and put his foot in it without a doubt.

'Pardon me' he said 'if I have overheard [part >] some words that you were saying. I cannot pretend to understand it all, but I think I am right in believing that you think I am no good. I am not – but I will be. I have no magic signs on my door and I am sure you have come to the wrong house – but treat it as the right one. Tell me what you wish me to do and I will try it – if I have to walk from here to [*cancelled*: Hindu Kush] the Great Desert of Gobi and fight the Wild Wire worm<s> of the Chinese. I had a great-great-great uncle Bullroarer Took and –'

'We know we know' said Gloin (in embarrassment) 'holed out [*added*: -checkmated] in one in the battle of the Green Fields. But I assure you the mark was on the door. The mark was here last night. Oin found it and we gathered tonight as soon as we could for the mark was fresh.'

'I put it there' said Bladorthin from the darkest corner. 'With my little stick I put it there. For very good reasons. [*cancelled*: Now let's get on] – I chose [*cancelled*: this] Mr Baggins for the fourteenth man and let anyone say He is the wrong man or his house the wrong house who dares. Then I will have no more to do with your adventure, and you can all go and dig [*added*: for] turnips or coal.'

'Bilbo my boy,' he said turning to the hobbit. 'Fetch the lamp, and let's have a little light on this dark matter.'

On the table in the light of a big lamp with a red shade he spread a parchment map. 'This I had from Fimbulfambi (?)[TN11] – your grandfather, Gandalf,' he said in answer to the dwarves' excited questions. 'It shows the Black Mountain and the surrounding country.[TN12] There it is, that dark blob [> lump > tangle]. Over here is the Wild Wood and far beyond to the North, only the edge of it is on the map, is the Withered Heath where the Great Dragons used to live.'

'We know all that' said Balin. 'This won't help – there is a picture of a dragon in red on the Mountain, but [that won't make it any ea[sier] >] it will be easy enough to find him without that.'

'There is one point' said the wizard 'which you haven't noticed, and that is the secret entrance. You see that rune† on the East side and <the> hand pointing to it from the runes below [*cancelled*: them]? That marks an old secret entrance to the Mountain's halls.'

Written at the bottom of this page is the following footnote:

† Don't ask what that is. Look at the map, and you will see [*added*: that] one

This clearly refers to the 'F' rune marking the secret door on Fimbulfambi's map (see Frontispiece).

'It may have been secret in the old days' said Gandalf 'but [how do you >] why should it be any longer. Pryftan has dwelt there long enough to find out all there is to know about those caves by now!'

'He may – but he can't have used it for years and years!'

'Why so [> Why]?'

'Because it is too small. "Five feet high is the door, and four abreast [> three abreast] may enter it" say the runes. But Pryftan could not creep in a hole that size, not even when he was a young dragon, certainly not in the [days >] after he had devoured so many of the maidens of the valley.'

'[How >] It seems a <pretty> big hole' piped up Bilbo. He loved maps, and in the hall there was a large one of the County Round (where he lived), with all his favourite walks marked on it in red ink. [This was quite exciting>] He was so interested he forgot to be shy and keep his mouth shut. 'How could such an enormous [hole >] door (he was a hobbit, remember) be secret'.

'Lots of ways' said Bl. 'but which one of them we don't know without looking.[TN13] From what it says on the map I should say that there is a closed door which looks just like the side of the mountain – the ordinary dwarf's way (I think I am night?)'

'Quite' said Gandalf.[TN14] '[*added*: But] This rather alters things. There are fourteen of us – unless you are coming, Bladorthin. I had thought of going up along Running River from the Long Lake – [if ever we could rea[ch] >] if we can get so far! – and so to the Ruins of Dale Town. But we none of us liked the idea of the Front Gate. The River runs out of that great door, and out of it the Dragon comes too. Far too often.'

'That would have been no good' said Bl. 'without a mighty warrior even a hero. I tried to find one but I had to fall back (I beg your pardon, but I am sure you will understand – [*cancelled*: this] dragon slaying is not I believe your hobby [> speciality]) – to fall back on Mr Baggins [> little Bilbo]'.

'A [> The] burglar' said Dwalin. 'Precisely' said Blad, not allowing Bilbo time to object.[TN15] 'I told you last Thursday it would have to be a burglary not a battle, and a burglar I promised to find – I hope no one is going to say I put the sign on the wrong door again.' He frowned so frightfully at Bilbo that the little man daren't say anything though he was bursting with questions.

'Warriors are very busy fighting one another in far lands' went on Bld. 'and in this neighbourhood [are >] there are none or few left of men dwarves elves or hobbits[TN16] not to speak of heroes. Swords <in the world> are mostly blunt, and axes used for [> on] trees and shields for dishcovers, and dragons comfortably far off. But burglary is <I think> indicated in any case by the <presence> of the back door.'

'What is your plan' then they all said. 'To go to the back door; sit on the step and think of one – if one does [*added*: not] sprout up on the way' said the wizard. 'There is no time to lose – You must be off before day break and well on your way – Dwarves

In the top margin of this sixth and final page of the fragment, Tolkien wrote the following list of dwarves' names:

Dwalin Balin Fili Kili Dori Nori Oi[TN17] Oin & Gloin
Bifur Bofur Bombur Gandalf

It will be noted that all the dwarves are named here, and in the order of their appearance in the typescript made from the now-vanished opening pages of this chapter, even down to the detail of Fili naming himself before Kili (their names being transposed in the final book; cf. DAA.39). From the ink, this list of names probably dates from the original period of composition or shortly thereafter. Much later, probably at the same time as he added the note to the other side of this sheet that it was the 'Only page preserved . . .' (cf. Note I above), Tolkien added the following in pencil at the end of the line:

NB *Gandalf* was originally
Chief Dwarf (=Thorin) and
Gandalf was called Bladorthin.

Here the fragment ends, in mid-sentence at the bottom of a page, and it is probable that no more was written at this stage. But from what we have we can, after the fashion of Sir Thomas Browne,[TN18] make some deductions about the contents of the missing pages that once preceded it; see the commentary that follows.

TEXT NOTES

1 This sentence originally continued with a semicolon followed by the word 'and', but these were cancelled and the period inserted.

2 Originally this was followed by the word 'and' and the beginning of another word that either started with *h-*, *tr-*, or possibly *th-*; these were cancelled at once and the sentence continued as shown.

3 Here 'go out to fetch it' was replaced by '*pretend to* fetch it'. Earlier in the sentence, in the haste of capturing the thoughts before they got away, Tolkien actually wrote 'and more and half a mind', which I have altered editorially to 'and more *than* half a mind'.

4 This sentence was revised to read 'Suddenly he found *the [singing >] music & song had stopped and they were* all looking at him . . .'

5 Tolkien originally began to write 'Bilbo' here – i.e., 'both halves of B[ilbo's mind]'.

6. This appositive, which originally followed 'fellow conspirator' on the next line in the manuscript, was bracketed and marked for insertion at this point. Tolkien originally began the line with 'Dwa' (i.e., Dwa*rves*), which was immediately cancelled; similarly, initially the name 'Bladorthin' was followed by an incomplete phrase ('Bladorthin of the'), but this too was immediately cancelled and we have no way of knowing what the wizard's completed title or derivation might have been.

7 The name of this battle (in the published book simply 'the Battle of the Green Fields') underwent several changes in this earliest manuscript mention. First Tolkien wrote 'the Battle of the' followed by a cancelled, illegible word of four or five letters that ended in *-ll* (possibly 'Bull-'?). Then he resumed with 'Green Fields of Fellin'. Later he cancelled 'Fellin' and wrote 'Fao' above it, but struck this out in turn (probably at once, without completing the word) and replaced it with 'Merria'. None of these names appear elsewhere in the legendarium, the closest approach being the Merrill, one of the rivers of Rivendell (HME VI.205). I cannot identify the meaning of these names, nor the language(s) to which they belong, although Taum Santoski left behind a linguistic note associating *Fellin* with Noldorin *fela* (cave) – cf. Finrod *Felagund* ('Finrod, lord of caves') – and suggesting a connection between *Merria* and Quenya *merka* ('wild'); cf. 'The Etymologies', HME V.381 (under the root PHÉLEG-) and 373 (under the root MERÉK-). In any case, it appears not to have been a direct translation of 'Green Fields', since the Elvish words for 'green' are *laeg* or *calen* (Sindarin) [*Letters* pp. 282 & 382] and *laiqa* (Quenya) ['The Etymologies', HME V.368], respectively, each of which has deep roots to the early days of the mythology.

8 The name 'King Fingolfin' is written in the left margin alongside this line. See pp. 15 & 24–5 for commentary on Tolkien's unexpected use here of this elven name, which in *The Silmarillion* is given to the High King of the Noldor, one of the greatest of the elf-princes fighting in the wars against Morgoth.

9 This long parenthetical kept expanding as Tolkien wrote; originally he intended it to end after 'exaggeration', then after 'any hobbit', but deleted the closing parenthesis each time and in the event failed to ever provide one, so I have added it editorially at what seems the appropriate place.

10 This sentence was altered through deletions to read 'In the meanwhile Bullroarer's gentler descendant was recovering in the drawing room.'

11 The question mark is in the original, and probably indicates Tolkien's uncertainty about the appropriateness of the name. Like the other dwarf-names in this chapter, 'Fimbulfambi' is Old Norse and comes from the *Elder Edda*; see pp. 15 & 24 for the name's source and meaning.

12 Here we have, for the first and only time, the original name for the landmark that plays such a large part in the second half of the book. Tolkien originally wrote 'the Black mountain', then capitalized 'Moun-

tain' and cancelled 'Black' to give just '*the Mountain*', the designation it thereafter retained within the opening chapter; unnamed on the map, it does not gain its full name as the *Lonely* Mountain until early in what is now Chapter III (cf. p. 111 for its first appearance in the draft manuscript, and DAA.87 for the corresponding published text).

Just before the word 'country' later in the same sentence, Tolkien began to write a word which seems to have started with a capital 'K'; if so, then this might be the first (abortive) reference to the Kingdom under the Mountain.

13 The rest of the page, from this point on, is the first map of the Mountain: see the Frontispiece and the commentary beginning on p. 17.

14 Here Tolkien originally began to write a name beginning with *D*, but immediately cancelled it and wrote *Gandalf* instead. While this might have been either Dwalin or Dori, the former is more likely, since the old dwarf had already taken part in the conversation and would do so again a few paragraphs later.

15 Tolkien originally began the next sentence

> 'Yes' said the

then changed this to

> 'It w[ould]

before finally settling on

> 'I told you last Thursday it would have to be a burglary not a battle . . .

16 Tolkien struck a line through part of this sentence: '. . . and there are none or few *left of men dwarves elves and hob*bits not to speak of heroes'. Presumably the cancellation of the word 'left' was inadvertent, and he intended the revised line to read 'and there are none or few left, not to speak of heroes'.

17 Christopher Tolkien reads this name as *Oi* rather than *Ori*, the name we would have expected, and notes (Foreword, page iv; personal correspondence, CT to JDR, 4th November 1994) that *Ái* is a dwarf-name appearing in the *Völuspá*, one of the component poems that make up *The Elder Edda*. See the commentary on the dwarves' names in Appendix III for more on this and other variants.

18 'What song the Sirens sang, or what name Achilles assumed among women, though puzzling questions, are not beyond all conjecture.' – Sir Thomas Browne, *Urn Burial* [1658].

(i)
The Lost Opening

In general structure, the lost opening must have paralleled that of subsequent versions fairly closely, however much it may have differed in detail. We know from other accounts that the opening line was either exactly the same as the familiar one in the published text or some close variation on it: e.g., 'In a hole in the ground lived a hobbit' or even 'At the edge of his hole stood the hobbit' (see 'The Chronology of Composition', pp. xii – xiii). References in the fragment to Bilbo's 'Tookish' side show that the Took/Baggins dichotomy was already well-established, even at this early stage, and the motif of the 'Unexpected Party' is clearly present. The two references to Bilbo as the fourteenth member of the party make it quite clear that Bladorthin's withdrawal from active participation at some point had been foreseen from the outset and was not a later development (although, as we shall see, the exact timing of his departure remained undecided for a considerable time). The dwarves' personalities are, for the most part, much as they remain in later drafts, though it is interesting to note that more of them participate in the discussion than will later be the case. Thus Dwalin, Gloin, Balin, and Gandalf all have speaking parts in rapid succession, and references to Fili and Kili's youth and Oin's having been the one to find the secret mark on Bilbo's door bring more of the full cast into play; Tolkien seems to be trying to make use of the full ensemble of his characters. Later streamlining will reduce the number of dwarven speakers in this passage from four to two, reassigning Dwalin's speech to Gloin and Balin's to Gandalf, retaining the reference to Fili and Kili while dropping all mention of Oin's contribution. While some interesting detail is thus lost, Tolkien's decision to focus the active roles on only a few of the dwarves (primarily Gandalf, Balin, Fili, and Kili, with lesser roles delegated to Dori and Bombur) makes it much easier for someone listening to the story to keep the characters straight. We might regret that some of the dwarves are relegated to such obscurity that they have virtually no speaking parts at all,[1] but overall the story is strengthened by the simplification.

At least one poem, the dwarves' song about their lost treasure, was already part of the story, as may be deduced from the opening line of the fragment. A single line of this song ('To claim our long forgotten gold') survives by chance, thanks to Tolkien's thrifty re-use of paper: he originally wrote this line on the first surviving sheet of the fragment (Marq. 1/1/22:2), then crossed it out, turned the page upside down and over, and used its reversed back (1/1/22:1) to draft the next bit of text (the section immediately following the now-lost poem; i.e., the beginning section of our fragment).

(ii)
Nomenclature in the Pryftan Fragment

The most startling thing about the fragment, from the point of view of readers familiar with the later published text, are the unfamiliar names given to several of the major characters and places: Pryftan instead of Smaug, the Black Mountain and Wild Wood instead of the Lonely Mountain and Mirkwood, Bladorthin instead of Gandalf, and especially Gandalf the dwarf instead of Thorin Oakenshield (son of Thrain son of Thror). Tolkien prided himself on his nomenclature (radio interview with Denys Gueroult, BBC, 1965; see also JRRT to SU, 16th December 1937; *Letters* p. 26), and rightly so; it is a point on which he excels any other writer of fantasy, even Dunsany and Morris – he was able to embrace the exoticism of the one and plainstyle of the other as the occasion warrants without ever losing his own distinctive touch. In point of fact, assigning the name 'Gandalf' to a dwarf and 'Bladorthin' to a wizard is quite appropriate. The dwarf-name comes from the same list in the *Elder Edda*, the *Dvergatal*, that provided the names of all but one of the dwarves who accompany Bilbo on this quest;[2] like them, it is Old Norse. Fimbulfambi, the original name tentatively given to the King under the Mountain, the character who would later become Thror the Old, likewise comes from Old Norse; this time from the bit of eddic lore known as the *Hávamál*.[3] Bladorthin, by contrast, is Elvish[4] – specifically, Sindarin, or 'Noldorin' as it was called at the time (see Note 13 below for the distinction between Gnomish, Noldorin, and Sindarin) – and as such helps distinguish the wizard from his associates, just as the very English-sounding 'Bilbo Baggins' sets the hobbit apart from the rest of the company.[5]

No less surprising is the use of the name *Fingolfin* for the goblin-king killed by Bullroarer Took: the first of many borrowings that explicitly link Mr Baggins's world to that of the mythology. While the name was undoubtedly appropriate in form, containing as it does the key 'golf' element necessary for the joke, it nonetheless comes as a great shock to readers familiar with the great elven-king as he appears in *The Silmarillion*, the 'Sketch of the Mythology', and 'The Lay of Leithian' to have it assigned, even briefly, to a goblin-king.[6]

It seems quite clear that Tolkien is here, as elsewhere in *The Hobbit*, drawing names from already-written tales and fragmentary sketches with little concern for how well their new use corresponds to that of their first appearance. This is quite understandable when we remember that these were, after all, unpublished and mostly unfinished stories known to (at most) two or three other people. We know from other evidence that Tolkien spent a great amount of time crafting names for his characters (in the *Lord of the Rings* papers, an entire page of rough workings survives to show how Tolkien worked his way through over thirty rejected names for his ranger Trotter (i.e., 'Strider') before eventually coming up with *Aragorn*). Any artist might want to find a way to reuse unpublished material arrived at with such effort, and Tolkien was thriftier than most; the totality of his work also has a unity unusual in any author. His mythology filled his mind to the extent that it is no surprise to find him borrowing names, ideas, and themes from it in a new work; indeed, it would be surprising if he did not. As he himself said in 1950, 'though shelved . . . the *Silmarillion* and all that has refused to be suppressed. It has bubbled up, infiltrated, and probably spoiled everything (that even remotely approached "Faery") which I have tried to write since. It was kept out of *Farmer Giles* with an effort, but stopped the continuation. Its shadow was deep on the later parts of *The Hobbit* . . .' (JRRT to SU, 24th February 1950; *Letters* p. 136).

Several other miscellaneous points of the fragment deserve commentary. The golf joke was redoubled by later additions so that the goblin king's death provided the occasion for the creation of not one but two new games for survivors of the battle: golf *and* chess. Fortunately, Tolkien soon thought better of this rather forced jollity and it vanishes without a trace at the next stage, where the original joke was restored to its full glory. References to 'the Water' and Bilbo's map of 'the County Round' (not, note, 'The Shire' – the latter conception did not yet exist) show that the essential neighborhood surrounding Bag-end (already so named) is much as it remains. Indeed, for all the small but significant differences, it is surprising how closely the final story follows this first hasty draft, sometimes even in phrasing. One interesting detail that did not survive is contained in Bladorthin's cancelled line about his efforts to find a hero or warrior to join the expedition, only to discover that the warriors are all 'busy fighting one another in far lands' – echoes of the wars of Beleriand in the Silmarillion tradition, perhaps? – while as for heroes 'in this neighbourhood . . . there are none or few left, of men, dwarves, elves, or hobbits'. The idea of heroic dragon-slaying hobbit warriors is an intriguing one, and may have influenced both the elusive figure in the *Lord of the Rings* manuscripts of Peregrin Boffin, or Trotter, the hobbit ranger who eventually metamorphosed into Strider (cf. HME VI.371 & 385), as well as Tolkien's original plan for the climax of *The Hobbit*, described in Plot Notes B & C, that it would be Bilbo himself who would slay the dragon (see pages 364 & 496).

(iii)
The Geography of the Tale & The First Map

One of the most remarkable things about this fragmentary draft, and one of the ways in which it most differs from the published text, is the casual use of place-names taken from the real world: China, the Gobi Desert, Hindu Kush, even the Shetland Islands (one assumes, from the mention of the ponies). At first, this gives the reader the impression that Mr Baggins' world is a totally different place from the legendary world of *The Silmarillion.* But this impression is deceptive, especially when we consider that in the early stages of the mythology Luthany, the lonely isle later known as Tol Eressëa, was England itself (BLT I.24–5); Kortirion among the trees the city of Warwick; Tavrobel the village in Staffordshire where the Tolkiens lived in the early days of their marriage. As Tolkien originally conceived it, his stories told the mythic history of England and the neighboring lands; a conception he never completely abandoned.[7] Christopher Tolkien warns us time and again in his edition of *The Book of Lost Tales* that just because an element drops out of the later versions of one of his father's stories does not necessarily mean that the conception had been abandoned; often it simply shifted into the background, held in abeyance. The same is undoubtedly true of this element of *The Hobbit.*

That Bilbo's world, the lands of *The Silmarillion*, and our own world are all one (albeit at different points in history) is demonstrable through many of Tolkien's explicit statements:

> 'Middle-earth', by the way, is not a name of a never-never land without relation to the world we live in (like the Mercury of Eddison[8]). It is just a use of Middle English *middel-erde* (or *erthe*), altered from Old English *Middangeard*: the name for the inhabited lands of Men 'between the seas'. And though I have not attempted to relate the shape of the mountains and land-masses to what geologists may say or surmise about the nearer past, imaginatively this 'history' is supposed to take place in a period of the actual Old World of this planet.
>
> —JRRT to Houghton Mifflin Co., 30th June 1955; *Letters* p. 220.

> Those days, the Third Age of Middle-earth, are now long past, and the shape of all lands has been changed; but the regions in which Hobbits then lived were doubtless the same as those in which they still linger: *the North-West of the Old World, east of the Sea.*
>
> —*LotR.* 14; italics mine.

> *The Lord of the Rings* . . . takes place in the Northern hemisphere of this earth: miles are miles, days are days, and weather is weather.
>
> —JRRT to Forrest J. Ackerman, June 1958; *Letters* p. 272.

Thus a real constellation like the Big Dipper (or, as Tolkien preferred to call it, the Sickle), set in the sky by Elbereth 'as a challenge to Melkor . . . and sign of doom' (*Silm*.48) appears on Fimbulfambi's map and can be seen by Frodo in the night sky over Bree (*LotR*.191); the calendars in Appendix D of *The Lord of the Rings* are calculated to fit a planet with exactly Earth's orbit, and so forth. It is dangerous to extrapolate backwards from *The Lord of the Rings* into *The Hobbit*, but it seems safe to conclude that Bilbo's story shares this one characteristic at least with the works that both preceded and follow it: all are assumed to take place in the legendary past of our planet. The 'legendary' part is worth stressing, since Tolkien was writing fantasy, not pseudo-history or pseudoscience à la Ignatius Donnelly or Immanuel Velikovsky. This liberates him from any obligation to make the details of his setting consistent with 'what geologists may say or surmise' and to replace real prehistory (insofar as we know it) with a feigned private history of his own devising.[9] Like the Britain of Geoffrey of Monmouth and Aegidius of Ham, Bilbo's world is full of anachronisms, from policemen on bicycles to mantle clocks; in this *The Hobbit* resembles works like Dunsany's 'The Bird of the Difficult Eye' and 'The Long Porter's Tale' (both in *The Last Book of Wonder* [1916]) more than, say, the neo-medieval romances of William Morris.

If Bilbo's impassioned 'Tookish' speech makes it clear that his world is firmly identified with our own, can it likewise be tied to the imaginative geography of Tolkien's earlier tales? The answer, I believe, can be found by turning to Fimbulfambi's Map. Although differing in significant details from the final version, it is remarkable how many permanent elements were already present and persisted from this first hasty sketch, which shows the mountain laid out two-dimensionally like a starfish. Among these details are the location of the Front Gate (labelled 'FG' on the map), the secret door (marked with an 'F' rune, as promised in Tolkien's footnote on the preceding Ms. page; see p. 9), the 'Ruins of Dale Town', and something of the surrounding countryside: the River Running (which originally had an eastward course), the 'WILD WOOD', and the 'WITHERED HEATH'.

The Mountain's north-east spur was only separated by a brief gap from another height that disappears off the map to the northeast, probably a chain of mountains – a feature that soon vanished from the Lonely Mountain maps (cf. 'Thror's Map I', Plate I [top]) but remains in both the earliest sketch Wilderland map (part of Plot Notes B; see pp. 366–7) and also in the more polished Wilderland Map that accompanied the 'Home Manuscript' (Plate I [bottom]), which brings the Iron Hills down to almost connect with the Lonely Mountain.

Later the original easterly course of the River Running was scratched out and the river is instead made to bend south once it passes the ruins of Dale Town. Several other new features are added as well: Lake Town upon the Long Lake (the former labeled on the map but not mentioned in the text, the latter named in the text but not labeled on the map), Mirkwood (originally along the bottom or southern border of the map, later expanded up the left margin to form the western border and then the whole southwest corner of the map), and the marshes between them. The Forest River, complete with northern bend before it empties into the lake, is present but not named. The addition of all these extra features makes this first map the ancestor not just of Thror's Map but of the larger-scale Wilderland map as well. Finally, a third stage of additions to this map, probably made when the story had reached what is now Chapter XI (i.e., about two years after this first drafting), pencils in the dwarves' first camp just to the west of the mountain's southernmost spur (the height that would later be called Ravenhill). At the same time, Tolkien added the side view of the mountain (also in pencil) in the lower right-hand corner of this page; compare it with the more careful, nuanced version directly based upon it, drawn to accompany the 'Home Manuscript', which is reproduced on Plate II (top).

Mirkwood and the Wild Wood are probably simply two names for the same place: the great primeval forest that once covered most of Europe, one of the remnants of which bears the name the Dark Forest to this day. As Tolkien notes in a letter to his eldest grandson,

> *Mirkwood* is not an invention of mine, but a very ancient name, weighted with legendary associations. It was probably the Primitive Germanic name for the great mountainous forest regions that anciently formed a barrier to the south of the lands of Germanic expansion. In some traditions it became used especially of the boundary between Goths and Huns . . .
>
> —JRRT to Michael George Tolkien, 29th July 1966; *Letters* p. 369.

However, this is not just a borrowing from historical scholarship, as in the case of the dwarf-names (although it is that as well), but also from Tolkien's literary roots: William Morris, perhaps his chief role model as an author, and one of the few whose influence he was proud to acknowledge,[10] used the name Mirkwood in his novel *The House of the Wolfings* [1888] for the name of the great forest where the Germanic woodsmen who are the heroes of the story won a battle against the invading Romans. Furthermore, Carpenter tells us that this book was one of those Tolkien bought with the prize money he received when he won the Skeat Prize for English in the spring of 1914 (Carpenter, p. 69), just at the time when he was creating the first poems of his mythology.

Can Mirkwood or the Wild Wood be tied to any of the great forests in Tolkien's early mythology? Certainly Beleriand itself was originally called 'Broseliand' (later emended to 'Broceliand') in 'The Lay of Leithian'

(HME III.160), the 1930 *Quenta* (HME IV, pages 107–8, 115, 122, 125, and 131), and on the first *Silmarillion* map (ibid., between pages 220 & 221); a name clearly borrowed from the great Forest of Broceliand of Arthurian legend.[11] A much better candidate, however, is Taur-na-Fuin (also known as Taur Fuin or simply Taurfuin), the Forest of Night. Comparison of the first *Silmarillion* map in Volume IV of *The History of Middle-earth* with Fimbulfambi's Map shows a striking parallelism in the former's placement of Taur-na-Fuin and Dor-na-Fauglith, the ruined plain to the north between Beleriand and Thangorodrim also known as Anfauglith, and the latter's Wild Wood and Withered Heath; if the two maps were blended, the Mountain would probably be to the southeast of the highlands later know as Dorthonion, just off the eastern edge of the map, near where Tolkien would later place the Hill of Himring (cf. the published *Silmarillion* map). We are told by Bladorthin that the Withered Heath is 'where the Great Dragons used to live', and I think it more than coincidence that Anfauglith is where Glorund, Ancalagon the Black, and all the rest of Morgoth's dragons are first seen by the outside world.

This parallelism is strengthened by the figure of the Necromancer. In 'The Lay of Leithian' we are told that, after his defeat by Luthien and Huan, Thû the necromancer took the shape of a vampire (that is, a vampire bat) and flew

to Taur-na-Fuin, a new throne
and darker stronghold there to build.
—'The Lay of Leithian', lines 2821–2822; HME III.255.

The *Quenta* (circa 1930) simply states laconically that 'Thû flew in bat's form to Taur-na-Fuin' and that after the destruction of his tower and Felagund's burial there 'Thû came there no more' (HME IV.111). In the published *Silmarillion* [1977] this becomes 'Sauron [= Thû] . . . took the form of a vampire, great as a dark cloud across the moon, and he fled, dripping blood from his throat upon the trees, and came to Taur-nu-Fuin, and dwelt there, filling it with horror' (*Silm.*175). As we shall see (p. 73), a cancelled manuscript reference early in the Second Phase makes explicit that the Necromancer whose tower Beren and Lúthien destroyed and the Necromancer in whose dungeons Bladorthin encountered Gandalf's father are one and the same. Hence the conclusion seems inescapable that Taur-nu-Fuin, the forest to which Thû the necromancer fled to build 'a new throne and darker stronghold' and Mirkwood, where the Necromancer defeated by Beren and Lúthien now dwells at the time of Mr Baggins' story, are one and the same. Its geographical location shifts as the 'Third Age' of Middle-earth slowly takes shape in its own right through the writing of *The Hobbit* itself, eventually (as the second layer of changes to Fimbulfambi's Map show) developing its own landscape that could no longer be fitted easily into the older geography, so that 'Mirkwood' comes to occupy a central position in Wilderland (which now seems quite distinct from Beleriand) closer to that of the Forest of Doriath on the old *Silmarillion* maps rather than Dorthonion (the place of which is eventually taken by the Grey Mountains on the later Wilderland maps).

A final piece of evidence for the original identification between the Mirkwood, Taur-na-Fuin, and the Wild Wood can be found in the illustrations. The first edition of *The Hobbit* featured a halftone of Mirkwood (see Plate VII [top]) that was unfortunately dropped from later reprintings. Comparison of this drawing with a painting Tolkien did of Taur-nu-Fuin (H-S#54) to illustrate the story of Túrin the Hapless shows that the two are identical, tree by tree. Only incidental details have changed: the two elves in the painting are not of course in the later drawing, replaced by a large spider and several extra mushrooms. By itself, this could be taken as just another example of Tolkien's characteristic self-borrowing, but in conjunction with the other evidence, it seems conclusive: the two forests look the same because they *are* the same; the same patch of woods at two different points in its history.

Two curious points about the map itself should be noted. The first is the compass rose:

Fig. 1: The compass rose from Fimbulfambi's Map

The pattern on top is clearly meant to represent the Big Dipper (the dark marks to the left of the constellation as reproduced in the Frontispiece are simply stray stains and splotches on the Ms.), and thus indicates north: the shift in orientation to turn the map on its side and place East at the top would not occur until much later. To the South is the sun. East is indicated by the sun rising above some sort of archway or gate, probably the Gates of Morn mentioned in 'The Tale of the Sun and Moon', which is described as 'a great arch . . . all of shining gold and barred with silver gates' (BLT I.216). West is marked by a three-tiered mountain, possibly meant to suggest the as-yet-unmentioned Misty Mountains (which do indeed lie west of the Lonely Mountain) but more probably the Mountain of the World, Taniquetil, in the Uttermost West. Only some two years earlier Tolkien had painted the magnificent picture of Mount Taniquetil

(H-S#52) featured on the front cover of both the Bodleian centenary exhibition catalogue *J. R. R. Tolkien: Life and Legend* and of *Artist & Illustrator*, having already appeared in *Pictures* (as Plate 31). This famous painting shows Taniquetil as a tall peak surrounded by lesser heights which, in profile, would look very like the small icon on the compass rose.[12]

The other puzzling feature about the map is that it does not, in fact, correspond to the one described in the accompanying text. Specifically, Balin points out 'a picture of a dragon in red on the Mountain', when there is neither dragon or any trace of red ink on this map. Furthermore, Bladorthin quotes the runic inscription, translating it as 'Five feet high is the door, and four [> three] abreast may enter it'. In fact, literally transcribed, the runes on the map itself read as follows:

> FANG THE
> SECRET PASAGE
> OF THE DWARVES

The runic system is the same as that followed in the published *Hobbit* – i.e., Tolkien used the historical Anglo-Saxon runes commonly known as the *futhark* rather than one of his invented alphabets such as the Cirth. The use of 'Fang' here is interesting, because it is an early example of his usage in *The Hobbit* of his invented languages (specifically, Gnomish, the language that eventually evolved into Sindarin).[13] It is also an explicit link of the new story back to Tolkien's earlier legendarium, the tales that were eventually published as *The Silmarillion*. In the earliest version of the legendarium, *The Book of Lost Tales* (1917–20), one of the two races of dwarves is known as the Indra*fang* or 'Longbeards'; indeed, use of the word 'fang' for 'beard' persisted into *The Lord of the Rings* (*Fang*orn, 'Tree-beard'). And, as we shall learn in the third chapter, Gandalf and all his companions belong to the Longbeards, or Durin's Folk as they were later called, a fact first adumbrated by this runic passage.

Below the runes and rather sinister-looking, long-nailed pointing hand was added a version of the text Bladorthin cited, along with the first draft of both the visible message on the map and what became the moon-runes passage:

> five feet high is the door and three may walk abreast
> Stand by the grey stone when the crow knocks and the rising sun [will >] at the moment of dawn on Durin's Day will shine upon the keyhole.

This second sentence was at some later point bracketed; the word 'crow' was replaced with 'thrush' and 'keyhole' changed to just 'key' (but the cancelled part of the word was underlined, possibly indicating it was to be retained after all). Then the whole sentence was cancelled and replaced with the following:

> Stand by the grey stone where the thrush knocks. Then the setting sun on the last light of Durin's Day will shine on the key hole.

The latter, of course, corresponds more closely to Elrond's spontaneous translation of what he reads from the map in Chapter III; see p. 116.

Taken together, these discrepancies in a rough draft text would mean little – even after publication, the words on the map and their translation in the text did not agree until this was put right in the second edition (see p. 749) – were it not for the specific reference to something that's not there; i.e., the image of the dragon in red on the mountain. Given Tolkien's fondness for 'handouts' – actual physical copies of documents seen by his characters, later examples of which include Bilbo's contract (plate two of the Frontispiece) and the pages from the Book of Mazarbul (a similar impulse can be seen expressed in the *Father Christmas Letters*) – it's quite possible that he made a fair copy map that is now lost. Perhaps Tolkien's choice of words in his comment to Auden that 'for some years I got no further than the *production* of Thror's Map' (see p. xii; italics mine) suggests a rather more elaborate map than this rough sketch drawn directly into the pages of the ongoing narrative, but this seems too slender a basis upon which to build much. If it ever existed, the lost map must have been quite similar to the next surviving map (Thror's Map I; see Plate I [top]), which bears the label 'Thror's Map. Copied by B. Baggins', retaining as it does the Northward orientation of Fimbulfambi's Map and representing the Mountain with a very similar style of hatching. Here the runes translated by Bladorthin are in place, and the back of the map has the moon-runes drafted on the first map. Furthermore, the newer map shows the dragon right on the center of the Mountain, exactly as described by Balin, in contrast with the final published version of the map (Thror's Map II), where the dragon is flying above the mountain, not resting on it, and the whole scene has been rotated 90 degrees to place East at the top of the map (contrast Plate I with DAA.50 & 97). But for all that, 'Thror's Map. Copied by B. Baggins' cannot be the map Balin and Bladorthin are referring to, since the proper names written on it (Thror and Thrain) did not arise until near the end of the Second Phase, some two years after the Pryftan Fragment was abandoned.

NOTES

1 For example, Bifur, Bofur, Oin, Ori, and Nori, whose combined dialogue would hardly fill a single page of this book.

2 For more on the *Dvergatal*, an interpolation into the *Völuspá*, the first poem in the *Elder Edda*, see Appendix III.

The sole exception is Balin, whose name is a bit of a mystery; why should his be the only dwarf-name among the party not to come from the list in the Edda? Moreover, in his letter to the *Observer* (Appendix II), Tolkien is explicit that 'the dwarf-names, and the wizard's [i.e., "Gandalf"], are from the Elder Edda.' In the absence of any statement to the contrary, this seems to imply that *all* the dwarf-names should be found in this list, making Balin's conspicuous absence all the more puzzling. Perhaps Tolkien felt that the dwarf-name usually rendered *Vali* (or sometimes *Nali*) should more properly be spelt *Bali* or *Balin*. Or he might have taken the name from *Bláin*, an obscure figure described in the line of the *Völuspá* immediately preceding the dwarf-list proper, said to be a giant from whose legs or bones the dwarves were made. More probably, he borrowed the name from Arthurian legend: Sir Balin was one of the best-known, most tragic, and most unlikable of the early heroes of the Round Table. He is the anti-hero of part two of Malory's *The Tale of King Arthur* (Book I of the work generally known as *Le Morte D'Arthur*); among his more notable achievements are the murder of the Lady of the Lake before the whole court of Camelot, the maiming of the Fisher-King (an act which creates The Waste Land and eventually requires the Grail quest to set right), and the killing of his own brother, Sir Balan, in a duel wherein each takes a mortal wound. If Malory's work is indeed the source from whence Tolkien borrowed the name, he took none of the knight's personality with it, as Balin the dwarf is easily the kindliest of Bilbo's companions.

3 *Hávamál*, strophe 103: *fimbulfambi heitir, saer fatt kann segja*: 'a *fimbulfambi* he is called, who can say little' – i.e., a mighty fool or great idiot. The *fimbul-* element is most famous through its appearance in *Fimbulvter*, the Great Winter whose coming signals the end of the world in Norse tradition. I am grateful to Christopher Tolkien for identifying the source and providing the translation.

4 For the probable meaning of Bladorthin's name, see 'The Name "Bladorthin",' on pp. 52–3.

5 For more on the name 'Bilbo', see pp. 47–8.

6 The story of Fingolfin, like so much else in the mythology, emerged gradually as the many-layered legends evolved. First in the *Lost Tales* we have *Golfinweg*, the Gnomish name for Finwë lord of the Gnomes (BLT I.115 & 132). Then in a prose fragment (probably written soon after 1920) recounting the arrival of the Elven host from Valinor in 'the Great Lands' (i.e., Middle-earth) we find the name *Golfin* given to one of the most prominent characters, the eldest of the three sons and captains of Gelmir, the king of the Gnomes (or Noldor). The fragment ends before we are told much about Golfin's deeds, but it is Christopher Tolkien's conclusion that Gelmir should be identified with Finwë and that 'It is certainly clear that *Golfin* here is the first appearance of Fingolfin' (HME IV.6–8).

The earliest use of the actual name 'Fingolfin' seems to be in the unfinished poem 'The Lay of the Fall of Gondolin' written shortly after the *Lost Tales* period (that is, sometime in the early 1920s). Here we are told of

> . . . Fingolfin, Gelmir's mighty heir.
> 'Twas the bent blades of the Glamhoth that drank Fingolfin's life
> as he stood alone by Fëanor . . .
>
> —HME III.146.

In the 1926 'Sketch of the Mythology', Fingolfin is the eldest son of Finn (= Finwë) and the older brother of Fëanor; in revisions he became Finn's second son, as he thereafter remained right through to the published *Silmarillion*. A reluctant participant in the rebellion of the Noldoli, this Fingolfin returns to Valinor after the Shipburning. In revisions to the 'Sketch', however, he leads the rest of the Host by foot over the Grinding Ice and is slain when Morgoth breaks the 'leaguer of Angband'; here his death takes place quite independently of Fëanor's, who had already been killed by a balrog before Fingolfin's host reached Middle-earth (see HME IV.14–15, 18–19, 22, 24). In a passage of 'The Lay of Leithian' written on 27th and 28th September 1930 (i.e., within a few months of the composition of the Pryftan Fragment), Tolkien describes Fingolfin's duel with Morgoth in epic terms (HME III.284–6, 292) that make the contemporaneous application of the name to a goblin king famous only for his spectacular decapitation all the more remarkable; the only thing the two have in common is the dramatic nature of their deaths.

7 For more on the importance of the real world as a setting underlying Tolkien's imagined prehistory, see my article '"And All the Days of Her Life Are Forgotten": *The Lord of the Rings* as Mythic Prehistory' in the Blackwelder Festschrift (*The Lord of the Rings*, 1954–2004*: Scholarship in Honor of Richard E. Blackwelder*, ed. Wayne G. Hammond & Christina Scull [2006], pages 67–100).

8 'like the Mercury of Eddison' – i.e., the setting of E. R. Eddison's *The Worm Ouroboros* [1922], a book Tolkien greatly admired and from which he borrowed some elements for *The Lord of the Rings*; Eddison himself was twice a guest at the Inklings. Eddison states that his fantasy lands – Demonland, Witchland, Zimiamvia, and the rest – are on the planet Mercury, to which his narrator travels in a dream at the start of the story, but this detail plays no importance to the story and is soon dropped; they are much more like the backdrops to an Elizabethan or Jacobean drama than science fictional.

9 'I cordially dislike allegory in all its manifestations, and always have done so since I grew old and wary enough to detect its presence. *I much prefer history, true or feigned* . . .' – JRRT, quoted in Carpenter, page 189; italics mine.

10 'The Dead Marshes and the approaches to the Morannon owe something to Northern France after the Battle of the Somme. They owe more to William Morris and his Huns and Romans, as in *The House*

of the Wolfings or *The Roots of the Mountains*' (JRRT to Professor L. W. Forster, 31st December 1960; *Letters* p. 303). Much earlier, Tolkien described his earliest surviving attempt at prose fiction by saying that 'I am trying to turn one of the stories [of the *Kalevala*] . . . into a short story somewhat on the lines of Morris' romances with chunks of poetry in between' (JRRT to Edith Bratt, October 1914; *Letters* p. 7). The resulting tale, 'The Story of Kullervo', was the direct inspiration for Tolkien's own tale of Túrin, one of the major component pieces that makes up *The Book of Lost Tales* (cf. Verlyn Flieger, *Interrupted Music: The Making of Tolkien's Mythology* [2005], pages 28–9), and *The Book of Lost Tales* itself strongly resembles the narrative framework of Morris's early masterpiece *The Earthly Paradise* [1865], in which a group of wanderers reach a far land where they exchange stories with their hosts, retelling Norse and Classical legends respectively. If Tolkien is the father of modern fantasy, then Morris and Dunsany are its grandfathers, the chief influences on Tolkien himself.

11 The fact that Tolkien himself had adopted Broceliand into his own mythology helps explain in part his rejection of Charles Williams' notably eccentric use of it in the latter's Arthurian cycle. It also casts an interesting light on Tolkien's comment in 'On Fairy-Stories' on the diminishment (both physically and imaginatively) of fairies in stories of the late sixteenth century: '. . . the great voyages had begun to make the world seem too narrow to hold both men and elves . . . the magic land of Hy Breasail in the West had become the mere Brazils, the land of red-dye-wood' (OFS.11) – 'Breasail' being an Irish variant on the Breton 'Broceliand'.

Within Tolkien's myth, an echo of the name survived even after its displacement by *Beleriand* as the name of the Great Lands, in the name 'Ossiriand', assigned to the extreme eastern portion of the former Broseliand; see also HME III.160, where Christopher Tolkien notes that 'Ossiriand' is twice pencilled alongside lines in 'The Lay of Leithian' as a suggested replacement for 'Broseliand'.

12 Dr Judith Priestman, author of the Bodleian catalogue, notes that the proper name of this picture (item #209 in the exhibition) is 'Halls of Manwe on the Mountains of the World above Faerie' and dates it to July 1928 (Priestman p. 74). Since as we have seen Tolkien probably began *The Hobbit* in the summer of 1930 (cf. 'The Chronology of Composition', p. xiii), this image would still have been quite fresh in his mind at the time he wrote the Pryftan Fragment and drew this first map.

13 For more on the relationship between Gnomish (i.e., the language of the Gnomes or Noldor), Noldorin (the slightly later form of the same language), and Sindarin (the final form of that language, now conceived not as the tongue brought back to Middle-earth by the Noldor but that of the Sindar who were already there), see p. 562 & ff. Technically the language was known as 'Noldorin' at the time Tolkien wrote *The Hobbit*, but in order to avoid confusing the nonphilological I have generally

used 'Gnomish' to mean the early (BLT-era) form of the language, as attested in *The Book of Lost Tales* and *The Gnomish Lexicon*, 'Noldorin' to mean the same language as reflected in the manuscript of *The Hobbit* from the early 1930s, and 'Sindarin' to mean the 'classical' form of the same language as it is reflected in the published *Hobbit* and in *The Lord of the Rings*.

For more on this ever-evolving language, see *The Gnomish Lexicon* (*Parma Eldalamberon* vol. XI [1995]) [Gnomish]; *The Lhammas* or 'Account of Tongues' (HME V.167–98 [1987]) and *Early Noldorin Fragments* (*Parma Eldalamberon* vol. XIII [2001]) [Noldorin]; *A Gateway to Sindarin* by David Salo [2004] [Sindarin], and the essay 'Gnomish *Is* Sindarin' by Christopher Gilson (*Tolkien's Legendarium: Essays on The History of Middle-earth* [2000], pages 95–104), which testifies to the continuity of the language despite shifting conceptions about its speakers.

Chapter I(b)

THE BLADORTHIN TYPESCRIPT

At some point before the first few pages of the Pryftan Fragment were lost, Tolkien made the following typescript (Marq. 1/1/27:1–12). Only twelve pages long, the portion near the end that overlaps the surviving pages of the manuscript shows that it follows the first rough draft very closely, incorporating changes and corrections jotted onto the Ms. pages, along with a few further revisions made in the course of typing (mainly slight improvements of phrasing and substitutions to avoid repetition). This, and the fact that the names have not yet undergone any changes (for example, the dragon's name is still 'Pryftan' and 'Fingolfin' is the goblin king), suggests it was made very shortly after the manuscript itself, probably as fair copy. This typescript is, then, the closest approximation we have to the lost opening and marks the fullest extent of the First Phase of the book's composition. The typescript was, typically, later revised itself, but I give it here as it was originally typed, aside from silently incorporating Tolkien's corrections of typos and omitted words necessary for the sense; the more interesting revisions are noted in the textual notes, followed by the commentary. A few eccentric spellings have been preserved, where they might be indications of pronunciations (e.g., 'particularrly').

The chapter originally had no title, but much later 'Chapter I: An Unexpected Party' was added to the first page.

In a hole in the ground there lived a hobbit. Not a nasty dirty wet hole filled with the ends of worms and an oozy smell, nor yet a dry bare sandy hole with nothing in it to eat or to sit down on; it was a hobbit's hole, and that means comfort. It had a perfectly round door like a porthole, painted green with a shiny yellow knob in the exact middle; and the door opened onto a tubeshaped hall like a tunnel, but a very comfortable tunnel without smoke, and lit by rows of little red lights and provided with polished seats against the walls and lots and lots of pegs for hats and coats: the hobbit was fond of visitors. The tunnel wound on and on, going fairly straight but not quite, under the hill (The Hill as all the people for many miles round called it), and many little round doors opened out first on one side then on another. No going upstairs for the hobbit: bedrooms, bathrooms, cellars, pantries (lots of these), wardrobes (he had whole rooms devoted to clothes), kitchens, dining rooms, all were on the same floor, and indeed on the same passage.

This hobbit was a very well-to-do hobbit and his name was Baggins. The Bagginses had lived in the neighbourhood of the Hill for time out of mind, and people considered them very respectable, not least because they never had any adventures, or did anything unexpected: you could tell what a Baggins would say about any question almost without the bother of asking him. This is the story of how a Baggins had an adventure and found himself doing things altogether unexpected; he lost the neighbours' respect, but he gained – well, you will see whether he gained anything in the end.

The mother of this hobbit – what is a hobbit? I meant you to find out, but if you must have everything explained at the beginning, I can only say that hobbits are small people, smaller than dwarves (and they have no beards), and on the whole larger than lilliputians. There is little or no magic about them, except the ordinary everyday sort which helps them to disappear quietly and quickly when ordinary big people like you or me come blundering along, making a noise like elephants which they can hear a mile off; they are inclined to be fat in the tummy, dress in bright colours (chiefly green and yellow), wear no shoes because their feet grow natural leathery soles and thick warm brown hair like the stuff on their heads (which is curly), have long clever brown fingers, goodnatured faces, and laugh deep fruity laughs (especially after dinner, which they have twice a day when they can get it). Now you know quite enough to go on with. The mother of this hobbit (of Bilbo Baggins, that is) was the famous Belladonna Took one of the three remarkable daughters of the Old Took, head of the hobbits who lived across the Water. It had always been said that long ago some or other of the Tooks had married into a fairy family (goblin family said severer critics); certainly there was something not entirely hobbitlike about them, and once in a while members of the Took hobbits would go and have adventures. They discreetly disappeared and the family hushed it up, but the fact remained that the Tooks were not as respectable as the Bagginses, though they were undoubtedly richer. Not that Belladonna Took ever had any adventure other than becoming Mrs Bungo Baggins and making Bungo (Bilbo's father) build the most luxurious hobbit-hole either under the Hill or over the Hill or across the Water. But it is possible that Bilbo, her only son, although he looked and behaved exactly like a second edition of his father, got through her something a bit queer from the Tooks, something that only waited for a chance to come out. And it never got its chance until Bilbo Baggins was grown up and living in the beautiful hole that I have just described to you, and in fact had settled down.

By some curious chance one morning long ago in the quiet of the world when there was less noise and more green and the hobbits were still numerous and prosperous, and Bilbo Baggins was standing at his door after breakfast smoking an enormous long wooden pipe that reached down nearly to his woolly toes (neatly brushed), Bladorthin came by. Bladorthin! If you had heard only a quarter of what I have (and I have heard only a little tiny bit of what there is to hear) about him you would be prepared for any sort of remarkable tale. Tales and adventures sprouted up all over the place wherever he went in the most extraordinary fashion. He hadn't been down this way under the Hill for ages and ages, and the hobbits had almost forgotten what he looked like; he had been away over the Hill and across the Water since their grandfather's time at least. All the unsuspecting Bilbo saw was a little old man with a tall pointed blue hat, a long grey cloak, a silver scarf over which his long white beard hung down below his waist, and immense black boots. 'Good morning' said Bilbo, and he meant it: the sun was shining and the grass was very green. But Bladorthin looked at him from under very long bushy eyebrows that stuck out farther than the brim of his shady hat.

'What do you mean' he said. 'Do you wish me a good morning, or mean that it is a good morning, or that you feel good this morning, or that it is a morning to be good on?'

'All of them at once' said Bilbo. 'And a very fine morning for a pipe of baccy out of doors into the bargain. If you have a pipe about you sit down and have a fill of mine; there's no hurry, you have got all the day in front of you!' And Bilbo sat down on a seat by his door, crossed his legs and blew out a beautiful grey ring of smoke that sailed up in the air without breaking and floated away over the Hill.

'Very pretty; but I have no time to blow smoke-rings, I am on the way to an adventure, and I am looking for some one to share it – very difficult to find'.

'I should think so – in these parts. We are plain quiet folk, and have no use for adventures. Nasty disturbing, uncomfortable things, make you late for dinner; can't think what anybody sees in them', said our Mr Baggins and stuck his thumbs in his waistcoat pockets and blew out another and even bigger smoke-ring. Then he took out his letters and began to read, pretending to take no more notice of the little old man; he had decided that he was not quite his sort, and wanted him to go away. But the old man didn't move. He stood leaning on his stick and gazing at the hobbit without saying anything, until he got quite uncomfortable and even a little cross.

'Good morning' the hobbit said at last. 'We don't want any adventures here, thank you. You might try over the Hill or across the Water'. By which he meant that the conversation was at an end.

'What a lot of things you do use "good morning" for' said Bladorthin. 'Now you mean you want to get rid of me, and that it won't be good until I move off!'

'Not at all, not at all! my dear sir (I don't think I know your name)'.

'Yes, yes! my dear sir – and I do know your name, Mr Bilbo Baggins, and you know mine though you don't know that I belong to it. I am Bladorthin and Bladorthin means me! And to think that I should have lived to be good-morninged by Belladonna Took's son, as if I were selling buttons at the door!'

'Bladorthin? Bladorthin? Let me see – not the wandering wizard who gave Old Took a pair of magic diamond studs that fastened themselves and never came undone – not the fellow who turned the dragon of the Far Mountains inside out, and rescued so many princesses, earls, dukes, widow's sons and fair maidens from unlamented giants – not the man who made such particularrly excellent fireworks (I remember them! Old Took used to let us have them on Midsummer's Eve. Splendid! They used to go up like great lilies and snapdragons and laburnums of fire and hang in the twilight all evening) dear me! – not the Bladorthin who was responsible for so many quiet lads and lasses going off into the blue for mad adventures, everything from climbing trees to stowing away aboard the ships that sail to the Other Side. Dear me, life used to be quite inter – I mean you used to upset things badly in these parts a while ago. I beg your pardon – but I had no idea you were still in business.'

'Where else should I be? I am pleased to see that you remember something about me. You seem to remember the fireworks kindly at any rate, and that is not without hope. Indeed for your Old grandfather Took's sake, and for the sake of poor Belladonna, I will give you what you have asked for'.

'I beg your pardon, I haven't asked for anything!'

'Yes you have. Twice. My pardon! I give it you. In fact I will go so far as to take you on my present adventure with me. Very amusing for me, very good for you.'

'Sorry. I don't want any adventures, thank you. Good morning. But please come to tea or dinner (beautiful dinner!) any time you like. Why not tomorrow? Come tomorrow! Good bye!' And the hobbit turned and scuttled inside his round green door, and shut it as quickly as he dared not to seem rude. 'What on earth did I ask him to tea for?' he thought to himself as he went to the pantry. He had only just had breakfast, but he thought a cake or two and something to drink would do him good after his fright. Bladorthin in the meanwhile was still standing outside the door and laughing long but quietly. After a while he stepped up and made a little magic sign on the hobbit's beautiful green front door and then he strode away, just about the time that the hobbit was finishing his second cake and beginning to think that he had escaped adventures very well.

The next day he had almost forgotten about Bladorthin. He didn't remember things very well unless he put them down on his engagement tablet (thus 'Bladorthin, tea Wednesday'), and yesterday he had been too flustered to do anything of the sort. Just before tea-time there came a tremendous ring at the front-door bell, and then he remembered! He rushed and put on the kettle and put out another cup and saucer and an extra cake or two, and went to the door.

'I am so sorry to keep you waiting' he was going to say, when he saw that it wasn't Bladorthin at all. It was a dwarf with a blue beard tucked into a golden belt, and very bright eyes under his dark green hood, and as soon as the door was open he pushed inside just as if he had been expected. He hung his hood on the nearest peg, and 'Dwalin at your service' he said with a bow.

'Bilbo Baggins at yours' said the hobbit, too surprised to say anything else. When the silence had become uncomfortable he added: 'I am just going to have tea; pray come and have some with me' – a little stiff perhaps but he meant it kindly; and what would you do if a dwarf came and hung his hat up in your hall without a word of explanation! They had not been at the table long, in fact they had hardly reached the third cake, when there came another even louder ring at the bell.

'Excuse me' said the hobbit, and off he went to the door. 'So you've got here at last' was what he was going to say to Bladorthin this time. But it wasn't Bladorthin. There was a very old-looking dwarf there with a yellow beard and a scarlet hood, and he too hopped inside as soon as the door was half open, just as if he had been invited.

'I see some of the others have come'[TN1] he said when he saw Dwalin's hood on the peg. He hung his yellow[TN2] one next to it, and 'Balin at your service' he said with his hand on his breast. 'Thank you' said Bilbo with a gasp. It was the wrong thing to say, but 'some of the others' had put him in a fright. He liked visitors, but he liked to know them before they arrived and he preferred to ask them himself. He had a horrible thought that the cakes might run short, and then he (as the host – he knew his duty as the host and stuck to it however painful) would have to go without.

'Come along in to tea' he managed to say after taking a deep breath.

'A little beer would suit me better, if it is all the same to you, my good sir' said Balin with the Yellow Beard, 'but I don't mind some cake – seed-cake if you have any'.

'Lots' Bilbo found himself answering to his own surprise, and scuttling off to the cellar to fill a pint beer-mug, and to the pantry to fetch two beautiful seed-cakes which he had baked that afternoon for his after-supper morsel.

Balin and Dwalin were talking like old friends at the table (as a matter of fact they were brothers, but he didn't know though he ought to have done) when he got back. He plumped down the beer and the cake, when loudly there came a ring at the bell [,] and then another. 'Bladorthin this time, for sure' he thought as he puffed along the passage. But it wasn't. It was two more dwarves, both with blue hoods, silver belts, and white beards; and both carried a bag of tools and a spade.

In they hopped as soon as the door began to open – Bilbo was quite expecting it. 'What can I do for you, my dwarves' he said.

'Fili at you service' said the one; 'and Kili' added the other, and they both swept off their blue hoods.[TN3]

'At yours and your family's' said Bilbo, remembering his manners this time.

'Dwalin and Balin here already I see' said Kili. 'Let us join the throng!'

'Throng!' thought the hobbit, 'I don't like the sound of that. I really must sit down for a minute and collect my wits and have a drink'. He had only just had a sip (in the corner while the dwarves sat round the table, and talked all about mines and gold and jewels and troubles with the goblins and the depredations of dragons, and lots of other things that he didn't understand, and didn't want to – they sounded highly adventurous) when, ding-dong-a-ling-lang, his bell rang again as if some naughty little hobbit-boy was trying to pull the handle off.

'Someone at the door' he said.

'Some four, I should say by the sound' said Fili, 'besides we saw them coming along in the distance behind us'.

And the poor little hobbit sat down in the hall and put his head in his hands, and [*added*: wondered] what had happened and what was going to happen and whether they would stay to supper.

Then the bell rang again louder than ever, and he had to run to the door. It wasn't four it was five; another one had come up while he was wondering. He had hardly turned the knob before they were all inside bowing and saying 'at your service' one after the other. Dor[i], Nori, Ori, Oin, and Gloin were their names, and very soon two purple hoods, a grey hood, a brown hood, and a white hood were hanging on the pegs, and off they marched with their broad hands stuck in their gold and silver belts to join the others. Some called for ale and some for stout, and one for coffee, and all of them for cake; and so the hobbit was kept very busy for a while. A big jug of coffee was just set in the hearth and the seed-cakes were almost gone, when there came – a loud knock. Not a ring, but a hard rat-tat on the hobbit's beautiful green door; somebody was banging with a stick. Bilbo rushed along the passage very angry and altogether bewildered and bewuthered (this was the most awkward Wednesday he ever remembered), and he pull[ed] open the door with a jerk. They all fell in one on top of the other. More dwarves; four more. And there was Bladorthin standing behind with his stick. He had made quite a dent in the beautiful door and, by the way, had knocked out the magic mark that he put there on the yesterday morning.

'Carefully, carefully' he said. 'This is not like you, Bilbo, to keep friends waiting and then open the door like a pop-gun. Let me introduce Bifur, Bofur, Bombur, and Gandalf'.

'At your service' they said, all standing in a row. Then they hung up two yellow hoods, a pale green one, and a sky-blue one with a silver tassel. This belonged to Gandalf, a very important dwarf,[TN4] and he wasn't very pleased at falling flat on Bilbo's mat with Bifur, Bofur and Bombur on top of him; but the hobbit said he was sorry so many times, that he forgave him.

'We are all here now' said Bladorthin, looking at the row of twelve[TN5] hoods on the pegs. 'Quite a merry party. I hope you have left something for us to eat and drink. What's that? Tea? No thank you. A little red wine, I think, if you don't mind, for me'.

'And for me' said Gandalf.

'And raspberry jam and apple-tart' said Bifur.

'And mince pies and cheese' said Bofur.

'And pork-pie and salad' said Bombur.

'And more beer – and tea – and coffee – if you don't mind' called the other dwarves [through][TN6] the door.

'Put on a few eggs, there's a good fellow' Bladorthin called after him, as the hobbit stumped off to the pantries; 'and just bring out the cold chicken and tomatoes'.

'Seems to know as much about the inside of my larder as I do myself' thought Mr Bilbo Baggins, who was now feeling positively flummuxed, and beginning to wonder whether a wretched adventure hadn't come right to his house. By the time he had all the bottles and dishes and knives and forks and plates and spoons and things piled up on big trays, he was beginning to feel very hot and red in the face and annoyed.

'Confusticate' (he was annoyed, I told you) 'and bebother those dwarves' he said aloud, 'why don't they come and lend a hand'.

Lo! and behold there stood Dwalin and Fili at the door of the kitchen, and Kili behind them; and before he could say 'knife' they had whisked the trays into the parlour, and set out the table all afresh.

Bladorthin sat at the head of the table and the twelve dwarves all round, and Bilbo sat on a stool at the fireside, nibbling a biscuit,[TN7] and trying to look as if this was all quite ordinary and not at all an adventure.

The dwarves ate and ate, and talked and talked, and time got on. At last they pushed their chairs back, and Bilbo made [a] move to collect the crocks.

'I suppose you will all stay to supper' he said in his politest unpressing tones.

'Of course' said Gandalf, 'and afterwards. We shan't get through the business till late, and we must have some music first. Now to clear up!'

Thereupon all the twelve dwarves (Gandalf was too important; he stayed talking to Bladorthin) got up and piled the things in tall piles. Off they went not waiting for trays, balancing columns of plates with bottles on the top on one hand, while the hobbit ran after them saying 'please be careful' and 'please don't trouble, I can manage' one after another. But the dwarves only started to sing:

Chip the glasses and crack the plates!
Blunt the knives and bend the forks!
That's what Bilbo Baggins hates –
Smash the bottles and burn the corks!

Cut the cloth and tread on the fat!
Pour the milk on the pantry floor!
Leave the bones on the bedroom mat!
Splash the wine on the cellar door!

Put the things in a boiling bowl
Pound them up with a thumping pole,
And when you've finished, if any are whole,
Send them down the hall to roll

That's what Bilbo Baggins hates –
So careful, carefully with the plates!![TN8]

And of course they did none of these dreadful things, and everything was put away quite safe while the hobbit was turning round and round in the middle of the kitchen trying to see what they were doing. Then they went back, and found Dwalin[TN9] with his feet on the fender with a pipe. He was blowing the most enormous smoke-rings, and wherever he told one to go it went – up the chimney or behind the clock on the mantelpiece or under the table or round and round the ceiling; but wherev[e]r it went it was not quick enough to escape Bladorthin. Pop! he sent a smaller one straight through it from his short clay pipe. Then Bladorthin's smoke-ring would go green with the joke and come back to hover over the wizard's head. He had quite a cloud of them about him already, and it made him look positively sorcerous.

Bilbo stood still and watched – he loved smoke-rings – and then he blushed to think how proud he had been yesterday morning of the smoke-ring he had sent up the wind over the Hill.

'Now for some music' said Gandalf. 'Bring out the instruments!'

Kili and Fili rushed for their bags and brought back little fiddles; Dori, Nori and Ori brought out flutes from somewhere inside their coats; Bombur produced a drum from nowhere; Bifur and Bofur went into the hall and came back with [their] walking-sticks and turned them into clarinets; Dwalin and Balin said 'excuse us we left ours in the porch'. 'Just bring mine in with you' said Gandalf. They came back with viols nearly as big as themselves, and with Gandalf's harp in a green cloth. It was a beautiful golden harp, and when Gandalf struck it the music began all at once, so sudden and sweet that Bilbo forgot everything else, and was swept away into dark lands under strange moons far over the Water and very far away from his hobbit-hole under the Hill.

The dark came into the room from the little window that opened in the side of the Hill; the firelight flickered – it was April – and still they played on, while the shadow of Bladorthin's beard wagged against the wall.

The dark filled all the room, and the fire died down, and the shadows were lost, and still they played on. And suddenly first one and then another began to sing as they played, deepthroated singing of the dwarves in the deep places of their ancient homes, and this is like a fragment of their song, if it can be like their song without their music.

Far over the misty mountains cold
To dungeons deep and caverns old
We must away, ere break of day,
To seek the pale enchanted gold.

The dwarves of yore made mighty spells,
As hammers fell like ringing bells
In places deep, where dark things sleep,
In hollow halls beneath the fells.

For ancient king and elvish lord
There many a gleaming golden hoard
They shaped and wrought; and light they caught
To hide in gems on hilt of sword.

On silver necklaces they strung
The flowering stars, on crowns they hung
The dragon-fire, in twisted wire
They meshed the light of moon and sun.

Far over the misty mountains cold
To dungeons deep and caverns old
We must away, ere break of day,
To claim our pale enchanted gold.

And cups they carved there for themselves
And harps of gold; where no man delves
There lay they long, and many a song
Was sung unheard of men or elves.

The pines were roaring on the height,
The winds were moaning in the night
The fire was red, it flaming spread;
The trees like torches blazed with light.

The bells were ringing in the vale
And men looked up with faces pale;
The dragon's ire more fierce than fire
Laid low their towers and houses frail.

The mountain smoked beneath the moon;
The dwarves, they heard the tramp of doom.
They fled their hall to dying fall
Beneath his feet, beneath the moon.

Far over the misty mountains grim
To dungeons deep and caverns dim
We must away, ere break of day,
To take our harps and gold from him![TN10]

As they sang the hobbit felt the love of beautiful things made by hands and by cunning and by magic moving through him, a fierce and jealous love, the desire of the hearts of dwarves. Then something Tookish woke up inside him and he wished to go and see the great mountains and hear the pinetrees and the waterfalls and explore the caves and wear a sword instead of a walking-stick. He looked out of the window. The stars were out in a dark sky above the trees. He thought of the jewels of the dwarves shining in dark caves. Suddenly in the wood beyond the Water a flame leapt up – somebody lighting a wood-fire, probably – and he thought of plundering dragons settling on his quiet Hill and kindling it all to flames. He shuddered, and very quickly he was plain Mr Baggins of Bag-End Under-Hill again.

He got up trembling; he had less than half a mind to fetch the lamp, and more than half a mind to pretend to, and go and hide behind the beer-barrel in the cellar and not come out again until all the dwarves had gone. Suddenly he found that the music and the singing had stopped and they were all looking at him with eyes shining in the dark.

'Where are you going?' said Gandalf, in a tone that seemed to show that he guessed both halves of the hobbit's mind.

'What about a little light?' he said apologetically.

'We like the dark' all the dwarves said. 'Dark for dark business! There are many hours before dawn'.

'Of course' said Bilbo and sat down in a hurry. He missed the stool and sat in the fender, knocking the poker and shovel over with a crash.

'Hush!' said Bladorthin. 'Let Gandalf speak!' And this is how he began.

'Bladorthin, dwarves and Mr Baggins, we are met together in the house of our friend and fellow conspirator, this most excellent and audacious hobbit – may the hair on his toes never grow less! – all praise to his wine and ale! –' He paused for breath and for a polite remark from the hobbit, but the praise was quite lost on poor Bilbo Baggins, who was wagging his mouth in protest at being called audacious and worst of all 'fellow conspirator'; but no noise would come he was so upsettled. So he went on:

'We are met to discuss our plans, our ways means, policy and devices. We shall soon, before the break of day, start on our long journey, a journey from which some of us, or perhaps all of us (except our friend and counsellor, the ingenious wizard Bladorthin), may never return. It is a solemn moment. The object is, I take it, well known to us all. To the estimable Mr Baggins, and to one or two of the younger dwarves (I think I should be right in naming Kili and Fili, for instance), the exact situation at the moment may require a little brief explanation –'

This was Gandalf's style – he was an important dwarf –; in the end he would probably have gone on like this, without telling anybody anything that he didn't know already, until he was out of breath. But this time he was rudely interrupted. Poor Bilbo couldn't bear it any longer. At 'may never return' he began to feel a shriek coming up inside, and very soon after it burst out like the whistle of an engine coming out of a tunnel.[TN11] All the dwarves sprang up, knocking over the table. Bladorthin struck a blue light on the end of his magic staff, and in its firework-glare the poor little hobbit could be seen kneeling on the hearthrug shaking like a jelly that was melting. Then he fell flat, and there he kept on calling out 'struck by lightning, struck by lightning' over and over again; and that was all they could get out of him for a long while.[TN12] So they took him and laid him out of the way on the drawingroom sofa, with a lamp and a drink beside him, and they went back to their dark business.

'Excitable little man' said Bladorthin, as they sat down again. 'Gets funny queer fits but he is one of the best, one of the best – as fierce as a dragon in a pinch'. If you have [ever] seen a dragon in a pinch you will realize that this was only poetical exaggeration applied to any hobbit – even to Old Took's great-uncle Bullroarer, who was so large that he could just ride a shetland pony, and charged the ranks of the goblins of Mount Gram in the Battle of the Green Fields. He knocked their king Fingolfin's[TN13] head clean off with a wooden club; it sailed a hundred yards through the air and went down a rabbit-hole, and in this way the battle was won and the game of Golf invented at the same moment.

In the meanwhile, however, Bullroarer's gentler descendant was reviving in the drawing-room. After a while, and a drink, he crept nervously to the door of the parlour. This is what he heard: Dwalin speaking.

'Humph! will he do it, d'you think? It is all very well for Bladorthin to talk about this hobbit being fierce, but one shriek like that in a moment of excitement would be enough to wake the dragon and all his relatives and kill the lot of us. Personally, I think there was more fright in it than excitement, and if it hadn't been for the secret sign on the door, I should have been sure I had come to the wrong house. As soon as I clapped eyes on the little fellow bobbing and puffing on the mat I had my doubts. He looks more like a grocer than a burglar!'[TN14]

Then Mr Baggins turned the handle and walked in. Took had won. He felt he would go [*added*: without] bed and breakfast to be thought fierce. As for 'little fellow bobbing on the mat' it almost made him feel really fierce. Many a time afterwards the Baggins part regretted what he did now, and he said to himself 'Bilbo, you were a fool, you walked right in and put your foot in it'. He did.

'Pardon me' he said 'if I have overheard some words that you were saying. I don't pretend to understand what you are all talking about, but I think I am right in believing' (this is what is called 'being on one's dignity') 'that you think I am no good. I will show you. I have no magic signs on my door – it was painted a week ago – and I am sure you have all come to the wrong house; as soon as I saw your funny faces on the door-step I had my doubts. But treat it as the right one. Tell me what you want me to do, and I will try it, if I have to walk from here to the last desert in the East and fight the Wild Wireworms of the Chinese. I had a great-great-great-uncle, Bullroarer Took, and –'[TN15]

'We know, we know' said Gloin (he was very fond of golf); 'holed out in one on the Green Fields! But I assure you the mark was on the door – "Burglar wants a good Job, plenty of Excitement and reasonable Reward" it means – it was there last night. Oin found it, and we all came tonight as soon as we could get together; for the mark was fresh. Bladorthin told us there was a man of the sort in this neighbourhood, and that he was seldom out of a job'.

'Of course' said the wizard. '[I] put the mark there myself. For very good reasons. I chose Mr Baggins for your fourteenth man, and let any one say I chose the wrong man who dares. If any one does you can stop at thirteen and have all the bad luck you like, or go back to digging coal. Bilbo, my boy' (he went on, turning to the hobbit), 'fetch the lamp and let's have a little light on this matter.'[TN16]

On the table in the light of a big lamp with a red shade he spread a parchment map.

'This I got from your grandfather, Gandalf' he said in answer to the dwarves' excited grunts. 'It shows the Mountain and the surrounding country. Here it is. Over there is the Wild Wood, and far beyond it to the North, only the edge of it is on the map, is the Withered Heath where the Great Dragons used to be'.

'We know all that' said Balin. 'I don't see that this will help us much. There is a picture of a Dragon in red on the Mountain, but it will be easy enough to find him without any picture – if ever we arrive at the Mountain'.[TN17]

'There is one point which you haven't noticed' said the wizard 'and that is the secret entrance. You see that rune* on the East side, and the hand pointing from it from the runes below? That marks the old secret entrance to the Lower Halls'.

Typed in the margin and marked for insertion at this point is the following authorial aside:

* Don't ask what that is. Look at the map and you will see.

'It may have been secret once' said Gandalf 'but why should it be any longer? Old Pryftan[TN18] has lived there long enough now to find out anything there is to know about those caves'.

'He may – but he can't have used it for years and years'.

'Why?'

'Because it is too small. "Five feet high is the door and three abreast may enter it" say the runes, but Pryftan could not creep into a hole that size, not even when he was a very young dragon, certainly not after he had devoured so many of the maidens of the valley'.

'It seems a great big hole' squeaked Bilbo (who had no experience of Dragons and only of hobbit-holes). He was getting excited and interested, so he forgot to be shy and keep his

The typescript ends here, at the bottom of the twelfth page but not, interestingly enough, the end of a line. The text is continued, resuming in the middle of the same sentence, by the first page of the Second Phase manuscript, Marq. 1/1/1:3, which continues the pagination of the Bladorthin Typescript; see p. 70.

TEXT NOTES

1 'some of the others have come' was later changed to the more precise '*one* of *them has come already!*'

2 The colour of Balin's hood was changed in ink from *yellow* to *red* (to match the mention of his 'scarlet hood' in the preceding paragraph), but this slip was probably not corrected until a much later date than the others noted in this section; not only is it made in a different colour of ink than that used in most of the other revisions to this typescript but Balin's hood is still mistakenly described as 'yellow' as late as Chapter VI (see pp. 198 & 210–11).

3 Note that here Fili names himself first, rather than Kili, just as in the list of names written across the top of the last page of the Pryftan fragment (see p. 11); the order was reversed in the Third Phase typescript (Marq. 1/1/51:6) and all subsequent texts, including the published book (DAA.39).

4 Added in the later ink: 'in fact none other than the great Thorin Oakenshield'. Since the name 'Thorin' did not arise in the Ms. until a much later stage – in fact, the arrival at Lake Town in Chapter X, although it had been suggested in Plot Notes A, written during the drafting of Chapter VII (see p. 293) – this is another late addition, made long after the original typescript.

5 Both here and at the next occurrence (when they all sit down to dinner), 'twelve' is corrected to 'thirteen'.

6 The word 'through' is hand-written over an erasure, but whatever word was originally typed here has been completely obliterated.

7 American readers should take note that the 'biscuit' Bilbo nibbles on is not a flaky wheat roll leavened with baking soda but a cookie (one

of the few points where English and American usage diverge, so far as understanding the book goes).

8 This, the first of what would be many poems in *The Hobbit*, appears here already in nearly final form, clearly preceded by drafting that does not survive (presumably in the lost pages of the Pryftan Fragment, although we cannot be certain it was included). Aside from minor adjustments to punctuation only three lines have any variants: (1) in the second half of line 8 'the cellar' would be replaced with 'every' ('Splash the wine on *every* door!'), (2) in the first half of line 9, 'Put the things' would be replaced by the more colourful 'Dump the crocks' ('*Dump the crocks* in a boiling bowl'), and (3) in the last line, 'careful, carefully' is replaced by 'carefully! carefully' ('So, careful*ly!* carefully with the plates!'). All these changes already appear in the next text of the poem, that appearing in the First Typescript (Marq. 1/1/51:8).

9 'Dwalin' was emended to 'Gandalf', a change necessitated by the fact that Dwalin, like the other twelve, was busy with the washing up; only Gandalf had stayed behind. The rather more prominent role Dwalin played in the First Stage texts may be due to his name having been taken from one of the most famous of all dwarves in Norse lore, *Dvalin*. As Christopher Tolkien notes in his edition and translation of *Heidreks Saga*,

> Dwalin seems to have been one of the most renowned of all dwarfs, and often appears in the Eddaic poetry (especially *Vǫlospá* 14, *Fáfnismál* 13, *Hávamál* 143).
>
> —*The Saga of King Heidrek the Wise* [1960], page 15.

In 'The Waking of Angantyr', one of several ancient poems incorporated into the much later (late twelfth/early thirteenth century) prose saga,† it is said that the cursed sword Tyrfing was forged by Dvalin (ibid., page 15). An alternate opening of the saga given as an appendix to Christopher Tolkien's edition gives the full story of how Dvalin and Durin, 'the most skillful of all dwarfs', were captured and forced to forge a magnificent magical sword, upon which they put a curse (*The Saga of King Heidrek the Wise*, page 68); the saga is essentially the story of the subsequent owners of the cursed sword. It is ironic that in Norse lore Dvalin was far better known than Durin, whereas through Tolkien's usage in *The Hobbit* and *The Lord of the Rings* that situation has now reversed.

† another being 'The Battle of the Goths and Huns', a probable remote inspiration for the character Éowyn in *The Lord of the Rings*.

10 Several small changes were made to the poem: '*to claim our long forgotten gold*' is written in the margin alongside the line '*To claim our pale enchanted gold*' in the fifth stanza. In the sixth stanza, 'cups' is changed to '*goblets*', in the eighth 'vale' is changed to '*dale*', and in the final line 'take' is changed to '*win*'. That these minor refinements were all that was needed to bring the poem into its final form was due to the fact

that the missing section of the Pryftan Fragment contained a draft of this poem, although only a single line of it survives; see p. 14.

11 As this line shows, *The Hobbit's* trademark mix of the familiar and the strange is perhaps at its strongest in this chapter: references to pop-guns, trains, tea-parties, and familiar names for days of the week lie alongside wizards, dwarves, dragons, and hobbits, just as the 'Wild Wireworms of the Chinese' is juxtaposed against the Battle of the Green Fields and the goblins of Mount Gram. Tolkien had good precedent for his mentions of tobacco and tomatoes;† even the Brothers Grimm allowed potatoes and contemporary coaches into their folk-tales. Some of the so-called anachronisms, however, are nothing of the sort; it is the narrator, not one of the characters in the story, who compares the scream welling up inside Bilbo to a train-whistle, just as in *The Lord of the Rings* it is again the narrator who compares the noise made by the firework dragon to an express train rushing by (*LotR*.40).

† In the third edition of 1966, Tolkien changed the tomatoes to pickles (see pp. 777 & 786) but let the tobacco stand, despite having used the less specific 'pipeweed' in the sequel. A devoted rather than a heavy smoker himself, Tolkien once recorded an amusing dialogue in praise of tobacco called 'At the Tobacconist's' for the Linguaphone Institute.

12 Bilbo's cry 'struck by lightning, struck by lightning' refers not to anything in Gandalf's speech but to Bladorthin's staff with its blue light and 'firework glare'. Compare the scene several chapters later when the goblins try to capture the wizard in the mountain-cave. There we are told 'there was a terrific flash like lightning in the cave and several fell dead' (p. 130); the goblin guards later report to the Great Goblin that 'Several of our people were struck by magic lightning in the cave, when we invited them to come below, and are dead as stones' (p. 132).

13 An ink revision here changes 'Fingolfin' to 'Golfimbul'.

14 Here 'burglar' was changed in ink to an illegible word, possibly 'hunter', which is then rejected in favor of 'burglar' once more.

15 References to the 'shetland' pony and the aforementioned wireworms 'of the Chinese' survive here from the previous draft, while the Gobi (famous at the time for Roy Chapman Andrews' fossil-hunting expeditions there throughout the 1920s, which led to the discovery of the first dinosaur eggs in 1923) has become 'the last desert in the East'; also gone is the Hindu Kush (already marked for deletion in the Pryftan Fragment). Through these exotic but real features, Bilbo's world remains firmly tied to our own.

16 Both this paragraph and the one before it were extensively reworked, with marginal additions in dark ink:

> . . . plenty of Excitement and reasonable Reward'; *that is how it is usually read. You can say 'Expert treasure-hunter', if you like, instead of 'Burglar'. Some of them do. It's all the same to us.* Bladorthin told us there was a man of the sort in *these parts looking for* a job *at once, and that he would arrange for a meeting this Wednesday tea-time.'*

'Of course *there is a mark*' said the wizard [*cancelled: not letting Bilbo speak*] *I* put *it* there myself. For very good reasons. I chose Mr Baggins for your fourteenth man, and let any one say I chose the wrong man who dares. If any one does you can stop at thirteen and have all the bad luck you like, or go back to digging coal.' *He scowled so angrily at Gloin, that the dwarf huddled back in his chair; and when Bilbo tried [to speak >] to open his mouth to ask questions, he turned and frowned at him and stuck out his <bushy> eyebrows, till Bilbo shut his mouth tight with a snap. 'That's right' said Bladorthin. 'Let's have no more argument. I have chosen Mr Baggins, and that ought to be enough for all of you. If I say he is a Burglar, a Burglar he is, or will be when the time comes. There is a lot more in him than you guess, and a lot more than he has any idea of himself. You may (possibly) all live to thank me yet. Now* Bilbo, my boy fetch the lamp and let's have a little light on this.'

17 These three paragraphs were reproduced with only minor changes in the First Typescript (that is, the first complete typescript of the entire book, begun after the manuscript draft had reached the scene on Ravenhill), but there they were recast by black ink revisions (indicated below in *italics*) written interlinearly in Tolkien's neatest script:

> On the table in the light of a big lamp with a red shade he spread a *piece of parchment rather like a map.*
>
> 'This I got from your grandfather, Thorin' he said in answer to the dwarves' excited questions. 'It *is a plan of* the Mountain.'
>
> *'I do'nt see that this will help us much' said Thorin disappointedly after a glance. 'I remember the Mountain well enough, and the lands about it. And I know where Mirkwood is, and the Withered Heath where the great dragons bred.'*
>
> *'There is a dragon marked in red on the Mountain', said Balin, 'but it will be easy enough to find him without that, if ever we arrive there.'*

As may be seen, this closely approaches the text of the published book, although the phrase 'This I got from your grandfather' was not replaced by 'This *was made by* your grandfather' until the final page proofs.

18 Both here and at its next occurrence 'Pryftan' was later changed in dark ink to 'Smaug'.

(i)

Baggins of Bag-End

From this typescript, we can see that while the story underwent considerable rewriting, its general outlines remained stable from the very earliest drafts. Actors and dialogue shifted around, names changed, and details were in flux, but the essential narrative remained from first germ to final flowering. Indeed, the evidence of this typescript shows that, once he turned his attention to finding out what that opening line meant, hobbits arrived fully developed in Tolkien's mind, right down to their eating habits and hairy feet.[1] The use of the present tense quietly establishes that although this story is set 'long ago in the quiet of the world when there was less noise and more green and hobbits were still numerous and prosperous,' hobbits are in fact still around today, if elusive and shy around 'ordinary big people like you and me.' The lighthearted comparison to lilliputians, surprising as it is to readers approaching *The Hobbit* from the more somber perspective of *The Lord of the Rings*, survived into the published text and was only removed almost three decades later, in the third edition of 1966.[2]

Bilbo himself is introduced gradually, almost casually, first as '*a* hobbit', then '*the* hobbit and '*he*'; not until the second paragraph do we find out that the name of '*This* hobbit' is *Baggins*, and we have to wait another paragraph before the full name is dropped in parenthetically in passing: '(*Bilbo Baggins*, that is)'. The gradual introduction of the main character is only one of Tolkien's many rhetorical devices that establish the relationship between the narrator and the reader; here Tolkien entices the reader's curiosity by feeding him or her information bit by bit. In contrast, Bladorthin's sudden intrusion, which begins the actual story, echoes the abruptness of the book's opening line, creating the feeling that the thing named exists before, and outside of, the tale about to be told.

The opening paragraphs are more concerned to introduce a context than a character, the background which Bilbo will at first seem part of and against which he will later stand out; hence the detailed description not of Bilbo but of his home, the neighborhood, and even bits of family gossip. The use of proper nouns made out of common nouns – The Hill, the Water – once again recalls William Morris, though it may be simple verisimilitude; well-known local landmarks are usually referred to in precisely this way, especially in small towns and rural communities. Some of the details of the description of Bag-End itself conjure up the civilized atmosphere of a comfortable sitting room in an old manor house, with 'little red lights' and 'polished' seats, while others suggest rather a railway tunnel from the days of steam trains: 'a tubeshaped hall like a tunnel, but . . . without smoke' (granting that train stations and underground tunnels had an elegance of their own in bygone days). While the name 'Bag-End' appears to be a family joke deriving from the nickname of the farm in Worcestershire where Tolkien's aunt Jane Neave and his grandfather Suffield lived in the 1920s (Carpenter, p. 106), on another level 'Bagg-ins of Bag-End' is a simple word-association joke of the golf/Fingolfin variety. The nearest *literary* antecedents for Bilbo's home come from Kenneth Grahame's *The Wind in the Willows* [1908]: the snugness of Mole End, the rambling underground passages of Badger's home, and the grandeur of Toad Hall (like Bag-End, the grandest dwelling of its type in the neighborhood, inherited by the present owner from his father) all contributed to the portrait of the hobbit-hole.[3]

Then there are the neighbors to consider, the other hobbits who while not appearing as characters nonetheless form the backdrop against which *the* hobbit begins his adventures. Like Giles, Niggle, Smith, and Mr. Bliss, Bilbo does not live in a void, and through reports of what 'people said', we soon learn what to expect of a Baggins and of a Took, cluing us in to Bilbo's typical behavior for the rest of the book. This is not to say that Tolkien had these later incidents in mind when he originally drafted these passages but rather the reverse: he jotted down details as they came to him and then, with typical attention to consistency, he later took those details into consideration as he came to write further chapters, developing the book along the lines he laid down very early on.

Much is made here and elsewhere of Bilbo's ancestry and its effect on his character. The rumor of fairy (i.e., elf[4]) or goblin blood is another point modified in the third edition, where all mention of the malicious slander about possible goblin ancestry was dropped and the idea of a Took ancestor having 'taken a fairy wife'[5] is dismissed as 'absurd'. This establishes that whereas the Bagginses are archetypical hobbits in being predictable, unadventurous, and respectable,[6] Tooks are 'not entirely hobbitlike'. That is, they are occasionally unpredictable, adventurous, and hence not 'respectable' – by hobbit standards, anyway.

Since Bilbo is both a Took and a Baggins, it is worthwhile stopping for a moment to consider what we are told here about his parents. We are never told what was so 'remarkable' about Belladonna and her sisters, nor why Bladorthin should refer to her as 'poor Belladonna', while we know little of Bungo besides a few of his favorite sayings (which Bilbo tends to repeat to himself when in a tight spot) and the fact that outwardly he looked, and acted, very like Bilbo (who is described as 'a second edition of his father' in appearance and behavior). That the Belladonna of the First Phase never had any adventure '*other than* becoming Mrs Bungo Baggins' makes one wonder if like his famous son Bungo was perhaps also not so 'prosy' as he seemed; in the published text 'other than' was changed to 'after', conjuring up images of a life of dreary respectability. Another First Phase phrasing not appearing in the finished book has Belladonna '*making* Bungo . . . build the most luxurious hobbit-hole either under the Hill or over the Hill or across the Water'; the published version has it that 'Bungo . . . built the most luxurious hobbit-hole for her (and partly with her money) that was to be found either under The Hill or over The Hill or across The Water, and there they remained to the end of their days'. Tolkien is deft at conveying characterization with extreme economy (so much so that careless readers and critics often miss it entirely); had it been retained we would have here in a single word the shadowy figure of

Belladonna T. Baggins indelibly delineated as the first in what becomes in *The Lord of the Rings* and after a line of indomitable hobbit matriarchs: Smeagol's grandmother, Lobelia B. Sackville-Baggins, Dora Baggins, and the tyrannical Lalia the Great.[7] Years later, when attempting to address all the loose threads left over from *The Hobbit* for the sequel, Tolkien returned to the question of 'poor Belladonna' and drafted a passage relating how Bilbo 'was left an orphan, when barely forty years old, by the untimely death of his father and mother (in a boating accident)' (HME VI.25), a fate later transferred to Frodo's parents rather than Bilbo's.

The Name 'Bilbo'

Like the similar hobbit names Bingo, Ponto, Bungo, and Drogo, all of which eventually end up in the Baggins family tree (see *LotR* page [1136] and HME XII.89–92), 'Bilbo' is both a short, simple, made-up name appropriate for the hero of a children's book or light-hearted fantasy story and also the sort of nickname that was actually in use in England at the time (or perhaps, more truthfully, a slightly earlier time), as preserved in the humorous tales of P. G. Wodehouse. Examples of the former include Gorbo, the main character in E. A. Wyke-Smith's *The Marvellous Land of Snergs* [1927], a book popular among the Tolkien children,[8] and Pombo, the anti-hero of one of Dunsany's short tales ('The Injudicious Prayers of Pombo the Idolater', in *The Book of Wonder* [1912]).[9] Examples of the latter can be found in Bingo (Richard) Little and Pongo (Reginald) Twisleton, both from Wodehouse's work.[10]

Bilbo is also, of course, a real surname which, while rare, survives into modern times: when my father was growing up near Hope, Arkansas in the early 1930s among his neighbors were the Bilbos, some of whom still lived in the area in the mid-1970s.[11] Unfortunately, the best-known person with that surname is the notorious Senator Theodore Bilbo of Mississippi (1877–1947), a politician infamous by the not too fastidious standards of the time for his racism and corruption; luckily, he cannot be the source for Tolkien's use of the name, since he did not rise to national prominence until 1934, by which time Tolkien had already completed the first draft of *The Hobbit*.

Finally, as the *Oxford English Dictionary* (OED) bears witness, 'bilbo' also exists, alone or in combination, in several archaic common nouns, the most important of which is the name of a type of well-tempered, flexible sword originating from Bilbao in Spain. Such 'bilbow blades' were often simply called a 'Bilbo', often uppercased (no doubt because of the proper noun nameplace that gave them their name) – e.g., Falstaff's 'compass'd like a good Bilbo in the circumference of a Pecke' (*The Merry Wives of Windsor* [1598], Act III. scene v. line 112) or Drayton's

'Downe their Bowes they threw/And forth their Bilbos drew' [1603], both cited by the OED. Similarly, a kind of shackles was also known from the mid-sixteenth century as a 'bilbo' or 'bilbow', and a cup-and-ball game popular in the eighteenth and nineteenth centuries was called 'bilbo-catch' (earlier *bilboquet*).[12] But it seems unlikely that our Bilbo's name derives from any of these: his acquiring a little sword early in his adventure is probably a case of the cart following the horse, as Tolkien brought in elements (such as a 'bilbo-blade') that would go well with the character he had already named Bilbo. Exploring linguistic associations no doubt gave Tolkien ideas of things he could do with the character, just as scholarly researches seem to have led him to later incorporate some elements of Plato's ring of Gyges into his own ring of invisibility (see p. 176 & ff), but they are not likely to have been the source of his name. Like *hobbit* itself, *Bilbo* is almost certainly Tolkien's own coinage.

(ii)
Bladorthin

After Bilbo, the most important character in this first chapter is Bladorthin. Bladorthin, the wizard in *The Hobbit*, later developed into the Gandalf the Grey of *The Lord of the Rings*, but it is difficult to tell in this first appearance how much of the later character was already present in Tolkien's mind in this first draft and how much he discovered in the course of writing, partly because the character is deliberately kept somewhat mysterious. Certainly the phrase 'Gandalf the Grey' is never used in *The Hobbit*, being part of the many layers of later accretions the character picked up over the years (a process which reached its peak in the 1954 essay 'The Istari', printed in *Unfinished Tales*). Bladorthin by contrast is never associated with any one colour; indeed, the first description of him offers quite a variety: blue hat, grey cloak, silver scarf, white beard, and black boots (we are not told the actual colour of his robe, only these accessories). Separating the ennobled Gandalf we know from *The Lord of the Rings* from the wandering wizard who flits in and out of the drafts of *The Hobbit* might be a difficult mental exercise, but it is a worthwhile one; otherwise we'll make assumptions that may not be justified, and bring things to *The Hobbit* that simply aren't there. In the interest of clarity, in this commentary I refer to the wizard in *The Hobbit* as 'Bladorthin', the name Tolkien used right up to the arrival at the Lonely Mountain (and indeed a bit beyond), and the wizard in *The Lord of the Rings* as 'Gandalf' or 'Gandalf the Grey' (not to be confused with Gandalf the dwarf, the character later renamed Thorin Oakenshield).

Late in life Tolkien described Gandalf the Grey as

> a figure strongly built with broad shoulder, though shorter than the average of men and now stooped with age, leaning on a thick rough-cut staff as he trudged along . . . Gandalf's hat was wide-brimmed (a shady hat, H. p. 14)[13] with a pointed conical crown, and it was *blue*; he wore a long *grey* cloak, but this would not reach much below his knees. It was of an elven silver-grey hue, though tarnished by wear – as is evident from the general use of grey in the book [i.e., in *The Lord of the Rings*] . . . But his colours were always white, silver-grey, and blue – except for the boots he wore when walking in the wild . . . Gandalf even bent must have been at least 5 ft. 6 . . . Which would make him a short man even in modern England, especially with the reduction of a bent back.[14]

This Odinic figure is an angel in incarnated form (i.e., a Maia), one of the five Istari, bearer of the Ring of Fire, whose other names are Mithrandir and Olórin, who passes through death and returns as Gandalf the White, the Enemy of Sauron; altogether a much more dignified, powerful, and political figure than the 'little old man' Bilbo meets on his doorstep one day 'in the quiet of the world'.

In the essay on the Istari, Tolkien states that 'they were supposed (at first) by those that had dealings with them to be Men who had acquired lore and arts by long and secret study' (*Unfinished Tales* p. 388). However, it is by no means clear whether or not Tolkien himself was of the same opinion when he first wrote *The Hobbit.* Like so much else in the story, Bladorthin's nature is ambiguous, no doubt deliberately so: he might be human, or he might already be something more. If we had only *The Hobbit* itself to go by, we should certainly have no reason to doubt that he was what he appeared, a 'little old man' – the phrase Tolkien twice uses to describe him when introducing the character (the second usage was later changed to 'old man' to avoid repetition, the first was likewise altered in the third edition, no doubt to increase the wizard's stature).[15] It might be objected that Tolkien also describes Bilbo as an 'excitable little man' in the Ms. and first edition, yet when children's author Arthur Ransome objected to the loose application of 'man' in the first edition, specifically as applied to Bilbo and in Thorin's concern for his 'men' (Ransome to Tolkien, 13th December 1937; see Appendix IV), Tolkien changed the description of Bilbo to 'excitable little fellow' and made similar adjustments regarding the dwarves but left the description of the wizard as a 'little old man' untouched, implying that it was literal and accurate.

However, *The Hobbit* does not stand alone, and once viewed in the context of the early Silmarillion material, Tolkien's other tales for his children, and its own sequel, the case for Bladorthin's being more than human grows somewhat stronger. Even if in the early drafts of the sequel Gandalf is still referred to as 'a little old man' (HME VI.20), a description retained as late as the sixth draft of the opening chapter (ibid.315), we must admit that within the published *Lord of the Rings* (where Gandalf's more-than-human status is firmly established) he is still twice described as an 'old man' (*LotR*.37). Presumably these last, whether literal or not at the time they were written, must within their published context be taken as reflecting the point of view of the hobbits rather than the reality beneath the appearances. In the brief account of the wizards' coming to Middle-earth that forms the headnote of the Third Age section of Appendix B: 'The Tale of Years', it is said that the wizards came 'in the *shape* of Men' (*LotR*.1121, italics mine), a statement that ties in closely with the viewpoint from the Istari essay already quoted. Moreover, Tolkien's reply to Ransome suggests that by that point (December 1937), several days before he wrote the first pages of what would become *The Lord of the Rings*, he was already thinking of Gandalf as something not quite human:

> The ancient English . . . would have felt no hesitation in using 'man' of elf, dwarf, goblin, troll, wizard or what not, since they were inclined to make Adam the father of them all . . .
>
> – Tolkien to Ransome, 15th December 1937; cf. Appendix IV.

Obviously, Tolkien's mythos provided the elves, dwarves, and others with their own creation myths, but the inclusion of 'wizard' here implies that they too stood apart in a separate category, distinct from Men (humans), whom Tolkien associates in his letter to Ransome with Elves as the Two Kindreds (anticipating here perhaps the five Free Peoples of *The Lord of the Rings*; *LotR*.485–6). Within this context, we should note that Tolkien's *Roverandom* [1925–7], which he wrote a few years before *The Hobbit*, begins with an unsuspecting innocent encountering an 'old man' who turns out to be a wizard (page 3), and the Man-in-the-Moon in the same story is repeatedly called 'an old man' (or, in one case, 'an old man with a long silvery beard'; page 22), as is his friend Father Christmas in the *Father Christmas Letters*, although the latter is certainly not human.

If Bladorthin, *Roverandom*'s Artaxerxes, and similar figures appearing in Tolkien's earlier writings are not human, is it possible to determine where they fit within the context of Tolkien's legendarium? Granted that the early stages of his mythology were less structured and more inclusive than it later became, the key figure in answering that question is Túvo the wizard, a figure who evolved into Tû the fay and eventually Thû the necromancer (see BLT I.232–5 and the discussion of this character beginning on p. 81 below). Túvo is emphatically neither elf nor human – in fact, he plays a part in the discovery and awakening of the first humans in Middle-earth – but rather a fay, the catch-all term Tolkien used at the time for beings created before the world and who came to inhabit it, including the Maiar. Thus from Tolkien's very first wizard, who existed in the unfinished 'Gilfanon's Tale' at least a decade before Bladorthin first came on the scene, can already be found the conceptual precedent for Tolkien's much, much later bald statement that 'Gandalf is an angel' – or at least, in the case of Bladorthin, a supernatural being incarnated within the world, neither human nor mortal but very human in his behavior and character.

Whether or not this was in Tolkien's mind when he wrote the opening scenes of *The Hobbit*, or indeed was merely present in the background as a potentiality, it is clear that, just as the power of Bilbo's ring was subtly altered between the original book and its sequel, so too were the wizard's powers enhanced. Contrasting Bladorthin's and Gandalf's behavior when battling wargs (pages 203–8 vs. *LotR*.314–16) shows that while Bladorthin is perhaps the more resourceful of the two, Gandalf's resources are greater; the wargs and goblins are almost too much for Bladorthin, while Gandalf can ignite a whole hillful of trees at a gesture. As Sam says, 'Whatever may be in store for old Gandalf, I'll wager it isn't a wolf's belly' (*LotR*.315), while Bladorthin is only saved from leaping to his death in a final blaze of glory by the timely intervention of the eagles. Bladorthin's greater vulnerability is also shown by the wound he receives in the final battle; it is hard to imagine the Gandalf of *The Lord of the Rings* walking around after the battle of Helm's Deep or siege of Minas Tirith with his arm in a sling.

Unlike Gandalf, Bladorthin is very much a traditional fairy-tale enchanter: among his recorded exploits are rescuing 'many princesses, earls, dukes, widow's sons and fair maidens' and slaying 'unlamented giants', exactly what we would expect of a hero from one of the old stories collected by Joseph Jacobs or Jacob & Wilhelm Grimm.[16] Although his magical skills extend far beyond fireworks – we learn that he 'turned the dragon of the Far Mountains inside out' – he prefers trickery and glamour, as in the troll-scene, to more obvious displays of magic.

When we first meet him, Bladorthin is busy organizing an adventure, and not having an easy time of it. From various hints in this first chapter we can reconstruct his movements in the days immediately preceding the unexpected party and conclude that Bilbo was not, in fact, his first choice. On 'last Thursday' the wizard met with the thirteen dwarves and convinced them to hire a professional burglar to help in their quest (having already tried and failed to find them a warrior or hero; cf. p. 10), assuring them he knew of one in the vicinity 'seldom out of a job'. The dwarves separate to look for the burglar. The following Tuesday, Bladorthin met Bilbo and put the sign on his door; that Bilbo was probably far down on his list[17] is indicated by the wizard's complaint that he is 'on the way to an adventure, and . . . looking for some one to share it – very difficult to find!' (to which Bilbo retorts 'I should think so – in these parts'). Later that same day, Oin spotted the sign and informed the others, who meet by appointment the next day ('as soon as we could get together'; cf. Gloin's speech on p. 40).

That Bladorthin's chief occupation lay in the organizing and expediting of adventures seems indicated not just by his role here but by Bilbo's recollection: 'dear me! – not the Bladorthin who was responsible for so many quiet lads and lasses going off into the blue for mad adventures, everything from climbing trees to stowing away aboard the ships that sail to the Other Side'.[18] We are not told his motivations, other than the passing hint that the adventure will be 'Very amusing for me, very good for you'; it is simply who he is and what he does ('I am Bladorthin, and Bladorthin means me!'). It is amusing to note that, before Bladorthin is through with him, Bilbo does indeed vanish on what his hobbit neighbors would call a mad adventure (eventually passing into hobbit legend as 'Mad Baggins'; cf. *LotR*.55), during the course of which he is forced to climb a tree not once but twice (to escape the wargs and to try to look for a way out of Mirkwood) and stow away invisibly on board a ship (actually a raft, on the way to Lake Town).[19] He does not, in the course of this book, ever reach the Other Side (i.e., Valinor),[20] although eventually, in the sequel, Bilbo ends his career by undertaking just such a voyage. At one point, early on in the composition of *The Lord of the Rings*, Tolkien even considered making the main focus of that story Bilbo's voyage into the West:

> . . . Elrond tells him of an island. Britain? Far west where the Elves still reign. Journey to perilous isle. (HME VI.41)

– i.e., Tol Eressëa or Elvenhome. Had this story-idea been carried out, the hobbit-hero might well have replaced Eriol/Ælfwine from the *Lost Tales* as the travelling adventurer who journeys to the Lonely Isle that later became Britain and hears there the tales that eventually make up *The Silmarillion*.[21] There is no reason to think Tolkien intended this when he drafted this passage in *The Hobbit* – indeed, it is clear he did not; rather, the possibilities implicit within it became one of the 'loose ends' he picked up on and ultimately addressed in the second book.

The Name 'Bladorthin'

The name *Bladorthin* is difficult to gloss, and Tolkien never explained its meaning, although it is clearly Gnomish (or perhaps Noldorin). We can best approach its meaning by comparison with other words in Tolkien's early writings containing the same elements.

The first of these, *Bladorwen*, appears in the *Gnomish Lexicon* [circa 1917] as the Gnomish equivalent for *Palúrien*, an early honorific for Yavanna, the goddess of the earth and all growing things. There *Bladorwen* is glossed as 'Mother Earth', as well as 'the wide earth. The world and all its plants and fruit' (*Parma Eldalamberon* XI.23); related words include *blath* ('floor'), *blant* ('flat, open, expansive, candid'), and *bladwen* ('a plain'). Hence *blador* probably applies to wide open country.

This guess is reinforced by the second name, *Bladorion*. In the earliest 'Annals of Valinor' and 'Annals of Beleriand' (which are associated with the 1930 *Quenta*, and hence contemporary with the First Phase of *The Hobbit*), this is the name given to the great grassy plain dividing Thangorodrim from the elven realms to the south before it is turned into a wasteland (Dor-na-Fauglith) in the Battle of Sudden Fire. Again the meaning seems to be something close to 'wide, flat, open country', with the added connotation of a green and growing place (since the name is changed after the plantlife is destroyed). Curiously enough, the *Qenya Lexicon* [circa 1915 & ff] gives *-wen* as the feminine patronymic, equivalent to the masculine *-ion* (BLT I.271 & *Parma Eldalamberon* XII.103), raising the possibility that *Bladorion* and *Bladorwen* are simply gender-specific alternatives that share exactly the same meaning, despite the different applications given to them.[22]

Finally, *-thin* is a familiar form: this word-element entered in at the very end of the *Lost Tales* period [circa 1919–20] when *Thingol* replaced the earlier *Tinwelint* as the name of Tinúviel's father in the typescript of 'The Tale of Tinúviel', the last of the *Lost Tales*. I have not found a gloss of 'Thingol' from this early period, but there is no reason to doubt that it would have been the same as the later Sindarin translation: 'grey-cloak', with *thin* = grey. A second, apparently unrelated, occurrence of this element can be found in the *Gnomish Lexicon* as a plural indicator; we are told that Qenya *silmaril, silmarilli* = Gnomish *silubrill/silubrilt, silubrilthin*, where it is clear that *-thin* is a plural suffix equivalent to the English *-s* (*Parma Eldalamberon* XI.67).

Given these various elements, what then is the meaning of *Bladorthin*? The simplest translation would be 'the Grey Country' (*blador+thin*). Alternatively, if we stress the *-or* element, this becomes 'Grey Plains Fay' or even 'Grey Master of the Plains'. If we interpret *blador* less literally and take 'wide' in the sense of 'far and wide', the name could even be interpreted as 'Grey Wanderer' (i.e., one who travels far and wide), thus becoming an early precursor of Gandalf's *Lord of the Rings*-era elven name, *Mithrandir*.[23] In any case, whatever its original meaning the name must have been capable of yielding a meaning appropriate to its re-assigned application to King Bladorthin, perhaps there meaning the ruler over wide (grey?) lands (see pp. 514 & 525).

(iii)
Dwarven Magic

The thirteen dwarves round out the rest of the main cast, and again the general outlines remained while phrasing and details were endlessly revised. Thus the motif of Bombur's obesity has not yet emerged[24] and it is still Dwalin, not Gloin, who bluntly expresses his doubts over whether Bilbo 'will do'. The most striking thing about this earliest draft lies in its emphasis on 'dwarven magic': whereas in later revisions Tolkien was at pains to make the opening scenes more realistic, particularly in the 1960 Hobbit (see pp. 778 & 812), in the early drafts he stressed the wonder and magic of the scene. Detail after detail – the dwarves' coloured beards, the musical instruments they pull out of thin air, the magical smoke rings – are all inessential to the plot but important to establish a sense of the uncanny, a world of wonder. The brightly-coloured hoods and beards are a good example of this light-hearted fairy-tale tone, obviously decorative rather than functional: thus Fili and Kili, the youngest of the dwarves, have white beards, while Balin, 'a very old-looking dwarf', has a yellow beard and no good reason is given for why Dwalin's beard is blue, like the fairy-tale villain (indeed, one of the *Lost Tales* features a dwarf named Fangluin the aged – literally 'Beard-blue'; cf. BLT II.229–30). We can rationalize that perhaps dwarves dye their beards or grow hair in tints that would be unnatural on a human head, but all that matters for the tale at hand is to make these strangers who have thrust their way into Bilbo's predictable little world as outlandish as possible, both from our point of view and that of the hobbit. The musical instruments provide another good example, where Bifur and Bofur turn their walking-sticks into clarinets while Bombur produces a drum 'from nowhere', as if they were travelling conjurers entertaining their host rather than seasoned adventurers about to depart on a desperate journey from which some or all may never return.[25]

But nothing is ever simple or one-dimensional in Tolkien's world, and the mood very quickly darkens. Once established, the uncanny wonder of dwarven magic is seasoned with somber warnings of the danger ahead; even the oddness of the visitors turns suddenly sinister with details like the dwarves' eyes shining in the dark ('dark for dark business'). The turning point is the dwarves' song 'Far Over The Misty Mountains Cold'. Against the comedy of confused expectations on all sides is set this poem describing the lost kingdom of the dwarves and its fiery destruction by the dragon. More than a reminder of the grim task awaiting them, although it is that too, like the passages about Tooks and Bagginses it opens up a sense of history behind the tale. What is more, it forms yet another link between this tale and the mythology, for the third and fourth stanzas of the poem clearly allude to the story of Tinwelint (Thingol) and the Nauglafring from the *Book of Lost Tales*, the 'old quarrel' referred to elsewhere in the book that soured relations between the dwarves and elves.[26]

(iv)
The Voice of the Narrator

Finally, there is the voice of the narrator, an essential element in establishing the overall tone of the story and hence of the book's success. In a way, the unnamed narrator, who blends seamlessly in and out of the story, leaving his mark behind everywhere, is one of the most important characters in the tale.[27] Through his interpolations in these opening pages, Tolkien develops several motifs that run throughout the book: a concern for etiquette, an ear for oral (and easily-visualized) elements, an interest in word-play. Intrusive narrators were once common in English fiction – Henry Fielding's *Tom Jones* [1749] uses one with great flair, and Laurence Sterne's *Tristram Shandy* [1759–67] raised it to an art form. Closer to Tolkien's own time and tastes, Lord Dunsany – after Morris, the chief influence on *The Book of Lost Tales* and Tolkien's other early work[28] – made adroit use of narrators who flitted in and out of their stories (e.g. in such tales as 'A Story of Land & Sea' [*The Last Book of Wonder*, 1916] and 'Bethmoora' [*A Dreamer's Tales*, 1910]). Tolkien himself also employed the same device elsewhere with great aplomb; as in *Farmer Giles of Ham* ('There was no getting round Queen Agatha – at least it was a long walk') and its famed definition of the blunderbuss, lifted directly from the OED. Critics who have dismissed the narrative voice in *The Hobbit* out of hand have overlooked its purpose: Tolkien uses it to interact with his audience, and much of the book's charm would be lost by its absence.

The voice of the narrator is by turns professorial and playful, now answering rhetorical questions from the reader ('what is a hobbit? I meant you to find out, but if you must have everything explained at the beginning, I can only say . . .'), now delivering a learned discourse on hobbit culture or wry comments on Bilbo's faulty memory. The narrator is not omniscient – he has heard only 'a little tiny bit of what there is to hear' regarding Bladorthin's exploits, and several chapters later he will introduce Gollum with the words 'I don't know where he came from, or who or what he was' (pp. 154–5). But he gives us the information we need to understand a scene, fills us in on the background as new people or places enter the narrative, and injects a great deal of humor into the book.

Aside from teasing the reader by foreshadowing or by withholding information, the narrator also frames the story by occasional direct addresses to the reader ('I imagine you know the answer, of course, or can guess it . . . since you are sitting comfortably at home and have not the danger of being eaten to disturb your thinking'; 'yes, I'm afraid trolls do talk like that, even ones with only one head'; 'Tom-noddy of course is insulting to anyone') and rhetorical interruptions; these help establish that the story is only a story and that the reader *is*, after all, 'sitting comfortably at home' – very important for any children's story as dark and nightmare-inducing as this one. They deliberately break the illusion of secondary reality that the rest of the story is creating, thus defying all Tolkien's rules and theories regarding the necessity of creating secondary belief, as later presented in his essay 'Of Fairy-Stories' (no doubt a major reason for his later strictures on the book).[29]

The playfulness of the narrative perhaps comes out best in the wordplay. *The Hobbit* delights in using odd, archaic words, intermixing them with neologisms of Tolkien's own invention, so that only a scholar familiar with the OED and various dialectical dictionaries (the special province of Joseph Wright, Tolkien's mentor in his undergraduate days; Tolkien himself had provided the Foreword to one such work, Walter E. Haigh's *A New Glossary of the Dialect of the Huddersfield District*, only a few years before, in 1928) could tell which was which: bewildered and bewuthered, upsettled, flummoxed, confusticate and bebother, cob, tomnoddy and attercop, hobbit. The blurb on *The Hobbit*'s original dustjacket compared Tolkien with Lewis Carroll, a point taken up by several early reviewers bemused by the idea of two academics writing fantasies for children; despite Tolkien's objection that *Through the Looking Glass* was a better parallel to his own work than *Alice's Adventures in Wonderland*,[30] the comparison is apt. Both authors share the trick of taking everyday expressions quite literally (as in Bladorthin's response to Bilbo's phrase 'I beg your pardon'). Even more Carrollingian is the use of the same word or expression to mean different things, as in Bilbo's three separate 'good mornings'.[31]

In addition to a fascination with wordplay, *The Hobbit* also shares with the Alice books a concern for etiquette. Whatever situation Alice finds herself in, she tries to mind her manners (often in the face of much provocation), and Bilbo is similarly careful to be polite even to uninvited guests:

> 'I am just going to have tea; pray come and have some with me' – *a little stiff perhaps but he meant it kindly*; and what would you do . . . ? (p. 32; italics mine)
>
> 'Thank you!' said Bilbo with a gasp. *It was the wrong thing to say*, but 'some of the others' had put him in a fright . . . He had a horrible thought that the cakes might run short, and then he (as the host – *he knew his duty as the host* and stuck to it however painful) would have to go without. (p. 32; italics mine)
>
> 'I suppose you will all stay to supper?' he said *in his politest unpressing tones*. (p. 35; italics mine)

The recurrent emphasis on good manners makes the exceptions stand out all the more strongly: Medwed, the trolls, Thorin's words at the gate ('Descendent of rats indeed'), or Bilbo's own occasional lapse, as at the eagles' eyrie or when provoked by Dwalin's description of him as a 'little fellow bobbing on the mat', to which he retorts 'as soon as I saw your funny faces on the door-step I had my doubts' (p. 40). And the effort of being polite to someone who is both rude and dangerous (Carroll's Queen of Hearts, *The Hobbit's* Smaug the Magnificent, Chiefest and Greatest of Calamities) only adds to the fun. This motif may owe something to the importance placed on politeness in traditional fairy tales, or simply to the fascination small children have in the manners, good and bad, of others.

Finally, there is a strong sense of oral narrative at work in this chapter (and indeed throughout the book): this is a book meant to be read aloud to an attentive audience, just as Tolkien read it aloud to John, Michael, and Christopher during the 'Winter Reads' while he was writing it. Scenes are deliberately described in such a way as to help a listener visualize them, and sound effects are provided to liven up the narrative. Sometimes the reliance on colour is deliberately overdone for comic effect, as with the dwarves' beards, belts, and hoods, where we get such a wealth of detail that the mind begins to boggle trying to keep track of it all; the joke seems to lie in the fact that there *is* no underlying pattern (significantly, we are never told the colours of the later arrivals' beards and belts). Here Tolkien may be echoing a famous medieval work, 'The Dream of Rhonabwy', in which precise visual detail is provided in such reckless profusion that the tale ends with the boast that

> no one, neither bard nor storyteller, knows the Dream without a book – by reason of the number of colours that were on the horses, and all the variety of rare colours both on the arms and their trappings, and on the precious mantles, and the magic stones.
>
> —*The Mabinogion*, tr. Jones & Jones [1949], page 152.

The sound effects vary from onomatopoeia (from the doorbell going *ding-dong-a-ling-lang* to the 'horrible swallowing noise', *gollum*, which gives that character his name) to simile ('he began to feel a shriek coming up inside, and very soon after it burst out like the whistle of an engine coming out of a tunnel') to song: all the 'poems' are in fact lyrics to songs, as the narrator is at pains to point out ('this is like a fragment of their song, if it can be like their song without their music'). Setting his own lyrics to traditional tunes was a favorite hobby of Tolkien's: *Songs for the Philologists*[32] includes both funny jingles like 'Éadig Béo þu' (a ditty in Old English set to the tune of 'Twinkle Twinkle Little Star') and serious pieces like 'Bagmē Bloma' (perhaps the finest of all his tree-poems, in Gothic) and 'Ides Ælfscýne' (Tolkien's own eerie and extremely effective take on the La Belle Dame Sans Merci legend). Thus 'The Stone Troll' (a piece appearing in different versions in both *Songs for the Philologists* and *The Lord of the Rings*, the latter reprinted in *The Adventures of Tom Bombadil* as ATB poem #7) borrows its tune from an old folk song called 'The Fox Went Out'. If the evidence of Tolkien's recordings of excerpts from *The Hobbit, The Adventures of Tom Bombadil*, and *The Lord of the Rings* (later released by Caedmon Records) may be trusted, more often Tolkien did not actually sing the pieces but used a sort of recitative.[33] All in all, his narrator employs a wide variety of devices, all with the common goal of making this a story to *listen* to, not just to read; the paragraphs preceding and following the dwarves' song about their lost home (pp. 36 & 37–8) show just how skilled Tolkien was in using word-music to evoke a mood.

NOTES

1 The hobbit point of view regarding food is masterfully summed up on the first page of the first draft for the 'New Hobbit' (the sequel that eventually turned into *The Lord of the Rings*), where Tolkien notes that Bilbo was famous among his fellow hobbits for having 'disappeared after breakfast one April 30th and not reappeared until lunchtime on June 22nd in the following year' (HME VI.13). The opening paragraphs of the Bladorthin Typescript establish that Bilbo is a thoroughly typical hobbit in his concern for steady meals and his frequent laments, as the story progresses, over short rations.

2 That Swift's bitingly satiric invention had come to be considered appropriate children's fare (albeit usually in carefully bowdlerized versions), a shift that seems to have occurred during the Victorian era, is also attested to by T. H. White's modern-day sequel, *Mistress Masham's Repose* [1946].

3 Tolkien was of course well acquainted with Grahame's work; in 'On Fairy-Stories' he cites the opening sentence of *The Wind in the Willows* ('this excellent book') approvingly and castigates A. A. Milne's adaptation, *Toad of Toad Hall* [1929] ('some children that I took to see [it] brought away as their chief memory nausea at the opening . . .') – OFS, Note A (pages 66–7). Nor was this a passing enthusiasm; when the letters from which Grahame composed the book were published by Grahame's widow in 1944 as *First Whispers of 'The Wind in the Willows'*, long after Tolkien's children had grown up, Tolkien wrote telling his son Christopher about reading the reviews and notes 'I must get hold of a copy, if poss.' (JRRT to CT, letter of 31 July and 1 August 1944; *Letters* p. 90). Finally, when a sharp-eyed proofreader queried the use of 'learn' instead of 'teach' in the scene at Bree ('Bob ought to learn his cat the fiddle . . .'), Tolkien rejected the proposed correction and scribbled in the margin: 'no indeed! Mr Badger in the Wind in the Willows would learn you better!' (Ms. annotation to Marq. 3/2/14 page 51).

It is perhaps also worthwhile to note that when Tolkien's fellow Inkling C. S. Lewis wanted to make a point about *The Hobbit*, he could find no better way to do so than by a comparison with *The Wind in the Willows*:

> *The Hobbit* escapes the danger of degenerating into mere plot and excitement by a very curious shift of tone. As the humour and homeliness of the early chapters, the sheer 'Hobbitry', dies away we pass insensibly into the world of epic. It is as if the battle of Toad Hall had become a serious *heimsókn* and Badger had begun to talk like Njal†
> —*Essays Presented to Charles Williams* [1947], 'On Stories', p. 104.

† the titular character of *The Saga of Burnt Njal*.

4 At first sight, fairies would seem, like the stone-giants, to be a race peculiar to *The Hobbit*, not found in *The Lord of the Rings*. But this is not the case: the usage in *The Book of Lost Tales* establishes 'fairy' as a synonym for 'elf'. Fairy should not, by the way, be confused with 'fay', the term applied in *The Book of Lost Tales* to beings created before the world – i.e., the angels, spirits, and elementals later grouped together under the general rubric of 'Maiar'. Thus Melian is a 'fay' (as, in all probability, are Goldberry and Bombadil; the one a nymph, the other a *genius loci*), while the elves of Rivendell are 'fairies'.

5 This late shift from the original 'married into a fairy family' to the more specific 'taken a fairy wife' is interesting, adding as it does yet another example to the long list of faerie brides in Tolkien's works. In every case of such marriages in Tolkien, it is the wife who belongs to the older, more powerful, and nobler race: Melian the Maia and Thingol the elf-king, Aredhel the elf-princess and Eöl the dark elf, Lúthien and Beren, Idril and Tuor, Mithrellas (Nimrodel's handmaiden) and Imrazôr the Númenórean (parents of the first Lord of Dol Amroth; *Unfinished Tales* p. 248), Arwen and Aragorn, and even the *belle dame sans merci* of 'Ides Ælfscýne' (*Songs for the Philologists*, pages 10–11 [1936]). In terms of folklore analogues, Tolkien clearly prefers the Thomas Rymer theme to Tam Lin.

6 In a 1968 interview with Charlotte and Denis Plimmer, Tolkien compared his hero to Babbitt, the main character in Sinclair Lewis's 1922 novel of the same name, and suggested that Lewis's character might have been a subconscious influence: 'Babbitt has the same bourgeois smugness that hobbits do. His world is the same limited place' ('The Man Who Understands Hobbits', *Daily Telegraph Magazine*, 22nd March 1968, p. 32); see p. xxxvii, Note 2.

7 Lalia Took's story is told in a letter to A. C. Nunn, c. 1958–9 (*Letters* p. 294–5).

8 The Tolkien children's fondness for *The Marvellous Land of Snergs*, and the probability that this work influenced *The Hobbit* in some details (primarily the characterization of the hobbits themselves), is discussed in the Introduction to Douglas Anderson's *The Annotated Hobbit* (DAA

6–7). Tolkien's own high regard for this now-forgotten story is recorded in Unwin's memorandum of October 1937, reproduced in Note 9 on pp. xxxix–xl.

9 This tale appears in the same collection as what seems to be Tolkien's favorite Dunsany tale, 'Chu-bu and Sheemish' (cf. *Letters* pp. 375 & 418), as well as 'The Hoard of the Gibbelins', the story that probably inspired his poem 'The Mewlips' (see pp. 370 & 376).

10 Wodehouse's breezy style, perfected just before World War I, remained unchanged throughout his long career: the Bertie and Jeeves stories are said to be the longest running series by a single author writing about the same characters, with very little evolution from the first story [published 1914] to the last [written in 1974]; see Kristin Thompson's *Wooster Proposes, Jeeves Disposes* [1992]. Other notable nicknames among Bertie (Bertram) Wooster's friends include Gussie (Augustus) Fink-Nottle, Barmy (Cyril) Fotheringay-Phipps, Boko (George Herbert) Fittleworth, Tuppy (Hildebrand) Glossop, and Catsmeat (Claude) Potter-Pirbright, as well as others more along the lines of *The Lord of the Rings*' Merry (Meriadoc) Brandybuck and Pippin (Peregrin) Took, such as Chuffy (Marmaduke†) Chuffnell and Biffy (Charles Edward) Biffen.

† Marmaduke was in fact the original name in the early *Lord of the Rings* drafts for the character who eventually became Merry; cf. HME VI.98–104.

11 Geographical locations such as Bilbo Cemetery in Lake Charles, Louisiana; Lake Bilbo near Warren, Arkansas; and Bilbo Island on the Tombigbee River in Alabama all seem, so far as I have been able to discern, to have drawn their names not from the literary character but from the family name; I have been able to trace a 'Bilboe's Landing' on the Tombigbee as far back as 1809.

12 Replicas of a variant of this game are still sold in museum shops and at colonial reconstructions; see www.historylives.com/toysandgames.htm.

13 The reference is to the following passage from the published book: '. . . Gandalf looked at him from under long bushy eyebrows that stuck out further than the brim of his shady hat' (DAA. 32).

14 These comments come from an essay Tolkien wrote circa 1970 in response to seeing Pauline Baynes' art for a poster-map of Middle-earth. In addition to ten vignettes on the map itself, Baynes added a headpiece at top showing all nine members of the Fellowship of the Ring (plus Bill the pony) and a tailpiece at bottom showing the Black Riders, Gollum, Shelob, and a horde of orcs. Although Tolkien greatly admired Baynes' work on the whole, he disliked this particular piece so much that, in addition to writing this essay he had the top and bottom cropped off the original painting when he had it framed for presentation to his longtime secretary, Joy Hill (personal communication, May 1987). The original essay is now in the Bodleian Library (Tolkien Papers A61 a, fol. 1–31).

15 In a 1958 letter to Forrest J. Ackerman commenting on Morton Grady Zimmerman's script for a proposed film of *The Lord of the Rings*, Tolkien

emphasized this point: 'Gandalf, please, should not "splutter". Though he may seem testy at times, has a sense of humour, and adopts a somewhat avuncular attitude to hobbits, he is a person of high and noble authority, and great dignity. The description on I p. 239† should never be forgotten' (*Letters* p. 271).

† 'Gandalf was shorter in stature than [Elrond and Glorfindel]; but his long white hair, his sweeping silver beard, and his broad shoulders, made him look like some wise king of ancient legend. In his aged face under great snowy brows his dark eyes were set like coals that could leap suddenly into fire.' (*LotR*, 1st edition, vol. I page 239)

16 One distinctive feature of English fairy tales, as opposed to German (Grimm) or French (Mother Goose), is their fascination with giants, a motif going back at least as far as Geoffrey of Monmouth and Arthur's battle with the giant of Mont St. Michel. The two most popular of all English fairy tales were 'Jack the Giant Killer' and 'Jack and the Beanstalk'.

17 Although Bilbo does not recognize him, the wizard and hobbit are already acquainted, as indicated by Bilbo's memories of Bladorthin's behavior and by Bladorthin's comment on the day of the Unexpected Party: 'This is not like you Bilbo' (p. 34) – obviously he could not comment that the hobbit was acting out of character unless he knew him well enough to predict his normal behavior.

Many years later, Tolkien returned to this scene and rewrote it (very much to Bilbo's disadvantage) from the wizard's and dwarves' point of view; see 'The Quest of Erebor' in *Unfinished Tales* pp. 321–36, DAA Appendix A pp. [367]–77, and HME XII pages 282–9.

18 We hear little more of these other beneficiaries (or victims, depending on one's point of view) of Bladorthin's attention, but Tolkien probably had this passage in mind when he finalized the Took family tree at the very end of the *LotR* period (i.e., c. 1952–4). The wizard was a close friend of Bilbo's grandfather, The Old Took ('the title Old was bestowed on him . . . not so much for his age as for his oddity', according to one draft passage in *The Lord of the Rings*; HME VI.245), and at least two of Bilbo's Took uncles had adventures that sound suspiciously like something Bladorthin/Gandalf had a hand in: Hildifons 'went off on a journey and never returned' – a 'there' without a 'back again', so to speak – and Isengar is 'said to have "gone to sea" in his youth'. In addition, a third brother, Hildigard, is laconically said to have 'died young', although no details are forthcoming (*LotR*.1137). Nor was Bilbo the only one of the Old Took's grandchildren to go adventuring; one of Bilbo's cousins – described in the published book as 'a great traveller' (DAA.145) – fared far enough afield to have 'visited the forests in the north of Bilbo's country' (p. 203), an area wild enough to be frequented by wolves. In retrospect, we can speculate that the wizard had already used up the more adventurous members of the preceding generation and was forced to rely upon Mr. Baggins to round out the party.

We should perhaps also note the phrase 'lads *and* lasses', suggesting as it does that Bladorthin was an equal-opportunity enchanter, responsible for young hobbits of both sexes going off on adventures; the all-male cast of *The Hobbit* might thus be due largely to chance rather than design.

19 It will be observed that the motif of hobbits' fear of water in *The Lord of the Rings* is another later accretion totally absent from this book: a hydrophobe would hardly propose barrelling down an underground river, and Bilbo shows no qualms about riding by boat from Lake Town across Long Lake and up the River Running (or indeed to staying in Lake Town, a city suspended above deep water).

20 The idea of hobbit stowaways on ships sailing to Valinor remained in the text until the third edition of 1966, when the passage was altered to read '. . . anything from climbing trees to visiting elves – or sailing in ships, sailing to other shores!'

21 Indeed, it is likely that here wc scc the first spark of an idea to which Tolkien later returned – that *The Silmarillion* would be a collection made by Bilbo at Rivendell from stories told to him there, just as Eriol the Wanderer and later Ælfwine of England had heard the 'lost tales' in the Cottage of Lost Play. A hint of this can be found in the 'three large volumes' of Bilbo's *Translations from the Elvish* described in the Prologue to *The Lord of the Rings* – 'a work of great skill and learning' 'almost entirely concerned with the Elder Days' 'in which . . . he had used all the sources available to him in Rivendell, both living and written' (*LotR*.26–7; see also *LotR*.1023).

22 The suffix *-wen* elsewhere means maiden, girl, daughter, in names such as *Morwen* ('daughter of night', a name for the planet Jupiter) and *Urwen/Urwendi*, the sun-maiden who guards the last fruit of the Golden Tree (and in the much later *Arwen*, Elrond's daughter); originally Qenya (the language that later evolved into High-Elven, or Quenya) rather than Gnomish (the language that eventually became Sindarin), the suffix was gradually adopted into the latter, where it displaced the earlier *-win* or *-gwen*. Thus Túrin's mother's name underwent a transformation from *Mavwin* in 'Turambar and the Foalóke', one of the Lost Tales (BLT II) to *Morwin* and then *Morwen* in 'The Lay of the Children of Húrin' (HME III).

Similarly, *-dor*, one of the most stable of Tolkien's linguistic inventions, meant 'land' or 'country' in the sense of an inhabited land, as far back as the *Gnomish Lexicon* (*Parma Eldalamberon* XI.30), a meaning that persisted right through to the 'classical' period of the published *Lord of the Rings* and *Silmarillion* in names such as Dor Lómin, Dorwinion, Dor-na-Fauglith, Mordor, and Gondor.

Finally, it is possible that *-or*, an early suffix meaning 'fay' in the *Gnomish Lexicon*, is present here; cf. *tavor* 'a wood fay' from *taur* wood + *-or* fay (*Parma Eldalamberon* XI.69). A similar but apparently unrelated suffix has the rough meaning 'one who is the master of X' – e.g.,

Gnomish *ind* ('house') > *indor* ('master of house') and Qenya *nand* ('field, acre') > *nandor* ('farmer') (ibid., pp. 51 & 59).

23 I have learned since writing this section that Tolkien linguist Chris Gilson has examined the possible meaning of the name *Bladorthin* in an early issue of *Vinyar Tengwar* (issue 17, pages 1–2 [May 1991]), arriving at similar conclusions regarding the name's appropriateness to Gandalf the Grey through somewhat different channels.

24 Bombur is not Tolkien's only obese character; other examples of his rather cruel sense of humor on this point (of a piece with the period) are Fatty Bolger in *The Lord of the Rings* and especially Fattie Dorkins in *Mr. Bliss*. We should note, however, that at least two of Tolkien's heroes – Farmer Giles and Bilbo himself – are distinctly on the tubby side.

25 Much, much later Tolkien jotted down as a note to himself two questions:

> What happened to the musical instruments used by the Dwarves at Bag-end?
> Why did they bring them to B-End?

Even thirty years later, he was unable to come up with a satisfactory answer; see p. 811.

26 This quarrel is discussed in more detail in 'The King of Wood and Stone'; see pages 411–13 following Chapter IX.

Briefly, the original version of the story runs thusly: Tinwelint [Thingol] the elvenking hires dwarves to work the treasure of Mîm (brought to his hall by Úrin [Húrin], and thus doubly cursed) into jewelry, agreeing to let them name their own 'small' reward when the work is done. He sends them half the gold, taking a hostage to ensure their good behavior. When they deliver the first shipment, he is delighted at the results of their craft and promptly takes all the dwarven smiths prisoner, forcing them to complete the work at his halls rather than risk letting any of the gold out of his sight again. They grudgingly finish the assigned task, and then demand a princely reward for the insult – including, among much gold, an elf-bride apiece. The king pays them a pittance (from which he extracts the cost of their food and board during the time of their captivity) and has them beaten for their insolence, driving them from his land. They return home, gather an army, and return to sack the elven kingdom and kill the elvenking. On the return march, they are ambushed by an elven force under the command of Beren; many dwarves are slain, the rest put to flight, and the treasure lost, except for the Nauglafring bearing the Silmaril, which Beren takes and gives to Lúthien.

This abbreviated account leaves out many betrayals and much treachery by elf against elf and dwarf against dwarf.

27 The narrator's importance to the story is usually slighted by critics who would prefer *The Hobbit* to conform to and resemble its sequel in every possible detail. In later years Tolkien came to regard the tone of the

intrusive narrator's remarks as condescending, feeling that it marked the book as targeted for children, and said over and over again in letters that he regretted this, considering it an error on his part and a severe flaw in the book. Taking their cue from Tolkien's afterthoughts, critics writing on *The Hobbit* have almost universally condemned the narrative interpolations, contenting themselves with pointing out how inappropriate the narrative voice in *The Hobbit* would be if used in *The Lord of the Rings*, rather than asking what role the narrator was originally designed to play in what was, after all, conceived as a stand-alone work (and did in fact stand alone for seventeen years). Taken on its own terms, the voice of the narrator is one of the most important elements in the success of the story. For a notable exception, and an insightful examination of the function of the intrusive narrator in *The Hobbit*, see Paul Thomas's essay 'Some of Tolkien's Narrators' in *Tolkien's Legendarium: Essays on* The History of Middle-earth, ed. Verlyn Flieger & Carl F. Hostetter [2000], pp. 161–81.

28 One of Dunsany's most important innovations was the creation of his own pantheon of gods – the first modern writer to ever do so – in *The Gods of Pegana* (1905); both Tolkien's Valar and H. P. Lovecraft's Cthulhu Mythos were directly inspired by this thin little book. This is not the place to enter into a full-scale description of the elder fantasist's impact, or to catalogue all Tolkien's references to Dunsany's work, but we should note that when Clyde Kilby arrived in Oxford in 1966 to offer his advice on *The Silmarillion*, Tolkien handed him a copy of Dunsany's *The Book of Wonder* [1912] and told him to read it in preparation for his task (C. S. Kilby, unpublished lecture, Marquette Tolkien Conference, September 1983).

For more on Dunsany, and his influence on early Tolkien, see *Beyond the Fields We Know: The Short Stories of Lord Dunsany* by John D. Rateliff, Ph.D. dissertation, December 1990, Marquette University.

29 In a letter to L. Sprague de Camp of 30th August 1964, Tolkien specifically criticized Dunsany for doing exactly the same thing – i.e., deliberately pricking his own illusion 'for the sake of a joke' – in the story 'The Distressing Tale of Thangobrind the Jeweller'; cf. de Camp, *Literary Swordsmen and Sorcerers* [1976], p. 243.

30 The relevant passage from Allen & Unwin's blurb read 'The birth of *The Hobbit* recalls very strongly that of *Alice in Wonderland*. Here again a professor of an abstruse subject is at play.' Tolkien objected that he did not consider Old English and Icelandic literature 'abstruse' ('Some folk may think so, but I do not like encouraging them') and pointed out that Dodgson never reached the rank of professor. He also expressed his doubts as to the validity of the comparison, maintaining that 'this stuff of mine is really more comparable to Dodgson's amateur photography' and the poem 'Hiawatha's Photographing',† although he speculated that 'the presence of "conundrums" in *Alice*' might be 'a parallel to echoes of Northern myth in *The Hobbit*.' He concluded that 'If you think it good, and fair (the compliment to *The Hobbit* is

rather high) to maintain the comparison – *Looking-glass* ought to be mentioned. It is much closer in every way' (JRRT to A&U, letter of 31st August 1937, *Letters* pp. 21–2).

In addition to the evidence of this letter, Christopher Tolkien testifies to his father's fondness for, and familiarity with, Carroll's work: in a gloss on a quote from Carroll's *Sylvie and Bruno* [1889] in Tolkien's *The Notion Club Papers*, Christopher says 'my father knew the work from which it comes well, and its verses formed part of his large repertoire of occasional recitation' (HME IX.x; see also p. 214 and Note 22 pp. 214 & 660). Another of Carroll's poems, 'What Tottles Meant', from *Sylvie and Bruno Concluded* [1893], seems to be echoed in the phrase '"Good morning" said Bilbo, *and he meant it*' (p. 30). One of Carroll's most famous poems, 'Jabberwocky' (from *Through the Looking Glass*), influenced Tolkien's vocabulary at one point when he is describing Smaug (see Text Note 9, p. 368), and another from *Alice's Adventures in Wonderland*,†† 'The Walrus and the Carpenter', was used by Tolkien to provide the text for an inscription in his invented 'Rúmilian' script, which predates the more familiar tengwar or 'Fëanorian' script; Arden Smith dates this inscription from the early 1930s (*Parma Eldalamberon* vol. XIII [2001], pages 82 & 84).

Finally, although this took place long after *The Hobbit* was finished, we should note that one of Tolkien's students, Roger Lancelyn Green (whose thesis Tolkien directed at Oxford), became a noted Carroll scholar and the editor of his diaries.

† This piece, written in the Kalevala meter, was collected in *Phantasmagoria and Other Poems* [1869]; Tolkien's knowledge of it reflects that his acquaintance with Carroll's work was more than casual, and extended well beyond the *Alice* books or even *Sylvie and Bruno/Sylvie and Bruno Concluded.*

†† *Alice's Adventures in Wonderland* [1865] and *Through the Looking-Glass* [1871] together make up the composite volume *Alice in Wonderland.*

31 W. H. Auden picked up on this point in his tribute to Tolkien, the poem 'A Short Ode to a Philologist', a meditation on words such as *Good-morning* and their uses and abuses that he contributed to Tolkien's festschrift, *English and Medieval Studies Presented to J. R. R. Tolkien on the Occasion of his Seventieth Birthday*, ed. Norman Davis & C. L. Wrenn [1962], which ends

a lot of us are grateful for
What J. R. R. Tolkien has done
As bard to Anglo-Saxon.

Tolkien returned the favor five years later with 'For W. H. A.', a dual-text poem in both Old English and Modern English, published in the journal *Shenandoah*'s tribute issue in honor of Auden's sixtieth birthday [Winter 1967].

32 Published in 1936, but most of whose contents dated back to Tolkien's time at Leeds [1920–25].

33 Thus Christopher Tolkien recalls 'I have a faint dim feeling that for some of them, at any rate, like "far over the misty mountains", he used some sort of recitative' (CT to JDR, November 1993).

THE SECOND PHASE

Chapter I (c)

THE ADVENTURE CONTINUES

The next stage of the manuscript begins in mid-sentence, resuming the story where the 'Bladorthin Typescript' ends, in the middle of Chapter I. This first page of manuscript in the Second Phase is numbered 13 (in the upper right-hand corner) because it followed directly on the final, or twelfth, page of the Bladorthin Typescript; see p. 41.[TN1] This marks the beginning of the Second Phase of composition, which carried the story from manuscript page 13 (Marq. 1/1/1:3) all the way to manuscript page 167 (Marq. 1/1/15:7) – that is, from the middle of the Unexpected Party in Chapter I to the scene on Ravenhill in what is now Chapter XV. Tolkien did not achieve this much of the story without several breaks or halts in composition, and occasionally stopped to sketch out several Plot Notes or outlines of what would follow in the as-yet unwritten chapters, each of which will be discussed in its appropriate location in the pages that follow.

While the text for the first page or so of this manuscript derives directly from the Pryftan Fragment, this would be difficult to deduce from the text itself – that is, had the Fragment not survived, there is nothing in this manuscript to indicate the point at which it ceases to be 'fair copy' and new drafting begins. This is because while clearly directly based on the earlier draft, incorporating revisions and the like written onto the old manuscript, the material has been rearranged and expanded in the course of creating this new draft. The suggestion found in the final paragraph of the Fragment to sit on the back door and think of a plan ('if one does not sprout up on the way') is deferred for several pages, while Bilbo's question to know 'a bit more about things' and his demand to have things made 'plain and clear' sets off a long interpolation by Gandalf the dwarf giving the history of the Mountain and describing the dragon's attack. This in turn leads to a second interpolation as Bladorthin the wizard answers Gandalf's questions about how he got the map. Only then, after almost four Ms. pages, does the story return to the suggestion (now transferred from the wizard to Bilbo) about sitting on the back doorstep. From this, we might conclude that the Fragment might not be so incomplete as it appears; it probably represents the entire latter half of the opening chapter as originally conceived, rather than roughly the middle third as we might otherwise assume.

As before, I give the text in its original form, silently supplying punctuation where necessary and noting interesting revisions and additions to the text in brackets. The present chapter divisions did not yet exist and were not inserted by Tolkien until much later, probably at the point when he was creating the First Typescript (that is, after he reached the end of the Second Phase). For ease of reference for readers familiar with the published text, I have, after considerable debate, decided it is best to break the Second and Third Phase manuscripts at the points where the eventual chapter divisions occur. While publishing several blocks of chapters together and only pausing when Tolkien broke off composition for one of the periodic interruptions that occurred over the two and a half years he spent writing the book (e.g., at pages 316 [Ms. p. 118] and 620 [Ms. p. 167]) would give a better idea of the smooth flow of the original story from incident to incident and site to site, the familiar chapter breaks help organize the material into short, convenient segments and enable notes and commentary to be much closer to the relevant passage than would otherwise be the case. But it must be emphasized that these chapter divisions are, so far as the manuscript of *The Hobbit* goes, purely artificial breaks which were not yet present when the text was written. Textual notes follow the transcription; these do not record every slip of the pen but instead remark upon variant readings that seem to me significant. Commentary follows the textual notes. Those who want to read the story as Tolkien wrote it without interrupting the flow of the narrative for notes and commentary can simply skip over these sections on an initial reading since I have distinguished typographically between the commentary (all of which is printed in this smaller font) and the original text.

his mouth shut. He loved maps, and in his hall there was a large one of the Country Round[TN2] with all his favourite walks marked on it in red ink. 'How could such an eenormous door (he was a hobbit, remember) be kept secret?', he asked.

'Lots of ways' said Bladorthin, 'but which one of them we don't know without looking. From what it says on the map I should say that there is a closed door which has been made to look exactly like the side of the mountain. That is the ordinary dwarves' method – I think I am right?'

'Quite' said Gandalf. 'This rather alters things – for the better. We had thought of going [up along the River Running >] East as quiet and careful as we could, until we came to the Long Lake. After that the trouble would begin. We might go up along the River Running, and so to the ruins of Dale – the old town in the valley there under the shadow of the Mountain – if we ever got so far! But we none of us liked the idea of the Front Door. The river runs right out of that great gate at the south of the mountain, and out of it comes the Dragon too – far too often.'

'That would have been no good' said the wizard, 'not without a mighty warrior, even a Hero. I tried to find one. But warriors are busy fighting one another in distant lands, and in this neighbourhood heroes are scarce – or simply not to be found. Swords in these parts are mostly blunt, and axes are used for trees, and shields for cradles or dish-covers, and dragons are comfortably far off (and therefore legendary).[TN3] Therefore *burglary* seemed indicated – especially when I remembered the existence of a side-door.'

'Yes, yes' said all the dwarves; 'Let's find a burglar!'

'Here he is' said Bladorthin; 'here is our little Bilbo, Bilbo Baggins the burglar!'

'The burglar[?]!' said Dwalin.

'Precisely', said Bladorthin not allowing poor Bilbo a chance to speak. 'Did not I tell you all last Thursday that it would have to be a burglary not a battle? And a burglar I promised to find – I hope no one is going to say I put the sign on the wrong door again!' He frowned so frightfully that Bilbo dared not say anything, though he was bursting with exclamations and questions.

'Well well' said all the dwarves, 'now we can make some plans. What do you suggest, Mr Baggins?' they asked, more respectfully than they had spoken to him yet.

'First I should like to know a bit more about things' said Bilbo feeling all confused and a bit shaky inside – though it was partly from excitement. 'About the gold and the dragon, and all that, and how it got there, and who it belongs to, and so on and further'.

'Bless me' said Gandalf, 'haven't you got a map, and didn't you hear our song, and haven't we been talking all about it for hours'.

'All the same I would like it all plain and clear' said Bilbo, putting on his business manner and doing his best to be wise and prudent, and live up to his new job.

'Very well' said Gandalf: 'long ago in my grandfather's day [the dwarves >] some dwarves were driven out of the far north and came with all their wealth and their tools to this Mountain on the map. There they mined and tunnelled and made huge halls and great workshops – and I believe in addition found a good deal of gold and of jewels too. Anyway they grew immensely rich and famous, and my grandfather was king under the mountain, and the mortal men who lived to the south, and even up the Running river as far as the valley beneath the mountain, where a merry town of Dale was in those days, treated them with great reverence.

Kings would send for our smiths, and reward even the least skilful richly. Fathers would beg of us to take on their sons as apprentices, and pay us well in excellent food – which we never bothered to grow or make. Altogether those were good days for us, and we had money to lend and to spend, and leisure to make beautiful things just for the fun of it, so that my grandfather's halls were full of marvellous jewels, and cups, and carvings.

Undoubtedly that was what brought the Dragon. They steal gold and jewels you know, from men and elves and dwarves, wherever they can find it. And they guard it as long as they live (which is practically forever if they are not killed) and never enjoy a brass-ring of it. They hardly know a good bit of work from a bad, though they have a good notion of the price, and they can't make anything for themselves, not even mend a loose scale of their armour.

There were lots of dragons in the North in those days, and gold was probably running short there with the dwarves flying south or getting killed, and all the general waste and destruction that dragons make going from bad to worse. There was a most especially strong, greedy and wicked worm called Smaug.[TN4] One day he flew up into the air, and came South. The first we heard of it was a noise like a hurricane coming from the North, and the pine trees on the mountain-sides creaking and cracking in the wind. Some of the dwarves outside (I was one, a fine lad in those days I was, always wandering about, and that saved me that day) – well from a good way off we saw in the middle of the wind the dragon settle on the mountain in a spout of flame. He came down the slopes, and when he reached the woods they all went up in fire. By that time the bells were all ringing in Dale, and warriors were arming. The dwarves rushed out of their great gate, but there was the dragon waiting for them. None escaped that way. The River rushed up in steam, and a fog fell on Dale, and in the fog the dragon came and [destroyed it >] destroyed most of the warriors. Then he went back and crept in through the Front Gate, and routed out all the halls, and lanes, and tunnels, alleys, cellars, mansions and passages. There were no dwarves left, and all their wealth he took for himself. Probably, for that is the dragons' way, he has piled it all up in [a] great heap in some hall far inside, and sleeps on it for a bed.[TN5]

Out of the gate he used to creep and come by night to Dale, and carry off people, especially maidens, to eat, until Dale was ruined, and all the people gone. What goes on now, I don't know, but I don't suppose anyone lives nearer the mountain than the Long Lake nowadays.

The few of us that were well outside sat and wept in hiding and cursed Smaug; and there we were very unexpectedly joined by my father and grandfather with singed beards. They looked very grim, but they said very little. When I asked how they had got away, they told me to hold my tongue, and one day, in the proper time, I would know.

After that we went away, and we have had to earn our living

as best we could up and down the lands – and often enough we have had to sink as low as black smithing and coal mining. But we have never forgotten our stolen treasure. And even now, when I will allow we have all a good deal laid by and are not so badly off,' (and Gandalf stroked the gold chain round his neck) 'we still mean to get it back, and bring our curses home to Smaug – if we can.

'I have often wondered about my father's and grandfather's escape – & now I see they made a map, and I should like to know how Bladorthin found it'.

'I didn't', said the wizard; 'I was given it. Your grandfather Gandalf you will remember was killed in the mines of Moria by a goblin'.[TN6]

'Curse [him >] the goblin, yes' said Gandalf.

'And your father went away on the third of March a hundred years ago last Tuesday, and has never been seen (by you) since.'

'True, true' said Gandalf.

'Your father gave me this' said Bladorthin, '[and >] to give to you, and if I have chosen my own time and way to give it to you, you can hardly blame me considering the trouble I had to find you.

'Here it is', said he and handed the map to Gandalf. 'Your father couldn't remember your name when he gave it me and never told me his own, so on the whole I think I am to be thanked.'

'I don't understand' said Gandalf. Neither did Bilbo, who felt that the explanation, which [was >] had begun by being given to him, was getting difficult once more.

'Your grandfather' said Bladorthin 'gave the map to his son for safety before he went to the mines of Moria. Your father went away to try his own luck with it after his father was killed; and lots of adventures he had, but he never got near the Mountain. How he ended up there I don't know; but I found him a prisoner in the dungeons of the Necromancer.'

'What were you doing there' said Gandalf with a shudder, and all the other dwarves [went >] shivered.

'Never you mind' said Bladorthin: 'I was finding things out, and a nasty dangerous business it was. Even I only just escaped. However I tried to save your father, but it was too late. He was witless and wandering, and had forgotten almost everything except the map'.

'The goblins of Moria have been repaid' said Gandalf; 'we must give a thought to the Necromancer'.

'Don't be absurd' said the wizard. 'That is a job quite beyond the powers of all the dwarves, if they could be all gathered together again from the four corners of the world. And anyway [others >] his castle stands no more and [his >] he is flown [*added*: to another darker place] – Beren and Tinúviel broke his power, but that is quite another story. Remember the one thing your father wished was for his son to read the map, and act on its message. The Mountain & the Dragon are quite big enough tasks for you'.

'Hear hear!' said Bilbo, and said it accidently aloud.

'Hear what?' they all said turning suddenly towards him, and he was so surprised that he answered:

'Hear what I have got to say!'

'What's that?' they asked.

'Well' said Bilbo 'I should say we [> you] ought to go East and have a look round, at least. After all there is the back door, and dragons must sleep sometimes.[TN7] If we [> you] sit on the back doorstep long enough I daresay we should [> you will] think of something. And well, don't you know, I think you have said [> talked] enough for one night, if you see what I mean. What about bed, and an early start. I will give you a good breakfast before you go'.

'Before *we* go' said Gandalf. 'Aren't you the burglar,[TN8] and isn't the side door your job? But I agree about bed and breakfast'.

So they all got up. And Bilbo had to find room for them all, and filled all his spare-rooms, and made beds on couches and chairs; and when he went to his own little bed very tired and not altogether happy, he could still hear Gandalf humming to himself in the best bedroom

'Far over the misty mountains cold
To dungeons deep and caverns old
We must away ere break of day
To find our long forgotten gold'

He went to sleep with that in his ears and it gave him uncomfortable dreams, and it was after break of day when he woke up.

TEXT NOTES

1 For another example of a composite typescript/manuscript text, see the initial draft of 'The Great Cake' (i.e., *Smith of Wootton Major*), published in facsimile on pages 102–29 of the Extended Edition of *SWM* edited by Verlyn Flieger [2005].

2 The 'County Round' of the Pryftan Fragment has now become the 'Country Round' of the published text, the precursor for what would, in the sequel, become the Shire.

3 A similar sentiment is expressed in *Farmer Giles of Ham*, which was first drafted either immediately before or immediately after *The Hobbit* (see pp. 492–3):

> . . . dragons on their side may have been forgetting about the knights and their swords, just as the knights were forgetting about the real dragons and getting used to imitation tails made in the kitchen.
>
> —FGH [50th anniversary extended edition, 1999], pp. 84–5.

This passage from the second draft text was recast in the third draft of the story ('The Lord of Thame'), about the time Tolkien was putting the final text of *The Hobbit* in order for submission to Allen & Unwin, into a form much more closely resembling the phrasing in *The Hobbit*:

> 'So knights are mythical!' said the younger and less experienced dragons. 'We always thought so.'
>
> 'At least they may be getting rare,' thought the older and wiser worms; 'far and few and no longer to be feared.'
>
> —ibid., p. 25.

4 Here the name 'Smaug' occurs for the first time as part of the original text (as opposed to a later revision); in the Bladorthin Typescript it appeared only as a revision replacing *Pryftan*. The name change may be taken as one indication of a gap in time between composition of these two (for more evidence, see the commentary on 'The Third of March' beginning on p. 84).

5 This habit of sleeping atop a mound of treasure is indeed traditional, and is shared by Beowulf's dragon, Sigurd's Fafnir, and dragons of medieval romance such as the dragon slain by Fulk Fitzwarrin (an exile from King John's court), of which we are told that its treasure consisted of 'the cool gold upon which alone it could sleep, because of the hot fire in its belly' (Jacqueline Simpson, *British Dragons* [1980; rev. ed. 2001], p. 57). It is also a hallmark of Tolkien's dragons: Glorund (see pp. 529–30), the nameless dragon of 'The Hoard' (first published in 1923 as 'Iúmonna Gold Galdre Bewunden'), and Snaug himself, and presumably also of Giles' Chrysophylax Dives (who certainly has a mort of treasure in his lair) and Scatha the Worm (from whose horde come heirlooms still treasured by the Rohirrim eleven centuries later).

6 Tolkien began to write another word, which may have begun with a capital letter, before cancelling it and writing 'a goblin', but the cancellation is so complete that I cannot make out any letter(s).

7 As originally drafted, this paragraph reads

> 'Well' said Bilbo 'I should say we ought to go East and have a look round, at least. After all there is the back door, and dragons must sleep sometimes, *and well, don't you know. I think we have talked as much as is good for us. What about bed, and an early start.* If we sit on the back doorstep long enough I daresay we should [> will] think of something. And well, don't you know, I think you have said [> talked] enough for one night, if you see what I mean. What about bed, and an early start. I will give you a good breakfast before you go'.

The portion printed in italics here was cancelled and that text repeated after the following sentence, incorporating the revision '. . . as much as is good for us [> you]' made before the cancellation. By the simple expedient of changing 'we' and 'us' to 'you' throughout the first few sentences, this whole passage was revised to mute Bilbo's newfound enthusiasm and distance the hobbit from the rest.

8 Gandalf's speech originally ended here after a short cancelled word or phrase, possibly 'after all' (i.e., 'aren't you the burglar *after all*').

(i)
The Dwarves

Through Bilbo's request for more information, and first Gandalf's and then Bladorthin's explanations, we learn a good deal more about the setting and characters, particularly about the dwarves.[1] This is important, for the most significant departure in *The Hobbit* from the old mythology of the Silmarillion texts lies in the new story's more or less sympathetic treatment of Durin's Folk. In their earlier appearances in Tolkien's tales, the dwarves had always been portrayed as an evil people: allies of goblins, mercenaries of Morgoth, pillagers of one of the great elven kingdoms.[2] Thus, their characterization here is totally at variance with what is said and shown of them in the old legends. And the break is both sudden and complete: no intermediate stages prepared the way. For them to be treated sympathetically as heroes of the new story is nothing short of amazing: no less surprising than if a company of goblin wolf-riders had ridden up to Bag-End seeking a really first-class burglar.

It seems impossible now to pinpoint exactly where dwarves entered the mythology, but it was sometime during the Lost Tales period (i.e., 1917–20). They played a major role in only one of the tales – 'The Nauglafring: The Necklace of the Dwarves' – but are mentioned, at least in passing, in three others: 'The Tale of Tinúviel' (the story of Beren & Lúthien), 'Turambar and the Foalókë' (the story of Túrin), and the unfinished 'Gilfanon's Tale' (the story of the Coming of Men). Throughout these early stories they are viewed exclusively from an (unflattering) elvish perspective, one best conveyed by an entry in the *Gnomish Lexicon*, where the Goldogrin/Gnomish word *nauglafel* is glossed as 'dwarf-natured, i.e. mean, avaricious' (BLT I.261; *Parma Eldalamberon* XI.59).

The Tale of Turambar's portrayal of Mîm the Fatherless, the first dwarf of note in the legendarium, establishes Tolkien's dwarves as guardians of vast treasure-hoards as well as the originators of inimical curses. The image of 'an old misshapen dwarf who sat ever on the pile of gold singing black songs of enchantment to himself' and who 'by many a dark spell . . . bound it to [him]self' (BLT II.113–14), along with the dying curse he lays upon the treasure, comes directly from the Icelandic legends which formed such a large part of Tolkien's professional repertoire. In particular, the old story of the famous hoard of the Nibelungs that plays a crucial part in works as different as the *Völsunga Saga*, Snorri's *Prose Edda*, the *Nibelungenlied*, and Wagner's Ring cycle provides the motif of a treasure stolen from the dwarves which later brings disaster upon all those who seek to claim it, even the descendants and kin of its original owners – the theme which dominates the final quarter of Tolkien's book.[3] Another work that Tolkien was much interested in for the glimpses it provided of ancient lore, *Heidreks Saga* (edited and translated into English by Christopher Tolkien as *The Saga of King Heidrek the Wise* [1960]), features an episode wherein a hero captures the dwarves Dvalin and Durin and forces them to forge him a magical sword; they do so but before departing lay a curse upon it so that once drawn it can never be resheathed until it has taken a human life.[4]

Of all these early references to dwarves, that in 'The Tale of Tinúviel' is the slightest and least judgmental. As part of her lengthening spell, Lúthien names 'the tallest and longest things upon Earth', foremost among which are 'the beards of the Indravangs' (BLT II.19). From the *Gnomish Lexicon* we learn that Indravang is 'a special name of the *nauglath* or dwarves' meaning Longbeards (ibid., p. 344; the 'vang/fang' element is the same as that occurring in the later *Fang*orn or 'Treebeard' and written on Fimbulfambi's Map). Here again we see a tie to Tolkien's philological studies: for the Langobards, or Longbeards, were one of the Germanic tribes who invaded the crumbling Roman Empire in the sixth century, settling in that area of Italy still called *Lombardy* in their memory. Tolkien was much interested in the Langobards' history and legend; in his unfinished time-travel story *The Lost Road* [circa 1936], he gave the main characters Lombardic names (Alboin and Audoin) and planned a chapter set in Lombardic times (HME V.37 & 77–8). This chapter was never written, but he did recast an episode from *Beowulf* into an alliterative poem he called 'King Sheave', presenting it as the mythical history of the Lombards (HME V.87–91; cf. Christopher Tolkien's comments on pages 53–5 and 93 regarding his father's fascination with Langobardic legends). Finally, Gandalf's curious phrase about 'money to lend and to spend' (p. 71) gains new significance in light of the fact that the Lombards became famed bankers, so much so that by the fourteenth century 'lombard' had became a common noun in Middle English meaning banker, money-lender, or pawnbroker.

We learn more of the Longbeards in 'The Nauglafring', the one of these early stories in which dwarves play the largest part. Here it is revealed that there are two main races of dwarves: the Nauglath of Nogrod and the Indrafangs (or Longbeards) of Belegost.[5] The dwarves in *The Hobbit* are descendants of the latter, as Gandalf states at Rivendell (p. 116):

> 'Durin, Durin' said Gandalf. 'He was the father of the fathers of one of the two races of dwarves, the Longbeards, and my grandfather's ancestor.'

The Indrafangs or Longbeards may have had some special tie to Mîm, for in 'The Nauglafring' they join in the planned raid on Tinwelint's kingdom (Artanor, the later Doriath) only when they hear of Mîm's death and the theft of his treasure (BLT II.230) – but what this tie may be, we do not know. At any rate, the King of Nogrod's vow 'to rest not ere Mîm was thrice avenged' (BLT II.230) is strikingly echoed in Gandalf's determination to 'bring our curses home to Smaug' and his reflection that 'The goblins of Moria have been repaid . . . we must give a thought to the Necromancer'.

Unedifying though it may be, 'The Nauglafring' does offer us the first extended view of Tolkien's dwarves – one so much at variance with that race as developed in *The Hobbit* that Tolkien was eventually obliged to create a new name for the old race, the 'petty dwarves', to distinguish the people of Mîm from Durin's Folk and their peers, the kindred of the Seven Houses of the dwarves.[6] According to the old story,

> The Nauglath are a strange race and none know surely whence they be; and they serve not Melko nor Manwë and reck not for Elf or Man, and some say that they have not heard of Ilúvatar, or hearing disbelieve. Howbeit in crafts and sciences and in the knowledge of the virtues of all things that are in the earth or under the water none excel them; yet they dwell beneath the ground in caves and tunnelled towns, and aforetime Nogrod was the mightiest of these. Old are they, and never comes a child among them, nor do they laugh. They are squat in stature, and yet are strong, and their beards reach even to their toes, but the beards of the Indrafangs are the longest of all, and are forked, and they bind them about their middles when they walk abroad. All these creatures have Men called 'Dwarves', and say that their crafts and cunning surpass that of the Gnomes [i.e., the Noldor or Deep-Elves] in marvellous contrivance, but of a truth there is little beauty in their works of themselves, for in those things of loveliness that they have wrought in ages past . . . renegade Gnomes . . . have ever had a hand. (BLT I.223–4)

Here we see the 'elvish' bias of the *Lost Tales* at its most blatant (a bias altogether missing from the more equitable narrative of *The Hobbit*), with the elvish narrator of the Tale unwilling even to give the dwarves credit for creating beautiful objects without elven help. Furthermore, we are told that as a result of the estrangement between the races that occurs in this tale (the 'old quarrel' referred to in passing in *The Hobbit*) 'the Dwarves [have] been severed in feud for ever since those days with the Elves, and drawn more nigh in friendship to the kin of Melko' (BLT II.230). Thus Naugladur, the dwarf-lord of Nogrod, hires Orc mercenaries to aid in the assault on Artanor, and in the outlines for the unfinished 'Gilfanon's Tale' it is a host of Dwarves and Goblins in the service of Melko-Morgoth who attack the first Men and their elven allies in the Battle of Palisor.

The mysteries surrounding the dwarves' origins expressed in 'The Nauglafring' endured to the time of *The Hobbit*'s composition and beyond;[7] the *Silmarillion* account of Aulë's creation of the dwarves did not enter the mythology until around the time of *The Hobbit*'s publication (and thus postdate the book's composition by roughly half a decade). Even here, in the (Later) 'Annals of Beleriand' (which are associated with the 1937 *Quenta Silmarillion*), it says that when dwarves die 'they go back into the stone of the mountains of which they were made' (HME V.129). The mystery about the dwarves' origins go all the way back to Norse myth: Snorri's *Prose Edda* mentions the old legend that dwarves 'had quickened in the earth and under the soil like maggots in flesh', acquiring 'human understanding and the appearance of men' through 'the decree of the gods . . . although they lived in the earth and in rocks' (*Prose Edda* p. 41). The essay 'Durin's Folk', which makes up the final third of Appendix A of *The Lord of the Rings*, mentions 'the foolish opinion among Men that there are no dwarf-women, and that the Dwarves "grow out of stone"' (*LotR*.1116) only to dismiss it out of hand, but this was clearly an afterthought: Tolkien's portrayal of dwarves exclusively as men, and usually old men, wherever they appear as characters in his works, from *The Book of Lost Tales* through to *The Lord of the Rings*, agrees with both Norse myth and folklore; the Brothers Grimm are as devoid of any female dwarves as are the two Eddas and the sagas.

In one important way, *The Hobbit* is closer to the original Norse lore than 'The Tale of the Nauglafring' had been: nomenclature. All but one of the dwarves in our story have Norse names, drawn directly from the *Elder Edda* (the sole apparent exception being Balin; cf. pp. 23–4), whereas in 'The Nauglafring' Tolkien had given them names in his invented languages. Fangluin the Aged, Naugladur king of Nogrod, Bodruith of Belegost, the Indrafangs and the Nauglath, the Nauglafring itself: all the nomenclature is Gnomish, the names the elven historians gave these people and places, not what they called themselves (in the *Gnomish Lexicon*, 'Bodruith' is glossed as 'revenge', while 'Naugladur' probably means simply 'Lord of the Dwarves'). By contrast, the name 'Mîm' harkens back to Old Norse, like Dwalin, Kili, Gandalf, and the rest.[8] Furthermore, there is no hint of any sort that Dwalin, Balin, &c., are not their real names: the 'secret language of the dwarves' and the motif of their hiding their true names had not yet arrived.

One curious motif that I believe was already present by the time this first chapter of *The Hobbit* was completed was the partial identification of the dwarves, in Tolkien's mind, with the Jewish people. Tolkien himself made the comparison in his 1965 BBC interview with Denys Gueroult[9] (much to the interviewer's astonishment). This is not to say that *The Hobbit* is an allegory of twentieth-century Zionism; rather that Tolkien drew selectively on the history of the medieval Jews when creating his dwarves. Some elements, such as the secret ancestral language (Khuzdul, Hebrew) reserved for use among themselves while they adopt the language of their neighbors (Common, Yiddish) for everyday use, were layered on later, during the *Lord of the Rings* stage.[10] But others were clearly present already. Like the ancient Hebrews, the dwarves have been driven from their homeland and suffered a diaspora; settling in scattered enclaves amongst other folk, yet still preserving their own culture. Their warlike nature could have come straight from *Joshua, Judges,* or *1st* & *2nd Maccabees,* while their great craftsmanship harkens back to the Jewish artisans of medieval Iberia, whose work was renowned throughout Christendom. Gandalf's phrase about 'money to lend and to spend' (p. 71) could apply equally to the Lombard-Longbeards, as we have already seen, and to the Jews – banking and money-lending being one of the reserved occupations for the Jews in most Christian countries. To his credit, Tolkien has been selective in his borrowings, omitting the pervasive anti-Semitism of the real Middle Ages expressed in such works as Chaucer's 'Prioress's Tale', Jocelyn of Brakelond's chronicle, or (to cite a somewhat later but all-too-relevant example) Shakespeare's *The Merchant of Venice.*[11]

(ii)
Moria

With Bladorthin's offhanded reference to 'the mines of Moria', a major element of Tolkien's dwarven mythology enters the legendarium. This is the first known mention anywhere in Tolkien's work of Moria, what would later become the Wonder of the Northern world, Khazad-dûm, the ancestral home of Durin's Folk. However, all this would come later: there is nothing in the text of *The Hobbit* to identify Moria as a *dwarrowdelf* (dwarf-delving) nor mark it as having any special significance for Gandalf's people, other than being the site of his grandfather's murder; from the context, it is far more likely a goblin-mine (we are told much of their 'mines' in the Misty Mountains chapter [Chapter IV]).

The geography is still murky, and seems to bear little relationship to the well-worked-out geography of the old tale. There is no indication of where Moria lay at this point – north, south, east, or west. In the old tale, the dwellings of the dwarves had lain in the far south: the map made in the mid- to late-1920s and printed in *The Shaping of Middle-earth* (HME IV, between pages 220 and 221) indicates that the dwarven strongholds Nogrod and Belegost lay far to the south-east of Broseliand/Beleriand, off the map itself; the later 'Eastward Extension' of this old map still places their dwellings off the mapped territory, with a note in the lower right corner that 'Southward in East feet of Blue Mountains are Belegost and Nogrod' (HME IV.231, 232). Against this is Gandalf's testimony that his ancestors came to the [Lonely] Mountain when they were driven out of the 'far north' by dragons. There is no mention in *The Hobbit* of Belegost, which in the old story had been the Longbeards' ancestral home, or of Nogrod. In *The Lord of the Rings* the dwarves' history is changed yet again and their movements greatly complicated: here Bilbo's companions are made descendants of the dwarves of Moria, now described as Durin's ancestral home, which had been 'enriched by many people and much lore and craft when the ancient cities of Nogrod and Belegost in the Blue Mountains were ruined at the breaking of Thangorodrim' at the end of the First Age (*LotR*.1108).[12] After being driven from Moria, the dwarves fled north first to the Lonely Mountain and then passed on to the Grey Mountains ('for those mountains were rich and little explored' – *LotR*.1109). When dragons forced them southward out of the Grey Mountains, some returned to the Lonely Mountain while others settled in the Iron Hills further to the east. Smaug's attack on the Lonely Mountain destroyed the Kingdom under the Mountain and caused the survivors to flee either east to the Iron Hills or far to the west to the Blue Mountains, not far from where Nogrod and Belegost had stood some six millennia before.

(iii)
The Necromancer

While Moria represents a new element in the legendarium, the Necromancer is an old acquaintance. The character goes back, in one form or another, all the way to the end of the 'Lost Tales' period. In the fragments and outlines that make up all we have of 'Gilfanon's Tale' – one of the truly 'lost' tales – appears 'a certain fay' (i.e., one of the Maiar) named Tû the wizard, 'for he was more skilled in magics than any that have dwelt ever yet beyond the land of Valinor'. According to one account, Tû or Túvo learned 'much black magic' from Melko in the Halls of Mandos during the latter's imprisonment there and 'entered the world' after Melko's destruction of the Two Trees and escape from Valinor, whereupon Tû 'set up a wizard kingship in the middle lands' (i.e., the center of the world, midway between East and West). Ruler of the Dark Elves of Palisor, the 'twilight people', the wizard-king dwelt underground in endless caverns beside a dark lake.

For all his sinister associations, this 'eldest of wizards' is not evil. In fact, he is god-fearing in the old-fashioned sense of the word; when one of his elves discovers the first Men sleeping in the Vale of Murmenalda, Tû forbids his people to waken them before their time, 'being frightened of the wrath of Ilúvatar'. Furthermore, perhaps from his earlier association with Mandos (the prophet of the Valar), he is aware that the humans are 'waiting for the light' and will not awaken until the first rising of the Sun. When one of his folk disobeys these orders, Tû takes the new Children of Ilúvatar under his protection and seeks to protect Men and Elves alike from 'evil fays'.

At this point a second, similar, figure appears upon the scene, variously called Fúkil or Fankil or Fangli, the servant (or, according to one version, the child) of Melko. Like Tû, Fangli is a fay or Maia, one of several who 'escaped into the world' at the time of Melko's chaining. Coming among the newly awakened humans, Fangli corrupts them, playing serpent in this Eden, and stirs up strife among the first Men. The result is the Battle of Palisor, where the Men corrupted by Fangli with their Dwarf and Goblin allies attack the twilight elves and the few Men still loyal to them. The outlines differ on whether Fangli's host or Tû's folk gain the victory, but most agree that 'the Men corrupted by Fangli fled away and became wild and savage tribes, worshipping Fangli and Melko'; some even specify that these Men become the 'dark and savage' peoples of the far south and east – the first hint of the Southron and Easterling, the Men of Harad and Khand and Rhûn (BLT I.232–7).

Neither Tû nor Fangli is mentioned again after the 'Lost Tales' were abandoned, but a new figure of great importance appears shortly afterwards who combines elements from both: Thû the necromancer. Also variously known as Gorthû and Sauron, this evil magician makes his first appearance in 'The Lay of Leithian'[13] and thereafter plays a major role in all of Tolkien's Middle-earth works:

Men called him Thû, and as a god
in after days beneath his rod
bewildered bowed to him, and made
his ghastly temples in the shade.
Not yet by Men enthralled adored,
now was he Morgoth's mightiest lord,
Master of Wolves, whose shivering howl
for ever echoed in the hills, and foul
enchantments and dark sigaldry
did weave and wield. In glamoury
that necromancer held his hosts
of phantoms and of wandering ghosts,
of misbegotten or spell-wronged
monsters that about him thronged,
working his bidding dark and vile:
the werewolves of the Wizard's Isle.

—Lay of Leithian, Canto VII, lines 2064–2079;
HME III.227–8.

While not yet as powerful as he later becomes, we have here the character of Sauron the Great fully developed: his undead servants (cf. *The Lord of the Rings*' Nazgûl); his desire for worship (prefigured in the Fangli story) and the dark temples which come to play so great a role in all versions of the Nūmenor story; his skill at sorcery, especially necromancy and mind-controlling enchantments. Elsewhere in the Lay there is even mention of his 'sleepless eyes of flame' (line 2055), with which he keeps endless watch on all comings and goings on the borders of Morgoth's land. The fate of those thrown into his dungeons is vividly described:

Thus came they unhappy into woe,
to dungeons no hope nor glimmer know,
where chained in chains that eat the flesh
and woven in webs of strangling mesh
they lay forgotten, in despair.

—Canto VII, lines 2210–2214;
HME III.231.

Bladorthin's comment that the Necromancer's castle 'stands no more, and he is flown to another darker place – Beren and Tinúviel broke his power, but that is quite another story' is an explicit reference back to events in 'The Lay of Leithian'. It is not surprising that the earlier work was still fresh in Tolkien's mind, nor that he would forge this connection between it and the new story taking shape. He had written the passages in the poem referring to Thû in March and April of 1928 – that is, just over two years before beginning *The Hobbit*. What's more, work on the two pieces overlapped: Tolkien began *The Hobbit* in the summer of 1930 and was still writing new lines for 'The Lay of Leithian' as late as September 1931 (HME III.304). Thus, if any part of the Silmarillion material were to have a direct impact on the new story, 'The Lay of Leithian' is the natural piece where we might expect to find it. And the influence is there, right down to verbal echoes: after Thû's defeat, the destruction of his tower, and the release of his captives, the Lay describes how Thû abandoned his body and took the form of a giant vampire bat

for Thû had flown
to Taur-na-Fuin, a new throne
and darker stronghold there to build.

—Canto IX, lines 2820–2822;
HME III.254–5.

Why, having made explicit ties between Mr. Baggins' story and that of Beren & Lúthien, did Tolkien later cut these lines? The answer, I think, lies in the problems of chronology they create. If, as Bladorthin says, Gandalf's father perished in the dungeons of the Necromancer but his castle has since been cast down by Beren and Tinuviel, then less than a century has passed between those events and the time of *our* story (since Gandalf's father set out on his ill-fated journey 'a hundred years ago last

Tuesday') – far too short a time to create the narrative distance from the Silmarillion tradition Tolkien seems to be striving for. It also involves the story in a serious contradiction later on, for we are told by Elrond in Chapter III that the swords from the troll lair are 'old swords, very old swords of the elves . . . made in Gondolin for the goblin-wars . . . dragons destroyed that city *many ages ago*' (p. 115; emphasis mine), yet the Fall of Gondolin came a generation or two *after* the time of Beren and Lúthien. The simplest way out of these difficulties was to eliminate one of the two references, either to Gondolin or to Beren & Tinúviel. Since the swords (and knife) from Gondolin play a crucial part in the narrative while the allusion to 'The Lay of Leithian' is essentially ornamental, it is no surprise that this is the reference which Tolkien decided to cut. Still, it is significant that it stood in the manuscript throughout the Second Phase – that is, for the bulk of the drafting of the story – and was only removed in the Third Phase with the creation of the First Typescript, after the story had been brought to the brink of the Siege of the Mountain; it is our strongest indicator that while writing *The Hobbit* Tolkien already considered it part of the mythology.

(iv)
The Third of March

Given Tolkien's scrupulous attention to detail, how are we to account for Bladorthin's remark that 'last Tuesday' was the third of March when only a few pages before the text had stated clearly and unambiguously that 'it was April' (see p. 36) – especially when we are told in the very next chapter that Bilbo's journey began 'one fine morning just before May', a date borne out by subsequent references (cf. p. 90: 'the weather . . . had off and on been as good as May can be . . . "To think it is June the first tomorrow" grumbled Bilbo')? The answer, of course, lies in the gap in composition between the first and last parts of this chapter: when Tolkien drafted this line as part of the Second Phase, he simply forgot that he had already set the scene for the Unexpected Party in April during the First Phase. The error remained in the book until the second edition of 1951, when Tolkien changed the starting date of Thrain's expedition to 'the twenty-first of April, a hundred years ago last Thursday' and toyed with ascribing the error to 'a misreading of the difficult hand and language of the original diary' (cf. p. 752).

From time to time efforts have been made to prove that Tolkien used the calendar for an actual year to construct the time-table for Bilbo's journey – see, for example, Mick Henry's 'The Hobbit Calendar' in the May 1993 issue of *Amon Hen* (pp. 14–15), which argues for 1932 on the grounds that April 21st fell on a Thursday that year. Interestingly enough, this error on Tolkien's part offers the best proof possible that he was *not* working from the calendar of a specific year, since it would have been easy for him to avoid this and other chronological anomalies if he was simply following the current calendar (again, see Tolkien's attempt years later to 'fix' the timeline of events in *The Hobbit* in the Fifth Phase). Furthermore, it is clear from reading his memorandum noting changes needed for the second edition that the change from Tuesday to Thursday was purely accidental; Tolkien simply forgot that the original text specified Tuesday rather than Thursday, and he was reluctant to abandon 'the comic precision' of 'one hundred years ago last Thursday' (see p. 750).

NOTES

1 In essence, 'The Unexpected Party' (to give Chapter I its eventual title) combines within its two halves parallels to both of the first two chapters in *The Lord of the Rings* ('A Long-Expected Party' and 'The Shadow of the Past', the latter originally named 'Ancient History'), with the light-hearted gathering immediately followed by a revelation of the somewhat sinister history underlying the quest that is about to begin.

2 Thus, they are included under the rubric *Úvanimor*, who are defined in 'The Coming of the Valar' as 'Úvanimor (who are monsters, giants, and ogres)' (BLT I.75); compare *ūvanimo* in the *Qenya Lexicon*, which is glossed as 'monster' (*Parma Eldalamberon* XII.98). An outline for the 'Story of the Nauglafring or the Necklace of the Dwarves' mentions how Linwë/Tinwelint, the figure who became Thingol Greycloak in later versions of the story, took a golden hoard 'and he had a great necklace made by certain Úvanimor (Nautar or Nauglath)' – i.e., dwarves (BLT II.136). Similarly, an outline for 'Gilfanon's Tale' tells how Úvanimor (goblins and dwarves) fought together under the command of Melko's servant, variously called Fangli, Fankil, and Fúkil, against men and elves at the Battle of Palisor (?Eden); see p. 82 and BLT I.236–7. For more on dwarves as part of what we might call the Children of Morgoth (that is, those forces allied with Melko/Melkor in the early stages of the mythology), see also BLT II.247.

3 For more on the theme of the cursed hoard, see pages 595–600 and also Tolkien's poem 'The Hoard' (ATB poem #14, pp. 53–6), which he himself explicitly ties back to 'the heroic days at the end of the First Age' (ATB, Preface, p. 8).

4 This saga is also the source of one of Gollum's riddles (see p. 173) and one of the sources for Dwalin's and Durin's names (see p. 42).

5 Elsewhere in the *Lost Tales*, Tolkien uses 'nauglath' in a less restrictive sense, to mean the whole of the dwarven race; cf. BLT II.223–4 and CT's commentary on p. 247.

Tolkien later commented to Stanley Unwin, apropos of the 'dwarfs/dwarves' issue, that *dwarf* and *gnome* 'are only translations into approximate equivalents of creatures with different names and rather different functions in their own world'; hence dwarf perhaps 'may be allowed a peculiar plural' ('Dwarrows' letter, JRRT to SU, 15th October 1937; *Letters* p. 23). Here he was no doubt referring to the use of the term *dwarf* rather than *nauglath* or *indrafang*.

6 This change came very late in the evolution of the legend(s), circa 1959–60. Cf. the essay 'Quendi and Eldar' in HME XI.

7 In the 1930 *Quenta* it is said 'There they [the elves] made war upon the Dwarves of Nogrod and Belegost; but they did not discover whence that strange race came, nor have any since. They are not friend of Valar or of Eldar or of Men, nor do they serve Morgoth; though they are in many things more like his people, and little did they love the Gnomes . . .' (HME IV.103–4); later 'made war upon' was changed to 'had converse with' (ibid.108). The 'Annals of Beleriand', composed slightly later, preserves the same idea in other words: 'in those mountains they met the Dwarves, and there was yet no enmity between them and nonetheless little love. For it is not known whence the Dwarves came, save that they are not of Elf-kin or mortal kind or of Morgoth's breed' (HME IV.331). See pp. 721–2 for more on dwarven origin myths.

8 Tolkien may have derived the name from *Mimir*, the Norse god of wisdom, but more likely this represents one of his very few borrowings from Wagner, who gave the name 'Mime' to the dwarven smith who counselled Siegfried how to slay the giant Fafnir (a role filled by Regin in the Eddas and *Völsunga Saga*).

9 The first reference to this analogue I have found is in Tolkien's 1947 'Thrym Thistlebeard' letter (see p. 757). More specifically, Tolkien says in the 1965 interview:

> The Dwarves of course are quite obviously a – wouldn't you say that in many ways they remind you of the Jews? All their words are Semitic, obviously; constructed to *be* Semitic. There's a tremendous love of the artefact. And of course the immense warlike passion of the Jews too, which we tend to forget nowadays.
>
> —JRRT to Denys Gueroult, 1965 BBC interview.

10 The first sign of this motif that I am aware of occurs in Tolkien's February 1938 letter to *The Observer*:

> These dwarves are not quite the dwarfs of better known lore. They have been given Scandinavian names, it is true; but that is an editorial concession. Too many names in the tongues proper to the period might have been alarming. Dwarvish was both complicated and cacophonous. Even early elvish philologists avoided it, and the dwarves were obliged to use other languages, except for entirely private conversations.
>
> —*Letters* p. 31; see Appendix II.

11 Tolkien's own attitude towards anti-Semitism was eloquently expressed in 1938 when he was asked by a German publisher to confirm his

arisch (Aryan) ancestry. To his own publisher he wrote 'I should object strongly to any such declaration appearing in print. I do not regard the (probable) absence of all Jewish blood as necessarily honourable; and I have many Jewish friends, and should regret giving any colour to the notion that I subscribed to the wholly pernicious and unscientific race-doctrine.' To the German publishers, he retorted 'if I am to understand that you are enquiring whether I am of *Jewish* origin, I can only reply that I regret that I appear to have *no* ancestors of that gifted people' (*Letters of J. R. R. Tolkien*, 25th July 1938, p. 37).

12 For Tolkien's eventual distinction between the good dwarves of Belegost and the less virtuous, more easily angered dwarves of Nogrod, see pp. 431–2.

13 Or, to give it its full title, 'The GEST of BEREN son of BARAHIR and LUTHIEN the FAY called TINUVIEL the NIGHTINGALE or the LAY OF LEITHIAN Release from Bondage' (HME III.153). Tolkien began this major work in the summer of 1925 and continued to work on it up through September 1931, so that it both precedes and is contemporaneous with his work on *The Hobbit*, particularly the First Phase (summer 1930) and the bulk of the Second Phase.

Chapter II

TROLLS

The text continues on the same page as before (manuscript page 18; Marq. 1/1/1:8), with its first paragraph comprising the last four lines on that page; no more than a single skipped line marks where the eventual chapter break would occur.

He jumped up and put on his dressing gown, and went out and saw all the signs of a very hurried breakfast. There was a dreadful lot of washing up in the kitchen, and crumbs and mess in the diningroom, and no fires. Nor were there any dwarves or wizard.

Bilbo would have thought it all a bad dream, if there hadn't been such a lot of washing up and mess to clear away.

Still he could not help feeling relieved, in a way, and yet in a way a bit disappointed to think they had all gone without him – 'and with never a thank you' he thought. So he put on an apron [and started on the washing up >] lit fires, boiled water, washed up, had a nice little breakfast, & did the dining room. By that time the sun was shining, and the front door was open letting in a jolly warm breeze. Bilbo began to whistle, and to forget about the night before. In fact he was just sitting down to a second breakfast by the kitchen window, when in walked Bladorthin.

'My dear fellow' he said, 'when ever are you going to [start >] come? What about an early start! – and here you are still having breakfast at half past ten. They left you the message because they could n't wait'.

'What message' said Bilbo all in a fluster.

'Great elephants' said Bladorthin 'you're not yourself at all this morning. You have never dusted the mantelpiece.'

'What's that got to do with it: I have had enough to do with washing up breakfast for thirteen.'[TN1]

'If you had dusted the mantelpiece you would have found this just under the clock.' And Bladorthin handed Bilbo a note (written of course on his own note paper). This is what he read:

'Gandalf and company to Burglar Bilbo, greetings! For your hospitality our sincerest thanks, and for your offer of professional assistance our grateful acceptance. Terms cash on delivery up to and not exceeding one fourteenth share of total profits. Thinking it unnecessary to disturb your esteemed repose we have proceeded in advance to make necessary preparations, and shall await your respected person at the Great Mill[TN2] across the river at 11 a.m sharp. Trusting you will be *punctual* we remain yours deeply G & Co.'

'That leaves you just ten minutes. It is a mile. You will have to run!' said Bladorthin.

'But – ' said Bilbo. 'No time for it' said the wizard. Even to this day Bilbo does not remember how he found himself outside without a hat, or a walking stick, or any money, and leaving half of his second breakfast unfinished and not washed up, and leaving his keys in Bladorthin's hand, and running as fast as his furry feet would carry him down the lane, and over the bridge, across the river, and so for a whole mile or more.

Very puffed he was when he got there on the stroke of eleven, and found he hadn't brought a pocket handkerchief!

'Bravo' said Balin who was standing by the mill door [*added*: looking out for him]. Just then all the others came round the corner of the lane from the village. They were on ponies, and each pony was slung about with all kinds of baggages, packages, parcels and paraphernalia. There was a pony for Bilbo.

'Up you two get' said Gandalf 'and off we go!'

'I am awfully sorry' said Bilbo 'but I have come without my hat, and I have left my pocket handkerchief behind, and my money. I didn't get your note till after 10.45, to be precise.'

'Don't be precise' said Dwalin, 'and don't worry. You will have to manage without pocket handkerchiefs, and lots of other things before we get to our journey's end. As for a hat I have a spare hood and cloak in my luggage.'

That's how they all came to start, jogging off from the mill one fine morning just before May, on laden ponies; and Bilbo was wearing a dark green hood (a little weather stained) and a dark green cloak borrowed from Dwalin. But he hadn't a gold chain, nor a beard so he couldn't be mistaken for a dwarf, not from close to.

They hadn't been riding very far[TN3] when up came Bladorthin very splendid on a white horse. He had brought a lot of pocket handkerchiefs and Bilbo's pipe and tobacco. So after that the party went very merrily, and they told stories and sang songs as they rode along all day, except of course when they stopped for picnic meals. These weren't quite as often as Bilbo was used to, but still he began to feel that he was enjoying himself.

Things went on like this for quite a long while. There was a good deal of wide respectable country to pass through inhabited by decent respectable folk, men or hobbits, or elves, or what not, with good roads, an inn or two, and every now and then a dwarf or a tinker or a farmer ambling by on business.

But after a time they came to places where people spoke strangely and sang songs Bilbo had never heard before. Inns were rare, the roads were not good, and there were hills in the distance rising higher and higher. There were castles on some of the hills, and some looked as if they had not been built for any good purpose. Also the weather, which had off and on been as good as May can be even in tales and legends, took a nasty turn.

'To think it is June the first tomorrow' grumbled Bilbo, as he splashed along behind the others in a very muddy track. It was after tea-time; it was pouring with rain (and had been all day); his hood was dripping into his eyes, his cloak was full of water; the pony was tired and stumbled [and shook >] on stones; the others were too grumpy to talk – 'and I am sure the rain has got at my dry clothes and into the food bags' thought Bilbo. 'Bother burglary and everything to do with it. I wish I was at home in my nice hole by the fire with the kettle just beginning to sing.' It was not the last time he wished that.

Still the dwarves jogged on, never turning round or taking any notice of the hobbit. Somewhere behind the grey clouds the sun must have gone down, for it began to get dark. Wind got up, and the willows along the riverbank [*added*: bent and sighed] – I don't know what river it was, a rushing red one swollen with the rains of the last few days that came down from the hills and mountains in front of them.

Soon it was nearly dark. The winds broke up the grey clouds, and a waning moon appeared above the hills between the flying rags. They stopped and Gandalf muttered something about 'supper, and where shall we get a dry patch to sleep on'.

Not until then did they notice that Bladorthin was missing. So far he had come all the way with them, never saying if he was in the adventure or merely keeping them company for a while. He had eaten most, talked most, and laughed most. But now he simply wasn't there at all.

'Just when a wizard would have been most useful too,' growled Dori & Nori (who shared the hobbit's opinions about regular meals, lots and often).

It seemed it would have to be a camp. They had camped before and knew they would soon have to camp regularly when they were among the misty mountains and beyond and far from the lands of respectable people, it seemed a bad wet evening to begin with.[TN4]

They moved to a clump of trees. It was drier underneath them, but the wind shook the rain off the leaves and the drip drip was most annoying. Also the mischief seemed to have got into the fire. Dwarves can make a fire almost anywhere out of almost anything, wind or no wind. But they couldn't do it that night.[TN5] Then one of the ponies took fright at nothing and bolted. He got in the river before they could catch him; and before they got him out again Fili & Kili were nearly drowned, and all the baggage was washed away off him. Of course it was mostly food, and there was mighty little left for supper, and less for breakfast.

There they all sat glum and wet and muttering while Bofur & Bombur tried to light a fire[TN6] and quarrelled about it. Bilbo was sadly reflecting that adventures are not all pony-rides in May sunshine, when Dwalin[TN7] who was always their look-out man said: 'There's a light over there'.

There was a hill some way off with some trees on, pretty thick in parts. Out of the trees shone a light, a reddish comfortable looking light, as it might be a fire or torches twinkling. When they had looked at it, they fell to arguing. Some said 'no' and some said 'yes'. Some said they could but go and see, and any thing was better than little supper less breakfast and wet clothes all night. Others said 'These parts are none too well known, and too near the mountains. Not even a policeman on a bicycle is ever seen this way; they have rarely heard of the king even; and the less inquisitive you are as you go along the less trouble you are likely to find'

Some said: 'After all there are fourteen of us'. Others said 'Where *has* Bladorthin got to.' This remark was repeated by all. Then they went at it again. Just then the rain began again, and Dori & Nori[TN8] began to fight. That settled it. 'After all we have got a burglar with us' they said, and so they made off leading their ponies (with all due & proper caution) in the direction of the light.

They came to the hill, and were soon in the wood. Up the hill they went, but there was no proper path to be seen, and do what they could they made a deal of rustling and crackling and creaking (and a lot of grumbling and dratting) as they went through the trees.

Suddenly the red light shone out very bright not far ahead. 'Now it is the burglar's turn' they said, meaning Bilbo. 'You must go on and find out all about that light, and what it is for, and if all is perfectly safe and canny' said Gandalf to the hobbit. 'Now scuttle off, and come back quick, if all is well. If not come back if you can. If you can't hoot twice like a barn owl and once like a white screech owl, and we will do what we can'.

Off Bilbo had to go, before he could explain that he couldn't hoot even once like any kind of owl, no more than fly like a bat.

At any rate hobbits can move quietly in woods, absolutely quietly.

They take a pride in it, and Bilbo had sniffed more than once at what he called 'all this dwarvish racket' as they went along – though I don't suppose you or I would have noticed anything at all on a windy night, not if the whole cavalcade had passed us two feet off.

As for Bilbo walking primly towards the red light, I don't suppose even a weasel would have stirred a whisker at it. So naturally he got right up to the fire – for fire it was – without disturbing anyone. And this is what he saw. Three very large persons sitting round a very large fire of beech logs; and they were toasting mutton on long spits of wood, and licking the gravy off their fingers. It smelt very fine and toothsome, and they had a barrel of good drink at hand, and were drinking out of jugs. But they were trolls. Obviously trolls. Even Bilbo, in spite of a sheltered life, could see that, from the great heavy faces of them, and their size and the shape of their legs, not to mention their language, which wasn't drawingroom fashion at all, at all.

'Mutton yesterday, mutton today, and blimey if it don't look like mutton again tomorrow' said one of the trolls.

'Never a blinking bit of manflesh have we had for long enough' said another. 'What the 'ell William was [a] thinking of in bringing us into these parts at all, beats me – and the drink running short, what's more' he said, jogging the elbow of William who was having a [drink >] pull at his jug.

William choked. 'Shut your mouth' he said, as soon as he could. 'You can't expect folk to stay here for ever just to be eaten [< et up] by you and Bert. You've et a village and a half between you since we came down from the mountains. Ow much more d'yer want. And time's been up our way when yerd have said "thank yer Bill" for a nice bit of valley-mutton like wot this is'. He took a big bite off a sheep's leg he was toasting, and wiped his lips on his sleeve.

Yes I am afraid trolls behave like that, even those with one head only. [TN9]

After hearing all this Bilbo ought to have done something. Either he ought to have gone back and warned his friends that there were three fairsized trolls at hand in a nasty mood when they would be quite likely to try toasted dwarf, or even pony as a change. Or else he should have gone on burglaring. A really good and legendary burglar would at this point have picked the Trolls' pockets – it is nearly always worth while, if you can do it – pinched the very mutton off their spits, purloined the beer, and walked off without their noticing him.[TN10]

Others more practical but with less professional pride would perhaps have stuck a dagger into each of them before they observed it. Then the night could have been spent cheerily.

Bilbo knew it. He had read a good deal more than he had seen or done. He was very much alarmed, and yet, and yet he did not somehow go straight back to Gandalf and company emptyhanded.

Of the various burglarious proceedings [*added*: he had heard of] picking the Trolls' pockets seemed the least difficult. He crept behind a tree, just behind William. Bert and Tom went off to the barrel. William was having a drink. [So >] Then Bilbo plucked up courage, and put his hand in William's pocket. There was a purse in it. 'Ha' thought Bilbo warming to his new work, and he lifted it carefully out, 'this is a beginning!'.

It was. Trolls' purses are the mischief, and this was no exception. 'Ere, oo are you' it squeaked as soon as he took it, and William turned round and grabbed him by the neck before he could duck behind the tree.

'Blimey, Bert look what I've copped' said William.

'What is it?' said the others.

'Lumme if I knows! What are yer?'

'Bilbo Baggins a bur – a hobbit' said poor Bilbo shaking all over and wondering how to make owl-noises, before they throttled him.

'A burrahobbit' said they a bit startled. Trolls are a bit slow in the uptake, and mighty suspicious about anything new to them.

'What's a burrahobbit got to do with my pocket, anyways', said William.

'And can yer cook 'em?' said Tom.

'You can try' said Bert picking up a skewer.

'He wouldn't make above a mouthful' said William who had already had a fine supper, 'not when he was skinned and boned.'

'Perhaps there are more of him round about' said Bert 'Ere you are there more of yer sneaking in these here wood, yer nassty little rabbit' said he looking at Bilbo's furry feet. And he picked him up by his toes and shook him.

'Yes lots' said Bilbo before he remembered not to give friends away. 'No none at all, not one' he said immediately afterwards.

'Wot d'yer mean' said Bert holding him right way up by the hair this time.

'What I say' said Bilbo gasping. 'And please don't cook me, kind sirs. I am a good cook myself, and cook better than I cook if you see what I mean. I'll cook beautifully for you a perfectly beautiful breakfast for you, if only you won't have me for supper.'

'Poor little blighter' said William (I told you he had already had supper, also he had had lots of beer). 'Let him go.'

'Not till he says what he means by "lots" and "none at all"' said Bert. 'I don't want my throat cut in me sleep. Hold his toes in the fire till he talks.'

'I won't 'ave it' said William. 'I caught him any way'.

'You're a fat fool William' said Bert 'as I said afore this evening'.

'And you're a lout'.

'And I won't take that from you' says Bert, and puts his fist in William's eye. Then there was a gorgeous row. Bilbo had just enough wits left to scramble out of the way of their feet, before they were fighting like dogs and calling each other all sorts of perfectly true and applicable names in very loud voices. Soon they were locked in one another's arms and rolling nearly into the fire kicking and thumping, while Tom whacked them both with a branch to bring them to their senses – and that of course made them madder than ever.

That would have been the time for Bilbo to have left. But his poor little feet were very squashed by Bert's big paw, and he had no breath left. So he lay for a while just outside the firelight.

In the middle of this fight up came Balin. The dwarves had heard the noise from afar, and waited, and when neither Bilbo came, nor the hoots were heard, they started off one by one to creep towards the fire.

No sooner did Tom see Balin come into the light, than he gave an awful howl. Trolls simply detest the sight of dwarves. Bert and William stopped fighting immediately, and 'a sack Tom quick' they said. Before Balin (who was wondering where Bilbo was in all this commotion) knew what was happening – a sack was over his head and he was down.

'There's more to come yet' said Tom 'or I'm [*added*: mighty] mistook. Lots and none at all, it is' said he. 'No burrahobbits, but lots of these ere dwarves. That's about the shape of it.'

'I reckon ye're right' said Bert, 'and we'd best get out of the firelight.' And so they did. With the sacks in their hands that they used for carrying off meat and other plunder they waited in the shadows. As each dwarf came up and looked at the fire and the spilled jugs and the gnawed mutton in surprise, pop went a nasty smelly sack over his head and he was down.

Soon Dwalin lay by Balin, and Fili and Kili together, and Dori Nori and Ori all in a heap, and Oin Gloin Bifur Bofur and Bombur uncomfortably near the fire.

'That'll teach 'em' said Tom; for Bofur and Bombur had given a lot of trouble, and fought like mad, as dwarves do when cornered. Gandalf came last – and he wasn't caught unawares. He came expecting mischief, and didn't need to see legs sticking out of sacks to tell him things were not all well.

He stood outside in the shadows a way off, and said:

'What's all this trouble. Who has been knocking my people about.'

'It's Trolls' said Bilbo from behind a tree. They had forgotten all about him. 'They're hiding in the bushes with sacks' said he.

'O are they' said Gandalf, 'Bladorthin will make them sorry for it when he comes back.' This was bluff, for he did not know whether Bladorthin ever was coming back; and he didn't know whether the Trolls knew his name well enough to be scared by it.[TN11] And he leaped forward to the fire before they could jump on him. He caught up a big branch all afire at one end and Bert got an end in his eye before he could step aside. That put him out of the battle for a bit. Bilbo did his best. He caught hold of Tom's leg (as well as he could, it was as fat as a young tree trunk) but was sent spinning off into the bushes when Tom kicked up the sparks into Gandalf's face.

He got the branch in his teeth for that, and lost one of the front ones. It made him howl, I can tell you; but William came up behind and popped a sack right over Gandalf's head. And so it ended. A nice pickle they were all in now, all nicely tied up in sacks, with three angry trolls (and two with burns and bruises to remember) sitting over them, and arguing whether they should roast them slowly, or mince them fine and boil them, or just sit on them one by one and squash them; And Bilbo up in a bush with his clothes and skin torn not daring to move for fear they should hear him.

It was just then that Bladorthin chose to come back. But no one saw him. The trolls had just decided to roast them and eat them later – that was Bert's idea.

'No good roasting 'em, it'd take all night' said a voice. Bert thought it was William's. 'Don't start the argument all over again, Bill' he said, 'or it *will* take all night'.

'Who's a-arguing?' said William who thought it was Bert that had spoken.

'You are' said Bert.

'You're a liar' said William.

And so the argument began all over again, and in the end they decided to mince them fine and boil 'em. So they got a big black pot, and they took out their knives.

'No good boiling 'em; we ain't got no water and it's a long way and all to the well' said a voice.

Bert and William thought it was Tom's. 'Shut up' said they 'or we'll never have done; and you can fetch the water yerself [*added*: if you argue]'.

'Shut up yerselves' said Tom, 'and get on with it, and fetch the bloody water.[TN12] Who's arguing but yerself, I'd like to know.'

'You are you booby' said William.

'Booby yourself' said Tom.

And so the argument began and went on hotter than ever again, until in the end they decided to sit on the sacks one by one and squash them, and boil them next time.

'Who shall we sit on first?' said the voice.

'Anyone,' said Bert [> William], who thought it was Tom speaking and didn't mind because he hadn't been hurt[TN13]

'Better sit on the last fellow first' said Tom [> Bert] whose eye was burnt by Gandalf; he thought Tom was talking.

'Don't talk to yourself' said William [> Tom]. 'Where is he?'

'The one with the yellow stockings' said Bert.

'Nonsense, the one with grey stockings' said his voice [> a voice like William's].

'I made sure it was yellow' said Bert.

'Yellow it was' said William.

'Then what did you say it was grey [*added*: for?].' said Bert.

'I never did, Tom said it'.

'That I didn't' said Tom 'it was you'.

'Two to one so shut your mouth' said Bert.

'Oo are you talking to' said William.

'Now stop it' said Tom and Bert together: 'the night's getting on and the dawn comes early. Let's get on with it'.

'Dawn take you both and be stone to you!' said a voice, that sounded like William's. But it wasn't. For just at that moment the light came over the hill, and there was a mighty twitter in the branches. William never spoke for he stood turned to stone as he stooped; and Bert and Tom were stuck like rocks as they looked at him. And there they stand to this day, I have no doubt, for Trolls as you know must be underground before dawn, or they go back to the stuff of the mountains they are made of, and never move again. That's what had happened to Bert and Tom and William.

'Excellent' said Bladorthin as he stepped from behind the bushes, and helped Bilbo to climb down out of the thorn [bush >] tree. Then Bilbo understood. It was Bladorthin's voice that had kept the trolls bickering and arguing till the dawn came and they were turned to stone.

The next thing was to untie the sacks and let out the dwarves. They were nearly suffocated, and very annoyed, and they hadn't [*added*: at all] liked lying there and listening to the trolls making plans for roasting them and squashing them and mincing them.

They had to hear Bilbo's account of what happened to him twice over before they were satisfied. 'Silly time to go practising burglary and pocket-picking,' said Bombur; 'when what we wanted was fire and food'.

'And that you couldn't have got [*added*: out of these fellows] without a struggle' said Bladorthin; 'and anyway you are wasting time now. You must [> don't seem to] realize that the Trolls must have a cave or a hole dug somewhere near to hide from the sun in. We must look into it'.

So now they searched about and found the mark of troll's stony boots, and followed them through the trees and further up the hill, until, hidden by bushes they came to a big door, and that they couldn't open. Not though they all pushed, and Bladorthin tried some magic.

'Would this be any good?' said Bilbo when they were getting tired. 'I found it on the ground where the Trolls were fighting'. He held out a largish key, but no doubt William thought it very small & secret. Out of his pocket it must have fallen before he was turned to stone, very luckily too.

'Why didn't you mention it before!' they said and Bladorthin grabbed it and fitted it in the key hole. Then the stone door swung back with a big push, and they all went inside. There were bones on the floor and a nasty smell in the air; but there was a deal of coins in earthen pots at the far end of the cave, and a sword or two on the walls, and a bunch of curious keys on a nail; and that was all they found.

The coins they carried out and loaded onto ponies and took them away and buried them very secretly not far from the track by the river, with a deal of spells and curses over them, just in case they ever had the chance to come back and cart them home. Bladorthin took a sword, and Gandalf another; and Bilbo took a little dagger in a leather sheath – little for a dwarf, but a big sword for Bilbo.[TN14] 'They have a good look [> look like good blades]' said Bladorthin, 'but if we can read the runes on 'em, we shall know more about 'em.'

'Let's get out of the smell' said Fili. And so they went, and would have left the keys.

'Hello!' said Bladorthin 'what are these do you suppose? There are no other locks or doors in here. These keys were not made for this place'. So he brought them out and hung them on his belt.

By that time it was breakfast time. They eat what they found of the trolls' that was good to eat – there was bread and cheese and ale to spare and bacon to roast in the embers of the fire. Then they slept, for their night had been disturbed. In the afternoon they got on their ponies, and jogged along the track [*added*: again Eastward].

'Where did you get to, if I may ask?' said Gandalf to Bladorthin as they went along. 'To look ahead' said he.

'What brought you back, in the nick of time?'

'Looking behind!' said he.

'Exactly' said Gandalf; 'but could you be more plain?'

'I went on to spy out our road, which will soon become dangerous and difficult – and I found out a good deal that will be of service (especially in the replenishment of our small stock of provisions). But also I heard about the three trolls from the mountains & their settlement in the woods near the track where they waylaid strangers. So I had a feeling I was needed back. And looking behind I saw a fire and came to it. That's that'.

'Thank you' said Gandalf.

TEXT NOTES

1 The correct number, fourteen (= the thirteen dwarves plus Bladorthin), appears in the first typescript (1/1/52:1).

2 The Great Mill remained the rendezvous spot right up until the page proofs (Marq. 1/2/1: page 41), where it was changed first to the Green Man and then to the familiar Green Dragon Inn. Note that even after these changes, the first illustration in the published book, 'The Hill: Hobbiton-across-the-Water', traces Bilbo's entire route from his round green door in the distance right down to the Mill, not the Inn. The Great Mill was based on Sarehole Mill, near which Tolkien lived when a boy (1896–1900); see 'The Mill on the River Cole' by Peter Klein in *An Afternoon in Middle-Earth* [1969], pages 15–16.

3 Immediately after the word 'far' appears another illegible, cancelled word. It appears that Tolkien originally wrote this line to read '. . . hadn't been riding very far <west>', but the final cancelled word is too blotted to be sure. If the cancelled word was initially 'west', then it shows just how fluid his conception of the tale's geography was at the time.

4 This sentence was changed to read 'They hadn't camped before & although they knew they would soon have to camp regularly . . . it seemed a bad wet evening to begin on.' Note that 'the misty mountains' remains a descriptive term, as in the dwarves' song, and has not yet become a proper noun (something which first occurs early in Chapter III; see p. 111).

5 Added at this point: 'not even Oin & Gloin who were especially good at it'.

6 Here 'Bofur & Bombur tried to light a fire' is changed to 'Oin & Gloin went on trying to light a fire' to tie in with the previous insertion (see TN5).

7 'Dwalin' is changed here to 'Balin', suggesting that Tolkien was initially undecided which of these brothers would be the group's look-out (a role that ultimately fell to Balin). Note that it was Dwalin who was first to arrive at Bilbo's house – as we might expect of a look-out man sent ahead to scout out their reception, while it is his brother who sees Bilbo arrive out-of-breath at the Mill; the addition of the phrase 'looking

out for him' there makes it clear that Balin was acting as look-out at the time.

8 'Dori & Nori' is changed to 'Oin & Gloin' here, as the climax of the little scene inserted in the preceding revisions noted in TN5 and TN6.

9 This observation was originally followed by the cancelled (and incomplete) lines: 'Bilbo had no idea what [to do >] a burglar ought to do, or how to do it. we can tell him what of course but how is'.

Trolls with multiple heads appear in many stories, perhaps the most famous of which is Dasent's 'Soria Moria Castle', where the hero must confront and defeat first a three-headed troll, then a six-headed troll, and finally a nine-headed troll (*East o' the Sun & West o' the Moon* [1888], pages 397–401). This same story might have contributed to the naming of *Moria*; see Tolkien's letter to Mr. Rang, August 1967; *Letters* p. 384.

10 This passage originally read: '. . . pinched the very mutton off their spits, purloined the beer, and *if he hadn't maybe stuck a dagger into each of them without their noticing it – After which the night could have been spent cheerily*' before the latter section was cancelled and moved into its own following paragraph.

For examples of 'really good and legendary' burglars, see Dunsany's thieves' tales such as 'The Bird of the Difficult Eye',† 'The Distressing Tale of Thangobrind the Jeweller',†† 'The Probable Adventure of the Three Literary Men',†† *A Night at an Inn* [1916], and especially 'How Nuth Would Have Practised His Art Upon the Gnoles'.††

† From *The Last Book of Wonder* [1916].
†† From *The Book of Wonder* [1912].

11 These two sentences relating Gandalf's bluff were cancelled sometime before the first typescript of this passage was made.

12 This passage was revised to read 'Shut up yerself' said Tom, *who thought it was William's voice*. 'Who's arguing . . .'

13 This paragraph was cancelled. Upside down on the bottom of the next page (the back of this same sheet) is preserved a scrap of draft dialogue that preceded this exchange – one of several occasions where Tolkien started a piece of draft, abandoned and cancelled it, then flipped the piece of paper over and began again on the other side. The entire cancelled passage reads as follows:

> 'Which shall we sit on first?' said the voice.
> 'Anyone,' said William,† who thought it was Tom speaking and didn't mind because he hadn't been hurt.
> Better sit on the last fellow

† Here Tolkien began to write 'Bert' but changed his mind after writing down only the first two letters and changed it to 'William'.

14 'little for a dwarf, but a big sword for Bilbo' was changed to 'a little penknife for a troll, but . . .'

(i)

The Trolls

We are dealing here with rough, first-draft text, yet the story is already well-advanced, both in general outline and in many details. Some of the wittiest lines and sharpest rejoinders are yet to come – e.g., 'trolls simply detest the sight of dwarves' lacks the parenthetical addendum '(uncooked)' – but the draft is recognizably the same book as the final polished text (as when the angry trolls call each other 'all sorts of perfectly true and applicable names'). Indeed, it is this closeness between first and final text which makes the divergences all the more interesting. As in the first chapter, there is much shifting of the roles assigned to the dwarves, with an eye toward consolidation and simplification. Thus it is originally Dwalin, not Balin, who is 'always their look-out man' (despite Balin's having apparently filled that role only a few pages before). Similarly, it is Bofur and Bombur who try to light the fire, and Dori and Nori who come to blows, before revisions assign both roles to Oin and Gloin, adding an earlier mention that these two dwarves were 'especially good at it' (firebuilding, that is), giving the scene a cumulative, cascading effect. Once again Tolkien's first impulse was to make use of his full cast, whereas the end result is to let a few of the dwarves make a strong impression on the reader while reducing the rest to nonentities.

Like so much else in Bilbo's world, trolls enter the mythology through the *Lost Tales*. However, they played no part in the story of the Elder Days, only appearing on the scene on the cusp of historical times, 'many ages of Men' after the War against Melko (Morgoth). They belong rather to the frame story, the tale of Eriol. In an early outline for what later became 'The History of Eriol', or 'Ælfwine of England', we are told that after the disaster of the Faring Forth and the final defeat and fading of the Elves, 'Men come to Tol Eressëa [i.e., the isle of Great Britain] and also Orcs, Dwarves, Gongs, *Trolls*, etc.' (BLT II.283, italics mine). And while Eriol is himself mythical, Tolkien took pains to tie him to historical figures, making him the father of Hengest and Horsa, the Jutes who led the English invasion of Britain in A.D. 449–455 (BLT II.290; *Finn and Hengest* [1982] p. 70). Thus, trolls did not enter England until the Germanic invasions (appropriately enough, since they derive from Scandinavian and not Celtic or Roman mythology) and are not yet conceived of as part of Melko the Morgoth's retinue.

A less oblique appearance, and more direct precursor for William, Bert, and Tom, comes not from the legendarium but in a poem Tolkien wrote while at Leeds (i.e., 1920–25), one of the 'Songs for the Philologists' later compiled by A. H. Smith in his 1936 booklet. Originally known as

'Pēro & Pōdex' (Latin for 'boot and bottom'), it appeared in *Songs for the Philologists* as 'The Root of the Boot'[1] and, in suitably revised form, in Chapter XII of *The Lord of the Rings*.[2] The text of the original manuscript, of interest because here we meet Tolkien's first troll character with a speaking part, differs slightly from any of the published versions:

Pēro & Pōdex

1. *A troll sat alone on his seat of stone*
And munched and mumbled a bare old bone,
And long and long he had sat there lone
And seen nor man nor mortal
Ortal!
portal!
And long and long he had sat there lone
And seen nor man nor mortal

2. *Up came Tom with his big boots on;*
'Hullo!' says he 'pray, what is yon?
It looks like the leg of me uncle John,
As should be a-lyin' in churchyard'.
Searchyard
birchyard &c.

3. *'Young man' says the troll, 'that bone I stole;*
But what be bones, when mayhap the soul
In heaven on high hath an aureole
As big and as bright as a bonfire?'
On fire
Yon fire &c.

4. *Says Tom 'Oddsteeth! 'tis my belief,*
If bonfire there be 'tis underneath;
For old man John was as proper a thief
As ever wore black on a Sunday,
Grundy
Monday &c.

5. *But still thou old swine 'tis no matter o'thine*
A-trying thy teeth on an uncle o' mine,
So get to Hell before thou dine
And ask thee leave of me nuncle
uncle
buncle &c.'

6. *In the proper place upon the base*
Tom boots him right – but alas that race
Hath as stony a seat as it is in face
And Pero was punished by Podex
Odex!
Codex! &c.

7. *Now Tom goes lame since home he came,*
And his bootless foot is grievous game;
But troll will not gnaw that bone for shame
To think it was boned of a boner
owner!
donor! &c.[3]

Note that while the troll's speech is somewhat archaic, it is loftier, more formal and correct, than Tom's, as when the troll speaks airily of an 'aureole' (halo), in contrast to Tom's dropped consonants and low curses.[4] The exact opposite applies to the trolls Bilbo meets in *The Hobbit*, who all speak a comic cockney slang in contrast to Bilbo's correct, rather formal way of speaking. It may seem odd, at first glance, that William, Bert, and Tom speak cockney rather than some rustic, rural dialect. The later character Sam Gamgee proves that Tolkien could write comic rustic extremely well: why, then, did he assign an urban dialect like cockney, the speech of lower-class Londoners, to these trolls rather than 'Mummerset' or some other country dialect?

The simplest explanation is that he adopted cockney because it was easily recognizable to his intended audience: i.e., John, Michael, and Christopher. As such, it need not be an accurate representation of actual Londoner speech to achieve his purpose, so long as it succeeds in creating the desired comic effect, as it certainly does.[5] Incongruity has a charm of its own, and the cockney trolls are of a piece with the anachronisms embedded in the text (the policeman on a bicycle in the current chapter is an obvious example, and very Dunsanian).[6] Then, too, with his love of the countryside and idealization of rural life Tolkien may have thought an urban dialect more appropriate to ruffians than any country dialect. In any case, it is hardly credible that marauders in parts where 'they have rarely heard of the king even' should speak the King's English.

More curious than their speech is the trolls' fate, the result of the first of a whole string of deceitful, misleading, or riddling conversations that run throughout the book. Despite Tolkien's breezy addition of 'as you know' to the description of their petrification, he seems to have introduced the motif to English fiction;[7] allergies to sunlight play no part in the most famous story involving trolls before Tolkien, 'The Three Billy Goats Gruff', nor in T.H. White's short story 'The Troll' [1935].

In Dasent's *East o' the Sun & West o' the Moon* [1859; expanded edition 1888], the trolls 'burst' with disappointment when defeated,[8] while Lang's *Pink Fairy Book* [1897] records a troll whose heart is hidden inside a fish; he dies when the fish is killed and cut up (as Tolkien noted, a very old motif, going back to Egyptian times; OFS.20). Katharine Briggs, who should certainly know, credits Tolkien with popularizing, but not inventing, the motif,[9] and the evidence of Stith Thompson's *Motif-Index of Folk-Literature*, with its massive listing of every 'motif' or plot-element in fairy tales and folklore, bears this out.[10]

Tolkien's source, insofar as he had a specific source, was probably one of two poems from the *Elder Edda*, *Helgaqviða Hjervarðzsonar* ('The Lay of Helgi Hjorvard's Son') and *Alvíssmál* ('The Lay of Alvis'). In the former, the heroes Atli and Helgi prolong a conversation with the giantess Hrimgerd, who seeks to destroy their ship and drown them all, until the sun rises and petrifies her:

> *Atli said:*
> *'Turn your eyes east, Hrimgerd, Helgi's runes*
> *have brought you down to death;*
> *at sea or in harbor the fleet is safe,*
> *and the warriors with it too.'*
>
> *Helgi said:*
> *'It's day now, Hrimgerd, Atli delayed you –*
> *now you must face your fate:*
> *you'll mark the harbor and make men laugh*
> *when they see you turned to stone.'*
>
> —*Helgaqviða Hjǫrvarðzsonar,* stanzas 30–31;
> *Poems from the Elder Edda,* tr. Patricia Terry
> [rev. ed., 1990], p. 110.

Similarly, in *Alvíssmál,* the dwarf Alvis ('All-wise') comes to Valhalla to claim his promised bride and is delayed by Thor, who questions him until sunrise, whereupon he is destroyed:

> *Thor said:*
> *'I never met another man*
> *so learned in ancient lore;*
> *but too much talk has trapped you, dwarf,*
> *for you must die in daylight.*
> *The sun now shines into the hall.'*
>
> —*Alvíssmál,* stanza 35;
> *Poems from the Elder Edda,* tr. Terry, p. 95.

Neither of these victims is what Tolkien would call a troll, but Jacob Grimm notes in his massive compendium and overview of religion and folklore, *Teutonic Mythology*, 'numerous approximations and overlappings between the giant-legend and those of dwarfs . . . as the comprehensive name *troll* in Scandinavian tradition would itself indicate. Dwarfs of the mountains are, like giants, liable to transformation into stone, as indeed they have sprung out of stone' (*Teutonic Mythology*, tr. James Stallybrass [1883], volume II p. 552). On page 551 in the same book Grimm alludes to the many legends of neolithic stone circles being petrified giants (indeed, although Grimm does not mention it, one of the old names for Stonehenge was 'The Giants' Dance'), and concludes (citing Hrimgerd's fate as his authority) that 'It would appear . . . that giants, like dwarfs, have reason to dread the daylight, and if surprised by the break of day, they *turn to stone*.' Tolkien obviously chose not to use this motif for his dwarves, but Grimm's comment about the inclusiveness of 'troll' as a descriptive term perhaps helps explain the presence of giants in some of his stories (the nameless giant who starts all the trouble in *Farmer Giles of Ham*, the stone-giants in Chapter IV of *The Hobbit*) yet their apparent absence from the final version of his mythology as presented in *The Lord of the Rings*; see p. 144.

So while Tolkien is on solid folk-lore ground in having his three trolls petrified by sunlight,† he is strongly at variance with what an English audience of his day had been taught to expect about trolls. In fact, he is ignoring or sidestepping a modern fairy-tale tradition in favor of reviving an ancient folk-lore belief once held by people who actually believed in such creatures, just as his elves (whom we shall shortly meet) are the elves of medieval Europe, not the 'flower fairies' of Conan Doyle's gullible imagination. When given a choice, Tolkien opts over and over again for folk-lore over fairy tale (as the term was understood before Tolkien redefined it in *On Fairy-Stories*), ancient belief over artificial invention.

The trolls' hoard is almost as interesting as its owners. Bladorthin's inability to read the runes on the swords is a simple set-up for the scene with Elrond in the next chapter, which was thus clearly already planned. Later development of the wizard as a peerless lore-master (as in, for example, the Moria gate and 'Scroll of Isildur' scenes in *The Lord of the Rings*) created a paradox that Elrond could read the runes while Gandalf the Grey could not, a puzzle that Tolkien resolved with typical panache in the 1960 Hobbit (see pp. 801 & 813). We will return to the swords and their explicit ties to the older mythology in the commentary following the next chapter.

In terms of plot, the troll hoard can be viewed as a simple means of getting needed items plausibly into the characters' hands – most notably the two swords and Bilbo's dagger. But in the manuscript they find a fourth treasure, ultimately more important than any of the others: the

† See page 110.

troll-key. This is a major departure from the published text, where the key to the secret door in the Lonely Mountain is given by the wizard to Thorin in the first chapter along with the map, having conveniently been overlooked by the Necromancer's jailers when they stripped his father and threw him into their dungeons. Tolkien's original plan, however, was to have the necessary key turn up by chance ('if chance we can call it') along the way. This scheme remained in place all through the first draft. This extraordinary bit of luck is really no greater than that involved in Bilbo's finding the ring or his happening in his wanderings below the mountains upon the one person who could show him the way out, and it avoids the puzzling carelessness of the Necromancer in the published version. Based upon the portrayal in 'The Lay of Leithian', Thû is a cunning, careful jailor who might conceivably miss a scrap of parchment or find it amusing to leave someone imprisoned without hope of escape with a map to a treasure he could never reach, but it seems utterly unlikely he would ever allow a prisoner to keep a key anywhere about his person.

In the odd behavior of the dwarves over the gold plundered from the trolls' lair, we see once again the dwarven association with curses and malefic magic:

> The coins they carried out and loaded onto ponies and took them away and buried them very secretly not far from the track by the river, with a deal of spells and curses over them, just in case (p. 97)

For more on dwarven curses, see pp. 598–9.

(ii)
Bilbo's Contract

As already noted in the discussion of Fimbulfambi's Map (p. 23), Tolkien delighted in providing his readers with physical objects from the world of the story. Some of these, such as the map of the Mountain, found their way into print as part of the books they were meant to accompany, although not as he had envisioned them. Others, such as the pages from the Book of Mazarbul meant to accompany the Moria chapters of *The Lord of the Rings*, proved too difficult to reproduce and languished for decades, only to be printed at last in art books, divorced from their proper context. Another fine example is the previously unpublished copy of Bilbo's contract (plate two of the Frontispiece), written in tengwar, the most famous of Tolkien's invented alphabets. Since it uses the name 'Thorin' for the chief dwarf rather than 'Gandalf', it obviously belongs to a later stage of composition and in fact was made sometime between February 1937 and February 1938.[11]

The tengwar text is a semiphonetical transcription (for example, the word 'honour', in Thorin's closing line is spelled 'onr'). The text is essentially that of the published book, differing from the draft mainly in the name-change from 'Gandalf and company' to 'Thorin & Co' (he even signs the facsimile with his initial, þ[orin] O[akenshield]) and in the addition of extra legalese. Thus 'necessary preparations' becomes 'requisite preparations'. More amusingly, the terms of the contract are expanded to cover a number of eventualities: after the phrase 'one fourteenth share of total profits' are added the following riders:

> . . . total profits (if any); all travelling expenses guaranteed in any event; funeral expenses to be defrayed by us or our representatives, if occasion arises and the matter is not otherwise arranged for.

– i.e., if the burglar has not been eaten or met with some similar fate. The comic precision of these terms later becomes important in the climax, when fair distribution of the treasure becomes the moral crux upon which the resolution of the story depends.

In addition to this facsimile, Tolkien also made three illustrations of the troll-scene, only one of which was used. Together, they illustrate the whole encounter. The first, and best, of the pictures, 'Trolls' Hill' (Plate IV [bottom]), shows the fire Dwalin spotted off in the distance as a single red spot on an otherwise black-and-white drawing; the necessity for colour reproduction was probably the key factor in this slightly ominous picture's exclusion. The second, the sinister picture included in *The Hobbit* ('The Trolls'), shows a dwarf approaching a forest clearing where three monstrous figures lurk just out of sight among the trees.[12] The third and final illustration (Plate V [top]) shows the great lumpish figures of the trolls turning to stone at sunrise; also clearly visible are the wizard with his staff, Bilbo hiding in the thorn bushes, and the captive dwarves.

Another illustration probably intended for this chapter is the 'The Hill: Hobbiton' (Plate IV [top]), which in one version or another has long served as a frontispiece for the published book; the whole sequence is reproduced in *Artist & Illustrator* (H-S#92–98), while Anderson places three examples in their proper place, near the beginning of 'Chapter 2: Roast Mutton' (DAA.62–3). As noted in Text Note 2 (p. 98), the placement of Bag-End at the top and the Great Mill at the bottom shows us the route Bilbo took in his mad dash to keep his appointment with Gandalf & Company. The change of the rendezvous from the Great Mill to first the Green Man and then the Green Dragon Inn obscured the picture's direct tie to the action, relegating it to a background piece. In all versions, we can see Bag-End centered in the distance, with the winding road Bilbo ran down ('a mile or more') before meeting the dwarves outside the Mill.

Text of Bilbo's Contract

For purposes of comparison, I give here the text from the Second Phase manuscript (pp. 88–9) followed by Taum Santoski's transcription of the tengwar document.

Manuscript text:

> Gandalf and company to Burglar Bilbo, greetings! For your hospitality our sincerest thanks, and for your offer of professional assistance our grateful acceptance. Terms cash on delivery up to and not exceeding one fourteenth share of total profits. Thinking it unnecessary to disturb your esteemed repose we have proceeded in advance to make necessary preparations, and shall await your respected person at the Great Mill across the river at 11 a.m sharp. Trusting you will be *punctual* we remain yours deeply G & Co.

Tengwar text from the facsimile document:

> Thorin and Company to Burglar Bilbo
>
> Greeting!
>
> For your hospitality our sincerest thanks, and for your offer of professional assistance our grateful acceptance. Terms: cash on delivery, up to and not exceeding one fourteenth of total profits (if any); all travelling expenses guaranteed in any event; funeral expenses to be defrayed by us or our representatives, if occasion arises and the matter is not otherwise arranged for.
>
> Thinking it unnecessary to disturb your esteemed repose, we have proceeded in advance to make requisite preparations, and shall await your respected person at the Green Dragon Inn, Bywater, at 11 a.m. sharp. Trusting that you will be *punctual,*
>
> —We have the honour to remain
> Yours deeply
> Thorin & Co.

NOTES

1 The 1936 text can be found in HME VI.143.

2 This final version (*LotR.*223–4) was reprinted in *The Adventures of Tom Bombadil* as 'The Stone Troll' (ATB poem #7, pp. 39–40); a recording of Tolkien singing the song to the tune of the old folk-song 'The Fox Went Out' appeared on the 1967 Caedmon record *Poems and Songs of Middle Earth.*

3 This poem underwent a great deal of revision and substitution even as it was being written: 'uncle' in the second stanza was changed to

'nuncle'; the entire fifth stanza was replaced by 'But still I don't see what is that to thee,/Wi' me kith and me kin a-makin' free/So get to Hell and ax leave o' he/Afore thou gnaws me uncle'. The third and fourth lines of the sixth stanza were changed to 'hath a more stony [> stonier] seat than its stony face' and 'and he [> Tom] rued that root on the rumpo/lumpo/bumpo'. Finally, the last lines of the poem seem to have given Tolkien special trouble: first he changed them to 'But troll's old seat is much the same/And the bone he boned from its owner/Donor/Boner' – the reading he adopted in *Songs for the Philologists*. But on the manuscript he follows this at once with 'That it was once in the boot of a burglar/Jurgler/<burgler>', taking quite literally Tom's earlier description of his Uncle John as 'a thief'. When Tolkien decided to adapt this poem for inclusion in *The Lord of the Rings*, he deleted the references to heaven, hell, and churchyard (since he conceived of Middle-earth as a pre-Christian world with no 'church' per se), changing the latter to the less specific 'graveyard'. In addition to completely rewriting the original sixth stanza into two new stanzas, Tolkien also added a whole new stanza between the original fifth and sixth stanzas, making the passive troll much more menacing:

'For a couple o' pins,' says Troll, and grins,
'I'll eat thee too, and gnaw thy shins.
A bit o' fresh meat will go down sweet!
I'll try my teeth on thee now.
Hee now! See now!
I'm tired o' gnawing old bones and skins;
I've a mind to dine on thee now.'

The new stanza is interesting because here we can see the chain of revisions come full circle. The depiction of William, Bert, and Tom in *The Hobbit* clearly derives from the old poem, but their characterization in the story in turn requires a rewriting of the poem to accommodate the changing conception, changing the Lonely Troll from a scavenger of carrion to a cannibalistic murderer. William's touches of good-nature are perfectly in keeping with the original troll of 'Pēro & Pōdex', a theme Tolkien also developed in the poem 'Perry-the-Winkle' (ATB poem #8, pp. 41–4). Later, when Tolkien had decided that trolls were creations of Morgoth (cf. *LotR*.507†), he revised this scene accordingly to remove the last traces of 'humanity': see pp. 799–800.

† 'Maybe you have heard of Trolls? They are mighty strong. But Trolls are only counterfeits, made by the Enemy in the Great Darkness, in mockery of Ents, as Orcs were of Elves. We are stronger than Trolls. We are made of the bones of the earth.' – Treebeard the Ent.

4 'Oddsteeth' (i.e., 'by God's teeth') is not attested by the OED, but many similar constructions are listed there, such as *Ods blood, Ods bodikins*, and *Ods wounds* (more frequently condensed still further to 'zounds!'). A fair number of examples occur in Shakespeare, and Chaucer mentions the practice of swearing by bits of God's body in 'The Pardoner's Tale':

With oaths so damnable in blasphemy
That it's a grisly thing to hear them swear
Our dear Lord's body they will rend and tear

—*The Canterbury Tales*, tr. Nevill Coghill [1962], p. 263

By the eighteenth and nineteenth centuries, the practice had ceased to be considered a strong blasphemy and become instead a mild way of swearing, eventually drifting into parody, as in this example by Tolkien.

5 Tolkien was professionally interested in dialects; his mentor when an undergraduate, Joseph Wright, was the editor and compiler of the massive *English Dialect Dictionary* [six volumes, 1898–1905], and Tolkien himself wrote the introduction to Haigh's *A New Glossary of the Dialect of the Huddersfield District* [1928]. The leading expert of his time on the medieval dialect of the West Midlands, he also ranged further afield. Thus, in 1931 Tolkien delivered a major paper published three years later as 'Chaucer as a Philologist: The Reeve's Tale', in which he examines Chaucer's spelling and word choice minutely through a number of manuscripts and concludes that in this Canterbury Tale Chaucer deliberately used dialect for comic effect. While giving Chaucer high marks for accuracy, he notes some lapses but judges them unimportant, so long as the general effect is conveyed to the intended audience.

6 Compare, for example, Dunsany's 'The Bird of the Difficult Eye' [*The Last Book of Wonder*, 1916], where Neepy Thang buys a special ticket at a London train station to the End of the World.

7 The only possible exception I have found comes in William Morris's *The Roots of the Mountains*, where at one point a character who believes in the existence of 'trolls and wood-wights' in the deep forest observes that 'trolls would not come out of the waste into the sunlight of the Dale' but does not specify why [1889; Newcastle Forgotten Fantasy re-issue, 1979, p. 175].

8 This occurs both in Dasent's title story and also in another story in his collection, 'Boots and the Troll', though not in a third, 'The Three Billy Goats Gruff.' In more recent times, Poul Anderson, in *Three Hearts and Three Lions* [1953], borrows the troll-turned-to-stone-by-daylight motif for a scene in his retelling of the story of Ogier the Dane. Terry Pratchett incorporated the idea into one of the early novels from his Discworld series, with the difference that his trolls come back to life again when the sun sets; cf. *The Light Fantastic* [1986] p. 98.

9 In her entry on *trow*, a variety of trolls found in the Shetlands, Briggs notes 'The gigantic trolls, it will be remembered, could not live in the light of the sun, but turned into stone. This trait has *been made familiar* to many readers by its introduction into J. R. R. TOLKIEN's *The Hobbit*. The Shetland trows also found the light of the sun dangerous, but not fatal. A trow who is above-ground at sunrise is earthbound and cannot return to its underground dwelling until sunset' (Briggs, *A Dictionary of Fairies: Hobgoblins, Brownies, Bogies, and other supernatural*

creatures. [1976; Penguin edition 1977], p. 413; emphasis mine).

10 Thompson cites several nineteenth- and early twentieth-century works on Norse mythology as his authorities for what he calls motif F531.6.12.2, 'Sunlight turns giant or troll to stone', as well as for motif F455.8.1, 'Trolls turn to stone at sunrise'. Grimm also cites, in his supplementary volume, 'Many Swed[ish] tales of giants whom the first beam of the sunrise turns into stone' (*Teutonic Mythology* vol. IV [1888], p. 1446).

11 These dates are established by two indicators. First, the rendezvous point given in the facsimile is 'the Green Dragon Inn, Bywater', a reading which replaced 'the Great Mill across The Water' in the marked page proofs Tolkien returned to Allen & Unwin shortly before 18th February 1937. Thus, the facsimile which incorporates this revision must postdate the page proofs. Second, the piece was in existence by February of 1938, since Tolkien refers to it in his letter to *The Observer*, in which he states that 'a facsimile of the original letter left on the mantelpiece can be supplied' (see Appendix II).

12 Brian Alderson, in the little booklet Blackwell Bookshops of Oxford issued commemorating the 50th anniversary of *The Hobbit* in 1987, was the first to note the close similarity of this picture to one by children's illustrator Jennie Harbour that had appeared in the 1921 collection *My Book of Favourite Fairy Tales* by Edric Vredenburg; Harbour's picture illustrates the Grimms' 'Hansel and Gretel'. Hammond & Scull print Harbour's and Tolkien's pictures on facing pages (H-S#101 & 102), as does Douglas Anderson in *The Annotated Hobbit*; Anderson also gives some background information on Harbour's career and states that Tolkien knew of Harbour's illustration through *The Fairy Tale Book* [1934].

† A possible source for this motif may come from *Grettir's Saga*, where Grettir fights a troll-woman in a scene parallel to Beowulf's encounters with Grendel and his Dam. After describing the she-troll's death, the saga then remarkably enough also gives an alternate version: '*Grettir said that the she-troll dived down into the gorge when she received the wound, but the men of Bardardale claim that* ***the day dawned upon her*** *as they were wrestling, and that she died when he cut off her arm –* ***and she still stands there*** *on the cliff,* ***turned into stone***' (*Grettir's Saga*, Chapter 65; tr. Denton Fox and Hermann Pálsson [1974; rpt 2005], page 138; emphasis mine). I am grateful to Marjorie Burns for drawing this passage to my attention.

A more proximate source probably lies in the work of Helen Buckhurst, a student and colleague of Tolkien's, and one of the people to whom he presented a signed copy of *The Hobbit* upon its first publication (see Appendix V). In a 1926 lecture on 'Icelandic Folklore' (later reprinted in *Saga-Book of the Viking Society*, Vol. X pages 216–263), Buckhurst retells several stories about 'Night-Trolls', who turn to stone at dawn – e.g.

> *'Dawn now hath caught thee, a stone shalt thou be,*
> *And no man henceforth shall be harmèd by thee'*
>
> —'The Night Troll' (*Saga-Book*, page 230)

and again in a story of two trolls ('old man' and 'old woman') moving an island:

> they were caught by the daylight, and the island came to rest there, where it remains to this day . . . And at that same moment the old man and old woman were turned to rocks . . . he is tall and thin, just as he was in life . . .
>
> —'Old Man and Old Woman' (ibid., page 231).

She also briefly summarizes a third such tale, based on a different rock formation, in which the island itself is 'a troll cow' flanked by its petrified troll owners (pages 231–232). For more on Buckhurst's work, including a compete reprint of 'The Night Troll', see DAA.80–82. I am grateful to Doug Anderson for drawing Buckhurst's work, and its importance, to my attention.

Chapter III

RIVENDELL

Once again the text continues without break, although this time what later became the third chapter starts at the top of a new page (manuscript page 32; Marq. 1/1/3:1); the chapter title for this short chapter ('A Short Rest') was added much later.

They did not sing or tell stories anymore that day, even though the weather improved; nor the next day, nor the day after.[TN1] They camped under the stars, and their horses had more to eat than they did. For there was plenty of grass, but their bags were getting low, even with what [Gandalf >] Bladorthin had brought back on his white horse.

One afternoon they forded the river at a wide shallow place full of the noise of stones and foam. The far bank was steep and slippery. When they got to the top leading their ponies, they saw the great mountains had marched down very near to them. Already they were [> seemed to be] only a day's amble from the feet of them [> the nearest mountain]. Dark and drear they looked, though there were patches of sunlight on their brown sides, and behind their shoulders the tips of snow peaks gleamed.

'Is that the mountain [> Mountain]' said Bilbo in a solemn voice; looking at the nearest one – a bigger thing than he had ever seen before.

'Of course not!' said Balin 'this is only the beginning of the Misty Mountains,[TN2] and we have got to get through or over or under them somehow, before we get to the wide land beyond. And it is the deal of a way and all from the tother side of these mountains to the Lonely Mountain in the East where Smaug lies on our treasure'.

'Oh!' said Bilbo, & just at that moment he felt tireder than he ever remembered. He was thinking once again of his comfy chair beside the fire in his favourite sitting room in his hobbit hole with the kettle singing. Not for the last time.

Now Bladorthin led the way. 'We must not miss it, or we shall be quite done for' he said. 'We need food for one thing, *and* rest (in reasonable safety) – *and* it is very necessary to tackle the misty mountains by the one and only proper path, or else we shall get lost in them, and never come back.[TN3]

They asked him where he was making for. 'You are now at the very

Edge of the Wild' he answered. 'Somewhere ahead is the Last Decent House[TN4] – I have been there already and they are expecting us.'

You would fancy it ought to have been easy to make straight for that house: There seemed no trees, and no hills, and no breaks in the ground, though it sloped up ahead to meet the feet of the mountain, the colour of heather and rock, with grass green and moss green where the rivers and rivulets were.[TN5]

That is what it looked like in the afternoon sun. Still you couldn't see a house. Then when you rode on a bit you began to understand that that house might be hidden anywhere at all between you and the mountains. There were quite unexpected valleys [full of trees >] narrow with steep sides that you came on all of a sudden, and look into surprised to find them full of trees and a rushing water at the bottom. There were gullies you could almost jump over, but very deep with waterfalls in them. There were ravines that you couldn't jump across, or get down into or climb out of. There were bogs, green pleasant sort of patches some of them with flowers growing; but ponies never came out again that walked on that grass with packs on their backs.

And it was a much much wider land from the ford to the mountain than ever you bargained for. And the only road [> path] was marked by white stones. Some of the stones were small enough,[TN6] and heather and moss were half over others. Altogether it was a slow business.

It seemed only a little way they had gone following Bladorthin, his head and beard wagging this way and that as he searched for the path, when the day began to fail. Tea time had long gone by, and it seemed suppertime soon would do the same. There were moths and flies about. There was no moon. Bilbo's pony began to stumble on the stones.

They came to the edge of a steep fall in the ground so suddenly that Bladorthin's horse nearly fell over it.[TN7] 'There it is' said the wizard and they came to the edge and looked, and they saw a valley far below. They could hear the noise of hurrying water rising from rocks at the bottom, the scent of trees was in the air, and there was a light on the valley side across the water.

Bilbo never forgot the way they slithered and slipped in the dark down the steep zigzag path into that valley. The air grew warmer as they got [*added*: lower] down, and the smell of the pine trees made him drowsy till he nodded and bumped his nose on his pony's neck, or got nearly shaken out of his seat when it slipped on [> by a sudden trip over] a stone or a root. But they all felt a deal more cheery when they came to the bottom. There was [a] comfortable sort of feeling in that valley in the twilight. The noise of the water under the bridge they crossed by had a wholesome sound.[TN8] There was green grass in patches among the rocks of the river's shores. 'Hm' said the hobbit; 'it feels like elves'[TN9] – and he looked up at the stars. They were burning bright; and just then there was a burst of laughter in the trees.

O what are you doing,
and where are you going?
Your ponies need shoeing!
The river is flowing!
O tra-la-la-lally
here down in the valley.

O what are you seeking,
and where are you making?
The faggots are reeking,
The bannocks are baking!
O tra-lil-lil-lolly
The valley is jolly
ha! ha.

O where are you going
with beards all a-wagging?
No knowing, no knowing
What brings Mister Baggins
And Balin and Dwalin
Down into the valley
In June
ha! ha!

O will you be staying,
Or will you be flying?
Your ponies are straying,
the daylight is dying.
To fly would be folly
To stay would be jolly
And listen and hark
To the end of the dark
To our tune
ha! ha!

So they laughed and sang in the trees. Elves of course, and soon Bilbo could see them as the dark deepened. He loved them as nice hobbits do, and he was a little bit frightened of them too.[TN10] Dwarves don't get on so well with them. Even decent enough dwarves like

Gandalf and his friends think them foolish (which is a very foolish thing to think) and get annoyed. But elves laugh at them, [and] most of all at their beards.

'Well well' said a voice, 'just look at dear old Bilbo the hobbit on a pony, my dear! Isn't it delicious!'

'Most astonishing and wonderful'

And then off they went into another song as ridiculous as the one I have written down in full.

At last one, a tall young fellow, came out from the trees and bowed to Bladorthin and to Gandalf.

'Welcome to the valley' he said.

'Thank you' said Gandalf a bit gruffly. Bladorthin was already off his horse and among the elves talking merrily to them.

'You are a bit off the path' said the elf, 'that is if you are making for <the> only way across the water, and the house beyond. We will set you right, but you had best [get off >] get on foot till you are over the bridge. Are you going to stay [*added*: a bit] and sing with us, or will you go straight on? Supper is preparing over yonder' he said 'I can smell the wood fires and the baking'.[TN11]

Tired as he was Bilbo would have liked to stay a while. Elvish singing is not a thing to miss, in June under the stars, not if you care for such things. Also he would have liked to find out how these people knew his name so pat and all, though Elves are wondrous people for news,[TN12] and know what is going on among the peoples of the lands as quick as water flows or quicker.

But the Dwarves were all for supper just then. So on they went, leading their ponies, [to a >] till they found a good path, and so in the end came down to the river's very brink. It was flowing fast as mountain streams do of a summer evening when sun has been on the snow far away all day. There was only a narrow bridge without parapet, and narrow as [a] pony could well walk on, and over it they had to go, slow and careful, one by one, each leading his pony by the bridle. The elves had brought bright lanterns to the shore, and they sang a merry song as the party went across.

'Don't dip thy beard in the foam father,' they cried to Gandalf who was bent almost on hands and knees. 'It is long enough without watering it. Mind Bilbo doesn't eat all the cakes' they called 'he is too fat to get through key-holes yet'.

'Hush hush good people, and good night' said Bladorthin who came last. 'Valley[s] have ears, and elves have over merry tongues. Good night'.

And so at last they came to the Last Homely House, and found its doors flung wide.

* * *

Now it is a strange thing, but things that are good to have and days that are good to spend are swift to tell about [> quickly told about], and not much to listen to; while things that are uncomfortable palpitating and even fearsome and gruesome to see or pass through make [> may make] a good tale, and take a deal of telling anyway. They stayed long in that good house, [all >] a week at least, and they found it hard to leave, and Bilbo would gladly have stopped there for ever and ever (not even supposing a wish would have taken him right back to his hobbit-hole without trouble). Yet there is not much to tell about it [> their stay].

The master of the house was an elf-friend – one of those people whose fathers came into the strange stories of the beginning of history and the wars of the Elves and goblins, and the brave men of the North.[TN13] There were still some people in those days [who were >] who had both elves and heroes of the North for ancestors, and Elrond the master of the house was one. He was as good to look at (almost) as an elf-lord, as strong as a warrior, as wise as a wizard, as venerable as a king of dwarves, and as kind as Christmas. And his house was perfect, whether you liked food or sleep or work or storytelling or singing or just sitting and thinking best. Bad things did not come into that valley.

I wish I had time [to] tell you even a few of the tales or one or two of the songs that they heard in his house. They all [> All of them], and the ponies as well, grew wonderfully rested and strong in a few days there. Their clothes were mended, *and* their bruises and tempers and hopes as well. Their bags were filled with food and provisions light to carry but strong to bring them over the mountain passes. Their plans were improved, and discussed and made better [> improved with the best advice]. And so the time came to midsummer eve, and they were to go on again with the early sun on midsummer morning. Elrond knew all about all runes of every kind. He looked at [their map >] the swords they had brought from the Trolls' lair, and he said:

'These are not troll-make. They are old swords, very old swords of the elves that are called Gnomes,[TN14] and they were made in Gondolin for the goblin-wars. They must have come from a dragon's hoard, for dragons it was that destroyed that city many ages ago.' He looked at the keys and he said 'these are [dwarf-make, and >] troll-keys, but there is one in the bunch that is not. It is a dwarf-key.'

'So it is' said Gandalf, when he looked at it. 'Now where did that come from.'

'I couldn't say', said Elrond 'but I should keep it safe and fast if I were you.' And Gandalf fastened it to a chain and put it round his neck under his jacket.

[He >] Elrond looked at their map, and he shook his head; for if he did not altogether approve of dwarves and their love of gold, he hated dragons and their cruel wickedness, and he did not like to think of the ruin of the town of dale, and its merry bells, and the burned banks of the bright river Running.

The moon was shining – it was now getting near the full [> a broad crescent]. He held up the map and its white light shone through it. 'What is this?' he said.

'There are moon-letters underneath the plain-runes, which say "five feet high the door and three may walk abreast"'.

'What are moon-letters?' asked Bilbo full of excitement. He loved maps (as I have told you before); and also he liked runes and letters and cunning hand writing, though his own hand was a bit thin and spidery.

'Moon-letters are rune-letters, but you can't see them' said Elrond 'not when you look straight at them. They can only be seen when the moon shines behind them, and what is more it must be [the same shaped >] a moon of the same shape and season as the day they were written. The dwarves invented them, and wrote them with silver pens. These must have been written on a midsummer's eve [with the moon >] in a crescent moon – a long while ago.'

'What do they say?' asked Bladorthin[TN15] – a bit vexed, perhaps, that even Elrond should have found this out first, though really there hadn't been a chance before, and [*added*: there] wouldn't have been another till goodness knows when.

'Stand by the grey stone where the thrush knocks. Then the [rising >] setting sun on the last light of Durin's Day will shine upon the key hole.'[TN16]

'Durin, Durin' said Gandalf. 'He was the father of the fathers of one of the two races of dwarves, the Longbeards, and my grandfather's ancestor.'

'Then what is Durin's Day?' said Elrond.

'The first day of the dwarves' New Year' said Gandalf 'and that is, as everyone knows, the day of the first moon of autumn. And Durin's day is that [*added in pencil*: first] day when the first moon of autumn and the sun are in the sky together. But I do not see that all this helps much.'[TN17]

'That remains to be seen', said Bladorthin. 'Is there any more writing?'.

'None to be seen by this moon' said Elrond, and he gave him back the map, and they went down the water to see the elves dance and sing.

The next morning was mid-summer morning and as fair as fair could be: blue sky and never a cloud and the sun dancing on the water.

Now they rode away with their hearts ready for more adventure, and a knowledge of the road they must follow over the mountains to the land beyond.

TEXT NOTES

1. Added in the top margin: 'They had begun to feel that danger was not far away on either side'.
2. This marks the first occurrence in the text of 'the Misty Mountains' used as a proper name; earlier (in the dwarves' song and on p. 90) it had been treated as a (lower-cased) description, not a name (as indeed it is again in Bladorthin's speech later on this same manuscript page).
3. This was altered to 'or else *you will* get lost in them, and *have to come back and start at the beginning again – if you ever even get back.*' Note that the change distances Bladorthin from the rest, implying that he will survive no matter what happens to the rest of them, an implication that ties in with Gandalf's words in the Pryftan Fragment about Bladorthin being the 'probable exception' to the possibility that they may all never return from the quest (p. 7).
4. The 'Last Decent House' was changed to the 'Last Homely House' by a revision in the right-hand margin. This change must have taken place very soon after this page was written, since 'Last Homely House' is the form used the next time Elrond's house is named.
5. This passage was revised to read as follows:

   There seemed no trees, and no hills, *or valleys to break the* ground *in front, which* sloped *ever* up ahead to meet the feet of the mountain, the colour of heather and rock, with grass green and moss green where the rivers and rivulets *might be.*

6. The word 'enough' here is circled, as if for deletion, but not actually cancelled.
7. As in the preceding note, the word 'it' here is circled but not cancelled.
8. This sentence was cancelled.
9. The word 'feels' here is written over another word, but I cannot make out the overwritten word it replaced (it may even have been the same word less legibly written). The sentence does raise the question of how Bilbo knows what elves 'feel' like; Bladorthin had not mentioned elves at all as having anything to do with their destination. The reading 'it feels like elves' also appears in the First Typescript (Marq. 1/1/53:2), where it is altered in ink to '*smells* like elves', the striking phrasing of the published book.
10. This sentence was revised to read 'He loved them as hobbits do, but he was a little bit frightened of them *as well*'; added in the top margin and marked for insertion at this point is the rather ominous phrase 'as people are who know most about them'. The original inclusion of

'nice hobbits' carries an implication of other, unnamed, not so nice hobbits, but we will not meet them (in the persons of the Sandyman family) until *The Lord of the Rings*.

11 This is an early example of the preternatural abilities of elven senses, best known through Legolas's phenomenal eyesight in *The Lord of the Rings* (*LotR*.443, 446, 450, [528]–529).

12 This sentence was slightly revised to read 'how these people knew his name *and all*. Elves are wondrous *folk* for news . . .'

13 These 'strange stories of the beginning of history and the wars of the Elves and goblins, and the brave men of the North' are, of course, the Lost Tales and Long Lays, another allusion by Tolkien within *The Hobbit* back to the core of the legendarium.

14 Pencilled additions change this phrase to read 'The elves that are *now* called Gnomes, *but were once called Noldor*'. Since most of the pencilled changes to the Second Phase manuscript date from the time when Tolkien was creating the First Typescript, this addition was probably made a year or two after this page was originally written.

15 Tolkien began to write 'Ga' – i.e., the name 'Ga[*ndalf*]' – here, then cancelled it and wrote the wizard's name instead.

16 At the end of this paragraph, Tolkien has added the following in smaller letters and within brackets:

> [I have marked the moon letters in red on the map]

Tolkien may be referring here to a lost copy of the Lonely Mountain map that came between Fimbulfambi's Map (see Frontispiece) and Thror's Map I (Plate I [top]); so far as I know no copy of Thror's Map with the moon-letters in red survives. See 'The First Map' (p. 23) for more evidence of this lost map.

Tolkien and, later, Allen & Unwin's production department, struggled over the best way to produce the secret writing on the map. The ideal solution would have been to have the moon letters as a watermark that only showed up when the page was held up to light, but this would have been prohibitively expensive. Tolkien's preferred solution was to write the moon-letters in reverse on the back of the page, producing a similar effect much more economically.† Unfortunately, Allen & Unwin decided to use both maps in *The Hobbit* as endpapers, meaning that they were glued into the inside front and back covers of the book, so that the 'secret writing' had to appear on the front of the map. In the end, the best compromise they could contrive was to have the letters of the 'invisible writing' be drawn in outline to show that they were different from the rest of the detail. Compare Douglas Anderson's simple but elegant low-tech solution in *The Annotated Hobbit* of printing the map twice, once in Chapter I without the hidden writing (DAA.50) and then again in Chapter III with the moon-letters revealed (DAA.97).

† Not until 1979 was Tolkien's idea finally put into practice, when the two

maps from *The Hobbit* were published in poster format; Thror's Map has the moon-runes printed in reverse on the back, clearly visible when the map is held up to the light [copyright 1979 Allen & Unwin, printed by Henry Stone & Sons, Banbury].

17 The next paragraph, on the top line of the next page (Ms. page 39; Marq. 1/1/3:7), began 'Well, well', but this was rubbed out in an inky smear and a new paragraph begun beneath ('That remains to be seen').

(i)
The Last Decent House

This brief chapter contains the most explicit references yet linking *The Hobbit* to the mythology out of which it grew. Elrond and Gondolin come directly from the Silmarillion tradition, while the 'Last Decent House' (renamed the Last *Homely* House before the end of the chapter) is clearly inspired by the Cottage of Lost Play that had appeared in the frame story of *The Book of Lost Tales*, where 'old tales, old songs, and elfin <sic> music are treasured and rehearsed' (BLT I.20) – a description strikingly like that of Elrond's house, which 'was perfect, whether you liked food or sleep or work or storytelling or singing or just sitting and thinking best' (p. 115), and of which the narrator says 'I wish I had time [to] tell you even a few of the tales or one or two of the songs that they heard in his house' (ibid.). It is in the House of Lost Play (as it is also called; cf. BLT I.189) that Eriol the wanderer hears all the stories that together make up the 'Lost Tales', just as much later it is in Elrond's House (not yet named 'Rivendell')[1] that Bilbo in his retirement collected the stories that made up *The Silmarillion* (cf. *LotR*.26–7 & 1023).

(ii)
Elves in the Moonlight

One can sympathize with the dwarves for thinking the elves of the valley foolish: despite the narrator's protest, nothing about their behavior in this chapter indicates anything differently. Their depiction owes something to the frivolous elves of much of *The Book of Lost Tales* – as for example the original version of 'The Tale of Tinúviel', where Lúthien dances among white moths in a 'silver-pearly dress' and hides herself 'beneath a very tall flower' after her brother bolts at the sight of Beren (BLT II.11). Alongside the grave, even grim, elves of some of the early tales – Fëanor and Turgon come readily to mind – are the stereotypical dancing fairies of Victorian and Edwardian children's literature[2] (for example, the Solosimpi or 'shoreland dancers' in BLT I.129). Tolkien is blending two traditions here. The one, of elves as sages and warriors and lovers, derives from medieval works such as *Sir Orfeo*, the *Mabinogion*, certain Arthurian romances, and the legends of the Tuatha de Danaan,[3] and is represented here by Elrond and later the Elvenking (and in *The Lord of the Rings* by Glorfindel, Elrond, Legolas, Galadriel, and Arwen). The other, the image of elves as delicate little fairy dancers or pipers, derives from Jacobean writers like Drayton and Shakespeare and is represented here by the elves in the trees. This latter strand found expression in Tolkien's work mainly through his poetry, especially poems such as 'The Princess Ni' (published 1924, revised as 'Princess Mee' ([ATB poem #4, pp. 28–30]), 'Tinfang Warble' (first published in 1927 and reprinted in BLT I.108), and 'Goblin Feet'.

'Goblin Feet' is of some importance, despite its stark contrast to Tolkien's subsequent treatment of Faerie,[4] because insofar as Tolkien had any reputation at all outside his own family as a writer for children prior to the publication of *The Hobbit*, it rested upon this slight little poem, which originally appeared in *Oxford Poetry* 1915[5] but was quickly reprinted in much less academic surroundings, such as *The Book of Fairy Poetry* (a lavishly-illustrated coffee-table book that appeared in 1920) and *Fifty New Poems for Children* [1922].[6] Tolkien later came to disavow the idea of elves as cute little fairies and moved his own elves firmly in the direction of medieval elf-lore; the Rivendell episodes in *The Hobbit* mark virtually its last appearance in the 'main line' of his legendarium.

Within Tolkien's own family, of course, there was already a well-established tradition of frivolous elves in *The Father Christmas Letters*, and these probably had a greater impact on the depiction of the elves in *The Hobbit* than any other single factor, since both those annual letters and Mr. Baggins' story were originally written for the same audience: Tolkien's own children. The 'Snow-elves' had already appeared in the annual letters by 1929,[7] before writing on *The Hobbit* itself had begun, and were soon joined by the 'Red Gnomes' in 1932 (written just when *The Hobbit* was reaching its climax). In later letters, we find various references to 'Elves and Red gnomes' [1934], 'Red Elves' who 'turn everything into a game' [1935] and 'Red and Green Elves' [1936]; while these postdate the drafting of our story, they predate its publication and reflect the attitude towards elves prevalent among its intended audience (some later elements, such as the elves' war with the goblins in 1932 and again in 1941, seem to derive from *The Hobbit* itself).

If in some features the elves of the valley echo the worst excesses of Edwardian and Georgian fairy sentimentality, other elements suggest traditional fairy lore – i.e., folk-lore rather than fairy tales. The approach to Rivendell mingles realistic detail, probably derived from Tolkien's 1911 Alpine walking tour,[8] with the eeriness traditionally associated with the borders of Elfland; we are clearly entering a secret world of heightened sights, sounds, and colours (cf. the smell of the trees). Another good example of the mix of realism and fantasy that is so much a hallmark of Tolkien's work are the stars that appear brighter when seen from Elrond's valley – a happy mix of myth (stars shine brighter on an elven place) and fact (stars can in fact be seen better when the observer is in a valley or pit looking up than when he or she is in a flat, open space). The chapter is filled with hints that elves can be dangerous, perfectly in keeping with the terror the Fair Folk inspired in most folk who believed in them – many of the recorded encounters with them in medieval lore are in the form of cautionary tales, like Tolkien's own 'Ides Ælfscýne' (see pp. 57–8 & 59), and charms against elf-shot remained current from Anglo-Saxon times to the nineteenth century.[9] Elves were blamed for everything from developmentally disabled children ('changelings') to sudden deaths, from lamed horses to mysterious pregnancies. Perilous yet fair, they were treated with the same wary respect as the Furies and God: to speak their proper name was to invite their attention and hence court disaster. Note Bladorthin's use of the traditional euphemism 'good people' (p. 114) and his 'laying' of them when he commands them to hush. Their mocking of others' difficulties (people who can't swim crossing the fast-running stream) shows a traditional heartlessness out of keeping with Tolkien's elves elsewhere;[10] Bilbo is wise to feel 'rather afraid' of them. Their being uncannily well-informed, even to the extent of knowing Bilbo's name (and, in the typescript and published text, his errand), is here just another example of elven magic; in later versions, where Bladorthin explicitly states at the end of the preceding chapter that during his scouting ahead he had spoken to some of Elrond's people and gotten word of the trolls from them (DAA.83), we can rationalize this away by assuming that the wizard had at that earlier meeting told the elves all about his companions and their quest.

(iii)
Elrond

The most important character in this chapter, however, is neither frivolous nor sinister, but 'kind as Christmas'.[11] Elrond, the Master of the House, comes directly to *The Hobbit* from the mythology, having first appeared in 'The Sketch of the Mythology' some four years previously (i.e., 1926), where he is described as 'half-mortal and half-elfin' <sic> (HME IV.38). It is remarkable how among the shifting names and relationships of the lords and ladies of the Noldor that Elrond's name and genealogy remained unchanged through all the various texts that comprise the Silmarillion tradition. From the first he is the son of Eärendel and Elwing,[12] saved by Maidros or Maglor[13] when the Sons of Fëanor destroyed the refugees of Gondolin and Doriath. We are further told that

> When later the Elves return to the West, bound by his mortal half he elects to stay on earth. Through him the blood of Húrin (his great-uncle)[14] and of the Elves is yet among Men, and is seen yet in valour and in beauty and in poetry.
>
> —'The Sketch of the Mythology', HME IV.38.

The number and kind of the half-elven or elf-friends had not yet been fixed when *The Hobbit* was written, and it took Tolkien several years and much experimentation to sort out their exact nature. For one thing, no clear distinction had yet been drawn between the elf-friends, or survivors of the elves' human allies, and the half-elven, the offspring of unions between elves and men – largely a moot point in any case, since inter-marriage between the human chieftains and rulers of the elves (Beren and Lúthien, Tuor and Idril, Eärendel and Elwing) and attrition in the wars against Morgoth had so drastically reduced the numbers of both that the few survivors could essentially be considered as one people. This point is made explicit in the 1930 *Quenta*, where after Morgoth's defeat the herald of the Valar

> summon[s] the remnants of the Gnomes and the Dark-elves that never yet had looked on Valinor to join with the captives released from Angband, and depart; and with the Elves should those of the race of Hador and Bëor alone be suffered to depart, if they would. But of these only Elrond was now left, the Half-elfin; and he elected to remain, being bound by his mortal blood in love to those of the younger race; and of Elrond alone has the blood of the elder race and of the seed divine of Valinor come among mortal Men.
>
> —1930 *Quenta*, HME IV.157–8.

The manuscript makes clear one puzzling point, first raised I think by Christina Scull, that arises in relation to Elrond's ancestry: since he is the direct descendant of Turgon, the king of Gondolin (father of Idril mother of Eärendel father of Elrond), why does Elrond not lay claim, as rightful heir, to Glamdring, his great-grandfather's sword? The answer, of course, is that when the scene was first drafted the swords were not named but merely identified as elf-blades from Gondolin, much as the hobbits' weapons in *The Lord of the Rings* are never given specific antecedents beyond being Númenórean blades forged during the war against Angmar. By the time the names and prior owner were added (in the First Typescript; Marq. 1/1/53:5) –

> This, Thorin, the runes name Orcrist, the Goblin-cleaver in the ancient tongue of Gondolin; it was a famous blade. This, Gandalf, was Glamdring, Foe-hammer that the king of Gondolin once wore

– Elrond's tacit abnegation was already part of the story. More importantly, Elrond's identification of the swords ties *The Hobbit* very explicitly to the very first of the Lost Tales Tolkien wrote, and evidently one of his favorites: 'The Fall of Gondolin'.[15] While it is very plausible that Turgon's sword would have fallen into goblin hands, given the scenario described in 'The Fall of Gondolin', Elrond's comment that 'dragons destroyed that city many ages ago' creates difficulties in the chronology. The reference only two chapters before to Beren and Lúthien's activities of less than a century ago – a mere nothing in the elvish scheme of things – and the very presence of Elrond himself, who is certainly not described as an elf (at the end of the chapter Elrond, the hobbit, the wizard, and the dwarves go outside 'to see the elves' dance and sing) and seems not to have been conceived of as an immortal or even particularly long-lived at this point, argues against a long gap in time between Gondolin's fall and Mr. Baggins' adventure. Indeed, in the first chronology of the war against Morgoth, the 'Annals of Beleriand' (which date from the early 1930s), dwarves first appear in the Year of the Sun 163; Thû is cast down by Beren and Lúthien about the same time, in A.B. 163–4; the Fall of Gondolin occurs just over forty years later, in A.B. 207; and the Age ends with Morgoth's downfall and the departure of Fionwë's host in A.B. 250 ('The [Earliest] Annals of Beleriand', HME IV.300, 307, & 309–10). By that scheme, Mr. Baggins' unexpected party would have occurred no more than 14 years after the fall of Thangorodrim, which is clearly exceedingly improbable. These difficulties probably led to Tolkien's deletion of the reference to Beren and Lúthien's adventure, which together with Elrond's undefined status and nature enable Gondolin and its ruin to recede into the distant, legendary past.

(iv)
Durin's Day

By contrast with the elvish material, Durin's Day represents a new element in the mythology. We have already touched on Durin himself (see commentary p. 77); now we learn a bit more about dwarven culture, and that their new year begins 'as everyone knows' (a typical Tolkienism) on 'the day of the first moon of autumn' – a detail probably inspired by the Jewish calendar, which is also lunar in nature and begins its new year in late September or early October (in contrast to the traditional medieval year, which began on the first day of spring).[16] Durin's Day was originally a much simpler affair than it later became, and the oddity of the dwarves' having a new year's day that they can't predict ('it passes our skill in these days to guess when such a time will come again' – DAA.96) is avoided. It is significant also that originally Durin's Day arrives on the *first* moon of autumn, changed before publication (actually in an emendation to the First Typescript) to the *last* new moon of autumn –

a date more in keeping with the Celtic calendar, which began the new year on 1st November. This change created an error or inconsistency in the next chapter that was not corrected until 1995: in Chapter III and Chapter XI, Durin's Day occurs on the last moon of autumn, as per the emendation. But Tolkien missed the reference in Chapter IV, where the dwarves upon leaving Elrond 'thought of coming to the secret door in the Lonely Mountain, perhaps that very next first moon of Autumn – "and perhaps it will be Durin's Day" they had said' (DAA.101–2).

Finally, a few miscellaneous points. This chapter reinforces (p. 111) the 'homesick' motif, first introduced in the previous chapter (p. 90) and later to play such a large part in Mr. Baggins' characterization. It is easy to understand the wizard's embarrassment over Elrond's discovery of the moon letters – Bladorthin had, after all, had the map in his possession for the better part of a century without discovering this vital clue – but the serendipity of Elrond's chance discovery is of an order comparable with the finding of the key in the troll lair in the previous chapter, or Bilbo's discovery of the Ring later on; one particular phase of the moon would only coincide with a specific night of the year roughly once per century. It is also noteworthy that Gandalf's hiding the key under his jacket enables him to keep it through the goblin and wood-elf encounters that are shortly to follow, suggesting that one or both of these plot-elements had already been anticipated.

NOTES

1 The name 'Rivendell' does not appear at all in the first draft, but it does occur in the first typescript of Chapter XIX (Marq. 1/1/69) and in replacement pages slipped into the first typescript of Chapters II and III (Marq. 1/1/53), and thus made its way into the first edition.

2 This tradition, which Tolkien deplored, was forever immortalized in the Cottingley fairy photographs authenticated and popularized by Conan Doyle (see *Pictures of Fairies: The Cottingley Photographs* by Edward L. Gardner [1966]†), more recently parodied by Terry Jones and Brian Froud in *Lady Cottington's Pressed Fairy Book* [1994].

† This book, Gardner's attempt to perpetuate the fraud by arguing that the photographs are genuine, was first published in 1945 under the title *The Cottingley Photographs and Their Sequel.*

3 The legends of the Tuatha de Danaan are most readily found in Lady Gregory's *Gods and Fighting Men* [1904]. The final expression of elves as doughty human-sized warriors and knights in mainstream literature is Edmund Spenser's *The Faerie Queene* [1590]; the hero of the first book, the Redcrosse Knight, is assumed throughout to be an elf and only revealed as a human foundling at the very end; the hero of the second book, Sir Guyon (Guy) is an elf.

4 Tolkien himself expressed a wish that 'the unhappy little thing, representing all that I came (so soon after) to fervently dislike, could be buried for ever' (HME I.32).

5 Along with poems by Tolkien's friends G. B. Smith and T. W. Earp, and future luminaries like Naomi M. Haldane (the future Naomi Mitchison), A. L. (Aldous) Huxley, and Dorothy L. Sayers.

6 This book of children's poetry fortuitously played a role in inspiring 'Bilbo's First Song'; see p. 725.

7 The Snow-elves were joined the next year by Snow-men (see the letter for 1930). The latter did not make it into *The Hobbit*, but they did make it into *The Lord of the Rings* as the Snowmen of Forochel, also known as the Lossoth or the Forodwaith (*LotR* Appendix A, pp. 1078–9).

8 See the section of commentary on 'Switzerland' beginning on p. 145, as well as *Letters* pp. 308–9 (letter of 4th November 1961 to Joyce Reeves) & pp. 391–3 (letter of 1967/1968 to Michael Tolkien).

9 For Anglo-Saxon references, see *The Exeter Book*; for nineteenth-century lore, see *The Denham Tracts*.

10 A possible exception is the green elves' behavior in 'The Nauglafring' when they laugh at and mock the desperate dwarves attempting to flee their ambush at the fords of Aros (BLT II.237).

11 In the first typescript (Marq. 1/1/53:5) the phrase 'as kind as Christmas' has been replaced by 'as kind as summer', the reading adopted in the published book – doubtless with an eye to Tolkien's everpresent concern with decorum and the avoidance of blatant anachronisms (there is no 'Christmas' yet because we are in a prehistoric world before the Christian era).

12 Originally, Elrond was Eärendel's only son ('Sketch of the Mythology', HME IV.38), and this was still the case in the 1930 *Quenta* as first written (HME IV.150) and also in the replacement text of this passage (*Quenta II*; HME IV.151). His brother Elros was only added in revisions to this replacement text; see HME IV.155, Notes 4, 9, & 10 and Christopher Tolkien's commentary on HME IV.196. Thus this passage in *The Hobbit* probably predates the creation of Elros.

13 In the earlier versions of the story, it is Maidros rather than Maglor who rescues young Elrond; contrast HME IV.38 ('Sketch') and HME IV.150 & 153 (1930 *Quenta & Quenta II*, respectively), both of which assign this role to Maidros the eldest brother, with HME IV.155 (revisions to *Quenta II*) and subsequent texts (e.g., *Silm*.247), which credit the deed to Maglor instead.

14 Actually, as Christopher Tolkien points out (HME IV.39), Húrin is Elrond's great-great-uncle.

15 'The Fall of Gondolin' was written circa 1916–17 (BLT II.146) but not published until the appearance of volume two of *The Book of Lost Tales* [1984]). That Tolkien thought highly of the story is shown by the fact that this was the only Silmarillion story he ever read aloud at

a public performance (to Exeter College's Essay Club, in 1920); cf. Nevill Coghill's account in Ann Bonsor's 1974 BBC Radio Oxford program and also Carpenter's brief mention (*Tolkien: A Biography* p. 102).

16 This custom continued up to the early eighteenth century; unwary scholars are sometimes tripped up by the fact that, for example, 24th March 1714 was followed the next day by 25th March 1715. The practice was phased out as the eighteenth century wore on, with the traditional usage often marked 'O.S.' (i.e., 'Old Style'); in modern editions of letters from the time the dates are often adjusted to reflect current practices. The change to our current system was not made in England and its colonies (including what became the United States) until 1752.

Chapter IV

GOBLINS

As before, the text continues on the same page (Ms. page 39; Marq. 1/1/3:7), with what would later become the chapter break indicated only by a short gap of a few lines in mid-page and a slightly larger opening letter on the first word of the new section.

There are many paths that lead up into those mountains and many passes over them. But most of the paths are cheats and deceptions, and lead nowhere or to bad ends; and most of the passes are infested by wicked things and dreadful dangers.

The dwarves and Bilbo helped by the good advice of Elrond and by the wisdom and memory of Bladorthin, took the right path to the right pass.

Long days after they climbed out of the valley and left the Last Homely House miles behind, they were still going up and up and up. It was a hard path and a dangerous path, a crooked way, and a lonely way and long. Now they could look back on the lands behind laid out below them. Far far away in the west where things were blue and faint Bilbo knew his own country was of safe and comfortable things, and his little hobbit-hole. He shivered. It was getting bitter cold up here, and the wind came shrill among the rocks. Also boulders came galloping down the mountain sides at times, and passed among them (which was lucky) or over their heads (which was alarming). And nights were comfortless and chill, and they did not dare to sing or talk loud, for the echoes were uncanny, and the silence did not seem to want [> seemed to dislike] being broken – except for [> by] the noise of water and the wail of wind, and the crack of stone.

'The summer is getting on' thought Bilbo, 'and haymaking is going on, and picnics. They will be harvesting and blackberrying before we are [> even begin to go] down the other side at this rate'.

And he was quite right. When they said goodbye to Elrond they had had the notion of coming to the side-door of the Lonely Mountain perhaps that very next first moon of autumn – and 'perhaps it will be Durin's Day' they had said. Perhaps. But they were not going to get there to see [> so soon to see].[TN1]

Even the good plans of wise wizards like Bladorthin and good friends like Elrond go wrong sometimes when you are off on such peculiarly dangerous adventures over the Edge of the Wild.

Now you will want to know what [*added*: really] happened; and I expect you guessed quite rightly that they would never get over those great tall mountains and those lonely [> with their lonely] peaks and valleys where no king ruled without some fearful adventure.

One day they met a thunderstorm – no not a thunderstorm a thunder-battle. You know how terrific a really big thunderstorm can be down in the land and in a river-valley; perhaps you have even seen two thunderstorms meet and clash. But have you seen thunder and lightening <sic> in the mountains at night, when storms meet and their warring shakes the rocks and . . . the valleys[TN2] [> when storms come up from East and West and make war]? The lightning splinters on the peaks, and rocks crash [> shiver], and the great crashes split the air and go rolling and tumbling into every cave and hollow; and the darkness is filled with fearful noise and sudden light.

Bilbo had never seen anything of the kind. They were high up on a narrow track, with a dreadful fall into a dim valley on one side. [The night was >] There they were sheltering under a hanging rock for the night, and he lay under a blanket and shook from head to toe.

He peeped out and in the lightning-flashes he saw that across the valley the stone-giants were out, and were hurling rocks at one another for a game, and catching them, and tossing them down into the darkness where they crashed among the trees far below or splintered into little bits with a dreadful noise.

Then came a wind and a rain, and the wind whipped the rain and hail about in every direction so that an overhanging rock was no protection at all. Soon they were getting drenched, and their ponies were standing with their heads down and their tails between their legs, and some were whinnying with fright. They could hear the giants guffawing and laughter and shouting all over the mountain-sides.

'This won't do at all' said Gandalf. 'If we don't get blown off, or drowned or struck by lightning, we shall be picked up by some giant and kicked sky high for a football'.

'Well if you [think we >] know of anywhere better take us there' said Bladorthin who was feeling very grumpy, and wasn't very happy about the giants either. And the end of their argument was that they sent Fili and Kili who had very sharp eyes – and being the youngest of the dwarves usually got these sort of jobs[TN3] (when they could see that it was absolutely no use sending Bilbo). There is nothing like looking if you want to find something. You usually find something if you look, though it may not be quite the something you were after. Soon Fili and Kili came crawling back holding on to the rocks in the wind.

'We have found a dry cave' they said 'not far round the corner, and ponies and all could get inside'.

'Have you *thoroughly* explored it?' asked the wizard, who knew that caves up in the mountains were not often unoccupied.

'Yes yes' they said, though everybody knew they couldn't have been long about it, they had been too quick. 'It isn't all that big, and it doesn't seem to go far back'.

That is of course the dangerous part about caves – you don't know how far they go back, or where a passage behind may lead to, or what is waiting for you inside.

In the end they went. The wind was howling, and the thunder still growling, and they had a business getting themselves and their ponies along. Still it wasn't very far, and before long they came to a big rock standing out into the path. If you slipped behind (there wasn't much room to do it, except perhaps for little Bilbo) you found a low arch in the side of the mountain, just high enough for a small pony to get under.[TN4] Under that arch they went, and it was good to hear the wind and the rain outside instead of all round them, and to feel safe from the giants and their rocks.

Bladorthin lit up his wand (like he did that day in Bilbo's dining room, if you remember) and they explored the cave. It seem quite a good size, but not too big and mysterious. It had a dry floor and some comfortable nooks. At one end there was room for the ponies, and there they stood (mighty glad to be there) and they had their nose bags on for a treat. Oin and Gloin [lit a fire near the arch >] wanted to light a fire at the door to dry their clothes, but Bladorthin wouldn't allow it. So they spread out their wet things on the floor, got dry ones out of their bundles, made their blankets comfy, got out their pipes, and blew smoke rings, which Bladorthin turned into different colours and set a dancing up on the roof to amuse them. They talked and talked and forgot about the storm, and [made plans >] discussed what they would each do with their share of the [gold >] treasure (when they got it which now seemed not so impossible), and so they dropped off to sleep one by one. And they never saw their ponies [*added*: alive] again, or most of their baggages packages tools and paraphernalia.[TN5]

It turned out a good thing that night that they had brought little Bilbo with them, after all. For somehow he could not go to sleep for a long time; and when he did sleep he had very nasty dreams. He dreamed that a crack in the wall at the back of the cave got bigger and bigger and bigger and opened wider and wider, and he was very afraid but couldn't call out or do anything save lie and look.

Then he dreamed that the floor of the cave was giving way, and he was slipping – beginning to fall down down goodness knows where. Then he woke up with a horrible start, and found that part of his dream was true. A crack had opened at the back of the cave, and was now a wide passage. He was just in time to see the last of the ponies' tails disappearing into it.

Of course he gave a very loud shout, as loud as hobbit could [cry >] make. Out jumped the goblins, big goblins, great ugly-looking goblins, lots of goblins before you could say 'rocks and blocks!'.

There were six to each dwarf (at least) and two even for Bilbo,[TN6] and they were all grabbed and carried through the crack before you could have said 'tinder and flint'. All except Bladorthin. Bilbo's yell had waked him up wide in a splintered second, and when goblins came to grab him there was a terrific flash like lightning in the cave and several fell dead.

The crack closed with a snap and Bilbo and the dwarves were on the wrong side of it. But where was Bladorthin? That neither they nor the goblins had any idea, and the goblins did not wait to find out.

They picked up Bilbo and the dwarves and hurried them along. It was deep deep dark such as only goblins who have taken to living in the heart of the mountains can see through.[TN7] The passages there were crossed and tangled, but the goblins seemed to know their way, as well as the way to the nearest post-office; and the way went down and down, and it was most horribly stuffy. The goblins were very rough and pinched unmercifully, and chuckled and laughed in their horrible stony voices, and Bilbo was more unhappy even than when William had picked him up by his toes. He wished again & again for his nice bright hobbit hole – not for the last time.

And now there came a glimmer of red light before them. Then the goblins began to sing, or croak, keeping time with the flap of their flat feet on the stone, and shaking their prisoners as well.

Clap! snap the black crack
grip, grab, pinch, nab,
and down down to goblin-town
You go, my lad!

Clash, crash, crush, smash!
Hammer and tongs, knocker and gongs;
pound, pound far under ground!
ho! ho! my lad.

Swish smack! whip crack.
Batter and beat, yammer and bleat;
work, work, nor dare to shirk.[TN8]
While goblins [laugh >] quaff
And goblins laugh

Round and round far under ground
Below, my lad!

It sounded very terrifying, and the walls echoed to the 'clap snap' and 'crash smash' and to the ugly laughter of their 'ho ho my lad'. The general meaning of the song was only too plain, for now the goblins took out whips and whipped them with a swish smack and set them running as fast as they could [*added*: go], and more than one of the dwarves were already yammering like anything when they came [> stumbled] into a big cavern.

It was lit with red fires & torches along the walls,[TN9] and was full of goblins. How they laughed and stamped and clapped their hands when the dwarves with poor little Bilbo came running in with the goblin-drivers cracking their whips behind. The ponies were already there, and all the packages and baggages broken open and were being rummaged by goblins, and smelt by goblins, and fingered by goblins, and quarrelled about by goblins.

I am afraid that was the last they ever saw of those excellent little ponies, for goblins eat horses and ponies and donkeys (and other worse things). Just now they had themselves to think of, though. The goblins chained their hands behind their backs, and chained [> linked] them all together in a line, and dragged them along, with Bilbo tugging at the end of the row, to the far shadows [> end of the cavern]. There in the shadows on a large flat stone sat a very big goblin, and armed goblins were standing round him carrying the axes and the bent swords that they use.

Now goblins are cruel, wicked, and bad hearted. They make no beautiful things, but make many clever things. They can tunnel and mine as well as any dwarves, and hammers, axes, swords, daggers, pickaxes, and also instruments of torture they make (or get other people to make – prisoners and slaves) very well. Also they make machines, all wheels and noise and stench, and doubtless they invented a great many of the machines – for wheels and engines, always delighted them, and also not working with their hands more than they were obliged[TN10] – but in those days and in those wild parts they had not yet advanced (as it is called) so far. They did not hate dwarves especially; in some parts wicked dwarves had even made alliances with them. But goblins did not care who they caught as long as it was done smart and secret, and the prisoners were not able to defend themselves.

'Who are these miserable persons?' said the big goblin.[TN11]

'Dwarves and this' said one of the drivers, pulling at Bilbo's chain so that he fell forward on to his knees. 'We found them sheltering in our front door'.

'What do you mean by it?' said the great goblin turning to Gandalf. 'Up to no good I will warrant or spying on the private business of my people, I expect! [Come, what have you got to say >] Thieves, I shouldn't be surprised to learn! Murderers and friends of elves, not unlikely! Come what have you got to say!'

'Gandalf the Dwarf' he replied 'at your service' (which is merely a polite nothing). '[Nothing of >] Of the things you suspect and imagine we had no idea at all. We sheltered from a storm in what appeared a convenient cave, and unused; nothing was further from our thought than inconveniencing goblins in any way whatever' (that was true enough).

'Um' said the great goblin 'so you say! Might I ask what you were doing up in the mountains at all, and where you were coming from, and [what >] where you were going to? – and in fact I should like to know all about you'.

'We were on a journey to our relatives, our nephews and nieces[TN12] and first, second and third cousins and other descendants of our grandfathers who live on the East side of these truly hospitable mountains' said Gandalf, not quite knowing what to say all at once in a moment, when obviously the exact truth [was > would have been no >] wouldn't do at all.

'He is a liar, O truly great and tremendous one' said one of the drivers. 'Several of our people were struck by magic lightning in the cave, when we invited them to come below, and are dead as stones. Also he has not explained this'. He held out the sword which Gandalf had worn, the sword which came from the Trolls' lair.

The great Goblin gave a truly awful howl of rage when he looked at it, and all the soldiers gnashed their teeth, clashed their swords, and stamped. They knew this sword at once. It had killed hundreds of goblins in its time, when the fair elves of Gondolin hunted them in the hills, or did battle before their walls. They had called it Orcrist, the goblin-slasher, as its runes said;[TN13] but the goblins called it simply Biter. They hated it, and hated worse anyone that carried it.

'Murderers and elf-friends!' the great-goblin shouted. 'Slash them, beat them, gash them – take them away to dark holes full of snakes, and let them never see the light again.'

He was [so in a >] in such a rage he jumped off his seat and rushed at Gandalf with his mouth open.

Just at that very moment all the lights went out in [the] cavern, and the great fire went off 'poof' into a tower of blue-glowing smoke right up to the roof, and scattered burning white sparks all among the goblins.

The yells and yammers, croaking, jibbering and jabbering, howls growls and curses, shrieks and skriking that followed passes all description.[TN14] Several hundred cats and wolves being roasted alive together could [> would] not have compared with it. The sparks were burning holes in the goblins, and the smoke made the dark too thick for even them to see in it, and soon they were falling over one another and rolling in heaps on the floor and biting and kicking and fighting [like >] as if they had all gone mad. Suddenly a sword flashed in its own light. Bilbo saw it go right through the great goblin where he stood dumbfounded in the middle of his rage. He fell dead, and the goblin soldiers fled before the sword shrieking into the darkness.

The sword went back into its sheath. 'Follow me quick!' said a voice fierce and quiet, and before Bilbo understood he was trotting along again at the end of the line as fast as he could trot, down more dark passages with the yells of the goblin-hall growing fainter behind him. A faint light was leading them on.

'Quicker quicker!' said the voice 'the torches will soon be relit'. [Now Dori who was at the back next to Bilbo, and a decent fellow, picked up the hobbit and put him on his shoulders, and off they went as >] 'Half a minute' said Dori. He made the hobbit scramble on his shoulders as best he could with his tied hands and chain and everything, and then off they went at a run with a clink clink of chains, and many a stumble, since they had no hands to steady them. Not for a long while did they stop, and they must have been right down in the very mountain's heart by that time.

Then Bladorthin lit up his wand. Of course it was Bladorthin, and wait a minute if you want to know how he got there. He took out his sword and it flashed in the dark all by itself. [It was refreshed after >] It burned with rage so that it shone [> gleamed] if goblins were about; and it was brighter then ever after killing the great goblin [> now it was as bright as pale blue flame for pleasure in the killing of the great lord of the cave]. Certainly it made no bother about cutting through the goblin-chains, and setting all the prisoners free as quick as possible. This sword's name was Glamdring (which means goblin-beater)[TN15] and it was if anything [<more> >] a better sword than Orcrist. Oh no Orcrist wasn't lost, Bladorthin had [<p>ut it >] brought it away all right. He thought of most things, and did what he could.

'Are we all here?' said he. 'Let me see: one,[TN16] two, three, four, five, six, seven, eight, nine, ten, eleven (where are Fili and Kili; here they are) twelve, thirteen, and here's Mr Baggins – fourteen. Well well, it might be worse, and then again it might be a deal better. No ponies, no food, and no knowing quite where we are, and hordes of angry goblins behind! On we go'.

On they went. He was quite right, they began to hear goblin-noises, and horrible cries far behind in the passages they had come through. That sent them on faster than ever, and as poor Bilbo couldn't possibly go half as fast (dwarves can shamble along a good pace, I can tell you, when they have to), they took it in turns to carry him on their backs.

Still goblins go faster, and also the goblins knew the ways <better> (they had made them themselves); so do what they would [> the dwarves would] the cries of the goblins got closer and closer. Now they could even hear the flap of their feet, many many feet, which seemed only just round the last corner. The blink of red torches could be seen [in the tunnel behind >] behind them in the tunnel they were following. They were getting deadly tired. 'Why o why did I ever leave my hobbit-hole' said poor Mr Baggins bumping up and down on Bombur's back; and 'why o why did I ever bring a wretched little hobbit on a treasure hunt' thought poor Bombur staggering along with the sweat dripping down his nose in heat and terror.

Now Bladorthin fell behind. They turned a sharp corner – 'about turn!' he said. 'Draw your sword Gandalf'. There was nothing else to be done. Nor did the goblins like it.

They came scurrying round the corner to find Goblin-slasher and Goblin-beater shining cold and bright right in their astonished eyes. They dropped their torches and gave one yell before they were killed. The others yelled still more behind, and ran back knocking over the ones that were running after them. 'Orcrist and Glamdring'[TN17] they shrieked and soon they were all in confusion, and most of them hustling back the way they had come.

It was quite a long time before they dared to turn that corner. By that time the dwarves had gone on again, a long long way on into the dark tunnels of the goblins' kingdom. When they found out that, they put out their torches and they put on soft soft shoes, and they chose out their very quickest runners. These ran on as quick as weasels in the dark with hardly as much noise as bats (of which there were lots in those nasty holes). That is why neither Bilbo, nor the dwarves, nor even Bladorthin heard them coming. Nor did they see them. But the goblins could see them when they had [come >] nearly overtaken them, for Bladorthin was letting his wand give out a faint light to help them as they went along.

Quite suddenly Dori at the back (with Bilbo on his shoulders) was grabbed from behind in the dark. He shouted and fell and Bilbo rolled off his shoulders into the dark, bumped his head and remembered nothing more.

TEXT NOTES

1 The narrator's observation that Bilbo's misgivings were 'quite right' (and that Gandalf & Company would not reach the mountain by Durin's Day) show that the expanded time scheme in which Bilbo and his companions would be more than a year on the road was already in place; see Plot Notes A. In the First Typescript (Marq. 1/1/54:1), this paragraph was merged with the one preceding it by the deletion (through erasure) of the narrator's comment and the addition (in ink, in the left margin) of the others' 'equally gloomy thoughts', and also merged with the one following it by the addition of a sentence about the wizard's foreboding and the dwarves' lack of recent experience in these parts. Finally, the paragraph after that was changed from second person to third, so the narrator's breezy segue ('Now you will want to know what really happened') becomes part of the wizard's forebodings ('He knew that something unexpected might happen . . .').

2 The illegible word before 'the valleys' starts with *r* and seems to end in *s*, perhaps *ruins*.

3 The typescript adds the detail 'the youngest of the dwarves *by some fifty years*' (Marq. 1/1/54:2). From this, combined with the information in the dwarven family tree in Appendix A of *The Lord of the Rings* (*LotR*.1117), we can deduce that the six dwarves among Bilbo's companions whose birth dates are not given (Dori, Nori, Ori, Bifur, Bofur, and Bombur) were all born after T.A. 2763 (Balin's birthdate, since we know he is the eldest after Thorin; see p. 380) but before about T.A. 2809 (fifty years before Fili's birth), although none of this precision of detail existed at the time *The Hobbit* was written.

4 Added in the left margin, and marked for insertion either within the parenthetical after 'little Bilbo' or at the end of the sentence: 'and they had to unpack the ponies or they would have stuck'.

5 This last line was cancelled and replaced by the following in the margin: 'And that was the last time they used their ponies, baggage, packages tools & paraphernalia they had brought with them.' – a change necessitated by their later sight of the ponies & baggage on p. 131.

6 Therefore there are presumably eighty-six goblins who take part in this ambush: 6 x 13 = 78 for the dwarves, + 2 for Bilbo = 80, + 6 for Bladorthin (all of whom are struck dead) = a total of 86; rather a lot for a cavern of 'quite a good size, but not too big', unless more of Bilbo's dream comes true than he realizes, and the cave actually does grow larger.

7 The phrase *taken to living* is interesting, since it implies that this was not their original habitat; presumably the fallen Dark Lord's minions are conceived as having hidden themselves in remote places to escape destruction, from which havens they have rebuilt their numbers and

are now beginning to assault others again; cf. a similar motif at the end of the Second Age and Third Age.

8 These three lines ('Swish smack . . . dare to shirk') were originally written at the beginning of the second stanza, then cancelled and moved to their present position. That is, lines 9–11 of the final poem were originally lines 5–7 of the draft. The poem is otherwise very neatly written into the page, indicating that this is fair copy from some rough drafting that does not survive; the replacement of 'laugh' by 'quaff' in line 12 was probably required because of a copying error, not a deliberate change.

9 This line was later changed to read '. . . with *a great* red fire *in the middle* & torches . . .'

10 This passage was revised via deletions and additions to read as follows: '. . . also instruments of torture they make *very well* (or get other people to make *to their design* – prisoners and slaves *that have to work till they die for want of air & light.) I have no doubt* they invented a great many of the machines – for wheels and engines, always delighted them, and also not working with their *own* hands more than they were obliged . . .'

11 The goblin-chief is referred to in lower case, variously as 'the big goblin', 'the great goblin', and 'the great-goblin'; not until the typescript (1/1/54:5) does his description become a proper name: the Great Goblin. Note, however, the reference to the goblin 'King' in the next chapter, p. 163.

12 This sentence was slightly altered to read '. . . on a journey to *visit* our relatives, our nephews and nieces . . .' Aside from the much later references to Fili and Kili's mother in Chapters X & XVIII, this is the only reference to female dwarves in *The Hobbit*.

13 This is the first appearance of the name *Orcrist*, a name which as the narrator says indeed means 'Goblin-slasher' in Gnomish; cf. the *Gnomish Lexicon*, page 63, which glosses *orc* as 'goblin. (children of *Melko*.)', and page 27, which glosses *crist* as 'knife. slash – slice'. The Noldorin equivalent given in 'The Etymologies' is similar but the slight difference is significant, since it glosses *crist* as 'a cleaver, sword' (HME V.365). The passage in which Elrond names the swords in Chapter III did not appear in the manuscript text of that chapter, entering there instead in the First Typescript (1/1/53:5):

> . . . many ages ago. This, Thorin, the runes name Orcrist, the Goblin-cleaver in the ancient tongue of Gondolin; it was a famous blade. This, Gandalf, was Glamdring, Foe-hammer that the king of Gondolin once wore. I wonder indeed where the trolls found them. Keep them well!

The word 'cleaver' here is written in ink over an erasure, but the word Tolkien originally typed has been obliterated and cannot be recovered. The penultimate sentence in this passage was cancelled in ink and does not appear in the Second Typescript (1/1/34:5).

14 As Douglas Anderson notes in *The Annotated Hobbit* (DAA.111), 'skriking' is not Tolkien's own coinage but a dialectical word meaning a shrill screeching; Anderson also notes that the word appears in Haigh's *A New Glossary of the Dialect of the Huddersfield District*, to which Tolkien contributed a Foreword.

15 This is the first appearance of the name *Glamdring*, which like 'Orcrist' is either Gnomish or Noldorin. The *Gnomish Lexicon* (page 39) gives 'glam · hoth' as the Gnomish word for the orcs. 'Glam' (*glâm*) itself means hatred or loathing, while 'hoth' (ibid. p. 49) means a folk, people, or army; thus glam+hoth = 'People of [the] dreadful Hate'. In 'The Etymologies' *glam* has come to mean 'shouting, confused noise' and though *glamhoth* is still a name for the orcs, in Noldorin the word is said to mean 'the barbaric host' (HME V.358). I cannot account for the second half of the name, *-dring*, in Gnomish, but 'The Etymologies' has an entry defining it as Noldorin for 'beat, strike' (HME V.355), which is close enough to 'hammer' that we can consider them equivalent. The later translation 'foe-hammer' is thus a slightly less literal and somewhat more poetic, though still accurate, translation than 'goblin-cleaver', and avoids confusing the unphilological reader as why two such different words (*Glam-*, *Orc-*) were, in the original, both translated as 'goblin'.

16 Added: '(that's Gandalf)'.

17 Penciled over the Elvish words are the orcish names for these swords: 'Biter and Beater'.

(i)
Goblins

In keeping with the pattern established in the preceding chapters, this chapter introduces yet another a new race: the goblins. Like the elves and dwarves, goblins already had a long history in Tolkien's writings predating *The Hobbit*. Even if we overlook the undifferentiated fairy-folk lumped under the 'goblin' label in 'Goblin Feet' [published 1915], goblins were featured prominently throughout the early Silmarillion material, especially in 'The Tale of Tinúviel', 'Turambar and the Foalókë', and 'The Fall of Gondolin' [all written 1916–20]. Goblins fought alongside balrogs and dragons in the sack of Gondolin, and goblin-mercenaries aided the dwarves in looting Tinwelint's caves in Artanor (the precursors in the legendarium to Thingol's Thousand Caves of Menegroth in Doriath). The terms 'goblin' and 'orc' were used more or less interchangeably in the early material – thus in 'The Fall of Gondolin' we hear of 'Melko's goblins, the Orcs of the hills' (BLT II.157), 'the Orcs who are Melko's goblins' (BLT II.159), and 'an innumerable host of the Orcs, the goblins of hatred' (BLT II.176), while in 'Turambar and the Foalókë' Beleg tracks 'the band of Orcs . . . a band of the goblins of Melko' (BLT II.77). It's possible to read Orc as the more specific term and goblin as the more generic, but often 'goblin' apparently replaces the more common 'orc' simply for the sake of variety, especially in the alliterative poetry. On the whole, the evidence suggests that Tolkien preferred 'orc' for works in the direct line of the Silmarillion tradition (such as 'The Sketch of the Mythology', the narrative poems that make up *The Lays of Beleriand*, the 1930 *Quenta*, and so forth) and used 'goblin' in more light-hearted contexts, such as *The Father Christmas Letters* and *The Hobbit*.

Also known as the Glamhoth (or 'people of hate'), goblins seem to be one of the *Úvanimor*, the monster-folk 'bred in the earth' by Melko; a category that includes 'monsters, giants, and ogres' and, early on, possibly the dwarves as well (BLT I.236 & 75). In the early myth, they seem to have been created by Melko – according to the elven narrator of 'The Fall of Gondolin', 'all that race were bred by Melko of the subterranean heats and slime' (BLT II.159).[1] Eventually Tolkien adopted the Augustinian view that evil cannot create but only corrupt and that therefore orcs must be one of the 'Free Peoples' who have been twisted and corrupted, probably elves (since orcs appear in the stories before the first humans awaken). Both views are present in *The Lord of the Rings*, where one character asserts that 'Trolls are only counterfeits, made by the Enemy in the Great Darkness, in mockery of Ents, as Orcs were of Elves' (*LotR*.507) and another 'The Shadow that bred them can only mock, it cannot make: not real new things of its own. I don't think it gave life to the orcs, it only ruined them and twisted them . . .' (*LotR*.948). In his later years, Tolkien wrestled with the problem and attempted to come to a definitive solution in a fascinating sequence of essays printed in *Morgoth's Ring* (HME X.409–22; these essays were written c. 1959–60 & 1969). Among the solutions he toyed with were (a) orcs are animals without souls; their speech is parrot-like and what little rational will they seem to have is part of Morgoth's dispersed personality;[2] (b) the original orcs were the least of the spirits corrupted by Morgoth, just as balrogs are greater spirits. Once incarnate, they could procreate (just as Melian could give birth to Lúthien and Morgoth could toy with the idea of taking Lúthien as his wife or concubine; cf. *Silm*.180) and the very act would trap them within the bodies they had assumed; their descendents would be weaker and weaker, perhaps dwindling in the end to mere poltergeists; (c) orcs are elves carried off by Morgoth from the awakening place, Cuiviénen, and corrupted. This is the position adopted in *The Silmarillion*:

> [T]his is held true by the wise of Eressëa, that all those of the Quendi [i.e., elves] who came into the hands of Melkor, ere Utumno was broken, were put there in prison, and by slow arts of cruelty were corrupted and enslaved; and thus did Melkor breed the hideous race

> of the Orcs in envy and mockery of the Elves, of whom they were afterwards the bitterest foes . . . This it may be was the vilest deed of Melkor, and the most hateful to Ilúvatar. (*Silm.*50)

and again:

> Whence they came, or what they were, the Elves knew not then, thinking them perhaps to be Avari [wild elves] who had become evil and savage in the wild; in which they guessed all too near, it is said. (*Silm.*94)

Furthermore, in later times a strong human strain was added to the mix; in the essay on the Drúedain, the Wild Men of the Woods, an author's note states that 'Doubtless Morgoth, since he can make no living thing, bred Orcs from various kinds of Men' and raises the possibility of some distant kinship between orcs and the Wild Men (or woodwoses), noting that 'Orcs and Drûgs each regarded the other as renegades' (*Unfinished Tales* p. 385). Finally, (d) some orc-leaders, the Great Orcs, were Maiar who took on orcish shape,[3] but the majority of their followers were mortal and short-lived by elven or Númenórean standards, being bred (by Sauron, not Morgoth)[4] from human stock. According to this last theory, orcs were capable of independent thought and even, theoretically, of repentance but were easily controlled by Morgoth or Sauron from afar, having been especially bred to be so dominated.

Whatever their origin, the goblins in *The Hobbit* seem as capable of free thought and action as any of the other races in the book, whether dwarves or elves or men or hobbits. There seems to be no connection between the goblins of the Misty Mountains and the Necromancer who lurks in Mirkwood – Thû the Necromancer may have been served by wolf-packs and orc-patrols in 'The Lay of Leithian', but not even a hint suggests that the Great Goblin owes the Necromancer of our story allegiance or is in any way under his sway. Instead, just as dwarves come into their own in this book, so too are the goblins presented for the first time as something more than swordfodder, having their own (admittedly wicked) culture and civilization, complete with poetry, commerce, an apparently thriving slave-labor industry[5], a hierarchical society (from the Great Goblin on top down through the warriors to the slaves), and xenophobia. In fact, they greatly resemble the goblins of one of Tolkien's precursors.

Up until this point in the story, Tolkien himself has been his own chief source – such once well-known works as Christina Rossetti's 'Goblin Market' [1861] and James Whitcomb Riley's 'Little Orphant Annie' [1885], with its famous refrain

> And the Gobble-uns'll git you ef you Don't Watch Out!

apparently having no discernible influence on him. Now, however, he draws directly from an outside writer popular to an earlier generation: George MacDonald. Tolkien himself freely acknowledged the debt in his 1938 letter to *The Observer*, noting that one of his chief sources had been 'fairy-story – not, however, Victorian in authorship, as a rule to which George Macdonald is the chief exception' (*Letters*, p. 31; see Appendix II). He was more explicit in the draft of his Andrew Lang Memorial Lecture, 'On Fairy-Stories':

> . . . But in the short time at my disposal I must say something about George Macdonald. George Macdonald, in that mixture of German and Scottish flavours (which makes him so inevitably attractive to myself), has depicted what will always be to me the classic goblin. By that standard I judge all goblins, old or new.[6]

Elsewhere he admitted that his goblins 'owe, I suppose, a good deal to the goblin tradition . . . especially as it appears in George MacDonald' (JRRT to Naomi Mitchison, 25th April 1954; *Letters* pp. 177–8) and again contrasted his own goblins with 'the goblins of George MacDonald, which they do to some extent resemble' (JRRT to Hugh Brogan, 18th Sept 1954; *Letters* p. 185).[7]

A look at MacDonald's *The Princess and the Goblin* [1872] confirms Tolkien's debt. MacDonald's goblins, like Tolkien's, are ugly, cunning, wicked,[8] and technologically advanced, delighting in waylaying benighted travellers or lone miners. At times they plan war or other mischief against the people who live nearby, aided by weird misshapen goblin animals called *cobs* – a possible inspiration for the goblin-warg and goblin-bat alliances in the chapters to follow later in *The Hobbit*. Moreover, MacDonald's goblins can interbreed with humans, although the only offspring of such a union that we see resembles his orc father more than his human mother – a probable forerunner of the half-orcs of *The Lord of the Rings* (some of whom, like Saruman's Uruk-hai, are orc-like, while others, like the spy at Bree, can pass for human). They greatly dislike daylight, being most active at night, and their homes are a mix of mines and caverns, just like the goblin-caves of the Misty Mountains.

However, Tolkien was nothing if not selective in his borrowings, picking and choosing to suit his own ends and the needs of his story. Even where his sources can be identified through his own admission, he adapted what he borrowed and made it his own. For example, although MacDonald's goblins are ruled over by a goblin king rather like the Great Goblin, there is nothing in Tolkien's story to parallel MacDonald's indomitable goblin queen, who stomps on her enemies' feet with her great stone shoes. MacDonald's goblins were originally humans who withdrew below-ground to escape persecution and now prefer a subterranean life, although they harbor a very understandable grudge against the king who wronged them and his descendants, including the princess of the title. All Tolkien's goblins remain nameless in the original draft, and when he did add names (Azog, Bolg) it was in one of his invented languages, while MacDonald's have comic names like Podge, Glump, Helfer, and Hairlip. *The Princess and the Goblin* even includes a comic scene of goblin family life that would be entirely inappropriate to the sense of menace Tolkien creates in this chapter, where the characters reel from peril to peril to peril. MacDonald's goblins have hard heads and soft, toeless feet – their one vulnerable point, which the hero of his story is quick to exploit. Tolkien gave this idea short shrift; in the letter to Naomi Mitchison already cited, he continues, after acknowledging his debt to MacDonald's goblin-lore, '. . . except for the soft feet which I never believed in' (JRRT to Mitchison, 25th April 1954; *Letters* p. 178). Tolkien's goblins, like hobbits, apparently go barefoot as a rule, only adopting footware at special need (such as to quiet the flapping of their feet when pursuing escaping guests).[9]

Most notably of all, MacDonald's goblins are afraid of singing. They can neither sing nor compose themselves, and the best way to drive them off is to shout out spontaneous rhyming nonsense. Not only are Tolkien's goblins, the goblins of the Misty Mountains, unafraid of a little verse, they seem as fond of breaking into a song as the villains in a Gilbert and Sullivan operetta. The goblin marching song in this chapter, with its alliteration and internal rhyme, might be a well-known chantey among the goblins for all we know, but the one they sing two chapters later ('Fifteen Birds') must be a spontaneous 'occasional' composition made up on the spot, so well does it fit the situation.

On one point, it's difficult to tell if Tolkien and MacDonald are in agreement or not. MacDonald's goblins are very long-lived (in the comic scene already referred to, the goblin-father remarks condescendingly to one goblin-child that 'You were only fifty last month' – *The Princess and the Goblin*, Chapter 8). The same may be true of Tolkien's goblins. Upon seeing the sword rescued from the Trolls' lair, they react instantly, howling and stamping and gnashing their teeth: they all recognize it at once (p. 132). And it is difficult to see how this could be so unless the majority of the goblins present in this scene took part in the siege of Gondolin.[10] Even so, this falls short of proof on the point of goblin longevity, as earlier chapters have disagreed on whether the events of our story are taking place ages and ages after the fall of Gondolin (Chapter III, p. 115) or in the same century (Chapter I, p. 73). Perhaps the sword had passed into legend, along with a detailed description of its appearance, though this seems unlikely; in any case, Tolkien never altered this detail in the scene, even when he later firmly embraced the vast separation of time between Mr. Baggins' world and the First Age.

No goblins appear in any of his illustrations for *The Hobbit*, but Tolkien did draw goblins in several of the *Father Christmas Letters* (see the illustrations for the letters from 1932, 1933, & 1935). These recurrent threats to the timely delivery of presents first enter the epistolary series in 1932, just about the time Tolkien was writing the final chapters of *The Hobbit*. Father Christmas describes them thusly:

> Goblins are to us very much what rats are to you, only worse, because they are very clever, and only better because there are, in these parts, very few. We thought there were none left. Long ago we had great trouble with them, that was about 1453, I believe, but we got the help of the Gnomes, who are their greatest enemies, and cleared them out.[11]

Initially they are drawn as small black figures with pointy heads and large pale eyes,[12] given to lurking and peering around corners (1932 Letter; see Plate VI [top left]); illustrations to later letters (1933 and 1935) reduce the size of the eyes somewhat and add a mouth and nose as well as showing them in much more active pursuits (battling elves, being squashed flat or thrown sky-high by the North Polar Bear, &c.). The later illustrations also replace the single crest or point atop the head with two very prominent ears, while the 1935 drawing gives them rather canine faces and very distinct tails. Their size throughout is the same as that of the 'Gnomes' or elves, or about half Father Christmas's height.

Like the goblins in *The Hobbit*, those encountered repeatedly by Father Christmas (in 1932, 1933, and 1941) are experts at tunnelling and mining, laying low for long periods then suddenly coming forth in rampaging hordes to loot and pillage. One of their favorite tricks is to make secret tunnels from which to launch sorties and ambushes, just like the waylayers of the Misty Mountains. They share the latter's alliances with bats and used to ride into battle on creatures named *drasils* (described as 'dwarf "dachshund" horse creatures') before these became extinct, a strong parallel both to MacDonald's cob and to the wolf-riders we are shortly to encounter (although there is no parallel in *The Hobbit* to the bat-riders of *The Father Christmas Letters*). Finally, goblins are *noisy*: except when sneaking up on somebody they make all kinds of racket. As Father Christmas observes, 'Goblins cannot help yelling and beating on drums when they mean to fight' – a characteristic shared by their cousins in the Misty Mountains; cf. p. 162:

> They saw him at once, and yelled with delight as they rushed at him . . . they yelled all the louder, only not quite so delighted . . . Whistles blew, armour clashed, swords rattled, goblins cursed and swore . . . There was a terrible outcry, to do and disturbance

and pp. 132–3:

> The yells and yammers, croaking, jibbering and jabbering, howls growls and curses, shrieks and skriking that followed passes all description. Several hundred cats and wolves being roasted alive together could not have compared with it.

Note, however, one characteristic feature of Tolkien's writings as a whole is not yet present: the goblins of *The Hobbit* do not have their own language but speak the same tongue as Bilbo and the dwarves. This feature never changed, so far as *The Hobbit* was concerned, but in the sequel Tolkien's love of words led him to create a few snatches of goblin (cf. *LotR*.466 – *Uglúk u bagronk sha pushdug Saruman-glob búbhosh skai* – and the discussion of orc-speech later on that same page and in Appendix F, pages 1165–6). But for now, this thoroughly typical expression of Tolkien's linguistic inventiveness lay in the future.

(ii)
The Giants

If the goblins open up a vast array of questions, the giants glimpsed from a distance during the crossing of the Misty Mountains remain on the fringes of the story. Giants occur in several of Tolkien's works, but we never learn a great deal about them. Lúthien's sleep-spell, already cited in reference to the beards of the dwarves (see p. 77), invokes 'the neck of Gilim the giant' and 'the sword of Nan' (BLT II.19) in its list of the longest things in the world, but little is known of either of these figures beyond the names. The version of this passage in 'The Lay of Leithian' names the sword as Glend and calls Gilim 'the giant of Eruman' (HME III.205). Christopher Tolkien notes that 'Gilim' is glossed as 'winter' in the Gnomish dictionary and cites an isolated note to the effect that Nan was a 'giant of summer of the South' like an elm (BLT II.67–8).[13] The contrast between summer and winter seems obvious, perhaps harkening back to the fire-giants and frost-giants of Eddic lore, but whatever story Tolkien may have had in mind behind these shadowy figures (if indeed he had any at all) was apparently never written down. Nevertheless, Nan may have been in the back of Tolkien's mind when he created the ents some twenty years later: for 'ent' simply means 'giant' in Old English, and it seems plain that the giant seen by Sam's cousin Hal up beyond the North Moors was an ent, described as being 'as big as an elm tree, and walking' (*LotR*.57).[14] The detail of the elm may be coincidental, but given Tolkien's creative reuse of material time and again it would be rash to dismiss the parallel as sheer chance.

The Book of Lost Tales had referred to giants as one of the Úvanimor, or monster-folk (BLT I.75), a thoroughly traditional touch on Tolkien's part; giants have a long, long tradition in folklore of being extremely dangerous if not downright wicked. Even Treebeard first appears in the *LotR* drafts as a distinctly sinister figure. It is initially 'the Giant Treebeard', not Saruman, who imprisons Gandalf the Grey and prevents him from warning Frodo to set out at once or accompanying him on his journey (HME VI.363), and an isolated draft passage survives describing Frodo's encounter with 'Giant Treebeard', who here seems entirely tree-like. The episode seems harmless enough, slightly reminiscent of Ransom's early adventures on Malacandra in Lewis's *Out of the Silent Planet* [1938], but Tolkien glossed it thusly in tengwar:

> Frodo meets Giant Treebeard in the Forest of Neldoreth while seeking for his lost companions: he is deceived by the giant who pretends to be friendly, but is really in league with the Enemy.
>
> —HME VI.382–4[15]

An outline for 'The Council of Elrond' contains yet another warning in the midst of notes regarding the route the Fellowship and Ring will take:

> 'Beware!' said Gandalf 'of the Giant Treebeard, who haunts the Forest between the River and the South Mts.'
>
> —ibid., page 397.

But then Tolkien had a change of heart, and an outline relating to events in Fangorn Forest contains the suggestion 'If Treebeard comes in at all – let him be kindly and rather good?' (HME VI.410), a suggestion taken up in the rest of the outline, where Treebeard not only rescues Frodo when the latter is wandering lost in the forest but takes him to Ond (= Gondor) and raises the siege of the city, thereby rescuing Trotter (= Strider) and the others. The last trace of ambiguity appears in a reversal of the original idea; here it is only after the 'tree-giant' (described in terms that sound something like a cross between the Green Man of medieval legend, Sir Bercilak, and an actual tree) has carried Frodo to his castle in the Black Mountains that he is revealed to be friendly, whereas in the earlier draft he had pretended friendship but been false.

While the ents went on to become one of Tolkien's most original and admired creations – attracting praise from critics as diverse as C. S. Lewis and Edmund Wilson[16] – giants in the traditional sense of large, dangerous monsters in more or less human form vanished from the more integrated Middle-earth of Tolkien's later work. Ents are one of the five Free Peoples; giants one of those races which may be called the Children of Morgoth. We have seen that both dwarves and goblins, who early on also fell under the '*úvanimor*' rubric, underwent further development in *The Hobbit*, with the goblins remaining a monster race ('cruel, wicked, and bad hearted') and dwarves undergoing a transformation into 'decent enough people', if 'commercial-minded' (cf. p. 505). What, then, of the stone-giants? Is it possible, from the scanty evidence presented in *The Hobbit*, to determine whether they should be classified as Children of Morgoth or free agents?

In purely practical terms, our heroes are less concerned with the giants' moral standing than the danger they pose. Their antics seem more the result of exuberance than malice, but that would be small consolation for any member of the party 'kicked sky high for a football'. Similarly, the dim-witted giant of *Farmer Giles of Ham* blunders about causing all sorts of damage – breaking hedges, trampling crops, knocking down trees, smashing houses, and squashing the farmer's favorite cow – yet all this destruction is merely the result of lack of attention on the part of the short-sighted and deaf giant, not active malice (unlike the dragon Chrysophylax Dives in the same story, whose depredations are quite intentional). The stone-giants of *The Hobbit* do not seem to be aware of the presence of the travellers, but then again there's no indication that they would have behaved any differently had they known; in short, they are portrayed as a perilous but almost impersonal force, rather like the thunder-storm itself.[17]

By contrast, a much more traditional view surfaces in the next chapter – when Bilbo is trying to think of the answer to Gollum's last riddle ('This thing all things devours'), his mind is filled with 'all the horrible names of all the giants and ogres he had ever heard told of in tales' (p. 158). Here we can plainly see the echoes of such traditional tales as 'Jack and the Beanstalk' and 'Jack the Giant Killer', with their murderous, man-eating giants.[18] Yet not all giants can be such monsters, for a chapter later Bladorthin casually suggests finding 'a more or less decent giant' to block up the goblins' front gate in the mountain pass. It seems, then, that giants occupy a neutral ground, neither good nor evil as a race but varying from individual to individual. Dangerous, certainly – but as Gandalf points out in speaking of Treebeard, powerful and perilous is not the same thing as evil (*LotR*.521; & cf. also ibid.706).

(iii)
Switzerland

While literature and his own earlier writings contributed much to *The Hobbit*, one element entered the story directly from personal experience: the descriptions of the mountain-crossing and thunderstorm in the Misty Mountains. As Tolkien recounted in a letter some fifty years after the event:

> . . . with a mixed party of about the same size as the company in *The Hobbit* . . . I journeyed on foot with a heavy pack through much of Switzerland, and over many high passes. It was approaching the Aletsch that we were nearly destroyed by boulders loosened in the sun rolling down a snow-slope. An enormous rock in fact passed between me and the next in front. That and the 'thunder-battle' – a bad night in which we lost our way and slept in a cattle-shed – appear in *The Hobbit*. It is long ago now . . .
>
> —JRRT to Joyce Reeves, 4th November 1961; *Letters* p. 309.

A later letter provides more details of the events underlying the early parts of Chapters III, IV, & VI:

> The hobbit's (Bilbo's) journey from Rivendell to the other side of the Misty Mountains, including the glissade down the slithering stones into the pine woods, is based on my adventures in 1911 . . . One day we went on a long march with guides up the Aletsch glacier – when I came near to perishing. We had guides, but either the effects of the hot summer were beyond their experience, or they did not much care, or we were late in starting. Any way at noon we were strung out in file along a narrow track with a snow-slope on the right going up to the horizon, and on the left a plunge down into a ravine. The summer of that year had melted away much snow, and stones and boulders were exposed that (I suppose) were normally covered. The heat of the day continued the melting and we were alarmed to see many of them starting to roll down the slope at gathering speed: anything from the size of oranges to large footballs, and a few much larger. They were whizzing across our path and plunging into the ravine . . . They started slowly, and then usually held a straight line of descent, but the path was rough and one had also to keep an eye on one's feet. I remember the member of the party just in front of me (an elderly schoolmistress) gave a sudden squeak and jumped forward as a large lump of rock shot between us. About a foot at most before my unmanly knees . . .
>
> —JRRT to Michael Tolkien, 1967–8; *Letters* pp. 391, 392–3.

It was this journey that enabled Tolkien to envision the Misty Mountain scenes with such a wealth of realistic detail, from the first approaches to Rivendell (cf. pages 112) through the *glissade* in Chapter VI (cf. p. 202),[19] and he may have drawn on these memories again in some of the Lonely Mountain scenes, such as the ascent of the 'fly-path' to the sheltered bay on the west slope (p. 473) or the march to Ravenhill (pp. 583 & 594).

(iv)

Bilbo's Dreams, and Other Matters

In addition to the main business of this chapter, several recurrent motifs make an appearance that should perhaps be noted before we move on to the next chapter. For the reference to Durin's Day, see Text Note I above. One motif that shows up here for the first time is Bilbo's prophetic dream (p. 129), which enables Bladorthin to evade capture and later rescue the others – thus marking the first time that the hobbit is responsible for the party's escape from peril, albeit indirectly. The first of several dreams in *The Hobbit*, this is also the most important to the plot (for other examples, see Bilbo's evocative dream at the end of Chapter VI, Bombur's dream of the elven feasts in the interpolation into Chapter VIII, and Smaug's nightmare of 'a small warrior, altogether insignificant in size, but provided with a bitter sword, and great courage').[20] As a student of medieval literature, Tolkien was of course familiar with the genre of dream-vision, being intimately acquainted with such an outstanding example as *The Pearl*. He not only translated this moving elegy into modern English but planned to edit the original with E. V. Gordon as a companion volume to their edition of *Sir Gawain & the Green Knight* (another work written by the same anonymous fourteenth-century author) – a plan forestalled by Gordon's sudden and untimely death in 1938 and Tolkien's increased academic responsibilities during the late 1930s and especially World War II.[21] Dreams also play important parts in two other works Tolkien was professionally concerned with: Chaucer's 'Nun's Priest's Tale' and the anonymous Breton lay *Sir Orfeo*.[22] Other important dream-visions Tolkien would have been familiar with include Cicero's *Somnium Scipionis* (*The Dream of Scipio*) [circa 50 BC];[23] Chaucer's *Book of the Duchess* [1368], *Parliament of Fowls* [c. 1370s], and *House of Fame* [c. 1380s]; Langland's *Vision of Piers Plowman* [1360s–80s]; Guillaume de Lorris's *Romance of the Rose* [c. 1230]; and the anonymous Welsh tales 'The Dream of Macsen Wledig' and 'The Dream of Rhonabwy' [early thirteenth century]. Tolkien's own remarks on the dream-vision genre can be found in the introduction to his translation of *Sir Gawain and the Green Knight, Pearl, and Sir Orfeo* (see especially page 20 of the 1978 edition). Nor should we neglect to consider the influence of life as well as literature: Tolkien himself was a lifelong dreamer, and the drowning of Númenor that figures so importantly in works such as 'The Fall of Númenor', *The Lost Road*, 'The Drowning of Anadûnê', and *The Notion Club Papers* is based on an actual recurrent dream (cf. *Letters* pp. 213 & 347).[24]

More important than its source, of course, is the use to which Tolkien put this motif. Some are mere dreams of no particular significance, as when a very hungry hobbit subsisting only on *cram* dreams of eggs and bacon during the siege of the Lonely Mountain (DAA.332). The dream in which he wanders from room to room of his home, looking for something he's forgotten (p. 210), is both believable as a dream and suggestive for what it reveals about his state of mind, but it has no direct bearing on the plot. Of the prophetic dreams, it is a curious fact that unlike Frodo's dreams in *The Lord of Rings*, which deal with distant events, the dreams in *The Hobbit* tend to relate to things which are either happening at the same time as they are being dreamed or follow in very short order. On the whole, dreams play a less important part in *The Hobbit* than in many of Tolkien's other works, but their very presence marks the recurrence of a favorite Tolkienian motif and thus helps link the story to other works that share this element, from *The Book of Lost Tales* and its Cottage of Lost Play, a place most men can only reach via 'the Path of Dreams' (BLT I.18), through *The Lost Road* (where the time-travel begins while the main character is dreaming) and *The Notion Club Papers* (which devotes most of Part I to a discussion of lucid dreaming) to *The Lord of the Rings* itself. More importantly, it places Bilbo firmly in the tradition of Tolkien's dreamers, alongside Eriol (whose name means 'One who dreams alone' – BLT I.14) and Ælfwine, Alboin and Audoin Errol, Michael Ramer and Arry Lowdham, Faramir, and Frodo Baggins.

Finally, we might note that admirable indirectness with which Gandalf responds to the Great Goblin's questions, 'not quite knowing what to say . . . when obviously the exact truth wouldn't do at all'. Lines such as these, even more than the moral ambiguity of the closing chapters, place Tolkien firmly in the modern tradition, beginning with Kenneth Grahame's *The Golden Age* [1895], that aligns itself with its audience and its foibles rather than preaches pieties in the Victorian manner. Tolkien is not directly parodying the older tradition, as Twain did in his lecture 'Advice to Youth' [1882] ('Always obey your parents, when they are present . . . Be respectful to your superiors, if you have any . . . You want to be very careful about lying; otherwise you are nearly sure to get caught . . .'), but his lack of condemnation of this white lie represents a stark contrast to, say, a MacDonald or Alcott or Knatchbull-Huggesson.

NOTES

1 Note that the trolls, when exposed to sunlight, 'go back to the stuff of the mountains they are made of' (see p. 96). Similarly, Treebeard claims that Ents are 'made of the bones of the earth' (i.e., stone† – cf. *LotR*.507), and we are told in *The Silmarillion* of the elvish belief that upon death dwarves 'returned to the earth and the stone of which they were made' (*Silm*.44). Thus, even if Melkor did form the first goblins from 'subterranean heats and slime', this would not in itself prevent them from being sentient; the Old Testament itself tells (*Genesis* 2.7) how 'the Lord God formed man of dust from the ground', and the very word 'Adam' simply means 'earth' or 'clay' in Hebrew (thus the burial service: 'ashes to ashes, dust to dust').

† This is at variance with the creation myth recounted in *The Silmarillion*, where Yavanna tells Manwë '. . . it was in the Song . . . For while thou wert in the heavens and with Ulmo built the clouds and poured out the rains, I lifted up the branches of great trees to receive them, and some sang to Ilúvatar amid the wind and the rain' ('Of Aule and Yavanna', *Silm*.45–6). Here it is clear that the Ents are trees ensouled by Ilúvatar: 'the hand of Ilúvatar . . . entered in, and from it came forth many wonders . . . the thought of Yavanna will awake . . . and it will summon spirits from afar, and they will go among . . . the *olvar* [plant life], and some will dwell therein' (ibid., p. 46).

2 Note Ilúvatar's rebuke to Aulë when he first makes the dwarves: 'the creatures of thy hand and mind can live only by that being, moving when thou thinkest to move them, and if thy thought be elsewhere, standing idle' (*Silm.*43). When Sauron is finally destroyed at the climax of *The Lord of the Rings* 'the creatures of Sauron, orc or troll or beast spell-enslaved, ran hither and thither mindless; and some slew themselves, or cast themselves in pits, or fled wailing back to hide in holes and dark lightless places far from hope' (*LotR.*985).

3 In a footnote to one of these mini-essays, Tolkien proposed the name *Boldog* for these Maiar-orcs, almost a kind of lesser balrog (HME X.418). According to this theory, presumably the Great Goblin of the Misty Mountains, Azog, and Bolg were either creatures of this type or descended from them.

4 According to this theory, the idea was Morgoth's but the actual execution was left to Sauron, who 'was often able to achieve things, first conceived by Melkor, which his master did not or could not complete in the furious haste of his malice' (HME X.420).

5 The slave-labor industry of Morgoth and his minions goes all the way back to *The Book of Lost Tales*. For example, in 'The Tale of Tinúviel' Beren is captured by Orcs, who 'thought that Melko might perchance be pleasured if he was brought before him and might set him to some heavy thrall-work in his mines or in his smithies' (BLT II.14–15), although in the event Beren winds up a kitchen-slave of Tevildo, Prince of Cats. Similarly, in 'Turambar and the Foalókë, we see in Flinding, the escaped prisoner from 'the mines of Melko', the effects of such servitude.

6 Ms. Tolkien 14, folio 19, verso. This draft is now in the Department of Western Manuscripts in the Bodleian Library in Oxford; I am grateful to Christina Scull for drawing this reference to my attention and providing me with a transcription.

7 Tolkien retained his good opinion of MacDonald right up until September of 1964, when he agreed to write a preface to a new edition of *The Golden Key* (JRRT to Mr. di Capua of Pantheon Books, 7th Sept 1964; *Letters* p. 351) – a task C. S. Lewis would no doubt have been asked to perform had he not died the year before. Unfortunately, actually rereading MacDonald again, probably for the first time in thirty years, filled Tolkien with dismay (cf. Carpenter page 242); the result was his writing 'an anti-G[eorge]. M[acDonald]. tract', the little story known as *Smith of Wootton Major* [1967] (SWM extended edition, ed. Verlyn Flieger [2005], pages 69–70).

8 MacDonald claims that goblins are not cruel for cruelty's sake, but the general tone of the text does not support this.

9 For more on hobbit footware, see p. 784 and *Letters* p. 35.

10 Similarly, in *The Lord of the Rings*, when Shagrat and Gorbag reminisce fondly about 'old times' when they could maraud freely before the 'Big Bosses' came back (*LotR.*765); they seem to be referring to the

period before Sauron's return to Mordor almost seventy years before, suggesting a lifespan longer than a human's or hobbit's.†

† However, Gorbag's allusion to 'the Great Siege' later in the same conversation (*LotR*.767) – that is, to the events of the Last Alliance just over three thousand years before – need not be from personal experience.

11 That Tolkien should have picked a specific year is typical of his comic precision ('100 years ago last Tuesday'), but it's not clear why he should have picked 1453, a year notorious in European history for two events: the fall of Constantinople and the end of the Hundred Years' War. The one event marked the final end of the Roman Empire and defeat of Christendom by Islam, while the other put an end to centuries of English attempts to gain territory on the European mainland. Both are seminal in the transition from the so-called 'Middle Ages' to modern times, and the disappearance of nonhuman monsters such as goblins might plausibly be thought of as another feature of modern times, but this is speculation.

12 Another cave-painting accompanying the 1932 letter is clearly based on the great Neolithic paintings of Altamira (discovered in 1879; those at Lascaux and Chauvet were not discovered until 1940 and 1994, respectively, too late to influence the *Father Christmas Letters*). In addition to drawings of bears, bison, horse, stags, boar, and mammoths, the page is littered with goblin graffiti. Just above the lower left corner are two figures, hand in hand – the one clearly meant to represent a goblin from its inky blackness and pointy head, but the other is red and has a flat head shaped rather like an inverted triangle. This may be a representational drawing of a female goblin; if so, it is the only one Tolkien drew known to me.

13 *Eruman* is a dark shady land bordering on Valinor; the name essentially means 'outside' (see Christopher Tolkien's discussion of both name and place, BLT I.252). For Gilim, see *Parma Eldalamberon* XI.38. Nan's name may be linked to the Qenya [early Quenya] word for woods or forest; cf. the *Qenya Lexicon's nan(d)* woodland, *nandin* dryad (*Parma Eldalamberon* XII.64).

14 The connection with the ents is strengthened by Sam's comment when he introduces the subject: 'what about these Tree-men, these giants, as you might call them?' (*LotR*.57).

15 This portrayal of an apparently friendly yet actually evil giant may owe something to Golithos, the most interesting character in Wyke-Smith's *The Marvellous Land of Snergs*. Formerly an ogre (the French equivalent of the Norse 'troll', and like it a term of wide applicability), he has taken the pledge and no longer eats people, but a visit from two tender young children proves too much for him after years of a strict vegetarian diet, and he attempts to revert to his former cannibalistic ways.

16 In his review of *The Fellowship of the Ring*, C. S. Lewis singled out 'the unforgettable Ents' for special praise – no doubt to the puzzlement of his original readers, since the ents do not enter the story until the

second volume, *The Two Towers*, published several months later. Similarly, Edmund Wilson, in his famous diatribe 'Oo, Those Awful Orcs', grudgingly admitted that the ents 'showed signs of imagination'.

17 As Doug Anderson points out (personal communication), the stone giants probably derive from the legend of the *rübezahl*, a German storm-spirit who, in the words of Andrew Lang, 'amused himself by rolling great rocks down into the desolate valleys, to hear the thunder of their fall echoing among the hills' (*The Brown Fairy Book* [1904] p. 283). Tolkien is not the only modern fantasist inspired by the legend; the game of nine-pins played by the strange little men in Washington Irving's 'Rip Van Winkle' [1819] was probably also inspired by the same German folk-lore.

18 Or, to go further back, the story of King Arthur's battle with the giant of Mont St. Michel, retold by both Geoffrey of Monmouth and Malory – or, further still, the story of Odysseus outwitting the cyclops. Whether called ogres, trolls, cyclopes, or giants, cannibalistic giant-folk loom large in the folklore of Europe.

19 For a detailed comparison of Tolkien's 1911 journey and its possible influences on *The Hobbit*, see Marie Barnfield's piece 'The Roots of Rivendell', published in the specialist Tolkien biography journal *Þe Lyfe ant þe Auncestrye* [1996], as well as Tolkien's letter to his son Michael (*Letters* pp. 391–3).

20 The first of these is realistic but inconsequential; the second blends enchanted dream with waking delusion; the third actually refers to a direction the plot was to have taken which was subsequently abandoned – cf. p. 507 and commentary page 519.

21 Gordon's edition, with some contributions by Tolkien, was completely redone by his widow, Ida Gordon, and eventually appeared from Oxford University Press in 1953. Tolkien's intimacy with the poem is further indicated by the fact that he not only translated and helped edit it but also wrote poetry in the extremely difficult stanza used by the *Pearl*-poet, which combines both rhyme and alliteration, merging the continental tradition of rhyming verse with the older English tradition of alliteration.† Tolkien's poem using the *Pearl* meter, 'The Nameless Land', was written in 1924. It originally appeared in 1927 in *Realities: An Anthology of Verse*, ed. G. S. Tancred and is reprinted in *The Lost Road* (HME V.98ff); Christopher Tolkien quotes there from a note of his father's that it was 'inspired by reading *Pearl* for examination purposes'.

† See Tolkien's discussion of the meter in his letter to Jane Neave, 18th July 1962; *Letters* p. 317.

22 Tolkien recited the first of these from memory in the original Middle English at the 1938 Oxford 'Summer Diversions' organized by his friend and fellow Inkling Nevill Coghill (who later translated all of *The Canterbury Tales* into modern English) and Poet Laureate John Masefield, while he both translated *Sir Orfeo* into modern English and prepared

a critical text that was released as a pamphlet by Oxford University in 1944; the latter, edited by Carl Hostetter, was published in *Tolkien Studies* (volume I [2004], pages 85–123).

23 It's easy to forget that Tolkien began his academic career as a classicist and only transferred his major to medieval studies in his second year at Oxford; the influence of classical literature on his work has been sadly neglected by Tolkien studies. For a notable exception, see Kenneth Reckford's excellent article 'There and Back Again: Odysseus and Bilbo Baggins' in *Mythlore* LIII [Spring 1988], pages 5–9.

As for *The Dream of Scipio,* Tolkien would not have had to rely upon hazy memories of undergraduate days for his knowledge of the work, since his friend and fellow Inkling C. S. Lewis discusses it at length in *The Discarded Image*,† pages 23–8, granting it great prominence for influencing the whole genre of medieval dream-vision.

† This book did not appear until 1964, the year after Lewis's death, but the lecture-series upon which it was based was in existence by 1934 (see *Letters of C. S. Lewis,* ed. W. H. Lewis [and Christopher Derrick]; rev. ed. 1988 ed. Fr. Walter Hooper, page 309, and also *The Collected Letters of C. S. Lewis*, ed. Walter Hooper, volume II [2004], page 141). Tolkien had sounded out Allen & Unwin about its publication as early as 1936 and they expressed an interest, although in the event Lewis demurred, apparently feeling it would reduce the appeal of his lectures if the material was readily available in print (Susan Dagnall to JRRT, letter of 10th December, 1936; Allen & Unwin Archives).

24 'Leaf by Niggle', that enigmatic little tale, might also have originated in a dream, as Tolkien says he 'woke one morning with it in my head' (JRRT to Jane Neave, 8–9th Sept 1962; *Letters* p. 320); he uses virtually identical language in the preface to *Tree and Leaf* and in a 1945 letter to Stanley Unwin (*Letters* p. 113).

Chapter V

GOLLUM

The text continues as before, near the bottom of manuscript page 49 (Marq. 1/1/4:9) with no more than a paragraph break to separate it from the preceding 'chapter'.

When he opened his eyes he wondered if he had, for it was just as dark as with them shut. No one was anywhere near him. Just imagine his fright. He could hear nothing, see nothing, nor could he feel anything except the stone of the wall and the floor. Very slowly he got up and groped about on all fours. And however far he went in either direction he couldn't find anything:[TN1] nothing at all, no sign of goblins, and no sign of dwarves. Certainly he did find what felt like a ring of metal lying on the floor in the tunnel. He put it in his pocket; but that didn't help much. So he sat down and gave himself up to complete miserableness for a long while. Of course he thought of himself frying bacon and eggs in his own kitchen at home (for his tummy told him it was very near to some meal-time), but that only made him miserabler. He couldn't think what to do, nor could he think what had happened, and if he had been left behind, and why if he had been left behind the goblins hadn't caught him.[TN2] The truth was he had been lying quiet in a very dark corner out of sight and mind for a good while.

After a while [> some time] he felt for his pipe. It wasn't broken and that was something. Then he felt for his bacca[TN3] pouch, and there was some bacca in it, and that was something more. Then he felt for matches, and he couldn't find any at all, and that [was a >] shattered his hopes completely. But in slapping all his pockets and feeling all round himself for matches his hand came on the hilt of [*added*: his] sword (a tiny dagger for the Trolls), and that he had forgotten, nor did the goblins seem to have noticed it. He drew it out and it shone pale and dim. 'So it is an elvish sword [> blade], too' he thought 'and goblins are not very near, nor yet far enough.' But somehow he was comforted. It was rather splendid to be wearing a blade made in Gondolin of which so many songs used to sing;[TN4] and also Bilbo had noticed that such weapons made a great impression upon Goblins.

'Go back?' he thought – 'no good at all! Go sideways – impossible! can't be done. Go forward – only thing to do'.

So up he got, and trotted along with his little sword in front of him, and one hand feeling the wall, and his heart all of a patter and a pitter.[TN5]

Now certainly Bilbo was in what is called a tight place. But you must remember it was not quite so tight for him as for you or me. Hobbits are not quite like ordinary people; and after all if their holes are nice cheery places quite different to the tunnels of goblins, still they are more used to tunnelling than we are, and they don't easily lose their sense of direction under ground. Also they can move very quietly, and hide easily, and recover wonderfully from bumps and bruises, and they have a fund of wisdom and wise sayings that men have mostly never heard of, or have forgotten long ago.

I shouldn't have liked to have been in Mr Baggins' place, all the same. The tunnel seemed to have no end. He knew it was going on down pretty steadily and keeping on in the same direction in spite of a twist [or a >] and a turn or two. There [seemed >] were passages leading off to the side every now and then, as he could see by the pale glimmer of his sword, and feel with his hand on the side-wall. Of these he took no notice, except to hurry past for fear of goblins or other things coming out of them. On and on he went down and down; and still he heard no sound of any one except the swish [> whirr] of bat near his ears occasionally (which startled him).[TN6]

Suddenly he trotted splash into water! Ugh! it was icy cold. That pulled him up sharp and short. He didn't know whether it was just a pool in the path, or the edge of an underground stream across [> that crossed] the passage, or the brink of a deep dark subterranean lake. He could hear water drip-drip-dripping from an unseen roof into the water below, but there seemed no other sort of sound; so he came to the conclusion that it was a pool or lake not a running river.[TN7] Still he did not dare to wade out into the darkness – he couldn't swim, and he thought of ghastly slimy things with big bulging eyes [like <lanterns> to >][TN8] wriggling in the water.

There are strange things living in the pools and lakes in the hearts of mountains: fish that swam in [> whose fathers swam in], goodness only knows how many years ago, and who never swam out again, while their eyes grew bigger and bigger and bigger from trying to see in the blackness; also other things more slimy than fish. And even in the tunnels and caves the goblins have made for themselves, there are other things living unbeknown, that have sneaked in from outside, and lie up in the dark. Also some of these caves go back ages before the coming of the goblins (who only widened them, and joined them up with passages), and the original owners were [> are] still there in odd corners.

Deep down here by the dark water lived old Gollum. I don't

know where he came from or who or what he was. He was Gollum, as dark as darkness except for two big round pale eyes. He had a boat, and he rowed about quiet quietly on the lake – for lake it was, wide and deep and deadly cold. He paddled it with large feet dangling over the side, but never a ripple did he make. Not he: he was looking out of his pale lamp-like eyes for blind fish, which he grabbed with his long fingers, as quick as thinking.

He liked meat too – goblins he thought good when he could get them; but He took care they never found [*added*: him] out: he just throttled them from behind if they came down alone anywhere near the edge of the water, while he was prowling about. They jolly seldom did, for they felt something not quite nice lived down there, down at the very roots of the mountain.[TN9]

As a matter of fact Gollum lived on a slimy island in the middle of the lake. He was watching Bilbo now with his pale eyes like telescopes from the distance. Bilbo couldn't see him, but he was wondering a lot about Bilbo, for he could see he was no goblin at all.

Gollum got onto his boat and shot off from the bank. There Bilbo was sitting altogether flummuxed[TN10] and at the end of his way and his wits. Suddenly up came Gollum and whispered and hissed:

'Bless us and blister us [> splash us], my precious! I guess 'tis a choice feast, a tasty morsel at least you'd be for Gollum [> it'd make us, Gollum]', and when he said 'Gollum' he swallowed unpleasantly in his throat – that's how he got his name. The hobbit jumped nearly out of his skin when the hiss came in his ears and he saw the pale eyes sticking out at him.

'Who are you?' he said, holding his sword in front of him.

'What is he?' said [> whispered] Gollum (who always spoke to himself not to you).

That is what he had come to find out, for he was not really hungry at the moment, or he would have grabbed first and whispered afterwards.

'I am Mr Bilbo Baggins. I have lost the dwarves and the wizard and I don't know where I am, and don't want to know, if I can only get away.'

'What's he got in his handses?' said Gollum looking at the sword, which he didn't quite like.

'A sword, a blade that came out of Gondolin' said Bilbo.

'Praps ye sits here[TN11] and chats with it a bitsy' said Gollum, 'Does he like riddles, does he praps?'[TN12] He was anxious to appear friendly, at any rate for the moment, and until he found out more about the hobbit, whether he was quite alone, whether he was good to eat, & whether Gollum was really hungry or not. Asking (and sometimes answering [> guessing]) riddles had been a game he played with other funny creatures sitting in their holes in the long long ago before the goblins came, and he was cut off from his friends far under the mountains.[TN13]

'Very well' said Bilbo, who thought it best to agree until he found out more about the fellow, and whether he was quite alone, whether he was fierce or hungry, and whether he was a friend of the goblins. 'You ask first' he said, because he hadn't had time to think of a riddle.

'What has roots [no >] as nobody sees, is taller than trees, and [do >][TN14] yet never grows?'

'Easy' said Bilbo – 'mountains, I suppose'.

'Does it guess easy? – it must have a competition with us, my precious. If precious asks, and it doesn't answer, we eats it my precious. If it ask us and we doesn't answer, we gives it a present: Gollum.'

'Alright' said Bilbo, not daring to disagree, and nearly bursting his brain to think of riddles that could save him from being eaten.[TN15]

'Thirty white horses on a red hill first they stamp, then they champ, then they stand still' he said [> asked] (the idea of eating was rather in his mind you see). This was rather a chestnut [> an old one], and Gollum knew the answer as well as you do.

'Chestnuts, chestnuts' he hissed: 'toosies, tooies[TN16] my precious but we has only six.[TN17]

Voiceless it cries
wingless flutters
toothless bites
mouthless mutters.'

'Half a moment' said Bilbo who was still thinking uncomfortably about eating. Fortunately he had heard this kind of thing before, and so soon got it [> his wits back]. 'Wind, wind' he said.

'An eye in a blue face
Saw an eye in a green face:
"[Tis like this >]
That eye is like to this eye"
Said the first eye
"But in low place
Not in high place."'

'Ss, ss, ss' said the Gollum[TN18] who had been underground a long long while and was forgetting that sort of thing. But just as Bilbo was [thinking >] wondering what Gollum's present would be like ['ss ss ss' he said >] Gollum [remembered >] brought up memories of long before when he lived with his grandmother in a hole in a bank by a river. 'Ss ss ss, my precious' he said: 'sun on the daisies it means, it does'.

But these ordinary above ground every day homely sort of riddles were tiring for him, and what is more reminded him of days when he was not so lonely and sneaky and nasty. Still he made another effort[TN19]

'It cannot be seen, cannot be felt
cannot be heard, cannot be smelt;
It lies [under >] behind stars and under hills
And empty holes it fills
Comes first and follows after[TN20]
Ends life kills laughter'

You notice he was hissing less as he got excited – also this was an easy one.[TN21]

'Dark' said Bilbo without scratching his head.

'A box without hinges key or lid
Yet golden treasure inside is hid'

he asked to gain time till he could think of a really hard one. All the same this proved a nasty poser for Gollum.[TN22] He sat and twiddled his fingers and toes [in the >] he hissed to himself and still he didn't answer. After some while Bilbo said 'Well, what is it?'

'Give us a chance; let it give us a chance, my precious'.

'Well' said Bilbo after giving him a good chance. 'What is your present?'

But suddenly the Gollum remembered sitting under the river bank long long ago teaching his grandmother, teaching his grandmother to suck —— 'Eggs' he [said >cried >] croaked 'eggs it is'.

Then he asked:

'Alive without breath
And cold as death
Never thirsty ever drinking
All in mail never clinking'

He [*added*: also] felt this was a dreadfully easy one, because he was always thinking of the answer; but he couldn't think of anything better at the moment [*added*: he was so flustered by the egg-question]. All the same it was a bit of a poser to [> for] Bilbo, who never had anything to do with water (I imagine of course you know the answer since you are sitting comfortably at home, and haven't the danger of being eaten to disturb your thinking).

After a while Gollum began to hiss with pleasure to himself: 'Is it nice, my precious; is it juicy; is it scrumptiously crunchable?' he said, peering at Bilbo out of the dark.

'Half a moment' said Bilbo. 'Give me a chance, I gave you a good long one'.

'It must make haste, haste' said Gollum, beginning to climb out of the boat to come at Bilbo. But when he put his long webby foot in the water, a fish jumped out in fright to get away from him and touched Bilbo's toe. 'Ugh' he said 'it's cold and clamy' – and so he guessed.

'Fish, fish' he said 'it is fish!'

Gollum was dreadfully disappointed, but Bilbo asked another riddle as quick as ever he could so that Gollum had to get back [*added*: in the boat] and think.

'No legs lay on one-leg; two-legs sat near on three legs; four-legs got some.' he said. It wasn't the right moment for this riddle at all, but he was a bit flurried. Very likely Gollum wouldn't have guessed it, if Bilbo had asked it at another time. As it was, talking of fish, 'no-legs' wasn't so very difficult, and after that the rest is easy.

Fish on little table; man at table on a stool. – gives bones to the cat – that is the answer of course, and Gollum soon gave it. Then he thought the time was come to ask something hard, and horrible.

'This thing all things devours:
birds, beasts, trees flowers;
gnaws iron bites steel
& grinds stones for meal;
slays kings ruins town
and beats high mountain down.'

Poor Bilbo sat in the dark thinking of all the horrible names of all the giants and ogres he had ever heard told of in tales; but never a one had done all these things. He began to feel frightened. The answer wouldn't come. Gollum began to get out of the boat. He flapped into the water and paddled to the bank; Bilbo could see his eyes coming towards him. His tongue seemed to stick to his mouth; he wanted to shout out 'give me more time, give me more time' but all that came out in a sudden squeal was

'Time, time'!

And that of course was the answer. Bilbo was saved by pure luck.

Gollum was dreadfully disappointed again. And now he was getting tired of the game, and also the game had begun to make him hungry once more. So he didn't go back to his boat. He sat down in the dark by Bilbo,[TN23] and that made the hobbit most horribly uncomfortable, and scattered his wits.

'It's got to ask us a question, my precious, yes yes just one more question to guess, yes, yes' said Gollum; but Bilbo simply couldn't think of one with that nasty wet cold thing sitting next to him poking him. He scratched his head, he pinched himself, still he couldn't think of anything.

'Ask us, ask us' said Gollum.

He pinched himself, he slapped himself, he gripped on his little sword, he even felt in his pocket with his other hand. There he found the ring he had picked up in the passage.

'What have I got in my pocket?' he said aloud (but he only meant it for himself). Gollum thought it was a riddle, and he was dreadfully upset.

'Not fair, not fair' he hissed 'it isn't fair, my precious, is it, to ask us what it's got in its nasty little pockets'.

Still Bilbo having nothing better to ask stuck to his question. 'What have I got in my pocket' he said louder.

'S-s-s-s' hissed Gollum. 'it must give us three guesses, my precious, three guesses'.

'Very well' said Bilbo 'guess away'.

'Hands' said Gollum.

'Wrong' said Bilbo 'guess again'. He had taken his hand out and held the ring [> with the ring in it] (which was lucky). [TN24]

'S-s-s' said Gollum, more upset than ever. He thought of all the things [people keep in pockets >] he kept in his pockets (fish bones), [TN25] goblins teeth, bits of stone to sharpen his teeth on and other nasty things) he tried to think and remember what other people kept in their pockets.

'Knife' he said.

'Wrong again' said Bilbo who had lost his some time ago (very luckily again). 'Last guess!'

Now Gollum was in a much worse state that when Bilbo asked him the egg-question. He hissed and spluttered, and rocked backwards and forwards, and slapped his feet on the floor and wiggled and squirmed – but still he did not dare to waste his last guess.

'Come on' said Bilbo 'I am waiting'. He tried to sound bold and cheerful, but he didn't feel at all sure how the game was going to end, whether Gollum guessed or no [> right or not].

'Time's up' he said.

'String, or Nothing' said [> shrieked] Gollum – which wasn't quite fair, [trying >] working in two answers at once: still it was a very nasty thing to answer.

'Both wrong!' said Bilbo very much relieved – and jumped to his feet and held out his little sword with his back to the wall. But funnily enough, he need not have been frightened. For one thing the Gollum had learned long long ago was never to cheat at the riddle-game. Also there was the sword. He simply sat and blubbered [> whimpered].

'What about the present?' said Bilbo, not that he cared very much; still he felt he had won it, and in very difficult circumstances too.

'Must we give it precious; yes we must – we must fetch it precious, and give it to the thing the present we promised.' So he paddled back into his boat, and Bilbo thought he had heard the last of him. But he hadn't. The hobbit was just thinking of going back up the passage (having had quite enough of the Gollum and that dark water-edge), when [Gollum came back >] he heard Gollum wailing and squeaking away in the dark [*cancelled*: on his island]. He was on his island (of which Bilbo, of course, knew nothing) scrabbling here and there, searching and seeking in vain, and turning out his pockets.

'Where is it, where is it' he heard him squeaking. 'Lost, lost, my precious, lost lost; bless us and splash us, we haven't the present we promised, and we haven't [*added*: even] got it for ourselves'.

Bilbo turned round and waited, wondering what it could be that the creature was making such a fuss about. This turned out very fortunately; For Gollum came back, and made a tremendous chatter and whispering and croaking; and in the end Bilbo [found >] understood, that Gollum had a ring, a wonderful beautiful ring, a ring that he had been given for a birthday-present ages and ages before in old days when such rings were less uncommon. Sometimes he had kept it in his pocket; usually he kept it in a little hole in the rock on his island; sometimes he wore it – wore it when he was very very hungry and tired of fish, and crept along the dark passages looking for stray goblins. Then (being very hungry) he ventured even into places where the torches were lit and made his eyes blink and smart; but he was safe. O yes quite [> very nearly] safe; for if you slipped that ring on your fingers, you were invisible; only in the strongest sunlight could you be seen, and then only by your shadow, and that was [a faint >] only a faint shaky sort of shadow.

I don't know how many times Gollum begged Bilbo's pardon. And he offered him fish caught fresh to eat instead (Bilbo shuddered at the thought of it); [but somehow or other he had to >] [TN26] but he said 'no thank you' quite politely.

He was thinking, thinking hard – and the idea came to him that[TN27] he must have found that ring, that he had that very ring in his pocket. But he had the wits not to tell Gollum. 'Finding's keeping' he said to himself; and being in a very tight place I think he was right, and anyway the ring belonged to him now.

But to Gollum he said: 'Never mind, the ring would have been mine now if you could have found it, so you haven't lost it. And I will forgive you on one condition'.

'Yes what is it, what does it wish us to do, my precious.'

'Help me to get out of these places', said Bilbo.

To this Gollum agreed, as he had to if he wasn't to cheat, though he would very much have liked to have just tasted what Bilbo was like. Still he had lost the game [> promised]; and also there was the sword, and also Bilbo was wide awake & on the look out, not unsuspecting as the Gollum liked to have things which he caught.

That is how Bilbo got to know that the tunnel ended at the water, and went on no further on the other side, where the mountain wall was dark and solid. He ought to have turned down one of the side passages before he came to the bottom, but he couldn't follow the directions he was given to find it. So he made Gollum come and show him.

As they went along up the tunnel together, Gollum flip-flapping along, Bilbo going very quietly, Bilbo thought he would try that ring. He slipped it on.

'Where are you [> is it], where is it gone to?' said Gollum at once, peering round with his long eyes.

'Here I am following behind' said Bilbo slipping off the ring, and feeling very pleased to have it in his pocket.[TN28] So on they went, while Gollum counted the passages to left and right: 'one left, one right, two right, three right, two left' and so on. He began to get very shaky and afraid as he got further from the water, and at last he stopped by a low opening on the left ('six right, four left').

'Here's the passage [*added*: he whispered]; it must squeeze in, and sneak down, – we durstn't go with it, my precious, no we durstn't: Gollum!'

So Bilbo slipped under the arch, and said goodbye to the nasty miserable creature, and very glad he was. He wasn't comfortable till he felt quite sure it was gone; and he kept his head out in the main tunnel listening until the flip flap of Gollum going back to his boat died away in the darkness.

Then he went down the new passage. It was a low narrow one, roughly made. It was all right for the hobbit, except when he stubbed his toes in the dark on nasty jags in the floor, but it must have been a bit low for Goblins. Perhaps it was not knowing that goblins are used to this sort of thing and go along quite fast stooping low with their hands almost on the floor, that made Bilbo forget the danger of meeting them, and go along a bit recklessly.

When he saw a glimmer of light in front of him, not red light of torch or fire or lantern, but pale ordinary out of doors sort of light that seemed to be filtering in round the comer of the passage, he began to really hurry. Scuttling along as fast as his little legs would take him, he came round a corner right into a wider place where the light seemed suddenly clear and bright after all that time in the black tunnel. Really the light was only <a ray> in through a door, a stone door, left a little way open. Bilbo blinked, and then he suddenly saw the goblins. Goblins in full armour with swords sitting just inside the door watching it and the passage that led to it. They saw him at once, and yelled with delight as they rushed at him.

Whether it was accident or presence of mind I don't know. Accident, I think, because Bilbo was not yet used to his new treasure. Anyway he slipped the ring on his left hand – and the goblins stopped. But they yelled all the louder, only not quite so delighted.

They couldn't see him any more. 'Where is he' they called. 'Go back in the passage' some shouted 'This way; that way' some said. 'Mind the door' said others. Whistles blew, armour clashed, swords rattled, goblins cursed and swore and ran hither and thither, getting in one another's way, and getting very angry. There was a terrible outcry, to do and disturbance.

Bilbo was very frightened, but he had the sense to understand what had happened, and to sneak behind a big barrel which held drink for the goblin-guards, and to get out of the way, and avoid being bumped into, trampled to death, or being caught by feel.

'I must get to the door! I must get to the Door' he kept on saying to himself, but it was a long time before he ventured to try. Then it was like a horrible game of blind-man's buff.[TN29] The place was full of goblins running about, and poor little Bilbo dodged this way, dodged that way; was knocked over by a goblin that could'nt make out what he had bumped into; scrambled away on all fours; slipped between the legs of a big goblin just in time; got up and ran for the door.

It was still ajar – but a goblin had pushed it nearly to. Bilbo struggled but he couldn't move it. He tried to squeeze through the crack; he squeezed and squeezed – and he stuck!

Wasn't that horrible! His buttons had got wedged on the edge of the door & the door post. He could see outside into the open air, there were steep steps running down into what seemed a valley; [there was the river shining bright>] the sun came out from behind a cloud & shone bright on the outside of the door – but he could'nt get through.

Suddenly one of the goblins inside shouted: 'There's a shadow by the door. Somebody's outside!' Bilbo's heart jumped into his mouth;

he gave terrific squirm, buttons burst off in all directions, and he was through with a torn coat and waistcoat, and leaping down the steps like a goat, while bewildered goblins were still picking up his nice brass buttons on the doorstep.

Of course they soon came down the steps, hooting and hollering, and hunting among the trees of the valley. But they don't like sun – it makes them quickly faint and feeble – and anyway they couldn't find Bilbo with the ring on, while he slipped in and out in the shadow of the trees, and took care not to throw any shadows. Soon they went back grumbling and cursing to guard the door, and Bilbo had escaped.

TEXT NOTES

1 This was altered to 'But however far he went [either back >] in either direction he couldn't find anything'.

2 Added in margin and marked for insertion at this point: 'nor even why his head was so sore'.

3 Both here and at the next occurrence, 'bacca' has been changed to 'baccy'.

4 Note that Bilbo is conversant with elven history to some extent even before his adventures began, as witnessed by his familiarity with the 'many songs' about Gondolin.

5 There is a slight change of ink at this point.

6 This line was changed to '. . . no sound of any one except *occasionally* the *whirr* of *a* bat near his ears, *which startled him at first*.' Also, a sentence was added in the top margin in very small letters and marked for insertion at this point: 'I don't know how long he kept on like this hating to go on, not daring to stop, on, on till he was tired as tired – it certainly seemed like all the way tomorrow and over it to the day beyond.'

7 This passage was revised to read 'so he *thought* that it *must be* a pool or *a* lake *&* not a *moving* river.'

8 The unfinished sentence presumably would have read something along the lines of 'like lanterns to see in the dark'.

9 Crowded into the top margin and marked for insertion at this point: 'They [made the >] came on the road [> lake] when they were tunnelling down long ago and they found they could go no further, so there their road ended in that direction, and there was no reason to go there unless the King sent them. Sometimes he took a fancy for fish from the lake. And sometimes neither goblin nor fish came back.'

10 The word 'flummuxed' (or flummoxed) is old slang for confused or perplexed or bewildered. Probably of dialectical origin (Gloucestershire, Herefordshire, Cheshire, Sheffield), it seems to have come into vogue

in early Victorian times (the OED's earliest citation is from Dickens' *Pickwick Papers* [1837]) and largely faded from use after mid-century (only one OED citation postdates 1857, and that is from 1892, the year of Tolkien's birth).

11 Added at this point: 'my precious,'. For more on 'ye' (dialectical for *you*), see p. 187 (Note 10).

12 This sentence was revised to read '*It* likes riddles, *does it* praps?' – with the dehumanizing shift from 'he' to 'it'. 'Praps' is of course a clipped form of *perhaps*; like *bitsy* it injects almost a touch of babytalk into the sinister conversation.

13 Added in pencil at the end of the paragraph: 'It was the only game <the old wretch> could remember.'

14 Added at this point: 'up rises > up up it goes'.

15 Tolkien originally followed this sentence with the single cancelled word, 'What'. Only two of the riddles begin with this word: the one Bilbo has just answered, and the final, unanswerable question that ends the contest – raising the possibility that Bilbo's first response was also to be his last and bring the exchange to a sudden, premature close. If such was the case, we can be grateful that Tolkien changed his mind and interpolated the full contest into this scene. It would also show that he had the scene's conclusion firmly in mind from the very beginning. An alternate explanation might be that he accidently began to repeat the first riddle but caught his mistake in time.

No separate drafts for the riddles have been found. All are written right into the text, but despite hesitations and minor variants these are so close to the final versions that it would be remarkable if they were all spontaneous compositions. It seems likely, then, that Tolkien may have been writing down riddles he had composed, perhaps orally, at some earlier point. At any rate, whether he was transcribing them from rough drafting (now lost) or recreating them from memory, the order in which he used them was not yet set (see p. 174).

16 Here 'toosies, tooies' were cancelled in ink, and 'teeth, teeth' written above them.

17 The next, cancelled words – 'Alive without breath' – indicate that originally the fish-riddle was to follow next.

18 This is the first of five references to Bilbo's opponent as 'the Gollum' rather than just Gollum; in three cases (pages 156, 157, & 160), Tolkien cancelled the article but in two others (pp. 160 & 161) he let it stand.

19 This last sentence was cancelled and replaced by the following, which was added in the top margin and marked for insertion at this point: 'On the other hand they made him hungry: So he tried something a bit more difficult, and more nasty.'

20 This line was originally preceded by a cancelled partial line: 'follows & comes a > Goes before &'.

21 This sentence was cancelled and the following crowded in at the end

of the line: 'Unfortunately for him Bilbo had heard one rather like that before.' At the same time, the following line was altered to read '"Dark" said *he* without *even* scratching his head, *or putting on his thinking cap.*'

22 The opening of this sentence was replaced by the following mostly marginal addition: '*He thought it a dreadfully easy chestnut; but it* proved a nasty poser for Gollum.'

23 Added in the top margin and marked for insertion at this point: 'and pinched [> prodded] him to feel if he was fat and munchable'.

24 This sentence was recast while being written, then changed again to read 'He had *just* taken his hand *out of his pocket again* (which was lucky).'

25 Here 'fish *bones*' is a revision, but I cannot make out the original short word that bones replaced, other than that it was short (perhaps three or four letters) and began with *p*-; *pin(s)* is my best guess.

Note that Gollum is not naked, as he is sometimes portrayed by inattentive illustrators, nor reduced to merely a loincloth, but has at least some clothing (however ragged), with pockets.

26 Written in small, neat letters in the bottom margin and marked for insertion at this point to replace everything in this paragraph after 'Bilbo's pardon':

> He kept on saying 'we are sorry, we didn't mean to cheat, we meant to give <our> only only present if it won the [game >] competition' He even offered to catch him some nice juicy fish to eat as a consolation. Bilbo shuddered at the thought of it.

27 Crowded in above the line and marked for insertion at this point: 'Gollum must have dropped that ring some time; that he'.

28 Added and marked for insertion at this point: 'and to find it really did what G. said it would'.

29 This game was originally called 'blind man's buff' but is more often now known as 'blind man's *bluff*'.

This chapter, the most famous in the entire book,[1] is paradoxically little-known in its original form. Only some 17,000 copies of the first edition were ever offered for sale,[2] and since 1951 those who wished to know how Tolkien originally conceived the crucial Gollum episode have had to consult sources such as Anderson's textual notes in *The Annotated Hobbit* or the parallel text presentation of excerpts from the two versions in Bonniejean Christensen's article 'Gollum's Character Transformation in *The Hobbit*'.[3] So far as I know, the first edition text of the chapter has been reprinted in its entirety only once in the last fifty-five years, in the anthology *Masterpieces of Terror and the Supernatural*, ed. Marvin Kaye & Saralee Kaye [1985].

The following commentary, therefore, while taking into account some features common to all versions of the chapter, from first draft through the third edition – such as the riddles – focuses primarily on the remarkable differences between the story as Tolkien first wrote it and the revised version he eventually, after much hesitation,[4] adopted as canonical.

(i)
The Gollum

One of Tolkien's greatest characters makes his auspicious debut in this chapter, and no point more firmly separates the draft and first edition on the one hand from the second and all subsequent editions on the other than their respective characterizations of Gollum. The most surprising difference, usually overlooked by the commentators, is that Gollum is clearly not a hobbit in the original – 'I don't know where he came from *or who or what he was*' says the narrator, and there's no reason not to think he speaks for the author here and take him at his word. It's not clear from the manuscript text whether Gollum is one of the 'original owners' who predate the goblins, 'still there in odd corners' or one of the 'other things' that 'sneaked in from outside'.[5] But in either case, all the details of his description argue against his being of hobbit-kin. Unlike Bilbo, *the* hobbit, Gollum is 'dark as darkness', with long fingers (p. 155), large webbed feet (p. 158) that flap when he walks (unlike the silent hobbit; cf. p. 161), and 'long eyes' (p. 161), huge and pale, that not only protrude 'like telescopes' but actually project light.[6] Small wonder that early illustrators like Horus Engels[7] depict a huge, monstrous creature rather than the small, emaciated figure Tolkien eventually envisioned.[8] Not until he came to write the sequel, *The Lord of the Rings*, and forced himself to confront all the unanswered questions in *The Hobbit* that might be exploited for further adventures, did Tolkien have the inspiration to make Gollum a hobbit. He subsequently very skillfully inserted the new idea into the earlier book through the addition of small details in the initial description of the creature. Thus the readings in the third edition [1966], with the interpolations highlighted in italics:

> 'Deep down here by the dark water lived old Gollum, *a small slimy creature* . . . as dark as darkness, except for two big round pale eyes *in his thin face*.'

Just as Tolkien changed his mind – or, rather, delved more deeply into the subject in the course of writing the sequel before finally committing himself – as to Gollum's origin, so too he changed the character's personality in the post-publication revisions. For Gollum is far more honorable in the draft and first edition than he later appears. He is perfectly willing, even eager, to eat Bilbo, should the hobbit lose the riddle-game, but abides by the results (cf. p. 160: '[Bilbo] need not have been frightened. For one thing the Gollum had learned long long ago was never to cheat at the riddle-game'). Without discounting his cowardice, or prudence, in the matter of the sword, we should nonetheless give him his due: having lost the contest, he is pathetically eager to make good on his debt of honour ('I don't know how many times Gollum begged Bilbo's pardon'), offering a substitute reward ('fish caught fresh to eat') in place of the missing ring. Remember too that Gollum had not yet specified what the 'present' was; a less scrupulous monster might have been tempted, upon discovering the ring's absence, to substitute some other prize, such as the fish, for the unnamed reward – but not Gollum. We are thus faced with the amusing depiction of a monster who is considerably more honorable than our hero. For Bilbo soon realizes that he already has Gollum's treasure but goes ahead and demands a second prize (being shown the way out) in addition to the one he has quietly pocketed – a neat parallel to Gollum's earlier trick of 'working in two answers at once' on that final attempt to answer the last question. The narrator, moreover, applauds his duplicity ('"Finding's keeping" he said to himself; and being in a very tight place I think he was right, and anyway the ring belonged to him now.') with spurious logic that sounds so much like special pleading that Tolkien eventually decided it was just that: Bilbo's own attempt, in writing this scene for his memoirs, to justify his claim to the ring (see the Fourth Phase of this book, beginning on p. 729, for Tolkien's eventual solution to this problem).

We should also note that Gollum's distinctive speech pattern – his hissing, overuse of sibilants, and peculiarity of referring to himself in the plural – was present from the very first, although greatly emphasised by revisions prior to publication.[9] As we might expect, though, it is somewhat more erratic in the draft, particularly in the matter of pronouns – thus he at first refers to Bilbo several times as 'he' before sliding into the depersonalized 'it', and once as 'you'. Similarly, he refers to himself as 'ye' at one point rather than his usual 'we/us'. Interestingly enough, it is quite clear that 'my precious' originally applied only to Gollum himself and not the ring: Gollum 'always spoke to himself not to you', usually in first person plural, yet he refers to the ring as 'it' ('bless us and splash us, we haven't the present we promised, and we haven't got it for ourselves'). Some of these aberrant elements remained in the published text,[10] even through Tolkien's careful revisions of 1947 and his recording of the Gollum-episode in 1952.[11]

One final point that we should perhaps consider before moving on is whether or not Gollum in some form predated *The Hobbit*. Carpenter notes that one of the poems Tolkien wrote as part of the series 'Tales and Songs of Bimble Bay', titled 'Glip', described 'a strange slimy creature who lives beneath the floor of a cave and has pale luminous eyes' (Carpenter, page 106). Carpenter mistakenly dates this poem to the Leeds period (1920–1925/6), while Anderson, who prints the entire poem for the first time (DAA.119), assigns it to 'around 1928'.[12] Glip seems to be yet another example of something escaping out of family folklore into one of Tolkien's books, like the Gaffer (cf. *Mr. Bliss),* the Dutch doll who became Tom Bombadil, the toy dog whose loss inspired *Roverandom,* or the teddy bears who helped inspire such figures as the three bears of *Mr. Bliss,* the North Polar Bear of the Father Christmas series, and of course Medwed/Beorn. The reverse is, of course, also equally possible: that Tolkien adapted a purely literary creation into the children's bedtime stories. In either case, the character did become a private bogeyman for the Tolkien children: Michael Tolkien recalled in a 1975 radio interview how John Tolkien, the oldest brother, terrified his younger siblings by 'playing Gollum', creeping into their room at night, with twin torches (flashlights) for the monster's shining eyes.[13]

(ii)
Riddles

> And what about the Riddles? There is work to be done here on the sources and analogues. I should not be at all surprised to learn that both the hobbit and Gollum will find their claim to have invented any of them disallowed.
>
> —JRRT to *The Observer,* 20th February 1938; see Appendix II.

Despite Tolkien's challenge nearly sixty years ago, relatively little has been done to date tracing the 'sources and analogues' of Bilbo's and Gollum's riddles, although many critics have offered suggestions of sources for specific riddles (the most thorough such treatment being Anderson's in *The Annotated Hobbit*) or drawn parallels between this riddle-contest and other wisdom-exchanges and question-challenges in medieval literature (including *Vafthrúthnismál*[14] and *Alvissmál* from the *Elder Edda,* 'The Deluding of Gylfi' from Snorri Sturluson's *Prose Edda,* Joukahainen's challenge to Vainamoinen in Runo III of the *Kalevala,* the Old English 'Second Dialogue of Solomon and Saturn',[15] and most importantly the riddle-contest in *The Saga of King Heidrek the Wise*).[16] Most of these contests involve one character questioning the other about obscure or mythological events, such as the origin of the earth, sun, and moon or the nature of the gods, or asking for prophecies of events still to come like the end of the world. Several have similarly high stakes as in Bilbo and Gollum's contest: the dwarf Alvis in *Alvissmál* is kept answering questions until day breaks and the sunlight kills him (an obvious source for Bladorthin's earlier trick with the trolls; cf. p. 103), while the wise old giant Vafþrúðnir warns his challenger (the disguised god Odin, operating under the *nom de guerre* of Gagnrad) that he never leaves alive those who cannot answer his questions, only to forfeit his own life in the end when Odin asks him an unanswerable question: 'What words did Odin whisper to his son/when Balder was placed on the pyre?' Only Odin himself knows the answer, just as only Bilbo knows what lies hidden in his pocket. The riddle-contest in *The Saga of King Heidrek the Wise*, Tolkien's direct model, ends with exactly the same question – Odin, disguised as Gestumblindi ('The Blind Stranger'), puts riddles to King Heidrek, who answers each with ease until the final question (*not* a riddle) is sprung on him. Again the stakes are high: Heidrek has promised to pardon any criminal who 'should propound riddles which the king could not solve', and when he realizes he has been tricked he goes into a rage and attacks Odin, who eludes him but curses the king to a shameful death at the hands of slaves, a curse quickly fulfilled (cf. the death of Tinwelint in 'The Nauglafring' and of Thingol in *The Silmarillion*). In his own story, Tolkien has combined features of both *Vafthrúthnismál* and the scene in *The Saga of King Heidrek the Wise*; like the former, both participants get a chance to ask and then answer; like the latter (where one character does all the asking and the other all the answering), the questions are in riddle-form. Indeed, one of Gollum's riddles derives directly from one answered by Heidrek (see below).

It should be stressed however that, whatever Tolkien's sources and inspiration, this striking scene and the riddles it is built around are almost entirely of Tolkien's own creation. Both frame (the back and forth interaction of the two contestants) and content (the riddles themselves) differ greatly from their precursors. This point was made strongly by Tolkien himself when, a decade after publication, Allen & Unwin suggested that Houghton Mifflin need not secure Tolkien's permission before reprinting several of the riddles in an anthology of poetry,[17] as 'the riddles were taken from common folk lore and were not invented by you'. Tolkien responded

> As for the Riddles: they are 'all my own work' except for 'Thirty White Horses' which is traditional, and 'No-legs'. The remainder, though their style and method is that of old literary (but not 'folk-lore') riddles, have *no models* as far as I am aware, save only the egg-riddle which is a reduction to a couplet (my own) of a longer literary riddle which appears in some 'Nursery Rhyme' books, notably American ones. So I feel that to try and use them without fee would be about as just as walking off with somebody's chair because it was a Chippendale copy, or drinking his wine because it was labelled 'port-type'. I feel also constrained to remark that 'Sun on the Daisies' is not in verse (any more than 'No-legs') being but the etymology of the word 'Daisy', expressed in riddle-form.
>
> —JRRT to Allen & Unwin, 20th September 1947; *Letters* p. 123.

Tolkien's delvings into riddle-lore parallel not just the great philologist

Jacob Grimm's work on fairy-tales but that of James O. Halliwell, the great Shakespearean scholar, who became deeply interested in nursery rhymes for the nuggets of ancient belief embedded in them, producing what was essentially the first critical edition of *The Nursery Rhymes of England* in 1842.[18] What of Tolkien's sources can be identified with some plausibility testify to his eclecticism, deriving as they do from Old English and Old Norse scholarship as well as Mother Goose. Of the ten 'riddles' in the exchange (counting the final, unanswered one, despite Gollum's quite reasonable objection that it's 'not a riddle, precious, no' – DAA.129),[19] only three can be shown to derive from nursery rhyme sources. The second riddle, 'thirty white horses', is a familiar nursery rhyme riddle still in common usage, and the eighth ('no-legs') is Tolkien's own variant of a once-familiar class of riddles that some have traced all the way back to The Riddle of the Sphinx;[20] the more common version reads

Two legs sat upon three legs
With one leg in his lap;
In comes four legs
And runs away with one leg;
Up jumps two legs,
Catches up three legs,
Throws it after four legs,
And makes him bring one leg back.

—Wm. S. & Cecil Baring-Gould, *The Annotated Mother Goose* [1962]; #709, page 276.[21]

As for the egg-riddle, we would be able to identify this with some certainty even without the letter already cited, for Tolkien had, years earlier, translated the aforementioned 'longer literary riddle' into Old English verse:

Meolchwitum sind marmanstane
wagas mine wundrum frœtwede;
is hrœgl ahongen hnesce on-innan,
seolce gelicost; siththan on-middan
is wylla geworht, waeter glaes-hluttor;
Thær glisnath gold-hladen on gytestreamum
æppla scienost. Infær n(æ)nig
nah min burg-fæsten; berstath hw(æ)thre
thriste theofas on thryth(æ)rn min,
ond thæt sinc reafiath – saga hwæt ic hatte![22]

The traditional form of this nursery-rhyme riddle appears in both Baring-Gould (p. 270) and the Opies (*The Oxford Dictionary of Nursery Rhymes* by Peter & Iona Opie, p. 152):

In marble walls as white as milk,
Lined with a skin as soft as silk,
Within a fountain crystal-clear,
A golden apple doth appear.
No doors are there to this stronghold,
Yet thieves break in and steal the gold.

I have found no specific parallel or antecedent for the first riddle ('mountain'), nor the third ('wind'), though Anderson notes that 'flying without wings' and 'speaking without a mouth' are common elements in wind-riddles (DAA.122). Nevertheless it is interesting to note that the very first riddle in that famous Anglo-Saxon collection of verse riddles known as the *Exeter Book* is a wind-riddle,[23] though it bears little resemblance to Tolkien's; careful examination of Old English sources, and the contemporary critical literature of the first third of the twentieth century debating their correct interpretation, would probably shed a good deal of light on Tolkien's exact sources and his treatment of them.

The fourth riddle ('daisy') is a straightforward example of the philologist at play, drawing on his knowledge of the history of our language (we should not forget that Tolkien's first professional job was researching word-origins for the OED). Just as he would later quote directly from the OED to define 'blunderbuss' in *Farmer Giles of Ham*, here he turns etymology into poetry, creating a riddle whose answer is self-evident to anyone who knows his or her own language well enough to see through the changes wrought by the years, that have slowly compressed *daeges eage* ('day's eye') through *day's e'e* to *daisy*.[24]

Several of the riddles seem to owe more to Scandinavian rather than Old English sources. Thus Taum Santoski pointed out that the fifth riddle ('dark') may owe something to a less sinister riddle found in Jón Árnason's *Ízlenzkar Gátur* ('Icelandic Riddles'), a nineteenth-century collection of contemporary riddles published in Copenhagen in 1887:

It will soon cover the roof of a high house.
It flies higher than the mountains
and causes the fall of many a man.
Everyone can see it, but no one can fetter it.
It can stand both blows and the wind, and it is not harmful.
—Árnason, riddle #352: Darkness.

Similarly, the ninth riddle ('time') has many parallels. Shippey (*The Road to Middle-earth*, page 112; revised edition, page 133) traces it back to 'The Second Dialogue of Solomon and Saturn':

Saturn said:
'But what is that strange thing that travels through this world, goes

on inexorably, beats at foundations, causes tears of sorrow, and often comes here? Neither star nor stone nor eye-catching jewel, neither water nor wild beast can deceive it at all, but into its hand go hard and soft, small and great. Every year there must go to feed it three times thirteen thousand of all that live on ground or fly in the air or swim in the sea.'

Solomon said:
'Old age has power over everything on earth. She reaches far and wide with her ravaging slave-chain, her fetters are broad, her rope is long, she subdues everything that she wants to. She smashes trees and breaks their branches, in her progress she uproots the standing trunk and fells it to the ground. After that she eats the wild bird. She fights better than a wolf, she waits longer than a stone, she proves stronger than steel, she bites iron with rust; she does the same to us.'

—*Poems of Wisdom and Learning* [1976], pages 91 & 93.

Taum Santoski, on the other hand, suggested the following Icelandic riddle as a source:

I am without beginning, yet I am born
I am also without ending, and yet I die
I have neither eyes nor ears, yet I see and hear
I am never seen, and yet my works are visible
I am long conquered, I am never conquered,
and yet I am vanquished
I labor ever, but am never tired
I am wise but dwell among the foolish
I am a lover of Providence, and yet it
may appear to me that it hates me
Often I die before I am born, and yet I am immortal
Without being aware of it, I often take by surprise
I live with Christians, I dwell among the heathen
among the cursed in Hell I am cursed, and I reign in the
Kingdom of Glory.

—Árnason, riddle #105: Time.

Tolkien would also have been familiar with the odd scene in the *Prose Edda* where Thor wrestles with, and is bested by, an old woman named Elli who turns out to be Old Age itself – in the words of Thor's wily host, 'there never has been, nor ever will be anyone (if he grows old enough to become aged) who is not tripped up by old age' (*Prose Edda*, 'The Deluding of Gylfi', pages 76 & 78). Finally, the strange little story that ends 'The Hiding of Valinor' in *The Book of Lost Tales* tells how the three children of Aluin (or Time), Danuin, Ranuin, and Fanuin (Day, Month, and Year), wind invisible chains that bind the sun and moon:

'. . . and so shall all the world and the dwellers within it, both Gods and Elves and Men, and all the creatures that go and the things that have roots thereon, be bound about in the bonds of Time.'

Then were all the Gods [i.e., the Valar] afraid, seeing what was come, and knowing that hereafter even they should in counted time be subject to slow eld and their bright days to waning, until Ilúvatar at the Great End calls them back.

—BLT I.219.

Beside this ferocious abstract riddle, the fish-riddle's source is simple: here Tolkien is quoting directly from *The Saga of King Heidrek the Wise*, where at one point Gestumblindi (the disguised Odin) asks King Heidrek

What lives on high fells?
What falls in deep dales?
What lives without breath?
What is never silent?
This riddle ponder,
O prince Heidrek!

'Your riddle is good, Gestumblindi,' said the king; 'I have guessed it. The raven lives ever on the high fells, the dew falls ever in the deep dales, *the fish lives without breath*, and the rushing waterfall is never silent.'

—*The Saga of King Heidrek the Wise*,
tr. Christopher Tolkien, page 80; italics mine.

Straightforward as this would seem, it also reveals something interesting about Tolkien's sources. As T. A. Shippey has noted, Tolkien seems drawn to the grey areas of scholarship – that is, his creative inspiration was sparked by debatable points. Thus the cup-stealing episode in *Beowulf*, which inspired the chapter 'Inside Information' (see p. 533), is based on a scholarly reconstruction of a badly-damaged section of the manuscript. Similarly, the name *Éomer* in *The Lord of the Rings* is borrowed, not from *Beowulf*, but from a scholar's emendation of the word which actually occurs in the *Beowulf* manuscript.[25] While *The Saga of King Heidrek the Wise* and its riddle-contest are well-known among Norse scholars, this particular riddle is found in only one of the three main versions of the saga, that found in the *Hauksbok* of Haukr Erlendsson (d. 1334). Furthermore, the page containing this riddle is lost from the original manuscript and only survives in two seventeenth-century copies made before the damage occurred – in short, making this exactly the kind of elusive, nearly-lost bit of ancient lore that Tolkien seems to have found most appealing.[26]

Finally, there is Bilbo's last, unanswerable question. It is true that it is not a riddle, but then Gollum's words – 'It's got to ask us a *question*, my precious, yes yes just one more *question* to guess, yes, yes' (italics mine) – open the door for a non-riddle: he asks for a question, and that is exactly what he got. This very neatly evades a problem: if, as Tolkien later said, 'the riddle game was sacred and of immense antiquity, and even wicked creatures were afraid to cheat when they played at it', then it is important that Bilbo himself not lie open to the accusation of cheating, that he win 'pretty fairly'. Comparison with Tolkien's sources is once again illuminating. In *Vafthrúthnismál*, the two contestants exchange questions to prove their knowledge; Bilbo's final question would be perfectly fair by the standards of that contest. By contrast, in *The Saga of King Heidrek the Wise* Odin (Gestumblindi) asks riddles and the king answers them all – until Odin asks a non-riddle that is unanswerable, 'winning' by an underhanded method that drives his opponent into a rage. As Christopher Tolkien notes, 'it is inapposite as the last question of a riddle-match, since it is not a riddle' and suggests that 'it was brought in . . . as the dramatic conclusion because it had become *the* traditional unanswerable question' (*The Saga of King Heidrek the Wise* p. 735). To be blunt, Odin wins by a cheat, just as Gollum accuses Bilbo of having done in the revised version of this chapter (see p. xx). But Tolkien has forestalled that objection by Gollum's careless wording just before the final puzzle, providing his hero with a valid out from the sticky situation.

One final curious feature about the riddles should be pointed out before moving on: as the narrator himself points out in a passage that did not survive into the published book, 'You notice he [Gollum] was hissing less as he got excited' (p. 157). In fact, he does not hiss at all when reciting his riddles; they are anomalous to his normal habits of speech. This fact, and the fact that all the riddles are written directly into the manuscript, in their final order, with little hesitation and with no preliminary drafting on scrap pages or the backs of pages (as is the case with the majority of the other poems in the book) – or at least none that survives – suggests that all these riddles predate the book. If this is the case, they may date from the Leeds period, like the two Anglo-Saxon riddles published in 1923, but the evidence is too slight to prove this one way or the other.

(iii)
The Ring

The most important point of connection between *The Hobbit* and its sequel, *The Lord of the Rings*, is the Ring itself. Just as hobbits, Gollum, the wizard, and the whole setting of Middle-earth grew and were transformed for the more ambitious requirements of the latter book, so too did the ring. For Bilbo's ring is not the same as Frodo's in its nature nor its powers, although the alteration was so smoothly done, with such subtlety and skill, that few readers grasp the extent of the change; many who read or re-read *The Hobbit* after *The Lord of the Rings* unconsciously import more sinister associations for the ring into the earlier book than the story itself supports. It is important to remember that Tolkien did not just expand the ring's effects for the sequel; he actually altered them. Bilbo's and Gollum's ring is a simple ring of invisibility with rather limited power – it cannot make its wearer's shadow disappear, for instance, and Bilbo has to be careful to avoid being given away by this flaw in the ring's power. By the time of *The Lord of the Rings*, this limitation has completely disappeared; the descriptions of its use there by Frodo give no hint that his shadow remains behind. Rather than simply making the wearer disappear, putting on the Ring plunges Frodo into an invisible, ethereal world, most notably in the scene on Weathertop, where it enables him to see the hitherto invisible features of the Ringwraiths. Bilbo experiences nothing of the kind; his remains a simple ring of invisibility, a 'very fine thing' (DAA.228) for a burglar to have, useful but limited in scope.

There is also in the original book no connection between Gollum's ring and The Necromancer who lurks on the fringes of the story – and indeed in 'The Lay of Leithian' this character had no special affinity with magical rings; only later, when Tolkien pondered possible connections between the various loose ends of Mr. Baggins' first adventure, did he forge a relationship between the elusive Necromancer and Gollum's ring. What's more, in the later tale he created a malign aura for the ring totally absent from the original book. The brooding presence Tolkien gives the One Ring throughout *The Lord of the Rings* – a masterstroke, insofar as its character can only be judged indirectly by the effect it has on the thoughts of its possessor – is absent here. Significantly, the curious episode of the ring's betrayal of its new master near the end of this chapter was not part of the original story and only came in with the revised version of 1947; in the original, the goblins saw Bilbo not because the ring had vanished from his finger without his knowledge but because he had taken it off immediately after playing his trick on Gollum to test its powers (contrast p. 161 with page 735). No shadow of murder hangs over it; the whole scene with Déagol had yet to be thought of. It is simply a magical ring that makes you (mostly) invisible: Gollum's birthday-present, given to him 'ages and ages before in old days when such rings were less uncommon.'

Tolkien's source for the ring has been much debated.[27] His exact source will probably never be known for the simple reason that he probably didn't have one in the sense of a single direct model. Magical rings are, after all, common in both literature and folk-lore, among the most famous being Aladdin's genie ring (with the same power as his magical lamp, and almost as powerful), Odin's Draupnir (which 'drops' eight identical gold rings every ninth night – cf. *The Prose Edda* p. 83), and the cursed Ring of the Nibelungs (which, like the Seven Rings of the dwarves, breeds wealth – cf. *The Prose Edda* pp. 111ff), none of which have the power to make their wearers invisible. Similarly, magical items that make one invisible are so common that Stith Thompson's *Motif-Index of Folk-Literature* has three full pages (rev. ed. [1955–8], Vol. II, pages 195–8) listing various forms such an item might take: a feather or herb, a belt or cap or hat, a sword or jewel or helmet, pills or a salve, a wand or staff or ring, a mirror or boots or stone or ashes, or any of a number of stranger means (such as being pregnant with a saint, or holding a Hand of Glory). The combination of these two motifs, however, are surprisingly rare: of the vast number of items that confer invisibility, and the huge number of magical rings, there are surprisingly few rings of invisibility before Tolkien popularized the idea.[28]

Of these rings the earliest, and widely (though I think mistakenly) thought the likeliest to have influenced Tolkien, is the Ring of Gyges. In Book II of Plato's *The Republic* [circa 390 BC], Plato's brother Glaucon tells Socrates a fable in order to make a point about power corrupting:

> They relate that he [the ancestor of Gyges the Lydian][29] was a shepherd in the service of the ruler at that time of Lydia, and that after a great deluge of rain and an earthquake the ground opened and a chasm appeared in the place where he was pasturing; and they say that he saw and wondered and went down into the chasm; and the story goes that he beheld other marvels there and a hollow bronze horse with little doors, and that he peeped in and saw a corpse within, as it seemed, of more than mortal stature, and that there was nothing else but a gold ring on its hand, which he took off and went forth. And when the shepherds held their customary assembly to make their monthly report to the king about the flocks, he also attended wearing the ring. So as he sat there it chanced that he turned the collet [i.e., setting] of the ring towards himself, towards the inner part of his hand, and when this took place they say that he became invisible to those who sat by him and they spoke of him as absent; and that he was amazed, and again fumbling with the ring turned the collet outwards and so became visible. On noting this he experimented with the ring to see if it possessed this virtue, and he found the result to be that when he turned the collet inwards he became invisible, and when outwards visible; and becoming aware of this, he immediately managed things so that he became one of the messengers who went up to the king, and on coming there he seduced the king's wife and with her aid set upon the king and slew him and possessed his kingdom. If now there should be two such rings, and the just man should put on one and the unjust the other, no one could be found, it would seem, of such adamantine temper as to persevere in justice and endure to refrain his hands from the possessions of others and not touch them, though he might with

> impunity take what he wished even from the market-place, and enter into houses and lie with whom he pleased, and slay and loose from bonds whomsoever he would, and in all other things conduct himself among mankind as the equal of a god. And in so acting he would do no differently from the other [i.e., unjust] man, but both would pursue the same course. And yet this is a great proof, one might argue, that no one is just of his own will but only from constraint . . .
>
> —Plato, *The Republic*, ed. & tr. Paul Shore [1930].

Were it not for the absence, in the manuscript and first edition of *The Hobbit*, of any hint that the ring corrupts its possessor, Plato's little tale would seem the obvious source for Tolkien's One Ring. Tolkien certainly knew his Plato – he had, after all, originally entered Oxford as a Classical scholar, and the whole Númenor story was, ultimately, inspired by passages in two others of Plato's dialogues[30] – and the story has a mythical air to it likely to catch in the memory and re-emerge years or decades later. Indeed, Gandalf's words in 'The Shadow of the Past' ('A mortal . . . who . . . often uses the Ring to make himself invisible . . . sooner or later – later, if he is strong or well-meaning to begin with, but neither strength nor good purpose will last – sooner or later the dark power will devour him') could almost be taken as a gloss on Plato's passage. But there is a fatal flaw in this theory: the One Ring 'to bring them all and in the darkness bind them' did not exist in *The Hobbit*. Tolkien might well have been inspired by Plato, or by H. G. Wells' *Invisible Man* [1897], which makes much the same point, when he was casting about in 1936–7 for a way of continuing the 'series' of Mr. Baggins' adventures at his publisher's request, but neither is likely to have inspired the original creation: the defining characteristics, the whole point of those stories – the inevitably corrupting nature of the power to move about invisibly – is totally absent from Tolkien's original conception. It seems much more likely, therefore, that the affinities between the Ring of Gyges and Sauron's ring are due to this passage having been drawn to Tolkien's attention *after* the publication of *The Hobbit* in 1937.[31]

Much more likely is the second possible source, occurring some millennium and a half later: Chrétien de Troyes' *Ywain: The Knight of the Lion*. In this Arthurian romance [circa 1177], Ywain is trapped in the castle of a man he has just mortally wounded, and escapes his foe's enraged retainers only because a maiden he had once befriended, the Lady Lunete, loans him a

> little ring, explaining that it had the same effect as the bark of a tree which covers the wood so that one cannot see it at all. It was necessary that one wear the ring with the stone inside the fist. Whoever had the ring on his finger need not be wary of anything, for no man

> could see him however wide his eyes were open any more than he could see the wood covered by the bark growing over it.
>
> —*Ywain: The Knight of the Lion*, tr. Ackerman, Locke, & Carroll [1957 & 1977], p. 18.

Ywain uses the ring to escape from a gatehouse (a good parallel to Bilbo's escape from the goblins' guardpost, although the knight makes his way *into* a stronghold filled with enemies, rather than escaping from one), easily evading their searches as they grope blindly for the unseen intruder in terms reminiscent of the goblin-guards at the Back Gate:

> . . . There was much floundering about, and they set up a great turmoil with their clubs just as does a blind man who stumblingly goes tapping about searching for something . . .
>
> —ibid., p. 19.

Like Plato's ring, and unlike Bilbo's, simply wearing this ring has no effect: the ring must be turned so that its stone or setting, which would normally rest on top of the finger, instead faces towards the palm (like turning a watch so that the face is on the inside of the wrist). It is implied, but not explicitly stated, that the hand wearing the ring must then be closed in a fist, concealing the stone within its grasp. There is thus no need to take the ring off to appear or to search frantically for it in a pocket when the sudden need to disappear arises, as when Bilbo encounters the goblin-guards.

The same is true of the magic rings in two romances directly based upon Chrétien's work, Hartmann von Aue's *Iwein* [circa 1210] and the anonymous 'The Lady of the Fountain' [mid-fourteenth-century or earlier]. Hartmann's romance is a translation of Chrétien's (Old) French story into his own Middle High German,[32] as comparison of the ring-description shows:

> '. . . Sir Iwein, take this ring and you will be safe from harm. The stone is of such a nature that whoever holds it in his bare hand cannot be seen or found as long as he keeps it there. You don't need to worry any longer: you will be hidden like wood under bark.
>
> '. . . Close your hand on the stone I gave you, and I'll pledge my soul that you won't be harmed, because truly no one will see you. What could be better? You will see all your enemies standing near you and going around you with ready weapons and yet so blinded that they can't find you even though you are right in their midst.'
>
> —*Iwein*, tr. J. W. Thomas [1979], p. 69.

The ring in 'The Lady of the Fountain', one of the three 'French Romances' that make up the final third of *The Mabinogion* in most editions and translations – in essence an adaptation of Chrétien's *Ywain* into Welsh – has a similar power and activation method: The Lady Luned (as she is called here) tells Owein (Ywain)

> 'Take this ring and put it on thy finger, and put this stone in thy hand, and close thy fist over the stone; and as long as thou conceal it, it will conceal thee too . . .'
>
> . . . And Owein did everything the maiden bade him . . . But when they came to look for him they saw nothing . . . And that vexed them. And Owein slipped away from their midst . . .
>
> —*The Mabinogion*, tr. Gwyn Jones & Th. Jones [1949; rev. ed. 1974], pp. 164–5.

Of these three closely related rings (or more accurately three versions of a tale about the same ring), Tolkien is most likely to have been familiar with the Welsh iteration, since this fell squarely within his fourteenth-century specialization (e.g., the same era as *Sir Gawain and the Green Knight*) and we know from other evidence that he was familiar with *The Mabinogion*.[33]

The third ring to consider also appears in works by multiple authors, but rather than translations here we have an unfinished romance by one author completed by a sequel written by another: M. M. Boiardo's *Orlando Innamorato* [Roland in Love, 1495] and Ludovico Ariosto's *Orlando Furioso* [Roland Gone Mad, 1516] – the latter being the work to which C. S. Lewis compared *The Lord of the Rings* when it first appeared, rather to Tolkien's annoyance.[34]

> *A ring . . .*
> *. . . of price and vertue great:*
> *This ring can make a man to go unseene,*
> *This ring can all inchantments quite defeat*
>
> —*Orlando Furioso*, Sir John Harington translation [1591]; Book III stanza 57.

Here the ring in question belongs to a femme fatale – Angelica, princess of Cathay, who uses it to sow chaos among Charlemagne's knights. Angelica's ring has the power not just of rendering her invisible, but her mount as well so long as she is touching it. More importantly, it has the additional power of making its wearer immune to any spell cast upon her, and as such is later used by the heroic virago (warrior-woman) Bradamante (the original of Spenser's Britomart and one of the possible inspirations for Tolkien's Éowyn) to defeat the evil wizard Atlante. Just as Angelica herself, in true 'perils of Pauline' fashion, is captured and rescued time and again, passing from knight to knight, so too does her ring pass from Angelica to Brunello to Bradamante to Rogero (Ruggiero) before it is finally regained by Angelica herself. Perhaps significantly, its separate powers each have a distinct activation method. To gain the invulnerability to spells, the ring must be worn on a finger; any finger will do, there is no mention of any stone or setting, and the ring's protection can be negated simply by pulling it off an opponent's hand. By contrast, to turn invisible a character must pop the ring into her mouth, and she remains invisible for as long as she keeps it there.

> *'Then see you set upon him . . .*
> *Nor give him any time, lest he convay*
> *The ring into his mouth, and so thereby*
> *Out of your sight he vanish quite away.'*
>
> —ibid., Book III stanza 61

> *Into her mouth the Ring she doth convay,*
> *And straight invisible she goeth away.*
>
> *Rogero . . .*
> *Found all too late, that by the Rings strange power,*
> *She had unseene convai'd her selfe away.*
>
> —ibid., Book XI stanzas 6–7.

With Angelica's ring, we see a theme that would become common among enchanted rings: a duplication (sometimes a multiplicity) of arbitrarily selected powers, making them devices able to protect the wearer from any harm and granting him whatever powers the dictates of the plot require. The stories in which characters possess these multi-purpose rings tend to treat those rings in perfunctory fashion, as self-consciously artificial plot-devices inserted to ease all the hero's challenges. This is certainly the case in our fourth ring, the first of the two rings of invisibility from relatively modern times discovered by Douglas Anderson (*The Annotated Hobbit*, page 133). Fr. François Fénelon's 'The Enchanted Ring' [late seventeenth century] is best known today through its appearance in Andrew Lang's collection *The Green Fairy Book* [1892], a volume Tolkien explicitly refers to in his Andrew Lang lecture that later became 'On Fairy-Stories' (OFS.38).

Archbishop Fénelon's story is an example of the highly artificial literary fairy tale that flourished in France in the late seventeenth and early eighteenth centuries in the hands of writers like Charles Perrault and Madame D'Aulnoy, and its titular Fairy's ring has a wide range of powers, the selection of which is decidedly eccentric:

> Take this ring, which will make you the happiest and most powerful of men . . . If you turn the diamond inside, you will become invisible. If you turn it outside, you will become visible again. If you place it on your little finger, you will take the shape of the King's son, followed by a splendid court [i.e., a group of richly dressed courtiers]. If you put it on your fourth finger, you will take your own shape.
>
> —'The Enchanted Ring', in *The Green Fairy Book*, page 138.

The turning of the ring clearly derives from the older examples of Plato's or Chrétien's rings, although either Fénelon or his translator (or both) are so careless that he or she forgets how the Fairy's ring works, and later in the story we are told that the hero *turns* the ring to assume the prince's form (ibid., p. 141). The reader is also left to wonder why it has specific powers on three of the hero's fingers, with no mention of the fourth. As with Plato's and Ariosto's rings, there is no sign that Fénelon's ring had any influence on *The Hobbit*, but it may have influenced the later development of the One Ring in *The Lord of the Rings*, particularly if Tolkien came across Fénelon's story while working on his Andrew Lang lecture in the period when he was beginning the sequel. Fénelon's tale in fact can be taken as a refutation of Plato's thesis (that such a ring would inevitably corrupt anyone who gained it): after the hero wisely decides he's achieved everything he wants and gives the ring back to the Fairy he got it from, she gives it to his brother. The brother promptly drives home the moral of the story by using it for vicious, selfish purposes, embarking on a mini crime spree strikingly reminiscent of Sméagol's behavior as retold by Gandalf:

> The only use he made of the ring was to find out family secrets and betray them, to commit murders and every sort of wickedness, and to gain wealth for himself unlawfully. All these crimes, which could be traced to nobody, filled the people with astonishment.
>
> —Fénelon, 'The Enchanted Ring'; *The Green Fairy Book*, pages 142–3.

Thus, in Fénelon's fairy tale the good character uses the ring primarily for good and the evil character for evil – not unlike the Gollum/Bilbo dichotomy noted by Gandalf in 'The Shadow of the Past'.

The fifth ring, also relatively modern, comes from an Estonian folktale [circa 1866] by Friedrich Kreutzwald, part of a group of nationalist writers who tried to do for Estonian what Elias Lönnrot had done for Finnish a generation earlier when he created the *Kalevala* [1835], writing down the surviving bits and pieces of old Baltic lore before they were entirely forgotten and constructing folk-tales and a national epic (the *Kalevipoeg*) from the remnants. Better known from its German translation in *Ehstnische Märchen* ['Estonian Fairytales'] as 'Der Norlands Drache', it was translated by one of Andrew Lang's assistants as 'The Dragon of the North' in *The Yellow Fairy Book* [1894]. Here the ring of invisibility is no less than King Solomon's signet-ring, now the property of a beautiful witch-maiden whom the hero beguiles until he gains the chance to steal it from her. Its full powers are unknown, but even the 'half-knowledge' of the witch-maiden unlocks a wide array of useful powers:

> If I put the ring upon the little finger of my left hand, then I can fly like a bird through the air wherever I wish to go.[35] If I put it on the

> third finger of my left hand I am invisible, and I can see everything that passes around me, though no one can see me. If I put the ring upon the middle finger of my left hand, then neither fire nor water nor any sharp weapon can hurt me. If I put it on the forefinger of my left hand, then I can with its help produce whatever I wish. I can in a single moment build houses or anything I desire. Finally, as long as I wear the ring on the thumb of my left hand, that hand is so strong that it can break down rocks and walls. Besides these, the ring has other secret signs which, as I said, no one can understand. No doubt it contains secrets of great importance. The ring formerly belonged to King Solomon, the wisest of kings . . . it is not known whether this ring was ever made by mortal hands: it is supposed that an angel gave it to the wise King.
>
> —'The Dragon of the North', in *The Yellow Fairy Book*, page 14.

Again, although the hero does use the ring to slay a dragon, there is little here that resembles Bilbo's ring, although there is a hint elsewhere in the tale that could be argued to anticipate *The Lord of the Rings*, when the witch-maiden offers the ring and herself to the hero:

> Here is my greatest treasure, whose like is not to be found in the whole world. It is a *precious* gold ring. When you marry me, I will give you this ring as a marriage gift, and it will make you the happiest of mortal men . . .
>
> —ibid., page 14 (italics mine).

Of all this array of five distinct rings of invisibility in eight separate works[36] – one classical (Plato), one medieval (Chrétien/Hartmann/*Mabinogion*), one renaissance (Boiardo/Ariosto), one from a literary fairy tale of the Enlightenment (Fénelon), and one from a reconstructed folk-tale of the Romantic era (Kreutzwald) – the one likeliest to have influenced Tolkien in *The Hobbit* is Owein's ring in 'The Lady of the Fountain', the Welsh version of Chrétien's tale. It seems very likely, however, that both Plato's account and perhaps Fénelon's as well contributed something to the One Ring as Tolkien developed it in *The Lord of the Rings* – never forgetting, however, that the primary influence on Frodo's ring is in fact *The Hobbit* itself: here, as so often, Tolkien is his own main source. Doubtless other rings of invisibility exist which have eluded my researches, but no ring exactly like Bilbo's has surfaced and it seems likely that this is because it was Tolkien's own invention, giving his hero an edge to offset his small size and lack of martial experience and given limitations because that improved the challenges the hobbit would face, creating a better story.

(iv)
The Invisible Monster

The idea of an invisible monster stalking its unwary prey and suddenly seizing upon it with dire results, such as Tolkien describes Gollum as having done for 'ages and ages', is of course not original with *The Hobbit*, but comparison with earlier examples casts some interesting light on Tolkien's treatment of the theme. It is a very old theme, going back at least to Malory's *Le Morte D'Arthur* [written by 1469, published 1485], which features as a recurrent villain in Book I (*The Tale of King Arthur*) Part ii ('Balin or the Knight with the Two Swords') Sir Garlon, the invisible knight, infamous for ambushing foes, striking them down, and then escaping under the cover of his invisibility. He is finally killed when struck down in turn by Sir Balin, who cares as little for the rules of chivalry as Garlon himself and seizes the chance of killing the apparently unarmed and visible Garlon while a guest of Garlon's brother. There is never any explanation of how Sir Garlon, the evil brother of King Pellam (the Fisher-King and guardian of the Graal), is able to become invisible; it seems to simply be one of the inexplicable wonders associated with the Graal's keepers. Tolkien was of course familiar with Malory and deeply interested in the rediscovery in 1934 of a manuscript version of *Le Morte D'Arthur* (cf. Verlyn Flieger's essay 'Tolkien and the Idea of the Book' in *The Lord of the Rings 1954–2004: Scholarship in Honor of Richard E. Blackwelder* [2006], especially pages 290–3), and the coincidence of an invisible villain and a character named Balin[37] in the same work is striking, but in the absence of any significant detailed parallels between Sir Garlon and Gollum it seems unlikely that Malory's work influenced *The Hobbit*.

In more modern treatments closer to Tolkien's own time, sometimes such a creature is human, as in Wells' *The Invisible Man* [1897], or very near it, as in de Maupassant's 'The Horla' [1887]. Other times it is starkly inhuman, as in Bierce's 'The Damned Thing' [1893] and Lovecraft's tale inspired by Bierce's story, 'The Dunwich Horror' [1928]. Wells' story is really a fable demonstrating the same moral as Plato – that the power to become invisible would inevitably be exploited for evil ends – with the Ring of Gyges replaced by modern chemicals and mathematical formulas, while de Maupassant's tale is more a variant on Edgar Poe's 'William Wilson' [1839], the story of an unseen *doppelgänger* who probably does not exist outside the narrator's deranged imagination. Gollum, while certainly unpleasant, is (as Gandalf later observes in 'The Shadow of the Past') not a monster per se but a creature more like Bilbo than unlike him, invisible only through the use of a magic ring. By contrast, Bierce's 'Damned Thing' is utterly alien, a creature whose size, shape, appearance, and nature can only be guessed from the viciousness with which it attacks and the horrible wounds it leaves on its victim (inspiring the subtitle of one part of the tale, 'A Man Though Naked May Be In Rags'). Bierce's Thing cannot be seen because it lies outside our frame of reference: one of his narrators suggests that, just as there are sounds audible to animals that we humans cannot hear, so too there are colours of the spectrum we cannot see. Since 'the Damned Thing is of such a colour!' it cannot be detected by human eyes.

The closest of all these invisible creatures to Tolkien's presentation of Gollum comes in Fitz-James O'Brien's 'What Was It?' [1859], a horror story by a little-known Irish writer who died fighting for the Union side in the Civil War. There is no record of Tolkien's reading O'Brien, but some of the parallels are striking, whether due to influence or parallel inspiration or an untraced common source. For example, the description of the creature's first attack in pitch-blackness sounds remarkably like what being attacked by Gollum must have been like. The narrator is lying down and trying to sleep when

> . . . an awful incident occurred. A Something dropped, as it seemed, from the ceiling, plumb upon my chest, and the next instant I felt two bony hands encircling my throat, endeavouring to choke me.
>
> —*The Fantastic Tales of Fitz-James O'Brien*, ed. Michael Hayes [1977], page 60.

Later, after the unseen creature has been captured and bound by the two main characters after it attacked, they are able to gain a general idea of its still-unseen appearance by touch:

> its outlines and lineaments were human. There was a mouth; a round, smooth head without hair; a nose, which, however, was little elevated above the cheeks; and its hands and feet felt like those of a boy.
>
> — ibid., page 65.

For Gollum's similarly smooth, round, hairless head, and relatively small size in the original conception, see Plate VI detail. Eventually O'Brien's protagonists are able to find out what the creature is like only by making a plaster cast of its form:

> It was shaped like a man, – distorted, uncouth, and horrible, but still like a man. It was small, not over four feet and some inches in height, and its limbs revealed a muscular development that was unparalleled. Its face surpassed in hideousness anything I have ever seen. Gustave Doré . . . never conceived anything so horrible . . . It was the physiognomy of what I should fancy a ghoul might be. It looked as if it was capable of feeding on human flesh.
>
> —ibid., page 66.

In the end, the creature starves to death because the narrator and his friend cannot find any food that it will eat (an echo of Gollum's rejection of *lembas* in *The Two Towers*?) and they dare not release it, given its initial murderous assault. O'Brien's creature sounds very like Gollum as Tolkien originally conceived him: small, wiry, and vicious; humanoid but not human; an invisible strangler lurking in total darkness who ambushes his prey, throttles them, and devours the corpses.[38]

NOTES

1 In its final, revised form it has been reprinted several times independently of the book (for example, in Boyer and Zahorski's 1977 anthology *The Fantastic Imagination*); see Hammond, *Descriptive Bibliography*, page 23, and Åke Jönsson, *En Tolkienbibliografi* 1911–1980; Verk av och om J. R. R. Tolkien [1984], pages 15–16.

2 According to Hammond (pp. 4, 15, 16, 18, 21, and 26), the first printing (September 1937) was only 1500 copies, followed three months later by a second of 2300 copies (423 of which were destroyed in a warehouse fire during the Blitz) and a third of 1500 printed simultaneously with a Children's Book Club edition of 3000 more (both late 1942/early 1943). The fourth printing (1946–7), the last to use the original text, was of 4000 copies. Finally, the first American edition of March 1938 accounts for another 5000 copies, for a grand total of 17,300, less the 423 destroyed before distribution, for an actual total of 16,877 books – a mere fraction compared with the 35,000 copies of the first paperback edition (Puffin, 1961), not to mention the vast numbers of the Ballantine, Allen & Unwin, Houghton Mifflin, and HarperCollins editions sold in the last forty years.

3 Printed in *A Tolkien Compass*, ed. Jared C. Lobdell [1975], pages 9–28; this article is excerpted from Chapter III ('The Descendant of Cain') of Christensen's dissertation, *Beowulf and The Hobbit: Elegy into Fantasy in J. R. R. Tolkien's Creative Technique* (Univ. of Southern California, 1969).

4 See Tolkien's letters to Allen & Unwin and Sir Stanley Unwin of 1st August, 10th September, and 14th September 1950 (*Letters* pp. 141 – 142), and the section of commentary titled 'The Fortunate Misunderstanding' beginning on p. 761.

5 On the face of it, the former seems more probable, especially since the first typescript adds a phrase to the line about the original owners to the effect that they 'were still there in odd corners, *slinking and nosing about*' – a description that seems very aptly to fit Gollum, silent throttler of any solitary goblins he catches 'while he was prowling about'. On the other hand, Gollum's 'memories of long before when he lived with his grandmother in a hole in a bank by a river' seems to hint that he belongs in the later category of post-goblin intruder. The matter is made still murkier by uncertainty over how long it has been since the goblins came into these mountains – certainly within Medwed-Beorn's

lifetime, since he bitterly resents his expulsion (cf. pp. 231–2), but we cannot rule out the possibility of his being unusually long-lived (on the analogy of the eldest of the Cave-bears in the 1932 Father Christmas letter, whom Father Christmas 'had not seen for centuries'; cf. the commentary to Chapter VII). In short, the narrator's words seem to sum up the original Gollum best: we don't know 'who or what he was'.

6 This detail is actually a bit of archaic science: Euclid and Ptolemy believed that light rays emanate from the eyes, and it was not until well into the Middle Ages that Ibn al-Haitham (c.965–1039, known in the West as 'Alhazen'), an Arabic scientist who specialized in optics, proved that we see by means of light reaching our eyes from luminous objects (*The Key to 'The Name of the Rose'* by Haft, White, & White [1987], page 40). Janice Coulter (private communication) raises the question of how could Gollum sneak up on prey when his 'lamp-like' eyes shone in the dark; the answer must be that the ring hid this projected light as well.

7 Engels sent a large (26? inches wide by 21 inches tall) illustrated letter to Tolkien on 1st November 1946; his Gollum-in-the-boat is huge, bloated, almost troll-sized (literally, since the other scene in the letter is of Bilbo and the trolls). Eventually a German translation, with illustrations by Engels, did appear in 1957; once again he depicted Gollum as large and rubbery, many times Bilbo's size, with beams radiating from his eyes. Engels' illustrations were removed from the revised 1971 German translation, but the original poster-sized letter can be seen on display in the Marquette Archives and is reproduced in *The Annotated Hobbit* as Plate Six (bottom).

8 The best description of Gollum as he appears in *The Lord of the Rings* comes in an unpublished commentary Tolkien made regarding Pauline Baynes' depiction of various characters from *The Lord of the Rings* in the headpiece and tailpiece to her 1970 'Map of Middle-earth'. While Tolkien's fondness for Baynes' earlier work on *Farmer Giles of Ham* [1949] had resulted in her being chosen to illustrate both *The Adventures of Tom Bombadil* [1962] and *Smith of Wootton Major* [1967], as well as providing the covers for *The Tolkien Reader* [1966] and the first paperback edition of *The Hobbit* (the Puffin edition of 1961, notorious for its 'correction' of *dwarves* to *dwarfs*, although *elves* remained), he disliked this piece so much that he wrote an essay critiquing her attempt in which he describes each member of the Fellowship of the Ring as he pictured them – an invaluable aid to any future illustrator of his work. In this he dismissed her Gollum as reminiscent of 'the Michelin tyre man' and included the following description of Gollum as he ultimately came to envision him:

> Gollum was according to Gandalf one of a riverside hobbit people – and therefore in origin a member of a small variety of the human race, although he had become deformed during his long inhabiting of the dark lake. His long hands are therefore more or less right.* [*Not his feet. They are exaggerated. They are described as *webby* (Hobbit

88), *like a swan's* (I. 398), but had prehensile toes (II 219).] But he was very thin – in The L.R. emaciated, not plump and rubbery; he had for his size a *large head* and a *long thin neck*, very large eyes (protuberant), and thin lank hair . . . He is often said to be dark or black (II 219, 220 where he was in moonlight).

Gollum was *never naked*. He had a pocket . . . He evidently had black garments in II 219 & eagle passage II 253: like 'the famished skeleton of some child of Men, its ragged garment still clinging to it, its long arms and legs almost bone-white and bone-thin.'

His skin was white, no doubt with a pallor increased by dwelling long in the dark, and later by hunger. He remained a human being, not an animal or a mere bogey, even if deformed in mind and body: an object of disgust, but also of pity – to the deep-sighted, such as Frodo had become. There is no need to wonder how he came by clothes or replaced them: any consideration of the tale will show that he had plenty of opportunities by theft, or charity (as of the Wood-elves), throughout his life.

—Bodleian, Department of Western Manuscripts, Tolkien Papers, A61 fols 1–31.

9 Most of these additions occur in the first typescript – i.e., the next stage of composition. Thus, the 'eggs' of the draft becomes 'eggs*es*', 'just one more question to guess, yes, yes' becomes 'Jus*s*t one more ques*s*tion to guess, yes, yes*s*', and the first mention of 'precious' is strung out to 'precious*ss*'. Other details were added to the printer's proofs ('It's got to ask us*s* a ques*s*tion, my precious, yes, yess, *yesss.*'). With very few exceptions, the text achieved in the proofs has remained unchanged, at least so far as Gollum's conversational peculiarities are concerned, ever since.

10 I.e., two of Gollum's references to Bilbo as 'he' rather than 'it' ('What iss he, my precious?' and 'What's he got in his handses?' – cf. DAA.120) and Gollum's reference to himself as 'ye' rather than 'we' ('Praps ye sits here and chats with it a bitsy, my preciouss.'). This latter was unfortunately changed in the fifth edition of 1995 from 'ye' to 'we' in the interests of consistency, despite the lack of manuscript authority; the two references to Bilbo as 'he', however, remain.

11 This extremely effective and rather impressive performance of the revised text, made at George Sayer's home in 1952 on an early home tape-recorder, was released by Caedmon Records in 1975 as *J. R. R. Tolkien reads and sings his The Hobbit and The Fellowship of the Ring* (Caedmon TC 1477) and is currently available from Harper Audio as part of the 'J. R. R. Tolkien Audio Collection'.

12 Anderson's date derives from Tolkien himself having written '1928' on one of the typescripts of another of the Bimble poems, which Carpenter seems to have misread as '1920'.

13 This interview on Radio Blackburn was broadcast in December 1975. I am grateful to Wayne Hammond and Christina Scull for drawing this

recording to my attention and playing a tape of it for me, and to Gary Hunnewell for helping me locate a transcription.

14 My attention was drawn to *Vafthrúthnismál* and its probable influence on this chapter, as well as to a possible parallel in the *Kalevala*, by Dr. Tim Machan's presentation at the 1987 Marquette Tolkien Conference, '*Vafthrúthnismal*, the *Kalevala* and "Riddles in the Dark"'. I am grateful to Dr. Machan for providing me with a copy of his unpublished paper. For more on the wisdom-challenge genre, see the introduction to his edition of *Vafthrúthnismal* (Durham Medieval Texts, Number 6 [1988]), especially pages 23–6.

15 So called to distinguish it from a shorter, unrelated, poem on the same subject. Both the original Old English text and a Modern English translation can be found in T. A. Shippey's *Poems of Wisdom and Learning in Old English* [1976], pages 86–103. See also Shippey's brief discussion of this work in *The Road to Middle-earth* [1982], page 112; rev. ed [2003], page 133. Note however that the Old English poem is less a 'riddle-contest' than a justification, via questions and answers, of God's wisdom in ordering the world as it is; it ends with Saturn (portrayed here as a Chaldean wizard rather than a Grecian Titan) laughing with delight at his defeat – a startling contrast to the grim endings of most of the other contests discussed in this section.

16 For an excellent discussion of this scene, and its affinities to other Norse lore, see the section entitled 'The Riddles of Gestumblindi' in Christopher Tolkien's introduction to his edition and translation of *The Saga of King Heidrek the Wise* [1960], pages xviii–xxi. The scene itself occupies pages 31–44 of the same edition, with additional riddles from one of the manuscripts given in an Appendix (pages 80–82).

17 This was almost certainly *An Inheritance of Poetry*, collected and arranged by Gladys L. Adshead and Annis Duff (Boston: Houghton Mifflin, 1948); cf. Åke Jönsson, *En Tolkienbibliografi*, see p. 185, pages 15 & 14.

18 Quite aside from the riddles, Tolkien was much influenced by nursery rhymes. While at Leeds he translated 'Who Killed Cock Robin' and 'I Love Sixpence' into Old English (as 'Ruddoc Hana' and 'Syx Mynet', respectively) and wrote new lyrics set to the tunes of several more well-known nursery rhymes: 'From One to Five' (to the tune of 'Three Wise Men of Gotham'), 'The Root of the Boot' (better known today as the troll song – see p. 101 – to 'The Fox Went Out'), '"Lit" and "Lang"' (to 'Polly Put the Kettle On'), and 'Éadig Béo þu!' (to 'Twinkle Twinkle Little Star'). All these were published years later in A. H. Smith's edition of *Songs for the Philologists* (University College London, 1936). Much earlier, as far back as March 1915 (cf. Christopher Tolkien's commentary in BLT I.202), Tolkien had expanded the little nursery rhyme 'The Man in the Moon' (The man in the moon/Came tumbling down/And ask'd his way to Norwich./He went by the south,/And burnt his mouth,/With supping cold plum porridge'†) into an 80-line piece (reprinted in BLT I.204–6) later revised into a 96-line version for *The*

Adventures of Tom Bombadil (ATB poem #6, pages 34–[38]). Similarly, he took 'Hey Diddle, Diddle,/The Cat and the Fiddle,/The Cow jump'd over the Moon;/The little Dog laughed/To see such Craft,††/And the Dish ran away with the Spoon.' – called by the Opies 'Probably the best-known nonsense verse in the language'; they go on to note that 'a considerable amount of nonsense has been written about it' – and created a 60-line poem around it that encompassed and incorporated the existing poem and 'explained' all its curious references. In fact, Tolkien's original title for his version was 'The Cat and the Fiddle, or A Nursery Rhyme Undone and its Scandalous Secret Unlocked' (HME VI.145–7). First published in 1923, this poem was later revised and incorporated in *The Lord of the Rings* (Chapter IX, 'At the Sign of the Prancing Pony'; *LotR*.174–6) and reprinted in *The Adventures of Tom Bombadil* (ATB poem #5, pages 31–3). Both of his man-in-the-moon poems start from familiar nursery rhyme lore and create a new poem based on it which paradoxically becomes, in the reader's mind, the 'lost original' of the nursery rhyme.

Finally, Tolkien rewrote one seemingly innocuous little nursery rhyme to chilling effect: 'Merrily sang the monks of Ely,/As King Canute came rowing by./"Row to the shore, knights," said the king/"And let us hear these churchmen sing."'††† Tolkien's version appears at the very end of *The Homecoming of Beorhtnoth Beorhthelm's Son* [1953] as 'Sadly they sing, the monks of Ely isle!/Row, men, row! Let us listen here a while!', transformed from a cheerful little bit of doggerel into a funereal dirge.

† The second line was later changed to 'Came down too soon' and the last line to 'supping hot pease porridge' – cf. Baring-Gould #79 (pp. 82–4) and Opies p. 294.

†† Later 'To see such sport' or 'To see such fun'. Cf. Baring-Gould #45, pp. 55–8.

††† Baring-Gould #203, p. 138. Tolkien quotes the Middle-English original of this rhyme at the end of part one of *The Homecoming*: 'Merie sungen ðe muneches binnen Ely,/ða Cnut ching reu ðerby./"Roweð, cnites, noer the land/and here we ther muneches saeng."'

19 The following chart of the ten riddles is provided for ease of comparison:

1st: mountain (Gollum).
2nd: teeth (Bilbo).
3rd: wind (Gollum).
4th: daisy (Bilbo).
5th: dark (Gollum).
6th: egg (Bilbo).
7th: fish (Gollum).
8th: no-legs (Bilbo).
9th: time (Gollum).
10th: ring (Bilbo).

20 'What walks on four legs in the morning, two legs at noon, and three legs in the evening?' The answer, as Sophocles knew, is a man, who crawls as an infant, walks upright as an adult, and hobbles along with a cane in old age. Note that, in keeping with the tradition of dangerous riddles, the Sphinx slays all who cannot answer her and, when foiled by Oedipus, kills herself (cf. *Oedipus Rex*).

21 The standard answer is a man at a table with a leg of mutton stolen by a dog; Tolkien adapts this to the circumstances by substituting 'no-legs' for one-leg (i.e., fish for mutton) and a cat (notoriously fond of fish) for the dog.

Baring-Gould also gives yet another variant (involving a milkmaid, cow, and stool) rather closer to Tolkien's in compression and general style:

> Two-legs sat on Three-legs by Four-legs.
> One leg knocked Two-legs off Three-legs.
> Two-legs hit Four-legs with Three-legs.
>
> —Baring-Gould p. 277.

22 This poem appeared in *A Northern Venture:* Verses by Members of the Leeds University English School Association [1923], p. 20. A rough translation of Tolkien's poem would run something like this: 'My walls are wonderfully adorned with milk-white marblestone; a soft garment is hung within, most like to silk; in the midst is a well of water clear as glass; there the most beautiful of apples glitters on the current. My fortress has no entrance; yet bold thieves break into my palace and plunder that treasure. Say what I am called!' My thanks to Dr. Tim Machan of Marquette University and Tolkien linguist David Salo for their help with this translation.

Tolkien also wrote a second Anglo-Saxon riddle which appears with 'Meolchwitum sind marmanstane' under the general title of 'Enigmata Saxonica Nuper Inventa Duo' – an ingenuous title, since in Latin 'inventa' can mean either 'invented' or 'discovered'. Thus, the title translates as 'Two Recently Discovered Saxon Riddles' or 'Two Recently Invented Saxon Riddles', nicely ambiguous. I give here the companion piece, 'Hild Hunecan':

> Hæfth Hild Hunecan hwite tunecan,
> ond swa read rose hæfth rudige nose;
> the leng heo bideth, the læss heo wrideth;
> hire tearas hate on tan blate
> biernende dreosath ond bearhtme freosath;
> hwæt heo sie saga, searothancla maga.

A literal translation would run something along these lines: 'Hild Hunecan hath a white tunican [tunic],/and a ruddy nose like a red rose;/the longer she bideth [waits], the less she thriveth [grows];/her hot tears on pale branch/fall burning and freeze 'in a twinkling';/say what she is, clever man.'

The answer, of course, is a candle. This is Tolkien's free adaptation of another once well-known nursery rhyme riddle, unusual in that it both alliterates in proper Old English fashion and yet also uses internal rhyme – a difficult metrical feat. The original riddle reads as follows:

Little Nancy Etticoat
With a white petticoat,
And a red nose;
She has no feet or hands,
The longer she stands
The shorter she grows.

—Baring-Gould p. 275; Opies p. 153.

'Hild' is the Old English word for 'battle', but it was also a common proper name (still in use today under the slightly altered form of 'Hilda'). I cannot explain 'hunecan', other than to suggest that it is a nonsense coinage and that 'Hild Hunecan' is, like 'Nancy Etticoat' (a candle) and 'Humpty Dumpty' (an egg), the name given in order to deceive the listener into thinking the riddle describes a person rather than an object. 'Hunecan' might therefore be a pun on 'honey-kin' (i.e., beeswax), which in a true Old English poem would have been spelled *hunig-cynn*. My thanks once again to Dr. Tim Machan and especially David Salo for providing much aid in this translation.

23 This first riddle is usually broken into three distinct riddles by editors (e.g., *The Anglo-Saxon Poetic Records*, Volume III: *The Exeter Book*, ed. Geo. P. Krapp [1936]; *Old English Riddles*, tr. Michael Alexander [1980]), each representing a different kind of storm. Craig Williamson, by contrast, in his detailed analysis of the Exeter Book riddles (*The Old English Riddles of the Exeter Book* [1977]), argues that the manuscript is correct and that all 104 lines represent a single riddle, whose solution is Wind.

24 Tolkien's riddle, of course, refers to the English daisy and not the larger American flower of the same name. English daisies are very small (usually about a half-inch in diameter), with white petals and a yellow center, the blossom lying flat on the grass. The name comes from the blossom's habit of opening in sunlight and closing in shade or darkness. The American daisy, a relative of the chrysanthemum, is more like a black-eyed susan in appearance and size, while the English daisy is similar to a chamomile (and to Tolkien's own elvish flower, the *elanor* or 'star-sun'). I am grateful to Anne al-Shahi for introducing me to the English daisy.

While Tolkien maintained that the daisy-riddle was not in verse, due no doubt to its metrical irregularity, it could easily be converted into a poem by very slight revision of the final line, e.g. '. . . in a low place/Not in a high' (which would give it the quite satisfactory rhyme scheme of *aabbab*).

25 For more on the cup-episode and the palimpsest page of the *Beowulf* manuscript, see p. 533. For the editorial addition of Prince Éomer to

the story (in place of *geomor*, the manuscript reading), see Kiernan's *Beowulf and the Beowulf Manuscript* [1981], page 184.

26 For more on the *Hauksbok* manuscript and its relationship to the other versions of the saga, see Christopher Tolkien's introduction to his translation and edition, *The Saga of King Heidrek the Wise* [1960], especially pages xxix–xxxi and 80.

27 Indeed, David Day has devoted an entire book, *Tolkien's Ring* [1994], to listing all the various ring-legends Tolkien might have drawn on for his One Ring, surveying and retelling Celtic, Greek, Tibetan, and Biblical myths, as well as stories from the Arthurian and Carolingian cycles, but focusing most on Norse and German myth, especially the story told variously in *The Volsunga Saga, The Nibelungenlied*, and Wagner's Ring cycle (*Das Rheingold, The Valkyrie, Siegfried*, and *Twilight of the Gods*). While Day's book is well written, wonderfully illustrated (by Alan Lee), and full of interesting stories, readers unfamiliar with the original legends should be warned that the book is factually worthless; Day has no compunction about making up details in order to magnify similarities between Tolkien and his 'sources'.

28 While rare, rings of invisibility are primarily to be found in medieval (Chrétien, Hartmann, the Welsh adaptor) and renaissance (Boiardo, Ariosto) romance, as the examples discussed in this section of commentary show. Curiously enough, they are extremely rare in one place where we might expect to find them plentiful: in fairy tales. Certainly magical items abound in such tales – from the Grimms' 'The Tinderbox' (which summons up three great dogs that do the owner's bidding) to 'The Worn-Out Dancing Shoes' (better known as 'The Twelve Dancing Princesses'), which features a cloak of invisibility – but so far only two have been discovered that feature rings of invisibility.

Since the success of *The Lord of the Rings*, magical rings of invisibility have become a generic part of post-Tolkienian fantasy, even to the extent of earning their own entry (along with *rings of djinn summoning* and *rings of three wishes*) in the Advanced Dungeons & Dragons *Dungeon Master's Guide* [1979; 2nd ed. 1989; 3rd ed. 2000]. Even so, they are generally avoided by fantasy authors as too blatantly borrowed from Tolkien – with the ironic result that they are more noted by their absence than their actual presence.

I would like to thank my friends 'The Burrahobbits', from whom I received much valuable help in uncovering ring-lore throughout this section.

29 Plato's text is quite clear that this adventure happened to an *ancestor* of Gyges; however, some commentators have argued that it was Gyges himself who rose from shepherd to king via the power of his magic ring (in the best fairy-tale tradition). Interestingly enough, Herodotus (*Histories*, Book I, parts 8–13) also tells a story about how this Gyges rose to become king through the contrivance of the queen, but his story lacks any magical apparatus. Gyges was actually a real person, who in historical fact founded a dynasty of kings and reigned over Lydia (a

neo-Hittite kingdom in western Anatolia) circa 687–652 BC. Aside from inspiring this legend, his chief claim to fame is that it was either in or immediately after his reign that the Lydians minted the world's first coins.

30 Atlantis features in two of Plato's late dialogues, *Timaeus* [circa 360 BC?] and more significantly in the late, unfinished *Critias* [circa 347 BC?], which contains a brief history and detailed description of Atlantis. Significantly, Plato does not claim to have invented the legend himself but has his character Critias state that his account was brought to Greece by Solon (who had died more than two centuries before), who in turn learned it from much earlier Egyptian accounts. Traditionally Plato scholarship has dismissed this claim as a fiction, but in recent years it has been revived as a serious possibility by iconoclasts such as Martin Bernal.

31 The passage in Plato might have been pointed out by C. S. Lewis, who considered himself a philosopher and one of whose three degrees was in 'Greats', or classical studies – cf. the figure of the Professor in the Narnia series, who keeps insisting 'It's all in Plato' – or by another of the early Inklings, Adam Fox, who later wrote a book *Plato for Pleasure* [1945].

32 Despite their names, 'High German' (*Hochdeutsch*) and 'Low German' (*Plattdeutsch*) refer not to social status but region: High German originated as the form of the language spoken in the highlands of what is now Austria and Bavaria, near the Alps in southern Germany, while Low German was spoken in the lowlands near the coast in northern Germany and modern-day Holland. Old English is closely related to Low German, particularly Old Saxon (sometimes also called Old Low German), the language of those Saxons who did not immigrate to the British Isles alongside the Angles and Jutes. Modern written German descends from High German, since Martin Luther chose it for his translation of the Bible, although many Germans in the north still use Low German in less formal contexts. Just as a work written in thirteenth-century English is in 'Middle English', a work written in the southern form of German in the thirteenth century is in 'Middle High German'. My thanks to Wolfgang, Brigitte, and Dr. Werner Baur for their help in sorting through the matter of modern vs. medieval German dialects.

33 The Red Book of Westmarch, Tolkien's fictional source for *The Hobbit* and *The Lord of the Rings*, takes its name from actual surviving medieval manuscripts such as The Red Book of Hergest and the White Book of Rhydderch, the two main texts of *The Mabinogion* [both fourteenth century]. Tolkien owned copies of both in the original Welsh, in the editions by J. Gwenogvryn Evans [The White Book, 1907; The Red Book, 1905†], along with Lady Charlotte Guest's famous translation [1837] (Verlyn Flieger, personal communication). Moreover, he taught Medieval Welsh at Leeds (*Letters* p. 12), and *The Mabinogion* is the greatest surviving work of literature in that language. Flieger also notes

that Tolkien 'made a transcription and partial translation of the First Branch, *Pwyll*',†† along with extensive notes on the name 'Annwn' (Flieger, *Interrupted Music* [2005], page 60). Tolkien also draws upon one of *The Mabinogion's* component stories, 'Culhwch and Olwen' – the oldest known Arthurian tale – in his essay 'The Name "Nodens"' [1932]. And of course the translator of the text given here, Gwyn Jones, was a friend of Tolkien's; see p. 281.

† Note that this was a limited edition of six hundred copies, testifying to the seriousness of Tolkien's interest in its text.

†† This text is now in the Bodleian Library's Dept. of Western Manuscripts (Mss. Tolkien A18/1. fols 134–56).

34 Lewis's remark, which in fact made the comparison to Ariosto's disadvantage, comes from the blurb he wrote for the first edition of *The Lord of the Rings* and which was included on the inside front flap of the dust jacket: 'If Ariosto rivalled it in invention (in fact he does not) he would still lack its heroic seriousness.' Tolkien was at first pleased by the comparisons in the blurbs to Spenser, Malory, and Ariosto, declaring them 'too much for my vanity!' (JRRT to Rayner Unwin, 13th May 1954; *Letters* p. 181). For Tolkien's later [circa 1967] disclaimer of any familiarity with the Italian mock-epic ('I don't know Ariosto, and I'd loathe him if I did'), see Carpenter, *Tolkien: A Biography*, page 218.

35 Again, either Kreutzwald or Lang's translator was careless or the original tradition this tale was based on confused, since we are told several times that one of the ring's powers is to enable the wearer to fly, yet the betrayed witch-maiden later avenges herself on the hero when he is 'in the form of a bird' (page 19) by changing herself into an eagle and capturing him; this is the only indication anywhere in the tale that the ring actually transforms its wearer, rather than (as on the three previous occasions) simply granting the power of flight.

36 Faux-Rings: In addition to these genuine rings of invisibility, the scholarly record is littered with references to magical rings, several of which are described as a 'ring of invisibility' but, upon examination of the original literature, turn out to be nothing of the sort. I include two such samples here, both appearing in *Brewer's Dictionary of Phrase and Fable*, since they demonstrate how errors perpetuate themselves.

The first false ring appears in *Ortnit*, a Middle High German romance [circa 1217–25] set in Lombardy, part of the Dietrich cycle or *Heldenbuch* inspired by legends of Theodoric the Great, king of the Ostrogoths. This ring is labelled 'Ornit's Ring of Invisibility' in *Brewer's* (e.g., 14th edition, [1989], page 938), but in fact it has no such power. Instead, Ortnit's ring would more accurately be called a ring to *detect* invisibility: it enables the wearer to see the 'wilderness dwarf' Alberich, a magical being who becomes Ortnit's helper. Those without the ring can hear the dwarf (or more properly midget, since he appears as a perfectly proportioned four-year-old child although as strong as a hardy knight), who sometimes pretends to be an unseen angel; only Ortnit or those to whom he loans the ring can see the dwarf-king:

> He saw [Alberich] . . . only by the power of the stone in the ring on his finger.
>
> . . . just as soon as the little one seized the ring, he disappeared and was nowhere to be seen.
>
> 'Speak! Where did you go?' cried the Lombard.
>
> 'Never mind where I am' replied the little one . . . 'You have given up a ring whose loss you will regret as long as you live. It was through the power of the stone that you were so lucky as to see and capture me, and I would always have had to serve you if you had kept it . . .'
>
> . . . [Ortnit] was crafty and strong and, as soon as Alberich held out the ring, he threw him onto the ground. Bending down over him, the king exclaimed: 'Well, evil spirit, before I let you go this time, you must tell me what you know.' When he put on the ring, he could see Alberich and he held him tightly.
>
> — Ortnit *and* Wolfdietrich: *Two Medieval Romances*, tr. J. W. Thomas [1986], pages 7, 10, & 11.

The second false ring appears in *Reynard the Fox* – a late twelfth- & early thirteenth-century Old French story-cycle of beast-fables so popular that the antihero's name, *renard*, replaced *goupil* as the standard French word for *fox*. At one point in one of the best-known Reynard stories, published by Caxton as *The History of Reynard the Fox* [1485], Reynard falsely claims to have owned a marvellous ring that, according to recent editions of *Brewer's*, among its many other powers 'rendered the wearer of the ring invisible'. In fact, the ring has no such power, although there was little else it could not do:

> . . . a ring of fine gold and within the ring next the finger were written letters enameled with sable and azure and there were three Hebrews' names therein . . . those three names that Seth brought out of Paradise when he brought to his father Adam the oil of mercy. And whosoever bears on him these three names, he shall never be hurt by thunder nor lightning, nor no witchcraft shall have power over him, nor be tempted to do sin. And also he shall never take harm by cold though he lay three winter's long nights in the field, though it snowed, stormed, or froze never so sore, so great might have these words . . . Without-forth on the ring stood a stone of three manner colours. The one part was like red crystal and shone like as fire had been therein in such wise that if anyone would go by night him behooved no other light, for the shining of the stone made and gave as great a light as it had been midday. That other part of the stone was white and clear as it had been burnished. Whoso had in his eyes any smart or soreness withoutforth, if he struck the stone on the place where the grief is, he shall anon be whole. Or if any man be sick in his body of venom or ill meat in his stomach, of colic, strangullion, stone, fistula, or canker or any other sickness, save only the very death, let him lay this stone in a little water and let him drink it and he shall forthwith be whole and all quit of his sickness.

> . . . the third colour was green like glass. But there were some sprinkles therein like purple . . . who that bore this stone upon him should never be hurt of his enemy and . . . no man, were he ever so strong and hardy . . . might misdo him. And wherever he fought, he should have victory, were it by night or by day, all so far as he beheld it fasting. And also thereto wheresomever he went and in what fellowship, he should be beloved though they had hated him tofore. If he had the ring upon him, they should forget their anger as soon as they saw him. And though he were all naked in a field against a hundred armed men, he should be well hearted and escape from them with worship.
>
> —*The History of Reynard the Fox*, tr. Wm Caxton [1485], ed. Donald B. Sands [1960], pages 141–2.

The misinformation about Reynard's ring entered in with the Centenary Edition of 1970, which replaced the correct earlier reading 'the *green* [portion of the stone] rendered the wearer of the ring invincible' (*Brewer's*, 8th ed. [1963], page 765) with the erroneous '. . . wearer of the ring *invisible*' (*Brewer's*, Centenary [12th] ed. [1970], page 920; emphasis mine). Sad to say, however, the error regarding 'Ornit's Ring' goes back to Rev. Ebenezer Cobham Brewer himself, and was present in every edition I checked, going back at least to 1890. Both these errors are still present in the most recent edition available to me (the 17th ed. [2005], 1st printing; cf. pp. 1165 & 1172).

My thanks to Gwendolyn Kestrel and Wolfgang Baur for aid in tracking down these errors in various editions of Brewer's book.

37 For my commentary on the probable origins of the name 'Balin', see pp. 23–4.

38 Two of the most famous invisible characters contemporary with *The Hobbit* slightly predate Tolkien's tale but did not become popular until after the manuscript of Mr. Baggins' adventures had been completed, so it seems unlikely that they contributed anything to Tolkien's portrayal of Gollum nor to Bilbo's behavior when invisible, although they do show how the idea was in the air and could take any of a number of forms. The first of these was Thorne Smith's *Topper* [1926], a story about playful ghosts whose invisible antics cause a staid, Bilbo-like character to gradually abandon his quiet dull life for a more enjoyable but less respectable existence. Smith's work was very popular in the 1930s, but *Topper* only gained wide renown when it was made into a film in 1937 (starring a young Cary Grant as one of the ghosts), so successfully as to inspire a number of sequels and eventually a television series (1953ff, starring Leo G. Carroll as Mr. Topper). The closest parallel between the ghosts' antics and Tolkien's work is in Bingo's pranks at Farmer Maggot's in draft versions of *The Lord of the Rings* (HME VI.96–7, 290–3, & 297).

The most famous invisible character of the 1930s, however, was The Shadow, the crimefighter who 'had the power to cloud men's minds, so that they could not see him'. The conjunction of invisibility and a shadow is suggestive, given the limitation of Bilbo's ring in hiding everything but his shadow, but while The Shadow's adventures as a pulp fiction hero began in 1929, it was not until 1937 that he gained his own radio series celebrating his exploits (with Orson Welles as Lamont Cranston, a.k.a. The Shadow, and Agnes Moorhead as his girl friday Margo Lane), so it seems unlikely that this icon of the old radio serials contributed anything to Tolkien's work.

Chapter Six

WARGS AND EAGLES

As before, the text continues on the same page (Ms. p. 61; Marq. 1/1/5:11), with no more than a skipped line in the middle of the page to mark where the later chapter break would be inserted.

He had escaped the goblins, but he didn't know where he was. He had lost hood, cloak, pony, food, and his friends. He wandered on and on, and the sun began to go down towards the west – sinking *towards the mountains*. Bilbo looked round and noticed it. He looked forward and could see no mountains in front of him, only ridge and slopes falling towards low lands and plains. 'I can't have got right to the other side of the Misty Mountains can I – right to the edge of the Land Beyond' he said. 'O where o where can Bladorthin and the dwarves be? I only hope they are not still back in there in the power of the goblins'. So he wandered on; he was wondering very much whether he oughtn't, now he had a magic ring, to go back into those horrible horrible tunnels and try and find his friends. He had almost made up his mind that he ought to, and was feeling very uncomfortable about it, when he heard voices.

He stopped and he listened. It didn't sound like goblins. So he crept forward carefully. He was following a downward path with a rocky wall on one side. On the other side the ground sloped away, and there were dells below the level of the path, fringed or filled with bushes and low trees. In one of these dells under the bushes people were talking, several people. Bilbo crept still nearer, and suddenly peering between two big boulders he saw a head with a yellow hood on – it was Balin doing look-out.[TN1] He could have clapped and shouted for surprise and joy, but he didn't. He had still got the ring out [> on], for fear of meeting something unexpected and unpleasant, and he noticed that Balin was looking straight at him without noticing him. 'I will give them all a surprise' he thought. He crawled into the bushes at the edge of the dell, and listened. Bladorthin was talking, and so were the dwarves: they were discussing all that happened to them in the goblin-tunnels, arguing, and wondering, and debating what they should do now. Bladorthin was saying they couldn't possibly leave Mr Baggins in the hands of the goblins without trying to find out if he was dead, or alive, and without trying to rescue him if they could.

'After all he is my friend' said the wizard, 'and not a bad little chap. I feel responsible for him. I can't think how you came to lose him'. The dwarves agreed, but they grumbled. They [didn't ca[re to] >] wanted to know why he had ever been brought at all, why he couldn't stick to his friends and come along with them, and said he had been more trouble than use so far – especially if they had got to go back into those abominable tunnels to look for him: they didn't like that at all.[TN2]

The wizard spoke <quite> crossly: 'I brought him, and I don't bring things that are of no use' he said. 'He would have been more use in the end to you people than you imagine – and will be if we can only discover him again. Whatever *did* you want to drop him for, Bombur?'[TN3]

'You would have dropped him' said Bombur 'if somebody suddenly grabbed you from behind in the dark, tripped up your feet, and kicked you in the back'.

'Why didn't you pick him up again?'

'Good heavens – can you ask! Goblins fighting and biting in the dark, everybody falling over things, and hitting one another. You nearly chopped off my head with Glamdring, and Gandalf was stabbing here and there with Orcrist. All of a sudden [he >] you gave one of your blinding flashes, we saw the goblins running back yelping – and you shouted "follow me everybody". Everybody followed, or so we thought; and we never had time to stop and count ourselves till we came to the lower gate, and found it open [> dashed into the gate-guards, drove them helter-skelter and rushed out]. And here we are – without the burglar, confusticate him!'

'And here's the burglar' said Bilbo stepping down into the middle of them and taking off the ring. Bless me, how they jumped. Then they shouted with surprise and [with a certain>][TN4] delight. Bladorthin was as surprised [> astonished] as any of them, and probably more pleased than all: but he called to Balin and told him what he thought of a look-out man that let people walk right into them without warning like that. It's a fact that Bilbo's reputation went up [even >] a very great deal with them[TN5] after that. If they had doubted before whether he was really a first-class burglar, they didn't doubt it any longer. Balin was very puzzled indeed, and they all said it was a very clever bit of work. Indeed Bilbo was so pleased with their praise that he just chuckled inside and said nothing whatever about the ring; and when they kept on asking him how he did it he said 'Oh, just crept along you know – carefully and quietly'. 'Well, it's the first time [even] a mouse has crept along quietly & carefully under my nose in broad daylight and not been spotted' said Balin 'and I take off my hood to you' which he did. 'Balin at your service' he said.

'Bilbo at yours' said Mr Baggins.

Then they wanted to know all about his adventures since they lost him; and he sat down and told them everything – about bumping his head when he fell off Bombur's back, and coming to himself all alone in the dark (but he didn't mention finding the ring – 'not just now' he thought). Then he described the horrible Gollum and the competition more or less how it happened, except that he pretended his pocket had been empty [> didn't say what had been in his pocket which Gollum couldn't guess, nor did he say what Gollum's lost present was].[TN 6]

'And then I couldn't think of any other question with him sitting beside me' he said. 'So I said "what's in my pocket?" And he couldn't guess [with >] in three times. So I asked for my present, and he went to look for it, and couldn't find it. So I said "very well help [*added*: me] to get out of this nasty place". "Very well" he said and he showed me the passage to the gate. "Goodbye" he [> I] said, and I went on down'.

'What about the guards?' they asked 'Weren't there any?'

'O yes lots of them, but I dodged 'em. I got stuck in the door, which was only open a crack, and I nearly got caught. In fact I lost lots of buttons' he said looking sadly at his coat and waistcoat 'but I managed to squeeze through in time – and here I am'.

The dwarves looked at him quite respectfully when he talked about dodging the guards and squeezing through, as if it wasn't very difficult or very alarming.

'What did I tell you?' said Bladorthin. 'Mr Baggins has more about him than you'd guess.' Bilbo didn't quite know what the wizard meant by that, but he smiled.

Then he had a few questions of his own to ask, for if Bladorthin had explained it all by now to the dwarves, he hadn't heard how the wizard had turned up again, or where they had come to now.

So Bladorthin explained that the goblins' presence [> the presence in the mountains of bad wicked goblins] was well known to Elrond.[TN7] But their main gate [was >] came out on a different pass to the one they had been following, a seemingly much easier road, and therefore one people more often followed (and got caught if they were anywhere near the gates at night-fall). They [can't >] couldn't have made that [new] entrance high up in the mountains almost at the top of the pass (which had [been] supposed to be safe) until quite recently: nobody knew about it before.

'I shall have to see if we can't find a more decent giant[TN8] to block it up' said Bladorthin 'or soon there will be no getting over these mountains at all'. Still as soon as the wizard heard Bilbo's yell he guessed what had happened.[TN9] In the flash [where >] which killed the goblins who were grabbing him, he had nipped inside the crack just before it snapped to. He followed after the drivers and prisoners right to the edge of the great hall, and there he sat down and worked up the best magic he could in the shadows. 'A very ticklish business' he said, 'touch and go it was'. But of course Bladorthin had made a special study of [fire and >] bewitchments with fire and lights ([you remember >] even Bilbo had never forgotten the magic fireworks at Old Took's mid-summer eve parties, as you probably remember). The rest we all know – except that Bladorthin knew about the goblin's back-gate; as a matter of fact anybody who knew anything about [these parts >] this part of the mountains was well aware of it, but it took a wizard to keep his head in the tunnels and guide them in the right direction.

'They made that gate ages ago' he said 'partly [to >] for a way of escape, if they needed it; partly as a way out into the Lands Beyond where they come in the dark and do a lot of damage. They guard it always, and no one has ever managed yet to block it up. They will guard it doubly after this' he laughed.[TN10] 'We must be getting on' he said. 'They will be out after us in hundreds [before >] when night comes on, and already it is getting teatimish.[TN11] They can smell our footsteps for [miles >] hours & hours after we have passed, and we must be miles on before dark. There will be a bit of moon, if it keeps fine, and that is lucky. Not that they mind the moon much, but we shall be able to see a bit better.'

'O yes' he said in answer to more questions from the hobbit 'you lose track of time inside goblins' tunnels. We were several days inside, and went miles & miles. We have come down through the heart of the mountains, and are right out on the other side. But we are not at the point where our pass would have brought us to; we are too far to the South[TN12] – and we have some awkward country ahead. We are still pretty high up. Let's get on'.

'I am so dreadfully hungry' said Bilbo, who suddenly remembered [> realized] he had been days inside the goblins' places, and had never had more than two biscuits which he had kept in his pocket. Just think of it for a hobbit. He certainly was breaking his old habits, all to bits; but it made his tummy feel horribly empty, and his legs all wobbly now the [*added*: worst] excitement was over.

'Can't help it' said Bladorthin '– unless you like to go back and ask the goblins nicely to let you have your pony and your luggage'.

'O No, no, certainly not' said Bilbo.

'Very well then, we must just trudge on, or we shall be made into supper which will be worse than having none ourselves.'

The blackberries were still in flower, so Bilbo looked in vain from side to side as they went along. [So <?were> >] Of course there weren't any nuts yet, nor even hawthorn-berries either. He nibbled a bit of sorrel, found a wild strawberry or two, and had a drink from a little[TN13] mountain stream that crossed the path. It was better than nothing, but it didn't do much good.

On they went. The bushes, and the short grass among the boulders, and the <thyme> and sage and marjoram and rockroses began to disappear. They scrambled and slipped down a dreadful long steep slope of fallen stones made in a landslide. First <rubbish> and little pebbles rolled away from them; then larger bits of split stone went clattering down; [soon >] then large lumps of rock were disturbed and bounded off crashing down the slope raising a dust and noise, soon they were sliding down all huddled together in a fearful fashion all among slipping rattling crashing stones and slabs.[TN14]

The pine trees at the bottom saved them. They slid into the edge of a dark wood of them standing right up the slope and going on down down darker and darker into the valley. They caught hold of the trunks and stopped themselves, while the sliding stones went on down in front crashing among the trees and bounding among the branches until they came to rest far below, and all was quiet.

'Well that has got us on a bit' said Bladorthin 'and [I would <?think>] even goblins tracking us will have a job to come down there quietly'.

'I dare say' said the dwarves [>Bombur],[TN15] 'but they won't find it difficult to send stones bouncing down on our heads.' They were rubbing their bruised legs and feet, and felt rather unhappy.

'Very well let's turn aside as soon as we can out of the path of the slide. Hurry up, look at the time.' The sun had gone behind the mountains; already they were in darkening shadow here, though far away through the trees & over the tops of those growing lower down they could still see evening light on the plains beyond.

They went on now more easily, down the gentler slope of the great pine forest,[TN16] picking out paths among the bracken (which was of course right high above Bilbo's head), and marching along quiet as quiet over the pine-needle floors, while all the time the forest-gloom got deeper, and the forest-silence more still. There seemed no wind that evening to bring the sea-sighing noise [*added*: even] into the upper boughs.

'Must we go any further?' asked Bilbo when it was so dark that he could only just see Gandalf's white beard wagging [in the >] by him, and so quiet he could hear their breathing like a loud noise. 'My feet [> toes] are all bruised, and my legs ache; and my tummy is simply wagging like an empty sack'.

'A bit further' said Bladorthin.

After what seemed ever such a lot further, they came to an open ring where no trees grew. The moon was up, and was shining into the clearing – somehow it struck all of them, as not at all a nice place, although there was nothing wrong to see.

All of a sudden they heard a howl away down hill, a long shuddering howl.

It was answered by another away on [> to] the side [> right] and a good deal nearer to them; then by another not far [on >] away to the left. It was wolves, howling at the moon, wolves gathering together!

There were no wolves living near Mr Baggins' hole at home, but he knew that noise. He had had it described to him. One of his cousins among the Tooks used to do it to frighten him – he had visited the forests in the north of Bilbo's country and heard it there.[TN17] To hear it out in the forest under the moon was too much for Bilbo; even magic-rings are not much use against wolves (and against probably very evil wolves, if they live under the shadow of goblin-infested mountains, in a country right on the edge of the wild and far into the unknown). Wolves of that sort smell keener than goblins, and don't need to see you to find you!

'What shall we do, what shall we do' he cried. 'Escaping goblins to be caught by wolves' he said – and it became a proverb, though we now say 'out of the frying pan into the fire' in the same sort of uncomfortable situations.

'Up the trees quick' said Bladorthin, and they ran to the trees at the edge of the glade, and hunted for ones that had branches fairly low, or were slender enough to swarm up. They found them only just in time, and up they went, up as high as ever they dare trust the branches. You could almost have laughed[TN18] to see the dwarves sitting up in the branches with their beards dangling down, like old gentlemen gone cracked and playing at being boys. Fili & Kili were right up a slender larch like a tall thin Christmas tree. Dori Nori Ori, Oin & Gloin were more comfortable in a big pine with branches even sticking out like the spokes of a wheel at intervals. Bifur Bofur Bombur and Gandalf were in another. Dwalin and Balin had swarmed up a tall slender fir with few branches, and were trying to find a comf[ortable] place to sit in the top bows among its thin greenery.

Bladorthin who was tallest[TN19] had found a tree which the others couldn't get into. A great big pine almost standing [> standing almost] at the edge of the ring. He was hidden in its branches, but you could see his eyes shining in the moon as he peeped out.

And Bilbo? He couldn't get into any tree, and was scuttling about from trunk to trunk like a rabbit that has lost its hole and has a dog after it.

'You've left the burglar behind again' said Bifur to Bombur, looking down.

'I can't be always carrying burglars on my back' said Bombur 'down tunnels, and up trees. What do you think I am, a porter?'[TN20]

'He'll be eaten if we don't do something' said Gandalf, for there were howls all round them now, getting nearer and nearer. 'Dori' he called, for Dori was lowest down in the easiest tree and also was a decent fellow 'give Mr Baggins a hand up'.

Dori really behaved very well; for Bilbo couldn't reach his hand when he climbed to the bottom branches and hung his arm down as far as ever he could reach. So Dori climbed out of the tree, let Bilbo climb up and stand on his back. Just then wolves [<?came> >] trotted howling into the glade. All of a sudden there were hundreds of eyes looking at them. Still Dori didn't let Bilbo down; he let him scramble off his shoulders into the branches, and then he jumped for the branches himself. Only just in time.

A wolf snapped at his cloak as he swung up and nearly got him. There were crowds of them all round the tree in a minute, yelping, and leaping up at the tree trunk, with eyes blazing and tongues hanging out. But even the wild [*added*: wicked] weorgs [> wargs][TN21] (for so the evil wolves [of >] beyond the edge of the unknown are called) can't climb trees. So for a time they were safe. Luckily it was warm and not windy, for trees are not very comfortable to sit in for long (with wolves all round below waiting for you) at any time, and in the cold and the wind they can be perfectly miserable places.

Evidently the ring was a meeting place of the wolves. They left guards at the foot of Dori's tree, and went snuffling about till they smelt out all the trees where the others were. These they guarded too; then all the rest went and sat (in hundreds it seemed) in a great circle in the glade. In the middle of their circle sat a great grey wolf. He spoke to them in the dreadful wolf-language of the wargs. Bladorthin may have understood it; Bilbo didn't, but it sounded as if it was all about cruel and wicked things, and probably was. The other wargs in the circle would answer their grey chief every now and again altogether, and the horrible cry almost made the hobbit fall out [*added*: of] his pine-tree.

I will tell you what Bladorthin heard, though Bilbo didn't understand it. The wargs and the goblins often helped one another in wicked deeds. Goblins do not usually venture very far away from their mountains, unless they are driven out, and are looking for new homes, or are marching to war (which I am glad to say hasn't happened for a long while). Sometimes they go on raids – especially to get slaves [> food or slaves] to work for them. Then they usually get the wargs' help. Sometimes they ride on wolves like men do on horses.

It seemed that a goblin-raid had been planned for that very night. The wargs had come to meet goblins, and the goblins were late. (I expect [*added*: the reason was] the death of the Great Goblin and all the excitement caused by the dwarves, Bilbo, and the wizard for whom they were probably still hunting). In spite of the dangers of this far land bold men had lately been pushing up into it from the south again,[TN22] and cutting down trees, and building themselves places to live in among the more pleasant woods farther down in the valleys away from the shadows of the hills, and along the river-shores. There were many of them and they were brave and well-armed and even the wargs dared not attack them if there were many together or in the bright day. But now they planned with the goblins' help to attack some of the villages nearest to the mountains by night. If they did there would probably be no one left next day – except some few the goblins kept from the wolves and carried back as prisoners to their caves.

This was dreadful talk to listen to, not only from the thought of the danger to the brave woodmen and their wives and children, but also because of the position of the [dwarves and >] Bladorthin & his friends.

The wargs were angry and puzzled at finding them here in their very meeting place. They thought they were friends of the woodmen, who had come to spy on them, and would take news of their plans down into the valley – and then of course the war-horns would blow, and people would arm in all the villages, and the goblins and wargs would have to fight a fearful battle instead of capturing prisoners and devouring people waked suddenly from their sleep. So the wolves had no intention of going away and letting the people up the trees escape – at any rate not until morning. And long before that, they said, the goblin soldiers would be coming down from the mountains; and goblins can climb trees, or cut them down.

Now you can understand why Bladorthin listening to their growling and yelping began to feel that they were in a very bad place, and had not yet escaped at all.[TN23] He wasn't going to let them have it all their own way all the same, though he could not do much up here in a tall tree with wolves all round on the ground below.

He gathered the great huge pine cones off the branches of his tree. He set one alight with bright blue fire and threw it whizzing down among the circle of wolves. It struck one on the back, and immediately his shaggy coat caught fire, and he was leaping to and fro yelping horribly. Then another came, and another, one [blue >] in blue-flames, one in red, another green. They burst on the ground in the middle of the circle and went off in coloured sparks and smoke. A very big one struck the chief wolf on the nose, and he leaped in the air ten feet – and then rushed round and round the circle biting even at the other wolves in anger, fright, and pain.

The dwarves and even Bilbo shouted [with >] and cheered. The rage of the wolves was terrific, and the commotion they made filled all the forest. Wolves are terrified of fire at all times, and this was a most horrible and uncanny fire. If a spark got in your coat it stuck and burned into you, and unless you rolled over quick you were soon all in flames. You should just have seen the wolves rolling over and over to put the sparks on their backs out, and those that were burning running about howling, and setting others alight, till their own friends chased them away, and they fled off into the forest crying and yammering and looking for water.

'What is all this uproar in the forest tonight?' said the Lord of the Eagles. He was sitting, black in the moonlight, on the top of a pinnacle of rock that stood out [from >] alone on the Eastern edge of the Mountains. 'I hear wolves' voices. Are the goblins busy at mischief in the woods?' He [called to two of his servants from >] swept up into the air, and immediately two of his army [> guards] leapt up to follow him from rocks on either hand. They circled in the sky and looked down upon the ring of the wargs, a tiny spot far far below. But eagles have keen eyes and can see a great distance, and the lord of the eagles of the misty mountains had eyes that could look straight at the sun unblinking, and could see anything moving on the ground a mile below even in the light of the moon.

So [they <?looked> >] though they could not see the people in the trees, they could [see >] make out the commotion among the wolves and the tiny flashes of fire, and hear the yelping and howling coming up faint from far beneath them. Also they could see the glint of the moon on goblin-spears and helmet, as long lines of wicked folk crept down the hill sides from their gate, and wound into the wood.

They knew then that some wickedness was going on, though they could not understand what was the matter with the wolves. [Eagles hate the goblins >] Eagles are not kind or gentle birds. They kill.[TN24] But they are proud and strong, and they do not love the [*cancelled*: ev[il]] goblins. When they take any notice of them at all (which is seldom, for they don't eat such creatures) they swoop on them and drive them shrieking to their caves, and stop whatever wickedness they are up to at the time. The Goblins [hate them and fear >] hate the eagles and fear them.

Tonight the Lord of the Eagles was filled with curiosity to know what was going on. So he summoned many of the eagles to him, and they flew slowly away from the mountains, and [sank slo[wly] >] then slowly circling ever round and round came down, down, down towards the ring of the wolves and the meeting place of the goblins.

A very good thing too. Dreadful things had been going on down there. The wolves that had caught fire and fled into the forest had set fire to it in places. It was summer[TN25] and there had been little rain on this side of the mountains for some time. Yellowing bracken, fallen branches, deep piled pine-needles, dead trees were soon burning here and there. All round the clearing of the wargs flames were leaping. But the wolves did not leave the trees. Maddened and angry they were leaping and howling round the trunks, and cursing the dwarves in their horrible language with their eyes shining as red and fierce as the flames.

Then suddenly the goblins came running up, yelling. They thought a battle with the woodmen was going on, but they soon learned what had really happened. Some of them actually sat down and laughed. The others waved their spears, and clashed their shafts against their shields.

Goblins are not particularly frightened by fire.[TN26] They got all the wolves together in a pack. They rushed round, and stamped, and beat, and beat and stamped until nearly all the flames were put out – but they did not put out the fire that was nearest to the trees where the dwarves were. No they fed that fire with branches, and bracken. Soon there was a ring of fire all round the dwarves, a ring which the goblins kept from spreading outwards; but it crept slowly on till it nearly licked those trees. Smoke was in Bilbo's eyes, he could feel the heat of the flames, and through the reek he could see the goblins dancing round & round it like people round a mid summer bonfire, and outside the dancers stood the wolves at a respectful distance watching & waiting.[TN27]

Horrible things the goblins sang; and then they would stop and call out.

'Fly away little birdies, fly away if you can
Come down little birds or [get roasted > get >] you will
get roasted in your nests.
Sing sing little birds, why don't you sing.

Fifteen birds in a five fir trees
their feathers were fanned by a fiery breeze.
[The goblins > They had >] But funny little birds they had
no wings
O what shall we do with the funny little things
Roast em alive; or stew em in a pot
Fry them, broil them, and eat em hot[TN18]

'Go away little boys' said Bladorthin. '[Birds >] It isn't bird-nesting time. Also naughty little boys that play with fire get punished'. He said it to make them angry, and show them he was not afraid of them (though of course he was, wizard though be might be); but they took no notice. They went on singing.

Burn, burn tree and fern!
Shrivel and scorch! A fizzling torch
To light the night for our delight.
Ya hey!

Bake and toast 'em fry and roast 'em,
Till beards blaze and eyes daze [> glaze],
Till hair smells, skins crack,
Fat melts, & bones black
In cinders lie
Beneath the sky.
So dwarves shall die
And light the night for our delight,
Ya hey!
Ya-harri-hey
Ya hoi.[TN29]

And with 'ya hoi' the flames were under Bladorthin's tree, and soon beneath the others. The bark caught fire, the lower branches crackled. [*cancelled*: Still they clung on – but]

Then Bladorthin climbed to the top of his tree; the light [> sudden splendour] flashed from his wand like lightning, and he got ready to spring down right amid the spears of the goblins. [They scrambled away from > gave back >] That would have been the end of him, even though he might have [got >] killed many as [he] came down among them like a thunder bolt. But he never leaped.

Just at that moment the lord of eagles swept above the scene, seized him in his talons and was gone.

The goblins howled, and began to scatter. That was the worst thing they could have done, but the sudden black shadow of the swooping eagle terrified them. If they had stuck near the fire the eagles would . . .[TN30]

At once he was back for Bladorthin had spoken to him; and he cried to his eagles. Some swept down upon the wolves and goblins that were not too near the fire. The goblins yelled the wolves howled; arrows and spears went up into the air. [*added*: But] Down swept some of the eagles; the black shadow of their wings struck terror into their enemies, their talons tore at them. Others flew to the tree-tops and seized the dwarfs,[TN31] as they scrambled up as high as they dared. Poor little Bilbo was nearly left behind again, but he caught hold of

Dori's legs as Dori was borne off, and up they went above the tumult & the flames, swinging in the air with his arms nearly breaking.

Far below the goblins and the wolves were scattering here and there in the woods. Eagles were still circling and sweeping above the battleground. The flames were leaping high, and crash fell the trees in which the dwarves had sheltered [*added*: in a flurry of sparks & smoke]. But the light was now faint below, [*added*: a red twinkle on the black floor].

They were high up in the sky, going up in strong sweeping circles ever upwards. Bilbo never forgot that flight, clinging on to Dori's ankles, while he moaned 'my arms my arms.' (and Dori kept on saying 'my poor legs my poor legs'). Heights made him [> Bilbo] giddy at the best of times.[TN32] His head swam if he looked down and saw the country [> dark lands] opening wide [*added*: underneath] touched here and there with the moonlight on a hillside or a stream. The pale peaks of the mountains were coming nearer, moonlit spikes of rock, with black shadows [> sticking out of black shadows]. Summer or not it seemed cold. The flight ended only just before poor Bilbo's arms gave way. He loosed Dori's ankles with a gasp and fell on to the rough platform of an eagle's eyrie. There he lay without speaking, and his only thought was [> his thoughts were] a mixture of surprise at being saved from the fire, and fear lest he fall off that narrow place into the dark shadows on each side.

He was feeling [*cancelled*: almost] very queer in his head after the dreadful adventures of the last few days (on only two biscuits!) and found himself asking [> saying]: 'Now I know what a piece of bacon feels like when it is suddenly picked out of the pan on a fork and put back on the shelf'.

'No you don't' he heard Dori saying: 'because the bacon knows it will get back into the pan sooner or later; [But I have a >] and it is to be hoped we shan't. Also Eagles are not forks'.

'O no, not a bit like storks, forks I mean' said Bilbo sitting up and looking anxiously at the Eagle who was perched closed by. He had wondered if he had been saying any thing rude. You oughtn't to be rude to an eagle, when you only the size of a hobbit, and are up in his eyries at night! But the eagle sharpened his beak on a stone, [*added*: and trimmed his feathers,] and took no notice.

Soon another eagle came flying up. 'The lord of eagles bids you to bring your prisoners down to the great shelf' he cried and was off. The other seized Dori and flew off into the night, leaving Bilbo all alone; he had hardly strength to wonder what they meant by calling them 'prisoners'. His own turn came soon. The eagle came back, seized Bilbo in his talons, and swooped off. Only a short way this time. Bilbo was laid down on a wide shelf of rock on the mountain side. There was no path down save by flying, and no path down from it except by jumping over a precipice. There he found all the others sitting with their backs to the wall. The Lord of Eagles also was there, and was speaking to Bladorthin.

It appeared they knew one another slightly, and were even on fairly friendly terms. Bladorthin had done one of them a service (healed him from an goblin's arrow's wound) once upon a time.[TN33] So after all 'prisoners' only meant prisoners rescued from the goblins after all. They really did seem to have escaped from those dreadful mountains after all, for the Great Eagle was discussing plans for carrying them far away and setting them down well on their way out in the plains below. But he would not take them near places where men lived.[TN34] 'They will shoot at us with great bows' he said, 'for they will think we are after their lambs – or their babies. And at other times they might be right. But glad though we are to cheat the goblins of their sport, we will not risk ourselves for dwarves in the plains.'

'Very well' said Bladorthin, 'we are already very much obliged to you. But we are nearly dead of [> famished with] hunger'.

'I am dead [> nearly dead] of it' said Bilbo in a weak voice.

'That can perhaps be arranged [> mended]' said the Lord of Eagles. And later on you might have seen a bright fire on the shelf of rock, and the figures of the dwarves gathered round it cooking, and smelt the smell of roasting. The eagles had brought up boughs of dry wood, and they had brought rabbits and hares and a lamb.

The dwarves managed all the preparations. Bilbo was too weak and weary (and he wasn't much good at skinning rabbits or cutting up meat anyway); Bladorthin had done his share in lighting up the fire for Oin & Gloin had lost their tinder boxes. (Dwarves have never taken to matches). So ended the adventures of the misty mountains. Bilbo slept (with his tummy feeling full again – though he would have liked a bit of bread and butter even better) curled up on the rock. He slept curled up on the hard rock more soundly than ever he had done on his feather bed in his own little hole at home. All night he dreamed of it [> his own home] and wandered about in his sleep into all the different rooms looking for something he couldn't find, & did not remember what it looked like.

TEXT NOTES

1 Note that Balin's hood is yellow here, an error carried over from the Bladorthin Typescript (cf. p. 32 and Text Note 2 on p. 41). This is significant, as in both typescripts for Chapter I (Marq. Ms. 1/1/51:5 & 1/1/32:5) the hood is described as 'scarlet' (and the beard yellow,

later changed in ink to 'white'). This corroborates the evidence of the names, and forms additional proof that the manuscript already extended to this point (and beyond) before the typescript was even begun. For more on the dating of the typescript(s), see the Third Phase.

Curiously enough, Balin's hood remained yellow in this chapter through both typescripts (1/1/56:1 & 1/1/37:1), even after the change to scarlet in the typescripts to Chapter I. This was clearly just a continuity slip on Tolkien's part which he caught in the galleys, correcting the colour to 'red' before publication.

2 This paragraph was originally followed by the sentence '"Whatever did you drop him for, Bombur" said the wizard.' which was cancelled and repeated (in slightly altered form) at the end of the following paragraph.

3 Both here and at the next two occurrences 'Bombur' was changed to 'Dori' in pencil – i.e., during the preparation of the First Typescript, a re-reading having apparently reminded Tolkien of what he had forgotten in the thirteen intervening manuscript pages: that, after the vivid description of Bombur's sweaty misery under his unhappy burden, the final paragraph of Chapter IV clearly states that at the time of the attack Bilbo was once more being carried by Dori (cf. p. 134).

4 The final word in this cancelled passage, following 'certain', was left incomplete: it seems to read 'amo' and is no doubt short for 'amo*unt* – i.e., 'with a certain amount of'.

5 'them' was later altered, in pencil, to 'the dwarves', making it clear that the wizard's estimation of the hobbit remained unchanged.

6 This passage was later simplified, through ink cancellations and additions, to read 'more or less how it happened, but not quite.'

7 Altered in pencil to read '*to himself &* to Elrond'.

Note the absence here of the phrasing from the book: 'The wizard, to tell the truth, never minded explaining his cleverness more than once, so now he told Bilbo . . .'; this character-defining passage replaced the more straightforward original in the First Typescript (1/1/56:3).

8 The original reading of this sentence, 'a more decent giant', was changed in pencil to 'a more *or less* decent giant', the reading of the typescripts.

9 The original account of the wizard's movements was quite different:

> Still as soon as the wizard heard Bilbo's yell he guessed what had happened. The crack closed and it was beyond his magic to open it. And he knew where the goblin's back-gate was – people who knew this part of the mountains at all well (& Bladorthin did) were well aware of it. Off he dashed

The apparent reason for the rejection of this version must have been Tolkien's realization of the time involved – for Bladorthin to have finished crossing the mountains, reached the gate, and run all of the way back up to the Goblin-King's chamber would have taken hours if not days, yet his timely rescue comes only moments after the captive dwarves and hobbit reach the room (having run there at the best pace goblin-whips could muster). Therefore Tolkien rejected the 're-entry through the back-door' rescue story as soon as he had written it, crossed out the passage, and on the same page continued with the replacement story wherein the wizard takes the same route as the captives, silently shadowing them and awaiting his chance.

10 Added in the bottom margin and marked for insertion at this point: 'and they all [did >] laughed too: after all they had killed the Great Goblin [*added:* as well as several others] & so might be said to have had the best of it so far'.

11 Teatimish: i.e., 'tea-time-ish', that is around tea-time, or late afternoon. See Bilbo's invitation to the dwarves in Chapter XVIII: 'If ever you are passing my way . . . don't forget to knock! *Tea is at four*, but any of you are welcome at any time!' (p. 681, emphasis mine; DAA.352).

Since the scene is set in summer – they had celebrated midsummer in Elrond's House, and the lack of nuts a few paragraphs later shows that autumn has not yet arrived† – that would still leave several hours of travel time before dark, but Bladorthin's analysis of the situation (borne out by subsequent events) shows that they will need those hours and must delay no longer.

† See also p. 207 and Text Note 25 on p. 214.

12 Note that while the manuscript text specifically states that they have been diverted further *south* than would have been the case had they not been ambushed in the mountains, the maps agree with the published text that they have actually come too far *north* (see Plate I [bottom]). This detail merely reinforces how fluid Tolkien's conception of the geography still was during the drafting of the story.

13 A partial cancelled word originally came between 'little' and 'mountain stream', perhaps 'bab' – that is, a little *babbling* mountain stream.

14 Like the approach to Elrond's house and the climb up into the Misty Mountains, this scene derives from memories of Tolkien's Alpine journey of 1911: 'The hobbit's (Bilbo's) journey from Rivendell to the other side of the Misty Mountains, *including the glissade down the slithering stones into the pine woods*, is based on my adventures in 1911' – JRRT to Michael Tolkien, c. 1967; *Letters* p. 391; italics mine.

15 Here 'the dwarves' is changed to 'Bombur' and then stetted back again to 'the dwarves'. However, both typescripts (1/1/56:4 and 1/1/37:4) give the reading 'Bombur', as does the published book.

16 Added at this point: 'Then they turned aside northward', changed in a darker ink to 'Southward'. See Text Note 12 above for the significance of this change.

Bracken, by the way, are dense stands of tall ferns, especially those found in wastelands.

17 This adventurous Took cousin is never identified in the later genealogies. The forests to the north of Bilbo's land never appear on the maps

in the sequel, although it's not safe to conclude they were deliberately removed from the later geography as some features disappeared or were not included in these maps through accident, not design. Indeed, the tree-men seen walking in the North Farthing (*LotR*.57) may be a relic of these unmapped forests.

The wolves from the north, at any rate, reappeared in the Prologue to *The Lord of the Rings*, where we are told that by Bilbo's time 'the wolves that had once come ravening out of the North in bitter white winters were now only a grandfather's tale' (*LotR*.17).

18 The typically Tolkienian parenthesis – 'you would have laughed (*from a safe distance*)' – was not added until the First Typescript (1/1/56:5).

19 In pencil, this phrase was changed to 'much the tallest', perhaps reflecting a shift of Gandalf from 'little old man' to a somewhat grander and more dignified figure. Compare the reading in the First Typescript (1/1/56:6), 'a good deal taller than the others', which is also that found in the published book (DAA.146).

20 In the First Typescript (1/1/56:6) and all subsequent texts, this conversation takes place between Nori and Dori, as in the published book; see Text Note 3 above for the shift from Bombur to Dori as Bilbo's chief 'porter'.

21 At its first occurrence the word was written 'weorg', then overwritten 'warg', the term used throughout thereafter. For more on the significance and origin of the name, see the commentary below.

22 Note the significance of the phrasing: that men are moving into those lands *again*. We were told as far back as Chapter I about 'the mortal men who lived to the south, and even up the Running river as far as the valley beneath the mountain' in Dale (see p. 71), but the real significance of Tolkien's phrasing is that it gives a sense of underlying history, of more story than can be told in this one book – cf. 'If you had heard only a quarter of what I have (and I have heard only a little tiny bit of what there is to hear)'. Tolkien later changed his ideas about the 'pre-history' of the Anduin vale, as it came to be called; see Appendix A of *The Lord of the Rings* and the essay printed as 'Cirion and Eorl' in *Unfinished Tales* for his final thoughts on the matter.

23 Note that the phrasing of the published text, where the wizard feels 'dreadfully afraid, wizard though he was' at hearing the warg-talk, is absent in the original, first appearing in the typescript (1/1/56:7). Bladorthin still calls the goblins 'naughty little boys' to 'show them he was not afraid of them (though of course he was, wizard though he might be)' a few pages later, in a passage that changed little from manuscript to publication aside from the alteration of 'afraid' to 'frightened' and a slight adjustment of the punctuation, both done at the time of the First Typescript. The epithet 'naughty little boys' was challenged by Arthur Ransome in his 1937 letter to Tolkien, but while he made most of the other changes Ransome suggested Tolkien kept the phrasing here. For more on the Ransome letter, see Appendix IV.

24 Originally this sentence ran 'They kill things for their food, but only'. Left unfinished, it was abbreviated to simply 'They kill.' Later, perhaps feeling that this was too bald, Tolkien added '& hunt' to the sentence above the cancelled passage.

25 Later 'summer' was changed to 'late summer' in pencil, probably at the time of the creation of the First Typescript. This change creates difficulties, however, as one would expect berries to be in fruit by 'late summer', and we are explicitly told earlier in this same chapter that it's too early for blackberries (cf. p. 201). Such a time-frame would also, given the length of their time in Mirkwood, give some nuts time to ripen while they were in the forest, yet we are told this is not the case. Tolkien solved this problem by changing the phrase 'late summer' – the original reading in the First Typescript (typescript page 56; 1/1/56:8) – to '*high* summer'; the later reading then appears in both the Second Typescript (1/1/37:8) and published book (DAA.150).

The comment about there having been 'little rain' also seems odd in light of the torrential storm of two days before, when 'two thunderstorms . . . come up from East *and West* and make war' (p. 128, emphasis mine). Still, Tolkien is careful to specify that he was speaking of 'this side of the mountains', and perhaps he was considering having the eastern slopes of the Misty Mountains fall into a rain shadow.

26 The typescript adds 'and they soon had a plan which seemed to them most amusing' (1/1/56:9).

27 This passage was revised and expanded to read as follows:

> . . . could see the goblins dancing round & round *in a ring* like people round a mid summer bonfire *while some were hacking at the trunks of the trees they were clinging to.* Outside the *ring of* dancers *and the goblins with axes* stood the wolves at a respectful distance . . .

The lines about the goblins hacking at the tree trunks survived into the page proofs, where this entire paragraph was so heavily revised that Tolkien recopied it neatly onto a separate page for the benefit of the typesetters, in the process achieving the text of this passage exactly as it stands today (see DAA.151): '. . . like people round a midsummer bonfire. Outside the ring of danc*ing warriors* with *spears and* axes stood the wolves at a respectful distance . . .' (Marq. 1/2/2: page 111 & rider). Thus the 'goblins . . . with axes' survive into the published book, although their significance had disappeared.

28 This poem is written directly into the manuscript and has its last two lines crowded into the right margin, with their proper placement indicated by an arrow. Given this roughness, it may represent the initial draft.

It's possible to catch an echo in these lines of Lewis Carroll's poem 'Little Birds' from *Sylvie and Bruno Concluded* [1893]. While the verbal echoes are slight, we know that Tolkien was fond of that poem (it 'formed part of his large repertoire of occasional recitation', according to Christopher Tolkien – HME IX, Foreword, page x), and he had one of his characters in *The Notion Club Papers* quote from it. See also p. 660 and Nt 30 on p. 65.

29 Unlike the preceding poem, which shows the hesitations of direct composition, this second goblin-poem is a clean copy with only one (marginal) change. It seems probable that it was copied into the manuscript from a separate rough draft that has not survived, as comparison with other poems in the *Hobbit* Ms. shows this was Tolkien's regular practice.

30 This incomplete sentence, the paragraph it is in, and the first three sentences of the following paragraph (everything before '[But] Down swept some of the eagles') were all struck out and replaced by the following, the first paragraph of which was written in the top margin and the second crowded into the left margin:

> There was a howl of anger and surprise [<when> >] from the goblins. But the Lord of Eagles swept back again. Bladorthin had spoken to him and he cried to [his >] the great birds that were with him, and down they came like huge black shadows.
>
> The wolves howled, and gnashed their teeth. The goblins yelled and stamped with rage, waving their tall spears in the air.

The unfinished thought clearly had been a tactical observation that the goblins would have been better able to resist the eagles' ambush had they stayed together and kept near the flames.

31 In a rare slip, Tolkien originally wrote 'dwarfs' and only later altered it to his characteristic spelling used elsewhere throughout the book: 'dwarves'.

This entire page (manuscript page 75; I/1/6:13) was subject to extensive small changes which bring the text closer to, but do not yet achieve, the final version.

32 Added in the left margin and marked for insertion at this point:

> He used to feel queer if he looked over the edge of quite a little cliff, & he had never liked climbing trees, (not having had to escape from wolves before). So you can guess how his head swam now,

33 'once upon a time' – despite his praise of this traditional fairy-tale line in 'On Fairy-Stories', Tolkien never used it to begin any of his published fiction, and its occurrence here is one of the very rare uses of it anywhere in his work.

34 In a revision to the manuscript (I/1/6:14), 'men' is changed to 'people', but this emendation is not picked up in either typescript, nor in the published book, all of which have 'men'.

This chapter introduces not one but two new races, both animal in shape but intelligent, having languages of their own. Each has strong ties to myth and folklore on the one hand and to Tolkien's earlier writings on the other; the wolves to Draugluin and Carcharoth, the great guardians of Morgoth and Sauron, and the eagles to Thorondor King of the Eagles and the messengers of Manwë.

(i)
The Wolves

Wolves do not, of course, eat people. But legend and folk-belief has maintained otherwise from time immemorial, from Aesop's fable of 'The Boy Who Cried Wolf' [sixth century BC] through fairy-stories like 'Little Red Riding-Hood' [seventeenth century French] and 'Peter & the Wolf'[1] to the modern day (Saki's 'Esme' and 'The Intruders', Willa Cather's *My Antonia*,[2] Bram Stoker's *Dracula*, and any number of Jack London stories). Perhaps the most famous literary account of a wolf-attack prior to Tolkien's occurs in Defoe's *Robinson Crusoe* [1719] – in the later chapters, after Crusoe's rescue from the island and return to civilization, he and Friday are set upon by a wolf-pack while travelling with a small group through the Pyrenees, repulsing the attack with great difficulty in a battle described with all Defoe's characteristic vigor and attention to detail. Tolkien himself cited S. R. Crockett's *The Black Douglas* [1899], a now justly forgotten novel, as his chief influence on the scene:

> the episode of the 'wargs' (I believe) is in part derived from a scene in S. R. Crockett's *The Black Douglas*, probably his best romance and anyway one that deeply impressed me in school-days, though I have never looked at it again. It includes Gil de Rez[3] as a Satanist.
>
> —JRRT to Michael Tolkien, c. 1967; *Letters* p. 391.

Closer examination of Crockett's book shows that while there is indeed a battle with wolves in it, the scene bears little resemblance to Tolkien's in *The Hobbit* (in fact, it is far closer to the battle outside Moria in *The Lord of the Rings*, which it probably did inspire). In Crockett's historical romance, Chapter XLIX: 'The Battle with the Were-wolves' is devoted to a detailed account of how three Scotsmen (two servants and a cousin of the late Lord of Douglas of the title) are set upon by evil wolves in the forest of Machecoul as they attempt to rescue their dead lord's sister and her maidservant from de Retz, who plans to sacrifice the two in a Satanic ceremony to regain his lost youth. The wolves are led by La Meffraye, a shape-changing witch in de Retz's service,[4] who takes the form of a great she-wolf. But rather than climb trees, as one of the servants prudently advises, the Scots put their backs against a bare lightning-struck pine and wait, watching the wolves muster in a ring all around them before finally charging for an eerily silent attack. The three of them eventually beat off the attack by sheer force of arms. Rather than actual fire, as in Tolkien, the scene is lit by 'the blue leme of summer lightning', also described as 'the wild-fire running about the tree-tops' and '[t]he leaping blue flame of the wild-fire'. The she-wolf (who does not personally take part in the charge, but directs her troops from a safe distance) eventually calls off the attack. The howls fade in the distance, becoming more human-like as they recede (one of the Scots remarks 'these are no common wolves . . . There will be many dead warlocks to-morrow throughout the lands of France'), finally ceasing suddenly at cock-crow.

As this summary should make clear, Tolkien did not follow Crockett's scene either in outline or detail: Tolkien's wolves attack pell-mell and his heroes lack the Scots' idiotic bravado (having considerably more sense), while Crockett's villains do not receive timely aid (as per the wargs' goblin-soldier allies) that requires a *deus ex machina* for the heroes' escape. The only points in common are a wolf-attack in a forest clearing, the uncanny fire (magical but real in Tolkien's case, merely illumination from distant lightning in Crockett's), and the idea that the wolves are a lesser evil in service or allegiance to the real enemy.[5]

Tolkien's wargs owe less to literary tradition than his own imagination, stimulated as always by philology. The word 'Warg' itself is derived from the Old English 'wearg',[6] a word meaning both a literal wolf and also a figurative one, i.e., an outlaw. Clark Hall's *Concise Anglo-Saxon Dictionary* [1894; rev. 4th ed., 1962] defines it as '(wolf), accursed one, outlaw, felon, criminal' and glosses its adjectival forms as 'wicked, cursed, wretched'. Tolkien himself, in a footnote to an unmailed letter, stated that

> The word *Warg* used in *The Hobbit* and the *L. R.* [i.e., *The Lord of the Rings*] for an evil breed of (demonic) wolves is not supposed to be A[nglo]-S[axon] specifically, and is given prim[itive] Germanic form as representing the noun common to the Northmen of these creatures.
>
> —JRRT to Mr. Rang, c. August 1967; *Letters*, p. 381.[7]

He reiterates this point, after distinguishing between the 'internal' history of names within the story[8] and their 'external' history ('the sources from which I, as an author, derived them') in a letter to fellow fantasy author Gene Wolfe:

> *Warg* . . . is an old word for wolf, which also had the sense of an outlaw or hunted criminal. This is its usual sense in surviving texts. [O[ld] E[nglish] *wearg*; O[ld] High German *warg*; O[ld] Norse *varg-r* (also = 'wolf', espec[ially] of legendary kind).] I adopted the word, which had a good sound for the meaning, as a name for this particular brand of demonic wolf in the story.[9]

Note that Tolkien stresses the demonic aspect of these creatures (and, in the Wolfe letter, that of their goblin allies: '*Orc* I derived from Anglo-Saxon, a word meaning a demon, usually supposed to be derived from the Latin Orcus – Hell. But I doubt this . . .'),[10] a feature which seems more in keeping with the wargs of *The Lord of the Rings*, whose bodies melt away with the daylight (cf. Note 5), than the wolves that tree

Gandalf & Company. It could be argued that Tolkien's thinking in the 1960s may have been influenced by his late speculations that the orcs, especially orc-leaders like the Great Goblin, Azog, and Bolg, might have been incarnated evil spirits similar in kind, if less in power, to the balrogs (for more on these 'boldog', see pp. 149 & 139). However, it can also be seen as a return to Tolkien's portrayal of wolves in the early Silmarillion tradition, especially in the figures of Draugluin and Carcharoth.

According to 'The Tale of Tinúviel', the race of wolves was bred by Melko from dogs (thus reversing the actual historical relationship between the two species), making the wargs Mr. Baggins encounters yet another of the Children of Morgoth, in accordance with the pattern throughout this book. In the earliest story, the Cerberus-like guardian of the gates of Angband (or Angamandi, as it was then called) was Karkaras ('Knifefang'), the Father of Wolves (eventually changed, through many intermediary stages, to Carcharoth, 'the Red Maw'). Some characteristics of this monster persisted through all the permutations of the story: that he was greatest of all wolves who ever lived; his role in biting off Beren's hand, swallowing the Silmaril, and eventually giving Beren his mortal wound; his death in the woods of Doriath (originally called Artanor) at the hands of Beren, Huan, and Lúthien's father, his vitals half-devoured by the Silmaril's 'holy magic' (BLT II.31, 33–4, 36–7, 38–9). The most important alteration, his loss of status as the first wolf or Father of Wolves, came through the introduction into the legendarium of a second great wolf, Draugluin, during the later development of the Beren & Lúthien story for 'The Lay of Leithian'. This 'old grey lord/of wolves and beasts of blood abhorred' (lines 2712–2713, HME III.252), whose authority even Carcharoth recognizes and respects (lines 3754ff, HME III.290), is Sauron/Thû's trusted pet 'that fed on flesh of Man and Elf/beneath the chair of Thû himself' (lines 2714–2715, HME III.252). Like Carcharoth, he can speak,[11] perhaps anticipating 'the dreadful wolf-language of the wargs' in *The Hobbit* (p. 204).

The most important of all the legendarium's wolves, however, is Sauron himself; Tolkien even considered having it be Thû the necromancer in wolf-form who devoured Beren's companions one by one in the dungeons beneath Tol-in-Gaurhoth, the Isle of Werewolves (cf. the plot-outline for 'The Lay of Leithian' that Christopher Tolkien refers to as 'Synopsis II', cited on HME III.233). Not only is Thû referred to as 'the Lord of Wolves' but after Draugluin's death at the hands (so to speak) of Huan, Thû takes the form of a demon wolf, hoping thus to fulfill the prophecy of Huan's being slain by 'the mightiest wolf of all'. Thû's identification with wolves in 'The Lay of Leithian', which Tolkien was working on simultaneously with the original drafting of *The Hobbit*, is so great that his title as 'Master of Wolves' almost tends to overwhelm his identification in that work as 'the necromancer'. We should also not forget that after his defeat by Huan and Lúthien he retreats to the forest of Taur-na-Fuin, which Tolkien elsewhere explicitly identified as Mirkwood ('Taur-na-Fuin, which is Mirkwood' – 1937 *Quenta Silmarillion*, HME V.282; see also 'The Disaster of the Gladden Fields', *Unfinished Tales*, page 281), the borders of which Gandalf and Company are approaching when they encounter the wargs. Thus, although Tolkien makes no explicit link in *The Hobbit* between the appearance of the wargs and the proximity of the necromancer's tower, any reader of the older tales and lays coming to *The Hobbit* for the first time would not be surprised to find wolf-packs allied with goblins prowling about near any refuge of The Necromancer.

(ii)
The Eagles

Unlike wolves, who have played the villain in any number of folk and fairy tales, from Aesop to the Reynard the Fox cycle to Brer Rabbit to modern-day stories of the type parodied by Saki's 'The Story of the Good Little Girl' (e.g., 'The Three Little Pigs'), eagles appear in surprisingly few well-known myths and folktales. There is the story of the eagle sent by Zeus to carry off Ganymede the Trojan to be his cup-bearer (a tale which gave its name to the Inklings' favorite pub, The Eagle and Child, whose street-sign illustrates the scene). There is also the grimmer story of another eagle, also sent by Zeus, which each day rips out the liver of the bound titan Prometheus as punishment for his having helped mankind against the Olympians' wishes. Descending from the level of myth to gossip, Sir Thomas Browne reports the old story that an eagle killed the Athenian playwright Æschylus (author of *Agamemnon* and *Prometheus Bound*, d. 456 BC) when, mistaking the great man's bald head for a rock, it dropped a turtle on it from a great height.[12]

Further west and slightly later, this emblem of the King of the Gods came not unnaturally to be identified with the Roman emperor and thence with the empire itself. The imperial eagle was carried on the standards of Roman legions and later adopted in heraldry by all those who claimed to be the heirs of the Caesars: the Holy Roman Emperors of the Middle Ages and later the Emperors of Austria, the German Kaisers, and the Russian Czars ('Kaiser,' 'Czar,' and 'Tsar' simply being the German, Russian, and Polish equivalents of 'Caesar'). Indeed, so prevalent was this usage that it is said one of Nostradamus's predictions about 'an eagle rising in the east' was taken in World War I as a sign of victory by superstitiously minded advocates of virtually all the combatants.

Meanwhile, Christian iconography associated the eagle with John the Evangelist, Tolkien's favorite apostle.[13] Tolkien also seems to have been influenced by the medieval bestiary tradition (from which he drew the inspiration for at least two of his poems written in the 1920s, 'Fastitocalon' and 'Oliphaunt'), with its curious and characteristic mix of allegorical significance and realistic detail – although much of the latter strikes a modern reader as decidedly fantastic. Bestiary lore (accurately) ascribed fantastically keen eyesight to the eagle: thus Chaucer's *Parliament of Fowls* [circa 1378–81], a literary work that combined the bestiary tradition with that of courtly love, described the eagle as 'the ryal [royal] egle . . . That with his sharpe lok perseth the sunne' (lines 330–331).[14] The idea that eagles could look at the sun without blinking, which derives from the Bestiaries,[15] made its way directly into Tolkien's text (cf. p. 206: 'eyes that could look straight at the sun unblinking'). Similarly, Chaucer describes the eagle as King of the Birds, a title Tolkien notes was later bestowed upon the eagle-lord of our story (cf. p. 229).

Outside the rather arcane bestiary tradition and Christian iconography (in, for example, *The Book of Kells* [eighth century]), however, eagles seem not to have figured greatly in the medieval imagination. While the eagle remained of great heraldic significance, medieval romance favored the hawk or falcon, those familiar birds used in the noble art of falconry, over their grander cousins.[16] Aside from American Indian traditions, there seems to have been little fairy-tale or folklore resonance to eagles, other than the widespread folk belief that eagles carry off lambs and even sheep (used even today by many ranchers to justify the illegal poisoning and shooting of protected endangered species). Tolkien incorporates this enduring superstition directly into his text, putting it into the mouth of the Lord of the Eagles himself: 'they will think we are after their lambs – or their babies. And at other times they might be right.' Interestingly enough, this alarming statement was toned down in the revisions, with the 'Ganymede' element being taken out before the First Typescript (where it's simply the lambs they're after – cf. Marq. 1/1/56:11 and 1/1/37:10–11) and the *lambs* changed to *sheep* in the page proofs (Marq. 1/2/2 page 116). Perhaps Tolkien wanted to emphasize the size and majesty of these great birds; perhaps he wanted to give another example of the divisions between the good peoples of the story (thus laying the groundwork for the wood-elf episode and Siege of the Lonely Mountain that were to follow). Still, he makes it clear that, while not 'kindly birds' (as the published text puts it), they are nevertheless foes of evil who put a stop to the goblins' 'wickedness' whenever they can.

Indeed, far from being Children of Morgoth (as has been the case with most of the other races the hobbit has encountered since leaving his home, always exempting the elves and elf-friends), a long-established tradition in Tolkien's work going back to *The Book of Lost Tales* portrays eagles as the messengers of Manwë,[17] guardians of Gondolin, bitter foes of Melko. We are told that Manwë created the eagles himself (1926 'Sketch of the Mythology', HME IV.23; cf. also the 1930 *Quenta*, HME IV.102), who thus stand in direct opposition to Melkor the Morgoth's forces. It was 'Sorontur King of Eagles' who delivered the message of banishment to Melko after the Two Trees were destroyed and the Silmarils stolen (and told him of the murder of his herald by the Valar):

> and between that evil one and Sorontur has there ever since been hate and war, and that was most bitter when Sorontur and his folk fared to the Iron Mountains and there abode, watching all that Melko did.
>
> —'The Theft of Melko', BLT I.149.

Sorontur (better known by his Gnomish name, Thorndor, and its later form Thorondor) and his eagles actually nest in Thangorodrim's upper regions, 'out of the reach of Orc and Balrog' ('Sketch of the Mythology', HME IV.23), the better to keep watch on Melko's doings. From here he witnesses Fingolfin's duel with Melko and sallies forth to mar the dark lord's face and rescue the fallen elvenking's body ('The Lay of Leithian', lines 3608–3639; HME III.286–7). Later the eagles move their eyries to the Encircling Mountains surrounding Gondolin, to help guard this last elven refuge against Melko's spies ('Sketch', HME IV.34). While they cannot prevent the fall of the city, the eagles do save the refugees from fallen Gondolin as they battle goblins and a balrog in a mountain pass in a scene strikingly similar to that in *The Hobbit* but predating it by more than a decade:

> . . . Now Galdor and Glorfindel held their own despite the surprise of assault, and many of the Orcs were struck into the abyss; but the falling of rocks was like to end all their valour, and the flight from Gondolin to come to ruin. The moon about that hour rose above the pass, and the gloom somewhat lifted, for his pale light filtered into dark places . . . Then arose Thorndor, King of the Eagles, and he loved not Melko, for Melko had caught many of his kindred and chained them against sharp rocks to squeeze from them the magic words whereby he might learn to fly . . .
>
> Now when the clamour from the pass rose to his great eyrie he said: 'Wherefore are these foul things, these Orcs of the hills, climbed near to my throne; and why do the sons of the Noldoli [the Noldor] cry out in the low places for fear of the children of Melko the accursed? Arise O Thornhoth ['eagle-folk'], whose beaks are of steel and whose talons swords!'
>
> Thereupon there was a rushing like a great wind in rocky places, and the Thornhoth, the people of the Eagles, fell on those Orcs who had scaled above the path, and tore their faces and their hands and flung them to the rocks of Thorn Sir far below . . .
>
> —'The Fall of Gondolin' [c. 1916–17]; BLT II.193.

The eagles even found their way into the story of Beren and Lúthien, rescuing them from certain capture after their escape from Morgoth's halls. Their entry into the story is a relatively late one, however – the unfinished 'Lay of Leithian' breaks off just at the point where Beren loses his hand, and the eagles enter in only via a pencilled rider to the outline for the three unwritten cantos that were to conclude the poem:

> . . . Thunder and lightning. Beren lies dying before the gate. Tinúviel's song as she kisses his hand and prepares to die. Thorondor comes down and bears them amid the lightning that <?stabs> at them like spears and a hail of arrows from the battlements. They pass above Gondolin and Lúthien sees the white city far below, <?gleaming> like a lily in the valley. Thorondor sets her down in Brethil.
>
> —HME III.309.

Tolkien himself felt that the eagles were a dangerous device, apt to be overused as a *deus ex machina*; he deplored their ubiquitous appearance throughout the first movie script for a potential *Lord of the Rings* movie sent to him in 1958 (JRRT to Forrest J. Ackerman, June 1958; cf. *Letters* p. 271).[18] Indeed, in *The Hobbit* they appear only twice and in *The Lord of the Rings* only three times, with two of those episodes being off-stage (the rescue of Gandalf from Orthanc and the retrieval of his body from atop Zirakzigil).

Close examination of the Silmarillion texts shows the danger: the more times Tolkien re-wrote the stories, the more new episodes featuring the eagles worked their way in. Thus in the 1930 *Quenta* not only are all but one of the previous references intact[19] – Manwë's sending forth the Eagles, Thorondor's maiming of Morgoth and rescue of Fingolfin's body, the rescue of Beren and Lúthien before the gates of Thangorodrim,[20] the removal from Thangorodrim to the Encircling Mountains to help ward Gondolin and guard the cairn of Fingolfin, their intervention at the pass on behalf of the fugitives of Gondolin – but we are also told that Melian summoned Thorondor to bear Lúthien to Valinor after Beren died (1930 *Quenta*, HME IV.115) and that the eagle-king aided in Fingon's rescue of Maidros when he hung chained to the cliff-face of Thangorodrim (1930 *Quenta*, HME IV.102) – the latter tale seems to have entered in via the 1926 'Sketch of the Mythology'; cf. HME IV.23).

Clearly, Tolkien was fond of his eagles and found it difficult to keep them out of each of the major stories that make up the Silmarillion cycle. When he was asked to add colour illustrations to *The Hobbit* for the first American edition, one of the five watercolours was devoted to a beautiful painting of an eagle of the Misty Mountains.[21] They also appear, of course, on the dust jacket – where they are placed in opposition to Smaug the dragon – and in the black and white interior illustration 'The Misty Mountains looking West from the Eyrie towards Goblin Gate', which serves as a tailpiece to Chapter VI (DAA.158, H-S#110 & #111).

Given Tolkien's continued interest in the eagles, it is odd that in The Battle of Five Armies the wargs and goblins each count as a 'people' for purposes of the tally yet the eagles do not. Perhaps there are simply too few eagles present to be described as an 'army' (as seems to be the case with Beorn/Medwed: doughty though he be, there is but one of him), but the designation is made all the more curious by the importance of the role they play in the combat, which is strikingly similar to that described in the passage from 'The Fall of Gondolin' quoted above.

The most unusual feature of the whole eagle scene, however, is the unusual shift in point of view away from Thorin & Company for four paragraphs – an entire Ms. page. For the most part, Tolkien is careful to stay with his main characters; the only similar shifts occur late in the book when the story divides between the dwarves and hobbit inside the Lonely Mountain and the dragon flying around outside before he flies away to attack Lake Town. The dramatic excellence of the cutaway shows that he was right in departing here from his usual practice, but we should not fail to notice how unusual it is, nor to give Tolkien credit for abandoning a favorite point-of-view when doing so will advance the story's dramatic impact.

Finally, we should note the mythic resonance of Bladorthin's parting words to the eagles on p. 229 in what became the early part of the next chapter. 'May the wind under your wings bear you where the sun sails and the moon walks' sounds fanciful, but in Tolkien's cosmology it has concrete aptness. His myth of the Sun and Moon, derived largely I believe from Egyptian cosmology (including the journey of the sun-boat through the Duat or Underworld from west to east each night), and his various geographical writings and drawings that make up the *Ambarkanta* or Shape of the World (reproduced in *The Shaping of Middle-earth,* HME IV) specify that in his subcreated world the atomosphere is divided into several discrete layers. The lower of these, Wilwa (later renamed Vista) composes the lowest level, the air that we breathe. Wilwa is furthermore subdivided into Aiwenórë or 'Birdland' and Fanyamar or 'Cloudhome'. Above this lies a region variously called Silma, Ilma, and Ilmen at different stages in the mythology's evolution. Silma/Ilmen is glossed 'Sky, Heaven' and defined as 'The region above the air . . . Here only the stars and Moon and Sun can fly' (HME IV.241). We are specifically told in the *Ambarkanta* that 'From [Wilwa >] Vista there is no outlet nor escape save for the servants of Manwë, or for such as he gives powers like to those of his people, that can sustain themselves in Ilmen . . .' (HME IV.236). The wizard's words thus obliquely tie into the cosmology of the created world and reaffirm that the Great Eagles are indeed the eagles of Manwë, either spirits incarnated as birds or their (mortal) descendants, just as the wargs are descended from spirits of evil that had taken wolf-form. The eagles and the wargs neatly counterpoise each other, and each play in our story what had already by 1930 become their 'traditional' roles in the stories that comprised Tolkien's legendarium: the one to threaten the heroes and the other to intervene when all hope had been lost and deliver them from evil, almost as a visible grace. *Deus ex* indeed.

NOTES

1 This Russian folktale inspired a famous musical work of the same name by Prokofiev that appeared in the same year that Tolkien submitted *The Hobbit* for publication [1936]; it is probably best known today through the Disney cartoon adaptation [1946].

2 Cather has a Russian immigrant describe a scene where a sledgeful of people chased by starving wolves were saved by tossing a baby overboard, a traditional scene that has often been the subject of melodramatic paintings and prints.

3 This historical figure, more accurately known as Gilles de Retz, was one of Joan of Arc's lieutenants who later became notorious as one of history's first recorded serial killers, being executed for sorcery, heresy, and the murder of children in 1440. De Retz, who may or may not have been guilty of the charges, is generally held to have been the original of the Bluebeard legend.

4 Crockett's La Meffraye (whose wolf-form is named Astarte) is reminiscent of the wolf-woman in MacDonald's 'Nycteris and Photogen' [1882] (a story also known as 'The Day Boy and the Night Girl'); MacDonald's tale probably inspired Crockett's characterization of the wolf-woman. MacDonald also wrote another story about a female werewolf, 'The Gray Wolf' [1871]; probably his single best short story, it depicts not an evil witch but a wistful, forlorn young woman cut off from love and normal human contact by her lycanthropy.

5 By contrast, the wolf-attack in 'A Journey in the Dark' (*LOTR*.314–17) is much closer to Crockett's in conception and detail. Forced by terrain to fight on the ground, the Company of the Ring see the wolves massing in a great circle beyond their defensive ring, with 'a great dark wolf-shape . . . summoning his pack to the assault'; we get the same sudden grey wall of attackers, the desperate thrusts and stabs by the defenders (in this case, Aragorn, Boromir, Gimli, and Legolas), and the withdrawal of the wolves before dawn. Also, it is made clear that these are no ordinary wolves, as their bodies melt away with the dawn (Crockett's 'were-wolves', while enchanted, left their bodies behind when killed, as did the wargs of *The Hobbit*).† The chief difference between the scene in *The Lord of the Rings* and that in *The Black Douglas* is in the presence of Gandalf and his use once again of magical fire to turn the tide in the heroes' favour.

† Otherwise Medwed could not skin one, as he does in the next chapter (cf. p. 241).

6 As noted above (Text Note 21), Tolkien originally wrote the word as 'weorg' on its first occurrence on manuscript page 69, then overwrote it as 'warg', the form used thereafter. It is possible that I have misread the ligatures and that the original word underneath the alteration was 'wearg' but I do not think so; both Taum Santoski and I independently read the second vowel as 'o'.

7 Tolkien himself goes on to note that the word *warg* seemed to have caught on' and cited its use in a science fiction story. This was Gene Wolfe's 'Trip, Trap', which appeared in the hardcover anthology *Orbit 2: The Best New Science Fiction of the Year*, ed. Damon Knight [1967], pages 110–44. The relevant passage occurs in a conversation between an archeologist and an alien:

> . . . I got a lesson in the zoology of the planet here, for the natives had been hunting and were returning with their butchered victims. Several of their specimens looked like creatures a wise young scholar would not want to study any other way, however much one might regret their demise. I particularly remember a naked-looking animal like a saber-toothed lemur. The natives called it *Gonoth-hag* – the Hunting-devil. There was also what looked like a very big wild dog or wolf, a *Warg*, formidable looking, but not beside the *Gonoth-hag*.

I am grateful to Richard West and Douglas Anderson for tracking down this reference for me.

Tolkien's wargs have since been disseminated to a wide audience through the medium of the fantasy role-playing game *Dungeons & Dragons* and its hundreds of associated novels and adventures, under the variant spelling 'worg' (defined in the *Monster Manual* as evil, intelligent wolves with their own language who sometime serve as goblin-mounts). This is only one of a number of Tolkienisms in the game, joining races like elves, half-elves, dwarves (so spelled), half-orcs, and halflings (divided into three types: 'Tallfellows' [= Fallohides], 'Hairfoots' [= Harfoots], & 'Stouts' [= Stoors]); monsters like wraiths, wights, orcs, goblins, 'treants' (tree-ents), and of course dragons, and treasures such as rings of invisibility and 'mithral' <sic> mail.

8 A good example is the change in the *Lord of the Rings* drafts from *the Kingdom of Ond* to *Ondor* to *Gondor*.

9 J. R. R. Tolkien, letter to Gene Wolfe, 7th November, 1966; reproduced in *Vector*, the Journal of the British SF Association, #67/68, Spring 1974, page 9. I am grateful to Douglas Anderson and Richard West for helping me confirm the exact quote.

10 Ibid. Tolkien may also have been influenced here by the bestiary tradition, which portrayed the wolf as an emblem of the devil; cf. this passage from a twelfth-century bestiary: 'The devil bears the similitude of a wolf: he who is always looking over the human race with his evil eye, and darkly prowling round the sheepfolds of the faithful so that he may afflict and ruin their souls' (Cambridge University Library Ms.

II.4.26, edited [1928] by M. R. James and translated [1954] by T. H. White as *The Book of Beasts*, p. 59).

11 Cf. BLT II.33 and HME III.290–1 (lines 3754–3789). This feature is absent from the 1930 *Quenta* (HME IV.112–13), perhaps due to compression rather than deliberate alteration, but it appears obliquely in the published 1977 *Silmarillion*:

> 'Carcharoth . . . was filled with doubt . . . Therefore . . . he denied them entry, *and bade them stand* . . .'
>
> —*Silm.*180; italics mine.

12 This bit of pseudohistory was picked up by fantasy author Terry Pratchett and woven into the climax of his Discworld novel *Small Gods* [1992].

13 JRRT to Amy Ronald, letter of 2nd January 1969, *Letters* p. 397; see also Humphrey Carpenter, *The Inklings* [1978], page 51. The four gospel writers were commonly depicted together as a man (Matthew), a lion (Mark), a bull (Luke), and an eagle (John).

14 Geoffrey Chaucer, *Parliament of Fowls*, in *The Complete Poetry and Prose of Geoffrey Chaucer*, ed. John H. Fisher [2nd edition, 1989]. All references are drawn from this excellent edition.

15 T. H. White, *The Book of Beasts*, page 107. White points out in a footnote that eagles can in fact look at the sun without blinking due to a nictitating membrane or inner eyelid (ibid.).

16 One example is the legend of the Watching of the Hawk; if a knight can stay awake beside the bird for a set period (usually seven days and nights, but sometimes three, and in one case a single night), a lady (a fay) will appear at the end of that time and grant him whatever he wishes. Sometimes, overwhelmed by her beauty, he asks for the lady's favors – she grants them, but such encounters always bring future disaster; the wiser ask for prosperity, a magic purse, or some other more worldly reward. This motif appears in *The Travels of Sir John Mandeville* [written before 1366] (Chapter 16), in William Morris's *The Earthly Paradise* [1865] ('July' section), and in E. R. Eddison's *The Worm Ouroboros* [1922] (Chapter X). I am indebted to Paul Thomas's endnotes to the 1991 edition of Eddison's work for drawing my attention to Mandeville.

17 '. . . upon Taniquetil was a great abode raised up for Manwë and a watchtower set. Thence did he speed his darting hawks and receive them on his return, and thither fared often in later days Sorontur King of Eagles whom Manwë gave much might and wisdom' ('The Coming of the Valar', BLT I.73).

Like Zeus, Manwë is both a sky-god and the king of the gods; both reign from atop a holy mountaintop (Olympus and Taniquetil, respectively) over a sometimes fractious family of gods, using great eagles as their messengers. The resemblance between the Valar and the Olympians was much greater in the earliest versions of the stories (e.g., *The Book of Lost Tales*), where the Valar were actually called 'gods' and their family relationships – e.g., who were the siblings, spouses, and children of whom – were much stronger. Later revisions made the Valar less 'human' and more remote, less like gods and more like angels – particularly Manwë, who is transformed from the well-intentioned but ineffectual figure of the early tales, much given to hand-wringing and lamentation, to the remote but wise viceroy of Ilúvatar in Arda.

18 The complete Zimmerman script, with Tolkien's annotations, is now in the Tolkien Collection at Marquette.

19 The exception is Thorondor's delivery of the message of banishment to Melkor, which dropped out of the story after *The Book of Lost Tales*; no mention is made of this episode in 'The Sketch of the Mythology' (cf. HME IV.16) or later texts.

20 Christopher Tolkien notes that this detail is a later addition to the manuscript; cf. HME IV.115, note 11.

21 This painting is included in the American 40th and 50th anniversary editions (the green and gold slipcased sets, respectively); it is also reproduced, with information of Tolkien's art sources for the piece, in *The Annotated Hobbit* (plate two [top]) and in *Artist & Illustrator* (H-S#113).

Chapter VII

MEDWED

The text continues on from the middle of the same page (manuscript page 77; Marq. 1/1/7:1), but at a slightly smaller indentation. This, and a skipped line with a short (1½ inch) horizontal line centered in it between this and the preceding paragraph, seem to indicate a slight pause in the composition – probably no more than a single night, but nevertheless marking a separation point that later grew to become a chapter opening.

The next morning he woke up with the eastern [> early] sun in his eyes. He jumped up to look at the time, and go and put his kettle on – and found he wasn't at home at all. So he sat down again, and wished he could have a wash, and a brush. He didn't get toast, nor tea, nor bacon. Only cold mutton. And after that he had to get ready for a fresh start. This time he was allowed to climb on an eagle's back and cling on between the wings. The air rushed over him, and he shut his eyes. The dwarves were crying farewells and promising to repay the Lord of Eagles if ever they could; then off went fifteen eagles into the air.

The sun was still close to the eastern edge of things. The morning was cool, and mists were in the valleys & hollows and twined here & there among the peaks & pinnacles of the mountains. [But soon >] When Bilbo opened an eye to peep they [> the eagles] were already very high up and the world was far away, and the mountains falling back behind them into the distance. He shut his eyes again and held on tighter.

'Don't pinch' said his eagle. 'You need not be frightened like a rabbit.[TN1] It is a fair morning, and little wind. What is finer than flying.' Bilbo would have liked to say 'a warm bath, and breakfast on the lawn afterwards'[TN2] but he said nothing at all, & let go his clutch just a teeny-weeny bit.

After a good while the eagles must have seen [far >] the point they were making for even from their great height. They began to go down circling round in great circles. For a long while they did this, then Bilbo opened his eyes again. The rough feet of the mountains were left behind. The earth was much nearer now, and below them were trees, oaks and elms probably, and wide green lands, and a river running through it all. But cropping out of the ground, right in the path of the stream which looped itself round it, was a rock

– almost a hill of stone, like a last outpost of the mountains, or a large piece cast miles into the plain by some giant among giants. Now quickly down to the top of this the eagles swooped one by one and set down their passengers.

'Farewell' they said 'where ever you fare, till your homes [> nests > eyries] receive you at the journey's end'. This is a polite thing to say among eagles.

'May the wind under your wings bear you [as >] where the sun sails and the moon walks' said Bladorthin, who knew the correct answer.[TN3]

And so they parted. And though the Lord of the Eagles became king of the [> all] Birds in after days and wore a gold crown[TN4] ([*added*: made] of the gold given him by Bladorthin in remembrance), Bilbo never saw them again.[TN5] But he didn't forget them.

There was [a] flat place on the top of the hill of stone, and a well worn path with many steps leading down it, to the river side, and a ford of huge boulders which led across to the grass land beyond the river. There was a little cave (a wholesome one) with a pebbly floor at the foot of the hill opposite the boulder-ford. Here the party gathered and discussed what was to be done.

The text continues without a break, but I interrupt it at this point to give the First Outline – at any rate, the earliest surviving one. Merely a brief, sketchy list of reminders to himself that Tolkien jotted down on a loose sheet of paper (Marq. 1/1/23:1),[TN6] it records episodes and some details that would occur in upcoming chapters.

Medwed the bear.
Mirkwood & <pygmies>.
disappearance of Bladorthin.
Long wanderings of the dwarves.
<chestnuts>
[spring >] Long Lake
<capture> by the <Sea> elves.

swans Mirkwood
<ball of twine>
dwarves beards

Not all of the ideas hinted at in this list of motifs and incidents are now recoverable, but the general outline of the tale is clear: the meeting with Medwed (Beorn) would shortly follow, prior to the wizard's departure and their subsequent travails in Mirkwood. If the ideas are more or less in sequence, as seems to be the case, the 'disappearance' of Bladorthin suggests that the wizard would leave the party *after* they had entered Mirkwood, and that his absence would occur suddenly and inexplicably. Originally the 'long wanderings' were intended to be of much greater duration than came to be the case in the published text; the cancelled reference to 'spring' probably refers to the coming of the next year's springtime while they are still lost without their guide in Mirkwood. The added reference to the dwarves' beards might be another allusion to this (i.e., their beards growing long in their travels, à la 'Rip Van Winkle'[TN7]), or it might be a glimpse of the spider-story (cf. Chapter VIII). The chestnuts (if that is indeed the correct reading for this nigh-illegible word) probably form their food during their wanderings once the provisions they brought with them give out; starvation in the forest remained a serious threat right into the published book (paralleling an important folklore motif found in 'Hansel & Gretel', 'The Babes in the Woods', and elsewhere).

The 'swans' vanished from the story without a trace; whether the dwarves were eventually to follow swans from the marshes to the Long Lake as Tuor follows swans in 'The Fall of Gondolin' (BLT II.152) or simply saw swans (or swan-boats; see the illustration on p. 244 of *The Annotated Hobbit*) on the lake once they got there is now impossible to say. The 'ball of twine' anticipates the Theseus theme with Bilbo's ball of spider-thread that plays a large part in the manuscript of the Mirkwood chapter – an important scene that did not make it into the published book. The party's capture by elves is already foreseen, but here it seems to follow their belated arrival at the Long Lake. The reference to the Sea-elves, rather than the Wood-elves, is at first surprising but upon closer examination turns out to fit well not just with Tolkien's concepts at the time but even with the published *Silmarillion*; see my commentary following Chapter IX. Note that the outline does not carry the story all the way to the end of the tale – it mentions nothing about the dragon and quest's end, for example – but it does contain the seeds for the next four chapters.

The text continues at the start of a fresh page (manuscript page 79; Marq. 1/1/7:3):

'I always meant to see you all safe [*added*: (if possible)] over the mountains' said the wizard. 'And more by good luck than by good management,[TN8] have done it. But we are now a deal further than I meant to go, for after all this is not my adventure.[TN9] I said I would get a burglar to help you, and I have, but I didn't say I would come burgling with you.'

'Still you are in an awkward plight, and so am I. We have no food, no ponies (except shanks'[TN10]) – and you don't know where you are. Now I can tell you that. You are miles south now [> still] of the path you would have followed, if we hadn't met the goblins. Very few

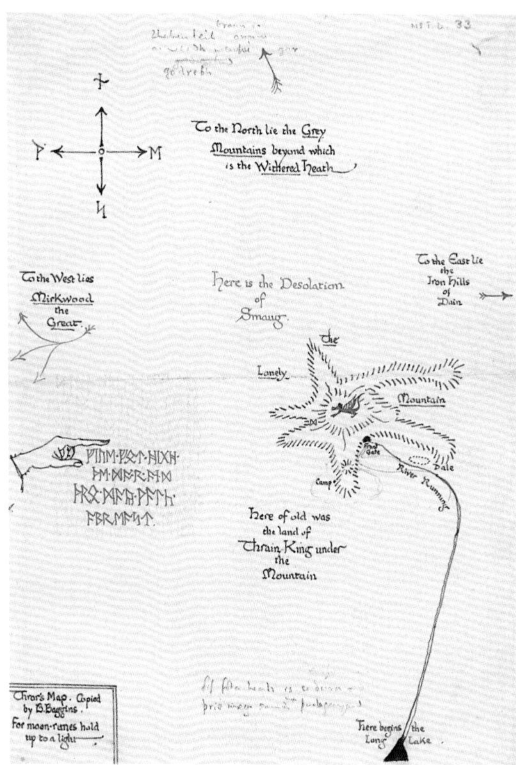

Left Thror's Map I.
This version ('Copied by B. Baggins') retains the northward orientation of Fimbulfambi's Map.

Below The 'home manuscript' version of the Mirkwood/Wilderland map, with Bilbo's outward journey marked in red.

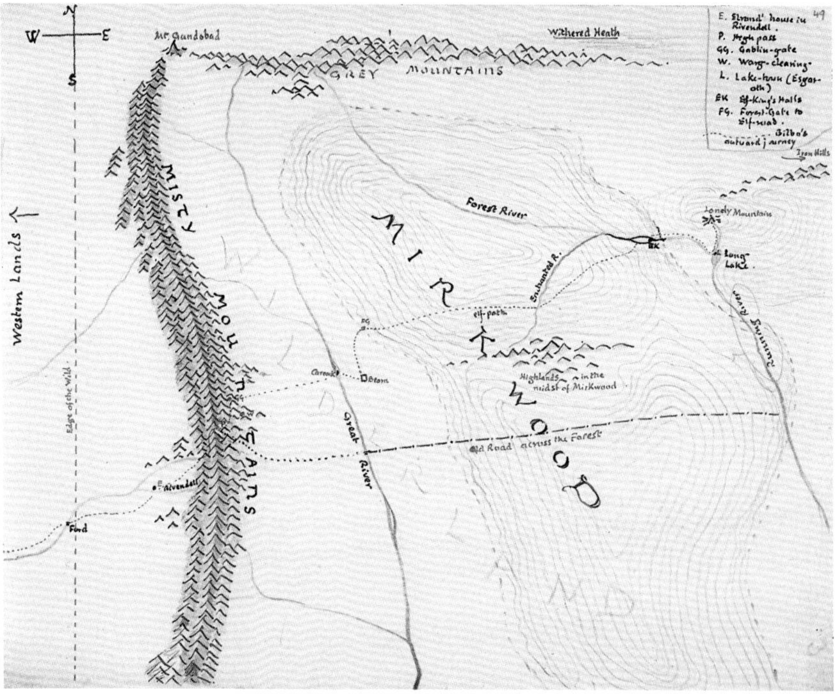

PLATE II

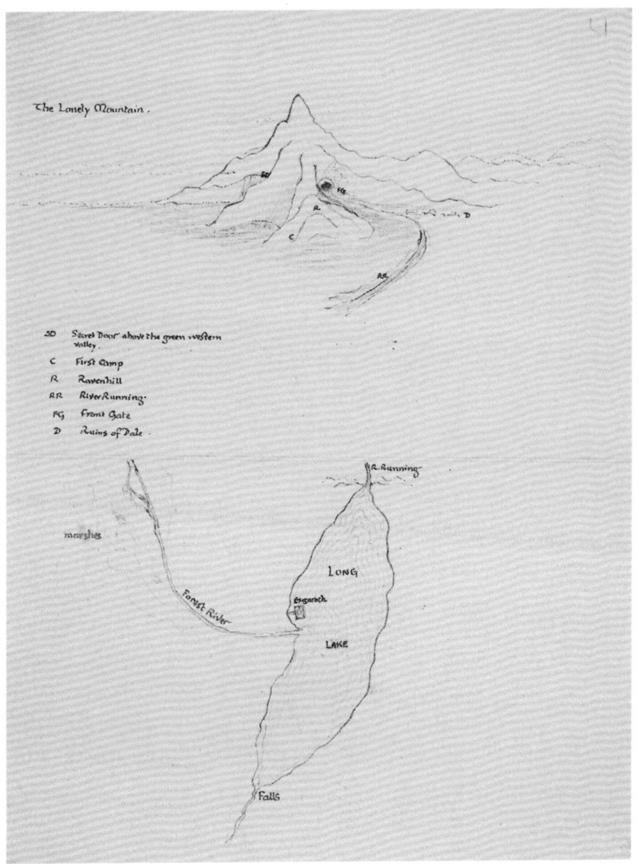

Above The Long Lake and Lonely Mountain. One of the set of maps accompanying the 'home manuscript'.

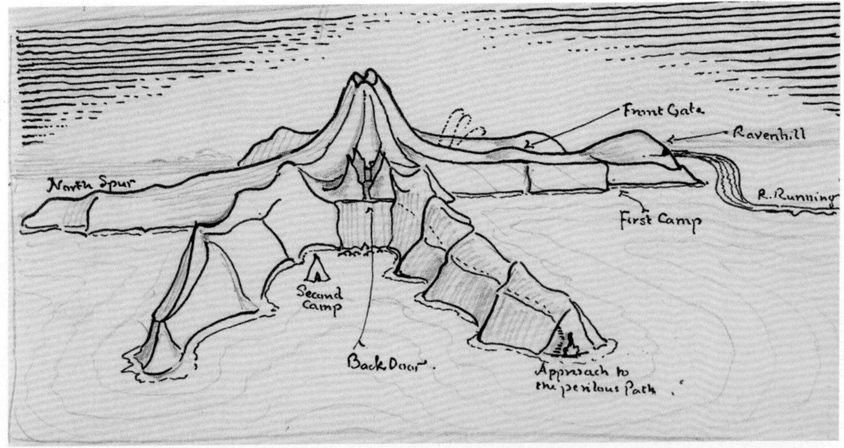

Above A schematic view of the Lonely Mountain from the West looking East.

PLATE III

Left 'One Morning early in the Quiet of the World': Gandalf (and adventure) approach the unsuspecting Bilbo's door.

Below Gandalf on the doorstep at Bag-End.

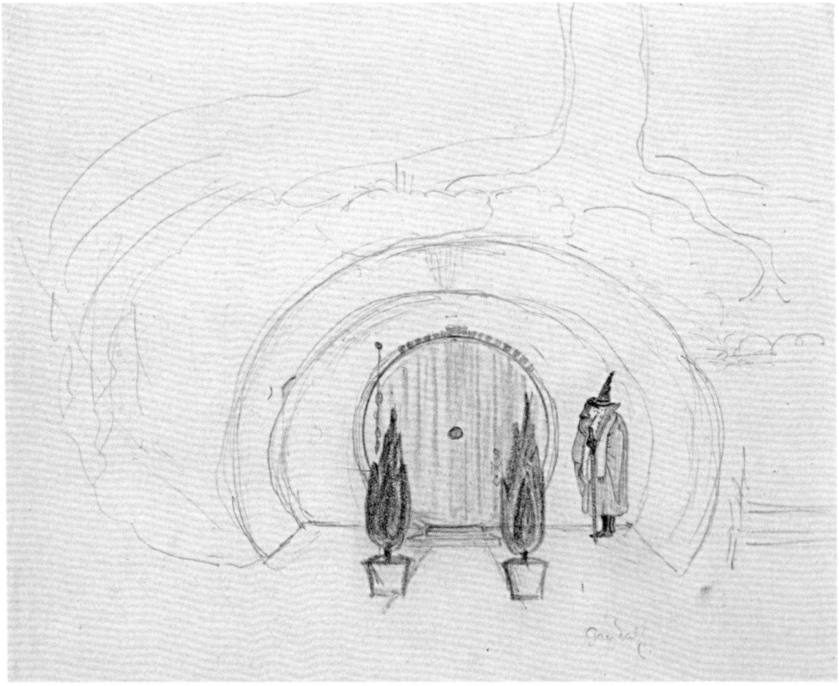

PLATE IV

Left 'The Hill: Hobbiton', showing the path Bilbo ran down from his front door in the distance to the Great Mill in the foreground.

Right 'Trolls' Hill': a mood piece showing the distant firelight that lured the dwarves to near-disaster.

The Three Trolls are turned to Stone

Above 'The Three Trolls are turned to Stone': note Bilbo caught in the bushes left of centre.

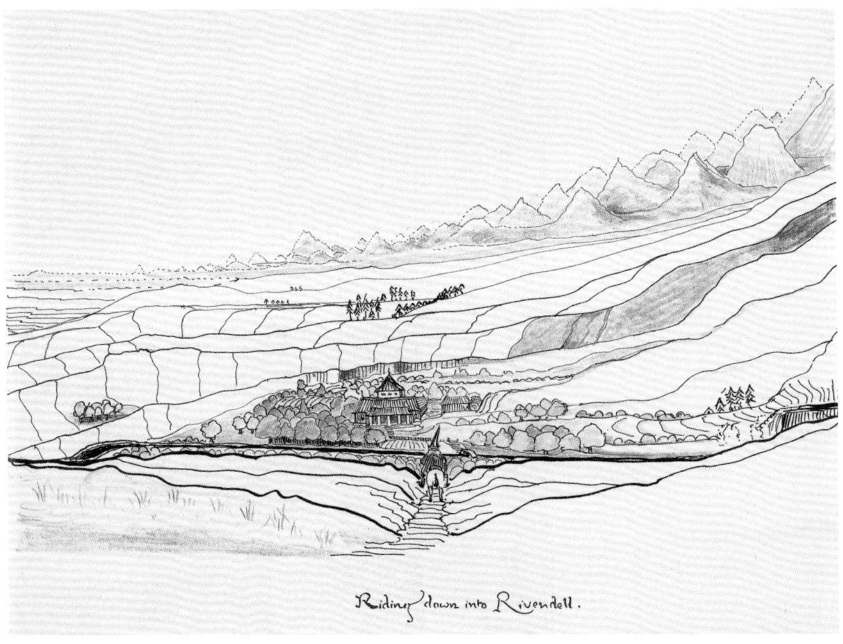
Riding down into Rivendell.

Above 'Riding down into Rivendell': Elrond's valley revealed among the desolate lands all around.

PLATE VI

Left The 1932 Father Christmas Letter.

Below Detail showing Smaug painted on the cave wall and Gollum peering around the corner.

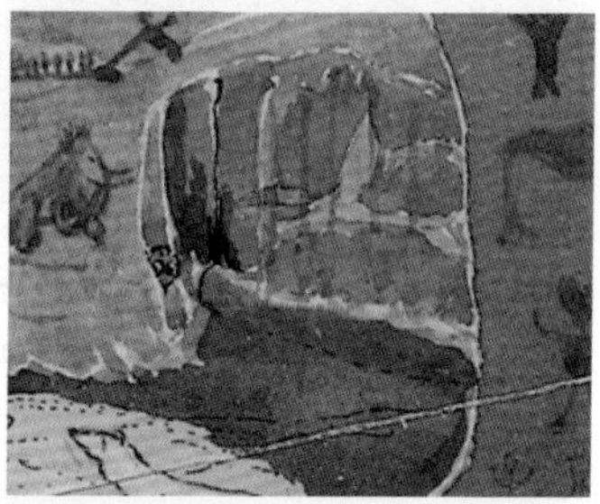

Right 'Firelight in Beorn's house': an alternate view, directly based on a re-creation of Hrolf Kraki's Hall (Heorot).

Above The lost Mirkwood halftone, based on Tolkien's earlier picture of Taur-na-Fuin.

Right Detail showing a Mirkwood spider.

Above Night-time view of the Elf-hill in Mirkwood. Note the cobwebs to left and right.

Above Barrel-rider: unfinished pastel of Bilbo's arrival at the huts of the raft-elves.

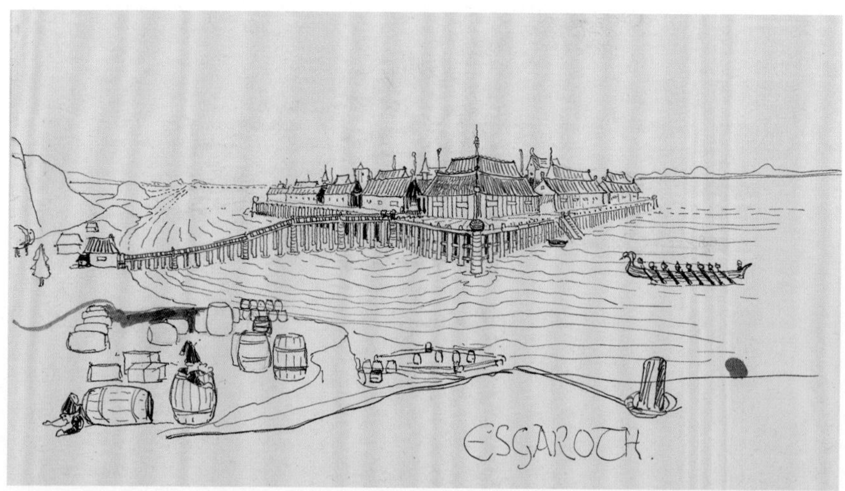

Above 'Esgaroth': alternate image of Lake Town. Note the dwarves' heads emerging from the barrels to the left.

people live in these parts, unless they have come into it since I was here last, which is some long years ago. But there is a person I know, who lives not far away.[TN11] He made these steps on the hill.[TN12] But he doesn't come here often, so it is no good waiting for him. We must go and find him; and if all goes well at our meeting, I think I shall be off and wish you like the eagles "farewell where ever you fare".'

They begged him, not to go [> not to leave them]. They offered him dragon-gold. But he wouldn't saying anything different. 'We shall see, we shall see' said he 'and I think I have earned some of your dragon-gold already – *when* you have got it'.

[*added*: Then] They took off their clothes and bathed in the river which was cool [>shallow] and clear and stony-bed. Then refreshed if still hungry they went on;[TN13] and over the ford, and marched through the long green grass and down the avenues of wide oaks and tall elms.

'What's <his> name, and why did he call it The Carrock?' asked Bilbo as they went along; he had been pondering the wizard's words.

'He calls it the carrock because carrock is his word for it' said Bladorthin 'he calls things like that carrocks, and this one *the* carrock because it is the only [one] near his home, & he knows it well.'

'Who calls it – who knows it[?]'

'The Somebody that I spoke about – a very great person. You must all be *very* polite when I introduce you. I shall introduce you slowly (one by one [> 2 by 2] in fact, I think) and you *must* be careful not to annoy him. He can be appalling when angry, though charming otherwise [> kind enough if humoured] – and [> but] he gets angry easily.

[Who is he>] The dwarves turned round when they heard Bladorthin talking like this to Bilbo. 'Is that the person you are taking us to now?' they asked. 'Wasn't there anybody more easy tempered! Hadn't you better explain a little bit clearer?' – and so on.

'[No there wasn't >] Yes it jolly well is! No there wasn't! I was just beginning to . . . [*added*: explain]' and so on, answered Bladorthin.

'His name is Medwed. He is very strong. He is a skin-changer'.

'What! a furrier; a man who calls rabbits conies and turns their skins into arctic fox??' said Bilbo.[TN14]

'Good gracious heavens no no no No!' said Bladorthin. 'In the name of thunder [> all wonder] don't mention the word furrier again as long as you are within a hundred miles of him, nor meat [> fur] rug, cape, tippet muff any other such idiotic words. He is a skin-changer – he is sometimes a huge black-bear, sometimes a great strong black-haired man with huge arms and a great beard.[TN15]

'I can't tell you much more. Whether he is a bear descended from the great bears of the mountains that lived there before the giants came,[TN16] or a man descended from the old men who lived there before Smaug invaded the land and the goblins came into the hills out of the North, I can't say. At any rate he is under no enchantment but his own.

'He lives [in] an oak-wood, and has a great wooden house; and as a man he keeps cattle and horses, which are nearly as marvellous as himself for they work for him and talk to him. But he does not eat them. He eats wild things often [> sometimes, not often]. He keeps hives and hives of great fierce bees. He likes cream and honey. As a bear he ranges far and wide. I have seen him sitting all alone on the top of the carrock at night watching the moon sinking towards the Misty Mountains. I believe he does that often, and I believe he sometimes sleeps in the little cave [> and that is why I believe he once came from the mountains].'

But Bilbo and the Dwarves had [*added*: now] plenty to think about; and they said [> spoke] very little any more. They had still a long long walk before them. Up slope and down slope [> up slope and down dale] they went. Sometimes they rested under the trees, and Bilbo was so hungry he would have eaten acorns, if they had been ripe enough yet to fall [> have fallen to the ground].

It was mid afternoon before they noticed that great patches of flowers had begun to spring up, all the same kinds growing together as if they had been planted. But especially there was clover, great waving patches of coxcomb clover, and ordinary red clover, and wide stretches of short white sweet honeysmelling clover. There was a buzzing and whirring and a droning in the air. Bees were busy every where. And such bees. Bilbo had never seen anything like them. 'If one was to sting me I should swell as big again as I am' he thought. They were bigger than hornets, much bigger. Why the drones were as big as a small thumb, and [their bands of gold shone >] the bands of yellow on their deep black bodies shone like fiery gold.

'We are getting near' said Bladorthin 'we are on the edge of his bee-pasture[s].'

After a while they came to a belt of tall old oaks, and beyond them to a high thorn hedge through which you could not see nor scramble.[TN17]

'You had better wait here' said the wizard [*added*: to the dwarves] 'and when I call or whistle come after me – one by one [> in pairs] mind, about five minutes between each [> each pair] of you. There is [a] gate somewhere round this way.' And with that he went off along the hedge taking Mr Baggins with him.[TN18]

They soon came to a high broad wooden gate, and beyond it they could see gardens, and a cluster of low wooden buildings, some made of unshaped logs, and thatched – barns, stables, sheds, and [a] long low house. All inside the hedge were rows and rows of hives with [fancy >] bell-shaped tops made of straw. The noise of the great bees flying to and fro and crawling in and out filled all the air.

The wizard and the hobbit pushed open the heavy creaking gate and went down a wide track towards the house. Some horses trotted up across the grass and looked at them intently with very intelligent faces, then off they galloped in front of them to the house. 'They have gone to tell him' said Bladorthin, and as he said it they came upon a courtyard three walls of which were made by the wooden house and its two wings. There was a great oak trunk lying, and many lopped branches beside it. Standing beside it [> near] was a huge man with a thick black-beard and hair, and great [bare] arms and legs with knotted muscles. He was dressed in loose black fur as low as his knees, and was leaning on a large axe. The horses were standing by him with their noses at his shoulder.

'Ugh, here they are' he said to the horses in a deep growling voice. 'They don't look dangerous – you can be off' and he laughed a great rolling laugh, put down his axe and came forward.

'Who are you and what do you want?' he asked [gruffly] standing in front of them and towering tall above even Bladorthin.[TN19] As for Bilbo he could have trotted through his legs without ducking his head to miss the bottom of the man's fur garment.

'I am Bladorthin' said the wizard.

'Never heard of him' growled the man. 'And what's this little fellow?' he said stooping down to frown at Mr Baggins with his bushy black eyebrows.

'That is Mr Baggins, a hobbit of good family and unimpeachable reputation' said Bladorthin (Bilbo bowed – he had no hat to take off, and was painfully conscious of his many missing buttons).[TN20] 'I am a wizard – I have heard of you, if you have not heard of me. But perhaps you have heard of my good cousin Radagast who lives near the borders of Mirkwood?'

'Yes yes: not a bad fellow. Now I know who you are.[TN21] What do you want?'

'To tell you the truth, we have lost our luggage, nearly lost our way, and are rather in need of help – or at least advice. I may say we have had rather a bad time with goblins in the mountains.

'Goblins?' said the big man, less gruffly. 'O! ho! so you've been having trouble with *them*, have you. What did you go near them for?'

'Did not mean to. They surprised us in the mountains, which we had to cross; we were coming out of the Lands over West[TN22] into these countries. It is a long tale.'

'You had better come inside and tell me some of it – if it won't take all day' said the man, and went in through his big door.

They found themselves in a wide hall with a fire [place] in the middle. Though it was summer there was a wood fire burning and the smoke was going up to the blackened rafters in search of the way out through a great opening in the roof. They passed through this hall and came through another [smaller] door into a sort of veranda with wooden pillars made of tree trunks. It faced south and was still warm, and filled with the light of the westering sun that slanted into it, and fell in gold on the garden full of flowers that came right up to the steps.

There they sat on wooden benches, while Bladorthin began his tale, and Bilbo [sat >] swung his dangling legs and looked at the flowers in the garden, wondering what their names could be – he had never seen half of them before.

'I was coming over the mountains with a friend or two . . .' said the wizard.

'Or two – I can only see one, and a little one at that' said Medwed.

'Well to tell you the truth I did not like to bother you with a lot of us, until I found out whether you were busy – I will give a call if I may'.

'Go on, call away!'

So Bladorthin gave a long shrill whistle, and presently Gandalf and Dori came into [> through] the hall and stood bowing low at the open door behind them.

'One or three, you meant, I see' said Medwed. 'But these aren't hobbits, these are dwarves!'

'Gandalf at your service!'

'Dori at your service' said the two dwarves bowing again.

'I don't need it [> your service]', said Medwed, 'but I expect you need mine. I am not over fond of dwarves, but if it is true that you are respectable dwarves & not friends of Goblins, [I will >] and are not up to any mischief in my lands – what *are* you up to, by the way?'

'They are on their way to visit the old country of their fathers, away east beyond Mirkwood' said Bladorthin, 'and it is entirely an accident that we are in your lands at all. We were crossing by the High Pass that should have been [> brought] us well to the north of your country, when we were attacked by the wicked goblins – as I was beginning to tell you'.[TN23]

'Go on telling then', said Medwed, who was never [very] polite

'There was a terrible storm, the stone-giants were out hurling rocks, and at the head of the Pass we found a cave. Into it we went for shelter, the hobbit and I and several of our dwarf friends . . .'

'Do you call two "several"?' asked Medwed.

'Well, no! as a matter of fact there were more than two'.

'Where are they – killed, eaten, gone home?'

'Well, no! to tell the truth they didn't all come when I whistled. Shy, I expect. [After >] You see, we are well aware that we are already rather a lot for you to entertain'.

'Go on! whistle again. I am in for a party, it seems; and one or two more won't matter much', growled Medwed.

Bladorthin whistled again, but Nori and Ori were there bowing in the doorway almost before he had stopped, for (if you remember) he had told them to come along every few [> five] minutes or so.

'Hello!' said the big man 'You came pretty quick – where were you hiding? Come on my jack-in-the-boxes!'

'Nori at your service. Ori at your . . .' they began, but 'Thank you! I will ask for it [> your help] when I need it' said he. 'Sit down, and let's get on with this tale, or it will [be] supper time before we end it.'

'As soon as we were asleep' went on Bladorthin 'a crack at the back of the cave opened, goblins came out, and grabbed the hobbit and the dwarves, and our troop of ponies . . .'

'Troop of ponies!' said Medwed 'What were you – a travelling circus? Or were you carrying lots of goods: – or do you call six a troop?'

'Well no! as a matter of fact there were more than six of us' said Bladorthin 'and well – here are two more'. Instant that moment Balin and Dwalin appeared, and bowed extremely low till their beards swept the stone floor. The big man was frowning, so they did their best to be very polite. They were so comically polite that after a good long frown he burst into a deep chuckling laugh.

'Troop is right' he said. 'A fine comic troupe. Come in my merry men, and what are *your* names. I don't want your service; just your names, and then sit down.'

'Balin & Dwalin' they said and sat on the floor looking a bit surprised but not daring to be offended.

'Now go on again!' said Medwed.

'Where was I?' said the wizard. 'O yes – I was *not* grabbed. I killed a goblin or two with a flash' ('good' growled Medwed 'it is some good being a wizard then.') 'and slipped inside the crack before it closed. I followed down the passages, and watched from the shadows while the prisoners were dragged before the Great Goblin. The hall was crammed with goblins. The king [> chief] was surrounded with [> by] thirty or forty armed soldiers, so it would have been pretty hopeless, even if they hadn't been all chained together. I thought "what can a dozen do against so many?" –'

'A dozen! – that is the first time I have heard eight called a dozen' said Medwed. 'Have you got some more jacks hiding in their boxes?'

'Well yes, to tell you the truth there is Fili and Kili here as well' said Bladorthin, as these two now appeared smiling and bowing.

'That's enough' said Medwed 'sit down and be quiet. [But before we go on – have we come to the end of the party or not. I am tired of these >] Now go on, Bladorthin!'

So Bladorthin went on [with the tale of that >] until he came to the fight in the dark and the loss of the hobbit [>, and the discovery of the lower entrance and their horror when they found that Mr Baggins had been mislaid]. 'We counted ourselves, & found there was no hobbit – there were only fourteen of us left'.

'Fourteen! That's the first time I have heard one from ten make fourteen' said Medwed. 'Do you mean nine, or do you mean [there are still some jacks that haven't >] that you haven't told me yet all the names of your party?'

'Well yes, to tell the truth I had not mentioned Oin and Gloin' said Bladorthin '– and well, here they are, if you will forgive them for bothering you.'

'O let 'em all come' said Medwed. 'Come along, come along! Sit down. But even now we have only got yourself and ten dwarves and the hobbit that was lost, and that only makes eleven (plus one mislaid) and not fourteen, unless wizards count differently to ordinary people. But get on with the tale!' He didn't show it any more than he could help, but really he was getting rather interested. As a matter of fact in old days he had known the very part of the mountains Bladorthin was now describing, and he nodded, and growled, when he heard of the hobbit's reappearance, of their scramble [*added*: down the mountain side] and of the wolf-ring [*added*: in the woods]. When he heard of their climbing their trees and the wolves all underneath, he got up and strode about muttering 'I wish I had been there; I would have given them more than fire works!'

'Well' said Bladorthin very relieved to see that his story was making a good impression 'there we were with the wolves gone mad under us, and the forest beginning to blaze in places, when the goblins came down from the mountains, & discovered us. They yelled with delight and sang songs making fun of us:

"fifteen birds in five fir trees"—'

'Good heavens' growled Medwed 'Don't pretend goblins can't count. They can. Twelve is'nt fourteen [> fifteen], and they know it.'

'Well no, of course not. There was Bifur and Bofur too. I haven't ventured to introduce them before, but here they are.'

In came Bifur and Bofur. 'And me' said Bombur puffing up last: he was rather fat, and he didn't like being left till last.

'Well now there *are* fifteen of you' said Medwed 'And since goblins can count, I suppose that is all there were up in the trees. Now perhaps we can finish the tale without more interruptions'. You see how clever Bladorthin had been – Medwed was really very excited by their story, just like you were, and so he forgot to be rude and gruff and grumpy, and did not send them all off quick (as he usually did with all strangers that come to his gates).

When the wizard had finished the story, and told of the eagles, and of their flight to the Carrock, the sun had [gone >] fallen to the tops of the Misty Mountains, & the shadows were long in Medwed's garden.

['Supper!' he said >] 'A very good tale' said Medwed. 'The best I have heard for a long while. You may be making it all up, of course, but you deserve a supper for the story all the same. Let's have something to eat!'

'Yes please' they all said. 'Thank you very much!'

This brings the text to the bottom of manuscript page 87 (Marq. 1/1/7:11). Sometime at or about this point, Tolkien paused briefly in the narrative to sketch out events for the following scene (and beyond) in what became the earliest of the surviving 'Plot-Notes' (Plot Notes A), the full text of which is given immediately following this chapter, beginning on p. 293. The text resumes, without apparent break, on the top of the next page (manuscript page 88, the back of the same unlined foolscap sheet).[TN24]

Inside the hall it was now grown dark. Medwed clapped his hands and in trotted four beautiful white ponies, and a number of large [f<urred> hound >] long-bodied grey dogs. Medwed said something to them in a queer language like animal-noises turned into talk. In a minute they went out and came back with torches in their mouths, lit them at the fire, and stuck them in low brackets on the pillars of the hall near to the fire. The dogs could walk on their hind-legs and carry things in their fore-paws marvellously cleverly. Soon they had got out tables and trestles from the side walls and set them up near the fire. Then 'baa! baa!' was heard and in came beautiful white sheep led by a large coal-black ram. Some bore white cloths on their backs, some trays of cups and bowls some platters and knives, which the dogs took and laid quickly on the tables. These were very low, and beside them the ponies pushed little low stools & chairs with wide seats and short legs. But at one end was an enormous black chair for Medwed.

Such a dinner they ate as they had not eaten since they left the house of Elrond. The light of the torches flickered on the walls, and there were candles on the table. All the while Medwed in his gruff voice told tales of the wildlands on this side of the mountains, and specially of the dark and dangerous wood – the Great Forest – that lay more than a day's long ride to the East. The Dwarves listened and shook their beards, for they knew they had to pass that forest, and that after the Mountains it was the worst of the dangers [> perils] they had to pass before they came to the dragon's stronghold. They also told many stories of their own, but Medwed did not seem very interested; most of them were about gold and silver and jewels and the making of them, and he did not appear to care for such things: there were no things of gold or silver in his house, and few save knives of any metal at all.

They sat long at table, till it was dark night outside. Then the fires in the middle of the hall were built up with fresh logs and the torches put out, and there they sat in the light of the flames with the pillars of the hall standing tall and dark at top like trees of the forest. Whether it was magic or not Bilbo heard what sounded like a wind in branches stirring in the rafters, and the hoot of owls. He began to nod because he was very sleepy and the voices seem[ed] far away, until he woke with a start and heard the end of a song of the dwarves.

'The wind was on the withered heath,
But in the forest stirred no leaf:
There shadows lay by night and day,
And dark things silent crept beneath.

The wind came down from mountains cold,
And like a tide it roared and rolled;
till branches groaned, the forest moaned,
and leaves were laid upon the mould.

The wind went on from West to East –
all movement in the Forest ceased,
But shrill and harsh across the marsh
Its whistling voices were released

The grasses hissed their plumes were bent
The reeds were rattling – on it went
o'er shaken pool neath heavens cool
[neath >] where racing clouds were torn & rent

It passed the lonely Mountain bare
And swept above the Dragons lair.
There black and dark lay boulders stark –
No light but of the moon was there'[TN25]

The[n] Medwed stood up and said that the time had come for sleep – 'for you' he said. 'In this hall you may sleep sound & safe, but I warn you not to stray outside its walls till the sun's up, on your peril'.

Beds were brought from the sides of the hall and ranged in a row at one side. For Bilbo there was a little mattress of straw, and coverings of fur. He snuggled into them, too, very gladly, summer-time though it was.

Then Medwed went out, and the great door creaked & slammed. The fire burnt low; and Bilbo fell asleep. But in the night he woke; and saw[TN26] the fire had burnt to nothing but a few embers; the dwarves were asleep (by their breathing); a splash of white on the floor came from the high moon which was peering down through the smoke-hole in the roof.

There was a growling sound outside, and a noise as of some great animal scuffling at the door. Bilbo wondered what it could be – whether it could be Medwed in enchanted shape and if he would come in as a bear, and kill them. He hid under the skins, and in spite of his fright went at last to sleep again.

It was full morning when he woke – the dwarves were moving about: one of them had fallen over him on the floor, as a matter of fact, and was grumbling about it. Bofur it was.

'Get up lazybones' he said, 'or there'll be no breakfast left for you.'

Up jumped Bilbo. 'Where is breakfast?' said he.

'Mostly inside us' said the dwarves; 'but what is left is out on the veranda. We have been about looking for Medwed, ever since the sun got up. But there is no sign of him anywhere. Breakfast we found laid on the veranda.'

'Where is Bladorthin[?]' said the hobbit, moving off to find breakfast, as quick as he could.

'O[!] out and about somewhere', they told him.

But Bilbo saw no sign of Bladorthin all day until evening. Just before sunset he came into the hall, where Bilbo and the dwarves were having supper – waited on by Medwed's marvellous animals, as they had been all day. Of Medwed they had seen nor heard a sound, since the night before; and they were getting puzzled.

'Where do you think he is?' they asked Bladorthin as he came in, 'and where have you been to all day, yourself?'

'One question at a time – and none till after supper: I haven't had a bite since breakfast'.

At last Bladorthin who had eaten two whole loaves (with butter and honey and clotted cream), and drunk a whole jug of mead (which is made out of honey) – pushed away his plates, and took out his pipe.

'I will answer the second question first' he said – 'but bless me this is a splendid place for smoke-rings!' And not for a long time could they get anymore out of him, he was so busy sending smokerings dodging round the pillars of the hall, changing them into all sorts of different colours, and setting them at last chasing one another out of the smoke hole in the roof. They must have looked very funny from outside – popping out into the air one after another green blue, red, silver-grey, yellow; big ones, little ones; little ones dodging through big ones, and joining into figures-of-eight, and going off like a flock of birds into the distance.

'I have been picking out bear-tracks' Bladorthin said at last. 'There must have been a regular bear-meeting outside here last night. I soon saw that Medwed could not have made them all – there were far too many of them, and they were of various sizes too: I should say little bears, big [> large] bears, ordinary bears, and gigantic big bears must have been dancing outside from dark to nearly dawn. They came from almost all directions except West from over the river, from the Misty Mountains. In that direction [led >] only one set of footprints went – none coming, only going away from here. They were the largest set of all. I followed them as far as the Carrock. There they disappeared into the river, but the water was too deep and strong for me to cross just there. [I had to > beyond the Carrock >] The Carrock, if you remember, stands nearly in the middle of the river, and is join[ed] to this bank by a ford and stepping stones, but on the other side a deep swirling channel runs under its overhanging side. I had to walk miles before I could find a [ford >] wide stretch where the water was slow and shallow enough for me to swim, and then miles back to pick up the tracks. By that time it was too late for me to follow them far. They went straight away in the direction of the pine woods on the east side of the Misty Mountains, where we had our pleasant little meeting with the wargs the night before last.

'And that I think has answered your first question, too' ended Bladorthin, and he sat a long time silent.

The hobbit thought he knew what Bladorthin meant. 'What shall we do', he cried '– if he brings all the wargs and goblins down here, we shall all be caught and killed. But I thought you said he was not a friend of theirs!'

'So I did – and don't be silly. You had better go to bed. Your wits are asleepy', said Bladorthin.[TN27]

There was nothing else to do, so Bilbo did go to bed, and while the dwarves sang songs he dropped asleep, still puzzling his little [head][TN28] about Medwed, till he dreamed a dream of hundreds of black bears dancing slow heavy dances round and round in the moonlight in the courtyard. Then he woke up and heard the same scuffling, scraping, snuffling, and growling as before.

Next morning, they were wakened by Medwed himself.

'So here you all are still!' he said. He picked up the hobbit and laughed: 'not eaten by wargs or goblins, yet I see'. And he poked Mr Baggins' waistcoat most disrespectfully. 'Little bunny getting nice and fat again on bread and honey, I see', he said. 'Come and have some more!'.

So they went and had breakfast. Medwed was most jolly. He seemed to be in a splendidly good temper, and set them all laughing with his funny stories. They did [not][TN29] have to wonder long where he had been, or why he was so nice to them; for he told them himself. He had been off over the river and right back to the mountains – from which you can guess he could travel quick, as a bear at any rate. He had soon found out, from the burnt clearing, that part of their story was true. But he had found out more than that. He had caught a warg and a goblin wandering in the woods – the goblin patrols were still hunting for the dwarves, and were fiercely angry because of the death of their great chief; and the wolves had not forgotten the burning of the chief warg's nose, and the killing of many of his servants by Bladorthin's fire.

So they told him. But they got no sympathy from him. He hurried home delighted to offer what help he could to Bladorthin & his friends.

'What did you do to the goblin and the warg?' said Bilbo.

'Come & see!'

A goblin's head was stuck on a pole outside Medwed's gate, and a warg skin was nailed to a tree just outside. Medwed could be a fierce enemy. But now he was their friend; and encouraged by his kindness, they told him all their story.

This is what he promised to do for them. He would provide ponies for each of them, and a horse for Bladorthin, and would lade them with food (nuts, flour in bags; twice-baked cakes of flour and honey; sealed jars of cream; dried fruits, and pots of honey) to last them with care for weeks, yet easy enough carry.[TN30] Water he said they would not want until they came to the forest, for there were stream and springs along the road. 'But your road through the forest is difficult and dangerous', he said; 'as difficult and dangerous as the path across the mountains. Water is not easy to find there, nor food. For the time is not come for nuts which is all there is growing there that can be eaten; and the wild things are dark queer and savage in there. I will provide you with skins for carrying water, which you had better fill before you enter the forest. You will see one stream, a strong black one, if you hold to the path, but I doubt if it is good to drink. I have heard that it carries enchantment, and brings a frightful drowziness. I will give you four bows and arrows,[TN31] but I doubt if you will shoot anything in the dim shadows of that place, without straying from the path – which you MUST NOT DO. And I doubt if it would be good to eat if you shot it.

'Beyond the edge of the forest I cannot help you. There at the edge I must ask you to send back my horse and my ponies.'[TN32]

They thanked him, of course, with many bows and sweepings of hoods and with many an 'at your service, O master of the wide wooden halls!'[TN33]

All the morning was busy with preparations. Soon after mid day they eat with Medwed for the last time and set off at a good pace, for said he: 'The goblins will not dare to cross the river at the Carrock or to come near my house – it is well protected at night! – but the river bends towards the forest northwards, and so do the [forest >] mountains, and I have heard of their raiding across the river and into the forest before now! If they should track [> have tracked] you, or tracked the warg and goblin that I captured and have found my trail, they might try to cut you off that way. I should be off now as quick as may be!'.

So they said goodbye, and rode out a little gate from his high hedges on the east side. The sun was behind them, and the meadow lands lay all golden before them.[TN34] They rode N.E. as Medwed directed them towards the beginning of the track through the forest. The sun was only just going westward & the meadowlands lay all golden about them. It was difficult to think of goblins behind them, or the Dark paths before them.

After [> In] several days riding in sunny weather they met with no adventure and saw nothing save grass and flowers and birds [*added*: & scattered trees] and occasionally herds of red deer browsing or sitting in the noon in the shade of trees, or in the long grass with only the antlers of the harts [showing >] sticking up like dead branches of trees (thought Bilbo).

So eager were they to press on that they often rode on after dusk and into night beneath the moon, before they camped under a big tree. Then Bilbo thought he saw away to the right or to the left, the shadowy form of a great bear prowling along in the same direction. But if he dared to mention it to Bladorthin, the wizard only said: 'Hush, hush – take no notice!'

At last one evening they camped at the very edge of the forest, which all day they could see as a black and <frowning> wall before them, getting ever nearer and nearer. The land began to slope up and up, and it seemed to Bilbo that a silence began to draw in upon them. Birds began to sing less. There were no more deer; not even rabbits to be seen. When they rested that evening, they were beneath the great overhanging trees at the edge. Their trunks were huge and gnarled, their branches twisted; their leaves were dark and long. Ivy grew about them, and trailed upon the ground.

'This is "Mirkwood"' said Bladorthin. 'The greatest of all forests of the North. And now we [> you] must send back [these excellent beasts that we >] the ponies you have borrowed'.

The dwarves were inclined to grumble at this – but Blad. told them they were fools. 'Medwed is not as far off as you think; and you had better keep your promises – to him at any rate. Mr Baggins' eyes are sharper than yours' said he, 'if you have not seen each night after dark a great bear going along with us. Medwed loves these [horses >] ponies as his children – you can hardly guess what a favour he has granted you in letting them ride so far [> in letting you ride them so far]!'

'What about your horse then?' said Gandalf. 'You don't mention sending it back!'

'I don't, because I am not sending it'.

'What about your promise then?'

'I am not sending it back, I am riding it back', said the wizard.[TN35] Nothing they could say would make him change his mind.

'No!' he said 'you won't catch me going through Mirkwood, unless I am obliged – and I am not. I told you some time ago that I was going to say goodbye, & that I had already come much further than I meant to.[TN36] You were lucky to have me to help you across the mountains! Not a step further this way, thank you! The rest is your affair – though if you ever find the dragon (& escape him again!) I hope you will remember your old friend. I have got other business on hand now that can wait no longer'.

And the next morning he said the same. The evening before the dwarves had turned the ponies' heads back homewards, and sent them galloping away. They did not seem to mind the gathering dark – but rather to be glad to turn their tails towards the gloom of Mirkwood. As they went off, Bilbo could have sworn that a thing like a black bear left the shadows of the wood and trotted after them.

Now Bladorthin sat on the horse Medwed had lent him, and said 'Farewell!' Bilbo felt very unhappy. He had gone just inside the forest after breakfast, & it seemed as dark inside there in the morning as at night, and very secret – 'a sort of watching & waiting feeling' said the hobbit to himself.

An interpolated section dealing with the troll-key is written into the top margin of manuscript page 98 and marked for insertion at this point. The writing of this additional text looks to be quicker and sloppier than the main passage and was thus probably added later:

'One minute' Bl. was saying. 'Here are the key from the troll-lair they might come in useful, Gandalf: And now Goodbye, Goodbye!'

'Goodbye, goodbye!' Bladorthin was saying – 'straight through the forest is your way now. Don't stray off the track – if you do it is a thousand to one you'll never find the path again, or ever get out of Mirkwood; and then I don't suppose I (or anyone else) will hear of you again!'

'Do we really have to go through?' said Bilbo

'Yes you do, if you want to get to the other side. You must either go through, or give up your quest. And I am not going to allow you to back out, Mr Baggins, now – I am sure you can't be thinking of it.'

'No, no!' the hobbit hastened to say (and between you and me I believe he really was speaking the truth: adventures were quite changing him) 'No, I meant – is there no way round?'

'There is if you care to go a hundred miles or so out of your way, north or south! But you wouldn't get a safe path, even then. Remember you're over the Edge of the Wild now, and in for all sorts of fun, wherever you go. Before you could get round Mirkwood to the North, you would be right among the slopes of the North End of the Misty Mountains – and they are stiff with Goblins, hobgoblins or orcs of the worst description.[TN37] Before you could get round the forest to the south, you would come into the land of the Great Necromancer, whose dark hidden tower watches over a wide land – I don't advise you to go that way, my dears![TN38]

'Stick to the forest track, keep your peckers up,[TN39] hope for the best, and with a tremendous slice of luck you will come out one day and see the Long Marshes lying below you – and beyond them faint and far the top of the Lonely Mountain in the East. There is a path too across the Marshes . . .'

'We know, we know!' said Gandalf. 'The marshes are on the borders of the lands we knew of old, and we have not forgotten. Thank you very much; goodbye! If you won't come, you had better be off; and so had we. Goodbye!'

And so they parted. Bladorthin rode off west, but before he had gone out of hearing, he turned his horse, put his hands to his mouth, and shouted. They heard his voice come faintly: 'Goodbye – Be good, take care of yourself [>yourselves] – and don't leave the path.'

'O Goodbye, and go away', grumbled the dwarves, who were really very worried at his going off. There was nothing for it, however, and so they shoulder each the heavy packs they had to carry as they were now without ponies. Then they plunged into the Forest.

TEXT NOTES

1 The phrase that completes this sentence in the published book, 'frightened like a rabbit, *even if you look rather like one*' (DAA.[161]), is absent in the manuscript but present in both typescripts (1/1/57 and 1/1/38). For Tolkien's denial of any connection between hobbits and rabbits, see his 1938 letter to *The Observer* (Appendix II) and also his 1971 letter to Roger Lancelyn Green (*Letters* p. 406). For T. A. Shippey's rebuttal, see *The Road to Middle-earth* (rev. ed. p. 62), where he lists five places in the published book where Bilbo is compared to a rabbit (these correspond to DAA.76, 156, [161], 181, & 334). Note, however, that not all of these are present in the original draft (cf. pp. 93, 209, 228, 241 & 667), which supports Tolkien's persistent and consistent denial of any connection in conception.

2 The sentence originally continued with the phrase 'when the sun is <a late>' followed by a final illegible word, the first letter of which seems to be *l-* and the fourth and fifth letters the ligature *-gh*, but I cannot make out the word itself.

3 For the significance of this passage in Tolkien's mythology, and hence its appropriateness as 'a polite thing to say among eagles', see the last paragraph of the Commentary to Chapter VI above (p. 223).

4 Added in the margin: 'and his fifteen chieftains [gold >] fine gold chains on their necks'.

5 This statement turned out not to be true, since in the manuscript of Chapter XVIII Bilbo encounters an eagle when he awakes on the battlefield after the Battle of Five Armies. However, there is no evidence that the battle had been foreseen this early on, and we may take this passage as evidence to the contrary. Later, after the manuscript was completed, Tolkien noticed the contradiction and changed the eagle in Chapter XVIII to a man of Lake Town (cf. pp. 678 & 683). He also changed the passage in this chapter to read as follows: 'Bilbo never saw them again – *except high and far off in the battle of Five Armies. But as that comes in at the end of this tale we will say no more about it just now*' (First Typescript, typescript page 61; Marq. 1/1/57:1), dropping the evocative final line of the original: 'But he didn't forget them'.

An ink emendation in the First Typescript changes the gold-giver from Gandalf (i.e., the wizard, replacing 'Bladorthin' in the manuscript) to 'the dwarves', so that 'the gold that Gandalf sent them in remembrance' becomes 'the gold that the dwarves gave them' – Tolkien having apparently decided it more appropriate for the gift to come from the surviving dwarves than the wizard.

6 This outline only takes up half of this page. The back of the sheet (1/1/23:2) is blank except for the following list of dwarf-names:

Gandalf
Dori Nori Ori

Oin Gloin
Bifur Bofur Bombur
Fili Kili
Dwalin & Balin

7 There might be an echo of this in the following passage from Tolkien's 'The Sea-Bell' (ATB poem #15; originally published in 1934 under the title of 'Looney'):

I crept to a wood: silent it stood
in its dead leaves; bare were its boughs.
There must I sit, wandering in wit . . .
For a year and a day there must I stay . . .

At last there came light in my long night,
and I saw my hair hanging grey.
'Bent though I be, I must find the sea!
I have lost myself, and I know not the way,
but let me be gone!'

8 This sentence was changed several times in the course of writing. Originally it read 'And more by good luck than by good management . . .', immediately changed to 'And by good management with good luck in plenty' before finally reaching wording almost the same as that of the published book (cf. DAA.163): 'And by good management and good luck, I have done it.'

9 The wizard's departure had been prefigured for careful readers as far back as the opening chapter; otherwise his partnership with the thirteen dwarves would preclude the need for Bilbo's addition as the lucky fourteenth member of the company.

10 Shanks' ponies (later altered by Tolkien to shankses' ponies), is an old expression meaning travel by foot – or, as the OED puts it, 'one's own legs as a means of conveyance'. Variants included Shanks' mare, Shanks' nag, etc., but Bladorthin chose the one most appropriate to hobbits and dwarves. Cf. the parallel term 'ash breeze' used by old-time sailors to refer to those dead calms when they must row their boats with ashwood oars.

11 This sentence and the one following it were altered to read 'But there is *somebody, that* I know of, who lives not far away. *That somebody* made *the* steps on *this* hill'. The word 'somebody' was probably inserted in order to tie in with the wizard's speech a few paragraphs later: 'The *Somebody* that I spoke about' (p. 231, emphasis mine). Similarly, the later line 'What's <his> name, and why did he call it The Carrock?' (ibid.) is changed into the passive 'And why is it called The Carrock?'

12 Added in top margin and marked for insertion at this point: 'which he calls Sorneldin > Sinrock > Lamrock > the *Carrock.*' For more on the significance of these invented names, see section iv of the Commentary below.

13 Tolkien revised the opening of this sentence to read 'Refreshed if still hungry they went on', then revised it again to read '*When they had dried in the sun now strong & warm they were* refreshed if still hungry; *and they crossed* over the ford . . .'

14 *Furrier:* a trapper, fur-trader. *Coney, Conies*: an archaic word for rabbit, still in use in rural dialects in England (cf. Sam Gamgee, *LotR*.680–82). Bilbo is thinking of a rustic trapper or poacher; his comment about 'turn[ing] their skins into arctic fox' probably contains not so much a view of the innate crookedness of fur-traders as a deliberate echo by Tolkien of Elizabethan slang, where 'coney-catching' meant a con game or swindle (the guileless victim being the rabbit or 'coney' to the conman's weasel or fox). The latter meaning is remembered today chiefly because of a series of pamphlets by an early rival of Shakespeare's, playwright Roger Greene, entitled *The Art of Conny-catching* [1591–2].

15 Several paragraphs followed this statement in the manuscript, each crossed out in turn (some before reaching the end of a sentence). Taken together, they reflect Tolkien's considerable uncertainty about just what sort of being Medwed was. I reproduce the entire sequence here as it was originally written.

> No one knows [> Most people disagree] > now knows whether he is an a magic bear with > a marvellous bear with magic > powers of magic, or a great man under an enchantment.
>
> 'Which is he?' said Bilbo who was becoming very interested: after all he had got to meet the 'person' before long.
>
> 'Neither' said the wizard 'He is a man [> an enchanter > a man.], one of <the> last of the old men who lived in these parts before the days of dragon. For it was in those days
>
> But he is under nobody's enchantment save his own. He is an enchanter himself, and can be a bear if he wishes. He often does wish, because in the days long ago he was a friend of the great bears of the mountains. The goblins drove them out of.

16 Initially this passage ran 'before the giants and goblins came', then the phrase 'and goblins' was deleted. This is significant in light of the rest of the sentence, which establishes a sequence of events: first came the great bears, then the giants, then the men of old, then Smaug and the goblins, the latter 'out of the North' (i.e., from Angband/Utumno/Thangorodrim). Either heritage, pre-giant mountain bear or pre-goblin man-of-old, marks Medwed as an aborigine (in the original sense), the last remnant of a displaced and vanished people.

For more on the werebear theme, see the Commentary below, section ii.

17 'a high thorn hedge through which you could not see nor scramble' – note that the thorn tree was traditionally linked with the faerie folk in English and Irish folklore. In a traditional fairy tale or ballad, such a detail would signal the eldritch nature of the setting and its denizens; by including it in his description of Medwed's house, Tolkien may

be reinforcing the otherworldly, slightly eerie, uncanny nature of its inhabitant.

18 Since Medwed had 'never heard' of Bladorthin, how was the wizard familiar with the layout of Medwed's yard and gate? Unless we assume Bladorthin frequently travelled incognito and in various guises – something we know is true of Gandalf the Grey as Tolkien later conceived him – then the simplest explanation is that he had not himself earlier visited the place but had had it described to him by his 'cousin', Radagast (the later Radagast the Brown).

19 In revisions, the word 'even' was deleted from the phrase 'towering tall above even Bladorthin', in keeping with the image of the wizard as merely a 'little old man' to the casual eye (cf. Bilbo's first impression back in Chapter I, p. 30). Tolkien may, of course, have been deliberately writing from Bilbo's perspective; after travelling so long with the dwarves and wizard, anyone taller than them all would stand out in the hobbit's mind. Anders Stenström has done extensive calculations based on this paragraph to determine just how tall Beorn must have been ('The Figure of Beorn', *Arda* 1987, volume VII [1992]), but this seems too elaborate a framework on too slender a basis, given the 'faerie magic' aspect of much of the tale's details.

20 'many missing buttons' – lost when he escaped through the goblins' 'back door' at the end of Chapter V (p. 163).

21 Medwed's reply was expanded to read 'Yes yes: not a bad fellow *I know him well*. Now I know who you are *or who you say you are*. What do you want?'

22 Bladorthin's use here of 'the Lands over West' (a phrase which persisted into the published book; DAA.168) seems to be juxtaposed with 'these countries' – that is, the lands beyond 'the Edge of the Wild' (p. 244); the settled country contrasted with Wilderland (or, to use the later *LotR* terminology, Eriador as opposed to Rhovanion). If this is indeed the case, Tolkien did not pick up on and reuse the name elsewhere, leaving this its sole appearance. Perhaps more significantly, 'Lands over West' seems to be *The Hobbit*'s equivalent of the later Western Lands, a phrase used in the 1937 *Quenta Silmarillion* (HME IV.159 & 161) and the '(Earliest) Annals of Valinor' (HME IV.264) to refer to Beleriand. By contrast, the earlier name 'the Great Lands' had applied to all lands East of the Sundering Sea although, like 'Middle-earth' itself, it seems to have sometimes been applied more to the westernmost of those lands. These parallels offer yet another hint that Bilbo's world is more than just closely tied to that of the heroes of the older legendarium; it is the same world at a slightly later date.

23 Note that the original geography is still in place, where Medwed's hall lay to the *south* of their intended route rather than to the *north* of it as in the published text.

24 The bottom of the next page (manuscript page 88; Marq. 1/1/7:12) is marked with a number of squiggles in ink, some of which are either

overwritten by the last few lines of text or else scribbled over them (it really is impossible to tell). It seems as if Tolkien's pen was giving him trouble, since he also traced over several words near the middle of the page with wider strokes in a darker ink.

These ink trills probably indicate a pause in composition, and I think it significant that similar doodling appears on the final page of Plot Notes A (Marq. 1/1/23:10). Since the rest of this chapter is based upon and derives directly from the very rough drafting of Plot Notes A, those Plot Notes were almost certainly written when the narrative had reached this exact spot.

25 This poem appears in the manuscript almost exactly as in the final text, with only a few minor changes. The replacement of 'till' with 'The' in the seventh line and the rephrasing of 'neath [clouds]' with 'where racing clouds' in line sixteen are made in ink in the manuscript, probably at the time of original composition. Such fluency in Tolkien's poetry generally means that the poem was probably drafted on loose sheets that have not survived. The alternate option, that the poem predates the current work and was incorporated into *The Hobbit* but not written especially for it, is rendered unlikely by the explicit mention within the poem of both 'the lonely Mountain' and 'the Dragons lair', the latter corrected to 'dragon's lair' in the typescript.

For the most part the earliest draft and published poem are word-for-word identical, aside from the addition of punctuation and adjustments of capitalization (and the replacement of 'plumes' with 'tassels' in line thirteen and 'neath' with 'under' in line fifteen). Curiously enough, though, the final line of the draft is later rejected and replaced by an additional five lines (that is, a new line to conclude the fifth stanza and a complete new sixth stanza to follow). The old line ('No light but of the moon was there') was replaced by the following in the typescript (typescript page 69; 1/1/67:9):

and flying smoke was in the air.

It left the world and took its flight
over the wide seas of the night.
The moon set sail upon the gale,
and stars were fanned to leaping lights.

This, of course, agrees exactly with the published text (DAA.178). As with the poem itself, no drafting of this additional stanza has been found among the *Hobbit* papers.

26 The words 'and saw' were cancelled, probably at the time of writing; their absence concentrates the effectiveness of the scene as Bilbo lies awake and listening in the dark.

Note that Bilbo here imagines himself as being in exactly the position of Beowulf's companions when they bed down in the great empty hall of Heorot waiting for Grendel to come:

> *. . . many*
> *valiant sea-fighters sank to hall-rest.*
> *None of them thought he would ever return*
> *from that long hall-floor to his native land,*
> *the people and home-fort where he'd been raised,*
> *for each one knew dark murder had taken*
> *too many men of the Danes already,*
> *killed in the wine-hall.*
>
> —*Beowulf*, tr. Howell Chickering, lines 689–696a.

27 The neologism 'asleepy' was almost at once changed to simply 'sleepy'.

28 This missing word has been supplied editorially on the basis of the typescript version of this passage (1/1/57:11); that Tolkien wrote 'little' at the end of one line and began the next with 'about Medwed' is an indication of the speed at which he was setting down the draft of the story.

29 Once again the missing [bracketed] word has been supplied editorially, as required by the sense of the passage. This agrees with the sense of the typescript text of this passage, which combines the two sentences with a semicolon and begins the second clause with 'nor did they have to wonder long . . .' (the exact reading that remained into the published book; cf. DAA.181).

30 This passage, detailing their provisions for the journey through Mirkwood, was changed to read as follows in the typescript:

> nuts, flour, twice-baked cakes of flour and honey, sealed jars of dried fruits, and red earthenware pots of honey, and various other foods which would last and the keep of which he had the secret (1/1/57:12).

This was then later revised in black ink on the typescripts to a reading very close to the final, published text:

> nuts, flour, sealed jars of dried fruits, and red earthenware pots of honey, and twice-baked cakes that would keep good a long time, and on a little of which they could march far. The making of these was one of his secrets; but honey was in them, as in most of his foods, and they were good to eat, though they made one thirsty. Water, he said, they would not want . . . (ibid.).

31 The specific detail of *four* bows was soon lost, replaced in the typescript by the more general 'some bows', the reading which remained thereafter. But the idea of the dwarves having only four bows resurfaced later, a good example of the phenomenon Christopher Tolkien points out (BLT I.9) where details which disappear between versions of one of Tolkien's stories are not necessarily rejected but sometimes merely omitted through compression; see p. 357 below.

32 Here the paragraph ends in the manuscript (on the bottom of manuscript page 94, the verso of manuscript page 93), but the typescript continues Medwed/Beorn's speech for one more significant sentence:

'But I wish you all speed, and my house is open to you, if ever you come back this way again.' – a bit of foreshadowing of Bilbo's return visit, perhaps, retrospectively tipped into the earlier scene.

33 In the typescript, this is followed with another sentence, tying their current activities into the quest as a whole: 'But their spirits sank at his grave words, and they all felt that the adventure was far more dangerous than they had thought, while all the time, even if they passed all perils the dragon was waiting at the end'. The final passage was later revised slightly, in ink, to read 'even if they passed all *the* perils *of the road*, the dragon was waiting at the end' (1/1/57:12).

34 At this point the text breaks off, and the bottom half of this page is a pencil map showing the relative positions of the mountain-pass (Chapter IV), Goblingate (Chapter V), the wargs' clearing in the pinewood (Chapter VI), the unnamed great river (later the Anduin) as well as a tributary thereto running down from the mountains, the Carrock and Medwed's steading, the borders of Mirkwood, and the path running northwest through the great forest. A dotted north/south line between Medwed's steading and the entrance of the forest path represents Gandalf & Company's route. This early sketch formed the basis for the more finished map appearing on Plate I [bottom] and hence ultimately the westerly portion of the Wilderland map that appeared as an endpaper in the published book (DAA.[399]).

In order to bring the text into accord with the map, a number of changes were made at the time of the typescript; no drafting of these changes survives. First, a penciled note was added to the end of the preceding paragraph in the manuscript: 'Beorn tells them of North<ern> paths'. Then the text was re-arranged (cf. DAA.184–6), and a new passage was added to reflect the new conception:

> . . . By his advice they were no longer making for the main forest-road to the south of his land. Had they followed the pass their path would have led them down a stream from the mountains that joined the great river miles south of the Carrock.† [*added*: At that point] there was a deep ford which they might have passed, if they had still had their ponies, and beyond [that] a track led to the skirts of the wood and to the entrance of the old forest road. But Beorn had warned them that that way was now often used by the goblins, while the forest-road itself he had heard was overgrown and disused at the eastern end and led to impassable marshes where the paths had long been lost. Its eastern opening had also always been far to the south of the Lonely Mountain and would have left them still with a long and difficult Northward march when they got to the other side. North of the Carrock the edge of Mirkwood drew closer to the borders of the Great River, and though here the Mountains too drew down nearer, Beorn advised them to take this way; for at a place a few days' ride due north of the Carrock was the gate of a little-known pathway through Mirkwood that led [almost] straight to[wards] the Lonely Mountain.

'The goblins' Beorn had said, 'will not dare to cross the Great River for a hundred miles north of the Carrock nor to come near my house – it is well protected at night! – but I should ride fast; for if they make their raid soon they will cross the river to the south and scour all the edge of the forest so as to cut you off, and Wargs run swifter than ponies. Still you are safer going north, even though you seem to be going back nearer to their strongholds; for that is what they will least expect, and they will have the longer ride to catch you. Be off now as quick as you may!'

That is why they were now riding in silence, galloping wherever the ground was grassy and smooth, with the mountains dark on their left, and in the distance the line of the river with its trees drawing ever closer. The sun had only just turned west when they started and till evening it lay golden on the land about them . . .

—typescript page 73; I/1/57:13.

† Editor's note: This stream appears as a southernly tributary to the Great River on the sketch-map.

35 There is a change in the handwriting at this point (the middle of manuscript page 97), indicating a slight pause in composition: the writing on the remainder of this page is smaller, darker, and neater than what precedes it.

36 Bladorthin's intended departure is made explicit on Ms. page 79 (p. 230 of this book, corresponding to DAA.163), but it had been prefigured as far back as the first chapter (see the commentary on the 'lucky number' on page 14). Note, however, that while in the published book the wizard stresses his pressing engagements elsewhere ('some pressing business away south; and I am already late through bothering with you people' – DAA.187), here he states less emphatically 'I have got other business on hand now that can wait no longer.' Bladorthin also rather tartly remarks 'you won't catch me going through Mirkwood, unless I am obliged – and I am not' – hardly words of reassurance to those about to undertake that very journey. Finally, Tolkien heightened the dwarves' dismay at his departure via the insertion of the following passage into the published book: 'Then they knew that Gandalf was going to leave them at the very edge of Mirkwood, and they were in despair' (DAA.187); this passage first appears in the typescript (typescript page 74; I/1/57:14). As we shall see subsequently, Tolkien at this point had no clear idea what Bladorthin's 'other business' might be, merely that the dramatic necessity of the story required his departure at this point.

37 'Goblins, hob-goblins, or orcs of the worst description' – in this, the only mention of hob-goblins or orcs in the original draft of *The Hobbit*, Tolkien established a false hierarchy between the three terms which he later explicitly spelled out in the prefatory note added to the revised paperback edition in 1966: '*Orc* is not an English word. It occurs in one or two places but is usually translated *goblin* (or *hobgoblin* for the larger kinds)' (DAA.[27]). As Tolkien himself later discovered when

researching possible origins of the word 'hobbit' for the OED, 'Alas! one conclusion is that the statement that *hobgoblins* were "a larger kind" is the reverse of the original truth' (JRRT to Roger Lancelyn Green, 8th January 1971; *Letters* p. 406) – that is, the 'hob' in *hob*goblin is probably a diminutive rather than the reverse. A hob-goblin, then, would in actual folklore usage be smaller than a regular goblin. So great is Tolkien's influence over the fantasy genre, however, that the distinction has persisted into other writers' work (such as that of the creators of the D&D game and the many novels derived thereof), even though based upon a fallacy.

For the distinction between 'goblin' and 'orc' in Tolkien's work, see the commentary on Chapter IV (pp. 137–8).

38 The Great Necromancer's 'dark hidden tower' was prefigured as far back as Chapter I. Gandalf & Company would certainly not want to go that way, since doing so spelled doom for his father's dwarven party a century before. During the writing of *The Lord of the Rings*, the place gained an elven (Sindarin) name, first *Dol Dúgol* ('The Dark Hill'), then *Dol Dúghul* (a refinement of essentially the same meaning), and finally *Dol Guldur* ('Hill of Sorcery', or perhaps 'Sorcerer's Hill' – a rough parallel to The Necromancer's Tower). See HME VII.178, 233–4, & 244 for the arising of the elven name, and Christopher Tolkien's discussion of the first Middle-earth map on pages 296, 298, and 306 of the same volume for its placement (originally the tower was placed further to the east and only shifted when the border of Mirkwood contracted on the evolving map). On the relationship between this tower and Sauron's tower in 'The Lay of Leithian', see the Commentary on pp. 20 & 83.

39 'Keep your peckers up' – probably the most startling phrase in the entire manuscript, this is not nearly as salacious as it sounds but was common British slang of a slightly earlier period (in keeping with the yesteryear air of most of the hobbit's accoutrements, especially in the Bag-End passage – all the OED's citations are from the 1850s through 1870s, and include a passage from Dickens and one from Gilbert & Sullivan). Like all slang, it's difficult to translate exactly but meant roughly 'keep your courage (spirits, resolution) up'. In short, it's the equivalent of the slightly later but much more familiar 'keep a stiff upper lip'.

(i)
Bears

An important fact people often overlook in discussing *The Hobbit* is that it was originally written for a very specific audience, Tolkien's three sons. While this is widely known as a biographical detail, few take into account the degree to which their likes and dislikes played a part in shaping the story.

As Tolkien himself said, an author writes primarily to please himself and uses his own interests as a guide – something we see time and again in *The Hobbit*, with its incorporation of favorite themes and frequent borrowings from Tolkien's professional subjects. Yet a writer is also naturally inclined to include things that he knows from first-hand experience will interest his audience, just as he may be tempted to exclude or down-play themes he knows bore them.[1] From the evidence of Tolkien's various children's stories, all of which originated as tales told to (or written down and then read to) John, Michael, and Christopher, we can emphatically conclude that one element they liked very much was Bears.[2]

Bears appear prominently in a number of Tolkien's stories for his children, most notably in the figure of the North Polar Bear (Karhu), Father Christmas's sidekick who provides most of the comic relief throughout the twenty-three-year series that makes up the *Father Christmas Letters*. Karhu's antics provide most of the plot elements in this episodic epistolary story, either to cause some disaster that endangered the arrival of some particular requested present or to save the day in the nick of time (most notably in the battles against the goblins). In time North Polar Bear (or NPB, as he is also sometimes called) is joined by two rapscallion nephews, Paksu and Valkotukka, who become continuing minor characters very much in their uncle's disaster-causing mode. Yet another bear, Cave-Bear, enters the story in the 1932 letter, and *his* progeny, the 'Cave-cubs', make an appearance a few years later in the letter for 1934.

Bears also play a prominent role in *Mr. Bliss*, whose unintended entourage runs afoul of the three bears: Archie, Teddy, and Bruno – based, according to Joan Tolkien, on the three teddy bears owned by Tolkien's three sons at the time.[3] In general the bear highwaymen are comic villains, mischievous rogues rather like the North Polar Bear in character, but openly larcenous in behavior. They are also, on the surface, considerably more threatening than the benign NPB, threatening at one point to eat our hero if he doesn't do what they want. Tolkien assures the reader that they wouldn't actually do it (*Mr. Bliss*, page 14), but even the possibility puts Mr. Bliss's bears somewhere between Karhu and Medwed on the danger meter. Interestingly enough, there is even one scene in *Mr. Bliss* reminiscent of *The Hobbit*, where the bears have Mr. Bliss's companions to supper at their house in the woods: 'quite a large house, long and low, with no upstairs' (*Mr. Bliss*, page 32). Even the illustration of the bears' dinner party, while completely different in detail (due to the inclusion of modern-day amenities such as chairs, tablecloth, cutlery, overhanging lamp, and curtains), bears a striking resemblance to the illustration of 'Beorn's Hall' in *The Hobbit*. In particular, both pictures use precisely the same point of view, looking down the length of the house or hall (compare DAA.170 [or H-S#116] with *Mr. Bliss*, page 31).

Medwed/Beorn does correspond to the bears in *The Father Christmas Letters* in two significant ways. Like Cave-Bear, Medwed is a survivor of an older, vanished world. Father Christmas describes Cave-Bear as 'the eldest of the few remaining Cave-bears' and casually remarks 'I had not seen him for centuries'. Furthermore, the walls of Cave-Bear's home are decorated with Neolithic cave-paintings strikingly similar to those found in the real world at Lascaux and Altamira. We are told that these have been in his family for over ninety generations, since before the time of Cave-men ('when the North Pole was somewhere else'). However, unlike Medwed, Cave-Bear has not been expelled from his ancestral home by the goblins but simply ignores their presence as nothing more than an annoyance. Presumably, therefore, he shares Polar Bear's immunity to goblin attacks – Father Christmas says in passing that 'of course Goblins can't hurt *him* [NPB], but their caves are very dangerous', and while North Polar Bear is lost in the darkness he 'boxed one or two [goblins] flat that came and poked him in the dark, and had said some very nasty things to them all' (FCL, 1932 letter). Even more reminiscent of *The Hobbit* (and the Battle of Five Armies in particular) is the description in the next year's letter of Polar Bear fighting a swarm of goblins that had invaded Father Christmas's home, Cliff House: 'Polar Bear was squeezing, squashing, trampling, boxing, and kicking Goblins sky-high, and roaring like a zoo, and the Goblins were yelling like engine whistles. He was splendid' (to which NPB modestly adds 'SAY NO MORE: I ENJOYED IT IMMENSELY!' – FCL, 1933 letter). The illustration of this letter shows the bear crushing a goblin in each hand while trampling another, knocking down a fourth, and kicking two more across the room. Interestingly enough, the North Polar Bear seems to have swelled to twice his normal size in this depiction of the battle-scene – cf. Tolkien's remark that Medwed/Beorn 'seemed to have grown almost to giant-size in his wrath' upon his appearance on the battlefield (DAA. 349). Clearly, the silly old bear could, upon provocation, become a dangerous foe – just as Tolkien says of Medwed, he is a good friend and a dangerous enemy ('Medwed could be a fierce enemy. But now he was their friend; and encouraged by his kindness, they told him all their story . . .' – p. 241).

This sense of danger held in check is very much present throughout the Medwed section, especially in its account of their first night in his hall (Bladorthin having already warned Gandalf & Company that the skin-changer can be 'appalling when angry'). After welcoming them into his hall and feeding them '[s]uch a dinner [as] they had not eaten since they left the house of Elrond',[4] he warns them not to go outside till sun is up 'on your peril' (p. 239). Add to this Bilbo's fears of being killed in his sleep when he hears growling in the night 'and a noise as of some great animal scuffling at the door' (ibid.), and the scene with the murdered orc and skinned warg (p. 241) which reveals just what Medwed does to those he considers his enemies.

All of this alarm is, of course, fully justified: unlike wolves and eagles, bears really DO eat people – a fact of which Shakespeare was well aware, hence his famous stage direction for one doomed character: 'Exit, pursued by a bear' (*A Winter's Tale*, Act III scene iii), followed by a gruesome off-stage mauling as the character is torn limb from limb. The largest land predators, bears maul people every year even today. Yet, perhaps due to the influence of the teddy bear,[5] they have ironically enough escaped the sinister reputation acquired by their lupine and aquiline cohorts. Many people who would be terrified to encounter a wolf in the wild actually approach bears they encounter in wilderness areas and national parks, often with tragic results. Bilbo knows better, and his attitude toward bears is wary caution, even after friendly relations with Medwed are firmly established.

(ii)
Bothvar Bjarki

Now that we know more about the dating of *The Hobbit* (see 'The Chronology of Composition'), we can see that Medwed's resemblance to the North Polar Bear is a case of source rather than influence. Indeed, NPB's transformation in the 1932–33 letters from a figure of fun to a heroic doughty warrior (a process paralleled in *The Hobbit* with the dwarves and Bilbo himself as the tone shifts in the final chapters to become less like a fairy-tale and more like a saga – as CSL put it, 'as if the battle of Toad Hall had become a serious *heimsókn* and Badger had begun to talk like Njal')[6] might be attributed to the influence of *The Hobbit* on the older series, particularly since it occurs just at the time when our best evidence suggests Tolkien was writing the story of Bilbo's adventures. A far more promising *source* (as opposed to parallel) for Tolkien's werebear lies in his professional interests. As so often, the figure of Medwed/Beorn marks one of those grounds where Tolkien's scholarship and his storytelling for his children meet.

In this case, the flash-point is the story of Bothvar Bjarki. The lost *Bjarkamál*, a poem apparently similar to those preserved in the *Elder Edda*, told the story of a man who could at times assume the form of a bear. The original story is lost, but elements of it can be glimpsed from works it influenced, including both *Beowulf* and *Hrolf Kraki's Saga*.[7] Underlying both the epic poem and the saga according to some theories is a folk-tale about a feral child raised by bears, the Bear's-Son Story. Tolkien himself was greatly interested in these speculations, and actually re-created the lost folktale in an unpublished short story, 'Sellic Spell'.[8]

Bothvar's story is only part of the greater saga of King Hrolf and his champions,[9] which has been compared to the King Arthur and Charlemagne cycles: the story of a great king and his magnificent court, his brave champions (of whom Bothvar is the greatest) and his vile, deadly foes. In the best tradition the saga is full of bravery, treachery, lust, incest, enchantments, transformations, and battles. Bothvar himself is one of three sons of an unlucky prince who, rejecting the improper advances of his stepmother (a Lappish witch), was turned into a bear by the evil queen. A bear by day and a man by night, he begets triplets on a childhood sweetheart[10] before being killed by hunters: the eldest child is only half-human, the middle one human save for a distorted foot, and the youngest, Bothvar, fully human – in appearance at least.[11] Eventually Bothvar grows up, avenges his father, and sets out on a heroic career, two of his greatest deeds being the transformation of a coward into a hero and the slaying of a Grendel-like beast that haunted King Hrolf's hall. Becoming the chief of Hrolf's champions, he marries the king's daughter and becomes literally his right-hand man ('Bothvar was prized and esteemed above them all, and sat on the king's right hand next to him'). The most extraordinary event of his career, however, comes at its very end: in the final battle where Hrolf Kraki's champions are besieged by an army of elves, norns, and evil men led by the king's half-sister (the elf-woman Skuld) and her husband Hjorvarth. Although vastly outnumbered the king and eleven of his twelve champions fight bravely, aided by a mysterious ally:

> . . . a huge bear advanced before king Hrolf's men, and always next at hand where the king was. He killed more men with [that] paw of his than any five of the king's champions. Blows and missiles rebounded from him, and he beat down both men and horses from king Hjorvarth's host, and everything within reach he crunched with his teeth, so that alarm and dismay arose in king Hjorvarth's host.
>
> — 'King Hrolf and His Champions', tr. Gwyn Jones, p. 313; cf. The Battle of Five Armies, pp. 679–80.

So long as the bear fights for them, Hrolf Kraki's forces triumph against overwhelming odds. However, one of the champions (the redeemed coward mentioned earlier, who has now become the most brutal of the champions) frets that Bothvar is nowhere to be seen on the battlefield and leaves the field seeking him. He finds Bothvar sitting in a trance and awakes him, urging him to be mindful of his glory, to join the battle and not hide like a coward. At that moment, Bothvar wakes and the bear vanishes. Bjarki berates his fellow champion ('You have not been so helpful to the king by this action of yours as you think') and the two men go outside, where they find that the tide of battle has turned against the heroes. Queen Skuld now begins to use black magic against them ('she . . . had not brought any of her tricks into play while the bear was in king Hrolf's host; but there was now such a change as when dark night follows the bright day' – Gwyn Jones, p. 315), summoning up a monstrous boar and causing the dead to rise again when slain and continue fighting. Bothvar, King Hrolf, and the rest are all slain, only to be later avenged by Bothvar's two brothers (the half-human outlaw Elgfrothi and King Thorir Houndsfoot) aided by a force sent by King Hrolf's other half-sister (who is also his mother – it's a complicated family tree), the Swedish Queen Yrsa.

Yet despite his apparent derivation from, or inspiration by, Bothvar Bjarki, Medwed/Beorn differs greatly from the ancient hero of the North. Medwed is a solitary, without wife or kin, living alone with his animals (indeed, it's hinted that he might *be* an animal, or at least as much animal as human). Bothvar is one of three brothers (in the best fairy-tale tradition), each as extraordinary in his own way as he. Bjarki has parents and grandparents, and his father's and mother's tragedy is directly responsible for his prowess and strange powers. By contrast, Medwed notably lacks the ancestry established for most other characters in Tolkien's story, including Bilbo, Gandalf/Thorin, Elrond, and later Bard. Wifeless and childless, he seems wholly without kinsmen or friends of his own kind (whatever that is), unless we count the unseen bears who rendezvous with him in the forest. Bothvar, by contrast, marries King Hrolf's daughter Drifa and has several children by her. In this, and in personality, Medwed/Beorn seems less like Bothvar and more like his eldest brother Elgfrothi, the wildest of the three.

This Elgfrothi is 'of a rather strange kind. He was a man above, but an elk from the navel down' (hence his name, Elk-Frothi or elk-Frodo).[12] Unlike Bothvar, who becomes the champion of Hrolf Kraki's court, Frothi becomes an outlaw, 'an evil-doer, killing men for their money,' living by himself in a hut in the mountains and waylaying travellers. Elgfrothi is unnaturally strong, beginning his exile after he has crippled many men and even killed some at wrestling games (in this he is slightly reminiscent of the hapless Túrin's early history as an outlaw and robber); however, we are also told (rather ambiguously) that while he kills men for their money, 'he had given peace to many men who were of little strength'. Despite this, however, he is not all bad: he bears no ill will to his more fortunate brothers and indeed offers to split all his gains with them (which by this point amounted to 'immense wealth' – Gwyn Jones, p. 271). After Bothvar has avenged their father, he visits his elder brother and Elgfrothi makes Bjarki drink his blood, making our hero stronger than ever. Together Elgfrothi and Bjarki seem to have provided hints that Tolkien combined into one character, who shares the elusive nature of his inspirations.

The dichotomy of Elgfrothi and Medwed's solitariness contrasted with Bjarki's gregariousness as a natural leader of men may explain one curious feature of the Beorn story: at the end of the book (here we are anticipating a bit), Tolkien breaks narrative continuity to tell us that Medwed/Beorn gathered the woodmen to him and 'became a great chief afterwards in those regions & ruled a wide land between the mountains & the wood; & it is said that for many generations the men of his line had the power of taking bear's shape, & some were grim men & bad' – shades of Elgfrothi, perhaps? – 'but most were in heart like Beorn, if less in size & strength. In their day the last goblins were hunted from the Misty Mountains & a new peace came over the edge of the Wild'.[13] We are also told, in *The Lord of the Rings*, that at the time of Frodo's journey some 80 years later the 'Beornings', as they were now called, were ruled by Beorn's son, Grimbeorn the Old (*LotR*.245).

The motif of Medwed-Beorn as a chieftain or leader of an independent people would seem to derive from the hitherto neglected middle brother, Thorir Houndsfoot ('He had hound's feet on him from the instep . . . though for the rest he was the most handsome of men' – Gwyn Jones pp. 268–9). When it comes his turn to set out and seek his fortune, he travels to the land of the Gauts, who make him their king 'by reason of his size' (the Gauts very practically pick whoever fits the throne best as their next king, rather than the other way around – Gwyn Jones, pp. 271–2). Thorir resembles Bothvar so much that when the latter shows up for a visit Thorir's wife the queen mistakes him for her husband, and only Bothvar's innate chivalry prevents him from cuckolding his brother the king in a scene strongly resembling an episode in the Welsh tale 'Pwyll Prince of Dyfed,' the first of the four branches of the *Mabinogi*. By incorporating echoes of the displaced prince becoming a king of men in his own right (or, in this case, creating a new people named after himself, along the lines of the historical Scyldings), Tolkien seems to be harkening back to the third of these three remarkable brothers.

One curious theme, hinted at in Tolkien's notes and outlines, was never fully realized in the finished book. As the section of drafting given in Text Note 15 above indicates, Tolkien hesitated over whether or not Medwed was under some sort of enchantment, finally coming down with the magnificently equivocal statement that he is 'under no enchantment but his own'. However, against this we must set the plot notes given between this and the next chapter, sketching out events between the guests bedding down for the night in Medwed's hall in what is now the middle of Chapter VII to their capture by wood-elves at the beginning of Chapter IX. Written while Chapter VII was still being drafted, in these plot notes Tolkien states unequivocally: 'Let bear be enchanted' (I/I/23:5; see p. 293), underlining the point for emphasis. Nor did he forget this motif: Plot Notes F, a half-page of late pencilled notes written on the back of an unsent letter, ends with a mention of 'Battle of Five armies and disenchantment of Beorn' (I/I/23:3; see p. 629).

The idea underlying these two isolated references is never made explicit, but taken in context with Medwed/Beorn's altered personality and behavior at the end of the book, they suggest that his 'disenchantment' and becoming a leader of men are linked. The exact nature of the enchantment, and the circumstances of its breaking, are obscure; mysteries like so much else about Medwed-Beorn. Perhaps it is even self-imposed ('under no enchantment but his own'). In any case, in some way his role in the battle – killing the goblin-chief, slaying and scattering his followers – apparently fulfills the unknown conditions for breaking his 'enchantment'. But unlike Bothvar, who projects his bear-form once and once only, Medwed/Beorn retains his shape-shifting ability and passes it along to his descendants. Even more curiously, the scanty information in *LotR* does not refer to his death but merely indicates that the rule has now passed to his son; from the text it is impossible to say that he did not eventually return at last to the mountains, vanishing back into his origins like Scyld Scefing (Shield Sheafing).[14]

(iii)
Beorn's Hall

Like the figure of Medwed/Beorn himself, the illustration of his hall that accompanies the published book marks another mingling of Tolkien's erudition with his storytelling gifts. A moody, evocative drawing in its own right, it exists in two distinct variants. The earlier, 'Firelight in Beorn's house', is the more striking of the two, making more use of shadows and having red flames emanate from the central fire-pit. It also presents the hall from a decided slant, leaving the far end out of the viewer's line of sight. A black and white reproduction of this piece appears in *Artist & Illustrator* (H-S#115) and in *The Annotated Hobbit* (DAA.171), but the original with its touch of colour has so far as I know never been published before: see Plate VI [bottom] in this book. The slight use of colour probably led to this original depiction of Beorn's hall being rejected for publication: even a speck of colour would require the entire picture to be produced in colour, a much more expensive process than that for black-and-white art. The similar 'Troll's Hill' – see Plate IV [bottom] – which was also not used in any edition of *The Hobbit* published in Tolkien's lifetime, was probably rejected for the same reason.[15]

The second or replacement illustration, 'Beorn's Hall' (DAA.170, H-S#116), offers a straightforward look down the length of the hall at more or less eye level, with a clear view of the long table (now with stump-seats), the fire-pit, a doorway at the far end, and a louver in the roof allowing smoke to escape. This drawing, being entirely in black and white, was used in the 1937 *Hobbit* and has been reproduced many times since.

A curious feature of the original, rejected illustration was discovered by Tolkien scholar J. S. Ryan in 1990:[16] Tolkien had modelled 'Firelight in Beorn's house' very closely on an illustration of a Norse mead-hall that had appeared in a work published just a few years before, *An Introduction to Old Norse* (1927), by his friend and collaborator, E. V. Gordon.[17] And not just any mead-hall: the illustration appears in the midst of Gordon's excerpt from *Hrolf Kraki's Saga*, a section he titles 'Bothvar Bjarki at the Court of King Hrolf' (EVG, pp. 27–8). What's more, since Hrolf Kraki is the same figure as *Beowulf*'s Hrothulf, nephew to the Danish king, his hall is better known to modern-day readers by its Old English name: *Heorot*, the Grendel-haunted seat of old King Hrothgar. Tolkien, then, has modeled Medwed-Beorn's hall on a building he had studied carefully – in fact, the most famous such hall in Old English literature, every detail of whose description had been scrutinized by generations of philologists and archeologists.[18] It's just another example of his fiction bringing vividly to life something that came out of his scholarship, offering us a re-creation of what it'd be like to spend the night in such a building.

(iv)
The Carrock

> [R]ight in the path of the stream which looped itself round it, was a rock – almost a hill of stone, like a last outpost of the mountains, or a large piece cast miles into the plain by some giant among giants . . . There was [a] flat place on the top of the hill of stone, and a well worn path with many steps leading down it, to the river side, and a ford of huge boulders which led across to the grass land beyond the river. There was a little cave (a wholesome one) with a pebbly floor at the foot of the hill opposite the boulder-ford. Here the party gathered and discussed what was to be done.

As noted above (cf. Text Note 12), Tolkien did not originally bestow upon this geographical feature the name it bears now. Instead in the top margin of the page (manuscript page 79; 1/1/7:3), he scribbled the sequence Sorneldin > Sinrock > Lamrock > the Carrock.

Sorneldin would seem to derive from Tolkien's invented languages, possibly the Gnomish (Sindarin) words for rock (*sarn*) and point (*nel*) – cf. the *Gnomish Lexicon* [1917], pp. 67, 60. More probably, it derives from the Qenya (Quenya) word for eagle (*sorn, sorne*), one of the derivatives of which is *soron* (high peak, pinnacle, crag) – cf. the *Qenya Lexicon* [1917–1920], p. 86. If so, then a memory of the rejected name might have influenced Tolkien when he came to illustrate the scene; see below.

Sinrock seems not to be Elvish at all, unless I have misread the (hastily scribbled) word and the third letter is actually -r-: *sir* being the Sindarin word for 'river' (*Gnomish Lexicon* p. 67) – cf. the great river of Beleriand, the *Sir*ion, and Moria's 'Gate-stream', the *Sir*annon. 'River-rock' suits the Carrock exceptionally well as a name, but it is unlike Tolkien to use mixed (Elven/English) forms by combining a Sindarin prefix with an English root, which may have lead to the word's rejection. It seems far more likely that the name is a modernization of Old English: *sin-* (great, huge) + *-rocc* (rock): 'The Great Rock'.

Lamrock I can find no explanation at all within the invented languages, the closest equivalents being Qenya *lama* (flock) and *lambe* (tongue), neither of which seems appropriate. Nor does the Old English word *lam* seem a likely candidate, as it means earth, dirt, or soil (all preserved in its modern descendant, *loam*). The answer probably lies, as in so much else of Tolkien's non-Elven geographic nomenclature, in the rich field of English place-names.

Carrock, the fourth in this hastily-written sequence and the name chosen from that point forward, derives from a dialectical Old English (Old Northumbrian) borrowing from the Celtic. That borrowed word, *carr*, came to be especially applied to isolated rocks standing in the sea just off the Scottish and Northumbrian coasts, a close parallel to the water-surrounded Carrock of our story. Curiously enough, the root Celtic word (from which our modern word *crag* also descends) is itself an anomaly that has caused scholars of the Celtic languages much puzzlement. The various forms of it in Welsh, Irish, Scots, and Manx, while obviously sharing a common ancestor, do not follow the normal laws of sound-changes that would enable philologists to establish exactly how that lost ancestor would have been spelled or pronounced. It is thus one of those 'asterisk words' which, as T. A. Shippey points out, is exactly the kind of thing that attracted Tolkien's attention.

As for the exact spelling 'carrock', Jim Allan's *An Introduction to Elvish* [1974] states that '*Carrock Fell* is a mountain peak in the Skiddaw group in Cumberland' (Allan p. 174). However, as Taum Santoski discovered, Tolkien's source was probably his old mentor, Joseph Wright,[19] who lists the word in Volume I of his monumental *English Dialect Dictionary*, noting that it was variously spelt *currick* (in Northumberland, Durham, and Cumberland), *carrock* (Northumberland, Cumberland), *corrock* ('North Country'), *currack* ('North Country', Durham), *curragh* (Durham), *currock* (Northumberland, Cumberland), and *kirock* ('North Country') and pronounced ke-rek. Wright defines the word as '1. A cairn, a heap of stones, used as a boundary mark, burial place, or guide for travellers' and '2. A distant mountain by which, when the sun appears over it, the country folk tell the time of day' (*English Dialect Dictionary*, Volume I, page 845).

We know that Tolkien was familiar with Wright's book and used it often; in 1923, fresh from completing his *A Middle English Vocabulary* [1922] and deep into the *Sir Gawain* project, he wrote to Mrs. Wright (herself a distinguished philologist):

> Middle English is an exciting field – almost uncharted I begin to think, because as soon as one turns detailed personal attention on to any little corner of it the received notions and ideas seem to crumple up and fall to pieces – as far as language goes at any rate. E.D.D. [= Wright's *English Dialect Dictionary*] is certainly indispensable, or 'unentbehrlich'† as really comes more natural to the philological mind, and I encourage people to browze in it.
>
> —JRRT to E. M. Wright, 13th February 1923; *Letters* p. 11.

† Editor's note: 'indispensable, essential, absolutely necessary'.

It seems likely that Tolkien's interest in the word is linked to his time at Leeds, when he was living near the region where the word had once been used and where remnants of it remained behind in the nomenclature of the area. Tolkien provided 'advice and encouragement' as well as a foreword to W. E. Haigh's book *A New Glossary of the Dialect of the Huddersfield District* in 1928, in which he talks about the value of such work (Hammond, *Descriptive Bibliography*, p. 290). That interest may also have been sparked by contact with A. H. Smith, one of his star pupils at Leeds and later the editor, compiler, and printer of *Songs for the Philologists*. Smith's special field of study was delving into the origins of English place-names and he eventually published a number of books on the subject, becoming one of his generation's leading experts in that field and serving as General Editor of the English Place-Name Society's multivolume series exploring and explicating the place names of each English county.[20] Smith himself contributed two volumes to this series (vols. XXV and XXVI, *English Place Name Elements*, Cambridge Univ. Press, [1956]), in which he gives *carrec* as a place-name element, citing Carrock Fell in Cumberland as an example. The Cumberland volumes of the series (*The Place Names of Cumberland* by A. M. Armstrong, A. Mawer, F. M. Stemton, & Bruce Dikins, English Place-Name Society vols XX, XXI, & XXII [1952]) discuss Carrock Fell, near Mosedale in Cumberland, and note that the name had variously been listed in historical records as *Carroc* [1208], *Carrok* [1261], *verticem de Carrock* [1568], *the mountain Carrak* or *Carrick* [1610], and *Carrock-Fell* [1794]. Armstrong et al. simply note that 'This is a British hill-name' (vol. XXI, p. 305). Thus, Carrock-Fell was once simply known as 'Carroc/Carrok/Carrock', *fell* being a word meaning a barren or rocky hill. Similarly, *verticem* (vertex, height) is merely Latin for a mountain peak or high place.

Curiously enough, one of the sources Wright cites in the *English Dialect Dictionary*, *The Denham Tracts*, also contains the only known occurrence of the word 'hobbit' before Tolkien; see Appendix I. We have no proof that Tolkien ever read this work, but its frequent citation by Wright – a work Tolkien consulted closely – offers indirect proof that Tolkien was probably at least aware of Denham's work, though it's unlikely he was familiar with it. Denham describes a currack known locally as 'The Lang [long] Man of Bollyhope' and retells the story relating to it (bracketed additions were probably supplied by the Folk-lore Society's editor, Dr Hardy):

THE LANG MAN O' BOLLYHOPE.

The warriors on the [mountain] high
Moving athwart the evening sky,
Seem'd forms of giant height:
Their armour as it caught the rays,
Flash'd back again the western blaze
In lines of dazzling light.

Bolliope, or Bollyhope, is a high ridge of black mountains, about four miles from Wolsingham. On the top of this dreary and sterile track is a *currack* or *curragh*† [a pillar of stones], known by the name of *March stones* on the Border. Tradition states that one clear summer's evening, many long years ago, two tall figures were seen to meet on the top of the ridge, and at once proceed to mortal strife. The clash of arms was heard in the valley, and their forms, being set in relief against the clear blue sky, seemed to dilate to that of the *giants of old*. One of them was at length seen to fall, and the other, after hovering about for a short space, vanished from sight. On the morrow the mangled corpse of a *tall man* was found on the spot. No person, however, knew him; neither was there any inquiry made after him. He was buried where he fell, and the *pile of stones* which was reared on his grave is now know as the

Lang man o' Bollyhope!

† [Denham's note:] This curragh is on the southernmost edge of Bollyhope.

—*The Denham Tracts*, Vol. I [1892], p. 112.

I have been unable to trace the March Stones, but it's suggestive that the cairn or currack in this case comes with suggestions of giantism, since the same hints apply to Medwed/Beorn himself. However, in the case of the 'Lang Man', Denham is at pains to point out that the dead man and his foe only seemed like 'giants of old' because of the length of their shadows, whereas Medwed turns out to be able to assume giant-size in truth (cf. Chapter XVIII).

Probably closely connected with this is the word *hurrock*, defined by Denham as '*a piled-up heap of loose stones* or rubbish; in fact, a collection of anything in a loose state' (*Denham Tracts*, vol. I, p. 105; italics mine);

Denham illustrates the word with a story about a shrewd Scots nobleman who bought a castle cheaply from King James by describing it as 'only a hurrock of stones' – only after he had sold it did the king visit and view the 'noble pile . . . the stately feudal castle, with its many tours [towers] and grete chaumbres [great chambers] and hawles [halls]', leading him to exclaim to the new owner: 'Did thou na' say that Raby Castle was only a hurrock of stanes! Ah! mon, I hae nae sic anither hurrock in a' ma' dominions.' Wright not only lists the word in his *English Dialect Dictionary* (Volume III, page 289) but cites Denham as his source and repeats the chagrined king's exclamation.

Even if we discount the 'heap of stones' definition for *currock* as due to confusion with the similar word *hurrock*, we still find that Tolkien has, for his own purposes, picked and chosen from among the cluster of meanings given in Joseph Wright and those preserved in modern-day Celtic words descended from it. THE Carrock of Tolkien's tale is clearly neither a cairn nor a burial place. It's distinctive enough to serve as a guide for travellers and could easily be used as a huge natural sundial whereby to judge the time of day, but Medwed would not have named it with the thought of strangers in mind, given how much he dislikes visitors, and there are no indications in the text that it serves any time-keeping purposes. A boundary marker seems closer to the mark – at the very least, it is within Medwed/Beorn's territory: a spot he visits often and one which goblins and wargs shun for that reason.

These very factors – being easily seen from a long way off, possibly marking the edge of Medwed's territory, and being within easy walking distance of his steading – account for its being a good place for the eagles to deposit their guests. Note, however, that Tolkien never commits himself to an actual definition of the word 'carrock', instead allowing his very detailed description ('he calls things like that carrocks') to stand in the place of a formal definition. Presumably the flat top that serves as a handy look-out, the carved steps, the little cave in its base, and even the ford across the river at its foot are all incidentals and it would still be a 'carrock' even without these: the key element seems to be an isolated hill surrounded by moving water, just as in the root-word *carr* (see above), except here transferred from coastal waters to standing alone in a great river that rushes by on either side. We know from the text that other carrocks exist (or what Medwed would call a carrock, which amounts to pretty much the same thing), and we do not have to look far on the map of Middle-earth to find another likely candidate: the island of Tol Brandir, a mountain standing alone in the same river further south (cf. *LotR*.393 & 414). And in fact in outlines for the chapter 'Farewell to Lórien' in *The Lord of the Rings* (Book Two Chapter VIII) we find the island later known as Tol Brandir was originally called 'Tolondren the Great Carrock' (*Tol*, island; *ondren*, of stone or perhaps great stone), contrasted by Christopher Tolkien with the 'Little Carrock' or 'Lesser Carrock' of *The Hobbit* (HME VII.268–9 & 287). The sheer peak rising out of fast-moving water was an image that appealed strongly to Tolkien, as is also testified by other 'carrocks' such as Tol Morwen (*Silm*.230) and perhaps Himling/Himring (cf. *Unfinished Tales*, pp. 13–14) left behind after the sinking of Beleriand, not to mention the great shoreless mountain rising from the sea glimpsed by St. Brendan the Navigator in 'Imram' (HME IX.297), apparently the remnant of Númenor's Meneltarma, and the Nameless Isle or Lonely Isle that figured in so much of his early poetry.[21] In July 1928, not long before beginning *The Hobbit*, Tolkien had painted Taniquetil as a great sheer mountain rising from the sea (see p. 21) – like Tol Brandir, a place where no human is allowed to step; like the Meneltarma and the Carrock itself, a climbable peak with a shrine or holy court or at least lookout spot on top.

Finally, we come to the curious illustration that Tolkien placed at the end of the preceding chapter in the final published book. Although labelled 'The Misty Mountains looking West from the Eyrie towards Goblin Gate', it seems to actually be a picture of the Eyrie itself (complete with eagle), with the main line of the Misty Mountains behind it, probably as viewed from atop the Carrock. It's also possible that it was originally intended as a depiction of the Carrock itself. For one thing, although it lacks the flattened top described in the text, this peak seems separated from the rest of the Misty Mountains by a considerable stretch of lowland. This separation was even more pronounced in the draft illustration (H-S#110) that preceded the one which actually saw print (H-S#111; DAA.158), in which the central mountain is also much nearer the viewer. Note also the rippling lines around the base of the mountain, connected to left and right with fine parallel lines that cross the picture horizontally; it's possible that these represent the river flowing from north to south, its waters lapping against the base of the Carrock as they flow around it. Finally, as Hammond & Scull point out, the central peak in this picture is a re-drawing of Mount Taniquetil itself (*Artist & Illustrator*, pp. 119 & 120), Tolkien's archetype for this recurrent image in his works.

(v)

The Dolittle Theme

One theme or motif that runs throughout the book, having been hinted at in the warg and eagle scenes and later to reappear with the spiders of Mirkwood and in the crow, raven, and thrush scenes at the Lonely Mountain, briefly takes center stage in this chapter: Medwed's ability to talk to his animals and understand their speech. This is an expression within *The Hobbit* of one of Tolkien's favorite themes: in Middle-earth, everything talks, from a passing fox (*LotR*.85) to Túrin's sword (*Silm*.225). Hence his ideal race, the elves, are linguists *par excellence* – Tolkien tells us in the final paragraph of *The Lord of the Rings* (Appendix F, *LotR*. 1171) that his elves' name for themselves is *Quendi*, or 'the speakers'. As Treebeard says, 'Elves began it, of course, waking trees up and teaching them to speak and learning their tree-talk. *They always wished to talk to everything, the old Elves did*' (*LotR*.489; italics mine). Just how accomplished the elves of old became at this is hinted at in Legolas's ability to hear the lament of the stones of Hollin for Celebrimbor's folk: *'deep they delved us, fair they wrought us, high they builded us; but they are gone'* (*LotR*.301); Legolas is also able to assert that 'the trees and the grass do not now remember them', so long has it been since the elven folk of that land were destroyed or driven away. Nor is the impulse to communicate limited to the elves: Caradhras, the doors of Moria-gate, and the Silent Watchers at Cirith Ungol may not be able to speak, but all can understand and respond to speech. This makes sense in a world where a mountain like Caradhras or tree like Old Man Willow can have a distinct (and malign) personality and some control over their surroundings, and where a river-spirit (nymph) like Goldberry or *genius loci* like Bombadil can take on tangible human forms. In all these cases, Tolkien is incorporating into his world over and over again what he called 'one of the primal "desires" that lie near the heart of Faërie: the desire of men to hold communion with other living things' (OFS.19).[22]

For readers the age of Tolkien's sons in 1930–31, the generation that formed the original audience for his tale, Medwed's ability to understand animal-language and his animal-friends acting as servants to set the table for their feast would immediately conjure up memories of another famous character in children's fantasy, Doctor John Dolittle. Hero of the very popular series beginning with *The Story of Doctor Dolittle* [1920] and its much more famous sequel, *The Voyages of Doctor Dolittle* ([1922], winner of the 1923 Newbery Award as the best children's book of the year), Dolittle too has animal friends who keep house for him, even setting the table just as Medwed's do in this chapter. Dolittle understands animal-language, not because he can assume their form or shares their nature, but because he is a great naturalist who can relate to animals on their own terms. He is in fact a philologist, although that term is never used: the whole focus of the series is on his ability to learn any language (such as, say, shellfish or fruit-fly), and on the unusual adventures to which his linguistic curiosity lead.

Dolittle himself and his assistant Stubbins (who joins the entourage in the second book and becomes the narrator thereafter, writing down these accounts at the end of a long and busy life – shades of Bilbo, perhaps?) are both very hobbit-like in personality, name, and habits. This is hardly surprising, since both Tolkien and Lofting were modeling their characters on the same originals: the English small-town and country folk of the previous century. Just as Tolkien drew on his childhood memories of growing up near Birmingham, so Lofting based Puddleby-on-the-Marsh on his native Berkshire (the county immediately south of Oxfordshire, whereas Tolkien's Warwickshire lies on Oxfordshire's northwest border). Tolkien is deliberately vague about the timing of his tale, as we have seen, although he did admit that 'The Shire . . . is in fact more or less a Warwickshire village of about the period of the Diamond Jubilee'[23] (JRRT to A&U, 12th December 1955; *Letters* p. 230), while Lofting says in the opening paragraph of the first book that his story takes place 'Once upon a time, many years ago – when our grandfathers were little children' (*Story*, page 1); a later reference tells us this was back in the days before one of the animals encountered in the book became extinct (ibid., page 81). The second book is more specific, informing us that if we were to visit the site of Stubbins' parents' home today, some seventy years later, we would find a historical marker on the wall stating that 'John Dolittle, the famous naturalist, played the flute in this house in the year 1839' (*Voyages*, page 43).[24] Thus Lofting's story is set in the very early years of Victoria's reign, while Tolkien's model for Bilbo's Shire comes from the very end of that same reign.

Given his own lifelong interest in languages, it is not surprising that Tolkien would incorporate the central theme of the Dolittle books, talking to animals, into his own story at several points, especially since Lofting's books were favorites of the Tolkien children,[25] his original audience for the new story. Of the many other features shared by both men's work, incidental and otherwise,[26] one in particular seems worth noting: that both *The Hobbit* and the Dolittle books were illustrated by their respective authors in highly distinctive and individualized style. All in all, the Dolittle books were probably the model most in Allen & Unwin's mind when they asked Tolkien for another hobbit book to turn *The Hobbit* from a stand-alone into a series, with results that they could not have foreseen.

(vi)
Radagast

> '. . . perhaps you have heard of my good cousin Radagast who lives near the borders of Mirkwood?'

With these words is introduced one of the most elusive of all Tolkien's characters, who never actually appears on-stage at any point in *The Hobbit* and even in *The Lord of the Rings* shows up only in references to his absence (*LotR*.291), one second-hand account that essentially serves as a flashback (*LotR.* 274–5), and a few brief and not wholly complimentary allusions to his skills and judgement (*LotR.*276, 278–9). The few additional references to him in *The Silmarillion* and *Unfinished Tales* do not add so much as a single line of dialogue, and he remains a sort of Godot about whom we hear but never really meet. Unusually for Tolkien, we do not even know what language his name may be in, or what it means (see below). Nevertheless, so vast is Tolkien's legendarium that all those short, passing references added together do tell us a good deal about the character as he evolved over time. In the face of Tolkien's changing conception, it seems best to approach Radagast layer by layer, to distinguish Tolkien's initial conception from the character's later development.

The first and most important fact about Radagast is that he is claimed by Bladorthin not just as a fellow wizard (apparently one of many) but as a relative: in fact, his cousin. While this claim does not reappear in *The Lord of the Rings*, where Gandalf simply identifies him as 'one of my order' (*LotR.*274), neither is it removed from later editions of *The Hobbit* (cf. DAA.167).[27] Certainly there is nothing impossible about a wizard like Bladorthin having relatives, any more than Gandalf/Thorin's having a cousin Dain (see Chapter XV) or Bilbo's heirs being his cousins the Alibone Baggins (see Chapter XIX). And this remains the case even if we think of Bladorthin as more than merely human (something which the original text cannot resolve one way or the other; cf. the Commentary beginning on p. 49) – note the references by Father Christmas, who is sometimes described as a wizard (p. xxxvi), to his Green Brother (*Letters from Father Christmas*, 1930 & 1931 letters), not to mention their father, Grandfather Yule (ibid., 1930 letter). In the earliest stage of the mythology, at least some among the Maiar were the Valar's children (cf. *The Book of Lost Tales*), and this conception lingered into the period when Tolkien was writing *The Hobbit*, as shown by references to 'Fionwë and the sons of the Valar' in the 1930 *Quenta* (HME IV.164) and to the 'Children of the Valar' in the '(Earliest) Annals of Valinor' (HME IV.293). Nevertheless, in a world where there seem to have been many wizards (see pp. 688 & 696–7), Radagast is the closest thing to another Bladorthin: the latter refers to him as his *good* cousin, and Radagast is liked even by the unsociable Medwed/Beorn ('not a bad fellow; I know him well'). And, while the plot notes make it clear that at the time he drafted this chapter Tolkien had no particular idea of where Bladorthin went or why, looking back from the end of the book we can see that in light of Tolkien's eventual answer to those questions it seems very likely in retrospect that Bladorthin leaves Bilbo & Company at this point in order to go see Radagast, since he lives nearby,[28] to plan together how to drive away the Necromancer (about whom Radagast could expect to be well-informed, since he lives near his dark tower).

The Lord of the Rings adds a good deal more information about Radagast – who now becomes Radagast *the Brown*,[29] no longer Gandalf's 'cousin' but *one of my order*; that is, one of the Five Wizards or Istari (*LotR*.606 & 1121; emphasis mine), and a fellow member of the White Council. The old idea that there are many wizards in the world gives way to the concept that there are only five, all Maiar (see also *Unfinished Tales* pp. 393 & 395). But the earlier concept is not entirely abandoned, and it reoccurs in Tolkien's essay on the Istari drafted in 1954–5 as part of the very final stage of his work on *The Lord of the Rings*, the unfinished Index:

> Of this Order the number is unknown; but of those that came to the North of Middle-earth . . . the chiefs were five.
>
> —*Unfinished Tales*, p. 389.

Tolkien intended at one point for Radagast to play a larger role in Bilbo's new adventure, but exactly what that role would have been cannot now be guessed. In outlines and plot notes written in August of 1939, when Tolkien was contemplating a fresh start on 'The New Hobbit' and thinking of such radical changes as recasting the story with Bilbo rather than Bingo/Frodo as the hero, he includes Radagast's name in a list of plot-elements, such as bringing a dragon to the Shire (shades of *Farmer Giles*!):

> Island in sea. Take Frodo there in end.
> Radagast?
> Battle is raging far off between armies of Elves and Men v. Lord.[30]
> Adventures . . . Stone-Men [i.e., Men of Gondor].
>
> —HME VI.379.

Unfortunately, in the absence of any development we cannot say what this episode would have been, nor how it would have fitted into the larger story. Radagast's presence here was no doubt inspired by a desire to include all the elements possible from *The Hobbit* that had not already been explored; it is perhaps significant, given the absence of *The Hobbit's* stone-giants from the sequel, that the 'Adventure with [the] Giant Tree Beard' appears in a similar list during this same period (HME VI.381).

A second reference to Radagast, during one of the early texts of the Council of Elrond, adds his name to an account of what would happen if they tried to send the One Ring overseas rather than destroy it: 'It would be too perilous – and [Sauron's] war would come over the Shire and destroy the Havens. [*added in margin*:] Radagast.' (HME VI.396–7) – but this is so allusive that there is no way to tell what Tolkien had in mind; whether it was Radagast who proposed the idea or voiced the objection (in which case he must have been one of those gathered in

Rivendell to discuss the crisis), or what part he might have played in such a scenario.

Within the published text, we learn from Gandalf's words at the Council of Elrond that he considers Radagast

> a worthy Wizard, a master of shapes and changes of hue; and he has much lore of herbs and beasts, and birds are especially his friends
>
> —*LotR*.274

but in the account that follows we also gain the impression that Radagast is somewhat careless of detail, if not a little dim, since he cannot get the name of the Shire right.[31] He comes across as a good fellow but not overbold, since he seems prepared to wash his hands of the dire business once he has fulfilled his task and delivered Saruman's message, riding off 'as if the Nine were after him' (as indeed they might well be) rather than accompanying Gandalf to Orthanc or taking direct action against the Nazgûl. More importantly, he comes across as gullible, since he is taken in by Saruman – but, to be fair, so too is Gandalf, who promptly rides into Saruman's trap. In his original draft of this passage, Tolkien considered the idea that Radagast was working with Saruman and had also turned to evil, deliberately luring Gandalf into their trap, but quickly rejected it (HME VII.131–4 & 138–9). When contrasted with Gandalf, all these shortcomings seriously diminish Radagast's stature. Yet Tolkien has a way of exalting the humble, and Radagast is no exception. Just as he undertook this errand for Saruman despite his aversion to travel and also pressing concerns of his own (see below), so he immediately promises his aid when Gandalf asks it. What's more, he delivers on his promise: it is 'honest Radagast' whose messenger delivers Gandalf from bondage and so foils Saruman's plot (*LotR*.278–9).[32]

After this point, Radagast vanishes altogether from the narrative, and his fate is one of the very few loose ends in a tightly-knit story. In some slightly later notes [circa 1940?] Tolkien considered giving Isengard to Radagast after Saruman is cast out from their order (HME VII.212), but this idea disappeared from the story before that scene was written. He does not attend the Council of Elrond, but then we are told he was 'never a traveller, unless driven by great need' (*LotR*.274). More ominously, when messengers from Rivendell reach his home at Rhosgobel in Mirkwood to bring him word of Frodo's mission they find it abandoned (*LotR*.291), and he does not appear at the Grey Havens to take ship back to the Undying Lands at the end of the story. While Rhosgobel is not shown on the Middle-earth map published with *The Fellowship of the Ring* and *The Two Towers*, we are told that it lay 'near the Southern borders of Mirkwood' (DAA.167; cf. also *LotR*.274), and it does appear on Tolkien's original draft for that map reproduced in *The Treason of Isengard* (HME VII.305), near the Gladden Fields (cf. *LotR*.291) under the western eaves of the great forest roughly halfway between the Forest Road and Dol Guldur (here still known as Dol Dúghul).

The explicit statement that Radagast failed in his mission comes not from the main text of *The Lord of the Rings* but the unused Index entry on the Istari:

> Indeed, of all the Istari, one only remained faithful [i.e., Gandalf], and he was the last-comer. For Radagast, the fourth, became enamoured of the many beasts and birds that dwelt in Middle-earth, and forsook Elves and Men, and spent his days among the wild creatures.
>
> —*Unfinished Tales*, p. 390.

This view is reinforced by a scrap of alliterative verse on the sending of the Istari, which includes the passage:

> of the Five that came from a far country . . .
> One only returned.
>
> —*Unfinished Tales*, p. 395.

In short, Radagast 'went native', and as such can be judged to have failed, but only if his mission is defined in the terms used in the Istari essay from the unpublished Index: to focus his attention on 'Elves and Men'. Moreover, this judgement seems uncharacteristically harsh in light of what is said about Radagast within the actual published text of *The Lord of the Rings*. Radagast never supported Sauron in any way, and other indications suggest that defending birds and beasts against the earth-destroying Darkness that had ravaged the Brown Lands (once the Garden of the Entwives), desecrated the landscape before the Black Gate ('Here neither spring nor summer would ever come again . . . a land defiled, diseased beyond all healing' – *LotR*.657), and left Mordor a dying land (cf. *LotR*.956) was in fact part of Radagast's mission – his special brief, as it were (see below). From 'The Tale of Years' (Appendix B, *LotR*.1127) and 'The Hunt for the Ring' (*Unfinished Tales* p. 338) we know that Sauron's forces in Dol Guldur attacked the wood-elves' realm in late June, or just before Radagast finally found Gandalf at Midsummer and hurried away homeward. In hindsight, it does not seem too much of a stretch to speculate that the cause of his haste to get Saruman's and Gandalf's business done was foreknowledge of the impending attack and concern over the denizens of the forest whom he had taken under his protection – a concern with which we would expect Tolkien to be altogether in sympathy, so long as it did not replace a concern for the greater world and its peoples (which, from the messengers he dispatched to Orthanc, it seems not to have done); cf. the sympathetic treatment of Treebeard, who transcends concern for his own forest into risking self-sacrifice for the good of others.

It seems that we have thus in Radagast someone who insofar as he is able opposes Sauron and all he stands for, and rightly values those creatures who are Yavanna's domain, but perhaps undervalues the children of Ilúvatar upon whom all the other Istari focus. His devotion to birds and beasts can be seen as parallel to Gandalf's fondness for hobbits, and his friendship with Beorn suggests that he aids not just the bears and other animals but also the wood-men who later become the Beornings. Perhaps Gandalf's words to Denethor can be applied more literally to Radagast:

> . . . for my part, I shall not wholly fail of my task . . . if anything passes through this night that can still grow fair or bear fruit and flower again in days to come.
>
> —*LotR*.788–9.

Tolkien's later, post-*Lord of the Rings* writings on Radagast bear out this view. Thus his being foisted upon Saruman as a companion at Yavanna's request in the account of the Valar choosing the Istari (date unknown; *Unfinished Tales* p. 393) need not be taken as a further diminishment of Radagast so much as yet another example of Saruman's pride from the very beginning of his mission (one of the great Vala should not have to 'beg' a Maia to take a companion on a dangerous mission). Then too there is a curious passage in a meditation on Sauron's motives written in the late 1950s, where Tolkien writes that Sauron believed others motivated wholly by self-interest like himself. The pronoun references in the following passage are unclear, but if I have interpreted them correctly then it casts both Gandalf and Radagast in a new light by closely associating them together in Sauron's mind and contrasting them both with Saruman.

> His [Sauron's] cynicism . . . seemed fully justified in Saruman. Gandalf he did not understand. But certainly he [Sauron] had already become evil, and therefore stupid, enough to imagine that his [Gandalf's] different behaviour [from Saruman's] was due simply to weaker intelligence and lack of firm masterful purpose. He [Gandalf] was only [in Sauron's view] a rather cleverer Radagast – cleverer, because it is more profitable (more productive of power) to become absorbed in the study of people than of animals.
>
> —'Myths Transformed', HME X.397.

This closer association with Gandalf – in fact, a full circle returning to the days when he was Bladorthin's only fellow wizard mentioned in *The Hobbit* – is reaffirmed in Tolkien's last writings on the subject [circa 1972/73]. Here Tolkien discards the idea, traceable back to the essay on the Istari from the unused *LotR* Index, that all the other wizards except Gandalf had failed – e.g., where he said of the two Blue Wizards that

> whether they remained in the East, pursuing there the purposes for which they were sent; or perished; or as some hold were ensnared by Sauron and became his servants, is not now known.
>
> —*Unfinished Tales* p. 390.

This idea had been most explicitly spelled out (albeit with no mention of Radagast, who once again proves the most elusive of all the wizards and the hardest to pin down) in Tolkien's 1958 letter to Rhona Beare, where he says of the two unnamed wizards

> I think they went as emissaries to distant regions, East and South, far out of Númenórean range: missionaries to 'enemy-occupied' lands, as it were. What success they had I do not know; but I fear that they failed, as Saruman did, though doubtless in different ways; and I suspect they were founders or beginners of secret cults and 'magic' traditions that outlasted the fall of Sauron.
>
> —JRRT to Rhona Beare, 14th October 1958; *Letters* p. 280.

In his final writings Tolkien reverses his earlier position, now suggesting instead that all four of the Istari except Saruman in some measure remained true to their missions. He affirms that Morinehtar ['Darkness-slayer'] and Rómestámo ['East-helper'], as he now names the two who journeyed into the East, were indeed sent into enemy-occupied territory [HME XII.384–5]. From what we now know of Radagast, we can surmise that the same must have been true of him, since he established his dwelling in southern Mirkwood, near the Necromancer's lair in Dol Guldur. Furthermore, Tolkien no longer believes that the other two Istari, who may have come as early as the middle of the Second Age (circa S.A.1600; cf. HME XII.382), failed:

> Their task was to circumvent Sauron: to bring help to the few tribes of Men that had rebelled from Melkor-worship, to stir up rebellion . . . They must have had very great influence on the history of the Second Age and Third Age in weakening and disarraying the forces of East . . . who would . . . otherwise have . . . outnumbered the West.[33]
>
> —HME XII.385.

Significantly, in these same notes Tolkien suggests that '[p]robably Gandalf and Radagast came together' to Middle-earth (HME XII.384), once again closely identifying the two as essentially kindred spirits. Certainly Radagast's close friendship with the Great Eagles (another characteristic he shares with Gandalf), depicted throughout the mythology as the noblest of all creatures and the representatives of Manwë the Elder King, speaks well of his overall character, as does his association with Yavanna, who along with Elbereth and Ulmo were the Valar whom Tolkien seems most to have admired. In the end Radagast should probably be viewed as a good fellow and a worthy wizard, but not an exceptional character like Gandalf, who transcends his original mission to become 'the Enemy of Sauron' (*LotR*.1007). A desire to stress Gandalf's achievement seems to have led Tolkien to denigrate the other Wizards in the period immediately following the completion of *The Lord of the Rings*, while a retrospective view many years later recognized that their contributions, while less than Gandalf's, were nonetheless worthy of praise.

The Name 'Radagast'

As with many of the names in *The Hobbit*, Tolkien never provided a satisfactory gloss on the name *Radagast*: we do not even know for certain what language he intended it to be in when he invented it: Slavic (like *Medwed*), Celtic (like the *Carrock*), Gothic (like the real-world models for the Wood-men), or Elvish (like *Bladorthin*). We might assume that Bladorthin and his cousin would share names in the same language, which would make 'Radagast' Gnomish/Noldorin (i.e., Sindarin), but there is little support in the glossaries of that language to support this assumption. It is true that *rada* appears as a pencilled addition to the *Gnomish Lexicon* [circa 1917], as a word meaning 'track, path, way' (*Parma Eldalamberon* XI.64), but this seems to be a temporary borrowing from Old English *rād* (= 'road'; see below) that was not, so far as I can tell, taken up in later forms of the language. In the *Etymologies*, which postdate *The Hobbit*, RAD- appears as a word-root meaning 'to return, to go back', with several derivatives meaning 'east': e.g., *radhon* 'east', *Radhrost* 'East-vale', *Radhrim* 'East-march' (HME V.382). Either of these might plausibly be applied to the wizard, who does live east of the Edge of the Wild, but I can find no satisfactory explanation of *-gast* in Elvish, and Tolkien's hesitance to identify the name suggests it could not be accommodated within Sindarin as it developed, whatever its origin. When Tolkien does provide an Elvish name for this wizard many years later, *Aiwendil* (= 'Lover of Birds'), it is in Quenya, not Sindarin.[34]

Both times when Tolkien did address the name's linguistic affiliation, he suggested a Mannish (i.e., human, as opposed to elven) tongue. The first of these occurs in the essay on the Istari from the unfinished *LotR* Index [circa 1954–5] – that is, almost a quarter-century after he invented the name – where Tolkien states that Radagast

> spent his days among the wild creatures. Thus he got his name (which is in the tongue of Númenor of old, and signifies, it is said, 'tender of beasts').
>
> —*Unfinished Tales* p. 390.

However, by this point in the legendarium Tolkien had established that the spoken language of Númenor was Adûnaic (cf. Appendix F, *LotR*.1163), and the name 'Radagast' predates the creation of the Adûnaic language by more than a dozen years. Nor does the word (almost certainly a compound, like *Gand-alf* and *Saru-man*) resemble the Adûnaic language known to us from other sources, such as the names of the last few Kings of Númenor (Ar-Adûnakhôr, Ar-Zimrathôn, Ar-Sakalthôr, Ar-Gimilzôr, Ar-Inziladûn, & Ar-Pharazôn; *LotR.* 1072–3) or the presentation of fragmentary texts in that language in *The Notion Club Papers* (see particularly HME IX.246–7 & 311–12, and 'Lowdham's Report on the Adûnaic Language', ibid.413–40).[35] Furthermore, it is highly unlikely that an Adûnaic name would be given to a wizard in Rhovanion in the latter half of the Third Age.

It is possible, however, that by 'the tongue of Númenor' Tolkien meant not what we might call classical Adûnaic as it was spoken in the Second Age but Westron, the Common Speech descended from it, represented by modern English in *The Lord of the Rings*. It is more probable still, given the linguistic situation of the region in which Radagast lived (as described in Appendix F), that the name is neither Adûnaic nor Westron but belongs to a different member of the same language family:

> Most of the Men of the northern regions of the West-lands were descended from the *Edain* [the *Atani* or Three Houses of the Elf-friends] of the First Age, or from their close kin. Their languages were, therefore, related to the Adûnaic, and some still preserved a likeness to the Common Speech. Of this kind were the peoples of the upper vales of Anduin: the Beornings, and the Woodmen of Western Mirkwood . . .
>
> —*LotR.*1163.

Probably for this reason, Tolkien states in a very late note [circa 1972]:

> Radagast a name of Mannish (Anduin vale) origin – but not now clearly interpretable
>
> —HME XII.384.

That is, 'Radagast' comes from one of the languages belonging to what we might call the *Atani* language family, just as Latin and English both belong to the Indo-European (or, more properly, Indo-Hittite). The question, then, becomes which one. And, since Tolkien equated each of the *Atani* languages with a real-world European tongue, which real world language he used in this particular instance. The three primary candidates are Old English, Gothic, and one of the Slavic languages like Russian.[36]

Of these, Old English fits best with Tolkien's final conception of the language spoken in that part of the world in his legendarium at the time of Bilbo's journey (or, if we take his system of parallels set down in Appendix F literally, the real-world language he chose to best represent the 'Mannish' language spoken in the Anduin Vale). It is the language spoken by the ancestors of the hobbits when they dwelt in that part of the world, it is the language spoken by the Eorlings, who also originated in that area, and best of all it is the language used in the (published) *Hobbit* itself for the werebear's name, *Beorn*. And, as it happens, the name can indeed be parsed in Old English: *rād* is the name for one of the Old English runes (Rune 5 in the *futhark*); it stands for the letter 'R' and means 'road'. And *gast* is the standard Old English word for 'spirit' (the direct ancestor of our modern *ghost*), with a range of meanings from 'angel' to 'human being';[37] 'Spirit of the Road' is not unlike the meaning I have suggested for *Bladorthin*, 'the Grey Traveller' (see p. 53).

However, despite the excellent fit in sound and etymology with Old English, there is the problem that Tolkien invented the name 'Radagast' before he changed Medwed's name from the original Slavic to an Old English replacement, just as it predates the change from Noldorin *Bladorthin* to Old Norse *Gandalf*. We must therefore consider the possibility that the name is not Germanic at all but rather Slavic, and in fact the evidence for a Slavic Radagast is surprisingly strong, given how little role the Slavic languages played in Tolkien's legendarium overall.[38] Adam of Bremen's *Gesta Hammaburgensis Ecclesiae Pontificum* ['Deeds of the Bishops of the Hamburg Church'; late eleventh century] mentions that the Wends, a West Slavic people who lived between the Elbe and Oder Rivers (in the area more recently known as East Germany), had a holy city named Rethra (Jacob Grimm calls it 'the chief place of Slav heathenism'; *Teutonic Mythology*, vol II. p. 663) in which there was a great temple devoted to the god *Radegast*; in fact, Johannes Skotus, Bishop of Mecklebury, was supposedly sacrificed to the god there in 1066. However, an earlier chronicler, Thietmar of Mersebury (whom Grimm calls 'Dietmar'; d. 1016), applied the name 'Rethra' to the people and gave 'Radegast' as the name of the town, not the deity worshipped there (who, from other evidence, was probably the well-attested Svarogich).

With the charming naiveté endemic among nineteenth- and early twentieth-century writers on mythology, who assume that all deities among any Indo-European people must correspond to some familiar figure in the Greek pantheon, Grimm confidently identified this Radegast as the Slavic equivalent to Wuotan (Wotan/Odin) in Germanic mythology, and Hermes (Mercury) in the classical pantheon (*Teutonic Mythology*, Preface pages xxx & liv, vol. I pages 130 & 248–9).[39] Nineteenth- and twentieth-century attempts to re-construct the lost Slavic pantheon eagerly seized upon the references in Adam of Bremen and a later chronicler, Helmold's *Chronica Slavorum* ['Chronicle of the Slavs'; later twelfth century], and the conclusions of Grimm to create a god, variously known as *Radegast*, *Ragidost*, *Redigast*, who may never have actually existed: a (modern) statue of him now stands on Mount Radhost in the Czech Republic near the Slovakian and Polish borders, and since the 1970s *Radegast* has been the name of a premium Czech beer named not for Tolkien's character but after the presumptive and possibly fictitious 'god of hospitality'.[40]

Tolkien, who was always intrigued by attempts to recapture lost myths and preserve the last fragments of a people's folklore (e.g., his fascination with Lönnrot's *Kalevala*), might have been drawn to the presumptive Slavic Radegast by the references in Grimm, an author for whom he had a great deal of respect and with whom he identified in some respects.[41] We have the example in his piece 'The Name "Nodens"' [1932] of his attempt to use all the tools of philology 'to recall forgotten gods from their twilight' (*Report on the Excavation . . . [at] Lydney Park, Gloucestershire*, page 135), and of course his borrowing of the name *Eärendel* from Cynewulf's *Crist*, so it is entirely possible that 'Radegast' is another borrowing of the same type, lifted from its shadowy and debatable original context and given a wholly new meaning within his legendarium by Tolkien.

A final plausible candidate for Tolkien's inspiration, and to my mind the most convincing of all, is the Gothic king or war-chieftain *Radagaisus* (died 406 AD), whose name is rendered *Rhadagast* in some eighteenth- and nineteenth-century sources.[42] Tolkien's great interest in the Goths (especially their language) was responsible for his vocation as a philologist specializing in the Germanic languages; his mentor when an undergraduate at Oxford was Joseph Wright, perhaps the world's leading expert in Gothic at the time, and Tolkien's first significant invented language was *Gautiska* or 'Neo-Gothic', in which he wrote one of his finest poems ('Bagmē Blōma', appearing in *Songs for the Philologists* [1936], page 12).[43] He was also, as might be expected, well-versed in Gothic history.[44] Radagaisus's story is told in Isidore of Seville's *History of the Goths, Vandals, and Suevi*, but the story was familiar to all readers of Edward Gibbon's monumental *The Decline and Fall of the Roman Empire* [1776–88]. As Isidore [d. 636 AD] describes it, in the year 405 AD:

> Radagaisus, king of the Goths, a Scythian by birth, a man devoted to the cult of idolatry and most savage in the fierceness of his barbaric cruelty, attacked with violent devastation the regions of Italy, together with two hundred thousand soldiers, vowing, in contempt of Christ, that he would make a libation of the Romans' blood to his god if he should win. His army, after being surrounded by the Roman general Stilicho on the mountainous ground of Tuscany, was destroyed by hunger rather than by battle. Finally the king was captured and killed.
>
> [Four years later] . . . now that Radagaisus was dead, Alaric, his colleague in kingship, who was a Christian in name but professed himself a heretic, grieving that so great a number of Goths had been

> slain by the Romans, waged war against Rome to avenge his countrymen's blood . . . and so the city which had been the conqueror of all nations was conquered and overpowered by the triumph of the Goths[.]
>
> —Isidore of Seville, *History of the Goths . . .*, tr. Guido Donini & Gordon B. Ford Jr. [1966], pp. 8–9.

Despite the obvious similarity of the names Radagaisus/Rhadagast and Radagast, the actual historical figure seems an odd choice to have inspired Tolkien to create his character, since one of the few things we know about Radagast in *The Hobbit* is that he gets along well with his neighbors, even the notoriously irascible Medwed. The historical Radagaisus was a sort of Gothic Boadicea, a pagan leader noted for his hostility to Christians, who fought Huns, Romans, and fellow Goths in a violent and ultimately disastrous campaign in 405–6 AD. Gibbon, for example, describes him as 'the implacable enemy of Rome' and 'a devout Pagan' who practiced human sacrifice.[45] However, we should note that Tolkien was quite willing to borrow a name from a less than attractive historical figure when it suited his purposes (that is, when something about the name attracted him), the best example being Alboin of the Lombards (Longbeards), whom even his namesake Alboin Errol in *The Lost Road* thinks less sympathetic than the rivals he destroyed, the Gepids (HME V.37; see also Christopher Tolkien's commentary in ibid.53–4). In fact, Alboin's career was remarkably like Radagaisus's some two and a half centuries before, except that Alboin was successful in leading his people (described as being both pagans and Arians) into Italy and conquering and settling a large section of it; compare also Tolkien's interest in and apparent admiration for Hengest, who led the (successful) Germanic invasion of Britain (*Finn and Hengest*, *The Book of Lost Tales*). Of course, there is always the possibility that Tolkien may simply have been amused by the comic possibilities of assigning a grandiose or otherwise inappropriate name, something he does over and over again in his works, from Galathea the cow (who shares the name of the statue brought to life in the story of Pygmalion) and Julius Agricola (the Roman general who conquered the part of Britain Tolkien considered his home county) in *Farmer Giles of Ham* to Fortinbras, Odovacar, and Sigismond as hobbit-names[46] (cf. the family trees in Appendix C of *The Lord of the Rings* [*LotR*.1137] and HME XII.85–118 for many more examples), not to mention using 'Fingolfin' as the name of the goblin-king whose decapitation created the game of golf.

In the end, it seems likely that Tolkien was attracted to the name precisely because of its ambiguity and uncertain status, just as he was to the cruxes in *Beowulf* and puzzling words preserved in old manuscripts like 'Earendel' and 'sigelwara' (see p. 719), to the explication of which he devoted much of his career, both philological and creative. The 'Radegast' of the chronicles probably represents an attempt to record in Old High German a now-lost Slavic name which might originally have referred to a place, or to a forgotten god, or been an epithet for another god that was later mistaken for a separate deity.[47] The 'Radagaisus' of late Roman history similarly represents an attempt to capture in Latin a Gothic name, possibly **Radagais* (Gothic: 'counsel-spear'),[48] rendered *Rœdgota* (OE: 'counsel-Goth') in Alfred's *Boethius* and *Rhadagast* by early modern writers. Out of these Tolkien chose *Radagast* as the name he wanted for his character, who proves just as elusive as his namesake(s).

NOTES

1 From the available evidence, one would assume this to have included romance, flirtation, and 'girl stuff'.

2 This is borne out in a passage appearing in the revised and extended edition of the *Father Christmas Letters*, where in the letter for 1928 Father Christmas says that he let the North Polar Bear pick out 11-year-old John's present this year: 'Polar Bear chose them; he says he knows what John likes because John likes bears' (*Letters from Father Christmas* [1999], p. 40).

3 This information comes from a letter by Joan Tolkien, Michael Tolkien's wife, published in *The Sunday Times* on 10th October 1982 under the heading 'Origin of a Tolkien Tale'. She asserts that 'the three bears are based on the teddy bears owned by the three boys. Archie was my husband's bear and survived until 1933.' However, we should also note that Priscilla in turn was very fond of teddy bears as a child; the later Father Christmas letters contain several references to 'the Bingos', her (vast) toy bear collection, numbering at least 60 bears by 1938 – cf. the letters for 1935 (*Letters from Father Christmas*, p. 104), 1937 (ibid. p. 120), 1938 (p. 124), and 1939 (p. 134) – but apparently reduced to a single favorite bear later on; cf. the letters for 1941 (p. 145), 1942 (p. 150), and 1943 (the last letter, p. 154); he even receives his own message from NPB one year ('Messige to Billy Bear from Polar Bear[.] Sorry I could not send you a really good bomb . . .') – 1942 letter (p. 151).

4 Note that, according to the code of conduct present in the medieval (and ancient) works to which so much of *The Hobbit* harkens back, Medwed's feeding of the wanderers establishes a host/guest relationship between them; this is a point of cultural etiquette as strong as the 'no cheating' rule that similarly governs the Riddle-game: 'sacred and of immense antiquity'. From that point on they are safe from the werebear, despite Bilbo's distrust continuing for a while longer.

5 The teddy bear is a twentieth-century phenomenon, said to have

acquired its name from the nickname of the U.S. president at the time, Theodore 'Teddy' Roosevelt (1901–9).

6 C. S. Lewis, 'On Stories', *Essays Presented to Charles Williams*, ed. C. S. Lewis [1947; 2nd edition, 1966], page 104. This piece is reprinted in the collection *On Stories and Other Essays on Literature*, ed. Walter Hooper [1982], page 18.

Heimsókn: an attack on a home or hall, as in the murder of Gunnar Hamundarson, who held out alone defending his home against forty men and very nearly prevailed (*Njal's Saga*, chapters 76–7), or the death of Njal himself, burned alive with his wife, sons, and grandson after a force of a hundred men could not overcome his sons' defense of the family hall (*Njal's Saga* chapters 127–30). The *Freswæl*, or Fight at Finnesburg, to which Tolkien devoted an entire lecture-series (published posthumously as *Finn and Hengest* [1982]), can also be seen as a *heimsókn* of sorts. As T.A. Shippey points out (*Tolkien Studies* V [2008], p. 220–21), the term survives into the modern day in Scottish legal jargon as *hamesucken*, '[t]he crime of assaulting a person in his own house or dwelling-place' (*Concise OED* vol. II, p. 1246–47), and as such finds its way into John Buchan's *Castle Gay* [1930]. I am grateful to Richard West and Prof. Shippey for clarifying Lewis's terminology for me.

7 *Hrólfs Saga Kraka* (*Hrolf Kraki's Saga*) was written in the latter half of the fourteenth-century and is thus contemporary with the *Gawain*-poet and Chaucer, but the work survives only in seventeenth-century paper copies. The Bothvar Bjarki story derives from the lost *Bjarkamál*, which influenced not only *Hrolf Kraki's Saga* but also the *Bjarkarimur* (a fifteenth-century Icelandic saga, now lost) and *Skjödunga Saga* (also lost, but not before Snorri Sturluson used two brief bits from it in his *Prose Edda* and a Latin summary of it had been made by Arngrím Jónsson in 1594). Some form of the story was also known to Saxo Grammaticus, who uses it in his late twelfth-century *Gesta Danorum* (better known as the source of the Hamlet story). And, of course, the *Beowulf*-poet (writing most probably in the eighth century but possibly later – the traditional dating of *Beowulf* having recently been challenged) knew either Bothvar's story or (more likely) some analogue thereto.

In short, as a once well-known tale now buried and partially lost, glimpsed today only through later versions and tantalizing references to lost manuscripts, the *Bjarkamál* is exactly the type of 'asterisk-tale' that most attracted Tolkien. And, appropriately, just as we shall never be able to read the *Bjarkamál*, so too we never get Medwed's full story but must reconstruct it from such glimpses into his history as we can get.

8 'Sellic Spell' has never been published, although Tolkien did submit it for publication and have it accepted; the magazine, *The Welsh Review*, ceased publication before the issue that was to contain the story saw print and the editor, Tolkien's friend Gwyn Jones (translator of both *The Mabinogion* and *Hrolf Kraki's Saga*), who had already published Tolkien's Breton lay ('The Lay of Aotrou and Itroun') in the same

magazine in 1945, regretfully returned the tale to Tolkien. The manuscript of the story is now in the Bodleian Library at Oxford.

For more on the Bear's Son story, see Klaeber, *Beowulf and The Fight at Finnsburg*, third edition, pages xiiiff.

9 Hrolf Kraki, or 'Rolf the Beanpole', makes an appearance in *Beowulf* as Hrothulf, King Hrothgar's nephew; both Hrothgar and Hrolf Kraki belong to the Danish royal line, the Skjoldungs or Scyldingas, descendants of Scyld Scefing ('Shield Sheafing'). Tolkien was deeply interested in the legends surrounding this royal house, and planned to devote a chapter of *The Lost Road* to 'The Legend of King Sheave'. Of all the unwritten chapters, this is one of the few that actually got partially drafted, as a prose text of a few hundred words retelling the story of the infant found on a ship who becomes a great king, returning to the sea again in the end. (The same story is told of Audoin the Lombard, from whom Tolkien took the name of one of the major characters in *The Lost Road*.) Tolkien also recast the legend as a poem, 'King Sheave', which he intended to insert in the Anglo-Saxon (Ælfwine) chapter of *The Lost Road;* Christopher Tolkien prints the poem in HME V.87–91.

Note that whereas in the English tradition as represented by *Beowulf* old King Hrothgar is remembered as the wise monarch overthrown by his treacherous nephew, in Danish tradition it is the nephew who overthrew the elderly tyrant and ushered in an all-too-brief golden age. For more on the tangled traditions concerning these historical figures, see Klaeber pp. xxxi–xxxv.

10 The doomed couple's names are significant: the cursed prince is Bjorn ('Bear') and the yeoman's daughter Bera ('She-Bear'); Bjarki means 'Little Bear' (bear-cub). Modern scholarship leans toward the theory that Bothvar Bjarki's given name is Bjarki, with 'Bothvar' ('Battle') being a nickname given for his prowess in combat. Also, as several Tolkien scholars have pointed out, *beorn* (bear) is a common substitution in Old English poetry for 'warrior', just as *wearg* (wolf) is for 'outlaw'; these probably had similar force to such usages today as referring to a woman as 'a fox' or a man as 'a weasel'. That usage in poetic diction should not disguise the fact that 'Beorn' is simply the Old English equivalent of Bjorn, still a common Swedish name, and that 'Bear' has continued in use as a nickname in America at least down to as recently as the middle of the twentieth century.

Several Beorns are found in English history and legend; cf. R. M. Wilson, *The Lost Literature of Medieval England* [1952, 2nd edition 1970], pp. 34–8). The most prominent of these is probably the son of Ragnar Lodbrok who, with his brothers Hælfdene and Ivarr the Boneless, led the Danish invasions that almost overwhelmed Alfred the Great in the ninth century, establishing a Danish kingdom in England (the Danelaw) that endured for generations. Significantly, his name is alternately given as Bjorn, Baerin (shades of Beren, perhaps?), or Beorn, depending on the nationality of the source.

11 The two elder brothers' part-monstrous forms is the result of the evil

stepmother, Queen White, having forced their pregnant mother to eat two bits of bear-meat taken from the slaughtered prince. Despite being warned by her lover before his death, Bera ate the first mouthful, resulting in Elgfrothi's half-human form. She spat out all but a morsel of the second mouthful, resulting in Thorir's almost-human form. Bera refused the third mouthful outright, resulting in Bothvar's being fully human to the eye despite his father's curse, the only heritage from which seems to be the bear-manifestation of his final battle.

12 Note that Frothi (*Froði*) can also be transliterated *Frodi*; it is the same name that Tolkien anglicized as *Frodo*, his hero of *The Lord of the Rings*. Frodo Baggins' name, however, probably comes not from Elgfrothi but from King Froði, in Icelandic tradition a legendary king of Denmark (grandson of the same Shield Sheafing about whom Tolkien wrote the poem referred to in Note 9 above), who reigned at the time of Christ's birth and established a reign of peace: 'Norsemen called it the Peace of Froði. No man injured another, even although he was confronted with the slayer of his father or brother, free or in bonds. Neither were there any thieves or robbers, so that a gold ring lay untouched for a long time on the Heath of Jelling' (*Prose Edda*, p. 118).

13 Note that this sunny future prophesied at the time of *The Hobbit* did not exactly come to pass in the actual future as revealed by *LotR* – 80 years later, the goblins seem worse than ever – unless we take it as applying to the period immediately *after* the end of the Third Age, when they have been scattered and decimated following Sauron's downfall.

14 To learn otherwise, we must go outside the book itself to Tolkien's letters, where in a letter of 24th April 1954 to Naomi Mitchison, answering a number of questions that arose out of her reading one of the review copies, he devotes a paragraph to the subject:

> Beorn is dead; see vol. I p. 241.† He appeared in *The Hobbit*. It was then the year Third Age 2940 (Shire-reckoning 1340). We are now in the years 3018–19 (1418–19). Though a skin-changer and no doubt a bit of a magician, Beorn was a Man.
>
> —*Letters*, p. 178.

† [Editor's note: this is the passage regarding Grimbeorn the Old alluded to above.]

It is only fair to note, however, that many of Tolkien's conceptions shifted between the time he wrote *The Hobbit* and when he put the finishing touches on *The Lord of the Rings* some twenty years later; his emphatic pronouncement on Beorn's fate may well be an afterthought rather than a deliberate linkage back to Scyld Scefing's arrival, establishment of an eponymous people, and departure back into mystery.

15 Stanley Unwin's *The Truth About Publishing*, an insider's look at the book publishing industry first published in 1926 and regularly updated over the next forty years, provides much insight into this and many other cost-conscious decisions made by Allen & Unwin when producing the book.

16 J. S. Ryan, 'Two Oxford Scholars' Perceptions of the Traditional Germanic Hall', *Minas Tirith Evening Star*, Spring 1990 issue, pages 8–11. I have since learned that this discovery was made independently by Wm H. Green as far back as 1969: in his dissertation, Green notes

> Beorn's 'wide hall' seems to suggest the great halls in ancient Northern literature, Heorot in *Beowulf* and Thorhall's house in *The Saga of Grettir the Strong*: except for the absence of weapons on the wall, Tolkien's drawing of the hall in the hardback edition of *The Hobbit* (p. 131) very strongly resembles the illustration of 'the interior of a Norse hall' in E. V. Gordon's *Introduction to Old Norse* (p. 27), a book which Tolkien helped to prepare for the press (p. ix).
>
> — Green, *'The Hobbit' and Other Fiction of J. R R. Tolkien: Their Roots in Medieval Heroic Literature and Language* (dissertation, Louisiana State University, 1969), pages 131–2.

Green's discovery failed to make its way into the general pool of Tolkien scholarship, but he deserves credit for having recognized the connection even without the benefit of ever seeing the unpublished version of Tolkien's illustration, which more strongly resembles the one in Gordon's book.

17 Eric Gordon (1896–1938) was first a student and then a colleague of Tolkien's at Leeds, collaborating with him on an edition of *Sir Gawain & the Green Knight* [1925, revised edition 1930] that for years stood as the definitive edition of that great Arthurian poem. Gordon also contributed to Tolkien's *Songs for the Philologists* [1936], a light-hearted collection of drinking songs in Old English, Old Norse, and Gothic set to nursery rhyme tunes. The two men planned several more collaborations and did a good deal of work on three more editions, of *Pearl* (a moving elegy in which a man meets his dead infant daughter in a dream-vision, believed to have been written by the same man who wrote *Sir Gawain & the Green Knight*), and two important Old English poems: *The Wanderer* (parts of which in time worked their way into *The Lord of the Rings*) and *The Seafarer*. After Gordon's untimely death, two of these three projects (*Pearl* and *Seafarer*) were eventually completed by his widow, Ida Gordon.

Hammond & Scull (*Artist & Illustrator*, pp. 122 & 124) attribute the illustration in Gordon's book to EVG himself, but this is merely an educated guess; the actual artist is unknown.

18 Since the publication of Ryan's original article, it has come to light that Gordon's drawing is based on an older one that had appeared in a number of academic works in the decades preceding it. Carl Hostetter discovered this earlier drawing, under the title 'Nordische Halle' [Norse Hall], in *Die Altgermanische Dichtung* ['Old Germanic Poetry'] by Dr. Andreas Heusler (Berlin, 1923), page 109. But Heusler in turn credits the drawing to a German translation (1908) of Axel Olrik's *Nordisk Aandsliv i Vikingetid og tidlig Middelalder* ['Norse Intellectual Life during the Viking Era', 1907], and when Arden Smith located Olrik's book

he discovered that Olrik in turn had taken the illustration from *Den islandske Bolig i Fristatstiden* ['The Icelandic Dwelling in the Time of the Republic'] by Valtyr Gudmundsson (Copenhaven, 1894). Alerted by the linguists, Douglas Anderson managed to find a copy of Gudmundsson's little book (an offprint from a piece published in the journal *Folkelaesning* the year before), which not only reproduces the drawing (page 12) but identifies the artist (page 26): E. Rondahl, who based it on a recently commissioned model in the National Museum of Copenhaven:

> . . . drawn by the painter E. Rondahl after a model which is found in the National Museum in Copenhagen and which shows a fully furnished Icelandic room from the time around the year 1000. This model was made in the year 1892 at the behest and expense of the Ministry of Culture under my [Gudmundsson's] direction and with assistance from architect Erik Schiodte and the directors of the National Museum in exact agreement with the information that is found in old writings about Icelandic rooms from the aforementioned time. The model was then exhibited at the Columbian Exposition in Spain.†.

> † [I.e., the 1892 Columbian Historical Exposition in Madrid, not to be confused with the 1893 Columbian Exposition, better known as the Chicago World's Fair.]

For a concise account, see DAA.171. I am grateful to Carl Hostetter and Arden Smith for sharing their discovery with me and to Arden Smith for the preceding quote, both text and translation.

19 The self-taught Joseph Wright rose from being a mill hand to Professor of Comparative Philology; see Carpenter pages 55–6. Tolkien studied under Wright at Oxford, and the older man was instrumental in convincing Tolkien to switch his focus from classical languages such as Latin and Greek to Old English, Old Norse, and Gothic. Indeed, it had been Tolkien's discovery of Wright's Gothic grammar that had set him on the road to becoming a philologist himself (see Carpenter p. 37 and *Letters* p. 357). For more on Wright, see *The Life of Joseph Wright* by E. M. Wright [1932], which contains a letter from Tolkien (Vol. II p. 651), and also Virginia Woolf's novel *The Years* [1937], which contains a lively fictional portrait of Wright and his family.

20 That this is a field that interested Tolkien greatly is shown by Christopher Tolkien's passing reference to 'my father's large collection of books on English place-names (including field-names, wood-names, stream-names, and their endlessly varying forms)', from which he drew when selecting place-names in the Shire (Christopher Tolkien, letter to Hammond & Scull, cited in *LotR: A Reader's Companion* [2005] page lvi).

21 See, for example, 'The Shores of Faëry' [1915], part of Tolkien's planned volume of poetry submitted to Sidgwick & Jackson in 1916, *The Trumpets of Faery*:

East of the Moon, west of the Sun
There stands a lonely hill;
Its feet are in the pale green sea,
Its towers are white and still . . .

—BLT II.271.

22 Tolkien also discusses 'the oldest and deepest desire', which he identifies as the Great Escape or Escape from Death – or, for immortals, Escape from Deathlessness (OFS.61). Hence, no doubt, the traditional ending for any number of classic fairy tales: '. . . *and they lived happily ever after.*'

23 The Diamond Jubilee was an elaborate celebration held in 1897 to mark the sixtieth anniversary of Queen Victoria's coming to the throne – and, incidentally, to recognize her as the longest-reigning English monarch by passing the previous record set by George III (reigned 1760–1820).

24 This passage was removed either when the books were re-written and expurgated by the American publisher in 1966 or shortly thereafter, or when it was further censored for the revised edition of 1988. The current text of the same chapter omits the entire paragraph (1988 Yearling edition p. 34).

While ostensively an attempt to remove any offensive stereotypes (for example, virtually all pictures of Dolittle's African friend Prince Bumpo were deleted),† the book was also changed in more subtle ways – for example, a comparison of Long Arrow, the world's greatest naturalist, to 'this young fellow Charles Darwin that people are talking about so much now' (1922 edition page 71) was silently dropped, so that no reference to Darwin appears in the current edition (1988 Yearling edition, page 57). For an account of the 1966 stealth censorship, which was made without any public announcement (or, so far as I have been able to discover, notice on the copyright page), see Diane Ravitch's *The Language Police: How Pressure Groups Restrict What Students Learn* [2003]. For an attempted justification of the 1988 rewriting, see the short afterword by Christopher Lofting, Hugh's youngest son, to the 1988 Yearling edition (pages 312–14).

I am grateful to Gary Hunnewell's presentation at the 1993 Mythcon for first making me aware of the changes between the original and later editions of the Dolittle books.

† Compare 1922 edition pages 175 & 353 with 1988 Yearling edition pages 149 & 302.

25 'Yes, the Doctor Dolittle books were central and deeply loved in our childhood, and we had the whole series, each new book as it appeared.' – personal communication, Christopher Tolkien to John D. Rateliff, 23rd February 1993.

26 For instance, Dolittle returns from the first of his famous journeys rich and settles down in his Puddleby home as the local eccentric bachelor at the end of the first book (*Story*, pp. 177–9) and the second book ends with another homecoming and a mention of arriving in time for

four o'clock tea (*Voyages*, p. 364). Then too there is the possibly accidental but suggestive resemblance of little *Stubbins* and *Baggins*, the point-of-view character who is initially the least important member of the party. Ironically, the most Tolkienesque of all the Dolittle books, *Doctor Dolittle and the Secret Lake*, did not appear until 1948, the year after Lofting's death, although a version of it had been serialized as early as 1923. Much of the similarities between Tolkien's and Lofting's works comes from shared experience of ordinary small-town or village English life,† a similar understated comic sensibility, an appreciation of the heroic potential of those who are decidedly unheroic in appearance and manner, and an unabashed fondness for an earlier, now-lost era just passing out of living memory. While not as direct an influence on Tolkien's work as Grahame's *The Wind in the Willows*, there seems no doubt that Lofting's series contributed its share to the 'leaf-mould' from which *The Hobbit* sprang.

† Lofting was only six years older than Tolkien and, while he spent much of his adult life in America, also served in the Somme and like Tolkien not only was invalided home from the Western Front but began what would turn out to be his life's work during that period; the first Dolittle book originated as letters written home to his children from the front.

27 It does still appear in early drafts of *The Lord of the Rings*, but was removed before publication; see HME VII.131 & 149.

It seems probable that Tolkien would have removed or altered this reference from *The Hobbit* as well had the 1960 'Fifth Phase' of his work on that book reached this far into the text, but we can never know for sure.

28 The original text simply notes that Radagast lives 'near the borders of Mirkwood'; changes in black ink to the First Typescript (Marq. 1/1/57:4) add the detail that this is the *southern* border (i.e., nearer the Necromancer than Bladorthin advises Bilbo is safe to travel). This change was made before the Second Typescript, which incorporates it (1/1/38:5).

Further changes bring Medwed/Beorn's comment on Radagast closer into line with the published text, but interestingly enough here the first and second typescripts were revised differently, and some of the revisions that now appear on them were added after Tolkien had received the page proofs. Since this offers valuable proof that Tolkien sometimes went back and entered revisions onto earlier drafts (no doubt as safety copies, and to prevent proliferation of variant texts that could occur if he failed to remember a later change), I give the whole sequence here:

Ms.: 'Yes yes: not a bad fellow [*added*: I know him well].'

Both Tss. as originally typed: 'Yes, yes; not a bad fellow. I know him well.'

1st Ts. (1/1/57:4), as revised in black ink: 'Yes, yes; not a bad fellow, I know him well. [*added*: as wizards go. I see him now and again', said Beorn]†

Tolkien's failure to cancel any of the existing text in the first typescript resulted in the following reading in the page proofs (Marq. 1/2/2: page 226): 'Yes, yes; not a bad fellow, I know him well as wizards go. I see him now and again,' said Beorn.

This was changed by black ink corrections to the page proofs to read 'Yes; not a bad fellow as wizards go, I believe. I used to see him now and again' said Beorn, thus achieving the text of the published book (DAA.167). At this same point, 'know him well' was replaced in pencil by 'believe' in the First Typescript.

† A pencilled addition is made at the same point in the Second Typescript (1/1/38:6), but it was later overwritten and cannot now be read. Later 'I know him well' was cancelled there in black ink and replaced by the same additional text as in the First Typescript, but the words 'I believe' do not appear.

29 In Tolkien's hierarchy of colours, Radagast's humble 'earthen brown' signifies that he is a being of less manifested power than Saruman the White or Gandalf the Grey, or even the two Blue Wizards Tolkien later added to round out the Five, Alatar and Pallando.

30 Here Tolkien seems to be thinking of the battle of the Last Alliance as a current event taking place as part of the War of the Ring.

31 Note that Saruman, for example, uses the correct form 'the Shire' ('What brings you now from your lurking-place in the Shire?'), although we later learn that he had the advantage of prior knowledge of the area through his spies. Interestingly enough, in the original draft of this encounter Radagast had correctly named the hobbits' country 'the Shire' (HME VII.131), but Tolkien changed this for the published version.

Also curious is the fact that Tolkien later made Radagast's usage seem more reasonable in one of the texts for 'The Hunt for the Ring' [circa 1954–5], where we are told that Sauron's torturers could get only two names out of Gollum: 'That is why the Black Riders seem to have had two main pieces of information only to go on: *Shire* and *Baggins*' (UT.342). Thus, when Radagast says 'wherever they go the Riders ask for news of a land called Shire' (*LotR*.274) he is being precisely accurate.

32 In all versions of Gandalf's story, Radagast's importance as a faithful messenger is juxtaposed with Butterbur's failure to keep his promise to deliver Gandalf's message to Frodo telling him to leave the Shire at once. The negligence of the unreliable messenger almost brings about Sauron's victory and is at least partly responsible for Frodo's incurable wound suffered on Weathertop, whereas Radagast's faithfulness as a messenger makes possible Gandalf's escape, a crucial factor in the victory of the West in the war against Sauron.

33 Tolkien does state that their one failure was 'to search out [Sauron's] hiding [place]' after his fall (whether in the destruction of Númenor or at the end of the Second Age is unclear). We could choose to see this paralleled by Radagast's establishing his home near Dol Guldur as

an attempt to keep watch on that sinister site, believed by the White Council to be occupied by one of Sauron's minions if not Sauron himself (Tale of Years entry for S.A.1100, *LotR*.1122). There seems to be an unstated agreement among the Istari that each will make a particular region his special concern – Radagast in Wilderland (Rhovanion), Gandalf in Eriador, Saruman in the Southlands once ruled by Gondor, and the other two either together or severally in the East (Rhûn), which in real-world analogy would encompass all of Asia.

34 See the account of the choosing of the Istari, a text probably written in the late 1950s, in *Unfinished Tales* (UT.393), and also Christopher Tolkien's explanation of the name (UT.401 Note 6).

By contrast, *Rhosgobel*, the name of Radagast's home, is unambiguously Noldorin/Sindarin: *rhosc* ('brown') + *gobel* ('fenced homestead'), translated by Tolkien as 'Brownhay' (with 'hay' here meaning a hedged enclosure). But this name dates from the middle stage of Tolkien's work on *The Lord of the Rings* in the early 1940s, at least a decade after Radagast himself was named. See HME VII.149, 164, & 172–3, as well as 'The Etymologies' (HME V.385 & 380) and Salo's *Gateway* pp. 390, 284, & 258.

35 The word *raba* ('dog') does occur in one rough draft passage of Lowdham's Report giving noun declensions, showing that at least the *rada-* part of the name has a parallel structure in Adûnaic, but this is far too slender to build upon and the whole name remains strikingly unlike any attested Adûnaic form in sound and orthography.

36 One of the Celtic languages, such as Welsh or pre-invasion British, would seem a possibility because of the presence in this same chapter of *Carrock*, which as we have seen derives from a lost Celtic original (see p. 262). But this assimilated form seems a solitary exception; Tolkien used Celtic languages in *The Lord of the Rings* for the languages of non-Edainic folk such as the Bree-Men and the Dunlendings, making them inappropriate as a source for place-names and personal names from Rhovanion (Wilderland) according to his thinking at the time he wrote the sequel. There is no way to know if this rather unusual departure from the *Atani*/Indo-European parallels already existed in his mind when he was writing *The Hobbit*. It may be that he avoided using Celtic in the earlier book simply because Welsh had been such a great influence on Noldorin/Sindarin (particularly its sound-system), which he did make use of in *The Hobbit*.

Old Norse is not an option here, despite the presence of *Gandalf* as a wizard-name in the published book, because (a) Old Norse had already been assigned to the area north-east of Mirkwood from whence the dwarves came and (b) the Bladorthin > Gandalf change postdates the creation of the name Radagast.

37 *Gast* is also an alternate spelling for *giest* (the ancestor of modern English *guest*), meaning 'stranger'. *Rœd* (OE: 'counsel') is sometimes cited as a possible element in Radagast's name, but Tolkien's usage elsewhere ('Rede oft is found at the rising of the Sun' – *LotR*.449)

shows that had this been the case he would probably have spelled the name *Redegast*. But this error, if it is one, is ancient; see p. 280 for evidence that Alfred the Great identified the first element in the name as *Ræd* rather than *Rād*.

38 The Slavic affinities of the name were first noted by Jim Allan as far back as 1978 (*An Introduction to Elvish*, p. 175). The only other Slavic origin for one of Tolkien's names suggested there is *variag* (the Variags of Khand; *LotR*.879), the Russian name for the Varangian Guard, the Viking bodyguards of the Emperor of Constantinople (*An Introduction to Elvish*, pp. 174–5).

I am grateful to Carl Hostetter for drawing my attention both to Grimm's work on this topic (personal communication, Hostetter to Rateliff, 23rd February 2000) and also to a long, learned, informative, and inconclusive on-line discussion about the possible Slavic antecedents of the name (TolkLang list, July 1996).

39 Some have seen Radagast's acting as a messenger as evidence that Tolkien accepted Grimm's identification of Radegast with Mercury, the messenger of the gods. However, against this must be set Gandalf's assertion that 'you were never a traveller' (*LotR*.274), which would seem to discount the identification.

40 This statue was created by sculptor Albin Polasek in Prague in 1929; an image of it can be found at http://en.wikipedia.org/wiki/Image:Radegastgod.jpg. In style it was no doubt inspired by the multi-faced statues unearthed by antiquarians and archeologists (e.g., cf. http://en.wikipedia.org/wiki/Image:SwiatowidZbrucz.jpg). Rev. H. H. Milman, in his notes to an 1845 annotated edition of Gibbon's *Decline and Fall*, mentions the discovery of one such statue, identified as '[a] statue of Radegast', between 1760 and 1770 'on the supposed site of Rhetra'.

Another modern use of the name in an unusual context, for the hapless teacher in *Mr. Radagast Makes an Unexpected Journey*, a children's book by Sharon Nastick (Thomas Y. Crowell; Weekly Reader Books, 1981), clearly derives not from Slavic lore but borrows the name from Tolkien, although it does not resemble Tolkien's work in any other respect.

41 Indeed, Grimm's *Teutonic Mythology*, which pulls together all that could be recovered of pre-medieval Germanic folklore and beliefs, is precisely the kind of thing Tolkien wished had been possible for the English, as he explained in his Letter to Waldman (*Letters* p. 143ff). Unfortunately the English folklorists started too late; his subcreated legendarium was a replacement for what had been forever lost. See Tolkien's little poem in a late [1969] letter comically claiming to be Grimm's heir:

J. R. R. Tolkien
had a cat called Grimalkin:
once a familiar of Herr Grimm,
now he spoke the law to him.

—JRRT to Amy Ronald, 2nd. January 1969; *Letters* p. 398.

For a serious and convincing argument that Tolkien, for his achievements in fairy-tale/fantasy, (reconstructed) mythology, and language, indeed deserves more than any other to be considered Jacob Grimm's modern-day successor, see Shippey's *The Road to Middle-earth*.

42 For example, J. S. Cardale's 1829 translation into modern English of Alfred the Great's Old English version of Boethius's *Consolation of Philosophy* [*King Alfred's Anglo-Saxon Version of Boethius' De Consolatione Philosophiae*] opens with the following:

> At the time when the Goths of the country of Scythia made war against the empire of the Romans, and, with their kings, who were called Rhadagast and Alaric, sacked the Roman city, and reduced to subjection all the kingdom of Italy . . .

This passage does not appear in Boethius's original Latin text. The form 'Rhadagast' also appears in a note in Chapter XXX of Edward Gibbon's *The Decline and Fall of the Roman Empire* [1776–1788], which connects the name to the Slavic Radegast:

> The name of Rhadagast was that of a local deity of the Obotrites† (in Mecklenburg). A hero might naturally assume the appellation of his tutelar god; but it is not probable that the Barbarians should worship an unsuccessful hero. See Mascou, Hist. of the Germans, viii.14.

> † [Editor's Note: The Obotrites were one of the Slavic peoples known as the Wends.]

Gibbon's source was Johann Jakob Mascov's *Geschichte der Teutschen bis zu Anfang der Franckischen Monarchie*, translated into English by Thomas Lediard as *History of the Ancient Germans* [1737]. Mascov's sources were no doubt the original chronicles by Adam of Bremen and Helmold, but I have been unable to confirm whether Mascov was the first to make the Radagaisus/Radegast connection or if some still earlier scholar had anticipated him in this.

I am grateful to David Salo for drawing my attention to Radagast's Gothic antecedents, for providing me with a photocopy of the relevant passage from Cardale's text, and for demonstrating how the intrusive 'h' in Rhadagast is an eighteenth-/nineteenth-century error – albeit one repeated by as august an authority as the Bosworth-Toller *Anglo-Saxon Dictionary*, which uses the form *Rhadgast* under its entry for *Gota* [Goth]; 1898 edition p. 486 (personal communication, Salo to Rateliff, 10th December 1998).

43 It is reprinted, with a translation, in Shippey's *The Road to Middle-earth*; Rhona Beare's earlier excellent translation unfortunately remains unpublished. Shippey points out that this is '[t]he only extant Gothic poem' (ibid., rev. ed. [2003] p. 26), but this is not quite true, since *Songs for the Philologists* also includes a Gothic translation by E. V. Gordon of the drinking ditty 'When I'm Dead' (*Songs for the Philologists* p. 26), dissatisfaction with which prompted Tolkien to create his own version (still unpublished). See also Arden Smith's essay 'Tolkienian

Gothic' in the Blackwelder festschrift (*The Lord of the Rings* 1954–2004: *Scholarship in Honor of Richard E. Blackwelder*, ed. Hammond & Scull [2006]), pages 267–81.

44 See the examples cited in Sandra Ballif Straubhaar's 'Myth, Late Roman History, and Multiculturalism in Tolkien's Middle-earth', esp. pages 104–5 & 108–9, in *Tolkien and the Invention of Myth*, ed. Jane Chance [2004].

45 For a historical account less highly coloured than Isidore's or Gibbon's, see Herwig Wolfram's *History of the Goths*, tr. Th. J. Dunlap [1988], especially pages 168–70. Unlike the pagan Radagaisus, the somewhat more successful Visigoth leader Alaric was Christian; by 'heretic' Isidore simply means that Alaric was an Arian (like most Goths) rather than a Trinitarian.

46 *Fortinbras* is familiar with all readers of *Hamlet* as one of the few characters actually still alive at the end of the play, the Norwegian prince who succeeds to the throne of Denmark after Hamlet's death. Odovacar (also known as Odoacer) is the Germanic chieftain who deposed the last emperor of Rome in 476 AD, marking the official end of the Roman Empire in the west. Sigismond (Sigismund, d. 523) was one of the last kings of the Burgundians, whose line plays such a large role in the Sigurd story, before their kingdom was destroyed by the Merovingians.

47 A more famous example of a non-German name of the era preserved only in a Germanic language is *Attila*, which is Gothic for 'Little Father' (i.e., 'Daddy'); the great Hun leader's original (probably similar) name in his own language is lost. For the appeal of such chance historical survivals to Tolkien, see *Letters* pp. 264 & 447.

48 Again I am grateful to David Salo for the probable Gothic form of Radagaisus' name.

PLOT NOTES A

These Plot Notes (Marq. 1/1/23:5–10) consist of six pages (three sheets), each numbered by Tolkien in the upper right-hand corner. I give the text of these plot notes in full, followed by textual notes and brief commentary.

Change name of Bladorthin > Gandalf.
Gandalf > Thorin (Oakenshield)
Medwed > to Beorn. Let bear be enchanted

Don't forget the key found in troll's lair.[TN1]

After visit to Beorn

They tell Beorn of their quest.[TN2]

Darkness falls. They are given beds in the hall. Moon shines in through the louver. Beorn stands up and bids them goodnight, but warns them they must not stray outside the hall till dawn on their peril. He goes out. They go to sleep.

Bilbo wakes up to hear growling outside, & scraping & snuffling at the doors. Next morning no sign of Beorn; but they find breakfast laid on the veranda. The sheep horses and dogs wait on them. Night comes again. More growling. Next morning Beorn is there. He is very pleasant to them. They find out he has been right away back to the mountains & found out their story was true. He has caught a warg and a goblin. He is delighted to think of the death of the chief goblin. So they tell him of their quest & ask his help. He lends them ponies and food. They are to ride these as far as the edge of the great forest, then to send them home; but to treat them well and not ride them fast.

They start off – [or so it >] and ride till dark. Bilbo thinks he sees a big bear sneaking in the trees at their side. Sh! says Gandalf[TN3] (=Blad) – take no notice.

They camp at edge of the great forest; and send back the ponies. In the moon they see them trotting back with a big bear trotting after them.

In the morning it is as dark in the forest almost as night.

'Do we have to go through?' says Bilbo.

Yes says Bladorthin – we shd. have to go[TN4] a hundred miles either way to get round it – and the North we should be back at the Misty Mountains again and [*added*: at the] south end the Necromancer lives. At this point there is a track through. But it is a narrow one. Don't stray off it – if you do you won't find the path again & I don't know what will happen. When you get to the other side you will come to the Long marshes[TN5] but you will already see far and faint the Lonely Mountain in the East. There is a path across the Marshes. We know, we know said Gandalf – that is on the borders of our own land, & we have not forgotten – beyond the marshes are the wide fields and then at last we come if we turn half south to Long Lake, but <hurrying> straight on we shall come to the <west> of the Mountain and the Secret Entrance.[TN6]

All right, then said Blad. Now off you go. Take care of yourselves & goodbye.

He wouldn't stay. No he said. This is your affair I have come much farther than I meant. I have other business on hand now that can wait no longer. And off he went back towards Medwed.[TN7]

The dwarves & Bilbo plunge into the forest. Very dark and silent. Black squirrels peep at them; and all kinds of queer <sneaky> creatures in the undergrowth. They see a sort of track like a rabbit track & stick to it – in a long line. They go on till their food is getting short (– stretch out with beechnuts[TN8] & acorns). Bilbo climbs a tree and <sees> Purple Emperors only they are black. but the forest seems still to stretch on far ahead. Night comes. They see a light not far from the track. peering through the trees they see people sitting in a clearing having a feast. They are so hungry that they disobey the warning and creep off towards the light to beg food. when they get there the lights go out and they are in pitch dark. They can't even see one another. Fall[TN9] over in dark trying to find one another. They cannot find track again. See light again. It goes out again as they creep up. This goes on till they are quite bewildered. At last they [get into spider's >] lose [track >] one another.[TN10] Voices all over wood answering and calling. Die away. Bilbo alone. Finds himself in a huge spiders web.

The spider comes at him. He kills her[TN11] – takes her thread and in dim light of day has marvellous luck to come across the track. Ties thread to a tree; puts ring on[TN12] and goes off. back towards spiderwebs – which he finds by thread.

He calls Dori Nori, Oinn & Gloinn, Balin Dwalin, Bivur & Bombr, Fili Kili Gandalf.[TN13] Faint answer comes, and he finds them all hung up, in webs twined round – like spider-meat. All except Gandalf who with orcrist had killed a spider & escaped. He cuts down Dori and with his help is releasing others when the spiders come back swinging from the branches of the trees.

Battle with spiders. When the spiders cannot overcome them they go off and spin black webs all round so that the dwarves are shut in – and hundreds more come up: poisonous spiders.[TN14]

The spiders are sitting up in the branches spinning black webs – and guarding their prisoners. Bilbo hears them talking about the nice <pretty> meat. Luckily he has his ring. He picks up a stone and <strikes> a spider down. Great <commotion>. They all come towards him. He slips off in another direction & knocks down another spider

Then when they have all swung down on the ground he sings a song.

Old fat spider spinning in a tree
" " " can't spy me
    Attercop! Attercop!
    Won't you stop,
Stop your spinning and seek for me?
Old Tom-noddy all big body
Old Tom noddy can't spy me
    Attercop! Attercop
    Down you drop,
You never will catch me in your tree.[TN15]

Then he threw another stone. Only <a few> spiders came down, others ran along the branches and swung from tree to tree. They wove webs all round the clearing[TN16] He went to a different place and sang.

Lazy lob and crazy Cob
Are weaving webs to wind me.

Then he <illegible>

<See the> tender meat is hanging sweet
but still they can not find me.
Here [am] I naughty little fly
[I go by and laughing fly >] You are fat and lazy
[Th I go by >] and [I] laughing fly as I go by
Through your cobwebs crazy[TN17]

Then he slashed one of their webs to pieces.

They all came in that direction and so he led them far away & then crept back and loosed the dwarves.

The spiders found out before he <finished> – and the dwarves found out his ring but they did not lose their respect because of his brave deed.

They had a dreadful time following Bilbo's thread. Spiders after them. Spiders in front weaving thick webs to stop them. But the dwarves beat them off with branches at the rear while Bilbo cut the webs ahead.

At last the spiders got tired of following. So they got back to the track.

Where was Gandalf?

Caught by wood elves. Took him to the caves of their king. they had had a battle with dwarves long ago and did not like them so he shut Gandalf up and sent people to look for the <others>.[TN18]

The dwarves were all captured by the woodelves but Bilbo popped on his ring and followed them into the caves.

Description of the woodelves caves.[TN19]

Bilbo stuffs his pockets <with> fairy cakes[TN20] & goes back for Bladorthin. <Frighten> by <big bear>. Medwed finds him and sends for Bladorthin. who has luckily been staying with him.[TN21]

Bladorthin angry. He comes and speaks to the woodelves king, and the dwarves are released, under pressure of <pledging> rich gifts when they go back that way <& they must>[TN22]

Bladorthin says 'Now really good bye.'

<Then> woodelves <guard> them to the end of the forest.

Over the marshes. First sight of the lonely Mountain All burnt.[TN23]

[*added in top margin*:]

In spring <he>

All shut up in it. Bilbo can't find his way out [> get out the magic gates].[TN24] lives by stealing food. Finds Dori's cell. <Must> get a message to Bladorthin (Dwarves made to work). Winter comes & Bilbo must go.

[*added at bottom of page*:]

In Spring

Bilbo escapes by <hiding> in a barrel which they are <wheeling> out Medwed – <agrees> to find <eagles> & send a message. Bladorthin found at last.

TEXT NOTES

1 The underlined phrase and the line about the troll-key are written in slightly smaller and hastier handwriting and may have been added later.

For the uncertainties about whether or not Medwed was enchanted, see p. 247 & 259. And for more on the enchanted bear theme, see the commentary on Bothvar Bjarki starting on p. 256 above and also Plot Notes F (p. 629).

2 This line and the one immediately preceding it each have a line drawn through them, indicating that they are false starts which were soon cancelled.

3 The word 'Gandalf' is struck through here. This first hesitant application to the wizard of the name under which he has long since become famous did not stick; within six lines Tolkien was once again calling the character 'Bladorthin'. Not until near the end of the Second Phase, in the Lonely Mountain chapters, was the wizard's new name actually adopted (see pp. 476 & 482 below).

4 A cancelled word or partial word follows 'to go' here which might read 'near' (i.e., *nearly*) or 'nor' (i.e., *north*).

In addition to Tolkien's reversion to the name 'Bladorthin' here and henceforth, only six lines after adopting 'Gandalf' as the name of the wizard and despite the confident listing of name changes at the start of the document, note the wizard's use of first person plural here: '*we* shd. have to go' and '*we* should be back'. This usage is curious, given his immediate departure from them at the top of the next page; along with the sketchy 'First Outline' given on p. 229 above this suggests that Tolkien was undecided about the exact point at which the wizard and the others would part company, although the departure itself had been foreseen from the very first chapter (see the references to 'Mr. Lucky Number'). In any case, his reversion to 'you' a few sentences later simply highlights the fluidity of these notes, with ideas emerging in the process of putting words to paper.

5 The 'Long Marshes', capitalized as if a proper name, appears in Chapter VII (p. 244; cf. also DAA.189) but the name appears nowhere else in the book. The marshes themselves go all the way back to 'The Pryftan Fragment', appearing on Fimbulfambi's Map (cf. Frontispiece), although in the event neither Bilbo nor the dwarves ever have any adventures there. See also p. 370 below.

6 The word I have read here as *hurrying* might instead be *keeping*.

Note that although this description of the terrain on the eastern side of Mirkwood does not quite match the final geography of the published book, it matches up perfectly with the first rough sketch of the lands near the Mountain which occurs as the last page of Plot Notes B (see pp. 366–7). It also fits tolerably well with the early version of the

Wilderland Map that appears on Plate I [bottom]. By contrast, in the Wilderland map that accompanies the published text (DAA.[399]) the 'Elf-path' leads from the 'Forest Gate' in the west to the Elvenking's Halls near the eastern edge of Mirkwood but does not actually reach the forest's border (travel further east presumably all being along the Forest River). Moreover, heading due east from the end of the path on this map would not bring the traveller to the Lonely Mountain but instead to Lake Town.

7 The detail that Bladorthin was heading back 'to Medwed' (whose name has already reverted back to the original after the 'Beorn' of the opening paragraphs) soon disappeared, but it remained implicit even in the published text: 'I am not sending the horse back, I am riding it' – [i.e., riding it back]. That Tolkien was uncertain about the wizard's activities and whereabouts after leaving Bilbo's company is clear from the various options and suggestions occurring in the final paragraphs of these Plot Notes; see below.

8 The second half of this word is unclear, and it's possible that Tolkien here wrote 'beech*mast*' (which means much the same thing), just as he did in the 'Enchanted Stream' episode he interpolated into the next chapter (see pages 351 & 357).

9 The second half of this word is obscured by an ink-blot, but Tolkien has written the missing letters in above it.

10 The cancellations and changes this line underwent were all made while it was first being written, a good indication of the speed with which Tolkien was setting down his thoughts.

11 The use of the female pronouns for the spider is significant, since this makes her the only female character to actually appear in *The Hobbit*; see Commentary following Chapter VIII.

12 The words 'puts ring on' are later struck through.

13 Tolkien later slightly revised this line, adding in the two missing dwarf-names as follows: Dori Nori [Ori], Oinn & Gloinn, Balin Dwalin, Bivur [Bovur] & Bombr, Fili Kili Gandalf. The rhythm of the original sentence is better, and once again the omissions testify to the speed with which these rough plot-notes were written.

The variant spellings of some of the dwarf-names here are not certain, given the roughness of the writing, but it seems as if Tolkien were experimenting with the idea of changing several of the other dwarf-names, no doubt as part of the Gandalf > Thorin / Bladorthin > Gandalf / Medwed > Beorn shift contemplated on the first page of these plot-notes. In each case the variant, which occurs only here, would de-Anglicize the name and bring it more into line with the form found in the Edda (see Appendix III).

14 When he had reached this point, Tolkien cancelled the four preceding sentences (everything from 'All except Gandalf' to 'poisonous spiders')

with a single slash through just over six lines (roughly a quarter of this manuscript page), then resumes in the middle of the page.

15 The spider-poem appears with no extant preliminary drafting, although some such probably existed. Tolkien made only two minor changes in the text here, changing 'spy' to 'see' in the second line and 'in' to 'up' in the final line. When he came to write this poem into the actual manuscript (see Chapter VIII, p. 311) in the fully developed text of the passage based upon these plot-notes, he made two further minor changes in wording: 'seek' in line five became 'look', and 'You never will' became 'You'll never' in the final line. Other than a few typographical changes, the poem otherwise remains unchanged from its first appearance here through into the published book.

For more on 'Attercop' (adder-spider) and 'Tom-noddy', see p. 321.

16 This sentence is written in the top margin and marked for insertion at this point.

17 In marked contrast to the first spider poem ('Attercop'), the second spider-poem ('Lazy lob') is full of changes and hesitations, seeming to indicate that what we have here might be the initial composition. Indeed, it looks as if Tolkien initially thought it might be as short as two lines: the cancelled line beginning 'Then he' was probably an anticipation of the line that follows the poem ('Then he slashed').

Even so, relatively few changes were needed to bring this draft into the form found in the full manuscript: a few typographic corrections, the deletion of a superfluous 'and' in the penultimate line, and a new version of line three: 'I am far more sweet than other meat' make it match the version found in the first full text of Chapter VIII (see p. 311 below). In the First Typescript, the poem appears divided into two stanzas, as in the published book, and the final two lines replaced by

> You cannot trap me, though you try,
> in your cobwebs crazy.

– again, the reading of the published text (which remained unaltered through all three editions in Tolkien's lifetime). No drafting survives for the typescript variations, which are typed cleanly into the text of both typescripts.

While presented as a piece of spontaneous doggerel, very much along the lines of the songs Curdie makes up to annoy the goblins in MacDonald's *The Princess and the Goblin* (see commentary on Chapter IV), this little bit of verse is actually quite sophisticated in its metrics, employing internal rhyme, alliteration, and a variable number of syllables per line, often an odd number. In fact, Tolkien seems to be employing a loose form that is almost a parody of the Old English line, with four beats per line and a caesura in each odd-numbered line; the actual number of syllables being of only minor importance.

18 The final word may instead be 'dwarves'.

19 The initial 'D' which begins this line is given a calligraphic treatment very like that of Father Christmas's tremulous script.

20 Fairy cake, or cupcakes, is a rather surprising light-hearted detail that was soon lost, but the idea of a special fairy-food associated with the elves re-emerged much later in *The Lord of the Rings* as elven waybread, or *lembas*. Known as cupcakes in the U.S., 'fairy cakes' are best known to American audiences from their appearance in Douglas Adams' *The Hitchhiker's Guide to the Galaxy* (episode 8); see *The Complete Hitchhiker Scripts* [1980, 1985], pages 165–6.

21 The phrase 'who has luckily been staying with him' was struck through, no doubt as too convenient, not to mention being out of accord with the 'pressing business' Bladorthin claimed prevented him from accompanying Gandalf and company into Mirkwood. It does, however, match with the idea that the wizard was riding back to Medwed with the borrowed horse; see Text Note 7 above.

22 'And they must': I take this to mean that there is no alternate route available, for the reasons Bladorthin lays out for Bilbo on the eaves of Mirkwood. If so, it may be an indication that Tolkien had not yet thought out the final section of the book and that the re-establishment of the Kingdom under the Mountain was not yet envisioned; it certainly suggests that the overthrow of the Necromancer and decimation of the goblins of the northern mountains were not yet part of the story.

23 It is probably not the Mountain itself that is 'all burnt' but the landscape surrounding it, the so-called Desolation of Smaug; see p. 483ff.

24 The revision regarding the magic gates appears at the top of the page and is marked for insertion following the line 'Description of the wood-elves caves'. It marks the introduction of this motif; see p. 380, where the Elvenking says 'There is no escape through my magic doors, for those who are once brought inside' (cf. DAA.223).

Tolkien's Plot Notes

Part of Tolkien's compositional method was from time to time to stop and write out in very rough summary form the events of the story to come. Sometimes, as in this case, the material covered a few chapters; in other cases, as with Plot Notes B (see pp. 361–6), it was an attempt to sketch out the rest of the story to the end. This pre-drafting then formed a basis for the actual first draft that followed, and sometimes (as with the two spider-taunting poems) here and there the actual words of the plot notes find their way into the final published book. This is however the exception; for the most part these plot notes are very rough, often filled with sentence fragments and incomplete words, contradictory ideas, and other examples of 'thinking on paper'. Since they represent the very first time Tolkien set down ideas about what was to happen in the book, and since those ideas sometimes diverge dramatically from what he finally settled on, they are among the most interesting and valuable sections of the entire manuscript. Unfortunately, because they are simply rough notes intended only for his own use and were typically written at great speed, they are also among the most illegible of all the *Hobbit* manuscripts. In this edition I have edited them as little as possible in order to convey something of the informality of this material: inserting all the quotation marks and similar punctuation would make these pages seem more finished and definitive than is in fact the case. As usual, doubtful readings are enclosed in French brackets: <thus>.

The most remarkable thing about these plot notes occurs in the first three lines, where Tolkien arrives at the final forms of the names for three major characters, then fails to implement that change (cf. his later reluctance to abandon *Bingo* for *Frodo* in the *Lord of the Rings* drafts, e.g. HME VI.221). Not until some time later, after a lengthy break in composition that may have lasted as long as a year, did he incorporate these name changes: see pages 437, 472, 476, & 679 below. It is particularly notable that the name *Thorin (Oakenshield)* emerged complete, with his cognomen or epithet already present, and indeed all the new names appear in their exact final forms, even though their adoption was delayed for several more chapters.

For the most part these plot notes adhere closely to the story as it actually came to be written, though with some significant departures. Unsurprisingly, the further into the story it goes the more it drifts from the familiar events, and the end of the tale is entirely absent. Thus, here Gandalf (= Thorin) evades capture by the spiders not because he has been enchanted by the wood-elves but by his own martial prowess, and his capture by the elves comes afterwards. Also, Tolkien was in considerable uncertainty about how Bilbo was to rescue the dwarves from the wood-elves' dungeons. The magic of the Elvenking's Gates seems to have been stronger in the initial conception, preventing even the unseen Bilbo from escaping that way, and hence leading to the episode of the barrels as a means of escape not for the dwarves but for Bilbo himself. In all three variants on the last page of these Plot Notes Tolkien re-introduces both Medwed and Bladorthin, the latter of whom re-enters the story just long enough to get Gandalf & Company out of one last tight spot before once again vanishing. Some of the ideas Tolkien considered here but ultimately rejected seem to have influenced the next set of plot notes as well; see pp. 361ff.

Finally, some apparent departures between the Plot Notes and the familiar text are the result of later changes to the latter – for example, Dori plays a more prominent role in the story in these projections. There is no mention of the enchanted stream here, but then that entire episode is similarly absent from the initial draft of what is now Chapter VIII, having only entered in later through an interpolation (see 'The Enchanted Stream', p. 347). Similarly, the idea that Bilbo would find the lost path again and use spider-thread to guide the dwarves back to it, although it does not appear in the published book, was part of the first full draft; see pages 309–14 and 'The Theseus Theme', p. 335.

Chapter VIII

MIRKWOOD

As before, the manuscript continues without anything more than a paragraph break between what are now Chapters VII ('Queer Lodgings') and VIII ('Flies & Spiders'), the new chapter starting in the middle of manuscript page 99 (Marq. 1/1/7:23).

They walked in single file. The entrance to the track was like a sort of arch leading to a gloomy tunnel made by two great trees that leant together, too old and hung with ivy and shaggy with lichen to bear many leaves of their own. The track [> path] itself was narrow, winding on among the great trunks of trees, about as wide and clear as a rabbit-track. Soon the light at the entrance was like a little bright hole far behind, and the quiet was so deep that their feet seemed to thump along, while all the trees listened. But their eyes were getting used to the dimness, and they could see some way to each side in a sort of darkened green light. Just occasionally a little beam of sun that had the luck to creep in through some opening in the leaves from above and still more luck in not being caught by the tangled boughs beneath, stabbed down thin and bright [. But >] before them, but this was seldom.

There were black squirrels in that wood.[TN1] As their eyes got used to seeing things they could see them whisking off the path and scuttling behind tree trunks. There were other quiet noises, grunts scuffles and hurryings in the undergrowth and among the leaves piled endlessly thick on the forest floor, but what made the noises they could not see.

The nastiest thing they saw was the cobwebs: Dark thick [> dense] cobwebs, with threads extraordinary thick, often stretched from tree to tree, or tangled in the lower branches on either side of them. But none were across their path; whether because some magic kept this path open or not they did not know.[TN2]

Very soon they got to hate the forest almost as heartily as they had disliked the tunnels of the goblins. But they had to go on and on long after they were sick for the sight of the sun and of the sky, and longed for the feeling [> feel] of the wind on their faces. It was still and dark and stuffy down under the unbroken forest roof. Nights were the worst.

It then became pitch dark – not what you call pitch-dark, but really pitch: so black you simply couldn't see anything. Bilbo tried flapping his hand in front of his nose, but he couldn't see [*added*: them] at all. It isn't true to say they couldn't see anything: they could – eyes. They slept all closely huddled together, and took it in turns to watch; and when it was Bilbo's turn he would see gleams in the darkness round them, and sometimes pairs and pairs of yellow or red or green eyes would stare at him from a little distance and then slowly fade and disappear. And they would sometimes look down from the branches above. That frightened him more still. But the eyes he liked least were horrible pale bulbous sort of eyes – 'insect eyes', he thought, 'not animal eyes, only they are much too big'.[TN3]

Although [he >] it was not cold at first they tried lighting a watch-fire at night, but they soon gave it up. It seemed to bring hundreds [of] eyes all round, only the creatures (whatever they were) were careful never to let their bodies show in the little flicker of the flames. Worse still it brought thousands of great dark grey and black moths, some nearly as big as your hand flapping and whirring round their ears. They could not stand that, nor the big bats (black as a top hat) either; so they gave up fires, and just sat or dozed in the enormous uncanny dark.[TN4]

This went on for what seemed ages and ages to the hobbit; and he was always hungry, for they were very very careful with their provisions. Yet as time went on, days and days, they began to get anxious. The food would not last forever, and was in fact already running low. Yet the path straggled on just as before, and there was no change in the forest. The only new thing that happened was the sound of laughter [*added*: often], and once of singing, in the distance. The laughter was the laughter of fair voices not of goblins, and the singing was beautiful, but it sounded so eerie and strange, that they were not at all comforted.

At last their food began to give out; and they could not find any thing in the wood to eat to eke out what they carried. Nothing wholesome seemed to grow here, [but >] only funguses, or [pale >] herbs with pale leaves and unpleasant smell. In parts where beech-nuts[TN5] grew, and were already dropping their mast (for autumn was now far on)[TN6] they tried gathering the nuts, but they were hard and bitter. Yet they liked the beechen part of the wood best for here there was no undergrowth, the shadows were less dense, the light was clearer, and sometimes they could see for a longish way all round them – an endless vista of great straight trunks like the pillars of huge dark hall. In these parts they heard the laughter.

Of course it was Bilbo that had to climb a tree. Not in the beech-grown parts, [but >] for their trunks were too smooth and their branches too high. But in what seemed a sort of valley mostly filled with oaks, when their food was nearly gone,[TN7] the dwarves said:

'Some one must take a look round, and the only way is to climb the tallest tree we can see'.

They chose the hobbit because of course to be of any use the Climber must get his head above the topmost leaves, and so he must be light enough for the highest and slenderest branches to bear him. Poor Bilbo hadn't had much practice in climbing trees; but they hoisted him up into the lowest branches of the tallest tree they could find near, and up he had to go as best he could.

He pushed his way up through the tangled twigs, getting slapped in the eye, and all greened and grimed [with >] from the old bark of the big boughs. All the time he was hoping there were no spiders in that tree.[TN8] He slipped and caught himself, he struggled up places were the branches grew difficult, and at last he got near the top. There he found spiders all right, but only small ordinary ones; and he found out why they were there. They were after the butterflies! When at last poor little Bilbo swaying Dangerously on the small top branches poked his head out of the leaves he was nearly blinded. He could hear the dwarves shouting up at him from far below, but he could not answer, only hold on and blink. The sun was shining brightly and it was a long time before he could bear it. Then he saw all round him a sea of dark green ruffled here and there by the breeze. And there were hundreds [of] butterflies. I expect they were a kind of 'purple emperor', but they were dark dark velvety black without any markings at all.

He looked at these for a long time, and he liked the breeze; but soon the shouts of the dwarves (who were simply [shouting >] stamping with impatience down below) reminded him of his real business. It was no good. He couldn't see any end to the trees and leaves in any direction. It was really very horrible with no food down below to go to.

Actually I believe they were coming fairly near to the end of the forest now, if they had only known it. (If they had it might have saved them a deal of trouble, as you will see). And if they or Bilbo had the sense to see it,[TN9] he had climbed a tree that was tall in itself but was standing near the bottom of a wide hollow or valley, and so from its top the trees seem to swell up all round it, like the edges of great bowl. No wonder [they >] he could not see very far.

Down Bilbo scrambled at last, scratched, hot, and miserable, and he could not hardly see anything in the gloom below when he got there. Very unhappy they all were when he told them [they>] 'this forest went on for ever and ever in all directions'. They were quite cross with him, as if it was his fault; and they didn't care tuppence[TN10] about the butterflies, and were only made more angry when he told them of the beautiful breeze (because they were too heavy to get their heads out and feel it).

That night they ate their last scraps of food, and woke up horribly hungry sometime next day (you could hardly call it morning it was so dim). All they could do was to tighten their belts round their empty tummies, and trudge along the track without much hope of ever seeing the end of it. You can perhaps guess how desperately hungry they were (especially Bilbo) when the blackness of night came on.

Bombur had just said 'I won't go a step farther. I am going to lie down here and sleep, and I don't care if I never wake up!'[TN11] When Balin[TN12] said.

'What's that? There's a twinkle of light'.

They all looked, and a longish way off (as far as they could guess) and to the left of their path, they saw a twinkle in the dark. Then they hurried along hardly caring whether it was trolls or goblins. The light did not seem to come any nearer, but first one and then another little twinkle came out. At last they had drawn level with it, and they could feel sure that lights (torches perhaps or small fires) were burning in some place in the forest along side of them, but a good way off their path.

They argued about it for a bit, but not for long. They did not forget the warnings of Medwed and Bladorthin, of course! But they all agreed, that they would starve to death quite soon if they stuck to the path, so that things could not be much worse if they left it and lost it. But [> Only] at first they could not agree whether to send out one or two spies or all go towards the light. In the end they all went (as quietly as they could, with the hobbit on the end of the line),[TN13] because nobody liked to go off into the forest alone, nor to be left alone on the path.

After a good deal of creeping and crawling along they peered round the trunks of trees and could see a place where it seem[ed] one or two trees had been cut down so that there was a more open space. And bless me if there were not people there, elvish looking folk all dressed in green and brown, sitting on logs. There was a little fire, and there were torches on some of the tree-trunks; but most splendid sight of all they were feasting, eating and drinking and laughing.

Without waiting to ask each other [> one another] each of them scrambled forwards with the same idea of begging some food and drink (for their water skins were as empty as their food bags).[TN14] But not one of them got into the clearing, before all the lights went out. Somebody kicked the fire and it went out in a shower of sparks, as if by magic. There they were in inky blackness, and they couldn't even find one another. Not for a long while at any rate. At last after blundering about falling over logs, bumping crash into trees, and shouting and calling till they must have waked all the things in the forest for miles round,[TN15] they managed to gather themselves together in a bundle and count themselves (fourteen) by touching. By that time of course they had no idea left as to where their track lay, and they were quite lost, until morning, at any rate.

There was nothing for it, but to lie down for the night where they were. They didn't even dare to grope about for any scrap of food for fear of getting separated again. But they had hardly settled down, before Dori (whose turn it was to watch first)[TN16] said in a loud whisper:

'The lights are coming out again over there!'

Up they all jumped again. There were the lights twinkling again not far off, and they could hear low voices and laughter quite plainly.

This time they crept even more slowly and carefully towards them; and Gandalf said 'No one is [to] stir from hiding, till I say. I shall step forward alone quietly first, and try to beg for food.'[TN17] They came right to the edge of the circle of light made by the torches this time, and they lay each behind a tree peering cautiously out.

Up got Gandalf finally and stepped into the ring. Out went all the lights again, and [they were >] if it was bad collecting themselves before it was worse still this time. Gandalf simply couldn't be found. Every time they counted it only made thirteen, and though they shouted [and called] 'Gandalf' there was no answer. Bilbo found him. He fell over what seemed a log, and found it was the dwarf lying down fast asleep.[TN18]

They soon woke him up, and until he understood what had happened he was very displeased [> annoyed]. 'I was having such a good dream, all about having a most gorgeous dinner' he said.[TN19]

'Dreaming about dinner won't do any good', said they. ['These people don't seem likely to offer us any more. But dreams about food is about all we seem likely to get in this place,' said he >] 'and we can't share it anyway.'

'But it is the best I seem likely to get in this place!' he grumbled.

But that was not the last of the lights. Once again, when the night must have been wearing on, Kili who was watching, came and waked them and said:

'There is a regular blaze of light not far away – just as if many torches and fires had all been lit up suddenly. And hark to the singing'.

This was too much for them, and so after lying and listening a little while they all got up once more. The result was worse than ever. This time Gandalf said he would step forward himself. [It was a >] The feast they looked on was larger and merrier than ever.

The elvish folk were passing bowls round and round as across the fires, and some were harping and many singing, but the language seemed strange and they could not catch the words.

Out stepped Gandalf. Out went the lights. The fires went up in dark smoke. Ashes and cinders were in his eyes. The wood was full of cries and voices.

This time they did not find one another at all. Bilbo found himself running round and round (or so he thought) calling and calling Dori Nori, [Ori] Oin Gloin, Fili, Kili, Bombur, Gandalf Dwalin Balin Bifur Bofur[TN20] – and other people all round seemed to be doing the same (with an occasional Bilbo thrown in). But the other voices got fainter and fainter, [till at last >] and he thought he heard far off cries for help, and shouts, but at last it all died away [and he was >] though he did his best to go in the direction of the calls; and he was quite alone in the dark.[TN21]

That was one of his most miserable moments. But he soon made up his mind that there was no help for it till 'morning'. It was no good blundering about tiring himself out, with no hope of breakfast. So he sat down with his back to a tree, and not for the last time fell to thinking of his far distant hobbit-hole, & its beautiful pantries.

He was deep in thoughts of [mutton >] bacon and eggs, and toast and butter, when he felt something touch him. Something like a [string or] sticky rope was against his left hand. He found his left leg was already wrapped in it. He leapt to his feet and fell over. Then the great spider who had been busy beginning to tie him up while he dozed & dreamed came from behind him, and made for him. He could only see the thing's eyes, but he could feel the hairy legs, as she[TN22] [> it] tried to wind <her> great abominable threads round and round him.

It was lucky he had come to his senses in time. Soon he would not have been able to move. As it was he had a horrible fight and struggle. He beat the creature off with his hands – it was trying to poison him to keep him quiet, as small spiders do to flies – until he remembered his sword, and drew it out.

The spider drew back and he had time to cut his leg free. Then it was his turn to attack. The spider was certainly not used to things that carried such stings at their sides, and before it could go off Bilbo came at it and stuck at it with his sword right at its eyes. Then it went mad and leapt and danced, in a horrible fashion, but soon he killed it with another stroke, and then he fell down and remembered no more for some time.

There was the usual grey light of the forest-day when he came to. The spider was dead beside him, and his sword blade was stained black.

Somehow the killing of the spider, winning his battle all by himself alone in the dark, without help of dwarves or wizard or anyone else, made quite a difference to Mr Baggins. He felt a different person, and much bolder and fiercer as he put his sword back into its sheath.[TN23] More still he sharpened up his wits and he gathered the horrible string of the great spider's thread together – there seemed an endless amount of it, that the creature had spun wildly out in the battle. Soon he had a huge ball, as much as he could carry. One end he tied to his tree, and then carrying his ball he set out to explore.

By some sort of luck it was not a very great while before in his casting round – and anyways hobbits are rather clever in woods, and can remember differences between trees and the way they grow which would all seem this same to you or me – he came upon the track that they had left. Soon he found the empty skins and bags they had put down before they crept towards the lights. Not that they were much use to him, though it certainly made him feel less lost.

'Perhaps some of the dwarves will find the way back here too' he thought as he turned the bags inside out for crumbs, 'and I suppose I ought to wait here, & not try to go on – or back.'

So he waited, but time went on & he heard no sounds at all. At last he made up his mind that it was his duty to look for his companions. I can tell you he didn't like it at all, but when he thought of his string he was a bit comforted. He cut it with his sword. Tied the new end to a tree close by the track, and then holding his ball, and also the old end he followed back along the thread he had himself laid until he came to the tree where he had fought the spider. From there he plunged into the forest clutching his ball with one hand, his little sword in the other. And luckily he remembered to put on his ring before he started.

That is why the spiders did not see him coming. Bilbo took care that nothing *heard* him. Hobbits can do that, as I have told you already. Creeping along in the direction – as far as he cd. guess – from which the cries had come in the night he saw a place of dense black shadow like a patch of night ahead.

It was made by spiders' webs one behind and over and tangled with another, as he saw as he drew near. There were [*added*: spiders] huge and horrible sitting in the branches above him, and ring or no ring he was terrified lest they should discover him. Standing behind a tree he watched some of them; and then in the stillness of the wood he suddenly realized that these loathsome and enchanted creatures were speaking one to another; with a sort of low creaking hissing sound, and he cd. make out many of the words.

They were talking about the dwarves![TN24]

'Fine eating they will make' said one 'when they have hung a bit'.

'Don't hang 'em too long' said another '– they are not as fat as they might be; not been feeding too well of late, I should say'.

'Well kill 'em then, kill 'em, and hang 'em again dead for a while.' said a third.

'They're dead now I'll warrant'.

'That they're not; I saw one a-struggling just now. Just coming round again, I should say, after a beautiful [> bee-autiful] sleep. I'll show you!'

Then one of the fat spiders ran along a rope till it came to a dozen bundles hanging up from a branch. Bilbo was horrified, now he noticed them for the first time in the shadows, to see a dwarvish foot stick out of the bottoms of some of these bundles, and here and there a tip of nose, and bit of beard, or hood. [*added*: The spider went to] One of the fattest of the bundles – 'that is poor old Bombur I'll bet' thought Bilbo – and nipped hard at the toe sticking out. There was muffled yelp inside and the toe shot out and kicked the old spider hard. There was a soft noise like kicking a flabby football, and the spider fell nearly to the ground before its thread caught it.

The others laughed. 'You were right' they said. 'The meat is still alive and kicking'.

'I'll soon stop that' said the angry spider climbing back.

Then Bilbo thought it was time he did something. He could not get up and [at] the brutes, but he found a stone. There was good many here among the leaves and moss on the floor. Now Bilbo was a fair shot. Yes he was. He could blow smoke-rings if you remember, and cook, and do lots of other things which I haven't told you of. As a boy he used to practise throwing stones [till rabbits >] – though he never meant any harm by it – still rabbits and squirrels and even birds got out of his way if he stooped in <those> days. Even grown up he went on being good at quoits, dart-throwing, shooting arrows at a wand, bowls, ninepins and other quiet games of the sort that he liked.[TN25] Now it came in useful for his first shot knocked a great spider senseless off its branch, and it fell flop to earth with its legs all curled up. The next went whistling through a big web, snapping its cords and knocking the spider sitting in the middle off with it, whack, dead.

There was a deal of commotion among the spiders then you can guess, and he forgot about the dwarves for a bit, I can tell you. They couldn't see Bilbo but they made a very good guess where <the> two shots had come from. They came running and swinging in that direction as quick as lighting, flinging out their long threads in all directions too, till the air seemed full of waving snares.

The Hobbit lost no time in slipping off to a different point. Now his idea was to get the spiders away from the dwarves, if he could. There seemed fifty of them at least. The only thing was to get them excited, curious, and angry all at once. So when a good many had gone off to his old place he threw another stone at those that stopped behind; and dancing among the trees he began to sing a song to infuriate them (and to let the dwarves hear his voice).

This is what he sang:–[TN26]

Old fat spider spinning in a tree,
old fat spider can't see me!
Attercop! Attercop!
Won't you stop,
Stop your spinning and look for me?

Old Tom-noddy, all big body,
Old Tom-noddy can't spy me!
Attercop! Attercop!
Down you drop,
You'll never catch me up your tree!

With that he threw some more stones, & stamped. Some more spiders came towards him. Some dropped to the ground; others ran along the branches, swung from tree to tree, or cast new ropes across the dark spaces. They were after his noise quicker than ever he expected. And they were angry. No spider likes being called Attercop;[TN27] Tom-noddy of course is insulting to anyone, spider or anybody else.[TN28]

The hobbit scuttled off to a new place, but others of the spiders were busy spinning webs across all the spaces between the trunks. Very soon the hobbit would be caught in a very hedge of them – that was their idea, anyway.

Still [in a new place>] standing in the middle of the hunting and spinning spiders he plucked up courage, and began a new song.

'Lazy lob [>Lob] and crazy Cob[TN29]
are weaving webs to wind me
I am far more sweet than other meat,
but still they cannot find me!
Here am I, naughty little fly;
You are fat and lazy.
I laughing fly as I go by
Through your cobwebs crazy!'

Then he turned and found the last space between two tall trees close together was closed with a web – not a proper web, but great strands of spider rope run quickly backwards and forwards from trunk to trunk. Out came his sword. He slashed the web to pieces and went off singing. The spiders heard, and they saw the sword I expect, though I don't suppose they knew what it was. At any rate they all came now hurry him after on ground and branch, hairy legs waving, nippers and spinners snapping, eyes popping, full of rage. They followed[TN30] him into the forest as far as Bilbo dared go. Then he went quicker than a mouse and stole back.

He had precious little time, he knew, before they were disgusted and came back. The worst of all the jobs was getting up into the tree where the dwarves were hung. Luckily a spider had left a rope dangling down and with its help though it stuck to his hand and hurt him, he reached the lowest branch, and got up at last – to meet an old slow wicked spider who had remained behind to guard the prisoners and was busy pinching them to see which was fattest. He[TN31] thought of trying one, while the others were away hunting the noise in the forest.

He hadn't much chance with Mr Baggins who was in a hurry – and he couldn't see him. But he saw and felt his little sword, and soon fell off the branch dead.

The next bad job was to loose a dwarf. If he cut the string which hung each up, the wretched dwarf would fall bump to the ground a good way below, but what else was he to do?

Wriggling along the branch (which made all the poor dwarves dance and dangle like ripe fruit) he reached one bundle.

'Fili or Kili' he thought, by the tip of a blue hood sticking out. 'Fili rather' by the long nose also sticking out.[TN32] He managed by leaning over to cut most of the strong sticky threads that bound him; and sure enough with a kick and a struggle most of Fili emerged. I am afraid Mr Baggins very nearly laughed at the sight of him jerking his stiff arms and legs as he danced on the spider string under the arm pits (like one of those funny toys hanging on a wire). But somehow or other he managed to help Fili up on to the branch. Then with his help they hauled up first one dwarf and then another, although poor Fili was feeling very sick and ill from the spider's poison, and hanging most of the night & the next day, and being wound round and round with only his nose to breathe through. It took him ages to get the beastly stuff out of his eyes and eyebrows – and as for his beard he had to cut most of it off.

None of them were better off. Some were worse, and had hardly been able to breathe at all. They rescued Kili, Bifur, Bofur, Dori and Nori. Poor old Bombur [had >] was so exhausted [he >] (he was the one that had kicked the spider) that he just rolled off the branch and fell plop on the ground (fortunately on leaves) and lay there.

There were still five dwarves hanging up at the far end of the branch when the spiders began to come back, as full of rage as ever.

Bilbo went to the end of the branch and kept off those that crawled up the tree.

'Now we see you, now we see you' they said 'you nasty little creature. We will eat you and leave your bones and skin hanging in a tree. Ugh! he's got a sting has he – we'll have him all the same'. [*added*: Of course Bilbo had taken off the ring when he rescued Fili, and forgotten all about it after.][TN33]

All this time the other dwarves were working at the rest of their friends, and cutting at the threads with their knives. Soon all would be free and sitting on the branch, [*added, in darker ink*: except Bombur] though they had not much idea what would happen next. The spiders had caught each of them easily enough the night before; but that was one by one and in the dark. This time there looked like being a terrible battle.

Then suddenly Bilbo noticed some of the spiders had got round old Bombur on the floor and had tied him up again, and were dragging him away.

He gave a shout and slashed at the spiders in front. They quickly made way, and he scrambled or fell down the tree into the middle of those on the floor. His little sword was something new in stings for them. It shone with delight as he stabbed at them.

He killed three, and the others left Bombur and drew away. 'Come down Come down'! he shouted to the dwarves 'don't stay up there and be netted'.

Down they scrambled or jumped or dropped, eleven of them all in a heap, most of them shaky and little use on their legs. Anyway there they were twelve together, for old Bombur was free again and held on his legs by his cousins Bifur and Bofur.[TN34]

Now spiders were [old >] all round them, and above them. There were more of them than before, in spite of the ones that had been killed; some of their horrible friends (there were a good many of the wretches about – though Bilbo and the dwarves had [not] struck one of their biggest colonies.) must have come up to see what the noise was about. It was then Bilbo thought he had lost his ball of guiding thread. He was ready to collapse, until he found he had stuck it in his pocket. Luckily it hadn't snapped, but of course it marked all the winding path he had gone, and went in and out round tree trunks backwards and forwards, and most ridiculous path to follow.[TN35]

Bilbo saw nothing for it, but to let the Dwarves into his ring secret. When he had done so very quickly and puffily, he made them stand where they were, while he very <bravely> followed up his own path, winding up his ball as he went. He put his ring on again; and that bothered the spiders once more. Because he kept on saying 'Attercop' and 'Lazy Lob' as he ran from tree [to] tree, and they [kept on >] did not like it, and couldn't tell where he would be next. In fact he kept them from attacking the dwarves in force, or doing more than drop lines from above down on to them, until he had found the point where his thread went off away from the spiders, back towards the track.

Then he dashed back to the dwarves, and got them to understand that he could lead them back to the track. With groans and moans they hobbled after him, and the spiders came too. They couldn't see Bilbo, and he tired himself out dashing to one side or to another or to the rear to keep them off. But soon they felt the sting so often they contented themselves with running ahead and barring the way with their sticky threads, which Bilbo and one or two of the dwarves who had knives and were more recovered had to cut and slash.

In some ways the most terrible time of all their adventures was that horrible fight back to the track. I am afraid they did not think just then how lucky they were ever to get there, when at last they did, leaving the angry and bewildered spiders behind. Only one or two followed them to the very edge of the path, and sat fuming and cursing at them from branches in the trees.

But the dwarves never forgot Bilbo's work. Even then they thanked him, and all bowed several times right to the ground, though some of them fell over with the effort and could not get up again for a long while. [There they >] They never forgot Bilbo, and though they knew now about his ring – Balin in particular had to have the whole tale[TN36] told him twice – they thought no less of him. In fact they praised him so much, Bilbo began to feel a great bold fellow – or would have done, if there had been anything to eat. There was nothing, and they were worn out. They just lay and looked at one another – except Balin, who kept on saying – 'so that is how he sneaked past me was it! Now I know. Little <terror> – good old Bilbo–Bilbo Bilbo-bo-bo-bo', till they told him to shut up.

All of a sudden Dwalin opened an eye and look round at them. 'Where is Gandalf?'[TN37] he said.

It was a terrible blow. Of course there were only thirteen of them: 12 dwarves, and the hobbit.[TN38] Where indeed was Gandalf?

If you want to know, read on and leave the rest of them sitting more or less hopeless on the forest path. They drowzed off into an uncomfortable sleep there, as evening came on; and they were too sick and weary to think of guards or taking watches. There you can leave them for the present.

[You rem<ember> >] Gandalf was caught much more fast than

those bound by spiders! You remember Bilbo falling like a log into sleep as he stepped into the feasting ring? Next time Gandalf had stepped forward; and as the lights went out he fell like a stone enchanted. All the noise of the dwarves lost in the night, their cries as the spiders caught them, and all the sounds of the battle next day, had passed over him. Till the wood-elves (and wood elves the people were of course) came to him and bound him, and carried him away.

Are the wood elves wicked? Well not particularly – indeed not at all. But most of them are descended from the ancient elves who never went to the great FairyLand of the west,[TN39] where the Light-elves, and the Deep-Elves (or Gnomes) and the Sea-elves lived,[TN40] and grew fair, and learned and invented their magic and their cunning craft and the making of beautiful and marvelous things.

The woodelves lingered in the world in the twilight before the raising of the sun and moon, and in the great woods that grew after sun rise,[TN41] but they loved the borders of the forest best, whence they could escape at times to hunt, or ride over the more open lands. In a great cave some miles within Mirkwood on its Eastern side, before whose huge doors of stone a river ran from out of the heights of forest and out into the marshes at the feet of the highlands, lived their king.

These caves wound far underground, and had many passages, and wide halls, but they were brighter and more wholesome and not so deep nor so dangerous as goblin-dwellings. In fact the wood elves themselves mostly lived in the woods in huts on the ground or in the branches. Their king lived in the great wood-cave because of his treasure, and [as] a defense against enemies.[TN42]

To this cave they dragged Gandalf. Not too gently, for they did not love dwarves. They had had wars in ancient days with dwarves, and accused them of stealing their treasure (& the dwarves accused them of the same, and [also] of hiring dwarves to shape their gold & silver, and refusing to pay them after!).[TN43]

The king of the Wood-elves looked sternly on Gandalf. But Gandalf would say nothing to all his questions, except that he was starving, and [or that he] knew nothing.

'Why did you and your friends burst three times upon my people[?]'

'Because we were starving' he said.

'Where are your friends now and what are they doing?'

'I don't know' said Gandalf – 'but I expect starving in the forest.'

'What brought you into our forest at all[?]' said the king.

But to that Gandalf shut his mouth and would not say a word.

'Take him away' said the king; and they put chains upon him, and put him in one of the inner caves and left him – they did give him food and drink, plenty if not very fine. Wood elves are not goblins, and are reasonably well-behaved even to their worst enemies when they have them as prisoners. Except to spiders. These they hate above all things,[TN44] and fear for few of them have swords of iron or steel at all. Hardly any at all even now. None I expect in those days. They fight chiefly with clubs, and bows, and arrows pointed with bone or stone.[TN45]

There poor Gandalf lay, and after he had got over the [> his] thankfulness for bread and meat and water, he began to wonder what had happened to his unfortunate friends . . .

He soon found out. The wood-elves were not going to have dwarves wandering about in their part of the forest, starving or not. So they went back to the place where they had caught Gandalf, and finding no one there they waylaid the track. They knew all about it, because they made it, and still guarded and kept [it] open most of the way. It was their only way of getting news of the western world.

It was not long before they found the hobbit and the dwarves staggering along – the day after the spider-battle – in a last effort to find a way out of the forest before they fell down and died of hunger and thirst. [Suddenly from behind the trees >] Such day as there was under the dark trees was fading into pitch blackness, when suddenly out sprang the light of torches on either side of them, like [<thousands> >] hundreds of red stars. Out leap the woodelves with their bows; and called the dwarves to halt.

There was no thought of a fight. The dwarves were exhausted; and their [*added*: small] knives, all the weapons they had, were no good [> use] against the bows of the woodelves that hit a bird's eye in the dark; and they knew it.

At this point in the manuscript (at the bottom of manuscript page 118; Marq. 1/1/8:18) there is a change in the kind of paper used that almost certainly marks one of the two major pauses or breaks in composition to which Tolkien referred in his 1938 letter (see Appendix II and 'The Chronology of Composition' on p. xviii). Accordingly, I have chosen to make the chapter break between what later became Chapter VIII: 'Flies and Spiders' and Chapter IX: 'Barrels Out of Bond' here, even though the last two paragraphs above eventually became the opening paragraph and a half of the following chapter (contrast DAA.221 & 222). Henceforth, instead of being written on both sides of the sheet on 'foolscap' paper, the rest of the Second Phase manuscript (manuscript pages 119–167) is written on one side only of the sheet. The new paper is also somewhat inferior to the old and has aged more; the unused backs are lined, which shows that these are probably unused sheets torn from student 'blue books' used in examinations. See p. 379 for a continuation of the text.

TEXT NOTES

1 Most of what little wildlife the dwarves and hobbit encounter in Mirkwood is dark in coloration, no doubt from protective camouflage in this dimly lit environment: the black squirrels, the 'great dark grey and black moths' attracted by their campfires, the big bats ('black as a top hat') presumably attracted by the moths, even the 'dark, dark velvety black' purple emperor butterflies Bilbo sees atop the oak canopy. The only exception seems to be the 'snowy white' deer (a hind and her fawns) seen in the enchanted stream episode and deliberately contrasted to the 'dark' hart seen immediately before, and that scene is itself a later interpolation added into the story, not part of the original draft (see p. 350).

For a speculation on the melanistic nature of Mirkwood's wildlife, see Henry Gee's column 'Melanism and Middle-earth', posted on the Tolkien site TheOneRing.net (http://greenbooks.theonering.net/guest/files/081104–01.html). Note that while Gee refers to the spiders as 'black', their coloration is actually not mentioned in the text. We are told that their cobwebs were 'dark' (p. 303) and it would certainly make sense that their dark coloration prevented their being seen when they came to stare at the campfires (p. 304), but the only indication that the spiders themselves are black comes not in the text but in an illustration: the lost halftone of Mirkwood (Plate VII [top]) that appeared in the first two printings of *The Hobbit* (and as a line drawing in the first printing of the American edition; see DAA.192–3) – a mere 8800 copies, some of which were destroyed unsold during the Blitz (Hammond, *Descriptive Bibliography*, pages 4, 15, & 18).

2 We are told much later that the elves built and maintain the forest road (p. 316), and that the elves and spiders are enemies (ibid.). We cannot say with certainty that the forest path was an elf-road from first conception, but it seems likely, given its quietly understated eeriness through all versions of the story.

The cobwebs are Bilbo and the dwarves' first hint of the spiders' existence. Later readers had more hints from three pieces of accompanying cartography and illustration: the final Thror's Map, one of whose labels reads 'West lies Mirkwood the Great – /there are Spiders' (DAA.50), the Wilderland Map, which clearly shows large spiders & cobwebs throughout northern Mirkwood (DAA.[399]), and the aforementioned Mirkwood halftone (Plate VII [top]), which shows a spider walking by prominently in the right foreground (ibid. [detail]).

3 These 'horrible pale bulbous . . . insect eyes' presumably belong to the Mirkwood spiders, since they stare down at Bilbo from the branches overhead. Tolkien does not actually describe the Mirkwood spiders, when we finally encounter them near the end of this chapter, as having compound insect eyes, but he did explicitly use that description for Shelob in *The Lord of the Rings* ('two great clusters of many-windowed

eyes . . . [with] their thousand facets' – *LotR*.747), whom he linked to the Mirkwood spiders as their progenitor. See Commentary, 'The Children of Ungoliant', p. 326ff.

4 'Black as a top hat' is the sort of detail often described by careless commentators on the book as anachronistic; it is not. Like the express-train in Chapter I of *The Lord of the Rings* or the whistling tea kettle it is merely a direct-address simile provided by the narrator (not Bilbo) to help his listeners, the modern-day audience, visualize the scene.

5 Tolkien originally wrote *beechnuts*, which he soon changed to *beechtrees*. For more on the role of beechnuts or beechmast in the story, see Plot Notes A, p. 294 and Text Note 8 page 298.

6 Much later, Tolkien changed 'far on' to 'getting on' in pencil (the first layer of revision in this chapter having been done in black ink, probably not long after the Ms. was written).

Note also the time-frame of the story; whereas in the published book they are already on the Mountain by late autumn, here they are still wandering in Mirkwood when 'autumn is far on', with the long captivity among the elves and rest of their journey still to come.

7 Curiously enough, the acorns eaten by the starving dwarves and hobbit in Plot Notes A dropped out of the story here and found no place in the published book. The beech-nuts (see Text Note 5) re-entered the story in the 'Enchanted Stream' interpolation in the form of bitter, inedible nuts thrown down from above at them by the black squirrels. In the published book the ground underneath the beech trees is littered only by 'the dead leaves of countless other autumns' (DAA.199).

8 Bilbo's concern about meeting a spider seems premature, given that the group's first encounter with the giant spiders of Mirkwood does not come until later in this chapter. However, he has already seen the great cobwebs stretched from tree to tree and sinister eyes staring down at him from the trees (see Text Notes 2 & 3 above), so his apprehension is understandable.

The smaller spiders chasing the butterflies enter the story for the first time here (at any rate they are not mentioned in the extremely compressed paragraph devoted to this scene in Plot Notes A); see p. 343 Note 19.

9 Once again the narrator draws the reader's attention to a small significant detail that has escaped the characters' notice: in this case the innocuous line earlier on the page *in what seemed a sort of valley mostly filled with oaks*. For more examples, see the careful enumeration of how many dwarves are present in the spider-webs (Text Note 38).

10 Tuppence: two pence (two pennies), roughly equivalent in buying power to the American nickel (or, earlier, dime). A proverbial phrase.

11 Bombur's sudden collapse here is motivated by nothing more than starvation, exhaustion, and despair, yet it is striking that almost the

same words remain in the story after Tolkien had made this speech the climax of the Enchanted Stream interpolation; see p. 352.

12 Tolkien originally wrote 'Ga' – i.e., the beginning of the name *Gandalf* (the chief dwarf), but immediately switched the role of sharp-eyed dwarf to Balin, who had been the group's look-out man during their council of war after their escape from the Misty Mountains (pp. 198 & 199). Back in Chapter II (p. 91) it had been Dwalin, not Balin, who had first spotted the campfire off in the distance that led to the disastrous but fateful encounter with the trolls, and Dwalin was even described there with the phrase 'Dwalin, who was always their look-out man' – the exact words ascribed to his brother Balin in the First Typescript (Marq. 1/1/33:3) and henceforth. The passage here, therefore, marks Tolkien's decision to keep to the decision in Chapter VI to have Balin be the group's most observant dwarf.

13 Note that the detail of the hobbit's going last at the end of the line, which did not survive into the next stage (the typescript) nor the published book, reverses the sequence used with the trolls and with Medwed, where the hobbit went first each time.

14 This is the first mention in the original text of the thirst suffered by the adventurers, a motif developed with great effect in the Enchanted Stream interpolation and published book (see p. 351).

15 The ominous implications of this last phrase do not become apparent until the spiders attack several pages later; note that in the next chapter the Elvenking rebukes the dwarves with having 'roused the spiders with your riot and clamour' (see p. 380).

16 Unlike the many shifts in assigning an action to a specific dwarf (e.g. Text Note 12 above), the detail of Dori as the watchman who next spotted the lights persisted unchanged from the first draft through into the published book. The same applies to Kili as the watcher for the third (ultimately disastrous) encounter with the elf-lights.

17 All but the first two words of this sentence was later cancelled and replacement text written in the top margin: 'send Mr Baggins forward alone first, to talk to them and ask for food. They won't be frightened of him – ('what about me of them?' thought Bilbo) – and I hope they won't do anything nasty to him!' The slightly revised version of this that appears in the First Typescript (1/1/58) corresponds exactly to the published text (DAA.205).

18 This paragraph was heavily revised to fit the change from Gandalf to Bilbo having been the one to step forward on the second try:

> *Then Gandalf pushed Bilbo forward and he quietly* stepped into the ring. Out went all the lights again, and if it was bad collecting themselves before it was worse still this time. *Bilbo* simply couldn't be found. Every time they counted *themselves* it only made thirteen, and though they shouted and called '*Bilbo Baggins. Hobbit. You dratted hobbit. Hi hobbit confusticate you' & other such things* there was no answer.

Dori found him. He fell over what seemed a log, and found it was the *hobbit* lying down fast asleep.

19 The motif of dreaming about a wondrous feast enters the story here, long before the 'enchanted stream' interpolation developed the idea, but it is not Bilbo or Bombur but Gandalf himself who is the dreamer. This passage is another striking example of how a scene, image, or speech could remain practically unchanged while its application and significance altered greatly. The shift from Gandalf to Bilbo must have occurred almost at once, since Gandalf's statement that this time he will step forward himself in their third attempt to beseech charity immediately follows only a few paragraphs later.

20 Tolkien seems have initially forgotten about Ori (who along with Bofur had also been omitted in the draft of this passage in Plot Notes A; see Text Note 13 on p. 298); the name appears as an addition to the line. The sequence of names is changed slightly in the typescript: the first eight are the same, but there *Bombur* is followed with 'Bifur, Bofur, Dwalin, Balin, Thorin Oakenshield.'

21 This point, the bottom of manuscript page 106 (1/1/8:6), marks the second of the three times in the story Bilbo will be all alone in the dark. This dramatic moment seems to correspond to a brief pause in the writing, since the top of the next page on a new sheet (manuscript page 107; 1/1/8:7) shows a marked change in Tolkien's handwriting style, which for the next page or two becomes thin and spidery but also more elaborate, with many more flourishes.

Only a few paragraphs into this new section, the text begins to show signs of being very quickly written, with many small mistakes (e.g., 'seemed an*d* endless', 'the*y* way they grow', 'before *it* his casting around', &c.). It clearly represents the very first stage of composition, the initial expansion of the skeleton given in Plot Notes A.

22 Remarkably enough, the spider that attacks Bilbo is initially referred to using female pronouns (she/her), though this is quickly switched to the gender-neutral pronouns (it/its) used in the published book. This carryover from the Plot Notes draft of the scene (see p. 294) is significant because it makes the giant spider the only female character to actually appear in the book.

See also Text Note 31 below.

23 Missing from this initial version of the scene is Bilbo's naming his blade: the name *Sting* does not appear until the First Typescript version of the scene (typescript page 85; 1/1/58:10).

24 Added in the top margin and marked for insertion at this point: 'It was a bit of struggle' said one '– but worth it. What nasty thick skins they have to be sure, but I'll wager there is good juice inside'. This addition called for small changes in the following lines; 'said one' becomes 'said *another*'; in the next line 'another' becomes '*a third*'; in the next 'said a third' becomes 'said a *fourth*', and finally the line after that ('They're

dead now I warrant') was ascribed back to the first spider (*'said the first'*).

25 Quoits, dart-throwing, shooting at the wand, bowls, and ninepins are all traditional English games.

Quoits: A game very similar to horseshoes, in which small hoops or rings are tossed at a spike or stake. Its modern descendant, the ring-toss, is still a favorite at carnivals and fairs.

Dart-throwing: Still a popular pastime, traditionally played in pubs.

Shooting at the Wand: According to Anderson (DAA.210), an archery game wherein players shoot at a 'wand', or flat slat of wood. If Bilbo were a good shot with a bow, one might expect him to have been given one of Medwed's bows (see p. 250). Probably Tolkien never linked the two passages, and there is in any case a great difference between a bow used in a game and a hunting-bow (comparable, say, to the difference between badminton and professional tennis); Bilbo could probably not even pull a heavy bow such as Medwed provided.

Bowls: Better known today as lawn bowling, this is played with wooden balls on a grassy lawn. The winner is usually the player whose ball ends closest to a specific point.

Ninepins: Also known as skittles, this is the ancestor of modern bowling. Tolkien originally wrote *ninepines*, but this seems a simple error rather than a variant. Ninepins is mainly famous in literature through its appearance in Washington Irving's 'Rip Van Winkle' [1819] as the game played by the magical dwarves in that story.

26 The spider-poem had already appeared in Plot Notes A; Tolkien clearly had his notes before him when writing this passage and simply copied the poem into the text here with only minor changes (see pp. 295 & 299).

27 Attercop is simply the Old English word for spider (*attercoppe*), first attested circa 1000 AD; a modernized spelling would be adder-cob (poison-spider). The 'coppe/cobbe' element is sometimes thought to mean 'head' but was more probably simply 'spider', which is still its meaning in some Germanic dialects (Flemish *cobbelcoppe*, Westphalian *cobbe*, Dutch *spinne-cob*); the word survives in modern English *cob*web (spider-web).

Our modern word *spider*, while also derived from an Old English root (in this case, one meaning 'spinner'), did not appear in English until around 1340 and was not definitely established for another century: early versions of Wycliffe's Bible [circa 1440] use *attercoppis* while later versions use *spiþers* in its place. Cf. the OED, pages 138, 451, & 2960.

More recently, 'attercop' was revived within a technical context when the name was given to the earliest known spider fossil, *Attercopus fimbriungis*, which lived in the Devonian Period some three hundred and eighty million years ago.

28 Tom-noddy: Tom-fool. While 'Tom-noddy' is nineteenth-century, 'noddy' (fool, simpleton) itself goes back to Henry VIII's time. Like booby, noddy is both a word for a fool and a seabird.

29 Like the first spider-taunting poem, this one originates in Plot Notes A; see p. 299 for comments on its composition. The only change made here in this version is the capitalization lob > Lob, which is in contemporary black ink.

'Cob' = spider (preserved in modern English *cobweb*: 'spider-web'); see Text Note 27 above.

'Lob' is a neat piece of Tolkienian linguistic doubling, since the word means both spider (OE *lobbe, loppe*) and also a rustic or country bumpkin. Hence it is both accurate and insulting at the same time. Its use here is interesting because, as Tolkien may have been aware, 'lob' is also a variant for 'hob' or house-spirit, the probable root-word for *hobbit*; examples include the Taynton Lob and Lob-Lie-by-the-Fire – cf. Katharine Briggs, *Hobberty Dick* [1955] and *A Dictionary of Fairies* [1976], especially the latter's entry under 'Lobs and Hobs'.

Much later, Tolkien used 'lob' as part of the name for his most fully realized spider character, Shelob (= 'she-spider').†

† 'Do you think *Shelob* is a good name for a monstrous spider creature? It is of course only "she+lob" (= spider), but written as one, it seems to be quite noisome' (JRRT to CT, 21st May 1944; *Letters* p. 81).

30 At this point, near the bottom of manuscript page 111 (1/1/8:11), Tolkien drew a line or bracket in red pencil between this and the next word, accompanied by a blue pencil annotation in the lower left margin:

<here> begins 88

– that is, the next word corresponds to the top of page 88 in the First Typescript (1/1/58:13).

31 The male pronouns (he, him) for this spider appear only in the manuscript; by the time of the First Typescript they have already shifted to neutral gender (it, its), which remained thereafter.

32 The minor detail of Fili's having a long nose is the only indication in the book that Fili and Kili are not, as many readers imagine them, identical in appearance; it is one of the very few bits of physical description of any character. The parenthetical comment about long noses proving useful first appears in the typescript.

33 The sentence about Bilbo's having taken his ring off before helping the dwarves, added to the Ms., was moved to the end of the preceding paragraph in the typescript, where it has remained ever since.

34 Throughout the manuscript of *The Hobbit* the exact relationship between Bifur, Bofur, and Bombur remained in flux. Here we learn for the first time that they are kinsmen, and it is specifically stated that Bifur and Bofur are Bombur's cousins, which in turn suggests that Bifur and Bofur are themselves brothers, given the analogy of the two brother-pairs Fili/Kili and Balin/Dwalin. For more on rhyming brother names, see Text Note 13 following Chapter XVII. When their relationship is mentioned again, in Chapter XII, all three dwarves have become brothers ('"Bombur and Bofur!" cried Bifur their brother. "They are

down in the valley!" "They will be slain . . ." moaned the others' – see p. 508 and Text Note 20 following Chapter XII.

Several pages in the original First Typescript of this chapter were replaced at some point before the Second Typescript was made,† including the page describing this scene (typescript page 89). The reading where Bifur and Bofur are Bombur's cousins persisted here through both the original and replacement pages in the First Typescript (1/1/30:2 and 1/1/58:14), as well as the Second Typescript (1/1/39:17); not until black ink revisions to the page proofs was 'his cousins Bifur and Bofur' replaced by 'his *cousin* Bifur and *his brother* Bofur' (1/2/2 page 169), the reading of the published book (DAA.215). Similarly, the passage wherein Bifur describes Bofur and Bombur as 'My brothers!' appeared in the First Typescript, where it was altered in ink to 'My *cousins*' (typescript page 118; 1/1/62:4). This change was made before the Second Typescript was created, since the latter gives 'My cousins' as originally typed (1/1/43:5), the reading in the published book (DAA.274). Thus the final relationship between these three is that Bombur and Bofur are brothers, and Bifur is their cousin.

† These were the bottom half of original typescript page 85 (now 1/1/30:1), the top half of which was retained and completed by new text pasted on to create a new composite page (1/1/58:10), and the original typescript conclusion to the chapter, original typescript pages 89–92 (now 1/1/30:2–5), which were replaced by new pages 89–92 (1/1/58:14–17). The replacement text expands upon the original somewhat, giving a more vivid account of the battle against the spiders. In addition, the bottom fifth of typescript page 83 (1/1/58:8) was covered by a pasteover of new text directly over the old; the three paragraphs of replacement text describe Bilbo's stepping into the elf-circle and the dwarves' search for him after he falls under the sleep enchantment. See Text Note 18 above and pp. 353–4 below for more on the evolution of this passage.

35 At this point, a pencil line is drawn in the left margin alongside four lines of text (from 'It was then' to 'went in and out round'), and the words

make him <find> it by a tree

written in the margin; this of course refers to the ball of spider-thread.

The other two changes to this paragraph – changing 'old' to 'all' and inserting the negative ('had struck one of their biggest colonies' > 'had *not* struck one of their biggest colonies') – are also in pencil and thus postdate the writing, probably by a considerable time.

36 'The whole tale': A revised version of this passage later introduced a crux into the text and became a disconnect between *The Hobbit* and its sequel *The Lord of the Rings:* see p. 739.

37 At this point, and on the next three mentions of the chief dwarf's name, 'Gandalf' has been changed to 'Thorin' in pencil. This is clearly a much later emendation, only made on this single page (Ms. page 116; 1/1/8:16), probably when Tolkien was looking over the chapter in anticipation of preparing the typescript, since Thorin did not become

the chief dwarf's name until he emerges out of the barrel outside Lake Town (see p. 437 & Text Note 7 on p. 444).

38 This revelation is a good example of Tolkien's narrative legerdemain, and the extent to which he rewards the attentive reader by letting them be in on the joke. He has been careful at three points in the preceding pages to enumerate the twelve dwarves without calling attention to the fact that there should have been thirteen: 'a dozen bundles hanging up from a branch' (p. 310), the fact that after having rescued seven dwarves (Kili, Fili, Bifur, Bofur, Dori, Nori, and poor old Bombur) there were 'still five dwarves hanging up at the far end of the branch' when the spiders returned (7+5=12, not 13; p. 313), and the final mention of eleven dwarves scrambling down to join Bombur on the ground ('there they were twelve together'; ibid.).

39 'The great FairyLand of the west': this is Eldamar or Elvenhome, also called 'Fairyland' in 'Ælfwine of England' [circa 1920] (BLT II.316) and in *Roverandom* [circa 1927] (pp. 103 & 73–74). Fairyland (so spelled) also originally appeared in the First Typescript of this chapter (original typescript page 91; 1/1/30:4), but the replacement typescript page (1/1/58:16) and the Second Typescript (1/1/39:20) has 'Faerie', the reading of the published book.

40 Light-elves, Deep-Elves (Gnomes), and Sea-elves: the Three Kindreds of the Elves go back to the earliest stages of Tolkien's mythology; in the *Book of Lost Tales* period they were called the Teleri, the Noldoli (or Gnomes), and the Solosimpi (or Shoreland Pipers). By the time of 'The Sketch of the Mythology' [1926] and the 1930 *Quenta*, these had shifted to become the Quendi or Light-elves, the Noldoli or Deep-elves (also called Gnomes), and the Teleri or Sea-elves (also called Solosimpi, the Shoreland Pipers). The dwarves' 'capture by the Sea-elves' had been foreseen in the very first rough outline, given back on p. 229 in the middle of Chapter VII. The wood-elves, according to this schema, are *Ilkorindi* or Dark-elves, those who never came to Valinor or saw the Two Trees (HME IV.85).

For more on the Wood-elves, see the section titled 'The Vanishing People' following the next chapter (pp. 395ff).

41 These lines about the raising of the sun and moon, and the great woods that grew *after* the sun's rise, make it clear that we are definitely in a world of Tolkien's mythology here; Bilbo's world shares the creation myth that underlies all the early versions of the legendarium. See in particular 'The Tale of the Sun and Moon' (BLT I.174–206), 'The Sketch of the Mythology' (HME IV.20), and the 1930 *Quenta* (HME IV.97).

42 The reference to the Elvenking's treasure is interesting; although there are a number of pointed hints throughout about the Elf-king's love of treasure, there is little indication that he already has much hoarded, aside from this passage. However, the opening canto of 'The Lay of Leithian' devotes several lines to Thingol's hoard, both in its first and

closing stanzas (see lines 15–18 and 93–5; HME III.155, 156, 157), and it seems clear that Tolkien's older conception of the Woodland King strongly influenced his description here and throughout the wood-elf section of *The Hobbit*.

The motif of elves living in caves not only harkens back to the ancient folklore tradition of fairy-mounds but was a firmly established part of Tolkien's elf-lore: the great woodland realm of Doriath, the oldest elf-realm in Middle-earth and the closest analogue in the older legendarium to the wood-elf realm of Mirkwood, was ruled from the great underground hall known as 'the Thousand Caves' ('Sketch', HME IV.13), later named *Menegroth*. Similarly, Nargothrond ('fair halls beneath the earth' – 'Sketch', HME IV.30) was a cave-kingdom, while Gondolin was a hidden city in a caldera that could only be reached through a natural tunnel. The late account of Tuor's coming to Turgon's abandoned halls in Nevrast also stresses the degree to which that was a hidden land, accessible from Hithlum only by a secret tunnel (*Unfinished Tales*, pp. 20–23).

43 This passage refers to the Nauglafring, or 'Necklace of the Dwarves', made by the dwarves of Nogrod for Tinwelint, king of Artanor (the figure who in later stages of the mythology came to be called Thingol Greycloak, King of Doriath); see 'The Nauglafring' (BLT II.221–51) and the commentary under the header 'The King of Wood and Stone' following Chapter IX.

44 Elves & Spiders: for the origins of this enmity, see commentary, p. 328.

45 Arrows pointed with bone or stone: a reference to the neolithic arrowheads occasionally uncovered in plowing, digging, or construction. In the United States, where they were still made by native peoples as recently as the early nineteenth century, these are called 'Indian arrowheads'; in medieval England such finds were called 'elf-shot' and believed to be the physical evidence left behind by an elf-stroke. Briggs (*A Dictionary of Fairies*, pp. 118 & 385) notes that our modern word *stroke* (for what is more technically termed a cardiovascular accident) is a shortened form of 'elf-stroke', itself the folk-explanation of why a person might be suddenly laid low with no apparent cause.

In addition, note the use of present tense here by Tolkien's narrator: *even now* few woodelves use metal weaponry – yet another of his subtle hints that the elves are still among us, though few know of or can detect their presence.

In this chapter, Tolkien depicts Mirkwood in ways that conjure up not just one but two archetypes: The Dark Wood and The Enchanted Forest. The realistic description of a desperate journey through primal woodlands, struggling against starvation and thirst, exhaustion and despair, dominates the first half of the chapter and represents yet another *tour de force* as Tolkien uses sensory details to build up a claustrophobic impression of a nightmarish journey in darkness and near-darkness that never seems to end. Tolkien's other journeys into darkness are relatively brief in duration: Bilbo's journey under the Misty Mountains, the Fellowship's trek through Moria, the Grey Company's passage of the Paths of the Dead, and Frodo and Sam's disastrous trip through Shelob's Lair all take a few days at most, in some cases only hours. By contrast, Bilbo and the dwarves' trip through Mirkwood lasts for weeks if not months; in some outlines Tolkien projected that as much as an entire year might pass while they remained lost or captive within the forest. For more on Mirkwood, or Taur-na-Fuin as it was sometimes called, as it had appeared in Tolkien's earlier works in the Silmarillion tradition, see the commentary on The Pryftan Fragment, p. 20.

The second half of the chapter shifts the descriptions to highlight the eerie aspects of the endless woods, dim rather than pitch-dark but full of disturbing features: the alluring sounds and smells and sights that lure the travellers off the path into disaster, the uncanny appearance and disappearance of the feasters, the spell of sleep that falls first upon the hobbit and then the chief dwarf. For more on this enchanted forest theme, see 'The Vanishing People' following Chapter IX.

(i)
The Children of Ungoliant

Like the dwarves, elves, goblins, wolves, and eagles, spiders had a long history in Tolkien's mythology going back more than a decade before he started *The Hobbit*. They are yet another link back to the legendarium, another example of the foes and friends Bilbo encounters on his unexpected journey turning out, on examination, to be descendents of the servants and servitors of the first great Dark Lord or his foes. Even the Necromancer Bilbo's group take pains to avoid (and rightly so, since he destroyed the previous dwarven expedition led by Gandalf's father a century before) fits into the same category, being Thû himself, Morgoth's lieutenant, who would soon gain the additional name of *Sauron*.[1] Unlike the goblins and wolves, however, the spiders cannot rightly be called Children of *Morgoth*, because they descend not from the first great Dark Lord himself but from his sometime ally Ungoliant, the Spider of Night. Significantly, when the goblins and wargs march to war at the book's climax, the spiders stay put, playing no part in the Battle of Five Armies – like Ungoliant before them and Shelob after they are essentially an unaligned evil (as Bombadil in *The Lord of the Rings* is an unaligned good).[2]

At first glance a spider, however large, does not seem a very epic opponent for our hero, but this is deceptive. Tolkien's use of spiders as major villains and dire threats goes back to an earlier layer of the mythology, when a hound (Huan) could defeat elf-lords, a cat (Tevildo) ably serve as one of Melko's more capable lieutenants, and a Spider (Ungoliant) plunge the entire world into darkness. Certainly Lord Dunsany, a major influence on Tolkien at that early stage, pits his heroes against huge man-sized spiders in 'The Fortress Unvanquishable, Save For Sacnoth' ([1907]; collected in *The Sword of Welleran* [1908]) and also in 'The Distressing Tale of Thangobrind the Jeweller' ([1910]; collected in *The Book of Wonder* [1912]). The monstrous spider-demon destroys the hero in the latter, while in the former the great spider is one of the few foes that evades the hero and escapes, defeated yet alive. These examples may underlie the prominence Tolkien gives in his own works to monstrous spiders and their slayers. By slaying one of the Great Spiders of Mirkwood, Bilbo joins a very select company of Tolkienian heroes: Eärendel the Mariner, the original character in Tolkien's mythos (featured in the 1914 poem that was the very first piece of writing set in what later became 'Middle-earth'; see below), was a spider-slayer. So too was Beren, the character Tolkien most identified with (even to the extent of having the name carved on his tombstone). And of course the inestimable Samwise Gamgee, whom Tolkien in some moods considered 'the chief hero' of *The Lord of the Rings* (Letter to Waldman; *Letters* p. 161), was if not a spider-slayer then certainly the victor in an epic battle with one, dealing her a near-mortal blow. As with Tolkien's eagles (see p. 222), the Spiders represented a mythological element that originally occupied an important but specific part in the story which, over time, grew as they found their way into other parts of the tales. In this case, Ungoliant's killing of the Two Trees of Valinor was the primal element going back to the original *Lost Tales*: the scene in which she and Melko make their alliance, sneak into Valinor, destroy the trees of light, and escape altered in details and tone over decades of revision but remained the same in essence all through the long evolution of the story.[3]

It is to this ur-story that our manuscript refers when, early in the next chapter (p. 380), Balin angers the Elvenking by asking

> 'Are the spiders your tame beasts or your pets, if killing them makes you angry?'
>
> Asking such a question made him angry at any rate, for the wood-elves think the spiders vile and unclean.

This elven distaste for spiders goes all the way back to 'The Tale of Tinúviel' (BLT II.10–11), where we are told

> Tinúviel danced until the evening faded late, and there were many white moths abroad. Tinúviel being a fairy[4] minded them not as many of the children of Men do, although she loved not beetles, and spiders will none of the Eldar touch because of Ungweliantë [Ungoliant].[5]

Of the four earlier appearances of monstrous spiders in the legendarium before *The Hobbit*, three involve Ungoliant, who in initial conception is less a physical creature than an embodiment of what an earlier century would have called 'Chaos and Old Night' (Alexander Pope, *The Dunciad*): Primal Night itself made incarnate in monstrous form. The *Gnomish Lexicon* of 1917 glosses one of her many names, *Muru*, as 'a name of the Primeval Night. personified as *Gwerlum* [Gloom-weaver], or *Gungliont* ['the Spider of Night'] (*Parma Eldalamberon*, vol. XI, pp. 58 & 43; BLT I.index & 153). Gwerlum and (Un)Gungliont are themselves two earlier forms of her Gnomish (Sindarin) and Qenya (Quenya) names; Ungwë Lianti/Ungweliante ('Spider-spinner') and Wirilómë ('weaver-of-shadows') are other variants of the latter, while Ungoliant is the ultimate form of her name in Sindarin. Christopher Tolkien's index to *The Book of Lost Tales* part I identifies *Móru* as 'The "Primeval Night" personified in the great Spider' (BLT I.288), and the earliest text describing her and her lair bears out this conception:

> a region of the deepest gloom . . . a dark cavern in the hills, and webs of darkness lie about so that the black air might be felt heavy and choking about one's face and hands . . . here on a time were the Moon and Sun imprisoned afterward; for here dwelt the primeval spirit Móru whom even the Valar know not whence or when she came . . . she has always been; and she it is who loveth still to dwell in that black place taking the guise of an unlovely spider, spinning a clinging gossamer of gloom that catches in its mesh stars and moons and all bright things that sail the airs . . . [S]he sucked light greedily, and it fed her, but she brought forth only that darkness that is a denial of all light. (BLT I.151–2)

Ungoliant's greatest deed beyond doubt was her destruction of the Two Trees of Valinor, which plunged the world into darkness. But in the early stages of the mythology she remained a threat even after withdrawing back into her underground lair in Eruman far to the south ('Melko held the North and Ungweliant the South'; BLT I.182); we are even told that the sun and moon travel an equatorial path to avoid the peril posed by these two archfoes (ibid.). The Valar's successful attempt to bring light to the world once again through the creation of the Sun and Moon ('The Tale of the Sun and Moon', BLT I.174–206; see also *Silm*.99–101) was almost undone by the Great Spider, according to Tolkien's outlines and notes for the (unwritten) 'Tale of Eärendel'.

In this original version of Tolkien's cosmology, implicitly evoked by the line in *The Hobbit* manuscript

> The woodelves lingered in the world in the twilight *before the raising of the sun and moon*, and in the great woods that grew after sun rise
>
> — p. 315; italics mine

(that is, after the sun's first rising in the West), the Sun and Moon were ships bearing the last lights of the Golden and the Silver Tree. Guided by a guardian Maia (Urwendi and Ilinsor, respectively), each sailed above the earth and out the Gates of Night in the west, then doubled back and sailed 'behind' or under the earth each night to re-emerge again in the east for the next dawn – a conception borrowed from Egyptian mythology, where Ra sails the sun-barge through the *Duat* or Underworld each night, battling his way past Apep the Devourer, a great serpent who was for the Egyptians the embodiment of Chaos, to emerge triumphant at dawn each day (a mythic journey celebrated in the so-called 'Book of the Dead', a set of ritual texts known to the Egyptians as *The Book of Going Forth by Day*). Similarly, Tolkien projected a tale wherein Ungoliant ensnared the Sun in her webs while it sailed under the earth: with the result that the Sun was no longer enchanted, only the Moon:

> Urwendi imprisoned by Móru (upset out of the boat by Melko and only the Moon has been magic since). The Faring Forth and the Battle of Erumáni would release her and rekindle the Magic Sun.
>
> —'The History of Eriol or Ælfwine and the End of the Tales' (BLT II.286).

Unfortunately, this elusive plot-thread, which underlay several major prophecies in *The Book of Lost Tales*, never found full expression in a written story.[6]

Ungoliant's only other major appearance in the mythos was to have occurred in 'The Tale of Eärendel' – but, as Christopher Tolkien observed, 'the great tale was never written' (BLT II.252) and the story is known to us only through extensive outlines and synopses in several Silmarillion texts. Thus, an early outline simply lists an encounter with 'Ungweliantë' as one of the major incidents on Eärendel's great voyage into the Firmament but gives no details. The 1926 'Sketch of the Mythology' is succinct, but specific, following Eärendel's decision to sail seeking Valinor:

> Here follow the marvellous adventures of Wingelot [Eärendel's ship] in the seas and isles, and of how Eärendel slew Ungoliant in the South.
>
> —HME IV.38.

The 1930 *Quenta* adds a little to this in its equally brief account:

> In the Lay of Eärendel is many a thing sung of his adventures in the deep and in lands untrodden, and in many seas and many isles. Ungoliant in the South he slew, and her darkness was destroyed, and light came to many regions which had yet long been hid.
>
> —HME IV.152.

But the Lay itself remained unwritten; the closest Tolkien ever came to telling Eärendel's story lay in two sets of poems, the first a group of four poems dating from the inception of the mythology [1914–15] telling of Eärendel's voyages to furthest East and West and his glimpses of the Gates of Night and of Valinor: 'Éalá Éarendel Engla Beorhtast', 'The Bidding of the Minstrel', 'The Shores of Faëry', and 'The Happy Mariners' (all printed in BLT II.267–76). The second group began as a single poem, 'Errantry' ([circa 1931–2]; published in *Oxford Magazine* in 1933 and later collected as poem #3 in *The Adventures of Tom Bombadil* [1962]). This was slowly transformed through a dozen intermediate stages into the poem Bilbo sings in the House of Elrond, 'Eärendil was a mariner' (*LotR*.250–53). In his analysis of the chapter for the *History of Middle-earth* series (HME VII.84–105), Christopher Tolkien shows how his father recast the poem stage by stage. Most significantly for our purpose, in one of the intermediate versions he prints is the following account of the battle with Ungoliant, one of Eärendel's greatest but most poorly documented deeds:

. . . unto Evernight [Eruman] he came,
and like a flaming star he fell:
his javelins of diamond
as fire into the darkness fell.
Ungoliant abiding there
in Spider-lair her thread entwined;
for endless years a gloom she spun
the Sun and Moon in web to wind.
She caught him in her stranglehold
entangled all in ebon thread,
and seven times with sting she smote
his ringéd coat with venom dread.[7]
His sword was like a flashing light
as flashing bright he smote with it;
he shore away her poisoned neb,
her noisome webs he broke with it.
Then shining as a risen star
from prison bars he sped away,
and borne upon a blowing wind
on flowing wings he fled away.

—lines 73–88 (HME VII.93).

This entire scene was deleted from the final typescripts of the poem, including the one that appeared in *The Lord of the Rings*.

The final appearance of the Great Spiders in the legendarium[8] before Bilbo's encounter with them in the wilds of Mirkwood is also the one closest to *The Hobbit* in tone and detail: Beren's battles with giant spiders, descendents of Ungoliant. This scene was absent from most early versions of the Beren and Lúthien story,[9] but it did feature prominently in the narrative poem 'The Lay of Leithian'. In Canto III, lines 569–574 and 583–592, Tolkien describes Beren's desperate journey from Taur-na-Fuin (the Forest of Night) to Doriath in these terms:

there mighty spiders wove their webs,
old creatures foul with birdlike nebs
that span their traps in dizzy air,
and filled it with clinging black despair,
and there they lived, and the sucked bones
lay white beneath on the dank stones—

. . . ever new
horizons stretched before his view,
as each blue ridge with bleeding feet
was climbed, and down he went to meet
battle with creatures old and strong
and monsters in the dark, and long,
long watches in the haunted night
while evil shapes with baleful light
in clustered eyes did crawl and snuff
beneath his tree

—(HME III.175–6).[10]

In the 1937 *Quenta Silmarillion*, which glosses Taur-na-Fuin as 'Mirkwood' (HME V.282), this is replaced by a similarly vivid passage written about the time *The Hobbit* was published:

> Terrible was his southward journey . . . There spiders of the fell race of Ungoliant abode, spinning their unseen webs in which all living things were snared; and monsters wandered there that were born in the long dark before the Sun, hunting silently with many eyes. No food for Elves or Men was there in that haunted land, but death only. That journey is not accounted least among the great deeds of Beren, but he spoke of it to no one after, lest the horror return into his mind . . . (*Silm.*164).[11]

Spiders or Spider-like?

As the preceding excerpts and quotes make clear, some of the details Tolkien gives when describing his spider-creatures do not correspond to real-world spiders. Leaving aside their size for the moment,[12] the Mirkwood spiders seem to have compound eyes like an insect (a feature they share with Shelob – cf. *LotR*.747 – and the things that beset Beren), whereas true arachnids have eight small separate eyes. Then too whereas spiders have tiny specialized legs that act as mandibles or mouthparts Tolkien's spiders are described as having a neb (a now-obsolete word meaning bill or beak; 'Lay of Leithian', Eärendil poem) or beak (*LotR*.756). We are not told specifically how the Mirkwood spiders poison their prey, but both Ungoliant (Eärendil poem) and Shelob (*LotR*.755) are described as having stings, another insect rather than spider feature (real spiders poison with their bite instead). Finally, spiders grow by shedding their carapaces, much as crustaceans do, yet we are told that Shelob has 'age-old hide . . . ever thickened from within with layer on layer of evil growth' (*LotR*.755). Not all of these features can be shown to be shared by all of Tolkien's monstrous spiders, but he takes pains to connect them: Shelob is explicitly linked to the Mirkwood spiders as their progenitor, and to Ungoliant as her progeny ('last child of Ungoliant to trouble the unhappy world' – *LotR*.750). Ungoliant, Shelob, and the Mirkwood Spiders all share the ability to spin black webs (hence Ungoliant's epithet 'Gloom-weaver'; note her 'ebon thread' on p. 330 and see also *LotR*.750 and p. 303 above), which is not so far as I am aware true of any real-world spider.[13]

It can (and has) been argued that when Tolkien describes Shelob as a 'monstrous spider creature' (*Letters* p. 81) or states that Ungoliant '[took] the *guise* of . . . [a] spider' (BLT I.152; emphasis mine) this implies his awareness of the deviation; they are meant to be spider-like rather than actual spiders. This is certainly possible, but the evidence (such as it is) is against it: in a letter to W. H. Auden, Tolkien wrote:

> . . . I knew that the way [into Mordor] was guarded by a Spider. And if that has anything to do with my being stung by a tarantula when a small child, people are welcome to the notion . . . I can only say that I remember nothing about it, should not know it if I had not been told; and I do not dislike spiders particularly, and have no urge to kill them. I usually rescue those whom I find in the bath!
>
> —JRRT to WHA, 7th June 1955; *Letters* p. 217.

This little bit of autobiography is important because tarantulas do not sting: they bite[14] – a small point, but nevertheless suggestive. Tolkien cannot be faulted for forgetting such a detail, since he was only a toddler when the incident occurred, but its significance is that his account shows that even years after writing *The Hobbit* he was under the impression that spiders have stings. This strongly suggests that Tolkien's other departures from spider physiology were simple mistakes, however uncharacteristic, rather than deliberate changes for effect – unlike, say, the Nazgûl's mounts, where he expressly stated that he was not attempting historical accuracy in his depiction but merely drawing on the 'semi-scientific mythology of the "Prehistoric"' as inspiration (JRRT to Rhona Beare, 14th October 1958; *Letters* p. 282).[15]

In point of fact, Tolkien could not have been 'stung by a tarantula' as a child because these spiders are not native to the Orange Free State or indeed southern Africa at all. Instead, the name is locally applied to *solifugae*, an aggressive arachnid also known as 'wind scorpions', 'sun-spiders', or 'camel spiders' but in fact neither a spider nor a scorpion but a cousin of both.[16] The true tarantula (L. *tarantula*) of southern Europe is a type of wolf spider, a free-ranging hunter very like the Mirkwood spider pictured in Tolkien's halftone of Mirkwood (Plate VII [top]; cf. also Plate VII [detail]). The name's most common usage today is through its application in the New World to various large hairy spiders of North, South, and Central America (*Theraphosidae*), some of which are so large that they can prey upon frogs, birds, and very small mammals (the so-called 'bird-eating spiders' and 'monkey spider').

In the end, it is perhaps unfair to hold Tolkien to a higher standard than God – or at least the authors of the Old Testament, which at one point describes grasshoppers as four-legged (*Leviticus* 11:20–23). After all, once the reader has accepted the idea of talking giant spiders (who speak in language that Bilbo can understand, unlike the wargs or even elves), quibbling over details seems, well, quibbling.

The Mirkwood Halftone

Finally, there is Tolkien's illustration of the forest of Mirkwood which appeared in the first two printings of the English edition of *The Hobbit* (see Plate VII [top]). The picture itself has a rather complicated history, first discussed in Christopher Tolkien's notes in *Pictures by J. R. R. Tolkien* (1979) [picture #37] and again by Hammond and Scull in *Artist & Illustrator* (1995), pages 96–8 and 54–5, 58. In essence, Tolkien took a painting of Taur-na-Fuin he had made in 1928 to illustrate a scene from the story of Túrin Turambar and redrew it in black, white, and delicate shades of grey to serve as an illustration of Mirkwood in *The Hobbit*.[17] While many of the trees in both pictures correspond exactly, point-by-point, he deleted the two elves from the original painting and instead inserted a big black spider in the foreground. While it's impossible to tell exactly how large the spider is in this picture, if the same scale holds here as in the original painting (as seems to be the case), then comparison between the two shows that it is about half as large as an elf. While this may not seem all that big, especially since Tolkien's elves were originally somewhat smaller than humans – after all, Bilbo is able to down one of these spiders with a single thrown stone – it still means they are a match for the halfling and dwarves, who are themselves considerably shorter than any full-grown man (Shelob and Ungoliant are, of course, much much larger).

It is not possible to make out many details of the spider as it appears in this picture, even with enlargement (see Plate VII [detail]), but it is interesting to note that it looks much more like a real spider than Tolkien's description discussed in detail above would seem to indicate. There is no sign of compound eyes, for example, or any sort of neb or beak. It even roughly resembles a wolf spider, who like the Mirkwood spiders are highly mobile and aggressive in chasing down prey rather than remaining in webs. A very similar spider appears in a drawing Tolkien made ten years earlier, in 1927, to accompany *Roverandom* (see the illustration opposite page 27 in Scull & Hammond's 1998 edition of this early work). Here we once again see a spider walking by, this time in pursuit of a lunar insect (probably a moonbeam or dragon-moth), its body about the same size as Rover, who we are told several times is a *small* dog. By contrast, both the lower left corner of the final version of Thrain's Map (DAA.97) and the upper half of the final Wilderland Map (DAA.[399]) show spiders which are much more stylized in appearance, almost insectlike (though still with the correct number of legs).

(ii)
Butterflies

If Tolkien's spiders are his own creation, not quite like anything else in fantasy literature before or since, the brief but memorable scene in which Bilbo discovers the 'black emperor' butterflies is by contrast a piece of strict fidelity to observed phenomena:

> When at last poor little Bilbo . . . poked his head out of the leaves he was nearly blinded . . . The sun was shining brightly . . . he saw all round him a sea of dark green ruffled here and there by the breeze. And there were hundreds [of] butterflies. I expect they were a kind of 'purple emperor', but they were dark dark velvety black without any markings at all. (p. 305)

Not only are purple emperors (*Apatura iris*) quite real, but their preferred habitat is the upper canopy of mature oak forests. Tolkien even gets the time of year right when they can be seen in the greatest numbers (late summer), and may have known about the occasional rare dark (melanic) specimens, an aberration known as *Apature iris ab. iole*.[18]

Among Britain's largest butterflies, with a wingspan of more than three inches (up to 84 mm), purple emperors are now almost extinct in England, limited mainly to the south-central portion of the isle (Wiltshire, Hampshire, and West Sussex). But at the time Tolkien was writing *The Hobbit* their range extended up into the Oxford area, and there are some indications that thirty or forty years earlier they could still be found in the Birmingham area when Tolkien was growing up there. It is entirely possible, therefore, that what Bilbo sees evokes such a vivid picture for the reader because Tolkien is drawing upon a real memory here, just as he used his memories of Switzerland in his descriptions of Rivendell and the Misty Mountains.

Where Tolkien departs from reality is not in his depiction of the butterflies but their predators, the tree-spiders ('small ordinary ones'). These are almost certainly huntsman spiders of some sort (that is, free-range hunters who chase down their prey), but they seem purely fictional: no English spider is large enough to bring down butterflies of this size.[19]

(iii)
The Theseus Theme

One of the most remarkable features of the manuscript of *The Hobbit*, as will be readily apparent from this edition, is the degree to which the story remained essentially the same from the very first time it was set down in words through into the published book. There was great variation of phrasing, and many details changed – and details matter greatly to an author whose fictional world is as fully realized as Tolkien's – but the essentials did not change. The Plot Notes and outlines show that at times he envisioned the story very differently from what he came to write, but once written it mostly stayed fixed.

This is not the case with the Mirkwood chapter, the only one in the book to undergo substantial re-writing before the book was published. In specific, Tolkien dropped what we may call the Theseus theme, wherein Bilbo uses a ball of spider-thread to find his way back to the path and, later, to help rescue his friends as well. At the same time, he inserted the story of the enchanted stream (which Medwed had warned them against before their entry into Mirkwood), Bombur's being cast into a sleep from which they cannot awaken him, and the dwarves' loss of their last arrows (thus providing an explanation for why they do not use them in their battles against the spiders or when ambushed by the elves). For more on the Enchanted Stream interpolation, see the section beginning on p. 347.

The Theseus theme derives from a very ancient folktale or myth, the story of Theseus and the minotaur.[20] In brief, like Bilbo Theseus set out with thirteen companions (in this case, as one of seven youths and seven maidens) from Athens, where his father was king, to travel to Crete as human sacrifices to the Minotaur, a bull-headed monster who preyed upon all who entered his Labyrinth. Ariadne, daughter of Crete's King Minos, gave Theseus a ball of thread (and, in some versions of the story, a knife), with which he was able to find his way to the heart of the maze, kill the monster, and then find his way back out again by following the thread.[21]

Tolkien was certainly familiar with this myth, one of the most famous in all Greek literature: it is often forgotten that, as previously stated, Tolkien began his career as a Classical scholar, and did not switch to Old English until near the end of his second year at Oxford (Carpenter, pages 54–5 & 62–3). He was so proficient in Latin and Greek as a schoolboy that he not only took active part in his school's Debating Society, where it was the custom to hold debates entirely in Latin, but once appeared as the 'Greek Ambassador', speaking entirely in (Classical) Greek (Carpenter, page 48). His very first published piece of creative writing, 'The Battle of the Eastern Field' [1911], was a parody of one of Macaulay's *Lays of Ancient Rome* [1842], wherein Lord Macaulay had attempted the very Tolkienesque enterprise of trying to re-create the lost ballads he believed lay behind the great legends of Roman history, the 'lost tales' behind once-familiar but now almost forgotten events – in short, an 'asterisk-text' of the kind that fascinated Tolkien.[22] Nor did he abandon interest in his former subject once he found his vocation in Gothic, Old English, Middle English, and Old Norse; as late as 1936, roughly half a decade after writing this chapter of *The Hobbit*, he compared Virgil's *Aeneid* to *Beowulf* as examples of 'greater and lesser things', respectively, clearly identifying the greatest work of Old English poetry as the lesser of the two ('Beowulf: The Monsters and the Critics', page 22).

Tolkien's use of the Theseus story is typically subtle: he never mentions any names from the classical tale, and knowledge of the myth is not necessary to follow his own tale. Rather than a gift from the princess Ariadne, his thread is a ball of spider-thread unintentionally left for him by the arachnid he killed, 'horrible string' wildly spun out in her battle with him, that enables Bilbo to find his way through the trackless forest – and it may be significant that this Spider is the only character in the book explicitly identified as female (see Text Note 11 for Plot Notes A and Text Note 22 following Chapter VIII),[23] or that Bladorthin, echoing Medwed's earlier warning (p. 242), speaks of Mirkwood in terms that make it sound very like a maze or labyrinth:

> 'Don't stray off the track – if you do it is a thousand to one you'll never find the path again, or ever get out of Mirkwood; and then I don't suppose I (or anyone else) will hear of you again!' (p. 244).

Aided by this thread, Bilbo *is* able to find the path again, whereupon he indulges in the very hobbitlike act of making a little feast on the few remaining overlooked crumbs among their abandoned food-bags. As with his earlier experience when separated from the dwarves under the Misty Mountains (p. 198), he decides he is duty-bound to try to find and rescue his lost comrades. That he is mounting a rescue expedition is a point made more strongly in the draft than in the book where, still lost himself, he decides to look for his missing companions in the direction from which he thinks he heard cries for help the night before; here he has already reached the safety of the path and decides to go back into the treacherous woods after them.

The scene where he names his little sword *Sting* is absent, being introduced for the first time in the typescript, although he is still changed by the experience of 'winning his battle all by himself alone in the dark' (words that could apply equally well to his earlier battle of wits with Gollum or his later struggle with himself in the tunnel leading to Smaug's lair). Bilbo is also comforted in his solitude by the thought of his string, which has already proven its usefulness. Equipped with sword in one hand, ball of string in the other, and his magic ring upon his finger he sets out to find the dwarves, first following the spider-thread back to the spot where he killed the spider and then exploring onwards until he finds 'a place of dense black shadow like a patch of night'. This was expanded in the typescript first to 'a place of dense black shadow, black even for that forest, like a patch of night that had [not >] never gone away' (Marq. 1/1/30:1), then that section of the page was cut away and new text pasted in its place: '. . . like a patch of midnight that had never been cleared away' (Marq. 1/1/58:10), the same reading as in the published book (DAA.209). This reference to primordial night is probably a deliberate evocation of Ungoliant, the Spider of Night; cf. p. 328.

Having found his friends, he proceeds to rescue them as in the published book, with the exception that he forgets to tie off the string first and is thus forced to retrace the wild zig-zag course he took while dodging about mocking the spiders before he can once again find the main thread leading back to the forest-path. In this original conception, Bilbo's revealing the secret of his ring to his fellow travellers was specifically tied up with the need for him to rewind the string beneath the eyes of the angry spiders, whereas in the published account it is so he can use it in his decoy mission to lure spiders away and improve their odds of escaping. The thread's importance is stressed by the fact that Bilbo is 'ready to collapse' at the thought of having lost it; with its assistance, he succeeds in bringing his rescued friends back to the path.[24]

That Bilbo and his friends regain the path has another significance. In the published book, when captured by the elves they are hopelessly lost in the woods, making 'one last despairing effort' to find the path before they die of thirst and hunger. The dwarves are not even sure of where they are or which way they are going, just 'stagger[ing] on in the direction which eight out of the thirteen of them guessed to be the one in which the path lay' (DAA.222). But in the draft, Bilbo and twelve of the dwarves are back on the path and on their way out of the forest when 'waylaid' by the wood-elves. They might indeed have '[fallen] down and died' of starvation before reaching their goal, particularly given the dangers of the Marsh ahead, but the fact remains that they were ambushed while pursuing their quest, not while off on a disastrous tangent; this somewhat undercuts the element of rescue-by-capture in the final version.[25]

Finally, we should note that this original version of events bears a striking similarity to another dwarven quest as Tolkien set it down some twenty-odd years later: the attempt of Thrain (as he was by then called) to regain his father's hoard. The opening chapter of *The Hobbit* included a brief account of how after the death of the former King under the Mountain in the mines of Moria, his son, Gandalf's father, 'went away on the third of March a hundred years ago last Tuesday, and has never been seen (by you) since'. As Bladorthin tells Gandalf,

> Your father went away to try his own luck with [the map] after his father was killed [in the mines of Moria]; and lots of adventures he had, but he never got near the Mountain.

– in fact, winding up a prisoner of the Necromancer (p. 73). Many years later, when drafting the section of Appendix A about Durin's Folk, Tolkien returned to Thrain's story to flesh out this episode with a few more details about the fate of the last bearer of one of the seven Rings of Power given to the dwarves:

> Partly by the . . . power of the Ring . . . Thráin after some years became restless and discontented. He could not put the thought of gold and gems out of his mind. Therefore at last when he could bear it no longer his heart turned again to Erebor and he resolved to return. He said little to Thorin of what was in his heart. But with Balin and Dwalin and a few others he arose and said farewell and departed ([Third Age year] 2841) [from their homes in the Blue Mountains].
>
> Little indeed is known of what happened to him afterwards. It would seem (from afterknowledge) that no sooner was he abroad with few companions (and certainly after he came at length back into Rhovanion) he was hunted by the emissaries of Sauron. Wolves pursued him, orcs waylaid him, evil birds shadowed his path, and the more he tried to go north the more he was driven back. One dark night, south of Gladden and the eaves of Mirkwood, he vanished out of their camp, and after long search in vain his companions gave up hope (and returned to Thorin). Only long after was it known that he had been taken alive and brought to the pits of Dol Guldur (2845). There he was tormented and the Ring taken from him; and there at last (2850) he died.
>
> —HME XII.280–81.

The parallel passage in the final book differs only by slightly improved clarity and phrasing:

> . . . the more he strove to go north the more misfortunes opposed him. There came a dark night when he and his companions were

> wandering in the land beyond Anduin, and they were driven by a black rain to take shelter under the eaves of Mirkwood. In the morning he was gone from the camp, and his companions called him in vain. They searched for him many days, until at last giving up hope they departed and came at length back to Thorin . . .
>
> —*LotR*. 1114.

Had Bilbo and the twelve remaining dwarves somehow made it through Mirkwood (and although in desperate straits we know they are very near the eastern border), they could hardly have continued their original quest any more than Thrain's companion did, though no outline continues the story in that direction to give a hint of what they might have done next: the capture by wood-elves had been foreseen as far back as the sketchy list of plot-points given back in Chapter VII (the First Outline, p. 229), although the means whereby the dwarves would escape remained undetermined for a long time (contrast the evolving ideas in Plot Notes A on p. 296 with Plot Notes B on p. 362). It is not unreasonable, however, to think the much later account of Thrain's loss an extrapolation by Tolkien, an author fond of reusing favorite motifs, from a plot-thread not followed up on in *The Hobbit*. Both dwarven expeditions, after encounters with wolves and orcs, lost their leaders in Mirkwood (and not far from the edges of the woods in both cases), neither group knew where their leader had gone or who had taken him, each captive was imprisoned in a dungeon, and father and son were even carrying the same map at the time they were captured.[26]

The one incongruity between this later account of Thrain's loss in Appendix A and that given earlier in the opening chapter of *The Hobbit* is the fact that Thorin should have known far more about his father's fate than seems to be the case, since two of Thrain's companions from that earlier expedition, Balin and Dwalin, are among his own companions on this quest. Although a relatively minor point, this is still notable as one of the very few points where the two books fail to completely sync up, like Bilbo's apology to Gloin at the Council of Elrond (see *LotR*.266 and also Text Note 36 following Chapter VIII).

(iv)
Bilbo the Warrior

Finally, we should also note a major threshold in Bilbo's character development that occurs in this chapter. Although Bilbo acquires his knife quite early in the story (in the troll's lair, near the end of what eventually came to be Chapter II), he does not use it in fight with the goblins (Chapter IV), or against the wolves (Chapter VI). He pulls it out but does nothing more than hold it ready during his encounter with Gollum (Chapter V).[27] Here in Chapter VIII he uses it to kill an enemy in self-defense, the spider having attacked first (an achievement which 'made quite a difference to Mr Baggins. He felt a different person . . .' – p. 309). That he is indeed 'much bolder and fiercer' is shortly borne out in the spider battle, where Bilbo attacks first, initiating combat to save his friends (specifically, Bombur) and kills great numbers of the giant spiders. This aspect of the hobbit's character will see its fullest development in Plot Notes B; see p. 361ff.

NOTES

1 This would occur about five years later, in *The Lost Road* and 'The Fall of Númenor' [both circa 1936].

2 For another example, compare Gandalf the Grey's statement that

> There are older and fouler things than Orcs in the deep places of the world. (*LotR*.327)

and also Gandalf the White's eyewitness account regarding the Things that lurk below the Mines of Moria:

> Far, far below the deepest delvings of the Dwarves, the world is gnawed by nameless things. Even Sauron knows them not. They are older than he. (*LotR*.523)

3 Compare 'The Theft of Melko and the Darkening of Valinor' [circa 1919?], BLT I, especially pages 151–4; the narrative poem fragment 'The Flight of the Noldoli from Valinor' [mid-1920s], HME III.132; the 'Sketch of the Mythology' [1926], HME IV.16–17; the 1930 *Quenta*, HME IV.91–3; the '(Earliest) Annals of Valinor' [early 1930s], HME IV.265–6; the '(Later) Annals of Valinor' [mid/late-1930s], HME V.114; the *Quenta Silmarillion* [1937], HME V.230–33; 'The Annals of Aman' [?1951], HME X.97–101 & 108–9; and the *Later Quenta Silmarillion* [late 1950s], HME X.190, 284–9, & 295–7.

For the 'definitive' version, see Chapter 8: 'Of the Darkening of Valinor' and the beginning of Chapter 9: 'Of the Flight of the Noldor', pages 73–7 and 80–81 of the published *Silmarillion* [1977].

4 fairy: that is, elf. See the passage in The Bladorthin Typescript about how 'one of the Tooks took a fairy wife' and my commentary, p. 59.

5 Perhaps significantly, spiders are absent from 'Goblin Feet', despite the presence there of bats ('flittermice'), beetles, glow-worms, and 'golden honey-flies' (which I take to be bees rather than butterflies), not to mention leprechauns, gnomes, fairies, goblins, and coney-rabbits. Cf. *Oxford Poetry 1915* pp. 64–5.

6 Elsewhere another prophecy is given stating that Melko will destroy the Door of Night while the Sunship is Outside, Urwendi will be lost

beyond recall, and Fionwë, the son of Manwë and Varda (the figure who later evolved into Ëonwë, Manwe's herald) destroys Melko to avenge the Sunmaiden. ('The Hiding of Valinor'; BLT I.219 & 222.)

7 The four lines I have indented here were cancelled in the original (HME VII.108 Note 18); I include them because they help flesh out this, the only blow-by-blow account we have of an epic battle in which one of Tolkien's most elusive characters slays one of his most powerful villains.

8 For an additional appearance *outside* the mythos, see Tolkien's children's story *Roverandom* [written circa 1927, published 1998]. Among Rover's adventures are a lengthy stay with the Man-in-the-Moon, during which he discovers that the light side of the moon is populated with fifty-seven varieties of spiders (along with other remarkable fauna), who are more or less under the Man-in-the-Moon's control, some of them 'great grey spiders' that spin webs from mountain to mountain and are easily large enough to catch and eat a dog. The Dark Side of the Moon, for its part, is home to a multitude of poisonous black spiders that even the pale spiders of the other side are afraid of, very like the Mirkwood Spiders (who are also large, poisonous, and sinister).

9 There is no mention of Beren's struggles with the spiders before his appearance in Doriath in 'The Tale of Tinúviel' (BLT II.11), for example, nor in the 'Sketch of the Mythology' (HME IV.24) or the 1930 *Quenta* (HME IV.109).

10 It is perhaps noteworthy that this entire passage was praised by CSL in his commentary on 'The Lay of Leithian' as 'truly worthy of the *Geste*' (HME III.322).

11 The 1937 *Quenta Silmarillion* text(s) for this chapter were used by Christopher Tolkien as the basis for the corresponding chapter in *The Silmarillion* [1977], so he did not reprint the material in the relevant *History of Middle-earth* volume; hence this quotation comes from the 1977 book.

12 For a technical explanation of why spiders cannot grow significantly larger than the largest known specimen, see 'Giant Spiders and "Mammoth" Oliphaunts' in Henry Gee's *The Science of Middle-earth* [2004] especially page 177; it's basically a matter of biomechanics (or hydraulics). The largest real world spider is a South American tarantula, whose body is only a few (3½) inches across, although its legs fan out to add several more inches to that (a maximum of about 11 inches). While this is certainly big for a spider, it's still tiny, smaller than all but the smallest birds and mammals, and would pose little threat to Tolkien's dwarves or even a hobbit. The largest spider known is generally thought to have been the fossil *Megarachne* ('large spider') of the Carboniferous Period, some 345 million years ago, but recently the theory has been advanced that this may actually not be a spider at all but a sea scorpion; I am indebted to Dr. Gee for the latter information (e-mail, Rateliff to Gee and Gee to Rateliff, 17th November 2004).

13 It might be thought that by making his spiders congregate and cooperate together Tolkien is departing from the reality, since most spiders are solitary hunters, but in point of fact communal spiders, while an exception to the norm, do exist. He is also correct in having his spiders subdue and hang up their prey: since spiders cannot eat solid food, they tend to let prey decompose a bit then drink its juices. Some of the larger spiders can indeed make a hissing noise (stridulation); cf. the 'sort of low creaking hissing sound' Tolkien ascribed to his creations. And although he never mentions it in his text he gets the most important fact of all right in all of his illustrations with spiders in them: eight legs (rather than an insect's six). This level of accurate detail is not surprising, given Tolkien's lifelong love of nature: someone who met him shortly before his death told me the conversation turned at one point to wasps, about which he proceeded to tell her an amazing amount of detailed information.

For an example of another author's inadvertent misdescription of spiders, see Nathaniel Hawthorne's *Dr. Grimshawe's Secret* [written circa 1858ff], which at one point describes the Doctor's pet 'great giant spider', with its 'six sprawling legs' – *Dr. Grimshawe's Secret*, ed. Edward H. Davidson [1954], page 52. Hawthorne also describes the spider as 'an insect', but in this he is correct in the usage of the time, the term *arachnid* not being coined by Huxley until 1869, five years after Hawthorne's death.

14 Note that Humphrey Carpenter, in retelling this episode in *Tolkien: A Biography* [1976], was careful to change 'stung' to 'bit': 'when Ronald was beginning to walk, he stumbled on a tarantula. It bit him, and he ran in terror across the garden until the nurse snatched him up and sucked out the poison. When he grew up he could remember a hot day and running in fear through long, dead grass, but the memory of the tarantula itself faded, and he said that the incident left him with no especial dislike of spiders. Nevertheless, in his stories he wrote more than once of monstrous spiders with venomous bites' (Carpenter, pages 13–14).

15 It can be argued that the Witch-King's mount is an 'asterisk creature', a modern reconstruction from bits and pieces of available evidence, very much corresponding to the 'asterisk words' that Tolkien drew such inspiration from in his philology, or the manuscript cruxes and lacunae that seem to have been the part of medieval stories that especially sparked his imagination.

16 I have since learned that the baboon spiders of South Africa (subfamily *Harpactirince*) are sometimes called 'tarantulas', and they do indeed closely resemble the tarantulas of South America in appearance and habits, being fellow members of the family *Theraphosidae*. I have been unable to confirm whether their range includes the area around Bloemfontein, or would have at the time Tolkien was living there (1892–1895).

17 Then, to complicate matters, Tolkien's halftone was redrawn by some anonymous American artist and this careful line drawing replaced his

original in the first printing of the American edition (contrast Tolkien's original on DAA.192 with the redrawn version on DAA.193). Finally, late in life Tolkien wrote a new title, 'Fangorn Forest', on his 1928 painting of Taur-na-Fuin so that it could appear in the 1974 Tolkien calendar as an illustration of Merry and Pippin in Fangorn. He did not, however, change the picture itself.

18 I am indebted for information about the purple emperor's dark variant to Andrew Middleton (e-mail, Rateliff to Middleton, 18th November 2004; Middleton to Rateliff, 19th November 2004), who along with Elizabeth Goodyear heads up a purple emperor conservation project: see the website www.btinternet.com/~michael.goodyear/BCHM/species_files/purple_emp.htm.

For a discussion of black (melanic) animals in Tolkien's writings, see the essay 'Melanism and Middle-earth' by Henry Gee, posted online at http://greenbooks.theonering.net/guest/files/081104_01.html.

19 Once again I am grateful to Andrew Middleton for this information. Mr. Middleton writes: '[A] spider of ordinary size or its web would probably not be able to take [a butterfly the size and strength of a Purple Emperor] . . . It would be hard to imagine how anything but a very special spider could secure an emperor around the tops of the oaks' (e-mail, Middleton to Rateliff, 19th November 2004).

20 Traditionally, Theseus is considered to have lived a generation or two before the Trojan War [circa 1200 BC]. Like Hercules and Jason, he was the hero of many tales, of which his adventure with the minotaur is only the most famous. No epic or coherent whole dealing with his exploits survives from Grecian times, but his story can be reconstructed from references in other tales, scenes on pottery and wall-friezes, and the like. Our main sources for the Theseus story are twofold. First, the Roman poet Ovid in his *Metamorphoses* [circa 8 AD] strings together vignettes drawn from myths and legends that were already old in his time, several of which feature Theseus. Second, the Roman biographer Plutarch (d. 120) wrote a biography of Theseus as one of his *Parallel Lives*, partnering him with Romulus (the legendary founder of Rome); this is much the longest surviving account but unfortunately also the least mythical, since Plutarch attempts to explain away or rationalize most of the fantastic elements.

For another indication of Tolkien's familiarity with the Theseus legend, it is perhaps significant that he once stated the piece of fan mail that had pleased him most was a note from Mary Renault, author of two historical novels that retold the Theseus story in light of what modern archeology knew of Minoan (Cretan) and Mycenaean (Greek) cultures: *The King Must Die* [1958] and its sequel *The Bull from the Sea* [1962]. Both Tolkien and Lewis greatly admired her books, especially these two; cf. JRRT to Charlotte & Denis Plimmer, 8th February 1967, where he reports being 'deeply engaged' in her books, 'especially the two about Theseus' (*Letters* p. 377). Similarly, in James Dundas-Grant's memoir of Lewis, this fellow Inkling recalls visiting CSL in the nursing home shortly before his death and listening to Lewis talk about Theseus from his hospital bed, recommending Renault's work (*C. S. Lewis at the Breakfast Table*, ed. James T. Como [1979], page 232).

We should also not forget that the Labyrinth was very much in the public eye in the early decades of the twentieth century, especially for those like Tolkien interested in the connections between myth, prehistory, and archeology, through Sir Arthur Evans' excavations at Knossos in Crete [1900–1940], where he claimed to have discovered the palace of King Minos and the actual passageways that inspired the Labyrinth legend. Evans brought back artifacts from these digs to Oxford's Ashmolean Museum (of which he was the curator), which is just down the street from the Eagle and Child, the Inklings' favorite pub.

21 The story ends in tragedy, however: Theseus abandoned Ariadne on the first island they came to, and his father, Aegeus, killed himself when he saw the ships returning. According to the legend, Theseus had promised before leaving home to switch the ships' black sails for white sails if he was still alive but in the event forgot to do so. Mistakenly seeing their black sails as a sign that his son had died, in his grief Aegeus leapt into the sea, which has ever since been called the *Aegean*.

Theseus's tragic homecoming is echoed in *The Lord of the Rings* Book V, Chapter VII: 'The Pyre of Denethor', where the combination of his son's impending death and the sight in the *palantír* of ships with black sails coming up the Anduin spark Denethor's suicide, just as very similar signs had King Aegeus's in the old tale. And just as in the myth, those ships bear the new ruler, Aragorn, who will shortly be crowned the new king of the city.

22 It is possible that Macaulay's work was a possible source for one scene in *The Hobbit*; compare Macaulay's retelling of Horatius' heroic deed holding a bridge alone against an oncoming army, with Bard the Bowman's final solitary stand against the dragon in Chapter XIII, including the last desperate swim after the structure each defends collapses into the water.

23 That is, among those who appear on the scene in the present day, as opposed to now-dead figures from the past like 'poor Belladonna'.

24 There is one more reference to the ball of spider's thread in the First Typescript. The last four pages of this chapter were removed and replaced with new pages at some point before the creation of the Second Typescript; the rejected sheets now make up Marq. 1/1/30:2–5 while the replacement pages complete the composite chapter 1/1/58. The rejected pages represent an intermediate stage between the manuscript text and the published version; the only section that concerns us here is a slightly rewritten account of Bilbo's regaining the thread after freeing his companions:

> . . . and hundreds of angry spiders were goggling at them all round and about and above. But some of them [> the dwarves] had knives,

and some had sticks, and all of them could get at stones; and Bilbo had his elvish dagger. So the battle began, and the spiders were held off. Indeed they soon saw that it was going to take a long time to recapture their prey.

That was all very well, but how were the dwarves going to escape? That is just what worried Bilbo, especially when he saw that the spiders were beginning to weave their webs from tree to tree all round them again. In the end he could think of no plan except to let the dwarves into the secret of his ring, though he was rather sorry about it. As quickly as he could, in between the shouts and the whacking of sticks and the throwing of stones, he explained it all to them; and when he had got them to understand, he told them to stay where they were and keep the spiders off, while he went to look for the ball of thread, which he had laid by a tree some distance off. Then he slipped on his ring and, to the great astonishment of the dwarves, he disappeared.

Very soon they heard the sound of 'Lazy Lob' and 'Attercop!' from among the trees. That upset the spiders very much, and helped the dwarves to press forward and attack them. In this way they drew slowly to the edge of the colony. Suddenly Bilbo reappeared again. He was carrying his ball of thread, 'Follow me!' he called, and off they all went after him, as fast as they could, though that was not much more than a hobble and a wobble.

The spiders followed too, of course; but the hobbit tired himself out dashing backwards and forwards slashing at their threads, hacking at their legs and stabbing at their heads and bodies if they came too near, so that although they swelled with rage and spluttered and frothed like mad they did not succeed in stopping the dwarves from moving steadily away. It was a terrible business and seemed to take hours, but in the end following the thread Bilbo got them all back to the tree where he had his first battle with the spider in the dark. There suddenly the last of the following spiders fell back and returned disappointed to their dark colony. They did not seem to like the place where the dwarves and Bilbo had come to. Perhaps some good magic still lingered there, for of course it was at the very edge of one of the rings where the strange feasting of the elvish people had been held.

They had escaped the spiders, but where were they, and where was their path, and where was there any food? They asked all these questions of course over and over again, as they lay miserably on the ground, too ill and exhausted to go any further . . .

This account eliminates the comic scene of Bilbo running all around trying to back-track the random zig-zags he made while taunting the spiders and substitutes a grim battle for freedom against desperate odds. In this version, once the retreat begins Bilbo does not leave the dwarves; his vanishment is only to find the thread, which here leads them back only as far as the spot where Bilbo defeated the first spider, the scene where he regained the path on his own having vanished. A few other details, such as the spiders who sit cursing in the trees after they have escaped, have also disappeared from the story, while an important new idea has entered it: that the areas where the elves had feasted retain some residue of 'good magic', a motif that in itself helps ennoble the elves and counteract some of the sinister connotations from the Plot Notes and manuscript draft.

25 However, it is possible that even had they reached the eastern end of the forest, further disaster still lay in wait for them; see 'Visiting the Mewlips' in the commentary following Plot Notes B (p. 370).

26 It has given some readers pause that the Necromancer (Sauron) could have missed the map or, in the published book, both the map and the magic key that accompanied it, but this is no more implausible than that the elves also failed to discover the secret map Gandalf was carrying.

27 Here I am referring to the story as it appeared in the first edition, where Bilbo uses the blade more as a light source than a weapon, rather than the recast version of the scene Tolkien sent to Allen & Unwin in 1947 which ends with Bilbo's internal struggle over whether or not to ambush and kill Gollum in order to escape. See Part Four of this book, beginning on p. 729.

'THE ENCHANTED STREAM'

The following interpolation represents the only significant scene not in the original handwritten manuscript to be added to *The Hobbit* before its publication. The text comes from the First Typescript (Marq. 1/1/58 & 1/1/30), starting about the middle of typescript page 77 (1/1/58:2). As noted in the introduction, this initial typescript was not made until after the manuscript draft had reached the scene on Ravenhill (about a third of the way through Chapter XV), and thus uses the later form of the characters' names (e.g., 'Beorn' for Medwed and 'Thorin' for Gandalf the dwarf-leader).

No drafting survives of this interpolated passage, though some must have existed: the text is too smooth and its insertion too regular to be the result of composition on the typewriter.

All this went on for what seemed to the hobbit ages upon ages; and he was always hungry, for they were very very careful with their provisions. Even so, as days followed days, and still the forest seemed just the same, they began to get anxious. The food would not last for ever: it was in fact already beginning to get low. They tried shooting at the squirrels, and they wasted many arrows before they managed to bring one down on the path. But when they roasted it it proved horrible to taste, and they shot no more squirrels.

They were thirsty too, for they had none too much water, and in all the time they had seen neither spring nor stream. This was their state when one day they found their path blocked by a running water. It flowed fast and strong but not very wide right across the way, and it was black, or looked it in the gloom. It was well that Beorn[TN1] had warned them against it, or they would have drunk from it, whatever its colour, and filled some of their emptied skins at its bank. As it was they only thought of how to cross it without wetting themselves in its water. There had been a bridge of wood across, but it had rotted and fallen leaving only the broken posts near the bank.[TN2]

Bilbo kneeling on the brink and peering forward cried: 'There is a boat against the far bank! Now why could it not have been on this side!'[TN3]

'How far do you think it is?' asked Thorin, for [*added*: by now] they knew Bilbo had the sharpest eyes among them.

'Not at all far. I shouldn't think above twelve yards.'[TN4]

'Twelve yards! I thought it was a river not a little stream,[TN5] but my eyes don't see as well as they used a hundred years ago. Still twelve yards is as good as a mile. We can't jump it and we daren't try to wade or swim.'

'Can any of you throw a rope?'

'What's the good of that? The boat is sure to be tied up, even if we could hook it, which I doubt.'

'I don't believe it is tied,' said Bilbo, 'though of course I can't be sure in this light; but it looks to me as if it was just drawn up on the bank, which is low just there where the path goes down to the water.'

'Dori is the strongest, but Fili is the youngest[TN6] and still has the best sight,' said Thorin. 'Come here Fili and see if you can see the boat Mr. Baggins is talking about.'

Fili thought he could; so when he had stared a long while to get an idea of the direction, the others brought him a rope. They had several with them, and on the end of the longest they fastened one of the large iron hooks they had used for catching their packs to the straps about their shoulders. Fili took this in his hand, balanced it for a moment, and then flung it across the stream.

Splash it fell in the water! 'Not far enough!' said Bilbo who was peering forward. 'A couple of feet and you would have dropped it onto the boat. Try again. I don't suppose the magic is strong enough to hurt you, if you just touch a bit of wet rope.'

Fili picked up the hook when he had drawn it back, rather doubtfully all the same. This time he threw it with all his strength.

'Steady!' said Bilbo, 'you have thrown it right into the wood on the other side now. Draw it back gently.' Fili hauled the rope back slowly, and after a while Bilbo said: 'Carefully! It is lying on the boat; let's hope the hook will catch.'

It did. The rope went taut, and Fili pulled in vain. Kili came to his help, and then Oin and Gloin. They tugged and tugged, and suddenly they all fell over on their backs. Bilbo was on the look out, however, caught the rope and with a piece of stick fended off the little black boat as it came rushing across the stream. 'Help!' he shouted, and Balin was just in time to seize the boat before it floated off down the current.

'It was tied after all,' said he, looking at the snapped painter[TN7] that was still dangling from it. 'That was a good pull, my lads; and a good job that our rope was the stronger.'

'Who'll cross first?' asked Bilbo.

'I shall,' said Thorin, 'and you will come with me and Fili and Balin. That's as many as the boat will hold at a time. After that Kili and Oin and Gloin and Dori, next Ori and Nori, Bifur and Bofur; and last Dwalin and Bombur.'

'I'm always last and I don't like it,' said Bombur. 'It's somebody's else's turn to-day.'

'You should not be so fat. As you are, you must be with the last and lightest boatload. Don't start grumbling against orders, or something bad will happen to you.'

'There aren't any oars. How are you going to push the boat back to the far bank?' asked the hobbit.

'Give me another length of rope and another hook,' said Fili, and when they had got it ready he cast it into the darkness ahead and as high as he could throw it. Since it did not fall down again they saw that it must have stuck in the branches. 'Get in now,' said Fili, 'and one of you haul on the rope that is stuck in a tree on the other side. One of the others must keep hold of the hook we used at first, and when you [> we] are safe on the other side he can hook it on and we [> you] can draw the boat back.'

In this way they were all soon on the far bank safe across the enchanted stream. Dwalin had just scrambled out with the coiled rope on his arm, and Bombur [*added*: (still grumbling)] was getting ready to follow, when something bad did happen. There was a flying sound of hooves on the path ahead. Out of the gloom came suddenly the shape of a flying deer. It charged into the dwarves and bowled them over, then gathered itself for a leap. High it sprang and cleared the water with a mighty jump. But it did not reach the other side in safety. Thorin was the only one who had kept his feet and his wits. As soon as they had landed he had bent his bow and fitted an arrow in case any hidden guardian of the boat appeared. Now he sent a swift and sure shot into the leaping beast. As it reached the further bank it stumbled. The shadows swallowed it up, but they heard the sound of hooves quickly falter and then grow still.

Before they could shout in praise of the shot, however, a dreadful wail from Bilbo put all thoughts of venison out of their minds. 'Bombur has fallen in! Bombur is drowning!' he cried. It was only too true. Bombur had only one foot on the land when the hart[TN8] bore down on him, and sprang over him. He had stumbled thrusting the boat away from the bank, and then toppled back into the dark water, his hands slipping off the slimy roots at the edge, while the boat span slowly off and disappeared.[TN9]

They could still see his hood above the water when they ran to the bank. Quickly they flung a rope with a hook towards him. His hand caught it, and they pulled him to the shore. He was drenched from hair to boots, of course, but that was not the worst. When they laid him on the bank he was already fast asleep with one hand clutching the rope so tight that they could not get it from his grasp; and fast asleep he remained in spite of all they could do.

They were still standing over him, cursing their ill luck and Bombur's clumsiness, and lamenting the loss of the boat which made it impossible for them to go back and look for the hart, when they became aware of the dim blowing of horns in the wood and the sound as of dogs baying far off.[TN10] Then they all fell silent; and as they sat it seemed they could hear the noise of a great hunt going by to the north[TN11] of the path, though they saw no sign of it.

There they sat for a long while and did not dare to make a move. Bombur slept on with a smile on his fat face, as if he no longer cared for all the troubles that vexed them. Suddenly on the path ahead appeared some white deer, a hind and fawns, as snowy white as the hart had been dark. They glimmered in the shadows. Before Thorin could cry out three[TN12] of the dwarves had leaped to their feet and loosed off arrows from their bows. None seemed to find their mark. The deer turned and vanished into the trees as silently as they had come, and in vain the dwarves shot their arrows after them.

'Stop! stop!' shouted Thorin; but it was too late, the excited dwarves had wasted their last arrows, and now the bows that Beorn had given them were useless.

They were a gloomy party that night, and the gloom gathered still deeper on them in the following days. They had crossed the enchanted stream; but beyond it the path seemed to straggle on just as before, and in the forest they could see no change. Yet if they had known more about it and considered the meaning of the hunt and the white deer that had appeared upon their path, they would have known that they were at last drawing towards the eastern edge, and would soon have come, if they could have kept up their courage and their hope, to thinner trees and places where the sunlight came again.

But they did not know this, and they were burdened with the heavy body of Bombur, which they had to carry along with them as best they could, taking the wearisome task in turns of four each while the others shared their packs. If these had not become all too light in the last few days they would never have managed it; but a slumbering and smiling Bombur was a poor exchange for packs filled with food however heavy. In a few days a time came when there was practically nothing left to eat or drink. Nothing wholesome could they see growing in the wood, only funguses and herbs with pale leaves and unpleasant smell.

About four days from the enchanted stream they came to a part where the trees seemed mostly beeches. They were at first inclined to be cheered by the change, for here there was no undergrowth and the shadow was not so deep. There was a greenish light about them and in places they could see some distance to either side of the path. Yet all they could see was an endless vista of straight grey trunks like the pillars of some huge twilight hall.[TN13] There was a breath of air and a noise of wind, but it had a sad sound. A few leaves came rustling down to remind them that outside the autumn was advancing fast; some beech-mast fell or was cast down by unseen squirrels high above, but it was hard and bitter and no use to them.[TN14]

Still Bombur slept and they grew very weary. Then they heard the disquieting laughter. Sometimes there was singing in the distance too. The laughter was the laughter of fair voices not of goblins, and the singing was beautiful, but it sounded eerie and strange, and they were not comforted, rather they hurried on from those parts with what strength they had left.

Two days later they found their path going downwards and before long they were in a valley filled almost entirely with a mighty growth of oaks.

'Is there no end to this accursed forest?' said Thorin. 'Someone must climb a tree . . .'

The scene where Bilbo climbs the tree and sees the Purple Emperors (and spiders), while differing in word choice and detail, is substantially the same in the manuscript as the typescripts and book. However, after Bilbo's descent the revised story once again departs from the original draft in order to cover Bombur's waking from his enchanted sleep. We resume with the final paragraph on typescript page 81 (1/1/58:6), coming after a gap of a skipped line:

Bombur Wakes

That night they ate their very last scraps and crumbs of food; and next morning when they woke the first thing they noticed was that they were still gnawingly hungry, and the next thing was that it was raining and that here and there the drip of it was dropping heavily on the forest floor. That only reminded them that they were also parchingly thirsty, without doing anything to relieve them: you cannot quench a terrible thirst by standing under giant oaks and waiting for a chance drip to fall on your tongue. The only scrap of comfort there was came unexpectedly from Bombur.

He woke up suddenly and sat up scratching his head. He could not make out where he was at all, nor why he felt so hungry; for he had forgotten everything that had happened since they started their journey that May[TN15] morning long past. The last thing he remembered was the party at the hobbit's house, and they had great difficulty in making him believe their tale of all the many adventures they had had since.

When he heard that there was nothing to eat, he sat down and wept, for he felt very weak and wobbly in the legs. 'Why ever did I wake up!' he cried. 'I was having such beautiful dreams. I dreamed I was walking in a forest rather like this one, only lit with torches on the trees and lamps swinging from the branches and fires burning on the ground; and there was a great feast going on, going on for ever. A woodland king was there with a crown of leaves, and there was a merry singing, and I could not count or describe the things there were to eat or drink'.

'You need not try,' said Thorin. 'In fact if you can't talk about something else, you had better shut up altogether [> be silent]. We are quite annoyed enough with you as it is. If you hadn't waked up, we should have left you[TN16] to your idiotic dreams in the forest; you are no joke to carry even after weeks of short commons'.

There was nothing now to be done but to tighten the belts round their empty tummies [> stomachs], and hoist their empty sacks and packs, and trudge along the track without any great hope of ever getting to the end before they lay down and died of starvation. This they did all that day, going very slowly and wearily, while Bombur kept on wailing that his legs wouldn't carry him and that he wanted to lie down and sleep.

'No you don't!' they said. 'Let your legs take their share, we have carried you far enough'.

All the same he suddenly refused to go a step further and flung himself on the ground. 'Go on, if you must', he said. 'I'm just going to lie here and sleep and dream of food, if I can't get it any other way. I hope I never wake up again'.

At that very moment Balin, who was a little way ahead, called out: 'What was that? I thought I saw a twinkle of light in the forest'.

They all looked, and a longish way off, it seemed, they saw a red twinkle in the dark; then another and another sprang out beside it. Even Bombur got up, and they hurried along then not caring if it was trolls or goblins. The light was in front of them and to the left of the path, and when at last they had drawn level with it, it seemed plain that torches and fires were burning under the trees, but a good way off their track.

'It looks as if my dreams were coming true', gasped Bombur puffing up behind. He wanted to rush straight off into the wood after the lights. But the others remembered only too well the warnings of the wizard and of Beorn.

'A feast would be no good, if we never got back alive from it', said Thorin.

'But without a feast we shan't remain alive much longer anyway' said Bombur, and Bilbo heartily agreed with him. They argued about it backwards and forwards for a long while, until they agreed in the end to send out a couple of spies to creep near the lights and find out more about them. But then they could not agree on who was to be sent: no one seemed keen [> anxious] to run the chance of being lost and never finding their friends again. And so it was that their hunger won in the end, because Bombur would keep on describing all the good things that were being eaten, according to his dream, in the woodland feast; and they all left the path and plunged into the forest together.

From this point on, the typescript continues much as in the published book, with only slight changes in wording. The passage about how 'The smell of the roast meats was so *enchanting*' (emphasis mine) first appears in the typescript, with all its (in retrospect) ominous connotations; especially when linked later in the same paragraph with the phrase 'as if by magic', which had already been present.

The account of their second attempt to petition the feasters for succor is developed further in the First Typescript than in the original manuscript: here the dwarves cannot find Bilbo because the hobbit is wearing his ring, and it's only by luck that Dori stumbles over him in the dark. And again it's luck that the dwarves do not discover his secret, since they can't tell in the 'inky darkness' that he was invisible when they found him. Also appearing for the first time in the typescript version is the expanded dialogue of Bilbo when they wake him from the spell of sleep that stepping into the elf-ring had cast on him:

When they got to the edge of the circle of lights, Bilbo was pushed forward, and he hastily slipped on the ring. But it was no good. Out went all the lights again; and if it had been difficult collecting themselves before it was far worse this time. They simply could not find the hobbit. Everytime they counted it only made thirteen, and though they shouted and called 'Bilbo Baggins! Hobbit! You dratted hobbit! Hi, hobbit, confusticate you!' and other things of that sort, there was no answer. In the end by good luck Dori found him. He fell over what he thought was a log, and he found it was the hobbit curled up fast asleep.

It took a deal of shaking to wake him, and when he was awake he was not pleased at all.[TN17]

'I was having such a lovely dream,' he grumbled, 'all about having a most gorgeous dinner'.

'Good heavens! he has gone like Bombur,' they said. 'Don't tell us about dreams. Dream dinners aren't any good, and we can't share them'.

'They are the best I am likely to get in this beastly place' he muttered as he lay down beside the dwarves and tried to go back to sleep and find his dream again.

Finally, the description of the third feast is recast to greatly enhance the level of detail and make the whole scene of what the hungry dwarves and hobbit see more vivid, and to include a glimpse of the woodland king mentioned by Bombur from his earlier dreams:

'There's a regular blaze of light begun not far away – hundreds of torches and many fires must have been lit suddenly and by magic. And hark to the singing and the harps!' [*added*: said Kili]

After lying and listening for a while, they found they could not resist the desire to go nearer and try once more to get help. Up they got again; and this time the result was disastrous. The feast was a far greater and more splendid one that they saw, this time; and at the head of a long line of feasters sat a woodland king with a crown of leaves upon his golden hair,[TN18] very much as Bombur had described the figure in his dream. The elvish folk were passing bowls from hand to hand and across the fires, and some were harping and many were singing. Their gleaming hair was twined with flowers; green and white gems glinted on their collars and their belts; and their faces and their songs were filled with mirth. Loud and clear and fair were those songs, and out stepped Thorin in to their midst.

Dead silence fell in the middle of a word . . .

From this point onward, the typescript for this chapter generally resembles the published book in its sequence of events, except for the changes to the spider-battle already discussed under Note 24 following the commentary on Chapter VIII (pp. 345–6).

TEXT NOTES

1 For the name change Medwed > Beorn, and Gandalf > Thorin (Oakenshield), see p. 293.

2 We never learn who built the bridge, but presumably it was the wood-elves, since when interrogating the captured dwarves in what became the next chapter the Elvenking states:

> you were in my realm, using the road my people have made
> —(p. 380)

This is all the more plausible, since both the path and the clearings where the elves feast share the property of keeping the noisome creatures of the forest at bay. However, if the elves made and maintain the path it is odd that they let it fall into decay; we learn later (DAA.242) that its eastern end is no longer passable, ending in debatable marshes, and it is unlike elves to simply let a bridge fall down rotten and leave the empty span. Perhaps the road's decay is simply part of the overall theme of worsening roads (already alluded to in Chapter II) and general decline. The increasing difficulties of travel is a persistent theme in Tolkien; cf. also the 1960 Hobbit (e.g. pp. 779, 794–5, 818), Boromir's account of his difficult journey north, particularly because of the ruined bridge at Tharbad (*LotR*.394), and 'The Hunt for the Ring' (UT.343–4).

By contrast, the Forest Road that appears on the Wilderland Map – the route Bladorthin originally intended Gandalf & Company to use before they got waylaid and driven off their planned path by the goblins – was presumably made and maintained by the Wood-men, one of whose woodland settlements appears just to the south of its western end (a feature missing from the draft map that appears on Plate I [bottom]).

3 'why could it not' changed to 'why couldn't it' (the reading in the book) in both typescripts, the better to match with the contractions (present from the start) in the dialogue that follows. 'There is' in the preceding sentence appears as 'There's' in the Second Typescript, a (no doubt unconscious) unauthorized change by Michael Tolkien, the typist, in keeping with the tone of the passage but not taken up into the published book.

As for the boat, we learn no details about it except for its colour (black, like most other things in Mirkwood – cf. Gee, 'Melanism and Middle-earth', published online at http://greenbooks.theonering.net/guest/files/081104_01.html) and roughly its size (big enough for four dwarves at a time but not more). This lack of information from the narrator here effectively echoes the limits of character knowledge, as in the Gollum scene ('I don't know where he came from or who or what he was'), in contrast to later in the same chapter where the narrator shares information with the reader not available to the characters (the nearness of the forest's eastern edge, the fate of Gandalf, &c).

4 The sentence continues in the First Typescript 'but it is so dark it almost looks'. This is then erased before the next line is typed; the deleted passage does not appear in the Second Typescript.

5 'I thought it was a river not a little stream', the reading in both typescripts, changed to 'I shd have thought it was thirty at least' (the reading in the published book) in the First Typescript only; this hasty ink revision accordingly belongs to the later stage of revision when Tolkien was preparing the book for publication.

6 This line is the only place where it is stated that Fili is younger than Kili, a fact not in the original draft of the story. It is also rather surprising, given Tolkien's usual practice of naming the elder of a pair first. In *The Lord of the Rings* Appendix A part iii: Durin's Folk, written more than twenty years later, Tolkien provides a family tree of Durin's line by which we learn that that Fili was born in Third Age 2859 and Kili five years later in T.A. 2864, contradicting the information given in *The Hobbit*. This is one of the few direct contradictions between *The Lord*

of the Rings and *The Hobbit*, even more overt than Bilbo's apology to Gloin at the Council of Elrond. Tolkien's failure to correct it in later editions undoubtedly means he never noticed the discrepancy – after all, the dwarven family tree in Appendix A probably did not exist when the second edition of *The Hobbit* was accidentally created in 1947. The thoroughgoing revisions that made up the 1960 Hobbit did not extend this far into the text, having halted at Thorin & Company's arrival at Elrond's House, and this small detail seems to have been overlooked in the great pressure to produce the third edition in the summer of 1965 in order to resecure the American copyright.

7 painter: A rope hanging from the bow of a boat and used to moor it. The speaker here is Balin.

8 Both here and at the next mention the word 'hart' is written in ink over an erasure. The original word underneath can no longer be made out, but since it was of the same length as its replacement it was probably 'deer', *hart* and *hind* being a male and a female deer, respectively.

The sudden, disastrous appearance of the hart, the motif of a white deer, and the distant sound of hounds evoke echoes of such medieval tales as *Pwyll, Prince of Dyfed* (the First Branch of the *Mabinogi*), *Sir Orfeo*, or the *lais* of Marie de France; see 'The Vanishing People' following Chapter IX.

9 span: One would expect 'spun' instead, but 'span' is the reading from the First Typescript through into the current edition of the published book.

10 dim horns blowing: No doubt a deliberate echo of Tennyson's 'the horns of elfland faintly blowing'. For more on the slightly sinister motif of the elven hunt, see 'The Vanishing People', p. 399.

By contrast with the horns, this is the only mention of dogs baying in the Mirkwood chapter. No dogs are referred to in the descriptions of the woodland feasts, nor are any encountered by Bilbo during his sojourn in and about the Elvenking's halls. Their absence in the elf-mound helps make plausible Bilbo's success in evading detection for weeks on end, and suggests that Tolkien inserted this reference to them for its evocation of old legends and then simply forgot to integrate it into the next chapter.

11 north of the path: Throughout the interpolated section Tolkien is consistent that all the sounds and sightings associated with the wood-elves take place north of the path. For example, when they spot the feast that ultimately lures them off the path, they see it 'in front of them and to the left of the path' – i.e., on the north as they are facing east.

12 three dwarves shooting arrows: This precision goes back to the original idea that Medwed (= Beorn) gave his guests four bows (see p. 241). One is in Thorin's possession, since he just used it to shoot the hart that leapt the stream; add in the three who shoot wildly at the hind and it equals four. The specific detail of how many bows Medwed/Beorn

gave them dropped out of Chapter VII, appearing in the corresponding passage of the First Typescript (1/1/57:12) merely as 'some bows', the reading preserved through into the published book (cf. DAA.183), but clearly it remained in Tolkien's mind and underlies the precision of the present passage, presumably written before that detail had dropped out of the Medwed section.

Rendering their bows useless, of course, was probably one of Tolkien's narrative goals in creating this interpolated passage; see commentary below.

13 trees in rows like grey columns: Cf. JRRT's illustration 'The Elven-king's Gate' (DAA.224 [top]), which appeared in the original and most subsequent editions of *The Hobbit*. Tolkien experimented with several different views of the forest surrounding the elf-mound, such as the one reproduced on Plate VII [bottom]; see *Pictures by Tolkien* plates 11 & 12, DAA.224, and H&S#s117–121. But only this one (the last in the sequence, apparently drawn over the 1936 Christmas vacation – cf. Hammond, *Descriptive Bibliography*, page 10) matched the description in the text of the elven section of the great forest.

14 beech-mast: beechnuts. See Chapter VIII, p. 304 and Text Notes 5 & 7 following that chapter.

15 May: The revised time-scheme introduced in the latter (Second Phase) half of Chapter I is in place here; see 'The Third of March', p. 84.

16 This rather startling threat is entirely unlike Thorin, whose team has all along taken great pains to leave no dwarf (or hobbit) behind; his snapping at the distraught and starving (but undeniably annoying) Bombur, who after all has not eaten for a full week, is a sign of just how stressed the entire party has become by this point: starving, desperately thirsty, and close to despair. Unfortunately, Bombur calls him on the empty threat at the end of that same day when he plops down and refuses to go forward any more, preferring enchanted dreams to a depressing reality (a recurring motif in legends and folklore about people stolen away or enchanted by the elves).

17 This passage was in turn replaced by yet another version of the scene, which approaches but does not quite achieve the text of the published book; Bilbo now is taken by surprise and does not have time to put on the ring. This new text was pasted over the old (typescript page 83, the bottom quarter of 1/1/58:8). The substitution predates the creation of the second typescript, since it follows the pasteover version (Bilbo does not use the ring), not the earlier version hidden beneath it (Bilbo uses the ring, to no avail).

My thanks to Matt Blessing of the Marquette Archives for providing a transcription of the two paragraphs covered by the pasteover.

18 The detail of the woodland king's golden hair, which only enters in with the typescript, is interesting, since it complicates his identification; see 'The Three Kindreds of the Elves', p. 407.

Mirkwood Reconsidered

The chief question posed by this extensive interpolated passage and the associated changes made to accommodate it in the text is the simple one of why. Why did Tolkien feel the need to add this complication to the story, the only major addition between the manuscript and typescript phases of the book? It's possible that he wanted to insert some folklore motifs (enchanted sleep, the white deer, the dire consequences of breaking a fairy-tale prohibition no matter what the temptation, echoes of the wild hunt) to make the dwarves' passage through Mirkwood even more eerie and unsettling than it already was, and quite distinct from the earlier journey in the dark through the Misty Mountains. Certainly the additions help enhance Bilbo's standing by providing another example of his usefulness with appropriate tasks in the episode of securing the boat, and they develop Bombur's character by making him a complainer and a drag upon the party, even more of a weak link than little Bilbo.[1]

The most likely answer, I think, is that the passage was created to pay a narrative debt once Tolkien realized he had incurred one. While he was dealing with that, he seems to have decided to settle several other points that had occurred to him after finishing the story, explaining why the dwarves didn't hunt food when they were starving (especially since the original draft already mentioned the black squirrels), or use the bows to defend themselves against the spiders or the elves.

Back in what ultimately became Chapter VII, Medwed warned his guests of the dangers they would face in Mirkwood:

> [Y]our road through the forest is difficult and dangerous . . . Water is not easy to find there, nor food. For the time is not come for nuts which is all there is growing there that can be eaten . . . I will provide you with skins for carrying water, which you had better fill before you enter the forest. *You will see one stream, a strong black one, if you hold to the path, but I doubt if it is good to drink. I have heard that it carries enchantment, and brings a frightful drowziness.* I will give you four bows and arrows, but I doubt if you will shoot anything in the dim shadows of that place, without straying from the path – which you MUST NOT DO. And I doubt if it would be good to eat if you shot it.
>
> —pp. 241–2 (emphasis mine).

There is no mention of the enchanted stream in the first rough outline (p. 229) nor in the Plot Notes describing their adventures in Mirkwood (Plot Notes A, pp. 294–6) which Tolkien used as his pre-draft guide when actually composing the chapter, but Medwed's warning suggests that this was an episode Tolkien intended to include and then simply forgot about. Re-reading the book as he was creating the First Typescript, he seems to have noticed the dropped motif and decided to recast the chapter to include it; hence the interpolation. While he was at it, he accounted for the dwarves not shooting food when they were starving by letting them try with the squirrels and discover them inedible, just as Medwed had predicted ('I doubt [anything] would be good to eat if you shot it').

The scene with the dark hart and white hind rather neatly first precipitates the disaster of Bombur's dunking and subsequent enchantment and then renders the bows useless when the desperate dwarves expend their last arrows.[2] And, although this may be unintentional on Tolkien's part, the revised text fits into the 'rule of three' that he consciously applies elsewhere (the three attempts to approach the feasting elves, Bilbo's three descents into Smaug's lair)[3] with the three warnings Gandalf's party receive. On Bladorthin's advice, the dwarves keep their first promise, to send Medwed's horse back. They try to keep their second promise not to drink from the enchanted stream, and only the thirteenth dwarf does so and then only by mischance, itself the result of an uncanny, unexpected intrusion; while inconvenienced the group is able to continue on with their quest afterwards. The third promise, to stay on the path, they finally break *in extremis*, and it brings disaster on their heads just as Bladorthin predicted:

> 'Don't stray off the track – if you do it is a thousand to one you'll never find the path again, or ever get out of Mirkwood; and then I don't suppose I (or anyone else) will hear of you again!'
>
> — p. 244.

However, had Tolkien kept to the manuscript version of events the wizard would have proved a false prophet, for Bilbo does find the path again, rather easily, and after rescuing his friends leads them back to it as well (see 'The Theseus Theme', pp. 337–8). With the revision, Medwed's and Bladorthin's dire warnings more closely resemble the results.

Finally, a few miscellaneous points. The 'little black boat' itself is interesting, since we are never given any indication whose boat it is nor how it came to be there. If the elves placed it there to replace the fallen bridge, it's surprising they would prefer to bring an oar with them (a seven days' journey) each time they wanted to cross the stream, rather than simply leaving one with the boat. Usually the narrator either provides the reader with information where the characters are stumped or admits to his own ignorance on a given point; here there is only silence. All we really know about the boat is that it is small (just large enough for four dwarves at a time), black, and has laid undisturbed for some time (since the painter snaps).[4] Thorin's prudence of standing guard lest 'any hidden guardian of the boat' appear not only shows him well-versed in fairy-tale tradition but proves justified by the event, though there's nothing to indicate that the hart itself, for all the misfortune it brings upon them, is anything but a fugitive from the elven hunt.

NOTES

1 This new emphasis on Bombur certainly makes him a more memorable character, but at the cost of making him considerably more petty; he essentially replaces Bilbo as the party's grumbler from this point on. In the original story he could hardly have contributed anything to the spider-battle, battered and debilitated as he was after mishandling by the spiders, not to mention being on the verge of starvation (remember that Bombur has had nothing to eat or drink at this point since falling into the enchanted stream seven days before). Then too his reluctance at the Lonely Mountain to climb narrow paths high in the air is not particularly unreasonable.

2 For more on the white deer and the invisible hunt, see 'The Vanishing People' in the commentary following Chapter IX.

3 For the proverb 'Third time pays for all', see Text Note 3 following Chapter XII.

4 This was clearly not an elven rope; compare the preternatural durability of Sam's rope, a gift of the elves of Lothlórien, in Book IV of *The Lord of the Rings*.

PLOT NOTES B

This rough drafting, which obviously preceded the first full draft of what is now Chapter IX, I have designated 'Plot Notes B.' It represents either Tolkien's attempt, after he had broken off composition at the start of a new school term, to jot down ideas for the continuation before he forgot them or, as seems more probable, his initial effort months later to get the story going again after having put it aside. For the break in composition, corresponding to the change in paper between manuscript page 118 (Marq. 1/1/8:18) and manuscript page 119 (1/1/9:1), see pages 316 and 379 and also 'The Chronology of Composition'; Plot Notes B is written on the later type of paper (lined on one side, unlined on the other). Each page except the final one bearing a map is numbered, by Tolkien, in the upper right-hand corner.

The three sheets (five pages plus a full-page draft map) that make up this outline[TN1] were later separated, long before the material came to Marquette, when the second sheet (original pages 316 & 379) was replaced by another sheet (new pages 3 & 4) giving a revised and further developed form of that section; I have given this newer material the name Plot Notes C to distinguish it from the original layer it replaced. At a still later date, the verso of this replacement sheet was in turn supplanted by the insertion of another two pages which I have designated as Plot Notes D.[TN2] In its final form, then, this set of plot notes (Plot Notes B/C/D; Marq. 1/1/10) is a composite document written in three distinct stages – the first layer (B) after Chapter VIII, the second layer (C) during or after Chapter XI, and the third and final layer (D) near the end of Chapter XIII. Since all the plot notes associated with *The Hobbit* are of interest mainly for what they reveal about Tolkien's ideas of what might happen in the as-yet-unwritten chapters ahead, I here present Plot Notes B as it was originally written, followed by commentary; for Plot Notes C (text and commentary) see pages 495–503 and for Plot Notes D (ibid.) see pages 568–76.

[page] 1

Bilbo follows party into the cave. Description of the Elfking and his halls. The dwarves are put into different cells. Bilbo cannot find the way out through the magic gates. He goes from cell to cell and manages to speak to the dwarves; and he tells them he has found Gandalf in a very deep dungeon. Gandalf will not tell the king his errand, because he will not share his treasure with the wood-elves.

The river flows under part of the caves & issues by a secret water gate. That way the wood-elves get many of their supplies, especially of wine. When the barrels were empty they dropped them into the river, and they floated out through the watergate until the current brought them to a place on the bank not far from the edge of the forest. There they were linked together and floated like a raft down past the marshes and the reedy places to the Long Lake.

<All/At> <times> Bilbo <illegible> <on> lurking in the king's passages, living on scraps of food. 'Living like a burglar that can't get out again' he thought. But in the end he had a desperate idea.

Steal jailers keys and lets out a dwarf at a time. Hides them in barrels. In this way they are all <?thrown> [in] water.

<Indeed> Bilbo escape only by sitting outside one. Difficulty of getting through watergate. the barrels assembled. Grumbles of elves.[TN3] Raft. Floating past the marshes. Raftsmen tell tales of the disappearance of the <rafts> and the loss of men & beasts in these places.

Reach Long Lake and a town of men. The dwarves leap out of their Barrels and gallop off with the waggons.[TN4] [But only go off towards the Mountain far with >] To the town.

Argument of Gandalf and the Mayor. They buy food, and waggons (but <how> to get the stuff back <large> quest!) and go off. The elves go back to the king who makes a plan.

[page] 2

All the land desert.[TN5]

The dwarves camped in a hollow near the skirts of the mountain. From here some went <taking> Bilbo up the river from the Lake, the Running river. They look on the Ruins of Dale. Smoke comes out of the Front Door.

Then Smaug is still alive? Doesn't <tell>. Inside of M. is probably pretty hot!

A whole year had now gone by since they stayed with Elrond. It was summer. But black bleak and lonely. They crept near<er> the mountain by stages but only saw crows and ravens, and were afraid of them as spies. The summer waned. After endless search on the west side of the mountain guided by the map they found a wall of rock standing in a kind of bay. <Strangely> flat with grass up to its feet. It was the door. But it had no key and nowhere could any crack or chink be seen. Nothing they could do would make any of it stir.

Bilbo was wandering disconsolately. The dwarves were silent <fierce> and unfriendly, and he wd. hear them muttering that the burglar – esp with his ring – ought to go in by F.G.[TN6] if necessary. He had <clombered> up the hill and <on> to the little flat terrace platform where the flat rock-face stood. Looking back he could see the line of the forest far to west, a yellow gleam of light on the marshes the trees in the distance going brown towards autumn. Suddenly he saw the orange sun setting and saw the new moon pale and sharp in the Western sky as well. At the very moment he heard a sharp crack. There on a grey stone was a huge and ancient thrush, coal black with white heart and black freckles. It was cracking snails upon the stone. Crack crack.

Bilbo <yells on> hill. <Fetches> dwarves. They watch excitedly as the sun sinks lower and lower. It goes behind a cloud to their despair. But suddenly just before it touches the rim of the forest a red ray shoots through a rent in the sky and falls on the rock-slab. There is a crack. There is a hole in the wall as if <illegible> by the sun as a flake of rock falls off.

The troll-key fits the door swings in. Darkness falls suddenly and the moon goes quickly after the sun.

[page] 3

—:Bilbo earns his reward:—[TN7]

The dwarves say he must go in. He begs them to come too. They won't, until he has explored: all save old Balin yellow-beard. Balin & the hobbit creep into the dark mountain.[TN8]

Not as difficult as they expected – the tunnel ran absolutely straight and slight[ly] Down. Down down down for ever. Soon they see a light at the end, growing steadily redder and redder. A bubbling snoring <burbling>[TN9] noise. It gets very hot. Vapors float up to them.

At last they peep into a <large> hall, the greatest of all the halls under mountain. It is nearly dark. Lit by a red glow. Coming from the large red [gold] dragon lying there fast asleep upon a pile of jems.[TN10] Crushed under him, as he lay half on his side. He steals a cup to show he has been there. He sees shields and spears.[TN11]

The dwarves pleased & pat him on the back.

Wrath of the dragon. He comes out – <of course>[TN12] he cannot get up the secret tunnel – and sniffs all round the mountain.[TN13] and settles flying on the mountain, fly fiercely round and round to find the thief. Terror of the dwarves as he flies over them in fire, while they crouch in holes and behind rocks. They dig holes to hide in.

Bilbo steals another cup.

Greater wrath of dragon – but this time, Dwarves have dug deep caves to hide in.[TN14]

Bilbo steals a gem.[TN15] Seen by dragon as he escapes up the tunnel. Dragon sends [fire >] fiery <spouts> up after him, and poor B. is burned badly. Dragon thinks that it is men from Long Lake. Goes off in a dreadful rage to destroy their town. The people see him coming [and fly. but he dare not come down >] and cut down the bridge to their lake-dwelling. [Dragon doesn't come out onto the water. >] Dragon flies over town trying to set the town on fire. They put fire out with water and shoot at him. He settles at end of lake and vast clouds of steam go up.

[page] 4

The dwarves and Bilbo can see this from the mountain side.

The dwarves go in while dragon is away and bring out a store of gold. Bilbo gets them to tell of all the treasure there. And he asks how they are going to get it all back[TN16]

Bilbo goes back a third time. [*added*: Steals a marvellous gem] Dragon wakes and speaks to him as he peers from mouth of tunnel into the hall.

'Who are you'

Says dwarves don't worry about him – how is he going to get his share home.

B. flatters dragon. D. says he is impregnable. Even on soft underside he is encrusted. B. makes him show. Sees there is a patch.

He goes back to the dwarves filled with misgivings and asks them about their future plans. They tell him of the Jem of Girion king of Dale the gem for the arming of his son. Bilbo keeps on looking at his gem. He must earn it.

He goes in and kills dragon as it sleeps [*added*: exhausted after battle] with a spear

The text stops here in the middle of the fourth page, with the bottom half of this page, reversed, being a draft of the river-barrel song from Chapter IX. These very rough workings are clearly the initial stage of composition: I have transcribed them as they appear, with cancelled passages here indicated with *italics* to avoid cluttering the lines with brackets. For the final form of the poem, see p. 386 and DAA.235.

O Down the swift dark stream you go
Back to woods you once did know.
Leave the northern forest deep
Leave the halls and caverns deep
Leave the northern mountains steep
Where the forest wide and dim
<Stoops> in shadow grey and grim.
Float beyond the world of trees
pass the out into the whispering breeze
past the rushes past the reeds
where past the marsh's waving weeds
through the mist that rises *pale* white
<from> <where> the land of lake and mere
up from meres and pools and night
<Then> find the lake of many isles
Gather at the town
Find the *town of <illegible>* the bridges and the piles
Where the town is

in lower left margin:

Follow follow <illegible> his leaping stars
Spring from the mists
<Spring> <illegible> from <his>
Up the heavens high & steep
<Illegible> Through the mist above the land
Over rapid over sand
South away and south away
Seek the sunlight and the day
Seek the <gardens> and field

in top margin:

<Find>
Seek the garden and the fields
Back to pasture, back to mead
back to where the *<herder> <fat>* kine & oxen feed
Back to gardens on the hills
where the berry swells and fills

in upper left margin:

Under sunlight and under day
South away and south away.

<Down the swift> <dark stream> go
Back to <illegible> you once did know

The following final page of Plot Notes B, originally numbered page 5, had its pagination cancelled in a lighter ink and was renumbered page 6; this occurred when Plot Notes D was incorporated into the composite Plot Notes B/C/D text (see Text Note 2). Significantly, even at that late date (when Tolkien was nearing the end of Chapter XIII) this projection of the ending of the book was still considered current, as indicated by the repagination. Not until the creation of Plot Notes E and F, at the very end of the Second Phase and beginning of the Third Phase, respectively (that is, written after the story broke off part way through Chapter XV) was the following page describing Bilbo's return journey superceded. The page begins with a small decorative flourish that seems intended to separate it from the preceding and mark the beginning of a new section.

[page] 5

With an army – a battle is gathering in the west. B. puts on [the >] a suit of silver mail made for an elf-king's son, and goes with the wood-elves to battle.

The men of the woods and the wood elves [and >] gather a great army, and men come from the south, and the goblins of the Misty Mountains & wargs are defeated[.] Beorn Medwed is there with a troop of bears. After the battle the way is clear over the mountains. Bilbo with only a little treasure – a nice set of golden dinner service – and the Gem of Girion – goes home.[TN17] The wizard won't have <any more>. They uncover the trolls' gold & leave it.

Brief stay at Elrond's. But in end B. <thinks> he will go home to his own hole. Took is getting tired.

Arrival at own home. 'Presumed dead'[.] In middle of an auction. Puts Gem in a safe but looks at it every day. Otherwise <just becomes> a hobbit again – but very different. Takes to writing poetry and is regarded as a bit queer.

Long after when he is very old he returns the Gem.[TN18]

His ring he used when unwelcome callers came.
Explanation of troll key
The wizard's reward.

The back of this page (Marq. 1/1/10:8) is a rough pencil map, forerunner of the finished map that accompanied the 'home manuscript', showing the relative locations of Mirkwood, the Marshes, the Forest River, Laketown, the Lonely Mountain, and the Withered Heath. As with the final map, this one shows mountains or spurs reaching down in a great crescent from the north-east until they almost touch the outstretched arm of the Mountain; these apparently form the eastern barrier to the Withered Heath.

TEXT NOTES

1 Marquette 1/1/10:1–2 (original pages 1 & 2), 1/1/25:1–2 (original pages 3 & 4), and 1/1/10:7–8 (original page 5 plus the draft penciled map).

2 That is, new page 4 from Plot Notes C was cancelled and replaced by a new sheet containing newer pages 4 and 5 (= Plot Notes D), at which point the final page of text from Plot Notes B (original page 5) was renumbered by Tolkien '[page] 6'. The full sequence of the composite manuscript can be shown thusly in tabular form:

original layer	**(Plot Notes B)**
original page 1 (1/1/10:1)	[B]
original page 2 (1/1/10:2)	[B]
original page 3 (1/1/25:1)	[B]
original page 4 (1/1/25:2)	[B]
original page 5 (1/1/10:7)	[B]
map (1/1/10:8)	[B]
replacement layer	**(Plot Notes B/C)**
original page 1 (1/1/10:1)	[B]
original page 2 (1/1/10:2)	[B]
new page 3 (1/1/10:3)	[C]
new page 4 (1/1/10:4)	[C]
original page 5 (1/1/10:7)	[B]
map (1/1/10:8)	[B]
final layer	**(Plot Notes B/C/D)**
original page 1 (1/1/10:1)	[B]
original page 2 (1/1/10:2)	[B]
new page 3 (1/1/10:3)	[C]
newer page 4 (1/1/10:5)	[D]
newer page 5 (1/1/10:6)	[D]
original page 5, now renumbered 6 (1/1/10:7)	[B]
map (1/1/10:8)	[B]

3 The last two words ('of elves') were cancelled.

4 Tolkien originally followed this sentence with the word 'Present' here at the end of a line and then immediately struck it out; perhaps it would have been the beginning of a line about the dwarves *present*ing themselves to the Mayor of Lake Town or simply some phrase beginning with the word '*Present*ly'.

5 This line, added at the top of the second page, uses 'desert' in the old sense of deserted and desolate ('a desert island'), not dotted with sand and cacti.

6 F.G.: that is, the Front Gate.

7 'Bilbo earns his reward' is written almost as a title, alone at the top of the page, preceded by an inverted triangle of three dots and followed by a small decoration that looks like a colon and a dash. The same words are repeated, like a catch-phrase, in the first line of Plot Notes C: see p. 495.

Although this sheet (I/I/25:I–2) is now brown with age, it is of the same paper and type as the somewhat more well-preserved sheet (I/I/10:I–2) that once preceded it.

8 This and the following two paragraphs were altered so that Bilbo would be forced to explore the tunnel alone, as in the published book, although the alteration was not consistently carried out (note the two accidental retentions of *they* which should have been changed in each case to *he*). The revised text reads:

> The dwarves say he must go in. He begs them to come too. They won't, until he has explored: *not even* old Balin yellow-beard. *the hobbit* creep*s* into the dark mountain.
>
> Not as difficult as they expected – the tunnel ran absolutely straight and slight[ly] down. Down down down for ever. Soon they see a light at the end, growing steadily redder and redder. A bubbling snoring <burbling> noise. It gets very hot. Vapors float up to *him*.
>
> At last *he* peeps into a large hall, the greatest of all the halls under mountain.

9 burbling: This word is nearly illegible, but certainly begins with a b, which seems to be followed by an -ur-, and ends in -ly or -ling. If my reading is correct, then it's a very old (Middle and Early Modern English) word meaning a bubbling, gurgling sound. Tolkien's use, however, probably derives not from the fourteenth- through sixteenth-century usages cited by the OED but from Lewis Carroll's 'Jabberwocky', from *Through the Looking-Glass* [1871]:

> And as in uffish thought he stood
> The Jabberwock, with eyes of flame,
> Came whiffling through the tulgey wood
> And burbled as it came!
>
> —lines 13–16.

For Tolkien's fondness for Carroll, and his propensity for quoting from Carroll's nonsense poetry (of which 'Jabberwocky' is perhaps the most famous), see p. 65, Nt 30.

10 Originally Smaug is described as red; the addition makes him a 'red gold dragon'.

It's possible that Tolkien's use of *jem* instead of *gem* in these plot notes was a deliberate archaism; the OED cites examples of that alternate spelling from c. 1400 to as late as 1799. If so he quickly rejected the idea and settled on the standardized spelling. Curiously enough, by the early eighteenth century 'jem' had become a slang term among the London underworld for a ring, particularly a valuable (gold or diamond) ring.

11 This last sentence may have been added later; it's written in a slightly smaller hand than the rest of the preceding paragraph. If so, its purpose was probably to help set up the dragon-killing episode on this outline's next page.

12 The word(s) immediately following the dash appear to be 'of course', but it could also be 'after', either of which makes sense in the context.

13 'sniffs all round the mountain' was struck out; originally the phrase was preceded by two words which appear to be 'flying' and 'camp', although this last is doubtful. The general sense, however, is clear even as Tolkien struggled with variant phrasing to best capture the scene of Smaug flying around, searching, attempting to sniff them out. Cf. Smaug's comment in the published book that he 'know[s] the smell (and taste) of dwarf – no one better' (DAA.280), and note also the reappearance of the motif of being hunted by scent in Frodo's first encounter with the Black Riders in Chapter III of *The Lord of the Rings* (*LotR*.88).

14 All the sentence following the dash is struck through, but Tolkien has underlined it with a dotted line and written 'stet' in the left margin, indicating that he withdrew the cancellation.

15 This line, which was probably struck through at the same time that the line 'Steals a marvellous gem' was added to the next page, represents the first appearance of what would become the Jem or Gem of Girion (the Arkenstone); see commentary below.

The entire paragraph, with its many hesitations and cancellations, was struck out with two parallel diagonal lines, but Tolkien also wrote 'stet' both above and to the left of the paragraph, indicating he restored the cancellation. It is not clear if this restoration applies to the cancelled first sentence or not.

16 This paragraph is cancelled by a stroke through it, and another set of cancellation lines extend up to include the preceding paragraph as well. Tolkien has written the word 'Stet' (i.e., do not delete) in the left margin opposite the preceding paragraph about Bilbo and the dwarves watching the mayhem from the mountain side, but presumably that restoration does not apply to the paragraph describing their removal of the gold.

17 This line was struck through and an arrow drawn from it to the middle of the penultimate paragraph, presumably to indicate that this topic was to be dealt with there. For more on the idea that Bilbo would either set out with very little treasure or would lose most of it on the way home, see Plot Notes F and also Text Note 11 to Chapter XIX.

18 This sentence is bracketed by Tolkien, usually a sign that the material thus marked needs to be moved, reconsidered, or deleted.

(i)
The Story Foreseen from the Capture by Wood-elves

As with Plot Notes A, this second set of Plot Notes begins with confidence and follows what would become the next chapter or so closely but increasingly diverges beyond that point. By contrast with Tolkien's indecision in the final paragraphs of Plot Notes A where he struggled to find an acceptable way of extricating his characters from the Elvenking's dungeons (see p. 296), here he starts by smoothly plotting out their escape from captivity; with Chapter VIII behind him the immediate road ahead had become clearer. It is no longer Bilbo who goes into the barrel but all his friends, while he must '[sit] outside one' (a complete reversal of the situation projected in Plot Notes A, where Bilbo escaped alone inside a barrel). Bilbo no longer has to retrace his steps back through Mirkwood to beseech help from Medwed, the great eagles, and Bladorthin, nor does Bladorthin reappear just long enough to solve all their problems before disappearing yet again. Instead, Bilbo's 'desperate' plan proves wholly successful and gets them all safely out of the forest and all the way to Long Lake, just as in the final book.

(ii)
Visiting the Mewlips

The rather ominous line about rafts, men (i.e., raft-elves), and beasts disappearing in the Long Marshes suggests that Tolkien had some adventure in mind for what unpleasantness would have befallen the hobbit and his companions had they found their way into the marshes. The disappearances described here might simply be the work of Smaug's foraging, but this seems unlikely – the dragon's hunting seems to have been far from subtle, and from later descriptions it sounds as if he has kept close to the Lonely Mountain for many years past. We do, however, have a description of sinister cannibalistic monsters lurking in a swamp in another of Tolkien's works: his poem 'The Mewlips' (ATB poem #9).[1] Given the degree to which Tolkien borrowed freely from his earlier works when writing *The Hobbit* – what I have elsewhere called his knack for autoplagiarism – it would be entirely in keeping for him to have done the same here, but in the event the story took a different direction and Bilbo luckily avoided having to slog through the marshes entirely.

(iii)
Lake Town

Tolkien originally conceived of the arrival at Lake Town (or, rather, at 'a town of men' on the shores of the Long Lake) somewhat more dramatically – rather than crawling from their barrels stiff and grumbling the dwarves boldly 'leap out', steal some wagons, and gallop off. At first Tolkien apparently thought to have them ride away from the lake towards the mountain, but on second thought he had them dash away from the elven rivermen (who might try to re-imprison them) and go to the human town instead, where they were no doubt able to claim sanctuary as in the published book. Interestingly enough, this settlement on the Long Lake is not yet named anywhere in the text but remains merely 'a town of men', although the label 'Lake Town' had appeared on the very first map drawn into the Pryftan Fragment in the initial stage of composition on the book: see the Frontispiece. After wrangling with the Mayor (who never does receive a name in any version of the story) and buying supplies, they set off toward the Mountain.

(iv)
The Original Time-Scheme

Another variance from the final story is revealed by the line 'A whole year had now gone by since they stayed with Elrond': as in Plot Notes A, the original conception whereby Bilbo's journey lasted more than a year, possibly two, was still in place. It was already late autumn when Bilbo climbed the tree in Mirkwood (cf. p. 304: 'for autumn was now far on' and Text Note 6 to Chapter VIII), while their captivity in the elf-mound lasted month after month, all through winter and into spring (again, see Plot Notes A, p. 296). Now more months pass as summer wears away while they slowly draw near the mountain, although whether fear or rough terrain is responsible for their slow progress is not made clear. When Durin's Day (which is not so named here) does arrive, it occurs on the *first* new moon of autumn, as in the original conception (an echo of which remained in the text of *The Hobbit* until 1995; see DAA.101–2 and my commentary on p. 135), not the *last* moon of autumn as in the published tale. The reference to crows and ravens indicates that the motif of the friendly ravens, Roäc and Carc, had not yet arisen (see Plot Notes D, p. 569, and Plot Notes E: 'Little Bird', p. 628).

(v)
Into the Dragon's Lair

The scene with the finding and opening of the secret door is in outline much the same as in the fuller version that was to follow; this episode had clearly been foreseen from at least as far back as the drafting of what is now Chapter III; see p. 116. The initial exploration of Smaug's lair is also similar, except for the all important fact that originally Tolkien thought that *two* of the party, Bilbo and Balin (who is beginning to emerge as the most sympathetic of the dwarves), would make the initial foray, before revising it to make Bilbo go alone. Bilbo steals the cup as in the final story (a detail inspired by *The Beowulf*; see p. 533) and the dragon emerges and goes on a rampage.

At this point, the outline begins to diverge from the story as it eventually developed, with the amusing detail of the dwarves digging holes to hide in (memories of WWI foxholes?) as the angry dragon flies over: a rather comic idea that did not survive. This is followed by mere repetition, with Bilbo stealing another cup, the dragon going on another prowl, and the dwarves hiding in deeper caves they have prepared (trenches like those on the Western Front?). Bilbo's third foray, where he steals a gem, ends in his being seriously injured ('burned badly') by the dragon; this injury survives into the final book – cf. DAA.283, where Bilbo is in 'great pain' – but is rather downplayed since Bilbo continues to act normally despite being scorched down to the skin.

The dragon's departure to attack the lake-men first occurs here, as does the first evidence that their settlement is actually on, not beside, the lake: we are explicitly told that once they have 'cut down the bridge to their lake-dwelling' the dragon cannot reach them because that would mean coming out over the water. The bifurcation of the story that later led to the resequencing and reversal of Chapters XIII and XIV (see pp. 547 & 577) has not yet occurred: here Bilbo and the dwarves know of Smaug's attack on the town because they can see it from the slopes of the Mountain – proof, by the way, that Smaug did not succeed in finding and sealing the secret door from outside. Indeed the dwarves, far from cowering in doubt for several days, seize this opportune moment to begin plundering Smaug's hoard; and it is seeing the first load ('a store of gold') on the mountain side that sparks Bilbo's doubts about the magnitude of the enterprise he has undertaken.

(vi)
Conversations with Smaug

At least some of the repetition in the account here of Bilbo's forays into Smaug's lair is more apparent than real, since Tolkien cancelled several paragraphs (everything between 'Dwarves have dug deep caves to hide in' and 'asks how they are going to get it all back'; see Text Notes 14, 15, & 16), after which the outline then goes back to sketch out a different way Bilbo's third descent into Smaug's lair might have gone, introducing the motif of 'conversation with Smaug'. Smaug's vulnerable patch appears here for the first time, a detail probably inspired by the Sigurd legend (where the dragon-slayer himself could only be slain if stabbed in one secret vulnerable spot; see pp. 500–501) and Tolkien's own earlier account of the dragon Glorund's death in 'Turambar and the Foalókë', stabbed suddenly by surprise in 'a very vital and unfended spot' (BLT II.107).[2] Bilbo's second thoughts and misgivings reappear but are now the result of his talk with the dragon.

(vii)
The Gem of Girion

As with the previous Plot Notes, the final sections of this outline mark the widest divergence from the eventual path the story took. The Arkenstone first appears here in Plot Notes B (although not yet under that name), initially prefigured by a simple statement that 'Bilbo steals a gem', then developed (or perhaps merely elaborated) as 'a marvellous gem' and finally given a name and history as the Gem of Girion.[3] Unlike the cup-theft motif borrowed from *Beowulf* (or, more accurately, from a scholarly reconstruction of a damaged page in the *Beowulf* manuscript), the pilfering of the jewel seems to be Tolkien's own invention, although no doubt influenced by folk-tales and legends.[4] But far from being a hidden treasure the 'expert treasure-hunter' smuggles out without the dwarves' knowledge and keeps concealed as a guilty secret, in this initial conception the dwarves openly offer it to Bilbo as his promised reward, which they apparently insist he has not yet earned. The Gem already has its strange allure and power to cause those who see and handle it to act in uncharacteristic ways to gain it[5] – a motif Tolkien transferred in the sequel to Bilbo's ring, which of course lacked that characteristic in *The Hobbit* itself – but here it is Bilbo, not the chief dwarf (Gandalf/Thorin), who is most affected. In retrospect, the phrase 'Bilbo keeps on looking at his gem' has a somewhat sinister aspect.[6] For more on the Gem of Girion, see Plot Notes C.

(viii)

Bilbo Kills Smaug

Most extraordinary of all is Tolkien's intention of casting Bilbo in the role of dragon-slayer. Admittedly, there is a certain amount of folk-tale logic to this: the eponymous hero of 'Jack and the Beanstalk' – one of the two most famous English fairy tales (the other being 'Jack the Giant Killer')[7] and a perfect example of 'There and Back Again' – is an apparently ordinary person who one day goes off on an unexpected adventure that culminates in his killing an evil monster and coming home with a marvelous treasure. It would mark the apotheosis of little Bilbo, *the* Hobbit, who has passed in the course of the story from 'fat little fellow bobbing on the mat' to reluctant traveller very much out of his depth, to effective warrior (and slayer of dozens of giant spiders), highly competent burglar (who evades the wood-elves in their own halls for weeks if not months), resourceful lucky number (whose plan gets all his companions out of their dungeons and safely away back on their adventure), to here being the only one who dares to do a deed that no hero or warrior could accomplish. It would also have had the effect of making Bladorthin's words from the first chapter deeply ironic:

> '. . . a mighty warrior even a hero. I tried to find one but I had to fall back (I beg your pardon, but I am sure you will understand – dragon slaying is not I believe your speciality) – to fall back on little Bilbo.'
>
> —'The Pryftan Fragment', p. 10.

The motif of Bilbo as dragon-slayer was developed more thoroughly in the next stage of outlines (Plot Notes C), which Humphrey Carpenter quoted from in his biography (*Tolkien: A Biography* [1977], page 179); see my commentary on Plot Notes C, pp. 499–501, for more on this projected plot-thread. For now I will only observe that the projected scheme of Bilbo stabbing the dragon 'as it sleeps, exhausted after battle', while very much in keeping with Jack the Giant Killer's ruthless practicality (see Note 7), has the drawback of creating sympathy in the reader's mind for the villain of the story. The eventual solution Tolkien ultimately arrived at, while much more complex and unexpected, smites down this mass-murderer in the midst of his villainy, which is far more satisfactory from the point of view of the story's moral code.[8]

(ix)
The Poem

The Raft-elves' song needs no explication here, other than to note that while this is evidently the very first rough drafting of the poem many lines emerge that remain exactly as in the final piece. It is worth noting, however, that the fact the plot-note material only takes up half this page and continues over onto the next page may indicate that the poem predates the plot notes. If so, this need not disrupt our projected sequence that Plot Notes B were written before Chapter IX, in which the finished poem appears: Tolkien had already decided by the end of Plot Notes A, written during the composition of Chapter VII, that at least one of the characters was going to escape the Elvenking's Halls by hiding in a barrel and may already by that point have decided on the water-route and hence the need for such a song; see p. 296.

(x)
A Battle Gathering in the West

One of the most remarkable departures between the story projected in this outline and that which Tolkien actually came to write was that the great battle near the end of the story did not take place at the Lonely Mountain, nor indeed did the dwarves play any part in it. Instead, Bilbo apparently parts from his companions after the dragon's death, presumably leaving them in possession of their ancestral home and treasure (although this is not actually stated; contrast Plot Notes C, p. 497) and taking his reward (the Gem of Girion) with him. Wearing his 'suit of silver mail' (which appears here for the first time; see p. 581), he joins the wood-elves and wood-men in their battle against the goblins and wargs, aided by 'a troop of bears' led by Medwed/Beorn.[9] Thus we see here the emergence of the climactic battle in which five armies take part – humans, elves, goblins, wargs, and bears – yet placed in a very different context, and apparently with somewhat different motivations (no doubt essentially to avenge the Great Goblin's death, subjugate the wood-men, and establish goblin/warg dominance over the region; cf. DAA.147–8). At some point the wizard reappears – he is casually mentioned in the immediate aftermath of the battle – but there is no indication of whether or not the eagles would intervene at the last moment, though given Tolkien's fondness for this motif I suspect it would have occurred in some form. Ultimately, rather than bringing Bilbo to the battle Tolkien decided in Phase Three to bring the battle to Bilbo, thus reducing the much more eventful return journey projected here to a long coda ('and back again').

In order to distinguish the battle projected here from the Battle of Five Armies taking place at the Lonely Mountain, I will refer to it as 'the Battle of Anduin Vale', this being the name for the area on either side of the Great River between Mirkwood and the Misty Mountains in the more developed geography of *The Lord of the Rings*.

(xi)

Just a Hobbit Again

Finally, the idea that Bilbo would come safely back home again after all his adventures is affirmed, along with the twin contradictory assurances that he on the one hand 'just becomes a hobbit again' yet on the other that he is 'very different', a writer of poetry, and regarded as 'a bit queer' (i.e., odd). That is, thereafter he is outwardly a normal hobbit but 'different' inside, with his writing poetry (one sample of which, 'Bilbo's first poem', is given as the last poem in the book – see commentary p. 693) as an outward manifestation of this. His journey has changed him, yet that change does not prevent him from putting his adventures behind him and picking up the thread of his daily life. Significantly for the later development of the story, a good deal of attention is given to his ultimate disposal of the Gem of Girion, yet his magic ring is only mentioned in the brief list of loose ends that need to be wrapped up, along with how the key to the Secret Door wound up in the trolls' lair and what the wizard got out of all this – outside of, presumably, amusement ('very amusing for me, very good for you'; see p. 31). And even at this very early stage Tolkien foresaw that in his extreme old age Bilbo would relinquish his greatest treasure ('when he is very old he returns the Gem'), as indeed becomes the case in the opening chapter of *The Lord of the Rings*.

Armed with this detailed five-page set of plot notes outlining the second half of the story, Tolkien was able to resume the Second Phase where he left off and smoothly carry the story forward; see p. 379.

NOTES

1 Originally published in 1937 under the title 'Knocking at the Door'. The date of composition of this poem is not known, but given the examples of two other poems Tolkien published in the same magazine that year ('The Dragon's Visit' [late 1920s?] and 'Iumonna Gold Galdre Bewunden' [1923 or earlier]) it could have been written years before this appearance in *The Oxford Magazine*. This is made more probable by the fact that the poem was clearly inspired by Dunsany's 'The Hoard of the Gibbelins', with perhaps some elements from 'How

Nuth Would Have Practised His Art Upon the Gnoles' as well (both in *The Book of Wonder* [1912]), and Dunsany's influence on Tolkien waned after the *Book of Lost Tales* period. Finally, Douglas Anderson points out that on the typescript of an earlier version of the poem which seems to belong to the 'Bimble Bay' period (late 1920s), Tolkien long afterwards wrote 'Ox. 1927? rev. 1937' (DAA to JDR personal communication, 29th October 2006), thus confirming that the poem's likeliest period of composition dates from just before Tolkien started *The Hobbit.*

2 This detail does not appear in the brief accounts of Glorund's death in the 1926 'Sketch of the Mythology', the 1930 *Quenta*, or the 'Annals of Beleriand'; the 1937 *Quenta Silmarillion* did not reach this point in the story.

3 The name 'Girion' might derive from Gnomish (Sindarin) *gîrin*, meaning 'bygone. old, belonging to former days. olden. former. ancient.' (*Gnomish Lexicon, Parma Eldalamberon* vol. XI.38 & 39). King Long-ago would be a good-enough placeholder name for the Gem's former owner, which in the event Tolkien wound up keeping into the published book.

4 For example, the *Arabian Nights* tale of Aladdin, who removes a single precious item from a vast underground hoard that is worth more than the rest of the treasure all together.

5 The Arkenstone thus entirely reverses its significance in the course of the story's development, from its creation here as a handy portable share of treasure the dwarves intend to give Bilbo to carry home with him as payment for fulfilling his contract, to ultimately being the one piece of treasure in all the horde that the dwarves would never willingly part with.

The problem of how is Bilbo to get a fair share of this vast treasure home again seems to have first occurred to Tolkien in the last paragraph of page 1 of Plot Notes B, with the parenthetical exclamation about 'how to get the stuff back . . . !', inspired by the practical concerns of the dwarves acquiring wagons for carrying food and supplies to the Mountain. The problem no sooner arises than it is solved, for the time being at least, by the creation of the Jem of Girion on page 4 of these same Plot Notes.

6 In specific, the description of how Bilbo, after his return to his home, 'Puts Gem in a safe but looks at it every day' sounds remarkably like Gollum and his ring on his little island. See Plot Notes C, p. 496, for more on the Gem's allure.

7 For unbowdlerized texts of these two folk tales, the best known to derive from native English tradition and not foreign sources such as Perrault, Andersen, or Grimm, see Iona & Peter Opie, *The Classic Fairy Tales* [1974], pages 47–65 and 162–74. Tolkien's reference in his Letter to Waldman grieving that all that had survived of the native English mythology was 'impoverished chap-book stuff' (*Letters* p. 144) is probably a direct reference to these two stories, the oldest surviving versions of which appeared in eighteenth- and early nineteenth-century chapbooks.

8 Note that Tolkien developed this idea at greater length in the 1947 Hobbit, where Bilbo, even in immediate peril of his life, concludes it would be wrong to stab his enemy from ambush; see p. 738.

9 For more on Tolkien's evolving ideas regarding this great battle, and just which armies would take part in it, see the commentary on 'The Battle of Five Armies' on p. 713ff following the Third Phase text.

Chapter IX

IN THE HALLS OF THE ELVENKING

Plot Notes B having done their work, Tolkien was able to resume writing the story at the point he had dropped it, probably having stopped at the beginning of the preceding school term and resuming in the next vacation.

As noted at the end of the preceding chapter, at this point in the manuscript there is a change in the kind of paper Tolkien used. By itself, this might not be enough to prove that a gap in composition had intervened between what are now Chapters VIII and IX of the book, but the presence of Plot Notes B, which cover precisely the material to which the next chapter was devoted, and Tolkien's statement that there were two points where he stopped writing for nearly a year, make it clear that this marks the first of those two major breaks in the composition.

The text resumes on manuscript page 119 (1/1/9:1); as previously noted, on this new kind of paper Tolkien wrote only on the front (as opposed to front-and-back, his practice with the preceding sheets). Therefore henceforth 1 page = 1 sheet.

So they just stopped dead, or sat down, and waited. But Bilbo slipped on his ring; and that is why, when the elves bound the dwarves with ropes in a long line (one behind the other), and counted them, they did not bind or count the little hobbit. Nor did they hear or feel him trotting along behind the torch-light as they led off their prisoners into the forest. Each dwarf was blindfold, and none of them had any idea of the way they were taking; but Bilbo had tied his thread to a tree by the path, and was unwinding it all the way along.[TN1]

At last it gave out. He had just time to fasten one end to a big stone and lay it beside an huge tree, when he saw that only a little way in front the torches had stopped. They had come to a wooden bridge, under which a dark river flowed swift and strong; and at the far end of the bridge on the other side of the water opened the dark mouth of a huge cave in the side of a steep slope of trees that ran down till their feet were in the stream.

Soon the elves and their prisoners began to cross the bridge. Bilbo did not like the look of the cave mouth, and for some time he hesitated; but in the end he scuttled over the bridge and was just in time to pass the gates of the Wood-elves Cavern before it closed behind them with a clang.

The passages were lit with torch light, and the woodelves sang as they marched along the twisting, crossing, and echoing paths. These were not like the goblin-cities: smaller, less deep underground, and filled with a cleaner air. In a great hall with pillars cut out of the living stone, the Elven-king sat on a chair of carven wood. On his head was [a] crown of red-berries, for the autumn was come again. In the spring he wore a crown of woodland flowers. In his hand he had a carven staff of oak.

The prisoners were brought before him, and he told his men to unbind them: 'for they need no ropes <in> here' said he, 'there is no escape through my magic doors, for those who [know not >] are brought once inside'.

Long and searchingly he questioned the dwarves[TN2] about their doings and where they were going, and where they were coming from.[TN3] But they were surly and wd. not answer him, any more than Gandalf had. Indeed less; for they were angry at their treatment.

'What have we done, O king' said Balin,[TN4] the eldest left now Gandalf was gone; 'Is it a crime to be lost in the forest, trapped by spiders; Are the spiders your tame beasts or your pets, if killing them makes you angry?'

[That made >] Asking such a question made him angry at any rate, for the woodelves think the spiders vile and unclean. 'It is a crime to walk in my realm without leave' said the king. 'Do you forget that you were in my realm, using the road my people have made? Do you forget you twice[TN5] pursued and vexed my people in the forest, and roused the spiders with your riot and clamour? At least I have a right to know what brings you here. And if you will not tell me now, I will keep you here until you have learnt sense and manners'.

So he ordered the dwarves each to be put in different cells, and given [drink &] food, but not allowed to pass the doors of their little prisons, until one at least of them was willing to tell him more.

Poor little Bilbo – it was a weary long time he lived in that deep place, all alone and always in hiding, never daring hardly to take off his ring, hardly daring to sleep, even tucked away in the darkest and remotest corners he could find. For something to do, he took to wandering about the wood-king's palace. Magic shut the gates, but he could sometimes get out, if he was quick. Companies of the wood-elves, sometimes with their king at their head would from time to time ride out [on >] to hunting, or to other business in the woods or the lands to the East.[TN6] Then if Bilbo was very nimble he could [nip >] slip out just behind them; though it was a dangerous business. More than once he was nearly caught in the doors as they crashed together when the last elf passed; yet he did not dare to march among them, because of his shadow,[TN7] and for fear of being bumped into and discovered. It was not often that he went out, because it was so difficult to get back[. If he >], and he did not wish to desert the dwarves; nor indeed did he know where in the world to go without them. Unless he kept up with the hunting elves all day – a hard and tiring task – he would somehow have to wander about miserably in the forest alone, until a chance of return came. Then he was very hungry, for he was no hunter. Inside the caves he could pick up a living of some sort by stealing food from store or table when no one was at hand. 'I am like a burglar that cannot get away, but must go on miserably burgling the same house day after day' he thought. 'This is the dreariest and dullest part of all this wretched, tiresome, uncomfortable adventure! I wish I was back in my hobbit-hole by my own warm fireside, with the lamp shining.'[TN8]

Eventually, however, Bilbo by watching and following the guards, and taking what chances he could, managed to find where each dwarf was. He found all their 12 cells in different parts of the underground palace, and soon he was beginning to know his way about quite well.

What was his surprise one day to overhear the guards talking, and to hear that there was another dwarf in prison too – in a specially deep dark place. He guessed, of course, that it was Gandalf. And he soon found out that he was right, though it was some time before he could manage to find the place [or >] when no one was about, and have a word with the chief dwarf.

Gandalf was too wretched to be angry any longer at his misfortune.[TN9] and he could hardly believe it when he heard one evening Bilbo's little voice at the keyhole. Very soon [they >], however, he came to the other side of the door, and spoke long and eagerly with the hobbit outside.

So it was that Bilbo was able in secret to take Gandalf's message to each of the other dwarves in prison, that the chief dwarf was there too, and that no one was to reveal their [business >] errand to the king – not yet, not till Gandalf gave the word. For Gandalf was determined not to ransom himself & his companions with promises of a share in the treasure, until all hope of escaping some other way had disappeared. The other dwarves were almost equally determined – they [knew >] feared the woodelves [share >] would claim all too big a share and the shares of each of them would suffer seriously. Often now they wished they had Bladorthin with them. Before he had always seemed to turn up to help them out of a fix, but now probably all the dark width of Mirkwood was between them. They hoped that one day he would turn up smiling and persuade the grim Elf-king, but they did not expect it. Nor did it happen. From this fix it was just purely Mr Baggins [entirely] on his own, who rescued them.[TN10]

This is how it happened. Bilbo nosing and wandering about had discovered a very interesting thing. The great gates were *not* the only entrance to the [Caves >] Caverns. A stream flowed under part of the lowest caves and joined the main forest-stream a little further to the East, beyond the steep slope [in >] from which the main mouth opened.

Where this underground water came forth out of the hillside there was a water-gate. The rocky roof came down close to the water, and from it a portcullis could be dropped right to the bed of the stream to prevent anyone coming in or out that way. But it was often open for a good deal of traffic went out by the water gate; and if anyone had come in by it, he would have found himself in a dark rough tunnel leading only into the hill. But at one point the roof of the tunnel had been cut away and covered with great oaken trap-doors. These [were in the >] opened up into the king's cellars. There were barrels and barrels and barrels; for the woodelves, and their king specially loved wine; but none grew in those parts,[TN11] and it was brought from far away, from their kindred in the south, or from the vineyards of men in distant lands. Hiding by one of the huge [> large] barrels Bilbo discovered the trapdoors and their use, and listening to the talk heard how wine came up the rivers or over land to the Long Lake and a town of men that had grown up there, built out on bridges far into the lake as a protection against enemies of all sorts and especially against the dragon of the Mountain.

From the Lake-town[TN12] it was brought up the Forest River. The barrels were often all just fastened together like big rafts and poled or rowed against the stream; sometimes they were piled on flat boats. When the barrels were empty they cast them through the trapdoors, opened the water-gate and out the barrels floated on the stream, bobbing along while they were carried by the current to a place where the bank jutted out far down the stream and near to the very Eastern edge of Mirkwood. There they were collected and tied together and floated back to Lake town which stood near the place where the Forest river ran into the Lake.

For a long time Bilbo used to think about this water gate, and wonder how [> if] it could be used for the escape of his friends. At last he had a desperate idea.

The evening meal had been taken to the prisoners. The guards were tramping away down the passages taking the torch-light with them leaving everything in darkness. Then Bilbo heard the king's butler, bidding the chief of the guards goodnight. 'And come down with me' he said 'and taste the new wine that has just come in. I shall be hard at work clearing the cellars of the empty wood [far into >] tonight; so let us have a drink first to help the labour'.[TN13]

Bilbo thought at last the chance had come when his idea might be tried. He followed the butler and the chief of the guards, until he saw them sit in one of the cellars; and soon they began to drink the wine and to make merry. What luck favoured him here, I cannot tell. It must be potent wine to make a wood-elf drowsy. But this it would seem was the heady brew of the great gardens of Dorwinion in the warm South, not meant for his soldiers or his servants, but for the king's feasts only, and for smaller bowls, not the butler's jugs. Soon the chief guard fell asleep and not long after the butler put his head on the table and snored beside him.[TN14]

Then in crept the hobbit, and soon the chief guard had no keys; but Bilbo was going as fast as he could, [though his bundle >] heavy though the great bunch seemed to his small arms, along the passages to the cells. His heart was in his mouth, in spite of his ring, for he could not prevent an occasional clink, which set him all a tremble.

First he unlocked Balin's door and locked it again as soon as the dwarf was outside. Balin was most surprised, I can tell you, for Bilbo had yet said nothing about his idea. [He wanted >] Glad though he was to get out of his wearisome little stony room, he wanted to know what Bilbo was going to do and all about it.

'No time just now' said the hobbit. 'You just follow me. We must all keep together, and not risk getting separated. [If you >] We all must go or none, and this is our last chance. If this is found out, we'll never have another. Goodness knows where the king will put you then, with chains on hand and feet, probably, too'.

So he went from door to door until his following had grown to twelve; and they were none too nimble after their long imprisonment. Bilbo's heart thumped every time they bumped into one another, or grumbled or whispered in the dark. 'Drat the dwarvish racket!' he said often to himself. Still nothing happened, and no one met them. As a matter of fact there was a great feast in the woods that night, ere the winter should come on; and in the halls above there was merrymaking too.[TN15]

[The last >] At last they came to Gandalf's dungeon, far down in a deep place, and fortunately [not far >] near to the cellars.

'Upon my word' said Gandalf, when Bilbo opened the door, and whispered to him to come out and join his friends, 'upon my word the wizard spoke true, as usual. A pretty fine burglar you make it seems, when the time comes. I'm sure we are at all forever at your service, whatever happens after this. But what comes next?'

At last Bilbo felt the time had come to explain his idea, but he did not feel at all sure how the dwarves would take it. And he was quite right. They did not like it at all at first.

'We shall be bruised and battered, or drowned, for certain' they [said >] muttered. 'We thought you had got some sensible idea, when you managed to get hold of the keys; but this is a mad notion'.

'Very well' said Bilbo very downcast, and also rather annoyed, 'Come along back to your nice cells, and I will lock you all in, and we shall be all happy and comfortable, and as we were, and no harm done'.

The [mere] thought of it was too much for them. So in the end they just had to do as he suggested, because of course it was out of the question for them to try to find their way up into the upper halls, or to fight their way out of the gates that closed by magic.

Into the cellar they crept past the door through which the chief guard and the butler cd be seen still happily snoring with smiles upon their faces. There would be a different expression on the chief guard's face next day; but before they went on Bilbo kindheartedly put the keys back on his belt.

'That will save him some of the trouble' he thought. 'He wasn't a bad fellow – and how it will puzzle 'em all too. They will [wonder >] think that we had a very strong magic indeed to pass between locked doors and disappear. Disappear! We have got to get busy very quick, if that is to happen.'

Balin was told off to watch the guard and the butler, and give warning if they stirred. There was little time to spare. Before long as Bilbo knew [the elves whose >] some elves were under orders to come down, and get the empty barrels through the trap-door into the stream. There they were already standing in rows in the middle of the floor waiting to be [stuffed >] pushed away.

Some were wine barrels, and these could not be opened without a deal of noise, or easily secured again.[TN16] But among them were many others that had been used for bringing other stuffs of all sorts to the king's palace. They soon found thirteen with plenty room enough for a dwarf each. In fact some were too roomy, and the dwarfs as they climbed in, thought anxiously of the shaking and bumping they would get inside. Bilbo did his best to find straw and such like stuff to pack them in as cosily as could be.[TN17] The last he had to stuff himself, and fasten on the lid. Soon twelve dwarves were packed. Gandalf[TN18] gave a lot of trouble, and turned and twisted in his tub and grumbled like a dog in a small kennel. Last came Balin, who now left his watch. Not a bit too soon. Bilbo had hardly finished fixing on his lid: when there came a sound of voices and lights. A number of elves came laughing and talking into the cellars, and singing snatches of song.

They had left a feast in one of the halls and were bent on returning as soon as they could.[TN19]

'Where is old Galion the butler' said one. 'I haven't seen him at the tables tonight. He ought to be here now, to show us what is to be done.'

'I shall be angry if the old slowcoach is late' said another. 'I have no wish to wait down here, while the song is up'.

'Ha! ha!' came a cry 'here is the old villain, with his head on a jug' Galion did not at all like being shaken and wakened; and still less being laughed at.

'You're late' he said. 'Here am I waiting and waiting while you fellows drink and enjoy yourselves and forget your tasks. Small wonder, if I fall asleep for weariness'.

'Small wonder' said they 'when the explanation stands close to hand. Come give us a draught of the same, and we will fall to. No need to wake the old turn-key guard. He has had his share by the looks of it.' So they drank once round and became mighty merry all of a sudden. 'Save us Galion' cried some. 'You began your feasting early. You have stacked some full casks here instead of empty ones, if there is anything in weight'.

'Get on with your job' grumbled the butler 'There is nothing in the feeling of weight in an idle toss-pot's arms. Those are the ones to go and no others. Do as I say'.

'[On > Well >] Very well very well' they cried 'On your own head be it, if you have the king's best wine pushed into the river, for the lake men to make merry on for nothing; or his full buttertubs.'[TN20]

Roll – roll – roll – roll.
roll-roll-rolling down the hole
Heave-ho Splash-plump
down they go! down they bump!

So they sang as first one [tub and then >] barrel then another rumbled to the dark opening, and was pushed off [with a >] into the dark water some feet below. Some were wine-barrels, or tubs really empty. Some were tubs neatly packed with a dwarf each. Down they all went together bump on top of one another, jostling in the water, bobbing away down the current and knocking against the walls of the tunnel.

It was at this point that Bilbo [wasn't in >] saw the weak point of his plan. Very likely you have already thought of it, and are laughing at him; but I don't suppose you would have done half as well yourself in his place. Of course he wasn't in a barrel himself[;

and so >]! It looked as if he would get left behind and lose his friends altogether (nearly all of them had disappeared through the dark trapdoor already) and have to stay lurking as a permanent burglar in the elf-caves for ever![TN21] For even suppose he could have got out of the front-gates at once (which he couldn't)[TN22] he had a precious small chance of [catching >] finding them all again before they came to the place where all the barrels were collected. Goodness knows, too, what would happen there, for he had not had time to tell the dwarves all he had learnt, or what his idea was of the best thing to do at that point.

The elves being very merry were beginning to sing a song round the river-door. Some had gone to haul on the ropes which pulled up the watergate ready to let out the barrels when they were all afloat below.

Down the swift dark stream you go
Back to woods you once did know
Leave the halls and caverns deep,
Leave the northern mountains steep,
where the forest wide and dim
Stoops in shadow grey and grim!
Float beyond the world of trees
Out into the whispering breeze,
past the rushes, past the reeds,
past the marsh's waving weeds;
through the mist that riseth white
Up from mere and pool at night!

Follow follow stars that leap,
Up the heavens high and steep
[Through the >] Turn when dawn comes over land
over rapid over sand

South away and south away
Seek the sunlight and the day,
back to pasture back to mead
where the kine and oxen feed
Back to gardens on the hills
where the berry swells and fills
under sunlight under day
South away and south away
Down the swift dark stream you go
Back to <woods> you once did know![TN23]

Now the last barrel was being rolled to the opening. In despair poor little Bilbo caught hold of it, and was pushed over the edge with it. Down into the water he fell, splash!, in the cold dark water. He came up spluttering clinging to the barrel; but he could not climb on top of it, for every time he tried, it rolled round and ducked him under again.

He heard the elves still singing in the cellars above. Then the trapdoors went to with a boom, and their voices faded away. He was in the dark tunnel, [cold >] floating in icy water, all alone – for you can't count friends that are all packed up in barrels, can you? Very soon a grey patch came in the darkness ahead. He heard the creak of the water gate being hauled up; and he found he was in the midst of a bobbing and bumping mass of casks and tubs all pressing together to pass through under the arch and out into the open stream. He had as much as he could do to prevent himself from being hustled and battered to bits. At last the jostling mass began to break up and swing off one by one under the stony arch and away away. He saw now that it could have been no good at all, if he had managed to sit on his barrel – there was no room to spare, not even for a hobbit, between the barrel and the stooping [> suddenly stooping] roof where the gate was.

Out they went under the overhanging branches of the trees on either bank. Bilbo wondered for a moment what the dwarves were feeling, and if a lot of water was getting inside their tubs. Some of the barrels that bobbed by him in the gloom seemed pretty low in the water; and he guessed these had dwarves inside. 'I hope I [> we] put the lids on well' thought he. But he was really far more anxious about himself. He was shivering with cold, and wondered if he would die of it, before the luck turned, and if he would be able to hang on much longer, even long enough for there to be a chance of getting near the bank, and slipping off onto dry land.[TN24]

His chance came all right. The [eddy] current carried several barrels close <ashore> at one point, and there they stuck for a while against some hidden root. Bilbo took the opportunity to scramble up the side of his barrel while it was held firm against another. Up he crawled like a drowned rat, and lay on the top spread out to keep the balance as best he could; and wondered whether he wouldn't be suddenly rolled off into the water again when they started. He did not have to wonder long. Soon they broke free and turn and twisted off down the stream again and out into the main current. He had a dreadful job to stick on, but he managed it. Luckily he was very light and the dwarf inside (actually it was Bombur) was fat, and probably too frightened to stir.[TN25] All the same it felt like trying to ride [a round-bellied >] without [*cancelled*: reins] bridle or stirrups a round-bellied pony that was always thinking of rolling on the grass.

So at last he came to a place where the trees on either side got thinner. The paler sky could be seen between them. The dark river opened out into a wider place and was joined by the main water of the Forest Stream flowing from [> past] the king's great doors.[TN26] There was a pale sheet of water no longer overshadowed but with dancing and broken reflections of cloud and star upon it. Here the incoming water of the Forest River swept them all away to the North Bank, where [a long shore of >] a regular bay had been eaten away walled by a jutting cape of hard rock. There was a stony gravely shore, where most of the casks ran aground, though some went on to thump against the stony pier. But there were people on the look-out on the banks. All the barrels were poled and pushed together into the shallows; and there they were left till morning. Poor dwarves! Bilbo slipped off and waded ashore, and sneaked off to the huts by the water's edge. He no longer thought twice about picking up a supper uninvited if he got the chance; he had been obliged to do it for so long; and he knew what it was now only too well to be really hungry not just interested in the dainties of a well-filled larder. He caught a glimpse of fire too, which appealed to him with his dripping and ragged clothes clinging to him cold & clammy.

There is no need to tell you of his adventures that night, for now we are drawing near the end of the journey, and the last great end of the adventure,[TN27] and we must be hurrying on. He was given away by his wet footsteps and the trail of the drippings and there was a fine commotion in the riverside village when he escaped with a loaf and flagon [> water-flask] and a pie which didn't belong to him into the woods. He had to pass the night wet as he was, but the flagon helped him to do that; actually he lay <on> some dry leaves and dozed although the year was getting late and the air was chilly.[TN28]

He woke with a sneeze! It was grey morning. There was a merry racket down by the river. They were making up a raft, and would soon be off down to the Lake. Bilbo sneezed again! He was no longer dripping, but he was cold all over. He scrambled down [as best he could >] as fast as his stiff legs would take him, and managed in the general business to get onto the mass of casks now all lashed together. Luckily there was no sun to cast awkward shadows.[TN29] There was a mighty pushing of poles, and a heaving and <illegible>[TN30] of men [> elves] standing in the shallow water.

'This is a heavy load' some grumbled. 'They float too deep – some of these are never empty, I'll swear' said another. 'Had they come ashore in the light we might have had a look inside' they said. 'No time now' <said> the raft-men 'Shove off.'

And off they went slowly at first until they passed the little point of rock fending off with their poles, and caught the main stream, and went swiftly off down down towards the Lake.[TN31]

Once again there is no chapter break between what became the end of Chapter IX and the start of Chapter X, which in the manuscript is a simple paragraph break in the middle of a page (Marq. 1/1/11:1). Even in the First Typescript, where the book has already been divided into chapters, the chapters start more often than not in the middle of a page (this being the case for both the start and stop of Chapter IX; cf. 1/1/59:1 and 1/1/60:1). By contrast, the Second Typescript, for all its shortcomings (see p. xxiv), does start new chapters on fresh pages (1/1/39:1, 1/1/40:1, &c.).

The text of the story resumes on p. 435 of this book.

TEXT NOTES

1 At this point, Tolkien wrote in the left margin 'not needed'. That is, he decided to drop the Theseus theme and omit all mention of the ball of spider-thread by which Bilbo navigated the dark maze of Mirkwood. Since this comment is written in pencil, it belongs to the period when he was creating the First Typescript.

This sentence was recast in the typescript to emphasize the hopelessness of the party's situation when captured: 'Each dwarf was blindfolded, but that did not make much difference, for even Bilbo with the use of his eyes could not see where they were going, and neither he nor the others knew where they had started from anyway.' – that is, in the revised version of the story (see 'The Enchanted Stream'), as opposed to the original where they were captured on the path.

Another typescript passage in the next sentence seems intended to paint the elves in a better light, more in keeping with their characterization in the final parts of the book: 'the elves were making the dwarves go as fast as ever they could (of course they did not know how ill and tired their prisoners were)' (typescript page 93†; 1/1/59:1–2). Similarly, in the typescript the king orders them unbound when he sees them 'for they were ragged and weary'. The first of these two passages was changed in page proofs (Marq. 1/2/2 page 178) to 'as fast as ever they could, *sick and weary as they were. The king had ordered them to make haste.*', the reading in the published book.

† This had originally been the bottom half of the original last page of the preceding chapter, but after the top half (now 1/1/30:5) was cut away the bottom half was renumbered from 92 to 93.

2 Tolkien originally wrote simply 'He questions the dwarves', then cancelled it and began the next paragraph with a new line. Note the use of present tense, which stylistically matches the Plot Notes more than the full text of the book.

3 This passage was recast slightly by an addition written in the upper margin and marked for insertion at this point: '. . . where they were going, and where they were coming from; *but he did not tell them that Gandalf was also in his hands. The dwarves* were surly and wd. not answer him . . .'

4 Originally another name was written before Balin's, then completely blotted out, leaving a square of solid ink. Use of a light table and careful examination of the few surviving ligatures leads me to believe the cancelled name to be either *Dwalin* or *Bifur*; *Bofur* is also a possibility. Unfortunately, the obliteration is too nearly complete for any certainty.

This is the first time that we are told Balin is the oldest of all the dwarves after Gandalf, or indeed that Gandalf their leader is even older than Balin (described the first time Bilbo sees him as 'a very old-looking dwarf' (p. 32) and often referred to as 'old Balin'. According to the House of Durin family tree (*LotR.*1117) – drawn up more than twenty years later and representing a different strata of the mythology – Thorin was 195 years old at the time of Bilbo's journey and Balin 178; Dwalin, the next eldest of whom we have any record, 169.

5 Note that the Elvenking makes no reference to having had his own revel disturbed by the dwarves, for the very good reason that the 'woodland king' scene did not enter into the story until the First Typescript (see 'The Enchanted Stream', p. 354). Still, it is curious that he refers to the dwarves' having '*twice* pursued and vexed my people' when in all versions of the Mirkwood chapter they encountered the elusive elven feasters *three* times, not twice. This slip is rectified in the typescripts, which correctly refer to three times that the starving dwarves 'pursue and trouble' the feasters.

6 'other business in . . . the lands to the East.': this phrase survived into the published book, but we never receive any explication of what that business might be.

7 his shadow: It seems worth emphasizing yet again that Bilbo's ring has different powers from Frodo's ring in the sequel, and cannot disguise his shadow when it makes the rest of him invisible. The image of Bilbo trapped inside the fortress of his enemies after a tricky gate closes behind him may derive at least in part from Chrétien's *Yvain: The Knight of the Lion*, which vividly places its hero in similar straits.

8 At the end of this paragraph, Tolkien later added the following, writing in small letters to squeeze it into the available space:

He often wished [to >] that he cd. get a message for help/B

– that is, a message for help to Bladorthin, this having been the means whereby they were rescued in the projections sketched out in Plot Notes A, wherein Bilbo set forth to fetch aid.

The typescript contains a new sentence developing this thought, only to firmly reject it:

> He often wished, too, that he could get a message for help sent to the wizard, but that of course was quite impossible, and he soon

> realized that if anything was to be done it would have to be done by his own small self.

The published book repeats this phrasing, except that at the end it substitutes 'it would have to be done by Mr. Baggins, alone and unaided.'

9 The typescript adds 'and was even beginning to think of telling the king all about his treasure and his quest (which shows how low-spirited he had become)'. In the original, even though imprisoned for much longer with no idea whether his companions had survived Gandalf showed no signs of yielding to his captor's demands.

10 The typescript expands upon this passage:

> For Thorin had taken heart again hearing how the hobbit had rescued his companions from the spiders, and was determined once more not to ransom himself with promises to the king of a share in the treasure, until all hope of escaping in any other way had disappeared, until in fact the remarkable Mr. Invisible Baggins (of whom he began to have a very high opinion after all) had altogether failed to think of something clever.
>
> The other dwarves quite agreed when they got the message. They all thought their own shares in the treasure (which they quite regarded as theirs, in spite of their plight and the still unconquered dragon) would suffer seriously if the woodelves claimed part of it, and they all trusted Bilbo. Just what Gandalf had said would happen, you see. Perhaps that was part of his reason for going off and leaving them.
>
> Bilbo however did not feel nearly so hopeful as they did. He did not like being depended on by everyone, and he wished he had the wizard at hand. But that was no use: probably all the dark distance of Mirkwood lay between them. He sat and thought and thought, until his head nearly burst, but no bright idea would come. One invisible ring was a jolly fine thing, but it was not much good among fourteen. But of course, as you have guessed, he did rescue his friends in the end, and this is how it happened.
>
> —Marq. 1/1/59:4.

11 In the First Typescript (1/1/59:4) this became '*was very fond of* wine, *though* none grew in those parts' – corrected in page proofs to '. . . though *no vines* grew'.

12 This sentence originally read 'From the Lake Town it was brought *on rafts, or else got floated up the Forest river that flowed also into the Lake which formed part of the course of the Running River*'.

This part of the story marks the emergence of the name Lake Town. First the story refers merely to 'the Long Lake and a town of men that had grown up there, built out on bridges far into the lake'. In the next sentence this settlement is referred to as 'the Lake-town', more as a common noun than a name. But by the end of this paragraph it has become a proper name as the phrase 'to Lake town' indicates. Remarkably enough, this name had appeared long before, in the very first stage of composition, when Tolkien used it as a label on the rough sketch-map incorporated into the Pryftan Fragment (see p. 19 and the Frontispiece). But when he came to write Plot Notes B he had either forgotten the name or chose not to use it; only now does it re-emerge. For a similar example of Tolkien proposing and then not using a name (at least, not for some time), see the opening of Plot Notes A.

13 The chief guard's reply first appears in the typescript, in exactly the same words that appear in the final book; he is without dialogue in the original.

14 The typescript includes the detail that the drunken butler went on talking without noticing that his friend was no longer listening, as in the final book.

15 This end-of-autumn feast 'ere the winter should come on' (probably corresponding to the Celtic feast of Samhain, roughly the 1st of November in our calendar), is another indication of the extended time-line of the original conception. Far from having already arrived in Lake Town by the beginning of autumn (in time for a feast on Bilbo's birthday, 22nd September, according to the much later chronology of *The Lord of the Rings*), they here escape from the elf-mound at the *end* of autumn.

For the theme of elves being taken unawares by intruders at festival time, see *The Silmarillion* (*Silm.*75, 242, & 248). This idea goes very far back in the mythology – cf. BLT I.144 & 146 (Melko's attack on Fëanor's home and slaying his father during Manwë's great reconciliation feast), BLT II.172 (Melko's attack on Gondolin as they prepare to celebrate the dawn festival known as the Gates of Summer), and HME IV.153 (1930 *Quenta*: 'and [Eärendel] came at a time of festival even as Morgoth and Ungoliant had in ages past'.

16 This sentence was originally preceded by 'Into twelve barrels, twelve dwarves got. There was plenty of room'. The typescript version of the following sentence adds details of the 'other stuffs' that came in barrels: 'butter, apples, and all sorts of things'.

17 This sentence was originally followed by 'It was an anxious and a busy time. Soon twelve dwarves were packed. Last came Balin whom'. The spelling 'dwarfs' in the preceding sentence is clear in the manuscript (Ms. page 124; Marq. 1/1/9:6), replaced in the typescript by the more familiar 'dwarves' (Ts. page 98; Marq. 1/1/59:6).

18 This marks the last appearance of Gandalf the dwarf – as the late Taum Santoski remarked, Gandalf goes into the barrel but it is Thorin who emerges six manuscript pages later.

19 This line was originally followed with 'The guard and the butler woke with the sound. Up they jumped with a start'.

The name Galion, in the next line, is significant, as he is the only elf named in *The Hobbit* (Elrond being half-elven, and the reference to Tinúviel not surviving into the published book). The name is probably Gnomish, composed of the elements *gal-*, or light (cf. the *Gnomish Lexicon*, page 37) – an element that also appears in the familiar names

*Gala*driel ('lady of light') and Gil*gal*ad ('star-light') – and *-ion*, here probably a patronymic suffix (cf. Salo, *A Gateway to Sindarin*, p. 165). If so, then it would mean something like 'son of light'.

'Galion' was immediately preceded in the manuscript by another cancelled name, probably incomplete, which looks to have been *Bong* or possibly *Bomg*. I can make nothing of this, unless it contains the element *bo(n)*, meaning 'son of' (*Gnomish Lexicon*, p. 23).

20 Tolkien originally began the next page with the line

'Those are no wine casks there' said Galion.

but he cancelled this, turned the page upside down, and began again with the elves' song.

21 This quick glimpse of Bilbo's possible fate is remarkably like what happened to Gollum, when 'the goblins came, and he was cut off from his friends far under the mountains.' (p. 156).

22 Deleted: 'he had only the faintest notion of the direction of the Forest Stream'.

23 For the first rough draft of this poem, see Plot Notes B (pp. 364–5). Aside from the addition of punctuation and capitalization, the version here corresponds exactly to that published in *The Hobbit*, with two exceptions: the substitution of the word 'cold' for 'high' in line fourteen ('Up the heavens *cold* and steep'), a change that first appears in the typescript, and the replacement of 'woods' – the reading in both typescripts – by 'lands' ('Back to *lands* you once did know') in the final line.

24 The typescript version of this passage reads '. . . able to hang on, and whether he should risk the chance of letting go and trying to swim to the bank'. This is notable not just for its realistic treatment of hypothermia (something everyone who, like Tolkien, lived through the era of the Titanic disaster and U-boat campaign of the Great War would have been familiar with) but because it plainly shows that the motif of Shire-hobbits being afraid of water and not able to swim was a late invention, belonging to *The Lord of the Rings* era, and not part of the original conception at all: Bilbo had shown no disquiet at riding in the little boat during the Enchanted Stream interpolation, and he is apparently at ease as no *LotR* hobbit would be in his stay at Lake Town, which would have struck one of the Shire hobbits of the later book as a profoundly unnatural and disquieting place. And of course no hydrophobe would conceive of a plan of escaping by barrel down an unknown river, much less be able to carry it out.

25 The detail that Bilbo rode atop Bombur's barrel disappeared; the typescript recasts both this and the preceding sentence, replacing them with

> . . . he had as bad a job as he feared to stick on; but he managed it somehow though it was miserably uncomfortable. Luckily he was very light and the barrel was a good big one and being a little leaky had shipped a small amount of water. All the same . . .

The first sentence was revised again sometime after the Second Typescript had been made (that is, probably at the time of revising the book to send it to the printer):

> he found it quite as difficult to stick on as he had feared; but he managed it somehow . . .

26 The intended correction to change 'the Forest Stream flowing from the king's great doors' to '. . . flowing *past* the king's great doors' either postdates the typescripts or else failed to get picked up by them and so does not appear in the final book (cf. DAA.237). Note, however, that this intended change would have made the text match the scene shown in the final picture of those doors ('The Elvenking's Gate'; DAA.224/H-S#121), which clearly depicts the water as flowing moat-like past the entrance, not issuing forth from it (a motif apparently displaced to the Lonely Mountain's Front Gate; contrast Plate VII [bottom] with 'The Front Gate', DAA.256/H-S#130).

27 The manuscript page was revised to read '. . . drawing near the end of the *Eastward* journey, and the last & great*est* end of the adventure' – i.e., the *and back again* element of 'there and back again' seems suppressed at this point. This is the first of several remarks by the narrator about the story's approaching end, which nevertheless remains farther off than it seemed, and doubtless further than the author anticipated, if we are to judge by the plot-notes.

28 Bilbo's nefarious adventures in the raft-elves' village were recast several times, first in the manuscript by the replacement of 'flagon' with *water-flask* on its first occurrence – though the second occurrence of 'flagon' remains unchanged in the next sentence, where it becomes all too clear it was not filled with water. By the First Typescript, the water-flask has become 'a leather bottle of wine' and it is the contents of 'the bottle' that enable Bilbo to sleep warmly, cold and wet as he is.

The pie Bilbo steals, by the way, is almost certainly a meat-pie – the original meaning of the word, according to the OED – rather than the fruit-pie that the word conjures up for modern American ears: marvellous as the elves may be, it's unlikely they have a pastry-chef making dessert among their huts for the raft-workers; cf. the simple travel-food (bread, fruit, and wine) Gildor and his fellows share with Frodo in Chapter III of *The Lord of the Rings*. Even the great open-air feasts that lured Gandalf and company from the path are noted more for free-flowing drink and smell of roasting meat than for sweets or dainties; cf. DAA/.204.

Bilbo's exploits in the typescript and final version are complicated by his catching a cold from his dunking: '. . . wet footsteps and the trail of drippings *that he left wherever he went or sat; and also he began to sneeze, and whenever he tried to hide he was found out by the terrific explosions of his suppressed sneezes. Very soon* there was a fine commotion . . .' (I/I/59:10).

29 This paragraph appears in the typescript in slightly revised form that exactly achieves the text of the published book; the most significant

changes are the splitting off of the final sentence to form the core of a short paragraph of its own and the addition to this sentence of the clause '*and for a mercy he did not sneeze again for a good while*'.

30 The corresponding word in the typescript and published book reads 'shoved', but the illegible word in the manuscript seems to begin with an *l* and to end with *ly*. Note also the indecision throughout this scene of whether the raft-workers were 'men' or 'elves', anticipating Arthur Ransome's objection (see Appendix IV) and creating some confusion whether men from the Long Lake or servants of the elven-king are intended here.

31 For the 'little point of rock' which they must round before getting fairly underway in the main current, see Plate VIII [top] and also Tolkien's painting 'Bilbo Comes to the Huts of the Raft-elves' (DAA plate II [bottom]; H-S#124); the point in question lies almost in the exact center of each picture but is more prominent in the coloured pencil sketch reproduced in this book. A slightly different depiction of the scene appears in his watercolour sketch for this scene (*Pictures by Tolkien* plate 13; H-S#122), where the point lies upstream of the little settlement (although the watercolour sketch is more accurate in showing Bilbo's arrival at night, not at sunrise as in the final piece).

Once Tolkien had divided the book up into chapters, during the Third Phase of his work on the book, he either re-wrote what became the final lines of each chapter to end on a more dramatic note or inserted short chapter-ending paragraphs. In this case, he chose to do the latter, with the following paragraph first appearing in the typescript. Note the use of present tense, which associates it with the (well-informed though not omniscient) narrator's voice rather than the story proper:

> They had escaped the dungeons of the king and were through the wood, but whether alive or dead still remains to be seen.

(i)
The Vanishing People

With the wood-elves, we have finally come full circle to what, had this been one of the Lost Tales, would have been either the starting point or the core of the book. With the inversion of Tolkien's invented races we have already discussed back in the commentary to the conclusion of Chapter I (see pp. 76 & 78), *The Hobbit* starts far from the elf-centric core of all Tolkien's earlier works in the legendarium[1] (perhaps one reason why he was sometimes ambivalent about whether it was or was not part of the mythology). Bilbo's story only comes to a sustained treatment of the elves mid-way through the book, and even then views them only from outside, and relatively briefly, before passing on. The flighty elves in the trees surrounding the Last Decent House (Rivendell) had been more like the fairies of Elizabethan and Victorian tales, a tradition Tolkien was probably first exposed to in Knatchbull-Hugesson's *Stories for My Children* [1870] – see *Letters* pp. 407 & 453 – and himself contributed to in 'Goblin Feet' [1915], 'Tinfang Warble' [1914], and similar early poems during the era when that tradition reached its lowest ebb in Barrie's Tinkerbell [1904] and Conan Doyle's flower-fairies of the Cottingley Photographs [1920]. By contrast, the wood-elves harken back to a more sinister side of faerie belief, one dominant throughout the Middle Ages and surviving into at least the nineteenth and possibly early twentieth century in Ireland and the more isolated parts of Britain.[2]

Tolkien professed, in his Andrew Lang lecture (revised and expanded as 'On Fairy-Stories'), not to be an expert in faerie lore,[3] but this is simply typical modesty on his part, as the essay itself shows; his definition of 'expert' required exhaustive, comprehensive knowledge of all the publications in a field (cf. his Beowulf essay, which although well-researched includes his disclaimer against having read every book ever written about his topic). His interest in elves dates back at least to his undergraduate days[4] and possibly much earlier – the wood-elves of Mirkwood display so many traditional traits ascribed to elves in folklore that it is clear Tolkien knew and directly drew on those folklore traditions.[5] Although he chose not to draw from modern works such as Lord Dunsany's *The King of Elfland's Daughter* (published in 1924, only some seven years earlier, by an author Tolkien admired and who had heavily influenced his earlier work),[6] even a cursory examination of traditional elf-behavior in folklore as described in Katharine Briggs' *A Dictionary of Fairies* [1976] or in *The Vanishing People: Fairy Lore and Legends* [1978] shows that Tolkien had not chosen to call his *Eldar* 'elves' haphazardly but, like the cooks in his metaphor of the great Cauldron of Story (OFS.31), had picked and chosen from among the various strands of tradition with a fine, discriminating eye: his wood-elves are recognizably the elves of folk-lore belief.

Consider, for example, the elves of British folk-lore as described by Briggs. Among their characteristics was their ability to vanish from mortals' sight in the blink of an eye (a characteristic Tolkien refers to pointedly early in 'On Fairy-Stories'; cf. OFS.11); this feature is in fact one of the reasons Briggs calls her book *The Vanishing People.*[7] In *The Hobbit* this is paralleled by the scenes where the elven feasters thrice disappear when all their lights are suddenly and simultaneously extinguished. In itself, this looks like a realistic rationalization of how the old legend might have started ('Somebody kicked the fire', p. 306), but an uncanny element remains: how to explain 'hundreds of torches and many fires' which on the one hand appear so suddenly that they 'must have been lit . . . by magic' ('The Enchanted Stream' p. 354), only to have all the lights disappear 'as if by magic' (Ch. VIII, pp. 306–7), all simultaneously snuffed out in an instant. These elf-lights seem to have something of the air of a will-o'-the-wisp about them; we have already been told that the feast thus illuminated had an 'enchanting' aroma (p. 353) that lured the travellers to stray from their way and meet disaster, and there are hints that the forest clearings are enchanted spots (e.g., elf-rings or fairy circles) – cf. a passage in the typescript when the spiders suddenly break off their pursuit of the fleeing dwarves as soon as the latter enter the fairy-ring:

> The dwarves then noticed that they had come to the edge of a ring where elf-fires had been. Whether it was one of those they had seen the night before, they could not tell. But *it seemed that some good magic lingered in such spots*, which the spiders did not like . . .
>
> —First Typescript 1/1/58:15; italics mine.

The motif of enchantment falling upon a mortal who steps into a fairy-ring, as happens to first Bilbo and then Gandalf (Thorin), also derives from traditional folklore: Briggs gives several examples, most of which involve the mortal joining briefly in a fairy dance (rather than, as here, a feast)[8] only to discover that vast stretches of time had passed in what seemed mere minutes – cf. Bombur's dream of 'a great feast going on, *going on for ever*' ('The Enchanted Stream' p. 352; emphasis mine).[9] To have the hobbit or dwarves caught up in a tarantella would hardly have suited the solemn mood Tolkien had worked so hard to establish for the Mirkwood chapter; the substitution of enchanted sleep makes a reasonable equivalent but raises some interesting questions of its own. Bombur's dream of enjoying a great feast while in fact he is slowly starving in an enchanted sleep, and Bilbo's dream of joining the feast when he too is enchanted upon stepping into the elf-ring and is in fact not eating but lying sleeping on the ground, suggests that we are seeing here examples of what Tolkien in 'On Fairy-Stories' called 'Faërian drama':

> If you are present at a Faërian drama . . . [t]he experience may be very similar to Dreaming . . . [b]ut in Faërian drama you are in a dream that some other mind is weaving, and the knowledge of that alarming fact may slip from your grasp . . . You are deluded – whether that is the intention of the elves . . . is another question. They at any rate are not themselves deluded. (OFS.49)

I take this to mean that what among the elves is a high art presents itself to mortal minds, like Bilbo's and Bombur's (and presumably Gandalf's), as a dream. In short, those who fall under the spell of the elves' enchantment are overwhelmed and can no longer distinguish fantasy from reality; they may even come to prefer the pleasant dream over the harsh reality:

> 'I was having such a lovely dream,' he grumbled, 'all about having a most gorgeous dinner'.
>
> 'Good heavens! he has gone like Bombur,' they said. 'Don't tell

> us about dreams. Dream dinners aren't any good, and we can't share them'.
>
> 'They are the best I am likely to get in this beastly place' he muttered as he lay down beside the dwarves and tried to go back to sleep and find his dream again.
>
> —First Typescript; see p. 354.

Casting people into a trance or sleep while they carried them off, as the elves do here with Gandalf, is yet another well-known fairy trick; Briggs cites a number of examples in her chapter 'Captives in Fairyland' in *The Vanishing People* (cf. page 104):

> Gandalf was caught much more fast than those bound by spiders! You remember Bilbo falling like a log into sleep as he stepped into the feasting ring? Next time Gandalf had stepped forward; and as the lights went out he fell like a stone enchanted. All the noise of the dwarves lost in the night, their cries as the spiders caught them, and all the sounds of the battle next day, had passed over him. Till the wood-elves (and wood elves the people were of course) came to him and bound him, and carried him away.
>
> —Chapter VIII, pp. 314–5.

Similarly, in *Sir Orfeo*, a thirteenth-century adaptation of the classical Orpheus story to fit medieval faerie-lore, Lady Heurodis (Eurydice) is first approached and claimed by the elves in her dreams, and only later carried off bodily; made to vanish in broad daylight when the elves come for her, disappearing 'by magic' (line 193) out of the middle of a circle of armed guards.[10]

The parallel to *Sir Orfeo* is significant, for while we cannot say that Tolkien was familiar with any specific folk tale about the elves in the more modern (nineteenth- and twentieth-century) collections cited by Briggs, he was intimately acquainted with medieval literature and seems to have drawn most of the inspiration for his elves from glimpses of elf-lore in works such as *Sir Orfeo*, *The Mabinogion* (more properly, *The Four Branches of the Mabinogi*; [fourteenth century]), the *Lais* of Marie de France [twelfth century], and the Breton lay 'Lord Nann & the Korrigan' [first recorded in the nineteenth century but embodying a legend that is presumably much, much older].[11] For example, *Sir Orfeo* not only has the association between elves and enchanted dreams and the motif of elven invisibility already mentioned, both of which fit very well with Tolkien's wood-elves, but also contains another motif introduced into *The Hobbit* as part of the typescript expansion to the Mirkwood chapter (see 'The Enchanted Stream'): the elven hunt. Elves were believed to be fond of hunting according to a very ancient tradition, and legends of trooping faeries, wild hunts, and the like are a constant feature of tales about the Fair Folk from the time of Walter

Map (twelfth century) onward.[12] Orfeo, during the long years he spent searching for his abducted wife, sees the elven hunt from afar:

> *There often by him would he see,*
> *when noon was hot on leaf and tree,*
> *the king of Faërie with his rout*
> *came hunting in the woods about*
> *with blowing far and crying dim,*
> *and barking hounds that were with him;*
> *yet never a beast they took nor slew,*
> *and where they went he never knew.*
>
> —*Sir Orfeo*, lines 281–288, pages 129–30.[13]

By contrast, Gandalf & company never *see* the elven hunt, but they hear it often, and are deeply disquieted by the sound:

> . . . they became aware of the dim blowing of horns in the wood and the sound as of dogs baying far off. Then they all fell silent; and as they sat it seemed they could hear the noise of a great hunt going by to the north of the path, though they saw no sign of it.
>
> There they sat for a long while and did not dare to make a move.
>
> —'The Enchanted Stream', p. 350.

In the original draft of the Mirkwood chapter, Tolkien vividly evoked the sense of unease the travellers felt at the discovery that they were surrounded by an unseen people:

> [T]he path straggled on just as before, and there was no change in the forest. The only new thing that happened was the sound of laughter often, and once of singing, in the distance. The laughter was the laughter of fair voices not of goblins, and the singing was beautiful, but it sounded so eerie and strange, that they were not at all comforted.
>
> —Chapter VIII, p. 304.[14]

Here the elves are simply unseen rather than actually invisible, perhaps in another realistic rationalization of how the old legends started, but it is nonetheless remarkable that the dwarves could journey for weeks and weeks within earshot of the elves, travelling on the main elf-road through the forest, and simply happen not to encounter the elves all around them in all that time (or indeed that the elves would remain unaware of their presence until the dwarves enter their elf-circles on the night of the festivals, as seems to be the case).

Significantly, the dwarves first hear the sounds of the unseen hunt just after they have crossed over the enchanted stream; many traditional tales place a stream as the border between the mortal world and Faerie (cf. Briggs, p. 86), and we should note that another stream flows immediately before the gates of the Elvenking's Hall which must be passed over by anyone entering the elf-mound (see plate VII [bottom]).[15] As for the hunt itself, the dark stag shot by Gandalf shares the dark coloration of almost all the other Mirkwood fauna and may or may not be a normal animal; its ability to jump a stream more than thirty feet wide suggests otherwise, as does the exchange-of-misfortunes motif (see below). The white doe and her snowy white fawns encountered immediately afterwards are clearly faerie creatures: they appear suddenly (unlike the hart, whose hoofbeats the dwarves heard before it ran into view), glimmer in the darkness, and somehow avoid being hit by all the arrows fired by the dwarves ('None seemed to find their mark'). Furthermore, white animals – specifically, white deer – are a well-known harbinger of faerie; encountering one is a sign that you have strayed out of our world into the borderlands of another realm. Thus, in 'Lord Nann and the Korrigan', the hero's encounter with the perilous fairy comes about because he follows a white deer to her lair:

By the skirts of the wood as he did go,
He was 'ware of a hind as white as snow;

Oh, fast she ran, and fast he rode,
That the earth it shook where his horse-hoofs trode.

Oh, fast he rode and fast she ran,
That the sweat to drop from his brow began –

That the sweat on his horse's flanks stood white;
So he rode and rode till the fall o' the night.

When he came to a stream that fed a lawn,
Hard by the grot of a Corrigaun.

The grass grew thick by the streamlet's brink,
And he lighted down off his horse to drink.[16]

Around 1930 – that is, about the same time that he started writing *The Hobbit*, or no more than a year or so before he was working on the Mirkwood chapter – Tolkien wrote his own version of this traditional poem, eventually published in 1945. Called 'The Lay of Aotrou and Itroun' (the names in Breton simply mean 'Lord' and 'Lady'), Tolkien's poem not only includes but expands the episode of the white doe:

Beneath the woodland's hanging eaves
a white doe startled under leaves;
strangely she glistered in the sun
as she leaped forth and turned to run.

Then reckless after her he spurred;
dim laughter in the woods he heard,
but heeded not, a longing strange
for deer that fair and fearless range
vexed him, for venison of the beast
whereon no mortal hunt shall feast,
for waters crystal-clear and cold
that never in holy fountain rolled.
He hunted her from the forest-eaves
into the twilight under leaves;
the earth was shaken under hoof,
till boughs were bent into a roof,
and the sun was woven in a snare;
and laughter still was on the air.

The sun was falling. In the dell
deep in the forest silence fell.
No sight nor slot of doe he found
but roots of trees upon the ground,
and trees like shadows waiting stood
for night to come upon the wood.

—'The Lay of Aotrou and Itroun'
[1945 version], lines 259–282.

Many of the elements in the Enchanted Stream scene in *The Hobbit* are here, albeit used very differently: the strange white hind, the fruitless hunt (as also in *Sir Orfeo*), the eerie laughter in the dark wood, even (in lines 69–76 and 151–155) the enchanted water that, when drunk, brings disaster upon the intruder.[17] Similarly, in Marie de France's 'Guigemar', the first in her collection of twelve Breton lays, her titular hero is out hunting one day when

Guigemar saw a hind with a fawn;
a completely white beast,
with deer's antlers on her head.
Spurred by the barking of the dogs, she sprang
into the open.
Guigemar took his bow and shot at her . . .

—*The Lais of Marie de France* tr. Rbt Hanning & Joan Ferrante [1978], 'Guigemar', lines 90–94.

In Guigemar's case, his shot does strike and mortally wound the deer, but he is unable to enjoy the meat because the arrow rebounds and injures him grievously as well; if there were any doubt that the 'completely white' hind with antlers like a stag were magical, they disappear when she speaks, laying a curse upon him for wounding her. Perhaps an echo of this appears in *The Hobbit*, when Bombur is stricken at the exact moment Thorin shoots the stag. Finally, in the Welsh tale 'Pwyll, Prince of Dyfed', the First Branch of the *Mabinogi*, Pwyll meets with misfortune while hunting a deer, although in this case it is not the deer but the hounds who are hunting it who are white:

> . . . of all the hunting dogs he had seen in the world, he had never seen dogs the colour of them: the redness of the ears glittered as brightly as the whiteness of their bodies.
>
> —*The Mabinogi and Other Medieval Welsh Tales*, tr. Patrick Ford [1977], page 37.

Naturally enough, since these particular hounds (the *cwn annwn*) belong to Arawn, King of Annwn, the Welsh Otherworld (which is conceived of as both Faerie and the Land of the Dead, depending on who is telling the story, rather like the faerie realm in *Sir Orfeo*).[18] White hounds also appear in Tolkien's ballad 'Ides Ælfscýne' ('Lady Elven-fair'), his own version of the *belle dame sans merci* legend which appeared in *Songs for the Philologists* [1936] but had been written at Leeds sometime in the first half of the 1920s as part of the *Scheme B Songbook*, where the narrator describes his beloved's unearthly homeland:

> þǽr gréne wæs grund, ond hwít hire hund,
> ond gylden wæs hwǽte on healme

This passage may be translated as

> There green was the ground and white her hound
> And golden was the wheat in the fields [*or*: on the stalk].[19]

Even the horses being ridden by the elvenking, his knights, and damsels in *Sir Orfeo* were 'snow-white steeds/and white as milk were all their weeds' [i.e., clothes] (lines 145–146), as is the horse ('her milk-white steed') upon which the Queen of Elfland takes Thomas Rhymer away with her after their tryst under the Eildon tree (Child Ballad number 37, text A, stanza six); according to some versions of the story, the two deer she sent years later to recall Thomas to Elfland were white as well. Note the repeated insistence not just on whiteness as a feature of creatures native to Faerie but on the strange intensity of the whiteness, which *glimmered* (*The Hobbit*), *glistered* ('The Lay of Aotrou & Itroun'), or *glittered* (*The Mabinogi*). And once again we have the motif of a fruitless hunt that leads the hero into danger – the deer Pwyll is hunting is actually killed before his pack reaches it by a strange pack of white hounds, whom he drives from the kill, thus deeply offending their lord, the King of the Underworld. Pwyll does not feast on deer-meat any more than Guigemar or Bilbo's companions, but instead rather than bear Arawn's enmity he willingly enters Faerie at

Arawn's bidding to take the faerie king's place for a year and, at the end of that time, kill Arawn's great enemy and rival – a deed he accomplishes so chivalrously that he thereafter to the end of his life bears the cognomen Pwyll Pen Annwfn ('Pwyll, Head of Annwn').

Pwyll enters Faerie willingly, in order to make good on a debt he has incurred, and perhaps for this reason comes back safely in the end to his own world and time, winning the friendship of the Faerie King in the process and, shortly afterwards, a faerie bride of his own, the Lady Rhiannon. More often, those who enter Faerie do so unwillingly or unwittingly, like Lady Heurodis in *Sir Orfeo*, Lord Nann in the old ballad, or the many prisoners carried off by the fairies – Briggs not only mentions many similar tales in passing but devotes an entire chapter to the topic (*The Vanishing People*, pages 104–17), as does Jacob Grimm in *Teutonic Mythology* (volume three, chapter XXXII). And this in turn brings us to Tolkien's final major borrowing from fairy tradition in his depiction of the wood-elves: the theme of imprisonment within an elf-mound.

For although Tolkien never calls it by that name, the Elvenking's Halls in many ways fit the folktale descriptions of an elf-mound or fairy hill. A number of the hills so identified in the British isles are barrow-mounds, and it is perhaps significant that in several of the pictures he drew of the scene Tolkien gave the entrance to the Elvenking's Halls a lintel gate (trilithon) such as those found on many real-world megalithic tombs.[20] Even without the neolithic associations, that Tolkien's wood-elves live in caves (as did the elves of Doriath and Nargothrond in *The Book of Lost Tales* and other stories in the Silmarillion tradition) may be yet another of his realistic touches rationalizing fairy mythology: many of the traditional tales feature a cave as the entrance into a fairy realm or, in at least one famous case, out of the fairy realm into our world.[21] The Tuatha dé Danaan, the fairy-folk of Ireland whose martial prowess seems to have been Tolkien's main model for the great warrior-elves of the *Quenta Silmarillion* (and who were to have featured in an unwritten chapter of *The Lost Road* [1936]; cf. HME V.77–8),[22] were so closely associated with the elf-mounds or fairy hills that they came to be more commonly known as *aes sidhe* or *daoine sidhe*, both literally meaning 'the people of the fairy hill', until *sidhe* shifted from its original meaning of 'elf-mound' to mean the elves themselves (as in the anglicized *banshee*, or *bean sidhe*: 'woman of the *sidhe*', faerie-woman). The *sidhe* were thought to live within the hollow hills, a conception that no doubt gave rise to the modern idea that fairies were smaller than humans in size, but in earlier lore these were simply the entrances to the Otherworld, as in *Sir Orfeo*, where the hero follows the faerie ladies when they enter an elf-mound:

with right good will his feet he sped,
for stock nor stone he stayed his tread.

Right into a rock the ladies rode,
and in behind he fearless strode.
He went into that rocky hill
a good three miles or more, until
he came into a country fair . . .

—*Sir Orfeo*, lines 345–351.[23]

One universal feature of elf-mounds, whatever else was believed about them, was the difficulty of escaping from one once inside – cf. the Elvenking's words (p. 380): 'there is no escape through my magic doors, for those who are brought once inside', a point later re-affirmed by Bilbo's experience ('Magic shut the gates', ibid.).[24] One motif often tied into this, as old as the myth of Persephone, is the idea that anyone who eats fairy food becomes trapped in fairy-land and cannot thereafter escape; Briggs recounts several tales of visitors being warned not to eat fairy-food, in at least one case by someone who had already done so and become trapped herself who prevents her beloved from sharing the same fate ('The Fairy Dwelling on Selena Moor', *British Folk-Tales and Legends* [1977; rpt. 2002], pages 181–4). It is therefore striking that *The Hobbit* contains no trace of this motif: the starving dwarves (and the hobbit as well) eat the elven food as soon as it is offered and suffer no ill effects whatsoever; in fact, it saves them from starvation and does not hinder their eventual escape in any way.[25]

That eventual escape – originally after months of captivity, reduced in the published version to a matter of weeks (see the calendaric reckonings accompanying Tolkien's notes for the 1960 Hobbit, p. 823) – comes after 'a weary long time'. In the folk-tales, those few captives in fairy-land who do succeed in escaping almost always do so by one of two means. They are either rescued by someone outside the elf-mound or fairy-circle – an idea Tolkien toyed with in Plot Notes A, as we have already seen, but ultimately rejected – or they escape on their own by means of a trick. Tolkien adopted the latter solution, and so far as I can discover the idea of escaping in barrels was his own invention;[26] there is nothing like it in the traditional literature, and it may be taken as a typical intrusion of practical hobbitry into the elven-dwarven impasse created by stubbornness, arrogance, and an unwillingness to let go of ancient history.

Out of these motifs, drawn together from scattered passing references in various medieval tales and some of their more modern descendents (e.g., the ballads) – all the record we have left of a once-widespread belief system now recoverable only through imaginative reconstruction of such remaining hints – Tolkien created a seamless and satisfactory whole. To borrow Verlyn Flieger's analogy, the individual pieces of elf-lore that have by chance and good luck survived but shorn of their original context are rather like broken pieces of ancient stained glass, retaining their striking evocative quality but their original pattern lost; Tolkien has taken these fragments and reassembled them, 'remounting, as it were, the stained glass into a new window' (*Interrupted Music*, page 131).

(ii)
The Three Kindreds of the Elves

Just as Tolkien's depiction of the elves in *The Hobbit* draws both on traditional medieval elf-lore and his own legendarium, so too do his larger groupings encompass both the old division between the *lios-alfar* and the *svart-alfar*, the light elves and the dark elves of Scandinavian myth, on the one hand[27] and his own myth of the threefold division of the Eldar into the Light-elves, the Deep-elves, and the Sea-elves (or, as they are known in *The Silmarillion*, the Vanyar, the Noldor, and the Teleri – *Silm*.53) on the other. Both these divisions underlie the passage from the manuscript on p. 315 already briefly discussed in Text Note 40 to Chapter VIII:

> . . . most of [the wood-elves] are descended from the ancient elves who never went to the great FairyLand of the west, where the Light-elves, and the Deep-elves (or Gnomes) and the Sea-elves lived, and grew fair, and learned and invented their magic and their cunning craft and the making of beautiful and marvelous things.

This passage was greatly expanded in the First Typescript:

> Are the wood-elves wicked? Well, not particularly, or indeed not at all, though they have their faults, and they don't like strangers. It is quite true that they are rather different from other elves; for most of them, as well as the few elves that live in hills and mountains, are descended from those of the ancient tribes of the elves of old who never went to the great Fairyland of the West, where the Light-elves and the Deep-elves (or Gnomes) and the Sea-elves lived for ages and grew fair and wise and learned and invented their magic and their cunning craft in the making of beautiful and marvellous things, before they came back into the Wide World. Here the wood-elves lingered in the twilight before the raising of the Sun and Moon, and afterwards they wandered in the forests that grew beneath the sunrise. They loved best the edges of the woods from which they could escape at times to hunt or to ride and run over the open lands by sun or moon or star; though after the coming of Men they took ever more and more to the gloaming and the dusk.
>
> —1/1/30:3–4, rejected ending to the First Typescript.[28]

There are two hierarchies of division here: first between those elves who went to Faerie (or Elvenhome, as Tolkien elsewhere calls it) and those who stayed behind, then a threefold division among those elves who set out on that great journey. But the actual situation is much more complicated than this, with many subdivisions and ever-evolving names. For example, the third group Tolkien mentions in *The Hobbit*, the Sea-elves, became divided between those who actually crossed the sea and reached Elvenhome (the Teleri) and those who remained behind in Beleriand with Thingol (the Sindar or Grey Elves); this latter group became the wood-elves of our story – cf. the reference in the first sketchy outline to the dwarves' 'capture by the Sea elves' (p. 229), meaning the wood-elves of Mirkwood.[29] Similarly, the term 'Dark Elf' was sometimes applied to those who refused the summons (the Dark Elves of Palisor; cf. BLT I.232–7 & 244) and sometimes to also include those who set out but fell by the wayside along the way (e.g., the Green Elves of Ossiriand), the Ilkorindi (i.e., 'Not of Kôr', the great elven city in Elvenhome known in later stages of the mythology as Tirion upon Túna); cf. page 112 of *The Silmarillion*, where Caranthir son of Fëanor refers (insultingly) to Thingol, the Lord of Beleriand, as 'this Dark Elf in his caves'.[30]

The interrelationship between the various groups of elves was one of the most complex elements in Tolkien's work, especially since each of these divisions had linguistic ramifications (cf. *The Lhammas* or 'Account of Tongues' [circa 1937], HME V.167–98). Philologist that he was, Tolkien was deeply interested in this aspect of elven history and returned to it over and over throughout his long years of work on the legendarium. Its essentials – the aforementioned twofold division of the elves – remained unchanged, but the names of the various groups were subject to constant change, along with other individual elements within that pattern. For example, the Three Kindreds, the People of the Great Journey (*LotR*.1171) here called the Light-elves, Deep-elves, and Sea-elves were known in *The Book of Lost Tales* [1917–1920] as the Teleri, the Noldoli (or Gnomes), and the Solosimpi (or Shoreland Pipers), respectively (BLT I.115, 119). By the time of the 1926 'Sketch of the Mythology,' these had become the Quendi or Light-elves, the Nodoli or Deep-elves (also known as Gnomes on account of their wisdom),[31] and the Teleri or Sea-elves (known in Valinor as the Solosimpi) (HME IV. 13). This same terminology carried over into the form of the Silmarillion that was most current when Tolkien wrote *The Hobbit*, the 1930 *Quenta* (HME IV.85), and he was clearly thinking of the passage in either the 'Sketch' or the 1930 *Quenta* when drafting this line in *The Hobbit*, since those names had already been superceded by the time of the book's publication – in the 1937 *Quenta Silmarillion* the Three Kindreds are the Lindar (the High Elves, no longer the 'Light-elves' of *The Hobbit*), the Noldor (the Deep Elves, also still known as the Gnomes), and the Teleri (the Sea Elves, here called the Soloneldi in Valinor) (HME V.214–5).[32]

By contrast, those elves who were lost along the road were originally known as the Lost Elves or the Shadow Folk (BLT I.119) and later as the Ilkorindi (1926 'Sketch', 1930 *Quenta*) or the Dark Elves (1930 *Quenta*). By the time of the 1937 *Quenta Silmarillion*, those lost along the way are known as the Lembi ('the Lingerers').

Finally, the detail of the woodland king's golden hair, which only enters in with the typescript, is interesting, given Tolkien's later statements that of the three kindreds of the elves it was the First Kindred or Vanyar (the Light-elves of p. 315) who are golden-haired, not the Third Kindred or Teleri (the Sea-elves); see Douglas Anderson's commentary in *The Annotated Hobbit* (DAA.206) and Christopher Tolkien's commentary in *The Peoples of Middle-earth* (HME XII.77 & 82). It is not known, however, at what point Tolkien made that decision, and there is some evidence that he originally conceived of the Second Kindred or Noldor (the Deep-elves) as golden-haired: in the genealogies meant to accompany the '(Earliest) Annals of Beleriand' [early 1930s] they are referred to as *Kuluqendi* or 'Golden-elves' (HME V.[403]); the 1937 *Quenta Silmarillion* includes 'the Golden' as one of their many descriptors (HME V.215) and Christopher Tolkien notes (BLT I.43–4, HME XII.77) that the passage in Appendix F of the first edition of *The Lord of the Rings* describing the Eldar (the Three Kindreds of the High Elves) as dark-haired, 'save in the golden house of Finrod' (i.e., the character known as Finarfin in the published *Silmarillion* and more recent editions of *The Lord of Rings* [cf. *LotR*.1171]: Galadriel's father not her brother, some of whose children were golden-haired because of his Vanyar mother), was written as a description of the Noldor (the Second Kindred) before being applied to the Eldar as a whole. It's possible the final determination that only the Vanyar (the First Kindred) were golden-haired actually postdates *The Lord of the Rings*: the earliest example cited by Christopher Tolkien dates from 1951, after *The Lord of the Rings* was finished but before its publication.

This still does not explain why the Elvenking, who is clearly neither one of the Light-elves (Vanyar) nor the Deep-elves (Noldor) but of the Sea-elves (the Sindar, or Teleri of Middle-earth) should be golden-haired. However, there is already precedent for golden-haired Sindar in Tolkien's earlier writings: in the A-text of 'The Lay of Leithian', written in August 1925, Lúthien herself is described as golden-haired (lines 10–16, HME III.157; see ibid. page 150 for the date). It is only in retrospect, then, after Tolkien had decided to restrict golden hair to a specific branch of the Eldar, that the problem of accounting for individual elves with gold hair who were not members of that specific group arose. Therefore we need not concern ourselves over the apparent violation of a rule or restriction that did not exist at the time this passage was written.

In any case, given the freedom which Tolkien allowed himself when drawing from his mythology in *The Hobbit* in this earliest draft (e.g., the application of 'Fingolfin' as a goblin name on p. 8), it's unreasonable to expect a strict consistency with his earlier material, especially given the fluid, shifting nature of details and concepts within that corpus. Tolkien often seems to have described scenes as he initially visualized them and worked out the details to make them consistent with the rest of the tale afterwards (e.g., contrast p. 90 with p. 828): in this case, 'golden-haired elf-lord' was a motif he decided to use when inserting this interpolation into *The Hobbit* and he did so, very effectively.

(iii)
The King of Wood and Stone

If Tolkien's wood-elves as a whole harken back to folklore beliefs about 'the Fair Folk', then in his depiction of the Elvenking he is drawing on a specific modern literary source: his own unpublished writings.[33] Certainly there are striking similarities between the Elvenking's halls and the caves of the Rodothlim, a shy and fugitive people who in the later evolution of the mythology became the elves of Nargothrond:

> . . . in the mountains there was a place of caves above a stream, and that stream ran down to feed the river Sirion, but grass grew before the doors of the caves, and these were cunningly concealed by trees and such magics as those scattered bands that dwelt therein remembered still. Indeed at this time this place had grown to be a strong dwelling of the folk . . . long ere [Túrin and his companion] drew nigh to that region . . . the spies and watchers of the Rodothlim (for so were that folk named) gave warning of their approach, and the folk withdrew before them, such as were abroad from their dwelling. Then they closed their doors and hoped that the strangers might not discover their caves, for they feared and mistrusted all unknown folk of whatever race, so evil were the lessons of that dreadful time.
>
> Now then Flinding and Túrin dared even to the caves' mouths, and perceiving that these twain knew now the paths thereto the Rodothlim sallied and made them prisoners and drew them within their rocky halls, and they were led before the chief, Orodreth.
>
> —'Turambar and the Foalókë' [circa 1919], BLT II.81–2.

While the wood-elves' dwelling [circa 1931] is not described as being located in mountains, it otherwise strongly resembles the Rodothlim's lair, being 'a great cave' alongside a river that 'ran from out of the heights of the forest'; these heights are also described as 'the highlands' (p. 315) and 'a steep slope' (p. 379). Like the Rodothlim, the wood-elves initially flee before the intruders (at the three feasts), only to waylay and capture the trespassers the next day and bring them before their king for judgement.

But aside from their dwelling the Rodothlim are not a very close parallel to the wood-elves: we are told the former are so industrious that 'there the ancient arts and works of the Noldoli [Deep Elves] came once more to life . . . There was smithying in secret and forging of good weapons, and even fashioning of some fair things beside, and the women spun once more and wove, and at times was gold quarried privily in places nigh . . . so that deep in those caverns might vessels of beauty be seen in the flame of secret lights' (BLT II.81). By contrast, we are specifically told that the Elvenking's treasure is small because his people 'neither mined nor worked metal or jewels, nor did they trade, nor till the earth more than they could help' (see below). Also, the wood-elves do not share the Rodothlim's aversion to marching off to war, as we shall see in later chapters, although admittedly this was a slightly later development.

A much closer parallel to the wood-elves can be found in the woodland realm of Doriath, located in the heart of a dark forest known for its impenetrability, a place where most travellers get lost and perish miserably. Like the elven kingdom in Mirkwood, Doriath is a realm of the Sea Elves (the Teleri), not the Deep Elves (the Noldoli or Noldor) as had been the case with the Rodothlim of Nargothrond. At the heart of Doriath lies their stronghold, Menegroth ('The Thousand Caves'), which can only be reached by crossing a guarded bridge over a stream that runs just past its gates – or, as *The Book of Lost Tales* put it, describing a scene strikingly like the one depicted in one of the illustrations for *The Hobbit* (DAA.224): 'his halls were builded in a deep cavern of great size, and they were nonetheless a kingly and a fair abode. This cavern was in the heart of the mighty forest of Artanor [Doriath] that is the mightiest of forests, and a stream ran before its doors, but none could enter that portal save across the stream, and a bridge spanned it narrow and well-guarded' ('The Tale of Tinúviel', BLT II.9–10).[34]

Furthermore, the wood-elves of Mirkwood are great archers, who can 'hit a bird's eye in the dark'; indeed, their extreme skill with the bow is so well known that the dwarves promptly and prudently surrender on the spot when faced with wood-elves armed with bows. Similarly, the most renowned warrior of Doriath was Beleg of the bow (also called Beleg the Bowman, the character known in *The Silmarillion* as Beleg Strongbow), Túrin's closest friend after whom the second canto of 'The Lay of the Children of Húrin' is named (HME III.29–48). The bow is also the weapon most associated with the Teleri of Eldamar, those of the Third Kindred who had immigrated to Valinor, with which they defend themselves against the Noldor during the Kinslaying (*Silm*.87).

The strongest parallel between Doriath and the wood-elves' realm, however, is the Elvenking himself, who strongly resembles one of the most famous characters in the legendarium: King Thingol Greycloak, ruler of the woodland realm of Doriath and high king of the Elves of Beleriand.

It is said in the 1937 *Quenta Silmarillion* that his name was 'held in awe' by the Lords of the Noldor (Fingolfin, Fingon, Maidros/Maedhros, and Inglor/Finrod) [HME V.266]. Thingol is unique in that he is a major character in not one but two of the 'great tales' that form the heart of the Silmarillion: 'The Lay of Leithian' (the story of his daughter, Lúthien Tinúviel, and her mortal lover Beren) and the story of the children of Húrin (as loyal foster-father to Túrin the Hapless). He is also one of the original elves, one of those who began life in Cuiviénen, the lost elven Eden far to the east of what we know as Middle-earth, and one of the three who travel to Valinor as representatives of their people. He thus became the leader of one of the three great divisions of the Eldar, the Sea Elves (see above), in their migration half-way across the world towards Elven-home. He is the only one of the Children of Ilúvatar to marry one of the Ainur or angels, Queen Melian, and ultimately became either ancestor or close kin to many of Tolkien's other important characters – for example, he is Elrond Halfelven's great-great-grandfather.[35] Later legends, not yet written at the time *The Hobbit* was drafted, would make him great-uncle to Galadriel (the most powerful elf depicted in *The Lord of the Rings*) and her brother Finrod Felagund (the first elf to befriend humans and perhaps the most appealing character in *The Silmarillion*), and the direct ancestor of the kings of Númenor and hence of Gondor and Arnor as well, including Aragorn/Strider.

Given the fluid nature of the unpublished myths, where Tolkien was willing to play around with concepts and occasionally contemplate major changes in the legends, we should ask the obvious question: is the elvenking Bilbo meets Thingol himself or an entirely new character closely modelled upon him – an analogue, as it were? The answer seems to be both: just as the status of *The Hobbit* itself hovered in Tolkien's mind between being part of the legendarium and standing apart from it, so too within the book the identification of the elvenking straddles both options and cannot conclusively be resolved either way. Even after Tolkien eventually, towards the end of work on *The Lord of the Rings*, committed to the decision that the wood-elf king was a separate character, he never fully reworked the original story to completely support that decision.

To understand, then, exactly how the wood-elf king in *The Hobbit* relates to the earlier stories, it is necessary (as so often) to make the mental effort to exclude from our minds knowledge of what Tolkien later resolved while working on the sequel, or that subsequent layer created as much as twenty years afterwards will prevent us from seeing clearly what he was doing at the time he created the character – that is, when writing the story of Mr. Baggins' adventures as a stand-alone work deriving in varying degrees from his already voluminous writings about Middle-earth. Seen in this light, while the Elvenking strongly resembles King Thingol in general, the evidence for and against the identification is contradictory.

Two elements Tolkien goes out of his way to include in the narrative support the argument that the two kings are one and the same, while two unstated facts argue against it because of the dissonance they would create between things we know to be true of Thingol that do not appear to apply to the Elvenking.

The first passage that strengthens the identification between the Elvenking and Thingol Greycloak is Tolkien's mention of the three kindreds of the elves (see part ii of this chapter's commentary, starting on p. 405 above). This places the wood-elves within the context of the old mythology, and we should not overlook the precision of Tolkien's phrasing that *most* of the wood-elves are descended from ancient elves who never went to 'the great FairyLand of the west'. In fact, only one Sea-elf in the whole legendarium ever visited Valinor and returned to live in Middle-earth, this being the figure originally known as Linwë Tinto (BLT I.106), then Tinwë Linto (ibid., pages 130–1) or Tinwelint ('The Tale of Tinúviel', BLT II.8), then from 'The Lay of Leithian', onwards as King Thingol. It's possible that this is an oblique allusion to the idea, expressed in the 1926 'Sketch of the Mythology', that some of the Gnomes (Noldor) returning to Middle-earth 'take service with Thingol and Melian of the Thousand Caves in Doriath' (HME IV.23).[36] It cannot, as it might first seem, be an early form of the idea presented in *The Lord of the Rings* that Sindar (grey-elf) lords settled among and ruled over Silvan (wood-elf) populations, since those rulers would be Sindar like Celeborn who had never left Middle-earth. Given the Elvenking's general similarity to Thingol, it seems far more likely then that this passage is a deliberate allusion to Thingol.

Thingol's story is even more explicitly evoked in the account of the old enmity between the dwarves and the elves (p. 315):

> . . . [the wood elves] did not love dwarves. They had had wars in ancient days with dwarves, and accused them of stealing their treasure (& the dwarves accused them of the same, and also of hiring dwarves to shape their gold & silver, and refusing to pay them after!).

The original ending to the first typescript of the Mirkwood chapter (1/1/30:4) expands upon this somewhat:

> . . . they did not love dwarves and thought he was an enemy. In ancient days they had had wars with some of the dwarves whom they accused of stealing their treasure. It is only fair to say that the dwarves gave a different account and said that they only took what was their due, for the elf-king had bargained with them to shape his raw gold and silver and had after refused to give them their pay. If the elf-king had a weakness it was for treasure, especially for silver and white gems, for though his hoard was rich yet he had not as

great a treasure as other elf-lords of old, since his people neither mined nor worked metal or jewels, nor did they trade, nor till the earth more than they could help. All this was well known to every dwarf, though Thorin's family[37] had had nothing to do with the old quarrel I have spoken of.

This in turn is followed closely in the revised ending of the Mirkwood chapter (1/1/58:17), which, in addition to a few small revisions of punctuation and phrasing, achieves the text of the published book:

> . . . though his hoard was rich, he was ever eager for more, since he had not yet as great a treasure as other elf-lords of old[38] . . . All this was well known to every dwarf, though Thorin's family had had nothing to do with the old quarrel I have spoken of. Consequently Thorin was angry at their treatment of him, when they took their spell off him and he came to his senses; and also he was determined that no word of gold or jewels should be dragged out of him.
>
> (compare DAA.220).

This quarrel is clearly an allusion to the Lost Tale known as 'The Nauglafring: The Necklace of the Dwarves', the last of the tales (in terms of the cycle's internal chronology) to be written out in full (BLT II.221–51). This story changed greatly in its details and tone but remained consistent in its overall outlines from *The Book of Lost Tales* through 'The Sketch of the Mythology' into the 1930 *Quenta*, the last completed version of the tale.[39]

The 1926 summary of the tale runs thusly:

> Húrin and outlaws come to Nargothrond, whom none dare plunder for dread of the spirit of Glórung [the dragon] or even of his memory. They slay Mîm the Dwarf who had taken possession and enchanted all the gold. [After transporting it to Doriath] Húrin casts the gold at Thingol's feet with reproaches. Thingol will not have it, and bears with Húrin, until goaded too far he bids him begone. Húrin wanders away . . .
>
> The enchanted gold lays its spell on Thingol. He summons the Dwarves of Nogrod and Belegost to come and fashion it into beautiful things, and to make a necklace of great wonder whereon the Silmaril shall hang. The Dwarves plot treachery, and Thingol bitter with the curse of the gold denies them their reward. After their smithying they are driven away without payment. The Dwarves come back; aided by treachery of some Gnomes [that is, Noldor or Deep Elves] who also were bitten by the lust of the gold, they surprise Thingol on a hunt, slay him, and surprise the Thousand Caves and plunder them. Melian they cannot touch . . .
>
> [On the return journey to their homelands] The Dwarves are ambushed at a ford by Beren and the brown and green Elves of the

> wood, and their king slain, from whose neck Beren takes the 'Nauglafring' or necklace of the Dwarves, with its Silmaril. It is said that Lúthien wearing that jewel is the most beautiful thing that eyes have ever seen outside Valinor. But Melian warned Beren of the curse of the gold and of the Silmaril. The rest of the gold is drowned in the river.
>
> But the 'Nauglafring' remains hoarded secretly in Beren's keeping . . .
>
> —'The Sketch of the Mythology' [1926] HME IV.32–3.

Besides prefiguring all the trouble that will erupt later in *The Hobbit* over Smaug's hoard, and the curse of possessiveness that falls upon Thorin in the end, this passage clearly describes the same quarrel which lay between the wood-elves and our dwarves in *The Hobbit*: dwarves hired to shape silver and gold (the *Book of Lost Tales* version stresses the amount of unwrought gold in the hoard; cf. Note 38) for an elvenking who then refuses them payment, an ensuing war, and lasting bitterness over the whole incident, with each side nursing grudges as to the rightness of their cause – the '(Later) Annals of Beleriand', which are associated with the 1937 *Quenta Silmarillion*, goes so far as to claim 'and there hath been war between Elf and Dwarf since that day.' If we were to go by Tolkien's later writings in *The Lord of the Rings* and published *Silmarillion* then in the account in *The Hobbit* the elf-king who bargained with the dwarves to shape his raw gold and silver and the elf-king of the next sentence who had a weakness for treasure are two separate people (Thingol and Thranduil, respectively), but this is clearly untenable: nothing in Tolkien's prose here justifies the assumption of a complete shift in antecedent between identical nouns used as the subjects of two consecutive sentences. Moreover the phrase 'as other elf-lords of old' clearly implies that our Elvenking is himself one among their number, not a newcomer of latter days but directly involved with the elf-dwarf wars of ancient days.[40] In short, there can be no doubt that here Tolkien is stating it was the same king of the wood-elves whom Bilbo meets who had quarreled and warred with the dwarves long ago, events that the Silmarillion tradition unequivocally ascribes to King Thingol. Furthermore, in a letter written many years later Tolkien explicitly said that this particular passage in *The Hobbit* is a reference to 'the quarrel of King Thingol, Lúthien's father, with the Dwarves' – JRRT to Christopher Bretherton, 16th July 1964; *Letters* p. 346.

This very identification, however, raises the first of the two disconnects between Thingol and the Elvenking that form the major objections to the possibility that the two characters might be one and the same at different points in Middle-earth's history. A key part of Thingol's legend was the account of his death at the hands of the dwarves he had cheated, the sudden and shameful death of one of the greatest of all the elves over a petty quarrel. If our Elvenking is Thingol, then how can he still be alive at the time of our story? Either Tolkien has removed the quarrel from the Thingol legend and given it to a new character, modifying it so that the chief elven protagonist survives, or he is making the same modification while leaving Thingol as its protagonist, thus extending Thingol's story forward into a much later era and setting aside the old account of Thingol's death and the destruction of Doriath. That he was willing to recast his stories in ways with far-reaching consequences we know from other evidence, a prime example being his decision no more than five years earlier between the original and revised versions of the 1926 'Sketch of the Mythology' to change Beren from an elf to a human (HME IV.23–5).

And indeed there is already precedent for ambiguity over Thingol's fate (or Tinwë Lintö/Tinwelint as he was then called) within *The Book of Lost Tales* itself. The story of the *Nauglafring* near the end of the collection recounts his violent death (offstage in the narrative, while on one of the hunts so beloved of the wood-elves – BLT II.231–2), yet in the section of *The Book of Lost Tales* that describes the origins of the elves and their coming to Valinor ('The Coming of the Elves and the Making of Kôr'), we are told 'yet 'tis said [Tinwë] lives still lord of the scattered Elves of Hisilómë [Hithlum, later a region in northwest Beleriand], dancing in its twilight places with Wendelin [Melian] his spouse' (BLT I.115) – that is, that according to this version of the story Tinwelint/Thingol is still alive at the time Eriol the narrator is being told the story in the early fifth century AD.

Unfortunately, none of the later versions of the legendarium recount the story of Thingol's death and the fall of Doriath, all breaking off incomplete before this point (see Note 39). So what evidence we have for Tolkien's intentions regarding the latter parts of the Silmarillion cycle must derive from sources such as the '(Later) Annals of Beleriand' [c. 1937] and 'The Tale of Years' ([c. 1951]; cf. HME XI.345), which recount the old story of Thingol's death at the hands of the dwarves in almost the same terms as in the the '(Earliest) Annals of Beleriand' [c. 1931]. In essence, then, between the time *The Hobbit* is drafted and its unexpected publication, and indeed well into the drafting of *The Lord of the Rings*,[41] we seem to have two competing traditions: one in which Thingol dies as in the old story (the Annals) and one in which the issue is left open (*The Hobbit*). Since both existed at that time only in unpublished manuscripts, it's impossible to say which of the parallel traditions was more definitive; *The Hobbit*'s version was certainly the first to reach print and might thus be thought to be more authoritative, yet it was at least partly superseded by the later account of the elvenking in *The Lord of the Rings*.

The second disconnect is an absence rather than a presence: namely, that there is no Faërie Queen at the Elvenking's side in Mirkwood. As great a figure as Thingol himself is in the legendarium, he is just as famous for his wife (and daughter) as for his own deeds, just as King Arthur is ultimately more famous for the deeds of the knights of his Round Table than for his own exploits (aside from the realm-establishing feat of drawing the sword from the stone). Thingol's daughter Lúthien Tinúviel is the fairest creature that ever walked the earth, and his wife Melian of Valinor (Wendelin/Gwendeling/Tindriel the fay in the earliest versions of the story) of another order of being altogether, as high above Thingol as Lúthien is above Beren (or Arwen above Aragorn). It is Melian's power that protects the woodland realm of Doriath from its enemies, just as Galadriel later protects Lothlórien in *The Lord of the Rings*. Such a figure could hardly escape Bilbo's notice during the weeks and months he was forced to lurk within the wood-elves' halls and 'go on burglaring', yet no queen is mentioned, either by the side of the woodland king in Bombur's visions and the description of the third great feast that followed in the Enchanted Stream interpolation, nor anywhere in this chapter's account of the wood-elves' halls. We can only infer her existence indirectly from much later evidence, long after the time of our book: the fact that in *The Lord of the Rings* we are told the Elvenking has a son, Legolas, who becomes one of the Fellowship of the Ring. If Tolkien's projected rewriting of our story in 1960 had proceeded as far as the Mirkwood chapters, we might have been able to discover whether he intended to bring Legolas into Mr. Baggins' story (after all, in the light of later knowledge we can say he would almost certainly have been present at the Battle of Five Armies); there is no sign of it in the admittedly sketchy notes that survive. But even this would hardly have resolved the question of what was in Tolkien's mind almost thirty years earlier when he wrote *The Hobbit*, since by that later date he was committed to the decision that Thingol and the Elvenking were two different characters.

The only possibility that would unite both traditions would be if Thingol did indeed die in the fall of Doriath but then later returned to Middle-earth after a suitable time in the Halls of Mandos.[42] Since elves experience serial immortality, it is quite possible in Tolkien's metaphysics for us to encounter in *The Hobbit* or *The Lord of the Rings* an elf who died during events in the First Age, spent time in the Halls of Mandos, was re-incarnated with the same personality and memories, and then returned to Middle-earth during the Second or Third Age. In fact, we have one specific example in the person of Glorfindel, Elrond's chief advisor in Rivendell, who dies fighting a balrog during the retreat from Gondolin near the end of the First Age ('The Fall of Gondolin', BLT II.194; *Silm*.243) yet re-appears in Middle-earth before the end of the second millennium of the Third Age (*LotR*.225–6; HME VI.214–5 & HME XII.377ff).

It might be argued that if the Elvenking in *The Hobbit* were indeed a figure returned from death then Tolkien would have drawn attention to this fact in some way, but the example of Glorfindel shows this is not necessarily the case; the same could be true of any elf we meet in *The Hobbit*. However, while entirely possible in terms of what we know to be true of the elves, one nonetheless cannot help feeling that it would be a coming down in the world for Thingol Greycloak, one of the most renowned elves of the First Age, to return to a diminished realm, *sans* wife and daughter, his original home sunk beneath the waves in lost Beleriand, his kingdom reduced to the wood-elf realm in Mirkwood. Glorfindel clearly had unfinished business drawing him back into the mortal world.[43] Thingol has no such motive; having only stayed in Middle-earth originally because of Melian, it seems unlikely that he would have left Valinor a second time without her. Instead, this sense of diminishment may be part of the very reason Thingol and the Elvenking ultimately did become separate characters. As Thingol grew in majesty and wisdom and stature during the long evolution of the legendarium – a process reaching its apotheosis in *Narn i Hîn Húrin* (cf. *Unfinished Tales*, page 83) but already well underway in 'The Lay of Leithian' (cf. Note 34) – the simple wood-elf king that had been Tinwelint became buried under the weight of glory; re-creating him in the person of the Elvenking enabled Tolkien to recapture something much more like the original character, regaining a quality that had been lost in the ennoblement of Thingol and one which made him much more suited to the role he was to play in *The Hobbit*.

In the end it seems clear that when he wrote *The Hobbit* Tolkien drew on the old story (which was, after all, unpublished and likely to remain so), changing it as he did so, to make the material more suited to his new purpose. But he left his options open as to whether the Elvenking was a new character or an old familiar character appearing in a new story, slightly altered to fit his new surroundings. In time he decided that the Elvenking was indeed a new character and gave him a name (see part iv below) and (sketchy) history of his own, but this decision postdated the publication of *The Hobbit*, probably by more than a decade, and he never went back and re-wrote the key passage in *The Hobbit* to distinguish what was now the analogue from the original. Thus to this day we are left with two contradictory accounts of which elvenking was responsible for provoking the elf–dwarf war, the one in the Silmarillion tradition and the other within *The Hobbit*.

(iv)
The Name 'Thranduil'

The Elvenking is never named within *The Hobbit*; like the Mayor of Lake Town (who never does acquire a name), he is always simply referred to by title throughout. Not until *The Lord of the Rings* is he given a name, Thranduil, and made father of the elven member of the Fellowship, Legolas Greenleaf. Even in *The Lord of the Rings* most of what we learn about him comes from Appendix B: 'The Tale of Years'; he never actually appears in the main story. His name is not easily explicated but seems to be in early Sindarin (that is, Gnomish/Noldorin, later rationalized as a dialectical form), and to contain the same element as the place-name Nargo*thrond*:[44] *Narog* + *othrond*, 'fortified cave by the river Narog' [Salo, p. 386; HME XI.414]. The *thrand/(o)thrond* element, meaning fortified cave (*ost* + *rond*), fits very well with the character as described in *The Hobbit*, where the chief thing we know about him is that he's a king dwelling in a cave; the *–uil* or *-duil* suffix might relate to *dûl* (hollow), but more likely links to *drui*, *drû* ('wood, forest') [*Gnomish Lexicon*, page 31]. If so, a possible gloss would be '(One who lives in) a (fortified) cave in the woods'.

(v)
The Wine of Dorwinion

> It must be potent wine to make a wood-elf drowsy. But this it would seem was the heady brew of the great gardens of Dorwinion in the warm South, not meant for his soldiers or his servants, but for the king's feasts only, and for smaller bowls, not the butler's jugs. Soon the chief guard fell asleep and not long after the butler put his head on the table and snored beside him.
>
> —p. 383.

The presence of wine from Dorwinion in the Elvenking's halls is yet another piece of circumstantial evidence demonstrating the affinity in Tolkien's mind between the elves of Mirkwood and those of Doriath, Thingol's people, since such wine appears in only two of Tolkien's works, *The Hobbit* and 'The Lay of the Children of Húrin' [begun circa 1918], and both times in connection with wood-elves. In the alliterative poem, Beleg the hunter gives this same wine to Túrin and his companions after he finds them lost in the woods of Doriath:

> *. . . their heads were mazed*
> *by the wine of Dor-Winion that went in their veins,*
> *and they soundly slept . . .*
>
> —'The Lay of the Children of Húrin',
> lines 229b–231a; HME III.11.

Furthermore, we are told that this wine

> *. . . is bruised from the berries of the burning South –*
> *and the Gnome-folk know it, and the nation of the Elves,*
> *and by long ways lead it to the lands of the North.*
>
> —ibid., lines 225–227.

That this wine would stupefy starving human travellers is no wonder, but its potency is also testified by its effect on Orgof, one of Thingol's high-ranking thanes (the figure known as Saeros in the published *Silmarillion*); it is when he is 'deep drunken' (line 484) on this same 'wine of Dor-Winion that went ungrudged/in their golden goblets' (lines 425–426a) that he taunts Túrin, resulting in his own death. These two incidents are the only two times in Tolkien's work when he describes an elf becoming drunk, and it can hardly be an accident that the same wine (potent indeed) was involved in both cases.

Unlike many names in *The Hobbit*, Dorwinion seems easy to explicate: *Dor*, land (as in Gon*dor*, Mor*dor*, *Dor*thonion); *winion*, wine: Wine-land or Vinland. David Salo (*A Gateway to Sindarin*, page 374) considers it a mixed Sindarin-Welsh form (Welsh *gwin*, wine) but it might as easily be taken as a case where Sindarin's inspiration in real-world Welsh has been less assimilated than usual; many similar instances are cited in *An Introduction to Elvish*, Jim Allan et al., pages 49–50. However, against this we must set a late linguistic essay Tolkien wrote glossing names in *The Fellowship of the Ring*, in which he gave a completely different explanation for the name:

> In the Hobbit all names are translated except *Galion* (the Butler), *Esgaroth*, and *Dorwinion. Galion* and *Esgaroth* are not Sindarin (though perhaps 'Sindarized' in shape) or are not recorded in *Sindarin*; but *Dorwinion* is *Sindarin* meaning 'Young-land country'.

Above the gloss he has later written in pencil 'or Land of Gwinion'. The *Gnomish Lexicon* gives *gwinwen* as a word meaning 'freshness' (*Parma Eldalamberon* XI.46), with *gwion* being one of the words meaning 'young' (ibid.42). The glosses given above, while authorial, postdate the creation of these names by decades and so may be afterthoughts rather than definitive explanations. But if they do indeed reveal what was in Tolkien's mind when he first created the name – that is, if *Dorwinion* in fact meant

'Land of Youth' rather than 'Wine-land' when Tolkien first created the name – then here he is deliberately drawing on Celtic (specifically Irish) myth. Not only is Tir na nÓg ('The Land of Youth') one of the most famous of the Celtic otherworlds that could be reached through *imrama* (voyages into the mythic West), but it was one that particularly interested Tolkien, who intended to devote a chapter of the unfinished *The Lost Road* [1936] to 'a Tuatha-de-Danaan story, or Tir-nan-Og' (HME V.77), having already mentioned it in his 1924 poem 'The Nameless Land', where he describes Tol Eressëa:

Than Tír na nÓg[45] *more fair and free,*
Than Paradise more faint and far,
O! shore beyond the Shadowy Sea,
O! land forlorn where lost things are,
O! mountians where no man may be!
—lines 49–53; HME V.99–100.

If these associations were present from an early date, it would explain the unusual potency of the wine from this magical land – compare Dunsany's Gorgondy, the wi`ne of the gnomes; so potent that drinking it can kill even a hardened sailor outright ('The Secret of the Sea'; *The Last Book of Wonder* [1916]), so superlative that it surpasses all other wines and its taste can lure a man into fatal risks to gain more ('The Opal Arrow-Head' [1920], collected in *The Man Who Ate the Phoenix* [1947]).

If *Dorwinion* indeed means 'The Land of Youth', then we would expect there to be only one such enchanted land in all the world. On the other hand, if it simply means 'Wine-land', that name could plausibly be applied to more than one country. Are we justified in considering the Dorwinion referred to in the Túrin story as the same land referred to in *The Hobbit*? Certainly Tolkien does seem to have re-used the name at least once, when he included in the final paragraph of the 1937 *Quenta Silmarillion* a reference to 'the undying flowers in the meads of Dorwinion' as part of Tol Eressëa, the Lonely Isle (HME V.334); while this fits in perfectly with the 'Land of Youth' gloss it cannot at the same time be accommodated to Dorwinion's mention in the alliterative poem and *The Hobbit* – however precious and potent the wine drunken in Menegroth and the Halls of the Elvenking, it certainly had not been imported all the way from Elvenhome. Moreover, in the revised version of *The Lay of the Children of Húrin* [circa 1923], it specifies that this wine reaches Doriath by way of dwarven traders:

. . . berries of the burning South–
the Gnome-folk know it, from Nogrod the Dwarves
by long ways lead it to the lands of the North

for the Elves in exile who by evil fate
the vine-clad valleys now view no more
in the land of Gods.

—lines 539–544a, HME III.111.

These two references could be reconciled if we assume that the vine-clad valleys of Valinor were known as Dorwinion, as per the 1937 *Quenta Silmarillion*, and the elves of Beleriand applied the name to a quite distinct wine district in Middle-earth in memory of that other Dorwinion, but it seems far more probable that Tolkien simply re-used the name in this section of the *Quenta Silmarillion* (which is more closely related to the 1930 *Quenta* than most of the 1937 text; see Note 32 on p. 429). By contrast, I think the two Dorwinions referred to in the alliterative poem and the wood-elf chapter of *The Hobbit* are one and the same, that Tolkien borrowed the name and concept entire from the old lay and that, given the geographical flexibility of lands 'off the map' to the south, the same referents would serve.

Dorwinion does not appear on any of Tolkien's Beleriand maps (see 'The First "Silmarillion" Map', HME.[219]–234), nor on the Wilderland map accompanying *The Hobbit* (see DAA.[399] and the maps on Plates I and II), nor on the large fold-out map of Middle-earth published with volumes one and two of *The Lord of the Rings*. However, it does appear on Pauline Baynes' version of the Middle-earth map published in 1970, at the mouth of the River Running on the north-west shore of the Sea of Rhûn (in the exact same spot where the label 'Sea of Rhûn' appears on Tolkien's own map, drawn for him by his son Christopher). This is one of a number of new names Tolkien provided Baynes for her map in 1969, not all of which were placed correctly, as noted by Christopher Tolkien (*Unfinished Tales*, pages 261–2),[46] but in this case we can confirm its placement thanks to the same unpublished late linguistic essay already cited, in which Tolkien comments that Dorwinion 'was probably far south down the R. Running, and its *Sindarin* name a testimony to the spread of *Sindarin*: in this case expectable since the cultivation of vines was not known originally to the *Nandor* or *Avari*'.[47] In any case, its placement here, even if in accordance with Tolkien's instructions, is a late accretion and almost certainly not what he intended at the time he wrote *The Hobbit*, when the surrounding geography was as yet undetermined; on Baynes' map, Dorwinion is no further south than the Necromancer's tower (Dol Guldur) and roughly equal to the southern edge of the Wilderland map – hardly 'in the warm South' (a location more like the later Ithilien would seem to be more in keeping with Tolkien's original conception, given his descriptions of the latter's climate in *The Lord of the Rings*).

NOTES

1 While a few of the other Tales start from non-elven (human) perspectives, they quickly shift to elven settings early in the story; see, for example, 'The Fall of Gondolin' and 'Turambar and the Foalókë' in *The Book of Lost Tales* (I do not use the example of 'The Tale of Tinúviel', which would otherwise fit this pattern, since in the earliest surviving version of this story, in *The Book of Lost Tales*, Beren is an elf). In *The Lays of Beleriand*, the same pattern holds: in 'The Children of Húrin' Túrin reaches Doriath by the middle of the first canto, while 'The Lay of Leithian' devotes its first canto to Thingol the elvenking, the second to Beren and Barahir the human outlaws, and the third to bringing the human and elven halves of the story together.

2 To give one famous example, in 1895, when Tolkien was three years old, a woman was burned to death by her husband in the belief she was a changeling and that, by abusing the substitute, he could force the fairies to bring back his real wife. After burying the corpse he spent the next several nights waiting at the crossroads for the fairies to ride by, hoping to seize and reclaim his wife from among them. His behavior, which horrified the nation and led to a famous murder trial in which a number of members of his wife's family were sent to jail for aiding and abetting in his faux-exorcism, was clearly in accordance with old beliefs regarding humans carried off by the elves reflected in stories recounted by Walter Scott, W. B. Yeats, and others, going at least as far back as the Tam Lin story [sixteenth century], if not Thomas Rhymer [thirteenth/fourteenth century] and Walter Map [twelfth century]; Briggs devotes an entire chapter to stories about humans carried off by the elves ('Captives in Fairyland'), some of whom are rescued and some lost forever, in her book *The Vanishing People* [1978]. For more on the historical episode, see *The Burning of Bridget Cleary* by Angela Bourke [2000].

Tolkien was probably aware of this episode, since it is alluded to in Roger Lancelyn Green's biography of Andrew Lang (*Andrew Lang: A Critical Biography* [1946], page 98), which had originated as Green's B. Litt. dissertation directed by Tolkien himself.

3 '. . . I am a reader and lover of fairy-stories, but not a student of them, as Andrew Lang was. I have not the learning, nor the still more necessary wisdom, which the subject demands.' – OFS, *Essays Presented to Charles Williams* [1947], page [38]. In the revised form of the essay that appeared in *Tree and Leaf* [1964], this passage is changed to read '. . . for though I have been a lover of fairy-stories since I learned to read, and have at times thought about them, I have not studied them professionally. I have been hardly more than a wandering explorer (or trespasser) in the land, full of wonder but not of information' (*Tree and Leaf*, expanded edition [1988], page [9]).

Note that Tolkien is here comparing himself against one of the world's top experts on fairy-stories, in a lecture-series named after that expert and intended to commemorate his achievements. Had Tolkien not already been considered something of an expert on fairy-stories himself, it seems unlikely he would have been asked to give the lecture, especially so shortly after *The Hobbit*'s first publication. The lecture was delivered in March 1939, but Tolkien seems to have already been at work on it as early as January–February 1938, since he promised to read 'a paper "on" fairy stories' to the Lovelace Society of Worcester College, Oxford at that time but since it was unfinished wound up reading them 'The Lord of Thame' (i.e., *Farmer Giles of Ham)* instead (FGH, expanded edition, page vi). This seems to indicate that he must have already received the invitation to deliver the lecture and selected its topic within months of *The Hobbit*'s publication, which had occurred only the preceding September [September 1937].

4 It may be significant that Mary Wright, the wife of his tutor and mentor, Joseph Wright, published a book in 1913 – that is, during the period of the Wrights' closest connection with JRRT, when he was visiting their home on a regular basis for his tutorials and socializing (cf. Carpenter, pages 55–6) – called *Rustic Speech and Folk-lore* which devoted a chapter to the survival of belief in fairy creatures such as hobs and fairies as reflected in rural dialects into modern times.

5 This is less true of the elves as he developed them in *The Lord of the Rings* or the later revisions of the Silmarillion material; for this reason, he came to prefer 'Eldar' over 'Elves' in his very late material.

6 For the argument that Tolkien's Valar were directly inspired by Dunsany's Gods of Pegana, see my dissertation, *Beyond the Fields We Know: The Short Stories of Lord Dunsany* (Ph.D. diss., Marquette University, [1990]).

7 Briggs, page [7]. Her other reason for the title is the persistent legend of the elves' withdrawal from mortal lands, or at least from contact with humans, something not at all evident in *The Hobbit* but very much a key feature of *The Book of Lost Tales* and a major background element of *The Lord of the Rings.*

8 Tolkien does use the motif of the fairy dance elsewhere, in *Smith of Wootton Major* [written circa 1964, published 1967]:

> [H]e heard elven voices singing, and on a lawn beside a river . . . he came upon many maidens dancing. The speed and the grace and the ever-changing modes of their movements enchanted him, and he stepped forward towards their ring. Then suddenly they stood still, and a young maiden with flowing hair and kilted skirt came out to meet him . . . 'Come! Now that you are here you shall dance with me'; and she took his hand and led him into the ring.
>
> There they danced together, and for a while he knew what it was to have the swiftness and the power and the joy to accompany her. For a while. But soon as it seemed they halted again . . . 'Farewell now!' she said. 'Maybe we shall meet again . . .'
>
> —SWM, pages 31–3.

Note the careful use of words with significant associations in fairy-lore: the sight of them *enchanted* him, she led him *into the* [faery] *ring*, and 'soon *as it seemed*' their dance was over, all of which the reader is free to read as much or as little significance into as he or she pleases, in accordance with Tolkien's championing of 'applicability' rather than allegory (cf. his Foreword to the second edition of *The Lord of the Rings*).

9 See also Tolkien's treatment of the enchanted forest of Lothlórien; when the Fellowship leave, they cannot agree on whether more time has passed than they thought or less (*LotR*.408). The best informed among those present, Legolas and Aragorn, argue that the difference was one of perception only, and this is borne out by the detailed calendar of events in Appendix B: 'The Tale of Years'. But Tolkien's rough drafts had reached a different conclusion, and one more in keeping with traditional folklore: 'Whether we were in the past or the future or in a time that does not pass, I cannot say: but not I think till Silverlode bore us back to Anduin did we return to the stream of time that flows through mortal lands to the Great Sea' (HME VII.355). See also page 286 (ibid.) for the conception of the elvenwood as a land outside of time, where travellers leave to find no time has passed in the outside world however long they remained within Lórien itself. For much more on time in Lórien, see 'Over a Bridge of Time', Chapter 4 in Verlyn Flieger's *A Question of Time: J. R. R. Tolkien's Road to Faërie* [1997].

10 The Middle English equivalent of the phrase Tolkien translates as 'by magic' is '*with fairie*' – that is, by means of faerie or elven arts. Later in the poem he translates the same phrase as 'by fairy magic' (line 404).

As Douglas Anderson points out in *The Annotated Hobbit* (DAA. 199–200), Tolkien knew *Sir Orfeo* very well, having prepared his own text of the original Middle English poem [1944] and also translated the poem into modern English [before 1945, published 1975]. All my citations come from Tolkien's translation. For a critical edition of Tolkien's Middle English text, and a discussion of the changes Tolkien made to the original manuscript, see '*Sir Orfeo*: A Middle English Version by J. R. R. Tolkien' by Carl Hostetter, in *Tolkien Studies*, Volume 1 [2004], pages 85–123.

11 It will be noted that all of these sources are, to some degree, 'Celtic' – that is, while some are written in (Old) French or (Middle) English, they all derive from Breton and Welsh legend. Tom Shippey has argued, in 'Tolkien and Iceland: The Philology of Envy',† that in creating his Mythology for England Tolkien 'wanted English myths, and English legends, and English fairy-stories, and these did not exist. He refused to borrow from Celtic tradition, which he regarded as alien.' This, I think, rather overstates the case. Certainly Tolkien did not choose Celtic legends for the core of his new myth, for reasons explained in his 'Letter to Waldman' (*Letters* p. 144), but he did explicitly state that he wanted it to possess 'the fair elusive beauty that some call Celtic (though it is rarely found in genuine ancient Celtic things)' and it could be said that any English mythology worthy of the name would have

to take into account the sense of vanished peoples and the lingering remnants of the former inhabitants of the land that is so much an element of England's history. It is true enough that one of the most fundamental core elements in Tolkien's imagined history of the elves derives from Norse tradition as recorded in the Eddas (see 'The Three Kindreds of the Elves' on p. 405), yet it is also true that those elves in Middle-earth speak a language (known at various points in its history as Gnomish, Noldorin, and finally Sindarin) that drew its inspiration and soundvalues from Welsh and that Tolkien's warrior-elves resemble not the Icelanders of the sagas but the Tuatha dé Danaan of Irish myth more closely than any other literary antecedent; the elven and human immigrations and invasions of Beleriand can even be loosely paralleled to the Irish *Leber Gabála Érenn* ('The Book of Invasions' [cmp. eleventh century]) and *Cath Maige Tuired* ('The Battle of Mag Tuired'; ninth/tenth century). As Verlyn Flieger says of *The Book of Lost Tales*, 'It doesn't take much to see in Tolkien's Fairies (soon to be developed into Elves) a near-direct replication of the Irish *Sidh*, the fairy folk of the Celtic Otherworld' (*Interrupted Music: The Making of Tolkien's Mythology* [2005], page 136). See also Marjorie Burns' *Perilous Realms: Celtic and Norse in Tolkien's Middle-earth* [2005] for a balanced argument on how Tolkien incorporated both Norse and Celtic elements into his mythology.

† This excellent and informative lecture, delivered at Icelandic National University [the Sigurður Nordal Institute] in September 2002, has not yet been published but is available online at http://www.nordals.hi.is/shippey.html.

12. Walter Map, *De Nugis Curialium* ('A Courtier's Trifles') [c. 1181–1193 AD], edited by M. R. James [1914] and 'Englished' (translated) by Frederick Tupper and Marbury Bladen Ogle as *Master Walter Map's Book* [1924]. While much of Map's miscellany is made up of gossip about kings and tirades about monastic orders he disliked, among the stories he records is that of King Herla, a British king who rode on a visit to Faerie and, returning to his own land the next day, found that more than two hundred years had passed and his realm had long since been conquered by the Anglo-Saxons. When one of his men dismounted, he crumbled into dust; for centuries afterwards Herla and his rout rode unceasingly up and down the land until the apparition suddenly ceased a few decades before Map's time (Map, pages 17–18).

Even more striking is the story of the woman who died whose husband later discovered her dancing in the woods with the Fair Folk and managed to rescue her and carry her back home again, a story Map likes so much he tells it twice (pages 97–8 & 218). The reunited couple resume their interrupted lives together, and Map notes that the descendants of her children born after her rescue were known to his day as 'sons of the dead woman'. The parallels to *Sir Orfeo* on the one hand, where Orfeo sees both the dead and the fairies together once he enters the elf-hill and reaches the fairy king's castle:

Then he began to gaze about,
and saw within the walls a rout
of folk that were thither drawn below,
and mourned as dead, but were not so.

— *Sir Orfeo*, lines 387–390

and the Bridget Cleary case on the other (see Note 2 above), are striking, considering that a century or more separates Map and *Sir Orfeo*, and another six centuries separates *Orfeo* from the Clearys, not to mention the geographical distance between Brittany, the setting of Map's story and source of the Breton lay from which *Sir Orfeo* derives, and rural Ireland where the Clearys lived.

13 In addition to the hunters, Orfeo also sometimes sees dancing (lines 297–302) and sometimes warriors riding by:

At other times he would descry
a mighty host, it seemed, go by,
ten hundred knights all fair arrayed
with many a banner proud displayed.
Each face and mien was fierce and bold,
each knight a drawn sword there did hold,
and all were armed in harness fair
and marching on he knew not where.

— *Sir Orfeo*, lines 289–296.

This latter passage may have helped inspire the marshalling of the elven army that occurs near the end of *The Hobbit*, first for the siege of the Lonely Mountain and then for the Battle of Five Armies. It also may account for the elusive scene in *Smith of Wootton Major* where Smith sees a host of elven mariners march past, while Smith himself later joins in just such a dancing scene as the Middle English poem describes when he dances with the Queen of Faery herself (see Note 8 above).

14 In the typescript interpolation, this passage is expanded somewhat:

> Then they heard the *disquieting* laughter. Sometimes there was singing in the distance too. The laughter was the laughter of fair voices not of goblins, and the singing was beautiful, but it sounded *eerie and strange*, and they were not comforted, *rather they hurried on from those parts with what strength they had left*.
>
> — 'The Enchanted Stream', page [4]; emphasis mine.

15 Indeed, Marjorie Burns goes so far as to assert that 'the inevitable water crossing . . . divides the rest of Middle-earth from the inner core of every Elven realm' – *Perilous Realms*, page 61.

16 'Lord Nann and the Fairy' ('Aotrou Nann Hag ar Gorrigan'), *Ballads and Songs of Brittany* by Tom Taylor [1865], pages [8]–14; translated from *Barsaz Breiz* by Vicomte Hersart de la Villemarque [1846].† An alternate translation, apparently the first into English, appears in Thomas Keightley's *The Fairy Mythology, Illustrative of the Romance and*

Superstition of Various Countries [revised and expanded 1850 edition] as 'Lord Nann and the Korrigan', pages 433–436.

† Verlyn Flieger notes that Tolkien owned a copy of the original 1846 edition of *Barsaz Breiz*, with his name and the date '1922' inscribed in it; this two-volume set is now in the English Faculty Library at Oxford (*Interrupted Music*, page 154).

17 In the original Breton lay, it is Lord Nann's drinking of the water from her fountain that puts him in the Korrigan's power. In Tolkien's more complex and subtle version, Aotrou has already visited her before and gotten a magic potion from her to give his wife; she now demands repayment for that earlier draught. In a possible parallel to the enchanted stream scene in *The Hobbit*, it may be significant that Aotrou does not see the Korrigan until after he has dismounted and 'laved his face in water cool' from 'the fountain of the fay' (lines 288 and 284), just as the dwarves do not hear the elven hunt until after Bombur has fallen into the enchanted stream.

18 For more on identification of the Fair Folk with the ancient dead, see Briggs, *The Vanishing People*, pages 31 and 37. This is only one of the many competing theories of fairy origins, both among folklore scholars and within the tales themselves (see Briggs, 'The Origins of Fairy Beliefs and Beliefs about Fairy Origins', Chapter 2 in *The Vanishing People*). Other suggestions advanced at various times are that they are gods reduced in stature after their former worshippers converted to Christianity (e.g., the Tuatha dé Danaan and the major characters in the Four Branches of the *Mabinogi* such as Manawydan, Aranrhod, and Rhiannon); that they are fallen angels, those who supported neither God nor Satan during Lucifer's rebellion and so were thrown out of Heaven but not driven into Hell; that they were a folk-memory of Neanderthals or other defeated peoples, earlier inhabitants of the land living on the margins of habitable lands (cf. Tolkien's Drúedain or woodwoses); that they are a cursed offshoot of the human race, either the children of Cain (*Beowulf*) or 'the hidden children of Eve' (Briggs, pages 30–31), &c.

19 I base this translation upon a full rhyming translation of the poem made by Dr. Rhona Beare (unpublished), modified by comparison with Shippey's prose translation (*The Road to Middle-earth*, expanded edition [2003], page 358) and my own consultation with Clark Hall's *Anglo-Saxon Dictionary*; any errors thus introduced are of course my own responsibility.

20 This feature can clearly be seen in two of Tolkien's drawings for the Elvenking's Halls in *The Hobbit*, one of which he chose to include for publication in the book; see DAA.224 (the top and bottommost drawings) or H-S#120, 121 (the lintel-gate shows up particularly well in the *Artist & Illustrator* reproductions). Interestingly enough, this same feature can also be seen in one of his drawings for the entrance to the underground elven city of Nargothrond (H-S#57); see

my commentary on pp. 408–9 on the links between the wood-elves' dwelling and Nargothrond.

For the intimate link between the elves and the dead, both of whom live in an 'other' world that is in some ways strikingly like our own and in others just as strikingly unlike, and both of whom can be perilous to deal with, see Note 18 above.

21 The Green Children. In this, the very first tale in the section on England in Keightley's *The Fairy Mythology* (pages 281–3), he recounts the story by Ralph of Coggeshall (died c. 1227) and also by William of Newbridge (died c. 1198) of two children with green skin who accidentally wandered out of their underground world into the sunlight realm of Suffolk in the time of King Stephen (reigned 1135–54). Overcome by the glaring light of the sun, they could not find their way back to their own world. For more on this unusual story, a rare case of elves intruding into and becoming trapped within the mortal world, see Briggs, *A Dictionary of Fairies*, pages 200–201.

22 Tolkien reveals extensive knowledge of the legends concerning the Tuatha dé Danaan and Welsh legends of the Fair Folk appearing in the *Mabinogion* and elsewhere in his short essay 'The Name "Nodens"', which appeared as a philological appendix to the archeological report published by R. E. M. Wheeler describing excavations at the Temple of Nodens in Gloucestershire [1932].

For more on the Tuatha dé Danaan, perhaps the best account is Lady Gregory's retelling of *Cath Maige Tuired* ('The Battle of Mag Tuired') in her book *Gods and Fighting Men* [1904], giving a vivid account of Nuada of the Silver Hand and Lug of the Long Arm and their battles against the Fir Bolg and Fomorians.

23 Faerie could also be reached by sailing across the sea: cf. *The Voyage of Bran* [Irish, eighth century], and Tolkien's own poems 'Ides Ælfscýne', 'Imram', and 'The Sea-Bell'. The voyages of Eärendel the Mariner in the earliest Middle-earth poems, Eriol in *The Book of Lost Tales*, and the unfinished 'Ælfwine of England' story [circa 1920] all draw on Tolkien's conception of an overseas Elvenhome reachable only by a chosen few.

24 On the face of it, the Elvenking's statement that none can escape back out through his gates seems to be contradicted by the fact that Bilbo can slip in and out undetected, but we should note that the hobbit was not 'brought' inside as were the dwarves but entered on his own volition. The literal truth or otherwise of his words goes untested, since the dwarves do not in the end escape through those gates but by another exit (the trapdoor over the river).

25 This is all the more remarkable because of Tolkien's earlier use of an enchanted drink motif (à la Rip Van Winkle) when Bombur is cast into a magical sleep after falling into (and presumably inadvertently drinking from) the dark waters of the enchanted stream. The motif of a stream bringing forgetfulness or drowsiness seems to derive more

from classical mythology (the river Lethe) than folklore, but Douglas Anderson points out (DAA.198) that it also occurs in the St. Brendan legend, which Tolkien recast as 'Imram'. In the original saint's life, one of the many marvels Brendan and his companions encounter comes when they land on an island with a clear well. Those who drink from it fall asleep for a full day and night for each cup of water they drank. Although this episode is not one of those Tolkien included in 'Imram' (which represents an extremely abbreviated version of the legend, with incidents selected for maximum effect), he would certainly have been aware of it. See 'The Soporific Well', part 13 in John J. O'Meara's translation of *Navigatio Sancti Brendani* ('The Voyage of St. Brendan' [1976; rpt. 1991]), pages 32–4.

26 The idea of hiding in barrels or crates is of course an ancient one (cf. the story of Ali Baba) that needs no specific source; even today newspapers occasionally carry the story of someone who has attempted to ship himself cross-country in a box. I have heard second-hand of one such story, a sixteenth-century account of an English traveller said to have escaped from a Turkish prison through means similar to those Bilbo employs in *The Hobbit* and which therefore might have inspired or influenced the episode in Tolkien's story, but I have been unable to confirm the existence of such a story in Hakluyt's *Voyages* or similar sources.

27 For a detailed look at the rather tangled matter of light-elves, dark-elves, and black-elves in the Eddas, and how they might interrelate with the wood-elves (*wudu-ælfen*) known from Old English sources, see Tom Shippey's 'Light-elves, Dark-elves, and Others', the lead article in *Tolkien Studies* Volume I [2004], pages 1–15. Tolkien has clearly taken a confused and contradictory tradition known to us only through fragmentary survivals and imposed a coherent (and, to millions of readers, wholly satisfactory) pattern of his own upon it.

28 This passage was further revised for the replacement ending to this Ts. (1/1/58:16). In addition to many minor changes in wording, the phrase 'different from other elves' was replaced by 'different from the high elves of the West, more dangerous and less wise'; 'as well as the few elves that live in hills and mountains' became '(together with their scattered relations in the hills and mountains)'; 'to the great Fairyland of the West' became 'to Faerie in the West'; and finally a new sentence is added to the end of the paragraph: 'Still elves they were and remain, and that is Good People'.

29 Compare the elven boat that appears in Tolkien's illustration of Lake-Town (Plate VIII [bottom]) with the one in his painting of Taniquetil ([1928]; *Pictures by JRRT* plate 31; Priestman, *Life and Legend*, cover illustration; H-S#52). Even though one is built by the Wood-elves of Mirkwood and the other by the Teleri of Tol Eressëa, the boats are almost identical – naturally enough, having been built by two branches of the same kindred, the Teleri of Middle-earth (the Sindar) and the Teleri of Valinor, respectively (cf. *Silm.*58 & 61).

30 In the published *Silmarillion* (pages 52–3), those who set out and reached Valinor are the Calaquendi ('Elves of the Light'); those who set out but failed to complete the journey the Úmanyar ('those not of Aman the Undying Land'); and those who never set out or refused the summons the Avari ('the Unwilling'). The Úmanyar and Avari together make up the Moriquendi ('Elves of the Darkness'), with the sole exception of Thingol Greycloak, since he did indeed visit Valinor once and became lost on his return journey to that land: 'king though he was of Úmanyar, he was not accounted among the Moriquendi, but with the Elves of the Light' (*Silm.*56). The wood-elves of *The Hobbit*, along with their kin who live scattered in the hills and mountains, seem to be a mix of Úmanyar and Avari (or, as the *Lhammas* called them, Lembi; cf. the 'family trees' of languages in HME V.182).

Caranthir's remark about Thingol is thus both deliberately insulting and untrue. However, it should be noted that this would not have been the case in earlier versions of the legend: in the 1930 *Quenta* it states explicitly that 'Of the Dark-elves the chief in renown was Thingol' (HME IV.85).

31 That is, the Deep-elves are so called because of their knowledge ('deep' in the sense of profound), not because they live underground. Similarly, their byname Gnome derives from the Greek *gnosis* (thought, knowledge, wisdom), a sense preserved today in gnomic literature (maxims, aphorisms, proverbs; literally 'wisdom writing') and Gnosticism (secret wisdom). Tolkien goes to some pains (*Letters* p. 318) to distinguish his Gnomes from the earth elementals created by Paracelsus [1658] and popularized by Alexander Pope's 'The Rape of the Lock' [1714], eventually abandoning 'gnome' altogether when he realized the popular association of the name with garden gnomes and the like was insurmountable.

The Light-elves are so called because of their devotion to the light of Valinor, which is so strong that they dwell among the Valar themselves at the foot of Mount Taniquetil rather than with their fellow elves in Elvenhome. The Sea-elves gained their name dwelling on the coasts of Beleriand before some of them removed first to Tol Eressëa and then Elvenhome itself; those left behind either withdrew into the woods of Middle-earth and became the wood-elves (Thingol's people) or stayed beside the ocean and became known as the Falathrim ('elves of the coasts', Círdan the Shipwright's people).

32 The old name 'Light-elves' was retained in the manuscript Christopher Tolkien refers to as 'The Conclusion of the *Quenta Silmarillion*' (HME V.323ff), but this text clearly is more closely linked to the 1930 *Quenta* than the 1937 *Quenta Silmarillion* as a whole, and it is not surprising that it retains some archaic elements, such as the retention of the old common name for the First Kindred that had appeared in the 1926 'Sketch,' the 1930 *Quenta,* and *The Hobbit* (this particular passage from which probably dates from 1931).

The final name for the First Kindred, 'Vanyar', seems to have arisen sometime in the late 1940s or early 1950s, possibly as late as 1958; cf. 'The Annals of Aman' ([circa 1958]; HME X.82–5) and 'The Grey Annals' ([1951 & 1958]; HME XI.6–7), as well as HME X.34 & 6 (Version D of the *Ainulindalë* [after 1951]).

33 One could say that Tolkien borrowed from Celtic legend and traditional folklore for the external description of the elves – that is, the elves as they appear to others (specifically, Bilbo and the dwarves) – and drew on his own legendarium once the focus shifts so that we can see the elves close up.

34 Unfortunately the elvenking's halls are never described in detail, either in *The Hobbit* or afterwards, but we can get some idea of what they might have looked like (albeit on a somewhat grander scale) from Tolkien's description in 'The Lay of Leithian' of King Thingol's halls in Menegroth:

> Downward . . .
> through corridors of carven dread
> whose turns were lit by lanterns hung
> or flames from torches that were flung
> on dragons hewn in the cold stone
> with jewelled eyes and teeth of bone.
> Then sudden, deep beneath the earth
> the silences with silver mirth
> were shaken and the rocks were ringing,
> the birds of Melian were singing;
> and wide the ways of shadow spread
> as into archéd halls [Lúthien] led
> Beren in wonder. There a light
> like day immortal and like night
> of stars unclouded, shone and gleamed.
> A vault of topless trees it seemed,
> whose trunks of carven stone there stood
> like towers of an enchanted wood
> in magic fast for ever bound,
> bearing a roof whose branches wound
> in endless tracery of green
> lit by some leaf-emprisoned sheen
> of moon and sun, and wrought of gems,
> and each leaf hung on golden stems.
> Lo! there amid immortal flowers
> the nightingales in shining bowers
> stand o'er the head of Melian,
> while water for ever dripped and ran
> from fountains in the rocky floor.
> There Thingol sat.

—'The Lay of Leithian', Canto IV, lines 980–1009; HME III.188–9.

35 Or, according to some versions of the legend, great-grandfather. Cf. Elrond's words to Bingo [= Frodo] in the earliest version of the Rivendell chapter: 'My mother was Elwing daughter of Lúthien daughter of King Thingol of Doriath' (HME VI.215–16). The same wording survived into the second version of 'The Council of Elrond' (HME VII.110) and does not seem to have been altered to include Dior, Lúthien's son, until the fourth draft (HME VII.127). Since Dior had already appeared as far back as *The Book of Lost Tales*, his absence here might be mere forgetfulness on Tolkien's part when drafting 'The New Hobbit', or it might represent the brief appearance of an alternate tradition which was rejected in favor of the long-established genealogy.

36 For an earlier form of the same concept of Doriath's mixed elven population, see *The Book of Lost Tales*: 'many a wild and woodland clan rallied beneath King Tinwelint [Thingol]. Of those the most were Ilkorindi – which is to say Eldar that never had beheld Valinor or the Two Trees or dwelt in Kôr – and eerie they were and strange beings, knowing little of light or loveliness or of musics save it be dark songs and chantings of a rugged wonder that faded in the wooded places or echoed in deep caves.† Different indeed did they become when the Sun arose, and indeed before that already were their numbers mingled with a many wandering Gnomes [Noldor], and wayward sprites [very minor Maiar] too there were of Lorien's host [i.e., the Vala Lórien or Irmo; cf. the *Valaquenta*, *Silm*.28] that dwelt in the courts of Tinwelint, being followers of Gwendeling [Melian], and these were not of the kindreds of the Eldalië [Eldar]', in addition to 'fugitives that fled to his protection' after the Battle of Unnumbered Tears ('The Tale of Tinúviel', BLT II.9).

† Compare the strange singing Bilbo and the dwarves heard in the forest – beautiful but eerie and strange and not at all comforting.

37 This assertion represents a new element entering into the mythology, since in all previous versions of the story Thorin's folk, the Longbeards or *Indrafangs*, had indeed taken part in the raid on Doriath and killing of the king; cf. BLT II.230 & 234–5, although in the original version of the story the dwarves of Nogrod (the *Nauglath*) rather than the dwarves of Belegost (the *Indrafangs*) had been the instigators of the attack. Both groups take part in the war in the 1926 'Sketch' (HME IV.32) and 1930 *Quenta* (HME IV.132–3), except in the latter we are now told that the Indrafangs or Longbeards are the dwarves of Nogrod, not Belegost (something also true of the 1937 *Quenta Silmarillion*, which unfortunately does not include an account of the elf-dwarf war due to its having been left incomplete). The '(Later) Annals of Beleriand' (post-*Hobbit*, pre-*LotR*) agrees with this tradition that both groups of dwarves invaded (HME V.141) but does not specify which is which.

In later material such as the 'Annals of Aman' ([1950s]; HME X.93), the 'Grey Annals' ([c. 1950–51]; HME XI.10), and the later *Quenta Silmarillion* ([post *LotR*/early 1950s]; HME XI.205), Tolkien reverted to the original identification of the dwarves of Belegost as the

Longbeards, but all of these works broke off before reaching the war, so the role of the Longbeards within it remains murky. In the published *Silmarillion*, the dwarves of Belegost not only refuse to join their kin from Nogrod in the attack but 'sought to dissuade them from their purpose' (*Silm*.233). However, by that point the name 'Longbeard' had been shifted to the dwarves of Khazad-dûm (Moria), though it seems clear that this shift postdated *The Hobbit* and that the association of Thorin's folk with the Blue Hills west of Bilbo's home, which were only their temporary homes in exile in the published book, had very ancient roots in the original conception.

38 'As great a treasure as other elf-lords of old.' The elf-lords specifically referred to here seem to be Orodreth of the Rodothlim (a figure whose role in the mythology was later greatly diminished, being largely superseded by Finrod Felagund of Nargothrond), Turgon of Gondolin, and, if he is not the same character as the Elvenking, Thingol of Doriath. Of Gondolin we are told the city held 'a wealth of jewels and metals and stuffs and of things wrought by the hands of the Gnomes to surpassing beauty' (BLT II.175).

For more on the great treasure of the Rodothlim, and the wonders the dwarves later crafted from it at Tinwelint's [Thingol's] bidding, see my commentary following Chapter XIV, starting on p. 595. Tinwelint's treasure, like the Elvenking's, was originally far too scanty for his liking (that is, before he gained the Rodothlim's hoard), although his wealth was greatly increased in later versions of the story, along with his majesty and dignity:

> Now the folk of Tinwelint were of the woodlands and had scant wealth, yet did they love fair and beauteous things, gold and silver and gems, as do all the Eldar . . . nor was the king of other mind in this, and his riches were small, save it be for that glorious Silmaril that many a king had given all his treasury contained if he might possess it. ('Turambar and the Foalókë, BLT II.95)

Furthermore, as Christopher Tolkien points out (BLT II.245 & 128), Tinwelint frankly admits that part of his motive for sending some of his elves to investigate the caves of the Rodothlim after they had become a dragon's lair is not just to find out what has become of his foster-son Túrin but the lure of dragon-treasure: 'Yet it is a truth that I have need and desire of treasury, and it may be that such shall come to me by this venture', although he magnanimously promises half of any treasure recovered to Túrin's mother (BLT II.95). Compare the Elvenking's similarly mixed motives in the final chapters of *The Hobbit*, where concern for the fate of the dwarves plays very little part and he chiefly wishes to claim Smaug's enormous hoard but nonetheless fully recognizes the Lake-men's claim to a large part of the treasure.

39 The 1937 *Quenta Silmarillion* broke off early in the Túrin story and so did not include the final quarter of the cycle, including the tales of the destruction of the great hidden elven kingdoms of Nargothrond,

Doriath, and Gondolin, corresponding to chapters 21, 22, and 23, respectively, of the published *Silmarillion*, which draws its text for these sections primarily from the 1930 *Quenta* instead.

For the three main versions of the destruction of Thingol's realm, see 'The Nauglafring' (BLT II.221-51), the 1926 'Sketch of the Mythology' (HME IV.32-3), and the 1930 *Quenta*, part 14 (HME IV.132–4, plus Christopher Tolkien's commentary thereon on IV.187–91). Shorter accounts may be found in the '(Earliest) Annals of Beleriand' (HME IV.306–7, V.141).

40 The plural 'wars' in this passage from *The Hobbit* is interesting but may simply refer to the early conception in *The Book of Lost Tales* of the dwarves as an evil people, like the goblins, who sometimes marched in Melko's armies; see commentary, pp. 76ff.† More probably, it refers to strife between the dwarves of the Blue Mountains and their neighbors the Sons of Fëanor mentioned in the 1930 *Quenta* (HME IV.103–4): '[The sons of Fëanor] made war upon the Dwarves of Nogrod and Belegost; but they did not discover whence that strange race came, nor have any since'.

† In fact, the dwarf-host that destroyed Tinwelint's realm was accompanied by 'a great host of Orcs, and wandering goblins', armed with dwarven weapons, attracted by 'a good wage' and the promise of much opportunity for looting and mayhem (BLT II.230, 232–3).

41 The name 'Thranduil' seems to have arisen quite late in the drafting of *The Lord of the Rings*, possibly during the construction of the Appendices after the main story had been completed; see part iv of this commentary on p. 417.

42 'Thither [i.e., to the Halls of Mandos] . . . fared the Elves . . . who were by illhap slain with weapons or did die of grief for those that were slain – and only so might the Eldar die, and then it was only for a while. There Mandos spake their doom, and there they waited in the darkness, dreaming of their past deeds, until such time as he appointed when they might again be born into their children, and go forth to laugh and sing again' ('The Coming of the Valar', BLT I.76).

Late in life Tolkien came to reject the concept that elves were literally reborn, preferring instead to have each elf's spirit (or *fëa*) once again be incarnated in a body (or *hröa*) identical to that he or she had inhabited before death rather than born into a new body as a child; the original (adult) body was either re-created by the memory of the spirit or created by the Valar, under dispensation from Ilúvatar, to house that spirit. In this conception, elves took up their bodies again immediately upon leaving the Halls of Mandos, and it is specifically stated that 'The re-housed *fëa* will normally remain in Aman [Valinor/ Elvenhome]. Only in very exceptional cases . . . will they be transported back to Middle-earth' (HME X.364).

43 It hardly seems a coincidence that Glorfindel, who died defending the seven-year-old Eärendil during the Fall of Gondolin, should turn up six

thousand years later in the retinue of Eärendil's son, Elrond Halfelven; he has clearly made it his task to guard the last scion of the house of Gondolin.

44 The name 'Nargothrond' itself arises for the first time in 'The Lay of the Children of Húrin', which predated *The Hobbit* by at least five years; see HME III.36 & 55.

45 For Tolkien's preferred spelling of this name, see HME V.98.

46 We know that Tolkien was unhappy with the results of Baynes' efforts (see Note 14 to the commentary following The Bladorthin Typescript), but he seems to have restricted his criticisms to the art-pieces she put at the top and bottom of her map; so far as I know his reservations did not extend to the map itself.

47 The Nandor are a group of Teleri who abandoned the westward march but later changed their mind and joined the Sindar in Beleriand, becoming the Green Elves of Ossiriand.

Chapter X
LAKE TOWN

As before, the story continues with nothing more than a paragraph break between what are now chapters IX and X in the middle of manuscript page 129 (Marq.1/1/11:1). On the back of this page is a faint sketch-map showing the forest's eastern edge, the precursor to the 'Home Manuscript' map shown on Plate I [bottom].

They rounded a steep shoulder of land that came down upon their right[TN1] under which the rocky feet [> under the rocky feet of which] the deepest stream flowed lapping and bubbling. Suddenly it fell away. The trees ended. Then Bilbo saw a sight. The land opened wide about them, filled with the waters of the river which broke up and wandered into marshes and pools and isles on either side, though a strong water flowed ever on through the midst. And far away, his dark head in cloud, there loomed the Mountain. Its nearest neighbors to the N.E. and the tumbled land that joined it to them could not be seen.[TN2] All alone it rose, and looked across the plain to the forest. The Lonely Mountain. Bilbo had come far and through many weary adventures to see it. And now he did not like the look of it at all!

Listening to the talk of the raftmen he soon realized that dreary as had been their emprisonment, and unpleasant as was their position even now, they were really more fortunate than they guessed.

They would have had small chance of doing more than glimpse that mountain from afar had they gone on and found the way out of the forest unhindered. The lands had changed since the days of the dwarves. Great floods and rains had swollen the waters. The marshes and bogs had spread wider and wider on either side. Paths had vanished, and many a wanderer and a rider too, who had tried to find his way across. Only by the river was there any longer a safe way from the skirts of Mirkwood to the mountain-shadowed plain beyond.[TN3] So they went on and on; and always the Mountain seem to threaten them more closely. At last late in the day its shores grew more rocky, the river gathered its wandering waters together; and then turning with a sweep southward it passed [*added*: through] a wide mouth with stony gates at either side piled with shingles at the feet into the Lake. The Long Lake! It was wide enough indeed, so that the far shore was small and far; but it was so long that its northern end pointing away towards the shoulders of the Mountain could only be guessed. At that end the Running river ran into it, and with the Forest stream filled what must once have been a great deep rocky valley, and then passed out again[TN4] southward with a doubled stream and ran away hurriedly to the South.

Not far from where the Forest Stream entered it, there was a strange town. It was not built upon the shore, though there were many huts and buildings there; but right out on the surface of the lake protected from the swirl of the moving river by a bay of rock. Great bridges[TN5] ran out into the water and to where on large piles made of the trunks of forest trees was built a busy wooden town. It was not a town of elves, but of men, who still dared to live under the shadow of the mountain, protected by the water, and the bridge that could be doubly defended or destroyed from enemies and even as they thought from dragons.

They grew rich [> still did well] on the trade that came up the great river from the south and was carted past the falls to their town, though the great days when Dale to the North was thriving and [they were rich >] there were <both> wars and a busy town of boats were now but a legend. The rotting piles of <another> greater <town> could be seen along the shores when there was a drought.

But they remembered little about it; though songs were still sung of the King Under the Mountain Thror and his son Thrain of the race of Durin, and of the coming of the Dragon, and the fall of the Lords of Dale.[TN6]

Added in the top margin and marked for insertion at this point: 'Some sang that Thror and Thrain would come back one day and gold would flow in rivers through the northern falls, and all that land would be filled with new song and new laughter. But that was a pleasant fable, which did not much affect their daily business, or their occasional quarrel with wood elves over tolls and such like troubles.'

Boats came out from the town and hailed the raftmen: [and soon the >] Ropes were cast, oars were pulled; and soon they were drawn out of the currents of the <merry> Forest River, and towed away to [the piles of >] round the shoulder of rock to lie ashore by the head [> some way from the head] of the chief bridge to Lake-town. Soon men would come up from the South and take some away, and fill others with stuffs they had brought to be taken back up to the wood elves' home. In the meanwhile the raftmen went to feast at [> in] Lake Town.

They would have been surprised if they could have seen what happened down by the shore as soon as evening fell. A barrel was opened by Bilbo (and the help of pushes and groans from inside); and out crept a most unhappy dwarf. Wet straw was in his draggled beard; he was so sore and stiff [*added*: so bruised & battered] he could scarcely stumble through the shallow water to lie groaning on the shore. He had a famished [*added*: & a savage] look like a dog that has been forgotten in a kennel for a week. It was Thorin[TN7] – but you can only have told it by his golden chain, and the colour of a now-tattered sky blue hood with a very tarnished silver tassel. It was some time before he would even be polite to the hobbit.

'Well are you alive or are you dead?' said Bilbo quite crossly at last. Perhaps he had rather forgotten that he had had at least one good meal more than the dwarves, and also the use of his legs and arms not to speak of air [> a greater allowance of air]. 'Are you still in prison or are you free? Have you arrived at last clear of the wood, and reached the Lake or not?'

'If you want food, and if you want to go on with this silly adventure, which is after all yours first not mine, you had better rub your legs and arms and try and help get the others out, [before >] while there is a chance!'

Thorin of course saw the sense of [> in] this. And after a few more groans he got up and helped the hobbit. They had a time of it in the gathering dark and the cold water finding which were the right barrels. Knocking outside and calling only discovered about six. These they got out. Some had to be helped or carried ashore and laid down helpless;[TN8] they were soaked as well as cramped and [?starved >] bruised and hungry [Dori and Nori were not much use yet nor Ori. >] Dwalin and Balin were two of the most unhappy. They were no use just yet. Bifur and Bofur were less knocked about, and drier but they couldn't be got to help. Fili and Kili, however, – who were young (for dwarves) – and had been packed more neatly with plenty of straw into smaller casks, came out more or less smiling, with only a bruise or two, and a stiffness that soon wore off.

'I hope I never smell the smell of [butter >] apples again', said Fili. 'My tub was full of it. To smell apples [when you can't move and can't >] everlastingly when you can scarcely move, and are getting cold and sick with hunger is exasperating. [But >] I could eat anything in the wide world now, for hours on end – but not an apple'. With the help of F. & K. they discovered the others at last and got them out. Poor fat Bombur was asleep or senseless. Dori Nori Ori Oin & Gloin were waterlogged, [*added*: only] half alive it seemed, and had to be carried and laid helpless on the shore.

'Well here we are!' said Thorin 'And I suppose we ought to

thank Mr Baggins. I am sure he expects it. But I wish he could have arranged a more comfortable journey. Still all very much at your service. No doubt we shall feel properly grateful when we are fed and recovered. In the meanwhile, what next?'

'I suggest lake-town' said Bilbo. 'what else is there?'

So Thorin and Fili and Kili went [> left the others and went] with Bilbo to [the] chief Bridge.

There were guards there, but they were [*added*: not] keeping careful watch; it was so long since there had been much need. Otherwise they would have heard [*added:* something of] the disembarking of the dwarves. Now their surprise was enormous when Thorin Oakenshield[TN9] stepped into the doorway of their hut.

'Who are you?' they shouted leaping to their feet.

'Thorin son of Thrain son of Thror king under the Mountain.' said he in a great deep voice and he looked it in spite of his torn and bedraggled dress. The gold and silver gleamed on his neck and waist; his eyes were dark and deep. 'I have come back. I wish to see the master of your town!'

Then there was a tremendous excitement. Some of the more foolish ran out as if they expected to see the mountain turned golden in the night and all the waters of the lake go yellow right away.

The captain of the guard came forward.[TN10] 'And who are these?' said he pointing to Fili and Kili and Bilbo. 'The sons of my father's daughter's son'[TN11] said Thorin 'Fili and Kili of the race of Durin, and Mr Baggins our guide from the lands of the West.'

'Lay down your arms' said the captain.

'We have none' said Thorin; and that was true enough. Their knives and the great sword Orcrist Goblin-slasher had been taken from them by the wood-elves. Bilbo had his knife, but he said nothing about that. 'What need of weapons we are not enemies, who return at last as spake of old. What use against so many. Take us to your master.'

'He is at feast' said the captain.

'All the more reason for taking us to him' said Fili who was getting impatient at these solemnities. 'We are wayworn and famished after our long road, and have sick comrades. Now make haste and let's have no more words, or your master may have something to say to you.'

'Follow me' said the captain, and with six men about them he led the way over the bridges to the market place of the town: a wide circle of still [> gentle] water surrounded with the greater homes, and great wide wooden quays with many steps and ladders going down to the surface of the lake.

From one great house there were many lights and a sound of

voices. They passed the door and stood blinking in the light looking at long tables filled with folk.

'I am Thorin son of Thrain son of Thror King Under the Mountain. I return' said Thorin in a loud voice from the door before the captain could say anything.

All leapt to their feet. The Master of the Town – the mayor perhaps we should call him – sprang from his great chair. But none knew greater surprise than the raftsmen of the elves, sitting at the end of the hall. They recognized Thorin and the two dwarves as the king's prisoners!

<Pressing> forward to the master they cried – 'these are prisoners of our king, that have escaped. Wandering and vagabond dwarves that could not give any good account of themselves; sneaking through the woods and pursuing our people.'

'Is this true?' asked the master.

'It is true that we were wrongfully waylaid by the Elf-king and emprisoned without cause, as we journeyed back to our own land' said Thorin. 'But locks nor bars may hinder the home coming spoken of old. Nor is this town in the wood-elves' realm. I speak to the Master of the Town of the men of the Lake, not to the boatmen of the king.'[TN12]

Then the master paused and looked from one to the other. The Woodelves' king was grown powerful in those parts; he did not wish for any enmity with him, and he did not trouble much about old songs; but about trade and tolls, cargoes and gold.

Others were of different mind, however, and soon [the dealing of his >] the matter was settled without him. The news spread from the doors of the hall like fire through all the town.[TN13] People were shouting within the hall and outside it. The quays were thronged with hurrying feet. Some began snatches of the old songs concerning the return of the King under the Mountain – that it was Thror's grandson not Thror himself bothered them not at all. Others took up this song and soon it rolled loud and high over the lake.

The King beneath the Mountain[s],
The King of carven stone,
The Lord of silver Fountain[s]
Shall come into his own!

His crown shall be upholden,
His harp shall be restrung,
His halls shall echo golden
To songs of yore re-sung.

The woods shall wave on mountains
The grass beneath the Sun;
His wealth shall flow like [> in] fountains,
[and the >] The rivers golden run.

The rivers run in gladness
The lakes shall shine and burn,
[And >] All sorrow fail and sadness
When the Mountain-kings return.[TN14]

So they sang – or very like that, only there was a great deal more of it; and much shouting as well as music of harps and fiddles mixed up with it. Such excitement had not been in the town in the memory of the oldest grandfather.

The woodelves themselves began to wonder greatly and even to be afraid. As yet they did not know how Thorin had escaped, and they were begin[ning] to think their King had made a grievous mistake. As for the master he saw there was nothing else for it, but to obey the general clamour for the moment at any rate.

In fact he gave up his chair to Thorin, and Fili and Kili and even Bilbo – whose presence [had >] was quite unexplained.[TN15]

Very soon the ten other dwarves were bought into the town [with >] amidst scenes of astonishing enthusiasm; and doctored, and fed, and housed, and pampered in the most delightful and satisfactory fashion.

A large house was given up to Thorin & his company; boats and rowers were put at their service, and crowds sat outside and sang songs all day. Some of them were quite new, and spoke confidently of the sudden death of the dragon, and cargoes of rich presents coming down the river to the Lake town. These were inspired largely by the Master & didn't particularly please the dwarves. But in the meantime they got fit & strong again. Indeed in a week they were more than recovered, fitted out in fine cloth, with well combed beards and proud steps. Thorin looked all he claimed to be and more;[TN16] and as he had said the dwarves' good-feeling towards the little hobbit grew stronger every day. They made a great fuss of him, which was just as well, for he had a shocking cold, and sneezed for <three> days, and couldn't go out; and his speeches at banquets were limited to 'Thag you very buch'.

In the meanwhile the wood-elves [were >] had gone back up the river with their cargoes; and there was not a little excitement in the king's palace. I never heard what happened to the guard and the butler. Nothing was ever said about keys or barrels while the dwarves stayed in Lake-Town, and B. was careful never to become invisible. Still I daresay more was guessed than was known. In any case the king [sent out >] knew the dwarfs [> dwarves][TN17] errand now or thought he did; and he thought also

'Very well, we'll see – no treasure will come back through Mirkwood without my having to say in the matter[, and I >]'. He at any rate did not believe in dwarves <illegible> dragons like Smaug, and he strongly suspected (being a wise elf) burglary or something like it[TN18] – which shows he was a wise-elf and wiser than the men of the Lake; and yet not as right as we may see. He sent out his spies [as far to >] about the shores of the lake end as far North towards the Mountain as they would go; and waited.

[Thorin > After >] At the end of a week Thorin began to think of departure. While the enthusiasm still lasted in the town was the time to get help. It would not do to let everything cool down with delay. So he spoke to the Master and his councillors, and [spoke >] said that soon he and his company must go on towards the Mountain.

Then for the first time the Master was surprised and a little frightened. I don't think he ever thought that the dwarves would dare to go [> approach Smaug];[TN19] he probably thought they were frauds who would sooner or later be discovered, and turned out. He was wrong. Thorin was really the grandson of the k. under the mountain; and there is no knowing what a dwarf will not dare and do for revenge or the recovery of his own.

At any rate the Master was not sorry to let them go. They were expensive, and their arrival had turned things into a long holiday; business was at a standstill. 'Let him go and bother Smaug, and see how he likes it' he thought. 'Certainly O Thorin Thrain's son Thror's son' was what he said. 'You must claim your own. The hour is at hand; what help we can offer shall be given'.

So one day – although autumn was already getting on, and winds were cold, and leaves were turn[ing] – three boats left Lake Town, laden with rowers, dwarves, Mr Baggins, and many provisions; horses went round by circuitous paths to meet them at their appointed landing place. The master and his counsellors bade the solemn farewell from the [steps of the >] great steps that went down to the lake. People sang on the quays and out of windows. The white oars dipped and splashed and off they went north up the Lake.

As before, the text continues with no indication in the manuscript of the point where the chapter break was later inserted – in this case, just before the last paragraph on manuscript page 136 (Marq. 1/1/12:1). As was so often the case, the last line was re-written and augmented in the typescript in order to make a more effective break: '. . . and off they went north up the lake *on the last stage of their long journey. The only person thoroughly unhappy was Bilbo'* (First Typescript, typescript page 109; 1/1/60:7).

TEXT NOTES

1 In the margin alongside this line is the single word 'left?' Since this is written in pencil, we know that it comes from the period when Tolkien was preparing the First Typescript, which takes up the proposed correction (as does every subsequent text). Note that the sudden bend to the right of the Forest River, suggesting that it was rounding some obstacle, dates all the way back to the very first *Hobbit* map incorporated into the Pryftan Fragment (Frontispiece) and can also be seen, though less prominently, in one of the five maps that accompanied Tolkien's original turnover of the completed text to Allen & Unwin in October 1936 (Plate I [bottom]). On the other hand, this feature has almost disappeared from another map in the same set, the precursor of the Wilderland map (given on Plate II [top]), indicating that Tolkien remained unsure about the course of the Forest River until relatively late in the process.

The final Wilderland map published in the original and all subsequent editions (DAA.[399]) does not entirely agree with the accompanying published text (DAA.241). The easternmost extension of the hills in which the Elvenking's halls are located does indeed appear on the left bank of the river† but the river does not 'round' any 'steep shoulder of land' but instead curves gradually to the right as it flows through marshlands.

† These same heights can also be seen rising on the left (north) bank of the Forest River in both of Tolkien's paintings illustrating Bilbo's arrival by barrel at the huts of the raft-elves (H-S#122 & 124). The unused coloured pencil sketch (Plate VIII [top]) clearly shows hills on the north bank of the river, while the published version (DAA plate two [bottom]) shows both these hills and the lack of any corresponding heights on the right (south) bank of the river.

2 This mention of these unseen landmarks in the midst of this vivid descriptive passage is remarkable, since our point-of-view character cannot see them and they have not yet appeared on any of the sketch-maps. These low hills or badlands show up most clearly on the early version of the Wilderland map that accompanied the submission of the completed book to Allen & Unwin in October 1936 (Plate I [bottom]), where they do indeed extend north-east from the Lonely Mountain instead of the more westerly orientation they are given in the final Wilderland map. They can also be seen depicted pictorially in the careful sketch of the Lonely Mountain that with the final map of the Long Lake made up another of the five maps accompanying the October 1936 submission (Plate II [top]).

3 In the next stage of the text, the first typescript, this section was greatly expanded to bring in a reference to the Dragon and a reminder of the missing wizard's mysterious business. Major changes are marked in *italics* to highlight the degree of expansion.

> . . . The talk *was all of the trade that came and went on the waterways and the growth of the traffic on the river, as the roads out of the East towards Mirkwood vanished or fell into disuse; and of the bickering of the lakemen and the wood-elves about the upkeep of the forest-river and the care of the banks*. Those lands had changed much since the days when dwarves *dwelt in the Mountain, days which nearly everybody [> most people now] remembered only as a very shadowy tradition. They had changed even in recent years, and since the last news Gandalf had had of them*. Great floods and rains had swollen the waters *that flowed East; and there had been an earthquake or two (which some were inclined to attribute to the dragon – alluding to him chiefly with a curse and an ominous nod in the direction of the Mountain)*. The marshes and bogs had spread wider and wider on either side. Paths had vanished, and many a rider and wanderer too, if they had tried to find the lost ways across. *The elf-road through the wood which the dwarves had followed on the advice of Beorn now came to a doubtful and little used end at the eastern edge of the forest;* only the river offered any longer a safe way from the skirts of Mirkwood in the North to the mountain-shadowed plains beyond, *and the river was guarded by the wood-elves' king*.
>
> *So you see Bilbo had come in the end by the only road that was any good. It might have been some comfort to Mr. Baggins shivering on the barrels, if he had known that news of this had reached Gandalf far away and given him great anxiety, and that he was in fact finishing his other business (which does not come into this tale) and getting ready to come in search of Thorin's company. But he [> Bilbo] did not know it.*
>
> *All he knew was that the river seemed to go on and on and on for ever, and he was hungry, and had a nasty cold in the nose, and did not like the way the Mountain seemed to frown at him and threaten him as they [> it] drew ever nearer . . .*
>
> —First Typescript, typescript pages 103–4 (Marq. 1/1/60:1–2).

For more on the theme of roads falling into disuse and the increasing difficulty of travel, see also the 1960 Hobbit (p. 818); for a lucid description of the theme of depopulation as settled lands turn into desolate wastelands, see Henry Gee 'The Gates of Minas Tirith', Chapter 14 in *The Science of Middle-earth* (page 151).

4 Added: 'over <illegible> waterfalls'. The single illegible word is not *high* (the reading of the typescript and published book) but probably *noisy*.

The reference to the drowned valley that has now become a great lake sounds like an echo of the many drowned lands in Tolkien's earlier tales, but here no actual tale seems to underlie the reference; like the ruins of the earlier, greater town and the reference to 'wars' (plural), it seems to be a deliberate layering of an untold prehistory for artistic effect.

5 Note the plural 'bridges' here and elsewhere in this chapter; back in Plot Notes B the reference had been to a single bridge; see p. 364. The plural here persists through both typescripts and was only changed to '*A* great bridge' in the page proofs (Marq. 1/2/2: page 198). At the same time, the 'chief bridge' on p. 436 became the 'great bridge' (1/2/2: page 199) and the plural was removed from the description of the bridges being thrown down during Smaug's attack (cf. p. 548; page proof 1/2/2: page 253). The decision for Lake Town to have only one great bridge seems to have been determined through the two illustrations Tolkien drew of the scene (Plate VIII [bottom] and DAA.244/H-S#127), apparently created over the Christmas 1936 vacation, the second of which he submitted to Allen & Unwin on January 4th, 1937 (the day after his 45th birthday). If so, the changes in page proof (made between February 24th and March 10th 1937) would have been made to bring the text into agreement with the illustration. The colour sketch 'Death of Smaug' (see Part Two) also shows the easternmost end of the fallen single Great Bridge and so definitely postdates the submission of the completed manuscript to Allen & Unwin in Oct. 1936; it was probably created between May and August 1937 along with the other colour pieces Tolkien made for the book at Houghton Mifflin's request (JRRT/Allen & Unwin correspondence, A&U Archives).

6 This marks the first appearance of the names *Thror* and *Thrain*. See part iii of the commentary, starting on p. 455.

7 This is the first appearance of the name *Thorin* used in the text as the chief dwarf's name, although the change had been anticipated as far back as Plot Notes A (see p. 293). Tolkien's rejection of 'Gandalf' as the name of the chief dwarf no doubt came because, on reflection, it offended Tolkien's sense of decorum to have a dwarf named 'elf' (Gand-*alf*: 'wand-*elf*'). For more on the name 'Thorin', see p. 455.

8 *Added*: where they sat and muttered or moaned.

9 This is the first appearance of Thorin's cognomen *Oakenshield* since Plot Notes A, where remarkably enough it had already been linked with Thorin's name. Like 'Thorin' itself, it comes from the list of dwarf-names that appear in both the *Völuspá* (in the *Elder Edda*) and the *Gylfaginning* ('The Deluding of Gylfi', in the *Prose Edda*) as *Eikinskjaldi*. However, there it is simply another dwarf-name and has no linkage to 'Thorin'; the two actually occur in different stanzas of *Völuspá* (Thorin in the third line of stanza 12 and Eikinskialdi in the last line of stanza 13, respectively). See Appendix III.

10 It is possible that this 'captain of the guard' is Bard, who later plays such a major role in the dwarves' fortunes; see p. 553.

11 This is the first mention that Fili and Kili are Thorin's close kin. Note that they are originally his great-nephews, his sister's grandsons, whereas in the final book their relationship is one generation closer (his sister's sons). The original relationship was still in place when the First Typescript was originally typed (cf. typescript page 106; 1/1/60:4)

but had already been changed before the Second Typescript (1/1/41:5) was created.

The uncle/nephew bond was extremely important in heroic medieval literature – cf. Roland and Charlemagne, Beowulf and Hygelac, Gawain and Arthur. This motif is more or less entirely absent from the Silmarillion tradition and only enters the legendarium at this point, but later became of great importance: cf. Éomer and Théoden, not to mention Frodo and Bilbo.

12 This was originally followed by a cancelled line that would have marked the beginning of a new paragraph: 'Yet at least the King of the woods gave us food, and sh[elter]' – a none-too-subtle hint on the hungry dwarf's part, in keeping with his earlier verbal sparring before the Elvenking (p. 315).

13 The simile may be significant, since within a few chapters the town will indeed burn, as had already been foreseen in Plot Notes B (although in the Plot Notes the dragon did not succeed in burning it to the waterline; see p. 364). Note also the line, ominous in retrospect, in the town-folk's song: 'The lakes shall shine *and burn*'.

14 An earlier draft of this poem can be found on the back of the next manuscript page; after this version was superseded Tolkien struck it through with a cancellation line, then turned the paper upside down and over to use the reversed back as a fresh sheet (manuscript page 135; Marq. 1/1/11:8). A large Roman numeral II appears at the top of this page, drawn directly over the first three cancelled lines:

II

When the king beneath the Mountains comes.
the Lord beneath the Hills
the lord of golden Fountains

This is followed by the draft:

The king beneath the Mountains
The king of carven stone
the lord of golden [> silver] Fortress
shall come into his own

[The >] His crown shall be uplifted
his harp shall be restrung
His halls shall be relighted
his praises shall be resung

His wealth shall flow like water
his gifts like light of sun
The river run in gladness
And the grass <stands> under sun [> beneath the sun]

He <sic> crown shall be upholden
his harp shall be restrung

his halls shall echo golden
to song[s] of yore resung.

[The >] His wealth shall flow like fountains
[The > like >] The rivers golden run
the grass [< woods] shall wave [> wax] on mountain
and the grass beneath the sun

The rivers run in gladness
[The > and men >]
the lake be filled with gems [> shall shine and burn]
[And men know no more >]
And sorrow fail and sadness
When the Mountain-kings return

The second draft fair copy incorporated into the main manuscript (see pp. 439–40) required only a very few minor changes (mostly typographical), made between the manuscript and typescript stages, to achieve the text of the published version (DAA.251). The most significant change comes in the final line, which shifts from the plural ('When the Mountain-kings return') to the singular ('At the *m*ountain king'*s* return'): compare Ms. 1/1/11:6 (manuscript page 134) with Ts. 1/1/60:5–6 (First Typescript, pages 107–8). One change marked in the manuscript which was not taken up into the typescript version is a pencilled change from 'kings' to 'lords' in the last line.

Curiously enough, between the first and second drafts the word *lake* (i.e., the Long Lake) in the third line from the end was changed to lake*s* (plural), a reading which has persisted ever since. While certainly justifiable from the point of view of poetic license, given the dominance of plurals in the closing stanza (it is Mountain-kings, not merely the King under the Mountain, whose return they praise and prophesy), it is nevertheless striking for Tolkien to move from the precise and accurate to the general and 'poetic'.

15 This passage was revised and expanded to read

> In fact he gave up his chair to Thorin, and Fili and Kili *sat beside him* and even Bilbo *was given a place at the high table – no explanation of where he came in (although no songs had alluded to him even in the obscurest way) [beyond >] was asked for in the general bustle.*

The cancelled 'beyond' suggests some such cover story as that which Thorin had offered the captain of the guard – that is, 'Mr. Baggins, our guide from the lands of the West'.

According to the much later chronology of *The Lord of the Rings*, this welcoming feast took place on September 22nd, but clearly no such specific time-scheme was present in the original conception; see 'Timeline and Chronology' in The 1960 Hobbit, especially pp. 823 & 832.

16 This sentence was recast between the manuscript and First Typescript to the reading in the published book: 'Thorin looked and walked as if

his kingdom was already regained and Smaug chopped up into little pieces.'

17 The apostrophe is missing in the original, but presumably Tolkien shifted from the singular (dwarf's) – that is, Thorin's – to the plural (dwarves') here rather than offered up an alternative plural (dwarfs').

18 The illegible word here might begin with a *k* and end in an *-ly* (or just possibly *-ing*), but it is certainly not 'killing'. The parenthetical '(being a wise elf)' was cancelled, presumably before the section following the dash was added.

19 This passage was cancelled and replaced by the following (written in the margin and marked for insertion at this point): 'I think that like the king he never believed . . .'

(i)
Lake Town

The vivid description of Lake Town that dominates this chapter is another example of Tolkien drawing upon his knowledge of history and prehistory as inspiration for his creative work. As Christina Scull was the first to point out,[1] archeological fact often underlies Tolkien's fiction – an aspect of his writing that is not surprising, given his avowed 'passion . . . for heroic legend on the brink of fairy-tale and history, of which there is far too little in the world' (letter to Waldman, 1951; *Letters* p. 144), as well as his emphatic preference for 'history, true or feigned' as a mode of writing (*LotR*.11, Foreword to the Second Edition). An interest in legends on the edge of recorded history naturally implies knowledge and interest in both sides of that borderland: a solid familiarity with early recorded history and a matching interest in unrecorded prehistory as well. By the same token, anyone who like Tolkien sets out to write 'feigned history' must be well acquainted with the real thing if his pseudohistory is to be plausible and persuasive. A good example can be found in the frame story for *The Book of Lost Tales*, the Eriol legend, set in the murky period just before the Jutes (closely followed by the Angles and the Saxons) invaded Britain and turned it into England, a period Tolkien revealed extensive historical knowledge of in his posthumously published lectures on the *Freswæl*, or 'Fight at Finnesburg' (*Finn and Hengest: The Fragment and the Episode*, ed. Alan Bliss [1982]). Furthermore, Tolkien's outline for the unwritten chapters of *The Lost Road* (HME V.77–8; see also JRRT to Christopher Bretherton, 16th July 1964, *Letters* p. 347) shows his intention to have that work, starting in the familiar present and ending in the wholly invented mythic world of lost Númenor, bridge the gap between the two through episodes set first in poorly-recorded historical periods (ninth-century England during the collapse of the Angles' kingdoms under Viking assault,[2] Lombardic Italy of the mid-sixth century AD), then in eras known only through legends (Norse lands in the time of Scyld Sceafing, Ireland during the legendary days of the Tuatha dé Danaan), then periods known from archeology but for which all legends and stories have been lost (the Ice Age, the era of the Paleolithic cave-paintings), and finally beyond, into his own imagined prehistory (Beleriand and finally Númenor).[3]

A closer look at the evidence shows that Tolkien was very well versed indeed in prehistory. We have already seen how he modeled Medwed's hall on modern archeological reconstructions of a Norse mead-hall (see commentary following Chapter VII, p. 261). Similarly, in his 1932 Father Christmas letter he drew on Paleolithic cave art, such as that found in the caves of Altamira, Spain [17,000 BC] (the similar caves at Lascaux and Chauvet not yet having been discovered). So too with Lake Town, which is closely modeled on the Neolithic lake-dwellings or *pfahlbauten* ('pile structures') first discovered in Switzerland in 1854 on the shores of Lake Zurich.[4] That Tolkien is drawing directly on accounts of the Swiss discovery, probably the classic *Die Keltische Pfahlbauten in den Schweizerseen* by Dr. Ferdinand Keller (literally 'The Celtic Pile-structures in the Swiss Lakes' [1854], translated into English by John Edward Lee as *The Lake Dwellings of Switzerland and Other Parts of Europe* [1866]), is shown by his reference (p. 436) to how

> The rotting piles of another greater town could be seen along the shores when there was a drought.

This reference to another, greater, Lake Town (what archeologists excavating the site would no doubt call Lake Town I, to distinguish it from the later Lake Town II visited by Thorin & Company and the still later Lake Town III that replaces it described in the final chapter) is unusual, because we learn nothing else about it; its destruction seems to belong to the distant past, long before Smaug's advent. It is striking, therefore, that the first prehistorical lake-dwelling was discovered because a dry winter lowered the water level of Lake Zurich, exposing the ancient wooden piles that had once supported the settlement; Tolkien's description seems to be a direct echo of the archeological discovery of some seventy-five years before. Scull ('The Influence of Archaeology and History' page 41; see Note 1), Anderson (DAA.245), and *Artist & Illustrator* (H-S#125) all reproduce nineteenth- and early twentieth-century images from various archeological texts showing artists' conceptions of what such Neolithic villages might have looked like; another, found in Bryony & John Coles' *Sweet Track to Glastonbury*, is an early twentieth-century depiction of the lake-dwellings closest to Tolkien's home, those at Meare and Glastonbury (some seventy-five miles from Oxford).[5] None of these images corresponds exactly to Lake Town as Tolkien describes it in his text or depicts it in his three drawings of the site ('Esgaroth' [Plate VIII, bottom], 'Lake Town'

[DAA.244/H-S#127], and 'Death of Smaug' [in plate section two], all of which clearly date from the time after he had already submitted the book to Allen & Unwin for publication (the first two to December 1936 and the third probably between May and August 1937), since they show only one bridge between Lake Town and the shore (see Text Note 5 above). The closest is that appearing in Robert Munro's *Les Stations Lacustres d'Europe aux Ages de la Pierre et du Bronze* [1908] ('The Lake Stations of Europe during the Stone and Bronze Ages'), said to have been based on an earlier drawing by A. de Mortillet[6] (DAA.245 [top], H-S#125). Given the exactness with which Tolkien based some of his drawings upon pre-existing sources – e.g., 'The Trolls' on Jennie Harbour's 'Hansel and Grethel Sat Down by the Fire', 'Bilbo Woke Up with the Early Sun in His Eyes' on Archibald Thorburn's chromolithograph of a golden eagle, and 'Firelight in Beorn's house', the original conception of Medwed's dwelling, on the picture of Hrolf Kraki's meadhall that had appeared in his friend E. V. Gordon's *An Introduction to Old Norse* – it is probable that he had a more direct source for his illustrations of Lake Town that has not yet been discovered.

As might be expected, the sequence of three drawings shows some variation as Tolkien refined his image of the city over the water: the hut beside the head of the bridge in the text wherein Bilbo, Thorin, Fili, and Kili meet the story's first humans to appear on-stage (see part ii of the commentary, below) becomes a gate-house attached to the bridge in the first drawing ('Esgaroth'), through which one must pass to enter the city. By contrast, a gap intrudes between gate-house and bridge in the second drawing ('Lake Town'), offering no explanation of how visitors climb up onto the elevated bridge. This same image also includes an archway in Lake Town's southern side, allowing access to the water-market at the city's center described in the text. The most dramatic of the three, 'Death of Smaug', depicts the burning city, its bridge already cast down (only the easternmost link can be seen, on the left). It also substitutes long rowhouses for the grander individual buildings shown along Lake Town's western edge in the two earlier drawings. Similar but smaller buildings had appeared in Lake Town's southeast quadrant in the second drawing ('Lake Town') and, less elongated, in the first ('Esgaroth'), but we can tell we are not simply looking at the lake-dwelling from a different angle by the position of the moon (just past new) in the upper left (i.e., the northwest) and a dim glimpse of the Lonely Mountain to the north, just left of the center of the picture.[7]

While Tolkien's debt to Keller et al. seems clear, it is interesting to note that by the time Tolkien was writing *The Hobbit* Keller's theory was under attack by a new generation of archeologists. It is now generally believed that the majority of 'lake-dwellings' were not actually out on platforms above the water but built on marshy ground along the shore or on low islands or peninsulas surrounded by marsh or bog; they were more wetland settlements than lake-dwellings per se, and this is definitely the case with the 'lake villages' of Somerset at Glastonbury [discovered 1892] and Meare [1895], the latter of which was actually still under excavation throughout the time Tolkien was working on *The Hobbit.*[8] However, we will badly misunderstand any influence on Tolkien from contemporary science and scholarship unless we look not at modern ideas and interpretations regarding a given field but instead at the scholarly consensus of Tolkien's day. For example, Keller asserted that many of the lake-dwellings seem to have been destroyed by fire (cf. Keller pages 8, 28–9, 33, 43–5, &c.), laying far less stress on the fact that, as modern archeology notes, many were simply abandoned. Tolkien, unrestrained by the demands of historical probability, took the lake-dwellings discovered by Keller, de Mortillet, Bulleid, and their peers and incorporated them into his fiction in their classic, raised-platform-on-pilings-above-the-water form. In the process, he provided a mythic explanation of why Neolithic folk sought such protection and undertook the enormous labor required to construct a lake-town: in a world inhabited by predatory dragons, it would be worth almost any pains to carve out a home in an environment dragons would instinctively avoid. Similarly, he picked up on the theme of destruction by fire, which has inspired many a speculation about warfare and pillage among the historians,[9] and gave it an epic interpretation of destruction by dragon in a holocaust worthy of the *Beowulf*-poet. Just as significantly, he departed from the archeological record when it suited his purpose – for example, while many lake-dwellings were destroyed and rebuilt several times, they were usually rebuilt on the same spot (the lake-dwelling at Robenhausen on Lake Pfaffikon just north of Lake Zurich, discovered in 1858 and described by Keller on pages 37–58, fits Tolkien's pattern particularly well, since it was built three times, burned down twice, and finally abandoned). By contrast, our Lake Town in *The Hobbit* shifted its site each time it was rebuilt, and the ultimate fate of its third incarnation is unknown, being beyond the scope of our story.

(ii)
'The Mayor & Corporation'

It is wholly remarkable that, in current editions of *The Hobbit*, incorporating Tolkien's second and third edition changes (as well as others made subsequently since Tolkien's lifetime), we come two-thirds of the way through the story before we meet our first humans, these being the guardsmen in the hut before Lake-town – and that when at last we do so little is made of the fact. The event is somewhat obscured by the description of Gandalf the wizard as 'an old man' (DAA.32), or Beorn as 'a huge man' (DAA.167), or of the raft-elves as 'raftmen' (cf.

DAA.240, 241, 250), whereas in fact none of these are truly human (Gandalf the Grey being one of the Istari, an incarnate Maia or angel, Beorn a werebear, and the 'raftmen' more properly 'raft-elves' – cf. 'the raftsmen of the elves', p. 439). The mention of the Men of Dale in Chapter I and the Men of the Long Lake on Thror's Map, and of the 'woodmen' in Chapter VI (see especially DAA.147–8) and on the Wilderland Map, has introduced the idea of off-stage humans from very early on, although the woodmen do not actually appear in the story until very near the end, at the Yuletide celebrations in Beorn's halls on Bilbo's return journey (see p. 682 and DAA.353). In addition, modern readers of the book as often as not come to it armed with knowledge from a prior reading of *The Lord of the Rings* and thus know that Bilbo would have passed through Bree on his journey east and encountered humans there, a fact Tolkien made explicit in the timeline he drew up to accompany the 1960 Hobbit (see 'Timelines & Itinerary', pp. 816, 818, 828, 834). Matters would of course have been quite different for a reader of the original manuscript, who would have no reason not to accept the text's description of Bladorthin as 'a little old man' quite literally and at any rate knew Bilbo and company had passed through lands inhabited by 'men or hobbits, or elves' in the early stages of their journey (contrast p. 90 with DAA.65). Hence the moment is momentous only because changes made in the course of later editions removed previous encounters with humans, and would itself have been superseded had Tolkien's proposed 1960 revision been carried to completion and seen print.

The woodmen, from what little we are told of them, are clearly very much in the vein of William Morris's Goths as described in works such as *The House of the Wolfings* [1888] and *The Roots of the Mountains* [1889], which pit Germanic tribesmen against expansionist Romans and marauding Huns, respectively. Compare Tolkien's account of the villages of the 'brave woodmen and their wives and children'

> In spite of the dangers of this far land bold men had lately been pushing up into it from the south again, and cutting down trees, and building themselves places to live in among the more pleasant woods farther down in the valleys away from the shadows of the hills, and along the river-shores. There were many of them and they were brave and well-armed (p. 205)

with Morris's Men of the Mark, who live in

> a dwelling of men beside a great wood . . . this great clearing in the woodland was not a matter of haphazard: though the river had driven a road whereby men might fare on either side of its hurrying stream. It was men who had made that isle in the woodland.
>
> . . . [T]hey had no lack of wares of iron and steel, whether they

> were tools of handicraft or weapons for hunting and for war. It was the men of the Folk, who coming adown by the river-side had made that clearing . . . they came adown the river . . . till they had a mind to abide; and there as it fell they stayed their travel, and . . . fought with the wood and its wild things, that they might make to themselves a dwelling-place on the face of the earth.
>
> So they cut down the trees, and burned their stumps that the grass might grow sweet for their kine and sheep and horse; and they diked the river where need was all through the plain . . . and they made them boats to ferry them over . . . and [the river] became their friend, and they . . . called it . . . the Mirkwood-water . . .
>
> In such wise that Folk had made an island amidst of the Mirkwood, and established a home there, and upheld it with manifold toil too long to tell of.
>
> —*The House of the Wolfings*, pages 1–2.[10]

In a sense, if Morris is describing the moment when prehistory (the Germanic-Roman strife from the point of view of the tribesmen resisting Roman encroachment) meets history (this war being known to history only from the other point of view through Roman writers such as Caesar and Tacitus), then Tolkien is offering a prequel to that transitional moment, when mythic monsters rather than ambitious empires were the greatest threat to existence; not the time when the Men of the Mark were defending their land against invaders but the earlier time when they themselves were first coming into that part of the world. Perhaps significantly, the Wolfings keep hanging from the roof of their hall a great work of art, the origins of which they have forgotten:

> a wondrous lamp fashioned of glass . . . clear green like an emerald, and all done with figures and knots in gold . . . and a warrior slaying a dragon . . . an ancient and holy thing
>
> —*The House of the Wolfings*, page 6.

This is probably a passing reference by Morris to the story of Sigurd dragon-slayer, which he had translated only the previous year, but within Tolkien's larger reconstructed prehistory it could just as easily be seen as preserving, like the Franks Casket, a fragment of the story of Bilbo dragon-slayer long after the details of what actually happened have been forgotten. Similarly, Tolkien may have decided to invent a different history for one of the Wolfings' neighbouring tribes, the Bearings, which is simply the modern English cognate of *Beornings*, the name bestowed upon those woodmen who later choose to take Beorn/Medwed as their leader; instead of merely being their totem-animal it would thus have been the name of the tribe's original leader, Beorn/Bear, who himself had long since been forgotten.

That the woodmen were an archetype that strongly appealed to Tolkien can be shown by the presence in the Silmarillion tradition during the First Age of the People of Haleth, a woodland folk who later become the Men of Brethil, the Second Kindred of the Elf-friends. Also very similar are the Northmen of eastern Rhovanion (Wilderland), whom Tolkien created to serve as the common ancestors for the Lake-men, the Men of Dale, the woodmen, and the Men of Rohan; they figure in the history of Gondor told in Appendix A of *The Lord of the Rings* and in 'Cirion and Eorl', especially part (i) 'The Northmen and the Wainriders' in *Unfinished Tales* (cf. UT.289–90 & 295, 297–8). Significantly, the woodmen's culture and way of life seem to have changed little in the seventeen hundred years that separates them from the Northmen of Vidugavia's day (a name which, as Christopher Tolkien points out, is itself Gothic for 'Wood-dweller', *Widu-gauja*; UT.311).

It is rather surprising, then, that the first humans we see close-up in the story are quite different. Rather than an Iron Age culture like the men on the other side of the forest (whom Tolkien makes their kinsmen when he comes to write Appendix A of *LotR*), the Men of Lake Town are urban, even urbane, with a culture right out of the High Middle Ages.[11] Lake Town is a free city (at least until the re-establishment of the Kingdom of Dale at the end of the story), belonging to no nation and owing allegiance to no king. It is also Tolkien's only oligarchy, ruled by a Master of the Town 'elected from the old and wise' (p. 551; cf. p. 639 & DAA.309) rather than a noble lord.[12] We are told about the Lake-men's concern with commerce, and how the Master has 'a good head for business – especially his own business' (p. 550) and a mind devoted to 'trade and tolls, cargoes and gold' (p. 439; the typescript rather tartly adds 'to which habit he owed his position' – cf. DAA.250). This, along with two references to 'the Master and his councillors' (p. 441), suggests that Lake Town is probably dominated by Merchant Guilds, the guildmasters of whom would choose one among their number to serve as Master of the Town ('the mayor perhaps we should call him'). As supporting evidence for this, note the Lake-men's disparagement of 'old men and money-counters' (p. 551) after the Master's poor showing during the attack by Smaug in contrast to Bard's heroism, and their cry in the typescript of 'Up the Bowman, and down with Moneybags' (typescript page 138; 1/1/64:4).

The Master of Lake Town is one of Tolkien's most interesting minor characters in his own right: an essentially unsympathetic figure who knows so little about his own town's history that he doubts there ever was a King under the Mountain yet who nonetheless helps our heroes a great deal when they need it most, giving them food and clothing and shelter and sanctuary when they most need it. Indeed, he treats them with a generosity that borders on extravagance, feasting them at banquets and clothing them in fine cloth ('of their proper colours' adds the First Typescript), granting them their own large house to stay in and even refusing the wood-elves' implied request for extradition despite the elvenking's being his primary trading partner. Yet in all this he is simply cynically going with the tide of public opinion; privately 'he believed they were frauds who would sooner or later be discovered and turned out'. Later he does them an ill turn just as crucial as the help he had given them earlier, when he defuses his people's criticism of his behavior during the attack on Lake Town by Smaug by shifting their anger onto the absent dwarves, stirring the lake-men up by reminding them that Thorin & Company must have disturbed the dragon and are thus responsible for his attack on the city (an accusation that is, of course, quite true, although inadvertent on their part) – though typically he frames the accusation in terms of profit and loss, payment and recompense. He thereby helps set in motion the conflict that soon results in the Battle of Five Armies. Yet he is not without skills, as the narrator himself notes (p. 639): it is he who plans out the new Lake Town that rises from the ashes of the old (pp. 552 & 641), and does it so well that the new is fairer than the old (DAA.313).

A wily politician (the only one in Tolkien's work),[13] the Master is sophisticated, subtle, and just a touch corrupt, and his advent on the scene is a harbinger of the ambivalence that is so much a feature of the final chapters, culminating in the tangle of rights and wrongs over ownership of the dragon-hoard. In fact, as Douglas Anderson points out, he is highly reminiscent of that touchstone of bureaucratic greed and double-dealing, the Mayor of Hamelin in Robert Browning's 'The Pied Piper of Hamelin' [1842].[14] Like the Mayor of Hamelin (who is similarly unnamed, identified only by title), the Master of Lake Town makes whatever bargain suits his goals at the time, and abandons it without conscience when circumstances change. It is possible that in this wholly unflattering depiction of a town official Tolkien may also owe something to the 'Town & Gown' rivalry that had divided Oxford since the thirteenth century; riots between students ('Gown') and shopkeepers ('Town') persisted until as late as the mid-nineteenth century,[15] and the Miller in *Farmer Giles of Ham* shows that Tolkien was quite willing to use medieval stereotypes when they would yield comic effect. Of course, if we are seeking for applicability it is only fair to point out that while Master of the Town (to give him his full title; cf. p. 439) is a title for what we would now call a mayor, more familiar today in its Middle English form *burgomaster* (literally 'town master'), the title Master is also used for the head of several Oxford colleges, including Pembroke, Tolkien's college at the time he was writing *The Hobbit*. Anyone who has witnessed academic politics can testify that here is a masterly portrait of a certain type of head of college, or department, or school, pleasant but not trustworthy, accommodating but not sincere.

In the end, though, what is important is not what the Master may or may not symbolize but his role within the story; to first help our heroes and then to greatly complicate their existence. He can fill both roles equally well because the keystone to his personality is that he is motivated entirely by self-interest, and it is a fitting though cruel fate that he winds up starving to death, entirely dependent upon his own too-inadequate resources and abilities, when he seizes for his own what should have been shared among his fellows.

(iii)
Thorin, son of Thrain, son of Thror

With this chapter, the sequence of names familiar from the published books finally makes its appearance, although as we have seen at least one of these changes (Gandalf > Thorin) was mooted as far back as Plot Notes A (see p. 293), written before the Mirkwood chapter had been tackled. And as we shall see, elements of this genealogy remained in flux even while the book was at the printers, with some associated issues not being finally resolved until many years later. Nonetheless, 'Thorin' henceforth replaces 'Gandalf' as the chief dwarf's name, and the father and grandfather of Bilbo's employer finally receive names.[16]

Like Thorin itself, both the names *Thrain* and *Thror* come from the same list of dwarf-names, known as the *Dvergatal* ('Dwarf-tally'), that provided the names of all the other dwarves who accompany Bilbo (with the sole exception of Balin); see Appendix III.[17] This list appears both in *Völuspá* ('The Sayings of the Sybil' [circa 1000 AD]), the first poem in the collection variously known as the *Elder Edda* or *Poetic Edda*, in what is generally considered to be an interpolation to the original poem,[18] as well as in *Gylfaginning*, 'The Deluding of Gylfi' in Snorri Sturluson's *Prose Edda* [1223].

Jean Young, in her translation of the *Prose Edda*, glosses 'Thorin' as 'Bold One' (page 41) but does not explain the meaning of the other two dwarf-names. Ursula Dronke, in her edition of *Völuspá*, translates the three names as 'Darer' (þorinn), 'Yearner' (þráinn), and 'Thrive' (þrór). Of the other dwarf-names associated with this family, 'Oakenshield' (Eikinskjaldi/Eikinskialdi) appears in both lists (indeed, it is repeated twice within the *Völuspá* itself, in stanza 13 line 8 and again in stanza 16 line 2; see Text Note 9), as does Gandalf (Ganndálf/Gandálfr). Young glosses the latter as 'Sorcerer-elf' but Dronke, rather surprisingly, prefers 'Sprite Elf'; the usual translation is 'Wand-elf', although Shippey prefers 'Staff-elf' (*The Road to Middle-Earth*, rev. edition [1992], page 88).

From this point onward, references to Thrain, Thorin's father, and to Thror, his grandfather and last King under the Mountain, appear frequently, as Thorin asserts his claim to the kingship and treasure and returns to the home of his youth.[19] It is now easy to overlook, but important to note, that in the original first edition of the book no mention of either Thror's or Thrain's name appeared in the text before the scene at Lake Town (see Note 16), with one notable exception which Tolkien had inserted into the text of Chapter VII when creating the typescript. This sole earlier occurrence is important, because remarkably enough it gave a reversed line of descent – i.e., *Thorin son of Thror son of Thrain* – and because this error was preserved through both typescripts and into the printer's proofs. Even more remarkably, when correcting those proofs Tolkien initially decided to change every other occurrence of the names to agree with this exception – that is, he adopted the reverse genealogy and decided to make Thror the father and Thrain the grandfather and Last King throughout – instead of simply altering this single anomalous case to match the rest. And, as Christopher Tolkien points out in his discussion of the two competing genealogies in *The Treason of Isengard* (HME VII.159–60), it is this reversed line of descent (Thorin–Thror–Thrain) which appears on the map with the moon-runes published in the book.

Since the resulting confusion persisted into the early stages of *The Lord of the Rings*[20] and required Tolkien to make adjustments and additions to *The Hobbit* as late as 1966 to fully resolve (and which he even then did not perfectly achieve), it seems worthwhile to go into the matter in some detail here to understand how two separate and competing genealogies – what we may call the 'text tradition' (father Thrain, grandfather Thror) and the reversed genealogy of the 'map tradition' (father Thror, grandfather Thrain) – arose, and how Tolkien ultimately solved the problem that traces of these competing traditions left in the story. The best way to do so seems to be to briefly rehearse the various stages by which Tolkien fixed upon the names of these two characters:

- First Phase: Gandalf is the chief dwarf; his father is unnamed; his grandfather is briefly named 'Fimbulfambi', then left unnamed. Bladorthin is the wizard (Pryftan Fragment, Bladorthin Typescript).
- Second Phase: Gandalf is the chief dwarf; his father and grandfather are unnamed; Bladorthin is the wizard; Medwed the werebear. (Second Phase manuscript from middle of Chapter I through what is now Chapter IX). In Plot Notes A, written during a brief pause between the composition of Chapters VII and VIII, Tolkien proposes changing several names (Gandalf > Thorin, Bladorthin > Gandalf, Medwed > Beorn) but does not carry out the changes.
- Second Phase, continued: Chief dwarf's name changes to Thorin (between Chapters IX and X). His father and grandfather are given the names Thrain and Thror, respectively (Chapter X). These names are used consistently throughout the rest of the Second Phase manuscript (through the scene on Ravenhill in Chapter XV).
- First Typescript: After breaking off the manuscript at the end of the

scene with Roäc, Tolkien returns to the beginning of the story and creates the First Typescript. The name changes proposed more than a year before in Plot Notes A are now carried out: Thorin (Oakenshield) is the chief dwarf throughout, Beorn the werebear, and Gandalf the wizard. Thorin's father and grandfather are unnamed anywhere before Chapter VII, where their names are accidentally reversed when Medwed's simple remark 'if it is true that you are respectable dwarves & not friends of Goblins' (p. 234) is changed to Beorn's 'if it is true that you are Thorin (son of Thror, son of Thrain, I believe), and that your companion is respectable . . .' (1/1/57:5). The typescript transposes two chapters (so that Ms. Chapters XIII and XIV become Ts. Chapters XIV and XIII, the latter represented by a thirteen-page 'fair copy') and breaks off shortly before the manuscript it is replacing did (in the middle of Ts. Chapter XIV rather than early in Ms. Chapter XV), but the majority of the references to Thrain and Thror in Chapters X through XV that had appeared in the Second Phase manuscript carry over unchanged, word-for-word, into the typescript (see Note 19), with Thrain the father and Thror the grandfather.

- Third Phase: Tolkien completes the book after a pause of about a year, writing a short, forty-five page manuscript conclusion from the point where the First Typescript broke off. The Thorin–Thrain–Thror line of descent is still in place. The Gem of Girion now becomes the Arkenstone, and in four places (once in a pasteover insertion into the typescript of Chapter XII,[21] twice in Chapter XVI, and once in Chapter XVII) it is called 'the Arkenstone of Thrain'. In one of these points in the new manuscript, and twice in the typescript that ultimately replaced it (the latter dating from autumn 1936), Thrain is explicitly Thorin's father rather than his *grand*father:

> 'What of the Arkenstone of Thrain?' said [Bard] . . .
>
> 'That stone was my father's, and is mine' [Thorin] said. '. . . how came you by the heirloom of my house'? (Chapter XVII: new Ms. page 21 & 1st Ts. 1/1/67:1)

and again

> . . . and now Thorin spoke of the Arkenstone of Thrain, and bade them eagerly to look for it in every corner.
>
> 'For the Arkenstone of my father,' he said, 'is worth more than a river of gold in itself, and to me it is beyond price . . .' (Chapter XVI: 1st Ts. 1/1/66:1)[22]

Significantly, Tolkien marked this passage in both the First and Second typescripts, changing 'father' to 'fathers' (i.e., 'For the Arkenstone of my *fathers*, 1/1/66:1 & 1/1/47:1), but for some reason he rescinded this correction in the page proofs – see the first set of proofs (1/2/2: page [273]), where Tolkien altered *fathers* to *father*, and the second set of proofs (1/2/3: page [273]), where he pencilled in an 's' after *father* but then erased it. Had he not done so, and had the reference in the following chapter been brought into line, the entire problem need never have arisen.

- Finally, at some point Tolkien makes 'Thror's Map' [Plate I; to distinguish this from the final version appearing in the published book, I will refer to this version as 'Thror's Map I' (TM.I)], based on the original 'Fimbulfambi's Map' that ended 'The Pryftan Fragment' [Frontispiece] (or on a now-lost intermediary map that closely resembled it; see p. 23). This earlier version of the map, which accompanied the submission of the completed book to Allen & Unwin on 3rd October 1936, is neatly labelled in the lower left corner: 'Thror's Map · Copied by B.Baggins · For moon-runes hold up to a light'. Beneath the Lonely Mountain in the center is the label 'Here of old was the land of Thrain King under the Mountain'. In the final version of Thror's Map ['Thror's Map II' (TM.II); DAA.97] published in the book, made in between 10th December 1936 and 4th January 1937, the label in the lower left has been simplified to 'Thror's Map' and the text beneath the mountain now reads 'Here of old was Thrain King under the Mountain'. This is the clearest expression of the reverse genealogy: Thrain is the grandfather who was the last King Under the Mountain and Thror is the son who years later made the map before setting out on his own final quest.

  Unfortunately, we do not know exactly when TM.I was made. It seems probable that it was during the creation of the First Typescript [e.g., sometime in 1932] – that is, after the emergence of the names Thror and Thrain during the writing of Chapter X and long enough afterwards that Tolkien had forgotten the original sequence, just as he did when typing the typescript version of Chapter VII. However, it might have been slightly later, during the composition of the final chapters [e.g., December 1932–January 1933], when the references to 'the Arkenstone of Thrain' seem to indicate that Tolkien had become either confused or ambivalent about the correct sequence. It could even be as late as the late summer and early fall of 1936, when Tolkien finally extended the typescript all the way to the end of the book (see Christopher Tolkien's letter to Father Christmas, December 1937, cited in the Foreword to the 50th anniversary edition, page vii).

In summary, then, the preponderance of evidence from what we may call the text tradition is overwhelmingly in favor of the original genealogy: Thorin, son of Thrain, son of Thror. However, in several places (Beorn's reference to Thorin's ancestry, at least some of the references to the Arkenstone of Thrain, and most importantly on the Map) Tolkien either explicitly or implicitly uses the reverse genealogy instead. Whether this was entirely the result of confusion on his part or deliberate choice is impossible to say, but the evidence suggests the former; it seems unlikely, for example, that Tolkien would deliberately revert to the rejected reverse genealogy when drafting the Council of Elrond scenes in 'The New Hobbit' (see Note 20) when he had already committed to the other line of descent in print just two years before (cf. HME VI.403). We have here, therefore, a rare case of Tolkien's losing track of some detail in the course of revising the book; he managed at the last minute to bring the text into accord (with the exception of two of the references to the Arkenstone) but failed to get the troublesome map to agree with it.

Not until years later did he return to the matter, when as part of the 1947 revisions that became the Second Edition of *The Hobbit* he resorted to what Taum Santoski called the typically Tolkienesque solution of leaving both contradictory pieces of information in place and adding a third element that took both into account and resolved their apparent contradiction: the invention of Thrain the Old. For a detailed discussion of this new character, and the reasons for his insertion into the story, see The Fourth Phase: The 1947 Hobbit, pp. 780, 788, & 791.

NOTES

1 Scull notes that for his work on medieval language and literature Tolkien needed

> . . . a deep understanding of the archaeology, history, and culture of the period in which the text is set . . . Tolkien's interest in such matters for the periods he studied and taught is clear in his writings and contributed much to the background of his fiction.

– 'The Influence of Archaeology and History on Tolkien's World', *Scholarship & Fantasy: Proceedings of The Tolkien Phenomenon, May 1992, Turku, Finland*, ed. K. J. Battarbee (page 33).

2 This era is recorded mainly through the records of the sole surviving Old English kingdom, the Saxon realm of Wessex, and naturally those records focus on the events from that perspective. Tolkien himself strongly identified with the Angles, considering himself 'a Mercian' (JRRT to CT, 18th January 1945; *Letters* p. 108) and at one point declaring a resolution 'to refuse to speak anything but Old Mercian' (JRRT to CT, 9th December 1943; *Letters* p. 65).

3 Tolkien was also influenced by other writers of 'feigned history', or pseudohistory, such as Geoffrey of Monmouth's *History of the Kings*

of Britain [1137], which covers the years from the time the Trojans defeated the giants down through King Arthur's time and into which he inserted his own excursion into that genre, *Farmer Giles of Ham*.

4. Actually, it was later discovered that workmen had first turned up prehistoric artifacts at the site in 1829 but discarded them without informing any antiquarian of their existence. Cf. Keller, *The Lake Dwellings of Switzerland*, page 10.

5. This image comes from a matchbox cover reproduced as illustration #68 [page 146, top] in Bryony & John Coles' *Sweet Track to Glastonbury: The Somerset Levels in Prehistory* [1986]; it seems to have been one of a series of twenty 'Historic Westcountry' images, in this case labelled 'No 8 GLASTONBURY LAKE VILLAGE'. For more on the Glastonbury and Meade lake-villages as they were understood at the time Tolkien wrote *The Hobbit*, see Arthur Bulleid's little booklet *The Lake-Villages of Somerset* [first published in 1924 and many times reprinted], Bulleid being the excavator of Glastonbury lake-village and, with George Gray, of the two minor lake-villages at Meade. My thanks to Jim Pietrusz for drawing the Coles' book and Bulleid's pamphlet to my attention and for loaning me both volumes, and to Bryony Coles for her courtesy in replying to my queries about this image.

6. I.e., Adrien de Mortillet, son of Gabriel de Mortillet, the leading French expert of his time on lake-dwellings (particularly the lake-dwelling at Lake Varese, Italy), famous today largely for his book *Le Prehistorique: Antiquité de l'Homme* [1882], which proposed a widely influential classification system for dividing prehistory into chronological epochs named after cultures identified through remains excavated at specific sites. Adrien himself was a distinguished archeologist and anthropologist in his own right.

7. The mountain is clearly larger here than the description in the published book would justify (for the manuscript version of this passage, see p. 548):

> From their town the Lonely Mountain was mostly screened by the low hills at the far end of the lake, through a gap in which the Running River came down from the North. Only its high peak could they see in clear weather, and they looked seldom at it . . .
>
> — DAA.[302].

However, it is far more aesthetically satisfying for the picture to show such an important feature somewhat larger than it might really appear; for another example, see the image of Thangorodrim in the background of Tolkien's 'Tol Sirion' (*Pictures by Tolkien*, plate 36 †. In the original drawing by Tolkien, Thangorodrim and the smoke clouds hanging over it are a menacing, looming presence; in the redrawn colourized version by H. E. Riddett, Morgoth's fortress has become a tiny dot in the far distance – more accurate perhaps but far less dramatic. (The two versions are presented on facing pages without comment in the first edition of *Pictures by Tolkien* [1979]; this change is noted in *Pictures*' second edition [1992].)

† Also known as 'The Vale of Sirion'; cf. H-S#55.

8 I can find no evidence that Tolkien ever visited the site, and in general he seems not to have felt any special interest in seeing for himself archeological digs, the results of which had inspired him when he read about them. For example, so far as I can determine he does not seem to have visited the site of any of the famous lake-dwellings discovered by Keller and his successors on his 1911 visit to Switzerland (for his route, see his 1967/68 letter to Michael Tolkien, *Letters* pp. 391–3). Nor can I find any evidence that he visited the site of Beorhtnoth's tomb in Ely while working on *The Homecoming of Beorhtnoth Beorhthelm's Son*, nor the temple of Nodens when writing his essay 'The Name "Nodens"', nor the burial mound at Sutton Hoo when writing the Rohirrim chapters of *The Lord of the Rings*. He did base places in his books on memorable spots he had visited, such as the Aglarond at Helm's Deep on Cheddar Gorge, or the description of Rivendell and the Misty Mountains on his one trip to snow-covered mountains, his 1911 visit to Switzerland (see Marie Barnfield's essay on Rivendell and Switzerland in *Þe Lyfe ant þe Auncestrye*, issue no. 3 [Spring 1996]), but this was a case of drawing inspiration from things he had happened to see years before, not of deliberately seeking out first-hand source material. In general, Tolkien seems to have drawn such inspiration more from imaginative reconstructions proposed in scholarly books than in on-site visits.

For more on possible real-world sites that might have inspired Tolkien, particularly in England and for *The Lord of the Rings*, see Mathew Lyons' *There and Back Again: In the Footsteps of J. R. R. Tolkien* (Cadogan Guides, 2004). For the current state of archeological thinking on the 'lake-dwellings', see Francesco Menotti's essay 'The *Pfahlbau-problem* and the History of Lake-Dwelling Research in the Alps' (*Oxford Journal of Archaeology*, vol. 20 number 4 [2001], pages 319–28).

9 For destruction by fire, see Keller, page 33: 'as in many other lake dwellings, the upper structure had been destroyed by fire'. The popularized idea of violent destruction by fire and assault lingered for a very long time: cf. the 're-enactment' of the 'Scythian' assault by dugout canoe on the reconstructed Polish lake-fortress of Biskupin staged in 1939. For a more moderate modern assessment, see the chapter devoted to Biskupin in *Exploring Prehistoric Europe* by Chris Scarre (part of the 'Places in Time' series [1998]) which, after admiring the high degree of organization required for a society to be able to create such a carefully planned structure, concludes 'It is not hard to see . . . that the close-packed timber buildings must have posed an enormous fire risk, even without enemy action, and it is possible that . . . Biskupin simply burned down by accident' (p. 170).

As for the persistent idea that only desperation would drive people to living in such dwellings, this ignores the wealth of resources available in wetlands. While generally viewed as wastelands, marshlands are actually prime hunting grounds for waterfowl (duck, geese, rails, snipe, &c.), not to mention fish and other animals that make their homes in or around the margins of lakes, bogs, and pools, providing a constant supply of food if the problem of shelter and access can be satisfactorily addressed.† Indeed, in the Middle Ages, the marsh later discovered to contain the ruins of the two ancient lake-villages was a prize possession of the Abbey of Glastonbury, which harvested large quantities of marshfowl from it every year; the Coles record that fisheries in the marshes near Meare alone paid the monks 7,000 eels each year (*Sweet Track*, page 21).

† The focus of the Coles' book is actually not on the lake-villages but on the wooden tracks constructed in ancient times to criss-cross the marshy areas and provide safe footing into and across the extensive wetlands; some of these tracks are more than 5,000 years old, including the 'Sweet Track' of the title.

10 For more on 'Mirkwood', see p. 19. While the juxtaposition of Morris's Wolfings with Tolkien's woodmen menaced by wolves is suggestive, the name in *The House of the Wolfings* simply refers to the totem animal that kindred has adopted: the Wolfings or people of the Wolf, to distinguish them from their neighbors the Bearings (folk of the Bear), the Elkings (Elk), the Hartings (Hart), and so forth.

11 Lake Town is really Tolkien's only High Medieval setting, which is curious from an author who spent most of his working life in a city dominated by that High Medieval institution known as Oxford University. By contrast, despite a few comic anachronistic touches the village of Ham in *Farmer Giles of Ham* is a Dark Ages village, while Minas Tirith in *The Lord of the Rings* strongly evokes a great Classical city from the end of antiquity, Byzantine rather than Roman (cf. *Letters* p. 157), already in decline and surrounded by barbarian hordes. Hobbiton is, by Tolkien's own description, a Victorian village from about the time of the Diamond Jubilee (i.e., Queen Victorian's 60th anniversary on the throne in 1897; *Letters* p. 230); this is one reason it has such affinities on the one hand with the world of Kenneth Grahame's *The Wind in the Willows* [1908], which draws on the same setting as it was a decade later, when the peace and quiet of the countryside was beginning to give way to the noise of the new century's motorcars,† and on the other with the Puddleby-on-the-Marsh of Hugh Lofting's *Dr. Dolittle* series [1922ff], which depict English village life six decades earlier, at the very beginning of the Victorian period. Wootton Major in *Smith of Wootton Major* is a deliberately timeless setting, while modern settings are relatively rare in Tolkien and are generally confined to single indoor locations: *Mr. Bliss* is a significant exception.

† For Tolkien's own parable of motorcars destroying Oxford, see 'The Bovadium Fragment' (unpublished; Bodleian Library, Department of Western Manuscripts, Mss. Tolkien, Series A, folder A62, pages 38–91).

12 This makes the Master of the Town one of the very few elected officials to appear anywhere in Tolkien's work, joined only by the Mayor of Michel Delving in *The Lord of the Rings*, the only elective office in the Shire (see part 3 of the Prologue to *The Lord of the Rings*, 'Of the Ordering of the Shire'). This essentially ceremonial role is held at the start of Frodo's story by Old Will Whitfoot, 'the fattest hobbit in the Westfarthing', who is treated more as an ineffectual figure of fun than a wily politician (*LotR*.172 & 1050), ill-equipped to deal with Lotho and Sharkey's usurpation. After the War of the Ring the position ('Deputy Mayor') is temporarily assumed by Frodo (*LotR*.1059) and afterwards held for many years by Sam (*LotR*.1067 & 1133–4). During Sam's tenure (seven consecutive terms, for a total of forty-nine years) the dignity and authority of the office undergo considerable expansion, as may be seen by King Elessar's letter (HME IX.117–18, 125–6, & 128–31), which treats the Mayor as the Shire's chief executive and official representative.

Neither Ham nor Bree seem to have mayors, while Minas Tirith and Meduseld are ruled directly by their resident lords (or, more accurately, by the appointed officials of those lords).

13 That is, 'politician' in the sense of an elected official who tries to be all things to all people while always looking out primarily for his own interests – unlike, say, Master Gríma Wormtongue, who while a master plotter is neither elected nor a mere weathervane but an evil councillor with a private agenda which he pursues with great skill and care. Similarly, while there is much plotting on all sides in 'The Wanderings of Húrin' (HME XI.251–310), it is the maneuvering of clever and ruthless men, more in the style of the Allthing moot in *Njal's Saga*, than politicians per se.

14 This was a work Tolkien professed to loathe yet seems to cite in one of his most cynical poems, 'Progress in Bimble Town', which is scathingly dedicated to 'the Mayor and Corporation', the phrase applied over and over in Browning's poem to the burgomeister of Hamelin and his council.

That Tolkien castigates Browning's poem late in life (JRRT to Jane Neave, 22nd November 1961; *Letters* p. 311) does not necessarily mean he was not influenced by it. This is particularly the case since his criticism of it comes in the context of a condemnation of works specifically written for children, in the course of which he severely criticizes *The Hobbit* itself as well as the works of Hans Christian Andersen, yet at the same time noting of the latter both that when young he 'disliked [them] intensely' and 'read them myself often', with what to an outsider 'may have looked like rapture' (ibid.). His praise of George MacDonald's work in the 1930s and condemnation of it in the 1960s (cf. his remarks to Clyde Kilby, printed in *Tolkien and the Silmarillion*, page 31) is of a piece with this, and shows that his occasional censoriousness always needs to be taken in context.

The similarity between Tolkien's 'the Master and his councillors' and

Browning's 'the Mayor and Corporation' was first explored by Douglas Anderson in *The Annotated Hobbit* (DAA.253), which reprints 'Progress in Bimble Town' (first published in *The Oxford Magazine* in October 1931, during the period when Tolkien was writing *The Hobbit* and quite possibly right around the time when he was writing this chapter). I am also grateful to Doug for helping me find Tolkien's 1966 characterization of MacDonald as an 'old grandmother'.

15 The worst such incident passing into legend as the 'St. Scholastic Day massacre' of February 10th 1354/55, which killed about ninety people, two-thirds of them students and the rest townspeople: the Mayor and town of Oxford were ordered by King Edward III to pay a fine of one silver penny for each student killed on the anniversary of that day, a ritual of public humiliation that was not abandoned until 1825.

16 Gandalf's grandfather, the last King under the Mountain, had of course briefly been named Fimbulfambi ('Great Fool') in the Pryftan Fragment (see p. 9), but this name had not survived into the Bladorthin Typescript, where the reference is simply to 'your grandfather'. Likewise, in the Second Phase continuation of Chapter I neither of Gandalf's forebears is named, simply being referred to as 'your father' and 'my grandfather' (e.g., p. 73). Indeed, this anonymity carried over into the first and second editions of the published book; not until the 1966 paperback third edition text were Thror and Thrain's names inserted into the first chapter:

- 'made by your grandfather' > 'made by Thror, your grandfather' (DAA.51)
- 'Long ago in my grandfather's time' > 'Long ago in my grandfather Thror's time' (DAA.54)
- 'Your grandfather was killed' > 'Your grandfather Thror was killed' (DAA.56)
- 'And your father went away' > 'And Thrain your father went away' (DAA.56)

One spot where we might expect these names to have been inserted but they were not comes in Chapter IV. In the manuscript text there is no indication that the goblin-chief realizes who his prisoner is (cf. p. 132), whereas in the exchange between Thorin and the Great Goblin in the First Typescript when the former gives his name ('Thorin the dwarf') the Great Goblin replies using his captive's full name, indicating that he knows just who his prisoner is:

> 'Not that it will do you much good, Thorin *Oakenshield*, I know too much about your folk already . . .'
>
> —typescript page 86; Marq. 1/1/54:5 (italics mine).

17 Tolkien was of course intimately familiar with this text, citing it as his direct source for the dwarf-names in his February 1938 letter to *The Observer* ('The dwarf-names . . . are from the Elder Edda'; see Appendix II). Cf. also his 29th March 1967 letter to W. H. Auden (*Letters* p. 379),

thanking Auden for sending his translation of this poem; Tolkien promises to send Auden his own (as yet unpublished) recasting of some of the *Elder Edda* material (the Volsunga/Sigurd story) in return.

18 For this reason, Patricia Terry omits the dwarf-names from her translation of *Völuspä* in her *Poems of the Elder Edda* (cf. pages 2–3), as did Gudbrand Vigfusson and F. York Powell from their dual-text edition *Corpus Poeticum Boreale* [1883], a once-standard tome that sought to bring together all surviving remnants of Old Icelandic poetry; see Vol. I pages 192 and 194–5. Dronke includes it in her edition of *Völuspá* but forebears to comment on this passage, although it comprises ten percent of the entire poem (*The Poetic Edda, Volume II: Mythological Poems* [1997]; see especially page 122), describing it as 'a unique record of unexpected tradition, made in an unfortunate place' (page 92). W. H. Auden does include the entire passage in his translation, *Völuspá: The Song of the Sybil* [published 1968], which Auden sent to Tolkien in 1967 (see Note 17) and later collected into *The Elder Edda: A Selection*, tr. Paul B. Taylor & W. H. Auden, with introduction by Peter H. Salus and Taylor and notes by Salus [1969], a volume dedicated 'For J. R. R. Tolkien'. Most significantly, Snorri Sturluson, who was better-informed on Eddic lore than it is possible for any modern scholar to be, selected this passage as one deserving preservation and explanation in his *Prose Edda*.

19 The full Thror–Thrain–Thorin genealogy occurs in the following passages:

- [p. 436]: 'songs were still sung of the King Under the Mountain Thror and his son Thrain of the race of Durin . . . Some sang that Thror and Thrain would come back one day' (Ms. page 131; corresponds to 1st ed. text page 199 and DAA.246).
- [p. 438]: 'Thorin son of Thrain son of Thror King Under the Mountain!' (Ms. page 132; 1st ed. page 202/DAA.248).
- [p. 439] 'I am Thorin son of Thrain son of Thror King Under the Mountain. I return' (Ms. page 133; 1st ed. page 203/DAA.249–50).
- [p. 441] 'Certainly O Thorin Thrain's son Thror's son' [the Master said] (Ms. page 136; 1st ed. page 207/DAA.253).
- [p. 504] 'O Thorin Thrain's son, may your beard grow ever longer' [Bilbo] said crossly (Ms. page 142; 1st ed. page 218/DAA.267).
- [p. 619] 'O Thorin Thrain's son Thror's son' [said Roäc] (Ms. page 166). This passage survived into the Third Phase manuscript conclusion (new Ms. page 6) but was simplified to 'O Thorin son of Thrain' (1/1/65:1), preserving the genealogy but omitting the grandfather's name, when the First Typescript was finally extended to include the final chapters of the story – e.g. immediately before the submission to Allen & Unwin on 3rd October 1936. This latter reading appears in the first and all subsequent editions of the book (cf. 1st ed. page 263/DAA.316).

There are also a number of references to Thror the grandfather:

- [p. 439] '. . . the King under the Mountain – that it was Thror's grandson not Thror himself . . .' (Ms. page 134; 1st ed. page 204/ DAA.250).
- [p. 509] 'Did you expect me to trot back with the whole treasure of Thror on my back?' (Ms. page 146; 1st ed. page 226/DAA.276).
- [p. 582] 'the Great Hall of Thror' (Ms. page 164; 1st ed. page 247/ DAA.297).
- [p. 619] 'the legend of the wealth of Thror has not lost in the telling' (Ts. 1/1/65:2; 1st ed. page 264/DAA.317).†

– and to Thrain the father:

- [p. 619] 'O Thorin son of Thrain' (Ts. 1/1/65:1; 1st ed. page 263/ DAA.316); see above.
- [p. 646] 'the gates of Thorin son of Thrain, King under the Mountain' (new Ms. page 9; 1st ed. page 267/DAA 320); this passage is repeated on 1st ed. page 269/DAA.322 whereas the manuscript simply says 'Again Thorin asked the same question as before' without actually repeating the text.
- [p. 656, Text Note 30] 'We speak unto Thorin Thrain's son calling himself King under the Mountain' (addition to new Ms. page 12; 1st ed. page 271/DAA.324).

Tolkien also deleted one reference to Thror and seems to have added one in a margin:

- [p. 473] 'Thror's map' (Ms. page 137; 1/1/12:2) > 'Thorin's map' (1st Ts. 1/1/61:2; 1st ed. page 212/DAA.260).
- [p. 588, Text Note 15] added: 'the gem of Girion, <Thror's> chief treasure' (marginal addition to Ms. page 162) (Ms. 1/1/15; 1st ed. page 245/DAA.295).

† This corresponds to Ms. page 167, but Thror is not mentioned in the original draft nor in the new Ms. page 6 of the continuation; Roäc's mention of 'the wealth of Thror' enters in for the first time in the First Typescript.

20 *The Return of the Shadow* (HME VI.403): 'It is said in secret that Thráin (father of Thrór father of Thorin who fell in battle) possessed [a Ring of Power] that had descended from his sires' [said Glóin]. In this volume Christopher Tolkien defers comment, simply pointing out 'In *The Hobbit* Thráin was not the father of Thrór but his son. This is a complex question which will be discussed in Vol. VII' (HME VI.414 Note 28). He returns to the point in *The Treason of Isengard* with a 'Note on Thrór and Thráin' (HME VII.159–60), which lucidly explains the problem of the competing genealogies and how his father ultimately solved it. One additional piece of evidence suggesting how Tolkien made the mistake is that the first portion of the book sent to him to proofread (signatures A–H) happened in its final pages to include the one place in the text where the genealogy was reversed, in Chapter VII. When he later received the remainder of the proofs,

he seems to have taken the (erroneous) reading in the section he had already proofed and returned to the printers as fixed and thus changed all the readings in the remainder of the book to match it. Then he reversed his decision, stetted every transposition he had pencilled in, and requested that the anomalous entry in Chapter VII be changed instead to match the rest, resulting in the text as published.

21 The pasteover in Chapter XII (1/1/62:11) occurred before the creation of the Second Typescript, which faithfully reproduces the replacement text. I have been unable to read the original text beneath the pasteover.

22 The manuscript version of this passage had read simply:

> and Thorin bade them eagerly to look for the Arkenstone of Thrain. 'For that' he said 'is worth more than a river of gold in itself and to me yet more' (new Ms. page 13; 1/1/17:7).

THE SECOND PHASE

[continued]

Chapter XI

THE LONELY MOUNTAIN

As before, the story continues without chapter break, in this case near the bottom of manuscript page 136 (1/1/12:1). This brief chapter is written quickly, with many abbreviations ('R. Running') and minor errors or omissions, which I have for the most part silently expanded or corrected. Perhaps significantly, it is a fairly clean text, with relatively few changes made in the course of composition; thanks to the brief sketch of these events in Plot Notes B (see pp. 362–3), Tolkien knew what he wanted to happen in this part of the story and seems to have simply concentrated on getting it down in full without for the moment worrying about details of phrasing.

They rowed right up it in two days' <journey> and passed out into the River Running, and saw now the Mountain towering grim and tall before them. The stream was strong and their going slow. At the end of the third day some miles up the River Running they halted on the bank to their left, the West bank, and disembarked. Here a store of provisions and other necessarys was made, but no men would stay there so near the shadow of the Mountain.[TN1]

'Not at any [rate] until the songs had come true' said they. Still there was no need for any guard. The lands were wide and empty. Here they joined the horses that had been sent for them; and bade farewell to their escort. The next day packing what they could carry on horseback they set out, Bilbo riding with Balin on one horse, leading another heavily laden beside them; the others were ahead in single file, picking [*added*: out] a slow road. They made due North, slanting away from the River Running and drawing nearer & nearer to a great spur of the Mountain that was flung out Southward towards them.

It was a weary journey, and a quiet and stealthy one. There was no laughter or song, and the pride and hopes which had stirred in all their hearts (esp. Thorin's) at the singing of the old songs by the lake had died away to a plodding gloom. They knew they were drawing near to the end of their journey – and that it might be a very horrible end. The land grew barren, though once, as Thorin said, it had been green and fair. There was little grass. Soon there were neither bush nor tree, and only broken stumps to speak of ones long vanished. They were come to the desolation of the Dragon, and they were come at the waning of the year.

They reached the skirts of the mountain without meeting serious danger, all the same. There was no sign of the dragon. The mountain lay dark and silent before them, and ever more above them. They made their first settled camp on the lowest slopes of the great southern spur – I have marked it on the copy of Thror's map; as he did himself, though of course it was not there when Bladorthin had it.[TN2] Before setting out to search the western slopes for the hidden door, on which all their hopes rested, Thorin sent out a scouting expedition to spy out the land to the east by the Front Gate. Bilbo went with them – and Balin and Fili and Kili. After a couple of days of silent journey they came back to the Running River, which here took a [?sudden >] great western turn and flowed towards the mountain, which stretched out great arms to meet it. The bank was rocky, tall, and steep here, and gazing out from the brink, over the narrow river, foaming and splashing over boulders, they could see in a wide valley shadowed by the mountain's arms, the grey ruins far-off of ancient [?towers >] houses, towers, and walls.

'There lies all that is left of Dale' said Balin. 'The mountain's sides were green with woods then, and all this valley rich and sheltered.' He looked both sad and grim as he said this: he had been one of Thorin's companions on the day the Dragon came.[TN3] They did not dare to follow the river much further towards the gate; but they went on until lying hidden behind a rock they could look out, and see the dark cavernous opening in a great wall between the mountain's arms, out of which the water ran. And out of which too there was coming steam and a dark smoke. Nothing else moved in the waste, save the vapour and the river [> water], and every now and again a dark and ominous raven. The only sound was the sound of stony water, and every now and again a raven's croak. Balin shuddered. 'Let us return' he said. 'We can do no good here! And I do not like those dark birds; they look like spies of evil'.[TN4]

'The dragon is still alive and in the halls under the Mountain then?' said the hobbit. 'Or I imagine so from the smoke'.

'That doesn't prove it' said Balin; 'though I don't doubt you are right. But he might be gone [*added*: away] some time, and [> or] he might be lying on the mountain's-side watching us [> keeping watch], and still I expect smokes and steams would come out of the gates because of the heat he leaves behind'.

With such gloomy thoughts, followed ever by croaking ravens, they made their weary way back to the others and the camp. A year and more had passed since they had been guests at the fair house of

Elrond, in June; and now the summer of the year after was drawing to a bleak end, and they were alone in the perilous waste.[TN5] They were at the end of their journey, but as far as ever it seemed from the end of their quest. None of them had much spirit left.

Now strange to say Bilbo had more than any of them. He would often borrow Thorin's map and gaze at it, pondering the runes, and the message of the moon-letters Elrond had read.[TN6] It was he who made them begin the dangerous search upon the western slopes for the secret door.[TN7] They moved their camp to a long valley deeper and narrower than that one where stood the great gates of the River, but hemmed in with lower spurs. Two of these here [sprouted >] thrust forward West from the main mass of the mountain, great long ridges with steep sides, [that] fell ever downwards towards the plain. Here there was less sign of the dragon's marauding feet, and there was grass for their ponies.[TN8] From their second camp, shadowed all day by cliff and wall until the sun began to sink west towards the forest, day by day they toiled in parties seeking for paths up the mountain side. If the map was true somewhere high above the cliff at the valley head must stand the secret door, now their only hope. Day by day they came back weary to the camp without success.

But at last they found what they were seeking. Fili and Kili and the hobbit went back one day near to the [end of the >] Southern corner of the valley, and here scrambling up some loose rocks they came suddenly on what looked like rough steps. Following these excitedly they came upon traces of a narrow track, often lost, often found again, that wandered onto the top of the sunken ridge and brought them at last to a narrow ledge. This turned north and looking down they saw they were at the top of the [valley >] cliff at the valley head, looking down on their own camp below.[TN9] Silently, clinging to the rocky wall on their right they went in single file along the ledge till the wall opened and they turned into a little steep walled bay, grassy floored, still and quiet. At its end a flat wall rose up at its lower part close to the ground as smooth and upright as man's work, but without a joint or crack. No sign was there of post nor lintel nor threshold; no sign of bar or bolt or key. Yet they did not doubt they had found the door at last. They beat on it, and they pushed, they implored it to open, they spoke fragments of broken magic, and nothing stirred. At last tired out they rested before their long climb down.[TN10]

There was excitement in the camp that night. In the morning they prepared to move. Bofur and Bombur were left behind to guard the ponies and the stores. The others went down the valley, and up the newly found path, and so to the narrow ledge, along which they cd. have carried no bundles or packs, so narrow and breathless was it, with a fall of a hundred and fifty feet beside them. But each of them carried a coil of rope tight about his waist. And so they reached the little grassy bay.[TN11]

There they made their third camp, hauling up what they needed by <knotted> ropes. Down the same way one or two of the most active, such as Fili, would go back from time to time to the valley, [and tell the others > Bofur and Bombur > of what was >] and bring such news as there was, or take a share in the guard, while Bofur climbed to the higher camp. Bombur would not go. 'I am too fat for such fly-paths' he said. 'I should [tread on a >] turn dizzy and tread on my beard and then you would be thirteen again!' Some of them explored the ledge beyond the opening and found a way leading higher onto the mountain; but that way they did not dare to go far.[TN12] Nor was there much use in it. All the while a silence reigned, broken by no bird or voice, nothing except the wind. They spoke low, and never shouted nor sang, for danger brooded in every rock.

Nor did they succeed in discovering the secret of the door, or where exactly it was in the flat face of rock. [*added in margin*: They had brought picks and tools of many sorts from Lake Town. But they soon gave up trying these on this part of the rock. Their handles splintered and jarred their arms with <illegible>, or the steel heads bent like lead. Mining work was no good at all.] Bilbo found that sitting on the doorstep [*added*: wearisome] – there wasn't one of course, really, but they used to call the little grassy space between the door and the opening onto the cliff edge 'the doorstep' in fun, remembering Bilbo's words long ago at the party in the hobbit-hole, that [they] could sit on the doorstep till they thought of something. And sit and think they did, or wandered aimlessly about, and glummer and glummer they became. Their spirits had risen a little, at the discovery of the path; but now they sank into their boots, and yet they wd. not give up and go away. The hobbit was no longer much brighter than the dwarves. He would do nothing but sit with his back to the rock-face staring away West through the opening over the cliff over the wide lands to the black wall of Mirkwood and the blue distances beyond in which he sometimes thought he cd. catch glimpses of the Misty Mountains.

'You said sitting on the doorstep [*added*: & thinking] would be my job, not to mention getting inside the door', said he, 'so I am sitting and thinking'. But I am afraid he was not often thinking of the job, but of what lay beyond the blue distances, the western land and The Hill and his hobbit-hole under it. A large grey stone lay in the centre of the grass, and he stared moodily at it; or watched the great snails that seemed to love this little shut in bay with its rocky wall [> sides] crawl slow and stickily along the sides.

'Autumn will be in tomorrow' said Thorin one day.

'And winter comes after autumn' said Bifur.

'And next year after that' said Dwalin. 'And our beards will grow till they hang down the cliff to the ground, before anything happens here.[TN13] What is our Burglar doing for us! Seeing he has got an invisible ring and so ought to be a specially excellent performer, I am beginning to think he ought to go through the Front Gate, and spy things out a bit.'

Bilbo heard this – he was on the rocks up above the enclosure. 'Good gracious!' thought he ' – So that's what they are beginning to think are they? What ever am I going to do. I might have known something dreadful would happen to me in the end. I don't think I could bear to see the ruined valley of Dale again, and as for that steam<ing> gate –.'

That night he was very miserable and hardly slept. Next day the dwarves went wandering off in various directions. Some were exercising the ponies down below; some were on the mountain side. All day Bilbo sat gloomily in the grassy bay gazing at the stone or out West through the opening.[TN14] He had a queer feeling that he was waiting for something. 'Perhaps the wizard will suddenly come back to day' he thought.[TN15]

He could see then a glimpse of the forest. As the sun turned west there was a gleam of yellow light upon its distant roof, going brown towards autumn. Suddenly [> At last] he saw the orange sun sinking towards the level of his eyes. He went to the opening and there pale and faint was a thin new moon above the rim of the earth. At that very moment he heard a sharp crack behind him. There on the [*added*: grey] stone in the grass was a large thrush, nearly coal black its pale yellow breast freckled with dark spots. Crack. it had caught a snail and was knocking it on the stone. Crack, crack!

Suddenly Bilbo understood. Forgetting all caution he stood on the ledge and hailed the dwarves, shouting and waving. Those that were nearest came tumbling over the rocks to him, wondering what on earth was happening, the others made for the path from the valley as fast as ever they could. You can just picture Bilbo standing now beside the thrushes' stone, and the dwarves with wagging beards watching excitedly by the walls. The sun sank lower and lower. Then their hopes fell. It sank into a belt of red-stained clouds and disappeared. The dwarves groaned, but still Bilbo stood almost without moving. The little moon was dipping to the [river >] horizon. Evening was coming on. Then suddenly when their hope was lowest, a red ray of the sun escaped like a finger through a rent in the bars of cloud. A gleam of light came straight through the opening in the bay, and fell on the smooth rock face. [There was a loud crack >] The old thrush which had been watching from a high perch with beady eyes [& head] cocked on one side gave a sudden trill. There was a loud crack. A flake of rock split from the face and fell. A hole appeared suddenly about three feet from the ground.

Quickly trembling lest the chance shd fade [Thorin fitted >] the dwarves rushed to the rock and pushed. 'A key a key' said Bilbo 'we need a key'.

'But we have no keys' said the desperate dwarves.

'Gandalf[TN16] gave me my father's map not keys of his' said Thorin. 'Gandalf –'

'Gandalf!' said Bilbo. 'He gave us [> you] the troll-keys.[TN17] Try them quick. You never know'.

Thorin stepped up and fitted [> put] in the only key that was small enough. It fitted it turned. Snap! and the sun gleam went out, the sun sank, and evening sprang into the sky. The moon was gone.

Now they all pushed together, and slowly a part of the rock-wall gave way. Long straight cracks appeared and widened. A door five feet high and three broad was outlined,[TN18] and slowly without a noise swung inwards. It almost seemed as if darkness flowed out like a vapour from the mountain side; deep darkness in which nothing could be seen lay before their eyes, a mouth leading in and down.

The manuscript continues on the same page (manuscript page 142; I/I/13:I), but after the next sentence (see page 504) the ink becomes noticeably darker, indicating at least a brief pause in composition.

TEXT NOTES

1 This store of provisions would later become important; see Plot Notes E ('Little Bird'), a hasty half-page of notes describing Tolkien's original conception of the Siege of the Mountain, page 626.

2 This 'camp' can be seen, in exactly the position described here, on Fimbulfambi's Map (see plate one of the Frontispiece). It also appears on Thror's Map I (Plate I [top]), which follows the earliest map very closely. However, it is probable that this and other details were added to Fimbulfambi's Map long after the Pryftan Fragment was originally drafted, as part of the drafting for Thror's Map I, and thus dates from the time the latter was created. The location of the camp does not appear on the final map (Thror's Map II, DAA.97) that appeared in the published book.

Note that *Bladorthin* is still the name of the wizard here – that is, although 'Gandalf' had been dropped as the name of the chief dwarf before Chapter X was written, it was not immediately transferred to the wizard, although that would in fact occur later in this same 'chapter'; see Text Note 16 below.

3. This is our first indication that Balin, like Thorin, is a survivor of 'the day the Dragon came'. Taken altogether, his is perhaps the most eventful life of any dwarf on record, rivaled only by the great Dain Ironfoot. He was not only one of the few† who survived Smaug's attack upon the Lonely Mountain and the destruction of the dwarven Kingdom there but almost certainly also fought in the Battle of Azanulbizar to avenge Thror's murder, where the death rate among the dwarven combatants approached 50% (a casualty rate exceeding that of the Battle of the Somme) – not only did his father die there but Balin is mentioned as being among Thrain's and Thorin's company immediately after the battle (cf. *LotR*.1113). He accompanied Thrain on his ill-fated quest that ended with Durin's heir imprisoned in the dungeons of the Necromancer (*LotR*.1114), fought alongside Thorin in the Battle of Five Armies (see page 672), and finally reconquered Moria for a time and reclaimed the crown of Durin himself (*LotR*.258 & 338–41).

All this is all the more remarkable because according to the family tree presented in 'Durin's Folk' (*LotR* Appendix A part iii), Balin would have been only seven years old at the time of Smaug's attack and thus an unlikely candidate to be a companion of the twenty-four-year-old Thorin. This is obviously too young to match the information given in *The Hobbit* by at least a decade and probably more; while it is implied that Balin must be younger than Thorin from a remark in Chapter IX ('"What have we done, O king?" said Balin, the oldest left now that Gandalf [Thorin] was gone' – cf. page 380 and Text Note 4 to Chapter IX), there's no indication that they're separated by more than a few years, nor any descriptions of Thorin to indicate that he is or looks old (unlike Balin, who from the first description of him on Bilbo's doorstep is 'a very old-looking dwarf' with a white beard, and whose age is reinforced by the many references to him throughout the story as 'old Balin'). By the official reckoning of *The Lord of the Rings*, Balin was thirty-six at the time of the Battle before Moria (when Dain, described as 'only a stripling', was himself thirty-two). He and his brother Dwalin – the latter not even born at the time of Smaug's attack – must therefore have been among the youngest members of Thrain's expedition, being at that time seventy-eight and sixty-nine respectively; compare Fili and Kili from Thorin's group, constantly referred to as youngsters, who are eighty-two and seventy-seven respectively, and Gimli, who at sixty-two was considered too young to accompany his father Glóin on Bilbo's adventure ('The Quest of Erebor', *Unfinished Tales* page 336 and DAA.376). At the time of his death in Moria, King Balin is officially two hundred and thirty-one, a respectable age considering that Thror, who is described as 'old' and 'crazed perhaps with age' (*LotR*.1110) is not that much older at the time of his murder (two hundred and forty-eight), nor is the 'old' and 'venerable' Dain (*LotR*.

245), whom Gandalf describes as being of a 'great age' (two hundred and fifty-one; *LotR*.1116). In fact, given the unlikelihood that he was only seven when the Kingdom under the Mountain fell or merely a dignified one hundred and seventy-eight at the time of Thorin's quest (when Thorin, who is never described as old, is himself one hundred and ninety-five), Balin was probably at least two hundred and forty at the time of his death and possibly, if we discount the reference in Chapter IX, much older; Thorin, had he lived, would then have been two hundred and forty-eight, the same age as old Thror at the time of his murder. See also *The Peoples of Middle-earth*, HME XII.284–5 & 288 for more on dwarven longevity.

† In the original conception as described in *The Hobbit*, it is clear that very few indeed escaped Smaug's attack, only Thror and Thrain (through the secret door) and 'the few' who like Thorin and Balin were outside at the time. When Tolkien revisited the history of the dwarves while constructing Appendix A of *LotR*, he greatly increased the number of survivors, stating (in contradiction to the account in *The Hobbit*) that 'many' of Thrór's kin escaped, including not just his son Thráin and grandson Thorin but Thorin's younger brother Frerin (later killed at the Mines of Moria) and his sister Dís (then only a child of ten, later the mother of Fíli and Kíli); furthermore, they were joined with 'a small company of their kinsmen and faithful followers' – the former including presumably Balin and his parents (Dwalin's having not yet been born until two years later indicates that their unnamed mother survived the disaster, and his father Fundin being among Thrain's company at the disastrous battle of Moria). A footnote adds that 'It was afterwards learned that more of the Folk under the Mountain had escaped than was at first hoped; but most of these went to the Iron Hills.' – *LotR*.1110.

4 Balin's distaste and distrust for the ravens shows that the idea of the ancient friendship between the dwarves and the ravens of the mountain had not yet arisen – there being no reference to conversations with either ravens or crows in Plot Notes B, nor in Plot Notes C (which followed immediately upon the writing of this chapter). There is however a very important reference to a crow in the earliest draft of the moon-runes passage all the way back in the Pryftan Fragment, where the secret writing had read 'Stand by the grey stone when the crow knocks and the rising sun at the moment of dawn on Durin's Day will shine upon the keyhole', but this had quickly been changed to a thrush (see page 22).

Crows do appear in Plot Notes D, but it seems that there the dwarves overhear the carrion fowl speaking rather than meet with them (see page 571). Not until Tolkien comes to write the last few pages of the Second Phase manuscript, the first third or so of what became Chapter XV – the last bit of writing Tolkien completed before breaking off the Second Phase and returning to the beginning of the story to create the First Typescript – do the ravens finally appear, with such suddenness that Bilbo himself comments upon it (see page 618). It is possible that they first appeared in the lost drafting of which the only surviving fragment is the half-page upon the back of which Tolkien jotted down Plot Notes E ('Little Bird'); at any rate, having introduced them as friends and allies of the dwarves, Tolkien initially projected the ravens of the mountain to play a larger part in the Siege; see page 626.

Since ravens appear in that later scene as much more sympathetic figures than those described here, Tolkien recast this passage in several stages to remove the incongruity. Thus 'a dark and ominous raven' becomes in the First Typescript 'a black and ominous crow' (1/1/61:2), while 'every now and again a raven's croak' becomes 'every now and again the harsh croak of a crow', which in turn at some point after the Second Typescript was made is changed to 'croak of a bird' (ibid. & 1/1/42:2). However, just a few paragraphs later 'followed ever by croaking ravens' was changed to 'by croaking crows and ravens', which did not resolve the problem at all. This latter reading survived into the page proofs (Marq. 1/2/2 page 211), where the words 'and ravens' was deleted (and 'above them' inserted so that the following lines would not need to be reset), thereby achieving the wording in the published book.

5 Tolkien originally wrote 'A year or more had passed since they had been guests at the fair house of Elrond, in June. The next . . .' before striking out the last two words and replacing the period with a semicolon and continuing '. . . and now [*added*: the] summer of the year after was drawing to a bleak end'. Once again, we see the more leisurely timeframe of the original draft is still in place; rather than it only being five or six months since their setting out as in the published book, here it is fifteen months or more since Bilbo left his hobbit-hole.

In the First Typescript (1/1/61:2), this passage was replaced with

> . . . made their weary way back to the camp. Only in June they had been guests in the fair house of Elrond, and though autumn was now crawling towards winter that pleasant time now seemed years ago. They were alone in the perilous waste without hope of further help . . .

See also Text Note 13.

6 In the text of Chapter II (page 116), these had read 'Stand by the grey stone where the thrush knocks. Then the rising [> setting] sun on the last light of Durin's Day will shine upon the key hole'. This is very similar to the revised text that appears on Fimbulfambi's map; see page 22.

7 This sentence was originally followed by an unfinished sentence beginning '[One day they >] Day by day they would toil in small parties up the lower slopes and'; a revised form of this sentence appears later in the paragraph.

8 This is the point at which the 'horses' described in the final paragraph of the preceding chapter and the opening paragraphs of this chapter become instead 'ponies', in keeping with Thorin and Company's two

previous sets of mounts (cf. pages 89 & 131, and 241–3). Despite much equivocation in later chapters, where Tolkien would occasionally write 'horses' and then alter it to 'ponies', they remained ponies henceforth.

9 This passage seems to ignore the idea, stated back in Chapter VI, that Bilbo is afraid of heights; see page 209 and Text Note 32 for Chapter VI. Possibly we are meant to conclude that Bilbo has simply learned how to face his fears better after his experiences in Mirkwood.

10 Later Tolkien created a schematic drawing of the mountain to help clarify the relationship of the first camp, second camp, hidden high path, and grassy bay hiding the secret door; see Plate II [top]. The second camp seems to be displaced in this illustration from the position described in the text; since 'looking down on their own camp below' suggests it was directly below the cliff they were atop – i.e., nestled against the right-hand spur (that is, the more southernly of the mountain's two short western spurs), not off on the other side of the valley below the left-hand (more northernly) spur, especially since they continue on past this point to reach the hidden bay at the head of the valley.

11 In the original (cancelled) drafting of this passage, the sequence of events was slightly more complicated:

> Bofur and Bombur were left below with the ponies. The rest carrying all they could went back by the newly found path, and came to the narrow ledge. But they could not carry bundles nor packs along there – as [they >] they ought to have thought of before. But luckily they had <illegible> brought ropes, a long coil each [slung over their >] about their waists. With these they lowered their packs.
>
> Bifur and Bomfur <sic>

Aside from the miscalculation of bringing baggage inappropriate to the route and the narrator's unsympathetic comment thereon, and the curious portmanteau combination of Bofur's and Bombur's names, the only significant difference here from the published text is Tolkien's apparent hesitation over whether Bifur or Bofur would be the dwarf who stayed below with Bombur.

12 Since Thorin & Company cannot explore the rest of this path for fear of exposing their presence to the dragon, we never learn anything more about where this path ultimately leads, though given the difficulty of building it, it must have some important purpose. Presumably it terminates in a lookout post at the mountain's peak, also accessible from other paths – cf. the account of the Battle of Five Armies in Chapter XVII, where the goblins scale the Mountain from the north and hence are able to attack the defenders' positions up against the spurs on either side of the river-valley, because '[e]ach of these could be reached by paths that ran down from the main mass of the Mountain in the centre' (DAA.343).

13 The original concept of Durin's Day coming on the first new moon of autumn, not the last, is still in place (see Chapter III, page 116). Accordingly, in the manuscript, this scene is envisioned as taking place just before the equinox, or around 21st–22nd September. By contrast,

in the First Typescript this passage is replaced by '"Tomorrow begins the last month [> week] of Autumn" said Thorin one day. "And winter comes after autumn" said Bifur. "And next year after that" said Dwalin . . .' (1/1/61:4). Similarly, the passage earlier in the chapter '. . . now the summer of the year after was drawing to a bleak end' is replaced in the typescript by '. . . autumn was now crawling towards winter' (1/1/61:2); see Text Note 5.

This revised timeline as it appears in the published book introduces a major difficulty into the chronology by placing this scene in December (around the end of the second week in December, or 14th–15th December to be precise, if we assume the winter solstice occurs on or around December 21st). This hardly seems to allow enough time for the death of the dragon, the siege, and the battle to all occur and yet leave Bilbo time to travel to the far side of Mirkwood (by a more circuitous route) and celebrate Yule with Medwed/Beorn (see page 682, Chapter XVIII). Even if we were to assume 'Yule-tide' here corresponds not to Christmas but to the last day of the year, as in the later Shire-calendar (see Appendix D, *LotR*.1143), still we are told that Bilbo and the wizard on their return journey reached Beorn's house 'by midwinter' – e.g., the solstice† – which cannot easily be reconciled with the statement here that Thorin & Company only gained entrance into the Mountain a week before, in the last week of autumn.

No such difficulty occurred in the original conception, of course, in which Durin's Day fell near the beginning of autumn (e.g., late September), allowing more than three months for the events of the final chapters to take place.

† 'Midwinter' traditionally means not halfway between the solstice (circa 21st December) and the vernal equinox (circa 21st March) – that is, around Groundhog's Day/Candlemas – but the day of the winter solstice itself, the shortest and darkest day of the year. Similarly 'midsummer' (cf. pp. 115–16 and DAA.95) means not the dog days of late July/early August but the longest day of the year, the day of the summer solstice (circa 21st June). This association is ancient; the OED traces it back for more than a thousand years. Essentially it dates back to a time when the year was divided into two seasons: summer (our spring and summer; the warm months of the year) and winter (our autumn and winter; the cold months of the year).

14 Given all the restless activity depicted in 'The Back Door' (Plate IX [top]), this sketch at first glance seems to be intended as an illustration for this scene, showing what Bilbo and the dwarves (some of whom are 'out of shot') were doing on Durin's Day. But, on closer examination, it is clear that the scene presented is a composite, not a single moment in time. Apparently unseen by any of the characters, the secret door stands open, revealing a dark tunnel going down into the mountain. We see Bilbo sitting between the door and the rock, apparently watching a dwarf at work with a pick-axe on the bay's wall who seems to be looking for the door in the wrong place (note that according to the text they couldn't tell exactly where it was).

In the background, higher up the mountain behind the door, we see two dwarves (no doubt the intrepid Fili and Kili) exploring the path's higher reaches. In the foreground, a dwarf is just arriving up the high path to the right, a coil of rope slung over his shoulder, while to the left another carefully raises or lowers something by rope from the base camp. A third dwarf lies flat between them, looking straight down the cliff, his beard hanging down over the edge. There is no sign of the third 'camp' in the little bay, and more importantly the rock is not 'in the centre of the grass' as described in the text but off-center to the left. Tolkien originally called this drawing 'The Back Gate' to correspond to 'The Front Gate' (DAA.256; H-S#130) but changed the name to the more accurate 'The Back Door'. See Plate IX [middle] for an unfinished companion piece to this drawing that shows the same scene facing west rather than east (that is, looking out from the secret door rather than looking towards it). While the rock outcroppings in these two companion pieces exactly correspond, 'View from Back Door' too omits the central thrush's stone and, while it shows the setting sun, there is no sign of the new moon.

15 Unfortunately for Bilbo, the wizard's return was still several chapters away (cf. the end of Chapter XVI) and in fact would not occur until well into the Third Phase manuscript; see page 663. This is the first reminder of the wizard since Chapter IX (the one in Chapter X having first appeared in the typescript) and reminds the reader of this off-stage character and so anticipates his eventual return.

16 This is the first appearance in text of Gandalf as the wizard's name – appropriately enough, in the mouth of the character who had originally been named 'Gandalf' himself; earlier in this same chapter (see page 472 and Text Note 2 above) it had still been 'Bladorthin'. After this scene the name 'Gandalf' only reappears once before the end of the Second Phase manuscript, near the end of Plot Notes D. When the name 'Bladorthin' next appears it has already been re-assigned to the long-dead King Bladorthin; cf. Chapter XII page 514. The directions set down in Plot Notes A (see page 293) to change several of the major characters' names had now finally been carried out.

17 Cf. the end of Chapter II, where among the items in the troll's lair they found '. . . a bunch of curious keys on a nail' which they almost left behind, until Bladorthin notices them and decides to take them along at the last minute (page 97). Elrond in Chapter III had identified one of these as a 'dwarf-key', not a troll-key, and advised Gandalf (the dwarf) to 'keep it safe and fast', which he does by 'fasten[ing] it to a chain and put[ting] it round his neck under his jacket' (page 115), hence incidentally preserving it from confiscation when he is captured first by goblins and later by elves. Tolkien seems to have forgotten this detail, since he added a rider into the parting scene in Chapter VI where at the last minute Bladorthin remembers the key and gives it to Gandalf (see the additional text on page 244). This

rider was probably added back into the manuscript of Chapter VII as a result of Tolkien's note to himself in Plot Notes A: 'Don't forget the key found in troll's lair.' (see page 293). Here in the present scene it is clear that Gandalf is carrying not a single key on a chain but the whole ring of keys; Bilbo says the wizard 'gave us [> you] the troll-key*s*' (emphasis mine), and this is borne out by the statement that '[he] . . . fitted in *the only key that was small enough*' (ibid.). Had Tolkien retained this plot-thread into the published book, he would have resolved these discrepancies, which are merely an artifact of the difficulty of keeping track of minor details in a complicated story composed in several distinct stages.

The idea that the key to the secret door was found somewhere along the journey survived into the First Typescript (1/1/61:5), where it is replaced by a pasteover ('The key that went with the map'); this revision was done before the Second Typescript was made, since the latter incorporates the pasteover silently into its text (1/1/42:6).

18 Interestingly enough, these dimensions, which have remained in the text of the published book to this day (cf. DAA.266), do not match those set down on Thror's Map: 'Five feet high is the door *and three may walk abreast*', a reading that goes all the way back to the Pryftan Fragment (see page 22 and the Frontispiece to Part One; italics mine) and remained remarkably stable through all iterations of the story. Granted that this 'seems like a great big hole' to Bilbo, and that dwarves are undoubtedly smaller than humans, still it seems unlikely that three dwarves could walk side-by-side in a passage only three feet wide.

(i)
The Desolation of the Dragon

> The land grew barren, though once, as Thorin said, it had been green and fair. There was little grass. Soon there were neither bush nor tree, and only broken stumps to speak of ones long vanished. They were come to the desolation of the Dragon . . .

One of the more interesting bits of Tolkien's dragon-lore, as presented in *The Hobbit* and elsewhere, is the idea that dragons are not only found in desolate places (like the 'Withered Heath' north of the Lonely Mountain),[1] but that they make places desolate simply by dwelling in them. The connection between dragons and wastelands is ancient, going all the way back to the *tannin* (*taninim*) of the Bible, the great dragons who were named in Genesis as the first created beings.[2] In most dragon-legends, however, the countryside surrounding the dragon's lair is not described as desolate or destroyed. This is certainly not the case with Beowulf's dragon, who until disturbed was sleeping peacefully in a barrow among the rich farms and fields of the Geatish lands. We might extrapolate and conclude that, once roused, if left unchecked he would eventually have reduced the kingdom to a wasteland as ruined as the moors surrounding Grendel's mere,[3] but the poem itself does not even hint at such an outcome. Nor does it apply to the most famous retelling of the St. George & the Dragon story, that found in Book I Canto XI of Spenser's *Faerie Queene* [1590], where the dragon lives in paradisial surroundings (in fact, the land that was once Eden) that seem to have escaped his depredations relatively unscathed. Nor, to speak of Tolkien's favorite dragon,[4] do the *Fáfnismál* and the *Reginsmál* in the *Elder Edda* hint that the area around Fafnir's lair is a barren wasteland, unless this is implied in its name, Gnitaheath ('The Glittering Heath'). It seems rather that dragons live in remote and hence wild areas than that they have reduced their surroundings to ruination.

Tolkien, on the other hand, goes beyond this. For him, dragons don't seek out wastelands to live in: areas *become* wastelands *because* dragons live there. This idea almost certainly derives from William Morris's treatment of the Fafnir story, first in his translation (with Eiríkr Magnússon) of the twelfth-century *Volsunga Saga* [1870], then in his long narrative poem *Sigurd the Volsung* (in full *The Story of Sigurd the Volsung and the Fall of the Niblungs* [1877]). Tolkien's first introduction to this work came when he was still a child, through the juvenilized redaction published as the final story in Andrew Lang's *The Red Fairy Book* [1890], 'The Story of Sigurd' (the only story in the volume adapted by Lang himself), which makes no mention of a desolation in its text though the accompanying pictures do suggest a barren, rocky landscape.[5] The actual saga, which derives directly from the Sigurd poems in the *Elder Edda* but greatly expands upon them, with typical saga conciseness does not talk much about the landscape any more than do the highly elliptical poems but does at one point say that Fafnir lies 'on the waste of Gnita-heath' (Morris & Magnússon, page 44). That this 'waste' (i.e., wasteland) is unnatural is established not in the saga itself but by Morris's expansion and adaptation of it into *Sigurd the Volsung*. In Morris's development of the tale, when Fafnir's brother Regin returns to his homeland long after being expelled by the greedy dragon, he finds all fallen into ruin and transformed into desolation:

And once . . .
I wandered away to the country from whence our stem did grow.
There methought the fells[6] *grown greater, but waste did the meadows lie,*
And the house was rent and ragged and open to the sky.
But lo, when I came to the doorway, great silence brooded there,
Nor bat nor owl would haunt it, nor the wood-wolves drew anear.

—*Sigurd the Volsung*, page 98.

Long years, and long years after, the tale of men-folk told
How up on the Glittering Heath was the house and the dwelling of gold,
And within that house was the Serpent . . .
Then I wondered sore of the desert; for I thought of the golden place
My hands of old had builded . . .
This was ages long ago, and yet in that desert[7] *he dwells.*

—*Sigurd the Volsung*, page 99.

In addition to Morris, the idea that dragons are bad for the surrounding countryside and, over time, reduce it to a desolate condition can also be found in various ballads and folktales, most notably 'The Laidly Worm' and 'The Lambton Worm'. In one nineteenth-century version of the former, it is said of the Laidly Worm that

For seven miles east and seven miles west,
And seven miles north and south,
No blade of grass was seen to grow,
So deadly was her mouth.

—Jacqueline Simpson, *British Dragons* [2nd ed., 2001], page 59.

Similarly, the hero of 'The Lambton Worm' returns from a seven years' absence to find 'the broad lands of his ancestors laid waste and desolate' and his aged father 'worn out with sorrow and grief . . . for the dreadful waste inflicted on his fair domain by the devastations of the worm' ('The Wonderful Legend of the Lambton Worm' [circa 1875]; reprinted in Simpson, *British Dragons* page 138). The same idea also appears in somewhat more whimsical form in the work of another of Tolkien's favorite fantasy writers, Lord Dunsany, who has one of his heroes seek out

> a dragon he knew of who if peasants' prayers are heeded deserved to die, not alone because of the number of maidens he cruelly slew, but because he was bad for the crops; he ravaged the very land and was the bane of a dukedom.

—'The Hoard of the Gibbelins',
The Book of Wonder [1912], page 77.

Building then from hints in Morris's work and perhaps also influenced to some degree by ballad and folktale tradition, Tolkien places his great wyrms in 'desolations' or wastelands of their own devising. Dragon-made wastes appear in three of Tolkien's works: in the story of Turin, in *The Hobbit*, and in *Farmer Giles of Ham*.[8] Of these, 'Turambar and the Foalókë' [circa 1919], the earliest version of the Turin story, predates *The Hobbit* by more than a decade and probably had the most influence on the depiction of the Desolation of Smaug and the lands around the Lonely Mountain. In *The Hobbit* itself, the effect is rather understated – for example, with the exception of birds (crows, ravens, and the thrush) and some snails there is no mention of Bilbo and the dwarves encountering a single living creature once they leave the Lake-Men behind other than the ponies they brought with them. Instead we have a careful description of a landscape so desolate that the presence of grass in one protected nook (see pp. 473–4 & DAA.285) is cause for comment, a point made more forceful by the contrast between the ruins of Dale and the once-prosperous town of farmers and craftsmen who had lived there in the days before the dragon came; we know this barren valley (depicted in 'The Front Gate', DAA.256) was once fertile enough to grow food for both the town of Men and the entire dwarven community within the Mountain as well (DAA.55). Finally, although it adds little to these two accounts, *Farmer Giles of Ham* (which in its original form is roughly contemporaneous with the composition of *The Hobbit*, either immediately preceding or immediately following it)[9] serves rather to confirm the pattern.

The Túrin story clearly sets a precedent: when Tinwelint [Thingol]'s band of would-be dragon-slayers warily scout out the area the dragon has made his own, they are appalled to discover that what had been 'a fair region' surrounding an underground city, a river-valley 'tree-grown' on one side and 'level and fertile' on the other, has been utterly ruined:

> . . . they saw that the land had become all barren and was blasted for a great distance about the ancient caverns of the Rodothlim [Nargothrond], and the trees were crushed to the earth or snapped. Toward the hills a black heath stretched and the lands were scored with the great slots that that loathly worm made in his creeping . . .
>
> Now was that band aghast as they looked upon that region from afar, yet they prepared them for battle, and drawing lots sent one of their number . . . to that high place upon the confines of the withered land . . .
>
> —'Turambar and the Foalókë', BLT II.96–7.

Indeed, so destructive is Glorund the firedrake that when he later sets forth to seek out Turambar (Túrin), he leaves behind him so great a 'path of desolation' and broken trees that from afar off can be seen 'that region now torn by the passage of the drake' (ibid.103–4). When Túrin and his band seek him out for a final combat they see 'a wide tract[10] where all the trees were broken and the lands were hurt and scorched and the earth black', and this scorched earth aspect of the dragon's passage is so pronounced that it complicates their tactics: 'not by day or by night shall men hope to take a dragon of Melko unawares . . . behold, this one hath made a waste about him, and the earth is beaten flat so that none may creep near and be hidden' (ibid.105).

This is entirely in keeping with the account of the kinds of damage Chrysophylax Dives does as he moves across the Middle Kingdom:

- 'He did a deal of damage in a short while, smashing and burning, and devouring sheep, cattle, and horses' (FGH, page 25)
- 'On the night of New Year's Day people could see a blaze in the distance. The dragon had settled in a wood about ten miles away, and it was burning merrily. He was a hot dragon when he felt in the mood' (page 28)
- '[In] the neighbouring village of Quercetum [Oakley] . . . [h]e ate not only sheep and cows and one or two persons of tender age, but . . . the parson too. Rather rashly the parson had sought to dissuade him from his evil ways . . .' (page 30)
- '[A]ll too soon they . . . came to parts that the dragon had visited. There were broken trees, burned hedges and blackened grass, and a nasty uncanny silence.' (pages 39–40)

Even closer is the description of the area around Chrysophylax's lair:

> . . . dragon-marks were now obvious and numerous.
>
> They had come, indeed, to the places where Chrysophylax often roamed, or alighted after taking his daily exercise in the air. The lower hills, and the slopes on either side of the path, had a scorched and trampled look. There was little grass, and the twisted stumps of heather and gorse stood up black amid wide patches of ash and burned earth. The region had been a dragons' playground for many a year.
>
> —*Farmer Giles of Ham*, page 58.[11]

Finally, we have one dragon-haunted region which is never described directly but which links the dragons of *The Silmarillion* with those of *The Hobbit*. For it seems likely that the Withered Heath,[12] from whence Smaug came, was originally none other than the ruined land known by many names in the various Silmarillion texts, including the Blasted Plain ('The Lay of the Children of Húrin', HME III.49 & 55), Dor-na-Fauglith ('the Land of Thirst'; ibid.), the Black Plain ('The First "Silmarillion" Map'; HME IV.220 and the colour plate ff), and ultimately the Anfauglith (translated as 'The Gasping Dust'; cf. 'The Grey Annals' and 'The Wanderings of Húrin', HME XI). Not only does the Withered Heath lie in a similar geographical position, north of the Grey Mountains just as the Land of Thirst had lain north of the highlands of Hithlum and Taur-na-Fuin (which, as we have seen elsewhere, is associated with Mirkwood; see page 20), but Tolkien actually describes Dor-na-Fauglith as 'withered' and 'the heath' ('The Lay of the Children of Húrin', lines 1054 and 1068 respectively; HME III.41 & 42). Close comparison of the respective locations of Taur-na-Fuin and the Thirsty Plain on the earliest Silmarillion map (HME IV) with the Wild Wood and Withered Heath on Fimbulfambi's Map (Frontispiece, plate one) reveals just how close the two were in initial conception. Moreover, whereas in the earliest versions of the tale this seems to be simply an arid volcanic region (cf. the Túrin poem and also the 1926 'Sketch'), starting with the 1930 *Quenta* (written about the same time Tolkien began writing *The Hobbit*) it is definitely depicted as a destroyed land, once fair and green[13] but now scorched bare, blackened and lifeless ('burnt and desolate', 'burned . . . to a desolate waste'; HME IV.101 & 105).

As we have seen, by its very name, the Withered Heath must be a similarly destroyed land – and we have no less an authority than Jacob Grimm for associating heaths with dragons; he notes in *Teutonic Mythology* (Stallybrass translation, vol. II page 689) that one of the old names for a dragon was *lyngormr* (*lyng-ormr*, that is 'ling-worm' or heath-dragon, *ling* being another name for heather). Furthermore, we are told that dragons first arose inside Morgoth's fortress of Angband beneath Thangorodrim in the Iron Mountains just to the north of the burned plain of Bladorion, and Gandalf the dwarf is quite definite that the Withered Heath is where dragons come from: 'Over here is the Wild Wood and far beyond to the North, only the edge of it is on the map, is the Withered Heath where the Great Dragons used to live' (Pryftan Fragment, page 9). In the manuscript continuation of the Bladorthin Typescript (that is, the first few pages of the Second Phase), the link between 'some dwarves [being] driven out of the far north' and coming to the Lonely Mountain and the presence of dragons is already implicit:

> There were lots of dragons in the North in those days, and gold was probably running short there with the dwarves flying south or getting killed, and all the general waste and destruction dragons make going from bad to worse.

Some two decades later Tolkien made it explicit with the story of the cold-drake killing Thror's father and younger brother ('Durin's Folk', *LotR*.1109): 'there were dragons in the waste beyond [the Grey Mountains]; and after many years they became strong again and multiplied, and they made war on the Dwarves, and plundered their works'.

The name 'Withered Heath' dates back to the very earliest stage of the story, appearing on Fimbulfambi's Map in the Pryftan Fragment, immediately to the north of the Wild Wood (Mirkwood); the Grey Mountains seem not to have arisen yet. By contrast, on Thror's Map I (which seems to have accompanied the original submission of the story to Allen & Unwin) it is off the map to the north, as indicated by an arrow next to the words 'To the North lie the Grey Mountains beyond which is the Withered Heath'. In short, it has become one of the four framing features, along with the Iron Hills to the east, Long Lake to the south, and Mirkwood the Great to the west, all surrounding the central area that was once the dwarf-kingdom ('Here of old was the land of Thrain[14] King under the Mountain') but is now the dragon's realm ('Here is the

Desolation of Smaug'). Thror's Map II, the final version published in the book, is even more explicit in its linkage of the dragons and Heath: 'Far to the North are the Grey Mountains & the Withered Heath *whence came the Great Worms*' (italics mine). On the final version of the Wilderland Map used in the published book, the label 'Withered Heath' is inserted into a long narrow valley between the two eastern arms of the Grey Mountains, this vale being marked with similar hatching to that used to indicate the Desolation of Smaug. We should note, however, that this was a late change; on the version of the Wilderland Map that had accompanied Tolkien's original turnover to Allen & Unwin (Plate I [bottom]), 'Withered Heath' is simply the land north of the low line of hills which are the Grey Mountains, with no indication of how far into the distance off the map it might extend – a depiction in keeping with the original conception.

Finally, we should note one curious feature of the Desolation of Smaug which the earlier Wilderland Map calls attention to, also prominent in Tolkien's picture of the Front Gate (DAA.256; H-S#130): the curious fact of Running River arising in the dragon's lair. In one sense this could merely be verisimilitude – most caverns are carved by underground rivers, after all, and its presence suggests that the dwarves expanded upon caves that were already there to create their underground kingdom, just as Gimli later does early in the Fourth Age at Aglarond (*LotR*.1118). However, it is worth noting that throughout world mythology dragons are associated with water – specifically, with springs, wells, and similar spots where streams and rivers begin (cf. Simpson, *British Dragons*, pages 48–50).

(ii)
The Thrush

> There on the grey stone in the grass was a large thrush, nearly coal black, its pale yellow breast freckled with dark spots . . . it had caught a snail and was knocking it on the stone . . . The old thrush, which had been watching from a high perch with beady eyes & head cocked on one side, gave a sudden trill (pp. 475–6).

> . . . The old thrush was sitting on a rock nearby with his head cocked on one side . . . (page 513).

> . . . [T]here was the old thrush, perched on a stone; and as soon as they looked towards him he flapped his wings and sang; then he cocked his head on one side as if to listen, and again he sang, and again he listened.
>
> 'I believe he is trying to tell us something' said Thorin . . . (page 618).

It is entirely characteristic of Tolkien that, even though he nowhere identifies the specific type of thrush that Bilbo, Bard, and the dwarves encounter, nonetheless he provides enough details of its appearance and behavior to make that identification certain. Out of the many thrush species native to England, the Lonely Mountain thrush is clearly a song thrush (*T. philomelos*),[15] a species particularly noted for its diet of snails and its habit of crushing their shells on a rock. Many song thrushes in fact choose a favorite rock as their 'snail anvil' and return to it again and again, making the clue on Thror's Map a plausible application of real-world avian behavior to the fantasy story. Song thrushes are also, as the name suggests, noted singers, whose voices can carry a half-mile, and often hold their head to one side as if listening (possibly in fact listening for prey such as earthworms beneath the soil).

The size and coloration (not to mention longevity) of the Lonely Mountain thrush indicates that he is an exceptional individual, but then Thorin does identify him as a member of 'a long lived and magical breed' (page 513). It seems very likely that Thror and Thrain set this particular thrush, one of those who 'came tame to the hands of my father and grandfather', the duty of watching the secret door so that others could use the instructions on the Map to find the secret door, should neither Thror nor Thrain return (as indeed through ill fortune proves to be the case). While there is a widespread tradition of helpful birds in folk and fairy tale, mythology and medieval romance, here Tolkien seems to be drawing on Celtic legendry, particularly the Welsh tale *Culhwch and Olwen* (the oldest surviving Arthurian story, found in *The Mabinogion*, and a tale with which we know Tolkien was familiar; see page 194), which depicts a bird performing the same innocuous action over and over for vast lengths of time – perhaps significantly, an ouzel or blackbird, depending on the translation[16] (each being another member of the thrush family, *T. torquatus* and *T. merula* respectively).

Initially the thrush existed merely to indicate the correct spot from which to find and open the secret door, but Tolkien later expanded his role in two crucial respects, first to bring the all-important information to Bard of Smaug's weak spot (in interpolations to Chapters XII and XIII), and then to introduce the dwarves to Roäc and so bring them news of Smaug's downfall (Chapter XVa). Somewhat curiously, the thrush disappears from the story after this point; presumably he either withdraws from the ensuing chaos of claims and counter-claims or else aligns himself with Bard, just as the ravens align themselves with Thorin and the dwarves, and hence is absent from our point-of-view character's perspective for the remainder of the Lonely Mountain chapters. In any case, he remains an extremely minor character without whom the major events of the story could not occur – a perfect example of the 'small hands turning the wheels of the world', as Tolkien put it.[17]

NOTES

1 A heath is a wilderness of open, uncultivated, treeless, uninhabited land, typically covered by tough dwarf shrubs such as heather (which gets its name from the fact it grows on heaths) and gorse. By contrast, a similar tract of marshy land is called a moor. It may be significant that most heaths are the result of deforestation and, left to themselves, regrow as forests over time – that is, the very word contains a suggestion of a land that was not always so barren as it now appears but was reduced to its current state by an outside agency (in this case, the dragons themselves).

2 Modern translations prefer 'great leviathan' or 'whale' or even 'crocodile' for the Biblical creatures haunting the wilderness and the deeps, but these were understood to be dragons in Medieval tradition – cf. Leslie Kordecki's *Tradition and Development of the Medieval English Dragon* (dissertation, Univ. of Toronto, 1980).

3 A scene which Tolkien twice illustrated; cf. H-S#50 & 51, both titled '*Wudu Wyrtum Faest*', or 'trees firm by the roots' (taken from line 1364a). For the poet's description of the moor, see in particular lines 1357 through 1376a.

4 See OFS, page 40: '. . . best of all the nameless North of Sigurd of the Völsungs, and the prince of all dragons', i.e. Fafnir. For more on the influence of Fafnir on Tolkien's depiction of Smaug, see the commentary following Chapter XII.

5 Although described as a 'heath' where 'no man dared go near', the *Red Fairy Book* version of the area surrounding Fafnir's lair apparently includes trees, since we are told the dying dragon 'lashed with his tail till stones broke and trees crashed about him' (*Red Fairy Book*, page 360). We should probably not put too much weight on this, since Lang seems more concerned with striking images than narrative consistency. Although Lang claimed his version was 'condensed by the Editor [i.e., Lang] from Mr. William Morris's prose version of the "Volsunga Saga"' (Preface, *Red Fairy Book*, page [vi]) – i.e., the Morris/Magnússon translation – in fact Lang draws as much from Morris's narrative poem, *Sigurd the Volsung*, as the saga account; his reticence to admit this may be due to the fact that Morris was still alive at the time (not dying until six years later, in 1896) and might have objected to liberties being taken with his own poem, which fleshed out the sparse saga story in his own inimitable fashion.

Carpenter claims that Tolkien as a child thought 'The Story of Sigurd' 'the best story he had ever read' (*Tolkien: A Biography*, page 22), which seems to be Carpenter's extrapolation from Tolkien's remark in 'On Fairy-Stories' ranking the story (or, more accurately, the *setting* of the story in 'the nameless North') of Sigurd and Fafnir above Lewis Carroll or pirate stories, above tales of 'Red Indians' and their great forests, and *even* above stories about Merlin and Arthur (OFS.39–40, emphasis mine). See also Note 4 above.

6 A fell is any rocky or barren heights or wasteland – in short, a heath or moor at a high elevation.

7 Morris, who loved archaic English and made much use of it in his narrative poems and pseudomedieval fantasy romances, is probably using 'desert' here in its older sense of a deserted or depopulated region, but with echoes of its more modern application of an arid, barren countryside incapable of supporting life no doubt also present.

8 There are of course many other wastelands in Tolkien's works, lands once fertile that have been destroyed by Morgoth's or Sauron's evil – not surprising, perhaps, in a man who had after all witnessed first-hand not just the scourges brought by industrialization and urbanization ('the country in which I lived in childhood was being shabbily destroyed before I was ten' – Foreword to *The Lord of the Rings,* page 12) but also had spent several months living next to the largest man-made desert in Europe, better known as No Man's Land,† parts of which were still treeless and not yet arable more than fifty years later. *The Lord of the Rings* alone has the Brown Lands (once the Gardens of the Entwives), the Dead Marshes, and Mordor itself, not to mention regions depopulated by the forces of evil and turned into wilderness, such as Hollin ('laid waste' more than four thousand years before in S.A. 1697 and still desolate during the time of Frodo's journey; cf. Book II Chapter 3: 'The Ring Goes South' and Appendix B 'The Tale of Years', *LotR*.1120), the Enedwaith, and most of the lands that had once made up the Kingdom of Arnor ('Tale of Years' entry for Third Age year 1636: 'many parts of Eriador become desolate'; *LotR*.1123).

† Tolkien actually included No Man's Land or Nomensland as a label on several of the *Lord of the Rings* maps in the early 1940s (see 'The First Map', HME VII, esp. pages 320–21). While the word vanished off the map after 1943, it appears in the text of the published book to describe the area between the Dead Marshes and the ashheaps before the Black Gate: 'a dismal waste . . . dead peats and wide flats of dry cracked mud. The land ahead rose in long shallow slopes, barren and pitiless, towards the desert that lay at Sauron's gate . . . the arid moors of the Noman-lands' (*LotR*.656–7).

9 It is not known when Tolkien wrote the earliest of the four versions of *Farmer Giles of Ham*, but since the story originated as an impromptu tale told during a family picnic according to his eldest son, Fr. John Tolkien, it was certainly after 1926 when his family returned from Leeds to Oxford, especially since part of the story's inspiration is to provide the 'real' explanation for Oxfordshire place-names such as Worminghall (and later Thame as well) and, I suspect, the nearby barrow known as Dragon Hoard (see Leslie Grinsell, *Folklore of Prehistoric Sites in Britain* [1976], pages 145 and 70). Since Tolkien was working on *Roverandom* from 1925–27 and *The Hobbit* from 1930–32/33, the most probable

dates for FGH's composition† are 1928–29 or 1933–34. And since the handwriting of the surviving pages of the Pryftan Fragment, the earliest part of *The Hobbit* to be set down, resembles that of the first draft of *Farmer Giles*, this makes it likely that Farmer Giles' story immediately preceded Mr. Baggins'.

† That is, of the first two drafts, in which the narrator is called 'Daddy' and the 'Family Jester', respectively; the third draft, the greatly expanded version known as *The Lord of Thame*, was written in 1936–7 and the final version shortly before the book's publication in 1949.

10 Christopher Tolkien notes that the word might be *track* instead of *tract* and that instead of 'the lands were hurt and scorched' his father might actually have written '. . . burnt and scorched' (BLT II.118). In either case, Tolkien is clearly drawing here on the Fafnir story – in the saga and subsequent versions Fafnir has over the years worn a track or path through the stone between his lair and the spot where he goes to drink, and it is in this slot or groove that Sigurd digs his pit and lies in wait to stab him as he goes by:

> Thou shalt find a path in the desert, and a road in the world of stone;
> It is smooth and deep and hollow, but the rain hath riven it not,
> And the wild wind hath not worn it, for it is Fafnir's slot,
> Whereby he wends to the water and the fathomless pool of old . . .
>
> —*Sigurd the Volsung*, page 122.

By contrast, Glorund is so terrible and destructive that he carves such a path simply by moving across the landscape.

11 These parallels were present from the very first draft of *Farmer Giles of Ham*, although the description of the destruction around the dragon's lair was much briefer in the original:

> There was no mistaking the dragon's tracks now. They were right in the parts where the dragon often walked or alighted from a little passage in the air. In fact all the smaller hills had a burned look about their brown tops as if these parts had been a dragon's playground for many an age. And so they had.
>
> —FGH, expanded edition, page 94.

12 This name had originally appeared with a different application in *The Book of Lost Tales*, where it was used for a spot near Tavrobel (Great Haywood in central England), site of the disastrous last battle wherein the Elves of Tol Eressëa were utterly defeated; cf. BLT II.284 & 287.

13 This fair green plain received the name *Bladorion* ('the Wide Land') in the '(Earliest) Annals of Valinor', written in 1930 or very shortly thereafter (cf. HME IV.280). This was eventually replaced (circa 1951) in 'The Grey Annals' and other late Silmarillion texts by *Ardgalen* ('the Green Region'); cf. HME XI.113. This latter name is the one used in *The Silmarillion*, in the hyphenated form *Ard-galen*; cf. *Silm.*119. Ardgalen was apparently similar in terrain to Rohan, since an inverted

form of the same name, Calenardhon (Calen+ardhon), was the original Gondorian name for that province (*Silm.*317).

14. For the inversion of Thror's and Thrain's names on the maps ('the map tradition'), see the commentary following Chapter X.

15. For those unfamiliar with birds who wouldn't know a thrush from a warbler, suffice it to say that the song thrush is about the same size as the (American) robin, a fellow thrush (*T. migratorius*),† and has much the same habits, except that it prefers snails to earthworms. Despite their particular association with snails, song thrushes are omnivores and also eat worms, bugs, and berries as available. I am grateful to Yvette Waters and especially Jacki Bricker for help in identifying the particular species of thrush Tolkien based his Lonely Mountain thrush upon.

   † not to be confused with the English robin, which is a different bird altogether, and only about the size of a sparrow.

16. In *Culhwch and Olwen*, Arthur sends Gwrhyr Gwastad Ieithoedd ('interpreter of tongues') with Cei (Kay) and Bedwyr (Bedivere), his two most trusted companions, on this quest because Gwrhyr 'know[s] all tongues, and can translate the language of birds and animals':

> They went forth until they came to the Blackbird of Cilgwri.
>
> 'For God's sake,' said Gwrhyr, 'do you know anything about Mabon son of Modron, who was stolen from between his mother and the wall when only three nights old?'
>
> 'When I first came here,' replied the Blackbird, 'a smith's anvil was here, and I was a young bird. No work was done on it except while my beak rested upon it each evening; today there is not so much as a nut-sized piece that isn't worn away, and God's revenge on me if I have heard anything of the man you want. But what is right and just for me to do for Arthur's messengers, I will do: there is a species of animal that God shaped before me, and I will guide you there.'
>
> —tr. Patrick Ford, *The Mabinogi and other Medieval Welsh Tales* [1977], page 147.

   This is merely the first of five encounters with progressively older creatures – a stag, an owl, an eagle, and finally a salmon – whom the questers question in turn before finding a clue to the location of the person they seek. Both Jones & Jones [1949] and Gantz [1976] prefer 'Ouzel' (page 124) and 'Ousel' (page 164), respectively, this being an old-fashioned term (along with water ouzel) for the bird also known as the dipper.

17. JRRT to Denys Gueroult, 1965 BBC radio interview. Tolkien's remark originally applied to the hobbits in *The Lord of the Rings* but is generally applicable throughout many of his works.

PLOT NOTES C

As noted on page 361, these two pages (I/I/10:3–4) form a single sheet which replaced the original third and fourth pages (I/I/25:1–2) of Plot Notes B, which had begun with the same four words (the fifth and final page, describing the end of the story, was left in place; see page 366). Significantly, Bladorthin '(Blad.)' is still the wizard's name, suggesting that this outline was written during the composition of Chapter XI (which had used Bladorthin for the wizard's name early in the chapter but shifted to using Gandalf by the chapter's end). For discussion of significant developments and variations from the Plot Notes it replaced, see the commentary following the transcription.

[page] 3

Bilbo earns his reward: – the dwarves say now he must go in, if he is to fulfil his contract. They won't go with him, only Balin Yellow-beard comes part of the way, in case he calls for help.

Hobbit creeps into dark mountain. Easier than he thought. Absol.[TN1] straight tunnel going gently down for a great way. Begins to see a light at end, getting redder and redder. A bubbling snoring sound. It gets v. warm. Vapours float up.

B. peeps into the great bottomost dungeon at Mountain's root nearly dark, save for glow from Smaug. The great red dragon is fast asleep upon a vast pile of precious things. He is partly on one side: B. can see he is crusted underneath with gems.

B. steals a cup to show he has been there.[TN2] [Describe some of things dimly seen especially swords and <u>spears</u>]

Dwarves pat him on the back. Wrath of Dragon, who comes out to hunt the thief, and settles flaming on the Mount. Then flies all round it roaring.

Terror of dwarves, hiding under rocks. They dig holes.

Bilbo goes back again. The D. is only pretending to be asleep. Bilbo catches glint in his eye and stays at mouth of tunnel. [*added*: slips on his ring. D. asks where he has gone to.] [*added in margin*: B. does not say who he is but says he came over the water in a barrel, D thinks he is one of LongLake men] (Riddling?).[TN3] D. tries to poison his mind with half-truths ag.[TN4] the dwarves. Says they don't worry about him or paying him. Supposing they could get treasure how cd. they carry it off? They <didn't> tell you <shares won't> work.

B. says they have not only come for treasure but revenge.

D. laughs.

B. flatters him, and says he cert. never imagined Smaug was so tremendous.

D says no warrior could kill him now. He is armoured with gems underneath. B. asks him to show – and sees a patch.[TN5] Then he escapes but D. sends fiery spurts after him.

B goes back and talks to dwarves. Warns them dragon knows of exit. <Asks> them about plans. They are a bit flummoxed. They tell him of the Jem of Girion king of Dale, which he paid for his sons' arming in gold & silver mail made like steel.[TN6]

[page] 4

B. creeps in third time and waits in shadows till Dragon creeps out of hall
He steals a bright gem which fascinates him
The dragon returning finds theft: and is awful rage.[TN7]

He goes to war with the Lake Men. The people sees him coming and cut bridges to lake-dwelling. D. flies over them and set houses alight, but dare not settle right in lake. They quench fire with water and shoot darts at him. Glint of gems in dragon's belly in light of fire. He settles at side of lake and tries to starve them out.

Dwarves see the steam from afar; and are bent on carrying out gold. B. watches them stagger out. But warns them D. will come back to entrance of tunnel? What can they do with gold.

Burglary is no good – a warrior in the end. But no one will go with him. Bilbo puts on ring and creeps into dungeon. and hides. Dragon comes back at last and sleeps exhausted by battle.

Bilbo [takes >] plunges in his little magic knife and it disappears. he cannot wield the swords or spears.

Throes of dragon. Smashes walls and entrance to tunnel. Bilbo floats <away> in a golden bowl on D's blood, till it comes to rest in a deep dark hole. When it is cool he wades out, and becomes hard & brave.

Discovers sources of Running River and floats out through Fro[nt] D[oor]. in a golden bowl.

Found by the scouts of the Lake-Men.

The dwarves dig through the tunnel and take possession of their old homes but the gold is mostly crushed, and they cannot use it because of the dragon's body

The men of <the> Lake and Woodelves come up and besiege the dwarves. Attempt to block F. Door.

Bilbo sorrowful meets Blad. in the <illegible> place of Laketown.[TN8]

Blad rebukes the besiegers. And makes dwarves pay Bilbo.

A share of his <part> he gives to Lake-men, and to wood-elves (though they may not deserve it).

They escort Blad & B back through Mirkwood.

This entire page, from 'B. creeps in third time' to 'back through Mirkwood', was struck through with a single slash. At the same time that this page was cancelled, Tolkien wrote in the left margin of this page and underlined:

Dragon killed in the battle of the Lake

This change almost certainly dates from the same time as the two new pages that replace the canceled page were written, which was demonstrably after the next chapter (Chapter XII) had already been drafted, and probably most of the following chapter as well. I treat this new material separately as Plot Notes D and have placed it following the next chapter, beginning on page 568.

TEXT NOTES

1 'Absol.': Absolutely (see Plot Notes B, page 363).

2 That is, he steals the cup to prove to the dwarves that he reached the treasure-chamber, not to alert Smaug to his presence.

The following sentence is bracketed by Tolkien in the original, and the word *spears* underlined for emphasis. Compare the parallel passage in Plot Notes B: 'He sees shields and spears', where one of these spears had been projected to play a crucial role in the climax as the weapon with which Bilbo was to kill the sleeping dragon (see page 364). Interestingly enough, while its significance disappeared after this point, these spears survive as an element in Smaug's horde and actually appear in the painting 'Conversation with Smaug' (Plate XI [top]), made some five years later after the book had been published.

3 'Riddling' here indicates not a riddle-game such as Bilbo had played with Gollum but instead the first indication of the 'riddling talk' whereby Bilbo identifies himself while refusing to tell the dragon his actual name. The 'barrel-rider' motif first emerges here in the interpolated passage (although puzzlingly enough Bilbo claims to have ridden *in* a barrel, not on one – perhaps Tolkien here is thinking of Bilbo's

solitary escape in a barrel from Plot Notes A; see page 296), along with Smaug's mistaken conclusion that the men of Lake Town are behind this intrusion.

4 'ag.': i.e., against.

5 'a patch': i.e., a bare patch.

6 'his sons arming': since the apostrophe is missing in this very lightly punctuated passage, we cannot tell for certain whether the right form is *sons* or *son's*. I have concluded that the former is more probable, since the manuscript of the next chapter (written from this outline) uses the plural – 'which he paid for the arming of his sons, in coats of dwarf mail the like of which had never before been made' – and is punctuated accordingly.

For the spelling 'Jem', carried over from Plot Notes B, see page 364.

'gold & silver mail made like steel': This passage further develops the mithril coat which later plays such an important part in *The Lord of the Rings*, although that term would not arise for almost another decade (see HME VI.465 & also 458). This remarkable piece of armor is not associated with Bilbo here, although it had been in page 5 of Plot Notes B (see page 366), nor is it a unique item since one was made for each of King Girion's sons. The presence of these suits of mail within Smaug's horde is incidentally proof of the mingling of 'much of the wealth of [Girion's] halls and towns' with the dwarves' goods mentioned by Bard in the parley before the Gate (see page 648).

7 Presumably Tolkien meant to write here either 'is [in an] awful rage' or possibly '[h]is awful rage' but in the haste of getting thoughts down on paper left the sentence compressed.

8 The illegible word is probably 'market', though it might also be 'smashed'.

Into the Lonely Mountain

Since the story sketched out in Plot Notes C represents Tolkien's projection of what would happen in Chapters XII and the chapters to follow, it was obviously written before Chapter XII (from which it notably diverges) was begun, probably while Chapter XI was still in progress – cf. the use of 'Bladorthin' near the beginning of Chapter XI on manuscript page 137 (page 472 in this book) and in these Plot Notes, whereas by manuscript page 141 near the end of Chapter XI (page 476 in this book) 'Gandalf' had finally replaced it as the wizard's name. Interestingly enough, rather than start a new outline Tolkien retained the same pagination and made the new material a replacement for the now-superseded middle section of Plot Notes B (which had been written at the end of Chapter VIII, probably the preceding year).

The new material at first follows the pages it replaced closely, particularly in the first six paragraphs, where many of the same words and phrases recur, although thereafter Plot Notes C develops and reshapes the material. Bilbo is still the dragon-slayer, but the sequence of events inside the Mountain is now somewhat different. Instead of stealing a cup on his first visit, another cup on his second, talking with the dragon on his third visit, and deliberately entering the tunnel a fourth time for the express purpose of killing Smaug in order to earn the Jem of Girion as his reward, as in Plot Notes B, Bilbo now steals a cup on his first visit, has an extended conversation with the dragon on his second visit, steals 'a bright gem' on his third visit when the dragon is (briefly) away, then hides within his lair on his fourth visit and stabs the weary dragon after Smaug returns from his attack on Lake Town – a sequence much closer to that of the published book, where the first three of these visits occur more or less as in this outline.

Instead of a spear found within the hoard (page 364), Bilbo now kills the dragon with his little knife (Sting, although that name has not yet arisen), apparently losing it in the process, driving it in so deeply that it 'disappears' within the dragon. His motivation now seems to be less pure greed, as in the preceding version of the Plot Notes, and more a desperate pragmatism: the dwarves are too busy carting gold up the secret passage to face the urgent question of what to do when Smaug returns, forcing Bilbo to take it upon himself. By contrast, Plot Notes B had stressed how 'Bilbo keeps on looking at his gem' (i.e., the Jem of Girion), which the dwarves tell him he must earn; the very next line describes his going to kill the sleeping dragon (page 364), strongly suggesting cause and effect: he wants the gem so badly he'd take on a dragon to get it. Plot Notes C thus somewhat downplay the theme of possessiveness in Bilbo himself, although we are told that the bright gem (presumably the Jem of Girion, which the dwarves had told him about shortly before) 'fascinates' him; this motif would later return strongly in Plot Notes D (see page 568).

It is interesting to note that the Lake-men fare rather better in their battle with Smaug here and in Plot Notes B than in any other version of the story, making them indeed the only community attacked by a dragon who succeed in driving it off in all of Tolkien's work: the Rodothlim of the early Túrin story and their later analogues the elves of Nargothrond, the dwarves of the Lonely Mountain and the men of Dale at the time of Smaug's advent, the Lake Men of the published tale, even the villagers of Bimble Bay in the poem 'The Dragon's Visit' [1937] all see their peoples decimated and their city or town destroyed.[1] By contrast, the people of Lake Town's spirited defense leaves the dragon temporarily stymied: once the bridges are destroyed he cannot reach his enemies, and any buildings he sets alight they 'quench with water'. Far from cowering or fleeing, they resolutely 'shoot darts[2] at him' whenever he flies over, although these cannot hurt him because of his gemstone armoring.

Given that they have an endless supply of fresh water and are presumably skilled as fishermen (which, given their boatcraft and the placement of their town over the water, seems a reasonable assumption), Smaug's attempt to 'starve them out' seems unlikely to succeed. Small wonder that the dragon eventually abandons his siege and returns exhausted to the mountain, no doubt to plot his next move.

Smaug's death-throes, which destroy Lake Town in the published version, here take place within the Mountain and are vividly depicted in terms partially derived from the old saga and partly from the death of Glorund in the Túrin story.[3] In particular, the enormous flood of blood that gushes out, enough to float Bilbo in a golden cup,[4] comes directly from *Volsunga Saga*, where Regin advises Sigurd to dig a pit in Fafnir's path to his favorite watering hole but treacherously plans for his protégé to drown in the dragon's blood, leaving Regin in sole possession of the treasure – a plan Odin foils by advising Sigurd to dig many pits, which drain off the excess blood.[5] In one particular the final book is closer to Tolkien's sources than are these Plot Notes: Morris has his dragon's last words be a lament that he dies 'far off from the Gold' (*Sigurd the Volsung* page 126), and in the published *Hobbit* of course Smaug dies at Lake Town ('he would never again return to his golden bed' – DAA.313) and his bones thereafter lie among its ruins.[6] Here, by contrast, Smaug dies atop his vast sleeping-bed of gold, and the tumult of his death-agonies collapses the secret tunnel[7] in which the dwarves had stored all the gold they had carted away from Smaug's lair during his absence.

One idea about Smaug's death from these Plot Notes did survive into the final book, albeit in a very different form. Here we are told that 'the gold is mostly crushed, and they cannot use it because of the dragon's body', whereas in the published tale the many gems attached to Smaug's underbelly are similarly lost to the dwarves when the dragon plummets into the lake; it is known where the gems lie deep in the water amid the ruins of Lake Town but none dare dive down through 'the shivering water' surrounding the dragon's bones to retrieve them (DAA.313).[8]

The idea that Bilbo becomes 'hard and brave' because he waded in dragonblood comes from yet another version of the Sigurd legend, not the Eddic poems nor the saga but the *Nibelungenlied* [circa 1200], which derives from German rather than Norse tradition:

> When he slew the dragon at the foot of the mountain the gallant knight bathed in its blood, as a result of which no weapon has pierced him in battle ever since . . . When the hot blood flowed from the dragon's wound and the good knight was bathing in it, a broad leaf fell from the linden between his shoulder-blades. It is there that he can be wounded . . .
>
> —*The Nibelungenlied*, tr. A. T. Hatto [rev. ed., 1969], page 121.[9]

Similarly, *Thidreks Saga*, a rambling thirteenth-century romance about Theodoric the Great, includes at one point a somewhat confused version of the Sigurd story (in which Regin is the dragon, rather than the dragon's brother), stating that after killing the dragon Sigurd 'smears his body with dragon's blood, except where he cannot reach between the shoulders, and his skin becomes horny' (ibid., page 375; cf. also *The Saga of Thidrek of Bern*, tr. Edward R. Haymes [1988], pages 107–8 & 210). Since Tolkien did not develop the theme, there's no way to know how Bilbo's becoming a great warrior, one of the few dragon-slayers in Tolkien's legendarium, would have influenced the end of the book, but it seems likely that having become 'hard and brave', 'a warrior in the end', he would play a significant role in the battle gathering in the east described on the last page of the composite Plot Notes B/C ('the Battle of Anduin Vale'; see pp. 366 & 375). The deft drawing-together of so many themes and characters who had appeared earlier in the book – Medwed/Beorn, the goblins, the woodmen, the wargs, and possibly the eagles – on the return journey would therefore in this projection still occur only after Bilbo had parted company with Thorin and the dwarves, forming the great adventure still to come on his homeward journey.

One point Plot Notes C does make clear that had been hazy in the original Plot Notes B material is exactly when Bladorthin re-enters the story. As in the final lines of Plot Notes A (page 296), here the wizard's reappearance is still enough to set things to rights and avoid bloodshed or further unpleasantness: Bladorthin rebukes the besiegers and makes the dwarves pay Bilbo the dragon-slayer his fair share, a portion of which Bilbo then parcels out to the Lake-men and wood-elves though, as Tolkien tartly observes, the latter 'may not deserve it' (a true enough statement based on what he had written about them so far in this book). Even with the major recastings and expansions to come, the linkage between Bilbo's share and the dragon-slayer's share (a large part of which gets turned over to the Men of the Lake and the wood-elves) remains, though after these had become two separate characters the scene of Bilbo giving the Gem of Girion (or Arkenstone, as it came to be called) to the character who had replaced him as dragon-slayer had to be invented.

Finally, the brief passage telling how the dwarves tunnel back through the partially collapsed secret passage 'and take possession of their old homes' seems to be our first glimpse of the re-establishment of the Kingdom under the Mountain. As corroboration of this, we are told that Bladorthin and Bilbo set out on the return journey, yet no mention is made of any of the dwarves accompanying them, suggesting that Thorin & Company remain behind at the Lonely Mountain (contrast Plot Notes B, page 366, where this could be inferred but was not actually stated). The deaths of Thorin, Fili, and Kili that darken the penultimate chapter of the published book had not yet arisen; there it is Thorin's cousin

Dain who becomes the new King under the Mountain, but here there is no reason to think that it is anyone other than Thorin himself, finally restored to his full inheritance.

NOTES

1 We might also include Gondolin in this tally, since Elrond says 'dragons it was that destroyed that city many ages ago' (page 115). I am not counting here Túrin's ambush of Glorund, which was achieved en route before the dragon reached the woodmen's settlement, nor Giles' encounter with Chrysophylax on a back-road several miles from Ham; these were essentially heroic or mock-heroic single combats à la Sigurd, not cooperative defenses by beleaguered townsfolk.

2 'darts': that is, arrows. The word was originally not restricted to the small darts thrown in pub games but also applied to javelins, to arrows shot from a bow, and even to projectiles from siege weapons.

3 Compare the three following passages:

- 'Now when that mighty worm was ware that he had his death-wound, then he lashed out head and tail, so that all things soever that were before him were broken to pieces' (*Volsunga Saga*, page 59).
- '[T]he Dragon lashed with his tail till stones broke and trees crashed about him' ('The Story of Sigurd', *The Red Fairy Book*, page 360).
- 'Then did that drake writhe horribly and the huge spires of his contortions were terrible to see, and all the trees he brake that stood nigh to the place of his agony' ('Turambar and the Foalókë', BLT II.107).

4 Although the gruesome, grotesque, and striking episode of Bilbo floating out through the Front Gate in a golden bowl vanished from the narrative, it is interesting to note that a huge cup appears both in the text ('the great cup of Thror'; see page 514 [= DAA.287]) and also in the colour painting 'Conversation with Smaug' (Plate XI [top]); these may owe something to the long-since-abandoned plot-thread.

5 In full, the passage in question (from Chapter XVIII: Of the Slaying of the Worm Fafnir) runs thusly:

> Then said Regin, 'Make thee a hole, and sit down therein, and whenas the worm comes to the water, smite him into the heart, and so do him to death, and win for thee great fame thereby.'
>
> But Sigurd said, 'What will betide me if I be before the blood of the worm?'
>
> Says Regin, 'Of what avail to counsel thee if thou art still afeard of everything? Little art thou like thy kin in stoutness of heart.'
>
> Then Sigurd rides right over the heath; but Regin gets him gone, sore afeard.

> But Sigurd fell to digging him a pit, and whiles he was at that work, there came to him an old man with a long beard, and asked what he wrought there, and he told him.
>
> Then answered the old man† and said, 'Thou doest after sorry counsel: rather dig thee many pits, and let the blood run therein; but sit thee down in one thereof, and so thrust the worm's heart through.'
>
> And therewithal he vanished away; but Sigurd made the pits even as it was shown to him.
>
> †[Morris's note:] i.e., Odin in one of his many guises.
>
> —*Volsunga Saga*, pages 58–9.

Morris's *Sigurd the Volsung* omits the detail of the many pits but does describe 'the rushing river of blood' (page 124) that gushes forth when Fafnir receives his death-wound. By contrast, Lang's 'The Story of Sigurd' includes the many pits but with typical carelessness omits any reason for their presence (Lang, *The Red Fairy Book,* page 360).

6 Glorund also died far away from his great bed of gold; cf. BLT II.87–8 & 107–9 ('Turambar and the Foalókë') and HME IV.127 & 129–30 (the 1930 *Quenta*).

7 Or, to be more accurate, part of the secret tunnel, presumably including that section in which the dwarves had stored their gold. The entire tunnel could not have collapsed, because it must have been within this passage that the dwarves hide when Smaug returns and thus escape being killed in the tumult. From the detail of Smaug smashing 'walls [of his lair] and entrance to tunnel', it seems clear that only the lower end of the passage is collapsed, which '[t]he dwarves dig through' to once more gain access to Smaug's great chamber.

8 The odd detail of the water around Smaug's death site 'shivering' perhaps relates to the idea, expressed in the description of Leviathan (the dragon in the sea) in the Book of Job chapter 41 verse 31, that dragons make the water around them boil ('like a pot'); see Text Note 33 following the next chapter (pp. 523–4) for more on this whole passage's possible influence on Tolkien's description of Smaug the Chiefest and Greatest of Calamities.

9 In this version of the story, Sigurd is called 'Siegfried', which led to Wagner's usage of that name in his opera-cycle *The Ring of the Nibelung* [1869–76]; in *Beowulf* (lines 874–898) the dragon-slayer is Sigemund, whom Norse tradition by contrast considered the dragon-slayer's father.

Chapter XII

CONVERSATIONS WITH SMAUG

The text continues on the same page as before (manuscript page 142, Marq. 1/1/13:1), with only a paragraph break to mark what would later become a new chapter. However, there seems to have been a pause in composition, probably quite brief, after the first sentence; with the words 'At last Thorin spoke' a new, darker ink and more deliberate and legible lettering begin.

The dwarves stood before the door and held long council.

At last Thorin spoke: 'Now is the time for our esteemed Mr Baggins, who has proved himself a good companion on our long road, and a hobbit full of courage and resource far exceeding his size, and if I may say so good luck far exceeding the usual allowance; – now is the time for him to perform the service for which he was included in our company: – now is the time for him to earn his Reward'. You are familiar by now with Thorin's style on important occasions. This cert. was one. But Bilbo felt impatient. [He >] By now he was familiar enough with Thorin and knew what he was driving at.

'If you mean you think it is my job to go into the [open tunnel >] secret passage first O Thorin Thrain's son,[TN1] may your beard grow ever longer' he said crossly. 'Say so at once and have done! I might refuse. I have got you ought of two messes already which were hardly in our original bargain,[TN2] and am I think already owed some reward. But somehow, I hardly think I shall refuse. Perhaps I have begun to trust my luck more than I used to in the old days (– he meant the spring before last, before he left his house, but it cert. seemed centuries ago –). But third time pays for all as my father used to say.[TN3] I think I will go and have a peep at once and get it over. Now who's coming in with me?'

He did not expect a chorus of volunteers, so he wasn't disappointed. Fili and Kili looked uncomfortable and stood on one leg. But the others frankly made no pretence about [> of] offering – except old Balin the look-out man, who was rather fond of the hobbit. He said he would come inside at least, and come a bit of the way, ready to call for help if needed. [One >] I can at least say this for the dwarves: they intended to pay Bilbo for his services, they had brought him to do a job, and didn't mind letting the poor little fellow do it; but they would have all done their best at any risk to get him out of trouble if they could [> if he got into it], as they did in the case of the trolls the year before.[TN4]

There it is: dwarves aren't heroes, but commercial-minded; some are [thoroughly bad >] tricky and treacherous and pretty bad lots; some are not, but are decent enough people like Thorin and Co. if not [filled with >] over high-minded.

The stars were coming out behind him in a pale sky barred with black, when the hobbit crept through the enchanted doors,[TN5] and stole into the M[ountain]. It was far easier going than he expected. This was no goblin-entrance, nor rough wood-elf cave. It was a passage made by dwarves at the height of their wealth and skill: straight as a ruler, smooth-floored and smooth-sided, going [direct >] with a gently never-varying slope direct – to some distant goal in the blackness below. After a while Balin bade Bilbo "good luck", and stopped, where he could still see the faint outline of the door, and by a trick of the echoes of the tunnel hear the rustle of the whispering voices of the others just outside.

Then the hobbit slipped on his ring, and warned by the echoes to [be >] take more than hobbit's care to make no noise [> sound], crept noiselessly down down down into the dark. He was trembling with fear, but his little face was set and grim. Already he was a very different hobbit to the one that had run out without a pockethandkerchief from Bag-end long ago. He hadn't had pocket hank. for a year. He loosed his dagger in its sheath, tightened his belt, and went on.

'Now you are in for it at last, Bilbo B.' he said to himself. 'You went and put your foot right in it that night of the party, and now you've got to pay for it.[TN6] Dear me what a fool I was and am' said the least Tookish part 'I have absolutely no use for dragon-guarded treasures, and the whole lot could stay here for ever, if only I could wake up and find this beastly tunnel was my own hall at home!'

He did not wake up, of course, but went on still, and on, till all sign of the door behind had faded away. He was altogether alone. Soon he thought it was beginning to feel warm.

'Is that a kind of glow I see on my right ahead down there?' he thought. It was. As he went forward it grew and grew, and [> till] there was no doubting it. It was a red light, steadily getting redder and redder. Now it was undoubtedly hot. Wisps of vapour floated up and past him, and he began to sweat. A sound began to throb in his ears, a sort of bubbling – like a large cat [*added*: purring][TN7] or like a big pot galloping on a fire. It grew to a most unmistakable gurgling snore of some great animal asleep somewhere in the red glow ahead.

It was this point that Bilbo stopped. Going on from that point was the bravest thing he ever did. The tremendous things that happened afterwards were as nothing compared to it. [Once he had made himself go on to the tunnel's end nothing else se[emed] >] He fought his real battle in the tunnel alone, before [the d. >] he even really saw this <vast>[TN8] danger that lay in wait.

At last you can picture the tunnel ending in a square opening [> a opening of much the same size as the door above].[TN9] Through it peeps the hobbit's little head. Before him lies the great bottommost [dungeon >] cellar or dungeon-hall of the ancient dwarves right at the Mountain's root. It was nearly dark so that its great size could only be dimly guessed, but rising from the floor there was a great glow. It was the glow of Smaug.

There he lay, a vast red-golden dragon fast asleep. A thrumming came from his jaws and nostrils and wisps of smoke, but his fires were low in slumber. Beneath him under all his limbs and huge-coiled tail and about him on all sides stretching away across the unseen floors, lay countless piles of precious things, gold wrought and unwrought, gems and jewels,[TN10] and silver red-stained in the ruddy light.

Smaug lay with wings folded like an immeasurable bat; he lay partly on one side and Bilbo could see his underparts, and his long belly were crusted with gems and fragments of gold stuck into his slime with his long lying on his costly bed. Behind him where the walls were nearest, could dimly be seen coats of mail and axes swords and spears hung, and great jars filled with wealth only to be guessed at.[TN11]

To say that Bilbo's breath was taken away is to say too little. There are no words to express his staggerment.[TN12] He had heard tell and sing of dragon-hoards before,[TN13] but the splendour the lust the glory of such treasure had never before come home to him. His heart was filled and pierced with the desire of dwarves – and he gazed, almost forgetting the frightful guardian, at the gold, gazed and gazed for what seemed ages, before drawn almost against his will he stole from the shadow of the door, across the floor, to the nearest edge of the mound of treasure. Above him the sleeping dragon lay, a fearful [> dire] menace even in his sleep. He grasped a great two handed cup[TN14] as heavy as he could carry; and cast one fearful eye upwards. The dragon stirred a wing, opened a claw, the rumble of his snoring changed its note. Then B. fled. But the dr. did not wake – yet – but shuffled into other dreams of greed and violence, lying there in his stolen hall, while the little hobbit toiled back up the path. His heart was beating faster, and his hands shaking & a more fevered shaking was in his legs than when he was going down; but still he clutched the cup, and his chief thought was 'Yes I've done it! This will show them. More like a grocer than a burglar indeed[TN15] – well we'll hear no more of that.'

Nor did he. To do Balin justice he was overjoyed, [when he >] to see Bilbo again. Fill[ed] with [great delight > delight greater than

>] delight as great as his surprise, and as great as his fear when he said goodbye. He picked Bilbo up indeed and carried him out to the open air. It was midnight. Clouds had masked the stars, and Bilbo sat gasping, taking pleasure only in the fresh air again, and hardly noticing the excitement of the dwarves, or how they praised him and patted him on the back, and put themselves and all their families for generations to come at his service.

A vast rumbling woke suddenly in the mountain underneath, as if it had been an extinct volcano that was suddenly [> unexpectedly] making up its mind to start eruptions once again.[TN16] The door was pulled nearly to, and blocked with a stone – they had not dared to risk closing it altogether – but up the long tunnel came the deep far echoes of a bellowing and a tramp that made the ground beneath them tremble.

Then the dwarves [stopped >] forgot their joy and their own confident boasts of a moment before, and cowered down in fright. Smaug was still to be reckoned with. It does not do to leave a live dragon out of your count if you live near him. Dragons may not have much real use for all their wealth, but they knew it to an ounce as a rule, especially after long possession: Smaug was no exception. He had passed from an uneasy dream in which a small warrior, altogether insignificant in size, but provided with a bitter sword, and great courage, figured most unpleasantly,[TN17] to a doze, and from a doze to wide waking. There was a breath of strange air in his cave. Cd there be a draught from that little hole? He had never felt quite happy about that hole, yet it was so small, but now he [liked it >][TN18] did not like the look of it at all. He stirred and missed his cup. Thieves fire murder! Such a thing had not happened since he first came there. His rage passes description – the sort of rage that is only seen when folk that have more than they can enjoy, suddenly lose something they have had before but have never before used or wanted. His fire belched forth, the hall smoked, he shook the mountain's roots. He thrust his head in vain at the little hole, and then coiling his length together, roaring like thunder underground he sped from his deep lair out through its great door, out and up towards the Front Gate.

To hunt the whole mountain till he [found >] caught the thief and burned and trampled him was his one thought. He issued from the gate, the water rose in fierce whistling steam, as up he soared into the air and settled on the mountain top in a spurt of flame. The dwarves heard the awful rumour of his flight. They ran and crouched against the rock walls of the grass terrace, <cringing> under the sides of boulders, hoping to escape the frightful eyes of the hunting dragon.[TN19] 'Quick Quick!' whispered Bilbo 'the door the tunnel'.

(So he saved their lives again) They crept inside the tunnel door and closed it as much as they dare. 'Bombur and Bofur!' cried Bifur their brother 'They are down in the valley!' 'They will be slain and all our ponies and all our stores'[TN20] moaned the others. 'You can't let them be' said Bilbo 'without a struggle. Where are the ropes?'

It was a terrible time. The worst they had ever been through. The horrible sound of the dragon's anger [*added*: was] echoing in the stony hollows far above; at any moment he might come down this side or fly whirling round; and there they were near the cliffs edge hauling like mad on the ropes. Up came Bofur and still all was safe; up came Bombur [added in pencil: puffing & blowing while the ropes creaked], and still all was safe; up came their [> some] bundles of tools and stores that had been left below – and danger came upon them. A whirring[TN21] roar was heard. A red light touched the points of standing rocks. The dragon was upon them.

They had barely time to get back in the tunnel. pulling and dragging in their bundles when Smaug came whirling from the North licking the mountain wall with flames,[TN22] beating his great wings with a noise like roaring wind.

His hot breath shrivelled the grass [in the >] before the door, and drove in through the crack and scorched them as they lay hid. Red light leapt up and black rock shadows danced. Then darkness fell as he flew south [> passed]. The [horses >] ponies shrieked with terror and galloped off for they were free. The dragon swooped & turned and hunted them.

'That'll be the end of our poor beasts' said Thorin. 'Nothing can escape him once he sees it.' They crept further down the tunnel, and there they lay and shivered till the dawn, hearing ever and anon the roar of the flying dragon grow and pass and fade as he hunted all the mountain sides. He guessed from the horses and from the tracks of the dwarves and their camps he had seen that men[TN23] had come up from the lake by the river and scaled the mountain side [<by> >] from the valley where the ponies had been, but the door withstood his searching eye, and the little walled bay kept out his fiercest flame; so that he hunted in vain, till dawn chilled his [fire >] wrath and he went back to his golden couch to sleep.

The dwarves even so [did not yet >] were not yet in the mood give up their quest; nor could they fly yet [*added in pencil*: had they wished]. The ponies were lost or killed, and they dare not march standing in the open while the dragon's wrath was still burning. They grumbled as is the nature of folk at Bilbo, of course, blaming him for what they had at first so praised him – for bringing away a cup and stirring up Smaug's wrath.

'What else do you suppose a burglar is to do?' said Bilbo 'I was not engaged to kill dragons, that's warrior's work, but steal treasure. [if you >] Did you expect me to trot back with the whole treasure of Thror on my back!'

The dwarves, of course, saw the sense of this; and begged his pardon. 'What do you propose we shd. do now, Mr Baggins?' said Thorin politely. 'Stay where we are by day and creep in the tunnel by night' said the hobbit '– in the meantime I will creep down and see what the dragon is doing [> Smaug is up to], if you like'.

This was too good an offer to be refused. [So when evening came with as yet >] So Bilbo got ready for another journey in the Mountain. He chose daytime this time, thinking Smaug would not rest for long, nor stay indoors for many a night – if he was to be caught napping (figuratively speaking: Bilbo had no thought of [*added*: really] catching him, of course!) about midday was the most likely time.

All the same it was as dark as night-time in the tunnel. The light from the door – almost closed behind him – soon failed as he went down. So silent was Bilbo's creeping that smoke on a gentle wind could hardly have beaten it, and he was inclined to feel a bit proud of himself as he drew near the lower door. The glow was very faint this time

'Old Smaug is weary and asleep' he thought. '[He'll neither hear nor >] He can't see me, and he won't hear me. Cheer up Bilbo'.

Smaug certainly looked fast asleep, almost dead[TN24] and dark with scarcely a rumble or a snore, as Bilbo peeped from the entrance. He was just about to step out on the floor, when he caught a sudden thin piercing ray of red from under the lids of the dragon's closed eyes [> the closed eyes of Smaug]. He was only pretending to sleep! He was watching the tunnel entrance.

Bilbo stepped back and [<?thanked> >] blessed the luck of his ring.[TN25] Then Smaug spoke.

'Well thief – I smell you, and I feel your air. I hear your breath. Come along! help yourself again. There is plenty and to spare.'

'No thank you O Smaug the tremendous!' said Bilbo. 'I did not come to take anything. I only wished to have a look at you and see if you were truly as great as tales say. I did not believe them.'

'Do you now?' said the dragon somewhat flattered, even though he did not believe a word of it.

'Truly songs and tales fall short of the truth O Smaug chiefest and greatest of calamities' said Bilbo.

'You have nice manners for a [lying >] thief and a liar' said the dragon. 'You seem familiar with my name – but I don't seem to remember smelling you before. Who are you, and where do you come from may I ask?'

'[I am he <that> walks unseen. >] I come from under the hill, and under the hills my paths led. And through the air – I am he that walks unseen.'

'So I can well believe' said Smaug, 'but that is hardly your name.'[TN26]

[*added in left margin*: 'I am the clue-finder the web-cutter the stinging fly, the']

'Lovely titles' sneered Smaug.

'[I am barrel-rider > I am friend >] I am he that buries his friends alive, that drowns them and [fishes them from water >] draws them alive from the water. I am come from the end of a bag, but no bag went over me.' [*added in left margin*: '[Those are not >] These don't sound so creditable' scoffed Smaug.] 'I am [barrel-rider >] the friend of bears and eagles. I am ring winner & luck wearer, and I am Barrel-rider,' went on Bilbo.

[*added, crowded in at end of paragraph*: 'That's better' said Smaug. 'But don't let your imagination run away with you.']

This of course is the way to talk to Dragons if you don't wish to reveal your name (which is wise), and don't want to infuriate them by a flat refusal (which is also wise). No dragon can resist the fascination of riddling talk, and of wasting time trying to understand it. There was a lot here Smaug didn't understand at all,[TN27] but he thought he understood enough and chuckled in his wicked inside – 'Lake-men, some nasty scheme of those nasty pier <handling> lake men' he thought 'I haven't been down there for an age and an age. I will soon put that right.

[Nor >] 'Very well O Barrel-rider' he said. 'Perhaps "barrel" is your pony's name. You may walk unseen, but you did not walk all the way. Let me tell you I ate six ponies last night, and shall [<soon> >] catch and eat the others before long. But I will give you one piece of advice for your good. Don't have more to do with dwarves than you can help.'

'Dwarves!?' said Bilbo in pretend surprise.

'[Yes >] Don't <tell> me' said Smaug. 'I know the smell (and taste) of dwarf extremely w[ell] – no one better. Don't tell me I can eat a dwarf-ridden pony – and not know it! You'll come to a bad end, if you go with such friends Thief Barrel-rider. I don't mind if you go back and tell them so from me.[TN28]

'I suppose you got a fair price for that cup last night – come now did you? Nothing at all! Well that's just like them. And I suppose they are skulking outside, and your job is to do all the dangerous work, and get what you can when I'm not looking – for them? And you will get a fair share? Don't you believe it. If you get off alive you will be lucky.'

Bilbo was beginning to feel really uncomfortable. Whenever Smaug's roving eye, seeking ever for him in the shadows, flashed across him, he trembled; and an unaccountable desire to reveal himself and tell all the truth to Smaug would seize hold of him. He was coming under the dragon-spell;[TN29] but plucking up courage he spoke again.

'You don't know everything O Smaug the mighty' said he. 'Not gold alone brought us hither'.

'Ha ha! you admit the "us"' said Smaug '– why not say us fourteen and be done with it. I am very pleased to hear that you had other business in these parts, besides my gold. Perhaps you will then not altogether waste your time. I don't know if it has occurred to you, but if you could steal all the gold bit by bit – a matter of a hundred years or so – you couldn't get it very far. Not much use on the mountain side? Not much use in the forest? Bless me – had you never thought of the catch! A fourteenth share I suppose or something like – that were the term<s> eh. But what about delivery, what about cartage.' And Smaug laughed. He had a wicked and [a] wily heart. He knew his guesses were not far out.

You will hardly believe it but poor Bilbo was really very taken aback. So far all their [> his] thoughts and energies had been concentrated on getting to the Mountain and finding the entrance. He had hardly even thought of how the treasure was to be removed, certainly never of how any part of it was to reach Bag-End Under Hill. Now a nasty suspicion began to cross his mind – had the dwarves forgotten this important point too, or were they, or were they laughing in their sleeves all the time? That is <the> effect dragon talk has on the inexperienced. Bilbo's really ought to have warned him;[TN30] but Smaug had [*added*: rather] an overwhelming personality.

'I tell you' he said in an <effort> to keep his end up 'that money [> gold] was no object or only a secondary one [> part].[TN31] We came over hill and under hill, by water and by wave and wind for revenge. Surely O Smaug the unassessably wealthy you must realize your success has made you some bitter enemies?'

Then Smaug really did laugh – A devastating sound which shook Bilbo to the floor, while far up in the tunnel the dwarves huddled together and imagined the hobbit had come to a sudden end.

'Revenge' he snorted and the red light lit the hall from floor to ceiling like scarlet lightning. 'The King under the Mountain is dead and where are his kin that dare take revenge. Girion lord of Dale is dead and I have eaten his people like a wolf among sheep and where are his sons' sons[TN32] who dare approach me. I kill where I wish and none dares resist. I laid low warriors of old and their like is not in the world today. Then I was young. Now I am old and strong, strong, strong – thief in the shadows' – he gloated. 'My armour is like tenfold shields, [my feet like >] my teeth are swords my claws spears, the shock of my tail a thunder bolt, my wings a hurricane, and my breath death!'[TN33]

'I have always understood' murmured Bilbo in an astonished squeak 'that dragons were tender underneath, especially in the region of the – er chest; but doubtless one so fortified has thought of that.'

The dragon stopped short in his boasts 'Your information is antiquated' he snapped. 'I am armoured above and below; with iron scales and hard gems. No blade can pierce me.'

'I might have guessed it' said Bilbo '– truly there can be no equal of Smaug the impenetrable. [Nor any waistcoat >] What wealth to possess a waistcoat of fine diamonds!'

'Yes it is rare and wonderful indeed' said Smaug absurdly pleased. He did not know that Bilbo had already had a glimpse of his peculiar adornment & was only itching for a closer view. He rolled over 'look' he said '– what do you say to that.'

'[Absolutely Perfectly dazzling >] Dazzlingly marvellous. Perfect. Flawless. Staggering.' said Bilbo, but what he thought was 'Old fool, and there is great patch in <the> left of his breast [> in a hollow of his left breast], [without >] as bare as snail out of its shell.'

'Well really I must not detain you any longer' he said aloud, 'or hinder your much needed rest. Ponies take some catching, I am told after a long start. And so do burglars' he added as a parting shot. Rather an unfortunate one for the dragon spouted flames after him, and fast as he ran up the tunnel, he had not gone far enough before the ghastly head of Smaug was [pressed >] thrust into the opening – no more would go – and fire and vapour pursued him and nearly overcame him.

He had been feeling rather pleased with his conversation with Smaug, but this [> his] mistake at the end shook him into better sense. 'Don't laugh at live dragons Bilbo my boy' he said, & a sound remark too. 'You aren't through this adventure yet.' That was equally true.

Inserted into the text at this point is a rider (manuscript page '151b'), seven paragraphs written on the back of the same page; the original page thereby changed from being '151' to being broken between '151a' (the two paragraphs before this point) and '151c' (the rest of the page following it) by Tolkien. This full page of additional text must have been added by Tolkien after he had finished the chapter, or else he would not have needed to resort to the unorthodox numeration or have drafted this on the back of a sheet; as noted earlier, all this section of the story, from manuscript page 119 (the capture by wood-elves) to 167 (the scene on Ravenhill), was written only on the front of each sheet, rather than on front and back as had been the case before (with the bulk of the Second Phase, manuscript pages 13–118) and after (the Third Phase manuscript pages with new numeration 1–45 concluding the book). Since it introduces the idea of the thrush learning of the immediate threat Smaug now poses to Lake Town, the information that some of the men of Dale could understand bird-speech, and the essential detail of Smaug's exposed weak spot, it must have been added after Smaug's death scene on manuscript page 155 (1/1/15: 3), where none of these details initially appear, and at the same time as the paragraph added to the bottom of that page incorporating all those details (see page 549).

The afternoon was getting late when he came out again. The dwarves were all sitting on the 'doorstep' and were delighted to see him, and made him sit down and tell them all that had passed.

But Bilbo was worried and uncomfortable – he was regretting some of the things he had said and did not like confessing [> repeating] them. The old thrush was sitting on a rock near by with his head cocked on one side [*added in margin*: listening to all that was said] and Bilbo crossly threw a stone at him; but he only fluttered out of the way and came back.

'Drat the bird!' said Bilbo 'I don't like the look of him.'

'Leave him alone' said Thorin. 'The thrushes are friendly – this is a very old bird, probably one of those that used to live here tame to the hands of my father and grandfather – they were a long lived and magical breed. The dwarves and the men of Dale used to have the trick of understanding their language and use them for messengers to fly to the Lake-town.'[TN34]

'Well he will have news to take there if he likes' now said Bilbo. 'Why what has happened?' cried the dwarves 'Get on with your tale' So B. told them – and he [told them > confessed a fear that <his> >] confessed an uncomfortable foreboding that the Dragon might go hunting back to the Lake, since he must guess from their camps and the ponies how they had come. 'O why did I ever say that about barrel-rider' he groaned.

['Yes and why did you let him find out your way of escape?' said they >] 'Well you found out one useful thing at any rate' Balin comforted him ' – the bare patch in old Smaug's diamond waistcoat may come in useful yet.' Then they fell to discussing stabs and jabs and weapons and the various dangers attending prodding a sleeping dragon.[TN35] [*added in margin*: and all the while the thrush listened, and at last as the sun sank towards the forest he flew away.] All the while as [evening drew > the sun went West >] the long shadows lengthened B. became more and more unhappy.

'I am sure we are very unsafe here' he said

The page of new material ('151b') ends here, and the text resumes with what had been the third paragraph on the original manuscript page 151, now marked by Tolkien '151 (c)'.

'You had better look out' said he – '[*added*: let's go on &] close the door and risk being shut in. The dragon [> Smaug] will <begin> going out before long [*added*: now] and I am very mistaken if he doesn't search this side of the mountain and break it bit by bit to find the outer entrance to the tunnel. What he doesn't know about it he guesses.'

The delight of the dwarves at seeing him was overwhelmed in terror [> fear]. 'What have you been saying' they asked him; and though B. gave them as close an account of all his words as he cd. they were far from satisfied.[TN36]

[All was now quiet, and >] [*added in margin*: Still the > The dwarves > The > When evening came on the dwarves took his advice as far as going inside the tunnel went.] But they delayed shutting the door – it seemed a desperate plan, and they were not willing yet to take the risk of cutting themselves off from the outer air with no way of escape except through the dragon's very lair. All was quiet below at any rate.[TN37] So for a while they sat near the tunnel's mouth and talked on.

Bilbo wished he cd. feel quite certain that they were being honest when they swore that they had never had any clear idea of what to do after the recovery of their treasure.

'As for your share Mr Baggins' said Thorin 'I assure you we are more than satisfied with your professional assistance; and you shall choose it yourself, as soon as we have it! I am sorry we were so stupid as to overlook the transport problem – it is many years since the eldest of us were in these lands, and the difficulties have not grown less with the passing of time. But what can be done [*added*: for you] we will do it. For ourselves well that is our affair. We shall see when the time come.'

There they sat and the talk drifted on to things they remembered, that must now be lying in the hall below – the spears that were made for the armies of Bladorthin,[TN38] each with a thrice forged head, each shaft <bound> with cunning gold [; the shields >], but they were never delivered nor paid for; shields for warriors long dead; coats of mail gilded and silvered; [the great cup of Thror two handled gold cold-wrought out of >] the great golden cup of Thror, hewn and carven like birds and flowers <with> eyes and petals made of pearls; and most fair of all the white gem of Girion Lord of Dale,[TN39] which he paid for the arming of his sons, in coats of dwarf mail the like of which had never before been made. [*added*: of silver wrought the power and strength of steel] The white gem of Girion like a globe with myriad facets shining like water in the sun, like snow in starlight [> under stars] like silver in firelight, like rain on the moon. [< Shining like silver in firelight, like water in the sun, like snow under stars, like rain upon the moon (like Sirius upon Earth).]

[Their speech was interrupted by the >] All the while Bilbo was only half-listening. He was near the door with an ear cocked for any sound without, his other was listening to the dwarves, but over and beyond straining for any sound from far below. Evening fell and deepened and became uneasy. 'Shut the door' he begged them. 'I fear that dragon in my bones. I like this silence less than the uproar of last night: Shut the door before it is too late'.

Something in his voice [made > moved >] gave the dwarves an uncomfortable feeling. Grumbling Thorin rose and pulled the door towards him 'How can we close it' he said 'without bar nor hand-hold this side?' He pushed the door and kicked [*added*: away] the stone that blocked the door. Then he thrust upon it and it closed with a snap and a clang. [They were shut >] No trace of a key hole was there left. They were shut in the Mountain. And not a moment too soon. A blow smote the side of the Mountain like a crash of battering rams made of forest oaks and swung by giants. The rocks boomed; stones fell on their heads. They fled far down the tunnel glad to be [*added*: still] alive, pursued by the roar without where Smaug was breaking the rocks to pieces smashing wall and cliff with his great tail till their little lofty camping ground, the thrush's stone the scorched grass the narrow ledge and all disappeared in a jumble of smashed boulders, and an avalanche of splintered stone fell over the cliff into the valley underneath.

Smaug had left his lair in silent stealth and crept to the west of the mountain [a heavy floating slow >] floating heavy and slow in dark like a crow down the wind, in the hopes of catching somebody or something there, or of spying the outlet to the tunnel which the thief had used. This was his outburst of wrath when he found nobody and could see nothing, even where he knew the outlet must in fact be.

Still he was well pleased; he thought in his heart that he would not be troubled again from that direction; [or he would hear and have ample warning >] or would have ample warning of any hammering or tunnelling.

But in the meanwhile he had revenge of his own to wreak. 'Barrel rider' thought he '– your feet came from the water side, and up the water you came without a doubt. If you are not one of those men of the Lake, you had their help; and now you shall see who is King [> They shall see me and remember who is King under the Mountain].' He rose in fire and went away South towards the Running River.

The text continues with only a line break before starting the account of Smaug's attack on Lake Town, what is now Chapter XIV of the published book but was Chapter XIII of the manuscript version of the tale. Much later, when preparing the First Typescript, Tolkien added in pencil at this point (between the first and second paragraphs of manuscript page 153 [Marq. 1/1/15:1]):

Here insert 'Not at home'

and at the same time added a chapter title – the first to appear in the manuscript:

Ch. Fire and Water

For more on the re-arrangement of the story that reversed the order in which the next two chapters appeared, see page 548.

TEXT NOTES

1 Note that the genealogy of the 'text tradition', with Thrain as Thorin's father rather than his grandfather, is firmly in place; see the section of commentary entitled 'Thorin, son of Thrain, son of Thror' following Chapter X.

2 'two messes already': Bilbo is referring of course to rescuing the dwarves (*sans* Gandalf/Thorin) from the Spiders of Mirkwood and also to freeing all the dwarves from the dungeon of the Elvenking.

3 This, the first of Bungo Baggins' sayings recounted by his adventurous son in the Lonely Mountain chapters, is Tolkien's adaptation of an actual medieval proverb occurring in line 1680 of the Tolkien-Gordon edition of *Sir Gawain & the Green Knight* (published in 1925, with a revised printing in 1930), where the phrase '*þrid tyme þrowe best*' is placed in quotation marks and glossed 'third time turn out best' (SGGK pages 52 & 201). Tolkien's note (page 109) slightly recasts it as an expression of hope rather than a statement of fact, 'third time, turn out best' and comments:

> *þrid tyme, þrowe best* is a proverbial expression which is quoted also in *Seven Sages* 2062 'Men sais þe þrid time þrowes best.' The modern equivalent is 'third time pays for all'.

The Seven Sages of Rome [fourteenth century] is another Middle English romance, about twice the length of SGGK, preserved in the famous Auchinleck Manuscript; this is an English translation of a French original of seven misogynistic tales within a frame narrative. For Tolkien's own commentary on the proverb as it appears in *The Hobbit* and *The Lord of the Rings*, see his letter of 31st July 1964 to Jared Lobdell, quoted in Anderson's *Annotated Hobbit*, page 267:

> It is an old alliterative saying using the word *throw:* time, period (unrelated to the verb *throw*); sc. this third occasion is the best time – the time for special effort and/or luck. It is used when a third try is needed to rectify two poor efforts, or when a third occurrence may surpass the others and finally prove a man's worth, or a thing's.

Anderson also notes that Tolkien translates *þrid tyme þrowe best* as 'third time pays for all' in his own translation of *Sir Gawain* (*Sir Gawain and the Green Knight, Pearl, Sir Orfeo*, tr. JRRT, ed. Christopher Tolkien [1975; 1978]; stanza 67, page 66).

4 'the year before': As elsewhere throughout the first draft, the extended time-scheme for Bilbo's adventures with a longer journey through Mirkwood and lengthy imprisonment by the elves is still in place. See also, for example, 'He hadn't had [a] pocket hank[erchief] for a year' three paragraphs later or the reference to his journey having begun 'the spring before last' a paragraph earlier.

5 The plural is remarkable, but the manuscript clearly reads *doors* not *door* at this point. I suspect that as usual Tolkien was describing the scene as he happened to envision it, ignoring for the moment possible contradictions until he had committed the scene to paper and trusting to the next draft to iron out any inconsistencies, as in fact it did: the First Typescript (1/1/62:1) reads 'door', along with all subsequent texts.

6 Added in pencil (i.e., at the time of the creation of the First Typescript): 'and now you've got *to pull it out or* pay for it.'

7 The idea that dragons purr is not Tolkien's invention, but derives from Kenneth Grahame's 'The Reluctant Dragon', a short tale originally published as part of *Dream Days* [1898] and later as a separate small book illustrated by Ernest Shepherd [1938], who is most famous for his work on *Winnie-the-Pooh*. Tolkien was conversant with Grahame's work; see the commentary following the Bladorthin Typescript (pp. 45–6) and Note 3 on page 58 for more on Tolkien's familiarity with, and admiration for, Grahame's writings. It is characteristic of Tolkien's eclecticism that he could combine in the figure of Smaug elements from sources as disparate as Grahame's whimsical little tale, the grim *Volsunga Saga*, and the Book of Job (see Text Note 33 below).

8 This word is very difficult to read in the manuscript and might just as well be 'worst'. 'Vast' is the reading of the First Typescript (1/1/62:2) and published book (DAA.270).

9 The sudden brief shift in perspective here to second person and present tense and then back again is anomalous and striking, but it persists through all subsequent versions of the passage (cf. DAA.270). The idea that the tunnel ended in a square opening was rejected at once, probably because he had already described the secret passage as 'straight as a ruler, smooth-floored and smooth-sided, going . . . with a gently never-varying slope direct . . . to some distant goal in the blackness below' and hence the exit should exactly match the entrance. The lower exit is not shown on Tolkien's painting of Smaug's chamber, 'Conversation

with Smaug' (Plate XI [top]), but its size and shape can be guessed by comparison with the upper entrance shown in 'The Back Door' (Plate IX [top]), which is definitely taller than it is wide – i.e., rectangular, not square.

10 Although often used interchangeably, 'gems' here indicate carved precious stones, while 'jewels' are gemstones set in items of jewelry. Thus the 'Gem of Girion' (the later Arkenstone), 'like a globe with myriad facets' is correctly named, while the 'five hundred emeralds green as grass' that make up the 'necklace of Girion' (which makes its first appearance in a pasteover in the First Typescript; Marq. 1/1/62:11) are jewels.

11 This sentence was slightly revised to read 'and *here* great jars *stood* filled with wealth . . .' Compare the painting 'Conversation with Smaug' (Plate XI [top]), where several such jars, one marked with Thror's rune (?), do indeed stand in an archway by the far wall. The two great jars in the foreground therefore probably stand against the near wall of the chamber, which would be out of our sight to the left; similar jars are probably hidden from our view behind the mound of Smaug's treasure. See 'The Dwarvenkings' Curse' in part i of the commentary following Chapter XIV (pp. 602–3).

12 See 'The Only Philological Remark', part iii of the commentary following this chapter.

13 Having spent months travelling on the road with dwarves, it would have been surprising if Bilbo had not 'heard tell and sing of dragon-hoards'. For example, the dwarves' first poem, 'Far Over the Misty Mountains Cold' – only 'a fragment' of which is set down in Chapter I – describes 'many a gleaming golden hoard' (page 37) and details of the wonderful things in them. Likewise, at Medwed's house the dwarves tell 'many stories . . . about gold and silver and jewels and the making of them' (page 238), and at Lake Town the townspeople are full of songs and speculation about the King under the Mountain's treasure (pp. 439–40). Also, of course, we know from his very first conversation with Bladorthin that Bilbo was already familiar, before he ever set out on the quest of Erebor, with stories about dragons (see page 31 and DAA.35); cf. his knowledge of their weak spot ('"I have always understood" murmured Bilbo . . . "that dragons were tender underneath, especially in the region of the – er chest"' [page 512]), which precedes the dwarves' discussion of the best way to attack a dragon by more than a page [page 513].

14 The detail of the stolen cup is a homage to a similar scene in *Beowulf*; see part ii of the commentary following this chapter.

15 'More like a grocer than a burglar': Dwalin's dismissive words (spoken by Gloin in the published book) go all the way back to the Pryftan Fragment (see page 8), as does Bilbo's reaction to them, his desire 'to be thought fierce', even if it meant travelling to a desert far to the east and fighting a dragon. Given that he is currently in the midst of the Desolation of the Dragon and soon to engage Smaug first in a battle of

wits and then, according to Plot Notes C, to kill him, his earlier words have in a sense come true, and would have done so more literally had Tolkien stuck to his original outline.

16 In fact, from its shape, general topography, and isolation from other heights, the Lonely Mountain is almost certainly an extinct volcano; compare its outline with that of such real-world volcanoes as Mt. Rainier or Mt. St. Helens.

17 Note that this description, which is amusingly ironic in the published book, was written when the idea of Bilbo killing the dragon himself with his little sword was still Tolkien's intention (see Plot Notes C). Hence, Smaug is in effect having a prophetic dream of his own approaching death here.

18 Added in left margin in cursive script and marked for insertion at this point: 'of late he had half fancied he had caught the din of echo of a knocking sound from far above.' This is marked for insertion at this point, but more properly goes at the end of the sentence, its corresponding placement in the published story.

19 The manuscript actually has 'frightened' here ('the frightened eyes of the hunting dragon'; 1/1/13:4); I have supplied the reading 'frightful' from the First Typescript (1/1/62:4).

20 This sentence was slightly altered with the addition of the word 'lost' following *ponies*, then replaced by 'They will be slain, and all our ponies *too*, and all our stores *lost*' in the typescript (since the stores could not be 'slain'). Note that in the next sentence in the manuscript it is Bilbo, not Thorin as in the published book, who makes the panic-strickened dwarves rescue their fellows. The paragraphs describing Thorin's coolly taking command to leave no dwarf behind while sending Bilbo, Balin, and Fili and Kili into the tunnel (so that if worse comes to worse 'the dragon shan't have all of us') first appear, without any surviving drafting, in the First Typescript (typescript page 118; 1/1/62:4), in exactly the words used in the final book (cf. DAA.274), except that Bifur at first refers to Bombur and Bofur as 'My brothers!', altered in ink to 'My cousins'. See Text Note 34 following Chapter VIII for more about this change in their family relationships.

21 'whirring': to make a continuous vibrating sound (OED). Note that this word falls within the portion of the OED upon which Tolkien worked during his time on the Dictionary staff in 1919–20, a decade before starting *The Hobbit*, although so far as we know 'whirr' was not one of the words which Tolkien personally researched; see Hammond, *Descriptive Bibliography*, page 278; Winchester, *The Meaning of Everything*, pages 206–8; and *Lexicography and the OED: Pioneers in the Untrodden Forest*, ed. Lynda Mugglestone, Appendix I (particularly pages 229–31). The best account of Tolkien's time on the Dictionary, and his contributions to that vast ongoing collaborative project, can be found in *The Ring of Words: Tolkien and the Oxford English Dictionary* by Gilliver, Marshall, and Weiner [2006].

22 A new ink begins at this point, indicating at least a short break in composition. The same ink was also used to touch up some words in the preceding lines and make them easier to read.

23 Tolkien is probably not using the word in the generic sense here (cf. the exchange with Arthur Ransome discussed in Appendix IV); although Smaug knows dwarves are present (see page 510), he also believes that lake-men are with them, of whom the unseen 'thief' is one (ibid.). Had he captured and eaten all fourteen ponies,† no doubt he would have been better informed about the composition of the intruders. Still, Smaug does know that there are fourteen individuals among the group camped on the mountain ('why not say "us fourteen"'? and 'a fourteenth share', both page 511).

† Apparently Thorin & Company have sixteen in the published book; contrast the manuscript account of their approach to the mountain described on page 471, where Bilbo and Balin are on the same pony leading a single pack-pony, with the account in the published book where Bilbo and Balin each lead a pack-pony and appear to be riding separate ponies themselves (DAA.255).

24 'almost dead and dark': That is, his fires seem to have died down, leaving the room almost dark.

25 This line, which survives into the published book, is one more indicator that Tolkien did not, when writing *The Hobbit*, regard Bilbo's ring as anything more than a harmless and useful treasure; the One Ring of the sequel cannot by any means be described as a luck-bringer. Cf. also Bilbo's riddling description of himself, a few paragraphs later, as 'luck-wearer'.

26 Bilbo's conversation with Smaug evolved and expanded in the very act of writing; in the lines originally following this sentence, the dragon immediately confronts the unseen intruder with his knowledge that dwarves were involved:

> Nor did you walk here unless > all the way here; unless you > let me tell you I ate six ponies last night, shall probably catch and eat the others before long. But never mind about your thirteen companions dwarves of course, don't tell me! I know the smell <u>and</u> taste of dwarf; and they had left tokens enough on the ponies for me. But

All this was struck through and the dialogue expanded in the telling in order to allow Bilbo to spin out his riddles and pseudo-names alluding to his adventures so far. Similarly, the only significant *nom de guerre* is 'barrel-rider', since it sparks Smaug's next remark (and determines the course of action that leads to his death); Tolkien twice wrote it and each time crossed it out, deferring it to the end of the passage.

Note that, like Odysseus (*The Odyssey*, Book IX), Bilbo refuses to tell his foe his real name (which, as Tolkien notes, is wise; cf. 'Turambar and the Foalókë', where knowledge of Túrin's true identity enabled Glorund to beguile the headstrong human into abandoning those who depended upon him and instead rushing off onto a fool's errand).

Sigurd also at first refuses to tell the mortally wounded Fafnir his name in both *Fáfnismál* (stanzas 1–3) and *Volsunga Saga* (Morris, page 59); the compiler of the Edda interrupts the poem to prosaically state that 'Sigurd concealed his name because it was believed in ancient times that the words of a man about to die had great power if he cursed his enemy by name'. Odysseus eventually does tell the Cyclops his true name, which brings down the curse of his long-delayed homecoming upon him; Sigurd likewise, after some hesitation ('A wanderer named for a noble beast,/the son of no mother,/I had no father as other men do;/always I go alone'), tells the dragon his true name but seems to escape any death-curse from the dragon; it is the treasure itself, Fafnir warns him, that dooms the man who claims it (*Fáfnismál*, stanzas 9 & 20). Bilbo, wiser than both, never does tell Smaug his name† but nonetheless reveals a little too much about himself ('barrel-rider'), thus bringing doom down upon the Lake-men – although, given the dragon's suspicions (page 508), he would sooner or later have attacked the town anyway.

† Note, however, that his having identified himself to Gollum (see page 155) led to much trouble in the sequel; see *The Lord of the Rings* Chapter II ('The Shadow of the Past') and Appendix B: 'The Tale of Years', as well as 'The Hunt for the Ring' in *Unfinished Tales.*

27 The typescript (1/1/62:7) adds, parenthetically, '(though I expect you do, since you know all about Bilbo's adventures to which he was referring)'. In fact each self-assumed epithet alludes to one specific episode earlier in the book:

- *I am he that walks unseen* – because of his magic ring (Chapters V & ff). Note that the shadow which had given Bilbo such trouble in the early days of his possessing the ring – cf. the episode with the goblin guards at the end of Chapter V, or the care needed to keep the sharp-eyed elves of Mirkwood from spotting it (page 381) – is no longer mentioned in the scene with Smaug, probably because the lighting here is dim enough (apparently coming entirely from Smaug himself)† that no shadows can be seen among the mirk, as had presumably been the case during his battle with the Mirkwood spiders.
- *I come from under the hill* – an allusion to the address of Bilbo's home, given in the first surviving paragraph of the Pryftan Fragment as 'Bag-end, Under-Hill' (page 7); see also Tolkien's drawing of the outside of Bilbo's home, labelled 'Bag-End, Underhill' (DAA.46).
- *and under the hills my paths led* – the goblin-caves (Chapter IV). The typescript adds '*and over the hills*' – i.e., the mountain-path (also Chapter IV, which in the First Typescript is given its now-familiar title, 'Over hill and Under hill' [1/1/54:1]).
- *And through the air* – when carried by Eagles (Chapters VI & VII).
- *I am the clue-finder* – this probably alludes to Bilbo's finding the spider-thread and using it to guide his friends through the tangle of Mirkwood in Chapter VIII, since 'clue' originally meant a ball of thread, specifically the one used by Theseus to navigate the laby-

rinth (*Concise OED* Vol I, page 434, under the spelling 'clew'). I am grateful to Anders Stenström for drawing this to my attention.

- *the web-cutter* – in his battle with the Spiders of Mirkwood (Chapter VIII).
- *the stinging fly* – Bilbo attacking the Spiders with his little sword; he calls himself a 'naughty little fly' in his spontaneous song 'Lazy lob and crazy Cob' (page 311) and the spiders refer to his little sword in terms they understand as 'a sting' (Chapter VIII). Later, of course, the sword would be given *Sting* as its proper name by Bilbo (DAA.208), but this would not occur until the First Typescript (see Text Note 23 for Chapter VIII).
- *I am he that buries his friends alive* – this might refer to Bilbo's getting all the dwarves safely underground inside the secret tunnel just before Smaug's attack the night before (Chapter XIII).
- *that drowns them* – i.e., Bilbo's hiding the thirteen dwarves in the barrels thrown into the Forest River to escape the dungeons of the Elvenking (Chapter IX).
- *and draws them alive from the water* – by opening the aforesaid barrels upon the arrival at the Long Lake (Chapter X).
- *I am come from the end of a bag* – cf. the name of Bilbo's home, Bag-End (Chapter I).
- *but no bag went over me* – Bilbo and Bladorthin were the only members of the expedition not to have bags thrown over their heads by the three trolls (Chapter II).
- *I am the friend of bears* – the visit with Medwed/Beorn (Chapter VII).
- *and eagles* – the rescue by Eagles, and brief sojourn in their eyries (Chapters VI & VII).
- *I am ring winner* – the riddle-contest with Gollum (Chapter V).
- *& luck wearer* – see the comment in Text Note 25 above about 'the luck of his ring', though we should also note that Bilbo was chosen as the lucky number (Chapter I) and that in the typescript version of Chapter VIII the dwarves come to recognize 'that he had some wits, as well as luck, and a magic ring' after he rescues them from the spiders (1/1/58:15; cf. DAA.217).
- *and I am Barrel-rider* – during the long, dark, cold ride down the Forest River in the first hours after escaping from the Elvenking's halls (Chapter IX). It is ironic that Smaug quips 'maybe "Barrel" is your pony's name', since at the time the narrator had likened Bilbo's attempt to stay atop the barrel 'like trying to ride without bridle or stirrups a roundbellied pony that was always thinking of rolling on the grass' (page 387).

† E.g., the chamber's being completely dark the third time Bilbo enters it, in Smaug's absence (see page 578).

Note that, unlike the actual riddles he had exchanged with Gollum, which rather resemble the riddle-contest in *Heidrek's Saga* (see page 168), these here are all tests of knowledge, like the final, fatal 'riddle' Odin asks the giant in *Vafthrúthnismál* (see page 169), where the speaker deliberately refers to events about which his listener is ignorant. It may be significant that in *Fáfnismál* Sigurd questions the dying dragon, very much as Odin questions the giant in *Vafthrúthnismál.*

28 The typescript (1/1/62:7) adds the following sentence at the end of this paragraph, which enables us to know that Bilbo's pony was one of the ones Smaug had eaten: 'But he did not tell Bilbo that there was one smell he could not make out at all, hobbit-smell; it was quite outside his experience and puzzled him mightily.'

29 This sentence was altered to read 'He was *in grievous danger of* coming under the dragon-spell'. Compare the Tale of Turambar, where the dragon's eye held the hero motionless: 'with the magic of his eyes he bound him hand and foot . . . and he turned the sinews of Túrin as it were to stone' (BLT II.85–6), while the dragon's voice beguiled him: 'for the lies of that worm were barbed with truth, and for the spell of his eyes he believed all that was said' (ibid., page 87).

30 Presumably the missing word should be something like 'friends': i.e., 'Bilbo's *friends* really ought to have warned him.' The words 'warned him' were canceled in pencil and replaced by 'put him on his guard', a reading similar to that in the First Typescript and published book ('Bilbo of course ought to have been on his guard'; 1/1/62:8 and DAA.281).

31 Added in top margin: 'gold was only an afterthought with us.'

32 The apostrophe marking the possessive is absent in the lightly punctuated original; I have chosen *sons'* over *son's* here because two pages later in the manuscript Tolkien unambiguously refers to King Girion's sons in the plural; see page 514 and also Text Note 6 for Plot Notes C.

33 Compare Smaug's boasts (manuscript page 150), and also the description of Smaug's attack on Lake Town that follows a few pages later (manuscript pages 154–155), with the description of the great dragon in the deeps in the Book of Job, chapter 41:

Can you draw out Leviathan . . . ?
Will he speak to you soft words? . . .
No one is so fierce that he dares to stir him up . . .
Who can penetrate his double coat of mail?

. . . Round about his teeth is terror.
His back is made of rows of shields,
shut up closely as with a seal.
One is so near to another
that no air can come between them.

. . . [H]is eyes are like the eyelids of the dawn.
Out of his mouth go flaming torches;
sparks of fire leap forth.
Out of his nostrils comes forth smoke,
as from a boiling pot and burning rushes.

His breath kindles coals,
and a flame comes forth from his mouth.
In his neck abides strength,
and terror dances before him . . .
His heart is hard as a stone . . .

When he raises himself up the mighty are afraid;
at the crashing they are beside themselves.
. . . [T]he sword . . . does not avail,
nor the spear, the dart, or the javelin.
He counts iron as straw,
and bronze as rotten wood.
The arrow cannot make him flee;
for him slingstones are turned to stubble.
. . . he laughs at the rattle of javelins.

His underparts are like sharp potsherds . . .
He makes the deep boil like a pot . . .
Behind him he leaves a shining wake . . .
Upon earth there is not his like,
a creature without fear . . .
[H]e is king over all the sons of pride.

Tolkien is reported by some sources to have worked on the translation of Job found in *The Jerusalem Bible* [first edition, 1966], in addition to his recognized role in translating Jonah; cf. Carpenter's checklist of Tolkien's publications (*Tolkien: A Biography*, page 274) and Tolkien's letter to Charlotte and Denis Plimmer (letter of 8th February 1967; *Letters*, p. 378). Hammond cites a letter from the bible's publisher stating that Tolkien 'also worked on the Book of Job, providing its initial draft and playing an important part in establishing its final text' (*Descriptive Bibliography*, page 279), but his role on that book seems to have been limited to reviewing an early draft by another translator. I am indebted to Wayne Hammond for this clarification. According to the *Reader's Guide*, vol. two of Christina Scull & Wayne G. Hammond's *The J.R.R. Tolkien Companion and Guide* [2006], Tolkien also did some work on Isaiah and probably Job as well, and was offered the Pentateuch or Books of Moses (Genesis, Exodus, Leviticus, Numbers, & Deuteronomy) as well as the historical books (Joshua, Judges, and 1st & 2nd Samuel), but ultimately had to decline because of the press of other work (*Reader's Guide* pages 437–9).† In any case, that work came many years after he had completed work on *The Hobbit*.

† Tolkien was of course also familiar with the Jonah story professionally through its vivid and amusing fourteenth-century Middle English retelling in the same manuscript as (and universally believed to be by the same author as) *Sir Gawain & the Green Knight* and *Pearl*: the Gawain-poet's adaptation is known as *Patience*.

34 'The dwarves and the men of Dale' was changed in the manuscript to simply 'The men of Dale'; otherwise, of course, some member of Thorin's company might be expected to be able to talk to the bird. The motif of the dwarves' special friendship with the Ravens of the Mountain may have originated by the displacement of this motif from the original thrushes to another breed of bird.

35 This sentence is replaced in the First Typescript by the passage essentially as it appears in the published book: '. . . they all began discussing dragonslayings historical, dubious, and mythical, and the various sorts of stabs and jabs and undercuts, and the different arts devices and stratagems by which they had been accomplished. The general opinion was that catching a dragon napping was not as easy as it sounded; and the attempt to stick one or prod one asleep was more likely to end in disaster than a bold frontal attack' (1/1/62:10; cf. DAA.285). The latter sentence, of course, postdates the abandonment of the Bilbo-as-dragon-slayer plot from Plot Notes B & C which had probably still been in place when this chapter was written: originally, the discussion of how to kill a sleeping dragon would have been immediately relevant to the upcoming chapters.

36 This paragraph was bracketed by Tolkien and marked for deletion, probably when the vast expansion represented by 151b replaced it.

37 As written, this sentence reads 'All was no quiet below at any rate'; this might be a slip for 'All was *now* quiet below . . .'

38 Only fourteen manuscript pages after it had been used as the wizard's name for the last time (see page 472), 'Bladorthin' has here been reassigned to an elusive figure who appears only in this single sentence. The First Typescript (1/1/62:11) makes this 'the great King Bladorthin (long since dead)', about whom nothing is otherwise told; a sad relic for what had been the name of one of the story's major characters.

39 The 'Gem of Girion' here makes its first appearance in the story, having been long anticipated in the Plot Notes (see page 364). Later this would be replaced by the Arkenstone, which would be given its own earlier history; see commentary following Chapter XIV. Similarly, the coats of mithril mail (although that term had not yet arisen and is in fact never used in *The Hobbit*), foreseen in Plot Notes C, also now appear in the narrative.

(i)
Tolkien's Dragons

I first tried to write a story when I was about seven. It was about a dragon. I remember nothing about it except a philological fact. My mother said nothing about the dragon, but pointed out that one could not say 'a green great dragon', but had to say 'a great green dragon'. I wondered why, and still do. The fact that I remember this is possibly significant, as I do not think I ever tried to write a story again for many years, and was taken up with language.

—JRRT to W. H. Auden, 7 June 1955 (*Letters* p. 214).[1]

Few elements in Tolkien's work have had as much influence on modern fantasy, the genre he himself essentially created, as his depiction of dragons. When Tolkien began writing, dragons had dwindled to whimsical fairy-tale creatures in the popular mind, treated more as figures of fun than the deadly menaces they had been in old legend. Even among scholars of those old legends, the feeling ran that dragons were pedestrian, unimaginative, and trivial, 'the merest commonplace of heroic legend' (W. P. Ker, *The Dark Ages* [1904]; quoted more in sorrow than in anger in Tolkien's 'Beowulf: The Monsters and the Critics' [1936], page 7). The great R. W. Chambers (*Widsith* [1912]) even lamented that the *Beowulf*-poet had given us a story about Grendel and the fire-drake when he and his fellow critics would have much preferred a melodrama of tangled loyalties at the Danish court above 'a wilderness of dragons' (quoted in 'Beowulf: The Monsters and the Critics', page 8).

There were, of course, notable exceptions to the general neglect; writers who fully appreciated the appeal and impact of what we may call dragons of the old school, such as Lord Dunsany ('The Fortress Unvanquishable Save For Sacnoth' [1907], 'The Hoard of the Gibbelins' [1912], 'Miss Cubbidge and the Dragon of Romance' [1912]) and Kenneth Morris (*The Book of Three Dragons* [1930]), but by and large the whimsical dragons of E. Nesbit (e.g., *The Book of Dragons* [1899] and 'The Last Dragon' [1925]) and above all Kenneth Grahame ('The Reluctant Dragon' [1898 and 1938]) had won the day. Tolkien, who considered dragons the quintessential fantasy creature ('The dragon had the trade-mark *Of Faërie* written plain upon him. In whatever world he had his being it was an Otherworld' – OFS.40), presented them so dramatically and successfully in his own work that he single-handedly reversed the trend of the preceding half-century and more, both in fantasy and in scholarship.[2]

Tolkien's interest in dragons was life-long: he recalled in his Andrew Lang lecture that his favorite fictional world when growing up had been 'the nameless North of Sigurd of the Völsungs, and the prince of all dragons . . . I desired dragons with a profound desire . . . [T]he world that contained even the imagination of Fáfnir was richer and more beautiful, at whatever cost of peril' (OFS.40).[3] In his 1965 radio interview with Denys Gueroult, he admitted to a fondness for these 'intelligent lizards':

> [D]ragons always attracted me as a mythological element. They seem to be able to comprise human malice and bestiality together . . . a sort of malicious wisdom and shrewdness. Terrifying creatures.

Writing to Christopher Bretherton a few months earlier [1964], he described how in his youth he had been 'interested in traditional tales (especially those concerning dragons)' in addition to philology and metrics, before '[t]hese things began to flow together when I was an undergraduate' (i.e., between 1911 and 1915; *Letters*, page 345). Indeed, so steeped in thinking about dragons was he that when as a child he found a fossil on the beach at Lyme Regis, he believed he had found a piece of petrified dragon.[4] It is no wonder, then, that when he came to write his mythology he filled it with dragons.

Dragons are one of the most persistent features in Tolkien's work, appearing in the Silmarillion tradition (Glorund the Golden, the 'dragons of the north' who destroy Gondolin, Ancalagon the Black), in both of his children's tales that preceded *The Hobbit* (*Roverandom*'s Great White Dragon of the Moon and *Farmer Giles of Ham*'s Chrysophylax Dives) as well as in the Father Christmas Letters (cf. the 1927 letter, the full version of which appears in *Letters from Father Christmas* pages 32–4), in several of his poems ('The Hoard', 'The Dragon's Visit'), in his scholarly essays ('On Fairy-Stories' and particularly 'Beowulf: The Monsters and the Critics'), and of course in his art: in addition to his illustrations for *The Hobbit*, *Roverandom*, and the Silmarillion tales, all of which have some featuring dragons, see the dragon-drawings reproduced in *Artist & Illustrator* (H-S#48 & 49), only two out of a number of uncollected pieces. A dragon (almost certainly Smaug himself) can even be seen in one of the Father Christmas Letters, painted on the cave walls along with prehistoric beasts in the letter for 1932 (see Plate VI [detail] and *Letters from Father Christmas*, page 75), and a tiny toy dragon belonging to a monster child appears in one untitled miscellaneous sketch (H-S#77). A recognized authority on the subject who even lectured on dragons at Oxford's Natural History Museum,[5] Tolkien argued that, far from being a worn-out folktale cliché, dragons were eminently fitted to serve as the supreme challenge for any hero. Like the elves, whom he rescued from being treated as dainty flower fairies, Tolkien also redeemed the dragon and re-established it as the greatest of all fantasy monsters. There is a reason that the world's pre-eminent role-playing game, which borrows liberally from folklore, mythology, legendry, and modern fantasy, is named *Dungeons & Dragons* rather than featuring any other monster in the title.

Turning from Tolkien's theory to his practice, we can divide the dragons appearing in his work into essentially three groups. The first, and least important, are those who remain undifferentiated from one another in the background of the stories, although their deeds *en masse* may be of importance: the dragons of the north who destroy the dwarves' settlements in the Grey Mountains (*LotR.* 1124, 1109), the host of dragons who destroyed Gondolin ('for dragons it was that destroyed that city many ages ago' – cf. page 115), those dragons in *Farmer Giles of Ham* who consider 'knights merely mythical' but nonetheless remain in their lairs far from Giles' land, the various lesser moon-dragons mentioned in *Roverandom* who wreak such havoc in the *Father Christmas Letters* when the Man in the Moon is temporarily absent (*Letters from Father Christmas*, 1927 letter), and of course the great host of winged dragons who nearly defeat the Army of the Valar in the final battle that once and for all ends the First Age. Although only described in general terms, these background dragons are important mainly because they provide a context, evidence that the few individual dragons with whom we meet are not the only ones of their kind but typical of the species.[6]

Secondly, there are those dragons who are merely a name (Ancalagon the Black, Scatha the Worm) or deed (the nameless cold-drake – that is, a flameless dragon – that forced Durin's Folk to flee the Grey Mountains) but who are given no line of dialogue or any characteristic that would mark them as individual personalities. While we would naturally like to know more about all of these, even in their abbreviated state they too serve an important purpose in the legendarium. Every collection of real-world myths is of necessity incomplete; there is always some story that has been lost, some figure who is reduced to a bare name or fact (e.g., the Old English 'Earendel', the 'recovery' of whose myth sparked Tolkien's creation of his legendarium). The inclusion of such figures, of obvious significance but shorn of all detail, helps make Tolkien's created myth seem much more like those surviving mythologies painstakingly compiled by generations of scholars. For example, we are fortunate that the story of Wayland the Smith has survived (e.g., in the poem 'The Lay of Völund' [*Völundarqviða*], part of the *Elder Edda*), so that we do not have to puzzle it out from such allusive evidence as the illustration of one scene from the legend on the Franks Casket (cf. the frontispiece to Dronke, *The Poetic Edda*, volume II [1997]), but the once-popular story of his father Wade the Giant has been lost (cf. R. M. Wilson, *The Lost Literature of Medieval England* [1952], pages 19–22). Similarly, we have lost the stories that once explained geographical features such as the chalk-figures now known as the White Horse of Uffington (which may in fact be intended to represent a dragon; cf. Paul Newman, *Lost Gods of Albion* [1997]), the Cerne Giant, or the Long Man of Wilmington, while image and story alike have vanished in the case of other hill-figures such as the Red Horse of Tysoe [destroyed 1800] or the pair of giants known as Gogmagog [destroyed in the 1660s] that once overlooked Plymouth harbour. In a chronicle or condensed account such as those represented by the appendices of *The Lord of the Rings* or the later parts of the 1977

Silmarillion there may be room for only the barest facts, but even here Tolkien makes sure that dragons are represented, including some that would be wholly unknown if we had only the major Silmarillion stories (e.g., the stories of Beren & Lúthien, Túrin, and Tuor) to go by or indeed the main story of *The Lord of the Rings* shorn of its Appendices.

Thirdly and most importantly, we have those dragons who are presented with fully developed personalities, true characters in their respective works: Smaug, Glorund, Chrysophylax Dives (whose name simply means 'Rich Treasure-Guardian'), and, to a lesser extent, the unnamed dragons appearing in 'The Dragon's Visit', 'The Hoard', and *Roverandom*. Of these, Glorund (also known at various times and in various texts as Glórung [1926 'Sketch'], Glómund [1930 *Quenta*], and finally Glaurung ['Grey Annals', published *Silmarillion*]), the Father of Dragons, is the most purely malicious; devious in preferring to inflict misery rather than indulge in straightforward destruction, as when he enspells Túrin and Nienor rather than simply killing them. He is also the most powerful of all Tolkien's dragons, save only Ancalagon the Black (of whom more later), and the one who has the most impact on the mythology, being not only deeply enmeshed in the Túrin story but fighting in two of the six great battles of Beleriand: the Fourth Battle, Dagor Bragollach ('the Battle of Sudden Flame'; *Silm.* Chapter XVIII) and the Fifth Battle, Nirnaeth Arnoediad ('[the Battle of] Unnumbered Tears'; *Silm.* Chapter XX) – incidentally, the only two in this sequence of battles which Morgoth won – as well as an earlier sally when he was 'yet young and scarce half-grown' (*Silm.* 116; cf. also Smaug's having been 'young and tender' at the time of his descent upon Dale, DAA.282). Smaug can destroy a dwarf-kingdom and powerful human city at the same time, while Chrysophylax, though not overbold (FGH 25 & 58), twice routs the knights of the Middle Kingdom ('all the King's horses and all the King's men'; FGH 59 & 72) and the green dragon of 'The Dragon's Visit' handily destroys the entire village of Bimble Bay when provoked, despite the best efforts of its fire brigade.[7] But Glorund is in a different league entirely: he leads balrogs into battle (*Silm.*151), destroys whole armies ('Elves and Men withered before him'; *Silm.*192), lays waste one of the great elven cities of old ('Glaurung came in full fire against the Doors of [Nargothrond], and overthrew them, and passed within'; *Silm.*213), and even commands orc armies and sets himself up as lord over his own realm under Morgoth's overlordship ('he gathered Orcs to him and ruled as a dragon-king'; 1930 *Quenta*, HME IV.129), rather like the much earlier Tevildo in 'The Tale of Tinúviel' and as Thû the Necromancer (i.e., Sauron) does from Wizard's Isle (Tol Sirion) in 'The Lay of Leithian'. And we should remember that these elven armies he opposed were not made up of wood-elves or wild-elves but Eldar; it takes Prince Fingon and a host of elven archers to repel him when he is still young and not yet at his full strength, and at his height he plays a devastating role in the Fourth and Fifth Battles and destroys the mighty Noldor of Nargothrond, a hidden city full of elven warriors, Finrod's men, who are probably the peers of those three Elrond sends out much later against the Nazgûl (Glorfindel and two others; cf. *LotR*.226). In his 'malicious wisdom', piercing eye and hypnotic voice, nigh-unstoppable might, gloating possessiveness over treasure, and vulnerable underbelly, Glorund obviously served as Tolkien's model for all the dragons who came after him, most especially Smaug, the greatest dragon of latter days (*LotR*.1109).

(ii)
Smaug the Magnificent

It is entirely in keeping with the 'Children of Morgoth' theme running throughout *The Hobbit* that, while Tolkien had established in the Silmarillion writings that dragons were created by Morgoth,[8] Smaug by contrast is solitary and independent. Unlike Glorund, he comes alone when he descends upon the Mountain, much as do Chrysophylax Dives in *Farmer Giles of Ham* and the green dragon in 'The Dragon's Visit'. And although like his progenitor Smaug too sets himself up as a king over his usurped halls – cf. 'They shall see me and remember who is King under the Mountain' (page 515; cf. DAA.288) and '"Which king?" said [Bard] . . . "As like as not it is . . . the dragon, the only King under the Mountain we have ever known"' (pages 547–8; cf. DAA.302–3) – his is a kingship in name only. Smaug is never seen commanding armies of orcs or following anybody's command; he has no connection with the other scattered survivors of Morgoth's minions who appear elsewhere in the book, such as the Necromancer, the goblins of the Misty Mountains, or the great bats of Mirkwood who later appear in the Battle of Five Armies (cf. Morgoth's messenger-bats in 'The Lay of Leithian' Canto XI lines 3402–3408a [HME III.278–9] and *Silm*.178).

This represents a different conception not just from the earlier Silmarillion stories, in which all evil things were united under Morgoth's command (although they also sought to advance their own interests, as when Glorund first serves Morgoth's bidding by destroying Nargothrond and then indulges himself by claiming all its treasures), but also from the *Lord of the Rings* era that followed, where once again the various evil races and beings of Middle-earth are falling under the command of (or at least into allegiance with) a Dark Lord: as Gandalf says of Gollum, 'Mordor draws all wicked things, and the Dark Power was bending all its will to gather them there' (*LotR*.72). In short, at the time *The Hobbit* was written (1930–32), Tolkien seems to have conceived of Middle-earth as no longer having a Dark Lord since Morgoth's fall. Morgoth's taint remained, but the evil creatures that once served him no longer had any unified purpose. Not until the creation of the Númenórean material (*The Lost Road* [circa 1936] and 'The Fall of Númenor' [ibid.]; cf. HME V and see also *The Notion Club Papers* [circa 1944–6] in HME IX), shortly before *The Hobbit*'s publication, does the idea of Sauron (whom Tolkien in his 1965 radio interview described as Morgoth's 'petty lieutenant') assuming Morgoth's mantle as a second Dark Lord seem to have arisen. This latter concept obviously underlies *The Lord of the Rings* (as reflected in that work's title), and later as part of his work to reconcile Bilbo's world to Middle-earth as it had developed in the sequel Tolkien deftly re-envisioned *The Hobbit* by presenting Bilbo's adventure as taking place during a lull in Sauron's activities, just before the long-banished Dark Lord (quiescent or incognito since the loss of the One Ring at the beginning of the Age) reasserted himself, dropping his guise as 'the Necromancer' and reclaiming his title as Lord of Mordor (cf. 'The Tale of Years', Appendix B to *The Lord of the Rings*).

In the post-*Lord of the Rings* period Tolkien would even speculate on how Sauron might have made use of Smaug, had the dragon survived to the time of the War of the Ring. Gandalf believed him fully capable of destroying Rivendell and ravaging Eriador, including the Shire ('The Quest of Erebor', *Unfinished Tales* pp. 322 & 326). In fact, Bilbo's sudden mental image while listening to the dwarves' song during the unexpected party –

> . . . in the wood beyond the Water a flame leapt up . . . and he thought of plundering dragons lighting on his quiet hill and setting it all in flames. Then he shuddered . . . (Pryftan Fragment, page 7)

– which almost dissuades him from going on the quest, becomes oddly prophetic when, a quarter-century after writing this passage, Tolkien decided that this is what *would* have come to pass had the hobbit *not* joined Thorin & Company and thus set in motion the chain of events that brought about the dragon's demise before the War of the Ring.[9] This is not to say that Smaug would have been under Sauron's command as Glorund had been under Morgoth's, any more than Shelob or Caradhras or the Watcher in the Water were, merely that Sauron would have been able to stir him up to new villainy that would surpass any destruction he wrought in his youth.

Thus, while clearly greatly influenced by Tolkien's earlier portrayal of Glorund – who in turn had been inspired by what was for Tolkien the quintessential dragon, Fafnir the great, guardian of the Nibelung treasure, a foe killable only by the greatest of all saga-heroes, Sigurd Fáfnirsbane – Smaug is also quite distinct from the great *foalókë* of the First Age.[10] One major cause of this divergence is that with Smaug Tolkien is drawing not just on his own legendry but also on another outside literary source, one which dominated his professional scholarship during the 1930s: *Beowulf*. Tolkien said in his Beowulf essay that there were only three great dragons in Old Norse and Old English literature: the Midgard Serpent (*Miðgarðsormr* or the Middle-earth Wyrm), Fafnir, and Beowulf's dragon ('Beowulf: The Monsters and the Critics', page 9). Fafnir, as we have already seen, became the primary model or inspiration for Glorund. The Midgard Serpent, whom Tolkien described as the fit adversary for the gods themselves rather than merely human heroes (it is foretold in *Völuspá* and the *Prose Edda* that in the battle after the destruction of the sun and moon, Ragnarök, he will slay and be slain by Thor, the greatest warrior of all the gods of Valhalla and most popular of all the Old English and Norse gods in pre-Christian times), found his analogue in Tolkien's legendarium in Ancalagon the Black, the greatest of all the winged dragons, who almost won the day for the Dark Lord in the apocalyptic battle that ended the Elder Days (the Great Battle or War of Wrath; cf. *Silm*.251–2). Dragons play an important role in this 'Battle of Battles' from its very first appearance in the 1926 'Sketch of the Mythology' (HME IV.39); Ancalagon makes his first appearance in the revised (Q II) version of the 1930 *Quenta* (contrast HME IV.160 with IV.157) and also features in such later works as the '(Earliest) Annals of Beleriand' ([circa 1930]; HME IV.309), the '(Later) Annals of Beleriand' ([circa 1937]; HME V.144) and the 'Conclusion' of the 1937 *Quenta Silmarillion* (HME V.329). Ancalagon's mythological significance within the legendarium, and his parallelism to the Midgard Serpent, were both significantly enhanced near the very end of Tolkien's life through a few late [post-1968] references in Tolkien's linguistic writings to 'the prophecy of Andreth' (a wise woman, one of the two main characters in *Athrabeth Finrod ah Andreth*, or 'The Debate of Finrod and Andreth', HME X.301–66), which foretells that 'the Great Dragon, Ancalagon the Black' was to return to fight in the Last Battle (*Dagor Dagorath*) when Morgoth returns from Outside to destroy the world at the end of time, where he was fated to be slain by Túrin, who would return from the dead for that final deed (HME XII.374–5).

The third of these great dragons, Beowulf's bane, dominates the final third of the Old English poem just as Grendel dominates the first third (and just as Smaug dominates the final third of *The Hobbit*, even after his demise). *Beowulf* was a major source for both *The Hobbit* and the Rohan sections of *The Lord of the Rings*, and we need not explore all the parallels here – indeed, a book-length study has been devoted to just the influence of *Beowulf* on *The Hobbit* (Bonniejean Christensen's *Beowulf and The Hobbit: Elegy into Fantasy in J. R. R. Tolkien's Creative Technique* [dissertation, Univ. of S. Calif., 1969]), a whole chapter of which is devoted to elements of Beowulf's dragon adapted to the Smaug chapters.[11] But the way in which Tolkien selected elements that fit what he needed for his story is instructive of his complex relationship with all his outside sources: he was neither a naive reader nor a passive borrower but transformed and remade what he chose to take (consciously or otherwise) from earlier authors.[12] For example, in both *Beowulf* and *The Hobbit* the dragon lairs in a hill or barrow where he guards ancient treasure for centuries, unmolested by any outsider, until stirred up by the theft of a cup from his hoard he embarks on an orgy of destruction which leads to the destruction of a nearby town and shortly thereafter his own death. But the Beowulf-dragon had discovered a hidden hoard and claimed it for his own, while Smaug, like the unnamed dragon in Tolkien's poem 'The Hoard',[13] steals his treasure and kills its previous owner(s); the Beowulf-dragon has as much right to the treasure as anybody, while Smaug's ownership is tainted with blood from the start. So too the dragon's arousal leads to the death of an old king (King Beowulf after half a century leading the Geats, old Thorin after a century as leading Durin's folk in exile and soon after his becoming King under the Mountain) and the emergence of a young warrior who suddenly steps forward to become hero and then king (Wiglaf the Wægmunding, Bard the Bowman). But again the differences are many: Beowulf proudly orders his honor-guard to hold back and not interfere in the fight and is only saved from throwing his life away when one young warrior disobeys his command and rushes to his aid, helping him to kill the dragon; Thorin is surrounded by his closest companions when mortally wounded in one last desperate heroic sally. Beowulf's dying thoughts are of the treasure he has won, but after his death his people bury it with him in his barrow; Thorin's death-speech renounces greed and gold in favor of the virtues Bilbo embodies (see page 679 & DAA.348), and his treasure (*sans* Orcrist and the Arkenstone) is distributed among his people and their neighbors, enriching the land.

Tolkien's debt to *Beowulf*, and the way he drew on (and played off of) the older work when making something new, are best revealed in three specific details. First, the cup which Bilbo steals from Smaug's lair (page 506) is a precise match for the cup (Old English *wæge*) which a thief steals from the dragon's lair in *Beowulf* (line 2216). Just as in *The Hobbit*, the thief in *Beowulf* manages to enter the dragon's lair stealthily, steal the jeweled cup, and escape. Second, whereas Bilbo is 'Mr. Lucky Number', included in the quest specifically so that Thorin and Company will not number thirteen (page 9), Beowulf chooses to confront the dragon with eleven picked warriors, forcing the nameless thief who had stolen the *maðþum-fæt* ('treasure-cup') to guide them to the spot as the thirteenth of their company. Third and perhaps most significantly, Tolkien felt that dragons in medieval literature suffered from being too abstract and not individual enough: '*draconitas* rather than *draco*', as he put it in his Beowulf essay (page 15) – i.e., representing 'dragon-ness' in an allegorical sense rather than just being a 'plain pure fairy-story dragon' (ibid., page

14). Leslie Kordecki, in *Tradition and Development of the Medieval English Dragon* [dissertation, 1980], notes that early medieval stories concerning dragons tend to portray them as living, breathing creatures, whereas later stories often reduce them to mere symbols vanquished by the sign of the cross, and Tolkien himself distinguished in his dragon lecture between 'the symbolic dragon', such as the one fought by St. George, and 'the legendary dragon', which he greatly preferred. Tolkien's allegiance and approval are wholly reserved for 'dragon [as] real worm, with a bestial life and thought of his own' (Beowulf essay, pages 14–15), albeit being willing to allow him to be invested with a certain amount of symbolism as an embodiment of 'malice, greed, destruction' (ibid., page 15). His most significant change that transforms Beowulf's bane into Smaug is granting the latter individuality, indeed a 'rather overwhelming personality'. Unlike the *Beowulf* dragon but like Fafnir, Smaug speaks; indeed, he has a highly individualistic turn of phrase that combines sarcasm with arrogance ('You have nice manners, for a thief and a liar'); his manner of speaking establishes him as an even more striking character than Glorund, one of the most vivid in *The Hobbit* despite the fact that he only appears in two chapters out of nineteen. It's hard to disagree with Christensen's judgment, made nearly four decades ago, that in Smaug Tolkien creates 'a "real" dragon unsurpassed in medieval or modern literature' (Christensen, page 121).

For the present, I defer discussion of Smaug's death until the commentary following Chapter XIII and a look at his hoard until Chapter XIV.

(iii)
'The Only Philological Remark'

In his comments on the proposed blurbs for the dust-jacket of *The Hobbit* that accompanied his 31st August 1937 letter to Allen & Unwin, Tolkien remarked that

> The only philological remark (I think) in *The Hobbit* is on p. 221 (lines 6–7 from end): an odd mythological way of referring to linguistic philosophy, and a point that will (happily) be missed by any who have not read Barfield (few have) and probably by those who have.
>
> —*Letters* p. 22.[14]

In the original manuscript, the specific passage in question reads

> To say that Bilbo's breath was taken away is to say too little. There are no words to express his staggerment. (page 506)

However, in the First Typescript this has been expanded:

> To say that Bilbo's breath was taken away is *no description at all.* There are no words to express his staggerment, *not even in the language of the pithecanthropes which consisted (we are told) largely of exclamations.*
> —typescript page 117, Marq. 1/1/62:3; italics mine.

This reading was preserved in the Second Typescript and represents the text as it was originally submitted to Allen & Unwin. However, the passage changed again in the page proofs, when 'left' was added to the first part of the second sentence to fill up a shortfall in the typeset line and the rest of that sentence cancelled and replaced:

> . . . no words *left* to express his staggerment, *since Men changed the language that they learned of elves in the days when all the world was wonderful.*
> —1/2/2: page 221; italics mine.

This achieves the reading of the first edition (page 221), which has remained unaltered ever since (cf. DAA.271).

Tolkien nowhere elucidates just what the underlying 'point' to which he refers might be, nor why only those familiar with Barfield's thought might grasp it, but his use of the nonstandard 'staggerment' does draw attention to the passage and suggests the essential point: that Bilbo cannot put what he feels at that moment into words. Quite literally, words fail him, falling short of the reality of the experience.[15] Barfield's theory (perhaps best expressed in his books *Poetic Diction* [1928] and *Unancestral Voice* [1965]),[16] that the history of language serves as a record of the evolution of human consciousness, is complex and subtle, and its application to Bilbo's experience here is not immediately obvious. An essential element of Barfield's theory, however, lies in his belief that nineteenth-century philologists such as Max Müller were entirely in error when they supposed that early humans had simple languages with small vocabularies in which all the words represented simple, concrete things, although they could be applied metaphorically to abstract concepts – for example, that the same word might be used for 'wind' and 'breath' (cf. Latin *spiritus*), and by extension figuratively to 'soul' or 'life-force' (modern 'spirit'). Barfield completely disagreed, arguing instead that in such languages a single word expressed a concept which we in later days cannot conceive of as a whole: hence in the more modern form of that language the 'breath of life' becomes *respiration*, the feeling of an outside force entering you becomes *inspiration*, the life-force within becomes *spirit*, and so forth, all thought of as distinct and separate things, whereas in the earlier language the ancestor-word had meant all these and more. Or, to pick another example, the O.E. word *mōd* (the direct ancestor of our modern word *mood*) puzzles most students who try to learn Old English, because it seems to mean so many different things: heart, mind, spirit, temper, courage, arrogance, pride (cf. Clark Hall, *A Concise Anglo-Saxon Dictionary* [4th ed., 1962], page 239). Thus in his translation of a passage from 'The Battle of Maldon' in *The Homecoming of Beorhtnoth Beorhthelm's Son*, Tolkien translates *mōd* as 'spirit', while in the essay 'Ofermod' which accompanies his verse-play he translated the compound *ofer-mōd* not as 'too much spirit' but as 'overmastering pride' or 'overboldness' (the latter a fair approximation of the original meaning of Tolkien's own surname, we might note, i.e. *tollkühn* = 'foolhardy' [*Letters* p. 218] or 'rashbold' [*The Notion Club Papers*, HME IX.151]).

While the 'ancient semantic unity' Barfield postulates may never have existed – after all, anyone learning a foreign language soon discovers that a similar phenomenon exists whenever we try to translate one language into another; we find some word which can be approximated by a cluster of words in one language but not exactly matched to any one word, since the concept it reflects doesn't exist as a whole in the other language (hence the popularity of the modern American word 'okay', which has been adopted into daily use in a number of unrelated languages around the world, such as Japanese) – Tolkien was wholly sympathetic at any rate to the idea that ancient languages could express more, in fewer words compact with meaning, than modern-day tongues. Such a concept fit in perfectly with his legendarium, where the Elven languages of Sindarin and Quenya are semantically rich despite having a relatively small recorded vocabulary (something already true of them in their earliest forms, as Gnomish and Qenya respectively). Tolkien's respect and admiration for the past meant he was wholly free of what Lewis called 'chronological snobbery';[17] he takes pains, for example, in 'On Fairy-Stories' to defend so-called 'primitive' peoples (footnote to OFS.27; see also OFS.39) and revolutionized *Beowulf* criticism by preferring and defending the aesthetic choices and literary judgments of the author, who had lived a thousand years or more before, above those of the critics of his own day ('Beowulf: The Monsters and the Critics'). Furthermore, from a very early stage of the legendarium the idea was already ensconced that humans were originally without language and learned how to speak from the elves:

> At the rising of the first Sun the younger children of earth [= humans] awoke in the far East . . . They meet Ilkorindi [Dark-Elves] and learn speech and other things of them, and become great friends of the Eldalië.
>
> —1926 'Sketch of the Mythology' (HME IV.20).

Similar statements appear in the 1930 *Quenta* (HME IV.99) and 1937 *Quenta Silmarillion* (HME V.246), and there seems little doubt that this is the 'mythological way' to which Tolkien refers in his letter to Allen & Unwin: like his later conception of the ents (*LotR*.489 & 494),[18] Tolkien initially conceived of humans as being without speech until they learned language from the elves (whose own name for themselves, Quendi, means simply 'the Speakers' – *LotR*.1171). And that language, once they acquired it, was not halting or primitive but full of meaning, subtlety, and beauty.

Finally, there is Tolkien's rather surprising use, in the typescript version of this passage, of the precise scientific technical name *pithecanthropus*. The term was first proposed by Ernst Haeckel, a disciple of Darwin, in 1866, just seven years after the publication of *On the Origin of Species* [1859]. Haeckel theorized that, if humans and apes truly shared a common ancestor, then there must once have existed an ancestral form which would combine human and ape characteristics, a 'missing link' which he called *pithecanthropus alulus*: 'speechless ape-man'. Several decades later, when Eugène Dubois discovered fossils of early humans that seemed to match Haeckel's prediction, he named his discovery *pithecanthropus erectus* ('upright ape-man' [1894]) – more popularly known as 'Java Man'. Today, Dubois' discovery is classified with 'Peking Man' [discovered in 1928ff] as *homo erectus*, along with the recently discovered hobbit-sized *homo floresiensis*. Significantly, not only is Tolkien's terminology correct in the contemporary usage of the time, but the skepticism expressed by his parenthetical '*which consisted (we are told) largely of exclamations*' makes it clear that he is well aware of the second part of Haeckel's proposed name, *alulus* or without language. Rather than enter into the paleoanthropological debate on just when humans acquired language (cf. for example Johanson & Edgar, *From Lucy to Language* [1996], page 106), Tolkien provided a mythological answer within his subcreated world, of mankind born mute (*alulus*) but then acquiring full-fledged language from our forerunners and sibling-race, the Elder Children or elves.

NOTES

1 This would have been about 1899, the year before Tolkien began his formal education at King Edward's School; by this time he had already been able to read and write for about three years, or since the age of four (Carpenter, page 21). Tolkien gave another account of this story a decade later in his piece 'Tolkien on Tolkien' printed in the October 1966 Tolkien issue of the magazine *Diplomat*: 'Somewhere about six years old I tried to write some verses on a *dragon* about which I now remember nothing except that it contained the expression a *green great dragon* and that I remained puzzled for a very long time at being told that this should be *great green*' (*Diplomat*, page 39; reprinted in *Letters* p. 221).

The next story we know of that Tolkien wrote after this piece of lost juvenilia, about fifteen years later [circa 1914], was 'The Story of Kullervo',† a William Morris-style adaptation from the *Kalevala*, which strongly influenced his slightly later Túrin story [circa 1919] written for

The Book of Lost Tales. While the original Finnish story has no dragon, Túrin's story featured one so prominently that it shared the title with the hero: 'Turambar and the Foalókë' (that is, Túrin and the Dragon).

In any case, by drawing his attention to the phenomenon known as the hierarchy of adjectives, the chance phrase 'green great dragon' seems to have played a role in Tolkien's becoming aware of the deep structure of his own language and helped him discover his vocation as a philologist. For more on hierarchy of adjectives, and why for example an adjective of colour (like 'green') idiomatically follows an adjective of size (like 'great') in English, see Jose A. Carillo's article 'The hierarchy of adjectives', available online at http://www.manilatimes.net/national/2003/may/21/top-stories/20030521top16.htm.

† It is unclear whether 'The Story of Kullervo' predates or postdates the Eärendel poems; the two seem to have been essentially contemporaneous, two different expressions of the same creative impulse (see Carpenter pages 71–3, BLT II.267, and John Garth's *Tolkien and the Great War* [2003] page 45).

2 For more on dragons in modern fantasy, and Tolkien's influence on the way they are depicted, see my article 'Dragons of Legend' in the June 1996 issue of *Dragon* magazine (*Dragon* #230). For more on dragons in children's literature from the 1890s to the 1950s, see Christina Scull's 'Dragons from Andrew Lang's retelling of Sigurd to Tolkien's Chrysophylax' in *Leaves from the Tree: J.R.R. Tolkien's Shorter Fiction* [1991]. For more on Tolkien's borrowing from, and transformation of, dragons in Old Norse and Old English literature and lore, see Jonathan Evans' 'The Dragon-Lore of Middle-earth: Tolkien and Old English and Old Norse Tradition', in *J.R.R. Tolkien and His Literary Resonances*, ed. George Clark & Daniel Timmons [2000]. Of particular note is Evans' observation that

> In Tolkien's Middle-earth the dragon-lore of our own Middle Ages is analyzed into its elementary components, rationalized and reconstituted, and then reassembled to fit the larger thematic purposes of Tolkien's grand narrative design. Tolkien treated the disjointed inferences and disparate motifs found in medieval literature as if they were the *disjecta membra* [i.e., scattered fragments] of a once-unified whole – that is, as if there really were a coherent underlying medieval conception of the dragon from which all scattered references drew information. This is in fact a fiction . . . an example of what Shippey has described as the reconstruction of a hypothetical . . . 'asterisk reality' that characterizes Tolkien's vision and method. It is analogous to, and for Tolkien part and parcel of, comparative historical linguistic reconstruction . . . of lost . . . languages and thus lost worlds . . . The dragon-lore embedded in the medieval literature of . . . our world . . . is *not* coherent: it springs from sources as diverse as medieval European geography, ancient Semitic and Hellenistic cosmology and cosmogony, Roman

> mythology and popular legend, Latin hagiography, and Germanic legend and folklore.
>
> —Evans, in Clark & Timmons, pages 27–8.

3 Tolkien seems to have had *The Hobbit* in mind when drafting this discussion of dragons in 'On Fairy-Stories', since part of what he says in the essay strongly parallels a passage in *The Hobbit* that goes all the way back to the Pryftan Fragment. Compare Tolkien's words in OFS

> I desired dragons with a profound desire. Of course, I in my timid body did not wish to have them in the neighbourhood, intruding into my relatively safe world, in which it was, for instance, possible to read stories in peace of mind, free from fear. But the world that contained even the imagination of Fáfnir was richer and more beautiful, at whatever cost of peril. The dweller in the quiet and fertile plains may hear of the tormented hills and the unharvested sea and long for them in his heart. For the heart is hard though the body be soft. (OFS.40)

with Bilbo's thoughts in the Pryftan Fragment:

> . . . something Tookish awoke within him, and he wished to go and see the great mountains and the seas, the pine trees and the waterfalls, and explore the caves and wear a sword instead of a walking stick. He looked out of the window. The stars were out in a dark sky above the trees. He thought of the jewels of the dwarves shining in dark caves. Then in the wood beyond the Water a flame leapt up – somebody lighting a wood fire probably – and he thought of plundering dragons lighting on his quiet hill and setting it all in flames. Then he shuddered, and quite suddenly he was plain Mr. Baggins of Bag-end Under-Hill again (page 7; cf. DAA.45–6 for the final published text).

4 Carpenter, page 38. Carpenter's source seems to have been Tolkien's 1938 Christmas Dragon lecture (see Note 5 below), in which as an aside Tolkien says:

> I [*added*: once as a boy] found a saurian jaw myself with nasty teeth at Lyme Regis – and thought I had stumbled on a bit of petrified dragon.†
>
> —Ms. Tolk. A 61. fols. 98–125.

Carpenter dates this as having occurred on a summer holiday with Father Francis after Mabel Tolkien's death, so probably in the summer of 1905, summer 1906, or summer 1907, when Tolkien was between thirteen and fifteen years old. However, this seems rather old for literal belief in dragons, especially given Tolkien's stated annoyance at the attempts during his childhood of condescending adults to conflate prehistoric animals with dragons (Note D, OFS.69). It seems likely, therefore, that the episode Tolkien recalls dates from an earlier unrecorded visit during his mother's lifetime – Hammond & Scull, for example, reproduce a seaside watercolour by Tolkien which they tentatively date to 1902, when Tolkien was only ten (*Artist & Illustrator*, pages 11 & 13), and Judith Priestman, in the centenary Bodleian catalogue, reproduces a two-page spread from the same sketchbook entitled 'Sea Weeds and Star Fishes' (*Life and Legend*, pages 12–13). Priestman does not date the piece, but places it between items from 1896 and 1900; in any case it was clearly painted by a child, not a teen. Hammond & Scull suggest the watercolour they reproduce might have been painted at Bournemouth or Poole, which are about forty miles east of Lyme Regis; all three are on the south English coast, a little over 200 miles south of Birmingham, where Tolkien was living at the time. At any rate, Tolkien's recollection about finding the fossil and the early watercolours taken together show that a visit to Lyme Regis during his mother's lifetime is certainly possible.

Lyme Regis is, incidentally, famous for its fossil finds, especially ichthyosaurs (which is probably what young JRRT found), plesiosaurs, and pterodactyls, many of which were discovered by amateur fossil-hunters in the early 1800s. For the role which actual fossils may have played in the rise of dragon-myths and legends of 'giants in the earth', see Simpson, *British Dragons*, pages 20–22.

†A faint echo of this 'bit of petrified dragon' might perhaps be found in the comment, added in the First Typescript of this chapter, that Smaug 'went back to his golden couch to sleep – and to gather new strength. He would not forget or forgive the theft, *not if a thousand years turned him to smouldering stone*, but he could afford to wait. Slow and silent he crept back to his lair and half closed his eyes' (typescript page 119, Marq. 1/1/62:5; compare page 508).

5 See Tolkien's 16th December 1937 letter to Stanley Unwin (*Letters* pp. 27 & 435). Rather than a learned disquisition, this was a light-hearted slide-show for children, where Tolkien showed slides of dinosaurs† and of dragons, including his own dragon-paintings such as 'Conversation with Smaug' (Plate XI [top]), of which he said 'This picture was made by my friend Mr Baggins or from his description . . . it shows a powerful lot of treasure'. Nonetheless, in the course of his lecture he makes a number of interesting points highly revealing of his personal dragon-lore. He describes the dragon as 'a very special creature: <u>draco fabulosus europaeus</u>, the "European fabulous dragon"', which he further divides into two kinds, '<u>repus</u> or creeping' and '<u>alatus</u> or winged'; clearly, Glorund and Fafnir would belong to the former category, while Smaug is most definitely in the latter.†† In addition to alluding to several famous dragon stories, such as Thora's dragon (from the legend of Ragnarr Shaggybreeks)††† and Thor's encounter with the *Miðgarðsormr* ('the Dragon of the Island-earth'), he observes of the dragon that 'he is largely man-made, and therefore very dangerous' and gives the admonition 'If you ever come across a dragon's egg, don't encourage it.' He describes dragons as 'legendary creatures founded on serpent and lizard', unlike the dinosaurs ('No one I suppose can tell . . . how long strange obsolete creatures may have survived lurking in odd corners. But even such accidents cannot affect the fact that the Dinosaurs passed away infinitely long before the adventures of Men began'). Of Smaug in particular he says 'A dragon made a desert. He

rejoiced in destruction' (see 'The Desolation of the Dragon' following Chapter XI).

Regarding encounters with dragons, Tolkien warns that a dragon will first try to catch your eye and then get your name in order to curse you before he dies with 'evil magic'; Smaug of course tries to do both, and Glorund succeeds on both counts, with disastrous results for the would-be dragon-slayer. Tolkien gives as a maxim that the right place to look for a dragon is in a burial mound, no doubt, basing this rule upon Beowulf's dragon, but Chrysophylax Dives is the only dragon of his known to me who actually follows this rule. He is emphatic that dragon-slaying is a solitary art, observing that 'It was the function of dragons to tax the skill of heroes, and still more to tax other things, especially courage [*added*: and fortune].' Armies, he maintains, are no use at all, nor would modern weaponry avail: '. . . machine-gun bullets are usually no more troublesome to them than a cloud of gnats; armies cannot overcome them; poison gas is a sweet breath to them (they invented it); bombs are their amusement'. Instead, 'Dragons can only be defeated by brave men – usually alone. Sometimes a faithful friend may help, but it is rare: friends have a way of deserting you when [you are faced >] a dragon comes'; this is certainly the experience of Beowulf and of Túrin. Finally, 'Dragons are the final test of heroes', requiring 'luck (or grace) . . . a blessing on your hand and heart'.

— Ms Tolkien A61 e., fols. 98–125.

†Stegosaur, brontosaurus ('only recently named'), pteranodon, triceratops ('a good name for a terrible creature'), and iguanodon, among others, including one slide he called 'two jolly dinosaurs at play'.

††Tolkien elsewhere notes that he is deliberately leaving out Chinese dragons, who are quite distinct from the European tradition, and symbolic dragons, such as St. George's dragon, although he notes that the latter appears on the English money of the time (the gold sovereign).

†††This is the same Ragnar Lodbrok one of whose sons was named Beorn (see page 282) and whose son Ivarr the Boneless led the viking invasion of England. In brief, Thora was given a dragon's egg or hatchling which grew up to be so fiercely protective of her that it endangered the whole area; Ragnar was the brave and clever hero who devised a scheme for challenging and defeating the dragon, thus winning her hand.

6 Two of these cases – e.g., in the attacks on Gondolin and on the host of the Valar – have additional significance because they depict dragons acting in groups. Tolkien is almost unique among fantasy authors in showing dragons working in unison towards some goal; the great legends always depicted them as solitary beasts, and most later authors have followed suit. The only post-Tolkien modern fantasy of note to deal with dragons *en masse* are the 'Dragonriders of Pern' series by Anne McCaffrey [1968ff] and the 'Dragonlance' novels by Margaret Weis & Tracy Hickman, et al. [1984ff]. Even here, the McCaffrey novels are not true fantasy but romance novels given fantasy trappings and a science-

fiction rationale: later books in the series reveal that the 'dragons' are in fact creatures genetically engineered by space colonists to fulfill a specific role in that planetary ecosystem. By contrast, the Dragonlance novels, although describing considerable numbers of dragons over the course of the series, only very rarely depict more than one dragon at a time; scenes in which dragons interact with each other are extremely rare. As a result, in modern fantasy dragons remain pre-eminently solitary creatures.

7 In the original [1937] version of this poem, the destruction is complete; in the version Tolkien re-wrote [circa 1961] for possible inclusion in *The Adventures of Tom Bombadil* the village's sole survivor (Miss Biggins) ambushes and slays the dragon. Even this modern-day dragon is not the last of his kind, however; the final lines of the original poem describe how, having destroyed the town, he flies back to his own land of Finis-Terre (or, as Dunsany liked to call it, the World's End):

Far over the sea he saw the peaks
round his own land ranging . . .
And the moon shone through his green wings
the night winds beating,
And he flew back over the dappled sea
to a green dragons' meeting.

It may be that in this poem Tolkien finally told the story of the 'green great dragon' he had begun circa 1899.

Note that Tolkien is explicit that dragons survived the Third Age (*Letters* p. 177); in the account of the Last Battle that overthrew Morgoth in the 1926 'Sketch of the Mythology', he is careful to include the detail that two (presumably one male and the other female, with this latter being the only female dragon to appear anywhere in Tolkien's work) escaped the slaughter to propagate their kind (HME IV.39). In the Father Christmas Letters, he describes the modern-day dragons on the moon who cause eclipses (*Letters from Father Christmas*, 1927 letter), and in his 1937 Dragon Lecture he calls the moon 'a refuge of dragons' and showed a slide of one of the Roverandom pictures (also from 1927), describing his own white dragon (called the Great White Dragon of the Moon in *Roverandom*) as 'a Saxon White Dragon that escaped from the Welsh borders† a long while ago.' Tolkien is here probably drawing on the old tradition, most notably embodied in Ariosto's *Orlando Furioso* [1516], that the moon is the home of lost things and hence an appropriate retreat for mythological monsters lost from the world before modern times, such as dragons.

†Chrysophylax's home in *Farmer Giles*, we should note – cf. *Letters* page 130.

8 Probably, as Paul Kocher speculated long ago (*A Reader's Guide to The Silmarillion* [1980], page 271), Morgoth created dragons from balrogs – who are, after all, fire demons – by a process similar to that which created the orcs; see page 138 and the section of *Morgoth's Ring* entitled 'Myths Transformed' (HME X). Particularly significant in this context

is the description in 'The Fall of Gondolin' of dragon-forms 'given hearts and spirits of blazing fire' (BLT II.170).

9 For another 'prophecy' in *The Hobbit* that does not come to pass, see Smaug's dreams of being slain by Bilbo (page 507 & Text Note 17 on page 519). This example is the exact obverse of Bilbo's sudden vision while sitting safely at home in the Shire, since at the time it was written it foretold what Tolkien expected to happen in the next chapters. When he actually came to write them the story shifted in unexpected directions, leaving the dragon's prophetic dream symbolically significant but no longer literally true.

10 Tolkien himself acknowledges both Smaug's affinities to Fafnir and his distinctiveness in his 1965 radio interview with Denys Gueroult:

> DG: I suppose Smaug might be interpreted as being a sort of Fafnir, is he?
>
> JRRT: Oh yes, very much so. Except no, Fafnir was a human or humanoid being who took this form, whereas Smaug is just pure intelligent lizard.

It should be noted that, unlike Sigurd's dragon, there is never any hint in *Beowulf* that its nameless dragon has ever been anything other than a 'real worm, with a bestial life and thought of his own . . . a foe more evil than any human enemy' (Beowulf essay, pages 14–15).

11 Christensen's dissertation is mainly important because one section from it was revised and published separately as the article 'Gollum's Character Transformation in *The Hobbit*', which appeared in *A Tolkien Compass*, ed. Jared Lobdell [1975], pages 9–28. A careful analysis of the changes Tolkien made between the first and second editions of *The Hobbit* (also covered in Part Four of this book), it gives the variant texts in parallel passages and remains one of the dozen or so best essays ever written on Tolkien's work.

For another detailed study of *Beowulf*'s influence on *The Hobbit*, see Roberta Albrecht Adams' *Gollum and Grendel as Cain's Kinsmen* (M.A. thesis, Stetson Univ., 1978).

12 A good example of this is the phrase 'the lord of the rings', which appears in William Morris's *The Tale of Beowulf* (tr. Wm Morris & A. J. Wyatt, Kelmscott Press [1895], page 82) as a translation of '*hringa fengel*' (*Beowulf*, line 2345b), a phrase usually translated as 'the prince of rings' – that is, King Beowulf himself as 'ring-giver' or distributor of treasure to his followers. We know Tolkien read, and disliked, Morris's translation (cf. his slighting reference to it in passing in the draft of his Beowulf essay given in Drout, *Beowulf and the Critics* [2002], page 97) – not surprising, given that Tolkien had probably already read *Beowulf* in the original before coming to Morris's deliberately archaic, not to say idiosyncratic, translation – and it is certainly possible that this phrase popped back into Tolkien's mind a quarter-century later when he was casting about for a suitable title to 'The New Hobbit'.

13 This poem was in existence by at least 1923, when it was published in the *Gryphon*, a Leeds University literary magazine. A revised version appeared in *The Oxford Magazine* in 1937 (only a month after 'The Dragon's Visit' had appeared in the same journal) and, further revised, was collected in *The Adventures of Tom Bombadil* [1962] as 'The Hoard' (poem #14); the original version can be found in *The Annotated Hobbit* (DAA.335–7). The original title, 'Iúmonna Gold Galdre Bewunden' (loosely 'The gold of men of old time was wound about with enchantment'), comes from line 3052 in *Beowulf* near the poem's end. The poem's links with *Beowulf* are strengthened by the fact that Tolkien included the entire poem in early drafts of his Beowulf essay (cf. Drout, *Beowulf and the Critics*, pages 56–8 and 199–205), along with C. S. Lewis's 'The Northern Dragon',† which had obviously been inspired by Tolkien's poem. Lewis's poem is given the title 'Atol inwit gæst' ['The Terrible Unwanted Guest'; *Beowulf* line 2670a] in the second draft of Tolkien's essay (see Drout pages 110–14), but it is unclear whether this title is assigned by Tolkien or Lewis's own. A slightly revised version is reprinted under the title 'The Dragon Speaks' in *Poems*, ed. Walter Hooper [1964], pages 92–3, but again it is unclear whether this title is Lewis's or provided by the editor.

† This title appears to be Drout's, taken from the chapter of Lewis's book in which the poem first appeared (*The Pilgrim's Regress* [1933], Book Ten, Chapter VIII).

14 Tolkien here was objecting to two sentences in the proposed blurb that compared his work to that of Lewis Carroll ('The birth of *The Hobbit* recalls very strongly that of *Alice in Wonderland*. Here again a professor of an abstruse subject is at play'), pointing out among other things that Rev. Charles Dodgson, the mathematics lecturer who wrote under the pen name of Carroll, never reached his own rank of professor. More importantly, Tolkien maintained that 'I do not profess an "abstruse" subject [e.g., Old English] . . . Some folk may think so, but I do not like encouraging them'. He did however concede that philology, which he called 'my real professional bag of tricks', might perhaps be 'more comparable to Dodgson's maths.' If so, then any parallel would lie in 'the fact that both these technical subjects in any overt form are absent' (*Letters* pp. 21–2). See Note 30, pp. 64–5.

15 Although the text of the rest of this paragraph gives a fair idea of how deeply Bilbo is moved by the sight, and hints at the enchantment that almost falls upon him (especially when compared with the dwarves' similar but even stronger reaction to the same sight a few chapters later; cf. page 580 & DAA.295–6). Note the lack of punctuation in the original text ('the spendour the lust the glory') where Tolkien piles on words to suggest aspects of the irreproducible experience:

> He had heard tell and sing of dragon-hoards before, but the splendour the lust the glory of such treasure had never before come home to him. His heart was filled and pierced with the desire of dwarves – and he gazed, almost forgetting the frightful guardian, at the gold,

> gazed and gazed for what seemed ages, before drawn almost against his will he stole from the shadow of the door, across the floor, to the nearest edge of the mound of treasure.

16 At the time Tolkien wrote *The Hobbit*, Barfield had published three books: *The Silver Trumpet* [1925], *History in English Words* [1926], and *Poetic Diction: A Study in Meaning* [1928]. We know that Tolkien read, and was deeply impressed by, *Poetic Diction*, since Lewis reported to Barfield:

> You might like to know that when Tolkien dined with me the other night he said *à propos* of something quite different that your conception of the ancient semantic unity had modified his whole outlook and that he was always just going to say something in a lecture when your conception stopped him in time. 'It is one of those things,' he said 'that when you've once seen it there are all sorts of things you can never say again.'
>
> —CSL to OB [date unknown],
> quoted in Carpenter, *The Inklings* [1978], page 42.

Based on this, Verlyn Flieger has eloquently argued that Barfield was a greater influence on Tolkien than any other writer excepting perhaps the *Beowulf*-poet (*Splintered Light: Logos and Language in Tolkien's World* [1983, rev. ed. 2002], page xxi). This is probably overstating the case, since there seems to be no great break or change in the late 1920s in the ongoing evolution of either Tolkien's invented languages nor in the myths expressed in the Silmarillion tradition of his legendarium (i.e., between the 1926 'Sketch of the Mythology' and the alliterative lays on the one hand and the 1930 *Quenta*, the Annals, and the 1937 *Quenta Silmarillion* on the other). It might be better to say that, like many other readers of Barfield, Tolkien found Barfield's ideas challenged his preconceptions and forced him to rethink the grounds upon which he based his ideas. As a result, Tolkien's work did not become Barfieldian but even more Tolkienesque, a process that was already a constant feature (indeed a hallmark) of the legendarium.

As for the other two books, we know that shortly before Tolkien submitted *The Hobbit* to Allen & Unwin, Lewis loaned him Barfield's little children's story *The Silver Trumpet*, which Tolkien read to his children to an enthusiastic reception – so much so that, when he had finished, the younger Tolkiens are said to have protested: 'You're not going to give it back to Mr. Lewis, are you?' (CSL to OB, June 28th 1936; *The Collected Letters of C. S. Lewis*, vol. II [2004], page 198).

By contrast, *History in English Words* lays out the groundwork and provides a good deal of the proofs for the ideas expressed in *Poetic Diction*. There is no direct evidence that Tolkien read this book, but it seems very likely; it may even have inspired the abortive Tolkien-Lewis collaboration *Language and Human Nature*, which Tolkien described as being 'on "Language" (Nature, Origins, Functions)' (*Letters* pp. 105 & 440); this project was first mooted in 1944 and abandoned circa 1949–50 (cf. *Letters of C. S. Lewis*, revised edition [1988], page 399).

In any case, *History in English Words* certainly served as the model of Lewis's *Studies in Words* [1960], a book which Tolkien greatly disliked.

Finally, we must not forget that Tolkien actually knew Barfield, although not well. The two men had first met through their mutual friend Lewis sometime in the late 1920s, when the Barfields were living in the village of Long Crendon a few miles from Lewis's home at the Kilns (in fact, near Thame and Worminghall, the sites where Tolkien set his Oxfordshire story, *Farmer Giles of Ham*), and both were founding members of the Inklings (circa 1933–34), although having by that time joined his family firm of solicitors (Barfield & Barfield) in London, Barfield could only rarely attend meetings. Tolkien particularly admired Barfield's knack of puncturing Lewis at his most dogmatic (cf. *Letters* p. 103), and felt that of all the memoirs of their joint friend in *Light on C.S. Lewis* [1965] that 'Barfield who knew him longest . . . gets nearest to the central point' (*Letters* p. 363).

17 One side effect of Barfield's theory is that it counters the assumption, implicit in almost all discussions of the past, that people who lived a long time ago were somehow stupider than those of us fortunate enough to live in the present day. The phrase 'chronological snobbery' represents C.S. Lewis's coinage to express this attitude and neatly encapsulates the concept he took from Barfield (cf. *Surprised by Joy: The Shape of My Early Life* [1955], page 208).

18 Barfield many also have contributed to the inspiration for Entish with his description in *Poetic Diction* of 'the "holophrase", or long, rambling conglomeration of sound and meaning, which is found among primitive and otherwise almost wordless peoples.' In the same context, he also mentions 'languages in which there are words for "gum-tree", "wattle-tree", etc., but none for "tree"' (*Poetic Diction*, 3rd ed. [1973], page 83). In its love of specificity over common nouns and its additive, repetitive word-building and syntax, Entish sounds very like a language of the type Barfield describes, except that Tolkien removes any pejorative sense of the language's being 'primitive' (it has, after all, been preserved and presumably developed over more than seven thousand years by the time Merry and Pippin hear Treebeard and the other ents use it).

Chapter XIII

THE DEATH OF SMAUG

As before, this chapter break was added at the time Tolkien created the First Typescript and divided the text of the original continuous manuscript into the familiar chapters of the published book. In this particular case, the new chapter began with what had been the third paragraph on Ms. page 153 (Marq. 1/1/15:1); between this and the preceding paragraph Tolkien inserted, in pencil, the directions:

Here insert 'Not at home'   Ch. Fire and Water

Thus, the decision to flip what are now chapters XIV ('Fire and Water') and XIII ('Not at Home') – or XIII ('Death of Smaug') and XIV ('While the Dragon's Away'), respectively, in the original draft and this edition – was made at the same time that Tolkien determined where the chapter breaks would fall.

This chapter also marks the spot where, later, the First Typescript broke off and the point to which Tolkien returned when he began the Third Phase drafting that completed the work; see page 638.

The men of the Lake-town were [sitting on the quays >] mostly indoors for the wind was from the North and chill, but some were walking on the quays, and watching as they were fond of doing the stars shine forth from the smooth patches of Lake as they opened in the sky.

From their town the Lonely Mountain was screened by the low hills at the far end of the lake, through a gap in which the R. Running came down from the North. Only its highest peak could they see and they looked seldom at it, for it was ominous and drear even in the morning light. Now it was lost and gone, blotted in the dark.[TN1]

Suddenly it flickered back to view, a brief glow touched it and faded. 'Look!' said one 'the lights again. Last night [they > I >] the watchmen saw them start and fade from midnight till dawn.[TN2] Something is happening up there.'

'Perhaps the King under the Mountain is forging gold' said another. 'It is long since he went North. It is time the songs began to prove themselves again.'

'Which king?' said another with a surly voice.[TN3] 'As like as not it is the marauding fire of the dragon – the only K. under the Mountain we have ever known.'

'You are always foreboding gloomy things' said the others 'from floods[TN4] to poisoned fish' they said. 'Think of something cheerful.'

Then suddenly a great light appeared red and golden in the low place in the hills [> the northern end of the lake turned golden]. 'The king beneath the Mountain' they shouted. '"[The rivers golden run >] His wealth is like the sun, his silver like a fountain. [his gold like rivers run >] his rivers golden run."[TN5] The river is running gold from the mountain' they cried, and everywhere windows opened and feet were hurrying. There was tremendous excitement and enthusiasm. But the surly fellow ran hot foot to the master. 'The dragon is coming or I am a fool' he cried: 'cut the bridges; to arms to arms!'

[So it was that >] The warning trumpets were sounded and the enthusiasm died away. So it was that the dragon did not find them quite unprepared. Before long they could see him as a spark of fire speeding towards them, and not the most foolish doubted that the prophecies had gone somewhat wrong. Still they had a little time. Every vessel in the town was filled with water; every warrior armed, every arrow ready and the bridges[TN6] to the land were cast down and destroyed before the roar of Smaug's terrible approach grew loud, [and the trees by the shore were >] and the lake rippled [red as] fire beneath his coming.

Amid the shrieks and wailing and the shouts of men he came over them, swept towards the bridges, and was foiled. The bridges were gone and his enemies were on an island in deep water – too deep and dark and cool for his liking: If he plunged therein a vapour and a steam wd rise enough to cover all the land with a mist for days, but the lake was mightier than he, it would quench him before he could pass through.

Roaring he swept by on the town. A hail of dark arrows swept up and snapped and rattled on his scales and jewels and their shafts fell back burning and hissing in the lake. No fireworks you ever imagined equalled the sight that night. Now the dragon's wrath blazed to its height till he was blind and mad with it. He circled high in the air lighting all the lake; and the trees by the shore shone like copper and like blood with many [*added*: <dancing>] black shadows at the feet. Now he swooped through the arrow storm taking no heed [for >] to turn his scales towards his foes, seeking only to set their town a blaze. Fire leapt from thatched roofs and wooden beams [But being <hurriedly> >] drenched though they had been with water. Water was flung by hundreds of hands wherever a spark appeared. Back swooped the dragon. A swirl of his tail and the roof of the Great House crumbled; fire unquenchable leapt up. Another swoop and more house[s] [leapt in >] sprang afire or fell. [Men were taking to boats or leaping into the water >] Men were leaping into the water on every side; women and children were being huddled into <?crowded> boats in the market-pool. [Soon all >] Weapons were flung down. The Master himself was <?brung> to his gilded boat. Soon all the town would b<e> burned down to the lake. That was the dragon's hope. They could stay in the boats till they starved, let them try to get to land and he would see. Soon he would set all the shoreland woods ablaze and wither every field and pasture. Just now he was enjoying such sport in town-baiting as he had not had for years.

Still a company of archers held their ground. Their captain was the surly man whose friends accused him of prophesying floods and poisoned fish. But [his >] Bard was his real name, a descendant as tales said of Girion lord of Dale. He shot with a great bow till all but one arrow was spent. The flames were near him, his companions were fleeing. He bent the bow for the last time.

'Arrow' he said ' – black arrow I have saved you to the last. I <ha>d you [from] my father and he from old. If ever you came from the forges of the true king of the Mountain go now and speed well.'[TN7] The dragon swooped once more lower than ever.[TN8] The great bow twanged. The black arrow sped [straight >] straight for the hollow by the left breast where his foreleg was flung wide. In it smote and vanished. barb shaft and feather. With a shriek that [cracked >] deafened men, felled stars and split stonc[TN9] the Dragon [> Smaug] shot into the air, turned over, and crashed down from a height in ruin. Full upon the town he fell. His last throes splintered it to gledes[TN10] and sparks. The lake roared in. A vast steam leapt up white into the sudden dark. And that was the end of Smaug and Esgaroth[TN11] and Bard.

The text breaks off here, about three-quarters of the way down the page (manuscript page 155; Marq. 1/1/15:3), indicating a pause in the composition. The last two words of this paragraph ('and Bard') were cancelled and replaced by 'but not of Bard'. Probably at the same time, the rest of the manuscript page was filled with the following paragraph, which was marked for insertion before the preceding paragraph (that is, between 'He bent his bow for the last time' and '"Arrow" he said'):

Suddenly out of the dark something fluttered to his shoulder – he started, but it was an old thrush and it perched by his shoulder and it brought him news. Marvelling he found he could understand its tongue – for he was of the Dale race. 'Wait wait' it said 'the moon is rising. Look for the hollow of the left breast as he flies and turns above you.' The[n] Bard drew his last arrow from his quiver. The dragon was circling back, and the moon rose above the eastern shore and silvered his great wings.

This addition clearly dates from the same time as the extended rider (manuscript page 151b) given on page 513, inserted into the end of the preceding chapter, where the old thrush is given a larger role in the story than simply being a passive signifier that they have found the right snail-stone marking the Secret Door.

The next page following the death of Smaug (manuscript page 156; Marq. 1/1/14:4) is marked by somewhat neater writing and also slightly more yellowed paper, indicating that the next thirteen pages probably came from a similar but slightly different batch of unused students' papers. Tolkien also starts further down the page than usual on this new sheet, leaving roughly enough room blank to have written another paragraph there, though in the end all he wrote were the words 'A great fog', which seem to have been partially erased. In both typescripts and the published book a blank line is skipped here to mark the break in the action.

A great fog

The moon [rises >] rose higher and higher, and the North wind grew loud and cold. It twisted the white fog upon the lake into bending pillars and hurrying clouds, and drove it off to the West to scatter in tattered wisps over the marshes before Mirkwood. Then the many boats could be seen dotted on the surface of the lake, and down the wind came the sound of the voices of the people of Esgaroth lamenting their lost town and goods and ruined homes. But they had really much to be thankful for, had they thought of it – which perhaps it was asking too much to expect them to do: [the dragon's was at end, >] three quarters of the people of the town had escaped at least alive, and their woods, fields, pastures and cattle, and most of their boats remained undamaged; and the Dragon was dead, and at an end. What that meant they had not yet realized.

They gathered in sorry crowds upon the western shores, shivering in the cold wind. The first grumbles were for the Master who had left the town so soon, while still [defenders were >] some were willing to defend it.

'He may have a good head for business – especially his own business – ' some murmured, 'but he is no good in a crisis!' And th<ey> praised and lamented Bard and his courage.

'If only he were not slain we would make him a king' they said 'Bard, [<King> >] the Dragon-shooter, of the line of Girion. Alas that he is lost!'

And in the very midst of their talk a tall figure stepped from the shadows. He was drenched[TN12] with water, his black hair hung wet over his face and shoulders; a fierce light was in his eyes.

'Bard is not lost' he cried. 'I am Bard the dragon-piercer of the race of Girion. I dived from Esgaroth only when none else was left, only when the enemy was slain. I will be your king!'

'King Bard, King Bard' they shouted, and the master ground his chattering teeth, as he sat upon the ground.

'Girion was Lord of Dale not King of Esgaroth' he said. 'In this lake town we have ever had masters elected from the old and the wise, and not endured the rough rule of mere fighting men. Let King Bard win [> take] back his own Kingdom – Dale is free, nor is more ruined now than Esgaroth. He has slain the slayer of his fathers and nothing hinders him. And those that like may go with him, though wise men will stay here and rebuild our town, and enjoy its richness and peace'.

'We will have king Bard' the people shouted. 'We have had enough of the old men & money-counters'.

'I am the last one to underpraise [> undervalue] Bard the Bowman' said the Master warily, for Bard was standing near him fierce and grim, 'and indeed his bravery tonight has made him the greatest benefactor the men of the Lake have known since the coming of the Smaug the unceasing Threat. But I don't quite see why I get all the blame. Who stirred up the dragon, I might ask? Who got rich gifts of us and ample help, and led us to believe that old songs would come true? What sort of gold have they sent down the river? To whom should we send a claim for the repair of all our damages and the help [*added*: & comfort] of widows and widowers and orphans?'

Cunning words. For the moment people forgot the idea of a new king and [were >] turned their thoughts and anger to Thorin and his company. Their hate flowed up against them, and their words grew ever more wild and bitter. Some of those who had sung the old songs loudest were now [singing parodies of them >] heard loudly to suggest that the dwarves had deliberately sent the Dragon down upon them.

Added later in the bottom and left margin and intended for insertion at this point: 'Fools' said Bard. 'And why waste hate on those unhappy creatures. They have doubtless perished in fire before Smaug came to us.' But even as he spoke, the thought of the treasure of the Mountain came into his heart, and he fell silent, thinking of the Master's words, and dr<eam>ing of Dale rebuilt, if he could find the men.

It was fortunate they [> that the lakemen] had something to discuss and to occupy their thoughts, for their night under the trees and in such rough shelter as could be contrived was miserable. Many [who >] took ill that night and afterwards died. Even Bard would have had a hard task in the following days to order them, and begin upon the rebuilding of the town, with such tools as were left in the huts upon the shore, if other help had not been at hand.

The spies of the woodelves had sent tidings of the dragon's rousing [> dwarves' north<ern> journey and of] to their King, and he was as astonished as the Master had been; but he too expected only a bad end for the dwarves [> yet he did not expect any other ending of their venture than their death in the jaws of Smaug]. When news of the rousing of the Dragon reached him, and of the fire upon the mountain tops, he thought that he had heard the last of Thorin Oakenshield.

Then came messengers telling him of the fall of Esgaroth and the death of Smaug. He knew then the time had come to move. 'It is an ill wind that blows no man any good' he said,[TN13] for he too had not forgotten the legend of the hoard of Thror.

So he led forth all the host he could muster, a great army of [woode<lves> >] the bowmen and spearmen of the woodelves. Some he sent North towards the Mountain; some he bid bring all the supplies they could gather down the river to the lake. It was a long march, for he had not rafts enough for all his folk, but in seven days he came upon the shores, and the unhappy men were glad indeed to see him, and ready to make any bargain for his help.

That is how it happened that while many were left behind with the women and the children, busily felling trees and making huts along the shore, and beginning under the direction of the Master (and with the help of woodelves) the replanning and building of their <restore>d town, [all the bravest warriors but those of the king, >] many gathered under Bard and marched away North with the Elven king.

The chapter comes to an end at the bottom of manuscript page 158 (Marq. 1/1/15:6), as the scene shifts back to the activities of Bilbo and the dwarves at the Mountain; see page 577.

TEXT NOTES

1 This paragraph was preceded on the page by a paragraph of drafting. I transcribe this cancelled passage just as it appears in the manuscript, since it offers a good example of Tolkien's seeking to visualize and properly describe a specific image – in this case, exactly what the people of Lake Town could see of Smaug's distant attack on the Mountain when he destroyed the Secret Door (cf. page 515).

> Suddenly a great light shone in the North and filled the low place in the hills which screened all but the top [> highest peak] of the lonely M. from the view. Though The highest peak of the Lonely Mountain was lost in dark – that was all they could see of it above

> the hills at the North end of the lake. Suddenly the low place in those hills through which came the R. Running from the North was filled with a great light, the Northern end
>
> The Mountain flickered with a glow of light such as

The gap between the hills at the northernmost point on the Long Lake at the inflow of the River Running out of the Lonely Mountain past Dale mentioned here can just be seen in 'Esgaroth' (Plate VIII [bottom]), on the horizon in a direct line above the dwarf popping his head up out of the barrel; it is slightly more evident in the finished version of this drawing ('Lake Town'; cf. DAA.244 & H-S#127).

2 'from midnight till dawn': this corresponds exactly with the account in Chapter XII, where it is midnight when Bilbo emerges from the tunnel with the stolen cup (page 507) and Smaug immediately thereafter discovers the theft and flies out '[t]o hunt the whole mountain till he caught the thief and burned and trampled him' (ibid.), scorching the mountain-side with his fiery breath 'till dawn chilled his wrath and he went back to his golden couch to sleep' (page 508).

3 This unpromising characterization marks the first appearance of Bard,† who will soon emerge as the hero of the coming battle. The description of his voice as 'surly' is distinctly unheroic; elsewhere the word is used of Ted Sandyman ('The Scouring of the Shire', *LotR*.1054) and Snaga the orc ('The Tower of Cirith Ungol', *LotR*.940). Within the published *Hobbit* itself, it appears only to describe the starving dwarves' attitude when questioned by their elven captors in Mirkwood (page 380) – the same elves who had the night before ignored their pleas for food and left them to the spiders' tender mercies.

There is certainly nothing in these paragraphs preceding the battle foretelling the heroic figure this as-yet-unnamed guardsman is about to become. In the First Typescript, *surly* has been replaced with *grim* (typescript page 127; Marq. 1/1/64:1), which conveys the same pessimism but leaves open heroic possibilities. Whereas 'surly' (which derives from Old French) usually means churlishly ill-humored, 'grim' (which comes from Old English) can mean not just fierce, cruel, or harsh but also determined or bold: in *Beowulf* it is used not just of Grendel (e.g., line 121) but of Wiglaf when he addresses his fellow guardsmen who deserted King Beowulf in his time of need (line 2860b); see commentary pp. 557–8.

† Unless this guard is the same character as the nameless guard captain who kept such a poor watch back in Chapter X; see Text Note 10 on page 444.

4 Tolkien originally wrote 'from a fi<re>' here but immediately changed it to 'from floods', perhaps in order to avoid anticipating the conflagration that erupts a few paragraphs later.

5 I have added the quotation marks here, since these lines would seem at first to be quoted from the poem in Chapter X (see pp. 439–40 and Text Note 14 on pp. 445–6), but not all of them actually occur there, nor in this sequence, either in the rough draft nor the final poem. We

must either imagine that the Lake-men are garbling their own song a few weeks later or, more probably, that this is a part of the song not recorded earlier, where we are told 'there was a great deal more of it'.

6 Note that Lake Town still has multiple bridges connecting it to the shore here and also in the accompanying First Typescript (1/1/64:1); cf. Text Notes to Chapter X, page 444.

7 An additional sentence appears in this passage in the First Typescript:

> *You have never failed me and always I have recovered you.*

This addition, along with some polishing, thus achieves in the First Typescript the text that appears in the published book. For more on the rather curious motif of an arrow that is always recovered until one final shot when it fulfills its destiny, see the commentary on page 558.

8 Added in the left margin and marked for insertion at this point:

> As he turned [*added*: and dived down] his belly glittered [with >] white with sparkling fire in the moon – but not in one spot.

For the role of moonlight in this scene, see the commentary on the picture 'The Death of Smaug', page 561.

9 The detail about Smaug's death cry causing stars to fall from the sky, while striking, disappeared by the time the First Typescript was made, where this passage reads '. . . a shriek that deafened men, *felled trees*, and split stone' (1/1/64:3). For a precedent elsewhere in Tolkien's work of falling stars being caused by dramatic earthly events, see the *Father Christmas Letters*, where in the 1925 letter two stars 'shot' (i.e., became shooting stars) when North Polar Bear broke the North Pole, and a third 'went red when [the] Pole snapped' (*Letters from Father Christmas*, 1925 Letter, page 23).

10 'Glede': a rare (dialectical) word more commonly spelled 'gleed' (Middle English *glede*, Old English *glēd*), meaning a glowing coal or ember. Douglas Anderson notes (DAA.308) that the word occurs both in *Beowulf* and in *Sir Gawain & the Green Knight*, as well as in Tolkien's translation of the latter (where it is once translated 'coals' and once left untranslated as 'gledes'; cf. SGGK line 891 [Tolkien translation page 47] and line 1609 [Tolkien translation page 65]).

11 This is the first appearance of the name *Esgaroth*. For the probable meaning of this elven name for Lake Town, see pp. 561–2. Several letters at the beginning and end of the word have been re-written in a darker ink, and it is possible that the original reading here was *Esgaron*, the form of the name found in Plot Notes D; see page 569 and Text Note 7 on page 571.

12 This marks the point at which the First Typescript broke off in the 'home manuscript' that Tolkien circulated among his friends; the next page which followed in that composite text was the first page of the Third Phase handwritten manuscript. For an explanation of how these texts fit together, see the headnote at the beginning of Chapter XVb: King Bard on pp. 637–8. Note that when Carpenter says that 'shortly

after he had described the death of the dragon' Tolkien broke off the story (*Tolkien: A Biography*, page 179), he is referring to the typescript. In fact, as the next two chapters show, Tolkien continued the story on past Smaug's death for the rest of that chapter, all the following chapter (which now precedes it in the re-arranged published sequence), and well into the chapter that followed – or, in the published book, for twenty-one out of the remaining sixty-five pages of the story (in the pagination of the first edition, not counting illustrations).

13 This proverb, while undoubtedly venerable, hardly dates back to the Third Age of Middle-earth. The earliest recorded usage, *an yll wynde that blowth no man to good, men saie*, appears in Henry VIII's time in John Heywood's *Proverbs* [1546], along with such still-familiar phrases as *no fire without some smoke, cart before the horse, more the merrier, penny for your thoughts*, and *hitteth the nail on the head*. Shakespeare uses slightly different forms of it twice (*Henry IV, Part II*, Act V, scene iii, line 87; *Henry VI, Part III*, Act II, scene v, line 55), and it has remained in use down to the present day. The most familiar form today is the eighteenth-century one, *'tis an ill wind which blows nobody any good* (cf. Laurence Sterne's *A Sentimental Journey* [1768]).

(i)

Bard the Dragon-Slayer

As we have seen in Plot Notes C, the idea that Smaug would die during the attack on Lake Town rather than be stabbed by Bilbo while he slept on his bed of gold emerged suddenly. Since Bilbo was no longer to be the dragon-slayer, Tolkien had to either re-assign the role to an already existing character within the book, such as Thorin or Gandalf, or create a new one with very little preamble.[1] Designating any other character already present as Smaug's bane would simply shift the problem without solving it, since all the dwarves were at the mountain with Bilbo and no other character who had appeared so far on their journey could be re-introduced to fill the role without usurping too large a part in the story and taking attention away from the main characters.[2]

Tolkien's solution was to introduce a new character to fill the necessary narrative role. Initially he planned to kill off this character as soon as his role of dragon-slayer was achieved: only two pages of manuscript separate his first appearance (manuscript page 153)[3] and his death in the ruin of Esgaroth (manuscript page 155), crushed beneath the dragon's fall. Before proceeding any further, however, Tolkien thought better of it and changed the line 'And that was the end of Smaug and Esgaroth and Bard' to '. . . the end of Smaug and Esgaroth *but not of Bard*' (italics mine) – as significant a change within such a small space of words as he achieved anywhere within the book.

Having decided to keep Bard alive was a crucial decision that greatly affected the concluding section of the book. The chapters immediately following the death of Smaug (Chapters XIV-XVIII in this edition, XIII and XV-XVIII in the published book) have long been noted as strikingly different in tone from all that had come before.[4] Initially, as we shall see, Tolkien's sympathies in the next several chapters were to remain with Thorin and the dwarves and no rift between Bilbo and his companions had been contemplated (see especially the 'little bird' outline, i.e. Plot Notes E), with the elves and their allies being cast in a much more hostile light (capturing and wounding Fili, pursing Kili, shooting arrows at the friendly ravens bringing food to enable the besieged dwarves and hobbit to hold out, etc.). Before the introduction of Bard, none of the outsiders described in the Plot Notes who descend upon the mountain after Smaug's death have any legitimate claim on the treasure there: certainly not the Elvenking who imprisoned the dwarves for months in solitary confinement merely for trespassing. Nor are the men of Lake Town, although certainly due generous recompense for all their aid in the dwarves' time of need (much of their sorry state having been due to the elves' mistreatment, it must be said), entitled thereby to any significant portion of Thorin's inheritance. That the elves and Lake-men were in the wrong in their attempts to steal or extort Thror's treasure and besiege his heir when he finally comes back into his own is shown by Bladorthin's words and actions when the wizard finally reappears:

> Blad[orthin] rebukes the besiegers . . .
> A share of his part [Bilbo] gives to Lake-men, and to wood-elves (*though they may not deserve it*).
>
> — Plot Notes C (page 497, italics mine).

But the introduction of survivors from Dale changes this: it gives those who like Bard are descended from the Dale-folk a rightful claim to at least part of the hoard – albeit probably a relatively small part: it is after all the gold of the King under the Mountain that has lived on in Lake-folk song and legend and likewise 'the legend of the hoard of Thror' that brings the Elvenking marching at top speed, not any legacy of Girion. Now Thorin faces a rightful claimant to any wealth of Girion's mixed into Smaug's treasure, and one who furthermore also legitimately serves as spokesman for the Lake-folk's claim for aid in time of need to reciprocate their own earlier generosity, plus a hero who by preventing Smaug's return has done the new King under the Mountain a great service and deserves his own reward as the dragon-slayer (cf. Bilbo's recognition of the essential fairness of Bard's presentation of his three-part claim in the latter part of Chapter XV, the first new text in the Third Phase drafting, on page 648 & DAA.323). Significantly enough, it was just at the point where Tolkien would either have to reject some of these new elements, particularly Bard, because of the complications they introduced into his projected conclusion, or else have to find a way to incorporate them by changing that conclusion, that he broke off the Second Phase of composition, just as Bilbo and the dwarves learn of the approaching elven and human armies (see page 620).

Bard is an important figure for another reason: he represents a turning point in Tolkien's legendarium. He is not the first of Tolkien's human heroes, having been preceded a decade and a half before by Beren, Húrin, Túrin, and Tuor, but unlike these tragic and rather remote figures, his is a fortunate fate. A dispossessed heir, he lives to achieve unexpected victory over the surpassingly strong hereditary foe who had destroyed his homeland, re-establishes the kingship, and founds a dynasty that renews alliances with nonhuman neighbors and helps bring renewed prosperity to the region.[5] In short, he is a precursor of Strider (Aragorn), who through his own efforts and the great deeds of others claims his ancestor's throne and re-establishes his kingdom; all that is lacking is the love story (a relatively late element of Aragorn's story; cf. HME VIII–IX). Bard is thus a pivotal figure, a turning point between the tragic figures of the First Age and the triumphant returning king of Volume III of *The Lord of the Rings*.

The sudden emergence of the unlikely hero, the one who dares to undertake some task or challenge which his apparent 'betters' shirk – as in, for example, the farmer who (twice) goes dragon-hunting in *Farmer Giles of Ham* or indeed Bilbo's exploration of Smaug's lair when Durin's heir dares not enter – is of course a traditional fairy-tale motif, frequently matched with the subsequent discovery that the new hero is in fact a lost prince or noble heir. However, the primary external influence for Bard's sudden emergence, aside from sheer narrative necessity, probably lies not in fairy tales but (as so often the case in the Smaug chapters) in *Beowulf*. When King Beowulf sets forth to fight the dragon that has burned down his royal hall, he brings along as companions eleven picked warriors but forbids them to take part in the battle, ordering them to stand back at a safe distance and serve as witnesses. But when it becomes clear that Beowulf is losing the fight, one of his companions springs into action. Heretofore merely one of eleven unnamed warriors, Wiglaf disobeys his king's orders and rushes to the old man's side; with his help, Beowulf is able to kill the dragon but is mortally wounded in turn. The dying king names Wiglaf as his heir, and it is he who takes charge of the disposition of the treasure and directs the construction of Beowulf's barrow. The differences from *The Hobbit* are considerable, but the essential points are the same: (1) an anonymous guard is first named when he shows the courage to fight a dragon, (2) all his fellows lack the courage to do likewise and abandon their duty (either by deserting their posts in *The Hobbit* or in *Beowulf* by failing to fulfill their oaths to defend the king, as Wiglaf angrily upbraids his fellows), (3) the newly named hero turns out to be of royal lineage (Bard being the descendant of Girion king of Dale and Wiglaf the last of the Wægmundings, Beowulf's kin; cf. *Beowulf* lines 2813–2816), and lastly (4) each becomes king as a direct result of his role in the dragon-slaying.

(ii)
The Black Arrow

The motif of the Black Arrow both harkens back to the alliterative poems of the 1920s and ahead to the Númenórean blades in *The Lord of the Rings*. In 'The Lay of the Children of Húrin', Beleg the Bowman carries a special arrow named *Dailir*,[6] of which we are told

> *. . . Dailir he drew, his dart beloved;*
> *howso far fared it, or fell unnoted,*
> *unsought he found it with sound feathers*
> *and barbs unbroken*
>
> —lines 1080–1083a (Canto II: 'Beleg') HME III.42.

When Beleg stumbles in the dark while rescuing Túrin and breaks this lucky arrow, injuring his hand in the process, the narrator makes clear this is an omen of disaster (ibid., lines 1187–1192; HME III.45), and indeed Túrin murders Beleg only minutes later in a tragic case of mistaken identity.

Bard is more fortunate, in that although his arrow too is ultimately lost, its final act is to exceed all hope by slaying his people's greatest foe, with a sense that it perishes in the act of fulfilling its destiny. This is hinted at by Bard's final words before that fateful shot: '*If ever you came from the forges of the true king of the Mountain go now and speed well*'; compare the narrator's comment when Merry's blade burns away after helping to slay the Witch-King of Angmar (that is, the Lord of the Nazgûl):

> So passed the sword of the Barrow-downs, work of Westernesse [Númenor]. But glad would he have been to know its fate who wrought it slowly long ages ago in the North-kingdom when the Dúnedain were young, and chief among their foes was the dread realm of Angmar and its sorcerer king. No other blade, not though mightier hands had wielded it, would have dealt that foe a wound so bitter, cleaving the undead flesh, breaking the spell that knit his unseen sinews to his will.
>
> —*LotR*.877–8.

Once again *Beowulf* may have contributed something to the idea of a weapon that achieves its goal but then perishes: in the battle with Grendel's dam, Beowulf finds that the sword he has brought cannot harm the monster, but he is able to slay her and to cut off Grendel's head with an ancient sword he finds within her lair. This *ealdsweord eotenisc* (*Beowulf* line 1558a; literally, 'old entish sword') then melts away (lines 1606b–1609), leaving only the hilt behind (1614b–1617). In any case, like Bard himself in the original draft, the Black Arrow is no sooner introduced than it fulfills its role in slaying the seemingly invulnerable dragon and leaves the story.

(iii)
The Death of Smaug

The great moment that would at first seem to be the climax of the entire book and the fulfillment of Thorin & Company's quest is remarkable because when it comes it not only occurs 'off-stage' so far as the main point-of-view characters are concerned[7] but it comes five-sixths of the way through the book, not in the last or even penultimate chapter, and what follows is far from dénouement. Indeed Smaug's sudden and permanent removal, while essential to any 'happy ending' for the story, immediately complicates the situation and leads to the tangle that takes another six chapters to resolve.

Unlike the traditional methods of dragon-slaying proposed in the Plot Notes but ultimately rejected, which derive primarily from the Sigurd legend and his own Glorund story, so far as I have been able to discover the method Tolkien chose for slaying The Dragon is unprecedented in fairy-tale, English folktale, or Old English/Old Norse lore. The closest parallel seems to be classical: the Eleventh Labour of Hercules, where in some forms of the story the demigod slays Ladon, the Dragon of the Hesperides, with an arrow or arrows in order to gain the Golden Apples it guards. Most stories seem to hold with the author of Job that arrows or darts are no good against a dragon's armor (Job 41.26–29; see Text Note 33 following Chapter XII), and, a few humorous folktales aside, traditionally only hand-to-hand combat has seemed sufficiently heroic for such an epic encounter. Simpson notes that while many dragons are described or depicted as winged, most storytellers and artists ignore this capacity for flight once battle is actually joined:

> . . . it is indeed only in literature, in Spenser's *Faerie Queene* that one can find a fully thought-out, detailed, visualized, blow-by-blow account of how a duel between an armed knight on horseback and a flying, fire-breathing dragon with claws and a spiked tail might be expected to unfold. In particular, Spenser makes good use of the dragon's power of flight.[8]
>
> —*British Dragons*, page 75.

Tolkien's account does not involve an armored knight, but it is complex, combining as it does the traditional motif of a dragon's weak spot (specifically the soft underbelly of the Sigurd/Fafnir legend, already seen in Glorund) with the Beowulf-dragon's fiery breath none can withstand (also present in Glorund; cf. BLT II.85, 'with the power of his breath he drove Túrin from those doors') and a tactically wily wyrm who uses his power of flight to attack foes on what is essentially a manmade island surrounded by deep water. Furthermore, Smaug has learned from his ancestor's mistake and armored himself so that a lurking assassin cannot ambush him (as Sigurd did Fafnir and Túrin Glorund). He does not know that there is a fatal weak spot in his 'jeweled waistcoat', but even so had he not lost his head to pride (allowing Bilbo to inspect his armaments) and to anger in the heat of battle he could have guarded against even that possibility.[9] The description of Smaug's attack – 'the dragon's wrath blazed . . . till he was blind and mad with it . . . *taking no heed to turn his scales towards his foes*' (italics mine) – implies he is so sinuous and serpentine (as indeed the illustrations bear out) that he could with care have kept his vulnerable belly turned away from his foes on each strafing pass. After all, he must have done so in his initial assault on Dale and Thror's halls, since at that time he lacked the embedded gemstones against which presumably even the Black Arrow was of no avail ('then I was young *and tender*' – DAA.282; italics mine).

We are fortunate that Tolkien illustrated this dramatic scene;[10] even though he left the picture unfinished it is full of interesting details (see Plate XII [top]), from an alternate view of Lake Town (viewed more from the south rather than in the westerly published view [DAA.244] or in the slightly earlier variant thereof ['Esgaroth', Plate VIII bottom]) and the Lonely Mountain looming ominously on the horizon like an erupting volcano (cf. Tolkien's [earlier] Thangorodrim and [later] Mount Doom in the backgrounds of his pictures of the vale of Sirion [H-S#55] and the Barad-dûr [H-S#145], respectively) to the dragon himself in his death agonies. Smaug is much yellower here than in the companion picture 'Conversation with Smaug' (Plate XI [top]) – in the text he is always described as 'red-golden' (cf. page 506) – but this may simply be an accident of the picture's having been left incomplete. Most notably of all, Tolkien annotated this picture, suggesting that he at one point thought of offering it as a guide to another artist, perhaps at the time Houghton Mifflin suggested hiring an American artist to illustrate their edition (cf. Hammond's *Descriptive Bibliography* page 18).[11] These annotations show that Tolkien drew a scene as he visualized it and only then worried about reconciling it to what he written and also his extreme precision in getting those details right during the revision stage:

left margin: The moon should be a crescent: it was only a few nights after the New Moon on 'Durin's Day'.[12]

lower left corner: Dragon should have a white naked spot where the arrow enters.

bottom margin: Bard the Bowman shd be standing after release of arrow at extreme left point of the piles.

Ultimately this picture did not appear in the first edition of *The Hobbit*, either redrawn by Tolkien or adapted by another hand, but it was published in Tolkien's lifetime as the cover of the second British paperback edition of *The Hobbit* (Unwin Books, trade paperback [1966]). In this publication the bottom of the illustration was trimmed slightly, cutting off those annotations, but the scrawled title 'Death of Smaug' did appear in the center of the drawing, along with the annotation concerning the moon to the far left (wrapped around on the back cover); the sharp-eyed could even catch the arrow on the bottom spine indicating where Bard stood, although there's no way they could have known its significance.[13] Tolkien himself was diffident about using this unfinished piece: with typical humility,[14] he wrote to Rayner Unwin: 'I am in your hands, but I am still not very happy about the use of this scrawl as a cover. It seems too much in the modern mode in which those who can draw try to conceal it. But perhaps there is a distinction between their productions and one by a man who obviously cannot draw *what he sees*' (JRRT to RU, 15th December 1965, *Letters* p. 365; italics mine). The final phrase is significant: Tolkien's chief concern is to capture the inner vision and convey to us in image as well as in words a scene from his story and his subcreated world.

(iv)
The Name 'Esgaroth'

This name is clearly Elvish, either Sindarin (Noldorin) or a dialect thereof; cf. *Esgal*duin (originally *Esga*duin),[15] the river that flowed past the door of Mene*groth* ('the Thousand Caves'), King Thingol's halls in Doriath. The simplest explanation is to assume that 'Esgaroth' and 'Lake Town' essentially say the same thing in different languages, and there is some support for this if we take the *–roth* element,[16] whose primary meaning is 'cave' (generally in the context of fortified cave-dwelling or underground city), as also having the more general meaning of 'dwelling' and could thus plausibly be extended to mean 'town'. Unfortunately, no such simple equivalence can be found for *esga-*. The river-name is not translated within the alliterative poems, and the only gloss I can find that Tolkien ever offered for it comes in 'The Etymologies' [1937–8, written to accompany the 1937 *Quenta Silmarillion*]. Under the root ESEK- comes the following entry:

> Ilk. *esg* sedge,[17] *esgar* reed-bed. Cf. *Esgaroth* Reedlake, because of reed-banks in west.
>
> —HME V, page 356.

This gloss is straightforward and clear, but unfortunately it is also certainly an afterthought. For one thing, Esgaroth is clearly *not* the name of the Lake, as this entry would indicate, but of the town itself: cf. the label on the published version of Thror's Map: '*In* Esgaroth *upon* the Long Lake dwell Men' (DAA.97; emphasis mine); perhaps Tolkien might have been misled by glancing at the final Wilderland Map (DAA.[399]), where the name 'Esgaroth' appears directly below the name 'Long Lake', and momentarily become confused and taken this to be another name for the same feature. Furthermore, this translation offers no explanation at all relating *-roth* to 'lake'. Finally, the *Esga-* element is clearly the same element that had appeared long before [circa 1918] in the river Esga(l) duin. In the Noldorin Word-lists, the oldest of which is contemporary with the name's first appearance (*Parma Eldalamberon* XIII [2001] page 133), *esk, esg* appears (ibid., page 143) and is glossed 'sharp upstanding rock in water' (e.g., a carrock – see page 265), apparently deriving from the *esc/aisc* (meaning 'sharp point, sharp edge') of the still earlier *Gnomish Lexicon* [circa 1917]; *Parma Eldalamberon* XI page 31. Combined with our earlier hypothesis that *-roth* could mean city, this provides a hypothetical but satisfactory gloss for 'Esgaroth': city standing in or rising up out of the water, perhaps with a suggestion of pilings like reeds.[18]

Finally, as already noted during our discussion of the name 'Dorwinion' (see page 418), years later Tolkien wrote regarding Elven names in *The Hobbit* that 'Esgaroth . . . [is] not Sindarin (though perhaps "Sindarized" in shape) or . . . not recorded in Sindarin'. Given its obvious affinities to Gnomish and Noldorin (the earlier forms of Sindarin within the real-world sequence of Tolkien's invented languages), I take this to mean that the name no longer fit Sindarin as he saw it at this late date and hence had to be relegated to a dialectical or aberrant form. But just as he clearly changed his mind several times regarding the name's meaning (see above), there seems little doubt that *Esgaroth* was Sindarin (i.e., Noldorin) when the name was created, like all the other Elven names in *The Hobbit*, although some were later disowned or orphaned, like *Esgaroth* and *Girion*. Unfortunately, Tolkien does not translate the name in this passage, in the end leaving us with no acceptable authorized gloss.

NOTES

1 That Smaug had to be slain by a single character rather than simply perish in a hail of arrows or smash into the lake in a misjudged dive or be crushed beneath the rockfalls that Tolkien intended would partially collapse the chamber within the Lonely Mountain (cf. Plot Notes C) goes without saying. To repeat what Tolkien said in his unpublished lecture on dragons (see Note 5 following the commentary to Chapter XII), Tolkien felt that

> Dragons can only be defeated by brave men – usually alone. Sometimes a faithful friend may help, but it is rare: friends have a way of deserting you when [you are faced >] a dragon comes. Dragons are the final test of heroes . . .

It follows that, if a dragon is the supreme challenge for a hero, it is only fitting that a dragon face a hero as his nemesis in turn, dying in single combat in the traditionally approved manner.

2 For example, if Gandalf re-appeared suddenly and struck the dragon dead in mid-flight, the reader would wonder why the wizard had bothered to involve the hobbit in Thorin's quest at all, and it would make hay of all Gandalf's earlier assertions that this is not *his* adventure after all (e.g., page 230).

3 I am assuming here that the surly-voiced watchman looking at the lights to the north is not the same character as the watch-captain who kept such poor look-out over the main bridge to Lake Town (cf. page 438 and Text Note 10 to Chapter X), who might have been expected to show a little more interest in the return of Thror's Heir if he himself were a descendant of Girion Lord of Dale. It seems likely that Tolkien would have clarified this point and introduced Bard into the earlier scenes in Lake Town (Chapter X) in the 1960 Hobbit, had his revisionary work reached this far into the story, paralleling his work in *The Lord of the Rings* drafts to insert brief appearances by or mentions of Arwen back into the earlier parts of the story before her first actual entry quite late in the story (see HME VIII.370, 386, & 425; HME IX.52, 58–9 & 66).

Even if we were to assume that the two characters are the same, then the point still applies, though then we should say that only two pages separate the character's sudden assumption of significance from his death.

4 See, for example, C. S. Lewis's comment in his review of *The Hobbit*, where he remarks upon 'the curious shift' between the earlier parts of the story and 'the saga-like tone of the later chapters' (*TLS* 2nd October 1937; reprinted in C. S. Lewis, *On Stories*, ed. Walter Hooper [1982], page 81). For more on Lewis's critique, see Note 3 following the commentary on the Bladorthin Typescript.

5 It is important that from the very first we are told that Bard is a descendant

of Girion (a fact that enters in with the same sentence as his name; see page 549); this gives a new application to Bilbo's words to Smaug about revenge and his reminder that 'your success has made you some bitter enemies' and a direct answer to Smaug's rhetorical question 'Girion lord of Dale is dead . . . and where are his sons' sons who dare approach me?' (page 511). Bard's heritage as Girion's heir gives him just as much right to revenge the Fall of Dale as Thorin would have for the destruction of Thror's kingdom; it keeps the scales of poetic justice balanced.

Dynasty: We know nothing about Bard's queen and little about his son Bain, who apparently ruled after him, but we do know that his grandson Brand is the king of Dale at the time of the War of the Ring some eighty years later and dies fighting alongside King Dain Ironfoot defending the Kingdom under the Mountain against Sauron's forces in the Battle of Dale (*LotR*.1116 & 1130). By King Brand's time, the Men of Dale are known as the Bardings (*LotR*.245; cf. the Beornings and Eorlings and *Beowulf*'s Scyldings) and the Kingdom of Dale extends down to include the lands surrounding the Long Lake: 'his realm now reaches far south and east of Esgaroth' (ibid.). Despite Glóin's description of him as 'a strong king', Brand seems to have been a less forceful personality than his progenitor, since Glóin reports at the Council of Elrond that messengers from Mordor seeking news of hobbits have come not just to Dain but 'also to King Brand in Dale, and he is afraid. We fear that he may yield. Already war is gathering on his eastern borders' (*LotR*.259) – that is, that Brand might try to appease the Dark Lord and buy peace by giving Sauron's emissaries news of Bilbo. After Brand's death fighting in battle alongside King Dain Ironfoot, his son Bard II becomes 'King in Dale', extending the dynasty into the Fourth Age (*LotR*.1131), partnered with Dain's son Thorin III Stonehelm as King under the Mountain.

6 *Dailir*: The word is Noldorin, Tolkien's more developed form of 'Gnomish' (i.e., what during the *Lord of the Rings* period would be renamed 'Sindarin'), and means 'cleaver' ('Noldorin Word-lists', *Parma Eldalamberon* XIII [2001], page 141). The *–ir* suffix here indicates a verb (*daila*, 'to cleave') transformed into an 'agent noun' (cf. Salo, *A Gateway to Sindarin* page 165), as in English pierce > Piercer, or the goblins' names for Orcrist and Glamdring ('Biter' and 'Beater', respectively).† If we accept Dailir as parallel to the contemporary names Dairon and Daideloth, then the *dai-* element would probably have become *dae-* in later Elvish (cf. Dairon > Daeron and Daideloth > Dor Daedeloth). In any case, while Beleg's arrow itself clearly served as a model for Bard's arrow, its name is not an Elvish parallel to 'Black Arrow', which in the Noldorin of *The Hobbit* would have been something like *Morlin* or *Morhlin* (*mor-* 'black', as in *Mor*ia and *Mor*dor, + *lhinn* 'arrow'; cf. *Parma Eldalamberon* XIII page 163).

† Note that Tolkien believed that the unknown god Nodens' name was also of this type, derived from a verbal form and thus meaning something like The Hunter or The Catcher ('The Name "Nodens"' [1932], pages 135–7).

7 This is not the only such passage in the book – cf. the Lord of the Eagles scene in Chapter VI or Gandalf/Thorin's capture by the wood-elves – but it is by far the longest, and the only one which complicates the narrative, forcing Tolkien to choose which of the two series of events to tell first: the story of what happened to Smaug or the adventures of Bilbo and the dwarves at the Mountain in his absence. Here we see Tolkien employing the interlace narrative technique which will come to be such a feature of *The Lord of the Rings*, especially in Book III and the early parts of Book V of that work (cf. Richard West's masterly article 'The Interlace Structure of *The Lord of the Rings*' in *A Tolkien Compass*, ed. Jared Lobdell [1975], pages 77–94). Initially Tolkien chose to follow the epic storyline, describing the dragon's death and its effect on Bard, the wood-elves, and the folk of Lake Town and only then turning back to the Lonely Mountain; in the published book he reversed this and transposed the two respective chapters.

8 Glorund, the only dragon described in detail in the older Silmarillion material, is of course wingless. Ancalagon the Black is the first great winged dragon, and his combination of flight, fiery breath, and draconic strength prove almost too much for the host the Valar send against Morgoth, so that he is only defeated by a similarly airborne foe, Eärendel in the flying ship Wingelot. Unfortunately, Ancalagon's battle is only described in remote and general terms. Spenser's archetypical dragon provides a better example, but like Chrysophylax his wing is injured early in the fight and thereafter his ability to fly plays no part in his combat. The Green Dragon in 'The Dragon's Visit', Chrysophylax in his battle against the Middle Kingdom's knights, and especially the White Dragon of the Moon in his pursuit of Roverandom all make full use of their wings; along with Smaug's devastating attacks on the Secret Door and Lake Town, these make it clear that flying combat is very much a feature of Tolkien's dragons.

9 That pride is the cardinal sin in Tolkien's ethos has been universally acknowledged among Tolkien scholars since Paul Kocher pointed it out more than thirty years ago (*Master of Middle-Earth* [1972]). It is perhaps less appreciated how often wrath accompanies it; the first sign of someone giving in to pride in Tolkien's work is usually his losing his temper – cf. the scenes between Gandalf and Saruman (*LotR*.605–6), Sam and Sméagol (*LotR*.742), Frodo and Boromir (*LotR*.419–20), etc.

10 This is unusual in itself, since Tolkien rarely did action shots; almost all of his illustrations to his Middle-earth works are landscapes or mood pieces, designed to help the reader more vividly visualize the places in the books. The three exceptions to this rule among his art for *The Hobbit* are 'The Three Trolls are turned to Stone' (Plate V [top]), 'Death of Smaug' (Plate XII [top]), and 'The Coming of the Eagles' (Plate XII [bottom]), of which the burning of Lake Town and the smiting of the dragon is by far the most dramatic.

11 This unfinished painting may have been created in July 1937, when Tolkien was working to make several colour illustrations of *The Hobbit*

for the American edition (see Note 10 following Chapter XIV on pp. 613–14). In addition to the five watercolours he submitted to Houghton Mifflin, illustrating The Hill (Hobbiton), Rivendell, the eagles' eyrie, the barrel-ride down the Forest River, and Bilbo's meeting with Smaug – all of which have appeared in many editions since – he also made or began colour pictures of Gandalf's approach to and arrival at Bag-End, the trolls' hill, four alternate depictions of Rivendell, Beorn's Hall, the elf-hill in Mirkwood, two alternate versions of the barrel-riding scene, Smaug flying around the Lonely Mountain, the Battle of Five Armies, and Smaug's death over Lake Town. Some of these were essentially black and white drawings enhanced with a very effective bit of colour, such as the firelight in 'Troll's Hill' (Plate IV [bottom]) and 'Firelight in Beorn's house' (Plate VI [bottom]).

12 In fact, it was the very next night, so even the crescent shown here should be far more slender.

13 The best reproduction of this picture appears in *Pictures by J. R. R. Tolkien*, plate 19.

14 Similarly, he had denigrated his own art in public during his 1937 dragon lecture, when he included slides of several of his own dragon-pictures among the images he showed, saying of his charming little drawing 'The White Dragon Pursues Roverandom & the Moondog' (reprinted in *Roverandom* on plate 3, facing page 27) that 'though a poor drawing' it clearly showed a Saxon White Dragon, and drawing attention to 'the world up in the sky' (i.e., the image of Earth as seen from the moon in the upper left corner). Similarly, he said of the magnificent 'Conversation with Smaug' (Plate XI [top]) that 'It is not very good – but it shows a powerful lot of treasure'. That is, in both cases the pictures included details he wanted to convey about dragons, whatever their merits (in his too-self-critical eyes) as art.

15 For the original spelling of this river-name as *Esgaduin*, rather than the later *Esgalduin*, see Christopher Tolkien's notes to 'The Lay of the Children of Húrin' (the A text and pre-revision B text, HME III.81) and 'The Lay of Leithian' (rough workings, ibid.158). 'Esgaduin' is also the form of the name that appears on the First Silmarillion Map [circa 1926], reproduced in HME IV between pages 220 and 221.

Esgaroth itself first appears in the text on manuscript page 155 (see page 549); an alternate spelling, *Esgaron*, appears in Plot Notes D. See Text Note 11 above and Text Note 7 following Plot Notes D (page 571).

16 The element *–roth* corresponds to *–(th)rond* '(fortified) cave', the same element that we have already seen in the personal name *Thrand*uil and the place-name Nargo*thrond*; see page 417. 'The Etymologies', HME V page 384, under the root ROD- (cave), gives *rondo* as the Quendian (Quenya) form, *rhond/rhonn* as the Noldorin (Sindarin) form, and *roth* as the Doriathrin equivalent – that is, the form the word would take in the dialect of Ilkorin or native Middle-earth Elvish spoken in Thingol's kingdom.

17 'Ilk.' here means Ilkorin, the language of the elves of Middle-earth who never made the Great Journey to Valinor; cf. 'The Three Kindreds of the Elves' on page 406.

18 By contrast, in 'The Etymologies' Tolkien glossed this same word-element twice in contradictory ways, neither of which agrees with the earlier 'Noldorin' nor with the ESKE-/reed entry given elsewhere within 'The Etymologies', which certainly suggests uncertainty on his part as to the word's meaning. First he gives it under the root EZGE- ('rustle, noise of leaves'): 'Q *eske*; Ilk. *esg*; cf. *Esgalduin*' (HME V.357), but then this is cancelled and the word given yet a third alternate explanation under the root SKAL- ('screen, hide [from light]'): 'Ilk. *esgal* screen, hiding, roof of leaves' with the derivative name 'Ilk. *Esgalduin* "River under Veil (of leaves)"'. The Quendian form includes the meanings 'veiled, hidden, shadowed, shady' (HME V.386), and accordingly Salo glosses it as 'the river of the veil' (e.g., the Veiled River), '"veiled" or screened by the trees that overhung it' (Salo, *A Gateway to Sindarin*, page 377). None of these meanings yields a satisfactory gloss for Lake Town, which is certainly not hidden nor overshadowed by trees and does not stand in the reedy part of the lake, as may plainly be seen by Tolkien's various illustrations of the scene.

Luckily, the *–duin* element of *Esgalduin* is relatively straightforward, meaning 'river', likewise described as an Ilkorin term in 'The Etymologies' (HME V.355). Its most familiar appearance is as part of the Sindarin name An*duin* ('the Great River') in *The Lord of the Rings*.

PLOT NOTES D

The following sheet (Marq. 1/1/10:5–6) replaced the fourth page or latter half of Plot Notes C (1/1/10:4; see page 497). It is difficult to date exactly when this occurred, but it seems to have been written immediately following the death of the dragon on manuscript page 155 (see page 549) and before the rider on manuscript page 151b and marginal addition on manuscript page 155 (see pages 512–13 & 549–50). A few elements from the cancelled page of Plot Notes C, particularly the last few lines (from 'The men of the lake and Woodelves come up and besiege the dwarves' through '[the wood-elves] escort Blad[orthin] & B[ilbo] back through Mirkwood'; see page 497), were incorporated into the new outline but expanded and developed in the process.

[page] 4

The Dwarves and Bilbo sit and <?quake>. Unable to tell passage of time. The silence goes on and on. and still they dare not move. They doze and wake and still the silence. The next day and next night and no sign of the dragon. They try to open the door – no good of course.

We are trapped they said and grumble at Bilbo.

[Only >] In desperation they go down the tunnel.

Bilbo slips on his ring. Absolute dark in the hall. no sign or <sound> of Smaug. The stillness is uncanny.

<Illegible> he gets [Oin to light >] Gloin to light him a little torch. He climbs the mound of gold – the dwarves see him from afar like a little spark. They see him stoop but don't know why. The gem of Girion & its fascination for him.

He explores all the hall. Peeps through its door into the vast passages above. The dwarves prepare to creep through the old halls.

Thorin is their guide

Dreading at every step to hear Smaug's return they climb the long stairs and passages <through> dark deserted halls <illegible>.[TN1]

At last <?they> reach the outer gate. <A whirl> of bats. A smooth and slimy passage worn by the dragon by the river-side.[TN2] They stand in the blessed light of day and see it is early morning in the east.

Crows are fly[ing] South in flocks

<Thorin> <?interprets> their speech.[TN3] There is great feasting <?&> a <slaughter> <?there>

[They <wonder> if <Smaug> <had> <?truly> has been <?destroy[ed]> >]

And armies are on the march. North.

In the evening [the crows >] a raven brings word. Bows to Thorin (now Smaug is dead)[TN4] and they learn of the Battle & Smaug's <overthrow>. The <illegible> of the Lake men & wood elves are coming to take the gold. The dwarves block the entrance <working> mightily?

The thrush reappears[TN5]

[page] *5* (verso and continuation of preceding)

Put this in on p 155? before the part about dwarves?[TN6]

What happened [<?when> >] at Esgaron ((Lake-town)).[TN7] <How> Bard escaped. The anguish of the Lake-men & <wrath> of the Master. They now hate the dwarves as source of the <trouble>: some even suggest the <?driving forth> of the dragon against them was deliberate.

<Messengers> go to the wood-elves; and the king's spies bring him news. He leads forth the soldiers and they join with the lake men <under> Bard. They go north to capture <the> dwarves and the gold.

Tolkien drew a line under this sentence, struck through the top part of the page, and put a check mark in the right margin next to the seven cancelled lines, indicating that this part of his instructions to himself had been carried out. As noted above this suggests that Plot Notes D were written during the pause that followed the destruction of Lake Town, and specifically immediately after the writing of the line 'the end of Smaug and Esgaroth and Bard [> but not of Bard]' on manuscript page 155 (page 549 of this edition).

The siege of the mountain.

Bilbo <sneaks> forth at night and comes to the camps. He calls <for> Bard and sits <amid> the counsellors. He says the Gem of Girion is his own since he <is> <illegible> <illegible> share. If it were all – and the dwarves prize it more dearly than all else – he would give it to Bard the heir of Girion to let his friends go in peace. The woodelves and other counsellors speak ag[ainst] him.

An old man rises from the floor. It is Gandalf!

He speaks to Bard. Prophecies often come true in diff. <guise>. Be not a greater fool than the fools who <illegible> the dragon <from> his wealth. Believe not prophecies less because you yourself have <aided> in their fulfilment. The gold is not yours. Prosperity shall reign if the real King under the M. comes back. Be not outdone in generosity by <plain> Mr. Baggins who has <?bargained> all his reward for his friends. [Girion >] Dale & Lake Town are to be rebuilt[TN8]

'Who are you?' says the king of the wood elves.

'I am Gandalf!'

Then he believed at last that Thorin is indeed Thorin son of Thrain son Thror. why did he not say so? [A >] Your own acts <?condemn> you. – because dwarves understood better than all others the <power> of the greed of gold. and fear therefore more <certainly> to <?extend> it. You owe <them> aid not <?enmity>.

Thus came the peace and pact of the Ruined <City>

Woodelves rich presents

<Huge> <?sums> of <money> for rebuilding of Esgaron.

Messengers are sent many dwarves from N S E W

<Thorin> has <?decided>[TN9] never more <forsaken the> western lands.

In the left margin:

<Since the> dragon was slain beyond hope. <Thorin> <?grieves> at first when he learns of Bilbo's dealing with the Gem of Girion – but after a while he says 'There is indeed more <in> you than you know yourself. We <have> <illegible> as seemed unlikely to be thankful to Gandalf. And yet perhaps you have more to thank him for than all – even though you went hence empty-handed.' They bid Bilbo take his share over & above the gem. He says he is sick of the sight of gold – yet in the end he accepts <illegible>[TN10] <dwarves> a set of golden dinner service and a silver kettle. With these he sets out home with Gandalf. An escort of wood-elves is found <through> Mirkwood. How Gandalf came here?

TEXT NOTES

1 The illegible phrase following 'dark deserted halls' may be '?followed his torch'.

2 This detail of a smooth slot worn in the rock derives from the Fafnir

story, in which Sigurd knows where to dig his pit-trap because of the groove worn in the stone where the dragon goes to drink; cf. page 493.

3 This line is very difficult to make out, and may actually read 'Their ?whispered <illegible> speech.' In either case, whatever the exact wording the situation is the same, that they overhear conversation among the passing crows that warns them of the coming crisis.

4 The interesting detail of the raven bowing to Thorin 'now [that] Smaug is dead' suggests that the birds recognized Smaug's suzerainty while he lived and only acknowledge Thorin as the new King under the Mountain when the all-powerful usurper is dead. This might account for Smaug's tolerance of their presence; aside from the furtive creatures who have crept Gollum-like into the outer reaches of his lair (see page 581), the crows and ravens are almost the only living things found within the Desolation of Smaug, a fact that becomes more explicable if he views them as subjects instead of interlopers – fellow birds of prey, as it were, yet posing no threat to his authority.

5 This phrase is scrawled in large letters across the lower right-hand portion of this page, the writing having otherwise stopped some five or six lines short of the bottom of the page.

6 This line, added in the top margin, seems to refer to the Thrush mentioned at the bottom of the preceding page. The manuscript page specified gives the account of Smaug's death, and in fact Tolkien added to the bottom of that page an account of the thrush appearing and bringing word to Bard of Smaug's weak point. The 'part about dwarves' would seem to be the Master's turning the townsfolk against the dwarves and blaming them for all their woes; either that or the section where the focus shifts back to the Mountain and what happened to Bilbo and the dwarves there (i.e., Chapter XIV).

7 *Esgaron*: Both here and again below Tolkien gives this earlier, alternate spelling of the Elven name for Lake Town, which is always Esgaro*th* in the main text (cf. page 549). The two names clearly have the same meaning (see commentary following Chapter XIII and especially Text Note 11 on page 554), with Esgaron being the Noldorin form (as opposed to Esgaroth, which is Doriathrin; see Note 16 following Chapter XIII on page 566). See below for the probable point Tolkien had reached in the text when he wrote these Plot Notes.

8 This sentence is crammed in at the end of the line and may have been added slightly later.

9 These three words are very difficult to make out, and may instead read 'Then his ?descendants . . .'

10 The illegible passage may read 'a bag &' – that is, a single bag filled with treasure; cf. the small chest of gold and another of silver he winds up accepting in the published book (DAA.351).

The Pact of the Ruined City

These two replacement pages, which form part of the Plot Notes B/C/D sequence,[1] are closely tied with changes Tolkien made to Chapters XII (the rider on page 513) and XIII (particularly to the important marginal additions given on pp. 549–50), and clearly preceded Chapter XIV, for which it provided the framework. While by its very nature sketchy and tentative, it is also, with Plot Notes E, the closest we can now come to recovering the details of the Siege of the Mountain as Tolkien originally intended them, before the decisions to retain Bard and introduce the Dragon-sickness complicated the plot and diverted his plans.

It is remarkable that, having come so far, Tolkien still at this stage seems to have kept to his original plan in which there was to be no battle at the Lonely Mountain; the Battle of Five Armies had not yet arisen, its place being filled by 'the Battle of Anduin Vale', a quite distinct conflict in which the dwarves were to play no part. Hence there is no need even now for the invention of Dain and his company of dwarven reinforcements: the Siege of the Mountain (elves and lake-men against Thorin & Company) is present, but Tolkien still expected Gandalf to be able to resolve the conflict by diplomacy. The only battle taking place in the east is that of Lake Town, which is already past by this point, and there is still no need to bring goblins, wolves, bears, or eagles out of the west to join the conflict. Tolkien did not yet know that Thorin or any of his companions were to die; instead, the story ended with him restored to his rightful place as King under the Mountain. Whereas in Plot Notes C Bilbo gives 'A part of his share' to the Lake-men and wood-elves, he now gives away his entire stake to save his friends. It is important to note that in the published tale Bilbo's attempt to buy peace fails,[2] and the battle between dwarves, wood-elves, and lake-men is averted only by the unexpected arrival of the goblin-warg army on the scene. By contrast, in Plot Notes D Bilbo's goodwill gesture provides Gandalf the opportunity he needs to reveal himself and talk sense to the dragon-slayer and his treasure-greedy allies, thus avoiding battle entirely.

This War for Gold

The anger of the lake-men is understandable enough, although their eagerness to fix blame and demand reparations smacks more of post-Great War politics than *wergild.* The recalcitrance of the wood-elf king, however, is especially notable; his reluctance in the published book to shed blood over something as trivial as dragon-gold[3] represents a complete reversal of his role in these events as Tolkien originally foresaw them in the Plot Notes. With no legitimate claim to the treasure himself, he tries to convince Bard to reject Bilbo's offer ('The wood-elves and other counsellors speak ag[ainst] him'), probably motivated by the knowledge that if his human allies recover the whole treasure his own share will of course be all the greater. Indeed, as far back as Chapter X, he had decided to seize any treasure the dwarves might gain from Smaug as it passed west through Mirkwood ('no treasure will come back through Mirkwood without my having to say in the matter', page 441). His behavior prompts Gandalf to remark 'Your own acts condemn you,' a judgment in keeping with Tolkien's earlier observation that although the wood-elves share in the treasure Bilbo gives to the Lake Men, they 'may not deserve it' (Plot Notes C, page 497).[4] However, since the woodelves and woodmen were to fight at Bilbo's side in the Battle of the Anduin Vale outlined in the final page of Plot Notes B/C/D/B, clearly the elvenking was to be given a chance to redeem himself before the story was over, as of course he does in the published book. Indeed, this projected final battle that Tolkien never came to write out would, in its alliance of elves and men against goblins, have been rather like one of the battles described in the early versions of the Silmarillion story (i.e., the wars against Melkor the Morgoth); in the more circumscribed world of *The Lord of the Rings* such battles are ascribed to the distant past, the last such being in the days of 'the Last Alliance' three thousand years before.[5]

During the Third Phase of composition on *The Hobbit* that brought the book to its conclusion, Tolkien was to shift this greed from the elvenking to the dwarves, which makes all the more fascinating the idea that can just be glimpsed here that, since dwarves 'understood better than all others the power of the greed of gold', for that very reason they try not to expose others to that temptation. This seems to suggest that long association with treasure has to some degree inoculated the dwarven people against dragon-sickness: certainly in the chapter that follows the dwarves are far less giddy and obsessive about the vast treasure, the very sight of which had moved Bilbo beyond words (and to the very uncharacteristic pocketing of the Gem of Girion when he has the chance), than in the published book – and far more practical about pocketing what they can of their temporarily recovered possessions while the opportunity lasts. In support of this, there is also the matter of Thorin's urging Bilbo to take a full share of the treasure 'over & above the gem'.[6]

Under the Mountain

Unfortunately, neither the relevant section of Plot Notes C nor this expansion and replacement of it tells us what the dwarves are doing between their blocking off the Front Gate in preparation of the siege and their deliverance when Bilbo and Gandalf between them break the deadlock. There is a hint of disagreement between Bilbo and the dwarves in the line 'Bladorthin . . . makes dwarves pay Bilbo' (Plot Notes C), the fact that Bilbo *sneaks* out to find Bard, and Thorin's later grief when he learns that Bilbo has bartered away the Gem of Girion, but this latter may simply be regret that Bilbo has lost the treasure Thorin intended him to take home with him as his reward for all he has done (see Plot Notes B and C for the Gem as Bilbo's portable payment). Given the lakemen's stated hatred for the dwarves (page 551) and the wood-elves' intention to 'capture' them and seize the gold (ibid.), Thorin & Company's failure to negotiate a satisfactory resolution with the besiegers may be due less to dwarvish stubbornness and more to a prudent desire not to surrender themselves to what might be a lynch mob accompanied by traditional enemies who would gladly take all Thror's treasure and condemn the dwarves to indefinite if not interminable imprisonment. If this is the case, then Bilbo's attempt to strike a deal may not be going against Thorin's wishes to circumvent an intractable dwarven king so much as the hobbit's simply taking the initiative when the dwarves are fearful to, the established pattern of all the hobbit's dealings with the dwarves from the time they send him off down the newly-opened secret tunnel alone at the beginning of Chapter XII to the end of the Second Phase text. In any case, we have Gandalf's word for it that their motivation is not unreasoning greed, but a salutary fear of what effect the dragon-sickness might have on the already aroused Lake-men and treasure-hungry elves.

The Gem of Girion

As in the earlier stages in this sequence of Plot Notes, the Gem of Girion continues to play a significant role in the events of these final chapters. Earlier it had served as a motivator for Bilbo to kill the dragon, his promised reward for delivering the treasure into Thorin & Company's hands. Now that the role of dragon-slayer has been split off and assigned to a new character, Bard, the Gem becomes a bargaining chip with which Bilbo hopes to satisfy Bard's claim for his rightful share of the treasure (what better way than with Girion's own Gem to Girion's heir?). Thus it has moved into the role it will play in the final story, although the events which followed in the Third Phase text (Bard's attempt to ransom it back to Thorin for a one-fourteenth share of the treasure, a transaction eventually completed by Dain) have not yet emerged. Instead of Bilbo bringing it home with him as his chief memento of his eventful journey, it has now become the peace-price he is willing to pay to save his friends, and the idea that Bilbo comes home with only a few token treasures to show for all his troubles, present since the earliest layer of Plot Notes B, nears its final form.

True, After a Fashion

In keeping with the general interest in dreams and prophecies in the latter section of the book, for the first time the 'pleasant fable' mentioned casually in an addition to Chapter X – 'Thror and Thrain would come back one day and gold would flow in rivers through the northern falls, and all that land would be filled with new song and new laughter' – has now been elevated to the dignity of a prophecy. But unlike in the final book here it is Bard, not Bilbo, who is surprised to find himself its fulfiller, and Gandalf's pointing out of this fact comes much earlier ('Believe not prophecies less because you yourself have aided in their fulfilment'), as part of the negotiations to resolve the conflict (the pact we might call 'the Peace of the Ruined City').

In any case, primed by the writing of these Plot Notes, Tolkien soon resumed the story and brought it within what he must have thought a chapter or two of the ending, not foreseeing the tangle that would require him to break off and reconsider the events of the climax.

NOTES

1 Actually, more accurately the B/C/D/B sequence, since the original final page of the earliest layer was renumbered 5 > 6 when Plot Notes D was inserted into the composite document, indicating that this page was still intended to outline the conclusion.

2 In this he is like Frodo, who in Tolkien's opinion actually fails in his mission to destroy the Ring (cf. JRRT 1965 BBC radio interview with Denys Gueroult), but who is a hero nevertheless for having made its destruction possible. Similarly, Bilbo in the published book fails to establish an accord between King Thorin and the besieging forces, loses for a time the friendship (or at least the trust) of the dwarves, and actually finds himself joining forces with the men and elves who are there to kill his travelling companions and take Smaug's gold by force; disaster is averted only through the unforeseen intrusion of the goblins.

3 'Long will I tarry, ere I begin this war for gold . . . Let us hope still for something that will bring reconciliation' (DAA. 338).

4 One must, however, sympathize with his outburst that, if Thorin was indeed the heir of Thrain and Thror, 'why did he not say so?' The comment that 'then he believed at last', which presents the wood-elf king in a slightly more favorable light, however contradicts his having already accepted Thorin's identity back near the end of Chapter XIII ('When news of the rousing of the Dragon reached him, and of the fire upon the mountain tops, he thought that he had heard the last of Thorin Oakenshield', and he certainly knew exactly who Thorin was since 'he . . . had not forgotten the legend of the hoard of Thror').

5 In *The Lord of the Rings*, Elrond makes clear that the Last Alliance is so called because 'Never again shall there be any such league of Elves and Men; for Men multiply and the Firstborn decrease, and the two kindreds are estranged' ('The Council of Elrond', *LotR*.261). It is unclear on the surface why the alliance here in *The Hobbit* of men and elves fighting side-by-side against first dwarves and then wargs and goblins does not count, unless by 'such league' Elrond meant something grander than the relatively small armies and localized battles of the Anduin Vale or Lonely Mountain projected here. In any case, his statement reflects a later conception than that described in *The Hobbit*, especially so far as the projected 'Battle of Anduin Vale' is concerned, and can only be accepted as true if we reserve the grand title of 'alliance' for massive struggles between great hosts (e.g., the surviving Númenoreans and Noldor against all Sauron's armies) resulting in the end of an Age of the world. Here again we see *The Hobbit* closer in conception to similar battles described in the early Silmarillion material than either is to *The Lord of the Rings* and the later Silmarillion material.

6 Although, strictly speaking, Thorin may just have been wanting to honor the letter as well as the spirit of the contract: 'one fourteenth share of total *profits* (if any)' and been willing to count the sacrifice of the Gem of Girion as a necessary 'expense' in achieving their goal. Even so, this reinforces the point that he shows no signs of contracting the dragon-sickness anywhere in these Plot Notes or in the few remaining pages of the Second Phase text that follow.

Chapter XIV

WHILE THE DRAGON'S AWAY . . .

This chapter start is one of the very few marked as such in the original manuscript, with 'Chapter XIV.' written in ink at the top of manuscript page 159 (Marq. 1/1/15:7). This forms the verso of manuscript page 158: for the few remaining pages of the Second Phase manuscript (manuscript pages 158–167), Tolkien writes on both the front and back of each sheet, as he had done in the original Pryftan Fragment and the earlier parts of the Second Phase but unlike his practice from manuscript page 119 (the capture by wood-elves) onward, where he had written only on the front of each sheet.

This chapter underwent considerable revision and expansion when it was recast (as new Chapter XIII: Not at Home) to better fit its new place preceding the chapter describing Smaug's death (original Chapter XIII, which now swapped places with it to become the new Chapter XIV: Fire and Water). Remarkably enough, a fair copy in manuscript exists of this chapter, titled '(Smaug is) Not at home' (manuscript pages 'a'–'m'; Marq. 1/1/14:1–14), which serves as an intermediate text between the original Second Phase manuscript draft of this chapter (manuscript pages 159–65; Marq. 1/1/15) and the First Typescript version of the chapter (typescript pages 127–34; Marq. 1/1/63). I have not reproduced this fair copy manuscript, which belongs to the early part of Tolkien's work on the Third Phase, because for most of its length it closely resembles the text of the First Typescript and thus of the published book, but in the Text Notes that follow I have noted the most significant changes between the manuscript and the fair copy, between the fair copy and the First Typescript, or between the typescript and the published book.

Their great foe was dead, and the hoard no longer had a keeper, but the dwarves did not know it. [Another danger was gathering about them, an army come > armies coming for the ransacking and plundering of the mountain palace. >] Nor would they have rejoiced had they known that the last great danger, the danger Thorin had dreaded all along, and which their silence before the Elvenking had not averted, was gathering about them – a host was marching up to ransack and plunder the halls of Thror. But they knew nothing of all this. They sat in the dark, and eventually silence fell round them. Little they ate and little they spoke. The passage of time they could not count, they scarcely dared to move, the whispers of their voices echoed and rustled in the tunnel. If they dozed they woke still to darkness and the silence going on unbroken.

At last after days [*added*: & days] <of waiting> as it seemed, when they were choked and dazed for want of air – it was but two [days >] nights and the day between in reality – they could bear it no longer. Almost they would have welcomed some sound of the dragon's return below. In the silence they feared his cunning devilry, not knowing that he would never again return to his golden bed, but was lying cold as stone [upon the twisted >] twisted upon the floor of the shallows of the lake, where forever after his great <bones> could be seen in calm weather, [and >] amid the ruined pile of the old town, [but no >] if any one dared to cross the accursed spot.

At last heedless of noise they went back to the door only to find by their groping that all the outer end of the tunnel was shattered. Neither they nor the magic which it had once obeyed – even if they had known it – would open it again.

'We are trapped!' they say. 'This is the end; we shall die here when our food is gone, or [choke >] stifle before that'.[TN1]

And yet somehow Bilbo felt a lightening of the heart. The gloom and foreboding that had settled on him on the night of the dragon's last assault was lifted. He felt as if a menace had departed [and] his courage returned (and trust in his proven and astonishing luck).

'Come come!' he said. '"While there's life there's hope," as my father used to say, and "third time pays for all".[TN2] I am going down the tunnel once more. I have been down twice when I knew there was a dragon at the other end, and I think I will risk a third visit, when I am no longer at all sure – and anyway <there> is no other way out of this.

'If you will take my advice you will all come with me this time; but do be careful and as quiet as you can be. There may be no dragon, but then again there may be. I am not going to take unnecessary risks with Smaug any more'.

[Something >] In desperation they agreed, and Thorin was the first to creep forward by Bilbo's side. Down down they went – but dwarves are not as good as hobbits when it comes to real stealth, and it was fortunate there was no listening ears at the far end of the echoing passage: the very puffing of their breath magnified in that place would have been enough for Smaug.[TN3] But no sound stirred below.

Near the bottom (as well as he could judge) Bilbo slipped on his ring again. But he scarcely needed it; the darkness was complete, and they were all invisible, with rings and without. So dark was it that Bilbo came to the opening unexpectedly put his hand on nothing, and stumbled forward and rolled headlong into the hall. There he lay still not daring to get up or even breathe. But nothing moved. There was not a gleam of light – unless far off, as his eyes [got >] stared fearfully into the blackness, he caught a pale white gleam. But certainly it was no spark of dragon-fire though the stench of the worm was still in the place, and it was hot and the taste of his vapour was on the tongue.[TN4]

At length B. could bear it no more. 'Confound you Smaug, you villain' he said aloud. 'Stop playing hide and seek. Give us a little light and eat me after if you must!'

Faint echoes ran about the unseen hall, but there was no answer. Bilbo got up, but he did not know in which direction to turn.

'Something seems to have happened to Smaug, I do believe' he said.[TN5] 'Now I hope Oin or Gloin has got a tinderbox, or can make a light. Let's have a look round before the luck turns!'

The dwarves were very alarmed when B. fell forward with a noise and were still frightened when they heard his voice, but Oin [> Gloin] was sent back as Bilbo asked to find some materials for light, if he could, among their goods near the upper end <of the> tunnel. Before long a little twinkle of light showed that he was returning with a small pine-torch alight and a bundle of others under his arm.[TN6]

Bilbo took the little lighted torch, but the Dwarves would not yet use the others, but preferred to stop inside the tunnel and see what would happen first. As Thorin explained [he > B >] Mr Baggins was still officially their expert burglar and investigator. If he liked to risk a light that was his affair: they would wait for his report.

So they sat near the opening and watched. They saw him steal[TN7] across the floor holding aloft his tiny light – a little flickering patch of red in the blackness. Every now and again there was a glint at his feet as he stumbled upon some golden thing. The light [<rose?> >] grew smaller as he wandered away into the huge hall, then it began to rise dancing into the air. Bilbo was climbing the great mound of treasure. Soon he stood near the top, and from afar they saw him stoop but they did not know the reason.

It was the Gem of Girion,[TN8] for such Bilbo guessed it to be from the description of the dwarves. Ever as he climbed forward the same [pale >] white gleam had shone before him like a small globe of pallid light; now as he approached it was tinged with [a] flickering sparkle of red [>splintering beams] reflected from his torch. At last he looked down upon it, and caught his breath. It held his eyes and he gazed in wonder. It was a great white gem, that shone of its own light within, and yet cut and fashioned by the dwarves to whom Girion had given it,[TN9] it caught and splintered all light that it received into a thousand sparkles of dazzling white. It was a large gem and heavy, larger than the hobbit's small hand – that was stretched out to it, drawn by its enchantment. Suddenly he stooped, lifted it and put it in his pocket.[TN10]

'Now I am Burglar indeed' thought B. ' – but I suppose I must tell the dwarves what I have done. Yet they said I could take my share as I could [> pick and choose my own share] – and I think I would choose this, if they took all the rest. But it remains to be seen, if I have won my share at all yet'.[TN11]

With that thought he went on. Down the mound he climbed, [and all round the walls he wandered >] and his spark was hidden from the watching dwarves. All round the walls he wandered, and they saw it dimly again in the distance, and then coming back [> Then they saw it red and far in the distance again].

On he went till he came to the great doors of the hall at the far side, and a draught of air nearly blew out his torch. He peeped through, shielding the flame with his hand, and caught a glimpse of vast passages, and stairs going up into the gloom.

Then a black shape flew [> swooped] <in the air> [> at him], brushed his hair; the flame flickered as he started, stumbled back, and fell. The torch dropped head downward & went out. 'Only a bat I suppose and hope' he said ruefully, 'but now what am I to do.'[TN12]

'Thorin Balin!' he cried out. 'The light's gone out. Some one come and help mc!' He didn't like being lost in the dark so far away from the tunnel at all and for the moment his courage failed altogether.

Faintly from far off the dwarves heard 'Thorin Balin!' echoing and 'help!' 'Now what on earth or under it has happened?' said Thorin. They waited a minute, but no dragon-like noises came. 'Come on one of you' said Th. 'strike another light. We must go and help Mr Baggins I suppose'.

'It does seem our turn' said Balin.

So when Gloin had lit a couple of torches they crept out[TN13] and went along the wall as hurriedly as they could; and before long they met Bilbo trying to feel his way round. They were very relieved to hear his account of what had happened, though what they would have said if he had told them at that moment about the gem of Girion I don't know. The mere fleeting glimpses of the treasure which they had caught had rekindled all the fire of their hearts; and when the fire of the heart of a dwarf is kindled by jewel and gold his courage grows.[TN14] They no longer needed any urging of Bilbo's. Both Balin and Thorin were eager now to explore, and willing to believe that at any rate for the present Smaug was not at home. Soon they had all the torches alight and all the party stole out of the tunnel and entered the hall which the dwarves had never [*cancelled*: again] entered since the days long ago [of] the dragon's coming.

Once they had started the exploration they forgot fear and

<caution>. They lifted old treasures from the mound and held them up in the light and felt them and fingered them. They took down mail and weapons from the walls and armed themselves.[TN15] Royal and princely Thorin looked in a coat of gold with a silver-hafted axe in his belt.

'Mr Baggins!' he said 'Here is the first payment of your reward! Cast off your old coat and put on this!' Then he put upon Bilbo a small coat of mail, <wr>ought for some elf-prince long ago.[TN16] It was of silvered steel,[TN17] [and pearls were <clustered> >] adorned with pearls, and a belt of pearls and crystals went with it. A light helm of figured leather strengthened within with hoops of steel, and studden about the rim with gems they set upon his head. An absurd desire to look at himself in a glass took hold of him: [He began to >] but he still kept his head more than the dwarves.[TN18]

[He grew >] 'Come!' he said 'we are armed, but what has any such armour availed against Smaug the Dreadful? The treasure is not yet regained. We are seeking not for gold but a way of escape. Let us get on.'

'True, true' said Thorin ' – and I will be your guide. Not in a thousand years shall I forget the ways of this palace.' So now the dwarves covered their glittering mail with their old[TN19] cloaks and the helms with <their> hoods, and followed behind Thorin, a line of little torches in the Dark.

Out [into the >] through the wide doors they went in single file. Dreading at every step to hear the rumour of Smaug's return, for Bilbo's words had recalled them only too well to their danger, they crept in single file into the passages <outside>. Though all was befouled [*added*: & <blackened>] with the dragon and all the old adornments rotten or torn away, Thorin knew every road and turn. They climbed long stairs, turned and went down <hollow> echoing ways, turned again and climbed yet more stairs, smooth carved and even in the long rock; and yet more stairs again, [Till Bilbo could go on no more. >] Up and up they went and met no sign or <word> of anything, save wild and fierce animal shapes,[TN20] and suchlike forms that slipped off into the shadows. At last Bilbo felt he could go on no more – the stairs were steep and high for him, although he alone was not carrying any <other> treasure than his armour.[TN21] The dwarves' pockets were stuffed with gold & gems (for fear this shd be their only chance of gaining anything); and besides they had all the bundles of such foods as they had got into the tunnel to carry on their backs.

'A little further still' said Thorin. 'We shall see the Day ere long. Cannot you feel the <sniff> of [> beginnings of] a new air?'

'Come on [> along] Bilbo' said Balin, taking his arm ' – if we get out safe and alive it will be due to you many times over; we cannot leave you here, nor can we wait.' So as they had done in the goblins cavern they picked him up and carried him[TN22] forward, until suddenly the roof sprang high far above the waning light of their torches. Light came in from an opening in the roof. Pale and white, and more light from great doors at the far end, one of which was fallen on the ground, the other was hanging on one broken hinge.

'This is the Great Hall of Thror, his hall of feasting and of council. And from the Gate it is not far off' said Thorin.

They passed out again[TN23] and soon [*cancelled*: before them the great arch of the Front Gate shone – blackened and ruined but still <?standing> <?firm> at the <illegible> and <splendid> at the <illegible> >] a sound of water fell upon their ears. Out of a dark tunnel issued, a boiling water and flowed in a built channel beside their road. 'There is the birth of the Running River' said Thorin, 'and it is hasting to the Gate. Let us follow!'

Round a wide turn they went and before them stood the [*added*: broad] light of day. A rising sun sent its light from the East between the arms of the mountain, and beams of gold came in and fell upon the floor. Before them was a great arch, still showing cunning work within, blackened and ruined & splintered as it was. They were come to Front Gate, and were looking forth to the East. A whirl of bats went up affrighted by their smoking torches which they had not put out. Their feet slipped upon the floors that were smooth and slimy with the passing of the great Dragon that had lived there long. The water rushed noisily past them [> below them] in its bed. They were dazzled by the morning light.

This paragraph and those that followed in the Second Phase manuscript were rearranged, rephrased, and expanded in the 'fair copy' (page 'i'; I/1/14:9), which has so many changes and crossouts in the course of writing that it here becomes essentially another draft, although still unusually legible by Tolkien's standards. The First Typescript here represents a polished and slightly revised version of the fair copy text. Parts of this section were also revised again at the page proofs stage (Marq. 1/2/2: pages 248–50 plus rider to page 249), with Tolkien (an experienced proofreader) taking care that each revision took exactly the same amount of space as the line(s) it replaced so that necessary changes would only affect those specific lines and not force the resetting of subsequent pages.

I do not reproduce the details of these three intermediate stages here, since the fair copy revision essentially achieves the familiar text of the published book except for geographical details regarding the orientation of the Front Gate with the rising sun and the path to the outlying watch-post; the most significant of these revisions are covered in the Text Notes.

Fair indeed was the morning <clear> with a cold North wind upon the threshold of winter when they looked out blinded with the light after the days and nights of dark; and sweet was the feel of the air on Bilbo's face. Far off he saw the ruins of Dale in the valley below, to which a long road wound down [*added*: <below> the stones], ruinous but still to be seen. On his right the clifflike bank of the Running River rose in the distance from which he and Balin had gazed. It was <only then> that he realized how hot the dragon's lair had been;[TN24] and that smokes and vapours were drifting out of the Gate <water>head and up into the morning air – which struck him now keen and piercing chilly.

'What are all those birds doing I wonder?' he said to Thorin, pointing up to great clouds of them that were circling in the sky southward over the river, while ever more seemed to be gathering <beyond> them, flying up dark from the South.

'There is something strange happening' said Thorin. 'The crows are all gathering as if after a battle, or as if a battle was afoot. I would give a good deal to know where Smaug is and what he is doing.'

'One thing we must do at any rate' said Bilbo '& that is get away from his Front Gate [as soon >] while we have a chance'.

'My Front Gate' corrected Thorin ' – still your advice is good. There is a place just beyond the Gate where [we can >] there used to be a bridge, and doubtless the river can anyway still be crossed, and there are steps beyond up the high South bank – and onto the long <Southern> Spur where [> under which] our first camp was made. [From there we may be able to find >] From there we can see far to South and West & East'.[TN25]

'More climbing!' groaned Bilbo.

'Your own advice!' said Thorin. 'We can have some food at the top.'[TN26]

The bridge was broken of course but they easily forded it. When they reached at last the top of the steps, and the winding upward path beyond, they found they were on an old flat look-out post with a wide view. There was a rocky opening there – 'steps lead down back into the mountain'[TN27] said Thorin 'or used to [> once did]. We used to keep watchmen here ever in the old days. If only it had had a northern view we might have [*added*: been ready in time to] kept [> keep] out Smaug & all this adventure wd never have been necessary! Still here we can lay hid and see without being seen.'[TN28]

They look [South >] West & there was nothing, nor East, and in the South there was no sign of man or dragon; but ever the birds were gathering.

The Second Phase text continues for another two manuscript pages, into what is now Chapter XV, but I halt here at the bottom of manuscript page 165, the spot Tolkien would later choose for his chapter-break.

TEXT NOTES

1 The opening paragraphs of this chapter were recast once the decision was made to make it precede, rather than follow, the account of Smaug's death. Accordingly, these paragraphs were replaced by the following in the intermediate fair copy manuscript:

> In the meantime the Dwarves sat in darkness and utter silence fell about them. Little they ate and little they spoke. They could not count the passing of time; and they scarcely dared to move, for the whisper of their voices echoed and rustled in the tunnel. If they dozed they woke still to darkness and to silence still unbroken.
>
> At last after days and days of waiting, as it seemed, when they were becoming choked and dazed for want of air, they could bear it no longer. Almost they would have welcomed some sound from below of the dragon's return. In the silence they feared some cunning devilry of his, but they could [not] sit still in hunger there for ever.
>
> Thorin spoke: 'Let us try the door' he said. 'I must feel the wind on my face soon or die. I think I would rather be smashed by Smaug in the open than suffocate in here'. So several of the dwarves got up and groped back to where the door had been. But they found that the upper end of the tunnel had been shattered, and blocked with broken rock. Neither key nor the magic it had once obeyed would ever open that door again.
>
> 'We are trapped' they groaned. 'This is the end. We shall all die here!'

This passage was slightly revised, both in contemporary ink and later pencil, bringing it more into line with the typescript (which is here identical with the published text; cf. DAA.289), but I have given it here as it was originally written.

2 For 'third time pays for all', Tolkien's (or, rather, Bungo Baggins') variant on a traditional but now unfamiliar maxim, see Text Note 3 following Chapter XII on page 516. We now learn a second saying of Bilbo's father, 'While there's life there's hope', a familiar proverb credited to the Roman orator Cicero [died 43 BC]. In its original form, appearing in a letter to his friend Atticus (*Epistolarum ad Atticum*, ix.10), the saying went 'While the sick man has life, there is hope'.

From these two proverbs, we can conclude a few things about the elusive Bungo, about whom very little indeed appears in the legendarium. First, he shared either his son's fondness for apt quotation or knack of coining proverbial sayings – cf. Bilbo's 'escaping goblins to be caught by wolves', which Tolkien equates to the later 'out of the frying pan into the fire' (Chapter VI page 203), and 'don't laugh at live dragons' (Chapter XII page 512), which in typescript became 'never laugh at live dragons' and 'passed into a proverb' (typescript page 128, Marq. 1/1/62:9; DAA.283). Furthermore, those sayings of his which Bilbo remembers reveal a sunny disposition; they are words of encouragement, the very opposite of the gloomy sayings 'Sunny Sam' the blacksmith is fond of airing in *Farmer Giles of Ham* (e.g., FGH expanded edition page 55). Secondly, he had the daring to court and marry Belladonna Took, who is not only 'famous' in her own right but 'one of the three remarkable daughters' of The Old Took, who himself seems merely a notable personality in *The Hobbit* but who we learn in *The Lord of the Rings* was in fact the ruler of his country at the time (i.e., the Took and Thain, a position held successively by Bilbo's grandfather, uncle, and, at the time of the Unexpected Party, his first cousin, according to the genealogical tables in Appendix C of *The Lord of the Rings*) – an example of solid upper middle-class stock marrying old nobility. Finally, Bungo had a gift for satisfying creature comforts (Bag-End, which he planned and built, is an exceptional hobbit-hole, enviously desired by Bilbo's and Frodo's relations) and the foresight to plan for future comforts, having laid down wine of such excellence (Old Winyards) that was fully mature seventy-five years after his death (*LotR*.50 & [1136]).

3 This sentence was replaced in the fair copy by

> . . . to real stealth, *and they made a deal of puffing and shuffling which the echoes magnified alarmingly. Every now and again in fear Bilbo would stop and listen*, but no sound stirred below.

This revision removes the reassurance that 'no listening ears' waited below and increases the suspense for readers who did not yet know Smaug was dead, which of course would now only be revealed in the following chapter.

4 At this point, there is a change in the handwriting, which becomes distinctly neater and more legible for the next three paragraphs (the last on manuscript page 160). The ink is also darker, and this same ink has been used to touch up some of the less legible words in the preceding paragraph. Clearly, this represents a pause in composition, but probably only a brief one, possibly no one than from one night's writing session to the next.

5 This sentence was replaced in the fair copy with '"Now I wonder what on earth Smaug is playing at" he said. "He is not at home to day (or tonight, or whatever it is) I do believe . . ."' (fair copy page 'c'; 1/1/14:3), once again increasing uncertainty about Smaug's inexplicable absence for the reader as well as the characters.

6 This paragraph serves as a good example of the sort of development parts of this chapter underwent, where the essential points change very little but their expression was expanded and polished. In both of the examples below I have indicated changes from the previous text in italics:

> The dwarves, *of course*, were very alarmed when Bilbo fell forward with a *bump into the dragon's hall*, and *they* were *both* frightened *&* *surprised* when they heard his voice. *At first they did not like the idea of striking a light at all; but Bilbo kept on squeaking out for light, so* [*added*: *that at last*] *Thorin* sent Oin *and* Gloin back *to the* goods *they had saved at the top* of the tunnel. Before long a little twinkle showed *them* returning, *Oin* with a small pine-torch [*added*: alight] *in his hand, and Gloin with* a bundle under his arm.
>
> *Then Bilbo knew again in what direction the tunnel was. Quickly he trotted back and took the* torch . . . (fair copy page 'c'; I/I/I4:3).

This passage was revised in both contemporary ink and later pencil, and developed further in the first typescript:

> The dwarves, of course, were very alarmed when Bilbo fell forward *down the step* with a bump into the hall, and they *sat* [*added*: *huddled*] *just where he had left them at the end of the tunnel.*
>
> '*Sh! sh!' they hissed*, when they heard his voice; *and though that helped the hobbit to find out where they were, it was some time before he could get anything else out of them.* But *in the end, when* Bilbo *actually began to stamp on the floor, and screamed out* 'light!' *at the top of his shrill voice*, Thorin *gave way, and* Oin and Gloin *were sent* back to *their bundles* at the top of the tunnel.
>
> *After a while* a twinkl*ing gleam* showed them returning, Oin with a small pine-torch alight in his hand, and Gloin with a bundle *of others* under his arm. Quickly Bilbo trotted *to the door* and took the torch . . . (typescript page 128; I/I/63:2).

For all the additional detail and fleshing out of the scene, the most significant change here is the addition of the idea that a step down separated the secret tunnel from the vast chamber that Smaug had made his lair; no such step had been mentioned in the earlier descriptions of Bilbo's two previous trips down the tunnel.

7 This highly suggestive word choice, coming as it does in the paragraph before he pockets the Gem of Girion and becomes 'a burglar indeed', survived into the intermediate fair copy text – 'They saw the little dark shape of the hobbit steal across the floor . . .' (page 'c') – but vanished thereafter; the First Typescript reads instead '. . . *start* across the floor'.

8 Here the manuscript reading, 'the Gem of Girion' (manuscript page 161; I/I/15), survives into the fair copy as 'the gem of Girion' (fair copy page 'd'; I/I/14), which is then changed in ink to 'the Arkenstone'. At some later time, probably at the time of the creation of the First Typescript, 'Heart of the Mountain' was added in pencil to the fair copy page alongside 'Arkenstone'. The typescript reading (I/I/63:2) is the same as that of the published book: 'the Arkenstone, the Heart of the Mountain'.

9 The original story, that Girion had given Thror the Gem in payment for the arming of his sons (see Plot Notes C), is reflected in the wording of the Second Phase manuscript here. Although this paragraph is developed and recast in the fair copy (so that it resembles the typescript and published

texts), the phrase 'the dwarves to whom Girion had given it' remained, until it was struck out and replaced in faint pencil which seems to read 'the dwarves who dug it from the mountain's heart' (fair copy page 'd'; 1/1/14:4). In the First Typescript this has become 'the dwarves, who had dug it from the heart of the mountain long ago' (typescript page 129; 1/1/63:3), the reading of the published book (DAA.293).

10 This passage was carefully revised to establish the qualities of the Gem or Arkenstone, both physical (that is, its size and weight) and magical, carefully balancing hints of Bilbo's being under the power of the wondrous stone versus his acting on his own volition when he takes and hides it. First, an addition to the original manuscript made the Gem somewhat smaller, so that 'larger than the hobbit's small hand' became 'larger than the hobbit's small hand *could close upon*' (manuscript page 161; 1/1/15). The passive tense of the Second Phase manuscript ('the hobbit's small hand . . . was stretched out to it') was initially retained into the fair copy, which devotes its own paragraph to Bilbo's taking the gem and becomes, for the moment, a new draft (albeit an unusually neat one) as Tolkien experiments with the phrasing:

> [Suddenly Bilbo's hand was drawn towards it. He >] Suddenly Bilbo's arm went towards it, drawn by its enchantment. [He could scarcely lift it, for it was large and heavy. >] His small hand would not close over it, for it was a large and heavy gem; but he lifted it, shut his eyes, and put it in his largest pocket.

The typescript stays very close to this, only dropping one comma and substituting *deepest* for *largest*, apparently over an erasure. The phrasing of this final version – where Bilbo's arm is 'drawn by its enchantment', but the actual passive tense has been removed, and ending in a string of simple active tenses (lifted, shut, put) – nicely captures the ambivalence of the passage.

11 For Thorin's assurance that Bilbo could choose his own share, see their discussion near the end of Chapter XII (page 514), from manuscript page 151c:

> 'As for your share Mr Baggins' said Thorin 'I assure you we are more than satisfied with your professional assistance; and you shall choose it yourself, as soon as we have it! I am sorry we were so stupid as to overlook the transport problem . . .'

The line about Bilbo's uneasy feeling over what he has just done first appears in the fair copy text, replacing the final sentence of the paragraph:

> '. . . I would choose this, if they took all the rest!' All the same, he had an uncomfortable feeling that the picking and choosing had not been really meant to include this marvellous gem, and that trouble would still come of it.

12 Here and throughout the original Second Phase manuscript depiction of the scene in Smaug's empty lair, Bilbo is much less panic-strickened than in the published account. We are told that 'his courage failed

altogether', but the actual description of his actions, both here and in his earlier stumble in the dark on page 578–9, does not really bear this out – for example, Bilbo is already feeling his way along the walls when the dwarves finally strike a light in the original draft, whereas in the fair copy 'his wits had returned as soon as he saw the twinkle of their lights' (fair copy page 'e'; 1/1/14:5). Many details added at the fair copy and First Typescript stages – e.g., the description of Bilbo's shouts after the loss of his torch as 'squeaking', his peeping *timidly* through the great doors, 'ruefully' being replaced by 'miserably', et al. – all have the cumulative effect of diminishing Bilbo's stature and courage throughout this scene, from the time he enters the dragon's lair for a third time until the dwarves rejoin him there.

13 The fair copy text (fair copy page 'e'; 1/1/14:5) adds 'crept out, *one by one*,' which marks a final appearance in the book of the Unexpected Party motif, which we have also seen in the troll scene, the arrival at Medwed and the Mirkwood bonfires scene along the way.

14 The effect that the sight of treasure has on dwarves shifts, from positive ('his courage grows') in the Second Phase manuscript to ambivalent (not just 'bold' but 'fierce', no longer 'kindled' but 'wakened')† in the fair copy:

> . . . when the fire of the heart of a dwarf is wakened by jewels and gold [> by gold and by jewels] he grows suddenly [fierce >] bold, and he may become fierce.

The typescript rearranges this slightly, and makes one significant addition:

> . . . when the heart of a dwarf, *even the most respectable*, is wakened by gold and by jewels, he grows suddenly bold, and he may become fierce.

These changes were obviously made to match the evolving conception and introduction of the idea of dragon-sickness taking hold on Bilbo's companions, which had been absent in the Second Phase story – cf. the mention of 'respectable' dwarves, a term specifically applied to Thorin & Company by Medwed (see page 234).

†Implying it was already there, though dormant.

15 Added in hasty script in the bottom margin, and marked for insertion first following 'in the light' in the preceding sentence and then at this point:

> They gathered gems in their hands & let them fall <with a sigh>. – and always Thorin sought from side to side for something he could not see. It was the gem of Girion <Thror's> chief treasure, but he did not speak of it <again>.

This passage accords well with the conception of the dragon-sickness taking hold on the dwarves and especially Thorin, a plot-point not present when this chapter was first drafted (that is, in the Second Phase story). Accordingly, although there is no appreciable difference in ink, this marginal addition probably dates from the Third Phase and represents drafting for the intermediate fair copy manuscript, a transition between the original story and the familiar one that appears in the typescript and subsequently the published book.

The passage about Fili and Kili playing the harps (cf. DAA.295) entered as a hasty pencilled addition onto the fair copy (page 'f'), appearing in more polished form in the First Typescript. Fili and Kili were obviously musical; back in the first chapter they had played fiddles (page 36) while it had been Gandalf (= Thorin) who played the harp; here they prove skilled at the harp as well.

16 Added in pencil, and thus appearing in the fair copy and typescript: 'for some *young* elf-prince long ago'. This is possibly of significance, because it suggests that Tolkien might have conceived of the elves as somewhat smaller than human size when he originally wrote this passage. Initially, in his early 'fairy poetry' such as 'Goblin Feet' and 'Tinfang Warble' and in *The Book of Lost Tales*, Tolkien had thought of the elves as much smaller than human, but by the mid-1920s came to reject this and envisioned them instead as of similar stature to humans (as in the feys of medieval romance, legends of the Tuatha dé Danaan, and Spenser's *Faerie Queene*).

17 This is of course the same suit of armor which will become Frodo's mithril coat in *The Lord of the Rings*, but the idea of 'mithril' had not yet arisen. In Plot Notes C, this had been 'gold & silver mail made like steel' – that is, soft precious metals somehow hardened by dwarven craft to serve as protection. Tolkien may have changed this upon realizing that such armor would be so heavy that its wearer could hardly move (gold being almost as heavy as lead, and silver roughly twice the weight of iron) – cf. the similar change of Thorin's armor from 'a coat of gold' (Second Phase manuscript and fair copy) to 'a coat of gold-plated rings' (First Typescript and published book).

Although it's tempting to view *The Hobbit*'s 'silvered steel' as simply mithril under another name, the only thing that indicates that Bilbo's armor is anything more than silver-plated steel here is the fact that it has not tarnished or disintegrated, as real silver does over time,† and the same is obviously true of the many other silver objects in the legendarium – e.g. the Sceptre of Annúminas (already more than five thousand years old when Elrond surrendered it to King Aragorn; cf. *LotR*.1009 & 1080), the Elendilmir (that is, the silver circlet bearing the Star of Elendil, some three thousand years old), the horn from Scatha's hoard presented to Meriadoc ('wrought all of fair silver' and at least a thousand years old; cf. *LotR*.1014, 1102, & 1123), and indeed the silver harpstrings Fili and Kili play (which we are specifically told are 'magical') – forcing us to conclude that Tolkien simply chose to ignore this detail of physics for aesthetic effect, since he preferred perishable silver to immutable gold.

† Hence we have many more items of gold than of silver from ancient Egypt not just because silver was rarer than gold in the Nile valley but because gold does not oxidize and thus can survive for millennia unharmed, while

silver tarnishes within a few years and eventually oxidizes away entirely over the course of centuries.

18 This simple statement is invested with ominous overtones in the fair copy version, which reads '*All the same Mr Baggins* kept his head more *clear of the bewitchment of the hoard* than the dwarves *did*' (fair copy pages 'f' – 'g'). Similarly, the reference to Thorin's 'recovering his wits' when he replies, which enters in with the First Typescript, emphasizes the dweomer the dragon-gold casts upon the unwary.

The reference to Beorn's refreshments (see DAA.296) also enters in at the fair copy stage; like Bilbo's thoughts of Gandalf in Chapter XI, this allusion helps remind the reader of this character (who has not appeared since Chapter VII) and helps set up his return a few chapters later.

19 The word *old* is cancelled in the manuscript but restored in the fair copy, so I have retained it here.

20 We never gain any more information about what wild animals might be warily sharing the outer regions of Smaug's lair than this brief reference. These 'animal shapes' became, in the fair copy, 'furtive shadows':

> . . . no sign of any living thing, save furtive shadows that fled from the approach of their fluttering torches [> torches fluttering in the draughts].(fair copy page 'g'; 1/1/14:7).

With the exception of one word changed in the typescript ('save furtive shadows' > ''*only* furtive shadows'), this is the reading in the published book (DAA.296), so we never learn any more about these Gollum-like lurkers in Thror's deserted halls.

21 This statement of course ignores the fact that Bilbo is carrying the Gem of Girion in his pocket; even though it had not yet gained the status it later reached of being worth 'a river of gold in itself' (DAA.326), it was nonetheless already the pre-eminent item of treasure within the hoard; cf. Chapter XII page 514 and Text Note 39 following that chapter. Compare the dwarves' reasonable behavior here of taking as much of the treasure as they can manage on what may be their only chance before the dragon returns (and only after arming themselves and as a last action before leaving the treasure-chamber), not forgetting the more practical business of preserving their supplies and remaining food (another practical detail that vanished after the Second Phase manuscript), with their more greedful behavior in the published account, where they caress the treasure longingly – e.g. the inserted passage cited in Text Note 15 above and its fair copy analogue:

> . . . they lifted old treasures from the mound and held them in the light, caressing and fingering them. They gathered gems and stuffed their pockets, and let what they could not carry fall back through their fingers with a sigh.
>
> —fair copy page 'f' (1/1/14:6); cf. DAA.295.

22 This rather touching scene of Balin's solicitude for the exhausted hobbit and the dwarves taking turns to carry him disappeared from the story, although it survived into the fair copy, which adds the detail 'as in the

goblin-caves, *but now more willingly*' (fair copy page 'h'; I/I/14:8). The fair copy text also makes clear that one element of Bilbo's exhaustion was the mail-coat: 'he felt dragged down by the unaccustomed weight of his mail coat, and his head swam. He sat down and panted on a step.' To this was added a hasty pencilled addition which seems to read '. . . of his mail coat, *and the stone weighing heavy in his pocket*.' – that is, the idea that the Arkenstone itself was a heavy burden was still present. The typescript omits this entire passage.

For the weight of the gem, see Text Note 10 above; for the weight of the 'silver-steel' armor, see Text Note 17.

23 The grisly detail of this chamber being littered with the skulls and bones of Thorin's people first appears in the fair copy (page 'h'; I/I/14:8):

> They passed through the ruined chamber. Tables were rotting here and chairs overturned and decaying. Skulls and bones were upon the floor among flagones and bowls and broken drinking-horns [*added*: and dust].

Oddly enough, neither in the fair copy nor in any later text is there any mention of distress among the dwarves at the sight of their murdered and unburied kinsmen, or of their afterwards seeing to the remains. Perhaps, given the dwarven tradition of entombment (cf. Chapter XVIII and *LotR*.1113) and the pressing circumstances (with, so far as they knew, the murderer still on the prowl), Thorin & Company felt that being in stone chambers underground was burial enough until more formal arrangements could be made – compare, in *The Lord of the Rings*, Gimli's grief at finding Balin's tomb with his apparent unconcern about the bones of Ori and his companions lying scattered about the chamber (*LotR*.338–44).

24 In comparing how hot and stuffy it was inside Smaug's lair with the chill outside, the fair copy text (page 'i'; I/I/14:9) specifies that it is not just cool but almost winter:

> 'Well' said Bilbo. 'I never expected to be looking <u>out</u> of this door. And I never expected to be so pleased to see the first sun on a cold wintry morning as I am now. [Ugh! >] But the wind is cold!'
>
> It was. A cold breeze from the North [> East], from the threshold of winter, [> A cold North-easterly breeze coming from the gates of winter] was slanting into the valley and sighing in the rocks. They shivered in the sun, after their long time in the stewing depths of the caves, yet the feel of the air was sweet upon their faces.

The change here from North first to East and then to North-easterly comes in order for the text to match the evolving map of the Lonely Mountain. In Fimbulfambi's Map (see Frontispiece, plate one), the eastern spur of the mountain already had its slight southward curl at the end but this would not have blocked direct line of sight between the Front Gate and the rising sun in the east, especially since in winter the sun rises somewhat to the south of East. In the redrawn version, Thror's Map I (Plate I [bottom]), the curl is less pronounced but the mountain's arm is longer, so that it would have blocked the view directly to the east but still has a clear south-east view.

This is not the case with the third and final map, Thror's Map II, which is printed in all copies of *The Hobbit* (for example, DAA.97). The map's orientation has changed, so that East rather than North now appears at the top (in keeping with the tradition of medieval and renaissance maps, rather than our modern practice of putting north at the top). Here that arm of the mountain has shifted from just south of east (ESE) to stretch just east of south (SES), completely blocking the view to the east. Similarly, the newly lengthened matching arm with the watch-post by this point known as Ravenhill on its southernmost tip (and which forms the other wall of the little valley that gives Dale its name) blocks off everything to the west, so that the Front Gate now has a clear view only to the south. Hence in the final text written onto the page proofs the relevant passage reads:

> . . . wind is cold!'
>
> It was. A bitter easterly breeze blew with a threat of oncoming winter. It swirled over and round the arms of the Mountain into the valley and sighed among the rocks. After their long time in the stewing depths of the dragon-haunted caverns, they shivered in the sun.

Accordingly, since they could no longer see the sunrise, in another set of last-minute page proof corrections the *rising* sun became the *misty* sun, its light changed from *red* to *pale*, the sunbeams changed from *ruddy gold* to simply *gold*, and it has now become *late* morning (I/2/2: page 248) rather than dawn.

The changes from 'wintry' and 'threshold of winter' are interesting, since they seem to reflect the revised time-scheme of the published book, in which Durin's Day fell on the *last* new moon before the onset of winter – i.e., no more than twenty-eight days before the solstice on or around December 21st, several days of which have already passed between the opening of the secret door and the dwarves' arrival at the Front Gate. Bilbo and company thus reach the Front Gate in early to mid December, just a few days before midwinter, whereas in the original time-scheme where Durin's Day falls on the *first* new moon of autumn it would be early autumn, sometime between the very end of September through mid-October. See page 481 for more on the unresolved difficulties created by the shift in timing.

25 This paragraph describing the lay-out of the valley was replaced by the following in the fair copy (page 'j'), with Balin as the speaker:

> 'Five hours' march or so. But we can have a rest on the way. Do you see there on the right? There is the high cliff-like bank of the river that we looked out from when we first came here, Bilbo.† Between that and this gate there used to be a bridge, and beyond it steps cut in the rock-wall that led to a path winding up on to the southern mountain-spur, above where our first camp was made.'

†See page 472 in Chapter XI.

Aside from the usual polishing of phrasing and the changing of the first sentence to 'Five hours march, I should think, as we are tired and it is mostly uphill', this is essentially the text of the First Typescript and the original page proof. It was replaced by Tolkien's emendations of the page proofs to:

> 'Five hours march, I should think. It will be rough going. The road from the Gate along the left edge of the stream seems all broken up. But look down there! The river loops suddenly east across the Dale in front of the ruined town. At that point there was once a bridge, leading to steep stairs that climbed up the right bank, and so to a road running towards Ravenhill.† There is (or was) a path that left the road and climbed up to the post. A hard climb, too, even if the old steps are still there.'

† See page 618 and Text Note 4 for Chapter XV(a) for the first mention of Ravenhill in the manuscript.

26 The eight paragraphs of dialogue that replaced this simple two-line exchange first appear in the fair copy (from the middle of page 'j' to the top of page 'k'). The fair copy is similar to the final text (see DAA.299–300), with the most interesting variant being a cancelled passage in Thorin's reply:

> 'Come come,' said Thorin, laughing his spirits rising *as he <thought> of his golden armour and his fists full of gems, and all the treasure yet to <?come>* [> with the hope of treasure].

This passage comes at the bottom of an unnumbered cancelled page (replaced by fair copy page 'j') which forms the verso of fair copy page 'k'.

27 This suggests that there might once have been a tunnel from the guard-post to the dwarven city in the mountain's heart, as was the case with the secret tunnel on the western side. No such implication survives into the published text, but see Plot Notes E (pp. 626 & 627) for a stronger indication of this possibility.

28 This paragraph's brief description of the journey from the Front Gate to Ravenhill, and their initial exploration of the old guard post, was greatly expanded in the fair copy (pages 'k'–'l'). In general the fair copy account closely resembles the typescript that followed aside from the usual small variations in phrasing and some reassignments of speeches: in the typescript Thorin's speech regarding the watchpost is reassigned to Balin, while Balin's reply is split between Dori and Thorin – although Balin's original reply ('"Small protection, if Smaug spots us, I fear" said Balin; "but we must take our chance of that. Anyway we can go no further to-day".') lacks Dori's apprehensions – and a brief rejoinder from Bilbo is inserted to close the conversation.

Aside from one addition regarding *cram* (see part iii of the commentary to this chapter), the typescript carried over almost verbatim into the page proofs, but the paragraphs describing their journey to the outpost were carefully revised at the proofs stage to better match the geography of the valley containing the Front Gate and ruins of Dale as they emerged in the final version of Thror's Map and also the various illustrations of the Lonely Mountain Tolkien made near the end of his work on the book. In particular, the altered course of the river results in shifting the ruins of Dale from the river's right (eastern) bank in Thror's Map I (Plate I [top]) and the painting 'Smaug flies round the Mountain' (Plate X [bottom]), to the river's left (west) bank in several other drawings such as 'The Lonely Mountain' (DAA.273, H-S#136; see also H-S#134 & 135) and the final map (DAA.50 & 97); note also the contrast between the boulder-strewn eastern bank of the Running River and the floodplain bordered by cliffs on the western bank in 'The Front Gate' (DAA.256; H-S#130). I here give the changes made to this section of the proofs (corresponding to DAA.300) in tabular form:

- So on again they trudged along the northern bank of the river – to the south the rocky wall above the water was sheer and pathless > So on they trudged *among the stones on the left side* of the river – to the *right* the rocky wall above the water was sheer and pathless (the reading of the first edition; Douglas Anderson notes that Tolkien revised this line again in the 1966 Ballantine paperback edition; cf. DAA.300).
- After going for a short distance eastward along the cliff top they came on a nook sheltered among rocks and there they rested for a while > After going a short *way they struck the old road, and before long* came *to a deep dell* sheltered among *the* rocks; there they rested . . .
- After that they went on again; and now the path struck southwards and left the river, and the great shoulder of the south-pointing mountain-spur drew ever nearer. Soon the narrow road wound and scrambled steeply up > After that they went on again; and now the *road* struck *west*wards and left the river, and the great shoulder of the south-pointing mountain-spur drew ever nearer. *At length they reached the hill-path. It* scrambled steeply up.

One interesting detail that should be mentioned here is that the Second Phase manuscript describes the southern arm of the mountain as 'the long Southern Spur'. However, on Thror's Map I (Plate I [top]), the arm of the mountain pointing directly south is rather short, certainly shorter than the two eastern arms extending towards the Iron Hills. By contrast, on the published map (DAA.50) the southern arm is much longer. It is certain that the published map (Thror's Map II) did not exist at the point when Tolkien drafted this chapter, so the description here of the southern spur being 'long' could mean that this draft served as an intermediate stage in its extension.

Finally, the last page of the fair copy (page 'm'; I/I/14:14) includes a single short paragraph that was moved to the start of the next chapter when the First Typescript was created, bridging the time-difference between these two chapters now that their original sequence had been reversed and the new Chapter XIV made into essentially one long flashback:

Now you will be wondering as much as the dwarves about Smaug and it is time to tell you. You must go back to the evening when the Smaug had burst forth in rage, two days before [*cancelled*: the end of].

(i)
Dragon-sickness ('The Hoard')

> [T]he last great danger, the danger Thorin had dreaded all along, and which their silence before the Elvenking had not averted, was gathering about them – a host was marching up to ransack and plunder the halls of Thror.

While greed over the dragon's treasure was to play an important part in the climax of the story from the earliest draft, as we see from the preceding text and also Plot Notes C & D, Tolkien's original intent was to portray this as essentially an external force acting upon Thorin & Company from outside. Bilbo's uncharacteristic behavior of pocketing the Gem of Girion for himself and hints of disagreement between the hobbit and the dwarves about how best to handle the crisis of being besieged by angry lake-men and greedy, calculating elves aside, there are no indications whatsoever in the Second Phase materials that Thorin or any of the other dwarves succumb to the dragon-sickness of lusting after 'gold upon which a dragon has long brooded' (page 648). In fact, a passage from Plot Notes D suggests the opposite, and that their silence before the Elvenking had not been anxiety over splitting the treasure but

> . . . because dwarves understood better than all others the power of the greed of gold and fear therefore more certainly to <?extend> it.

The wisdom of this reticence is shown by the unedifying scramble for the treasure that ensues immediately following Smaug's death among the lake-men, enraged by their losses and deliberately stirred up into a blood frenzy by the Master (to deflect attention from his own inglorious behavior during the defense of their city), and by the wood-elves' king's plan to coolly seize the treasure with no better claim to it than the goblins of the Third Phase text have, namely because he shows up with an army large enough to take it.

Thus although the idea of the dragon-sickness bringing together rival claimants for the treasure was already the motivating factor for the projected climax in the final pages of the Second Phase text, resolving that crisis in the unwritten chapters, had Tolkien proceeded according to his original plan, would have been a relatively straightforward matter of dealing with a wholly external threat (the besieging armies). All this was to change when the second of the two great complications that derailed the Second Phase narrative entered the text:[1] the idea that Bilbo's companions would themselves succumb to the 'dragon-sickness' more strongly than any other group present, whereas he himself would be able to throw off the 'bewitchment' and 'enchantment' of the dragon-hoard and thus take actions that would estrange him from his trusted companions of the last year and more,[2] and even ultimately place him on the opposite side of the coming battle, which could no longer be averted. The great moral complexity of the published book's final chapters and its bittersweet resolution were thus an innovation of the Third Phase; the original Second Phase ending would have been much more of a piece with the bulk of the book that preceded it – full of incident but morally unambiguous.

Given the heavy influence of the Túrin and Sigurd stories throughout the 'Lonely Mountain' section of *The Hobbit*, it is no surprise that they played an important role here as well. But as is usual with Tolkien, he was careful and creative in his borrowings, and here the Fafnir legend exerts much less influence over *The Hobbit* than it does over the earlier Túrin's story and Tolkien's borrowings are mainly from his own earlier unpublished work (as would henceforth be the case with all his subsequent work, from *The Lord of the Rings* onward). The theme of cursed treasure had been a powerful narrative thread in *The Book of Lost Tales* (especially in the tale of 'The Nauglafring' or Necklace of the Dwarves) and no doubt owed much to the story of Fafnir's and Sigurd's treasure (also known as Andvari's Hoard after its original owner, or the Gold of the Nibelungs, or Das Rheingold, depending on which version of the legend one consults). The Völsungs' treasure on the one hand (in Germanic and Norse myth) and the gold of the Rodothlim, the Silmarils, and indeed the One Ring on the other (within Tolkien's legendarium) indiscriminately bring doom to all their owners one by one, although a few (like Bilbo, Beren, and Eärendel) escape the curse's full effects.

So strongly did this theme appeal to Tolkien that it inspired one of his finest poems, 'The Hoard' (ATB poem #14), earlier known as 'Iúmonna Gold Galdre Bewunden' – a title ('ancient gold, entangled with enchantment') which itself laid equal emphasis, in two metrically balanced Old English half-lines, on the gold and on the spell or curse it was under (see Note 13 following Chapter XII). The poem tells of a wonderful treasure of gold and silver and jewels owned successively by elves, a lone dwarf, a dragon, and a hero who becomes a king, all of whom perish miserably, leaving the hoard in the end lost forever, buried in a grassy mound. Furthermore, the poem makes clear that all but the original owners are chained to the hoard, possessed by their own possession. Tolkien explicitly drew a connection between 'The Hoard' and the Túrin/Nauglafring legend in his Preface to *The Adventures of Tom Bombadil* [1962], where he assigned the poem's authorship to Bilbo (who after all knew a thing or two about possessive possessions – cf. the first chapter in both Book I and Book II of *The Lord of the Rings* ['A Long-Expected Party' and 'Many Meetings', respectively] – but who had not been created as a character until at least seven years after this poem had first appeared in print!) during his years at Rivendell and said 'it seems to contain echoes of the Númenorean tale of Túrin and Mim the Dwarf' (ATB page 8). This tale is told in its fullest form in *The Book of Lost Tales* in the two stories 'Turambar and the Foalókë' (BLT II.69–143) and even more in 'The Nauglafring' (BLT II.221–51). We have already briefly touched on the Nauglafring story in Chapter IX (see 'The King of Wood and Stone', pp. 412–13), but the extraordinary degree to which the Rodothlim's treasure blights all who come into contact with it, a fate narrowly averted by most of the various claimants in *The Hobbit*, deserves revisiting, since the earlier story seems to have acted as a template underlying our tale.

The treasure's original owners, the Rodothlim elves (who in later forms of the legend became the Noldor of Nargothrond, Finrod Felagund's people), were destroyed by Glorund and his goblin [Orc] army, largely because of the arrogance and *ofermod* of Túrin before the battle. After his victory, Glorund claims all the treasure for himself and uses it for his bed, just as Smaug will later do with the wealth of Girion's and Thror's people:[3]

> all the mighty treasure that [the Orcs] had brought from the rocky halls and heaped glistering in the sun before the doors he coveted for himself and forbade them set finger on it, and they durst not withstand him, nor could they have done so an they would . . . (BLT II.85).

> . . . the dragon gloated upon the hoard and lay coiled upon it, and the fame of that great treasure of golden vessels and of unwrought gold that lay by the caves above the stream fared far and wide about; yet the great worm slept before it . . . and fumes of smoke went up from his nostrils as he slept (BLT II.87–8).[4]

As in *The Hobbit*, a small group later dares to venture into the dragon's territory to see if they can gain the treasure, but in the earlier tale these are not any survivors of the dragon's attack but an outside group, a picked band of wood-elves[5] sent by Tinwelint the elvenking, who is frank about his motivations:

> Now the folk of Tinwelint were of the woodlands and had scant wealth, yet did they love fair and beauteous things, gold and silver and gems . . . nor was the king of other mind in this, and his riches were small . . .
>
> Therefore did Tinwelint answer: '. . . it is a truth that I have need and desire of treasury, and it may be that such shall come to me by this venture . . .' (BLT II.95).

In the event, the expedition ends in disaster and achieves nothing besides stirring up the dragon and exposing Nienóri, Túrin's sister, directly to the dragon's curse.[6] Some time later, after Glorund's death at Túrin's hands far to the north (see commentary following Chapter XIII), the treasure passes into the keeping of Mîm the dwarf, who is here a figure of much greater stature than the petty-dwarf of the same name in the published *Silmarillion* (*Silm.*202–6 & 230). Indeed in the early tale Mîm is almost a Durin figure, called 'Mîm the fatherless', whose slaying is one of the factors that cause the dwarves of Nogrod (the Nauglath) and those of Belegost (the Indrafangs, a name later applied to Thorin's kin) to unite in a war of vengeance 'vow[ing] to rest not ere Mîm was thrice avenged' – a situation strongly reminiscent of the seven kindreds of the dwarves uniting to avenge the death of Thror, Durin's heir; cf. pp. 73 & 782 and *LotR.* 1111. Mîm's warnings to Úrin of the Woods (the later Húrin, Túrin's father, who comes with a band of elven outlaws to carry off the treasure), are very much in keeping with the ideas expressed more than a decade later in Plot Notes D:

> . . . one only dwelt there [in the caves of the Rodothlim] still, an old misshapen dwarf who sat ever on the pile of gold singing black songs of enchantment to himself . . . when those Elves approached the dwarf stood before the doors of the cave . . . and he cried: '. . . Hearken now to the words of Mîm the fatherless, and depart, touching not this gold no more than were it venomous fires. *For has not Glorund lain long years upon it, and the evil of the drakes of Melko is on it, and no good can it bring to Man or Elf*, but I, only I, can ward it, Mîm the dwarf, and by many a dark spell have I bound it to myself' (BLT II.113–14; italics mine).[7]

Thus the twin motifs of dragon-haunted gold bringing bad luck and a dwarven claim to immunity from the dragon-sickness were established very early on in the legendarium (although in the end both would be almost entirely reversed; see below). Glorund's hoard, doubly cursed by the dragon-sickness and Mîm's dying curse upon it – the one attracting people irresistibly to the gold and the other striking down those who give in to its allure and claim it – brings disaster to all its subsequent owners: the outlaws who carry it away (slain by the wood-elves), the wood-elves and Tinwelint himself (slain and their realm overthrown by angry dwarven smiths cheated of their payment for recasting the gold into treasures), the victorious dwarves (who fall to fighting among themselves over the treasure and are ultimately ambushed and killed by Beren's green elves), and even Tinúviel (i.e., Lúthien, whose second, human, life is cut short by the Nauglafring Beren gives her, the only piece of treasure he retained).[8] And although 'The Nauglafring' stresses Mîm's curse as the chief agent at work in the betrayals and murders that follow (cf. Christopher Tolkien's comment on BLT II.246), the dragon-sickness is also definitely at work:

> Now came Gwenniel [Melian] to Tinwelint [Thingol] and said: 'Touch not this gold, for my heart tells me it is trebly cursed. Cursed indeed by the dragon's breath, and cursed by thy lieges' blood that moistens it, and the death of those they slew; but some more bitter and more binding ill methinks hangs over it that I may not see' (BLT II.223).[9]

Over and over again the tale stresses the unnatural power that sight of this gold has over the actions of those who come into contact with it: 'he [Tinwelint] might not shake off its spell' (BLT II.223), 'the spell of the gold had pierced [Ufedhin's] heart' (ibid., page 224), 'by reason of the glamour of the gold the king repented his agreement' (ibid., page 225), 'he [Narthseg] was bitten by the gold-lust of Glorund's hoard' (ibid., page 231). Late in the Tale, Gwendelin [Melian] reaffirms the complex nature of the curse, including 'the dragon's ban upon the gold' (BLT II.239), while it is explicitly stated that the elf-on-elf battle wherein the Sons of Fëanor kill Dior, Beren's son, and destroy the green-elves' kingdom is not only because of their remorseless pursuit of the Silmaril but also 'nor indeed was the spell of Mîm and of the dragon wanting' (BLT II.241).

Perhaps this long and complicated story offers a salutary lesson into what might have happened had Bilbo and the wizard not intervened: the dwarves in possession of the dragon-treasure slain by the men of Lake Town, who in turn might soon have found themselves at odds with the wood-elves over its distribution, if the earlier story is any guide. Dragon-treasure has a way of arousing treachery and setting allies at each other's throats. Even within the Sigurd story, the hero's first act after slaying the dragon is to murder his foster-father, Regin, who had taught him how to kill Fafnir but was now expressing remorse over the deed (Fafnir having been his own brother before his transformation into a dragon after killing their father and stealing the entire treasure for himself). In words that sound remarkably like internal paranoia, the birds warn Sigurd that 'Regin [is] minded to beguile the man who trusts him' (i.e., young Sigurd himself): 'Let him [Sigurd] smite the head from off him then, and be only lord of all that gold . . . not so wise is he if he spareth him, whose brother he hath slain already . . . Handy and good rede to slay him, and be lord of the treasure!' (Morris & Magnússon, pages 64–5).

Luckily, Smaug's hoard is not cursed to the same degree: the dragon-sickness is there, but not the additional death-curse. It's true that the dwarves cursed Smaug himself ('[we] sat and wept in hiding and cursed Smaug' and '. . . we still mean to get it back, and bring our curses home to Smaug' – Chapter I (c), pp. 72–3), but it is specifically the dragon that they curse, not the treasure itself (which was, after all, their own). Then too there is the curse inscribed on the treasure-jar in the painting 'Conversation with Smaug' (see Plate XI [detail] and commentary below), but this would not apply to Thorin & Company, who are Thror and Thrain's rightful heirs, nor Bilbo, who is their contracted representative. Despite the later devlopment of the 'dragon-sickness' theme in the Third Phase and published book, relatively few succumb to it: Bilbo (very briefly), Thorin himself (who heroically throws off its influence during the Battle of Five Armies and dies free of it), most of Thorin's fellow dwarves to a lesser degree, and the Master of Lake Town at some later date. Ultimately, in fact, Thror's recovered treasure brings prosperity and peace to the region in the hands of those who can resist the dragon-sickness: Dain (who renews the Kingdom under the Mountain) and Bard (who re-establishes and rebuilds Dale and eventually extends his realm all the way down to include the rebuilt Lake Town); those who cannot resist meet with personal disaster but their fate has little effect on others (e.g., the Master of Lake Town's death from starvation does not harm Esgaroth's thriving recovery). This forms a stark contrast with Tolkien's models: the Völsung hoard is lost (knowledge of its location perishing with the execution of Sigurd's murderers), as is the gold of the Rodothlim (which Beren casts into the river, since it is tainted with all the injustices and murders committed over its possession), and also the treasure guarded by Beowulf's dragon (which is promptly buried once again, this time in Beowulf's barrow, and does his people no good whatsoever). Tolkien here creates a near-catastrophe followed by a happy ending appropriate to a fairy-story, in keeping with his ideas of eucatastrophe (cf. OFS): our hero may himself not wind up with a river of gold, but that gold is used instead of hoarded and makes his world a better place, so that in the end 'prophecies do come true, after a fashion'.

Such Mighty Heaps of Gold

Curiously enough, for all the mentions of the vastness and splendour of Smaug's hoard, relatively little space is devoted to describing it, and most of that is added in the expanded account of the dwarves reveling in their recovered treasure in the fair copy and First Typescript. Bilbo's awe at first seeing it robs him of all descriptive power, while the account of his later climbing the treasure-mound is almost casual, and the manuscript's description of the dwarves' exploration is more practical than sensuous, describing their choice of arms and armor and only then loading up on the most portable precious items (jewels and gemstones). To find a verbal portrait of such a hoard, a true Scrooge McDuck moment, we must go all the way back to *The Book of Lost Tales* and its description of the hoard of the Rodothlim:

> . . . such mighty heaps of gold have never since been gathered in one place; and some thereof was wrought to cups, to basons, and to

> dishes, and hilts there were for swords, and scabbards, and sheaths for daggers; but for the most part was of red gold unwrought lying in masses and in bars. The value of that hoard no man could count, for amid the gold lay many gems, and these were very beautiful to look upon . . . (BLT II.223).

After the great dwarven craftsmen have laboured for months at it, the hoard's beauty and splendor are exponentially increased:

> . . . in silken cloths, and boxes of rare woods carven cunningly . . . Cups and goblets did the king behold, and some had double bowls or curious handles interlaced, and horns there were of strange shape, dishes and trenchers, flagons and ewers, and all appurtenances of a kingly feast. Candlesticks there were and sconces for the torches, and none might count the rings and armlets, the bracelets and collars, and the coronets of gold; and all . . . subtly made and . . . cunningly adorned . . .
>
> A golden crown they made . . . and a helm too most glorious . . . and a sword of dwarven steel brought from afar that was hilted with bright gold and damascened in gold and silver with strange figurings . . . a coat of linked mail of steel and gold . . . and a belt of gold . . . a silver crown . . . [and] slippers of silver crusted with diamonds, and the silver thereof was fashioned in delicate scales, so that it yielded as soft leather to the foot, and a girdle . . . too of silver blended with pale gold. Yet were these things but a tithe of their works, and no tale tells a full count of them (BLT II.226–7).

The gem of the collection, quite literally, is the Nauglafring itself:

> Gems uncounted were there in that carcanet of gold, yet only as a setting that did prepare for its great central glory, and led the eye thereto, for amidmost hung like a little lamp of limpid fire the Silmaril of Fëanor, jewel of the Gods (BLT II.228).

This imbalance was more than rectified with the inclusion, beginning with the first American edition of 1938, of Tolkien's painting 'Conversation with Smaug' (Plate XI [top]), which not only shows the treasure-hoard in all its glory but is full of specific detail from the text.[10] First and foremost there is Smaug himself – clearly a favorite of Tolkien's, whom he illustrated more times than any other character in the entire legendarium – red-gold and resplendent, looking very sly and self-satisfied in a smiling crocodilian way, the very picture of 'malicious wisdom'. The Arkenstone also draws the eye, shining brightly from the very peak of the treasure-mound. The emerald necklace, the Necklace of Girion (which arose in the Third Phase text when the Arkenstone became too precious for the old story of Girion's having given it to Thror in exchange for his sons' armour to remain credible – see pages 364 & 496), stretches between Smaug's head and tail. Directly below the Arkenstone can be seen a two-handled cup, no doubt just like the one

Bilbo made off with on his first venture into the dragon-lair; horns, swords, shields, helmets and at least one crown, bowls, goblets, chests, many, many gems, and of course a mort of gold and silver coins, along with a few less identifiable objects,[11] make up the rest of Smaug's bed. Bilbo's mail coat and accompanying cap can be seen on the far wall, above Smaug's folded wings, along with a pair of spears that might be a relic of the spear with which Bilbo was to kill the dragon in Plot Notes B (page 364) but which along with the shields and spears seen to the right is more probably the 'mail and weapons' with which the dwarves arm themselves. The 'great jars' standing along the walls 'filled with wealth only to be guessed at' are here as well (see commentary below). Even the bats who later extinguish Bilbo's torch (not to be confused with the more bloodthirsty bats who accompany the goblin army) and the passage up are included, as is of course Bilbo himself (who, Tolkien noted, was much too large in proportion – *Letters* p. 35). The one element remarkable for its presence here when nothing in the text so much as mentions it are the dwarven bones that lie scattered about, many of them alongside the sword, axe, shield, or helm that all too obviously failed to avail them against the dragon. The only feature of the hoard specifically mentioned in the text which this picture fails to include are the golden harps with silver strings that so delight Fili and Kili; doubtless these were hung on the walls to the left or right outside our field of view.

The Dwarvenkings' Curse

Among the most interesting details of this painting is the inscription on the massive treasure-cup in the lower left (see Plate XI [detail]). The words are English but the alphabet used is Tolkien's Tengwar except for the initials at the bottom, which use the same Old English runes employed for Fimbulfambi's Map (Frontispiece to Part One) and Thror's Map I (Plate I [top]). It is unusual for Tolkien to combine both writing systems in a single illustration but not absolutely unprecedented; see the title page for *The Lord of the Rings* itself, with runes at the top (this time in Tolkien's own runic arrangement, which he called the *cirth*) and continuing in Tengwar at the bottom. Tolkien nowhere translates the writing on the cup and the inscription is partially obscured by the ladder, but the missing ligatures can be restored with confidence:

A literal transcription, with vowels indicated by diacritical marks in the original enclosed in parentheses and restored letters obscured by the ladder given in italics, reads as follows:

G (O) L D TH R (O) *R* TH R A (I) N
A K (E) R S T *B* (E) *THE* TH (E) F
TH [ror] TH [rain]

– that is, '. . . gold [of] Thror [and] Thrain . . . accursed be the thief', signed with the initials of THror and THrain. Note that this is only half of the full inscription, since the writing encircles the jar and we cannot know what appeared on the far side.

(ii)
The Arkenstone as Silmaril

The evolution of the Gem of Girion into the Arkenstone of Thrain, the Heart of the Mountain and supreme treasure of Durin's line,[12] was a gradual process throughout the latter parts of Tolkien's work on the Second Phase story from Plot Notes B on, until it finally reached its now-familiar form in the Third Phase texts. Initially invented to serve as a portable one-fourteenth share of the hoard to give the lie to Smaug's insinuation that the dwarves knew all along that Bilbo could never carry away his fair share, its value and allure were greatly increased with each iteration, until instead of Bilbo's designated portion it became the one item from the hoard Thorin most wanted to reclaim (DAA.326) and, in an ironic reversal, the one item he would have forbidden Bilbo to take.

In the original conception, the Gem of Girion is so named because it was given by Girion, King of Dale, to the dwarves of the Lonely Mountain in payment for the arming of his sons; we are never told how it came into Girion's possession. And just as a new character had to be introduced to fill the role of dragon-slayer once Tolkien decided it strained credulity to have little Bilbo in that role (Bard, whom Tolkien economically made the heir of Girion, thus opening up new plot-threads and possibilities even as he resolved one issue), so too the elevation of the 'Gem of Girion' into the Arkenstone led to the introduction of the Necklace of Girion to assume some of the plot-elements no longer suitable for the original item as it had evolved. For example, it is no more plausible that a human king would surrender a wonder like the Arkenstone for his son and heir's armor, however finely wrought, than that Gollum's grandmother gave away Rings of Power as birthday-presents (*LotR*.70), and the stories had to be changed to match the later conceptions. It is interesting, given the other echoes of the old 'Nauglafring' story in this cluster of chapters, that having split the Gem of Girion into two items,

Tolkien chose to make this new item a necklace, since the Nauglafring itself had combined a wondrous necklace with a fabulous gem.

In the new conception, as represented by the First Typescript and associated Third Phase manuscript(s), the Arkenstone was found by dwarves and had never been owned by men. The account of its discovery in fact appears in the same piece of text that introduces the Necklace of Girion:

> . . . the necklace of Girion, Lord of Dale, made of five hundred emeralds green as grass, which he gave for the arming of his eldest son in a coat of dwarf-linked rings the like of which had never been made before, for it was wrought of pure silver to the power and strength of triple steel. But fairest of all was the great white gem, which the dwarves had found beneath the roots of the Mountain, the Heart of the Mountain, the Arkenstone of Thrain.[13]

Obviously, since in the revised story this gem had never been owned by Girion, the old name 'Gem of Girion' had to be replaced. The choice of *Arkenstone* is significant, since in other writings Tolkien was making at the same time he was using a variant of this same name as a term for the Silmarils themselves, forging a link between the Jewels of Fëanor and the Arkenstone of Thrain in the legendarium.

Thus, in the '(Earliest) Annals of Valinor', the entry for the Valian Year 2500 (that is, the equivalent of 25,000 solar years from the time the Valar entered Arda), reads:

> About **2500** the Noldoli [Noldor] invented and began the fashioning of gems; and after a while Fëanor the smith, eldest son of Finwë chief of the Noldoli, devised the thrice-renowned Silmarils, concerning the fates of which these tales tell. They shone of their own light, being filled with the radiance of the Two Trees, the holy light of Valinor, blended to a marvellous fire (HME IV.265).

This work is associated with the 1930 *Quenta* and only very slightly later in date – that is, contemporaneous with Tolkien's work on *The Hobbit* (HME IV.262). And among the very earliest work Tolkien did on the Annals (ibid., page 281) was an Old English version by Ælfwine/Eriol, the frame narrator of *The Book of Lost Tales*, in which the entry given above is translated thusly:

> **MMD** Hér þurh searucræftas aþóhton and beworhton þá Nold-ielfe gimmas missenlice, 7 Féanor Noldena hláford worhte þá Silmarillas, þæt wæron Eorclanstánas (ibid. 282).

Literally translated, this remarkable passage reads:

> [The Year] 2500. Here through cunning craft/artistic skill the Noldor elves devised ('a-thought') and created ('be-worked') many gems, &

> Fëanor the Noldor lord wrought the Silmarils, that were precious/holy stones [*Eorclanstánas* or 'Arkenstones'].

Furthermore, in a later draft of the same work in Mercian dialect, the fictional translator 'Ælfwine of Ongulcynne' (Elf-friend of England) lists the three parts that make up 'The Silmarillion' – The Annals of Valinor, the Annals of Beleriand, and the Quenta – noting 'and þes þridda dǽl man éac nemneð *Silmarillion* þæt is Eorclanstána gewyrd', which translates as 'and this third part is also named "Silmarillion"'; that is '[the] history/fate [of the] Precious/Holy Stones' (HME IV.291). The equivalent Eorclanstána = Silmarils also appears in Ælfwine's Old English translation of part of the 'Annals of Beleriand', which date from about the same time as the complementary 'Annals of Valinor':

> Morgoþ . . . genóm þá eorclanstánas Féanóres . . . ond þá eorclanstánas sette he on his isernan helme ['Morgoth . . . stole the silmarils of Fëanor . . . and the silmarils he set in his iron crown'].
>
> —HME IV.338.

The idea that the Arkenstone could be a Silmaril, or was at least somehow linked to the Silmarils in Tolkien's mind, has additional support from the philological roots of the word. As Jacob Grimm pointed out back in 1844, there was little stone-lore in Teutonic mythology, but foremost among what he discovered he cites the 'time-honoured myth' of the holy *iarkna-steinn* of the Elder Edda, listing the Old English equivalent (*eorcan-stân*) and postulating Gothic (*áirkna-stáins*), and Old High German (*erchan-stein*) forms (Jacob Grimm, *Teutonic Mythology*, tr. Stallybrass [1883]; vol. III page 1217).[14] Furthermore, within the Edda, the term is at one point applied to gems made by craft, not natural stones.[15] In Old English, the most famous usage of *eorcan-stan* occurs in *Beowulf* (line 1208a), where it appears under the variant spelling *eorclanstānas*; interestingly enough, it is used there to describe a wonderful jeweled necklace of gold and gems given to Beowulf by Queen Wealhtheow (Hrothgar's consort).[16] Tolkien's source, however, may have lain not in *Beowulf* but in Cynewulf's *Christ* – the same work from which he took the name 'earendel' (line 104) some twenty years earlier – where *earcnanstān* ('precious/holy stone') appears in line 1194 as a metaphor for Christ [cf. Gollancz's edition, pages 100–101, and Cook's edition, pages 45 & 200]. This is made somewhat more likely by the spelling found in Cynewulf's poem, and the fact that words in Old English which began with *eor-* (eorl, eorth, eornoste) generally became *ear-* in modern English (earl, earth, earnest), whereas words beginning *ear-* typically became *ar-* (e.g., earc > ark [= Noah's Ark]). Alternately, rather than modernization of the Old English, 'Arkenstone' as it appears in *The Hobbit* could represent an anglicization from the Old Norse. It is, after all, a dwarven stone and hence should have a dwarven name, and all the names Tolkien gives the dwarves in *The Hobbit* (this being several years before the creation of a distinctive Dwarven language, e.g., Khuzdul), from Fimbulfambi to Dain, are Old Norse.

One element worth stressing that would link the Arkenstone even more closely with the Silmarils is the implication of the *eorcan* element in its name. Although usually translated simply as 'precious' (that is, highly valuable) and generally applied to any gemstone (e.g., at various times to topaz, opal, and pearl), Grimm stressed that the Gothic equivalent *airkna* meant rather 'holy', and was so used in the Gothic translation of the New Testament (the oldest surviving document in any Germanic language). G. H. Balg (*A Comparative Glossary of the Gothic Language*, 1887)[17] goes further, linking *airkns* to the Greek *argos* or *'apyós* ('bright') and Sanskrit *arjuna* ('bright, pure').[18] The Silmarils are referred to over and over again in the legendarium as the 'holy jewels', who burn evil-doers (such as Melkor the Morgoth, Karkaras/Carcharoth, Maidros/Maedhros and Maglor) at the touch. We have no way of knowing if the Arkenstone shares this same power, since within our story it never comes into direct contact with any evil-doer (or, if we do assume it shares this characteristic with the other Silmarils, then its failure to scorch Bilbo is a testament to the integrity of his intentions and the rightness of his action in purloining it, concealing it from Thorin, and giving it to Bard as a hostage for the dragon-slayer's due portion of the treasure). Certainly, although like Beren's Silmaril the Arkenstone inspires fierce possessiveness in all who behold it, so that not even Bilbo can give it up without a pang, it seems nonetheless pure and innocent (again, like the Silmarils); no pejorative or sinister terms are ever employed in describing it (not even the obvious one within Tolkien's moral lexicography, 'precious', a word never applied to the Arkenstone within *The Hobbit*). Like the Silmarils in the main branch of the legendarium, and unlike the One Ring in the sequel, the Arkenstone inspires greed but is not itself malicious in any way:

> 'The Arkenstone! The Arkenstone!' murmured Thorin in the dark, half dreaming with his chin upon his knees. 'It was like a globe with a thousand facets; it shone like silver in the fire-light, like water in the sun, like snow under the stars, like rain upon the Moon!'
>
> —First Typescript, pasteover on typescript page 125 (1/1/62:11).

The original description of the Gem of Girion as a bright, shining jewel, a globe with many facets (pp. 514–15), which shone of its own light yet catches and magnifies all light that falls on it (page 579), sounds remarkably like Tolkien's descriptions of the Silmarils. Unfortunately we cannot compare them in detail, because for all their importance to the story Tolkien only rarely describes the Silmarils themselves, and then more in terms of their effect on the viewer than in appearance. For example, the earliest account of their creation (BLT I.128) lists the materials Fëanor assembled – the sheen of pearls, phosphorescence, lamp- and candle-light reflected through other gems, the half-colours of opals, and the all-important Light of the Two Trees – but aside from their radiance the only specific detail about their appearance is that '[he gave] all those magic lights a body to dwell in of such perfect glass as he alone could make', implying that they were clear.[19] Although we are told Fëanor started by acquiring 'a great pearl' we could not even tell from this account whether the Silmarils were smooth or faceted (the pearl cannot have provided the actual body for the first Silmaril, since he has only one such pearl yet makes three Silmarils before he runs out of materials). References in the alliterative poems to 'fair enchanted globes of crystal' ('The Flight of the Noldor from Valinor', lines 139b-140a; HME III.135) and 'thrice-enchanted globes of light' ('The Lay of Leithian', line 1642; HME III.212) imply a smooth sphere, but the descriptions of them in the 1926 'Sketch' (HME IV.14) and 1930 *Quenta* (e.g., HME IV.88) are too cursory to provide any details beyond that they shine with their own inner light. Not until the 1937 *Quenta Silmarillion*, which of course postdates *The Hobbit* and hence the Arkenstone, do we learn that 'all lights that fell upon them . . . they took and reflected in marvellous hues to which their own inner fire gave a surpassing loveliness' (HME V.227), implying that they had facets that refracted incoming light. Compare Bilbo's first sight of the Arkenstone as 'a small globe . . . that shone of its own light within . . . *cut and fashioned by the dwarves* . . . it caught and splintered all light that it received' (page 579; emphasis mine). It thus seems that some of the most characteristic features of a Silmaril's appearance familiar to us from the published *Silmarillion*[20] – that it magnifies incoming light and that it splinters this light like a magnificent prism – derive not from the direct line of descent (BLT > 'Sketch' + alliterative poems > 1930 *Quenta* + earliest Annals > 1937 *QS* + later Annals > later *QS* + final Annals) but first appeared in the description of the Arkenstone in *The Hobbit* and from there were imported back into what had been the 'main line' of the legendarium. This does not prove, of course, that the Arkenstone is a Silmaril, but it does show that not only was the description of the Gem of Girion based upon the Silmarils but that it in turn influenced the way the Silmarils were described henceforth.

If however the Arkenstone is indeed a Silmaril, the question arises: which one? Is there any way to reconcile the presence of a Silmaril within the fabled Hoard of Thror with what is said of the Jewels of Fëanor elsewhere in the legendarium? It is out of the question that it might be a 'fourth Silmaril', since all accounts from *The Book of Lost Tales* onwards are unanimous that Fëanor made only three and could never repeat his achievement, but might one of the Three have found its way hence? The answer, just as with the identification of the Elvenking with Thingol Greycloak, is both 'yes' and 'no'.

The fate of the Silmarils is not addressed in *The Book of Lost Tales*, aside from the one rescued by Beren and Tinúviel and later incorporated within the Nauglafring, which according to Tolkien's outlines for the unwritten 'Tale of Eärendel' was lost in the sea when Elwing drowned.[21] Tolkien himself left the fate of the other two an open question, jotting 'What became of the Silmarils after the capture of Melko?' in his notebook, and Christopher Tolkien observes: '. . . the question is itself a testimony to the relatively minor importance of the jewels of Fëanor' at the time (BLT II.259; see also BLT I.156). The matter was not addressed until Tolkien came to write the 1926 'Sketch of the Mythology', where Elwing's Silmaril is still lost at sea, while of the two recovered from Morgoth's crown one is stolen by Fëanor's son Maglor the minstrel who, finding that the holy jewel burns him, 'casts himself into a pit' – presumably with the Silmaril, since the next sentence states 'One Silmaril is now in the sea [i.e., Elwing's], and one in the earth [i.e., Maglor's]' (HME IV.39). The third is claimed by Maidros the maimed, Fëanor's last surviving son, but the Valar deny his right to it because of the Fëanoreans' many evil deeds and grant it instead to Eärendel, who with Maidros's aid finds Elwing and transforms her from a seabird back into her own form again: 'thus it was that the last Silmaril came into the air' (HME IV.41). As Christopher Tolkien observes (HME IV.201–2), this was shuffled about in the 1930 *Quenta*: first (QI) Elwing's is still lost in the sea 'whence it shall not return until the End' (HME IV.150), while Maidros and Maglor seize the other two (IV.158). Both are scorched by the holy jewels: Maglor throws himself and his jewel 'into a yawning gap filled with fire . . . and the jewel vanished into the bosom of the Earth' (IV.159), while Maidros throws his to the ground and kills himself (IV.158) and his Silmaril is reclaimed by Fionwë the Valar's herald; this text breaks off just before the jewel was presumably given to Eärendel (IV.164). The revised version of the 1930 *Quenta* (QII) has Elwing surviving and bringing her Silmaril to Eärendel (IV.153), who sails the night sky with the Silmaril on his brow (IV.164), while Maidros 'cast himself into a gaping chasm filled with fire', taking his Silmaril 'into the bosom of the Earth', and Maglor 'cast [his] . . . into the sea' (IV.162); this idea was retained, in much the same words, in the Conclusion to the 1937 *Quenta Silmarillion* (HME V.331) except that here instead of simply stating that the three Silmarils came to rest in 'sea and earth and air' (HME IV.40 & 165),[22] as had been the case in the three earlier versions (1926 'Sketch', 1930 *Quenta*, and revised 1930 *Quenta*), they now 'found their long homes: one in the airs of heaven, and one in the fires of the heart of the world, and one in the deep waters' (HME V.331), words that would be carried over verbatim into the published *Silmarillion* four decades later (*Silm*.254).

Thus while to us, thirty years after the posthumous publication of *The Silmarillion*, it seems inevitable that the three jewels would be lost beyond recovery – in fact, an addition to the revised 1930 *Quenta* is explicit on this point, stating that 'the Silmarils . . . could not be again found, unless the world was broken and re-made anew' (HME IV.163) – in 1931–2 when Tolkien created the 'Gem of Girion' or in late 1932 when he was writing about the Arkenstone in the Third Phase text of *The Hobbit*, this was most definitely not the case. Despite the sense of finality in the passage just quoted, Tolkien had in fact at that point changed his mind four times in the previous fifteen years about the holy jewels' fate, all in a series of unpublished works that remained in flux and were each to be replaced by a new version of the story. There is no way any observer at that time could have told that this one point would henceforward remain relatively fixed within the Silmarillion texts; the one constant had been that the story ended with all three of the jewels remote and inaccessible. Just as the sword of Turgon King of Gondolin had somehow survived the fall of his city and found its way through the ages into that troll-lair and hence Bladorthin/Gandalf's hands, it is thus more than possible that Tolkien was playing in *The Hobbit* with the idea of having one of Fëanor's wondrous Jewels re-appear, no doubt the one that had been thrown into a fiery chasm and lost deep within the earth – which is, after all, exactly where the dwarves find the Arkenstone, buried at the roots of an extinct volcano. As with his borrowings regarding Tinwelint's quarrel with the dwarves in 'The Nauglafring' for the chapter about the wood-elves and their king's 'old quarrel' with the dwarves, Tolkien drew on his legendarium without committing himself: it was a one-way borrowing in which elements from the 1930 *Quenta* and Early Annals found their way into *The Hobbit* but that 'unofficial' usage did not in turn force changes in what Tolkien was still thinking of as the main line of the legendarium. By avoiding the use of the word *silmaril* and instead using the ingenious and agreeable synonym Arkenstone (*Eorcanstán*), Tolkien got to draw on his rich homebrew mythology, which by the early 1930s had developed a remarkable depth and sophistication, without worrying what the effect of his new story would be on that mythology (and hence could blithely include such statements as 'indeed there could not be two such gems, even in so marvellous a hoard, even in all the world'). It was probably this idea of one-way borrowing to which Tolkien referred when, on occasion, he denied that *The Hobbit* was part of his mythology (e.g., *Letters* pp. 215 & 346). Not until the publication, and success, of *The Hobbit* called for a sequel did the new side-line of Middle-earth's story displace the old legend of the war against Morgoth as the main story of the legendarium and the events of *The Hobbit* and *The Lord of the Rings* require the older stories to be rewritten and revised with the published chronicles in mind.

(iii)
A Note on Cram

The first mention of *cram* appears in the First Typescript (typescript page 133; 1/1/63:7); the line about its being made by the Lake-men is added there in ink at some point before the corresponding passage in the Second Typescript (1/1/44:8) was created, and it was taken up into the page proofs and published book. Douglas Anderson notes (DAA.300) that Tolkien gave 'cram' an Elvish derivation in 'The Etymologies' (which seems to have been mostly written in late 1937 and early 1938, or at least five years after this part of the First Typescript):

> **KRAB**- press. N[oldorin] *cramb*, *cram* cake of compressed flour or meal (often containing honey and milk) used on long journey.
>
> —HME V.365.

This is however almost certainly an afterthought on Tolkien's part, like the entry there regarding 'Esgaroth' (see the commentary following Chapter XIII on page 562). Not only would it be extraordinary for the Noldorin (Sindarin) and English words to be so similar in both form and meaning – the elvish meaning being due to the ingredients being pressed together and the Old English ancestor (*crammian*) of the modern-day familiar word 'cram' meaning to squeeze in or stuff, itself in turn deriving from an Indo-European root (**grem-*) meaning 'to press or compress' – but Tolkien explicitly states in a draft passage for *The Lord of the Rings* that

> *Cram* was, as you may remember, *a word in the language of the men of Dale* and the Long-lake . . . Bilbo Baggins brought back the recipe – he used *cram* after he got home on some of his long and mysterious walks. Gandalf also took to using it on his perpetual journeys . . . (HME VI.177; emphasis mine).

Furthermore, the entry regarding the Elvish root KRAB- and its derivation *cram* is a later addition to 'The Etymologies' (HME V.365), and neither appears in the earlier Noldorin, Qenya, or Gnomish material (cf. *Parma Eldalamberon* volumes XIII, XII, and XI), whereas the *Lord of the Rings* passage just cited was written before the summer of 1938 (cf. HME VI.214) and may predate it. Indeed, the passage in *The Lord of the Rings* Book III Chapter VIII: Farewell to Lórien (written sometime after August 1940 – cf. HME VII.271 & 267) makes it clear that this hardtack is called 'cram' by the men of Dale and dwarves (i.e., in the human language of the North) whereas the elves of Lórien have no direct knowledge of *cram* and call their trail rations by the Sindarin name *lembas* (= literally 'journey-bread'; HME XII.404):

> 'I thought it was only a kind of *cram*, such as the Dale-men make for journeys in the wild,' said [Gimli].
>
> 'So it is,' [the elves] answered. 'But we call it *lembas* or waybread, and it is more strengthening than any food made by Men, and it is more pleasant than *cram*, by all accounts.'
>
> —*LotR*.389.

Thus it seems certain that Tolkien's final decision was to have *cram* be a 'Mannish' word, just as it had been in its original appearance, and the proposed Elvish etymology was simply a mooted alternative that was quickly abandoned.

NOTES

1 The other being the introduction of Bard, the legitimate heir of Girion.

2 That is, according to the original time-scheme, in which Bilbo with Thorin & Company spent more than a year on the road.

3 So ancient is the idea of dragons sleeping on gold that Jacob Grimm noted *ormbedr* or 'worm's bed' as a standard kenning (traditional metaphor) for gold in Old Norse poetry; *Teutonic Mythology* (tr. James Stallybrass [1883], vol. II, page 689).

4 The later developments of this passage in subsequent Silmarillion texts bring it much closer into line with Smaug's situation. Thus, in the 1926 'Sketch of the Mythology', the rather odd detail of the dragon's gold-bed being outside the caves out in the open is dropped:

> Glórung lies in the caves of Narog and gathers beneath him all the gold and silver and gems there hoarded (HME IV.30).

This brings the Glorund story back into accord with the Sigurd story, in which Fafnir's 'abiding place' is 'dug down deep into the earth: there found Sigurd gold exceeding plenteous . . .' (*Völsunga Saga*, tr. Morris & Magnússon, page 67). The 1930 *Quenta* refines this still further, until it becomes a very close approximation of Smaug's practice:

> Glómund . . . gathered unto himself the greater part of its wealth of gold and gems, and he lay thereon in its deepest hall, and desolation was about him (HME IV.127).

It would have been on the basis of a line such as this that Gandalf the dwarf can say with such confidence that '. . . all their wealth he took for himself. Probably, for that is the dragon's way, he has piled it all up in [a] great heap in some hall far inside, and sleeps on it for a bed' (page 72). Like Glorund, Smaug chooses the deepest chamber within the Lonely Mountain for his lair: every stair Thorin & Company take after leaving it leads up (cf. page 581).

5 It is true that the elves are accompanied by Túrin's mother and sister, who might be thought to serve as a parallel for the presence in *The*

Hobbit of Thorin, Fili, and Kili, since Mavwin and Nienóri were close kin of the man who had been acting as the Rodothlim's champion while the three dwarves are all descendants (grandchild and great-great-grandchildren, respectively) of Thror, whose people had been destroyed or dispossessed by Smaug. It might also be noted that disaster comes about in every iteration of the Túrin story because of the presence of the two women in the group, just as it is Thorin's behavior under the dragon-sickness that almost brings disaster in the Third Phase *Hobbit* story, but this might be pressing the point too far. Finally, Tinwelint's sending a group whose brief is not just to take the treasure but also slay the dragon (a point made explicit on BLT II.96, where they are described as 'that band of dragon-slayers') could be taken as a parallel for the projected Bilbo-as-dragon-slayer theme of Plot Notes B & C.

6 This curse, the dragon's ability to directly manipulate the minds of those who look into his eyes and to individually curse any whose name he knows, is distinct from the more general dragon-sickness attached to treasure that has come into contact with a dragon. Both Túrin and Nienóri make the mistake of making eye contact with the wyrm and are beguiled, and his knowledge of who they are enables Glorund to craft specific curses that set both on the road to incest and suicide. There is no mention of whether Sigurd looks into Fafnir's eyes while the dragon is still alive, but the *Fáfnismál* and *Völsunga Saga* both agree that he initially gives a false name to avoid Fafnir's dying curse; Bilbo wisely both avoids meeting Smaug's gaze and giving him his real name. Both motifs are lacking in *Beowulf*, whose dragon is more animalistic and less of a personality, but note that even in *Farmer Giles of Ham* Chrysophylax wants to know the farmer's name at their first meeting and the farmer refuses to tell him until he has gained the upper hand (FGH 41 & 43). See also Tolkien's dragon lecture summarized in Note 5 following the commentary to Chapter XII.

7 Later Tolkien inserted a reference earlier in the text to Glorund having 'set a guard that he might trust to watch his dwelling and his treasury, and the captain of these was Mîm the dwarf' before he set forth on his final fatal mission to seek Túrin (BLT II.103 & 118).

8 The curse might be so relentlessly effective in part because, as Tinwelint concedes, none of the initial claimants have any real right to this treasure: 'the Rodothlim who won it from the earth long time ago are no more, and no one has especial claim to so much as a handful save only Úrin by reason of his son Túrin, who slew the Worm, the robber of the Elves' (BLT II.222). He advances his own claim on the fact that (a) 'this gold belongs to the kindred of the Elves in common' (a particularly specious argument, given that he is using it to deny Úrin's elven companions more than a token share†) and (b) 'Túrin is dead and Úrin will have none of it; and Túrin was my man' (who had murdered a kinsman of the king and fled Tinwelint's halls, abandoning his allegiance). The latter suggests additional complications that could have arisen in the scramble over Smaug's gold had Bard not survived,

as had been Tolkien's original intent (see page 549), and the Master of Lake Town and Elvenking been left to settle matters between them.

†These outlaws had been human in the original draft of this tale but became elves in the revision, from which this sentence is taken; see BLT II.242.

9 I.e., Mîm's curse: 'Now Elves and Men shall rue this deed, and because of the death of Mîm the dwarf shall death follow this gold so long as it remain on Earth, and a like fate shall every part and portion share with the whole' (BLT II.114). Mîm's dying curse in 'Turambar and the Foalókë' pointedly excludes his own people, the dwarves, but a later passage in 'The Nauglafring' implies that whatever immunity they might have to the dragon-sickness does not protect them from Mîm's all-encompassing curse: 'Indeed all that folk love gold and silver more dearly than aught else on Earth, while that treasury was haunted by a spell and by no means were they armed against it' (BLT II.229).

To this might be added yet a third curse, that laid upon the Nauglafring itself by the dwarven-smiths held in prison by Tinwelint and forced to expend their craft in slave-labor on his behalf: 'even had that gold of the Rodothlim held no evil spell still had that carcanet been a thing of little luck, for the Dwarves were full of bitterness, and all its links were twined with baleful thoughts' (BLT II.228) – not to mention that they incorporate into the necklace the Silmaril Beren and Tinúviel took from Morgoth's crown, with the additional perils that gem (and its proximity to the original Dark Lord) might bring.

10 This piece was painted between 8th and 24th July 1937, too late for inclusion in the first printing but late enough that the text had already been typeset and thus finalized. The idea that Tolkien might himself provide additional illustrations, in colour, for the American edition was first mooted in May in a brief exchange between Charles Furth of Allen & Unwin and Tolkien (Furth to JRRT 11th May 1937, JRRT to Furth 13th May, Furth to JRRT 14th May), at which point Tolkien dispatched several Silmarillion illustrations as examples of his colour artwork. Unfortunately Houghton Mifflin mistook these for the actual pieces to be used, resulting in several months of confusion. In a letter written on or soon after 8th July, Tolkien says 'I have done nothing about the new ones. I will now set about them, if they are still required, or it is not too late' (JRRT to Furth, undated reply to Furth's letters of 1st June & 8th July). In another undated letter, probably written on 24th or 23rd July, Tolkien asks for an update ('I do not want to labour in vain') and arranges to call on Stanley Unwin in London 'on Wednesday next, 28th July' to 'submit what I have done' and see if A&U's production department thinks them 'passable, & . . . suitable for reproduction'. Although HM had still not replied by 24th July (SU to JRRT), Tolkien seems by this point to have finished the four paintings,† since in his reply of 25th July (JRRT to SU) discussing their upcoming meeting he says '. . . I shall not take much of your time, as it will not take long to tell me if what I have done is suitable, & if unsuitable what is wrong', suggesting that he was going to bring

the paintings along for Unwin to vet them. Apparently the pieces were deemed acceptable, since the next mention of them is in Tolkien's letter to Furth of 13th August, written while on vacation at Sidmouth in Devon, stating that 'You are very welcome to use the coloured drawings at any time' (that is, in any future reprint), suggesting the originals be stored at A&U's offices once they are returned by the Americans, and concluding 'I have completed the coloured version of the frontispiece. †† Would you care to have it to lay by (hopefully)?' (JRRT to Furth, August 13th) – an offer which Furth, in his reply, gratefully accepts (Furth to JRRT, 16th August).

†These four were 'Bilbo Comes to the Huts of the Raft-elves', 'Bilbo Woke Up with the Early Sun in His Eyes', 'Conversation with Smaug', and 'Rivendell' (H-S#124, 113, 133, & 108 ; DAA plates 2B, 2A, 3A, and 1B)

††This fifth painting is 'The Hill: Hobbiton-across-the Water' (H-S#98; DAA plate 1A).

11 For example, the glowing cone-shaped object directly above the bowing hobbit, or the three glowing low mounds to the left behind Smaug's elbow.

12 Supreme, that is, within the context of *The Hobbit*; in *The Lord of the Rings* it is eclipsed by the Ring of Power belonging to Durin's house, one of the Seven. After all, while they left the Arkenstone behind when they fled the Lonely Mountain Thror and Thrain managed to save their house's Ring, just as their ancestors had done even from the Balrog's rampage that drove them from Khazad-dûm (Moria); it later passed from Thror to Thrain and was not lost until the Necromancer captured Thorin's father, a hundred years before the time of Bilbo's journey (*LotR*.286, 1110, & 1113–14). But this is a *Lord of the Rings*-era innovation, not present at the time *The Hobbit* was written. For more on the emergence of Durin's Ring, see the draft of Gloin's speech at Rivendell in HME VI.398.

13 This passage appears on a piece of typescript pasted over the original text of the First Typescript (typescript page 125; 1/1/62:11); the underlying text cannot now be read even when the page is held up to the light, due to the darkening of the glue or paste Tolkien used. This replacement occurred before the Second Typescript was made, since the latter faithfully reproduces the pasteover text; presumably the obscured text closely resembled the manuscript version on page 515 of this book describing 'the white gem of Girion Lord of Dale'.

Even though less is made of the Necklace of Girion than of the Arkenstone, it must be stressed that this was a rare and wonderful treasure in its own right: emeralds are far rarer and more valuable than diamonds or even rubies.

The description here of silver with a strength three times that of steel sounds very like the later *mithril*, but Tolkien never made this connection in later editions of *The Hobbit* after the introduction of mithril in *The Lord of the Rings*, although he did insert a single mention of mithril into the earlier book in his 1966 revision for the Ballantine paperback with regard to Bilbo's 'silvered steel' mail-coat (DAA.295). It might be expected that the wondrous suit of mithril-mail, whose value is revealed in *The Lord of the Rings* to be greater than the Shire and everything in it (*LotR*.335), would turn out to be the very suit of armor King Girion surrendered his wondrous necklace for, but the connection is never made (perhaps because then the conscientious Bilbo would feel obliged to give Bard his mail-coat as well in the end).

The 'Thrain' here, by the way, is Thorin's grandfather, the King under the Mountain; the reversed genealogy was in place when Tolkien made this addendum to the typescript (see page 458). In later years rather than simply making it the 'Arkenstone of Thror' he instead resolved the inconsistency by ascribing it to a distant ancestor, Thrain I, Thorin's great-great-great-great-great-great-grandfather. In the later story, it was this Thrain I who led the exodus from Moria after his father and grandfather had been killed by the Balrog and the ancestral kingdom overthrown, founding the realm-in-exile at the Lonely Mountain, and discovered the Arkenstone there deep beneath the mountain (*LotR*.1117 & 1109).

14 For more on Eorcanstan and the cognate names in other Germanic languages, see Christopher Tolkien's discussion in *The Shaping of Middle-earth* (HME IV.283) and Douglas Anderson's note in *The Annotated Hobbit* (DAA.293–4). I am grateful to Doug's entry for drawing my attention to Grimm.

15 In the rather gruesome story of Wayland the Smith's captivity, crippling, revenge, and escape, he murders the sons of his captor and makes goblets of their skulls, brooches of their teeth, and 'pure gems' (Old Norse *iarknasteina*) of their eyes *Vǫlundarkviða*, stanzas 25 & 35; cf. Dronke, vol II. pages 250 & 252).

16 So beautiful is this piece of jewelry that the poet compares it to the legendary *Brosinga mene* ('necklace of the Brosings', line 1199b), familiar in Old Norse legend as the Brisingamen, the goddess Freya's most valued treasure (cf. 'The Deluding of Gylfi' [*Gylfaginning*] in Snorri's *Prose Edda*, 'The Lay of Thrym' [*Þrymsqviða*] in the *Elder Edda*, and the tale of Loki's theft of the necklace hinted at in the surviving fragments of the *Húsdrapa* ['House Song'] of Ulf Uggason). Like the *Book of Lost Tales*' Nauglafring ('Necklace of the Dwarves'), which it no doubt inspired, the Brisingamen was made by great dwarven craftsmen working at the behest of others. Interestingly enough, Tinwelint's captive dwarven jewelsmiths demand an elven maiden apiece as payment (which the elvenking refuses, having them beaten instead); Freya had to promise to sleep with each of the four dwarves who make her necklace and honors her agreement.

17 Christopher Wiseman told me (interview, August 1981) that Tolkien used to come to Rugby practice with a great big Gothic book under his arm, which he would apparently read in snatches when not engrossed in the game or actually on the field. This could not have been either Joseph Wright's *Gothic Grammar* or *Gothic Primer*, both of which are

smallish (octavo) volumes. I suspect Balg's massive quarto (more than ten inches tall, seven inches wide, and over six hundred pages thick), simultaneously published in New York, London, Germany, and Mayville Wisconsin, to have been the book Wiseman remembered.

18 The Greek word is best known as the name of the hundred-eyed monster Argos (more commonly spelt *Argus*), who was so-named because of the clarity and sharpness of his vision. The Greek, Sanskrit, and Gothic words all probably go back to the same Indo-European root **ar(e)g-* meaning 'shining' or 'bright' – the same root, in fact, which seems to underlie the word *elf* (Germanic **alba-* or **albinjo*, which seem to have meant 'white' and 'shining' – cf. 'the White People' as one of the euphemisms of the Fair Folk and the discussion of an uncanny whiteness as a defining elven characteristic in the commentary following Chapter IX). The Latin word for silver, *argenta*, also derives from the same root, and it may underlie the names for the Alps ('the Whites', so called for their snow-cover; cf. the White Mountains of Gondor) and Albion, a traditional name for Britain in old legends ('The White Land', from the White Cliffs of Dover, the first part of the island seen by someone approaching from mainland Europe).

19 By 'glass' Tolkien here probably means some sort of clear crystal, since the Silmarils survive many encounters that would have shattered mere glass. Cf. also the reference in the alliterative poems to the Silmarils as crystal, such as the allusion to Beren's Silmaril as 'the Gnome-crystal' in *The Lay of the Children of Húrin* (line 379; HME III.107).

The appearance of pearls and opals here may owe something to Jacob Grimm's guess, in *Teutonic Mythology*, that *eorcanstan* probably originally was applied either to 'the oval milk-white opal' and/or to the pearl (Grimm/Stallybrass, vol. III pages 1217–18).

20 The passage from the 1977 *Silmarillion* derives primarily not from the *Later Quenta* (X.187), which closely resembles the passage in the 1937 *Quenta Silmarillion*, but from the 'Annals of Aman' (the final version of the 'Annals of Valinor', supplemented by a few details taken from the *Later Quenta*):

> . . . As three great jewels they were in form . . . Like the crystal of diamonds it appeared and yet was more strong than adamant, so that no violence within the walls of this world could mar it or break it. Yet that crystal was to the Silmarils but as is the body to the Children of Ilúvatar: the house of its inner fire, that is within it and yet in all parts of it, and is its life. And the inner fire of the Silmarils Fëanor made of the blended Light of the Trees of Valinor . . . Therefore even in the uttermost darkness the Silmarils of their own radiance shone like the stars of Varda; and yet, as were they indeed living things, they rejoiced in light and received it, and gave it back in hues more lovely than before.
>
> —HME X.94–5.

21 The *Gnomish Lexicon*'s entry for 'Nauglafring' agrees, stating plainly that the Necklace of the Dwarves was '[m]ade for *Ellu* [= Tinwelint/

Thingol] by the dwarves from the gold of *Glorund*, that Mîm, the fatherless, cursed and that brought ruin on *Beren Ermabwed* [the One-Handed], and *Damrod* [Dior], his son, and was not appeased till it sank with *Elwing*, beloved of *Earendel*, to the bottom of the seas' (*Parma Eldalamberon* XI.59).

22 Note that the Three Rings of the Elves were originally to have been 'of earth, sea, and sky' (e.g., in the draft of the Ring-verse [HME VI.269] and also the 'third phase' text of 'Ancient History' [VI.319]: 'the Three Rings of Earth, Sea, and Sky'). In the original draft of the Lothlórien chapter(s), it is plainly stated that Galadriel's ring is the Ring of Earth (HME VII.252) and an associated page of drafting speculates that Fëanor himself made the three elven rings, 'the Rings of Earth, Sea and Sky' (ibid., page 255).

In the published book, of course, *Kemen* the Ring of Earth is replaced by *Narya* the Ring of Fire, Galadriel holds *Nenya*, the Ring of Water, and Elrond *Vilya* the Ring of Air, so that Earth, Sea and Sky have been replaced by Air, Water, and Fire. This later arrangement better matches the later (1937) *Quenta Silmarillion*, in which the three Silmarils are lost in the sky (Air), the fires in the depth of the earth (Earth > Fire), and the sea (Water).

Chapter XVa

THE KINDNESS OF RAVENS

As before, the text continues onward without anything more than a page break, with the section that later became Chapter XV starting at the top of manuscript page 166 (Marq. 1/1/15). This last sheet of the Second Phase manuscript, along with the associated Plot Notes that follow, represents the point the story had reached when Tolkien broke off to go back to the beginning and create the First Typescript.

Suddenly Bilbo said: 'There is that old thrush again – he seems to have escaped when the dragon smashed the terrace, though I don't suppose his beloved snails have!'[TN1]

Sure enough, there was thc old thrush, perched on a stone; and as soon as they looked towards him he flapped his wings and sang; then he cocked his head on one side as if to listen, and again he sang, and again he listened.

'I believe he is trying to tell us something' said Thorin 'but I do not understand the tongue of small-birds – it is very quick and difficult. Do you Mr Baggins?'

'Not very well' said Bilbo, 'and I can't make this old fellow out at all, except that he is very excited.'[TN2]

'I only wish he was a raven!' said Balin.

'I thought you did not like the ravens of these parts, when we came this way before' said Bilbo to him.

'Those were crows!' said Balin, 'and nasty suspicious-looking ones at that, and rude as well. You must have heard the ugly things they were calling after us – there was one old raven, you remember how he flew after us a long way home [> towards camp],[TN3] but he never said anything beyond a croak. But there are some ravens still about here, though, for I have seen them in my wanderings about, that remember the old friendship between us in Thror's day. They used to live on many many years, and their memories are long, and they hand their wisdom on to their children. I had many a friend among the Ravens of the Mountain when I was a boy – this very ridge we stand on was called Ravenhill[TN4] by many, for it was a favourite place of theirs close to the watchmen's seat. There's never a sign of them now: I suppose they are off to see what all this gathering forebodes, though they are not birds for company, unless great things are brewing. If we had one here now we shd soon have news'.

Loud shrilled the Old Thrush and off it flew.

'That old bird understood all you said, at any rate' said Thorin. 'Keep watch now and see what happens!'

Before long there was a flutter of wings and back came the thrush. With it came another most decrepit old bird: it was getting blind, it could hardly fly and the top of its head was almost bald. It was a very aged raven of great size. It alighted stiffly on the ground, flapped its wings slowly & bobbed towards Thorin and Balin, and began to croak. – 'O Thorin Thrain's son Thror's son [and Balin son of Fundin]' it began [> said], & Bilbo to his surprise could understand all it said. 'I am Roäc son of Carc.[TN5] Carc is dead, but once he was well known to you. It is one hundred years and three and fifty since I came out of the egg, but I do not forget what my father told me. I am the chief of the old [> great] Ravens of the Mountain, who remember still the king that was of old. I bring tidings of joy to you and yet other tidings not so good. Behold the birds are gathering back again to the Mountain from South and East and West, for word has gone forth that Smaug is dead! The Thrush, may his feathers never fall, has seen it and we trust his words. He saw him fall in battle with the men of Esgaroth on Tuesday night, that is the night before the night before last [> eight nights ago at the rising of the moon]. So much for joy O Thorin Oakenshield! You may go back to your palace in safety, all the treasure of your fathers is yours once more – for the moment. But there is more to tell. Among the flocking birds are many crows and birds of carrion – indeed ravens are among them though they fly by themselves – for they espy a gathering of arms, and to our minds an army and a hoard means dead men ere long. The Lake-town of Esgaroth is destroyed, but the men of the lake, most of whom have escaped, and the Elven king have joined together, and their warriors are marching north to plunder the mountain, and it is said that they trouble not whether the dwarves of Durin are alive or dead.

'I have spoken. I and the Thrush have looked for you in the West and we feared you dead.[TN6] We rejoice to see you safe, but a hard strife looms ahead. Thirteen is [not >] but a small remnant of the great folk of Durin that [was wont >] once was here. The <thrush> says that he who shot the Dragon, one Bard of the race of Dale and of the line of Girion is among the host, and he is a grim man yet true. Fear him not so much as the Elven king and the Master that remains behind. We would see peace once more between dwarves and men after the long desolation. But it may cost you dear in gold.'

Then Thorin's wrath blazed forth 'Our thanks Roäc Carcson' he said. 'You and your people shall not be forgotten. But none of our gold shall the thieves of [the] Lake and the Wood get from us alive. If you would earn [*added*: our thanks] still more bring us tidings at once of their approach. Now we have work to do. Back to the Mountain' he cried to the dwarves 'For we must stand a siege'.

'But we have no food' cried Bilbo always practical on such <points>.

At this point, at the bottom of manuscript page 167, the Second Phase text ends.

However, associated with this material is a half-page fragment of rough drafting (Marq. 1/1/24b) that preceded manuscript pages 166–7; this survives only because Tolkien tore the sheet in two, turned it over, rotated it 90 degrees counterclockwise, and used the blank space on what had been the bottom half of its verso to hastily sketch out events that were to occur during the Siege of the Mountain (Marq. 1/1/24a, or Plot Notes E). We do not know how much such rough drafting preceded the 'first draft' of the Second Phase manuscript, but by good fortune this small surviving fragment offers us a rare chance for comparison, suggesting that it strongly resembled what followed in storyline but only generally corresponded in word choice and expression.

The line just above the tear has vanished almost completely, but a large descending ligature at the beginning of the line indicates that it began with a capital 'L' and from the context it almost certainly read 'Loud trilled the Thrush' or something very like it. Similarly, since the lines slant slightly upward across the page the last two or three words at the end of the first line below the tear are lost but probably read 'we said'.

L<oud> . . .

'[If that >] That old bird understood all that <we> . . .' Thorin. 'Keep watch now and see what happens!'

Before long there was a flutter of wings, and back came the Thrush. With it came a most decrepit old bird, nearly blind. It could hardly fly and the top of its head was almost bald. It was a very aged raven. It lighted stiffly on the ground, flapped its wings and bobbed towards Thorin and Balin; then it began to croak. Bilbo did not know what it was saying, but Balin seemed to. Afterward he told them all that he had learned.

'O Thorin Thrain's Son, Thror's son' he said 'this is a most Venerable Raven, Roäk [> Roäc] by name, the son of Carc. Carc I knew in the old days when I was young, but alas he is now dead. Röac his son must be 180 years old if he is a day – he is the last raven of the Mountain left who [we can understand the language >] who can understand our language, being taught by his father, or make himself understood by me. He brings tidings truly tremendous and <astonishing> and bewildering: joy and sorrow.

The birds are gathering back again to the mountain from S. E and W. for word has gone forth that the Dragon is dead!

This brings the text to the bottom of 1/1/24b. The top half of the back of this sheet (1/1/24a) is missing, having been discarded by Tolkien himself, but two lines below the tear remain:

Loud the Thrush trilled again. Roac croaked.
'It seems that the Thrush

At this point, the draft breaks off in mid-sentence half-way through a line of dialogue. The rest of this page is devoted to the 'little bird' outline (Plot Notes E); see page 626.

Besides seeing the emergence of the raven's name – the exact form of which, Roäk/Roäc/Röac, remained unfixed for the present[TN7] – and having the venerable bird being even older than in the published book,[TN8] the most significant difference between the draft and the text that replaced it is that originally only Balin could understand the raven's speech, and translates it for the benefit of his friends. While reminiscent of their meeting with Medwed/Beorn and his horses, this was replaced in the main draft with the simpler and more direct route of allowing the raven to speak directly to Thorin & Company without an interpreter.[TN9] Tolkien may have felt that having two tiers of interpreters – the Thrush speaking to the Raven, the Raven to Balin, and Balin to the rest – was too cumbersome and so simplified it, especially since ravens, like parrots, are famous for their ability to speak (in the words of Edgar Poe, 'quoth the raven: "Nevermore"').

TEXT NOTES

1 Crowded into the left margin, and presumably meant for insertion preceding this paragraph, is the following:

> For several days they remained there on the Mountain, keeping watch by day and guard at night. Nothing happened, and they became sorely puzzled. At last their supplies began to run low, and [in] the morning they began to discuss whether they should send some of their number down to the riverside store, or whether all should go, or whether they should again seek the aid of the men of Lake-town. [Thorin > Bilbo >] The hobbit was looking about him taking no part in the discussion. Already he was wondering what had happened to [> in] Lake-town, for he had not forgotten his fear that Smaug would go <thither>. He was looking about him idly when suddenly he saw a fluttering on his right.

This additional text not only stresses Thorin & Company's bafflement about the dragon's continued absence but expands the time-frame, no doubt to allow the elven and human host time to gather and begin its march north; before its addition the story moves directly from the dwarves' arrival at Ravenhill to their encounters with the thrush and raven. The published text compromises between these two, having them arrive at the watch-post at sunset (DAA.301) and encountering the birds early the next morning (DAA.314). See the added reference a few paragraphs later about it now having been eight days since Smaug's death, whereas in the original texts only three nights had passed (the Battle of Lake Town taking place on Tuesday night and the conversation with Roäc on Friday morning). The original timeline thus ran like this:

- Monday, Durin's Day: Bilbo enters the secret tunnel just after sunset, emerging again at midnight. (pp. 505 & 507–8)
- Tuesday: Smaug destroys the secret door almost exactly twenty-four hours later, flies south, and dies in the attack on Esgaroth. (pp. 513 & 515, 549)
- Wednesday: Bilbo and the dwarves spend all the previous night, all this day, and this night huddled in the tunnel. (page 578)
- Thursday: Bilbo and the dwarves explore Smaug's lair and traverse the dwarven city. (page 578ff)
- Friday: Thorin & Company reach the Front Gate at sunrise; Balin leads them to Ravenhill, where they soon encounter the thrush and raven, who tells them Smaug died 'the night before the night before last'. (pages 582, 619).

The expanded time-scheme of eight days better matches the statement in Chapter XIII that the Elvenking's army reached Lake Town seven days after Smaug's fall (page 552), presumably setting forth for the Mountain the next day.

For the 'riverside store' (that is, storage site or supplies depot beside the river-bank), this lay three days' journey north of Lake Town where they disembarked from the boats; see the first paragraph of Chapter XI on page 471.

2 Note that the implication here is that Bilbo can understand bird-talk; in the Third Phase and subsequent texts he merely diplomatically pretends to; see page 642.

3 No such incident in fact occurred during the earlier chapter. Had he retained this passage, Tolkien would no doubt have inserted this event back in Chapter XI on or about the section represented by page 472 in the Second Phase text. By contrast, Balin's claim to have already made contact with the ravens of the mountain during their earlier explorations, while significant, would simply have served to set up the encounter which follows and could have been retained as is.

4 This is the first appearance of the name 'Ravenhill', one of those names that like Bag-End and Rivendell and Lake Town remained unchanged from its first recorded appearance onward.

5 As Douglas Anderson notes, both these names are 'marvelously onomatopoeic' (DAA.316), being approximations of the croaks these birds themselves might make (roughly *rroahkk* and *kahrrkk*, respectively). This is all the more appropriate since the very word 'raven' itself

(OE *hræfn*, ON *hrafn*) is believed to derive from an Indo-European root imitating the bird's cry (**kor-*, **ker-*), just as the modern English 'crow' represents the sound now more usually spelled *caw* (i.e., *kraw! kraw!*).

6 'I and the Thrush have looked for you in the West' – that is, on the western side of the Lonely Mountain, where they had last been seen before Smaug destroyed the Secret Door. As with the mention of Balin's earlier contact with the ravens, this suggests a more active role for the Ravens of the Mountain somewhat earlier than in the final text.

7 The dieresis (¨) indicates that both vowels are to be pronounced, not blended into a diphthong – for example, as in *cooperate* (formerly spelled 'coöperate'), rather than *coop*. The name's final appearance in the penultimate line of this rough draft also has a dieresis, but from its placement it is not possible to tell which vowel it is meant to cover and thus whether Roäc or Röac is intended.

8 In fact, according to the chronology in 'The Tale of Years' (*LotR*.1125–6), old enough to remember the days of King Thror and to have known Balin personally before the dragon came one hundred and seventy years earlier. This chronology of course post-dates *The Hobbit* and it is clear that Roäc was taught dwarf-speech after those days were past, so it simply indicates that Tolkien initially had an even greater span of time in mind between the fall of the Kingdom under the Mountain and its restoration under Thorin.

9 For all the linguistic richness of his work and the many (mutually incomprehensible) invented languages included in its narratives, scenes where an interpreter must mediate between two groups who do not share a common tongue are rare in Tolkien, the chief example being Legolas speaking with the border-guards of Lórien on behalf of the Fellowship (*LotR*.360 & 362).

(i)
The Ravens of the Mountain

Helpful birds had played an important part in Tolkien's writing from the earliest days: the Eagles of Manwë (cf. Chapter VI), the swans of Ulmo, the birds of Melian, even Mew the seagull in *Roverandom*, so it is no surprise to see the wise Thrush and old Raven figure prominently in the Lonely Mountain chapters, from the discovery of the Secret Door to the revealing of Smaug's weak spot and setting in motion preparations for the Siege of the Mountain. In particular there had long been a traditional association of talking birds with the aftermath of a dragon-slaying: by accidentally tasting Fafnir's heart Sigurd was able to understand the language of birds and discovered that the woodpeckers in the nearby trees were actually discussing him and how his foster-father planned to kill him and, after he kills Regin on their advice, tell him how to find Brynhild the valkyrie (*Fáfnismál* stanzas 32–44; *Völsunga Saga* Chapter XIX, esp. pages 64–6). Tolkien had referred to this motif as far back as the tale of Túrin, where it is said that eating the heart of a dragon grants knowledge of 'all tongues of Gods or Men, of birds or beasts' (BLT II.85), a philologist's dream which Christopher Tolkien in his commentary explicitly credits to the story of Sigurd Fafnisbane (BLT II.125). But here in Tolkien's story it is *because* the dragon-slayer has the ability to speak with birds (Bard and the Thrush) that he is able to kill the dragon, and Thorin & Company's only encountering the raven after Smaug's fall seems more a matter of chance than necessity, the result of not having earlier visited the part of the mountain frequented by ravens (i.e., Ravenhill).

Tolkien's specific choice of ravens combines both elements of traditional myth and real-world fact. Not only are ravens and crows traditionally associated with battles, but they are the smartest of all birds, exceptionally long-lived (one of the ravens at the Tower of London lived to be forty-four years old, and a less-well-attested individual is said to have reached eighty), and capable of speech, at least to the extent of being able to learn and intelligibly repeat several words or phrases. Tolkien has exaggerated or rather enhanced their intelligence, longevity, and loquaciousness or linguistic ability for the purposes of his story, but his fantasy builds on a solid factual basis here. He combines their rather sinister reputation as harbingers of battle (they are, after all, carrion birds, as Roäc admits) with their legendary exploits as messengers: Odin's two ravens, Hugin and Munin ('Thought' and 'Memory'), fly forth every day and report back to him all that passes in the world (*Prose Edda* pages 63–4). He also rather surprisingly in the Plot Notes which follow (Plot Notes E) draws on the Biblical account of ravens feeding the prophet Elijah 'bread and meat' in the Wilderness (1st Kings, Chapter 17, verses 1–7) and has the Ravens of the Mountain bring 'meat and bread' to the besieged dwarves until (even more surprisingly) they are driven away by elven archers.[1]

Once present in the story, the ravens may also have inspired Tolkien's re-introduction of the eagles in the final chapters as the Siege of the Mountain evolved into the Battle of Five Armies, but since this development belongs rather to the Third Phase I postpone discussion of it for now; see page 715.

NOTES

1 It might seem unlikely that birds could carry enough food to make any appreciable difference, but ravens are quite large, typically about two feet in length and with a wingspan of some four feet. They are not

only quite capable of killing and carrying off small animals but also sometimes carry off small items that attract their curiosity (a habit for which their smaller cousins the jackdaws are notorious).

THE SIEGE OF THE MOUNTAIN

I now give the 'little bird' outline, or Plot Notes E, the final piece of text unambiguously associated with the Second Phase storyline. In these hasty jottings we see how the events of the next chapter would have unfurled had the Second Phase text not been abandoned.

Plot Notes E

'Little Bird'

Raven tells of 2 or 3 ponies still alive. Offers also to <assemble> <their> folk[TN1] and bring food from far and wide.

Fili and Kili go off to catch ponies: Others go into Mountain. Great <labours> day and night at the great door. Bilbo keeps watch on Ravenhill.

The birds bring news of approach of the men of lake and the Elvenking and the <joining> of the host with that of <?men> host of the Elves. Fili and Kili have not come back they are pursued by warriors

The dwarves gather weapons and a store of arrows to the G.D.[TN2] which is now blocked with stones <with crevices> for shooting from. The opening on Ravenhill is guarded by Dori & Nori.[TN3]

Three days later Kili [rides up >] comes to the G.D. & begs for admitance. Their horses were shot under them but they have laid all the stores they could carry near the foot of the great spur, but as they climbed the hillside Fili was wounded & captured.[TN4] The host is already at the foot of the mountain.

Each of the ravens fly bringing meat and bread. But that night the dwarves steal out and recover the <bags>. The camp fires start up in the <ruins> of Dale.

The parley at the Gates. Thorin's scornful words. He will give nothing to <u>demand</u>. What got they out of the last K.u.M?[TN5] The Elvenking on behalf of the Lake men demands payment <for/from> <illegible> of Smaug, the destruction of the town, all <?slain>. Thorin says first remove your menace from my <?palace>. Stores run low for the elves shoot at the ravens.

There seems little doubt that these hastily scribbled words comprise Tolkien's final work on the Second Phase, differing greatly as they do from the events as they would appear in the actual written texts of the chapters that followed. At this point, he probably thought that no more than two or three chapters would be needed to complete the story: one to resolve events at the Mountain, a second to cover the Battle of Anduin Vale (see page 713) on the return journey, and a third to see Bilbo safely home afterwards. And it must be stressed that in one sense he was right. Even with the folding together of the projected 'Battle of the Anduin Vale' with the Siege of the Mountain and the greater complexity and added complications that Bard's legitimate claim on the treasure and Thorin's succumbing to dragon-sickness would bring in the Third Phase text, Tolkien here has come within forty-five pages of the end,[TN6] and nearly half of the book's earlier chapters had reached twenty pages or more.[TN7] In the final book the remaining material would be divided into five chapters (out of the book's total of nineteen), making it seem at first glance that Tolkien abandoned the book less than three-quarters of the way through. But this does not take into account the extreme brevity of these closing chapters, three of which are among the shortest in the book. If we go by page count, then, Tolkien was more than five-sixths of the way through the story when he broke off, not abandoning the book as Carpenter claimed but instead going back to the beginning and embarking on the creation of the First Typescript.

TEXT NOTES

1 By offering to assemble their folk, Roäc does not mean the dwarves but ravens; neither Plot Notes B/C/D nor E contain any reference to Dain, who had not yet been invented, and no dwarven army was to march to their relief.

2 That is, the Great Door, usually referred to as the 'Front Gate'.

3 Since it seems unlikely that any dwarves would be posted where they would be cut off from their fellows once the valley was occupied, the idea of a tunnel leading from within the guard-post back into the dwarven city behind the Front Gate, suggested in Chapter XIV, must still be present.

4 The first seven words of this sentence were cancelled.

5 Here Thorin seems to be referring to Smaug, not Thror; cf. the surly watchman's words in Chapter XIII (pp. 547–8). This is surprising, both for the threat implied and for its recognition of Smaug's suzerainty – not to mention unwise, since he is speaking to survivors of Smaug's attack who have all too much reason to blame him for their sufferings. Thorin's refusal to hand over his family treasures to an angry mob or

to negotiate at swords-point is in itself an admirable display of courage. Even though with hindsight provided by Third Phase developments we might see his 'scornful' reply to the massed army outside his gate as the first signs of dragon-sickness, within the context of the Second Phase story it is entirely in keeping with the heroic saga tradition.

6 That is, near the bottom of page 265 of the first edition, which had 310 pages.

7 In order to better see just how variable the chapter lengths are in the book, and how the longer chapters tend to cluster in the earlier half, the following chart lists all the chapters in order from longest to shortest, given the pagination of the first edition. I have used a copy of the third (wartime) printing from 1942 [cf. Hammond, *Descriptive Bibliography*, page 16] to determine these figures, which lacks the 'Mirkwood' half-tone and colour plates (none of which were included in the original pagination in any case).

i. Chapter VIII. Flies and Spiders (30 pages)
ii. Chapter VII. Queer Lodgings (27 pages plus one illustration)
iii. Chapter I. An Unexpected Party (27 pages)

iv. Chapter XII. Inside Information (22 pages)
v. Chapter VI. Out of the Frying-Pan into the Fire (21 pages)
vi. Chapter IX. Barrels Out of Bond (18 pages plus one illustration)
vii. Chapter V. Riddles in the Dark (17 pages)
viii. Chapter II. Roast Mutton (17 pages plus one illustration)

ix. Chapter IV. Over Hill and Under Hill (13 pages plus one illustration)
x. Chapter XVII. The Clouds Burst (12 pages plus one illustration)
xi. Chapter XIII. Not at Home (12 pages) [= manuscript chapter XIV]
xii. Chapter X. A Warm Welcome (12 pages plus one illustration)
xiii. Chapter XV. The Gathering of the Clouds (11 pages)

xiv. Chapter XIV. Fire and Water (10 pages) [= manuscript chapter XIII]
xv. Chapter III. A Short Rest (10 pages)
xvi. Chapter XI. On the Doorstep (9 pages plus one illustration)
xvii. Chapter XVIII. The Return Journey (9 pages)
xviii. Chapter XIX. The Last Stage (9 pages plus one illustration)
xix. Chapter XVI. A Thief in the Night (7 pages)

Plot Notes F

This brief outline (Marq. 1/1/23:3), scribbled on a torn sheet of good paper (in fact, the back of an unsent letter[TN1]), is little more than a collection of notes in now-faint pencil on miscellaneous points that Tolkien jotted down as a reminder to himself of loose plot-points that would need to be addressed in the wrapping-up. Unlike Plot Notes E, which represent the final work on the Second Phase, these notes seem to belong to the beginning of the Third Phase.

Bilbo's treasure all lost on the way home – except his kettle & a pair of studs.

And were the dwarves forever at his service?

Send message back by Thrush to Lake Town – it arrives too late but reaches Bard before his last shot.

Bring him <?word> in last <moment>.

Wood-elf king gives back orcrist
How troll-key fitted – Gandalf explains.
Trolls had <?even> <illegible>[TN2] Moria, where Thrain son of Thror <was> prisoner

Bilbo hangs his sword over mantlepiece & has his mail put on a stand

Prophecy came true for the Dale became rich, and the Dwarves of Thror for long were good till their race faded, and gold flowed down the river & <fountains> were made.

Battle of Five armies and disenchantment of Beorn

Written in the left margin:

1 2 3 4 5
woodelves, dwarves,[TN3] eagles, men, bears – goblins wolves
6 7

But <illegible> Bilbo got out of it was a set of useful proverbs

Written in the right margin:

Lost his <reputation> & found another.
Digs up <?trolls'> treasure, <distributes> it.

The most notable feature of Plot Notes F is that the inclusion of dwarves among the participants in 'The Battle of Five Armies' (which is finally and for the first time given that name) suggests this event might have now shifted from taking place not far to the west as part of Bilbo's return journey, but as the culmination of the events at the Lonely Mountain. Even so, Tolkien remained in difficulties deciding just which of the forces present counted as one of the 'Five'; cf. the commentary on page 714 following the Third Phase text. Beorn's bear army is still present, as in the final page of Plot Notes B. One significant and intriguing new element here is the brief mention of the 'disenchantment of Beorn'; see the commentary on Bothvar Bjarki following Chapter VII for more on this unrealized motif. Otherwise, these notes closely correspond to what Tolkien actually came to set down once he began writing the Third Phase text; the two significant departures are the absence of Beorn's bear-army (his prowess being upgraded until followers would have been superfluous),[TN4] and of the loss of Bilbo's treasure (a scene which Tolkien began to write but then crossed out; see page 690 & Text Note 11 on page 698).

TEXT NOTES

1 The unsent letter (I/I/23:4), written in Tolkien's neatest script, is undated; Tolkien tore the page in half and only the top half survives (because of its blank verso's reuse for plot-notes). It represents Tolkien's reader's report for some unidentified publisher on a book he had been sent to evaluate for possible publication. Despite the letter's lack of context, Tolkien's opinion is clear, as he definitely advises against publication: '. . . published without a competent revision it would receive ungentle handling from any reviewer in this country who knew anything about Old English. I hardly like to think of what I should say about it, if I was a reviewer myself, and not your adviser.' Possibly this letter was not sent because it was superseded by a more circumspect replacement.

2 This illegible word seems to begin with *p-* and end with *-d*, but it is clearly not *plundered*, the reading of the Third Phase text (see page 688), because it lacks the ascender for the *-l-* and has an ascender immediately followed by a descender in the middle; possibly it is two short words run together, the first of which ends in *-ly*. The doubtful word preceding this word or phrase might be *been* rather than *even*.

3 This word is circled, but the significance of this is unclear: possibly Tolkien hesitated between the old idea of the Battle of Anduin Vale (without the dwarves' presence) and the new idea that seems to be emerging of bringing the battle to the Lonely Mountain (where he could segue between the Siege of the Mountain directly into the battle). For more on the Battle of Five Armies, see the commentary on page 713ff following the Third Phase text.

4 See the North Polar Bear's similar immunity to goblins ('for of course goblins can't hurt *him*') and similar tactic of wading into battle with a sea ('more like 1000') of goblins in the Father Christmas Letters for 1932 and 1933: 'squeezing, squashing, trampling, boxing, and kicking Goblins sky-high'; see *Letters from Father Christmas* pages 74 and 87 and the commentary following Chapter VII.

THE THIRD PHASE

'A THIEF INDEED'

Perhaps the most important misconception about the writing of *The Hobbit*, even more significant than its alleged lack of connection to the earlier legendarium (which is self-evidently false from the various allusions within the original manuscript, not to mention explicitly refuted by Tolkien himself in his first statement in print about the book after *The Hobbit* was published),[1] is the claim that Tolkien abandoned the story unfinished in the early 1930s, only resuming work on it sometime in the summer or fall of 1936 at the prodding of a publisher. This claim was first advanced by Humphrey Carpenter in his authorized biography, and since all subsequent accounts derive from Carpenter's, it seems best to examine his argument and assertions in some detail:

> The writing of the story progressed fluently until the passage not far from the end where the dragon Smaug is about to die. Here Tolkien hesitated, and tried out the narrative in rough notes – something he was often to do in *The Lord of the Rings* but seems to have done only rarely in *The Hobbit*. These notes suggest that Bilbo Baggins might creep into the dragon's lair and stab him . . . But this idea, which scarcely suited the character of the hobbit or provided a grand enough death for Smaug, was rejected in favour of the published version where the dragon is slain by the archer Bard. And then, shortly after he had described the death of the dragon, Tolkien abandoned the story. Or to be more accurate, he did not write any more of it down. For the benefit of his children he had narrated an impromptu conclusion to the story, but, as Christopher Tolkien expressed it, 'the ending chapters were rather roughly done, and not typed out at all'. Indeed they were not even written in manuscript. The typescript of the nearly finished story . . . was occasionally shown to favoured friends, together with its accompanying maps (and perhaps already a few illustrations). But it did not often leave Tolkien's study, where it sat, incomplete and now likely to remain so. The boys were growing up and no longer asked for 'Winter Reads', so there was no reason why *The Hobbit* should ever be finished.
>
> —Humphrey Carpenter, *Tolkien: A Biography*, pages 179–80.

In addition to a great deal of information conveyed succinctly and clearly, this account unfortunately also includes a good deal of misinformation, details that Carpenter, who has to cover a great deal of territory in very little space, all of it without any prior scholarship on the point to guide him, got wrong, misinterpreted, or oversimplified. For example, while he clearly alludes to Plot Notes B & C, he takes no account of the first outline (page 229), the extensive Plot Notes A, the 'little bird' outline (Plot Notes E), Plot Notes F, nor the complicated evolution that produced the composite, multilayered document that is Plot Notes B/C/D/B. His account ignores one of the three major breaks in the book's composition, discussing the ones at the end of Chapter I (that is, at the end of the First Phase) and early in Chapter XV (although failing to convey exactly where this break takes place) but not the break at the beginning of Chapter IX (at their capture by wood-elves, which like the other two is marked by a change of paper). Carpenter's account is also unintentionally misleading to readers who do not know that Chapters XIII and XIV were later switched, so that in the manuscript the story continued for about another chapter and a half beyond Smaug's death.

Similarly, there is no evidence known to me of these impromptu oral conclusions; certainly Tolkien never mentions them in any of his later recollections, nor are they alluded to in any of the memoirs by his sons that I have seen. Carpenter may be relying here on information he received directly from John and Michael Tolkien (whose evidence, while valuable, is demonstrably wrong on some points). It is more probable that, given his stage background[2] and not having the benefit of the *History of Middle-earth* series before him with its many examples of Tolkien working out difficulties foreseen in upcoming sections through plot-notes before undertaking the actual writing of those chapters, Carpenter mistook the plot-notes as cues for an oral performance.

More importantly, there is no evidence to support Carpenter's assertion that the concluding chapters 'were not even written in manuscript'; indeed, such evidence as there is, is to the contrary. For my argument that we should take young Christopher's words literally as an accurate description of the Third Phase text (129 pages of typescript completed by a 13-page 'fair copy' interpolation and the 45 pages of Third Phase manuscript) as it stood between January 1933 and summer 1936 (see page xx). As a refutation of the claim that the story was abandoned because the 'Winter Reads' ceased, see Note 16 to the commentary following Chapter XII for evidence that Tolkien's sessions of reading aloud to his children were still ongoing at the time Tolkien was preparing *The Hobbit* for publication in the summer of 1936.

Tolkien himself contradicts Carpenter's claim that the manuscript 'did not often leave Tolkien's study' when he noted that 'the MS. certainly wandered about' (*Letters* p. 21); over the course of some three and a half years he loaned it not only to C. S. Lewis but at least three other people that we know of: Rev. Mother St. Teresa Gale (the Mother Superior at Cherwell Edge), his graduate student Elaine Griffiths, and a twelve-to-thirteen-year-old girl (possibly Aileen Jennings, daughter of a family friend who attended the same church; Aileen and her younger sister Elizabeth [later a moderately well-known poet] both received presentation copies from Tolkien as soon as the book was published),[3] and there might of course have been others. The Inklings might count among their number: Tolkien noted that the story had been read to the group but did not specify when this occurred;[4] certainly before publication, and it seems likely that it would have been during the period when Tolkien was preparing the book for publication in 1936 – that is, after Dagnall had returned the 'home manuscript' to him but before he sent the completed typescript to Allen & Unwin for official submission in early October 1936. And of course he proved quite willing to loan it to Dagnall herself, who clearly borrowed it in an informal capacity, whatever hope she might have been able to hold out to him of putting in a good word regarding the book with her employers.

In short, we should view the Third Phase text, and the final chapters of the book, as still part of the original two-to-three-year impetus of composition, written after a gap of no more than a year from where he left off, not as the return to an abandoned work that had languished untouched for three years or more. The very fact that Tolkien had in the meantime decided to go back to the beginning of the story and create the First Typescript – at 129 single-spaced pages a significant investment of time and energy for a ten-fingered typist like himself who carefully revised as he typed – is a testament to his faith in the story. Far from lying abandoned between the breaking off of the Second Phase and the drafting of the Third Phase, during that period all he had so far achieved of the story was in fact laboriously being put into legible form where it could be shared with others. The great differences between these final chapters and the early parts of the book are the result of internal development within the story, the working out of the twin complications Tolkien introduced late in the Second Phase. Tolkien's decision to cut the Gordian knot of Bard's legitimate claim to an indeterminate portion of the treasure versus Thorin's inability to accept any negotiation or compromise that meant parting with any of the treasure because of his succumbing to dragon-sickness, and his decision to raise the stakes by re-introducing virtually all the creatures encountered earlier in the book into one grand melee, avoids the anticlimax of a long dénouement following the dragon's death and creates a climax even more comprehensive and, ultimately, more satisfactory than the dragon-quest Bilbo had originally set out on.

NOTES

1 'My tale is not consciously based on any other book – save one . . . the "Silmarillion", a history of the Elves, to which frequent allusion is made' – JRRT, letter to *The Observer*; see Appendix II. Although at times Tolkien sought to distance *The Hobbit* from the pre-existing legendarium, at others he freely admitted or even laid stress upon the connection.

2 Carpenter's first involvement with Tolkien's work was to direct a children's theater adaptation of *The Hobbit*, and he later wrote a radio-play depicting Tolkien as a detached eccentric ('In a Hole in the Ground, There Lived a Tolkien' [1992]); most of my second meeting with him (in Oxford, in 1985) was spent watching him direct a rather odd adaptation of *The Wizard of Oz* for an all-teen cast. For more on Carpenter's interests and background in drama, see the obituary by Charles Noad and Jessica Yates, published in the March 2005 issue of *Amen Hen*; I am grateful to its authors for sharing a pre-publication copy with me. See also Douglas A. Anderson's detailed account of Carpenter's work with Tolkien in Volume II of *Tolkien Studies* (pages 217–24).

3 See the Introduction to Douglas Anderson's *The Annotated Hobbit* for more on the identities of those who read the book before its publication (DAA.12).

4 See Tolkien's 4th June 1938 letter to Stanley Unwin telling him of 'our literary club . . . before whom the *Hobbit*, and other works (such as *The Silent Planet*) have been read' (*Letters* p. 36). Our best evidence suggests that the Inklings did not yet exist in January 1933 when Tolkien completed the story, but came together very shortly thereafter, one of the significant factors that led to the group's formation being the retirement of Major (then Captain) Warnie Lewis in December 1932, his return from Shanghai to live with his brother at the Kilns, and his joining Tolkien and Lewis at some of their regular gatherings. The Inklings seem to have come about from the two men's desire to include Warnie in their meetings while providing a comfortable environment for less exclusively academic discussion; the late Dr. Humphrey Havard told me he was invited to join the group upon returning to Oxford and meeting the Lewis brothers in 1934. The first documentary evidence for the group's existence comes in C. S. Lewis's first letter to Charles Williams (11th March 1936) inviting him to attend a meeting of 'a sort of informal club called the Inklings' (*Collected Letters of C. S. Lewis*, ed. Walter Hooper, vol. II, page 183). The early members of the group included Tolkien, Lewis, Warnie, and Havard (the four who formed the core of the group throughout its existence), as well as Nevill Coghill (a fellow member with Lewis in Tolkien's Kolbítars, and specially mentioned along with Tolkien and Warnie in Lewis's letter to Williams), Hugo Dyson, Owen Barfield (usually *in absentia*, since he lived in London), Adam Fox (who seems to have promptly quit the group after they got him elected Professor of Poetry in 1938), and C. L. Wrenn.

Chapter XVb

KING BARD

The Third Phase text began with the creation of the First Typescript, when Tolkien returned to the beginning of the story and produced a legible, polished version of almost all the material he had written so far, incorporating into earlier chapters changes made necessary by developments in later chapters, such as the changes in names of some characters, and inserting the chapter breaks for the first time into the hitherto continuous text. This typescript reached as far as typescript page 129, the page describing the death of Smaug (Marq. 1/1/64:3; the third page in Chapter XIII [> XIV]). Tolkien then created the 'fair copy' version of the chapter describing Bilbo and the dwarves' adventures inside the mountain (Chapter XIV [> XIII]; Marq. 1/1/14), carefully written on good paper, numbering the pages a-m to show that they formed a separate sequence. We can show that this 'fair copy' text of what is now Chapter XIII is *later* than the first few pages of the typescript of what is now Chapter XIV by the pagination of the latter: the First Typescript has sequential page numbers neatly typed in the upper left corner of each page from Chapter I through the third page of Chapter XIII [> XIV]. When Chapter XIII (The Death of Smaug) became Chapter XIV ('Fire and Water') and later a typed version of the new Chapter XIII ('Not at Home'; Marq. 1/1/63) was inserted in place of the 'fair copy' text, the new typed pages lacked any typed page numbers and are instead numbered 127–34 in black ink, while the first three pages of 'Fire and Water' were re-numbered in the same ink: 127 > 135, 128 > 136, and 129 > 137, followed by page 1 of the Third Phase manuscript. Similarly, we know the next typescript page in 'Fire and Water' (Marq. 1/1/64:4) is *later* than the new typescript of the transposed chapter because it lacks any typed page number and instead is numbered in ink '138'; close comparison of the text also confirms that it derives from the Third Phase manuscript, not the earlier Second Phase version of this passage. In short, it was here that the 'beautifully typed copy' Elaine Griffiths recalled borrowing (Ann Bonsor radio interview; see also DAA.12) ended and the 'rather roughly done' ending chapters described by thirteen-year-old Christopher (see page xvii) began.

Thus, the circulating copy of Bilbo's adventures which Tolkien loaned to Lewis, Griffiths, the Reverend Mother, the thirteen-year-old girl, and possibly others, which he called the 'home manuscript' in a later letter to Allen & Unwin, was a composite of typescript and fair copy manuscript:

- typescript pages 1 through 126 (Chapters I through XII)
- fair copy pages 'a' through 'm' (Chapter XIV > XIII)
- typescript pages 127 through 129 plus Third Phase manuscript pages 1 through 45 (Chapters XIII > XIV through XIX/end).

The First Typescript carried the story up to the words *'And in the very midst of their talk a tall figure stepped from the shadows. He was drenched'* at the bottom of typescript page 129 (Marq. 1/1/64:3). The Third Phase manuscript begins in mid-sentence with the next word on page 1 *'with water'* (the Second Phase text has a pencilled mark at this exact point indicating where the First Typescript ceased and the Third Phase manuscript took its place; see page 551 and Text Note 12 following Chapter XIII on page 554).

Like the first half of the Second Phase manuscript (manuscript pages 13–117), the Third Phase manuscript is written on good-quality 'foolscap' paper, unlike the larger pages (lined on one side and torn from student exam books) which had supplied the paper for the latter half of the Second Phase (i.e., manuscript pages 118–67 and the 'little bird' fragment).

The first seven pages of this new manuscript present a new draft of material which has already appeared in Chapters XIII and XVa of this book, but I include the overlap and give the entire Third Phase manuscript here for purposes of comparison to show how Tolkien expanded and polished the material in the course of making a fresh draft.

As with so many of Tolkien's manuscripts, the Third Phase text began as fair copy, very neatly and legibly written in Tolkien's best script on good paper. And as is also typical with Tolkien's fair copies, the handwriting begins to deteriorate (in this case, after the first twenty pages or so), but even so this text remains much more legible than most.

Finally, the Third Phase manuscript includes a number of cancelled pages; those that survive after they had been superseded by replacement text do so because after he struck through the rejected text Tolkien re-used the verso for a later page. Thus, for example, what seem to be the original second, third, and fourth pages of the Third Phase were all cancelled but survive because they form the versos of pages 14, 9, and 8, respectively. See Text Notes 3, 4, and 7 for the cancelled texts. There is evidence that other cancelled pages once existed but did not survive.

with water, his black hair hung wet over his face and shoulders, and a fierce light was in his eyes.

'Bard is not lost!' he cried. 'I am Bard, slayer of the dragon. I dived from Esgaroth only when no one else was left, and only when the enemy was slain. I am of the race of Girion, Lord of Dale. I will be your king!'

'King Bard! King Bard!' they shouted; and the Master ground his chattering teeth, as he sat upon the earth.

'Girion was Lord of Dale, not king of Esgaroth', he said. 'In this lake-town we have always elected masters from the old and wise, and have not endured the rule of mere fighting men. Let King Bard go back to his own kingdom; and anyone go with him that wish to. Dale is [*added*: now] free; and he has slain the slayer of his fathers; nothing hinders his return. But the wise will stay here and rebuild our town, and hope to enjoy again in time its riches and its peace, any that prefer the mountain-shadowed valley to this water-side can go with him!'[TN1]

'We will have King Bard!' the people clamoured. 'We have had enough of the old men and money-counters'.

'I am the last man to undervalue Bard the bowman' said the Master warily (for Bard had come & stood now close beside him). 'He has tonight earned a chief place in the list of our benefactors, and is worthy of many imperishable songs. But, why, O people?' – and here the Master rose and spoke very loud and clear – 'why do I get all your blame? Who aroused the dragon from his <illegible> slumber,[TN2] I might ask?[TN3] Who obtained of us rich gifts and ample help, and led us to believe that old songs could come true? Who played on our soft hearts and pleasant fancies? What sort of gold have they sent down the river to reward us? Fire and ruin! From whom shall we claim the recompense of our damage, and aid for our widows and orphans?'

As you see the Master had not earned his position for nothing. For the moment the people quite forgot the idea of a new king, and turned their angry thoughts towards Thorin and his company. Wild and bitter words were shouted from many sides; and some of those who before had sung the old songs loudest, were now heard as loudly crying that the dwarves had stirred the Dragon up against them deliberately!

'Fools!' said Bard. 'Why waste words and wrath on those unhappy creatures? Doubtless they perished first in fire, before Smaug came to us.' Then even as he was speaking, the thought of the fabled treasure of the Mountain came [suddenly >] into his heart, and he fell suddenly silent; and he thought of the Master's words, and of Dale rebuilt, and filled with golden bells, if he could but find the men.

At last he spoke again: 'This is no time Master for angry words, or for considering weighty plans and great changes. There is work to do. I serve you still – though after a while, I may think again of your words, and go North with any that will follow me'.[TN4] Then he strode off to help in the ordering of the camps and in the care of the sick and wounded. But the Master scowled at his back as he went, and remained sitting on the ground. He thought much, but he said little, unless it was to call loudly for men to bring him fire and food.

Now everywhere Bard went he found talk running like fire among the people concerning the vast treasure that was now without a guard. Men spoke of the recompense for all their harm that they would soon get from it, and wealth over and to spare wherewith to buy rich things from the South;[TN5] and it cheered them greatly in their plight. That was fortunate, for their night was bitter and miserable. Shelters could be contrived for few, and there was little food. Many took ill of wet and cold and anguish [> sorrow] that night, and afterwards died, who had escaped uninjured from the town; and in the days that followed there was much sickness and great hunger. Meanwhile Bard took the lead, and ordered things as he wished, though always in the Master's name; but he had a hard task to govern the people, and to arrange [> direct] the preparations for their protection and recovery. Probably most of them would have perished in the winter that now hurried [onwards >] after autumn, if help had not been to hand.[TN6]

But help came swiftly; for Bard had at once had [swift >] speedy messengers sent up the river to the Forest to ask help of the King of the Elves, and these messengers had found a host already on the move, although it was only the second day after the fall of Smaug.[TN7]

The Elven king had received news of what passed from his scouts and from the birds that loved his folk. Very great indeed was the commotion among all things with wings that dwelt on the borders of the desolation of the dragon. The air was filled with circling flocks, and swift-flying messengers sped here and there across the sky. Above the borders of the forest the air was filled with the noise of birds whistling, crying and piping. Far over Mirkwood the tidings spread: [*added*: 'Smaug is dead'] Leaves rustled and startled ears were lifted. Even before the Elvenking rode [from his <?halls> >] forth the news had passed west even to the pinewoods of the Misty Mountains, and the Goblins were at council in their halls.

[But >] 'That will be the last we shall hear of Thorin Oakenshield, [*added*: I fear]' said the king. 'He would have done better to remain my guest. It is an ill wind all the same' he added 'that blows no one good', for he too had not forgotten the legend of the wealth of Thror. So it was that Bard's men found him now riding [> marching] with all the spearmen and bowmen he could muster; and all the crows were gathered above him, for they thought they saw signs of <?battle and> wars awakening again, such as had not been for a long time. [*cancelled*: But some of the woodelves were gone <a route> direct towards the Mountain:]

Now the king when he received the prayers of the Bard because of his old friendship with the men of the lake; and because he was a lord of good and kindly race turned his march[TN8] which had been purposed to go direct toward the mountain, and turned [> went] along the river towards Lake-Town [> the Long lake]. He had not boats or rafts enough for all his host and they had [> were forced] to go the slower road [> way] by foot, but great store of goods he sent ahead by water. Still elves are light-footed, and though [they] were not much used to the marshes and treacherous lands between the Forest and the Lake, their going was swift; and but four days from the fall of Smaug the[y] came upon the shores of the Lake, and looked on the burnt ruins of the town. Their welcome was good, as may be expected, and the men & their Master were ready to make any bargain for the future in return for the Elvenking's aid.

Their [<?dangers> were s[oon] >] plans were soon made. With the women and children, the old and the unfit the Master remained behind, & with him were some men of crafts and many skilled elves; and they busied themselves felling trees and with these and such timber as was sent from the Forest they set about the raising of many huts by the shore against the oncoming winter; also under the Master's direction [farther >] they began the planning of a new town, designed more fairly and more large even than before, but in a place removed somewhat [> a little] northward, for they liked not the water where the body of the dragon lay.

A rider (1/1/15:11), written in pencil on a loose, unnumbered sheet of lined student notepaper, was clearly meant to be inserted at this spot, although there is no indication of its existence or exact placement on the page it supplements:

He would never again to his golden bed, but was lying cold [*added*: as stone, his bones > twisted] upon the floor of the shallows of the Lake – where forever after his great bones could be seen in calm weather amid the ruined pile<s> of the old town if any dared to cross the accursed spot. But [<?men> >] they rebuilt the town in a different place and none ever <dared> afterwards to gather the precious stones that were [<?fallen> >] fell out from his rotting carcass – not even the Master

A second rider (1/1/15:12), more carefully written in ink on a small piece of good paper, replaces this with a more polished form of the same passage:

He would never again return to his golden bed but was lying cold as stone, twisted upon the floor of the shallows of the lake, where for ever after his great bones could be seen in calm weather amid the ruined piles of the old town, if any one dared to cross the accursed spot.[TN9]

At the bottom of this text appear the penciled words 'new p. 4.', indicating that this rider is meant to go with Third Phase page 4 (1/1/16:1), which began with the words 'four days from the fall of Smaug' a paragraph and a half earlier.

But all the men of arms who were still able, and the most of the host of the king, got ready to march north to the Mountain. It was thus that in seven days from the death of Smaug that the head of their host passed the rock-gates at the end of the lake and came to the desolate lands.

At this point, Tolkien later began a new chapter (Chapter XV: 'The Gathering of the Clouds'). On the manuscript page itself, in the middle of Third Phase manuscript page 4 (1/1/16:1), only a double skipped line between the third and fourth paragraphs marks the shift in scene. There is some evidence that Tolkien did not intend a chapter break to come here in the 'home manuscript'; see page 666 below.

Now we will return to Bilbo and the Dwarves. All night one of them in turn had watched, but when morning came no sign of danger had been seen. But still yet more thickly the birds were gathering. Their companies came flying from the south, and the crows that still lived about the mountain were wheeling <&> crying unceasingly [*added*: above].[TN10]

'Something strange is happening' said Thorin. 'The time has gone for the autumn wanderings; and there are birds that dwell ever in the land, starlings and flocks of finches – and there are many crows [> carrion birds far off] as if a battle were afoot.'

Suddenly Bilbo pointed: 'There is that old thrush again' he cried. 'He seems to have escaped when Smaug smashed the mountain-side; but I don't suppose the snails have!'

Sure enough the old thrush was there, and as Bilbo pointed he flew towards them and perched on a stone nearby. Then he fluttered his wings and sang; then he cocked his head as if to listen; and again he sang and again he listened.

'I believe he is trying to tell us something' said Balin; 'but I don't understand the tongue of small [> such] birds, it is very quick and difficult. Do you, Mr Baggins?'

'Not very well' said Bilbo (he did not know anything about it as a matter of fact),[TN11] 'but this old fellow seems very excited.'

'I only wish he was a raven' said Balin.

'I thought you did not like them' said Bilbo. You seemed to be very nervous [> shy] of them when we came this way before.'

'Those were crows! And nasty suspicious-looking creatures at that, & rude as well. You must have heard the ugly names they were calling after us. But the ravens are different. There used to be a [*added*: great] friendship between them and the people of Thror, and they were often our scouts and news-bringers [> bringers of secret news to us]. [There are some that still linger here, I know, for I have seen > But I do not suppose there > any of that wise race that linger here now. >] They live many a year and their memories are long, and they hand [on] their wisdom to their children. I had many friends [> knew many] among the ravens of the rocks when I was a dwarf-lad. This very ridge we are on was once named 'Ravenhill' for there was a wise and famous pair [*added*: old Kark and his wife] that dwelt here above the guard-chamber. But I do not suppose that any of that ancient race linger here now.'[TN12]

No sooner had he finished speaking than the old thrush gave a loud call, and immediately flew away.

'[That old bird >] We may not understand him, but that old bird understood [> understands] us, I am sure' said Thorin. 'Keep watch now, & see what happens!'

Before long there was a fluttering of wings, and back came the Thrush; but with him came another most decrepit old bird. He was getting blind, he could hardly fly, and the top of his head was bald. He was an aged raven of great size. He alighted stiffly on the ground before them, slowly flapped his wings and bobbed towards Thorin.

'O Thorin, Thrain's son, Thror's son, & Balin son of Fundin' he croaked, and Bilbo found he could understand what he said. 'I am Roäc son of Carc. Carc is dead, but he was well-known to you once. It is a hundred years and three and fifty since I came out of the egg, but I do not forget what my father told me. [Now] I am the chief of the great Ravens of the Mountain. We are few [and we >] but we remember still the King that was of old. The others are mostly gone south, where there are great tidings – some are tidings of joy to you, and some you will not think so good. Behold! the birds are gathering back again to the Mountain from South and East and West, for word has gone forth that Smaug is dead!'

'Dead?' shouted the dwarves. 'Dead! Then we have been in needless fear – and the treasure is ours!' They sprang up and began to caper about for joy.

'Yes, dead' said Roäc. 'The thrush, may his feathers never fail, has seen it [> saw him die], and we may trust his words. He saw him fall in battle with the men of Esgaroth the third night back from now, at the rising of the moon. So much for joy, Thorin Oakenshield. You may go back to your halls in safety; all the treasure is yours – for the moment. But many are gathering hither other than [> besides] the birds. The news of the death of the guardian has gone far and wide, & many are eager for a share of the spoil. Already an army is on the way, and carrion birds are with them, hoping for battle and slaughter. The Elvenking is coming hither; and by the Lake men murmur that their sorrows are due to you; For they are homeless and many are dead, & Smaug has destroyed their town. They purpose too to find amends from your treasure, whether you are alive or dead (as they expect). [I have sp[oken] > I have <nought> >] Your own wisdom must decide your course; but thirteen is small remnant of the great folk of Durin that now is scattered far. If you will hearken to my advice you will trust [rather Bard the bow-man; for he it was that shot >] not the Master of the lake-men, but rather him that shot the dragon with his bow. Bard is he, of the race of Dale, of the line of Girion; he is a grim man but true. We would see peace once more among dwarves and men and elves after the long desolation; but it may cost you dear in gold. I have spoken.'

Then Thorin burst forth in wrath [> anger]: 'our thanks Roäc Carc's son. You and your people shall not be forgotten. But none of our gold shall thieves or the violent have while we are still alive. If you would earn our thanks still more bring us news of any approach [> that draw near]. Also I would beg you, if any of you are yet young and strong of wing, that you would send messengers to our kin in the mountains of the North, both west from here and East, and tell them of our plight. But go specially to my cousin Dain at [> in] the Iron hills, for he has many people well armed and bid him hasten [> and dwells nearest to this place; and bid him hasten].'[TN13]

'I will not say if this plan be good or bad' [said >] croaked Roäc; but I will [*cancelled*: try to] do what can be done,' and off he slowly flew.

'Back now to the mountain' said Thorin. 'We have little time to lose.'

'And little food to use!' cried Bilbo, always practical on such points. In any case he felt that the adventure was properly speaking over with the death of Smaug – in which he was much[TN14] mistaken – and would have given much of his share of the profits for a peaceful winding-up of these affairs.

'Back to the mountain' cried the dwarves, as if they had not heard; so back with them he had to go.

As you have heard some of the events that were going on about already you will see that the dwarves still had some days before them. They laboured hard, for tools were still to be found in plenty in their old halls [*added*: and at such work they were greatly skilled] and [*added*: as they worked] the ravens brought them constant tidings.

This last sentence was cancelled and replaced by an expanded passage crowded into the left margin:

> They explored the halls once more, & found as they had expected that, but the main Gate remained open. All the others save the more [> smaller] secret door, had long ago been broken and blocked by smaug. So now they laboured hard in fortifying the Eastern Gate. Tools were to still be had in plenty that the miners and quarriers and builders of old had used, and at such work they were greatly skilled. As they worked the Ravens brought them constant tidings.

Thus they learned [after four days' toil that the joined host of the elves >] that the Elvenking had turned aside to [the] Lake, and they still had breathing space. Better still they heard that three of their ponies were wandering wild far down upon the river banks, not far from where their stores had been left. So while the others went on with their chief task of fortifying the gate, Fili and Kili were sent guided by a raven to [bring in such suppl[ies] >] find the ponies and bring back all they could.

[It was four days >] They were four days gone, and by that time they knew that the joined armies of the lake-men and Elves were hastening towards them. But now their hopes were more high, for they had food for some weeks with care, and the gate was block[ed] with a wall of squared stones laid dry but very thick and high across the opening. There were holes in it [for see >] from which they could see or shoot, but no entrance. They climbed in and out by ladders, or hauled stuff up with ropes. For the issuing of the river [> stream] they had contrived an arch [> a small arch], [but they so altered its bed near the entrance that >] under the new wall, but near the entrance they so altered its [narrow] bed that a wide pool [stood >] stretched from the mountain wall to the head of the falls over which it went on towards Dale, and approach to the Gate was only by a narrow path that wound close to the high [bank >] cliff southward. [There was no pasture for the ponies, so these they took >] The ponies they had brought only to the head of the steps above the old bridge[TN15] and unloading them had bidden return to their mortal masters,[TN16] and sent them back riderless to the south.

The[re] came an evening [> a night] when suddenly there were many lights as of fires and torches away East [<out> the >] in Dale before them. 'They have come,' called Balin 'and their camp is great. They must have come into the valley under the covering of dusk; and most are on the north side of the River.'

That night they [> the dwarves] slept little. The morning was still pale when they saw a company approaching. From behind their wall they watch[ed] them come up the valley's head and climb [<the rock> >] slowly up. Soon they saw that both men of the lake armed as for war, and elvish bowmen were among them. At last they climbed the rocks and appeared at the fall's head; and great was their surprise to see the pool before them, and the [blocked gate >] gate blocked with a wall of new-hewn stone.

Then Thorin hailed them: 'Who are you' he called in a loud voice 'that come as if to war to the gates of Thorin son of Thrain, king under the Mountain, and what do you desire?'

But they answered nothing; some turned swiftly back and [the] others after gazing long at the gate and its defences soon followed them. That day the camp was moved, and came right between the arms of the mountain. The rocks echoed then with voices and with song, as they had not done for many a day. There was sound [too] of elven-harps and sweet music; and Bilbo longed to escape and go forth and join in the feasting by the fires. Even the dwarves [> Thorin was] moved, & muttered that he would things had fallen out other-wise, and that he might welcome such folk as friends.[TN17] But Thorin scowled.

A pencilled addition, scribbled at the end of the paragraph and in the left margin, introduces the idea of dwarven music as a counter to the elven song outside:

But the dwarves themselves brought forth the[ir] harps and <?instruments> regained from the hoard & made music to heart[en] <him> and they sang again songs as they had done in B's <home>.

There is no indication here that Tolkien intended to include an actual song at this point, but an unnumbered page in pencil on a loose sheet of student paper (1/1/16:12) survives that is clearly the very first rough workings for the poem that was later inserted here (i.e., in the resumed First Typescript). The typescript version of the preceding paragraph notes that 'their song . . . was much like the song they had sung long before in Bilbo's little hobbit-hole' (1/1/65:4), and indeed one stanza of the final poem is identical (the third in the new poem and the second in the old) and another reproduces three lines out of four (the fourth in both poems, differing only in one line and one word), while the other stanzas reuse some of the rhymes and phrasing from the earlier poem (compare DAA.321–2 with DAA.44–5). The two are clearly meant to be companion pieces, depicting the hoped-for goal at the onset of the quest and its apparent achievement at what Bilbo had optimistically hoped would be its end.

Under the Mountain dark and tall
[The King is > returns <to> his ha[ll] >] The King is come unto his hall
The [<?thane> >] worm of dread
This foe is dead the worm of dread <illegible>
[And so shall his foes >] And ever so his foes shall fall

[The Gate is strong, the >]
The sword is sharp the spear is long
The arrow swift the Gate is strong
The heart is bold that looks on gold [TN18]
That *wrong.*[TN19]
[It <brooks> . >]
It fears not
The <illegible> is swift the [> No more the dwarves]
The king shall suffer <no>[TN20] *[> shall suffer wrong]*

The Dwarves lift up the hearts afar
Where ever folk of Durin are.
Come haste come haste across the waste
The king has need of friend <&> [> friend and k.][TN21]

[The dwarves >] The mountain throne once more is freed
O folk of Durin O wandering folk the summons heed
The king of kin and friend hast need.
the melody of harp they wrung

Now call their voices over mountains cold
Come back unto the cavern old
Rejoice where [added: hoarded] silver lies and gold
Here at the gates the king [added: now] awaits
his hands [are <illegible> >] with silver > with gifts of silver and of gold

Despite its extreme roughness, this first draft is recognizably the same poem as the final piece in the published book, the main differences being the insertion of two stanzas from the companion poem in Chapter I (one of which was slightly altered in the process), thus expanding it from the five stanzas of the draft to the seven of the final poem, the combination of the draft's third and fourth stanzas into a single stanza (the fifth) in the final, and the addition of a final stanza that recaps the first but with its lines in slightly different order. The poem appears in its final form in the continuation of the First Typescript exactly as in the published book and, like all the other poems in *The Hobbit*, Tolkien left it unaltered from the first printing onwards.

The next morning a company of spearmen came and they bore amid them the green banner of the Elvenking and the blue banner of the Lake; and they came by the narrow path [and >] until the[y] stood right before the wall at the gate.

Again Thorin asked the same question[TN22] as before, and this time it was answered. A tall man stood forward dark of hair and he cried:

'Hail Thorin! [We >] Why do you fence yourself like a robber in his hold. We are not [*added*: yet] foes, and we rejoice that you are alive beyond our hope. [But still > We come hither > we came hither not >] We came expecting to find none living here, yet now that we are met there seems to be much matter for a parley and & a council.'

'Who are you and of what would you parley' answered Thorin.

'I am Bard and by my hand was the Dragon slain and your treasure delivered. Is not that a matter that concerns you? Moreover I am by right descent the heir of Girion of Dale, and in your hoard is mingled much of the wealth of his halls and towers, which of old Smaug stole. Is not that a matter of which we may speak? Further in his last battle Smaug destroyed the town of Esgaroth, and I am yet the servant of its master. I would speak for him and ask whether you have no thought for the sorrow and misery of his people, who aided you in your distress, and on whom you have thus far brought ruin only, if undesigned, in recompense.'

Now these were fair and true words, if [hars[h] >] proudly and grimly spoken, and Bilbo thought that Thorin would admit what justice was in them. But he did not reckon with the power that gold [*added*: has] upon which a dragon has long brooded, nor with dwarvish hearts.[TN23] Long hours in the past days had Thorin spent in the treasury, and the lust of it was heavy upon him. Though he hunted chiefly for the Arkenstone, yet he had an eye for every other thing that here was gathered, and about most were wound old memories of the labours and the sorrows of his race.[TN24]

'You put your worst cause in [last >] the chief place he answered.[TN25] To the treasure of my people you have no claim because Smaug who stole it from us also robbed you of life and home. The treasure is not Smaug's that his heirs should pay for his evil deeds with it![TN26] The price of the goods that we had of the lake-men we will fairly pay [and > in due time > hour] – but nothing will we give, not a loaf's worth, under threat of force. While an armed host lies before our doors, we look on you as thieves and foes.

'It is in my mind to ask what [recompense you >] share of their inheritance you would have paid to our kindred had you found the hoard unguarded and us dead.'[TN27]

'A just question' replied Bard. 'Yet you are not dead, and we have no thought at least of robbing you alive. [And still >] Moreover the wealthy may have pity on the needy [*added*: that helped [> befriended] them when they needed help]. And still my other claims remain unanswered.'[TN28]

'I will not parley, as I have said, with armed men at my gate. Nor at all with the people of the Elvenking, whom I remember with small kindness. In this debate they have no place. Begone now ere our arrows fly. And if you would speak with me again, [*added*: first] dismiss the elvish host [*added*: to the woods where it belongs] and come [hither >] to my gates and lay down [first >] your arms upon the threshold.'

'The Elvenking is my friend, and he has succoured the people of Esgaroth in their need, though we have [> they had] no claim but friendship on him,' answered Bard. 'We will give you time to repent your words. Gather your wisdom ere we return.' Then he departed and went back to the camp.[TN29]

Ere many hours were past, the banner bearers [and trumpeters >] returned and trumpeters stood forth and blew a blast. 'In the name of Esgaroth and the Elvenking' one cried[TN30] 'we bid you [> him] consider the claims that have been urged, or be declared our foes [> foe]. At least shall you deliver one twelfth portion of the treasure unto Bard, as the dragon-slayer, and as the heir of Girion. From that he will himself contribute to the aid of Esgaroth; but if you will have the friendship of the lands about you, as your sires of old, then you will add also somewhat of your own beside.'[TN31]

Then Thorin seized a bow of horn, and shot an arrow at the speaker. It smote in his shield and stuck quivering there.[TN32]

'Since such is your answer' he called in return 'I [can >] declare this Mountain besieged. You shall not depart from it until you call [> ask] on your side for a truce and a parley. We bear no weapons against you, but we leave you to your gold; and you may eat that, if you will.'

With that the messengers departed swiftly, and the dwarves were left to consider their case. So [fie[rce] >] grim had Thorin become that they did not dare to murmur against him.[TN33] Indeed most of them seem to share his mind, except perhaps for old fat Bombur, and Fili and Kili; and of course for Bilbo. He had by now had more than enough of the Mountain, and being besieged in it was not at all to his taste. It still smelt hatefully of dragon anyway; and food was short and poor.

TEXT NOTES

1 The latter half of this paragraph, all the words following 'his own kingdom', was cancelled and replaced at once by 'Dale is now free – but wise men will stay here' which in turn was changed to ' – Dale is now free, and nothing hinders his return. And any that wish can go with him, if they prefer the cold stones under the mountain-shadow to this waterside. The wise will stay here and hope to rebuild our town, and enjoy again in time its peace and riches.'

2 I cannot read the cancelled word preceding 'slumber', but it ends in *-dable*, possibly *mendable*.

3 A cancelled page (1/1/17:3) survives that represents an earlier draft of the Third Phase text that originally followed this passage. Undoubtedly once the second page in the Third Phase text, it survives because its blank verso was used shortly thereafter to become new page 14 [= 1/1/17:2].

> his slumber, I might ask? Who obtained of us rich gifts and ample help, and led us to believe that our old songs would come true? Who played upon our foolish [*added*: soft hearts] generosity and our pleasant dreams? What sort of gold have they sent down the river to recompense [> reward] us? Dragon-fire and ruin! From whom shall we claim the recompense of our damage, and the help of our widows and orphans?'
>
> [From which >] You can easily see that the Master had not earned his position for nothing. For the moment the people quite forgot their idea of a new king, and turned their angry thoughts towards Thorin and his company. Hate flared up against them, and wild and bitter words were shouted. Some of those who had sung the old songs loudest were now heard as loudly crying that the dwarves had sent the dragon down upon them deliberately!
>
> 'Fools!' said Bard. 'Why waste words or hate on those unhappy creatures. Doubtless they have perished in fire before Smaug came to us.' Yet even as he spoke, the thought of the fabled treasure of the mountain came into his heart, and he fell suddenly silent; and he thought of the Master's words, and of Dale rebuilt and filled with golden bells, if he could but find the men.
>
> At last he spoke again. 'This is no time, Master, he said for [<illegible> >] counsels of change. There is work to do. I serve you yet; though after a while I may think again of your words and go north with such folk

This passage marks the point at which the detail of Dale's 'golden bells' enter the story, although the destroyed city had been linked with bells as far back as the first poem (Bladorthin Typescript, page 37; DAA.45), all accounts of Smaug's attack (page 72; DAA.56), and Balin's sad memories upon seeing the ruins (where the mention of bells first appears in the typescript, contrast page 472 with DAA.258). The contrast between alarm bells and these golden bells recalls Edgar Poe's poem 'The Bells' [1849], which successively contrasts the sounds and associations of silver, golden, brass, and iron bells (delight, happiness, alarm, and melancholy, respectively); the juxtaposition of golden bells ringing on happy occasions immediately followed by brazen alarm bells sounding warning at times of sudden danger/disaster is particularly suggestive.

4 A cancelled page (1/1/16:10) survives that represents an earlier draft of the Third Phase text that originally followed this passage. Originally the third page in the Third Phase text, as with the text given in Text Note 3 above it survives because its blank verso was used shortly thereafter (in this case, to become page 9 [= 1/1/16:6]).

> as will follow me.' Then he strode off to help in the ordering of the camps, and in the helping of the injured; [*added, then cancelled*: but first he sent messengers as swift as <illegible> find to ask for the help of the king of the Elves] But the Master scowled at his back, and sat still upon the ground. If he thought much, he said little save to call loudly for men to bring him fire and food.
>
> But now the talk ran ever among the people of the fabled hoard of the mountain that lay now without a guardian. And men spoke of [the] recompense and to spare for all their harm that they should get from it; and it cheered them much in their plight. And that was fortunate, for their night was bitter and miserable. Shelters could be contrived for few, and there was little food. Many took ill then and afterwards died, who had escaped unhurt from the town. In the days that followed there was much sickness and hunger, and even Bard would have had a hard task to order the people, for now he took the lead [> . . . and hunger. Bard now took the lead] and ordered things as he wished, though always in the Master's name. But he had a hard task to govern the people and direct the preparations for [the] rebuilding of their town. Probably the most of them would have perished in the winter, if other help had not been to hand <in> <this/their> <illegible> the help of the Elves. [*Added, in smaller letters at the end of the paragraph and continued in the bottom margin*: It was not long before the wood-elves came. Swift messengers were sent > But help soon came, for Bard had at once had swift messages sent to the Forest to ask help of the King of the Elves.]
>
> The spies of the wood elves [> Their spies] had sent news of the dwarves' northward journey to their King; and he was as astonished as the Master of the town had been to learn of it, but he expected no other ending than their death in the jaws of the dragon.

5 The image of rich, warm lands to the South, the source of unimagined luxuries, that underlies *The Hobbit* (and to a lesser extent some passages in the early legendarium) is very much in keeping with the Old English,

Gothic, and Scandinavian view of the Mediterranean. Cf. my commentary on the trade in the wine of Dorwinion (Chapter IX) and also the reference in Chapter X to 'the trade that came up the great river from the south'.

6 'the winter that now hurried after autumn': This reference, which survives into the published book (DAA.311), shows that this scene is set in the days immediately before the onset of winter, in keeping with the shift of Durin's Day to the *last* full moon of autumn. For the problems this creates in the story's chronology, see Text Note 13 following Chapter XI.

7 Again the text that follows was preceded by a cancelled page (1/1/16:11), now the verso of new page 8 [= 1/1/16:5]; this earlier draft was once the fourth page of the Third Phase text, following immediately the text given in Text Note 4 above.

> When news reached him of the rousing of the dragon and of fire upon the mountain-top, he became alarmed, and fear for his woods fell on him; but he thought at least he had heard the last of Thorin Oakenshield.
>
> But soon other messengers came in rowing madly up the Forest River, and they told of the fall of Esgaroth and the death of Smaug. Then he thought the time had come to move. 'It is an ill wind that blows no one any good' he said; for he too had not forgotten the legend of the wealth of Thror.
>
> So now he led forth all the host he could muster, or that would follow him beyond the eaves of their beloved forest. It was a great army of bowmen and spearmen, and they were robed in green and brown, and their going was exceedingly swift. Some were sent with speed North towards the Mountain; some he led bearing great store of goods down the river towards the lake. These had a long march for they were not used to the marshes and the lands beyond the forest, and they had not boats or rafts enough to carry them. Yet elves are quick and light-footed, and [in] but four days from the fall of Smaug he reached the lake-shores, and the unhappy men were glad indeed to welcome him; and ready (as he had expected) to make any bargain for the future in return for his help.
>
> [So >] This is how it came about that while many, both men and skilful elves, were left behind upon the [<?lake> >] shores, with the women and children, busily felling trees [and gathering >] for the making of huts against the winter, and beginning under the direction of the Master to re-plan and re-fashion a town like the one destroyed, yet in a place removed further north, and planned [> designed] even more fairly and more large

While this corresponds in general to the more polished text that replaced it, some interesting details are worth noting. The inelegant detail of elves frantically rowing up-river was dropped, replaced by swift-footed messengers and, more significantly, birds 'that loved his folk', a parallel to the ravens and thrush who are shortly thereafter telling Thorin & Company the same news, and more. The statement that he brings 'all . . . that would follow him beyond the eaves of their beloved forest' suggests for the first and only time that he is not an absolute monarch; there are commands he could give that at least some of his people would not obey. This assumes, of course, that all the elves who march under his banner belong to his kingdom: the description that 'they were robed in green and brown' recalls the 'elfin folk all clad in green and brown' (BLT II.234) that Beren summoned to lead against the dwarven host in 'The Nauglafring', ambushing them and taking away all the treasure those dwarves had just claimed. It seems possible, even likely, that 'the brown Elves and the green', a phrase used three times in 'The Nauglafring' (BLT II.237, 240, & 242), distinguishes between the elves who dwelt in the caves of Artanor (Doriath) with King Tinwelint/Thingol (= the brown elves or wood-elves) and those wanderers who live in the woods (later in revisions to the 1930 *Quenta* specifically identified as the Green Elves of Ossiriand, wandering the woods in the south-east corner of Beleriand just as the wood-elves of *The Hobbit* live in the northeast corner of the area shown on the Wilderland map). The dichotomy is maintained in the 1926 'Sketch' ('the brown and green Elves of the wood', HME IV.33) but vanishes thereafter. Finally, the mercenary aspect of the elvenking's charity, explicit in this draft, was still present but de-emphasized in the main Third Phase manuscript that replaced it and in the published book (DAA.312–13). Indeed, the replacement text goes out of its way to stress that he diverted his host from marching straight to the mountain to instead helping the lake-men 'because he was a lord of good and kindly race' – a statement not in harmony with his role as projected in the Plot Notes associated with the end of the Second Phase and the first indicator that Tolkien has shifted the book's attitude towards the wood-elves to something much more favorable than their depiction in the Second Phase texts.

8 This passage initially read 'Now the king *divided his forces* because of his old friendship with the men of the lake; *some he sent westward to skirt the marshes and come more direct upon the Mountain* and because he was a lord of good and kindly race turned his march *and went so[uth]*'.

9 Although this more nearly approaches the text of the published book (DAA.313), that familiar text is not achieved until the continuation of the First Typescript (compiled when Tolkien was preparing the book for submission to Allen & Unwin in summer-autumn 1936), where it appears as first typed exactly as in the printed book (1/1/64:6, revised typescript pagination page '140').

10 The following was written neatly in the left margin in black ink, but it was neither completed nor was the specific point at which it was to be inserted indicated; presumably it would have replaced part of the paragraph just given, probably the second sentence: 'Three nights and days they dwelt in the watch-chamber, and did not dare to go far afield. Ever they grew more puzzled, and though they debated ever the matter of'.

11 Compare the equivocation of the Parson in *Farmer Giles of Ham*, when faced with an inscription on a sword he cannot make out: the reader is told 'he could not make head or tail of them', but rather than admit this, 'to gain time' he tells the sword's owner that '[t]he characters are archaic and the language barbaric . . . [a] little closer inspection will be required' (FGH 32). In the Second Phase version of this passage (page 618), there was no hint of Bilbo's deliberate evasiveness on this point.

The idea that different animals all have their own individual languages harkens back to the Dr. Dolittle books, which were favorites of the Tolkien children; see page 266ff.

12 This variant spelling of the more usual *Carc* appears only this once. The first typescript, which also gives this line as a later (ink) addition, has the more usual 'old Carc and his wife' (1/1/65:1). The second typescript (1/1/46:1) includes 'old Carc and his wife' (who never receives a name in any version of the tale) as first typed.

13 This sentence marks the first mention of Dain Ironfoot; for more on this remarkable figure, see page 702ff.

The statement that Thorin has kin in the mountains of the north first appears here, and remains unchanged into the published text (cf. DAA.318). The later account in *The Lord of the Rings*, however, seems to contradict this by stating that after the great cold-drake killed Thror's father and brother 'most of Durin's Folk abandoned the Grey Mountains' for the Lonely Mountain and Iron Hills, an event that the Tale of Years states took place some one hundred and eighty years before Smaug overthrew the Kingdom Under the Mountain, or some three hundred and fifty years before Thorin's return (*LotR*.1124–26).

14 Tolkien inserted an end-bracket in the text at this point; the only significance I can see for this is that this marks the end of later typescript page '142' (1/1/65:2) and was, of course, very near the point at which the Second Phase manuscript had broken off. It thus presumably marks a pause in the creation of the later typescript in summer-autumn 1936.

15 There is no mention of this bridge in their first view of the ruined valley in Chapter XI (page 472), but Thorin mentions it near the end of (original) Chapter XIV and they ford the spot where it once stood on their way to Ravenhill; see page 583. The support-stones for this bridge are also visible in several pictures Tolkien drew of the Lonely Mountain, such as 'The Front Door' (plate X [top]), but not in the black and white drawing 'The Front Gate' which appeared in the published book (this picture's point of view being from the valley floor, where the bridge would be behind the viewer).

16 This phrase, reminiscent of the 'mortal men, doomed to die' in the Ring-verse of the sequel, suggests that the dwarves are not mortal in the same sense. This agrees with what is said of the dwarves in *The Book of Lost Tales* ('. . . a strange race and none know surely whence

they be . . . Old are they, and never comes a child among them' – BLT II.223–4). See 'The Halls of Waiting' starting on page 720.

17 Changed by later ink to '*Some of the younger dwarves also were* moved, & muttered that *they* would things had fallen out otherwise . . .'

18 'The heart is bold that looks on gold': cf. Text Note 14 following Chapter XIV on page 588.

19 Tolkien wrote only the first and last (rhyming) word on this line, leaving the space between them blank. Similarly, the next two lines were left incomplete.

20 These two half-lines were replaced by

> *No more the dwarves*
> *shall suffer wrong.*

21 I.e., 'friend and k[in]'.

In the right margin above this point, Tolkien has jotted down several rhyming words as an aid to composition: bar, car, <?char>, far, jar, shar, scar, tar. He was apparently unable to come up with a suitable third line with this rhyme (to match with *afar* and *are*) and so dropped both of the earlier lines from the final poem.

22 Tolkien underlined the words same question in pencil and wrote 'repeat' above them, indicating that Thorin's actual words were to be given here, as indeed they are in the typescript that followed (1/1/65:5), although not phrased exactly the same as on the previous day; compare DAA.320 and 322.

23 As the reference to 'dwarvish hearts' shows, Tolkien has now reversed his original idea about dwarves and dragon-gold; instead of being at least partially immune to the dragon-sickness, he now sees dwarves as particularly susceptible to it. See the commentary ('Dragon-sickness') following Chapter XIV, starting on page 595.

24 This passage was slightly revised to read 'he had an eye for *many an*other thing . . . and about *each* were wound . . .'. Tolkien also added at the end of the paragraph 'Also he remembered the Elvenking with small kindness and was little pleased to see the elves among' but cancelled this, no doubt when he incorporated it into the discussion that followed. Finally, Tolkien seems to have originally begun to write 'the sorrows of his *people'* before changing this to 'of his race'.

25 Thorin's rejection of charity, which should be a legitimate concern whatever the legitimacy or otherwise of all the other claims, is a warning sign of just how deeply sunk in dragon-sickness he has fallen. The Elvenking's delaying his expedition to seize the treasure in order to help the victims of the disaster at Lake-town gives him the high moral ground in the Third Phase text over Thorin, who will not even repay the charity he received a few weeks earlier when he was similarly cold, hungry, destitute, and homeless. Note also that in contrast to the final Second Phase Plot Notes, here the Elvenking makes no claim but merely supports the claims of Bard and the lake-men.

26 This sentence was revised several times, probably to eliminate the problematic concept of 'Smaug's heirs':

> To the treasure of my people *no one has a* claim because Smaug who stole it from us also robbed *him of* life *or* home. The treasure is not Smaug's that *from it his* evil deeds *should be paid for*

This second sentence was then cancelled in its entirety and replaced with the following in the left margin:

> The treasure [is not >] was never [Smaug's >] his that his evil deeds should be amended with [> his evil deeds should be atoned for with] a share of it.

27 Tolkien later answered this question for us with the story of Scatha the Worm, which can be found in Appendix A of *The Lord of the Rings*. After Fram of the Éothéod [Horse-folk], one of the ancestors of Eorl the Young, kills 'the great dragon of Ered Mithrin' [Grey Mountains], the dwarves claim his hoard, which had been stolen from them by the dragon (as evidence of which, note that Merry's horn, which came from that hoard, 'was made by the Dwarves'; *LotR*.1014). Fram 'would not yield them a penny, and sent to them instead the teeth of Scatha made into a necklace, saying "Jewels such as these you will not match in your treasuries, for they are hard to come by." Some say that the Dwarves slew Fram for this insult. There was no great love between Éothéod and the Dwarves' – *LotR*.1102. Note that this incident probably did not involve Durin's folk, since these events took place more than a century before Thorin I removed from Erebor to the Grey Mountains.

28 Thorin's rejection of the appeal to pity, especially on those in desperate need who had aided him when his folk were in similar straits, is a second warning sign of his moral corruption.

29 This paragraph replaced Bard's original, much simpler, response:

> 'We will give you time to repent your words' said Bard and then he departed.

This type of expansion in the course of writing is typical of the Third Phase manuscript.

30 Added in the bottom margin, and marked for insertion at this point: 'We speak unto Thorin Thrain's son calling himself King under the Mountain.'

31 Changed to 'but if you *would* have friendship *and honour in* the lands about you, as your sires *had* of old, then you will *give* also somewhat of your own beside.' The detail that Bard and his allies requested one-twelfth of the treasure remained constant through the typescripts and various editions of the published book, but there is no indication how they determined that this figure would represent the proportion of Girion's wealth to Thror's hoard.

32 Attacking a herald, even symbolically like this, was of course a gross violation of the heroic code and hence significant. It shows that even

if Thorin is within his rights to withhold charity and not to negotiate under threat, and quite justified in his resentment of the Elvenking, he is still, in Gandalf's words, 'not making a very splendid figure as King under the Mountain' (see page 668).

This point also marks a slight pause in composition; the next paragraph is more neatly written and in darker ink.

33 This sentence was changed several times in the course of writing it: 'murmur against him > offer him other counsel, and indeed > that had they wished they would not have dared to grumble at > find fault with him.' That Thorin's most trusted companions dare not speak their mind is of course another sign that Thorin is no longer the person he was, and sets the stage for his threats against them in the next chapter and his assault on Bilbo in the chapter after that. It is rather surprising that Balin, the most reasonable of all the dwarves, is not listed as having mental reservations à la Bilbo, Bombur, Fili, and Kili; perhaps his disdain for the Elvenking (made plain in his bluntness before him back in Chapter IX) affected his judgment here.

Chapter XVI

DIVIDED LOYALTIES

As before, there was initially no chapter division in the manuscript, merely a paragraph break between the third and fourth paragraphs (of five) on this page (Third Phase manuscript page 14; 1/1/17:1). However, at some later date, probably during the continuation and completion of the First Typescript in summer–autumn 1936, Tolkien wrote 'Ch' (i.e., 'Ch[apter]') in the left margin in pencil and marked it for insertion at this point, indicating where he had decided the chapter break should occur. There is some evidence that Tolkien initially considered this the fifteenth chapter, not having yet inserted the chapter-break on page 642; see page 666 below.

Now the days passed slowly and wearily. Many of the dwarves spent their time piling and ordering the treasure, and Thorin [asked >] bade them eagerly to look for the Arkenstone of Thrain. 'For that' he said 'is worth more than a river of gold in itself and to me yet more.'

Added in pencil at the bottom of the page and marked for insertion here:

> That of all the treasure I name unto myself and I will slay any one that [*added*: finds it > takes it <&>] withholds it.[TN1]

Bilbo heard these words and he grew afraid wondering what would happen if the stone was found – wrapped in an old bundle of tattered oddments that he used as a pillow. Yet he did not yet speak of it, and as the weariness of the days grew heavier [he thought of >] a plan came into his little head.

Things had gone on thus for some while, when the Ravens brought news that Dain and five hundred dwarves were hurrying from the Iron Hills in the N.E. and in a few days' time would be coming to Dale.

'But [I >] they cannot [come >] reach the Mountain unmarked' said Roäc. 'And I fear lest there be battle in Dale. Nor do I call this counsel good. Though they are a grim folk they are not likely to overcome the host that besets you, and even should they do so what will you gain? [*added*: Winter and snow is hastening behind them.] [TN2] [Without >] How shall you be fed without the friendship and good will of the lands about you?[TN3] The treasure is likely to be your death though Smaug is dead!'

But Thorin would not listen [> was not moved]. 'Winter and snow will bite [the >] both men and elves' he said, 'and they may find their dwelling in the vale too grievous to bear. With my friends [upon their >] behind them and winter upon them they will perchance be in better mood [for >] to parley with.'

That night B. made up his mind. Bofur & Bombur were the watchmen about the middle of the night. The sky was dark and moonless. As soon as it was full dark he slipped on his ring and going to a <illegible>[TN4] corner he drew from his bundle a rope and the Arkenstone. Then he climbed to the top of the wall. Bifur & Bombur were there, for the dwarves kept but tw[o] watchmen. Bilbo sat beside him and after a while he sneezed 'It is mighty cold' said Bombur. 'I wish we could have a fire as they have in the camp.'

'It's warm enough inside' said Bilbo.

The paragraph describing his preparations for departure was re-written even while it was being set down, eventually becoming as follows:

That night B. made up his mind. The sky was dark [> black] and moonless. As soon as it was full dark he went to a corner of an inner chamber and drew from his bundle a rope and the Arkenstone [*added*: <wrapped in a rag>]. Then he climbed to the top of the wall. Bombur was there, for the dwarves kept but one watchman [*added*: and it <was> his turn]. 'It is mighty cold' said Bombur. 'I wish we could have a fire as they have in the camp.'

It is warm enough inside' said Bilbo.

Originally Bilbo's exit from the group was both more whimsical and more dramatic, as the following cancelled draft (I/I/17:6), which survives as the verso of new page 17 (=I/I/17:7), demonstrates:

'But I am bound here until midnight' grumbled Bombur 'A sorry business altogether. Not that I say a word against Thorin may his beard grow ever longer; yet he was ever a dwarf stiff in the neck!'

'My eyes are sharp' said Bilbo '[and I have >] it is long since I did watch. [Lend me your >] Let us sing songs to cheer us up.' said Bilbo.

'Singing is thirsty work and calls for more than water.'

'I will sing to you' said Bilbo.

And he began to sing in his small voice an absurd song one that used to be sung to him long ago in the green of the world when he was a small hobbit in a little bed in his father's hole.

Birds are

[For which we have >]

At this point, all but the first paragraph on this page was cancelled, after which the drafting continued:

'Not as stiff as my legs' said Bilbo. 'I am tired of stairs and stone-passages. I will be going to bed, I think.'

Bombur gave a shiver and a sneeze. 'Stay here a moment' he begged. 'I will fetch <us> another cloak and some wraps, against the Eastwind. There is no need to freeze at one's post.'

No sooner had B. gone than Bilbo [fastened >] slipped [> put] on his ring secured his rope slipped over the wall and was gone.

'Confound that hobbit!' said Bombur when he returned. '[I should be >] What Thorin would say if he knew the watch were broken I don't know.' But in the dark he did not see the rope & it was not until morning

At this point the drafting breaks off, well shy of the bottom of the page. Clearly, Bilbo absconds in the night without meaning to come back, taking the Arkenstone with him. His further movements would probably have been along the lines of those outlined in Plot Notes D (see pp. 569–70).

The drafting actually gives two variants of the scene with Bombur (Bifur/Bofur having already been eliminated), shifting focus in the middle; the writing is somewhat neater in the second half, perhaps indicating a brief pause in composition. Initially the idea seems to be that Bilbo sings a lullaby that sends Bombur to sleep, perhaps with the aid of strong drink; cf. Bombur's reference to the need for something 'more than water' (i.e., alcohol). It is regrettable that only the first two words of Bungo's lullaby were written down, since this is our only opportunity to hear what sort of bedtime songs Bilbo's father sang his son; from the subject matter (a lullaby) and the tiny scrap preserved here, I suspect it would have resembled the choruses (e.g., 'little birds are sleeping') from Lewis Carroll's poem 'The Pig Tale' in *Sylvie and Bruno Concluded*, from which Arry Lowdham quotes in *The Notion Club Papers* (HME IX.179 & x–xi).

All this is changed in the latter half, so that instead of singing Bilbo now slips off while Bombur's back is turned, much to the latter's chagrin. However, the guileless dwarf does not suspect that Bilbo has crept out toward the enemy and simply assumes Bilbo has gone off to sleep, as had been his stated intention ('I will be going to bed, I think'); his concern is merely for the watchpost's having been left unmanned for a brief interval. When Tolkien decided that Bilbo would be able to conclude his business that same night and rejoin the dwarves before his disappearance had become known, he recast the scene on the replacement page (Third Phase manuscript page 15; 1/1/17:4) into a very close approximation of its familiar final form:

'But I am bound here till midnight' grumbled Bombur. 'A sorry business altogether. Not that I venture to disagree with Thorin, may his beard grow ever longer; yet he was ever a dwarf [with a stiff neck >] stiff in the neck!'

'Not as stiff as my legs' said Bilbo. 'I am tired of stairs and stone-passages. I would give a good deal for the feel of grass at my toes.'

'I would give a good deal for [*added*: the feel of] a strong drink in my throat and a soft bed after good supper' said Bombur.

'I can't give you those' said Bilbo; 'but it is long since I watched, and I will [watch for >] take your turn for you, if you wish. I have no sleep in me tonight.'

'You are a good fellow Mr Baggins. I will take your offer kindly. [I will >] If there should be anything to note, rouse me first, mind you. I [sha[ll] >] will lie in the inner chamber to the left not far away.'

'Off you go' said Bilbo. 'I will wake you at midnight, and you can wake the next watchman.'

As soon as Bombur had gone Bilbo put on his ring secured the rope, slipped over the wall and was gone. He had [*added in pencil*: nearly] six hours before him.[TN5] It was very dark and the road after a while when he left the narrow path and climbed down towards the [riv[er] >] stream in its lower course below the falls was strange to him. Fording the river narrow and shallow as it was was not easy for the little hobbit. He missed his footing on a boulder & fell into the cold water with a splash; and he had barely scrambled out on the northern bank, shivering and spluttering, when up came elves in the gloom and seized him.

To this was added in bottom margin: '. . . up came elves in the gloom *with lanterns* and *searched for* him.' This sentence was recast as:

'That was no fish' one said. 'There is a spy abroad. Hide your lights they will help him more than us.'

Suddenly Bilbo sneezed and they gathered towards the sound. 'Let's have a light' he said. 'I am here if you want me' and he slipped off his ring.

Quickly they seized him. 'How have you got so far past our sentinels' they asked.

'Who are you' they asked 'and what are you doing?'

'I am Bilbo Baggins' he answered, 'companion of Thorin. I know your king well by sight though he does not know me; but Bard perhaps will remember me, and it's he that I wish to see.'

'[O ho >] Indeed' said they 'and what may be your business?'

'That's my own affair, my good elves' he answered. 'But if you wish ever to get back to your woods from this cold cheerless place,' he answered shivering, 'you will take me along quickly to a fire where I can get dry – and let me speak with your chiefs as quick as may be. I have only a hour or two to spare.'

So it came about that about 2 hours from his escape B. was sitting beside a large [> warm] fire before a large tent, and there sat gazing curiously at him both the Elvenking and Bard. An [>A] hobbit in elvish armour (covered with the tatters of a coat and waistcoat) was something new to them.

'Really you know' Bilbo was saying [*added*: in his best business-manner] 'Things are impossible. Personally I am tired of the whole affair. I wish I was back in [my >] the West in my own home, where folk are more reasonable. But I have an interest in this matter – a fourteenth share to be precise according to a letter which I think I have kept.'[TN6] He drew out from a pocket the [> a] crumpled and much folded Thorin's letter that had been put under his clock on the mantelpiece in May! 'A share of profits, mind you.' he went on. 'I am aware of that. Personally I am only too ready to consider all your claims, and deduct them from the total before putting in my own claim. However you probably don't know Mr Thorin O. as well as I do now.

'I assure you he is quite ready [to starve sitting >] to sit on a heap of gold and starve as long as you sit here.'

'Well let him' said Bard. 'Such a fool deserves to starve'.

'Quite so' said Bilbo. 'I see your point of view. At the same time winter is coming on fast. Before long you will be having snow [and all sorts >] and what not, and supplies will be difficult. Also there will be other difficulties. I think you may not know quite all I do. You have not heard of Dain and the dwarves of the Iron Hills?'

'No we have not, and what has he to do with us' The king asked.[TN7]

'I thought not. Well here is now but a few [> less than 2] days' march off and has at least five hundred grim dwarves with him, not a few that have [> had] experience in the dreadful dwarf and goblin wars of which you may have heard.[TN8] When he arrives there may be serious trouble.'

'What do you tell us this for? [> Why do you tell us this?] Are you betraying your friends or are you threatening us?' asked Bard grimly.

'My dear Bard' squeaked Bilbo 'don't be so hasty. I merely wish to [avoid all trouble >] stop trouble for all concerned. Now I will make you an offer – '

'What offer' said they.

'This!' said he and he drew forth the Arken stone. The Elvenking himself whose eyes were not unused to things of wonder and of beauty stood up in amaze. Even Bard gazed a while in silent wonder. It was as if the moon lit water had caught the sharp glitter [*added*: netted all the glinting] of all the frosty stars and risen radiant in the <illegible> before [them].[TN9]

'This is the Arkenstone of Thrain' said Bilbo, 'and it is the heart of Thorin. He will value it above a river of gold.[TN10] I give it to you. It will aid you in your bargaining.'

Then Bilbo not without a shudder, not without a longing glance handed the marvellous stone to Bard, and he <held> it [in] his hand as though dazed.

'But how is it yours to give' he asked at last with an effort.

'O well' said the hobbit uncomfortably. 'It isn't exactly, but, well I am willing to let it stand against all my claim, don't you know. I may be a burglar (or so they say: [I never >] personally I never really felt like one) but I am a honest one, I hope, more or less. Anyway I am going back now, and the dwarves can do what they like to me.'[TN11]

Then the Elvenking looked on B. in a new wonder. 'Bilbo Baggins' he said. 'You are more worthy to wear the armour of elf princes than many who have looked more comely in it. But I wonder if Thorin Oakenshield will see it so. I have perhaps more knowledge of dwarves in general than have you. I counsel you to remain with us, and here you shall be honoured & twice welcome.'

'Thank you very much' said Bilbo 'I am sure. But I don't think I could leave my friends [*added*: like that] after [such a lot we >] all we have gone through together. And I promised to wake old Bombur by midnight too. Really I must be going, and quickly.'

And nothing they could say would stop him. [So h[e] >] So an escort was provided for him, and as he went both the Elvenking & Bard saluted him with honour. Guided to a safe ford and set safely across Bilbo soon scrambled back to the Gate, and it was well before midnight when he climbed his rope again, untied it and hid it, and sat down upon the wall.

This last sentence detailing Bilbo's return to the lookout post was cancelled and a new scene inserted:

As they passed through the camp, an old man sitting by a tent door rose and came towards them.

'Well done Mr Baggins!' he said clapping B. on the back. 'There is always more about you than any one expects![TN12] [*cancelled*: There is a]'

It was Gandalf!

For the first time for many a day B. was really delighted; but there was no time for all the questions that he wished suddenly to ask.

'All in good time' said Gandalf. 'Things are drawing towards an end, now. There is an unpleasant time just before you, but [be of >] keep your heart up. There is news brewing that even the ravens have not yet heard. Good night.'

Puzzled but cheered Bilbo hurried on. Guided to a safe ford and set across dry he said farewell to the elves, & climbed back towards the Gate. Great weariness began to come over him; but it was well before midnight when he climbed his rope again, untied [it >] and hid it, and sat down on the wall to wonder what would happen now.

At midnight he woke up Bombur, and then in turn rolled himself up in his corner, without listening to the old dwarf's thanks (which he felt he had hardly earned); and soon he was fast asleep, forgetting all his worries till the morning.

TEXT NOTES

1 This hastily pencilled addition is significant, since it shows that Thorin is slipping into madness and can no longer be trusted. That he would threaten capital punishment over a piece of treasure to one of the loyal companions he has led for a year and more is completely out of character (cf. his courage in the face of Smaug's attack in Chapter XII, sending others to safety while risking his life to save Bofur and Bombur from danger) and foreshadows his attack on Bilbo in the next chapter.

2 This sentence is added at the bottom of the paragraph and marked for insertion here; it recasts the unfinished and cancelled sentence that originally began this paragraph:

> 'But winter and snow is hastening behind them' said Roäc and their food is

3 By Thorin's own account in Chapter I, the Kingdom under the Mountain depended upon the nearby human communities for food, trading worked goods in order to gain all the produce and other foodstuffs they needed. Remarkably enough, here we have a carrion bird advising against a battle, something which we have just been told (through a later interpolation) none of Thorin's fellow dwarves dared to do.

4 This cancelled unfinished word seems to be either *stor[eroom]* or *stai[r]*.

5 It is one indication of just how late in the year it is that it is already full dark shortly after six in the evening – again a detail more in keeping with the revised timing of Durin's Day (the last new moon before winter) rather than the original version (the first new moon of autumn).

6 Tolkien later created a facsimile of this very letter that Bilbo had carried with him on his trip; see Frontispiece, plate two, for a reproduction of Bilbo's contract, and page 107 for a transcription.

7 This sentence was preceded by a fragment of another, cancelled paragraph in which Bilbo continued speaking:

> 'Quite so. I thought not' he

When Tolkien decided to include the others' reply, it is originally 'B' (i.e., B[ard]) not the Elvenking who asks this question. The First Typescript changes this to the familiar

> 'We have, a long time ago; but what has he got to do with us?' asked the king.
>
> —new typescript page 150; 1/1/66:3.

8 See Chapter I (c) for an earlier reference to the dwarf-goblin war and the battle of the mines of Moria.

9 The illegible word might be *heart*, but this is doubtful. This sentence was revised, then cancelled and replaced:

> It was as if the moon lit water had *netted all the glinting* of all the frosty stars . . . > It was [as] if a globe had been filled with moonlight and hung in a net woven of the glint of all the frosty stars before them.

10 Here Bilbo echoes Thorin's words from the beginning of this chapter; cf. page 658.

11 Written in the left margin alongside this paragraph is an additional sentence: 'I only wish to save trouble and foolishness all round, and this seemed to me a possible way'. There is no indication of its exact placement, but it is probably intended to follow the words 'don't you know'. This sentence was not picked up on in the typescripts and thus does not appear in the published book.

12 Bladorthin here is more or less repeating his words to Bilbo the last time they were unexpectedly reunited (at which time the wizard's name was of course still Bladorthin) – 'Mr Baggins has more about him than you'd guess'; cf. page 200.

Chapter XVII

THE BATTLE OF FIVE ARMIES

As before, there is no chapter break in the original Third Phase manuscript, merely a gap of one skipped line between the first and second paragraphs on new manuscript page 20 (1/1/18:1). Later Tolkien wrote, in pencil, 'Ch. XVI' in this gap. That he wrote *XVI* rather than *XVII* might be inadvertence, but that would be very uncharacteristic. It seems more likely that the break between what are now chapters XIV and XV had not yet been inserted (see page 642); no such break having existed in the Third Phase ms., either as originally written or in later markings as had been the case for the starts for what are now chapters XVI (page 658), XVII (this page), or XIX (page 687).

Next day the trumpets rang early in the camp. Soon a single runner was seen hurrying along the narrow path. At a distance he stood and hailed them, asking whether Thorin would hearken [*added*: now] to [an embassy as new tiding had occurred, which >] another embassy since new [things >] tiding had occurred & matters were changed.

'That will be Dain' said Thorin when he heard. 'They will have got wind of his coming. I thought that would soften their mood. Bid them come few in number and weaponless and I will hear.'

About mid morning the banners of the Wood and Lake were seen to be borne forth again. [Behold > As they drew > <As the entire> >] A company of twenty was approaching. At the beginning of the narrow path they laid aside sword & spear, and [behold among them >] drew near. <Wondering> the Dwarves saw that among them was [*added*: both] Bard & the Elvenking, and before them one carried a strong casket of iron bound wood.

'Hail Thorin' said [> cried] Bard. 'Are you still of the same mind?'

'[A>] My mind changes not with the rising & setting of a few suns' said Thorin 'And [<did> > see >] not yet has the elfhost departed as I [sai[d] >] bade. Till then no bargaining will you have of me.'

'Is there nothing for which you would yield any of your gold?'

'Nothing that you or your friends have to offer?'

'What of the Arkenstone of Thrain' said he and he bade open [> opened] the box and held aloft the jewel in his opened hand. The light leapt from his palm bright even in the morning.[TN1]

Then Thorin was stricken dumb with amazement & confusion. No one spoke for a long while.

[That stone >] At length Thorin spoke and his voice was thick with wrath. 'That stone was my father's and is mine'[TN2] he said. 'Why should I purchase mine own? [*cancelled*: Yet I knew you were thieves.]' But wonder got the better of his anger [> him] and he added. 'And how came you by the heirloom of my house – if there is need to ask such a question of robbers.'

'We are not robbers' Bard said. 'Your own we will yield in return for our own.'

'How came you by it' shouted Thorin in gathering rage.

'I gave it them!' squeaked Bilbo, who was peeping over the wall, by now in a dreadful fright.

'You, you' cried Thorin turning upon him and grasping him with both hands. 'You miserable hobbit, you you burglar' he shouted at a loss for words, and he shook poor B. like a rabbit.[TN3] 'By the beard of Durinn[TN4] I wish I had Gandalf here. But I will wring your neck first' he said.[TN5]

'Your wish is granted' said a voice and Thorin paused. From the company a man stood forth, and cast aside his hood & cloak.[TN6] 'Here is Gandalf – and not too soon it seems! If you don't like my burglar please don't damage him.[TN7] Put him down and listen first to what he has to say.'

'You all seem in league' said Thorin putting Bilbo down. 'Never again will I have dealing with a wizard or his friends. What have you to say you descendant of rats.'

'Dear me dear me!' said Bilbo. 'I am sure this is all very [unfor[tunate] >] uncomfortable: [If>] You may remember saying that I might choose my own fourteenth [*added in pencil*: share]. Perhaps I took it too literally though the time was when you seemed to think I was of some service. Descendant of rats indeed. Is this all the service of you and your family that I was promised, Thorin. Take it that I have disposed of my share as I wished, and let it go at that.'

'I will' said Thorin grimly. 'And I will let you go.'[TN8] Then he turned and spoke over the wall. 'I am betrayed' he said. 'It was rightly guessed that I could not forbear to redeem the Arkenstone the treasure of my house. For it I will render one fourteenth of the hoard in silver and gold, but that shall be for the share of this cre[ature] – hobbit, and with that reward he shall depart. [But to you I will >] I will give him to you and [> but] no friendship of mine goes with him.'[TN9]

'Get down now to your friends' he said [*added in pencil*: to B.] 'or I will throw you down.'

'What about the gold' said Bilbo.

'That shall follow after' said he. [*added in different ink*: as can be arranged.]

'Until it does [> then] we keep the stone' said Bard.

'You are not making a very splendid figure as King under the Mountain' said Gandalf. 'Still matters may change yet.'

'They may indeed' said Thorin – and already so strong was the bewilderment of the treasure upon him, that he was pondering whether by the help of Dain he could not recapture the Arkenstone and withhold the share of the hoard.

And so Bilbo was swung down from the wall and departed without any reward for all his trouble, except for the armour which [he >] Thorin had given him before. [Many of the hearts of the dwarves felt >] More than one of the dwarves in the[ir] hearts felt shame and pity at his going.

'Farewell' he cried to them. 'We may [meet] again, as friends'

'Be off' cried Thorin. '[If you had not mail upon you. >] You have mail on you which was made by my folk and is not to be pierced with arrows. But if you do not hasten I will sting your miserable feet. So be swift.'

In the bottom margin of this page (Third Phase manuscript page 23; Marq. 1/1/18:4) is a pencilled note 'see 23b' and an arrow, indicating that a new paragraph numbered '23b' on the verso (= Marq. 1/1/18:5) should be inserted at this point:

> 'Not so hasty' said Gandalf [> Bard] '[in three days >] we will give you until the day after tomorrow. At noon on that day we will return, and see if you have brought from the hoard the gold and silver that is to be set against the stone. If that is done without deceit, then we'll depart, and the elfhost shall go back to the Forest. In the meantime, farewell.'[TN10]

With that they departed to the camp, but Thorin sent messages by Roäc[TN11] telling Dain of what had passed, and bidding him come [with > warily and >] with wary speed.

That day passed, and the night. The next day [came a bitter >] the wind shifted west and it was a dark morning [> and the air was dark and gloomy]. The morning was still early when a cry was heard in the camp. Messengers ran in to tell that a host of dwarves [were marching >] had suddenly appeared round the east spur of the Mountain, and were hastening into Dale!

Dain was come. [The > At dusk he had reached the first >] He had hurried through the night and came thus suddenly upon them. His five hundred were [armed >] clad in steel-mail and wielded heavy mattocks [with >] two-handed in battle; yet each had also a short sword at his side and a round shield slung at his back. Their beards were [plaited

>] forked and plaited and thrust into their belts. Their caps were of steel and their shoes were of iron,[TN12] and their faces were grim.

Trumpets called men and elves to arms, and before long the dwarves could be seen from the camp coming [down >] up the valley till they halted about a mile to the East. Some [> A few] still went on their way until they drew near the camp, and there they laid down their arms [> weapons] and lifted up their hands, in sign of peace.

Bard went out to meet them and with him went Bilbo. 'We are sent from Dain son of Nain'[TN13] they said when questioned. 'We are hastening to our kinsmen in the Mountain, since we learn that the kingdom of old is renewed. But who are ye that sit in the plain as foes before defended walls?'

By now you will know well enough the sort of things that are said at such parleyings; and I will not recount all that was said on either side.[TN14]

On Bard's side the dwarves were refused passage to the Mountain until Thorin had paid for the Arkenstone; but the dwarves muttered angrily and retired. Later they moved their camp yet nearer.[TN15]

But when messengers were sent to the Gate they found no gold or payment; and arrows came forth as soon as they drew within shot. Returning they found all astir, as if for battle; for the dwarves of Dain had advanced almost to within hail of their camp.

'Fools!' said Bard ' – to come thus within the mountain's arms. They do not understand war above ground! There are many of our archers [*added*: & spearmen hid] now in the rocks upon both their flanks. Dwarf-mail may be good, yet they will [> <?would>] soon be in [<illegible> >] hard put to it. Let us at them now from the front, ere they be fully rested.'

But the Elvenking said: 'Long will I tarry [even though the advantage slip from us, save what we have in numbers which is very > and that is sufficient >] ere I begin this war for gold. The dwarves cannot pass us unless we will, and our advantage of numbers will be sufficient [> enough] if it must come to unhappy blows.'

But he reckoned without the dwarves. The knowledge that the Arkenstone was in the hands of the besiegers burned in their minds; and they guessed the hesitation of Bard and his allies.

Suddenly without a signal they began to advance and sprang silently forward to attack. [Arrows >] Bows twanged and arrows whistled, and well-nigh battle had begun.

Suddenly a darkness came on with dreadful swiftness. A dark cloud hurried over the sky. Thunder rolled in the mountain and lightning lit its peaks. Beneath it another cloud could be seen whirling forward; but like a cloud of birds so dense that [it could >] light cd. not be seen [beneath their >] between their wings.[TN16]

'Halt!' cried Gandalf and he ran and stood suddenly [before >] between the advancing dwarves and the ranks awaiting them. 'Halt!' he cried and his staff blazed with a sudden flash. '[The dread >] Dread has come upon you all more swiftly than I guessed. The Goblins are upon you. Bolg of the North is coming, whose father you slew in Moria.[TN17] Behold the bats are above his army like a sea of locusts[TN18] [and the wargs & wolves of >] They ride upon wargs [> wolves] and wolves [> wargs] are in their train.'

Amazement and confusion fell upon them all; and even as [they >] he spoke the darkness grew. 'Come' shouted Gandalf 'there is yet time for counsel. Let Dain son of Nain come swiftly to us.'

So began the battle in a fashion none had expected. And it was called after the Battle of Five Armies, and it was very terrible. For upon one side were the Goblins and the Wolves and upon the other were men elves and dwarves.[TN19]

This is how it fell out. [The Goblins <had> >] ever since the fall of the Great goblin of the M. Mountains the hatred of their race for the dwarves had been aroused [> rekindled] to fury. Tidings in secret ways they had gathered; and in all the Northern Mountains there was forging and an arming. [When they learned of the fall of Smaug their plan was soon made. >] They marched and gathered by hill and mountain [and till in the great >] going ever by tunnel or under dark until [<under> >] around and beneath the great mountain Gondobad of the North[TN20] a vast host was assembled, ready to sweep down upon the South. Then they learned of the death of Smaug and joy was in their hearts; and they hastened night after night through the mountains, and came thus at last on a sudden from the North East, and not even the Ravens knew of their coming until [the broken >] they issued in the broken lands which divided the Lonely M. from the [lands >] hills behind.[TN21]

This was the plan of Gandalf and of Bard and the Elvenking and of Dain who now joined them, for the Goblins were the foes of all and at their coming all other quarrels were forgotten.[TN22] Their only hope was to lure the goblins into the valley between the mountain's arms; and themselves to man the great spurs that stuck [> struck] S. and East. Yet this would be perilous if the goblins were in sufficient numbers to overrun the mountain itself and so attack them also from above. But there was no time to devise anything else. Soon the thunder passed rolling away to the SE, but the bats cloud came [down >] flying over the mountain and whirled above them. 'To the mountain' said Bard 'Let us take our places while there is time.'

On the Southern spur [were arranged the Elves >] in its lower slopes and in the rocks at its feet the Elves [took >] were set, on the

Eastern were men and dwarves (since there was less <cover>). But Bard and some of the nimblest of men and elves climbed [higher >] to the height of the E. shoulder to look out [> forward] to the North.

Soon they could see all the lands to the north and the M. foot black with the hurrying hosts. Ere long they swirled round <illegible> and came into Dale – the swifter wolfriders and their howls rent the air. A few brave men were there to make feint of resistance, [but >] and many there fell ere the rest drew off to either side. As G. had hoped the goblins' army [enraged >] had gathered behind the resisted vanguard, and poured now in rage into the valley, seeking for the foe. Their banners were countless black and red and <they> came on like a tide, but their order was wild.

This was a terrible battle: the most dreadful of all B's experiences & the one he hated most (& which is also to say the one he was after most proud of, & most fond of recalling).[TN23] Yet actually I may say he put on his ring early in the business and vanished from sight if not from danger. A magic ring of that sort is no complete protection in a goblin charge, nor does it stop flying arrows and wild spears; but it does help in getting out of the way, and prevents your head from being chosen [by a goblin swordsman for >] for a sweep stroke by a goblin swordsman.

The Elves were the first to charge. As soon as the g. host was dense in the valley they sent into it a shower of arrows [*added in pencil*: set afire by magic]. And behind [*added*: five hundred > a thousand spearmen] they leapt down and charged the enemy. The yells were deafening, and the rocks [were] stained black with goblin blood. But just as the goblins were recovering and the elf-charge halted; there rose from across the valley a deep throated roar. With a cry [> cries] of 'Moria' [and] 'Dain Dain' the dwarves of the Iron Hills plunged in wielding great Mattocks upon the other side. And beside them came the lake men with long swords.

Panic came on the goblins and even as they turned to meet this new foe the elves charged again. Already some of the goblins were turning back down the river to escape from the valley, and victory seemed at hand, when a cry was raised above.

The Goblins had scaled the mountain and were on the heights above the Gate and many were streaming down to attack the spurs from above. They had only stemmed the first attack. [Now the bats flew down >] Now darkness was coming early in a stormy sky, and the bats wheeled darkly over the field [&] heedless of arrows they swirled about the heads and ears of elves and men. Behind in the valley a host of wargs came running [> ravening] and with them a new host of goblins of huge size. Already [their >] Bard was fighting on the Eastern slopes and the Elves were withdrawing to stand about the king upon the <southern> arm near the watch-place of Ravenhill. Suddenly there was a shout and from the Gate came a trumpet call. Part of the wall moved by levers from within fell outward with a crash into the pool. Down leapt Thorin and his companions no longer in hood and cloak but all in royal armour, and in the gloom Thorin shone like gold in a dying fire. Rocks were hurled down from on high by the goblins above, but they held on, leapt down the fall's foot and rushed forward against their foes. Wolf and rider fell before them. Thorin wielded an axe with <huge> strokes and nothing seemed to harm him. 'To me to me elves and men to me O my kinsfolk' he cried and his voice shook like a horn [between the >] in the valley.

Down rushed all the dwarves of Dain heedless to his help and down came such men as Bard would spare with him; down upon the other side came elvish spearmen. Once again the goblins were stricken in the valley and they were slaughtered in heaps till Dale was dark with them; but among them lay many men, many men and dwarves, and many a fair elf that should have lived yet many an age merrily in the <borders> of the woods.

But as the valley widened they made slower progress and soon the attackers were attacked, and slowly they were forced into [a ring >] a mighty ring all hemmed about with goblins and with wolves. But their friends could not succour them for they were fighting bitterly on the hillsides and slowly they were being beaten down.

'It will not be long' thought Bilbo 'before they win the gate; and then goodness knows what will happen. I would rather old Smaug had all the [gold >] treasure tha[n] these <hateful> Goblins. I have heard songs of many battles, and I have always understood defeat may be glorious. It seems very very uncomfortable. I wish I was well out of it.'

[*cancelled*: Suddenly high and far off he saw]

The clouds were torn by the wind and a red sunset slashed the west. Suddenly high and far off B saw a sight that made his heart leap: dark shapes small yet majestic against the distant glow.[TN24] 'The Eagles the Eagles' he cried – he was among elves up Ravenhill ' – the Eagles the Eagles are coming.' And happily his eyes were seldom wrong. The Eagles were coming.

The Very rumour of them changed the day. The Goblins on the mountain wavered and hesitated.[TN25]

'The Eagles are coming' he cried again [> shouted] and the elves took up the cry and it echoed across the valley. [Even the Goblins looked up, but it >] and <many> eyes [were >] looked up. [But only >] 'The Eagles' cried Bilbo once more, but at that moment a rock [> stone] hurled from above smote heavily on his helm and he fell with a crash & knew no more.[TN26]

TEXT NOTES

1 That is, the Arkenstone casts enough light that even in the full daylight it can be seen to shine brightly. This passage was emended to read 'bright & *white* in the morning'.

2 The apostrophe indicating singular possessive (*father's* rather than *fathers'*) is clear here (Third Phase manuscript page 21; Marq. 1/1/18:2), and also in both typescripts (1/1/67:1 and 1/1/48:1). See the discussion of Thrain and Thror following Chapter X.

3 See Text Note I following Chapter VII (page 245) for Shippey's claim that this line and others like it show that Tolkien associated hobbits with rabbits. While Shippey's argument is intriguing, it does not take into account the fact that the majority of references to rabbits in the final book (eleven out of sixteen) do not refer to Bilbo, or that Bilbo is also compared to other animals (e.g., 'descendant of rats!').

4 The alternative spelling here of *Durinn* rather than the more usual *Durin* is perhaps in order to more closely reproduce the Old Norse original. Dronke, for example, gives *Durinn* in her edition of *Völuspá* (*The Poetic Edda*, Vol II: Mythological Poems [1997], page 9), while Young gives *Durin* in her edition of Snorri's *The Prose Edda* (page 41), for reasons given in her foreword (ibid., page 19). The typescript (1/1/67:1) reverts to the familiar *Durin*.

5 This sentence was cancelled and replaced by the following:

> 'I wish I had Gandalf here. I will [> would] have words for him and his choice. But I will throw you on the rocks first [> But now I will throw you on the rocks],' he said, and lifted B. in his arms.

The idea that Thorin might actually attempt to murder Bilbo in a fit of rage, which would have been unthinkable in the Second Phase text, has been carefully prepared for over the last two chapters; cf. Text Notes 1 & 3 for Chapter XVI and Text Notes 23, 25, 28, 32, & 33 for Chapter XVb, as well as Text Notes 14 & 18 for the fair copy and typescript revisions to Chapter XIV.

6 Added in pencil: '. . . his *tall* hood & *long* cloak'.

7 Tolkien initially wrote 'please don't h[arm] . . .'; shifting the word choice to *damage* casts Bilbo in the role of Gandalf's property ('*my* burglar'), thus subtly enhancing his value in the treasure-smitten dwarf's eyes. Perhaps the implication is that Thorin might have killed a traitor, but in the grip of the dragon-sickness he would be unable to destroy anything of (monetary) value.

8 This sentence was altered slightly so that Thorin's words became parallel with Bilbo's: 'And I will let you go *at that*.' The added clause ' – and may we never meet again!' first appears in the extended typescript (1/1/67:2).

9 The last two sentences of this paragraph were cancelled and the words 'What will you have for it > What price will you have for it? > What

price will you set upon for it?' written below them. This was then cancelled in turn and the word 'stet.' written next to the paragraph to indicate that the cancellation of those sentences was rescinded. Later, in pencil, Tolkien added '. . . he shall depart; *and you can divide it as you wish.* I will give him to you . . .'

10 An earlier draft of both this paragraph and the first paragraph on the following page (Third Phase ms. page 24; Marq. 1/1/18:6) can also be found on this page's unnumbered verso (1/1/18:5):

> 'Not so hasty' said Gandalf. 'Tomorrow the elf-host will prepare to depart as you desire. But at noon we will return with the stone, and by that time you must have ready [within >] outside the wall or near within all the gold and silver that is its price.'
>
> That day passed. Evening was come [> approaching], when sudden there was a cry in the camp. Messengers ran in. 'A host is marching with speed into Dale' [he >] they cried. It was the dwarves of Dain, and they were armed with steel. From afar the men of Bard and the elves watched them until they halted about a mile [fr[om] >] to the east. Dusk was deepening, when three dwarves came

11 This is the last mention of Roäc in the book, but we can assume that he survived the upcoming battle, since Tolkien would have told us otherwise.

12 Changed to 'Their caps and their shoes were of iron'. Hence, no doubt, Dain's later *encomium* or epithet 'Dain Ironfoot'. This name does not however arise within *The Hobbit* and is never used in the earlier book (or indeed until Tolkien was at work on the Appendices of *The Lord of the Rings* – cf. HME XII.281 where it first occurs, in a passage apparently not written until 1948–9 or shortly thereafter).

13 Dain's ancestry, unlike Thorin's (with the two competing Thror-Thrain-Thorin and Thrain-Thror-Thorin genealogies) or later Balin's (who briefly went from 'son of Fundin' to 'son of Burin' and then back again; cf. HME VI.443–4 & 460), never varied: he remained 'Dain son of Nain' from this first mention through to the final references in Appendix A of *The Lord of the Rings*. As with Dain, Thorin, and all the other dwarf-names in *The Hobbit* except Fimbulfambi (and possibly Balin), *Nain* comes from the *Dvergatal* or dwarven name-list in the *Voluspá*, although it does not appear in all manuscripts (cf. Dronke page 90); Snorri also includes it in the *Prose Edda* (page 41). The pattern of giving brothers rhyming names (Fili/Kili, Balin/Dwalin, Oin/Gloin) is also evident here; since Dain is Thorin's cousin (page 644), then Thror's sons were *Thrain* and *Nain*. Like 'Dain', 'Nain' is unusual in that it has a wider meaning and circulation beyond the *Dvergatal*; see the commentary on 'Dain son of Nain' beginning on page 702.

14 This simple statement is replaced in the typescript (1/1/67:3) by a greatly expanded account of what was said at the parley and also of the dwarves' plans; cf. DAA.337–8.

15 Tolkien originally followed the semicolon with 'on' (i.e., on [the dwarves' side] . . .). This paragraph was recast to read:

> Bard refused the Dwarves' passage to the Mountain until Thorin had exchanged gold for the Arkenstone; but the dwarves muttered angrily and retired.

16 This paragraph was revised, in several layers, to eventually read:

> *Then still more* suddenly a darkness came on with dreadful swiftness. A dark cloud hurried over the sky. *[A winter > Winter >]* Thunder *& a wild wind rolled up and rumbled in the* mountain and lightning lit its peaks. Beneath it another *blackness* could be seen whirling forward; *from the North* like a cloud of birds so dense that light cd. not be seen between their wings.

17 This is the first appearance of Bolg, whose name remained unchanged thereafter; see the commentary starting on page 708.

18 For bats as yet another of the 'Children of Morgoth', see commentary on pp. 716–18.

19 See Plot Notes F for Tolkien's earlier hesitation about just who did and did not count as one of the 'five armies'.

20 The spelling was later changed to *Gundobad* in pencil (Third Phase manuscript page 27; 1/1/18:9) and this form appears in both typescripts (1/1/67:4 & 1/1/48:5); the published book has *Gundabad*. This is the only mention of Gondobad in *The Hobbit*, although 'Gundobad' does appear on the draft Mirkwood map [Plate I (bottom)] and 'Gundabad' on the final Wilderland map (DAA.[399]), in both cases at the juncture of the north-south Misty Mountains and the east-west Grey Mountains. The name is Gnomish-Noldorin (i.e., early Sindarin); cf. *Gondobar* ('City of Stone'), one of the alternate names for Gondolin in *The Book of Lost Tales* ([1917–20]; BLT II.158), the unfinished 'Lay of the Fall of Gondolin' ([early 1920s]; HME III.145), and the poem 'The Nameless Land' ([written 1924, published 1927]; HME V.100 & 104). I can find no place where Tolkien defines Gondobad, but GON-/GOND-/GONDO- means 'stone' or 'of stone' (*Gondo-lin*, 'Song of Stone'; *Gon-dor*, 'Stone-land') and the -BAD element may relate to the Gnomish word *bad* meaning 'way, path' (*Gnomish Lexicon, Parma Eldalamberon* vol.XI.21; 'Noldorin Dictionary' and 'Noldorin Word-lists', *Parma Eldalamberon* vol.XIII.160 & 137). If so, 'Gondobad' might mean something like 'the crossroads of stone', which would suit its position at the meeting of these two great mountain ranges riddled with dwarven and goblin mines and tunnels, but this is only a guess. Much later [1969 or after] Tolkien decided that *Gundabad* was a dwarven (Khuzdul) name (HME XII.301), but this clearly could not have been the case at the time *The Hobbit* was written, since the idea of a dwarven language and nomenclature distinct from Old Norse seems to have first arisen several years after *The Hobbit* was finished, in the 1937 *Quenta Silmarillion* (HME V.273–4) and the *Lhammas*, which

dates from about the same period (HME V.178–9). Tolkien also in this late essay created a new backstory for Mount Gundabad, deciding that this was the spot where Durin had woken from sleep and that it was thus, like Moria, originally a revered dwarven stronghold now fallen into orcish hands (HME XII.301). Of all this later development there is of course no trace in *The Hobbit*, unless its seeds lie in Gandalf/Thorin's remark that his ancestors first came to the Lonely Mountain when they were 'driven out of the far north' (page 71); *The Lord of the Rings* suggests that Khazad-dûm (Moria), if anywhere, was the stronghold revered for its associations with Durin the Deathless.

21 Fimbulfambi's Map [see Frontispiece of Part One], the original Mirkwood map (Plate I [bottom]), and the pictorial view of the Lonely Mountain on the Long Lake map (Plate II [top]) – the latter two of which accompanied the 'home manuscript' (i.e., the composite First Typescript/Third Phase manuscript) when it was loaned out to Tolkien's friends – all agree in showing the foothills to the northeast as coming within a short distance of the mountain; these hills can also be seen in the background to the right of the drawing 'The Lonely Mountain' (H-S#136).

The typescript alters the account of their approach slightly:

> . . . came thus at last on a sudden from the North hard on the heels of Dain. Not even the ravens knew of their coming until they came out in the broken lands which divided the Lonely Mountain from the hills behind. How much Gandalf knew cannot be said, but it is plain that he had not expected this sudden assault. (1/1/67:4)

This account made it into the published book (cf. DAA.340) but unfortunately does not match the final version of the Wilderland Map (DAA.[399]), where the line of hills is to the east, not north-east as in the earlier map. Here the goblins would have been entirely in the open from the time they left the Grey Mountains, a distance much too far to have marched in a single night (it is some four times the distance between the Lonely Mountain and the Long Lake), and their north-to-south march would not have overlapped Dain's east-to-west march from the Iron Hills.

22 This idea of enemies uniting when faced with a threat from true evil resurfaced a decade later when Tolkien was drafting the early parts of what became Book V of *The Lord of the Rings*; when King Théoden arrives at Dunharrow to muster his troops for the ride to Minas Tirith, he finds among the forces gathered some of the Dunlendings he has just defeated at Helm's Deep a few days earlier, men willing to set aside a five-hundred-year feud in the face of the threat of Sauron (HME VIII.249 & 247).

23 The closing parenthesis is lacking in the manuscript; I have supplied it editorially in what seems the appropriate place.

24 For Tolkien's own depiction of this scene from Bilbo's point of view, see the unfinished drawing labelled 'The Coming of the Eagles' in tengwar (Plate XII [bottom]).

25 This sentence was left unfinished, ending in a semicolon, and the paragraph cancelled.

26 It will be seen that this earliest account of the Battle of Five Armies, while following the same lines as the published version, leaves out many details, especially as relate to the role that Bolg of the North and his bodyguard play in the fight – indeed, there is no indication that Bolg's forces differ from any other goblins. A few such details are added in pencil to this Third Phase manuscript, but most appear for the first time in the typescript (1/1/67:4–7) with no intermediate drafting (or at least none which survives), and except in typographical details and the spelling of the name 'Gundobad' the typescript exactly achieves the text of the published book in its description of the actual battle (although some of the preliminary scenes, such as that describing the parley with Dain's dwarves, were revised considerably in the page proofs). Of particular note is the fact that Thorin's charge, which is ambiguously depicted as glorious but perhaps unwise in the published text (cf. DAA.343, where Bard is unable to restrain his men from abandoning their positions to join it), is here unambiguously heroic. For more on this climactic scene, see my commentary beginning on page 713.

Chapter XVIII

'AND BACK AGAIN'

As usual with the Third Phase manuscript (or indeed with *The Hobbit* manuscripts as a whole), the text originally continued with no chapter break. In fact, Tolkien at first simply indented and began a new paragraph, but had not even completed the first word ('Wh[en]') when he stopped, crossed it out, and drew a squiggle in the middle of the (blank) line that followed, and skipped the line after that. Thus he clearly intended a section break to come at this point. The text for what became the new chapter begins matter-of-factly with its description of the battle's aftermath, about one-third of the way down the manuscript page (Third Phase manuscript page 31; Marq. 1/1/19:1).

When he came to himself he was lying on the flat rock [> stones] of Ravenhill, and no one was near. Night was fading from the sky. [Dawn >] A cloudless dawn but cold was pale in the East.[TN1] He was shaking with cold [> & chilled as stone], but his head burned like fire.

'Now I wonder what has happened' he said to himself 'At any rate I am glad to find that I am not yet one of the glorious dead – but I may be soon enough yet.'

He sat up painfully. Looking into the valley he saw no goblins. After a while as the light grew he thought he saw elves moving in the rocks below; and suddenly he was aware of a great eagle perched upon a mountain just above.

'Hullo there!' he called 'Hail O Eagle, may your wings be ever blessed. I am hurt'.

'[Who is it that speaks >] What voice is it that speaks unseen among the stones' said the Eagle, <tak>ing to his wings and circling above Bilbo. Suddenly Bilbo remembered his ring. 'Well I am blessed' said he. 'This invisibility has its drawbacks after all! I suppose otherwise [> Otherwise I suppose] I should [> might] have spent a warm and comfortable night in bed!'

'It's me Bilbo Baggins companion of Thorin' he said, hurriedly taking off the ring.

'It is well that I have found you; you are needed and long sought' said the Eagle: and it was that [> the] very selfsame eagle, as it proved that had borne him from the [> to the] Carrock long before. 'I will bear you.'[TN2]

PLATE IX

Left 'The Back Door': A flurry of dwarven activity in the hidden bay on the western side of the Mountain.

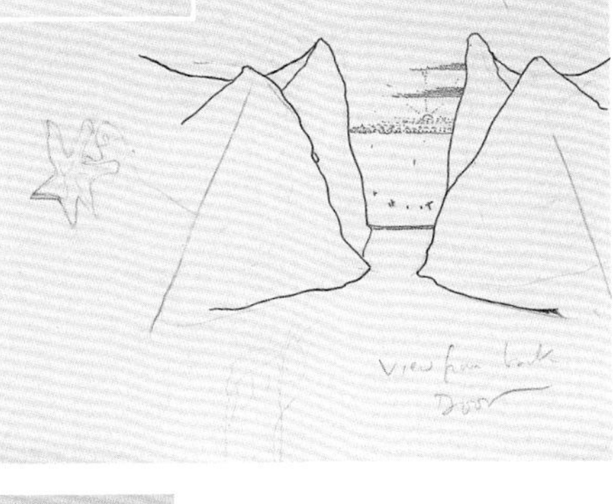

Right 'View from Back Door': companion piece to the preceding, showing the view from inside the secret tunnel looking out towards the setting sun.

Left Dwarves marching, with sketch of Smaug flying overhead.

PLATE X

Above 'The Front Door': the Lonely Mountain by daylight. Note the smoke-rings above the Mountain, the river looping around the ruins of Dale, and the opening on Ravenhill.

Above 'Smaug flies round the Mountain': a night-time scene in muted colour. Note placement of Dale and aberrant phase of the moon.

Above 'Conversation with Smaug': Bilbo's meeting with the Dragon in a picture full of significant detail. Note the dwarven curse on the jar to the lower left.

Left 'The wrong way to do it': even before he began writing *The Hobbit*, Tolkien was thinking about dragons, and this drawing from 1928 shows one of the 'creeping' kind being attacked in 'the wrong way'.

PLATE XII

Above 'Death of Smaug': Tolkien's annotated sketch showing the destruction of Lake Town.

Above 'Not competent produce drawings required. Can send rough sketch and directions [to] artist': previously unpublished sketch of Bilbo.

Above 'The Coming of the Eagles': this rough sketch shows the only known depiction of the Battle of the Five Armies, with the figure in the foreground possibly that of Bilbo.

In this way Bilbo was borne swiftly down into the valley, and set down before a tent. Gandalf greeted him [*added*: at the door].[TN3] 'Baggins!' he said. 'Well I never alive after all. [Who >] But come' he said more gravely. 'tidings may wait: you are called for;' and leading the hobbit he took him within.

'Hail Thorin' said Gandalf 'I have brought him.'

There lay Thorin wounded with many wounds, and his rent armour and notched axe were cast upon the floor.

'Farewell o gracious thief' said Thorin. 'I go now to the halls of waiting to sit beside my fathers until the world is renewed. The goblins have slain me.[TN4] Since I leave now all gold and silver and go where it is of little worth, I wish to part in friendship with [> from] you, and would take back my words and deeds at the Gate.'

Bilbo knelt on one knee filled with sorrow. 'Farewell O king [> my king]' he said. 'This is a bitter adventure if it must end so; and not a mountain of gold can amend it. Yet I am glad that I have been of your servants & your company [> shared in your perils] – and that has been more than any Baggins deserves [> might hope for].'

'Nay' said Thorin. 'There is more <to> you than you know descendent of [> son of] the <kindly> West – [sure and >] valour & wisdom and little greed. [> wisdom in good & blended measure]. If more valued food and cheer above hoarded gold [that >] it wd be a merrier world. But sad or merry I must leave it now. Farewell.'

Then Bilbo turned away and he went by himself and sat alone in a tent, and whether you believe it or not he wept until his eyes were red and his voice hoarse. He was a kindly little soul. Indeed it was very long before he had the heart to make a joke again.[TN5]

'Thank go[odness] > M[ercy] > A mercy it was' he said to himself at last 'that I awoke when I did. I [wish] Thorin were living, but I am glad that we parted in kindness'.

All that happened Bilbo learned of course bit by bit, though he was no longer as interested as I hope you are. He was aching in his bones for his homeward journey.

The Eagles [had > in great number >] had had suspicion of the Goblins gathering [> mustering] and they had gathered in great numbers and come down upon the wind in the nick of time. They it was that dislodged the Goblins from the Mountain and cast them over precipices or drove them shrieking down among their foes; [Soon the Elves and men could turn and go to the help of the battle in the valley. >] so that soon all those on the mountain were overcome or in flight. Then Elves and Men turned to [> came at last to] the help of the battle in the valley. But they were still outnumbered. In that hour Beorn had himself appeared – no one knew how or whence, [<saved> >] and he seemed to have grown to half-giant size in his wrath. The roar of his voice was like thunder and he tossed goblin and wolf from his path like straws and feathers.[TN6] He fell upon their rear and broke into the ring and there he lifted Thorin who had fallen pierced with spears and bore him out of the fray. Then he returned and none could withstand his onslaught.[TN7] Thus enheartened the weary companies had fallen on and soon the goblins <?they were> [scattered >] broken. The <most> were driven into the river and such as escaped across were hunted into [> right to] the marshes about the Forest River and there most perished, or coming into the wood-elves' realm were slain or driven to die deep in the trackless dark of Mirkwood.

[All this had befallen ere full >] The victory had been assured before night fall, but the pursuit was still on foot when B. returned to the camp, and not many were there save the wounded.[TN8]

'Where are the eagles?' he said to Gandalf that evening as he lay rolled in many warm blankets. 'They are gone' said G. 'for they [do not love >] will not tarry here, [But they are >] now that they have hunted the last fugitives from the mountain.'

'[Good >] I am sorry: I should have liked to see them again,' said B. sleepily. '[When d[o] >] I suppose I shall be going home soon?'

'As soon as you like' said Gandalf.

[But >] Actually it was some days [before Bilbo was strong again on his legs. He left the Mountain >] before Bilbo left the place. They buried Thorin deep beneath the Mountain, and Bard laid the Arkenstone upon his heart.[TN9] 'There let it lie with the last of the kings' he said, 'and may it guard [bring good fortune to >] all his folk that dwell here after.'

Two more sentences are squeezed in at the end of the paragraph, running over into the bottom margin:

And by him [*added*: upon his tomb.] the Elven king laid Orcrist the <illegible> sword that had been taken from Thorin in captivity. It is said it gleamed ever in the dark if foes approached.[TN10]

But Dain son of Nain took up his abode there, and all his dwarves; and [many >] he became king under the Mountain and <?many> dwarves of the race of Durin [were >] came back to <illegible> old halls. The twelve dwarves[TN11] chose also to remain there; and [> for] Dain dealt his treasure well. [Yet >] There was, of course, no longer any question of dividing it in shares among Balin Dwalin, Bifur Bofur & Bombur [(or Bilbo) >] and the rest or Bilbo.

Yet a fourteenth share [> part] of all the gold and silver made & unmade was given up to Bard; for Dain said 'we will honour the agreement of the dead, and he has now the Arkenstone in his keeping.' [*Added*: And even a fourteenth share was wealth exceeding rich.]

And of that Bilbo was given a chest full of silver and a chest full of gold by Bard himself – he would take no more. 'And it will be difficult enough to get that home as it is' he said; which proved true enough.[TN12] To the Elven king for his aid many jewels such as he loved were given, and <?among them> the emeralds of Girion that Dain gave to Bard.[TN13]

<Now> the hour came to say farewell to his friends. 'Farewell Dwalin' he said 'and Farewell Fili & Kili, and Farewell Dori and Nori, and Oin and Gloin, and Bifur & Bofur and Bombur' he said. And turning towards the mountain 'Fairwell king Thorin Oakenshield.'[TN14]

And the Dwarves bowed low and their words stuck in <their throats> '[Farewell >] Goodbye and good luck' they said ' – if ever you visit us again when these halls are made fair again, the feast shall indeed be splendid' said Balin.[TN15]

'If ever you pass my way' said Bilbo 'don't wait to knock. Tea is at four, but any time [is time for >] will do for you! Goodbye'.

And he rode [> turned] away.

The Elfhost was on the march and if it was sadly lessened yet many were glad, for now the world would be merrier for many a day. [T]he dragon was dead and the goblins would [be >] have small power in the North for many ages of m.[TN16] and their hearts look forward [to a >] over winter to a spring of joy.

Gandalf and Bilbo rode behind the Elvenking.[TN17] But when they drew within sight of Mirkwood they halted; for the wizard and hobbit were going [to str >] north <along> the Forest and towards the Hills. Now that the Goblins were overcome it was a safer road if long[er] than the dark & dreadful pathways under the trees.

'Farewell O Elvenking' said Gandalf, 'Merry be the greenwood while the world is yet young; and merry be all your folk.'

'Farewell Gandalf. May you ever turn up [> appear] where you are [wanted >] most needed; and the oftener you appear in my halls the better shall I be pleased' said the king.

'I beg you' said Bilbo stammering 'to accept a gift,' and he brought out a silver necklace [> necklace of silver and pearls].

'In what way have I earned gifts of you [> such a gift] O hobbit' said the king.

'Well er' said Bilbo 'I thought don't you know that some little return for your hospitality should be made. I mean even a burglar has his feelings, and I drank a deal of your wine and eat much of your bread [– though >] without by your leave.'

'I will take it O Bilbo the magnificent' said the king gravely. 'And I name you elf-friend[TN18] and blessed: may your shadow never grow less (or we should [> might] all be ruined). Farewell.'

Then the Elves [wen[t] >] turned toward the Forest and
Bilbo <went> home.

Indeed yes! He had many adventures ere [> before] he got there. The wild was still the wild, and the Battle had not changed it much, but he was never in any great danger again. The wizard was with him and for long Beorn too.

The following two paragraphs (and the first sentence of the third paragraph) were later bracketed and then cancelled, and the words 'Put in Later' written beside them in the margin, no doubt when the passage was moved to its present position near the end of the next chapter.

If you would have all things settled I will tell you this: Bard brought Men back to Dale and rebuilt a town there and all the valley became in time rich and tilled, and many boats were on the running river which [fell >] ran less swift below [> after] its sudden Southern turn. and much folk gathered there And Lake Town was rebuilt in time and became prosperous once more; but the Master came to a bad end.

He stole what treasure he could lay ha[nds on] > Bard sent much treasure to him for the help of the town; and being of the sort that is easily <illegible> he fell under the spell of it, and took it and fled with it; and those who went with him, murdered him for it, and threw him in to > left him > and he died of starvation in the waste.

But that was long after Bilbo went away . . .

. . . Christmas [> Yule-time] he spent in Beorn's house – <with> Gandalf and it was warm and merry, and men came from far and wide for the Misty Mountains were now freed.[TN19] And Beorn became a great chief [*added*: afterward] and ruled the [> a] wide land between the mountains & the wood; and it is said that for many a generation the men of his line had the power of taking bear's shape; and some were grim men [*added*: and bad], but [some were of rough >] most were just such as Beorn, if less in size and strength. [As long as they ruled >] In their day the last goblins were hunted from the Misty Mountains, and new peace came over the edge of the wild.[TN20]

[And after that Bilbo crossed the mountai[ns] > When Yule was over Beorn invited them to stay here >] It was spring and a fair one with mild weather and bright sun before Bilbo and Gandalf left;

and B. left then with regret for the flowers of the gardens of Beorn were in spring [mo [re] >] no less marvelous than in high summer.

At last they came [over the >] up the long road and to the very pass where the goblins had captured them before; but they came there at morning, and looking back a white sun was shining over the distant [> outstretched] lands, and mirkwood, darkly green even in spring, stretched across the lands laid out below away from left to right and blue. [> There behind lay Mirkwood blue in the distance and darkly green even in spring at the nearer edge.] There far away was [a glint of s[now] >] the Lonely Mountain on the edge of eyesight. On its highest peak snow yet unmelted glinted pale.

'So comes snow after fire, and even dragons have an ending' said Bilbo and he turned his back on his adventure. The tookish part was getting very tired and Baggins was daily coming forward. 'I now wish only to be in my home' he said.

TEXT NOTES

1 This is changed to 'A cloudless day [*added*: but cold] was broad above.' That is, the amount of time Bilbo spends unconscious on the battlefield is increased; originally he is wounded and passes out at sunset, waking with the next day's dawn. In the final version, it is already well into the next day when he recovers consciousness.

2 These five paragraphs were re-written to remove the eagle and replace him with one of the lake-men:

> . . . suddenly he was aware of a man standing at the door of the watch-chamber nearby.
>
> 'Hullo there!' he called '[How goes >] hullo! what news?'
>
> 'What voice is it that speaks unseen among the stones' said the man peering forward. Suddenly Bilbo remembered his ring. 'Well I am blessed' said he. 'This invisibility has its drawbacks after all! Otherwise I suppose I might have spent a warm and comfortable night in bed!'
>
> 'It's me Bilbo Baggins companion of Thorin' he said, hurriedly taking off the ring.
>
> 'It is well that I have found you; you are needed and long sought' said the man: 'Are you hurt?' 'A knock on the head' said Bilbo, 'but I have a helm and a hard skull. All the same I feel sick. My legs are weak.' 'Then I will carry you,' said the man, 'to the camp in the valley' (Third Phase manuscript pages 31–32; I/I/19:1–2).

This change was no doubt made because Tolkien remembered that earlier he had written of the eagles that 'Bilbo never saw them again. But he didn't forget them' (see page 229 and Text Note 5 following Chapter VII).

3 The idea that Gandalf was wounded in the battle, which seems so out of keeping with the character as he was later developed in *The Lord of the Rings*, did not appear in the original manuscript but entered in with the typescript: '. . . set down before a tent in Dale; and there stood Gandalf, with his arm in a sling. Even the wizard had not escaped all hurt; and there was scarcely one unharmed in some way in all the host [> and there were few unharmed in all the host].' (I/I/68:I).

4 This line was cancelled. For more on 'the halls of waiting' and the dwarven afterlife, see part four of the commentary (iv. 'The Halls of Waiting') following the Third Phase manuscript, beginning on page 720.

5 The ink of the following lines is darker, again indicating a slight pause in composition.

6 It took Tolkien several tries to find the right simile. He tried first 'like a dog amo[ng]', then broke off and replaced this with 'as if they were but yapping pupp[ies]', before settling on 'like straws and feathers'.

7 Bolg's fate is not mentioned here, instead first entering in with the typescript: 'Swiftly he [Beorn] returned and his wrath was redoubled, so that nothing could withstand him, and no weapon seemed to bite upon him. He scattered the bodyguard, and pulled down Bolg himself and crushed him. Then dismay fell on the Goblins and they fled in all directions . . .' (I/I/68:2–3); see Text Note 26 to Ch. XVII and also the commentary starting on page 708.

8 This sentence was originally followed with 'The eagles were all off on the mountain hunt > Bilbo > Among these Bilbo found himself counted' – i.e., among the wounded.

9 This word looks like *heart* in the manuscript (Third Phase manuscript page 34; I/I/19:4) but might instead be *breast*, the reading of the typescript (I/I/68:3).

10 The word preceding 'sword' is difficult to make out but may be *Elfin*.

11 In the original story neither Fili nor Kili died fighting alongside their great-uncle but survived to the end of the tale. The idea that the two most likeable of all Bilbo's companions should also die in the battle – one of the saddest moments in the whole story, even though it occurs offstage while our narrator is *hors de combat* – first appears in the continuation of the typescript that eventually (autumn 1936) replaced the Third Phase manuscript: 'Of the twelve companions of Thorin ten remained. Fili and Kili had fallen defending him with shield and body, for he was their mother's elder brother' (I/I/68:3). This change thus postdates the completion of the book by some three and a half years. Thorin had still been their great-uncle when the First Typescript reached Chapter X (cf. I/I/60:4), where at some point after the page was typed 'sons of my father's daughter's son' was changed to 'sons of my father's daughter'. The phrase 'their mother's *elder* brother' perhaps suggested the presence of another brother as well, as would indeed eventually be the case, although the unfortunate Frerin was not invented until late

in Tolkien's work on *The Lord of the Rings* (*LotR*.1110–11 & 1117 and HME XII.276, 281, & 287); note his absence from the family tree given on HME XII.277. For more on issues of dwarven inheritance and the kingship, see the section of commentary entitled 'Dain son of Nain' beginning on page 702.

12 Several cancelled words originally came between 'full of gold' and 'by Bard himself', but I cannot make any of them out. That Bilbo would return home with little or no treasure had long been foreseen in the Plot Notes – cf. the last page of Plot Notes B, as well as Plot Notes D & F, particularly the last, where he loses most of his treasure on the return journey. Ironically, setting off with two chests full of treasure (here a sign of modest restraint) may derive from *Fáfnismál*, where Sigurd finds so much gold in Fafnir's hoard that it fills two chests, with which he loads down Grani, his faithful horse (Terry, *Poems of the Elder Edda* page 159). This becomes 'two great chests' in Morris & Magnússon's translation of the *Völsunga Saga* (page 67), and Snorri Sturluson tells us that 'Grani's burden' became a kenning for 'gold' from this incident (*Prose Edda*, page 113), while Bilbo's chests became 'two *small* chests . . . *such as one strong pony could carry*' in the typescript (1/1/68:4). Of course Bilbo also kept his little sword, his mail coat, and the Ring, and it seems a parallel beyond coincidence that the three additional treasures Sigurd took with him from Fafnir's hoard were a famous sword, a gold byrnie (mail-coat), and the *ægishjálmr* or 'Helm of Awe' – an item famed for its power to make the wearer invisible.†

†Also known as the Helm of Terror, the *ægishjálmr* is better known today by the name Wagner used in *Das Rheingold*, the *Tarnhelm*.

13 This sentence was preceded by the line '"I beg of you" said Bilbo to the Elvenking', which was cancelled and the replacement text squeezed into place, with many hesitations. Originally the insertion seems to have read 'To the Elven king for his aid many jewels such as he loved were given, but the emeralds of Girion were given to Bard, and by him <illegible> that B. were' before this broke off and was altered rather illegibly to read as I have given it in the main text. The typescript clarifies the sequence of events: 'To the Elvenking he [Bard] gave the emeralds of Girion, such jewels as he most loved, which Dain had restored to him' (1/1/68:3).

14 Aside from the inadvertent omission of Balin and Ori, Bilbo here takes his leave of the dwarves in exactly the same order in which he was first introduced to them back in the first chapter. Fili and Kili are of course alive and present (see Text Note 11 above). The line where he bids farewell to their memory (cf. DAA.352) first appears in the typescript (1/1/68:4), where both Balin and Ori are included in their proper order, except that Balin precedes his brother Dwalin in this listing (no doubt as Bilbo's special friend among all the remaining dwarves, and the Company's leader now that Thorin is gone), whereas he had been the second to arrive at the 'unexpected party'.

15 *The Lord of the Rings* records that Bilbo did indeed take them up on this invitation and pay them a visit many years later, after he had vanished from the Shire and before settling down to his retirement at Rivendell (*LotR*.247).

16 That is, 'many ages of m*en*'; the elision is an example of the speed with which Tolkien set down the latter half of the Third Phase manuscript in his hurry to reach the end of the story. Cf. young Christopher Tolkien's description of this material as 'rather roughly done' in his 1937 letter to Father Christmas (reprinted in the Foreword to the Fiftieth Anniversary *Hobbit*, page vii).

17 Added above the line, but not marked specifically where it should be inserted: 'and Beorn strode beside'.

18 This seemingly casual remark gains great significance in the sequel, where both Bilbo and Frodo enjoy special privileges because they are known to be 'elf-friends' (cf. *LotR*.94). More significantly, it ties Bilbo into a long tradition of Tolkien's elf-friends, a line of figures stretching back to Eriol in *The Book of Lost Tales* [1917–20] and his slightly later counterpart Ælfwine in 'Ælfwine of England' [circa 1920 & afterwards], through the elf-friends of the Silmarillion tales such as Tuor, Húrin, and Beren, and onward to those time-travellers Oswin and Alboin Errol of *The Lost Road* [1936] and Arry Lowdham and Young Jeremy in *The Notion Club Papers* [1944–6], and ultimately Smith Smithson in *Smith of Wootton Major*, Tolkien's last completed story [1964].

19 These sentences were revised to read:

> But that was long after Bilbo went away. Anyway By Mid winter Bilbo & Gandalf had reached Beorn's house – And there they stayed. Yule tide was warm and merry there, and men came from far and wide to feast for the goblins of the Misty Mountains were now few and <terrified>, &nd men went abroad without fear.

20 Unlike Gandalf's prediction a few pages later (see Text Note 4 for Chapter XIX), this statement does come true, since the goblins suffer catastrophic losses upon Sauron's downfall at the climax of *The Lord of the Rings* which seem to leave them near extinction (cf. *LotR*.985: 'the creatures of Sauron . . . ran hither and thither mindless; and some slew themselves, or cast themselves in pits, or fled wailing back to hide in holes and dark lightless places far from hope'), although we have the testimony of the *Father Christmas Letters* that a few still linger in remote spots even in our time (see in particular the 1932 letter).

Chapter XIX

THE END OF THE JOURNEY

As before, no break separated the paragraphs in the original manuscript (Third Phase manuscript page 38; Marq. 1/1/19:8), but Tolkien later inserted 'Ch' in pencil here to mark where he had decided that the final chapter should begin.

[So homesick was he that even the House of Elrond could not long delay him. He called there of course and spoke with the elves > It was already May and >] It was on May the 1st that he came back to that valley of the last homely house. Again it was evening and as he rode down beside the wizard the elves were still singing in the trees. As soon as Bilbo and Gandalf [came >] appeared they burst into song very much as before

Put in a song like the one on p 28.[TN1]

The page which follows, providing a very neat handwritten copy of the poem that ultimately appeared here, was interpolated later, since all the remaining pages of the Third Phase manuscript that follow (Third Phase manuscript pages 39–45; Marq. 1/1/20:2–8) were later renumbered to accommodate the addition of a new page '39' bearing the poem (1/1/20:1).

O where are you going,
so late in returning?
The river is flowing,
the stars are all burning!
O whither so laden
so sad and so dreary?
Here elf and elf-maidenTN2
Now welcome the weary

Come, tra-la-la lally,
Come back to the valley

The stars are far brighter
than gems without measure,
The moon is far whiter
than silver in treasure;

The fire is more shining
on hearth in the gloaming
Than gold won in mining!
So cease from your roaming!

Come tra-la-lalley
come back to the valley!

The dragon is withered
His bones are now crumbled,
His armour is shivered,
his splendour is humbled.
Though swords shall be rusted,
and crown and throne perish,
with strength that men trusted
and wealth that they cherish
Here [grass] is yet growing
And leaves are yet swinging,
the white water flowing
and elves are all singing

Come tra la lally
come back to the valley[TN3]

A warm welcome was made there in the house of Elrond. and [*added*: <there> were many] eager ears to hear the tale of all their adventures. Gandalf it was who spoke, for Bilbo was fallen quiet and drowsy; but every now and again he would open an eye and listen when some part of the story he did not know came in.

Written following the next paragraph but marked for insertion here, following 'quiet and drowsy':

Most of the tale he knew, for he told much of it to the wizard himself on the homeward way. But

So he learned that Gandalf had been to a council of good wizards; and that the Necromancer had been driven from his hold in the south of Mirkwood, and had fled to other lands. 'The North is freed from that horror for many an age' said G. 'yet I wish he were banished from the world'. [*cancelled*: Also one thing that had often puzzled him was explained – the trolls had been traced by Elrond. They had plundered > been <buried>][TN4]

'It would be well indeed' he said [> said Elrond] 'but I fear that will not be [> come about] in this age of the world, or for many after.' After the tale of their journeys there were other tales, and yet more tales, tales of long ago, and tales of new things, and tales of no time at all: till Bilbo's head fell on his chest, and he <snored> comfortably in a corner.[TN5]

He woke to find himself in bed, and the moon shining through an open window. Below the elves were still singing.[TN6]

[Song]

This instruction is written in pencil in the top margin of Third Phase manuscript page 40 [>41] (=1/1/20:3); the actual text of the poem appears on a separate sheet later inserted into the manuscript, as may be seen from its being given a sequence of page numbers (39 > 40 > 41):

Sing all ye joyful, now sing all together!
The wind's in the tree-top the wind's in the heather;
The stars are in blossom, the moon is in flower,
Bright are the windows of night in her tower!

Dance all ye joyful, now dance all together!
Soft is the grass, and let foot be like feather!
The river is silver, the shadows are fleeting,
Merry is Maytime and merry our meeting.

Sing we now softly, and dreams let us weave him,
Wind him in slumber and there let us leave him!
The wanderer sleepeth, now soft be his pillow!
Lullaby, lullaby, alder and willow!

Hush, hush, oak ash and thorn!
Sigh no more pine till the wind [that >] of the morn;
Fall Moon, dark be the land,
Hushed be all water, till dawn is at hand![TN7]

The original manuscript continued with Bilbo's reaction to the elven singing:

'Well merry people' said Bilbo looking out. 'What time under [> by] the moon is this? Your lullaby would wake a drunken goblin. Yet I thank you.'

'And your snores would wake a stone dragon' [they answered. 'Yet for your >] 'Yet we thank you' they answered with laughter. 'It is but midnight; and you have slept now since early evening. Tomorrow perhaps you will be cured of weariness.'

'Maybe. A little sleep [goes >] does a great cure in the house of Elrond' said he. 'But I will take all I can get. Good night fair friends.' And he went back to bed, and slept till late morning.

Weariness fell from him soon in that house and he had many a merry jest and dance[TN8] with the elves of the valley. Yet even that place could not long delay him now. He thought ever of his home.[TN9]

In but [> After but] three days therefore he said farewell to Elrond and giving him many gifts of gold and receiving much he rode away on a fine morning with Gandalf.[TN10] But even as they left the valley the sky darkened behind them [> in the west] and wind and rain came up to meet them.

'Merry is may time' said Bilbo as the rain beat on his face 'but <?our> back is to legends and we are coming home. I suppose this is a first taste of home coming.'

'There is a long road yet' said Gandalf.

'[But >] Yet it is the last road' said Bilbo.

Soon they reached the ford in the river with the steep bank and down this they slithered.

Gandalf did not like the look of the river.

The river was somewhat swollen, and as they plunged in soon came above their feet as they sat their ponies. They were but halfway across when Bilbo's pony slipped on a stone and floundered into the water.[TN11]

Soon they were over the ford and had left the wild behind. At each stage in the road Bilbo recalled the happenings of a year ago (which now seemed so [far >] long ago).[TN12] It was not long before they came to where they had laid the troll-gold [*added*: they had hidden]. 'I have enough to last me my time' said Bilbo. '[This had better be >] You had better take this Gandalf.'

'Share and share alike' said Gandalf 'You may have more needs than you expect.' So they slung the bags [> gold in bags] upon the ponies and after that their going was slow, for most of the time they walked.

But the weather soon mended & as it drew near to June became warm and hot. The land was green and fair about them.

And as all things come at last to an end even this story a day came when they came to the mill by the river and passed the bridge and came right back to Bilbo's own door.[TN13]

'Bless me what is going on' said he! For there was a great commotion and people were thick round the door and many were coming and going in & out – not even wiping their feet as Bilbo noticed with disgust.

If he was surprized they were more surprized still. He had arrived back in the middle of an auction! Nearly all his things had [*added*:

already] been sold for little money or old songs and his cousins the Allibone Baggins[TN14] were busy measuring the rooms to see if their furniture would fit.

Bilbo in fact was 'Presumed Dead' and not everybody that said so was sorry to find the presumption wrong.

The return of Bilbo in fact created quite a [comm[otion] >] disturbance both under hill and across the water and was a great deal more than a nine days wonder.[TN15] The legal bother indeed lasted for months [> years]. It was a long time indeed before Mr Baggins was admitted to be alive, and even then, to save time, he had to buy back a lot of his own furniture. The Allibone Baggins never fully admitted it [*added in pencil*: that he was genuine], and at any rate they were never on speaking terms with him again.

Indeed Bilbo found he had lost <one> thing altogether – and that was his reputation.

[Nothing he > He was no longer res[pectable] >] It is true that for ever after he remained an elf-friend and had the honour of dwarves wizards and all such folk as ever passed his way; but he was no longer respectable.[TN16]

Indeed he was held by all the hobbits to be 'queer' – except his nephews & nieces[TN17] on the Took-side and even they were not encouraged in the friendship by their elders.

I am sorry to say he did not mind very much. [His sw[ord] >] He was perfectly happy [> quite content]; and the sound of his own kettle on the hearth was ever after more musical than it had been in the quiet days before the unexpected party.[TN18] His sword he hung on the mantlepiece. His armour was arranged on a stand in the hall [*added in pencil in left margin*: till he lent it to a museum]. His gold and silver was large[ly] [> mostly] spent in presents both useful and extravagant and his [*added*: invisible] ring was chiefly employed when unpleasant callers came.[TN19]

He took to writing poetry and visiting the elves and [<if> >] though many shook their heads and said 'poor old Baggins', and only few believed any of his tales, he remained perfectly happy to the end of his days and those were extraordinarily long.

At this point a line was drawn across the page and the rest of this manuscript page (Third Phase manuscript page 43 [> 44]; Marq. 1/1/20:6) cancelled. I give the original text here:

One day [when >] long long after
put in visit of Gandalf <here> news of dwarves
So the prophecy came true?
Yes of course – don't disbelieve in them because you helped to bring them about.

To this is added in hasty pencil:

> After all you don't really suppose [that you contrived all your adventures and all your escape[s] >] that all your adventures and all your escapes were <contrived> by you do you [> by you yourself]. You are a very [*added*: fine] person Mr Baggins & I am very fond of you, but you are only quite a little fellow in a wide world after all.
>
> Thank goodness said Bilbo.

All this material, forming as it does the rough draft for the brief epilogue, was cancelled and replaced by an additional sheet (Marq. 1/1/20:7–8) of fair copy text (Third Phase manuscript pages 45 and 45 [> 46]) written in a very neat hand:

One day [> autumn evening] long afterwards Bilbo was sitting in his study writing his memoirs – he thought of calling them 'There and Back Again'[TN20] – when there was a ring at the door.

It was Gandalf and a dwarf; and the dwarf was actually Balin.

'Come in, come in!' said Bilbo, and soon they were settled in chairs by his fire. If Balin noticed that Mr Baggins' waistcoat was more extensive (and had real gold buttons) he [> Bilbo] also noticed that Balin's beard was several inches longer, and his jewelled clothes [> belt] of great magnificence. They fell to talking of their times together of course, and Bilbo asked how things were going in the Lands of the Mountain. It seemed they were going very well.

Bard had rebuilt a town in Dale and men had gathered to him from the Lake and from South and West, and all the valley had become tilled again and rich, and the desolation was now filled with birds and blossom in spring and fruit and feasting in autumn. And Lake-town had been refounded more prosperous than ever, and much wealth went up and down the Running River; and there was friendship in those parts between elves and dwarves and men. The Master had come to a bad end; for Bard had sent much gold for the help of the lake-people, and being of the kind that [is >] easily catches such disease he fell under the dragon-sickness and took it [> the gold] and fled with it, and died of starvation in the waste. 'The new Master was [> is] of [more >] wiser kind,' said Balin 'and very popular; for of course he gets most of the credit of the present prosperity. They say that in his day the river runs with gold.'

'Then the prophecies of the old songs have [accidentally >] come all right by [*added*: happy] accident,' said Bilbo.

'Of course!' said Gandalf. 'How else would they come true? Surely you don't disbelieve the prophecies because you had a share in bringing them about yourself? After all you don't really suppose, do you, that all your adventures and all your wonderful escapes were managed by you yourself, do you? You are a very fine person, Mr Baggins, and I am very fond of you; but you are only quite a little fellow in a wide world, after all.'

'Thank goodness!' said Bilbo and pushed over the tobacco-jar.[TN21]

END

Roads go ever ever on
under [> over] rock and under tree
by caves where never sun has shone
by streams that never find the sea.

[R>] over grass and over stone
and under mountains in the moon
over snow by winter sown
and through the merry flowers of June[TN22]

Roads go ever ever on
under cloud and under sun [> star],
But [never >] <foot> <?hath> never never gone
Beyond the seas to <?Gondobar>[TN23]
    [Yet feet that wandering have gone]
    [turn at last to home afar.]

Eyes that [have >] fire and sword have seen
and terror walking in the wild[TN24]
Look at last on meadows green
and trees and hills they long have known.[TN25]

* * * * *

This represents the end of the composite typescript/manuscript of the completed story (i.e., the Third Phase) which Tolkien reached in December 1932 or, more likely, January 1933, loaning it to C. S. Lewis by February. For more on its 'wander[ing] about' over the next three and a half years, see page 635. For the well-known story of how the book came to Allen & Unwin's attention and the subsequent stages that led to its acceptance and publication, see Carpenter (*Tolkien: A Biography*, pages 180–1), Anderson (DAA.12–13, including a facsimile of ten-year-old Rayner Unwin's reader's report on DAA.14), Hammond (*Descriptive Bibliography*, pages 7–8), and especially Elaine Griffith's account.[TN26]

It is probable, however, that this had not been Allen & Unwin's first contact with Tolkien. The project which Dagnall travelled to Oxford to pick up from Griffiths on the day that she was persuaded by Griffiths, who had not actually yet done the promised work, to ask to borrow

Professor Tolkien's 'frightfully good' story rather than return to London empty-handed, was probably the Clark Hall *Beowulf*. This prose translation[TN27] had originally been published in 1901 by Swan Sonnenschein, a firm that had later [1911] merged with George Allen & Sons, which in turn had been acquired [1914] by young Stanley Unwin and renamed George Allen & Unwin. Although reprinted in 1911 and popular among students who wanted to avoid actually reading *Beowulf* in the original (an attitude Tolkien deplored), it now badly needed updating, and Stanley Unwin or one of his staff (e.g., Charles Furth) seems to have approached Tolkien to see if he would undertake the job (see Hammond, *Descriptive Bibliography*, page 296, who dates this contact to 'probably in early or mid-1936).[TN28] Tolkien, who expresses a low opinion of Clark Hall's translation in his own Prefatory Remarks to the eventual reprint (Clark Hall, page xv), declined the job (possibly because he had already translated *Beowulf* himself into both verse and prose) but with typical generosity seems to have recommended his former graduate student, Elaine Griffiths, for the job. Griffiths eventually proved unequal to the task (throughout her long career she published very little, concentrating her energies instead on teaching) and two years later the project reverted back to Tolkien, who passed it along to fellow Inkling Charles Wrenn; Wrenn completed the work within a year and the revised edition, with Tolkien's essay on Old English prosody, appeared in 1940. An updated version followed in 1950 that was still being reprinted thirty years later (Hammond, page 299), though its longevity owes far more to the presence of Tolkien's essay than the quality of Clark Hall's translation or Wrenn's notes.

The acceptance, publication, and success of *The Hobbit* quickly led to Allen & Unwin's decision to publish more Tolkien: *Mr. Bliss* (with the proviso that he needed to redraw the pictures into a more easily, and cheaply, reproducible format), *Farmer Giles of Ham* (as soon as he could flesh out the volume with the addition of similar stories), and most of all a sequel to *The Hobbit* (as soon as he could write it). They probably envisioned the latter either as stories about Bilbo's further adventures, rather like Lofting's Dr. Dolittle books – to which Tolkien objected that 'he remained very happy to the end of his days, and those were extraordinarily long' (DAA.361) left very little wiggle room for further exploits (cf. *Letters* p. 38) – or else as a series of stories each about a different hobbit, which is in fact what they eventually got. In the event all these projects were delayed in their publication for many years, but within three months of *The Hobbit*'s publication in September 1937 Tolkien had begun work on 'The New Hobbit', which at one point he thought of calling *The Magic Ring* (a handwritten title-page bearing this title survives among the papers at Marquette, Marq. 3/1/2:2). Eventually the sequel, far from being the thinner repetition of Bilbo's adventure he had feared ('For nearly all the "motives" [i.e., motifs] that I can use were packed into the original book' – *Letters* p. 38) was such an engrossing project that it took him fourteen years to complete, and picked up on all the unanswered questions from the earlier book – Gollum, the ring, the Necromancer, Moria, et al. (the chief exception being no mention of Beorn's earlier history), as well as elements from *The Lost Road*, the 1937 *Quenta Silmarillion*, Tolkien's 'fairy poetry', his scholarly work, &c., until it became the definitive masterpiece of his subcreated world.

More importantly from the point of view of *The Hobbit*, *The Lord of the Rings* turned out to be quite different from its predecessor, although clearly linked to it in story, style, and characters. And as his ideas developed Tolkien came to reject some of what was said in the original book, particularly in the crucial encounter with Gollum. Once he had established that Bilbo's ring inspired possessiveness even beyond what the Arkenstone (and, earlier yet, the Silmarils) evoked, the idea that Gollum honestly intended to give Bilbo his ring when he lost the riddle-game became untenable. At first Tolkien decided to reveal in *The Lord of the Rings* that the account that appeared in *The Hobbit* was not what actually happened, and he had Gandalf recount the true story in the new book. Eventually, however, he realized that it would be a simpler solution if he could actually alter what was said in the first book, which would have the added benefit of not casting his earlier book into the status of unreliable narrative. Accordingly, in 1944 he drafted replacement text for a large portion of Chapter V: Riddles in the Dark, and in 1947 sent it off to Allen & Unwin to see if they thought inserting it into the next printing would be feasible. Due to a miscommunication (see Hammond, *Descriptive Bibliography*, pages 22–3, and *Letters* p. 120–4) Tolkien thought the publisher had decided not to make the change and so was taken by surprise when three years later in 1950 he was sent proofs for the next printing which incorporated his replacement text (*Letters* p. 141). This of course became the second edition of 1951, the form of the story that has been familiar to readers ever since. For the complete text of this new material Tolkien sent Allen & Unwin in 1947, the Fourth Phase of his work on the book, see the section beginning on page 729.

TEXT NOTES

1 Tolkien's note to himself here refers to page 28 of the First Typescript (Marq. 1/1/53:3), corresponding to page 113 in Chapter III of this book. This is yet another piece of evidence that the First Typescript for chapters I through XII and part of XIV, replacing the bulk of the Second Phase text, already existed before the Third Phase manuscript was written.

2 Elf-maiden: This is the only reference to female elves within *The Hobbit*, aside from the (cancelled) mention of (Lúthien) Tinúviel.

3 The poem as we have it here is a fair copy obviously preceded by drafting that does not survive. It strongly resembles the version published in the book, the main variance being, as any comparison soon shows, that the three stanzas appear in reverse order in the manuscript from how they appear in the typescript and published book (the typescript text – 1/1/69:1–2 – being exactly that which saw print). Tolkien later numbered the stanzas from top to bottom '3', '2', and '1' respectively in pencil in the left margin, indicating that the decision to reverse their sequence belongs not to the Third Phase but a somewhat later stage of work on the book, the period of the completion of the typescript (summer-autumn 1936).

Aside from the re-sequencing of the stanzas, Tolkien also made a few other changes. The line 'Here is yet growing' near the end I have treated as a miscopying from the lost draft for an intended 'Here *grass* is yet growing', since the line is otherwise short one syllable; in any case, Tolkien altered it in contemporary ink to read 'Here *grass* is *still* growing'. In the final line (sans chorus) of the poem, 'and elves are all singing', he underlined the words are singing and wrote 'are yet/ at their' in the right margin. This I take as offering two variant revisions, so that instead of 'and elves *are yet at their* singing', which is euphonious but metrically irregular, he was weighing the respective merits of 'and elves *are yet* singing' versus 'and elves *at their* singing'; comparison with the typescript and published book (DAA.[355]) show he decided upon the former.

In addition to these changes on the manuscript itself, between the fair copy manuscript and the typescript 'So cease from your roaming' (line 8 in the middle stanza) became 'So why go a-roaming?'. The slight indentation of every other line was abandoned, and the chorus elaborated somewhat, especially in the final refrain. So that instead of 'Come' being repeated three times we instead get 'Come! . . .', 'O! . . .', and 'With . . .', followed in the last case with an additional flourish of fa-la-las.

4 These last two sentences were cancelled, leaving the second one (an attempt to pick up a loose thread from Plot Notes F) unfinished. The rest of the paragraph was extensively revised and supplemented with marginal additions until it read as follows:

> So he learned that Gandalf had been to a council of *many magicians and wise and learned men masters of lore and beneficial wizardry [> white wizardry]*; and that the Necromancer had *at last* been driven from his hold in the south of Mirkwood, and had fled to other lands. 'The North is freed from that horror for many an age' said G. 'yet I wish he were banished from the world'.

It is remarkable to find Tolkien using the word 'magician' in a favorable context; cf. his more usual negative associations with the term in *On Fairy-Stories* (OFS.15 & 49) and *Letters* (page 200), and indeed the phrase 'magicians and' was cancelled in ink. The presence of enough wizards and magicians to form a council is less surprising: Tolkien's early work was filled with wizards, from *The Book of Lost Tales*' Tû the wizard ('Gilfanon's Tale', BLT I.232–3) to the *Father Christmas Letters*' Man in the Moon, Father Christmas himself, and presumably Fr. Christmas's Green Brother as well, to *Roverandom*'s same Man in the Moon, Psamathos Psamathides the sand-sorcerer, and Artaxerxes the wandering wizard. The idea that Middle-earth in the Third Age had only five wizards (Saruman, Gandalf, Radagast, and the two Blue Wizards of the east), none of whom are human, was like the concept of the Third Age itself a much later development; cf. HME VIII.64 & 67, the essay 'The Istari' in *Unfinished Tales* (UT.388–402), and 'The Five Wizards' (HME XII.384–5). Tolkien's final thoughts on this 'council of good wizards' transformed it in *The Lord of the Rings* into the White Council, composed of three wizards (Saruman the White, Gandalf the Grey, and Radagast the Brown) and the most powerful of the Elves (Galadriel of Lothlórien, Elrond of Rivendell, Círdan of the Havens, and a few others who are not identified but probably included Glorfindel; cf. *LotR*.61, 267–8, & 376 and 'Of the Rings of Power and the Third Age'; *Silm*.299–300).

Thus, while it is clear from the various Plot Notes that mere dramatic necessity required the wizard to leave Thorin and Company to their own devices for most of the second half of the story and that Tolkien had no particular idea of what the wizard was doing in the meantime (cf. Plot Notes A, page 296),† Tolkien's ultimate decision regarding what Gandalf had been up to evolved from a neat tying up of loose ends in the original *Hobbit* to have significant ramifications in the sequel. Ultimately, of course, it proved untrue (or at least premature) that 'the North [was] freed from that horror for many an age', since during the War of the Ring there was war in Mirkwood ('long battle under the trees and great ruin of fire' – *LotR*.1131), an invasion that occupied Dale (and presumably Esgaroth), and a second deadlier Siege of the Lonely Mountain that ended in the deaths of both the Lord of Dale and the King under the Mountain (ibid.), so it was not until the beginning of the Fourth Age some eighty years later, at the very end of Bilbo's extraordinarily long life, that Gandalf's prediction comes true.

†He never does provide any explanation of the means by which Gandalf reaches the far side of Mirkwood; presumably, given his aversion to entering the forest itself (see page 243), he rode not through but around the great forest by the south once Sauron had been defeated.

5 Compare the account of the Cottage of Lost Play, wherein Eriol hears all the stories that were to make up *The Book of Lost Tales* (BLT I.13ff).

6 Changed in pencil to 'Many elves were singing clear beside the river below his window'.

7 This earliest surviving text of the poem ('Sing All Ye Joyful') is a careful fair copy, clearly preceded by drafting that does not survive. Aside from changes in capitalization, punctuation, and indentation, all its lines are

identical to the published version, but the sequence of the last four was shifted:

Sigh no more Pine, till the wind of the morn!
Fall Moon! Dark be the land!
Hush! Hush! Oak, Ash, and Thorn!
Hushed be all water, till dawn is at hand!

Their re-arrangement was a late change, since the original sequence occurs in both the continuation of the First Typescript (1/1/69:2–3) and the corresponding page from the Second Typescript (1/1/50:3), both made in 1936.

The only other notable feature of this poem is its reference to the moon being 'in flower'. Rather than a poetical conceit of a piece with the flowering stars, this may be an allusion back to 'The Tale of the Sun and Moon', where the Moon was formed from the last blossom of Silpion the Silver Tree (BLT I.191).

8 It is perhaps an indicator of the change in Bilbo brought about by his adventures that whereas at the end of Chapter III he goes 'to see the elves dance and sing' (page 116), now he joins in with their dancing.

9 Added here in pencil are the words 'B.'s first poem'. This refers of course to 'Roads Go Ever Ever On', which Tolkien apparently considered inserting at this point. For more on this, the third interpolated poem in this final chapter, see Text Note 13 below.

10 Added at this point, mostly in the left margin:

> Each was on a pony and they led also a third [> another] laden with many things – including Bilbo's little treasure chests.

This was apparently added to set up a scene a few paragraphs later wherein Bilbo's treasure would be swept away during a river-crossing; see Text Note 11.

11 The three preceding paragraphs, which would have culminated in Bilbo's pack pony losing the treasure in the rushing water (see the first line of Plot Notes F: 'Bilbo's treasure all lost on the way home'), were all cancelled in the manuscript (Third Phase manuscript page 41 [> 42]; 1/1/20:4). The word 'pony' is changed to 'pack-pony' in the last line, and there is a cancelled partial word, 'wh', after 'the steep bank'; I suspect that Tolkien began to write 'wh*ere*' – that is, where they had trouble with the ponies just before meeting the trolls on the outward journey. At any rate, this is clearly the same river described in Chapter II, as Tolkien makes explicit in the typescript: 'They came to the river that marked the very edge of the borderland of the Wild, and to the ford beneath the steep bank, which you may remember' (Marq. 1/1/69:3; cf. DAA.358). It may be significant that when Tolkien returned to re-envision *The Hobbit* in 1960, the first new scene he inserted into the story dealt with Bilbo's troubles at a river-crossing; perhaps the idea of this abandoned scene stayed in his mind for the almost thirty years that intervened.

12 The one-year's journey of the published book is finally unambiguously in effect, as opposed to the longer time-frame of the original (Second Phase) draft; cf. Bilbo's remark about may-time a few lines earlier. '. . . so long ago' was later altered to 'ten <illegible> at least'; the illegible word does not look like *years* but might possibly be *may*[s] – i.e., that ten Mays rather than just one have passed since he was last here.

13 At the bottom of this page (Third Phase manuscript page 41 [> 42]; Marq. 1/1/20:4), immediately below this paragraph, Tolkien has added in hasty pencil

> and could see the woods upon the Hill. The[n] Bilbo
> stopped & said suddenly – the poem
> 'Something is the matter with you Bilbo' said G.
> 'You are not the hobbit you were.'
> And so they passed

– i.e., 'passed *the bridge and came right back to Bilbo's own door*'. The poem alluded to here (see also Text Note 9 above) is 'Roads Go Ever Ever On'; see part v of the commentary following this chapter, beginning on page 723.

Note that it is still the Mill (clearly to be seen in the foreground of all Tolkien's versions of the Hobbiton illustration; cf. Plate IV [top]), which is the landmark here and not the Green Man or the Green Dragon Inn.

14 The original name of Bilbo's cousins, the Allibone Baggins, was altered to *Sackville* Baggins in pencil here and *Sackville*-Baggins (that is, with the hyphen) two paragraphs later; this change probably dates to the period of the book's preparation for publication in 1936, and the latter form appears in the typescript (1/1/69:5). I am unable to explain the exact significance of 'Allibone', which probably originated not as part of their surname but in reference to a place (i.e., to distinguish between the *Allibone* Bagginses and the *Bag-End* Bagginses). Certainly it seems unlikely that Tolkien here was alluding to any real person with this name, such as Samuel Austin Allibone (a leading figure in the Sunday School movement and compiler of the *Critical Dictionary of English Literature and British and American Authors* [1854 & 1871]), journalist and travel/nature writer Thomas Allibone Janvier [d.1913], or physicist T. E. Allibone (a much younger colleague of Rutherford), just as *Sackville* almost certainly derives not from the Elizabethan poet Thomas Sackville (*A Mirror for Magistrates*, *Gorboduc*) nor literary personality V. Sackville-West (a friend of Virginia Woolf's) but rather is simply as T. A. Shippey points out a comic variant between *sack* and *bag*: *Sack*ville vs. *Bag*gins (*The Road to Middle-earth*, expanded edition [2003], page 72). Rather, I would argue that 'Allibone' is a variant of *Alboin*, the name Tolkien gave one of the two main characters in his time-travel story *The Lost Road* [circa 1936] in which one of the main characters states 'at school . . . they call me All-bone' (HME V.37). If so, its application to Bilbo's stay-at-home relatives is deeply ironic, for *Alboin* is the sixth-century Lombardic equivalent of the Old English *Ælfwine*

or 'Elf-friend',† and it is Bilbo rather than his cousins who has earned such a title.

†For more on Alboin the Lombard, a Germanic prince whose people gave their name to Italy's Lombardy region, see Christopher Tolkien's commentary on *The Lost Road*, HME V.53–5.

15 The very first page of the earliest draft of the sequel puts the matter nicely: '[Bilbo] had disappeared after breakfast one April 30th and not reappeared until lunchtime on June 22nd in the following year' (HME VI.13). As an encapsulation of his hobbit neighbors' point of view, this can hardly be bettered. According to the typescript of this final chapter (1/1/69:5) Bilbo returned home on June 2nd; this was changed to June 22nd in the page proofs (1/2/2: page 306).

16 The statement that among Bilbo's visitors in later years were *wizards* (note the plural) remains even in the most recent texts of the published book although the later conception makes it extremely unlikely that Radagast or Saruman, not to mention either of the long-missing Blue Wizards, dropped by during the years following Bilbo's return.

17 Just as with the 'lads *and lasses*' whom Bladorthin/Gandalf encouraged to go off and have their own adventures, we hear very little about Bilbo's nieces in the sequel; a few who would probably qualify for the title in the looser sense used in *The Lord of the Rings* appear or are referred to briefly (Caramella Took,† Angelica Baggins, Melilot Brandybuck, Pearl Took††) but play no role in the main story.

†HME VI.15. ††Cf. *Letters* page 295.

18 This is the first usage in the manuscript of the phrase that would give its name to the first chapter of the book, but it had already occurred in the First Typescript for Chapter XI:

> they used to call the little grassy space between the wall and the opening the 'doorstep' in fun, remembering Bilbo's words long ago at the unexpected party in his hobbit-hole
>
> —typescript page 113; Marq. 1/1/61:4.

19 At this point Tolkien started a new paragraph and wrote 'It was one of his jokes to put it on and open the door and if' but left the sentence unfinished and cancelled it. Cf. Bingo's tricks with Farmer Maggot in early drafts of 'A Short Cut to Mushrooms' (HME VI.96–7 & 292–3).

20 This marks the first appearance of the phrase that later became the book's subtitle.

21 In this final line 'pushed over' remained the reading in both typescripts (1/1/69:6 and 1/1/50:7), not being changed to 'handed him' until the page proofs (1/2/2: page 310), probably to avoid having readers think that Bilbo had accidentally knocked the jar over.

22 These four lines were re-sequenced by Tolkien, who wrote the numbers 3, 4, 1, and 2, respectively, in the left margin alongside them, shifting the lines to the order they have in the typescript version of this poem and the published book (DAA.359).

23 These last two lines, which seem to have formed the original conclusion of the poem, were cancelled in ink. The two lines that follow ('Yet feet . . . to home afar'), which I have bracketed and slightly indented here to set them apart, are written in ink over pencil underwriting, indicating a pause in composition before these replacements were drafted. The final four lines that follow the replacement lines have no such underwriting.

Unfortunately, the two highly interesting cancelled lines – with their parallel of 'never never gone' for journeys not taken with the 'ever ever on' of those that are now coming to an end – are in parts nearly illegible; the final *-h* of <?hath> is particularly dubious. Similarly, the word or words that end the next line could also be read '*find the bar*', which might be an allusion to the old notion of 'crossing the bar', made famous by Tennyson's poem of the same name ('Crossing the Bar' [1889]), with its imagery of sailing beyond the world into eternity; Tolkien had already used similar phrasing in the final stanza of his poem 'The Nameless Land' [written 1924, published 1927]; cf. Text Note 20 following Chapter XVII (page 675) and HME V.100.

On the other hand, if I am correct in reading this final, nearly illegible series of ligatures as 'Gondobar', then we have here another reference to the city more commonly known as *Gondolin*, one of the great elven kingdoms of the legendarium, which had already been mentioned by Elrond in Chapter III. At first glance its reappearance here might seem rather unlikely, but this variant of the name was particularly associated with Tolkien's poetry about voyaging to the Undying Land and glimpsing Tol Eressëa, as in the revised version of 'The Nameless Land' retitled 'The Song of Ælfwine', the two texts of which seem to date from circa 1936 and circa 1945, respectively:

O! Haven where my heart would be!
the waves that beat upon thy bar
For ever echo endlessly,
when longing leads my thoughts afar,
And rising west of West I see
beyond the world the wayward Star,
Than beacons bright in Gondobar
more clear and keen, more fair and high . . .

—'The Song of Ælfwine', 1936 version,
lines 51–58; emphasis mine†

and the later version of 'The Happy Mariners' [circa 1940]:

O happy mariners upon a journey far,
beyond the grey islands and past Gondobar,
to those great portals on the final shores . . .

—lines 23–25; HME II.275.††

†See HME V.100–104.
††See also Christopher Tolkien's commentary HME II.274 and HME V.104.

24 This line was partially cancelled and replaced by 'And [terror >] horror in the halls of stone', written at the end of the poem and marked for insertion at this point.

25 The text of this poem, which is given the pencilled title 'Bilbo's first poem', appears on a separate piece of paper (1/1/31) meant to be inserted into the final chapter somewhere around page 690; Tolkien wrote '41' in pencil in the upper right corner, making this the third 'page 41' in the Third Phase manuscript.† Its actual placement wavered; first Tolkien thought to insert it just before Bilbo's departure from Rivendell (see Text Note 9), then instead to give it on Bilbo's doorstep (see Text Note 13). Ultimately it is given its final placement, just as Bilbo glimpses 'his own Hill in the distance', in the first typescript (1/1/69:4); cf. DAA.359. Given his uncertainty, I have thought it best to offer it here as an appropriate coda for the story as a whole.

†The others being in the main Third Phase text just before the middle of the final chapter (numbered '40 > 41'; 1/1/20:3) and also the page bearing the inserted poem 'Sing All Ye Joyful' (numbered '<?top> 39 > 40 > 41').

26 Griffiths' (oral) account was initially broadcast as part of Ann Bonsor's 1974 Radio BBC Oxford tribute to Tolkien (produced by Humphrey Carpenter), along with other memoirs of Tolkien by friends (e.g., Nevill Coghill) and family; a transcription of Griffiths' contribution is reprinted in *The Annotated Hobbit* (DAA.12) and the original audiotrack was incorporated into Brian Sibley's *J.R.R. Tolkien: An Audio Portrait* (BBC [2001]) as part of CD 1, track 12.

27 Not to be confused with Clark Hall's 'Metrical' (verse) translation, published in 1914 and again in 1926 by Cambridge University Press.

28 That Allen & Unwin would contact an author they had never worked with before out of the blue like this to see if he was interested in undertaking a project for them was not unprecedented; coming across E. R. Eddison's translation of *Egil's Saga* (Cambridge University Press, [1930]), Stanley Unwin wrote to him asking if he would be interested in translating more sagas for Allen & Unwin. Engrossed in his own creative work, Eddison declined, but the episode shows Unwin's willingness to seek out potential authors and scholars rather than wait for them to come to him. This correspondence is now in the Bodleian (Ms. Eng. Misc. e 456/1, fol. 123 & 124).

(i)

Dain son of Nain

One of the most appealing of all Tolkien's dwarven characters, Dain of the Iron Hills plays a small but crucial role in *The Hobbit*, essentially stepping in to fulfill Thorin's role after Thorin is no longer capable of doing so himself, first because he succumbed to dragon-sickness and then because of his death. That Thorin was to die was a late development, not present at all in the Second Phase: there is no hint of it in any of the Plot Notes, and clear indication to the contrary as late as Bilbo's discussion with Thorin after the battle in Plot Notes D. Even when Tolkien concluded that Bilbo would be unable to resolve the crisis and lift the siege without a battle (Plot Notes F), the idea of bringing a dwarven army to the scene was one of the last plot-points to emerge: no such army is described as playing a part in the Plot Notes B/C/D sequence or Plot Notes E, and their listing among the seven forces present in Plot Notes F could mean just the thirteen members of Thorin & Company; in any case the word 'dwarves' on that list is circled in pencil, as if for removal or further development: Dain himself nowhere appears until the Third Phase. Like Bard (or, later, Arwen in *The Lord of the Rings*), Dain is a character Tolkien introduces abruptly to fill a specific plot-function – in this case, to bring a dwarven army to the fight at the Mountain – but with his usual keen eye to potentialities, once the character is present Tolkien makes good use of him. Nothing in fact anticipates Thorin's death scene in the original manuscript until Gandalf actually ushers Bilbo into the dying dwarvenking's tent, but once Tolkien had made the surprising decision to drive home the cost of victory with the tragic but heroic death of the second most important character in the book,[1] he needed someone else to fill Thorin's role as the new King under the Mountain, dealing out treasure and restoring the lost realm so that the prophecies could come true.

In a sense, Dain is to Thorin as Faramir is to Boromir in *The Lord of the Rings*: the close kinsman who avoids the fall from grace of his elder. Even Gandalf at one point describes himself after his return as Gandalf the White as being Saruman as he was supposed to be ('The White Rider', *LotR*.516). It is easy, in retrospect, to forget Thorin's or Boromir's virtues even after their heroic deaths and dying renunciations of their misdeeds, but an unprejudiced reading of the First Phase and Second Phase *Hobbit* (and indeed the bulk of the published book, right up to the dwarves' discussion of the treasure at the end of Chapter XII) shows Thorin as a capable leader, fair in his judgments, determined to leave none behind, and courageous (although not to the point of being willing to beard the dragon who destroyed his people in its lair). Dain is all this and more: Thorin as he is meant to be, who either because of the example of Thorin's fall before him or more likely because of an unshakable bedrock of good sense and a lack of *ofermod* (again, cf. Faramir's ability to avoid repeating Boromir's mistakes) is able to resist the dragon-sickness. Dain deals out the treasure fairly, keeps his bargains, and establishes good relations with his neighbors – all the things Thorin should have done and that we like Bilbo expected him to do based on our experience of him prior to his glimpsing the dragon-gold. The good effects of King Dain's reign are already apparent by the time of the Epilogue – a brief glance ahead ten years that enables us to see the fulfillment of Thorin's dream to re-establish the Kingdom under the Mountain as a thriving dwarven haven for Durin's Folk at peace with its neighbors and no longer surrounded by desolation – and Glóin in 'Many Meetings' (*LotR* Bk II Ch. I) gives a glowing report of their progress in the decades since.

That Thorin's heir proves to be a new character, Dain, and not one of Thorin's companions – say, his second-in-command Balin or perhaps Fili and Kili, already established as his great-nephews – might have surprised some readers among whom Tolkien circulated the original version of the story (e.g., C. S. Lewis), especially since *Beowulf*, which had a marked influence on the closing chapters, provided the parallel of an old king dying and being succeeded by a relatively unknown much younger kinsman. But the two young dwarves' descent is through the female line, being the grandsons of Thorin's sister (the sons of his sister in the published text and later family trees), whereas the patriarchal dwarves obviously trace the kingship through the male line; it is indeed possible that the deaths of Fili and Kili were added to the story during the typescript stage precisely to avoid such confusion. Then too whereas strict patrilineal descent became the norm during feudalism (with sometimes disastrous results when a small child inherited the throne and left a country with a decade or two of regencies while he grew up), in the 'heroic' cultures that preceded feudalism a closely-related capable adult male (brother, uncle, nephew) often succeeded instead of a son.[2] As Thorin's first cousin,[3] the battle-hardened Dain, who proved himself a loyal kinsman by coming at once to Thorin's aid and who had already accomplished heroic deeds in killing Bolg's father in the goblin war, is obviously an eminently suitable candidate to re-establish the Kingdom under the Mountain.

For all his importance to the resolution of the story, however, Dain remains almost entirely in the background, his words and deeds reported at second hand. Despite this, like so many of Tolkien's 'minor' characters his personality and character come across clearly, revealing him as the most sensible and ultimately quite possibly the most fortunate of all Tolkien's dwarves (with the exception of the legendary Durin and possibly also of Gimli Glóinson in his later career as described in the Appendices of *The Lord of the Rings*). We know he proves to be an excellent king and have already noted his fairness in sharing out treasure (the *sine qua non* for being a great king or 'ring-giver' according to the Anglo-Saxon heroic code – at least according to the surviving poetry);[4] that his generosity and sense of fair-play go beyond merely keeping his word or fulfilling Thorin's bargains is shown by his giving Bard the Necklace of Girion, clearly a fabulous treasure, above and beyond the one-fourteenth share that was supposed to settle Bard's claim on the treasure. His chief defining characteristics seem to have been an unshakable practicality, a keen appreciation of his own limits, and willingness to aggressively defend a good cause. In the later story ('Durin's Folk', *LotR* Appendix A part iii) he answers Thrain's call to avenge Thror's murder and fights heroically at Moria, killing Bolg's father (clearly a great feat, even within the context of the original *Hobbit*, since Gandalf has heard of it) but stops short of over-reaching and prevents Thrain from re-claiming Moria since the peril that originally drove them from Durin's halls remains (i.e., the Balrog). Similarly, within *The Hobbit* he comes at once to aid Thorin but does not hesitate to ally with the Elvenking and Bard when the goblins arrive, nor to drop old grudges and negotiate a fair peace after the battle. Later (*LotR*.257–8) he allows Balin to found his own dwarf-colony, despite his personal misgivings, which prove to have been fully justified. At one point Tolkien even considered making him the keeper of one of the dwarven Rings of Power (HME VI.398); although this proved to be only a passing thought it shows his high regard for the character. And Dain is wise enough to resist temptation when Sauron sends messengers with promises of Rings of Power and, unlike his ally King Brand, to realize that attempts to appease the Dark Lord are useless; instead he sends warnings to Bilbo and representatives to the Council of Elrond. One could argue that Gimli goes with the Fellowship not just as a representative of dwarves in general but as one of Dain's folk, the people of Durin, in particular.

As Tolkien eventually developed him, Dain thus plays a large role in the history of his people throughout the last two and a half centuries of the Third Age, contributing in no small part to their survival into the Fourth Age through a remarkable career on a par with those of Thorin and Balin: fighting heroically at Moria when young and killing the leader of the goblin army, thus personally avenging Thror's murder ('held a great feat, for Dáin was then only a stripling in the reckoning of the Dwarves' – *LotR*.1112), leading one of the namesake armies in The Battle of Five Armies (where victory enables him to re-establish the Kingdom under the Mountain with the survivors), and finally dying heroically in the War of the Ring fighting over the body of his fallen friend defending the Front Gate from Sauron's armies (*LotR*.1116; 'The Quest of Erebor', *Unfinished Tales*, page 326). Even more important was his maintenance of a safe haven for Durin's Folk first in the Iron Hills and then later in the Lonely Mountain, since we are told 'It is because of the fewness of women among them that the kind of the Dwarves increases slowly, and is in peril when they have no secure dwellings' (*LotR*.1116), especially when we juxtapose this with Thrain and Thorin's group in the Blue Hills whose numbers were apparently few and increased only very slowly, a fact directly linked to the statement that 'They had very few women-folk' (ibid.1113), Thorin's sister Dís being a rare exception.

Since we do not know how old Dain was supposed to be in the original story, we cannot say whether he like Thror, Thrain, Thorin, and Balin was a survivor of Smaug's attack or whether he was born in the Iron Hills after the event; from the lack of any statement to the contrary it seems probable that in the original conception the Iron Hills settlement was founded by refugees from Erebor, whereas in the later story the colony in the Iron Hills had been founded by Thror's brother (Grór) at the time the dwarves were driven out of the far North (i.e., the Grey Mountains) long before Dain's birth (*LotR*.1109 & 1117), meaning that Dain was certainly born there and was still a small child (only three years old) when Smaug destroyed Thror's nearby kingdom. In this later story, most of the survivors of the catastrophe join Grór in the Iron Hills ('It was afterwards learned that more of the Folk under the Mountain had escaped than was at first hoped; but most of these went to the Iron Hills' – *LotR*.1110), and it is clear that the Iron Hills settlement was the largest and most thriving community of the Longbeards, much larger than Thorin's smaller halls in the distant Blue Hills. For example, Thorin dreams in 'The Quest of Erebor' (*Unfinished Tales*, page 322) of raising a dwarven army to reclaim his lost kingdom but is advised by Gandalf to take only a small trustworthy group, whereas in the original story there is nothing to contradict the conclusion that the Heir of Durin can only manage to gather a band of a dozen followers; by contrast Dain at short notice can bring five hundred warriors to the spot.[5]

Finally, there is the matter of Dain's name, nomenclature always being important in Tolkien's stories. Like the rest of *The Hobbit*'s dwarves (with the possible exception of Balin, already noted), Dain and his father both take their names from the *Dvergatal*; although they do not appear in all manuscripts of the *Voluspá* (see Dronke, pages 10 & 90) they are both in Snorri's list (*Prose Edda* page 41). However, unlike most of these dwarf-names, Dain's name also appears elsewhere, in a variety of different contexts and applications, some rather puzzling. Thus while we are told in *Heidreks Saga*[6] that Tyrfing, a cursed sword which must kill somebody every time it is unsheathed, was made by the dwarfs *Durin* and *Dvalin* (i.e., Tolkien's 'Dwalin'), Snorri in the *Skáldskaparmál* tells a very similar story of a sword called *Dainslaf* ('Dain's heirloom'), used in the Endless Battle between Hedin and Högni (*Prose Edda* page 121);[7] the sword's title implies that 'Dain' was recognized in Norse lore as a famous dwarven maker of weapons. Oddly enough, another of the *Elder Edda*'s poems, the *Hávamál*,[8] tells of another Dain who is the king of elves:

> *Odin for the Æsir [gods], Dain for the elves,*
> *Dvalin for the dwarfs,*
> *Asvid for the giants . . .*
>
> —*Hávamál*, stanza 143; Terry, *Poems of the Elder Edda*, page 31.

We are also told, in the *Gylfaginning*, that the World-Tree Yggdrasil has four harts living in its branches, named Dáin, Dvalin, Duneyr, and Durathrór (*Prose Edda*, page 45). By contrast, I have found no other references to *Nain*, a name which neither Dronke nor Young translates but which probably means 'near' (cf. E. V. Gordon, *An Introduction to Old Norse*, page 371), although it is certainly a remarkable coincidence that *nain* is actually the French word for 'dwarf' (e.g., cf. Madame D'Aulnoy's 1698 fairy tale *Le Nain Jaune*, translated into English as 'The Yellow Dwarf'). While the scattered references to Dain in the Old Norse sources do not seem to cohere into a single figure, someone who like Tolkien was creating a new mythology out of the incoherent fragments of lost myth[9] might well have concluded that the original Dain had once been a figure of some significance, associated in some way with kingship and with those famous dwarves Durin and Dvalin, but whose story had been wholly lost.

NOTES

1 As the leader of the expedition, Thorin has more lines of dialogue than any other character except Bilbo, and he is present through far more chapters than, say, Gandalf. At first Thorin's sudden death – shocking within the traditions of classic British children's fantasy (e.g., Carroll, Grahame, Milne, Lofting, Nesbit)† – would seem to reverse Tolkien's theory of eucatastrophe, the sudden unexpected happy ending to the tale, but in fact the eagles' arrival that turns the tide serves as the eucatastrophe that makes *The Hobbit* a successful fairy-story within Tolkien's own conception of the genre. Thorin's death, and the later addition of those of Fili and Kili, serve rather to ground the eucatastrophe and prevent the book from being 'escapist' in a negative sense: in Tolkien's terms they confirm 'the existence of *dyscatastrophe*, of sorrow and failure: the possibility of these is necessary to the joy of deliverance; [eucatastrophe] denies (in the face of much evidence, if you will) universal final defeat' (OFS.62).

† MacDonald, who shared the late Victorian sentimentality over early death, is the chief and notable exception to this rule, but Thorin's death is quite unlike anything in MacDonald except perhaps the death-in-combat of the narrator of *Phantastes* [1858], and even there the author's interest is primarily in the character's first-person description of what happens to him immediately following his death.

2 See for instance in *Beowulf*, where Beowulf is offered the throne after his uncle Hygelac's death but insists it go to his young cousin, Hygelac's son, instead. Similar non-direct successions can be found in sources as widely ranged as *Hamlet* (based on Saxo Grammaticus's twelfth-century *Geste Danorum*), where Prince Hamlet is passed over for his father's throne in favor of his uncle Claudius, the early history of Islam (where Mohammad is succeeded as the first caliph by his father-in-law, not by his closest male relative, his cousin and son-in-law), and English history, which especially in early Norman times provides all too many examples.

3 That is, if I am right in my guess that Thrain and Nain were brothers in Tolkien's original conception; see Text Note 13 following chapter XVII. Already by the time of the earliest family tree in the late 1940s Thorin and Dain had become the children of cousins – that is, third cousins or as hobbits would no doubt say each was the other's 'second cousin once removed', descendants of a common great-grandfather – which they remained thereafter; see HME XII.277 and *LotR*.1117. For the idea of Thorin having close kin somewhere in the area that he could call upon in extremity, see his remark to the Great Goblin in Chapter IV: 'We [are] on a journey to our relatives, our nephews and nieces and first, second, and third cousins and other descendants of our grandfathers who live on the East side of these truly hospitable mountains' (page 132); this passage contains the first germ that eventually led to Dain and his band of five hundred hardened warriors marching from the Iron Hills.

4 See for example in *Beowulf* the elaborate comparison between Sigemund the dragon-slayer (= Sigurd) and bad King Heremod (lines 875–915), of whom it is said *nallas beagas geaf Denum aefter dome* – translated by Howell Chickering as 'never a ring did he give, for glory, to the Danish men', adding 'Joyless he lived and unhappy he died' (*Beowulf: A Dual-Language Edition*, lines 1719–1721, tr. Howell D. Chickering Jr. [1977]).

5 Thus the question arises: why did Thror, Thrain, and Thorin not themselves settle in the Iron Hills and merge their group with the larger settlement of their kin already established there? Tolkien nowhere addresses this issue, but one suspects that King Thror wished neither to usurp his brother's halls nor dwell in them as a guest and that his son and grandson were similarly proud and independent.

6 *The Saga of King Heidrek the Wise*, ed. & tr. Christopher Tolkien [1960], page 68.

7 Tolkien explicitly refers to the story of Högni and Hedin's endless battle in his essay 'The Name "Nodens"' (*Report on the Excavation . . . in Lydney Park* [1932], page 133).

8 This is the same source from which Tolkien had two or three years earlier taken the name 'Fimbulfambi' as the last King under the Mountain; see page 15.

9 Cf. Jonathan Evans on Tolkien's dragon-lore; see Note 2 to the commentary on 'Tolkien's Dragons' following Chapter XII (page 538).

(ii)
Bolg of the North

Bolg of the North plays a far less dramatic part in the Third Phase manuscript than will eventually develop in the typescript (see below) and final book. Nonetheless he is remarkable as one of only two goblins to gain the distinction of a name in the original edition of *The Hobbit* (if we exempt

'The Great Goblin' as a title).[1] The parallelism between 'Bolg of the North' and 'Gondobad of the North', when laid alongside Bladorthin's earlier admonition that the North End of the Misty Mountains was 'stiff with goblins, hobgoblins, and orcs of the worst description' (page 244), suggests that Mount Gundabad might have been Bolg's capital. In any case, like Morgoth's forces in the earlier tales in the legendarium, the goblins of Bilbo's time seem clustered in the north; only after their devastating defeat in the Battle of Five Armies do Bilbo and Gandalf, accompanied by Beorn, dare to take the northern route around Mirkwood.

Also in the Third Phase, we learn more about the famed goblin-dwarf war, although the full story has to wait until 'Durin's Folk' (specifically *LotR*.1110–13). That it was fought to avenge the death of Thror was already clear from Thorin's comment in Chapter I that the 'goblins of Moria have been repaid' as he considers going after the Necromancer to exact similar vengeance for Thrain (page 73). It is not yet revealed that Moria is an ancestral dwarven city overrun by goblins, and on the whole it seems likely that this idea had not yet arisen when Tolkien was working on *The Hobbit*; he may have conceived of Moria at this time as simply a goblin stronghold, probably mines worked by those unfortunates who have been captured and made slaves by the goblins (a fate Bilbo and the others narrowly escaped thanks to Bladorthin's timely intervention). Certainly similar mines were an omnipresent threat to the elves of Beleriand in early versions of the legendarium: Flinding bo-Dhuilin (known in the published *Silmarillion* as Gwindor of Nargothrond) is one example of the terrible changes wrought by long captivity in 'the mines of the north' (cf. 'Turambar and the Foalókë' [BLT II.78–79], 'The Lay of the Children of Húrin' [HME III.36], the 1926 'Sketch' [HME IV.29], the 1930 *Quenta* [HME IV.124], *Silm*.207, et al.). All we know for certain is that the goblin-dwarf war took place more than a century ago (page 73), was famous (Bilbo expects Bard and the Elvenking to have heard of it – page 662) and that the Battle of the Mines of Moria was a significant encounter in that campaign, since it was there that Dain killed Bolg's father (page 670) – although we could probably also have guessed this from the fact that 'Moria! Moria!' is one of the battle-cries of Dain's dwarves when they attack Bolg's goblins.[2] Finally, we can reasonably conclude that the dwarves must have won the war, since Thrain, Thorin, and Dain all survived and Bolg's father did not; more significantly, Thorin considers that it settled the score over his grandfather's death (which would not have been the case with a dwarven defeat or even stalemate). In the later development of the Moria story, the battle was made more devastating for both sides (Thorin's brother, Dain's father, and Balin's father all died there, and Thrain was permanently disfigured – *LotR*.1117 & 1112), and the mortality so high as to make it unlikely that a significant portion of the forces Dain brings with him a century and more later in answer to Thorin's call could be survivors of that battle (or that many, if any, of the goblins now facing them were veterans of the same combat).

Magol

One of the most interesting things about Bolg is of course his name, which is neither Norse (like the dwarves') nor Sindarin/Noldorin (like most of the other personal and place names within *The Hobbit*). Instead, it comes from one of Tolkien's minor invented languages, called *Mago* or *Magol*, about which little is known other than that at one point Tolkien considered making it the Orkish language, only to reject this idea. In that tongue, *bolg* is an adjective meaning 'strong' (Magol document, page 3) – an eminently suitable name for a great goblin-chief.[3]

However, it may be significant that another similar name, later identified as Noldorin, is given to an Orc leader in 'The Lay of Leithian' and the 1930 *Quenta*. This *Boldog*[4] was a captain whom Morgoth sent to raid Doriath to capture Lúthien; his importance may be guessed not just from the fact that he is one of only two orcs (the other being Bolg) named in the legendarium before *The Lord of the Rings*. Even more significantly, originally Morgoth had ordered Thû (the Necromancer; the later Sauron) to undertake that mission ('The Lay of the Children of Húrin', HME III.16 [lines 391–394] & 117 [lines 763–766]), which in slightly later parts of the legendarium was reassigned to Boldog instead:

> *A captain dire,*
> *Boldog, he sent with sword and fire*
> *to Doriath's march; but battle fell*
> *sudden upon him: news to tell*
> *never one returned of Boldog's host,*
> *and Thingol humbled Morgoth's boast.*
>
> —'*The Lay of Leithian*', lines 3670b–3675 – HME III.288.

In fact, Beren and his elven companions, trying to enter the Dark Lord's land disguised as orcs, claim to be part of Boldog's host when captured and questioned by Thû (ibid., lines 2121–2136; HME III.229). That Boldog's raid was no minor skirmish but a major battle is indicated by the account in the 1930 *Quenta*:

> Assaults . . . there were on Doriath's borders, for rumours that Lúthien was astray had reached Angband. Boldog captain of the Orcs was there slain in battle by Thingol, and his great warriors Beleg the Bowman and Mablung Heavyhand were with Thingol in that battle.
>
> —HME IV.113.

A synopsis for the unwritten cantos of 'The Lay of Leithian' adds still more details:

> Thingol's army meets with the host of Boldog on the borders of Doriath. Morgoth has heard of the beauty of Lúthien, and the rumour of her wandering. He has ordered Thú and the Orcs to capture her. A battle is fought and Thingol is victorious. The Orcs are driven into Taur-na-Fuin† or slain. Thingol himself slays Boldog. Mablung Heavyhand was Thingol's chief warrior and fought at his side; Beleg was the chief of his scouts. Though victorious Thingol is filled with still more disquiet at Morgoth's hunt for Lúthien.
>
> †Mirkwood; cf. page 20.
>
> — HME III.311.

Obviously, Bolg in *The Hobbit* cannot be the same character as Boldog in the Silmarillion stories contemporary with its drafting (since the latter is killed by Thingol), but the parallel is interesting. Perhaps significant in this context is a late note [circa 1960] Tolkien wrote on the name 'Boldog' in which he stated that 'it is possible that *Boldog* was not a personal name, and either a title, or else the name of a kind of creature: the Orc-formed Maiar, only less formidable than the Balrogs' (X.418). That is, according to this line of thought, evil Maiar in Morgoth's service sometimes incarnated themselves into orcish form in order to command orc troops, and 'boldog' was the generic term for these, no more individualized than, say, *Nazgûl*. For more on Maiar incarnating themselves as super-orcs ('orcs of the worst description', perhaps?), see commentary on page 138.

Orcs

Finally, there is the question of whether Bolg was a normal goblin, despite his rank as leader of the goblin-horde, or something more. The original Third Phase text offers no clues on this point, but the account of the Battle of Five Armies as developed in the typescript that followed does, and suggests that he was in fact an Orc, not merely a goblin (cf. in a later account the contrast between the rather puny goblins of the Misty Mountains against the much more dangerous Orcs of Mordor – not to mention Saruman's Uruk-hai – in *LotR*.467–8, 472, 473–4). Thus in the typescript and published book, the core of the goblin army around which it rallies after the elf-dwarf-human alliance stems the first onslaught is 'the bodyguard of Bolg, goblins of huge size with scimitars of steel' (typescript 1/1/67:6, DAA.343; contrast page 671 of this book). Similarly, Thorin's charge fails when he comes up against Bolg's honour guard: 'Thorin drove right against the bodyguard of Bolg. But he could not pierce their ranks . . . The bodyguard of Bolg came howling against them, and drove in upon their ranks like waves upon cliffs of sand' (DAA.344). Later Bilbo learns that after Thorin fell, presumably because of injuries inflicted by Bolg's guard if not Bolg himself, Beorn arrives and attacks like an unstoppable force: 'He scattered the bodyguard, and pulled down Bolg himself and crushed him. Then dismay fell on the Goblins and they fled in all directions' (typescript 1/1/68:2–3, DAA.349–50; contrast pp. 679–80 in this book).

The clear distinction between Bolg and his guard on the one hand and the average goblin of the horde on the other certainly carries over into the description of the Battle of Moria in Appendix A of *The Lord of the Rings*, where it is said of his father that Azog 'was a great Orc with a huge iron-clad head, and yet agile and strong. With him came many like him, the fighters of his guard' (*LotR*.1112). Thus the preponderance of evidence, though indirect, shows that Bolg in *The Hobbit* is far more than a mere goblin – in fact an Orc in all but name.

NOTES

1 The other, of course, being *Golfimbul* (or, in the First Phase text, *Fingolfin*) of Mount Gram, killed by Bullroarer Took in the Battle of the Green Fields. Mount Gram appears only in this context, but this may merely be another name for Gondobad/Gundabad, not least because 'Gram' is a Norse name (famous as the name of Sigurd's sword forged or reforged by Regin) and thus would seem to belong to the area north and east of Bilbo's home and because the Misty Mountains, which are particularly associated with the goblins throughout *The Hobbit*, also seem to be the mountains closest to Bilbo's home (cf. Bilbo's never having seen a mountain before, page 111).

As for *Azog*, while we are told in the manuscript that Dain killed Bolg's father at Moria, Azog's name does not enter the story until the 1960 Hobbit (see page 781), nor see print within *The Hobbit* until the third edition of 1966 (cf. DAA.56 and 339), having arisen during the creation of the Appendices for *The Lord of the Rings* (contrast HME XII.276, where in early drafts of this material old Thror is 'slain in the dark by an Orc' in Moria, with the specific references to Azog in HME XII.284 and *LotR*.1110–12).

2 Note that Nain's forces chant 'Azog! Azog!', the name of their hated enemy, when they join the attack at the Battle of Moria (*LotR*.1112); hence, Dain's dwarves in *The Hobbit* chant 'Moria! Moria!' as a reminder of the atrocity they wish to avenge on Bolg's goblins (that is, the death of Thror). There is of course a long tradition of battle-cries that evoke famous defeats ('Remember the Maine!' 'The Alamo!') as well as victories.

3 A probable real-world source for the name comes from the *Fir Bolg*, one of the mythical races of Ireland whose deeds are retold in the

twelfth-century *Lebor Gabála Érenn* (or Book of Invasions) along with those of the *Fomorians* and the *Tuatha dé Danaan*. Tolkien was well-versed in this mythic material (see page 427), and his attention might have been drawn to the name by John Rhys's claim in *Celtic Britain* [1884] that *Bolg* was probably an Ivernian name – that is, that it came from the pre-Indo-European language of the British Isles (Rhys, pp. 268 & 281).† Since this is the same book from which Tolkien took the word *ond* (Ivernian for 'stone') and adapted it into Sindarin, it is entirely plausible that it may have influenced him in other borrowings as well.

†Rhys's theory has since been rejected, and scholars now believe that Ivernian, like Pictish, was a Celtic language closely related to British (the ancestor of Welsh), superseded by Gaelic (Irish).

4 David Salo glosses the name 'soldier of torment' (*A Gateway to Sindarin*, page 344) and points out that *The Etymologies*, written circa 1937–8, contain two entries on *Boldog*. The first (HME V.375, under the root **NDAK-**) identifies the *-dog* element as a variant of *daug*, meaning 'warrior' ('chiefly used of Orcs'), and suggests that Boldog might simply be a generic term for orc-warrior, although this last point seems rather doubtful. The second (HME V.377, under the root **ÑGWAL-**) gives *bol-* as a variant of *baul*, 'torment', as in the more familiar *bal*rog and states flatly that 'Orc-name *Boldog* = Orc-warrior "Torment-slayer"'.

(iii)
The Battle of Five Armies

As we have seen in the various Plot Notes, Tolkien's original idea was to have the Lonely Mountain chapters end with the Siege of the Mountain, where Thorin & Company (aided by the ravens) would be besieged by the wood-elves and lake-men until Bilbo and Gandalf could negotiate a peaceful ending to the impasse. This would then have been followed on Bilbo's return journey by the unnamed battle I have dubbed for ease of reference 'the Battle of Anduin Vale', which did not involve the dwarves but 'goblins of the Misty Mountains' and their allies the wargs, versus the wood-elves (with whom Bilbo goes to battle, armed in his elven mail), 'the men of the woods' (e.g., the wood-men dwelling on the western side of Mirkwood, described back in Chapter VI), 'men . . . from the south' (presumably the kin of the wood-men, who are said to have moved into the area from the south – page 205), and 'Beorn Medwed' leading 'a troop of bears'.[1] Conspicuous by their absence are the Eagles; more startling to readers familiar with the published story is the absence of any mention of the dwarves, Thorin and Company having remained in the east and Dain not yet having entered the story. Since this battle is said to take place 'in the west', it is no surprise that most of the participants are those associated with what later came to be known as the Vale of the Anduin: goblins, wargs, wood-men, and Beorn-Medwed (from Chapters IV, VI, & VII), plus the wood-elves from deeper in Mirkwood (Chapters VIII–IX). Hence the great climactic battle in the original conception (maintained throughout the Second Phase manuscript)[2] did not take place at the Lonely Mountain at all but somewhere between the Misty Mountains and Mirkwood; only with the advent of the Third Phase did Tolkien reach the decision to transform the stand-off at the Mountain into a dramatic all-out battle, which in turn necessitated the addition of Dain's five hundred dwarves.

Having ultimately decided upon a battle at the Lonely Mountain, initially Tolkien was in great uncertainty as to just who its participants would be. The name 'Battle of Five Armies' first appears in Plot Notes F, along with a marginal addition that seems to represent Tolkien's attempt to decide on which of the forces present counted as an 'army':

1	2	3	4	5			
woodelves,	dwarves,	eagles,	men,	bears	–	goblins	wolves
						6	7

From this, it seems rather that seven armies actually took part and the battle took its name from the five allies who oppose the forces of darkness (perhaps a distant precursor of the later Five Free Peoples who oppose Sauron in *The Lord of the Rings*: ents, elves, dwarves, men, and hobbits). We do not know for sure that 'men' here means only the Lake-men nor that 'dwarves' means Dain's army and not just Thorin & Company's heroic charge, but both seem likely. The plural in 'bears' implies that the idea of Beorn-Medwed's troop of bears is still present, but by the time Tolkien came to write the Third Phase text describing Beorn's role in the battle (which is then expanded upon in the typescript) the great were-bear had become solitary, as he remained in the published text. Neither the bats nor the sole hobbit are taken into account, apparently having negligible effect on the outcome; rather more surprisingly, the wizard is also omitted, while the ravens of the mountain (whom we might expect to battle the bats) make no appearance in any account of the battle, whether draft or outline.

Eventually Tolkien would determine that *the* five armies who gave the battle its name were the elves, the dwarves, the men, the goblins, and the wargs; the eagles and Beorn, while significant, did not really qualify as an 'army' per se.[3] Still, it is interesting that between the forces listed in the last page of Plot Notes B, in Plot Notes F, and in the Third Phase draft, almost all those Bilbo had encountered on his journey out were projected to be caught up in the grand climactic battle: only the trolls (who had been turned to stone), the storm-giants (who luckily for all concerned – cf. *Farmer Giles of Ham* – seem to have few dealings with others or to come down from their mountains), Gollum (who, according to the sequel, actually belatedly did make the journey seeking 'Baggins' in hopes of recovering his Ring; cf. *LotR*.70–71), and the spiders of Mirkwood (who clearly never range far from their own territory) are absent.

Herefugolas & Wælceasega

The idea of re-introducing some of the races and creatures who had appeared earlier in the story into the battle at the end (whether that battle took place at Erebor or west of Mirkwood), specifically the wolves and the eagles, may have a philological inspiration; if so it would be just another example of elements in *The Hobbit* arising out of Tolkien's professional work as an Anglo-Saxon scholar (he was, after all, at the time holder of the Rawlinson and Bosworth chair as Professor of Anglo-Saxon at Oxford, one of the most prestigious academic posts in Old English in the world). In his edition of the Old English *Exodus*, a spirited retelling in heroic alliterative verse of the Biblical story, Tolkien includes notes on the words *herefugolas* (literally, 'battle-birds') and *wælceasega* ('chooser of the slain' i.e. carrion-picker).[4] He notes the ancient and pervasive association in Old English heroic verse of wolves, ravens, and eagles (*The Old English* Exodus [1981], page 49), all eaters of carrion who are attracted to battlefields and all of whom he believed to be present in the scene thus described.[5] In these notes, he is careful to distinguish the carrion-pickers (*wælceasega* – a kenning for ravens) from the closely related *wælcyrige*, a word better known in its Old Norse form, *valkyrie*, 'derived partly from the actual carrion-birds of battle, transformed in mythological imagination; partly from the necromantic practices of female followers of Odinic magicians' (ibid., page 50). There are certainly no such followers at the Battle of Five Armies (but see below), but the association of ravens with wolves and with eagles may have turned Tolkien's mind back to earlier parts of the story and made him decide that rather than defusing one conflict only to follow it up with another, he could bring that traditional cluster of creatures together, along with others Bilbo had faced on his journey as enemies or allies to the Mountain itself, elevating the Siege into the great climactic battle of the book and expanding its scope beyond a merely local squabble into a great regional conflict that will decide the fate of that part of the world for years to come.

Bats as 'Children of Morgoth'

Finally, there are the bats, whose presence adds a note of horror to the proceedings. Indeed, the verbal image of them darkening the sky 'like a sea of locusts' was so vivid that Tolkien began a black, white, and red drawing of the scene (Plate XII [bottom]), although he did not complete it. That these are no ordinary bats is clear – for one thing, real-world bats are shy around people and only bite when grabbed and panic-strickened (in fact, they act exactly like the bats inside Smaug's lair, seen in Plate XI [top], who rather than swarming the solitary hobbit only bother him by accidentally making him drop his torch when he startles one). And of course blood-drinking 'vampire' bats are a very small sub-group (only three out of the eleven hundred known species of bats drink blood; two of those prey on birds, not mammals, and all three lap blood oozing from wounds rather than suck it) found only in Central and South America, certainly not part of the fauna of England (past and present) upon which Tolkien based almost all the other animals appearing in *The Hobbit*. Like the spiders of Mirkwood, the other conspicuous exception to Tolkien's general practice, these are clearly not natural animals but evil creatures in animal form, corresponding to real-world bats as wargs do to wolves. They are in fact yet another of the Children of Morgoth, who nowhere else take center stage but had lurked around the edges of the legendarium from 'The Lay of Leithian' onward.[6] For example, when Lúthien casts down Thû's tower,

bats unclean
went skimming dark through the cold airs
shrieking thinly to find new lairs
in Deadly Nightshade's branches dread.
—lines 2805b–2807; HME III.254

and Thû himself flees in bat-form:

A vampire shape with pinions vast
screeching leaped from the ground, and passed,
its dark blood dripping on the trees;
. . . for Thû had flown
to Taur-na-Fuin, a new throne
and darker stronghold there to build.[7]
—lines 2816–2818, 2820b–2822; HME III. 254–5.

Not long afterwards Lúthien herself assumes bat-form in order to sneak into Thangorodrim in disguise:

a batlike garb
with mighty fingered wings, a barb
like iron nail at each joint's end –
such wings as their dark cloud extend
against the moon, when in the sky
from Deadly Nightshade screeching fly
Thû's messengers.

—lines 3402–3408a; HME III.278–9.

These references to Thû's taking bat-form and Lúthien adopting the disguise of a great bat (specifically alluded to as an 'evil fay') also appear in the 1930 *Quenta* (HME IV.111–12), the form of the legendarium most closely associated with the original *Hobbit*, and were retained into the published *Silmarillion* (*Silm*.175, 178–9), in a text largely derived from the 1937 *Quenta Silmarillion* (HME V.295).

Within *The Hobbit* itself, the unnatural behavior of the bats (who although they do sometimes flock in great numbers are not carrion-eaters and thus would not follow an army as crows or ravens often did) was accentuated. Not only do they blot out the sun when they descend into the valley but 'swirled about the heads and ears of elves and men', adding to the chaos and confusion of the scene. Tolkien later (in the typescript, 1/1/67:5–6) added details that make the bats much more sinister, such as the bat-cloud's 'filling them with dread' as it whirls above the defenders, or most notably later in the battle when the bats 'fastened vampire-like on the stricken'.

One other example of bats allying with goblins to stage an attack very slightly postdates *The Hobbit*, having been written in December 1933, but is so nearly contemporaneous and so striking that it deserves special mention here. In the 1933 Father Christmas Letter, Fr. Christmas awakes to see a goblin looking in his window, despite the fact that that window faces out above a cliff several hundred feet high. He realizes that this 'meant there were bat-riding Goblins about – which we haven't seen since the goblin-war in 1453'. The goblins of the *Father Christmas Letters* are smaller than human-size (as are the elves whom we see in combat with them in this same letter's illustrations), but still these must have been extremely large bats, larger than any existing in the real world. The bat-messengers of Morgoth in the legendarium, such as Thuringwethil ('the messenger of Sauron', whose name means 'Woman of Secret Shadow'; *Silm*.178), were clearly of more or less human size, but these might have been were-bats rather than actual animals however enhanced since Lúthien can assume Thuringwethil's form and flying ability by putting on her 'bat-fell' (literally a bat-skin or bat-hide). We cannot tell exactly how large the bats accompanying Bolg's army were, but between the manuscript and the published book Tolkien did change the description of the bats in western Mirkwood from 'big' to 'huge'

(Chapter VIII) and those fastening on the fallen became not merely bats but 'great' bats (Chapter XVII). At any rate, they were certainly not large enough for goblins to ride or to combat eagles (in either of which cases they would have counted as an 'army' in themselves), and mainly served to darken the sky (thus providing cover for the sun-shy goblins), to prevent effective arrow-fire from the elves (who are, after all, legendary archers), and disconcert and dismay the defenders – at all of which they succeeded all too well.

NOTES

1 See the last page of the original Plot Notes B and the associated commentary (pp. 366 & 375–6) for more on 'the Battle of Anduin Vale' and its projected participants. The evidence that Beorn-Medwed associated with a large number of other bears, whom he could call upon at need, goes all the way back to the Second Phase text of Chapter VII, where Bladorthin describes following their host in secret and finds

> 'There must have been a regular bear-meeting outside here last night. I soon saw that Medwed could not have made them all – there were far too many of them, and they were of various sizes too: I should say little bears, big bears, ordinary bears, and gigantic big bears must have been dancing outside from dark to nearly dawn. They came from almost all directions except West from over the river, from the Misty Mountains.'

That night Bilbo sees this bear-moot in his dreams when he

> dreamed a dream of hundreds of black bears dancing slow heavy dances round and round in the moonlight in the courtyard.

For Tolkien's original audience's enthusiasm for bears, see the commentary following Chapter VII, page 253ff.

2 It is possible that this idea first arose in Plot Notes F, which represents a transitional stage between the Second and Third Phases. Here there is no hint that the battle might take place elsewhere, but that detail might simply not have been set down in these very sketchy notes; neither is it specifically stated that the battle described takes place at the Mountain, although that is the implication.

3 'So began the battle . . . And it was called after [i.e., afterwards] the Battle of Five Armies . . . For upon one side were the Goblins and the Wolves and upon the other were men, elves, and dwarves' (page 670; cf. DAA.339). This is remarkable, since the text is clear that the eagles played a decisive role in depriving the goblins of the devastating advantage they had claimed by seizing the high ground and that Beorn's intervention turned the tide; the typescript and published book differ from the Third Phase manuscript in denying the eagles a full share of credit for the victory, ascribing it chiefly to Beorn's assault.

4 This edition was not published in Tolkien's lifetime but appeared in 1981, edited by Joan Turville-Petre. Its exact dating is unknown; Turville-Petre simply says it was 'based on full notes for a series of lectures delivered to a specialist class in the 1930s and 1940s' (*The Old English* Exodus*: Text, Translation, and Commentary* by J. R. R. Tolkien, ed. Joan Turville-Petre [1981], page v). However, Tolkien had already given some of the poem's vocabulary a very close look during the period when he was drafting *The Hobbit* (i.e., the very early 1930s): he begins his detailed study of the unusual phrase *Sigelwara land* with a quote from *Exodus* in an article that appeared in the December 1932 issue of *Medium Ævum* (that is, published during the weeks when Tolkien was writing the Third Phase text) and had been announced in the journal's first issue back in May 1932† It thus seems quite possible that Tolkien's notes on *herefugolas* and *wælceasega*, or at least the thinking that underlies them, dates from the very early thirties.

†The second part of Tolkien's article did not appear until the June 1934 issue (Vol.III No.2).

5 In real life, ravens and wolves often form a symbiotic relationship: the ravens help spot the prey, the wolves make the kill, and the ravens get to feast on the carrion after the wolves have eaten their fill. See Bernd Heinrich's *Mind of the Raven* [1999], particularly the chapters describing ravens as 'wolf-birds' because of the close association between the two in the wild ('Ravens and Wolves in Yellowstone' and 'From Wolf-Birds to Human-Birds'). Bernd also includes a number of accounts of eagles feasting alongside ravens from the same corpses despite the generally hostile relations between the two types of bird (the predator-scavenger eagles and the scavenger-predator ravens).

6 Bats had of course already appeared in 'Goblin Feet', arguably the first piece of what became Tolkien's 'legendarium' to see print (*Oxford Poetry 1915*, pages 64–5; cf. DAA.113). But here they are not threatening ('pretty little flittermice'); like the 'goblins' themselves they are simply one more element of the elusive, gone-before-it-can-be-grasped little people. Hammond & Scull also see 'bat-like faces' on the curtains in Tolkien's early drawing 'Wickedness' [H-S#32], one of the pieces in *The Book of Ishness* [1911–13], but given these images' similarity to the Siamese cat that can just be glimpsed between the parted curtains of this image I suspect they are actually cats' heads instead (cf. *Artist & Illustrator*, pages 37 and 36).

7 'Deadly Nightshade' and Taur-na-Fuin are both alternative names for the same place, the dark forest elsewhere called Mirkwood. The tower Thû the Necromancer builds there after the escape described here is clearly the same Necromancer's tower in southern Mirkwood in *The Hobbit*, where Thrain died and which Bladorthin advises Bilbo to avoid; see page 244.

(iv)
'The Halls of Waiting'

'Farewell o gracious thief' said Thorin. 'I go now to the halls of waiting to sit beside my fathers until the world is renewed. The goblins have slain me. Since I leave now all gold and silver and go where it is of little worth, I wish to part in friendship with you, and would take back my words and deeds at the Gate.'

— page 679; cf. DAA.348.

This passage, with its interesting glimpse into the dwarven afterlife (or at least the dwarves' beliefs about what would happen to them after death), was completely without parallel in the legendarium when it was first written. Nothing so marks the distance between Tolkien's initial conception of the dwarves as set down in *The Book of Lost Tales*[1] and dwarves as presented in *The Hobbit* and *The Lord of the Rings* as this disagreement over their fate. From very early on in the legendarium the divergent fates of Men and Elves were a key part in the story: humans who die depart from the world and do not return; their souls leave Arda (Creation) altogether, whereas elves travel to the Halls of Mandos in Valinor to wait until they can be re-incarnated. Dwarves initially fit into neither of these categories – the occasional references in *The Hobbit* to 'Mortal Men' and the extremely long lifespans indicated for dwarves (Thrain having gone away a hundred years ago, many of Dain's band being hale and hearty veterans of a war that took place well before that, Thorin and Balin remembering events that the 153-year-old raven is too young to have experienced first-hand, the elvenking's threat to imprison Gandalf/Thorin for a hundred years before questioning him again) show they are not exactly mortal, or at least have a lifespan far, far beyond human years. As all readers of *The Lord of the Rings* know, Tolkien had his own definitions of mortal and immortal: 'Mortal Men' are 'doomed to die' (*LotR* ring-verse) because they have a finite lifespan and eventually die of sheer old age, unlike dragons (who 'live . . . practically for ever, unless they are killed' – DAA.55; cf. page 72) and elves (on the battlefield 'lay . . . many a fair elf that should have lived yet long ages merrily in the wood' – DAA.344; cf. page 672). Tolkien's elves are 'immortal' in that they do not die of age, disease, or natural causes, although they can be killed; as Tolkien says in his 1965 radio interview with Denys Gueroult, their life-spans extend to the habitability of this planet and 'longeval' might have been a better choice than 'immortal' as most understand the term.[2] And even if killed, elves are re-incarnated with the same memories, personalities, and (apparently) appearance, so that death is for them a temporary state, an interruption of their 'serial longevity' (*Letters* p. 267).

With the dwarves, in *The Hobbit* and subsequent works Tolkien created a third alternative. The early legendarium texts, in which dwarves play a relatively minor part, do not address the question of what happens after dwarves die, making Thorin's dying words (written in December 1932 or January 1933) the first time this issue had been addressed. Oddly enough, several years later (circa 1937), when Tolkien inserted several references to the dwarves' fate in various component texts that he hoped would go together to make up *The Silmarillion* (cf. HME V.167 & 202 and HME IV.284), his comments flatly contradict what had already been stated in *The Hobbit* and instead harken back to the *Book of Lost Tales* and 1930 *Quenta*. These new legendarium texts, written from an elvish point of view, suggest that dwarves are soulless and simply cease to exist upon death:

> Dwarves have no spirit indwelling, as have the Children of the Creator [i.e., elves and men], and they have skill but not art; and they go back into the stone of the mountains of which they were made.
>
> —'(Later) Annals of Beleriand', HME V.129.

Similar comments are made in the *Lhammas* (HME V.178), and the 1937 *Quenta Silmarillion* agrees that dwarves 'return unto the earth and the stone of the hills of which they were fashioned' (HME V.273). This is clearly an allusion back to Old Norse lore which we have already touched on back in the commentary following Chapter II (see Note 9 on page 109), particularly the fate of the dwarf Alvis in the *Elder Edda*, who is turned to stone at the end of the *Alvíssmál*. It also clearly cannot be reconciled with Thorin's dying words, and it was not long before the *Quenta Silmarillion* text was altered to bring it into accord with the concept alluded to in *The Hobbit*. The revised *QS* text reads

> *the Noldor believed* that the Dwarves have no spirit indwelling . . . and that they go back into the stone of the mountains of which they were made. *Yet others say that Aulë cares for them, and that Ilúvatar will accept from him the work of his desire, so that the Dwarves shall not perish.*
>
> —HME V.146; emphasis mine.

This is remarkable as the first instance[3] of the older legendarium being altered to match Bilbo's story; the newly published book clearly has gained an authority over as-yet unpublished material within what had till then been the more venerable main lineage, just as *The Lord of the Rings* would later gain authority over both, requiring further work on *The Hobbit* that became the Fourth Phase and Fifth Phase (the 1947 Hobbit and 1960 Hobbit, respectively). Further development of the ideas suggested in Thorin's dying speech appears in *The Lord of the Rings*' Appendix A ('Durin's Folk'), where it is noted that 'strange tales' of the dwarves' origins are told 'both by the Eldar and by the Dwarves themselves' (*LotR*.1108), one of which is the idea 'that there are no dwarf-women, and that the Dwarves "grow out of stone"' (*LotR*.1116) – so that what was once an authoritative statement is now dismissed as a 'foolish opinion' (ibid.). We also now meet with the story of Durin the Deathless (Durin I), who has been reincarnated five times (Durin II–VI) and has one remaining incarnation yet to come ('Durin VII & Last'; *LotR*.1108 & 1117); although each body dies, his time between lives is referred to as 'sleep' ('Till Durin wakes again from sleep' – *LotR*.334).

A full explication of Thorin's words, if any was needed, had to wait until the *Later Quenta* [circa 1951], which magisterially embraces and places into harmony all the previous discordant thoughts on the subject:

> [The Dwarves] live long, far beyond the span of Men, and yet not for ever. Aforetime the Noldor held that dying they returned unto the earth and the stone of which they were made; yet that is not their own belief. For they say that Aulë cares for them and gathers them in Mandos in halls set apart for them, and there they wait, not in idleness but in the practice of crafts and the learning of yet deeper lore. And Aulë, they say, declared to their Fathers of old that Ilúvatar . . . will . . . give them a place among the Children in the End. Then their part shall be to serve Aulë and to aid him in the re-making of Arda after the Last Battle.
>
> —HME XI.204.

With the exception of the passage about the dwarven spirits' activity during the period after their deaths – which seems to me to harken back to glimpses of the busy *swart-álfar* in some Norse sources, such as Snorri's *Prose Edda* – this corresponds exactly with Thorin's words, and provides the final clue of what he and the others will be waiting for: a challenge truly worthy of their skill, the chance to rebuild the world (Arda Marred) the way it should have been.[4]

NOTES

1 See the passage quoted on page 78 in the commentary following Chapter I (c). This is echoed in the 1930 *Quenta*, written about the time Tolkien wrote the First Phase of *The Hobbit* (i.e., the bulk of the opening chapter): 'the sons of Fëanor . . . made war upon the Dwarves of Nogrod and Belegost; but they did not discover whence that strange race came, nor have any since' (HME IV.103–4). The story of Aulë's creation of the dwarves (cf. *Silm*.43–4) did not arise until about the time of *The Hobbit*'s publication (i.e., a year or so after the completed typescript had been submitted to Allen & Unwin) in the '(Later) Annals of Beleriand'; see HME V.129 and 149. For the brief later development of the original negative, elven-centric view of the dwarves, see the passages cited on page 721 from the '(Later) Annals of Beleriand', the *Lhammas*, and the 1937 *Quenta Silmarillion*.

2 Note that Tolkien's friend C. S. Lewis, in what is perhaps his best book, *The Discarded Image* [posthumously published in 1964], names the chapter devoted to elves, nymphs, fauns, and fairies 'The Longaevi'; i.e., 'long-livers'.

3 That is, the first if we except the Arkenstone affecting the description of the Silmarils; cf. page 607.

4 For Tolkien, the chance for an artist to take part in actual Creation was the highest reward; cf. 'Leaf by Niggle'. For Tolkien's opinion that our own world was itself a sub-creation and that a writer might be able to contribute through his imaginative works in enriching the post-apocalyptic world that would succeed it, see my essay '"And All the Days of Her Life Are Forgotten": *The Lord of the Rings* as Mythic Prehistory', especially part v: '"We Make Because We Are Made": Tolkien's Sub-creative Theology', in *The Lord of the Rings 1954–2004: Scholarship in Honor of Richard E. Blackwelder*, ed. Wayne G. Hammond & Christina Scull [Marquette University Press, 2006].

(v)
Bilbo's First Poem

The decision to incorporate not one, not two, but *three* poems into the final pages of the story not only fleshed out the brevity of this part of the book (even with three poems inserted into the text, the final chapter is still one of the shortest) but marked a return to the lighter mood of the early chapters after the sadness of Thorin's death. We are told that 'it was very long before [Bilbo] had the heart to make a joke again' (page 679), and although we are told in passing that Yuletide was 'warm and merry' at Beorn's house (page 682), not until after the elves' second song are we shown that Bilbo has fully recovered, making 'many a merry jest and dance' (page 690). The inclusion of these songs also re-asserts a stylistic feature of the first half of the book: prose interrupted at unpredictable but frequent intervals by verse – a highly characteristic feature of both *The Hobbit* and *The Lord of the Rings* that sets them apart from all Tolkien's other work. Of the twenty-three poems in the published book, all but four occur in the first ten chapters, and only one of those chapters is altogether without a song (Chapter II).[1] The addition of the poems thus helps create a sense of 'back again' by paralleling a stylistic reversion with Bilbo's return to familiar regions.

Of these three poems, the first is more or less a continuation in much the same spirit of the elves' song in the trees back in Chapter III. The sense that the song has gone on all the time Bilbo has been away juxtaposed with its now incorporating details from Bilbo's adventures highlights the mix of timelessness and time's passing that is characteristic of Rivendell throughout *The Hobbit* and *The Lord of the Rings*; it also reinforces the message that life goes on. The next poem is notable chiefly for the exuberance of its opening stanzas (particularly the striking image of the lights in the night sky as 'windows of Night in her tower'), which segue into the lullaby of the second half. But it is the third poem, 'Roads Go Ever Ever On', which is most notable: a celebration of both the allure of possibilities of unending travel and the joy of homecoming by someone whose journeys are now ending.

Roads go ever ever on,
Over rock and under tree,
By caves where never sun has shone,
By streams that never find the sea;
Over snow by winter sown,
And through the merry flowers of June,
over grass and over stone,
And under mountains in the moon.

Roads go ever ever on
Under cloud and under star,
Yet feet that wandering have gone
Turn at last to home afar.
Eyes that fire and sword have seen
And horror in the halls of stone
Look at last on meadows green
and trees and hills they long have known.[2]

Poems about roads and wanderlust and homecoming ('there and back again', as it were) are of course not uncommon: the very first line of the very first published poem of the legendarium began 'I am off down the road', and the same poem's second half with 'I must follow' ('Goblin Feet', in *Oxford Poetry 1915*, page 64); the same volume contained fellow T.C.B.S. member G. B. Smith's poem about a Roman road, probably Smith's best poem and his most Tolkienesque piece:

This is the road the Romans made,
This track half lost in the green hills,
Or fading in a forest-glade
'Mid violets and daffodils.

The years have fallen like dead leaves,
Unwept, uncounted, and unstayed
(Such as the autumn tempest thieves)
Since first this road the Romans made.'[3]

A much closer parallel, however, to Bilbo's poem is E. F. A. Geach's 'Romance', which appeared in the same book as a reprint of 'Goblin Feet' (in fact, on the very next page following Tolkien's poem):

Round the next corner and in the next street
Adventure lies in wait for you.
Oh, who can tell what you may meet
Round the next corner and in the next street!
Could life be anything but sweet
When all is hazardous and new
Round the next corner and in the next street?
Adventure lies in wait for you.[4]

Geach's poem, while different in expression from Bilbo's, nonetheless nicely anticipates its spirit and also that of two similar poems in the sequel, 'The Road Goes Ever On' (see below) and the hobbits' walking song:

Still round the corner there may wait
A new road or a secret gate,
And though we pass them by today,
Tomorrow we may come this way
And take the hidden paths that run
Towards the Moon or to the Sun.

—*The Lord of the Rings*, page 91.

Similarly, Martin Simonson has pointed out how another of Tolkien's fellow Georgian poets, Edward Thomas (sometimes known as 'the English Frost' from his friendship and affinities with his American contemporary, poet Robert Frost, who outlived him by almost half a century) seems to anticipate Tolkien's poems in his own aptly-titled 'Roads':

Roads go on
While we forget, and are
Forgotten like a star
That shoots and is gone

The next turn may reveal
Heaven: upon the crest
The close pine clump, at rest
And black, may Hell conceal

Often footsore, never
Yet of the road I weary
Though long and steep and dreary
As it winds on forever[5]

In the end, whatever his inspirations for 'Roads Go Ever Ever On', once it was in existence it offered a prime example of Tolkien once again being his own most important source through creative recycling of earlier material. For the most significant poem that resembles 'Roads Go Ever Ever On' is of course Tolkien's own 'The Road Goes Ever On', which essentially provides a third and final stanza to the earlier poem, recited by Bilbo when he finally takes to the road again (*LotR*.48) and also by Frodo when he at length sets off on his own adventure (*LotR*.86–7):

The Road goes ever on and on
Down from the door where it began.
Now far ahead the Road has gone,
And I must follow, if I can,
Pursuing it with eager feet,
Until it joins some larger way,
Where many paths and errands meet.
And whither then? I cannot say.[6]

NOTES

1 The poems in *The Hobbit* are distributed thusly: two in Chapter I ('Chip the Glasses' and 'Far Over the Misty Mountains Cold', plus a refrain from the latter), 'O Where Are You Going' in Chapter III, the goblin song in Chapter IV ('Ho Ho My Lad'), the riddles (eight in all) in Chapter V, the second goblin song in Chapter VI ('Fifteen Birds'), the dwarf song in Chapter VII ('The Wind was on the Withered Heath'), Bilbo's spider songs ('Attercop' and 'Lazy Lob') in Chapter VIII, two river songs in Chapter IX ('Heave Ho Splash-plump' and 'Down the Swift Dark Stream You Go'), the Lake-men's song in Chapter X ('At the Mountain-king's Return'), then a gap before the dwarven song in Chapter XV ('The King is Come Unto His Hall', a reworked version of the second song from Chapter I), and then a second gap before the three songs in Chapter XIX ('Tra-la-la-lally Come Back to the Valley', 'Sing All Ye Joyful', and 'Roads Go Ever Ever On').

Thus Chapter II is the only one of the first ten to lack a poem, while Chapter XV is the only one of the next eight to have one, followed by a sudden burst of three poems in the final chapter.

2 I give here the typescript text (1/1/69:4) for ease of reference; see page 693 above for the initial rough drafting of this poem. The only changes between the First Typescript version and the published text are the latter's capitalization of the first words in the two lines not capitalized here (both are capitalized in the Second Typescript [1/1/50:4–5], a rare case where Michael's typescript more closely resembles the published text than the main typescript) and the indenting of every other line in the published text (cf. DAA.359–60). The third line of the poem has

been erased and retyped in the original, but I think this was simply to correct a carriage return error or some similar typing mistake.

Note that by referring to it as 'Bilbo's first poem' Tolkien has either forgotten about the two spider-songs Bilbo spontaneously composed in Mirkwood ('Attercop' and 'Lazy Lob') or does not consider them 'poems' per se so much as rhyming nonsense to annoy his foes.

3 This is the first of the two 'Songs on the Downs' (*Oxford Poetry 1915*, page 60). Smith was one of Tolkien's closest friends, and the poem is included in *A Spring Harvest* [1918], the book of Smith's poems edited by Tolkien after GBS's death in the Battle of the Somme.

4 Both Tolkien's and Geach's poems appear in *Fifty New Poems for Children: An Anthology*, Selected from Books Recently Published by Basil Blackwell (Basil Blackwell, Oxford [1922]). 'Goblin Feet' appears on pages 26–27 and 'Romance' on page 28; a bibliographic note on page 62 notes that Geach's poem first appeared in *Oxford Poetry 1918*. For more on Geach, see *The Annotated Hobbit* (DAA.360–1).

5 These are stanzas two, twelve, and thirteen from Thomas's poem, which continues with an all-too-timely application:

Now all roads lead to France
And heavy is the tread
Of the living; but the dead
Returning lightly dance;

Whatever the road bring
To me or take from me
They keep me company
With their pattering . . .

Simonson's piece, '*The Lord of the Rings* in the Wake of the Great War', appears in *Reconsidering Tolkien*, edited by Thomas Honegger (Walking Tree Press [2005]); see in particular pages 161–163. So far as I have been able to discover, no substantial comparison has yet been written of Tolkien with Thomas, who like Tolkien celebrated the quiet English countryside in his work, wrote fairy-tales, and fought on the Western Front, where he died in 1917.

6 The only difference between the two versions in *The Lord of the Rings* is that when Frodo repeats the poem two chapters later, he changes the word *eager* in line five to *weary*; Christopher Tolkien reveals in *The Return of the Shadow* that 'weary' is in fact the wording of the original draft (HME VI.47).

THE FOURTH PHASE

THE 1947 HOBBIT

The 1947 Hobbit – that is, the material Tolkien created around 1944 while working on *The Lord of the Rings* and sent to Allen & Unwin in 1947 as a way to bring the earlier book into harmony with its sequel – marks the first of a sequence of revisionings that led first to the second edition of *The Hobbit* [1951], then to 'The Quest of Erebor' [1954], and then finally to the 1960 Hobbit (the never-before published Fifth Phase). The first of these made adjustments within the original book to make it better match the sequel, the second retold a small portion of Bilbo's story within the new book (or would have, had it been published as part of Appendix A as Tolkien originally intended), while the third re-envisioned a complete recasting of the old book to agree with the new in minute detail. Unlike these three, the 'third edition' Hobbit of 1966 was imposed upon him by outside circumstance (that is, the need to quickly produce an 'authorized' edition to belatedly assert the American copyright); by contrast, the others had all arisen from Tolkien's internal compulsion to bring the old story of Bilbo's adventure more strongly into accord with the new one of Frodo's quest.

The Fourth Phase material exists in three states: ten sheets of fair copy manuscript numbered 1 to 10 in the upper right corner (Ad.Ms.H.34–53),[TN1] followed by six pages of single-spaced typescript numbered 1 through 6 in the upper right corner (Ad.Ms.H.77–82), followed by eight typeset sheets (sixteen pages) from Allen & Unwin showing how the new material looked when typeset and allowing Tolkien to proofread the changes (Ad.Ms.H.54–61). The first of these dates from 1944; the second either from 1944 or 1947; the third from 1950. They represent, respectively, Tolkien's manuscript of the rewritten passages; his 'home copy' of the typescript of this material that he sent to Allen & Unwin; and Allen & Unwin's page proofs of the changed sections returned to Tolkien for proofing.

Aside from a few ink-over-pencil additions, no drafting survives for these changes, though the fair copy text is far too neatly written to have been spontaneously generated without careful preparation – for one thing, as was his usual practice when revising material already set in type, Tolkien has taken great pains to keep many of his changes as localized as possible, so that only that specific line or lines would have to be re-set without affecting the rest of the page (and thus upsetting the layout of every subsequent page). Although the greatly expanded encounter with

Gollum did add five extra pages to the book's length, it added *exactly* five pages, so that for instance where page 99 in the first edition began with the words '"You would have dropped him," said Dori', page 104 in the second edition now began with those exact words; everything from the beginning of Chapter VI on has simply shifted five pages.

All Tolkien's substitutions are preceded by a page and line number indicating exactly where each correction should be inserted into the existing (first edition) text. I have retained these, since even for those without access to a copy of the first or second edition they give a proportional sense of where a passage may be found. In any case, it should be easy for anyone familiar with Tolkien's book in any of its permutations to locate these passages. Since this material transforms what was already an impressive chapter into one of the most moving and memorable scenes Tolkien ever wrote, I have provided unusually full annotation for this section, giving variations between the fair copy and the typescript (and proof pages) in the Text Notes, aside from changes in punctuation or paragraph breaks.

The fair copy page has no title, but in the left margin of the first page (Ad.Ms.H.34) Tolkien has hastily written in pencil:

(i)

Proposed correction of Hobbit
to simplify Sequel *(Gollum*
does not give *ring).*

The typescript (Ad.Ms.H.77) has the following header instead:

Corrections required in THE HOBBIT in order to bring the story into line with the sequel, THE LORD OF THE RINGS.

Above this is written in ink:

or rather if The Hobbit ran so the Sequel would be a little easier to <conduct> as a narrative (in Ch II), though not necessarily 'truer'.

– that is, Chapter II in *The Lord of the Rings*, i.e. 'The Shadow of the Past' (or, as to give it its original title, 'Ancient History'). I now give the fair copy manuscript, beginning on page Ad.Ms.H.34.

p. 85 l. 9. Before he lost all his friends and was driven away, alone, and crept down, down into the dark under the mountains.[TN2]

l. 25–26. We does what it wants, eh? We shows it the way out, yes[TN3]

p. 91 l. [14>]15ff.[TN4] He knew, of course, that the riddle-game was sacred and of immense antiquity, and even wicked creatures were afraid to cheat when they played at it. But he felt [*cancelled*: that] he could not trust this slimy thing to keep any promise at a pinch. Any excuse would do for him to slide out of it. And after all that last question had not been a genuine riddle according to the ancient rules.[TN5]

But at any rate Gollum did not at once attack him. He could see the sword in Bilbo's hand. He sat still, shivering and whispering. At last Bilbo could wait no longer.

'Well?' he said. 'What about your promise? I want to go. You must show me the way'.

'Did we say so, precious? Show the nasty little [noser >] baggins[TN6] the way out, yes, yes. But what has it got in its pocketses, eh? Not string, precious, but not nothing. Oh no! gollum'.

'Never you mind', said Bilbo. 'A promise is a promise'.

'Cross it is, precious, impatient',[TN7] hissed Gollum. 'But it must wait, yes it must. We can't go up the tunnels so hasty. We must go and get some things first, yes, things to help us'.

'Well, hurry up!' said Bilbo, relieved to think of Gollum going away. He thought he was just making an excuse, and did not mean to come back. What was Gollum talking about? What useful thing could he keep out on the dark lake? But he was wrong. Gollum did meant to come back. He was angry now and hungry. And he was a miserable wicked creature, and already he had a plan.[TN8]

Not far away was his island, of which Bilbo knew nothing, and there in his hiding-place he kept a few wretched oddments, and one very beautiful thing, very beautiful, very wonderful. He had a ring, a golden ring, a precious ring.

'My birthday-present!' he whispered to himself, as he had often done in the endless dark day.[TN9] 'That's what we wants now, yes; we wants it!'

He wanted it because it was a ring of power, and if you slipped [it >] that ring on your finger, you were invisible; only in the full sunlight could you be seen, and then only by your shadow, and that would be faint and shaky.[TN10]

[Who knows >] 'My birthday-present' he whispered;[TN11] but who knows how Gollum came by that present, ages ago in the old days when such rings were still at large in the world. Perhaps even the Necromancer [> Master][TN12] who made them could not have said. Gollum used to wear it at first, till it tired him; and then he kept it in a pouch next his skin, till it galled him; and now usually he hid it in a hole in the rock on his island, and went back [> was always going back] to look at it. And still sometimes he put it on, when he could not bear to be parted from it any longer, or when he was very, very, hungry, and tired of fish. Then he would creep along dark passages, looking for stray goblins. He might even venture into places where the torches were lit and made his eyes blink and smart; for he would be safe, oh yes, quite safe. No one would see him, no one would notice him, till he had his fingers on their throat. Only yesterday [> a few hours before][TN13] he had worn it, and caught a small goblin-imp. How it squeaked! He still had a bone or two left to gnaw, but he wanted something softer.

'Quite safe, yes', he whispered [*added*: to himself]. 'It won't see us, will it my precious? No! It won't see us, and its nassty little sword will be useless, yes quite'[TN14]

That is what was in his wicked little mind, as he slipped suddenly from Bilbo's side, and flapped back to his boat, and went off into the dark.

Bilbo thought he had heard the last of him, and he <felt in his bones ?that> Gollum did not meant to keep his promise.[TN15] Still he waited [*added*: a while;] for he had no idea how to find his way out alone. Suddenly he heard a screech. It sent a shiver down his back. Gollum was cursing and wailing away in the gloom, not very far off by the sound of it. He was on his island, scrabbling here and there, searching and seeking in vain.

'Where iss it? Where iss it?'[TN16] Bilbo heard him crying. 'Lost it is, my precious, lost, lost! Curse us, and crush us, my precious is lost!'

'What's the matter', Bilbo called. 'What have you lost?'

'It mustn't ask us', [screech >] shrieked Gollum. 'Not its business, no, gollum. It's lost,[TN17] gollum, gollum, gollum'.

'Well, so am I', said [> cried] Bilbo, 'and I want to get unlost. And I won the game, and you promised. So come along! Come and let me out, and then go on with your looking!' Utterly miserable as Gollum sounded, Bilbo could not find much pity in his heart, and he had a feeling that anything Gollum wanted so much [*cancelled*: and missed so badly] could hardly be something good [*cancelled*: – for Gollum at any rate].[TN18] 'Come along!' he shouted.

'No, not yet, precious!' said Gollum [> Gollum answered]. 'We must search for it, it's lost, gollum'.

'But you [promised >] never guessed my last question, and you promised', said Bilbo.

'Never guessed!' said Gollum. Then suddenly out of the gloom came a sharp hiss. 'What has it got in its pocketses? Tell us that. It must tell us first'.[TN19]

As far as Bilbo knew, there was no particular reason why he should not tell – Gollum's mind had jumped to a guess quicker than his:

naturally, for Gollum had brooded on one thing for ages, and he was always afraid of it being stolen.[TN20] But Bilbo was annoyed at the delay; after all he had won the game, pretty fairly, and among awkward circumstances [> at a horrible risk]. 'Answers were to be guessed not given', he said.

'But it wasn't a fair question', said Gollum. 'Not a riddle, precious, no!'

'Oh well, if it's a matter of ordinary questions' Bilbo replied, 'then I asked one first. What have you lost? Tell me that!'

'What has it got in its pocketses?' The sound came hissing loud and sharp [> louder and sharper], and as he looked towards it, to his alarm Bilbo saw now [> now saw] two small points of light peering at him. As suspicion grew in Gollum's mind, the light of his eyes burned with a pale flame.

'What have you lost?' Bilbo persisted.

But now the light in Gollum's eyes had become a green fire, and it was coming swiftly nearer. Gollum was in his boat again, paddling wildly back to the dark shore; and such a rage [in his heart that >] of fear and suspicion in his heart[TN21] that no sword held any more terror for him.

Bilbo could not guess what had excited the wretched creature <so madly>, but he saw that all was up, and that Gollum had forgotten all promises.[TN22] Just in time he turned and ran blindly back up the [*added*: dark] passage down which he had come, keeping close to the wall and feeling it with his left hand.

'What has it got in its pocketses?' he heard the hiss loud behind him, and the splash as Gollum leaped from his boat.[TN23]

'What have I, I wonder?' he said to himself, as he panted and stumbled along. He put his [*added*: left] hand in his pocket. The ring felt very cold as it [*added*: quietly] slipped on to his groping forefinger.[TN24]

The hiss was close behind him. He turned and saw Gollum's eyes like small green lamps coming up the slope. Terrified he tried to run faster, but suddenly he struck his toes on a snag in the floor and fell flat, with his little sword under him.

At that moment Gollum came up. But before Bilbo could do anything shout, pick himself up, wave his sword, Gollum passed on, taking no notice of him, cursing and whispering in the dark.[TN25]

What could it mean? Gollum could see in the dark. Bilbo could see the light of eyes palely shining even from behind. Painfully he got up,[TN26] and very cautiously he followed. There seemed nothing else to do. It was no good crawling back down to Gollum's water. Perhaps, if he followed him, Gollum might lead him to some way of escape without meaning to.

'Curse it, curse it, curse it!' hissed Gollum. 'Curse it [> the Baggins]! It's gone! What has it got in its pocketses? Oh we guess[es], we guess, my precious.[TN27] He's found it, yes he must have, my birthday-present.

Bilbo pricked up his ears. [This was so interesting >] He was [*added*: at last] beginning to guess himself. He hurried a little, getting as close as he dared behind Gollum, who was still going quickly, not looking back, but turning his head from side to side, as Bilbo could see from the faint glimmer on the walls.

'My birthday-present! Curse it! How did we lose it, my precious? Yes, that's it, when we came this way yesterday[TN28] catching that nassty little squeaker. That's it. Curse it. It slipped from us, after all these ages and ages. It's gone, gollum!

Suddenly Gollum sat down and began to weep, a <horrible> wheezing and gurgling sound [> a whistling and gurgling sound horrible to listen to]. Bilbo halted, and flattened himself against the tunnel-wall; and hid his sword, which was now glowing faintly again.[TN29] [Then Gollum began to curse >] After a while Gollum stopped weeping and began to talk. He seemed to be having an argument with himself.

'It's no good going back there to search, no. We can't [> doesn't] remember all the places we've visited. And it's no use. It's [> The baggins has] got it in its pocketses; the nassty noser has, we says [> the nassty noser has found it].'

'We guesses, precious, only guesses. We can't know till we finds the nasty creature and squeezes it.'

'But if it's got in its <?pocketses>, we shan't find it, we shan't see it. It'll escape us, gollum! It'll go away, away with our present, gollum!'

'Perhaps, precious. But it doesn't know about the present.[TN30] It doesn't know what the present can do, does it! It'll just leave[TN31] it in its pocketses. It doesn't know; and it can't go far – it's losst itself, the nassty nosey thing. It doesn't know the way out. It said so.'

'It said so, yes; but it's tricksy. It doesn't say what it means. It won't say what it's got in its pocketses. It knows. It's off now, we guess, to the back-door, yes to the back door.'[TN32]

'The goblins[es] will catch it then. It can't get out that way, precious.'

'Sss, sss, gollum! [*added in pencil*: Goblinses!] Yes, but if it's got the present, our precious present, then goblins[es] will get it, gollum! They'll find it, they'll find out what it does. We shan't ever be safe again, never, gollum. One of the goblins[es] will put it on, and [then] no one will see him. He'll be there but not seen. Not even our clever eyeses will notice him; and he'll [creep >] come creepsy and tricksy and catch us: Gollum, gollum!'

'Then let's stop talking, precious, and make haste. If <illegible> [> the baggins has] gone that way we must go quick and see. Go! Not far now. Make haste!'

With a spring Gollum got up and started shambling off at a great pace. Bilbo hurried after him, still as cautiously as he could [> cautiously], though his chief fear now was of tripping on another snag and falling with a noise. His head was in a whirl of hope and wonder. It seemed that the ring he had was a magic ring: it made you invisible! He had heard of such things, of course, in old old tales; but he found it hard to believe [> it was hard to believe] that he really had found one, by accident. Still, there it was: Gollum with his bright eyes had passed him by, only a yard to one side.

On they went, Gollum flip-flapping ahead, wailing [> hissing] and cursing; Bilbo behind going as softly as a hobbit can. Soon they came to places where, as Bilbo had noticed on the way down, [*added*: side-] passages opened, this way and that. Gollum began at once to count them.

'One left, yes! One right, yes! Two left, yes, yes! Two right, yes, yes';[TN33] and so on and on. As the count grew, [he began before <looking> to get slow >] he slowed down, and he began to get shaky and weepy. For they were [> he was] leaving the water further and further behind, and he was getting afraid. Goblins were [> might be] about, and he had lost his ring.

At last he stopped by a low opening, on their left as they went up. 'Six [> Seven] right, yes; four [> six] left, yes!'[TN34] he whispered. '[That's it >] This is it. This is the way to the back door, yes. Here's the passage. [*added*: He peered in *and shrank back*] But we dursn't go in, precious; no we dursn't. Goblins[es] down there, lots of goblins [> Goblinses]! We smells them – sss!'

'What shall we do, curse them and crush them? We must wait here precious, wait a bit and see!'[TN35]

So they came to a dead stop. Gollum had brought Bilbo to the way out after all, but he [> Bilbo] could not get in! There was Gollum sitting humped up right in the opening, and his eyes gleamed cold in his head, as he swayed it from side to side between his knees.

Bilbo crept out from the wall more quietly than a mouse; but Gollum stiffened at once, and he sniffed; and his eyes went green. He hissed softly but menacingly. He could not see the hobbit, but other senses he had, sharpened too by the darkness: hearing and smell. Now he seemed to be crouched right down with his flat hands splayed on the floor [*added*: and his head thrust out, nose almost to the stone]. Though he was only a black shadow in the gleam of his own eyes, Bilbo could see or feel that he was tense as a bow string, gathered for a spring.[TN36]

Bilbo stopped breathing and went stiff himself. He was desperate. He must get away, out of this horrible darkness, while he had any strength left. Thoughts flashed through his mind. He must fight. He must stab Gollum, kill the foul orc-<illegible>,[TN37] put his eyes out, kill him. It meant to kill him. But no, not a fair fight. He was invisible now. Gollum had no sword. Gollum had not actually tried to kill him yet. And he was miserable, alone, lost. A sudden understanding, a pity mixed with horror, welled up in Bilbo's heart; a glimpse of endless unmarked days [of >] without light, hard stone, cold fish, sneaking and whispering. He trembled. All this passed in his mind in a flash of a second. And then quite suddenly in another flash, as if lifted by a sudden strength and resolve, he leaped.[TN38]

No great leap perhaps for a man, but a leap in the dark. Straight over Gollum's head he sprang [> jumped], about seven feet forward and three in the air: indeed he only just missed cracking his skull, had he known it, on the low arch of the passage.[TN39]

Gollum threw himself backwards and <grabbed> as the hobbit fled[TN40] over, but too late: his hands snapped on thin air, and Bilbo falling fair on his sturdy feet sped off down the new passage [> tunnel]. He did not turn to see what Gollum was doing. There was a hissing and a cursing almost at his heels at first, then it stopped. Suddenly [> All at once] there was [> came] a bloodcurdling shriek, filled with hatred and despair. Gollum was beaten [> defeated]. He dared go no further. He had lost: lost his prey, and lost too the only thing he had ever cared for: his precious. The cry brought Bilbo's heart to his mouth, but still he held on. Now faint like [> as] an echo, but menacing the voice came behind:

'Thief, thief, thief! [*added*: baggins!] We hates it, we hates it, we hates it for ever.'[TN41]

Then there was a silence. But that too seemed menacing to Bilbo. 'If Goblins are so near that he smelt them' he thought, 'then they'll have heard his shrieking and cursing. Careful now, or this will [> this way will] lead you to worse things'. The passage was low and roughly made. It was not too difficult for the hobbit, except when in spite of all care he stubbed his poor toes [once again >] again, several times, on nasty jagged stones [*cancelled*: in the floor, but it must have been a bit too low for goblins.] 'A bit low for goblins, at least for the big ones', thought Bilbo, not knowing that even the big ones, the orcs of the mountains, are used to that sort of thing

[> go along at great speed stooping low with their hands almost on the floor].TN42

Soon the passage, that had been sloping down, began to go up again, and after a while it climbed steeply. That slowed Bilbo down. But at last the slope stopped, the passage turned a corner, and dipped down again, and there at the bottom of a short incline he saw, filtering round another corner – a glimmer of light. Not red light as of fire or lantern, but [a] pale ordinary out-of-doors sort of light. Then he began to run. Scuttling along as fast as his legs would carry him he turned the last corner and came suddenly right into an open place, where the light, after all that time in the dark, seemed dazzlingly bright. Really it was only a leak of sunshine in through a doorway, where a great door, a stone door, was left standing a little open.TN43

Bilbo blinked, and then suddenly he saw the goblins: goblins in full armour with drawn swords sitting just inside the door, and watching it with wide eyes, and watching the passage that led to it. They were aroused, alert, ready for anything.

They saw him sooner than he saw them. Yes they saw him. Whether it was an accident or a last trick of the ring before it took a new master, it was not on his finger! With yells of delight the goblins rushed upon him.TN44

A pang of fear and loss, like an echo of Gollum's,TN45 smote Bilbo, and forgetting even to draw his sword he stuck his hand[s] in his pocket[s], And there was the ring still, in his left pocket, and it slipped on his finger. The goblins stopped short. They could not see a sign of him. [The >] He had vanished! They yelled twice as loud as before, but not so delightedly.

p.100 l.14 in three goes.] So I said what about your promise? Show me the way out! But he came at me to kill me, and I ran [*added*: & fell over] and he missed me in the dark. Then I followed him, because I heard him talking to himself. He thought I really knew the way out, and so he was making for it. And then he sat down in the entrance and I couldn't get by. So I jumped over him and escaped, and ran on down to the gate.TN46

l.26 respect, when he talked] about jumping over Gollum, [dodging guards . . .TN47

p.101 l.6 from bottom Gandalf knew all about] the back-door as the goblins called the lower gate [where Bilbo

This marks the end of the new Gollum-story Tolkien drafted in 1944 and sent to Allen & Unwin in 1947. Accompanying the typescript pages of new text was a sheet (Ad.Ms.H.76–7) listing errata Tolkien had discovered and wished for them to fix in the next printing, as was their usual practice. To distinguish it from the 'Proposed correction of Hobbit' (see page 732) of the next six sheets, this sheet is given its own title, 'Errors in "The Hobbit"'; see page 749 below.

Note that close comparison of this fair copy and typescript with Tolkien's spirited reading of the entire encounter with Gollum, recorded in July 1952 at George Sayer's home, reveals that Tolkien used a copy of the newly published book as his text on that occasion.

TEXT NOTES

1 These pages are neatly written with a minimum of cancellations and revisions (at least until the last three paragraphs, which are ink over pencil drafting and seem to have been added slightly later; see Text Note 46 below). They are written on the back of torn half-pages that were once mimeographs detailing the language of the C-scribe of *The Owl and the Nightingale*; Christopher Tolkien notes that this paper was 'extensively used in the later chapters of *The Two Towers*' [annotation to Ad.Ms.H.34]. He also points out, in his introduction to *The Notion Club Papers*, that his father borrowed the name 'Nicholas Guildford' for one of the prominent members of the pseudo-Inklings 'Notion Club' from a character in this early Middle English dialogue [circa 1200] (HME IX.150).

2 This replaced 'before the goblins came, and he was cut off from his friends far under under the mountains' <sic>, the reading of the first edition.

3 In the typescript, 'If it asks us, and we doesn't answer, then we does what it wants, eh? We shows it the way out, yes!' replaces 'If it asks us, and we doesn't answer, we gives it a present, gollum!' from the first edition.

4 The typescript introduces this extended passage with 'For the passage from page 91, l. 15 beginning But funnily enough and ending with not so delightedly on page 95, l. 8 substitute the following account'. For the text thus replaced, see page 160 & ff of this book, the parallel-text presentation in Bonniejean Christensen's 'Gollum's Character Transformation in *The Hobbit*' in *A Tolkien Compass*, ed. Jared Lobdell [1975, abridged edition 2003], and the textual marginalia in Douglas Anderson's *The Annotated Hobbit* (rev. ed.) pages 128–31.

5 The typescript replaces 'the ancient rules' with 'the ancient laws'.

6 Here and on all but one subsequent occurrences the word 'baggins' was written in lowercase in the manuscript but was carefully hand-corrected to 'Baggins' in ink in the typescript; only in Gollum's parting curse was it typed 'Baggins' from the start.

7 The words 'cross' and 'impatient' were reversed in the typescript.

8 This passage originally read

> 'Well, hurry up!' said Bilbo, relieved to think of Gollum going away at least. He thought this was just an excuse, and did not mean to come back, but <he wondered what> things Gollum talking about. What useful thing could he keep out on the dark lake? He guessed but he did <not> <illegible> He was out in his guesses, for Gollum did meant to come back. He was angry and hungry. And he was a miserable wicked creature, and already he had a plan.

9 The typescript reads 'endless dark days'; the original image perhaps more strongly captured the horrific eternal present in which the unaging Gollum has become trapped by the Ring.

10 Here 'faint and shaky' was changed to 'shaky and faint'. The idea that the ring-wearer's shadow can be seen in strong light is still present in the second and subsequent editions of *The Hobbit*, although this feature of the Ring came to be altogether ignored in *The Lord of the Rings*.

11 The opening of this paragraph was recast and supplemented by ink over pencil drafting in the margin to read

> 'My birthday-present! It came to me on my birthday, my precious!' So he had always said to himself, but who knows . . .

12 Although heavily cancelled the word 'Necromancer' is clear here, but was struck out at once and replaced with 'Master'. The typescript includes a second significant change, where *made* is erased and replaced in ink with *ruled*. So that instead of 'the Necromancer [> Master] who made them' we get 'the Master who ruled them'. Had the original name survived it would have been the only time in *The Hobbit* that a specific connection would have been drawn between the sinister Necromancer in his tower and Gollum's ring. Even the replacement offers a subtle link between the two books, since 'the Master who ruled them' is a close synonym of the second book's title, 'the lord of the rings'.

13 This is further changed in ink on the typescript to 'a few hours *ago*'. The removal of 'yesterday' was necessitated by the fact that there was no way of keeping track of the passage of days in the dark beneath the mountains; cf. the 'endless unmarked days' on page 738. See also Text Note 28 below.

The 'small goblin-imp' captured, throttled, and eaten by Gollum is probably our only encounter in the legendarium with an orc-child. Again, see Text Note 28 for Tolkien's description of it as not just 'little' but 'young'.

14 There are no skipped lines, such as the one following this paragraph, in the manuscript; all the ones in this chapter I have taken from the typescript, none of which carry over into Allen & Unwin's page proofs.

15 The last half of this sentence, everything after 'the last of him,' was bracketed and then cancelled.

16 In the typescript, the extra sibilant is absent from the first 'iss' but an

additional one appears in the first 'Lost', so that the line now reads 'Where *is* it? Where iss it? . . . *Losst* it is, my precious . . .' (emphasis mine).

17 Again, the typescript changes 'lost' to '*losst*'.

18 This sentence was revised to read 'anything Gollum wanted so much could hardly be something good.'

19 This last sentence was slightly simplified in the typescript, to 'It must tell first'.

20 This sentence was only achieved after three attempts. Originally Tolkien wrote:

> . . . should not tell – naturally his [<?guessing> >] suspicion awoke slower than Gollum's, who had brooded on this one thing for ages and ages – Gollum's mind had jumped to a guess quicker

Then he stopped, cancelled everything between the dashes, and continued:

> . . . should not tell – Gollum's mind had jumped to a guess quicker than Bilbo's naturally – Gollum had brooded on this one thing for ages and ages

Then again everything after 'quicker than' was cancelled, and the text given on page 735 written in the left margin. The typescript, along with some adjustments in punctuation and capitalization, changes the wording and arrangement slightly:

> . . . for Gollum had brooded *for ages* on *this* one thing, and he was always afraid of *its* being stolen.

21 This sentence was later altered to read '. . . such a rage of *loss* and suspicion *was* in his heart . . .'. The replacement of Gollum's first instinctive response of *fear* by the more covetous *loss* is in ink over pencil.

22 This sentence was changed to read 'Bilbo could not guess *what had maddened the wretched creature*, but he saw that all was up, and that Gollum *meant to murder him after all.*'

23 The typescript changes *leaped* to *leapt* here, but 'leaped' was retained on Ad.Ms.H.48 (Ms) and Ad.Ms.H.81 (Ts). See page 738: 'as if lifted by a new strength and resolve, he leaped', and contrast DAA.130 ('Gollum leapt from his boat') with DAA.133 ('[Bilbo] leaped. No great leap for a man . . .').

24 Both of these changes are made in ink over pencil. The phrasing of this sentence is thematically significant: Bilbo does not put on the ring (subject-active verb-object) nor is a passive construction used but rather *it* slips on his finger (again subject-active verb-object, but with the Ring being the actor and Bilbo the acted upon). See Text Note 44 below.

25 This paragraph was revised in pencil, some of which was overwritten in ink:

> *In a* moment Gollum *reached him*. But before Bilbo could do anything *recover his breath*, pick himself up, *or* wave his sword,

> Gollum passed on, taking no notice of him, cursing and whispering *as he ran*.

The typescript refines the phrasing slightly:

> In a moment Gollum *was on him* . . . Gollum passed *by*, taking no notice . . .

26 Later Tolkien added in the margin 'and sheathed his sword <which>', then canceled it. This is clearly drafting for the passage that appears in pencil in the left margin of the corresponding page of typescript, which changes the passage to read 'Painfully he got up, *and sheathed his sword, which was now glowing faintly again. Then* very cautiously he followed . . .'

Originally this action had occurred several paragraphs later; see page 736 and Text Note 29.

27 The change from 'guess' to 'guesses' was not taken up in the typescript and does not appear in the published second edition. The change from 'Curse it!' to 'Curse the Baggins' is added above the line in ink over pencil.

28 This 'yesterday' escaped Tolkien's attention (see Text Note 13 above) and thus made its way into the typescript and then the page proofs, where it was corrected to read 'When we came this way *last, when we twisted* that nassty *young* squeaker' (Ad.Ms.H.56). On the bottom of this page Tolkien explained:

> yesterday won't do. G. knew no days
> cf. unmarked days p. 98

This last is a reference to 'endless unmarked days without light'; see page 738 above.

29 The typescript has '*sheathed* his sword' rather than the manuscript's 'hid his sword', then all of the sentence after 'the tunnel wall' is cancelled (in ink) and the passage entered (in pencil) several paragraphs earlier; see Text Note 26. The original idea that Bilbo kept his sword in hand while following the person who is trying to kill him presents the hobbit as wary in a desperate situation; the revision lays more stress on his wishing to move silently and undetected in dangerous circumstances.

30 These sentences were altered to read

> 'But if *the baggins has found the present*, we shan't see it. It'll escape us, gollum! It'll go away, away with our present, gollum!
>
> '*But* it doesn't know about the present [> precious > present].'

These lines were then bracketed and the word 'omit' written beside them; these sentences are indeed absent from the typescript, which merges the rest of this paragraph with the one preceding it ('. . . and squeezes it. But it doesn't know what the present can do . . .').

31 The word I read as 'leave' here might also be 'have' ('It'll just *have* it in its pocketses'); at any rate, over it Tolkien pencilled '*keep*', and this became the reading in the typescript.

In a rare case of a dropped sibilant, the typescript and proof read 'lost' for the 'losst' in the following sentence.

32 Changed to 'It knows. *It knows a way in, it must know a way out, yes.* It's *off to* the back-door, yes to the back door, *that's it.*'

33 The typescript reverses this: 'Two *right*, yes, yes. Two *left*, yes', probably to avoid the impression that the tunnels fall into a neat unvarying pattern of right, left, right, left, &c.

34 This sentence was changed to read '*Seven* right, yes; *six* left, yes!'

35 On the typescript, Tolkien marked for these two sentences to be transposed. This direction was not carried out for some reason, for they appear in the original order in the page proofs. He seems to have begun to mark the proof page in pencil requesting this change and then erased his directions.

36 This paragraph was revised, both in ink and pencil, to read

> Bilbo crept *away* from the wall more quietly than a mouse; but Gollum stiffened at once, *and sniffed*; and his eyes went green. He hissed softly but menacingly. He could not see the hobbit, but *now he was on the alert and he had* other senses *that* the darkness *had sharpened*: hearing and smell. *He* seemed to be crouched right down with his flat hands splayed on the floor and his head thrust out, nose almost to the stone. Though he was only a black shadow in the gleam of his own eyes, Bilbo could see or feel that he was tense as a bow string, gathered for a spring.

37 I cannot read this cancelled word, but it lacks a descender at the end and thus is not orc-*thing*; orc-*hun*[ter] is more probable. The typescript (Ad.Ms.H.81) replaces this with the familiar '. . . He must stab *the foul thing*, put its eyes out'.

38 This paragraph was carefully revised, and since it is perhaps the most important in the book from the point of view of the sequel – certainly, at least, the key passage in the second edition revisions – I reproduce the whole paragraph as revised here for comparison with the original in the text.

> Bilbo stopped breathing and went stiff himself. He was desperate. He must get away, out of this horrible darkness, while he had any strength left. He must fight. He must stab *the foul thing*, put *its* eyes out, kill *it*. It meant to kill him. But no, not a fair fight. He was invisible now. Gollum had no sword. Gollum had not actually tried to kill him yet. And he was miserable, alone, lost. A sudden understanding, a pity mixed with horror, welled up in Bilbo's heart; a glimpse of endless unmarked days without light, hard stone, cold fish, sneaking and whispering. All *these thoughts* passed *in* a flash of a second. *He trembled.* And then quite suddenly in another flash, as if lifted by a *new* strength and resolve, he leaped.

The typescript again revises this slightly but significantly ('. . . *almost* stopped breathing . . . *No*, not a fair fight . . . had not actually *threatened* to kill him, *or tried to* yet . . . without light *or hope of betterment* . . .'), achieving the text of the published second edition (see DAA.133).

Bilbo's sudden insight into Gollum's inner life here is on par with the unwitnessed moment outside Shelob's lair when Gollum briefly appears as 'an old weary hobbit, shrunken by the years that had carried him far beyond his time, beyond friends and kin, and the fields and streams of youth, an old starved pitiable thing' (*LotR*.742) – not surprisingly, because both were written at about the same time (cf. HME VIII.183–184, when Christopher dates this chapter in *The Lord of the Rings* to May 1944).† Most significant here is the change in the original of *his*, *he* to *its*, *it* when Bilbo is preparing to kill 'It', literally depersonalizing his intended victim, and the shift preserved in the final text back to his using *he* to describe Gollum, along with once again using his name, once Bilbo begins to treat Gollum as a fellow creature again and therefore is unable to murder him, even in self-defense.

†Assuming, of course, that this scene was in the original manuscript of that chapter, which is now lacking that section – cf. HME VIII.192.

39 Several small abridgments and some re-arrangement produced the familiar final version of this paragraph (cf. DAA.133).

40 The manuscript here (page 8, Ad.Ms.H.48) clearly reads 'fled over', while the typescript (page 5, Ad.Ms.H.81) has 'fled over him'. The proofs (page 98, Ad.Ms.H.58) give instead '*flew* over *him*'. Tolkien marked for this to be changed to *fled*, but for some reason the change was not made and the printer's reading persisted into the published book (second edition page 98; DAA.133).

The typescript of this paragraph includes one very minor departure from the fair copy: the replacement of 'a hissing and a cursing' with 'a hissing and cursing'.

41 This marks the spot at which Tolkien's 1952 audio recording of the Gollum chapter ends.

42 Once again the paragraph underwent minor changes for the typescript: 'Goblins' became 'goblins' (lower-cased), part of the cancelled passage was restored so that it was once more 'nasty jagged stones *in the floor*' that Bilbo stubbed his toes on, and the goblins are said to run 'at *a* great speed'. More significantly, the use of the word *orcs* in the fair copy to describe 'the big ones' doubles the number of times this *Silmarillion* and *Lord of the Rings* term appears in the published *Hobbit*, †its only appearance in the original edition or manuscript being Bladorthin/Gandalf's warnings about trying to travel northward around Mirkwood (see page 244 and DAA.188); it also confirms our guesses about Bolg and his bodyguard (see page 711).

†The third mention, discussed in Text Note 37 above, not having survived into the typescript.

43 Only four minor changes differentiate the typescript from the fair copy in this paragraph: the replacement of *glimmer* by *glimpse*, the omission of *ordinary* ('a pale out-of-doors sort of light'), the substitution of a

proper noun for the pronoun ('Then *Bilbo* began to run'), and the omission of *along* ('Scuttling as fast as'). See the commentary on 'The Vanishing People' (page 402) for connotations of 'glimmer' Tolkien may have wished to avoid here.

A single page (Marq. 1/1/21:1) survives among the *Lord of the Rings* papers that corresponds almost exactly to the last page (page 6) of the typescript, beginning at the exact same point ('a stone door') and also stopping at the identical spot ('. . . the lower gate [where Bilbo'). Comparison reveals that this neat pencil text is an intermediary stage between the manuscript (Ad.Ms.H.52) and typescript (Ad.Ms.H.82), probably drawn up by Tolkien as a guide to the creation of the latter. This page became separated from the rest of the *Hobbit* revision material, probably because the back of this sheet (1/1/21:2) bears some nearly illegible notes and rough drafting for a passage from *The Lord of the Rings*, dealing with calculations regarding the time needed for Boromir and the Nazgûl to travel from Gondor or Minas Tirith to Rivendell.

These notes are written on a page bearing the letterhead of the Oxford Circle of The Catenian Association, listing 'Prof. J.R.R. Tolkien' as the group's Vice-President and giving his address as 20 Northmoor Road (a house the Tolkiens occupied from 1930 to 1947). According to a history of this brotherhood for Catholic laymen, Tolkien was one of the founders of the group's Oxford Circle in 1944 and served as that branch's first Vice-President. Accordingly, it seems likely that these notes date from 1944, although of course they could have been written later, anytime up to 1947 when he sent the typescript version of this material to Allen & Unwin.

44 This paragraph ends with a cancelled incomplete sentence: 'With a sudden <illegible> of fear or loss,' which was plainly cancelled when Tolkien decided to begin a new paragraph instead with a more poignant form of the same sentiment.

In the original (first edition) version of this scene, Bilbo was not wearing the ring when he parted on neutral if not friendly terms from Gollum and so naturally it was not on his finger when he stumbled upon the goblins. The new version of the scene has to account for the facts that (a) Bilbo had to have had the ring on when he escaped from Gollum, and (b) he could not be wearing it when he encountered the goblins (or else they would not have seen him and the encounter would have been far less dramatic), yet (c) he had no reason to take it off in the meantime. Tolkien's solution, to have the ring simply vanish from Bilbo's finger, is the only time it seems to vanish from one place under its own power and reappear in another, unless we assume that it forced Bilbo to unconsciously slip it in his pocket without being aware of the act. It could not have come off accidentally, since someone feeling his way in total darkness with one hand on the wall would hold the other hand out in front, not put it in his pocket.

In any case, its attempt to get Bilbo killed by the goblins and itself into the hands of an orc (cf. Frodo's glib words, 'What . . . Wouldn't an Orc have suited it better?' – *LotR*.69), and hence eventually to the

Necromancer (Sauron), is foiled by Bilbo's luck (he is, after all, Mr. Lucky Number, has just been saved three times by luck during the riddle-game, and later admits 'I have begun to trust my luck' – cf. page 504) or presence of mind. The episode does, no doubt deliberately, call up echoes of its betrayal of Isildur (*LotR*.66 & *UT*.275) and, of course, its purposeful abandonment of Gollum: cf. Gandalf's words to Frodo in 'The Shadow of the Past': 'A Ring of Power looks after itself . . . *It* may slip off treacherously, but its keeper never abandons it . . . The Ring was trying to get back to its master.† It had slipped from Isildur's hand and betrayed him . . . it caught poor Déagol . . . it had devoured [Gollum] . . . So now, when its master was awake once more . . . it abandoned Gollum' (*LotR*.68–69).

†Note here Gandalf's use of the term *master*, the same as that used within *The Hobbit* for Sauron as the Ring-lord: 'even the Master who ruled them'. See also Text Note 12 above.

45 The typescript elaborates this slightly: 'like an echo of Gollum's *misery*'. This is the only time within *The Hobbit*, even the second edition text, where Bilbo's being in danger of succumbing to the 'Ring-sickness', if we may so call it, is hinted at; everywhere else within the story it remains just a magic ring with no sinister connotations.

46 The text being replaced here read, in the first edition, 'And he couldn't guess in three goes. *So I asked for my present, and he went to look for it, and couldn't find it. So I said, "very well, help me to get out of this nasty place!" and he showed me the passage to the door. "Good-bye" I said, and I went on down.*'

This entry and the two that follow it are crowded on the bottom of the last manuscript page (page 10, Ad.Ms.H.51); all are ink over pencil underwriting and probably slightly later than the fair copy text of the rest of the manuscript. The pencil has not been erased, and enough of it can be read under or around the ink to make it clear that it was simply drafting for the text that overwrote it, somewhat different in phrasing but close to it:

> . . . me the way out. But he came at me . . . in the dark . . . it. And he sat down in the passage, and I could not get by so I jumped over him and escaped, and ran on down to the doorway . . . the goblins called the lower <gate> – where

The first of these three entries seems to have given Tolkien a good deal of trouble – not so much in finding what he wanted to say but in getting it to fit in as small a space as possible (even so, its inclusion wound up adding lines to this page; see Text Note 47 below). In addition to the ink-over-pencil text at the end of the last of these ten manuscript pages, two pencilled versions take up the bottom half of the last typescript sheet as well, along with pencilled notations as Tolkien added up letters, adjusting his totals with each change or deletion.

The first of the pencilled drafts reads

[what's in my pocket >] So I [asked >] said 'what about your

> promise?' But he came at me [and I ran >] to kill me and I [*cancelled*: ran. But he missed me and I] dodged him. Then I followed him to the passage to the back-gate. and I jumped over . . .

before trailing off into illegibility. The next pencil draft, written below it, reads

> So I said 'what about your promise?' But he came at me, to kill me, and [I ran >] I dodged him. Then I followed him [*cancelled*: to the passage] till he came [*cancelled*: to the passage] the way out, and I jumped over him, and ran down to the back-gate.

By contrast, although the typed final version in the typescript above this drafting has an 'X' beside it in the margin, it represents the second edition text exactly as it appears in the page proof and subsequently published book. The only difference between the ink-over-pencil text (page 739) and the typescript is the latter's omission of 'on' from the last sentence, so that 'jumped over him and escaped, and ran on down to the gate' becomes '. . . and ran down to the gate'.

47 The usually vigilant typesetters at Unwin Brothers dropped the phrase 'dodging guards' when they inserted 'jumping over Gollum'. Tolkien wrote in the missing words on the proof page but, although the printers did subsequently enter it, they did so in the wrong place, reversing the order of the phrases from what Tolkien intended, and this transposition persists into the published book, so that instead of 'when he talked about jumping over Gollum, dodging guards, and squeezing through' – that is, the events in their chronological sequence – we get 'when he talked about dodging guards, jumping over Gollum, and squeezing through' (second edition page 105; cf. DAA.140). The original first edition text had simply read 'when he talked about dodging guards, and squeezing through' (first edition page 100; cf. page 200).

It should be noted that the changes discussed in Text Notes 46 & 47 were the only ones that created an overrun, since the first expanded its paragraph from seven lines to ten and the second from three lines to four. Once they finally implemented both changes, the typesetters compensated for the expanded page 100/105 by moving one line to the bottom of the preceding page (new page 104, corresponding to old page 99) and two lines to the top of the following page (new page 106, corresponding to old page 101); by the time the second edition text reaches page 107, the second edition text once again corresponds page-by-page to the first edition text (in this case, to old page 102).

(ii)

Errors in 'The Hobbit'.
Misprints, or uncorrected verbal errors in the Ms.

[added in pencil: previously sent in]

In addition to a list of purely typographical errors (e.g., then > than, nay > any, find > fine, above stream > above the stream), most of which are noted by Hammond (*Descriptive Bibliography*, pages 4, 7, 16, & 22), Tolkien also wanted to take advantage of the opportunity offered by a new printing to address some issues arising from problems within *The Hobbit* itself. After listing seventeen misprints, Tolkien himself notes:

These are not important, except for precision. Though back p. 104 for black is unfortunate; while when [p.64] is required to match the runes on the map.[TN1]

Most of the various corrections Tolkien requests are included in short excerpts on the proofs sent back to him (Ad.Ms.H.59–61) so that the author could check them in context. This list of typos is then followed on the same sheet by the more significant category, with a new header written in ink:

(iii)

Other corrections.

On page 30, ll. 26,27 by inadvertence (that has annoyed some of the 'fans' who have solved all the runes) the text: five feet high is the door and three abreast may enter it does not correspond with the actual runes, and should read: five feet high the door and three may walk abreast. I think the map-maker did not read his text properly,[TN2] but since his map cannot be altered, and his version is better, I hope the text can be adjusted.

The Map-maker has also placed on his map the words HERE OF OLD WAS THRAIN KING UNDER THE MOUNTAIN, in defiance of the fact that his father [> Thrain's father] Thror was still alive and dwarf-kings do not abdicate. I am afraid that nothing can here be done, except to point out in the Sequel that the Thrain referred to was a yet more ancient king.[TN3]

On pages 27 (l. 28) man; and 294 (l. 11) men. Arthur Ransome[TN4] and others pointed out the desirability of not using man, men as 'person, people' in a story in which other rational creatures than Men appear. On p. 27 read 'fellow'; and on p. 294 read 'of us'.[TN5]

More annoying to me is the carelessness on p. 35 And your father went away on the third of March, a hundred years ago last Thursday. Now the Unexpected Party occurred on a Wednesday (as is stated). If this remark is true, then the Party must have occurred on March 9th. But that is impossible. Not only does it make the time far too long before the travellers reach the trolls on the night of May 31st (p. 41); but also they are supposed to start off the next morning, and that is 'just before May'. For 'third of March' we must read 'twenty-first of April' – or regretfully abandon the comic precision of 'last Thursday'. For since Bilbo's birthday was the 22nd of September and fell that year on a Thursday, a party held on a Wednesday near the end of April must have occurred on the 20th [> 27th]. Read therefore either 'on the third of March, a hundred years ago last month' or 'on the twenty first of April, a hundred years ago last Thursday'. [*added in ?pencil*: The latter is better.]

In the event, the printers adopted 'the twenty-first of April, a hundred years ago last Thursday' (Ad.Ms.H.60), although this did not end Tolkien's attempts to reconcile the dates and moons of Bilbo's story to the twin constraints imposed by the reduction of the original journey to a single year and also new complications introduced in *The Lord of the Rings* (e.g., the specific date of Bilbo's birthday, which occurred while they were in Lake Town, and the time required to journey from Bilbo's home to Rivendell). To this was later added the additional constraint of trying to adjust events written by the modern Gregorian calendar to fit the Shire-calendar instead; see 'Timeline and Itinerary' in the 1960 Hobbit, starting on page 815.

TEXT NOTES

1 That is, the text that currently read 'Already the shadows were deepening about them, though far away through the trees and over *the back tops* of those growing lower down' (first edition page 104 line 16) should instead have read '. . . over the *black* tops . . .' Similarly, in Rivendell Elrond states that the moon-letters read 'Stand by the grey stone *where* the thrush knocks', whereas the runes on the actual map provided with the book say instead '. . . *when* the thrush knocks'. Since he could not change the printed map without great trouble and expense and did not wish to have a loremaster like Master Elrond appear careless or in error, the latter error was more significant than the former (which at worst would merely puzzle some readers). Both of these corrections appear in the proofs Tolkien was sent in 1950 (Ad.Ms.H.61) and in subsequent editions of the book from the fifth printing onward.

2 The 'map-maker' whose work Tolkien disparages here is, of course, himself, not the production departments at Unwin Brothers and Allen & Unwin. Compare his similar humorous self-deprecatory remarks in lectures at Oxford about his definitive edition of *Sir Gawain & the Green Knight*, still in print more than eighty years after its first publication: 'Tolkien and Gordon were quite wrong, quite wrong when they said that! Can't imagine what they were thinking of!' (Carpenter, *Tolkien: A Biography*, page 105).

The correction requested was indeed made, bringing the story's text into agreement with the map's runes: *five feet high the door and three may walk abreast* (Ad.Ms.H.60; DAA.52).

3 This paragraph was bracketed, usually a sign that the material so treated needs further attention, either cancellation or replacement. In this case, the point was addressed in the brief prefatory note Tolkien added to the book, starting with the second edition; see part (iv) below.

The matter was further developed in *The Lord of the Rings*, where 'Thráin I' became the dwarf-king who led his people away from Moria after the Balrog killed his father (Náin I) and grandfather (Durin VI), founding the Kingdom under the Mountain at the Lonely Mountain, and discovering the Arkenstone (thus explaining its hitherto puzzling title as 'the Arkenstone of Thrain' and explaining away the remnants in the text of the Thror-Thrain-Thorin/Thrain-Thror-Thorin confusion); see *LotR*.1109 & 1117. For the original drafts of this material, see HME XII.275–7 and Note 5 on HME XII.286.

4 For Ransome's letter, and Tolkien's reply, see Appendix IV.

5 The specific passages in question are Gandalf's description of Bilbo as an 'Excitable little man' (changed in the page proofs to 'Excitable little *fellow*'; Ad.Ms.H.60) and Thorin's dying words 'If more men valued food and cheer and song above hoarded gold' (changed to 'If more *of us* valued . . .'; Ad.Ms.H.59).

Tolkien had suggested these two changes as far back as December 1937 (see *Letters*, p. 28), only three months after the book was first published; they finally appeared in the fifth printing (i.e., the second edition) of 1951.

(iv)
Prefatory Note

One additional significant piece of new writing associated with the second edition is the prefatory note Tolkien wrote to explain why this printing differed from those that had gone before. This note, which first appeared in the fifth printing (i.e., the second edition) of 1951, exists in two states, a long and a short version, each of which is preserved in fair copy manuscript and single-spaced typescript. I give first the fair-copy manuscript text of the long version (A) [Ad.Ms.H.87–8]. The typescript (B)

[Ad.Ms.H.89] based upon this has a number of variations in phrasing, the more significant of which are given in the Text Notes that follow.

This reprint has been revised. Some small inaccuracies have been corrected: such as the failure of the text on pages 30 and 64 to translate precisely the runes on Thror's Map; and the date twenty first of April, previously on page 35 given wrongly as the third of March. The last error was due to a misreading of the difficult hand and language of the original diary [*cancelled*: or memoir].[TN1]

More important is the matter of Chapter Five. I have thought it desirable to give now the true story of the ending of the Riddle Game, in place of the somewhat 'altered' account of it that Bilbo gave to his friends (and put down in his diary). This weighed on his conscience, as notes in his private papers show, and he was uneasily aware that Gandalf did not believe it.[TN2] His story – that Gollum had promised to give the Ring to him as a gift, if he won the game – seemed of course to the wizard most unlikely from the first, and in the light of later developments [*cancelled*: was] simply incredible. But it was not until many years after Bilbo's journey that he pressed the old hobbit to tell him the truth; for the truth about the Ring had become desperately important.

If ever it proves possible to arrange extracts from the Red Book and present them in English to students of hobbit-lore,[TN3] it will be made clear how it was that Bilbo, as honest a hobbit by nature as could be found, came to put out a false tale; and how by that game at the dark roots of the Misty Mountains the history of the Western world and the end of the Third Age was changed. For the Red Book of Westmarch, not long ago rediscovered and deciphered, contains a chronicle (of great length and by many hands) of that perilous time,[TN4] as it was seen by hobbits; and its earlier parts are largely made up of extracts from Bilbo's writings, including the various secret or private papers that he [handed >] gave to his heir.

However, in the meanwhile none of this need trouble those who in this edition make their first acquaintance with hobbit-lore.[TN5] It has little bearing on the tale of the dragon-hoard. Yet I felt that some immediate explanation was due to those who may possess older copies, and might suspect me of wilfully [rewriting >] altering the story, in one version or the other. I have not. The older version is the account in Bilbo's diary;[TN6] the later is the truth as told to Gandalf and revealed in the Red Book. And there for the present I will leave the matter.

I will end with one further note, on a point that several readers have raised. Thorin Oakenshield was the son of Thráin, and Thráin was son of Thrór King under the Mountain. But upon the Map is written here of old was Thrain King under the Mountain Yet dwarf-kings do not abdicate, and Thror was still alive when Smaug put an end to the kingdom for that time. Nonetheless the Map is not at fault. Names [*added*: often] repeat themselves in dwarvish dynasties, and the genealogies of the Red Book show that the Thráin referred to was Thráin I, a distant ancestor of Thrór, who had long before ruled the same realm, before his people passed on to the remoter mountains of the North. Thrór and his son were thus in fact re-entering old [*cancelled*: incomplete] delvings of their kin when, driven out of the North again, they returned to the Lonely Mountain of Erebor.[TN7] Dwarves had been long in the world and known much troublous history before the days of Thrór,[TN8] and when he wrote of old he meant it: in the ancient past remembered still in those deep throated[TN9] songs of lore that the dwarf-kin sang in their secret tongue at feasts to which none but dwarves were bidden. Some say that they sing still.

The 'long version' was followed by another typescript (C) [Ad.Ms.H.86], a 'short version', derived primarily from (B) but incorporating some elements from (A). This in turn was followed by a fair copy (D) [Ad. Ms.H.85], which became the version actually printed (cf. DAA.28). I here conflate (C) and (D) together, with passages present in the typescript but omitted in the manuscript that followed given in italics; the title given here appears only on the fair copy.

Note on corrections and alterations in reprint 1950

In this reprint several minor inaccuracies, most of them noted by readers, have been corrected. For example, the text on pages 30 and 64 now corresponds exactly with the runes on Thror's Map. *On page 35 the third of March, a misreading of the difficult hand and language of the original, is replaced by the correct reading the twenty first of April, a date borne out by the fact that the expedition started on a fine morning 'just before May'.*[TN10] More important is the matter of Chapter Five. There the true story of the ending of the Riddle Game, as it was eventually revealed (under pressure) by Bilbo to Gandalf, is now given according to the Red Book, in place of the version Bilbo first gave to his friends, and actually set down in his diary. This *strange* departure from truth on the part of a most honest hobbit was a portent of great significance. It does not, however, concern the present story, and those who in this edition make their first acquaintance with hobbit-lore need not trouble about it. Its explanation lies in the history of the Ring, as it is set out in the chronicles of the Red Book of Westmarch, and it must await their publication.

A final note may be added, on a point raised by several students of the lore of the period. On Thror's Map is written Here of old was Thrain King under the Mountain; Thrain was the son of Thror, the last King under the Mountain before the coming of the dragon. The Map, however, is not in error. Names are often repeated in dynasties, and the genealogies show that a distant ancestor of Thror was referred to, Thrain I, a fugitive from Moria, who first discovered the Lonely Mountain, Erebor, and ruled there for a while, before his people moved on to the remoter mountains of the North – *Dwarves had already known a long and troublous history in the world before the days of Thror, and when he wrote of old he meant it: in the ancient past, remembered still in the songs of lore that the dwarf-kin sang in their secret tongue at feasts to which none but dwarves were bidden. Some say that they sing them still, and with the lengthening of the years the songs have become very long indeed.*[TN11]

JRRT
9/9/50

At the bottom of the typescript page, Tolkien added the notation in pencil:

Suggested specimen of a prefatory note
to a revised edition of The Hobbit

The fair copy page (D) is stamped '18 SEP 1950' by the printer, showing that this and not the typescript is actually the text sent to be typeset. By the omission of the passages I have italicized, the Note was shortened to the point where it could fit on a single page (in fact, on the hitherto-blank back of the table of contents) and thus not disrupt the pagination; had Tolkien known earlier that such a note would be needed, the pagination could no doubt have been adjusted as it was for the Gollum chapter (see page 732 above).

The Prefatory Notes as published did establish a rationale for changing one of the key chapters in the book, the encounter with Gollum, in a way that served the purposes of the sequel without harm to the coherence and independence of the original book: the replaced passage is revealed to be authentic but inaccurate. And for its part, the passage on Thrain I at last resolves the inconsistency created by the earlier confusion between the two competing Thror-Thrain-Thorin/Thrain-Thror-Thorin genealogies. In a masterly demonstration of his preferred method, Tolkien leaves intact both pieces of information – that Thror was the last King under the Mountain (text) and that 'Here of old was Thrain King . . .' (map) – by adding a third new piece of information alongside them that places them into harmony as part of a larger picture.

The abbreviated published version of this Prefatory Note provides the necessary information to place the new edition in context, but the more extended versions that had to be trimmed down had done more. For example, the closing sentences ('when he wrote of old he meant it') conjure up a vast sense of time only remembered in songs which we, not being dwarves, can never be privileged to hear. More remarkably, like some of the remarks about hobbits in the Prologue to *The Lord of the Rings*, they bring the story down to the present day (e.g., '[Hobbits] *now* avoid us with dismay', 'the regions in which Hobbits then lived were doubtless the same as those *in which they still linger*' – *LotR*.13 & 14, italics mine): 'Some say *they sing them still* . . .' Also, the idea that Thror returned to incomplete delvings from long ago enhances his stature as the founder (rather than merely re-occupier) of the Kingdom under the Mountain.

Significant in another sense, as a road not taken, is Tolkien's proffered explanation that a change here is simply a correction of an 'error due to a misreading of the difficult hand and language of the original'. Had he adopted this simple expedient, which was entirely in keeping with his authorial pose as editor and translator of Bilbo's story (cf. the runic border on the dust jacket, where Tolkien referred to himself as the translator of Bilbo's memoir), it would have served him well when he tried to resolve the conundrum of recalcitrant phases of the moon in the 1960 Hobbit.

TEXT NOTES

1 In the typescript, the example and explanation are both dropped and the paragraphs run together: '. . . have been corrected, *many of them long noted by readers and students of hobbit-lore*. More important *than these details* is the matter . . .'

2 'Gandalf did not believe it' > 'Gandalf *had never* believed it'.

3 The opening of this paragraph was replaced by '*When, if ever, a selection from the matter of the Red Book is presented to students of the period*'.

4 The typescript reads '. . . how by that game at the dark roots of the *mountains* the *fortunes* of the Western World . . . of Westmarch, *a hobbit-heirloom* not long ago re-discovered and deciphered, contains *chronicles* [*cancelled: and commentaries*] of that perilous time . . .'

5 Changed to 'with *hobbitry*'.

6 The typescript reads '. . . the account in Bilbo's *memoirs, my primary source*'. This distinction is significant because there is no mention in *The Hobbit* of Bilbo's jotting down what happened to him each day, while we are told in the Epilogue that Gandalf and Balin visit him while he is writing 'his memoirs'.

7 This sentence was bracketed in the manuscript.

The typescript expands slightly upon the career of Thráin I: 'a distant ancestor of Thrór, *a fugitive from Moria, and the first discoverer of the Lonely Mountain, Erebor, who ruled that land for a while,* before his people . . .'; the sentence about Thror and his son re-entering old delvings upon their return is absent in the typescript. The inclusion of 'and his son' shows how closely Thror and Thrain are linked in Tolkien's mind; the genealogy in *The Lord of the Rings*, which probably postdates this prefatory note, gives the date of Thrain's birth as fifty-four years after Thror's re-establishment of the Kingdom under the Mountain (*LotR*.1117).

8 For the details of this 'troublous history', see Appendix A part iii: 'Durin's Folk' in *The Lord of the Rings*. Even within the context of the original *Hobbit*, note Thorin's thoughts during the Siege of the Mountain: how each piece of treasure had associations for him with 'old memories of the labours and sorrows of his race' (page 648).

9 The words 'deep throated', bracketed in the fair copy, do not appear in the typescript.

10 This passage is bracketed in the typescript and absent in the fair copy. The next sentence began a new paragraph in the typescript but becomes part of the first paragraph in the fair copy.

11 The fair copy might well have once included these sentences, since it ends rather abruptly at the bottom of a page. If so, although bracketed in the typescript they were probably curtailed for reasons of space rather than any dissatisfaction with their content.

(v)
Thrym Thistlebeard

Finally, the following unpublished letter casts an interesting light on Tolkien's thinking about *The Hobbit* at the time he sent the corrections and proposed re-casting of Chapter V in to Allen & Unwin, offering slightly different solutions to some of the problems than the ones he sent to the publisher. Written on 26th September 1947 to Jennifer Paxman, whose father had been one of Tolkien's companions in that memorable 1911 visit to Switzerland from which Tolkien drew memories many years later when writing the Misty Mountain sequences in Chapters IV and VI, the letter first addresses her question about applying to various Oxford colleges, then turns to *The Hobbit*:

As for 'the Hobbit'. There are a fair number of errors in it; and though I keep on sending corrections in to Allen & Unwin they don't seem to get put right . . .

But the author also made errors. On p. 30 the text to agree with red runes should read '<u>five feet high the door and three may walk abreast</u>'

The chief error otherwise is on p. 25: the third of March a hundred years ago last Thursday. The party was on a Wednesday (p. 17, 20). If this was true, therefore, the party must have been on March 9 and the expedition must have set out on March 10. But that was not so: it was just before May (p. 40), and also it would only have taken about a month's slow going to reach the Trolls on 31st May (p. 41). As Bilbo's birthday was Sept. 22nd and a Thursday that year, the party must actually have occurred on Wednesday April 27th. The text should read twenty-first of April /or/ a hundred years [*added*: ago] last month. The latter is correct. . . .

Runes. The whole linguistic situation of 'The Hobbit' has become rather complicated owing to the necessity for translation. The language of the time, or the Common Speech of the West, is represented by English. This particular variety of Dwarf came from the North where a more northerly language was locally spoken. Now Dwarves have their own secret language, but like Jews and Gypsies use the language of the country. So all these Dwarves have Norse dwarf-names to represent the relations of the country and people of Dale (Bard the Bowman) etc. to the Common Language. The Dwarves used a more inscriptional alphabet – and I am now rather sorry that I used instead the Anglo-Saxon Runes (on the translation principle). The dwarf-alphabet was much better. The Elvish Alphabets do not come into the Hobbit – unless you have the full English edn. with coloured pictures, in which case you will see a bit of an inscription in an Elvish alphabet (the Alphabet of Fëanor) on the great jars in the left-foreground. This alphabet plays a considerable part in the sequel 'The Lord of the Rings'. I can let you have all these things, if you want them. They were not, of course, invented for the Hobbit or its sequel, since these things are only fragments torn out of 'the Silmarillion' or The History of the Elves, which no one will publish.

As for the actual runes in the book and your question. Þ·Þ stands for Thror son of Thrain. But that is an error that besides myself you alone have spotted. On p. 202–3, the order is given as Thorin – Thrain – Thror. The map-maker was confused and had the order Thorin – Thror – Thrain. But even that was erroneous as dwarf-kings don't abdicate, and the 'grandfather' was still alive when the map was made. In the sequel it will appear that the grandfather Thror was son of an older King Thrym (Thistlebeard). So that Þ·Þ stands for Thrór Thrym's son. All these dwarf-names (except Thrym and Thistilbarði (Thistlebeard), which is in another list) come out of the list of dwarf-names inserted into the Völuspá or 'Prophecy of the Sibyl' that is the first poem of the Elder Edda.[TN1]

After this, he continues with a discussion on the actual Anglo Saxon runes, his recent visit to Lincolnshire on college business, a dubious reliquary of 'Little Saint Hugh (the supposed martyr)', Chaucer's 'Prologue', and the various editions available of *The Hobbit*.

The logic underlying the problem with 'the third of March' is the same as in part (iii) above, although interestingly enough here, only five days after sending off (i), (ii), and (iii) to Stanley Unwin, Tolkien now prefers a different phrasing in the replacement text. The reference to dwarves adopting the language of the country they live in 'like Jews and Gypsies' shows that this idea was already present long before Tolkien compared his dwarves with the Jews in his 1965 radio interview with Denys Gueroult (see page 86, Note 9 and also page 859), although so far as I am aware the comparison to the Gypsies (an apt parallel to the wandering dwarves mentioned in early parts of *The Lord of the Rings*) occurs nowhere else.

The most interesting passage, of course, is that dealing with Thrym Thistlebeard, a hitherto unknown king of Durin's line. Although like Fimbulfambi he was destined never to appear in canonical form, having already been replaced by Dain (I) in the earliest surviving dwarven family-trees (see Marq. 3/9/1 and also HME XII.277), in this case he was probably not rejected so much as simply forgotten. I have already noted, on pp. 602–3, that the runic initials þ·þ on the inscribed jar in the foreground of the painting 'Conversation with Smaug' (Plate XI [top]) must refer to Þror and Þrain (or possibly Þrain and Þror), and that the presence of both's initials here presents some problems. This unpublished letter is proof first that the Thrain-Thror-Thorin genealogy was simply an error ('the map-maker was confused') and that Tolkien himself came to be well aware of the problem inherent in the initials on the inscribed jar. In this paragraph he offers a satisfactory and ingenious solution to their meaning, once again solving a problem in the received text by addition, not contradiction or replacement.

Why then was it never implemented? My guess is that Tolkien had not yet thought of this solution when he sent the errata off to Allen & Unwin on 21st September and that he generated the character on the spot in response to Paxman's question five days later. But he neglected to keep a copy of this letter for his files,[TN2] so that when he came to create the dwarven family tree, he had by that point forgotten about Thrym Thistlebeard.[TN3]

TEXT NOTES

1 Thrym ('Uproar') comes from the *Þrymskviða*, part of the *Elder Edda*, while Thistilbarði ('Thistlebeard') is part of a *þulur* (thulur) or namelist, one of many sometimes appended to Snorri's *Prose Edda*. However, in the original each is the name of a giant, not a dwarf.

Thrym is indeed the famous King Thrym of Jötunheim ('giantland'), lord of the frost-giants; *Þrymskviða* is the story of how he stole Mjöllnir (Thor's hammer, the bane of all giants) and demanded Freya's hand for its return. Loki convinced Thor to disguise himself as the bride-to-be, enabling the angry storm god to get close enough to reclaim his weapon, whereupon he killed most of the wedding party. This story has an unusual personal connection to Tolkien, for it was retold by his friend Rob Gilson as a short Christmas play in 1903, when the future fellow T.C.B.S. member was about ten years old. Called 'Thor's Journey to Fetch His Hammer', something of its precocious nature can be conveyed through its list of characters, scenes, and the mock-Shakespearian diction of its closing lines:

Characters
Loki: The God of evil
Thor: The God of thunder
Thrym: A wicked giant

Scenes
Scene I: Thor's bedroom
Scene II: Jötunheim
Scene III: The Hall of Valhalla
Scene IV: Dining-Hall in Thrym's castle

Thrym. And now I will fetch the hammer from its hiding-place.
(Exit Thrym)
Thor. Ha, ha, Thrym will soon lie prostrate on the ground.
(Enter Thrym)
(He places Miölnir in Thor's lap)
Thrym. Here is Miölnir.
(Thor rises from his seat and throws off his veil)
Thor. Now giant thou shalt die.
(He kills Thrym)
(curtain)

I am grateful to David Bratman for drawing my attention to R. Q. Gilson's early interest in Eddic myths and providing me with a copy of both this mini-play and 'The Wooing of Gerda', a similar retelling of *Skírnismál* from the year before (Christmas 1902).

As for *Thistilbardi*, Dronke (*The Poetic Edda*, vol. II, page 183) cites it as part of a list of giant names: Þistilbarði, Hrímnir, and Ganglati (Thistle-beard, Sootface, and Slowcoach) all being among the names for giants and Hengikepta, Loþinfingra, and Grottintanna (Hangjaw, Hairyfingers, and Grittingteeth) those for giantesses. The full list, one of a number of verse name-lists or *thulur* appearing in some manuscripts of Snorri's Edda – including lists of names for Odin, Thor, Freya, dwarves (deriving mainly from the *Dvergatal*), valkyrie, giants, giantesses, and the like – is printed in the massive collection *Corpvs Poeticum Boreale: The Poetry of the Old Northern Tongue*, ed. Gudbrand Vigfusson & F. York Powell [2 vols.,

1883], which attempts to bring together virtually all Old Norse heroic and mythological verse still in existence. The 'Thulor' appear in Bk X, §6: 'Rhymed Glossaries' (Vol. II, pages 422–39), and Thistilbardi's name in line 64 on page 425, in the same line with Thrym himself:

Þrymr, Þrúð-gelmir, Þistil-barði.

2 In his letter of 10th September 1950 to Stanley Unwin, announcing his decision to accept the 'second edition' Hobbit as the true and authentic version of the story and sending him the new Prefatory Note, Tolkien mentioned that 'as I have no secretary I rarely keep copies of my own letters, and I do not suppose that my recollections of them at long remove are necessarily accurate' (Ad.Ms.H.83; a portion of this letter, but not this passage, appears in *Letters* p. 142).

3 The absence of any mention of Thrym Thistlebeard from the 1950 Prefatory Note probably indicates that Tolkien had forgotten about him at this point, but in any case it would have been awkward to bring up a point hinging on a detail in an illustration in the introduction to a printing of the book that did not contain that picture.

The Fortunate Misunderstanding

In the end, Allen & Unwin's failure to recognize that although the two batches of material Tolkien sent them on 21st September 1947 were similar in appearance they were different in kind, each having its own title or subtitle, proved to be a fortunate misunderstanding. Eager to please one of their authors when they could, especially at a time when Tolkien was becoming increasingly distressed over the length of the as-yet-unpublished *Lord of the Rings* in a time of paper shortages and by their lack of interest in *The Silmarillion*, they scrupulously incorporated all his changes into the next printing, even to the extent of replacing a five-page section of the old edition with a ten-page section in the new. As Christopher Tolkien points out (letter to Taum Santoski, 3rd March 1989), when Tolkien wrote in his cover letter of 21st September 1947 that he was sending Allen & Unwin '. . . some notes on The Hobbit; *and* (for the possible amusement of yourself and Rayner) a specimen of re-writing of Chapter V . . .' (*Letters* p. 124; emphasis mine),[1] the publisher failed to grasp that the 'and' linked two entirely distinct categories of material. When Stanley Unwin informed Tolkien on 27th September that he was 'passing on The Hobbit corrections to our Production Department', Tolkien naturally assumed he meant the first sheet – that is, parts (ii) and (iii) above and further assumed, since Unwin said nothing further about the 'specimen of re-writing', that its inclusion had proved impossible. Not until Unwin sent him the proofs of the revised sections the next time the book was up for reprint on 26th July 1950 did Tolkien discover that (i), (ii), and (iii) had all been accepted and, although surprised, he quickly decided to make any necessary changes in *The Lord of the Rings* manuscript to match this change:

> . . . I have now made up my mind to accept the change and its consequences. The thing is now old enough for me to take a fairly impartial view, and it seems to me that the revised version is in itself better, in motive and narrative – and certainly would make the sequel (if ever published) much more natural.
>
> —JRRT to SU, 1st August 1950; *Letters* p. 141.

He further noted that

> Such people as I have consulted think that the alteration is in itself an improvement . . .
>
> —ibid., 10th September 1950; *Letters* p. 142.

He had now begun work on the prefatory note requested by Allen & Unwin to explain the difference between the first and second editions, sending them one version of it with his 10th September letter – being careful to specify that this was

> . . . a *specimen* of the kind of thing that I should want to insert . . . *This is not intended as copy*; but if you would return it, with any comment you like, it would be helpful.
>
> —ibid., italics mine.

This was probably the 'long version' – i.e., (A) or (B) – which was replaced by the 'short version' a few days later:

> I enclose . . . a copy of the briefest form of the prefatory note: which is intended as copy, if you should think it well to use it in the reprint.
>
> —JRRT to SU, 14th September 1950; *Letters* p. 142.

Thus, the original first edition text was replaced by a new and improved text which so overwhelmed its predecessor in sales that the existence of the earlier version of the Gollum chapter soon came to be known only through references to it in the editions that supplanted it. The experience also showed Tolkien that he could revisit the book more than a decade later (1944 vs. 1930–33) and improve it while also binding it more closely to what had become his masterwork: *The Lord of the Rings*. This discovery would in turn lead first to 'The Quest of Erebor' in 1954 and ultimately to the Fifth Phase, the abortive third edition now known as the 1960 Hobbit.

NOTES

1 Tolkien had earlier described this material to Unwin in a letter written on 31st July 1947 but not sent until 21st September along with the Fourth Phase Hobbit material:

> . . . when I revise chapter II [of *LotR*] for press: I intend, in any case, to shorten it. The proper way to negotiate the difficulty would be slightly to remodel the former story [*The Hobbit*] in its chapter V. That is not a practical question; though I certainly hope to leave behind me the whole thing revised and in final form . . .
>
> —*Letters*, page 121.

THE FIFTH PHASE

THE 1960 HOBBIT

The second edition Hobbit showed Tolkien that he could revisit Bilbo's story, even after a gap of years, and improve upon the original, while at the same time binding the story and its sequel more closely together. Roughly a decade after drafting that material, and several years after its publication, he returned to the story of the Unexpected Party and wrote 'The Quest of Erebor' [1954] – not a replacement for the opening chapter but in effect a complement to (and commentary on) it, retelling the story from Gandalf's and the dwarves' point of view. Focusing on the events that led Gandalf with Thorin & Company to Bilbo's doorstep, it places Bilbo's adventure in a larger – what we may call 'strategic' – context, as Gandalf considers how to counter the threat of Smaug in a war against Sauron, which he already foresees as impending some eighty years before the event. Fascinating though it is, 'The Quest of Erebor' does set one unfortunate precedent: it diminishes Bilbo in the reader's eyes, casting him very much as a silly fellow puffing and bobbing on the mat. Gandalf, after describing Bilbo as 'rather greedy and fat', says the hobbit 'made a complete fool of himself' and 'did not realize . . . how fatuous the Dwarves thought him . . . Thorin was much more . . . contemptuous than he perceived' (UT.323–4).

Ultimately, only a few paragraphs of 'The Quest of Erebor' made their way into the published *Lord of the Rings* (*LotR*.1115 & 1116), but clearly Tolkien did not so much reject this material as merely find himself forced to cut it for reasons of space. When, around 1960, he decided to undertake a detailed revision of *The Hobbit* and fully reconcile it to the later story in chronology, geography, and style, he drew upon this unpublished material when recasting *The Hobbit* into *The Lord of the Rings*' image. This is not to say that he inserted passages from the alternative opener into the earlier book, or even that he had the 1954 material before him as he worked, but rather that he approached Bilbo's story from the point of view of the rejected Appendix material, very much to Bilbo's disadvantage.

It has long been known that the last work Tolkien did on *The Hobbit*, the third edition of 1966, came about at his publisher's request, since the appearance of the unauthorized Ace paperbacks of *The Lord of the Rings* in the summer of 1965 meant that Houghton Mifflin and now Ballantine Books needed him to produce a revised authorized text in order to belatedly assert the American copyright. Humphrey Carpenter describes how Tolkien began, and

> spent many hours searching for some revision notes that he had already made, but he could not find them . . . When the next day he did get down to *The Hobbit* he found a good deal of it 'very poor' and had to restrain himself from rewriting the entire book.
>
> — *Tolkien: A Biography*, pages 227–8.

These 'revision notes', the Fifth Phase or 1960 Hobbit, are far more extensive than Carpenter's account indicates, in fact nothing less than a wholesale recasting of the book into the mold of its sequel. Aside from this passing mention in Carpenter's book, this material remained wholly unknown until Christopher Tolkien read a substantial section from it as his Guest of Honor presentation at the 1987 Marquette Tolkien Conference (Mythcon XVIII). It is here published, in its entirety, for the first time.

The 1960 Hobbit does not form a continuous text, but rather a series of passages, some brief and some extensive, intended to replace their second edition equivalents – very much as the Fourth Phase replaced superseded passages from the first edition. As with that material (see page 732), I have retained Tolkien's page and line numbers, on the theory that these chapters of *The Hobbit* are so familiar, and the range of pages so short, that it is easy for readers with any edition to locate the specific passage Tolkien means for comparison. Like the 1947 Hobbit, the Fifth Phase greatly expands upon the original in some places. Most of the material exists only in a single typescript, and it seems to have been composed on the typewriter. Although there are extensive plot-notes associated with the timeline and phases of the moon, very little rough drafting of the actual chapters survives; I give the few exceptions at the end of this chapter. I have divided the typescript and associated material into three groups:

- **New Chapter I**, which consists of fourteen pages of typescript [Ad.Ms.H.62–75], numbered 1 through 14 in the center at the top of each page; the first eight pages are double-spaced, the last six single-spaced. Appended to this I give excerpts from the two isolated sheets [Ad.Ms.H.12 & Ad.Ms.H.18] which contain very rough drafting for a few individual lines.
- **New Chapter II,** eight crowded single-spaced pages of typescript [Ad.Ms.H.25–32], numbered 'II 1', 'II 2', and the like in the upper right corner. This is immediately followed by about a single page's worth of text (single-spaced typescript) for New Chapter III, starting in the middle of the last page of New Chapter II and halting about a third of the way down the next page [Ad.Ms.H.32–3] but given its own pagination ('III 1' and 'III 2', respectively). I follow this with the text of a single sheet of notes [Ad.Ms.H.11] which contains

a few queries or reminders of points that need addressing in the preceding New Chapters.

- **Timelines and Itinerary**, which consists of four pages of single-spaced typescript [Ad.Ms.H.21–4] giving a detailed, day-by-day summary of Thorin & Company's trip from Bag-End to Rivendell; four pages of manuscript notes [Ad.Ms.H.19, 20, 13] covering the same ground in rougher form; and six pages of rough notes [Ad.Ms.H.15–18], not wholly legible, dealing with problems in the tale's chronology, particularly focusing on the phases of the moon.

Since this text is wholly unknown, aside from those fortunate enough to have been present at Christopher Tolkien's reading at Marquette in 1987, I have here reversed my normal procedure. In all the earlier sections of this book I give the earliest recoverable version of a text, striving to record the first glimpses as Tolkien puts words down on the page, since the final polished form of that text is familiar to all his readers from the published book. Here by contrast I give the *final* text in all cases, with all significant earlier readings given in Text Notes. A number of ellipses or rows of dots are in the original; these are given in closed format as Tolkien typed them (...), to distinguish them from omissions made in the notes or transcriptions by myself as editor (. . .).

New Chapter I

A WELL-PLANNED PARTY

In a hole in the ground there lived a hobbit. Not a nasty wet hole, filled with worms and an oozy smell, nor a dry hole, bare and sandy, with nothing in it to sit down on or to eat: it was a hobbit-hole, and that means comfort.

It had a round door like a porthole, painted green, with a yellow brass knob in the exact middle. The door opened into a long hall, shaped like a tunnel, airy, but dark when the lamps were not lit. Its floor was tiled and carpeted, there were polished chairs against the walls, and rows of pegs for hats and coats – the hobbit was fond of visitors. The tunnel went on a good way into the side of the hill, the Hill of Hobbiton, near the top of which the hobbit lived; and many little round doors opened out of it, first on one side and then on the other. No going upstairs for the hobbit: bedrooms, bathrooms, cellars, pantries, wardrobes (rooms full of clothes), kitchens, breakfast-room, dining-room, drawing room, all were on the same floor. The best rooms were all on the lefthand side as you went in, for only these had windows, deep-set round windows looking over the garden to meadows beyond, sloping down to the river.

The hobbit was very well-to-do, it was said, and his name was Baggins. The Bagginses had lived in the neighbourhood of Hobbiton for time out of mind, and people considered them very respectable, not only because most of them were rich, but also because they never had any adventures nor did anything unexpected: you could tell what a Baggins would say on any question without the trouble of asking him. But this story tells how a Baggins had an adventure, and found himself saying and doing things altogether unexpected. He got caught up in great events, which he never understood; and he became enormously important, though he never realized it.

How astonishing this was will be better understood by those who know something about hobbits; and some account of them is really needed nowadays for they are becoming rare, and they avoid the Big People, as they call us. They were a small people, about half our height or less, often smaller than the Dwarves of those days, to whom they were quite unrelated: hobbits never have beards. They loved peace and the quiet of a well-ordered and well-farmed countryside; most of them were in fact farmers in a small way, though many were clever with tools. They had long and skilful fingers and made many useful and well-shaped things, mostly of wood or clay or leather [> glass]. But there were very few shoemakers among them, for they seldom wore either shoes or boots. They did not need them, for their feet had tough leathery soles, and were covered as high as the ankles in thick curling hair, warm and brown like the hair on their heads. They had good-natured faces, broad, bright-eyed and red-cheeked, and mouths shaped for laughter. And laugh they did, and eat, and drink, often and heartily; for they were fond of jests at all times, and liked six meals a day (when they could get them).

They dressed in bright colours, especially yellow and green, for they delighted in fields and trees. Though they were inclined to grow rather fat, and did not hurry unnecessarily,[TN1] they were nimble; and quick of hearing too, and sharp-eyed. They had from the first the art of moving swiftly and silently, disappearing when large folk or beasts that they did not wish to meet came blundering by. To us that might seem magical; but Hobbits have never in fact studied magic of any kind, their skill is a gift improved by long practice and helped by their friendship with the earth and all growing things.

More could be said, but for the present that is a good enough description of Hobbits, or at least of that kind that in those days lived, as they had done for hundreds of years, in the little land that they called the Shire, away in the North-west of the world.

The chief family in the Shire were the Tooks, whose lands lay across The Water, the small river that ran at the foot of the Hill. Now that is important, for[TN2] the mother of the hobbit of this tale, Bilbo Baggins, was Belladonna Took, eldest of the three remarkable daughters of the Old Took, head of all the Tooks, and famous for having lived to the age of one hundred and thirty. It was often said (in other families) that the Tooks must have some elvish blood in them: which was of course absurd, but there was undoubtedly some thing queer about them, something not quite hobbitlike, according to the manners of the Shire: an outlandish strain maybe from long ago.[TN3] Every now and again Tooks would go off on adventures. They disappeared, and the family hushed it up.

Not that Belladonna Took ever had any adventures after she married Bungo Baggins. Bungo, that was Bilbo's father, built for her the most commodious hobbit-hole that was to be found in that part of the Shire, always excepting the vast and many-tunneled dwelling of the Tooks. It was meant, of course, to house a large family. But Bilbo was their only son, and they both died young – for hobbits – being still in their early eighties. And there now was Bilbo, in the commodious hole, looking and behaving like a second edition of his solid and comfortable father. But maybe there was something a little peculiar in his make-up coming from the Took side, hidden, but waiting for a chance to come out. The chance never arrived, until Bilbo Baggins was grown up, indeed about fifty years old, and had apparently settled down immovably.

One morning long ago in the quiet of the world, when the hobbits were still numerous and prosperous, and their green corner of the great lands was still enjoying its long peace,[TN4] Bilbo Baggins was standing at his door after breakfast, smoking a long wooden pipe.[TN5] At that moment Gandalf appeared. Gandalf![TN6] Those who go in for Ancient History will prick up their ears, though few know all there is to tell about him. Wherever he went strange things happened, and he left behind him marvellous tales. All the same he seemed fond of hobbits, and at one time he had often visited the Shire. But it was now many years since he had appeared there, except for a brief visit when his friend the Old Took died, and that was now at least twenty years ago. So most even of the older folk in Hobbiton had almost forgotten what he looked like. He had been far away, 'over the Hill and across the Water' as they said, on business of his own,[TN7] since they were young. To little hobbits he was just a character in fireside tales.

All that Bilbo saw that morning was an old man with a tall pointed blue hat, a long grey cloak, and a silver scarf, over which his white beard hung down below his waist. He had tall black boots, and leaned on a staff.

'Good morning!' said Bilbo cheerily. The sun was shining and the grass was very green. But Gandalf looked at him from under his bushy eyebrows that bristled beneath the brim of his hat.

'What do you mean?' he said. 'That it is a fine morning, and you feel pleased with yourself? Perhaps you wish me to feel pleased too. I may. We'll see'.

'Indeed I hope you will', said Bilbo. 'Why not? It is a fine morning anyway for a pipe of tobacco out of doors.[TN8] If you have a pipe with you, pray take a seat and try some of my weed: it is "Old Toby". There is no hurry. All the day's before us'. Then Bilbo sat down on the bench by his door, crossed his legs, and blew out a beautiful grey ring of smoke that sailed up into the air without breaking and floated away over the Hill.

'Very pretty!' said Gandalf. 'But I have no time to blow smoke-rings today. I am looking for someone to share in an adventure that I am arranging, and it is very difficult to find anyone suitable'.

'I should think so – in these parts. We are plain quiet folk and have no use for adventures. Nasty disturbing things! Make you late for dinner! I can't think why anybody has them'. With that Mr. Baggins stuck a thumb behind his braces, and blew out another even bigger smoke-ring. Then he took out his morning letters, and began to read, pretending to take no more notice of the old man. He was not the kind of visitor he liked; he made him feel uncomfortable. He wished he would go away. But the old man did not move. He stood leaning on his staff and gazing at the hobbit without saying a word, till Bilbo began to feel annoyed.

'Good morning!' he said at last. 'We don't want any adventures here, thank you! You might try over the Hill or across the Water. Good morning!'

'Now I understand what you mean by *Good morning*', said Gandalf. 'You mean that you want to get rid of me, and that it won't be good till I move off'.

'Not at all, not at all, my dear sir! Let me see, I don't think I know your name?'

'Yes, yes, my dear sir! But I do know your name, Mr. Bilbo Baggins. And you knew my name once, when you were younger and brighter. It is Gandalf, in this part of the world.[TN9] Gandalf! Do you hear? To think that I should live to be good-morninged by Belladonna Took's son, as if I was selling buttons at the door!'

'Gandalf, Gandalf! Not the old wizard who used to visit the Tooks? Good gracious me! He used to make marvellous fireworks for the Old Took's parties on Midsummer's Eve. I remember them! Splendid! They used to go up like great roses and lilies and snap-dragons of fire, and hang in the sky like flowers of golden-rain in the twilight!' Mr. Baggins was not quite so prosy as he liked to believe, and any way he delighted in flowers. 'Bless me!' he went on. 'Not the Gandalf who used to tell such wonderful tales about dragons, and goblins, and giants, and mountains in far countries – and the Sea. They used to send many quiet lads, and lasses, off on *adventures*, it is said: any mad thing from climbing tall trees to visiting Elves, and even trying to sail in ships'.[TN10] Bilbo's voice fell almost to a whisper. 'To sail, sail away to the Other Shore. Dear me!' he sighed. 'Life used to be quite interest– I mean, you used to upset things badly in the Shire, once upon a time. I beg your pardon, but I had no idea you were still in business'.

'Where else should I be?' said the wizard. 'But you have my pardon. Indeed I am pleased, and it *is* a good morning.[TN11] You do remember something about me; and what you say is very promising. For your old grandfather Took's sake, and for poor Belladonna's, I will do something for you'.

'You are very kind; but I have not asked for anything, thank you all the same!'

'That doesn't matter. I have made up *my* mind. Yes, I think you will do. Yes, I will send *you* on this adventure. You may be useful; and anyway it will do you good, if you come through'.

'No, no! I am sorry. I don't want any adventures. Not today, thank you! Good morning!' Bilbo backed towards his doorstep. 'But please come to tea, any time you like', he stammered.[TN12] 'Why not tomorrow? Come tomorrow! Good bye!' With that he scuttled inside his round green door, and shut it as quickly as he dared, not to seem too rude. Wizards are after all wizards.

Bilbo had only just had breakfast, but he felt that a cake or two and a drink would do him good after his fright. 'What on earth did I ask him to tea for!' he said to himself in the pantry. 'But perhaps he won't come. I am sure wizards don't like hobbit-tea'.

Gandalf in the meantime was still standing deep in thought outside the door. At last he laughed softly, and stepping up with the spike on his staff he scratched a curious sign on the hobbit's beautiful green door. Then he strode away, just about the time when Bilbo was finishing his second cake and was beginning to think he had escaped adventures very well.

The next day he had almost forgotten about Gandalf. His letters had brought him much news of his many relations, and some of them were troublesome. And anyway yesterday he had been too upset to mark his invitation on his Engagement Tablet: today, Wednesday, was blank.

Just before his tea-time there came a tremendous ring of the front-door bell; and then he remembered! He rushed and put on the kettle, and put out another cup and saucer, and an extra cake or two, and ran to the door.

'I am so sorry to keep you waiting!' he was going to say, when he saw that it was not Gandalf at all. It was a dwarf, with a blue beard tucked into a golden belt and very bright eyes under his dark green hood. As soon as the door was opened, he pushed inside, just as if he had been expected. He hung his hooded cloak on the nearest peg, and 'Dwalin at your service!' he said with a low bow.

'Bilbo Baggins at yours!' said the hobbit, too surprised to ask any questions for the moment. When the silence that followed had become uncomfortable, he added: 'I am just about to take tea; pray come and join me'. He was a little stiff, perhaps; but he was not used to having uninvited dwarves come and hang up their things in his hall. Without a word of explanation. That would follow, he hoped.

They had not been long at the table, in fact they had hardly reached the third cake, when there came another even louder ring at the bell.

'Excuse me!' said the hobbit, and off he went to the door.

'So you have got here at last!' he meant to say to Gandalf this time. But it was not Gandalf. Instead there was a very old-looking dwarf on the step, with a white beard and a scarlet hood; and he too hopped inside as soon as the door was open, just as if he had been invited.

'I see they have begun to arrive already', he said when he caught sight of Dwalin's green hood. He hung his red one next to it, and 'Balin at your service!' he said with his hand on his breast.

'Thank you!' said Bilbo with a gasp. It was not the correct thing to say, but *they have begun to arrive* had flustered him badly. He liked visitors, but he liked to know them before they arrived, and he preferred to invite them himself. He had a horrible thought that the cakes might run short, and then he – as the host: he knew his duty and stuck to it, however painful – he might have to go without.

'Come along in, and have some tea!' he managed to say after taking a deep breath.

'A little beer would suit me better, if it is all the same to you, my good sir', said Balin with the white beard. 'But I don't mind some cake – seed-cake, if you have any'.

'Lots!' Bilbo found himself answering, to his own surprise; and he found himself scuttling off, too, to the cellar to fill a beer-mug, and to the small pantry to fetch two beautiful round seed-cakes that he had meant to have last thing, before he went to bed.

When he got back Balin and Dwalin were talking at the table like old friends (as a matter of fact they were brothers). Bilbo plumped down the beer and the cakes in front of them, when loud came a ring at the bell again, and then another ring.

'Gandalf for certain this time', he thought as he puffed along the passage. But it was not. It was two more dwarves, both with blue hoods, silver belts, and yellow beards; and each of them carried a bag of tools and a spade. In they hopped, as soon as the door began to open. Bilbo was hardly surprised at all.

'What can I do for you, my dwarves?' he said.

'Kili at your service!' said the one. 'And Fili!' added the other; and they both swept off their blue hoods and bowed.

'At yours and your family's' replied Bilbo with a bow, remembering his manners this time.

'Dwalin and Balin here already, I see', said Kili. 'Let us join the throng!'

'Throng!' thought Mr. Baggins. 'I don't like the sound of that. I really must sit down for a minute and collect my wits. It's my turn for a drink!' He had only just had a sip – by the fire, while the dwarves sat round the table, and talked about mines and gold and troubles with the goblins, and the depredations of dragons, and many other things which he did not understand, and did not wish to, for they sounded much too adventurous – when *ding-dong-a-ling-dang*, his bell rang again, as if some naughty little hobbit-boy was trying to pull the handle off.

'Someone at the door!' he said, blinking.

'Some four, I should say by the sound', said Fili. 'Besides, we saw them in the distance, coming along behind us'.

The poor little hobbit sat down in the hall and put his head in his hands, and wondered what had happened, and what was going to happen, and whether they would all stay to supper. Then the bell rang again louder than ever, and he had to run to the door. It was not four after all, it was FIVE. Another dwarf had come up while he was wondering in the hall. He had hardly turned the knob before they were all inside, bowing and saying 'at your service' one after another. Dori, Nori, Ori, Oin and Gloin were their names; and very soon two purple hoods, a grey hood, a brown hood, and a white hood were hanging on the pegs, and off they marched, with their broad hands stuck in their gold and silver belts, to join the others. Already it had almost become a throng.

Two called for cider, and two called for beer; and Gloin called for old ale. 'Bring some honey and spices!' he said. 'I like mine mulled by the fire'. And all the nine called for more cakes, and for butter as well;[TN13] so the poor hobbit was kept very busy for a while.

Great jugs of beer and cider had been set on the table, Gloin's ale was in a pan on the fire, the seed-cakes had gone, and the dwarves were busy toasting buttered cake,[TN14] when there came – a loud knock. Not a ring, but a hard rat-tat on Bilbo's beautiful green door. Somebody was banging with a stick!

Bilbo rushed along the passage, very angry, and altogether bothered and bewildered – this was the most awkward Wednesday he ever remembered. He pulled open the door with a jerk, and they all fell in, one on top of the other. More dwarves, four more! And there was Gandalf behind, leaning on his staff and laughing. He had made quite a dent on the beautiful door, but he had also, by the way, knocked out the secret mark that he had put there the morning before.

'Carefully! Carefully!' he said. 'It is not like you, Bilbo, to keep friends waiting on the mat and then open the door like a trap! Let me introduce Bifur, Bofur, and Bombur, and especially Thorin!'

'At your service!' said Bifur, Bofur, and Bombur, a little coolly, standing in a row. [*added*: They brought in a large bag, and what looked like sticks wrapped in cloths, which they put in the hall-stand.][TN15] Then they hung up two yellow hoods and a pale green one; and also a sky-blue hood with a long liripipe[TN16] ending in a silver tassel. This belonged to Thorin, a dwarf of immense dignity, in fact no other than the great Thorin Oakenshield himself, renowned in history. He was not at all pleased at falling flat on Bilbo's mat with his attendants, Bifur, Bofur, and Bombur, on top of him. For one thing Bombur was enormously fat and heavy. Thorin indeed was very haughty, and he said nothing about <u>service</u>; but poor Mr.

Baggins bowed so low and said he was sorry so many times that at last he grunted 'pray do not mention it', and stopped frowning.

'Now we are all here!' said Gandalf, looking at the row of thirteen hoods, and his own hat and cloak, hanging on the pegs. 'Quite a merry gathering! I hope there is something left for the late-comers to eat and drink! What's that? Tea! No thank you! A little red wine, I think, for me'.

'And for me', said Thorin.

'And raspberry jam and pastry', said Bifur.

'And mince-pie and cheese', said Bofur.

'And pork-pie and onions', said Bombur.

'And more cakes, and ale, and cider, if you don't mind', called the other dwarves from the parlour.[TN17]

'Put on a few eggs, there's a good fellow!' Gandalf called after him, as the hobbit stumped off to the pantries. 'And just bring out the cold chicken and pickles!'[TN18]

'He seems to know as much about the inside of my larders[TN19] as I do myself!' thought Mr. Baggins, who was altogether flummoxed, and was beginning to feel alarmed: he wondered whether a most wretched adventure had not come right into his house. By the time he had got all the bottles and dishes and knives and forks and glasses and plates and spoons, not to mention the food, piled up on big trays, he was getting very hot, and red in the face, and annoyed.

'Confound and bother these dwarves!' he said aloud. 'Why don't they come and lend a hand?' Lo and behold! there stood Balin and Dwalin at the door of the kitchen, and Fili and Kili behind them; and before he could say *knife* they had whisked the trays and a couple of small tables into the parlour and set out everything afresh.

Gandalf sat at the head of the party, with Thorin at his right, and the other twelve dwarves round the joined tables; but Bilbo sat on a stool at the fireside, nibbling at a biscuit (his appetite was quite taken away), and trying to look unconcerned, as if this was all just an everyday affair and not in the least like an adventure. The dwarves ate and ate, and talked and talked, and time got on. At last they pushed their chairs back, and Bilbo made a move to collect the plates and glasses.

'I suppose you will all stay to supper?' he said in his politest unpressing tones.

'Of course!' said Thorin. 'And after. We shall not get through our business till late, and we must have some music first. Now to clear up!'

. . . . . .

At this point, the continuous narrative stops and the text becomes a series of replacement passages, very much like the Phase Four typescript (the

1947 Hobbit material). In each case, Tolkien has provided a page number (using the second edition pagination) and line number as well; a minus sign in front of the line number means lines counted up from the bottom.

p. 22/bottom line to 23/top.[TN20] safe and quick, while the hobbit was turning round like a top in the middle of the kitchen, shouting out directions and trying to see that things were put in the right places.

p. 23/4 He was blowing enormous smoke-rings

p. 23/ 22 from inside their jackets; Bombur produced a drum from his bag in the hall; Bifur and Bofur[TN21] went out too, and came back with the clarinets that they had left . . .

p. 26/ –2 [2 up] he was so overwhelmed

p. 27/3 us (even our friend...
/10–13. important dwarf, and he thought it an important occasion.[TN22]
/16 it burst out like the whee of a rocket going up in the sky
/19 delete magic
/–7 'Excitable little fellow[TN23]
/–5 one of the best – as brave as Bandobras at a pinch'. No doubt an exaggeration; but Gandalf was doing his best in a difficult situation. For Bandobras had been the Old Took's great-granduncle, and usually called Bullroarer. He was so huge (for a hobbit) that he rode a small horse. At the Battle of the Green Fields, when the hobbits were driven back, he charged the ranks of the Goblins of Mount Gram, and smote their king Golfimbul [> Gulfimbul][TN24] to the earth with his great wooden club. So the battle was won, and there had been none since in the Shire. Even the dwarves had heard of Bullroarer Took.

In the meantime, however, Bullroarer's gentler relative

p. 28/13 being brave
/14 a stone dragon out of an enchanted sleep.[TN25]
/20 He looks more of a fool than a burglar
/23 to be thought brave. As for little fellow puffing on the mat it made his blood hot
/26 you were a fool

p. 29/1 strange faces.[TN26]
/9 And I assure you there is a mark on this door – the sign we were told to look for: Tracker and Treasure-hunter it means to

those who know the Dwarf-runes. Burglar we say in these days; it is shorter. The fees are the same. Gandalf said there was a hobbit of the sort, living quietly in these parts, waiting for a job – needing one soon. Only yesterday he told us he had arranged a meeting here for today. 'Four o'clock' he said, 'but don't all arrive at once!'

'Of course there was a mark', said Gandalf. 'I put it there myself. You asked me to find a treasure-hunter for your expedition, and I chose Mr. Baggins

/–7 I have chosen Mr. Baggins, and that must be enough for all of you. If I say he is a Burglar, a Burglar he is, or will be when the time comes. If I say he needs a job soon, I know what I am talking about. There is a lot more in him than you see, and a deal more than he guesses himself.

p. 30/3 This was made by Thror, your grandfather, he said to Thorin. Bilbo and the other dwarves gathered round. 'It is a plan of the Mountain'.

'I don't see that this will help me much' said Thorin, after a glance.

/18 Delete (Look...red). Substitute * and a footnote *See the copy of the plan at the beginning of this book.[TN27]

/–6 devouring so many dwarves and most of the Men of Dale'

p. 30/–4 to 31/ top. 'It seems a great big hole to me' said Bilbo, deeply interested. He loved maps, and in his hall there hung a large one of The Hobbiton Country which he had drawn himself, marking all his favourite walks in red. 'How could such a large door be kept secret from everybody outside, apart from the dragon?' he asked. He had of course no experience of dragons, and very little of dwarves.

'In many ways', said Gandalf.........method, I believe'.[TN28]

'It is', said Thorin.

/–14 ...what to do. We must go east, of course, by as straight roads as we can find, quietly, attracting as little notice as possible – until we come to the Long Lake. After that the trouble will begin'.

'A long while before that', interrupted Gandalf. 'Things have not changed for the better since you came to the West. Few roads are straight, and none are safe, and the East is full of danger.'

'From the Long Lake we might go up the Running River', Thorin went on, taking no notice, 'and so to the ruins of Dale...

p. 31/–2 to 32/ top 'That would be no good', said the wizard, 'not even for warriors of the Elder Days, who cannot now be matched.[TN29] But we have discussed all that; and anyway we are not looking for a warrior in the Shire: their little swords are blunt; their axes are used for trees, and their bows for small deer.[TN30] We decided that you must use stealth; and I chose your helper. Here he is, Bilbo Baggins: the "burglar", specially selected. So now let us get on'.

'Very well then', said Thorin, turning to Bilbo with mock-politeness. 'Let the selected expert give us some ideas and suggestions!'......

p. 32/18. 'Bless me!' said Thorin. 'Haven't you looked at the map? And didn't you hear our song? And haven't we been talking about all this for hours?'

'All the same, I should like it plain and clear', said Bilbo obstinately, trying to appear prudent and professional. 'Also I should like to know about...' By which he meant: 'What chance is there of my coming back alive? and what am I going to get out of it, if I do?'

'O very well', said Thorin. 'Many years ago, in my great-grandfather's days, our family was driven out of the far North.[TN31] Some went east to the Iron Hills. But Thror my grandfather returned with most of our kin to this Mountain on the map, where Thrain the Old[TN32] his ancestor had lived for a while, once upon a time. There they mined and they tunnelled, and they made deeper halls and greater workshops;[TN33] and they found a wealth of gold and many gems. They grew rich and famous, and Thror became King under the Mountain, and was treated with great reverence by the Men who lived further south, and were spreading up the Running River. In those days they built the merry town of Dale in the valley over-shadowed by the Mountain. Their lords used to send for our smiths, and reward even the least skilful most richly. Fathers would beg us to take their sons as apprentices, and paid us handsomely. It was always for food and wine that we asked, so that we had no need to grow it or get it for ourselves. The land was fat and fruitful in those days [> then]. Those were good years for us, and the least of us had gold to spend and to lend, and leisure to make beautiful things for our delight. The young dwarves made marvellous and cunning toys, the like of which are not to be found in the world today. So the halls of Thror were filled with armour and harps and drinking-horns and cups and things carven and hammered and inlaid, and with jewels like stars; and the toy-market of Dale was one of the wonders of the North.

Alas! that brought the dragon upon us! Greed has long ears.[TN34] Dragons, as no doubt a treasure-hunter will know, steal gold and jewels from elves and dwarves and men, wherever they can find them; and they guard their plunder as long as they live, a thousand years[TN35] maybe, unless they are killed, though they never enjoy one small ring of it. They cannot use it, and they do not know good work from bad; but they remember the least thing that they have ever possessed, and woe to anyone who tries to set a finger on it! Curse them!

There were still many dragons in the North in those days,[TN36] and treasure was becoming so scarce that they fell to fighting among themselves, and the waste and destruction that dragons make was going from bad to worse. There was beyond the Grey Mountains a most greedy, strong, and wicked worm called Smaug. One day he flew up in the air and came south

p. 34/ bottom. After that, when we had set our curse on the dragon, we went away; and we

p. 35/2 as low as coalmining, or even road-mending...[TN37]

/6. 'I still mean to get it back, and to bring my curse home to Smaug – if I can'.

/9, 10. had a secret Side-door

/14 'I did not get hold of it, it was given to me', said the wizard with a flash of his eyes. 'Thror, your grandfather was murdered in the mines of Moria by Azog the Goblin – '[TN38]

'Yes, curse Azog!' said Thorin.

'And Thrain, your father, went away on the twenty-first of April, a hundred years ago last Thursday, and has never been seen by you since –'

'Too true, alas!' said Thorin.

'Well your father gave me this map,[TN39] ninety one years ago, and I have guarded it ever since'.

'Ninety one years!' cried Thorin. 'For ninety one years you have kept my property?'

'Thorin', said Gandalf quietly, 'though your fame had reached me, I first met you only a few weeks ago.[TN40] Until then the use and meaning of this map was quite unknown to me; and I did not know who it belonged to. [*added in margin*: Your father could not remember his own name, nor yours, when he gave me the parchment.] If I have chosen my own time for restoring it, you have no right to be angry: I came by it only at the peril of my life, for which I think you owe me some thanks. I give it to you now', he said, handing the map to Thorin with a bow.

'I thank you' said Thorin. 'I would thank you more, maybe, if your words were not dark. I do not understand them at all!' Bilbo felt that he would like to say the same; but he wisely said nothing.

'You are slow', said Gandalf tartly [> sharply]. 'Until I heard your tale, I did not know how Thror and Thrain escaped from the Mountain. Thrain was dying when I found him. I guess that your grandfather gave this map to him for safety before he himself went to the mines of Moria. Then later Thrain, your father, went away, as you have told, though you did not know why. I think he took the map and went to [spy on >] try his luck in the Mountain. But he had no luck; he was caught in dark perils, and never came in sight of his home. How he came there, I cannot tell; but I found him a prisoner in the dungeons of the Necromancer'.[TN41]

'Whatever were you doing there!' said Thorin with a shudder, going pale, and the dwarves hid their faces.

'Do not ask! Not at night.' said Gandalf. 'I will not speak of it.[TN42] But it was my task to search in the shadows, and a dark and dangerous quest it was. Even I, Gandalf, hardly escaped. I tried to save your father, though he was a nameless dwarf to me, alone, in misery. It was too late. He was witless and wandering, and had forgotten almost all that he had known, except a map, and a key'.

Thorin ground his teeth. 'Thror was avenged: we paid the goblins in Moria long ago. We must give a thought to this Necromancer!'

'Hush!' said Gandalf. 'Grief has robbed you of your wits. He[TN43] is an enemy far beyond the powers of all the dwarves in the world, if they could all be gathered again from the four corners of Earth, even from their tombs. The one thing that your father wished was that you should read the map and use the key. *Give them to my son*[TN44] were his last words, though he did not speak your name. They are burden enough. The Dragon of the Mountain is as big a task as you can manage; too big, maybe'.

'Hear, hear!' said Bilbo to himself, but he said it aloud.

'Hear what?' they all said, turning suddenly towards him; and he was so flustered that he answered: 'hear what I have got to say!'

'What's that?' they asked.

'Well, I should say that you must go east, which will take several days,[TN45] no doubt – '. Gandalf smiled, and Thorin snorted. 'Well, then you must have a quiet look round. After all, there is the Side-door, and dragons must sleep sometimes, I suppose. If you sit on the door-step long enough, I daresay you will think of some plan, or something will turn up. And well, don't you know, I think we have talked long enough for one night, if you see what I mean. What about bed, and an early start, and all that? You can have a good breakfast before you go.'

'Before *we* go, I suppose you mean', said Thorin. 'Aren't you the burglar? And what about *stealth*? Isn't sitting on the door-step your job, not to speak of getting inside? But I agree about bed and breakfast. I like six eggs with my ham, when starting on a journey: fried not poached, and mind you don't break 'em'.

p. 37/14 ..., and he was not at all sure now

As will readily be seen, much of the wording of the original book remains, yet the tone is greatly altered. In particular, the voice of the narrator is muted and editorial asides omitted. Word-play is greatly reduced – for example, 'confusticate and bebother' becomes simply 'confound and bother', and 'bewildered and bewuthered' becomes instead 'bothered and bewildered' – and in general the playfulness of the original gives way to a more stately style. Perhaps more significantly, characterization is also changed: Gandalf, for example, now speaks with more authority. He could no longer be mistaken for 'a little old man' in a pointed hat, but this enhanced dignity does come with a price: he is also more remote, less a figure the reader is likely to sympathize with.

The change in Thorin is greater. In keeping with his portrayal in 'The Quest of Erebor', the dwarven leader has become much more abrupt and brusque, and he shows an unhealthy concern over property that anticipates his later fall in the Lonely Mountain chapters. In the original book his succumbing to the dragon-sickness had been a sudden and surprising departure from his usual self, a distortion of his fundamentally admirable personality and a frightening lesson in the corrupting power of dragon-haunted gold; here an obsession with his property and grievance over his rights has simply become part of his character, an innate flaw. Like the anticipations of Saruman's fall Tolkien inserted into some of his later writings, these have the effect of hinting that the character was corrupt from the beginning, which was very much not the case in the original book.

Finally, Bilbo is made more foolish – someone who 'loved maps' and had his favorite walks all marked out on the neighborhood map (made by himself) would know that the dragon-haunted mountain they speak of is more than a day or two, or even a few days' walk away; maps made in the Shire might tend to end at its borders (*LotR*.56), but he would certainly know that Thror's kingdom and Smaug's lair must lie outside those borders. And this naivety is extended beyond the end of the book. We are told that 'He got caught up in great events, which he never understood; and he became enormously important, though he never realized it', but this contradicts *The Lord of the Rings*, where Bilbo took part in the Council of Elrond and learned (if he did not know already from Gandalf) that his ring was the One Ring, who its maker and master was, and what would happen if He regained it. He even volunteered to undertake the Quest of Mount Doom himself, which is not so quixotic as it sounds, given that the quest was to rely on luck and stealth, not martial prowess. More importantly, it contradicts the closing lines of *The Hobbit* itself, where Gandalf, who serves as Tolkien's spokesman more than any other character, assures Bilbo that he played only a small role in all these events. This diminishment of Bilbo, a central feature of 'The Quest of Erebor', becomes even more pronounced in the next chapter.

TEXT NOTES

1 originally: 'Though inclined to grow rather fat, they did not hurry unnecessarily'.

Several small variants from the published text in the section describing hobbits are interesting to note: most significantly, the shift from present tense (all published editions) to past tense (1960 Hobbit); e.g., 'hobbits are (or were) a small people' becomes simply 'hobbits *were* a small people'. The sentence about how hobbits are half our height, introduced into print in the third edition (cf. DAA.30 & 31), makes its first appearance here, but the 1960 text has 'half our height *or less*'; this is a direct link to *halflings*, the generic name for hobbits among other peoples in *The Lord of the Rings*. Finally, the allusion to their 'seldom' wearing shoes or boots seems to refer back to an idea Tolkien had mentioned in a 1938 letter to Houghton Mifflin but never managed to incorporate into any text:

> There is in the text no mention of [Bilbo's] acquiring of boots. There should be! It has dropped out somehow or other in the various revisions – the bootings occurred at Rivendell; and he was again bootless after leaving Rivendell on the way home. But since leathery soles, and well-brushed furry feet are a feature of essential hobbitness, he ought really to appear unbooted, except in special illustrations of episodes.
>
> —JRRT to HM, March/April 1938; *Letters* p. 35.

This comment seems to have arisen from comparison between the various pictures and drawings of Bilbo in the book: he is clearly barefoot in 'The Hall at Bag-End' (DAA.363; H-S#139) but just as clearly booted in the eagle picture (DAA plate two [top]; H-S#113). He seems barefooted in the Barrel-Rider sketch (plate VIII [top]) but clearly has some sort of footwear in both of the finished versions of that scene (DAA.238–9 & plate two [bottom]; H-S#122 & 124) and in 'Conversation with Smaug' (plate XI [top]).

Tolkien is in error in saying that text mentioning Bilbo's boots 'dropped out'; in fact, what seems to have occurred is that he must have thought of adding such text at some point but failed to write it down (at least in any form that survives) and so forgot to implement the change.

2 The words 'that is important, for' were bracketed but not cancelled.

3 Immediately after the sentence about the Old Took originally came the sentence 'There was something queer about the Tooks, something not quite hobbitlike. It was whispered that they had some fairy blood from long ago'; the replacement sentence that followed originally ran 'It was often said (in other families) that the Tooks must have some elvish blood in them: or some outlandish strain, which was of course

absurd; but there was undoubtedly some thing queer about them, something not quite hobbitlike . . .'

4 The phrase 'its long peace' was changed to 'its peace', possibly to avoid what had presumably been the deliberate reiteration in 'long ago' 'long peace' 'long wooden pipe' all in the same sentence.

5 This was originally followed by 'a long wooden pipe *that reached nearly down to his well-brushed toes*'; the latter phrase was bracketed, apparently for omission as a too-whimsical touch.

6 An entire sentence was cancelled here: 'Gandalf! *If you had heard a quarter of what even the hobbits had heard about him, and that was not a hundredth part of all that there was to hear, you would be prepared for any sort of remarkable tale*'. The sentence that followed originally read 'will prick up their ears *expecting remarkable things to happen* . . .'

7 The phrase 'on business of his own' is bracketed as if for removal, but then the brackets were scratched out and the words retained.

8 'a pipe of tobacco': it is mildly surprising that Tolkien has retained the apparent anachronism of 'tobacco' here, given the circumlocution of the more ambiguous 'pipe-weed'† used in *The Lord of the Rings*. But even there he had specified that this was 'a variety . . . of *Nicotiana* . . . not native to our part of the world, but . . . brought over Sea by the Men of [Númenor]' ('Concerning Pipe-weed', *LotR*.20–21). Since *Nicotiana* is a class of New World plants, including tobacco, its presence in Middle-earth is presented not as an anachronism but a piece of lost history.

†The original Carib word (rendered by Spanish explorers as *tabaca*) is generally thought to have meant the pipe, not the plant smoked in it, but the OED notes that the point is disputed: Tolkien's 'pipe-weed' nicely bridges the ambiguity by embracing both.

9 This is an oblique reference to a passage from *The Two Towers*, where Faramir reports Gandalf as once saying '*Many are my names in many countries . . . Mithrandir among the Elves, Tharkûn to the Dwarves; Olórin I was in my youth in the West that is forgotten, in the South Incánus, in the North Gandalf; to the East I go not*' (*LotR*.697).

10 Added, but then omitted: 'to sail in *their* ships'. The passage in the next sentence about Bilbo's wistfully thinking of sailing 'away to the Other Shore' (here significantly capitalized to make it clear that Elvenhome is meant) is of course a foreshadowing, in this first encounter, of his eventual fate in the final chapter of *The Lord of the Rings*.

11 Originally this sentence read 'Indeed I am pleased, *as you wished* . . .'

12 The words 'he stammered' were bracketed, then removed.

13 Originally they called 'for *bread and* butter'; this cancellation probably was made at the same time as the toast was removed from the following paragraph (see Text Note 14).

14 Originally 'busy *making rounds of buttered toast*'; this pencilled change would have been made at the same time as that noted in Text Note 13.

15 This sentence is typed in the left margin and marked for insertion at this point; the bag contains their musical instruments. See the Draftings section at the end of this chapter.

16 A *liripipe* is a long narrow extension at the point of a hood; the word is of unknown (fourteenth-century) origin but seems to have originally been applied to academic costume (a graduate's hood). In Pauline Baynes' illustrations to Tolkien's *Smith of Wootton Major* [1967], Alf the Master Cook wears a liripipe (SWM, expanded edition, page [42]).

17 Originally the other dwarves are in the sitting room rather than the parlour; this change seems to have been made right away in the course of typing, before Tolkien moved on to the next line (Ad.Ms.H.71).

18 In the first and second editions, Bifur asked for 'raspberry jam and *apple-tart*', Bofur for 'mince-*pies* [plural] and cheese', Bombur for 'pork-pie and *salad*', the other dwarves for 'more cakes, and ale, and *coffee*', and Gandalf reminded Bilbo to 'bring out the cold chicken and *tomatoes*'.

Tolkien incorporated one of the changes that first appeared here into the third edition of 1966 (DAA.41), where *tomatoes* did indeed become *pickles*. This change has been the subject of much debate; see, for example, Shippey's *The Road to Middle-earth* (expanded edition, page 69), Anderson's *Annotated Hobbit* (DAA.41), et al. The general consensus has been that 'tomato' was removed as foreign to the time and place, though this did not prevent Tolkien's including tobacco earlier in this same chapter, or potatoes in Bilbo's garden in *The Lord of the Rings* (*LotR*.34), or, for that matter, *coffee* in the same sentence.† More likely, Tolkien (a keen gardener) thought it too early in the year for tomatoes and simply decided that preserved goods like pickles were more likely to be found in Bilbo's larder that early in the year.

† Although an Old World plant (being native to Africa), coffee as a drink dates from early modern times and was unknown in Europe before the sixteenth century, first appearing in England in 1652, about the same time (circa 1650) that tea arrived in England, having made its way westward from Asia.

19 The replacement of the first and second editions' *larder* by *larders* (plural) is another 1960 Hobbit revision taken up into the third edition of 1966; cf. DAA.41, annotation #27. This change was probably made to match the pantries (plural) of the book's second paragraph.

20 That is, from the bottom line on (second edition) page 22 through the top line on page 23.

21 Tolkien actually wrote 'Bombur produced a drum from the [> his] bag in the hall; Bifur and Bombur went out too', but it is clear that *Bofur*, the reading in all published editions, is meant for the second occurrence (for one thing, 'bombur' means *drum* in Old Norse).

22 This entry is added to the typescript, having been preceded by rough drafting on a separate sheet of paper; see the Draftings section at the end of this chapter.

23 This change, from the first edition's 'Excitable little *man*', had already been made in the fifth printing of 1951; see page 749. For the changes in the preceding lines, compare the suggested replacement or correction with the published text (e.g., DAA.47). For example, '/19 delete magic' (which is added at the same time as the entries discussed in Text Notes 22 & 25) means that the line 'Gandalf struck a blue light on the end of his magic staff' should now read '. . . the end of his staff'. The replacement of 'the whistle of an engine coming out of a tunnel' (page 27, line 16) by 'the whee of a rocket going up in the sky' was no doubt to remove a perceived anachronism, fireworks being firmly established as part of Middle-earth in a way mechanisms like steam engines were not.

24 Golfimbul is changed to 'Gulfimbul', either because of the further evolution of Tolkien's languages (cf. Mt. Gondobad > Gundabad, page 675) or because Tolkien had now dropped the 'golf' joke and so no longer needed (or wanted) the *-golf-* element to appear in the goblin-king's name.

25 This phrase, added to the typescript at the same time as the entry noted in Text Note 22, is one of the few for which drafting exists; see the Draftings section at the end of this chapter.

26 Written in pencil beside this, apparently as a possible replacement: 'funny beards?'

27 That is, for the reading in the second edition '(Look at the map at the beginning of this book, and you will see there the runes in red.)', Tolkien now proposed that an asterisk be inserted in the text and a footnote added to the bottom of the page which would read '*See the copy of the plan at the beginning of this book.'

28 The extended row of ellipses, here and throughout this chapter, is in Tolkien's original.

29 This was originally followed with 'And anyway there are no more battle', then this unfinished sentence was cancelled.

30 By small deer, Tolkien does not mean hobbit-sized deer, appealing though the image is, but 'small game' – that is, creatures such as rabbits, squirrels, and the like. Cf. Shakespeare's *King Lear*: 'Mice, and Rats, and such small Deare, Haue been Tom's food for seuen long yeare' (Act III, scene iv, lines 144–145).

The conversation to which Gandalf refers ('we have discussed all that . . . we decided . . .') is described in more detail in 'The Quest of Erebor'.

31 Several lines of typed drafting, which gave more information about the dwarven exodus from the Grey Mountains, were deleted following this sentence:

> Many years ago, in [Dain >] my great-grandfather's time, our family was driven out of the far North, and [Dain was slain by a dragon >] returned to this Mountain on the map, where their ancestors had

> lived for a while long ago [> once upon a time]. They brought such wealth as they could save >

This seems to have been replaced with

> . . . driven out of the far North, and return with their goods and their tools to this Mountain on the map where our ancestors had lived for a while once upon a time.

This Dain is of course Dáin I, the figure who replaced Thrym Thistlebeard as Thrór's father in the published dwarven genealogy, said in 'Durin's Folk' to have been killed by 'a great cold-drake' (*LotR*.1109) and in the family tree by 'a dragon' (ibid.1117). His youngest son, Grór, founded the dwarven colony in the Iron Hills at the same time his heir, Thrór, re-established the Kingdom under the Mountain at Erebor.

See also the Draftings section at the end of this chapter for rough drafts on a separate sheet [Ad.Ms.H.18] of this passage relating to Thrain the Old and Thror's return to the Lonely Mountain.

32 This marks the first appearance in the main text of 'Thrain the Old' by that name (an appellation that arose during the drafting given at the end of this chapter); in 'Durin's Folk' (*LotR*.1109 & 1117) and the 1950 Prefatory Note to the second edition he had been simply 'Thráin I'. This is yet another of the proposed 1960 Hobbit changes that got carried over into the 1966 third edition; cf. DAA.54.

33 This passage originally read

> . . . to this Mountain on the map, where our ancestors had lived for a while, once upon a time. There they mined and they tunnelled, and they made [great halls >] wide halls and great workshops

The changes from 'wide' to *deeper* and 'great' to *greater* emphasize the continuity of the dwarven community building on and expanding what had come before, whereas the original readings convey the impression that the earlier settlement was completely dwarfed (so to speak) by the magnificence of the new establishment.

34 Originally these sentences read 'Alas! *Undoubtedly that was what* brought the dragon upon us! *Their* greed has long ears.'

35 Originally this read 'as long as they live, *five thousand years* maybe'.

36 The addition of *still*, typed in the margin and marked for insertion here, suggests that the battles between dragons mentioned in the next clause seriously reduced their numbers. Compare *Farmer Giles of Ham*, which suggests a number of dragons dwelling close together in the mountains, at least one of whom is killed and eaten (by the returning C. Dives) by the end of the story.

The specific detail a few lines later that Smaug came from *beyond* the Grey Mountains appears here for the first time, but this is merely a confirmation of the legend on Thror's Map: 'Far to the North are the <u>Grey Mountains</u> & the Withered Heath whence came the Great Worms.'

37 'as low as coalmining, or even road-mending' replaces 'as low as blacksmith-work or even coalmining', either because Tolkien wished not to disparage blacksmithing (which he celebrates in passing in *Smith of Wootton Major* only a few years later [circa 1964] as a useful craft that is also an appealing art), or because he wished to allude to the association between dwarves and stone roads that appears elsewhere in the legendarium.

38 Azog's name enters *The Hobbit* at this point, this being one of the 1960 changes that carried over into the published third edition of six years later; cf. DAA.56–7 and 339. The name first appeared in 'Durin's Folk' (*LotR*.1110–12) and was now imported back into *The Hobbit* retroactively, replacing the anonymous goblin of the first and second editions.

I have been unable to locate any authoritative gloss for the meaning of Azog's name; even the language it is in is unknown. It may be Magol, like his son Bolg (see page 710), but given the gap of years between their invention and the linguistic situation as it stood at the time Tolkien was writing the *Lord of the Rings* Appendices, *azog* is more probably a word in Black Speech (cf. *LotR*.1165) – cf. for instance the similarity between *azog* and n*azg*, attested from the Ring-inscription (ibid., 271), which share three out of four letters all in the same sequence.

39 To this Tolkien added, then deleted 'and the key' (i.e., 'this map *and the key*'). For more on his hesitancy over whether the wizard gained one item or two from the dying dwarf, note that when two paragraphs later Gandalf ceremoniously hands Thorin the map there is no mention of the key, although in the paragraphs that follow Gandalf mentions the key twice. See also Text Note 44.

40 'a few weeks ago': their first meeting is described in 'Durin's Folk' (*LotR*.1115). For a different account of that encounter, see 'The Quest of Erebor'; cf. *Unfinished Tales* (UT.322 & 332–5) and *The Annotated Hobbit* (DAA.368–77).

41 Rather surprisingly, Tolkien did not at this point have several of the dwarves present – e.g., Balin and Dwalin, and possibly others – reveal that they had accompanied Thrain on his unfortunate expedition; cf. *LotR*.1114. This is all the more unexpected, because while they did not know what ultimately became of Thrain, they certainly could have revealed to his son the purpose of his final mission rather than leave him completely in the dark for a full century about his missing father.

42 In full, including cancellations, Gandalf's reply reads:

> 'Do not ask! Not at night. *NO, not even at noon!*' said Gandalf. [*Only those whom* >] I will not speak of it.'

It is interesting that Gandalf refers to this remarkable achievement – in which he joins Beren, Lúthien, and Sméagol as the only characters in the whole legendarium known to have escaped from a Dark Lord's lair – as a 'task'; presumably one laid upon him by the White Council.

43 Originally Gandalf's reply began:

'*Don't speak as a fool!*' said Gandalf. 'Grief has robbed you of your wits. *The one that you name* is an enemy . . .'

44 Tolkien first wrote 'Give *it* to my son', meaning the map; when Tolkien decided that this should include the key mentioned in the previous sentence as well, he changed the pronoun to match, although no account of the wizard presenting Thorin with the key, as in the published book, was added back to the text above.

Interestingly, the four words 'even from their tombs' are typed over pencil drafting, suggesting that the typescript at some point halted in the middle of this page (Ts. page 14; Ad.Ms.H.75) after the words 'four corners of the Earth', which was originally followed by a full stop.

45 Bilbo's remark was originally the even more naive 'which will take *a day or two*'.

Draftings

New Chapter I was composed on the typewriter and, like New Chapter II and the fragment of New Chapter III which follow, is itself the sole text of this new version of the book's opening. However, drafting for three individual passages does survive, on two separate sheets. The first, Ad.Ms.H.12, is the back of a page whose brief text I give at the end of the next chapter under the heading 'Queries and Reminders' (see page 811). Ad.Ms.H.12 has some nearly illegible drafting for two passages that appeared in New Chapter I. The first passage reads:

and he thought it an important occasion. If it had been allowed he might have come at last to the explanation. <But> it would not have been brief.

This is clearly a suggested replacement for 'He was an important dwarf. *If he had been allowed, he would probably have gone on like this until he was out of breath, without telling any one there anything that was not known already*. But he was rudely interrupted . . .' (second edition page 27, lines 10ff; DAA.47). See page 778 and Text Note 22 above for the addition to the typescript which seems to be Tolkien's final version of this passage. The second passage reads:

a dragon of nine spells of
a dragon out of [> under] nine spells of sleep
even [the >] a drunken dragon.
would be the end of us: it would wake a stone dragon out of an enchanted sleep

These in turn are clearly an attempt to arrive at a satisfactory replacement for Gloin's 'one shriek like that in a moment of excitement *would be enough to wake the dragon and all his relatives, and kill the lot of us*' (second edition page 28, lines 13ff; DAA.48). See page 778 and Text Note 25 above for Tolkien's actual addition to the typescript for this passage.

The second sheet with drafting, Ad.Ms.H.18, forms the verso of the notes on phases of the moon that I give as section (iv) in the 'Timelines and Itinerary' chapter below (Ad.Ms.H.17; see page 831). Here Tolkien is bringing material from the Prefatory Note to the second edition about Thrain I (see page 753) and working it into harmony with what Thorin says about his family on pages 32 and 242 of the second edition (the passages about long ago being driven out of the far north and about the discovery of the Arkenstone, respectively; cf. DAA.54 & 287). Not all of this drafting, most of it hastily written in faded pencil, is legible; I give what I can make out of it to show how Tolkien worked his way to the final wording, with illegible words or passages replaced by ellipses (. . .) and doubtful words enclosed by french brackets < > as usual. At one point Tolkien himself uses an ellipsis to indicate an omitted passage; this is given below as a closed ellipsis (.....) without spaces between the dots.

p. 242[2] [TN1] Thrain Arkenstone . . .

[*cancelled*: back >] my family was driven out far north . . . came back . . .
. . . Old Thrain my ancestor. Long ago . . . . . .
It was discovered by my far ancestor Thrain the Old [but >] . . . they mined <tunneled> . . . and . . . grandfather Thror

[*added in blue ball-point ink*: 32, 242]

. . . grandfather Thror's time my family were driven out of the North [*added*: back] and.....Map. <It> had been discovered long before by my [> our] far ancestor Thrain the Old, but now they <mined> . . . [*cancelled*: great] <hall> . . . they mined <them> they tunneled <them>. <He became> King under Mountain

[p. 24 >] 32 and 242[2]

Unlike the preceding, which is written in pencil, the final paragraph of drafting on this page is in blue ball-point ink:

Long ago in my grandfather Thror's time my [> his] family were [> was] driven out of the Far North and [they] came back with all their wealth and <their> tools to the Mountain on the Map. It had been discovered by our far ancestor Thrain the Old, but now they <mined> they <tunnelled> and they made deeper halls and greater workshops – and Thror became K u M again and his

This final paragraph of drafting in turn directly underlies those passages given in Text Notes 31, 32, and 33 above. Not only do these draftings, sketchy though they are, mark the emergence of the name 'Thrain the Old' (see pp. 780 & 788) but they resolve one lingering question from Tolkien's earlier confusion of the two competing Thror-Thrain-Thorin/Thrain-Thror-Thorin genealogies: why, if Thror was the last King under the Mountain, did Thorin refer to the Arkenstone as 'the Arkenstone of Thrain' (second edition page 242)? The now-familiar answer appears here for the first time in a typically Tolkienian resolution: Thror was indeed Last King, yet the appellation 'Arkenstone of Thrain' is also correct because it refers to a different Thrain, just as the Prefatory Note established was the case on Thror's Map.

Thus Tolkien finally resolved a contradiction accidentally introduced into the text before its first publication; all that would have been required to remove the last traces of the confusion would have been to substitute *fathers* for *father* in the second paragraph of Chapter XVI ('For the Arkenstone of my father . . . I name unto myself') and *fathers'* for *father's* in Chapter XVII ('That stone was my father's, and is mine . . . how came you by the heirloom of my house . . . ?'). But unfortunately Tolkien either did not realize that these two small changes remained to be made (since the 1960 Hobbit never reached so far) or, as seems more likely, he was well aware of it but made no note to that effect at the time and had forgotten this detail when forced to hastily revisit the book in 1965 for the 1966 third edition.

TEXT NOTES

1 I cannot explain the superscript here, which also occurs again further down the page. It does not refer to the second paragraph on that page, which describes the Arkenstone; it is the first paragraph which alludes to its discovery 'beneath the roots of the Mountain'.

New Chapter II

THE BROKEN BRIDGE

The typescript for New Chapter II starts at the top of a new page [Ad. Ms.H.25] but otherwise strongly resembles the last six pages of New Chapter I and clearly marks a continuation of the same text. As before, rather than a continuous narrative this Fifth Phase material varies between short bits of replacement text and longer extended scenes. The most notable addition is the scene of crossing the river beside the broken bridge, necessitated by discrepancies that arose when Bilbo's adventure, which had taken place 'off the map' (literally, since they had not yet entered the area covered by the Wilderland map at this point),† had to be superimposed upon Frodo's well-mapped journey covering the same terrain. Tolkien's solution was to alter both *The Hobbit* (see below) and the second edition of *The Lord of the Rings* (see HME VI.199–203) to match if possible the final published *LotR* map.

†It is not until they reach the ford early in Chapter III that Gandalf informs them that they 'are come to the very edge of the Wild' (DAA.88), and indeed the 'Edge of the Wild' is helpfully drawn as a double red line on the Wilderland Map published as the back endpaper of the second edition.

p. 40/13. and each pony was slung about with bundles and blankets and saddlebags. Four were without riders: two laden with foodbags and gear for cooking and camping; one more for Balin; and last a very small pony (with no baggage), evidently for Bilbo. The whole expedition had clearly been prepared long before[TN1]

p. 41/2 white horse called Rohald.[TN2] He brought no pocket-handkerchiefs, but he did bring a couple of blankets and Bilbo's pipe and tobacco...... rode forward all that day and the next. <u>After this substitute for</u> except <u>line 5 to</u> William <u>p 46/5 the following</u>:[TN3]

They were still in the Shire, of course, and went at a leisurely pace, spending the nights in good inns; not until the Saturday afternoon did they cross the great bridge over the Brandywine River and enter what Bilbo called the Outlands, where outlandish things might be expected at any turn. At last he felt that his Adventure had begun.

But beyond the Bridge the road was still good, and there were wide lands looking wholesome enough. They met or came up with a number of folk on lawful business: dwarves for the most part going east or west with packs on their backs. Some belonged to Thorin's people of the western mountains, and they saluted him with a low bow; some were of poorer sort, pedlars of iron-ware, tinkers, or road-menders. There were a few Men, farmers mostly, ambling along on large fat horses; and several hobbits on foot. They stared at Thorin's company, but gave them no more than a grin and a nod.

In a day or two they came to Bree on the Hill. There they spent their last comfortable night for many a day to come, in the great inn of Bree, the Prancing Pony, well-known to the hobbits of the east side of the Shire.[TN4] Bree was as far as Bilbo's knowledge reached, even by hearsay. Beyond it the lands had been desolate for many long years. When in a day's journey more they came to the Last Inn, they found it deserted. They camped in its ruins, and next day they passed into a barren country with great marshes on their left as far as eye could see. They went very slowly now, sparing their laden ponies and often trudging on foot, for the road became very bad, rutted and pitted, and in places almost[TN5] lost in soft bog. The weather remained dry – as far as Bree it had been as fair as May can be, even in legends – but it was grey now and rather sad.

Bilbo's spirits fell, and he said very little, thinking always of the next stop for food, though meals came much more seldom (and more scanty) than he would have liked. So they went on for many days,[TN6] and each day they became more silent and wary; for there was a stillness all round them – as if the land was listening (so Bilbo thought to himself). After a time the flat lands began to rise before them; still far away there were hills looming up, and as they drew nearer Bilbo saw that they were clad in dark trees, and on some there seemed to be the ruins of grim towers and walls. They had an evil look, as if men of evil days had built them.[TN7]

It was at about this time that things took a bad turn. One morning cold wind from the east met them with a breath of far mountains, bringing low clouds and driving rain. Bilbo shivered. 'Not what I call June!' he grumbled as he splashed along behind all the others in a deep muddy track that was fast becoming a stream. Poor hobbit, he was quite out of his reckoning; it was the nineteenth of May,[TN8] but the three weeks on the road began to seem endless. 'Bother adventures and everything to do with them!' he thought. 'I wish I was at home by the fire with the kettle just beginning to sing!' It was not the last time that he wished that.

The track[TN9] climbed to the top of a ridge, and then went down steeply into a narrow valley. They all halted and looked ahead. Through the valley a strong river flowed from the North, cutting across their road. Beyond it the dark hills frowned, and the road faded from sight under the shadows at their feet.

'Ha!' said Gandalf, peering through the rain. 'The bridge! The bridge is broken!' He turned away snapping his fingers and muttering to himself: 'there is mischief here! Elrond must be told'.

They did not know what he meant. This country was not well known[TN10] to the dwarves, and they could not see far before them. But Bilbo, whose eyes were keen, if not so keen as the wizard's, looked down and he thought he could see a grey stone bridge with a single arch over the river; but the arch was broken in the middle.

'Well, what's to be done?' said Gandalf. 'None are better at bridge-building than dwarves'.

'Maybe', said Thorin. 'But not in the wilds, without the tools or the tackle, nor in a storm of rain!'

'Just so' said Gandalf. 'But there is no other bridge over this river. A hundred miles away north you might jump it, but I should not go that way if I were you: it is troll-country.[TN11] Well, let us go down, and see the worst!'

They came to the bridge-end, and found that the river was not yet very wide. But it was swift: at the point where the bridge had been built it flowed over a rocky shelf, and then slid down long rapids away to their right. Here it foamed and swirled round the broken stones of the arch that were tumbled in the midst of its cold grey stream.

'It might be worse', said Gandalf. 'A dangerous ford, but the only one. It is this way, or go back. Unless you think of turning south, where there are no roads at all, and no way to pass the Misty Mountains,[TN12] which still lie ahead. Except, of course, by the Mines of Moria'.

The dwarves stared at him sullenly, muttering in their beards. 'It was you that advised us to come this way', said Thorin. 'What is your advice now?'

'I also said that no roads are now safe' answered the wizard. 'But I have given my advice: we must try to ford the river'. With that he mounted his horse and rode forward. As Bilbo had already noticed Gandalf used no stirrups, and seldom held the reins: Rohald[TN13] answered his commands, spoken softly in a strange tongue. The white horse tried the water and then walked on, slowly but without fear. The ponies lifted their dejected heads and watched him, like hobbit-children staring at some large lad showing off for their benefit. He skirted the tumbled bridge-stones in midstream, where the water was up to his hocks, and waded carefully to the further side. There he slipped, and recovered, for the far bank was steeper and more slimy: at last he scrambled up, and turned back, and neighed.

The ponies snorted. Plainly he had said as much as: 'There you are. Quite easy. You try it!'; but they were not so sure. Neither were the dwarves.

'Now or never!' Gandalf called across the water. No one moved for a moment. Then Thorin mounted and rode forward, beckoning the others to follow. Fili and Kili at once obeyed, but the rest were more reluctant. One behind the other they passed into the dangerous stream, the dwarves hiding their fear under the eyes of the wizard; the ponies going warily but stoutly watched by the white horse. The water in places swirled under their bellies, and some slipped and were nearly carried away, in the end they all reached the far bank without disaster.[TN14] Last of all came the pony bearing Bombur, and he had a heavier task than any, even the pack-ponies.

Thorin mopped his face, wet with sweat, rain and spray. 'Well, we've managed that', he said. 'On we go! There's no shelter here'.

'Don't you want the hobbit any more?' said Gandalf. 'I think you may need him'.

They had quite forgotten poor Bilbo! There he was still on the other side, sitting and shivering, more frightened than he had yet been in his life.

'Confound your hobbit!' said Thorin, 'When will he learn to look after himself?'

'In time', said Gandalf. 'Sooner than you expect'. 'Mr. Baggins!' he called. 'Don't try the crossing by yourself; your pony is small. I will come and help'.

Then the wizard went back over the stream, and set Bilbo behind him on the horse.[TN15] 'Hold on to your pony's reins' he said, 'and keep him on our right, if you can. He may make it, with Rohald[TN16] to break the force of the current'. 'Steady now', he said to the horse. 'Over once more, and your own land is not so far ahead!'

At last they had all crossed: but now the ponies were restive. They seemed unwilling to go further, turning their noses north towards the hills, the lower slopes of which were now close at hand, as if something there alarmed them. Suddenly one of the pack-ponies wrenched the reins from Bombur's hand, and bolted back towards the river. The other dwarves were busy calming their mounts, and before they could help, the wild pony was floundering in the stream, and struggling to cast off all his burdens. In the confusion that followed Fili and Kili were nearly drowned, and the pony was only saved at the cost of most of its baggage. Of course this proved to be the best part of all their food-supplies: away it went towards the rapids, and <u>donk donk</u> was the last they heard of their best cooking-pot as it was rolled among the boulders.

Gandalf spoke in the ear of the white horse, and he strode on to the road beyond the bridge-end. There he stood facing north, arching his neck and neighing loudly. Whatever that meant, it seemed to calm the ponies, or cow them. They allowed themselves to be led forward to his side. There all the company mounted again.

'Well', said Gandalf, 'now you must go on, much faster than before. And on short commons. Nothing more to eat until evening and a meal less each day!'

Bilbo groaned, but they took no notice of him. At once they started to jog along as fast as they could make the ponies go. The road was now much better; it was indeed a road, not a track, and seemed to be kept in some order.[TN17] But before they halted for midday, having covered several miles, they were skirting the hills,[TN18] and dark thickets over-hung the steep bank on their right. Tightening their belts, they went doggedly on again, hungry and ill at ease, speaking hardly at all.

The wind rose, seething in the trees, rain drove in their faces, and the light began to fade. Far behind there was a brief stab of red, as the sun sank westwards;[TN19] shadow loomed before them. Still they went on. And last in the line came Bilbo; his hood was dripping in his eyes, and his cloak was full of water, he was empty and cold; but no one turned to look at him, not even to shout 'keep up!' 'I wonder if they would care, if I vanished?' thought Bilbo [> he thought]. It would not have been difficult in the gloom.

At last when it was night-dark under the trees,[TN20] Thorin called a halt. The wind was still blowing, but the rain-storm was passing. The clouds were breaking, and away in the East before them a waning moon was tilted between the flying rags.

'We must eat a little now', said Thorin; 'but where we shall find a dry patch for a bed, I don't know. At least we will have a fire, if we can. Oin, Gloin, look about for fuel!'

'I don't like the look of the woods' said Balin. 'The shelter may be better, but the thinner trees on the right feel more friendly'.

'What would you advise, Gandalf?' said Thorin, looking round. And only then did they discover that Gandalf was missing. So far he had always been with them, never saying if he was in the adventure, or merely keeping them company as long as his road and theirs went the same way.[TN21] But he had been there, always at hand to help, talking most, laughing most, and eating almost as much as Bombur. He was not there now!

'Just when a wizard would have been most useful!' grumbled Bombur, who seemed to think Gandalf might have conjured up roast mutton all hot, if he had been at hand.

They moved to a clump of trees just off the road; but the mould[TN22] was sodden beneath them, and the wind shook the water off the leaves, everything was dripping all round them. Oin and Gloin had gathered fuel, but the mischief was in it, or in their tinder-boxes.[TN23] Dwarves can make a fire for their needs almost anywhere out of almost anything, wind or no wind; but they could not kindle one that night, not even Oin and Gloin who were specially skilful. The others sat round, glum and wet, muttering at them, as they tried in vain to wake a flame; and they lost their tempers and began to quarrel. Bilbo sat huddled against a tree-trunk, hardly caring: he was reflecting that an adventure may start with pony-rides in May sunshine, but it will soon lead you into the Unknown – if it is really an adventure.

Suddenly Balin, who was always the dwarves' look-out man, called softly: 'There's a light over there!' He pointed across the road to a hill-slope thick with bushes and trees. A good way up, they could all now see a light shining out of the dark mass of the forest: a reddish comfortable light, as it might be a fire or torches twinkling.

When they had stared at it for some time in silence, they fell into an argument. Some said no and some said yes. Some said they might at least go and see, and anything was better than little supper, less breakfast, and wet clothes all the night. Gloin said he could think of many things that were much worse. 'You get on with your fire, then', the others answered.

Balin was the most doubtful. 'These are strange parts and not canny', he muttered. 'They are too near the great mountains, if I reckon right. This is Noman's kingdom, without charts, or guards or watchmen.'[TN24]

'Do you mean they haven't heard of the king here?' asked Bilbo with a sinking of the heart, for in the Shire they said that only of wild and wicked things.[TN25]

'The king is long gone', answered Balin. 'There is no law, and the less inquisitive you are, the less trouble you are likely to find'.

'There are fourteen of us' said Fili. 'We could give some account of ourselves'. 'Where has Gandalf got to?' said Bombur, looking about, as if he expected him to pop out from behind a tree.[TN26] That question they all repeated, Bilbo several times. Then the rain began to pour down again, and Oin and Gloin began to fight one another with the sticks that would not burn.

That settled it. 'After all we have got a burglar with us', they said; 'a little stealth is what we need!' And so they made a move, leading their ponies across the road, and beginning, very cautiously, to climb up the hill. There was no proper path to be seen, such as might lead, say, to a woodman's house, and the trees were thick with much undergrowth about them. Do what they could, they made a deal of rustling and crackling and creaking, with much stumbling and muttering, in the pitch dark.

Suddenly the red light shone out very bright through the tree-trunks not far ahead. They halted, for the ponies who had come very unwillingly took fright again, and tried to bolt back down the hill. The dwarves covered the beasts' eyes with their cloaks and tried to calm them.

'Now it's the burglar's turn to do something' they said, looking towards Bilbo, who was standing shivering in the gleam of the fire. 'You must go and find out all about that light', said Thorin, 'what it is, and if it is all quite safe and canny. Off you go, stealthy mind you! Come back quick, if all is well. If not, come back, if you can. If you can't, give a signal: the cry of a night-hawk, and two hoots like an owl, and we will do what we can'. With that he pushed the hobbit forward.

So off Bilbo had to go, before he could explain that he had never heard a night-hawk. 'I wish I could fly like a bat', he thought. He could not, but he could move on the ground as quietly, if not so quick. Hobbits can walk in woods without any sound at all. They take a pride in it, and Bilbo had sniffed more than once at what he called 'all this dwarvish racket' as they went up the hill, though on a windy night Big People would probably have heard nothing at all.[TN27] As for Bilbo walking primly towards the red light, even a weasel would hardly have stirred a whisker as he passed. So naturally he got right up to the fire – for fire it was – quite unnoticed. And this is what he saw.

Three very large persons were sitting round a very large fire of beech-logs. They were toasting mutton on long spits of wood, and licking the gravy off their fingers. There was a fine toothsome smell. Also there was a barrel of ale at hand, and they were drinking out of large jugs. But they were trolls! Obviously trolls. Even Bilbo, in spite of his sheltered life, could tell that: from the great heavy faces on them, and their huge size, and the shape of their legs – and their language! It was not decent Shire-fashion at all.

'Mutton yesterday, mutton today, and blimey, if it don't look like mutton again tomorrer', said one of the trolls.

'Never a blinking bit of manflesh have we had for long enough' said a second. 'What was the blasted good of knocking down the bridge? It ain't caught nobody. Nobody hasn't passed for days and days'.

'Ah, that was William', said the first troll. 'What the ell he was a thinkin of to bring us down into these parts at all, beats me. And the drink runnin short what's more', he said, jogging the elbow of William, who was taking a pull at his jug.

William choked. 'Shut yer foul mouth!' he said as soon as he could. 'Yer can't expect folk to stop here for ever just to be et by you and Bert. You've et a village and a half each, since we came down from the mountains, and folk have all skedaddled. What d'yer expect? But time's been up our way when yer'd have said "thank yer, Bill" for a nice bit o' fat valley mutton like what this is'. He took a big bite off a sheep's leg he was toasting, and wiped his mouth on his sleeve.

That is the way of trolls of their sort.[TN28] Great greedy slow-witted brutes. There are other kinds, more cunning and dangerous; but Tom and Bert and Bill were quite dangerous enough. As soon as he saw them Bilbo ought to have done something at once. Either he should have gone back quickly and warned his friends that there were three large trolls at hand in a nasty mood, quite likely to eat pony, or even try toasted dwarf for a change; or else he should have done a bit of good quick stealing. In legends a really first-class thief would at this point have picked the trolls' pockets, pinched the mutton off the spits, purloined the beer, and escaped while they were still wondering what had happened. Or better still and more practical, he might have stuck a dagger into each of them before they observed it, and then he and his friends could have spent the night cheerily.

Bilbo knew it. He had read or heard tell of many things that he had never seen or done. He was very much alarmed, as well as disgusted; he wished himself a hundred miles away, and yet – and yet somehow he could not go straight back to Thorin and Company emptyhanded. He stood and hesitated in the shadows on the edge of the clearing. Of the various stealthy proceedings that he had heard of picking the trolls' pockets seemed the least difficult, so at last he crept to a tree just behind William...

pp. 46/6 onwards, as in text, except as corrected.

p. 47/13 Delete I told you.

47/–10 He rose with a roar and bashed Bert on the nose; and a rampaging row began. Bilbo had just enough wits left when Bert dropped....[TN29]

p. 48/8 (after owl, they)[TN30] left Bombur to mind the ponies as best he could, and one by one they started to creep towards the light. Deserting their companions was not one of their faults.[TN31] Now Balin stood peering and wondering where in all this commotion Bilbo was; but Tom caught sight of his face in the firelight, and he gave a wild howl. Trolls detest the very sight of dwarves (uncooked). Bert and Bill stopped fighting at once, and 'a sack, Tom, quick' they shouted. Before Balin could slip off, a sack was over his head, and he was down.

p.48/–8 Soon Dwalin lay by Balin, and Bifur and Bofur together, and Dori and Nori and Ori all in a heap, and Oin and Gloin and Fili and Kili piled uncomfortably near the fire. 'That'll teach 'em,' said Tom; for Fili and Kili had given trouble, fighting fiercely as dwarves will when cornered.[TN32]

p. 49 is blank[TN33]

p. 50/15 into the top of a thorn-bush,

/18 and lost one of his fangs. He fell back howling and cursing, but at that moment William

p. 52/3 'The night's getting old. I can smell the dawn coming. Let's get on with it quick!'

'Dawn strike you all, and be stone to you!' said a voice that sounded like William's, but it was not. For at that moment the dawn came, light gleamed pale through the branches, and there was a mighty twitter of birds.

/13 Delete, as you probably know,

/18 a great tree, and helped Bilbo to climb out of the thorn-bush

/–12 for annoyed read angry

/–8 twice over, and still Thorin was not satisfied.

'Silly time to go practising your pocket-picking!' he said. 'What we wanted was fire and food'.

'And you wouldn't have got that from trolls without a struggle, in any case', said Gandalf. 'It might have turned out a great deal worse. Anyhow...

p. 53/14 for grabbed read seized

/19 plunder, of all sorts from buttons and rusty brooches to pots of gold coins standing in a corner. There were lots of clothes, too, hanging on the walls – all that was left of many poor wood-men and shepherds who had still lived here and there in the wild lands near-by. But hidden behind the door they found a number of swords and knives of various sizes and strange shapes. Two caught their eyes, because of their beautiful scabbards and their jewelled hilts that seemed to shine in the shadows.

Gandalf took one, and presented the other to Thorin. To Bilbo he gave a knife with a silver pommel. 'A gift for a good hobbit!' he said with a bow, which pleased Bilbo very much, though he did not himself feel that he had earned any praise. He looked at the knife: it had a sheath of black figured leather, and when he drew it, he saw that the blade was bright and unstained. It was long enough to serve a hobbit as a sword.

'These look like good blades too', said the wizard, half drawing the swords and examining them closely. 'They were not made by any troll, nor by any smith among Men of these days. But there's black blood on them, goblin-blood. When they are cleaned and the runes on them can be read, we shall know more about them'. end of page. p.54/ after l. 8 insert:

'Now you had better look for Bombur', said Gandalf: 'and we shall need the ponies, if you can find them'.

Bifur and Bofur went off, and soon came back with the old fat dwarf. He looked rather glum. Not that he minded at all having missed the affair of the sacks, but they had found him fast asleep, and no sign of the ponies. Thorin was not pleased.

Gandalf laughed. 'Never mind!' he said. 'Let's have breakfast! You were fools to bring them across the road. I wonder you got them so far. No one could have held them when all the noise started. But they'll be all right: my Rohald is looking after them'.

So they all set to, and had a great breakfast, or a feast as it seemed; and after that they slept (even Bombur), for their night had been disturbed. They did not make a move until the afternoon. Then Gandalf got up and went down the hill, and soon he came back leading his white horse, and all the ponies coming meekly behind.

Then the dwarves packed up all the food that was left fit to eat, and other things that might prove useful, and they carried away the pots of gold. These they buried very secretly in a thicket not far from the road, and set many spells on them, and a stone cut with dwarf-runes to mark the place,[TN34] in case they ever had the chance to come back and recover them. When that was done, they all mounted once more and jogged along again on the road to the East.

'Where did you go to without a word, if I may ask?' said Thorin to Gandalf as they rode along.

'To look ahead', said he.

'And what brought you back in the nick of time?'

'Looking behind', said he.

'No doubt', said Thorin, 'but would you mind saying a little more!'

'Well, I hurried on ahead, to find some friends, if I could. The broken bridge was a bad sign; and there was not enough food to see you through the next few days. As I hoped, before long I met some folk from Rivendell'.

'Where's that?' asked Bilbo, who was keeping as close to the wizard as he could.

'Don't interrupt!' said Gandalf. 'You'll get there in a few days now, if we're lucky, and then you'll find out all about it. As I was saying, Elrond had heard of the trouble. The Rangers were out, and he had sent two of his own people to report. They told me that trolls had come down from the North, and they feared that three had settled in the woods not far above the road. Men had fled away south, and they were waylaying strangers.

'"Back you go then, and quick", I said to myself. Looking behind I saw a fire in the distance, and I came as fast as Rohald could carry me. I found all your ponies huddled on the road with their heads down and their tails to the north. The rest you can guess. But please be more careful, or we shall never get anywhere. My friends had no food to spare, for they are hunting: there are other wicked things abroad.[TN35] The trolls' larder is a piece of luck that you hardly deserve. But for Mr. Baggins you might have been lying among the bones on the floor!'[TN36]

'Pray don't mention it!' said Thorin.

This marks the end of New Chapter II, in the middle of the page [Ad. Ms.H.32]. The brief fragment of New Chapter III follows immediately on the same page after only a gap of a few skipped lines, albeit with a new pagination ('III 1'); see page 802.

New Chapter III

ARRIVAL IN RIVENDELL

p. 56/3 They felt that danger was lurking on both sides of their road. They camped where they could, and set watches; and their[TN37]

/7 trolls. On the fourth day from the Bridge[TN38] they passed the shadow of the dark hills. Gandalf laughed and pointed ahead; and still far off they saw another river before them, gleaming in the morning [> evening] sunshine, but all the lands beyond were shrouded in mist.

In the afternoon of the next day[TN39] they came to the river, and found a great ford over wide shallows, and there was a causeway of huge stepping-stones against which the stream gurgled and foamed; but on the far side the path wound steeply up a high frowning bank. When they had climbed to the top, leading their horses, they saw that the great mountains had marched down to meet them. The day was hot and clear and there was no mist, and it seemed only a day's easy journey now to the feet of the nearest.

p. 57/3 'You must not miss the path, or that will be the end of you',[TN40] he said. 'You need food, for one thing, and rest in safety for a while, <u>and</u> advice. None of you have ever tried the north passes, I think. Their perils are always changing, and you must consult one who knows, if you are to make the right choice. Those who take the wrong way in the Misty Mountains never come back to try again!'

/10 'You have come to the last fences of the Westland. Ahead of us [> Over there] lies hidden the fair valley of Rivendell, of which no doubt some of you have heard tell, though few dwarves have ever seen it.[TN41] There Master Elrond lives in the Last Homely House. I sent a message by my friends, and we are expected'.

That sounded comforting; but they had not got there yet, and it was not easy to find the way to the secret valley and the Last Homely House west of the Mountains

p. 58/ 10 <u>Delete</u> about pretty well.[TN42]

/11 They went on until moonless night [> twilight] overtook them, and they lay that night under the bright stars. The next day was failing, and they were still following Gandalf, whose head and beard wagged this way and that as he searched for the white stones in the dusk. White [> Pale] moths were fluttering in the whins[TN43] and long heather, and twilight deepened like a mist about the horses' feet.

'Supper-time and past it!' thought Bilbo, who had not eaten since midday. His tired pony began to stumble over roots and stones.[TN44] Then just ahead Rohald neighed, and he hurried forward, and came to [a] steep fall in the ground so suddenly that he nearly slipped headlong down it.

'Here it is at last!' cried Gandalf, as the dwarves came up and stared over the edge

At this point, the Fifth Phase typescript comes to an end, leaving about two-thirds of the final page [Ad.Ms.H.33] blank. On the blank space, Tolkien wrote a note regarding the projected contents of the rest of this chapter, had he continued beyond this point:

Ch. III should make clear
Elrond's care for roads etc. from
Greyflood to <Mountains>
Also insert the white horse
Róhald belonged to Rivendell, & had
been lent by Elrond to Gandalf.

This final point should perhaps be taken to indicate that Rohald would be left behind in Rivendell when Thorin & Company set out again to attempt the mountain-passes. Certainly it is disquieting enough to think of all the ponies being eaten by the goblins in Chapter IV, now that they have been given a sort of corporate personality and even pseudo dialogue (cf. pages 793–94), much less an elven horse such as Rohald. See also 'Queries and Reminders' below.

TEXT NOTES

1 This last sentence is bracketed for removal.

2 Gandalf's white horse dates all the way back to the earliest pages of the Second Phase manuscript, but he only now gains a name: Rohald. Again I have found no authorized gloss, but the name is clearly Sindarin, with the *ro-* element meaning 'horse'; cf. Aragorn's horse, Roheryn (*LotR*.809), which means 'horse of the lady' (*roch* + *heru*; so named from being Arwen's gift – cf. *Silm*.363), and Rochallor, High King Fingolfin's great horse (*Silm*.153). Salo's *A Gateway to Sindarin* lists no *hald* in its Sindarin-English Glossary, but it does have *hall*, which can mean either 'exalted, high' or 'veiled, hidden, shadowed, shady' (Salo, page 263).

In any case, the line adding the name of Gandalf's white horse was not part of the original typescript here but was added later; Rohald's name does not appear as originally typed until page 796 (see Text Notes 13 & 16).

3 Originally Tolkien intended the replacement text that follows to take the place of the passage beginning on line 5 of page 41 in the second edition ('. . . rode forward all day, *except of course when they stopped for meals* . . .') and continuing through line 22, ending with '*the weather which had often been as good as May can be, even in tales and legends*, took a nasty turn'. Much of this passage would in fact be replaced by Tolkien in the 1966 Hobbit (see DAA.65–6), although in briefer form than the text given here. When Tolkien came to actually write the replacement text, it flowed so fluently that by the time he stopped rather than sixteen lines later on page 41 he had reached the fifth line on page 46 ('. . . *crept behind a tree just behind* William'). I have added the underlinings here and throughout this chapter, matching Tolkien's own practice in New Chapter I, to help distinguish between Tolkien's instructions and the words to which they apply. As with New Chapter I, ellipses without spaces separating the periods (e.g. .....) are Tolkien's own.

4 A pencilled notation in the left margin along these lines seeks to establish a timeline of their trip. The first few words are too faint to read, but the rest of the note reads '. . . 2½ days' journey arriving at evening on May 2.' This corresponds to the entry in the Itinerary, which has them crossing the Brandywine Bridge early on 30th April and arriving at Bree on 2nd May; see page 818.

5 The word *almost* is cancelled in pencil and replaced by a passage in light pencil in the right margin, but I cannot make out any of this marginalia.

6 In the left margin along this line is written '16 days', which is then changed to '15 days'. See entries 7 and 8 in the timeline (page 818), which between them equal fifteen days.

7 In the original story, some of these hills had castles on them, of which 'many looked as if they had not been built for any good purpose'. In the more developed history of *The Lord of the Rings*, this area had now come to be the territory of the fallen evil kingdom of Rhudaur (one of the inheritor-kingdoms of fractured Arnor), which had been destroyed more than a millennium before. Accordingly, the slightly sinister castles become evil-looking ruins in the 1960 Hobbit, a change carried over (though not in the same words) into the 1966 Hobbit (the published third edition); cf. DAA.66.

8 See Itinerary, page 819.

9 Originally 'The *deep* track'.

10 Originally this sentence read 'This country was *unknown* to the dwarves', obviously altered because it has already been established that Thorin's people traded and travelled up and down the Great East Road. In addition, Thorin's people could not have passed through Moria on their flight west after Smaug destroyed the Kingdom under the Mountain, nor is it likely that they came by way of the goblin-haunted Mount Gram, or took the extreme long away around through the Gap of Rohan.

Instead, they almost certainly came by way of the Forest Road to the same passes Thorin and Company will attempt in Chapter IV and hence westward down the same East-West road they are now travelling all the way to the Blue Mountains west of the Shire. Furthermore, it seems extremely unlikely that Thorin's dwarf-colony in Harlindon has no contact at all with Dain's people in the Iron Hills, which would also imply east-west travel along this route.

11 The area in question is marked the 'Ettenmoors' on the *Lord of the Rings* map, *etten* (ettin) being an old word for 'giants' (descended from the Old English *eoten*, ent) that remained in use up until the early 1600s. Strider, in 'Flight to the Ford', glosses the term as 'the troll-fells' (*LotR*.216), *troll* being a mid-nineteenth-century borrowing from the Scandinavian which supplemented but did not replace *giant* (itself Anglo-Norman in origin). Also on the *LotR* map, the area in which Bilbo and the dwarves encounter the trolls is called the 'Trollshaws', *shaw* being an archaic word for woods or thicket; cf. the thick woods in all three of Tolkien's pictures of the troll-episode, most notably 'Trolls' Hill' (Plate IV [bottom]) and the black and white drawing 'The Trolls' (DAA.74).

12 Originally this passage read 'no way to pass *the great mountains*, which still lie ahead'. Significantly, not even Balin (who, as *The Lord of the Rings* reveals, did later dare to enter Moria) takes Gandalf up on his taunt about trying the Mines of Moria as an alternate route past the mountains. Nonetheless its mention helps tie the geography of the two books (and the two journeys, of Bilbo and the Ring-bearer) together; like the earlier mention of the Prancing Pony at Bree, it emphasizes to those who have read *The Lord of the Rings* before (this version of) *The Hobbit* that both take place in the same world and, in this passage at least, traverse the same territory.

13 Again 'Rohald' is added later, replacing *his white horse* in the original.

14 This was originally followed by a cancelled line, 'Last of all came the pack ponies'.

15 In this passage, Bilbo becomes the first of three hobbits who at one point or another ride with Gandalf on a great pale horse, the other two being Pippin in the ride from Rohan to Minas Tirith (*The Lord of the Rings*, last chapter of Book III and first chapter of Book V) and Odo, the latter in the rejected storyline from early drafts of *The Lord of the Rings* where Gandalf rescued him from the Black Riders at Crickhollow (HME VI.304) and Odo accompanied the wizard as far as Weathertop (HME VI.352, 355–6); none of the Odo material made it into the published book.

16 This marks the first time that Rohald has appeared in the text as first typed; on previous occasions the name had been added in later as replacement text.

17 This was initially followed by the cancelled line 'The rain too had almost stopped.'

18 Originally this passage read 'But before they halted for midday, having covered several miles, they were *under the shadow of the dark hills*'.

19 Originally this sentence read 'Far behind *in the West* there was a brief stab of red, as the sun *sank*'.

20 Originally this passage read 'when it was *nearly night*', which was altered first to 'the dark' (i.e., 'when *the dark* . . .') and then to 'when *the tree-shadowed road was dark*', before finally reaching the form given in the text.

21 In fact, 'The Quest of Erebor' makes this explicit. When Thorin reluctantly agrees in the wee hours of the morning following the Unexpected Party to take Bilbo, at Gandalf's urging (and threats), Thorin makes it a condition that Gandalf shall then accompany them as well:

> 'Very well,' Thorin said at last after a silence. 'He shall set out with my company, if he dares (which I doubt). But if you insist on burdening me with him, you must come too and look after your darling.'
>
> 'Good!' I answered. 'I will come, and stay with you as long as I can: at least until you have discovered his worth.' It proved well in the end, but at the time I was troubled, for I had the urgent matter of the White Council on my hands.
>
> —*Unfinished Tales*, pp. 325–6.

This account finally makes clear therefore that Gandalf does indeed have 'pressing business' of his own (DAA.187) and must leave Thorin & Company as soon as he decently can to deal with a different crisis elsewhere: marshalling the Wizards and the Wise – that is, Radagast and the Elven-princes – to join him in overruling Saruman and attacking the Necromancer before the latter can destroy Rivendell or Lórien (UT.321–2, 326; see also 350–51).

22 *Mould* here means not 'mold' in the sense of mildew or fungus (its most common usage today) but dirt rich with organic decay (in this case, from generations of fallen leaves).

23 The penultimate paragraph of Chapter VI observes that 'Dwarves have never taken to matches even yet' (DAA.159). Whether this line, and the relatively modern touch of Bilbo's pocket-matches in Chapter V (DAA.116), would have survived in the 1960 Hobbit, had the Fifth Phase reached so far, is an unanswerable question; at any rate, they survived unchanged through the third edition changes of 1966.

24 Originally Balin describes this area as 'Noman's *land*', a phrase Tolkien used several times in *The Lord of the Rings* for the area better known as the Brown Lands (*LotR*.394 & 657). The addition of these lines of dialogue by Balin and Gloin, like Fili and Kili's promptly springing into action after Thorin's decision at the fallen bridge and Bombur's fumbling and grumbling, all help characterize the dwarves – for example, Balin's distrust of the woods north of the road helps establish his good judgment, since it is soon revealed that trolls are lurking there. Had Tolkien continued the 1960 Hobbit all the way to the end he would

no doubt have added similar bits of action or dialogue for the less differentiated members of Thorin & Company; i.e., Nori, Oin, Bofur, Bifur, and Ori.

25 Bilbo originally referred to 'the kings' (plural) here, but this may be no more than a typing error, which in any case was quickly corrected to 'king'. This referent replaced the 'They have seldom even heard of the king round here' of the first and second (and ultimately third) editions. In the Prologue to *The Lord of the Rings*, Tolkien explain that this was an allusion to the fallen Dúnedain kingdoms of Arnor, in words he is clearly echoing here in the 1960 Hobbit:

> there had been no king for nearly a thousand years . . . Yet the Hobbits still said of wild folk and wicked things (such as trolls) that they had not heard of the king. For they attributed to the king of old all their essential laws . . . The Rules (as they said), both ancient and just.
>
> —*LotR*.21–2.

There is an irony in this mention of the king here, when with hindsight from *The Lord of the Rings*' Appendices A and B we realize that within a few days they will be arriving in Rivendell, where ten-year-old Aragorn, the rightful king of Arnor and Gondor, is living under the name of Estel ('Hope') in Elrond's household.

26 Bombur's expectation is amusing, given that Gandalf at his reappearance indeed 'stepped from behind a great tree'; see DAA.80 and Tolkien's correction for page 52 line 18 on page 799.

27 Note that the rephrasing here eliminates the direct address to the reader of all the published editions at this point: 'though I don't suppose you or I would have noticed anything . . . I don't suppose even a weasel would have stirred a whisker' (DAA.70); the formerly intrusive narrator ceases to be a character in the story, which now lacks a storyteller.

28 Originally, 'trolls of *that* sort'. In a 1954 letter, Tolkien described the trolls appearing in *The Hobbit* as 'Stone-trolls' (JRRT to Peter Hastings, *Letters* p.191). The 'other kinds' mentioned in the following sentences include the cave-troll that almost forces its way into Balin's burial chamber in Moria (*LotR*.342–3) and the *Olog-hai* (*LotR*.1166), described in the rumors circulating in the Shire in 'The Shadow of the Past': 'Trolls were abroad, no longer dull-witted, but cunning and armed with dreadful weapons' (*LotR*.57).

29 This entry is a late addition, written in the left margin.

30 That is, in place of the original passage that read '. . . after waiting for some time for Bilbo to come back, or to hoot like an owl, they *started off one by one*', the text should now read '. . . hoot like an owl, they *left Bombur to mind the ponies. . .*'

31 This sentence is bracketed in pencil but not deleted. Presumably what called it into question was the new scene earlier in this same chapter

where they had in fact left behind one of their number (the overlooked hobbit) on the far bank of the swollen river.

32 The sequence in which the dwarves arrived at the troll's campfire is altered from the original, which mimicked the order in which they arrived on Bilbo's doorstep (and included the surprising information that Bifur, Bofur, and Bombur were the Heir of Durin's 'attendants' – i.e. either courtiers or an honor-guard). Now the surprisingly good account the last two captured gave of themselves is transferred from the unlikely Bifur and Bombur (not elsewhere distinguished for their valour) to the more active and effective Fili and Kili.

33 This page is not literally blank but it does lack any text, being devoted to the black-and-white picture 'The Trolls' (cf. DAA.74).

34 Originally 'set *a stone over them with dwarf runes*'.

35 Originally Tolkien typed 'there are *more trolls about*' before changing it to the less specific and more evocative 'other wicked things abroad'.

36 Gandalf's final statement, absent from earlier editions, is curious, since nothing added here indicates that Bilbo played any part in saving them from the cannibal feast.

37 The unchanged skipped text that bridges the gap between this revision and the next is 'and their *horses had more to eat than they had; for there was plenty of grass, but there was not much in their bags, even with what they had got from the* trolls.' This actually misses an opportunity to correct an error going all the way back to the first edition, since 'horses' should in fact read *ponies* here. The original book had switched back and forth between 'horse' and 'pony', especially in the Lonely Mountain chapters (see page 479), as if the two were interchangeable, but the dichotomy between the dwarves' ponies and the wizard's horse has been stressed throughout New Chapter II.

38 Written in the left margin alongside this: 'May 22'. See Itinerary, page 819.

39 Written in the left margin alongside this: 'May 23'. See Itinerary, page 819.

40 The shift from first person plural ('We must not . . . we shall be . . . We need') in the published editions (cf. DAA.88) to second person ('You must not . . . the end of you . . . You need') here has the effect of exempting the wizard himself, suggesting that whatever dire peril they may find themselves in he at least will come through unscathed. This is in keeping with his enhanced stature in *The Lord of the Rings*, but again it leaves him detached, not really a part of the group struggling to survive the adventure he arranged.

41 The idea that dwarves were not particularly welcome at Rivendell is a new and somewhat disconcerting idea, apparently imported back into *The Hobbit* to match the initially chilly relations between Gimli's people and the elves of Lórien in *The Lord of the Rings*. The version of this passage Tolkien originally drafted, '*no dwarf has*', was even more

uncompromising (i.e., 'though *no dwarf has* [ever seen it]). It is also out of keeping with their extended stay there, which in the 1960 Hobbit is expanded from the two weeks ('a fortnight') of the published book to at least five (see Itinerary, page 823).

42 The passage being altered reads 'Gandalf, who seemed to know his way about pretty well', which would now become 'Gandalf, who seemed to know his way.'

43 *whin*, like heather, is a tough prickly shrub, more commonly known as *furze*, that grows in European wastelands.

44 This sentence was followed by several lines of drafting:

> Suddenly he came to the brink of a steep fall in the ground, so sharp that [he] nearly slipped headlong down it. 'Steady!' said Gandalf. 'You have better come last.'

Although cancelled, this passage shows us that the 'he' who hurried forward in the next sentence is Bilbo, not Gandalf or his horse.

Queries and Reminders

Nothing in the nature of Plot Notes exists for New Chapters I, II, & III – naturally enough, given that Tolkien had already long since completed the story and instead was now trying to bring it into accord with its sequel, and his own revised opinions about how such a story should be told. However, a single page of notes [Ad.Ms.H.11] does exist, clearly meant to serve as reminders to Tolkien of points he had not yet addressed in this revision, and I give those here:

Hobbit

There is no mention in The Hobbit of Gandalf's horse after Rivendell. What did he ride on?

What happened to the musical instruments used by the Dwarves at Bag-end?

Why did they bring them to B-End?

Since the Fifth Phase was abandoned at this point, ultimately none of these points was resolved. The fate of Rohald is suggested by Tolkien's note at the end of New Chapter III (see page 803 above); since the horse was from Rivendell, Gandalf presumably left him there when Thorin & Company departed and headed up into the mountains. The musical instruments are a thornier issue, since these notes indicate Tolkien's dissatisfaction with the text as it stands but give no hint of how he might have resolved the problem. Given his attempt throughout the 1960 Hobbit to reduce the whimsy and comic touches of the original, however, it seems likely that in the end this bit of dwarven exuberance would have been sacrificed to probability and all but the most portable instruments deleted.

The End of the Fifth Phase

The goal of this chapter's revision was not so much to flesh out the rather sketchy account of Bilbo and the dwarves' journey from Bag-end to Rivendell, although it does do that, as to make it fit with the later, more detailed description of travelling over some of that same territory (between Bree and the Last Homely House) in *The Lord of the Rings*. As the late Karen Wynn Fonstad observed in *The Atlas of Middle-earth* [1981]:

> The Troll's fire was so close to the river that it could be seen 'some way off,' and it probably took the Dwarves no more than an hour to reach; whereas Strider led the Hobbits north of the road, where they lost their way and spent almost six days reaching the clearing where they found the Stone-trolls. Lost or not, it seems almost impossible that the time-pressed ranger would have spent six days reaching a point the Dwarves found in an hour . . . the two stories seemed irreconcilable.
>
> —Fonstad, page 97.

As the 'Timelines and Itinerary' show, Tolkien was well aware of this problem, and Christopher Tolkien discusses in *The Return of the Shadow* (HME VI.203–4) how the 1960 Hobbit revisions would have redressed this dilemma. The fact that the 1966 third edition changes failed to do so is, I think, a persuasive bit of evidence that Carpenter is correct in stating that Tolkien did not have the 1960 material before him when he made those final changes to the text. Instead, he was almost certainly working from his memory of this material: the third edition introduces the stone bridge found in *The Lord of the Rings*, but since it is intact in this final authorized edition of *The Hobbit* (DAA.66) its presence only exacerbates the problem of the discrepancy in the time their respective journeys took.

In addition to more diminishment of Bilbo's character – the hapless hobbit now cannot even keep track of what month it is – the new revisions firmly place Bilbo in Frodo's world: to mentions of the Shire and Hobbiton and Moria in New Chapter I are now added another mention of Moria and references to the Prancing Pony at Bree and to the Rangers operating in the area around Rivendell (in fact, hunting down monsters like the trolls). The bridge across the Mitheithel (Hoarwell) upon which Glorfindel leaves a token for Strider (*LotR*.217) now appears in *The Hobbit*, but broken by trolls; clearly Elrond must have restored it sometime in the intervening years (see Tolkien's note on Elrond's maintenance of the road at the end of the New Chapter III fragment, on page 803).[1]

Small wonder, in the face of such specificity, that statements by the narrator such as 'I don't know what river it was' (second edition page 42) vanish in the 1960 revision. In fact, all first person references by the narrator are excised from the text, along with all direct (second person) addresses by the narrator to the reader; Tolkien had come to feel that these were a stylistic flaw and removed them throughout.

What is surprising is that, even with all these changes, large sections of the story remained intact and indeed unaltered. For example, Tolkien had stated in 1954 that 'I might not (if *The Hobbit* had been more carefully written, and my world so much thought about 20 years ago) have used the expression "poor little blighter",[2] just as I should not have called the troll *William*' (JRRT to Peter Hastings, Sept 1954; *Letters* p. 191), yet aside from some additions at the beginning of the encounter the troll's dialogue survived virtually untouched in this extensive 1960 recasting of the chapter, and the now-inappropriate names William (or Bill), Bert, and Tom were all retained.

One other long-standing point is resolved in this revision: the vexing question of why Elrond could read the writing on the swords but Gandalf could not. Now we are told that the runes are obscured by old dried goblin-blood; not until they are cleaned can the letters be seen. Presumably their hosts perform this task for them during their stay, and the scene of Elrond's viewing the swords in Chapter III would probably have been slightly recast to incorporate a presentation of their newly polished swords.

We cannot know what else Tolkien would have added to the story, had the 1960 Hobbit or Fifth Phase continued beyond this point. Bilbo could not have met Arwen at Rivendell, for we know she was at that time in the middle of a decades-long visit to her grandparents, Galadriel and Celeborn, in Lórien. But did Bilbo's lifelong friendship with Aragorn (then a ten-year-old living in Rivendell with his mother and being raised by Elrond) begin during his visit there, either on the outgoing or the return trip? Did Legolas Greenleaf fight in the Battle of Five Armies? Would more light have been cast upon the storm-giants of the Misty Mountains, or the source of Beorn's enchantment, or would we have learned a little more about the elusive Radagast? Would the Spiders of Mirkwood have been made more horrific, à la Shelob, and the wood-elves absolved of all blame in their treatment of the dwarves? Would Balin's visit in the Epilogue include some mention of his plans for Moria? And most importantly, would the Ring have been presented in more sinister terms throughout, with hints of its corruptive influence even on one such as Bilbo?

We will never know the answers to any of these questions. According to Christopher Tolkien, when his father had reached this point in the recasting he loaned the material to a friend to get an outside opinion on it. We do not know this person's identity, but apparently her response was something along the lines of 'this is wonderful, but it's not *The Hobbit*'. She must have been someone whose judgment Tolkien respected, for he abandoned the work and decided to let *The Hobbit* retain its own autonomy and voice rather than completely incorporate it into *The Lord of the Rings* as a lesser 'prelude' to the greater work. When he briefly returned to it in 1965 for the third edition revisions, he restricted himself in the main to the correction of errors and egregious departures from Middle-earth as it had developed (e.g., the policemen of Chapter II; DAA.69) and left matters of style and tone alone. Thus the work begun in a flash of inspiration thirty-five years before – 'in a hole in the ground lived a hobbit' – saw periodic revisioning through several distinct phases over a period of thirty years (1930 to 1960), until in the last decade of its author's life it reached the final form we know and love today.

NOTES

1 While Elrond's maintenance of the road makes sense and is in keeping with his role as the preserver of the last vestiges of the North Kingdom, it is hard to picture the elves of Rivendell working at road-mending, since throughout the legendarium the elves are never associated with road-making. We might speculate that he hires dwarves to do the work without actually permitting these contractors to know Rivendell's exact location (lying as it does some way off the main road), but that solution runs afoul of this text's statements that dwarves were not welcome here and did not know this part of the world well. No doubt if Tolkien had fully developed this idea we would know the answers to these apparent difficulties.

2 Hastings had argued that this phrase implied that William was capable of feeling pity and thus making a moral judgment. This would of course run counter to the legendarium's presentation of the Creatures of Morgoth as irredeemably wicked. Tolkien however disagreed: 'I do not say William felt *pity* – a word to me of moral and imaginative worth . . . Pity must restrain one from doing something immediately desirable and seemingly advantageous. There is no more "pity" here than in a beast of prey yawning, or lazily patting a creature it could eat, but does not want to, since it is not hungry' (*Letters* p. 191). Thus there was no need to rewrite the scene of William's actions, and Tolkien left his little comic masterpiece of the trolls' dialogue intact, even preserving the mild profanity of 'what the 'ell'.

TIMELINES AND ITINERARY

The final group of texts associated with the 1960 Hobbit are concerned with distances and dates, particularly as they relate to time of travel between various points and to the phases of the moon. Primarily, Tolkien was concerned with four main points: (1) the date of Thorin & Company's departure from Bag-End, (2) the date and place of their encounter with the trolls (with its associated phase of the moon), (3) the time of their stay in Rivendell (with *its* associated moon-phase on the eve of their departure), and (4) the timing of Durin's Day. Through the changes incorporated into New Chapter I and New Chapter II, he had managed to bring some of these points into sufficient harmony to satisfy himself; the itinerary below beautifully lays out the specifics, along with many interesting hitherto unknown details about their journey. However, reconciling all of these points, and others that arose as a result of his revisions, ultimately proved impossible without even more radical alterations than he had already carried out, for reasons that will become evident in the material that follows.

(i)
Distances and Itinerary

These two sheets of single-spaced typescript, or three and a half pages of text [Ad.Ms.H.21–4], lay out with admirable clarity the day-by-day details of Bilbo's first journey, from his rendezvous with the dwarves outside the inn in Bywater to their arrival in Rivendell. This document is later than New Chapter I and New Chapter II as they were originally typed, since the latter text is quoted from within it, but before some of the alterations and revisions to those documents.

The Hobbit.

Distances and itinerary of the journey from Bywater Inn to Rivendell. This has been altered to fit the more precise geography of the 'Lord of the Rings', the first Book of which covers the same ground. Also to make more credible and explicable Gandalf's disappearance before the Troll-episode.

The maps in the L.R.[TN1] have been taken as more or less correct and to scale. The scale of the large map is 1 centimetre to 50 miles. That of the Shire-map is not stated, but is approximately 9 times as large (1 millimetre to 5/9 of a mile). But note** in this map Bywater and its pool is somewhat too far east. There should be no houses of Hobbiton on the south side of 'The Water'. Or rather none at the time of The Hobbit. At time of L.R. ('Scouring of the Shire') there should be a small block of 'new houses' to the right of the road-junction, 'a mile beyond Bywater'; but none to the left.[TN2] It was not more than a mile and a quarter from the footbridge just south of the Mill to the first houses of Bywater, among which was the 'Green Dragon' Inn.

The episode of the broken bridge (The Bridge of Mitheithel in L.R.) is inserted, to fit geography, which does not allow for any part of the East Road running beside a river. It also suggests, though this is not explained (unless perhaps in Ch. III)[TN3] that Elrond exercised some supervision over the road and the territory between the Grey-flood and the Mountains. This makes it more credible that Gandalf should go in search of help, and should actually meet people from Rivendell. The Rangers are just mentioned, as a link with L.R. but not further explained.

As for the journey, before that point (the troll-meeting), the text of The Hobbit, Ch.II, obviously cannot be equated with the L.R., not even if based on the confused memories of Bilbo (who covered the road twice, to and fro).[TN4] But fair speed of narrative is still needed, and even apart from competing with the L.R., no such detail as is given in the later book should be given. It is however impossible that Bilbo would have forgotten Bree, or that he should not have heard of it before:[TN5] it was well-known in hobbit-history. Though he may not have heard the name of the Inn (which in the L.R. is evidently only known to and visited by people from Buckland and the neighbourhood of the Brandywine Bridge).

Bree is therefore just mentioned as a last stopping place before the real wilds began. The Last Inn (by the time of the L.R. called the Forsaken Inn: L.R. I 200)[TN6] a day's journey east of Bree is brought in to emphasize the growing desolation between Bree and the Grey-flood. But Weathertop is not mentioned; nor are the rivers Greyflood and Loudwater named.

Distances.

1. SHIRE. Junction of the Hill Road in Hobbiton and the main East Road to Brandywine Bridge: about 50 miles.
2. Brandywine Bridge to Bree (by road) 50 miles. +
   + called (L.R. I. 162) 'not much [further] than a day's riding' but that refers to quick <journeys> on <unhampered> mounts.[TN7]
3. Wild. Bree Eastgate to ruined Last Inn about 20 miles
4. Last Inn to Weathertop (by road) 80 miles.
   100 miles Bree to Weathertop.
5. Weathertop to Bridge of Mitheithel (by road) 110 miles
6. Bridge of Mitheithel to Ford of Bruinen about 80 miles
   Bridge to point where Troll-fire seen: 20 miles.
   From that point to Ford 60 miles.
7. Ford of Bruinen to entrance to Rivendell, about 22 miles.

The whole journey from Bywater in the Shire to Rivendell was about 412 miles. Time allowed: from morning of April 28 to evening of May 24th. That is, according to the Shire Calendar (followed but nowhere alluded to in The Hobbit),[TN8] from Astron 28 to Thrimidge 24 inclusive: 27 days. That is an average of 16 miles a day. This is slow, but accounted for by leisurely pace at the beginning, and slow progress in the Wilds, especially before passing the Greyflood. But is clear that it could not be 'June the first tomorrow' (i.e. in Shire reckoning May/Thrimidge 30), as in text, p. 41, on the day of the troll-adventure. This is accounted for by Bilbo's loss of reckoning, without the help of any calendar, during the 22 days of the journey up to that point. Hence new text: 'Not what I call June, etc.'

Itinerary.

1. April 28. Spend night at the All-welcome Inn, at junction of the Northway and East Road (on Hobbiton side of Frogmorton). So-called because much used by travellers through the Shire, especially by dwarves on the way to Thorin's home in exile, which was in the west-side of the Blue mountains (southern part, in Harlindon). None of this is mentioned in text, but The All-welcome Inn should be marked on the needed Shire-map in any new edition of The Hobbit.[TN9] It has to be remembered that the East Road though it ran through the Shire was not the property of the hobbits:

it was an ancient 'royal road', and they maintained the traditional duty of keeping it in repair and providing hospitality for travellers. This was of course profitable. It also provided their chief source of 'outside news'. Dwarves were therefore not a rare sight on the East Road or in its inns (It would also appear that they were sometimes employed as roadmenders and bridge-repairers), but they seldom turned off it, and their appearance in a company in Bywater and Hobbiton must have caused a lot of talk.[TN10] They cared very little about hobbits, and had little to do with them, except as a source of food in exchange for metal, or sometimes forged articles (knives, ploughshares, arrowheads, axe-heads and the like). The poorer sort (or Thorin's folk in their earlier time of poverty) might accept employment, as masons and roadmakers for example. But they had the notion that hobbits were a slow stupid folk, with few artefacts, and simpleminded – because the hobbits were generous, never haggled, and gave what was asked.

2. April 29. Night at Whitfurrows.

3. April 30. Early start. They cross the Brandywine Bridge (about 12 miles from Whitfurrows) in the late afternoon, and camp by the road about 10 miles on from the B. Bridge.

4. May 1. They ride another 20 miles, taking their time, with longish halts and good meals (but only three), since there are still supplies ahead.

5. May 2. They reach Bree (another 20 miles). There they stay the night, and also purchase a good many supplies (including pipe-weed).

6. May 3. Early start. They enter the wild. They reach the Last Inn early in the evening, but are depressed at finding it deserted and go no further. [*added in pencil*: Another 20 miles.]

7. May 4 to May 10: 7 days.

Their progress is now very slow, owing to the badness and dangerousness of the road, esp. in the marshy region. They barely manage 12 miles a day, and by evening of May 10 have only reached Weathertop (80 miles from the Last Inn). They camp on its east side.[TN11] This is not mentioned at all in text.

8. May 11 to May 18: 8 days.

It was about 109 miles (for they started on the far side of Weathertop) to the Bridge of Mitheithel (over the Greyflood). By the evening of May 18 they had covered only 106 miles, and camped beside the road, on drier and rising ground, actually only about 3 miles from the Bridge, which could not be seen as it was in a deep narrow valley. In the night the weather took a bad turn.

9. May 19. Wakened in the early morning by wind and rain, they make a hurried meal. Soon reach the top of the ridge and look down. Episode of the broken bridge. They get across Greyflood about 10.30 a.m. 3 miles. They make two foodless halts, at midday about 5 miles on from Bridge, and another (not mentioned in text) about 4. p.m.; and then go on till darkness. Say about 8.30 p.m. (sun-set about 8 p.m.) but the road was under dark trees.[TN12] Ponies become more and more reluctant to proceed, so that in spite of improved road they are slow. Going from 1 p.m. to 4 and 4.30 to 8. (6 1/2 hours) they only cover about 17 miles.[TN13] Episode of the Trolls occurs night of May 19, at a point about 25 miles from the Bridge. 55 miles to go to Ford of Bruinen.

10. May 20. Do not start until afternoon, say 3.30 p.m. Journey till 8 p.m. with one halt: about 4 hours in which they covered about 12 miles: 43 to Bruinen.[TN14]

11. May 21. They go another [20 >] 18 miles. 25 from Bruinen.

12. May 22. 'Fourth day from the Bridge' (19, 20, 21, 22). The weather is clearing up, and the ponies are willing, but they are tired and short of food. They start late, and make a long midday halt. They have only covered about another 15 miles, when in the evening sunshine they see Bruinen gleaming. It is 10 miles away. They go no further that day, for they have passed out of the shadow of the Trollshaws, and feel safer.

13. May 23. They reach the Ford in the afternoon. Probably halting for midday meal on the west bank of the river, though that is not mentioned in text. Further progress is very slow in the heathland. They did not go on when the light failed, and halted when only about 10 miles further on. 12 miles to entrance to Rivendell.

14. May 24. Progress still slow and difficult. Nightfall was near when, after covering 12 more miles, they reached the head of the path down into Rivendell.

The journey of 27 days is over

The typed text ends here about half-way down the fourth typescript page [Ad.Ms.H.24]. Beneath it is written the following penciled note:

But. It is said p. 62 that they stayed in Rivendell 'at least 14 days'. On their last evening it is Midsummers eve if Shire calendar is used that is the Lithe of June. Next day after June 30th (our calendar July 1) On that day there was a broad crescent moon Sc. at or near FQuarter

The abbreviation 'Sc.', used here and elsewhere in Tolkien's notes on phases of the moon, is short for *scilicet*, meaning 'namely' or 'that is to say'.

As for 'Lithe of June', in the Shire Calendar three days fall between June 30th and July 1st. These 'Summerdays' are known as *Lithe* (the day after June 30th, known as the 'June Lithe' or 'June 30+1' as Tolkien expresses it in some of the notes below), *Midyear's Day* (two days after June 30th, or 'June 30+2'), and *Lithe* (the day before July 1st, three days after June 30th, or the July Lithe). Their presence, and that of the two days of Yule at midwinter (between December 30th and January 1st), enable the Shire Calendar to have twelve months of thirty days each (12 x 30 = 360, +5 midwinter/midsummer days).

TEXT NOTES

1 'L.R.': That is, *The Lord of the Rings*. The 'large map' Tolkien refers to is the fold-out map of Middle-earth pasted in the back of *The Fellowship of the Ring* and also *The Two Towers*. The 'Shire-map' is the map labelled 'A Part of the Shire' appearing just after the Prologue (*LotR*. [30]). By 'Book' in the preceding paragraph Tolkien means of course Book 1, the first half of the first volume.

2 This sentence and the one before it ('Or rather none . . . to the left') are bracketed but not deleted; this passage may have been singled out because it relates to features of the locale that did not exist at the time of Bilbo's story. See *LotR*.1041 & 1049. Note, however, that several such houses in fact appear on the Shire map printed in *The Lord of the Rings*, where in fact most of Hobbiton is situated south of The Water, with only a very few buildings (primarily those seen in Tolkien's painting of The Hill: Hobbiton [DAA plate 1 (top), H-S#98]) north of the little river.†

†This feature is much clearer in the first edition, which prints this map in two colours (black for the river and houses, red for the roads).

3 An ink note over the parenthetical seems to read 'no explanation <is> <there>'. See Tolkien's note written on page 'III.2' just after the New Chapter III text broke off (Ad.Ms.H.33; see page 803), which may be Tolkien's reminder to himself to insert such an explanation into the text of Chapter III, no doubt as something Bilbo would have learned at Rivendell had the recasting continued beyond this point.

4 Actually Bilbo covered it a third time after his spectacular departure from Hobbiton at the end of the Long-Expected Party, though by that time he had already written at least the earlier portions of his book; cf. *LotR*.247 for the journey and DAA.361 & *LotR*.119 for the book.

5 This sentence originally read '. . . impossible that Bilbo would have forgotten Bree, *and very improbable* that he *had not heard* of it before'.

6 The reference is to page 200 of volume one (*The Fellowship of the Ring*) of the first edition of *The Lord of the Rings* ['L.R.']; emphasis mine:

> 'How far is Rivendell?' asked Merry . . . The world looked wild and wide from Weathertop.
>
> 'I don't know if the Road has ever been measured in miles beyond the *Forsaken Inn*, a day's journey east of Bree,' answered Strider. 'Some say it is so far, and some say otherwise. It is a strange road, and folk are glad to reach their journey's end, whether the time is long or short. But I know how long it would take me on my own feet, with fair weather and no ill fortune: twelve days from here [Weathertop] to the Ford of Bruinen, where the Road crosses the Loudwater that runs out of Rivendell. We have at least a fortnight's journey before us, for I do not think we shall be able to use the Road.'
>
> —*LotR*.204.†

† = Page 200 of *The Fellowship of the Ring* in the first edition.

7 This passage is added in pencil in the top margin and marked as a note applying to this entry. The full passage cited here can be found on *LotR*.166.

8 Tolkien here introduces a new complication: the idea that all dates given in *The Hobbit* are really according to the Shire Calendar described in Appendix D of *The Lord of the Rings* (see *LotR*.1140–46). *The Hobbit* of course had not been written with the Shire Calendar in mind, as the latter had not yet been created when the story was published, and the decision here to adapt the story from one calendar to another would lead him into insoluble paradoxes: see section (iii) below, esp. Text Note 1 on page 828.

9 Added in left margin in pencil: '<Also> Thorin's Dwelling' – i.e., Thorin's halls in exile in the Blue Mountains south of the Gulf of Lune should also appear. Since these lay well outside the Shire, Tolkien presumably means that they should be added to the large foldout map of Middle-earth.

10 This line harkens back to one of the texts of 'The Quest of Erebor', where Gandalf notes that '[Bilbo] did not know . . . the care . . . that I took so that the coming of a large party of Dwarves to Bywater, off the main road and their usual beat, should not come to his ears too soon' (UT.335).

11 Here 'east side' was typed over an erasure; the phrase originally typed seems to have been 'west side'.

12 The text here originally ran 'and then go on till *nearly night*. Say about 8 p.m. (sun-set about *that time*). Ponies . . .' All these changes are in ink, with 'but the road was under dark trees' in the left margin and marked for insertion at this point.

13 This sentence originally read 'Going from 12.00 to 4 and 4.30 to 8.30 (7 1/2 hours) they only cover about 20 miles.'

14 The original version of the next few entries read:

11. May 21, 22.	2 days. Each day they cover about 16 miles (36) and at night are only 7 from the Ford, which they cannot yet see.
12. May 23.	In the morning after a short ride they see the Bruinen ahead and below them in another (less steep) valley.

These were cancelled and replaced by separate entries for all three days giving a somewhat different account of their progress.

(ii)

Timetable from Rivendell to Lake Town

This single sheet of notes (Ad.Ms.H.13), written in ink on the back of an unused page taken from a 'blue book' (student's exam booklet),[TN1] extends the timeline and itinerary from Rivendell through Mirkwood to Thorin & Company's departure from Lake Town. It thus forms a suitable companion piece to the more formal 'Distances and Itinerary' given as section (i) above, which focuses on the first stage of Bilbo's journey (Bag-End to Rivendell), the part covered by New Chapter II and the fragment of New Chapter III. However, it is probably much earlier: all the page references here are to the first edition (i.e., pre-1951), and dates are given in the Gregorian calendar, not the Shire Calendar developed during work on *The Lord of the Rings*. Christopher Tolkien notes (private communication) that this same kind of paper was used for drafting portions of *The Lord of the Rings* pre-1944. So these notes may date from as early as the Fourth Phase. But since annotations with ball-point pens show that if so he was still carefully considering and updating them long afterwards, in the period of the 1960 Hobbit, and since they deal with the same concerns as all the material in this chapter, here seems the natural place to give them.

Hobbit Time table is not very clear.[TN2]

[Written in top margin in dark ink:]

Mirkwood is too small on map it must be 300 miles across

Adventure with Trolls night of 31 May/1 June. reach R'dell appar. about June 3rd. Leave on Midsummer morning: say June 24.

Long days after still climbing p. 66.
On map R'dell is about 50 miles direct to top of the range or pass. Make it more? going <will be> slow and actual distance possibly twice as far as forward distance. Say 100 at 10 miles per day, 10 days. They therefore reach Cave of Goblins on night of July 4th. Summer is getting on down below – haymaking p. 67.[TN3]
Adventure with Goblins takes 3 days. night before night before last. p. 102. They assemble therefore on July 7th
Adv. with wargs night July 7/8.
Reach Beorn afternoon July 8
Depart 3 days later. July 11th (p. 141)
Take 4 days riding to the Forest Entrance (p. 142)
Enter Forest therefore 15 or 16 July.

Ages and ages p. 148 They reach Enchanted River (which is about 1/2 way to Elvenking's hall). And after they have gone on again about as long leaf falls suggesting autumn is coming on p. 153. The Forest is largely dark and they are laden – later carrying Bombur. But must allow at least an average of 12 miles per day. Say 12 days to Enchanted River. 144 miles. July 28th.
12 days to adventure with Spiders.
144 miles. August 9th[TN4]
[total] 288 [miles]
Weary long time in King's Hall. say 3 weeks.[TN5] Aug 30th.
Reach Lake Town about Sept 2/3.
9 days gap
We know Bilbo's Birthday Sept 22 was at Lake Town. They were there about 24 days. Birthday would come after 10 days. Leaves about October 6th?
Reach Lake town on 8th. Stay 10 days. Sept 18.

Rivendell must be further off.[TN6] Reach Cave about July 9th. Therefore enter Forest 21 July. Forest journey must be 300 miles (150 each) and take about 25 days. 15 August. [*cancelled*: leave King's Halls 5 Sept.]

[Text continued in left margin:]

Taken prisoner on 16 August. Escape <9th> Sept.[TN7] Reach L.T. 12th Sept. B. <illegible>[TN8] Sep 22. Leave <about> 6th of October.

[Added in margin in green ink:]

Use Hobbit Calendar as in L.R.[TN9]

In this time-table, Tolkien attempts to retroactively apply a scale to the Wilderland map published in *The Hobbit* but is not able to do so consistently. If the distance from Rivendell to the Cave of the Goblins atop the Misty Mountains pass (about an inch and a half on the Wilderland map) [TN10] is 50 miles (as the crow flies, 100 miles of actual travel), then the route Thorin & Company wound up taking through Mirkwood (three and a half inches) cannot equal 300 miles but is more like 175 miles (the last part of it in barrels), meaning the dwarves averaged only about six miles a day before their capture. The large Middle-earth map,[TN11] while different in scale, faithfully reproduces the proportions of the earlier map in their overlapping sections: here their route through the dark forest measures about $3\frac{1}{2}$ cm (roughly $1\frac{3}{8}$ inches), which again equals about 175 miles by the scale Tolkien decided on in the 'distances' typescript given as section (i) above. By contrast, Gimli in *The Lord of the Rings* as one of the Three Walkers managed to travel roughly the same distance in only five days (albeit as an epic feat under much better conditions, spurred on by both competition from Man and Elf and the desperate necessity to rescue his friends).

Or to pick a less extreme example, Dain and his company of dwarves from the Iron Hills arrive within a very short time – clearly only a matter of days[TN12] – from the time Thorin sent Roäc to summon them. The Iron Hills are not shown on the Wilderland Map in *The Hobbit*, being off the edge of the map to the east, and thus more than one inch [= about 35 miles] away. We are not told exactly where Dain's halls are within the Hills, but since the Hills themselves are clearly nearby, the Wilderland Map leaves it plausible that Dain is easily within the distance of a rapid forced march. But applying this part of *The Hobbit's* story to *The Lord of the Rings* immediately creates difficulties. According to the Middle-earth Map in *The Lord of the Rings*, we can see that at their nearest point, the Iron Hills are double the distance from the Lonely Mountain that Rivendell is to the top of the mountain-pass; at their furthest point they are seven times that distance. Since we know the latter distance to be at least fifty miles, then Dain had to travel somewhere between a hundred to three hundred and fifty miles to come to Thorin's aid (the latter if coming from the far eastern side of the Hills), after having first taken at least some time to gather and equip his troops. Furthermore the fact that Thorin & Company are heavy-laden cannot be a significant factor, for we are told within *The Hobbit* itself of Dain's army that

> They had brought with them a great store of supplies; for the dwarves can carry very heavy burdens, and nearly all of Dain's folk, in spite of their rapid march, bore huge packs on their backs in addition to their weapons.
>
> —DAA.337.

Fonstad observed that doubling the scale on the Wilderland map found in *The Hobbit* would resolve many difficulties (*Atlas of Middle-earth*, page 97), and it is clear that Tolkien himself had arrived at the same realization long before from the note he added at the top of this manuscript page. That would not however have fixed the problem of the speed of Dain's travel versus the slowness of Thorin's journey; only by redrawing the map to make Mirkwood much, much wider could he have resolved the problem of how long it took Bilbo and his companions to travel though the forest. Here then we come to an example – not the last – of a solution (doubling the map scale to make Thorin & Company's travel time more credible) that would in turn create a new problem (doubling the distance Dain's five hundred dwarves travel in much less time), something that proved endemic in the 1960 Hobbit (see below) and no doubt played a part in the project's abandonment: a story written without a specific timetable simply could not in the end be fitted within a fairly narrow time frame without radical alteration of either the existing maps or the time-references and description of scenes within the published text.

TEXT NOTES

1 Actually, a large (8½ by 5½ inch) fragment of such a page, with 'Prifysgol Cymru' (i.e., University of Wales) in the upper left corner and the header 'DEGREE EXA[mination]'. Tolkien worked for many years as an external examiner for other universities, and one of the side benefits was the opportunity to accumulate a supply of scrap paper from unfilled booklets.

2 This line is written in pencil at the top of the page.

3 Above 'haymaking', Tolkien has written *harvest* in red ball-point pen. This is a reference to Bilbo's gloomy prediction regarding their slow rate of travel: 'down below . . . haymaking is going on and picnics. They will be harvesting and blackberrying, before we even begin to go down the other side at this rate' (first edition, page 66; DAA.101).

4 The original numbers in this passage are overwritten in darker ink, but seem to have originally read

Say *10* days to Enchanted River. *120* miles. July *26th*.
12 days to adventure with Spiders.
144 miles. August <*5th*>

The final date is largely obscured by the overwriting but seems to be '5th', where one would have expected to see instead 'August 7th'.

5 Note that here an imprisonment that had once been meant to last for months (from fall to spring – cf. Plot Notes A) has now shrunk to a mere three weeks – just enough time, one would think, for the dwarves and Bilbo to recover from their privations before becoming restless to press on with the next stage of their journey, and the same amount of time he now intended for them to spend in Lake Town.

6 The rule across the bottom of the page preceding this sentence indicates that Tolkien had reached a decision and that what followed stood apart from and would modify what came before (in this case, supplanting their dates).

7 The number for the day of the month has been overwritten in ink, obscuring whatever date originally stood here.

8 The illegible word here might be *presents*; it is certainly not 'birthday'.

9 This final instruction added to the page is written with a green ball point pen and thus dates from relatively late in Tolkien's life (post-*LotR*), probably added when he revisited this material as part of his work on the Fifth Phase/1960 Hobbit. It would also soon involve Tolkien in difficulties over the story's chronology; see section (iii) below, specifically Text Note I on page 828.

10 Here I use the map appearing as the back endpaper of the second edition (thirteenth printing, 1961), the earliest printing of the map available to me, since my reference copy of the first edition (3rd printing, wartime edition of 1942) lacks the maps. The proportions, however, hold true to any copy of the book including the map; cf. DAA.[399], which is reduced by about one-third, so that from Rivendell to the Mountain is about one inch, the distance across Mirkwood roughly two inches, and so forth.

11 Here I use the fold-out map in the first edition, first printing *The Fellowship of the Rings* as my standard for reference.

12 We know Dain's trip was very rapid, since less than a month passed between Durin's Day (the beginning of the last moon of autumn) and Bilbo's arrival at Beorn's Hall on the far side of Mirkwood in time for Yule.

(iii)

The Timeline Revisited
(moons taken into consideration)

These two sheets [Ad.Ms.H.19–20] contain three pages of text, the second sheet having been rotated ninety degrees and folded in half to divide it into two side-by-side half-pages: .20a (left) and .20b (right); the writing comes to an end about halfway through the last half-page. The text is written in ink and legible for the most part but a few lines have faded into illegibility; I indicate illegible words and passages with ellipses (. . .). Several sentences in this text are bracketed by Tolkien, but here I think it was not because of dissatisfaction with the bracketed material but rather for emphasis, to highlight those passages and make those points stand out for when he came back to put this material to use in the intended continuation of the Fifth Phase Hobbit. In order to avoid confusion with brackets added editorially, I have substituted double parentheses ((thus)) for authorial brackets in this section. Also, to improve readability, I have replaced some marks Tolkien used as shorthand: thus ∴ has been replaced by 'therefore', > by 'to' and in some places a slash (/) separating two numbers by 'to' where I thought the results might otherwise be mistaken for a fraction (e.g., '3/4 days' is here printed as '3 to 4 days' where that was Tolkien's intent). I have left the following of Tolkien's abbreviations in place: 'H' for *The Hobbit*, 'L.R.' or 'LR' for *The Lord of the Rings*, 'SC' for Shire Calendar (for the month, day, and day of the week), and 'SR' for Shire Reckoning (for the year).

This text clearly postdates the 'Distances and Itinerary' document given as section (i), since it refers to it and to the rewritten version of Chapter II (New Chapter II), but it was probably written at about the same time.

The Hobbit

The times and distances of the journey from Hobbiton to Rivendell are in great confusion, and it is difficult to make sense of them. But it is important to do so, if possible, owing to the L.R., which covers same ground in more detail. The 'moons' too are out of order – but this cannot be tolerated, since Durin's Day and the incidence of New Moon is integral to the plot.

Something, of course, could be done by attributing inaccuracy to Bilbo's memory. ((This would need a note in some future edition.))

The calendar used must evidently be the Shire Calendar ((though that is not and need not be alluded to)).

Fixed points that cannot be altered are the following

1. By calculation from H p. 35 [*added*: 21 April] '100 years ago last Thursday' – since weekday-date relation did not change in SC. – The Unexpected Party occurred on Wed. 27 April SC, 1341 SR Start of journey therefore 28 April (morning) SC.[TN1]

2. By L.R. Map distance from Hobbiton to Rivendell by road was approx 412 miles. From Troll-place to Ford of Bruinen [50 >] 60 miles; ((from Ford to head of path down into Rivendell 20 miles: 80 miles from Trolls to Rivendell)).

3. Company left Rivendell on Midsummer Day (= in SC. June 30 + 2) The Moon on the previous day (Lithe: June 30 + 1) was a broad silver crescent: therefore 3 to 4 days old. NM must have been June 27/28.

NB This fits tolerably well with later narrative. For if NM occurred on June 28 it would next occur on July 23 [29, 30, Lithe, Mid Year, Lithe] = 5 days + 23 = 28.[TN2] <Next> since all months have 30 days: on Aug. 21, on Sept. 19, October 17th. There is probably time for the events after Bilbo's Birthday (Sep 22) in Lake Town before the discovery of the Key-hole – Durin's Day[TN3]

It is said (p. 62) that the Dwarves &c. stayed at least 14 days in Rivendell. As they departed on Midsummer's Day, they must therefore have arrived on June 17th <about> at earliest, say, June 15 [*added*: or late on 17].

Question is (1) how did they take April 3 days, May 30 [days], June 15/17 [days] = 48/50 days in journey of 412 miles = an average rate (on ponies mostly) of only 8 1/2 miles (or a little more or less) per diem?

At any rate on day before the Troll-adventure (it being 80 miles only from that point to Rivendell) it cannot have been only May 30th. ((Bilbo says 'tomorrow it will be June 1st')).

The itinerary worked out in 'revision' of The Hobbit[TN4] is well enough in itself but it brings the company to Rivendell in 27 days on May 24 without regard to Moons!

? Something must be said about halts etc. esp. Bree, Last Inn ((later The Forsaken Inn)).

<Ponies> very reluctant after Bree & Last Inn. <most of the time> they had to be led.

The Bridge of <?Mitheithel> is broken . . . It was here . . . Ponies had be led . . .[TN5]

As for moons: if the moon was new on June 28 it would be New on June 1st, approx. but is said to be waning p. 42 and yet get . . . <soon> after dark like a NM or early crescent.[TN6]

? Say young and thin or *wandering ((because of the <hurrying> clouds))

If, however, they arrived in Rivendell <by> June 15/17 after a journey of 80 miles (slow and wary, and in the heathland very slow) of say 6 days – not much more than 13 miles a day! – they would be at Troll-place on June 9/11: 8 to 10 days after NM. June I and the moon would have <appeared> full – be in the wane – but would rise late at night!

The journey from Trolls to Bruinen needs lengthening in some way.[TN7]

Here we see problems introduced in the work Tolkien had already accomplished in the Fifth Phase begin to complicate the revision process, something that no doubt helped contribute to the Fifth Phase's abandonment. Here the specific problem is that by bringing Bilbo to Rivendell two weeks earlier than had been the case in the original Hobbit, he has taken a problem already present in the text and made it worse. Specifically, if the moon is a thin crescent in the evening sky on Midsummer Eve – that is, just a few days after the New Moon – and if they spent two weeks in Rivendell (DAA.93), then it would have been a gibbous moon – that is, a moon a few days past full[TN8] but more than half – at the time of their arrival. Bilbo sees just such a moon on the night of the troll-adventure, but that takes place several days *before* their arrival, when the moon should actually have been Full or rapidly approaching Full (and hence not 'waning'). And while Tolkien had at one point considered having time pass differently or not at all within elven enclaves (cf. HME VII.353–5, 363–5, and 'Note on Time in Lórien' in HME VII.367–9), he had firmly rejected this idea by the time of the published *Lord of the Rings*. It was an important part of Tolkien's legendarium that the story took place in the imagined past of the real world – as he wrote to Forrie Ackerman, '*The Lord of the Rings* . . . takes place in the Northern hemisphere of this earth: miles are miles, days are days, and weather is weather' (JRRT to Ackerman, June 1958; *Letters* p. 272). And, one might add, moons are moons; cf. Tolkien's modest boast, in his interview with Denys Gueroult that 'I don't think the moons rise or are in the wrong place at any point in [*The Lord of the Rings*]' (1965 BBC radio interview), a feat he only achieved during the book's revision by drawing up many-columned sheets listing where each character was on each day of the story.[TN9] No such charts exist for *The Hobbit*, since its narrative never split into multiple storylines following different sets of characters, but in the Fifth Phase Tolkien decided to treat its text with the same rigour, and the materials given below in sections (iv) and (v) probably represent the rough notes from which he could have generated such a chart correlating date, moon-phase, and action.

TEXT NOTES

1 That is, since the story is purportedly set down by Bilbo, it must use the Shire Calendar. Unfortunately, Tolkien failed to notice that *Thursday, 21st of April* is a date that cannot occur in the Shire Calendar, where the 21st always falls on a Friday (see Appendix D of *The Lord of the Rings*). It is probably for this reason that Fonstad silently shifts the Unexpected Party from Wed. 27th April and their departure on Th. 28th April to 26th April (= Wednesday) and 27th April (= Thursday), respectively in *The Atlas of Middle-earth* (page 98). Thus preservation of the 'comic precision' (see page 750) of 'a hundred years ago last Thursday' and '*Gandalf Tea Wednesday*' on the one hand and the much later decision to adapt the story to the Shire Calendar on the other set up a paradox: either Bilbo's adventure began on Thursday the 28th *or* the story was using the Shire Calendar, but both could not be true.

2 All these dates were shifted by one day, the passage having originally read:

> . . . if NM occurred on June 27/28 it would next occur on July 22/23 [28, 29, 30, Lithe, Mid Year, Lithe] July 1 = 7 days + 21 = 28.

More importantly, here and elsewhere in this material (see pages 826, 827, 832 & 834) Tolkien is treating the moon's cycle as if it lasted exactly twenty-eight days, rather than the actual twenty-nine-and-a-half of the real world's lunar cycle. My thanks to Tolkienian astronomer Kristine Larsen for drawing this to my attention.

3 Below this sentence Tolkien drew a line across the page, as if marking the beginning of a new section – i.e., shifting from the timetable after their departure from Rivendell back to their arrival and the events preceding it.

Note that the reference to a new moon on 19th October and the statement that 'There is probably time' between Bilbo's birthday (three days after the previous New Moon, which fell on 19th September just before the start of autumn) and 'the discovery of the Key-hole' suggest that Tolkien here is thinking of Durin's Day as falling on the *first* new moon of autumn, as in the original manuscript, rather than on the *last* new moon before the start of winter as in the published book. This would have solved the problem of Dain's too-rapid relief expedition and Bilbo's amazing rate of progress on the first stage of the return journey, but it would also have required the re-writing of several descriptive passages vividly conveying the rapid onset of winter; see Text Note 2 following section (iv) below.

4 This is a reference to section (i) above [Ad.Ms.H.21–4], which therefore already existed when Tolkien drafted these further notes (cf. also the specific reference a few lines earlier to '412 miles', the exact tally given in the Distances document (page 817).

Tolkien is pointing out here that by bringing Thorin & Company to Rivendell two weeks earlier than in the published book he has replaced one anomaly in the phases of the moon with another, so that the waning moon glimpsed on the night of the troll-adventure could not be at the right time of its cycle on Midsummer Eve to be a crescent moon, as required by the scene in which Elrond reads the moon-letters. See Text Note 6 below.

5 This passage of five lines (the last three on Ad.Ms.H.20a and the first two of Ad.Ms.H.20b) is very faint, but taken with the preceding paragraph the general sense is clear. Tolkien is searching for reasons to make their journey slower and delay their arrival in Rivendell to something closer to the original book (that is, about three weeks after the date given in New Chapter II and the Itinerary), and here suggests longer stays at Bree and the Last Inn, and the distress of their ponies in the wild, which in turn would lead to a slower rate of progress on the road after leaving Bree-land.

6 Tolkien's point is that if the moon were a few days past new on Midsummer's Eve, then the time specified for the troll-encounter (whether May 19th or the day before June 1st) cannot have a waning moon – that is, one past full. In addition, such a moon would not rise until well after dark (since the full moon rises at the same time that the sun sets), and the published book specifies that 'it was *nearly* dark' (i.e., the sun had not yet set) when 'a waning moon appeared' – characteristic of a waxing, not a waning, moon. His proposed solution, given in the next line, is to convert the moon Bilbo glimpsed that night into a waxing moon ('young and thin') or else evade the problem by simply describing it as 'a *wandering* moon' and avoid specifying its phase at all. The former would require the troll encounter to take place about thirty days before Elrond's discovery of the moon-runes the night the moon had just passed the same phase at Midsummer. The latter is the solution he adopted in the 1966 Hobbit (DAA.66).

7 Actually, it is the journey from the Hoarwell to the trolls that needs lengthening, if *The Hobbit* is to agree with *The Lord of the Rings*; cf. Fonstad, *The Atlas of Middle-earth* page 97 and the tailnote to section (iv) below.

8 Technically a gibbous moon can be either waxing (between First Quarter and Full Moon) or waning (between Full Moon and Last Quarter), but the text is specific here that it was the latter, a *waning* moon.

9 These charts are now (since 1997) part of the Tolkien collection at Marquette (Additional Tolkien Manuscripts, Fourth Installment, Envelope 6, items 2, 3, & 4).

(iv)
Waxing and Waning

This single page of notes [Ad.Ms.H.17] shows Tolkien looking not backwards from Rivendell to the troll-encounter but ahead to the other crucial moon-scene, that of the new moon on Durin's Day. Once again, as with section (iii) above, Tolkien seems to be treating Durin's Day as if it fell in the first month of autumn rather than the last; whether this is inadvertence or a deliberate decision which he nowhere expressed in writing cannot now be determined.

The 'broad crescent' moon on Midsummer eve in Elrond's house fits very well with Durin's Day in Chapter XI (2nd edn p. 221) – acc. to Shire Calendar Midsummer even was the June Lithe = June 30 + 1

A broad crescent would indicate that moon was approaching First Quarter therefore New Moon would be about June 26 (say) in Shire Calendar. Five [*added*: calendar] months later it would bring New Moon about Oct 19. This fits well enough with such time indicators as there are. They had been in Lake Town a week (+ 2 or 3 days?) when Bilbo had his cold – from LR we know that <this> was his birthday = Sep 22 (SC).[TN1] They were about another week in L. Town before Thorin spoke of going. Say Sep 29. Their departure was not at once. say Oct 5. Two days rowing (Oct 7) and then their journey to the Mountain and the search for the Door could well take more than 12 days, but could be accomplished in that time.[TN2]

As for <earlier> Moon. Just before Troll adventure . . . moon was waning. It had not <?gone> (it was said not to have risen) as they arrived at Rivendell. A fortnight must be allowed from NM to FM or LQ to NM

FQ. FM. LQ.| |NM

|NM^7 FQ^7 O^7 LQ|[TN3]

The final lines of these notes just begin to explore the calculations which Tolkien developed further in section (v); see below. This little chart provided Tolkien with two months' worth of moon-phases for him to work out the problem bedeviling him, and in fact nicely demonstrates that the period between the Last Quarter moon and New Moon, during which Bilbo met the trolls almost a week's journey away from Rivendell, could not be followed three weeks later by a moon that had advanced only about a week in its cycle (that is, now being somewhere between the NM and FQ on the second line). Tolkien's earlier solution (in New Chapter II and 'Distances and Itinerary') to move their arrival in Rivendell back from early June (circa June 7th in the original conception) to at least two weeks earlier (May 24th) also pushes 'midsummer' from around June 21st (modern calendar) to two days after June 30th (Shire Calendar).[TN4] This does give the moons in their right phases but forces the company to stay a full month in Elrond's House and fails to address the compatibility problem with *The Lord of the Rings* of why Bilbo got from the river to the trolls so quickly when Strider, the best hunter and tracker of his time, took so long. It also ignores the problem that a moon between last quarter and new cannot be seen in the early evening hours (as specified in the troll-encounter) but would only rise long after midnight.

TEXT NOTES

1 For the banquet where Bilbo had the cold (from his soaking in the Forest River while barrel-riding), see DAA.252. There is no mention in *The Hobbit* that this was Bilbo's birthday; that detail, and the date (22nd September) both come from the opening chapter of *The Lord of the Rings* (*LotR*.42). Tolkien's statement in these notes that this banquet came seven to ten days after their arrival in Lake Town (repeated from section ii above) is contradicted by Bilbo in his Farewell Speech, where Mr. Baggins is explicit that both his arrival in Esgaroth and that banquet took place on the same day, his fifty-first birthday. Even without this, circumstantial evidence from within *The Hobbit* itself would place the banquet much earlier than halfway through their stay: Bilbo was already sneezing in the early morning hours before their arrival in Esgaroth (DAA.242), so the 'three days' that his 'shocking cold' lasted are presumably the first three he spent in Lake Town (DAA.252); if these three days included his birthday then by that reckoning alone their arrival could have come no earlier than 19th September and the banquet no later than 25th September.

2 That is, Tolkien here intends for Durin's Day to fall on 19th October. This avoids the cramming together of too much incident in the last weeks of the year (see page 481) and could be achieved with the change of a single word on page 64 in the second edition (cf. DAA.96), although had he carried out a thorough revision Tolkien would also have had to deal with the various comments about the rapid approach of winter in Chapters X, XI, & XIII. I have found no explicit statement from Tolkien about any decision regarding shifting Durin's Day. As with the two competing Thror-Thrain/Thrain-Thror genealogies, Tolkien may have become confused by a single divergent passage in the text – in this case, one near the beginning of Chapter IV that still (until its post-authorial correction in the fourth edition of 1995) referred to Durin's Day as occurring in the first month of autumn. But it seems extraordinary that he would have been guided by this passing remark,

which he nowhere draws attention to in the Fifth Phase (1960) material, and not by the statement on a page he repeatedly cites from the end of Chapter III, literally divided from the other in the second edition only by a turn of the page.

3 These abbreviations stand, in proper sequence, for New Moon (NM), First Quarter (FQ), Full Moon (FM or the symbol O), and Last Quarter (LQ). The superscripts represent Tolkien's notation of the number of days to allot for each phase of the moon in its twenty-eight day monthly cycle. The significance of the vertical lines (|) seems to be to mark off the phase he wishes to highlight (i.e., the period of the waning moon between last quarter and new moon).

4 Tolkien noted that astronomically the Shire Calendar was about ten days off from our modern calendar – that is, that a date given as Mid-summer in the Shire Calendar, the actual solstice, would correspond to about 21st or 22nd June in our Gregorian calendar (*LotR*.1144).

(v)
Phases of the Moon

This single sheet of paper [Ad.Ms.H.15–16], the final piece of manuscript associated with the Fifth Phase or 1960 Hobbit, is covered with rough notes on both sides. The page has been folded in half and rotated ninety degrees so that it forms four half-pages: .15a (left), .15b (right), .16a (verso left), and .16b (verso right). The first half-page is written in red ball-point ink; the remaining three half-pages are in pencil, which unfortunately in some places has become illegible through the speed of the writing and its faintness after more than four and a half decades. As before I replace illegible words and passages by ellipses (. . .) and expand contractions where necessary to avoid confusion but have let stand the following authorial contractions: 'L.R.' or 'LR' stands for *The Lord of the Rings*, 'SR' for Shire Reckoning, and 'SC' for Shire Calendar.

<Waning> Moon June 1. sc. 4 past full
June 8. 2 before LQ.
June 15. 3 before NM[TN1]

NM June 28
LQ June 21
FM June 14
FQ June 7
NM May 30

1 <Ride> sleep in Shire . . . stay a night . . . in Bree.
. . . to F. Inn. <stay> . . . <night>

lose way in the Marshes <?Hay> ran <?low>
. . . <in> road is <?awash> . . . <least>
<Mitheithel> Bridge is broken (by Trolls.) . . .[TN2]

This marks the end of the ink text at the bottom of half-page Ad.Ms.H.15a. The top of the right-hand portion of the same page, Ad.Ms.H.15b, begins a new section or sub-section with its own header. From here on out the text is written in pencil, which is difficult to read throughout and becomes wholly illegible towards the end.

Hobbit [*added*:] Time table of journey will not work out?
• Time indications in text.
It was Wednesday when dwarves came to Bag End.

p. 35. Thrain went away 100 years last Thursday on 21st April. Since week-day relative to date did not change in Shire Calendar, 21st April was a Thursday in 2941 (= 1341 SR) the year of the Visit of the Dwarves. Therefore the U.P. occurred on 27 April (Wed.) 1341 SR. The journey to Erebor started on Thursday 28th April.[TN3]

p. 41 Bilbo says it is June 1st tomorrow at tea time on the [day >] before the adventure with the Trolls.
*It would be better to make this correct if possible (rather than assume B. was out of his reckoning) . . . . that in Shire Calendar [they >] The Company had now been 32 days on the road (April 29, 30) 2; (May 1–30) 30. They had still a long way to go before Rivendell. They set out on the afternoon of June 1. After that the following time/distance <indications> occur:

p. 42 a waning moon was in the sky on the evening of May 30. On the eve of Midsummer (= Lithe June 30 + 1) and the eve of their departure from Rivendell, there was a broad silver crescent

p. 56 No singing first day = afternoon to night of June 1. nor next day June 2, nor day after June 3. 3 1/2 days journey. 'One afternoon' – gap of time <undefined> – they came to Ford of Bruinen. p. 58 that Day began to fail. it was very dim because moon had not risen.

<His> plan that they were supposed to reach the head of path down into Rivendell during early night of the day in which they had crossed the Ford (in afternoon). As they were going . . . wearily[TN4] and were in difficult country they could not have done more than 10–12 miles. In L.R. it was not made clear how far Ford was from Rivendell[TN5] (along the river course). But in the LR map 1 centimetre = 50 miles the distance from Ford to head of path down is 4 mm = 4/10 of 50 miles = 20 miles.

Alter p. 56 One afternoon to One fine morning [p. 57 they rode slowly on >][TN6] and adjust narrative to . . . long day lasting on into early night. <Or> <made> a camp in the <heather> above Rivendell.

At p. 58/11 They went on until moonless twilight overtook them, and they lay that night under the bright stars. The next day was failing But <then> perhaps . . . <the journey> too . . .[TN7]

p. 62 They stay in Rivendell at least 14 days. Therefore if they left on SC Midsummer = June 30 + 2 they arrived not earlier <than> June 16 night.
How could they spend 16 days on way from Trollshaw to Rivendell? On LR map it is 1 cm 2 mm from Troll place to Ford & 20 miles on beyond = [75 >] 60 + 20 = 80. Thus = [less than 5 miles a day >] exactly 5 miles on good days

If the Moon was waning sc. at least a day or two past full on May 30 it would be approx. same . . . on June 28. But if it were <really> waxing <for> [. . . it might be only 20/21days from June 1 & LQ to NM. <so> New Moon. >] There <might> be no moon at all after . . .[TN8]

FQ= half moon [7 days] ◗ = <moon> before <full> [7 days] (. . . FM O
LQ [7 days] = ◖[TN9] We must start from p. 63[TN10] which fits (by chance!) fairly well . . . the New Moon would appear about Oct 19th. (SC)

The moon is a broad silver crescent therefore about halfway to FQ, <only> 3 to 4 days from NM. It is June 30+1 therefore NM was about June 28/(27) There would therefore be a NM about June 1 but <it was> called a waning moon p. 42 [And the >] <New Moon> . . . ?

Or we must shorten the time of the journey from the Trollshaw to Rivendell. LQ on night of the Troll-adventure NM. [June 28 Therefore LQ. >] Waning moon = only just going off <full> . . . therefore say on May 28

If N.Moon was on June 27. [LQ was on June 20. The F.M. >] FM was June 12/13
<Waning moon> must be . . . about June 15–16
They arrived Rivendell on June 16
But they <must> . . . <taken> . . . <?Say> in 4–6 days <?also> for journey from Trollshaw <?to> <?River>

<This> <is> <from> LQ <but> <?has> . . . to Waxing. <?Just> say <wandering> for waning . . . <?having> <after> <?appeared> . . .[TN11]

In this final section of the 1960 Hobbit material, we see Tolkien returning once again to the time indicators in the published text to see if setting them out would suggest a solution to the tangle. Highly significant, therefore, is the lightly pencilled message written alongside the title – *Time table of journey will not work out?* – signaling as it does his realization that the ends he wanted to achieve could only come at the cost of an even more radical revision and recasting than he had already drafted for New Chapters I and II, and that New Chapter II would itself need to be re-done. And even with this, he had still not addressed the problem of matching the dwarves' relatively swift trip from river to trolls (a matter of hours) with Strider's urgent journey over the same ground (taking the better part of a week).

TEXT NOTES

1 This line is cancelled; I retain it here because it continues and clarifies the sequence of the two preceding lines.

2 The final line on this half-page, roughly three words following '(by Trolls)', is illegible.

3 Tolkien is correct that days of the week are fixed to specific days of the month in the Shire Calendar year after year, but here he still has not noticed that since April (Astron) always begins on a Saturday, the 21st and 28th can never fall on a Thursday. U.P. = Unexpected Party.

4 This partially illegible sentence originally read 'As they were *walking (evidently <illegible> the ponies)* – that is, Tolkien seems to have fixed on the idea that Bilbo and the dwarves were walking, not riding, at this point, which could help delay their arrival in Rivendell.

5 This is because Frodo, our point of view character for this section of the story, is unconscious when he travels that distance in *The Lord of the Rings*; Book I ends with his collapse at the Ford and Book II begins with him awakening already safe in Rivendell some days later. He of course covers this ground again on his return journey, but compression in the denouement of a very long story prevents the inclusion of much detail of that trip other than a few vivid encounters along the way.

6 The text of the first and second editions read 'The afternoon sun shone down; but in all the silent waste there was no sign of any dwelling. *They rode on for a while*, and they soon saw that the house might be hidden almost anywhere between them and the mountains'. This passage was recast for the third edition to address the concerns raised in the 1960 Hobbit, although not in the same words: '*Morning passed, afternoon came*; but in all the silent waste there was no sign of any dwelling.

They *were growing anxious, for they saw now* that the house might be hidden . . .' (DAA.88 & 90).

7 Only a single short word, starting with a capital 'T', follows 'too', but I cannot make out what it might be.

8 The last word following 'after' is illegible and probably unfinished, but the gist of the sentence is clear: a new crescent would set shortly after sunset, leaving the night dark.

9 Here I think Tolkien is reminding himself of the rather confusing terminology whereby 'quarter' is applied to a half-moon (because it is a quarter of the way through its twenty-eight day cycle), and also which way the crescent faces when the moon is waxing (◗) and waning (◖), for purposes of description.

10 The allusion is to the line 'The moon was shining in a broad silver crescent' on midsummer eve – cf. DAA.95.

11 I cannot make out anything in the last two lines following this point except the words 'June 15' and the final phrase ' – not . . . waning'.

See also section (iii) above for Tolkien's decision to simplify his problem by replacing 'waning' with 'wandering', a change he carried out in the 1966 third edition.

(vi)
The Wandering Moon

In all these notes and compilations on distances, dates, and moons, we see Tolkien attempting to take *The Hobbit*, a story written out of one storytelling tradition of long ago and far away, where details are only included when dramatically relevant or aesthetically effective and things work according to their own narrative logic,[1] and make it into a story like *The Lord of the Rings*, which is written in a very different tradition, where each mile of each day of each character's journey can be followed on a map and plotted on a timetable. Tolkien himself is largely responsible for creating the latter,[2] and making it the standard by which modern fantasies are judged, but he also excelled at writing the former, a traditional mode going all the way back to the Middle Ages and beyond. There is a qualitative difference between the narrator's admission that 'I don't know what river it was' (DAA.67) or 'I don't know where he came from, nor who or what he was' (DAA.118) and Gandalf's well-informed speculation about the whereabouts of the lost *palantíri* (*LotR*.621), or his partial knowledge about 'older and fouler things than Orcs in the deep places of the world' (*LotR*.327).

The Hobbit harkens back to an older tradition, where forests seem endless, a period of captivity is a *weary long time* rather than twenty-one days (August 9th–30th), dragons and goblins destroyed Gondolin 'many ages ago' (rather than exactly 6,472 years before to the very day),[3] and it is the passing of seasons rather than the counting of days that mark the passage of time. Bilbo's is a world where the moon only just past new can rise after the sun sets (an astronomical impossibility) rather than becoming visible in the west just after the sun goes down (DAA.307–8, 312),[4] because that's how Tolkien envisions the scene, and the chill moonlight falling on the now-quieting scene of devastation sets just the right note to follow the noise and flames and flashes of light and sudden violence of the immediately preceding pages.

If *The Lord of the Rings* is, as some have claimed, the 'Book of the Century', then *The Hobbit* is more than the book that made it all possible. A major contribution to the Golden Age of children's literature, it is a rare example of a work that transcends age boundaries in its readership, like Grahame's *The Golden Age*, Carroll's two *Alice* books, Twain's *Huckleberry Finn*, and very few others. It is, like Joyce's *A Portrait of the Artist as a Young Man* in relation to his *Ulysses*, or Carroll's *The Hunting of the Snark* in relation to *Alice in Wonderland*, a case of a masterpiece overshadowed by another masterpiece on a grander scale from the same author. Had Tolkien never completed *The Lord of the Rings*, he would still be remembered as one of the great fantasy authors. The achievement of the sequel has eclipsed the accomplishment of writing *The Hobbit* itself, but we should not deny the distinct appeal and charm of the original book. In the end, I think it was more than just the intractable nature of the problems facing him in recasting the book that caused Tolkien to abandon the 1960 Hobbit. Rather, he decided to trust his friend's judgment that what he was doing was 'wonderful, but not *The Hobbit*'. That is, he came to recognize that *The Hobbit* was more than *The Lord of the Rings* writ small, more than a 'charming prelude': indeed, a work deserving to stand on its own merits.

And with that realization, aside from the 'Sixth Phase' of 1965/66 forced upon him by his publishers – which he took as the opportunity for correction of some errors and the incorporation of some fixes he had settled upon during his work on the 1960 Hobbit – Tolkien's decades-long work on *The Hobbit* finally came to an end.

NOTES

1 For example, as Janice Coulter has pointed out (private communication), if Gollum's eyes glowed in the dark how did he sneak up on goblins? Or, to repeat a question Tolkien himself asked and left unanswered, why did the dwarves bring their musical instruments, some of which would have been quite bulky, to Bag-End? Overthinking such points is a hallmark of approaching a work in the first of these two traditions as if it were in the second.

2 Tolkien of course was not alone in creating this shift: Joyce's *Ulysses*, where both of the major characters' actions can be followed hour-by-hour and street-by-street through a single day on a Dublin city map, pioneered this mode in the realistic novel a decade and a half before Tolkien began work on his magnum opus. One might expect the detective novel or mystery to have pioneered this approach, but in fact Conan Doyle's Sherlock Holmes series, which defined the genre, is very much written in the old school, with a fine carelessness about dates, Holmes' fields of expertise and expert knowledge, the location of Watson's war wound (leg or shoulder), the dates (and number) of Watson's marriage(s) and bereavement(s), and even the narrator's first name (variously James or John). Before Tolkien, most fantasy novels followed the example of one of those two great masters, Dunsany and Morris, and took place in either dreamworlds à la Dunsany or deliberately unmapped and borderless medieval settings à la Morris (frameless tapestries, as it were). Post-Tolkien, world-building has become a key defining part of the genre: elaborate histories ('backstory') and chronologies, invented languages, multiple cultures and distinct humanesque races, fantasy pantheons, creation myths, and above all maps are all essential elements that make a work recognizably 'fantasy'.

3 According to the '(Later) Annals of Beleriand', the city was destroyed ninety years before the end of the First Age (HME V.142 & 144); 90 + the 3441 years of the Second Age (*LotR*.1121) + the 2941 years of the Third Age that had passed before Bilbo reached Rivendell (*LotR*.1126) = 6,472 years. The 1930 *Quenta* states that the attack came before dawn as the people were preparing to celebrate a festival known as the Gates of Summer (HME IV.144), which I take to mean greeting the dawn on midsummer's day. Appendix D of *The Lord of the Rings* states that the elven day starts at sunset (*LotR*.1141); therefore the midsummer's eve on which Elrond reads these runes is the anniversary of the day when his father's city was destroyed.

4 Note that Tolkien's friend C. S. Lewis makes the same mistake in his narrative poem *The Queen of Drum* [1927], as was pointed out to him by John Masefield, the poet laureate, to whom he sent the unpublished poem in 1938. Cf. Canto V, line 123 (page 170) and Masefield's correction on page 178 (CSL, *Narrative Poems*, ed. Walter Hooper [1969]).

If we were to pursue a mythological explanation, of course, we could do so by noting that Tilion, the Maia who steers the moon, is well-known for his wayward behavior and difficulty in keeping a regular course, being easily distracted by the beauty of the Sun-maiden (*Silm*.99–100) or overindulgence in beer or brandy (1927 Father Christmas letter, ATB poem #5, *LotR*.174–6). But while this would be a perfectly reasonable explanation in Bilbo's world, it would be special pleading in Frodo's.

APPENDICES

Appendix I

THE DENHAM TRACTS

One of the recurring questions Tolkien faced from the first publication of *The Hobbit* to the end of his life was 'where did you get the name "hobbits"?' While there seems little doubt that he was telling the truth when he said he simply made it up, the issue was confused in the mid-1970s by the discovery, in a nineteenth-century collection of North Country folklore, of the word 'hobbit' among a long list of fairies, spirits, creatures from classical mythology, and other imaginary beings. The discovery was made by Katharine Briggs, the leading expert of her time on traditional fairy folklore (and author of a superb fantasy novel, *Hobberdy Dick* [1955], incorporating many of those beliefs), who reprinted the list in her *A Dictionary of Fairies: Hobgoblins, Brownies, Bogies, and Other Supernatural Creatures* [1976], pages 93–94. Briggs herself did not comment on the appearance of hobbits in the list,[1] but her discovery was soon picked up on by an outside reader for the OED and thence reported in various newspapers (including most notably Philip Howard's piece 'Tracking the Hobbit Down to Earth', which appeared in *The Times* on 31st May 1977), but for the most part without crediting Briggs for her role in the discovery.

The list itself had appeared in a miscellany published by the Folk-Lore Society, the full title of which was *The Denham Tracts: A Collection of Folklore by Michael Aislabie Denham, and reprinted from the original tracts and pamphlets printed by Mr. Denham between 1846 and 1859.* Edited by Dr. James Hardy (with the assistance of Laurence Gomme, who also wrote the prefaces), this had been issued in two volumes in 1892 and 1895, with our list appearing as the final item in Tract VIII, 'Folklore, or Manners and Customs, of the North of England' (Vol. II pages [1]–80). Denham himself had been a mid-19th-century amateur antiquarian who collected sayings, tales, and customs from the north of England, issuing them in little self-published pamphlets or 'tracts'. These tracts went through multiple editions, expanding as he came across new material – for example, the specific tract in which our list appears went through several versions, and the word 'hobbit' did not appear in the earliest of these.[2] It thus becomes important to look at Denham's sources and the way he put these lists together.

In this particular case, the list of fantastic and folklore creatures had originally† been published as an article in the 23rd December

†see Note page 854.

1848 issue of *The Literary Gazette: Journal of the Belles Lettres, Arts, Sciences, &c.* (London; No. 1666, page 849). Denham's primary source was a list of 'vaine apparitions' compiled by the skeptic Reginald Scot more than two and a half centuries before in *The Discoverie of Witchcraft* [1584], an eloquent and impassioned refutation of the superstitions of his day. In Book VII of that work, after discussing the Oracle at Delphi and the Witch of Endor (1st Samuel 28. 3–25), Scot gives the following mingling of classical lore with old wives' tales:

> Chapter XV. *Of vaine apparitions, how people have beene brought to feare bugges, which is partlie reformed by preaching of the gospell, the true effect of Christes miracle.*
>
> . . . It is a common saieng [saying]; A lion feareth no bugs [bugbears, boogiemen]. But in our childhood our mothers maids have so terrified us with an ouglie [ugly] divell having hornes on this head, fier in his mouth, and a taile in his breech . . . and a voice roring like a lion, whereby we start and are afraid when we heare one crie Bough [Boo!]: and they have so fraied us with bull beggers, spirits, witches, urchens, elves, hags, fairies, satyrs, pans, faunes, sylens, kit with the cansticke, tritons, centaurs, dwarfes, giants, imps, calcars, conjurors, nymphes, changlings, *Incubus*, Robin good-fellowe, the spoorne, the mare [i.e., nightmare], the man in the oke [oak], the hell waine, the fierdrake [firedrake, dragon], the puckle [puck, pooka], Tom thome, hob gobblin, Tom tumbler, boneles, and such other bugs, that we are afraid of our owne shadowes . . . [S]ome never feare the divell, but in a darke night . . . speciallie in a churchyard, where a right hardie man heretofore scant durst passe by night, but his haire would stand upright.
>
> —1972 Dover facsimile reproduction of the 1930 Montague Summers edition, page 86

Denham took Scot's list and expanded it from thirty-three items (thirty-four if we follow Denham in including the generic name 'bugs') to a hundred and twenty-nine, adding in new names from literary sources (e.g. the poetry of Robert Burns, from which he took *cutties*),[3] the folklore researches of others (including, for later versions of the list, Th. Keightley's *The Fairy Mythology* [1850], from which he derived *korigan*), and his own researches, which had focused on the local beliefs in Durham, Northumberland, Cumberland, and Westmoreland. His inclusion of every item from Scot's list explains the otherwise rather odd appearance of conjurors alongside (classical) nymphs and (faerie) changlings. Denham also took from Scot the deliberate jumbling of material from very different sources: his organizational principle seems not to group together related material but instead to deliberately juxtapose creatures from different traditions to stress their diversity, although small clumps of related creatures do appear here and there in the mix. Denham also seems to have deliberately padded out his list by including simple variants in spelling as separate entries, as in the case of *hobthrush* and *hobthurst* (both covered by a single footnote), *freith* and *freit*, *hobby-lanthorn* and *hob-and-lanthorn*, &c. In other cases, he takes the name of an individual (e.g., Tom Thumb, Peg Powler, Robin Goodfellow, Dick-a-Tuesday, Gyl-burnt-tail, &c.) and 'genericizes' it, so to speak, extrapolating from a proper name into a creature type.

In the following text of the final form of Denham's piece (from the 1895 posthumous collection), I have marked items deriving from Reginald Scot's 1584 list with an asterisk (*); those appearing in Denham's original 1848 list appear in normal (roman) type, while those added by the time of the final (1895) version are given in *italics*. I do not, however, record all the minor variants between Denham's earliest and latest versions – e.g. hobgoblins [1848] vs hob-goblins [1895], Pans vs. pans, pegpoulers vs. Peg-powlers, &c. Two names appearing in the 1848 list (breen, bull-bears) disappear from the final version, three (fairies, thrummy-caps, and cutties) are displaced from early in the old list to near the end of the newer one for reasons that are not apparent, and the total is increased to one hundred and ninety-seven names, four of which (fiends, hobgoblins, imps, and korreds) are duplications of names already found elsewhere in the list (as opposed to only one duplication – imps – in the original list); these repetitions are a sign that, as Tolkien wrote of Bilbo, Denham was 'not . . . an orderly narrator, and his account is involved and discursive, and sometimes confused' (Foreword to the first edition of *The Lord of the Rings*, Vol. I page [7]). To distinguish authorial comments from my own annotation, Denham's notes from the 1895 reprint are given as [D1], [D2], and so forth, while my own notes on his material are given as[1], [2].

GHOSTS NEVER APPEAR ON CHRISTMAS EVE!

'Some say that ever 'gainst that season comes
Wherein our Saviour's birth is celebrated,
The bird of dawning singeth all night long;
And then they say no spirit dares stir abroad;
The nights are wholesome; then no planet strikes,
No fairy takes, nor witch hath power to charm,
So hallowed and so gracious is the time.'
Marcellus.

'So have I heard and do in part believe it.'
Horatio.

So says the immortal Shakespeare;[4] and the truth thereof few now-a-days, I hope, will call in question. Grose observes,[5] too, that those born on Christmas Day cannot see spirits; which is another incontrovertible fact. What a happiness this must have been seventy or eighty years ago[6] and upwards, to those chosen few who had the good luck to be born on the eve of this festival of all festivals; when the whole earth was so overrun with ghosts, boggles,[D1] bloody-bones, spirits,★ demons, ignis fatui,[7] brownies,[D2] bugbears, black dogs, spectres, shellycoats, scarecrows, witches,★ wizards, barguests,[D3] Robin-Goodfellows,★[D4] hags,★[D5] night-bats, scrags, breaknecks, fantasms, hob-goblins, hobhoulards, boggy-boes, dobbies,[D6] hob-thrusts,[D7] fetches,[D8] kelpies, warlocks, mock-beggars,[D9] mum-pokers, Jemmy-burties, urchins,★ satyrs,★ pans,★ fauns,★ sirens,(★)[8] tritons,★ centaurs,★ calcars,★ nymphs,★ imps,★ incubusses,★ spoorns,★ men-in-the-oak,★ hell-wains,★ fire-drakes,★ kit-a-can-sticks,★ Tom-tumblers, melch-dicks, larrs, kitty-witches, hobby-lanthorns, Dick-a-Tuesdays, Elf-fires, Gyl-burnt-tails, knockers, elves,★[D10] raw-heads, Meg-with-the-wads, old-shocks, ouphs, pad-fooits, pixies, pictrees,[D11] giants,★ dwarfs,★[9] Tom-pokers, tutgots, snapdragons, sprets,[10] spunks, conjurers,★ thurses, spurns, tantarrabobs, swaithes,[D12] tints, tod-lowries,[11] Jack-in-the-Wads, mormos, changelings,★ redcaps, yeth-hounds, colt-pixies, Tom-thumbs,★ black-bugs, boggarts, scar-bugs, shag-foals, hodge-pochers, hob-thrushes, bugs,★ bull-beggars,★ bygorns, bolls, caddies, bomen, brags,[12] wraithes,[D13] waffs,[D14] flay-boggarts, fiends, gallytrots, imps, gytrashes, patches, hob-and-lanthorns, gringes, boguests, bonelesses,★ Peg-powlers,[D15] pucks, fays, kidnappers, gally-beggars, hudskins, nickers, madcaps, trolls, robinets, friars' lanthorns, silkies,[D16] cauld-lads,[D17] death-hearses, goblins,[D18] *hob-headlesses,*[D19] *buggaboes, kows*[D20] *or cowes, nickies, nacks [necks], waiths,*[D21] *miffies, buckies, gholes, sylphs, guests, swarths, freiths, freits, gy-carlins [Gyre-carling], pigmies, chittifaces, nixies,*[D22] *Jinny-burnt-tails, dudmen, hell-hounds, dopple-gangers,*[D23] *boggleboes, bogies, redmen, portunes, grants,* ***hobbits,*** *hobgoblins, brown-men,*[D24] *cowies, dunnies,*[D25] *wirrikows,*[D26] *alholdes, mannikins, follets, korreds, lubberkins, cluricauns, kobolds, leprechauns, kors, mares,*★ *korreds, puckles,*★ *korigans, sylvans, succubuses, black-men, shadows, banshees, lian-hanshees, clabbernappers, Gabriel-hounds, mawkins, doubles,*[D27] *corpse lights or candles, scrats, mahounds, trows, gnomes, sprites, fates, fiends, sybils, nick-nevins,*[D28] *whitewomen,* fairies,★[D29] thrummy-caps,[D30] cutties,[D31] *and nisses,* and apparitions of every shape, make, form, fashion, kind, and description, that there was not a village in England that had not its own peculiar ghost. Nay, every lone tenement, castle, or mansion-house, which could boast of any antiquity had its bogle, its spectre, or its knocker. The churches, churchyards, and cross-roads, were all haunted. Every green lane had its boulder-stone on which an apparition kept watch at night. Every common had its circle of fairies belonging to it. And there was scarcely a shepherd to be met with who had not seen a spirit! [See *Lit. Gaz.* for December 1848, p. 849.]

DENHAM'S NOTES

D1 Boggle-house, parish of Sedgefield. Bellingham Boggle-Hole, Northd. [Bogle-houses in Lowick Forest, Northumberland.]

D2 There is also a river of this name in the Bishopric of Durham. Also at York is Browny Dike, a portion of the Foss.

D3 The York Barguest. See *Memoirs of R. Surtees, Esq.*; new ed., p. 80, 1852.

D4 This merry fay acted the part of fool or jester, at the court of Oberon, the fairy monarch.

D5 Hag-House. A farmstead near Brancepeth.

D6 The Mortham Dobby. A Teesdale goblin.

D7 Hob-o-t'-Hursts, *i.e.* spirits of the woods. Hobthrush Rook, Farndale, Yorkshire.

D8 The spirit or double of a dying person.

D9 Mock-beggar Hall. Of houses, rocks, etc., bearing this name we meet with many instances.

D10 Elf-Hills, parish of Hutton-in-the-Forest, Cumberland. Elf-How, parish of Kendal. Elf-Hills, near Cambo.

D11 There is a village of this name near Chester-le-Street; and singular enough a ghost story, called the 'Picktree Bragg,' is attached to it. See Keightley's *Fairy Mythology*, Bohn's ed. p. 310.[13]

D12 *The spirit or double of a dying person.*[14]

D13 *The spirit or double of a dying person.*

D14 *The spirit or double of a dying person.*

D15 This oulde ladye is the evil goddess of the Tees. I also meet with a Nanny Powler, at Darlington, who from the identity of their sirnames, is, I judge, a sister, or it may be a daughter of Peg's. Nanny Powler, aforesaid, haunts the Skerne, a tributary of the Tees.

D16 The Heddon Silky, and Silky's Brig, near Heddon. See Richardson's *Table Book*, Leg.Div., vol. ii., p. 181.

D17 Occasionally, we may hear Cowed, or rather Cowd Lad. The meaning, however, is the same; Cowd being a variation of the more refined word, cold.

D18 Goblin Field, near Mold, Flintshire.

D19 Hob-Cross-Hill. A place near Doncaster.

D20 'The Hedley Kow,' a Northumberland ghost story.

D21 *The spirit or double of a dying person.*

D22 'Know you the nixies, gay and fair?
Their eyes are black, and green their hair,
They lurk in sedgy waters.'

—*Keightley*

D23 *The spirit or double of a dying person.*

D24 See ghost story of the 'Brown Man of the Moor.' Richardson's *Table Book.*

D25 The Hazelrigg Dunny. An excellent Northumberland ghost story.

D26 'Frae gudame's mouth auld warld tale they hear,
O' warlocks louping round the wirriknow.'

—The works of Robt. Fergusson, ed. by A. B. Grossart, Edin., 1851, p. 61.

D27 *The spirit or double of a dying person.*

D28 Mother witches.

D29 Fairy Dean, two miles above Melrose. Fairy Stone, near Fourstones, in the parish of Warden, Northumberland. This stone, in which is a secret cavity, has attained a celebrity in history owing to the letters being placed therein, to and from the unfortunate Earl of Derwentwater, during the '15.[15]

D30 Thrummy Hills, near Catterick. The name of this sprite is met with in the Fairy tales of Northumberland.

D31 These are a certain class of female Boggles, not altogether peculiar to Scotland, who wore their lower robes, at least, *a-la-bloomer*. They are named by Burns, in his inimitable poem Tam-o'-Shanter. Mr. Halliwell gives the word as localized in Somersetshire.

Mr. Denham's Hobbit

Given the evidence of Denham's list, and the inclusion of 'hobbits' within it, the question then becomes threefold: what were these hobbits, where did Denham get the word, and did Tolkien know about Denham's work? So far as the first point goes, there is no doubt that hobbits were a kind of hob (also sometimes known as brownies or, more rarely, lobs), like the hob-goblins, hob-thrushes/hob-thrusts,[16] hobhoulards, hob-headless, and hob-and-lanthorns/hobby-lanthorns (a kind of Will o' the Wisp) who also appear in the list – in fact, hob names make up nine of the hundred and ninety-seven items, or roughly five percent of the whole, the largest grouping within the entire list, whereas they had been represented by a single entry (hob gobblin) in Reginald Scot's 1584 account. The traditional hob of English folklore was a solitary creature, sometimes described as a little brown man a few feet high, who attached himself to a farm or manor and, although seldom if ever seen, did chores and sometimes helped the family in times of crisis. His payment was traditionally a small cake or bannock or a bowl of milk or cream left out each night; if this was ever neglected or if he was given a gift of clothes he left forever. *Hobbit* seems to be a typical variation on the name, but one recorded nowhere else, so we cannot tell if it was a proper name of a specific hob 'genericized' by Denham (as he demonstratably does in the case of Hob Headless, another in his list, whose story is briefly retold by Briggs – *A Dictionary of Fairies* page 222) or a type of hob, like hobthrusts or hobgoblins.

As for Denham's immediate source, unfortunately the industrious folklore collector provided no note explaining where he had found the name *hobbit*. Since like several others in Denham's list the name is not recorded elsewhere, it almost certainly came through his own first-hand collection of old folklore in the Durham region or its neighboring counties – a region particularly rich in hob-stories, as Briggs notes (ibid.).[17] But the exact source has proved elusive and will probably remain so. As Tolkien says of his own hobbits, 'it is clear that Hobbits had, in fact, lived quietly in Middle-earth for many long years before other folk became even aware of them . . . the world being after all full of strange creatures beyond count' (Prologue to *The Lord of the Rings*, p.14), and the same is analogous of the actual folklore creature that shared the name of Tolkien's creation, which was recorded only by chance in this single instance; any associated story or stories have long since been forgotten beyond recovery.

Adding to the mystery, as we have already noted the name does not appear in the original [1848] article but was added to the list sometime between then and its posthumous appearance, long after Denham's death in 1859, in the Folk-Lore Society volumes. Given the free hand the miscellany's editor, Dr. Hardy, allowed himself for silently adding or re-arranging material (see Note 2), for a time I investigated the possibility that it had been added by Hardy himself as late as 1892–1895, but this turns out not to have been the case. As discovered by Peter Gilliver, Jeremy Marshall, & Edmund Weiner, who examined some of the original tracts from which the book was compiled (the most complete collection of which is a single bound volume assembled by one 'W.S.' in 1860, now part of the Opie Collection in the Lilly Library at Indiana University, Bloomington), the 1848 article was followed by an independent 1851 tract in which *hobbit* is still absent, but the word does appear in an 1853 version of that same tract, which in turn seems to have provided the base copy for the 1895 text (*The Ring of Words: Tolkien and the Oxford English Dictionary* [2006], pages 147–148); this pushes back the word's first recorded appearance from 1895 to 1853, beyond which its origins once again fade into obscurity.[18]

The final question of whether Tolkien knew about Denham's inclusion of the name is equally murky. Certainly he knew about Reginald Scot's list, which was reproduced and discussed by C. S. Lewis in *The Discarded Image*.[19] In addition, *The Denham Tracts* was one of the primary sources from which Joseph Wright drew for his *English Dialect Dictionary* [six volumes, 1898 –1905], a work Tolkien greatly admired,[20] but this is not to say that Tolkien ever had reason to examine this specific source-volume for himself. If he had (and this is a big *if*), then he would almost certainly have discovered Denham's list, since Gomme explicitly draws attention to it in the Preface to the second volume in tantalizing terms:

> . . . the only way to study folk-lore is to treat each recorded item separately. For this purpose there will be found very interesting features here which are not to be found elsewhere. The names for the different classes of spirits (on pp. 77–78) is very full, and needs some investigation philologically and mythologically . . .
>
> —Preface, Vol. II page ix

The names in question are of course those making up Denham's list reprinted on pages 844–46 above. And, of course, one might say that taking a single item from that list (the otherwise unknown name 'hobbit') and investigating it philologically (what might the word mean? what might a 'hobbit' be like?) and mythologically (what sort of tales might be told about such a creature?) is exactly what Tolkien does in *The Hobbit*. Such a chain of events would make Tolkien's hobbits his personal adaptation of actual folklore survivals just like the elves, dwarfs (or dwarves), wizards, goblins, giants, fire-drakes (dragons), trolls and hob-goblins, all of which occur both in *The Hobbit* and in Denham's list and all of which are given distinctly Tolkienian interpretations.[21] The possibility is tantalizing, but it remains only a possibility, with no direct evidence to back it up. Certainly if Tolkien did ever read *The Denham Tracts*, it must have been during his early years studying with Wright [1911–1915] or when himself compiling *A Middle English Vocabulary* [1919ff] or editing Middle English texts like *Sir Gawain & the Green Knight* [circa 1922–1925] at Leeds, since he had forgotten about it completely by 1930 when he actually came to write down that solitary sentence *In a hole in the ground there lived a hobbit.*

Unfortunately, this attractive little scenario can hardly represent what really happened, for it runs counter to the most important evidence of all: Tolkien's own account of how he created the name, repeated over and over with great consistency over a number of years (see pages xii–xiii), and his attempts late in life (detailed in Appendix II) to find any possible earlier occurance of the name. Had Tolkien deliberately acted on the hint in Gomme's preface, it is wildly improbable that he would have completely forgotten about it and gone to such lengths, which included not just his own researches into the topic but corresponding with his old pupils Robert Burchfield, then the editor of the OED, and Roger Lancelyn Green, whom he recruited to try to track down any nineteenth-century fairy-story that might have included the name (see pp. 860–62). Therefore, despite its apparent plausibility, it is highly unlikely that *The Denham Tracts* was actually Tolkien's source for *hobbit*.

How then do we explain the coincidence? For one thing, English folklore traditions about hobs obviously played a part in Tolkien's creation, including the name, and since this is the case it is not so very surprising to find that Tolkien's invention, his own personal variant, can be matched by an actual example from the historical record, albeit an obscure one. Tolkien's gift for nomenclature was posited on creating words that sounded like real ones, creating matches of sound and sense that felt as if they were actual words drawn from the vast body of old lore that had somehow failed to otherwise be recorded. That his invention should match actual obscure historical words was inevitable provided he did his work well enough, as is also attested by the accidental resemblance of his place-name *Gondor* (inspired by the actual historic word *ond* ['stone'], which had once been thought to be a fragment of a lost pre-IndoEuropean language of the British isles)[22] to both the real-world Gondar (a city in northern Ethiopia, also sometimes spelled Gonder, once that country's capital; see *Letters* p. 409) and the imaginary Gondour (a utopia invented by Mark Twain in the story 'The Curious Republic of Gondour' [1870]; see my essay in the Blackwelder festschrift, p. 93 Note 24, for more detail). It is a tribute to Tolkien's skill with word-building that his invented *hobbit* should prove to have indeed had a real-world predecessor, though Tolkien himself probably never knew of it. For more on Tolkien's investigation into real-world antecedents of the hobbit, see Appendix II.

JDR NOTES

1 Although she was surely aware of it, since in her entry on Tolkien within the same book she praises his work for being 'deepened by the use of traditional folklore which gave it that sense of being rooted in the earth which is the gift of folklore to literature' – Briggs, *A Dictionary of Fairies*, page 401. In her various entries on hobs and hobmen – 'Hob, or Hobthrust' (p. 222–223), 'Lobs and Hobs' (p. 270–271) and 'Brownie' (or little brown men, p. 45–49) – she summarizes traditional beliefs and in so doing helps us see the extent to which Tolkien was influenced by them. For example, her description of the brown men (brownies) as 'small men, about three feet in height, very raggedly dressed in brown clothes, with brown faces and shaggy heads' would take very little adjustment to serve as a description of hobbits in their latter days, when they have become a shy and fugitive people who 'avoid us with dismay and are becoming hard to find' (Prologue, *LotR*.[13]). Even though Denham's groupings are somewhat erratic, it is suggestive that 'hobbit' is immediately followed by hobgoblin and brown-man (i.e., brownie) as items number one hundred and fifty-four, one hundred and fifty-five, and one hundred and fifty-six, respectively, in his final list. Elsewhere in *The Denham Tracts* he retells stories about several hobs, most notably the Cauld Lad o' Hylton ('the Cold Lad of Hilton'; Vol. I pages 55–57), Hob Thrush (Vol. II pages 355–356), and the Hazelrigg Dunnie (ibid. pages 157–163).

Denham's own closeness to the material may be judged from his admission of his childhood terror of Peg Powler, a local drowning spirit,† and the precautions he took as a child to avoid attracting the attention of the fairies.††

†'the writer still perfectly recollects being dreadfully alarmed in the days of his childhood lest, more particularly when he chanced to be alone on the margin of those waters, she should issue from the stream and snatch him into her watery chambers' – Vol. II page 42.

††'I well remember that on more occasions than one, when a schoolboy, I have turned my coat inside out in passing through a wood in order to avoid the good people' – Vol. II page 88.

2 Gomme's preface to the second volume sums up the difficulties thusly: 'Mr. Denham['s] . . . peculiar practice of issuing these tracts sometimes without date or other means of identification makes it extremely difficult to ascertain whether all he published on folk-lore has been recovered. There is no complete collection . . . It often happened that a tract was issued as a simple leaflet, and that later on this would be included in another tract without any alteration of or allusion to the original publication' (Vol. II page x). Indeed, the bulk of 'Tract VIII' (ibid. pages [1]–80) in the Folk-Lore Society's compilation turns out to be from another tract (pages 21–80) titled 'Folklore; or Manners, Customs, Weather Proverbs, Popular Charms, Juvenile Rhymes, Ballads, &c. &c.

in the north of England' (see the editorial footnote on the bottom of Vol. II page 21), whose title accurately reflects the miscellaneous nature of the compilation.

To compound the problem, the Folk-Lore Society volumes were carelessly edited and at several points inadvertently reprint slightly different versions of the same material – e.g., the long annotated list of items associated with fairies given as examples of 'The not yet wholly exploded belief in fairies, fays, and elves', which appears both as its own short tract (Tract XIV: 'A Few Fragments of Fairy Folklore'; Vol. II pages 110–115) and in briefer form without explanatory notes on page 30 in the same volume as a single paragraph within what the editor designated as Tract VIII. Furthermore, at a number of points the editor either rewrote passages or inserted new material. Gomme's preface (Vol. I page xi) promises that additional notes by Hardy would all be carefully identified with the latter's bracketed initials ('[J.H.]'), but in practice this is rarely the case. Contrast, for example, Denham's first-person account of the strange behavior of his mother's cat after its mistress died (Vol. II page 74) with the third-person reference to Denham on page 12 of the same volume, or quotations from letters by Denham (apparently to Hardy himself) woven into the main text on page 270 and elsewhere, not to mention many examples given in the text that are taken from works published after Denham's death (e.g. Vol. II pages 182, 226, 257, 272, 287, 356, 357, &c.), the latest of these dating from 1888, when Denham had been dead almost thirty years. In short, the published text of these two volumes has undergone massive interference at the hands of its editor(s) and cannot reliably be taken as representing exactly what Denham wrote on specific points without outside confirmation from the original tracts.

3 This almost certainly involves a misapprehension on Denham's part, since in Burns' poem 'Tam O'Shanter' [1791] Cutty Sark ('short skirt/smock') is the name of a beautiful witch so called from her revealing garments, not (as he puts it in a footnote to the 1895 list) 'a certain class of female Boggles'; see note [D31].

4 Specifically, the lines that open Denham's piece† come from *Hamlet*, Act I, Scene 1, lines 158–165. Horatio and the guards are discussing the effect of the cock's crow on the ghost of King Hamlet, whose manifestation they have just witnessed.

†These lines of dialogue are absent in the 1848 article, which is simply headed 'SEASONAL INFORMATION' (a title possibly provided by the journal's editor) followed by the line 'Ghosts never appear on Christmas eve!' in quotation marks; the latter was probably Denham's title, since it reappears in *The Denham Tracts* version.

5 This would presumably be the antiquarian Captain Francis Grose, author of *The Antiquities of England and Wales* [six volumes, 1773–1787], *Antiquities of Scotland* [two volumes, 1789 & 1791], and the unfinished *Antiquities of Ireland* [1791].

6 That is, seventy or eighty years before this piece's first publication in 1848, not from the time of its collection in *The Denham Tracts* – that is, in the 1770s and before.

7 Originally, in the 1848 list, *fairies* appeared here between *ignis-fatui* and *brownies*, before being moved to near the end of the 1895 list.

8 Denham prints *sirens* here instead of R. Scot's *sylens*, both in the 1848 and the 1895 lists. Some folklorists have suspected that the word should be read *sylvans* instead, meaning some woodland creature such as the satyrs, Pans, and fauns that precede it, but the point is debatable.

9 The 1895 printing actually reads *dwafs* here, but it is clear from the 1848 reading (*dwarfs*) that this is a simple misprint. Note that while Denham (and Scot) use *elves* instead of *elfs* (as indeed did Tolkien's slightly elder contemporary, Lord Dunsany), neither used the purely Tolkienesque *dwarves*.

10 Originally, in the 1848 list, *thrummy-caps* appeared here between *sprets* and *spunks*, before being moved to near the end of the 1895 list.

11 tod-lowries: In his 1848 piece, Denham glosses this as 'Phantom foxes', one of only two footnotes to the original article and the only one not picked up and repeated in the final piece.

12 Originally, in the 1848 list, *cutties* appeared here between *brags* and *wraiths*, before being moved to the penultimate position in the 1895 list.

13 A simpler version of this footnote appears in the 1848 article: 'There is a village of this name near Chester-le-street, in the county of Durham.'

14 Denham's note actually reads '12, 13, 21, 23, 27. The same with note 8.' (e.g., [D8]). That is, he interprets these six as different names for the same concept. I have repeated the text of Denham's note ([D8]) at each occurrence for the sake of clarity.

15 That is, the Jacobite Uprising of 1715; the said earl was executed for treason in 1716 for his role in supporting the Old Pretender (James Stuart, son of the deposed James II).

16 While Denham himself accepted the theory that 'hob-thrush' is a contraction of 'hob-o'-t'-hurst' (i.e., hob in the woods – see note[D7]), Briggs follows Gillian Edwards in suggesting that 'hobthrust' derives instead from hob-thyrs, *thyrs* being one of the Old English words for giant† (*A Dictionary of Fairies*, page 223); thurse (thurses) itself appears elsewhere in Denham's list. Since as Tolkien notes *hob-* is a diminutive (see page 862), the name essentially means 'little giant'.

†along with the more familiar (to the ears of Tolkien's readers, at any rate) *eoten*.

17 A secondary possibility is that the word was drawn to his attention by one of his many correspondents (one of whom was Dr. Hardy, the editor more than thirty years after Denham's death of *The Denham Tracts* themselves – see the Preface to Volume I page viii). If this is the case, the name may have come from somewhat further afield, either the northern Midlands or just over the border in southern Scotland

(e.g., Berwickshire), both areas being similarly well-provided with hob legends.

18 Gilliver, Marshall, & Weiner give the title page for the 1851 tract:

> To all and singular the Ghosts, Hobgoblins, and Phantasms, of the United Kingdom of Great Britain and Ireland, These brief Pages are Fearlessly Inscribed, In utter defiance of their Power and Influence, By their verie hvmble Seruaunte, To Com'aund, M:A:D.
>
> —*The Ring of Words*, page 147.

This is almost certainly the same tract given in a listing of Denham's works drawn up by Denham himself just before his death. The listing, published as the first item ('A List of Antiquarian Tomes, Tracts and Trifles') in an 1858 collection of Denham's work titled *Denham Tracts, or a few Pictures of the Olden Time in connection with The North of England* [1858; facsimile reprint 1974], gives as the first item of section XI ('Sundry Minor Tracts, &c.') a piece titled 'Ghosts, Hobgoblins, and Phantasms', stating that the first edition of fifty copies was printed in 1852 and ran six pages long; the second item in the same list is the second edition of the same title (eight pages, 1853). The listing may be found on page 7 of the 1858 *Denham Tracts*, which unfortunately does not include that tract among its 142 pages.

19 For Tolkien's attempt to get this book by his friend published by Allen & Unwin in 1936, see Note 23 to the commentary following Chapter IV, page 152. In the event, it was not published until 1964, the year following Lewis's death.

20 For more on Tolkien's admiration for, and usage of, Wright's book, see the commentary on Wright as a source for 'the carrock', pages 202–203.

21 Other creatures from Denham's list appearing in Tolkien's other works include wraithes (wraiths), corpse-candles, gnomes, fairies, fays, and korigans (as the Corrigan in 'The Lay of Aotrou and Itroun').

22 See *Letters* p. 410. Tolkien's probable source for this information† was John Rhys's *Celtic Britain* [1884], page 270.†† Modern scholarship has concluded that the so-called 'Ivernian' language, like the similarly once-mysterious Pictish, was in fact simply an earlier form of Celtic.

† First uncovered by Carl Hostetter and Pat Wynne in their article 'Stone Towers' (*Mythlore* #74, Autumn 1993), page 48.

†† The other 'Ivernian' word to which Tolkien refers in his letter that he had forgotten was *fern*, meaning (according to Rhys) 'anything good'. Rhys also thought he detected Ivernian words underlying proper and place names such as *Bolg* (pages 268, 281) and *Nét/Nuada/Nodens* (page 263).

Note

I have since learned of a still earlier appearance of Denham's list, in his little book bearing the rather unwieldy title *A Collection of Proverbs and Popular Sayings Relating to the Seasons, the Weather, and Agricultural Pursuits; Gathered Chiefly from Oral Tradition* [Percy Society, 1846]. The longest section (pages 23–68 out of a slim volume of only 79 pages, including frontmatter) is devoted to sayings organized by month; our now-familiar list appears (*sans* hobbit) as a long footnote in the December section, pegged to the saying 'Ghosts never appear on Christmas-eve' (which appears between 'Christmas comes but once a year' and 'Busy as an oven at Christmas'). I here give Denham's note in its entirety; italicization, spelling (e.g., 'Shakspeare'), and the like are as in the original:

‡So says Shakspeare; and the truth thereof few, *now-a-days*, will call into question. Grose observes, too, that those born on Christmas-day *cannot* see spirits.

What a happiness this must have been seventy or eighty years ago and upwards, to those chosen few who had the good luck to be born on this day; when the whole world was so over-run with ghosts, boggles, bloody-bones, spirits, demons, ignis-fatui, fairies, brownies, bug-bears, black-dogs, spectres, spelly-coats,* scare-crows, witches, wizards, barguests, Robin-goodfellows, hags, night-bats, scrags, break-necks, fantasms, hobgoblins, hobhoulards, boggy-boes, dobbys, hobthrusts, fetches, kelpies, warlocks, mock-beggars, mumpokers, jemmy-burties, and apparitions, that there was not a village in England that had not its peculiar ghost! Nay, every lone tenement or mansion which could boast of any antiquity, had its boggle or spectre. The church-yards were all haunted. Every green lane had its boulder-stone, on which an apparition kept watch by night; every common had a circle of fairies belonging to it; and there was scarce a shepherd to be met with who had not seen a spirit!

*These were Scotch boggles: they wore garments of shells, which made a horrid rattling when they appeared abroad. [Denham's Note]

Denham states in his Preface that his work of collection began 'as far back as the year 1825' (p. i) and was done 'chiefly orally' (ibid.); this might account for his later recording the word *hobbit*, for which no prior written source has yet been found before Denham's own 1853 publication.

Appendix II

TOLKIEN'S LETTER TO *THE OBSERVER* (THE HOBYAHS)

In addition to the undoubted appearance of the word *hobbits* in Denham's list, although Tolkien probably was not aware of the fact (see Appendix I), the issue of whether or not Tolkien invented the name outright has long been confused by a vague claim that it might have come from a late nineteenth- or early twentieth-century fairy tale. This claim was first raised by a pseudonymous letter to the editor of the British newspaper *The Observer*, printed on 16th January 1938, just four months after *The Hobbit* had been published.

Sir: Dr. Julian Huxley, in one of his recent lectures, referred to the 'little furry men' seen in Africa by natives and, although dimly in moonlight, by at least one scientist.

What I should like to know is whether these creatures provided the inspiration for Professor Tolkien's attractive hobbit, the newest visitor to so many of our nurseries this Christmas. Naturally, I always read my children's books before giving them to them, and I noticed that the characters in the hobbit were nearly all drawn from real animal life or from real mythology. Few of them appeared to be invented.

On mentioning the hairy-footed hobbit, rather like a rabbit, to one of my contemporaries, I was amazed to see her shudder. She said she remembered an old fairy tale called 'The Hobbit' in a collection read about 1904. This creature, she said, was definitely frightening, unlike Professor Tolkien's. Would the Professor be persuaded to tell us some more about the name and inception of the intriguing hero of his book? It would save so many research students so very much trouble in the generations to come. And, by the way, is the hobbit's stealing of the dragon's cup based on the cup-stealing episode in Beowulf? I hope so, since one of the book's charms appears to be its Spenserian harmonising of the brilliant threads of so many branches of epic, mythology, and Victorian fairy literature. – Yours, etc.

'HABIT.'

This brief letter inspired a long, detailed reply which is so important as a statement of how Tolkien felt about *The Hobbit* immediately following its first publication, and so full of information about his sources and the writing of the book, that I give it here in full.

Although written within days of the publication of Habit's letter (*Letters* p. 35), Tolkien's reply was not printed until the Sunday, 20th February 1938 issue.[1]

HOBBITS

Sir. – I need no persuasion: I am as susceptible as a dragon to flattery, and would gladly show off my diamond waistcoat, and even discuss its sources, since the Habit (more inquisitive than the Hobbit) has not only professed to admire it, but has also asked where I got it from. But would not that be rather unfair to the research students? To save them trouble is to rob them of any excuse for existing.

However, with regard to the Habit's principal question, there is no danger: I do not remember anything about the name and inception of the hero. I could guess, of course, but the guesses would have no more authority than those of future researchers, and I leave the game to them.

I was born in Africa, and have read several books on African exploration. I have, since about 1896, read even more books of fairy-tales of the genuine kind. Both the facts produced by the Habit would appear, therefore, to be significant. But are they? I have no waking recollection of furry pygmies (in book or moonlight), nor of any Hobbit bogey in print by 1904. I suspect that the two hobbits are accidental homophones, and am content† that they are not (it would seem) synonyms.[2] And I protest that my hobbit did not live in Africa, and was not furry, except about the feet. Nor indeed was he like a rabbit. He was a prosperous, well-fed young bachelor of independent means. Calling him a 'nasty little rabbit' was a piece of vulgar trollery, just as 'descendant of rats' was a piece of dwarfish malice – deliberate insults to his size and feet, which he deeply resented. His feet, if conveniently clad and shod by nature, were as elegant as his long, clever fingers.

As for the rest of the tale it is, as the Habit suggests, derived from (previously digested) epic, mythology, and fairy-story – not, however, Victorian in authorship, as a rule to which George Macdonald is the chief exception. *Beowulf* is among my most valued sources, though it was not consciously present to the mind in the process of writing, in which the episode of the theft arose naturally (and almost inevitably) from the circumstances. It is difficult to think of any other way of conducting the story at that point. I fancy the author of *Beowulf* would say much the same.

My tale is not consciously based on any other book – save one, and that is unpublished: the 'Silmarillion', a history of the Elves, to which frequent allusion is made. I had not thought of the future researchers, and as there is only one manuscript there seems at the moment small chance of this reference proving useful.

But these questions are mere preliminaries. Now that I have been made to see Mr. Baggins's adventures as the subject of future enquiry I realise that a lot of work will be needed. There is the question of nomenclature. The dwarf-names, and the wizard's, are from the Elder Edda. The hobbit-names from Obvious Sources proper to their kind. The full list of their wealthier families is: Baggins, Boffin, Bolger, Bracegirdle, Brandybuck, Burrowes, Chubb, Grubb, Hornblower, Proudfoot, Sackville, and Took. The dragon bears as name – a pseudonym – the past tense of the primitive Germanic verb *Smugan**, to squeeze through a hole: a low philological jest. The rest of the names are of the Ancient and Elvish World, and have not been modernized.

And why *dwarves*? Grammar prescribes *dwarfs*; philology suggests that *dwarrows* would be the historical form. The real answer is that I knew no better. But *dwarves* goes well with *elves*; and, in any case, *elf*, *gnome*, *goblin*, *dwarf* are only approximate translations of the Old Elvish names[3] for beings of not quite the same kinds and functions.

These dwarves are not quite the dwarfs of better known lore. They have been given Scandinavian names, it is true; but that is an editorial concession. Too many names in the tongues proper to the period might have been alarming. Dwarvish was both complicated and cacophonous. Even early elvish philologists avoided it, and the dwarves were obliged to use other languages, except for entirely private conversations. The language of hobbits was remarkably like English, as one would expect: they only lived on the borders of the Wild, and were mostly unaware of it. Their family names remain for the most part well known and justly respected in this island as they were in Hobbiton and Bywater.

There is the matter of the Runes. Those used by Thorin and Co., for special purpose, were comprised in an alphabet of thirty-two letters (full list on application), similar to, but not identical, with the runes of Anglo-Saxon inscriptions. There is doubtless an historical connection between the two. The Feanorian alphabet, generally used at the time, was of Elvish origin. It appears in the curse inscribed on the pot of gold in the picture of Smaug's lair, but had otherwise been transcribed (a facsimile of the original letter left on the mantelpiece can be supplied).[4]

And what of the Riddles? There is work to be done here on the sources and analogues. I should not be at all surprised to learn that both the hobbit and Gollum will find their claim to have invented any of them disallowed.

Finally, I present the future researcher with a little problem. The tale halted in the telling for about a year at two separate points: where are they? But probably that would have been discovered anyway. And suddenly I remember that the hobbit thought 'Old fool,' when the dragon succumbed to blandishment. I fear that the Habit's comment (and yours) will already be the same. But you must admit that the temptation was strong. – Yours, etc.

J. R. R. Tolkien

20 Northmoor-road, Oxford.

†[Tolkien's note:] Not quite. I should like, if possible, to learn more about the fairy-tale connection, c. 1904.

No reply being forthcoming from 'Habit', there the matter rested for more than thirty years. It was only in the last years of Tolkien's life that he turned again to the question of possible antecedents to his invention of the word *hobbit*, as testified in letters to two of his former pupils, Robert Burchfield and Roger Lancelyn Green. The immediate impetus was the decision by Burchfield, now the senior Editor of the OED, to include 'hobbit' in the *Supplement to the OED* he was preparing. According to Gilliver, Marshall, & Weiner's *The Ring of Words: Tolkien and the Oxford English Dictionary* [2006], Burchfield sent Tolkien a proposed entry on the word in December 1969 to see if it met with his approval. Tolkien replied on 11th September 1970:

The matter of *hobbits* is not very important, but I may be forgiven for taking a personal interest in it and being anxious that the meaning intended by me should be made clear.

Unfortunately, as all lexicographers know, 'don't look into things, unless you are looking for trouble: they nearly always turn out to be less simple than you thought'. You will shortly be receiving a long letter on *hobbit* and related matters, of which, even if it is in time, only a small part may be useful or interesting to you.

For the moment this is held up, because I am having the matter of the etymology: 'invented by J. R. R. Tolkien': investigated by experts. I knew that the claim was not clear, but I had not troubled to look into it, until faced by the inclusion of *hobbit* in the Supplement.

In the meanwhile I submit for your consideration the following definition:

> One of an imaginary people, a small variety of the human race, that gave themselves this name (meaning 'hole-dweller') but were called by others *halflings*, since they were half the height of normal Men.

This assumes that the etymology can stand.[5] If not it may be necessary to modify it: e.g. by substituting after 'race'

; in the tales of J. R. R. Tolkien said to have given themselves this name, though others called them . . .

If it stands, as I think it will even if an alleged older story called 'The Hobbit' can be traced, then the '(meaning "hole-dweller")' could be transferred to the etymology.

This definition, since it is more than twice as long as the one that you submitted and differs from it widely, will need some justification. I will supply it.[6]

Unfortunately, the promised 'long letter on *hobbit* and related matters' never followed, and probably was never written. It is not clear who the experts Tolkien engaged to research the matter for him were, but within a few months he consulted with Roger Lancelyn Green, another former pupil who had become the biographer of such important Victorian and Edwardian writers for children as Lewis Carroll, James Barrie, and Andrew Lang (and later, of course, of C. S. Lewis), as well as a recognized authority on the history of children's literature in England; cf. his book *Tellers of Tales: Favourite Children's Authors and Their Books of the Last* 100 *Years* [1946; updated, revised, and expanded in five distinct editions between 1946 and 1969 to eventually cover the period 1800–1968], which contained short biographies of the life and works of both major (Lear, Nesbit, MacDonald) and relatively minor (Mrs. Molesworth, S. R. Crockett) figures. Accordingly, Tolkien wrote to Green on 8th January 1971 (*Letters* p. 406–407):

The Ox. E. D. has in preparation of its Second Supplement got to *Hobbit*, which it proposes to include together with its progeny: *hobbitry*, *-ish*, etc. I have had, therefore, to justify my claim to have invented the word. My claim rests really on my 'nude parole' or unsupported assertion that I remember the occasion of its invention (by me); and that I had not *then* any knowledge of *Hobberdy*, *Hobbaty*, *Hobberdy Dick* etc. (for 'house-sprites');† and that my 'hobbits' were in any case of wholly dissimilar sort, a diminutive branch of the human race. Also that the only E.[nglish] word that influenced the invention was 'hole'; that granted the description of *hobbits*, the trolls' use of *rabbit* was merely an obvious insult, of no more etymological significance than Thorin's insult to Bilbo 'descendant of rats!' However, doubt was cast on this as far back as 1938. A review appeared in *The Observer* 16 Jan 1938, signed *'Habit'* . . . 'Habit' asserted that a friend claimed to have read, about 20 years earlier (sc. c. 1918)[7] an old 'fairy story' (in a collection of such tales) called *The Hobbit*, though the creature was very 'frightening'. I asked for more information, but have never received any; and recent intensive research has not discovered the 'collection'. I think it is probable that the friend's memory was inaccurate (after 20 years), and the creature probably had a name of the *Hobberdy, Hobbaty* class. However, one cannot exclude the possibility that buried childhood memories might suddenly rise to the surface long after (in my case after 35–40 years), though they might be quite differently applied. I told the researchers that I used (before 1900) to be read to from an 'old collection' – tattered and without cover or title-page – of which all I can now remember was that (I think) it was by Bulwer Lytton, and contained one story I was then very fond of called '*Puss Cat Mew*'. They have not discovered it. I wonder if you, the most learned of living scholars in this region, can say anything. Esp. for my own satisfaction about *Puss Cat Mew* – I do not suppose you have found a name precisely *hobbit* or you would have mentioned it. Oh what a tangled web they weave who try a new word to conceive!

†[Tolkien's note:] I have now! Probably more than most other folk; and find myself in a v. tangled wood – the clue to which is, however, the belief in *incubi* and 'changelings'. Alas! one conclusion is that the statement that *hobgoblins* were 'a larger kind' is the reverse of the original truth.

Green was able to identify the collection from which 'Puss Cat Mew' came as Edward Knatchbull-Hugessen's *Stories for My Children* [1869] (*Letters* p. 453), the American edition of which is actually titled *Puss-Cat Mew, and other Stories for my Children* [1871]. Knatchbull-Hugessen (1829–1893) was, in addition to the author of several such books of stories for children, the son of one of Jane Austen's nieces (Fanny Knight) and a reasonably prominent politician of his day, serving in Parliament and as Under-Secretary of State under several administrations, including Gladstone's, eventually being ennobled [1880] as the first Lord Brabourne. But Green's identification did not resolve the issue, since there is no story in this collection remotely answering the description of Habit's friend and no hobbits to be found therein.[8]

In fact, the story to which Habit's friend referred was almost certainly 'The Hobyahs',[9] which appeared in Joseph Jacobs' *More English Fairy Tales* [1894]. Jacobs' work, along with its earlier companion volume *English Fairy Tales* [1891], were once almost as well known as that of his rival Andrew Lang's coloured fairy book series [1889ff] but much more sharply focused in their contents, including only stories once current in Great Britain (thus the inclusion of 'The Hobyahs' which, although collected in America, clearly harkens back to the north-of-England/southern Scotland range of traditional hobs and hobgoblins, Perth being just some forty miles north and slightly west of Edinburgh). And, just as Tolkien had suspected, the hobyahs of this tale are indeed goblins who in no way resemble his hobbits. Since it is quite brief, for purposes of comparison I give here the entire tale as it appeared in Jacobs' source, a piece submitted by anthropologist and archeologist S. V. Proudfit to *The Journal of American Folklore*, vol. iv no. xiii (April-June 1891), pages 173–174.[10]

THE HOBYAHS: A SCOTCH NURSERY TALE. – When a child, I used to hear the following story told in a Scotch family that came from the vicinity of Perth. Whether the story came with the family I am unable to say. I have spelled the word 'Hobyah' as it was pronounced.

The effectiveness of the story lies in a certain sepulchral monotone in rendering the cry of the Hobyah, and his terrible 'look me.'

S. V. Proudfit

WASHINGTON, D. C.

Once there was an old man and woman and a little girl, and they all lived in a house made of hempstalks. Now the old man had a little dog named Turpie; and one night the Hobyahs came and said, 'Hobyah! Hobyah! Hobyah! Tear down the hempstalks, eat up the old man and woman, and carry off the little girl!' But little dog Turpie barked so that the Hobyahs ran off; and the old man said, 'Little dog Turpie barks so that I cannot sleep nor slumber, and if I live till morning I will cut off his tail.' So in the morning the old man cut off little dog Turpie's tail.

The next night the Hobyahs came again, and said, 'Hobyah! Hobyah! Hobyah! Tear down the hempstalks, eat up the old man and woman, and carry off the little girl!' But little dog Turpie barked so that the Hobyahs ran off; and the old man said, 'Little dog Turpie barks so that I cannot sleep nor slumber, and if I live till morning I will cut off one of his legs.' So in the morning the old man cut off one of little dog Turpie's legs.

The next night the Hobyahs came again, and said, 'Hobyah! Hobyah! Hobyah! Tear down the hempstalks, eat up the old man and woman, and carry off the little girl!' But little dog Turpie barked so that the Hobyahs ran off; and the old man said, 'Little dog Turpie barks so that I cannot sleep nor slumber, and if I live till morning I will cut off another of his legs.' So in the morning the old man cut off another of little dog Turpie's legs.

The next night the Hobyahs came again, and said, 'Hobyah! Hobyah! Hobyah! Tear down the hempstalks, eat up the old man and woman, and carry off the little girl!' But little dog Turpie barked so that the Hobyahs ran off; and the old man said, 'Little dog Turpie barks so that I cannot sleep nor slumber, and if I live till morning I will cut off another of his legs.' So in the morning the old man cut off another of little dog Turpie's legs.

The next night the Hobyahs came again, and said, 'Hobyah! Hobyah! Hobyah! Tear down the hempstalks, eat up the old man and woman, and carry off the little girl!' But little dog Turpie barked so that the Hobyahs ran off; and the old man said, 'Little dog Turpie barks so that I cannot sleep nor slumber, and if I live till morning I will cut off another of his legs.' So in the morning the old man cut off another of little dog Turpie's legs.

The next night the Hobyahs came again, and said, 'Hobyah! Hobyah! Hobyah! Tear down the hempstalks, eat up the old man and woman, and carry off the little girl!' But little dog Turpie barked so that the Hobyahs ran off; and the old man said, 'Little dog Turpie barks so that I cannot sleep nor slumber, and if I live till morning I will cut off little dog Turpie's head.' So in the morning the old man cut off little dog Turpie's head.

The next night the Hobyahs came and said, 'Hobyah! Hobyah! Hobyah! Tear down the hempstalks, eat up the old man and woman, and carry off the little girl!' And when the Hobyahs found that little dog Turpie's head was off they tore down the hempstalks, ate up the old man and woman, and carried the little girl off in a bag.

And when the Hobyahs came to their home they hung up the bag with the little girl in it, and every Hobyah knocked on top of the bag and said, 'Look me! look me!' and then they went to sleep until the next night, for the Hobyahs slept in the daytime.

The little girl cried a great deal, and a man with a big dog came that way and heard her crying. When he asked her how she came there and she had told him, he put the dog in the bag and took the little girl to his home.

The next night the Hobyahs took down the bag and knocked on the top of it and said, 'Look me! look me!' and when they opened the bag the big dog jumped out and ate them all up; so there are no Hobyahs now.

Although almost forgotten in the United States and England, this gruesome little tale remained well-known in Australia, thanks to an adaptation that appeared in the *Victorian Readers Second Book*, a second-grade reader used in elementary schools in the southeast Australian state of Victoria for decades, from the mid-1920s until the early 1950s. Unsurprisingly, this version took liberties with the story, replacing little dog Turpie with yellow dog Dingo, the house made of hempstalks with a hut made of bark, and leaving out the little girl altogether; instead of simply 'the Hobyahs came' its hobyahs came 'creep, creep, creeping'. There have also been several modern versions in recent years, by far the best of which is that by Simon Stern [1977], which draws its visual imagery of what hobyahs look like from the original illustrations (by John D. Batten) to Jacobs' version but moderates the brutality of the original story towards little dog Turpie.

In the end, it is clear that neither Proudfit's folk tale nor Knatchbull-Hugessen's fairy story has a prior claim to the invention of the name 'hobbit'. Both are in fact red herrings, neither of which had any influence on our story at all, making it overwhelmingly likely that no story called 'The Hobbit' existed until Tolkien himself wrote one. It is however interesting to note that by Proudfit's account he is the first to set down a previously oral tale. Without his having done so, all trace of hobyahs would have vanished, just as whatever story originally underlay Denham's hobbit (see Appendix I) *did* vanish forever. All we can say is that it was almost certainly wholly unlike Tolkien's story; his claim to have invented hobbits as we know them stands unassailed.

NOTES

1 According to Tolkien's disclaimer to Unwin on 4th March 1938 (*Letters* p. 34), he had written 'a short and fairly sane reply for publication' and sent it in with 'this jesting reply', the latter accompanied by a stamped envelope to forward its contents to 'Habit'. The contents of the now-lost shorter version are not known, but presumably it would have covered much the same points in less detailed form (and in less entertainingly playful language).

Tolkien's letter to *The Observer* is reproduced in *Letters* pp. 30–32, but I reproduce it here as it appeared on page 9 of the original newspaper.

2 'accidental homophones . . . [and] not . . . synonyms': That is, having the same sound but not the same meaning and sharing no common origin, such as *weak* (which derives from the Old Norse *veikr*) and *week* (which derives from Old English *wicu*).

3 I.e., *quende*, *noldo*, *orc*, and *naug*, respectively.

4 This passing reference enables us to date Bilbo's contract, reproduced for the first time as plate two of the Frontispiece to this volume, as already having been in existence by mid-January 1938.

5 Etymology: that is, research into the origin of a word, tracing it as far back to its original source(s) as possible. At issue is whether Tolkien's claim to have invented the word is accepted by the OED, although apparently it was questioned by no one except Tolkien himself, solely on the basis of the 'Habit' letter thirty-two years before.

6 Slightly different excerpts from this letter appear in both *Letters* pp. 404–405 and Gilliver et al.'s *The Ring of Words* pages 143–144; the first paragraph given here appears only in *Letters* and the final paragraph only in *The Ring of Words*. The latter goes on to give the OED entry as it was actually published in 1976:

> In the tales of J. R. R. Tolkien (1892–1973): one of an imaginary people, a small variety of the human race, that gave themselves this name (meaning 'hole-dweller') but were called by others *halflings*, since they were half the height of normal men.

7 Tolkien is obviously writing from memory here without the original clipping in front of him, since 'Habit' had in fact specified a somewhat earlier date (i.e., circa 1904).

8 The story 'Puss-Cat Mew' can most readily be found in Douglas A. Anderson's collection *Tales Before Tolkien: The Roots of Modern Fantasy* [2003], pages 46–86. It is unfortunate, given Tolkien's early fondness for the tale, that Knatchbull-Hugessen did not inherit any of the writing talent of his illustrious great-aunt. Instead, *Stories for My Children* in general and 'Puss-Cat Mew' in particular exhibit all the characteristics in children's stories that Tolkien came to loathe: a facetious narrator, smug moralizing, jarring anachronisms, and prettified fairies that would have been right at home in 'Tinfang Warble' or 'Goblin Feet'. In short, Knatchbull-Hugessen's best is more or less on par with Tolkien's worst.

However, as Anderson notes (*Tales*, page 47), it is possible to see a few parallels to scenes in *The Hobbit* in its narrative; examples include the hero's fight with three dwarves in which he knocks out the tooth of one and bashes the second in the face, only to be struck down by the third (compare Thorin's fight with the three trolls, in which he knocks out Tom's fang, pokes Bert in the eye, and is then nabbed by William), the hero's acquisition of a glove of invisibility (which he uses to assassinate his various foes, just like the 'practical' burglars of whom Bilbo has heard tell – see page 92), or the hero's sitting down and turning out his pockets for crumbs when lost in the forest after escaping a deadly foe. But none of the parallels is particularly compelling, and all could be the result of simple coincidence. More interesting is that Knatchbull-Hugessen starts with a bit of nursery rhyme:

Puss-cat Mew jumped over a coal;
In her best petticoat burnt a great hole;
Puss-cat Mew shan't have any milk
Till her best petticoat's mended with silk.†

and writes his story to explain the events behind it, a very Tolkienesque enterprise.

Far more important, although not of relevance for *The Hobbit*, is that 'Puss-Cat Mew' marks the first time we know of that Tolkien was exposed to what became one of the signature motifs in his legendarium: the winning of a faerie bride by a worthy mortal (the titular cat of Knatchbull-Hugessen's story is in fact a fairy under an enchantment). This theme appears over and over again in Tolkien's work, from the story of Beren and Lúthien to that of Aragorn and Arwen, from Tuor and Idril or the story of Mithrellas of Lórien and Imrazôr the Númenórean (UT.248) to the nameless temptress of 'Ides Ælfscýne' and her equally nameless victim.

†Baring-Gould gives a somewhat different version of this same poem, which he derives from the work of James O. Halliwell (i.e., either one of the editions of *The Nursery Rhymes of England* [1842ff] or *Popular Rhymes and Nursery Tales* [1849]):

Pussy cat Mole jumped over a coal
And in her best petticoat burnt a great hole
Poor Pussy's weeping, she'll have no more milk
Until her best petticoat's mended with silk.

—*The Annotated Mother Goose* [1962],
page 171; rhyme #300

9 This identification was made as far back as 1988 in the first edition of Douglas Anderson's *The Annotated Hobbit* (page 5); more information appears in the revised edition (DAA.9).

10 Reprinted in Joseph Jacobs, *More English Fairy Tales* [1894], tale number LXIX, pages [118]–124, plus notes page 232. Despite Jacobs' carelessness – he gets both the name of the journal ('American Folk-Lore Journal') and the volume ('iii') in which the story appeared wrong – he reproduced the tale itself word-for-word as it had appeared in Proudfit's version, aside from a few minor changes in punctuation (some inadvertent).

Proudfit himself, in addition to his splendidly hobbit-like name, was a distinguished archeologist and anthropologist, with a special interest in the preColumbian settlements in the Washington DC area. A career bureaucrat, he seems to have drafted the first version of what later became the Antiquities Act when a lawyer working for the McKinley administration [1899] and later as Acting Commissioner of the Bureau of Indian Affairs under Taft intervened decisively to preserve Navaho sites in the Southwest [1909].

Briggs observes (*A Dictionary of Fairies* page 223) that although derived from Scots immigrants, the story as told by Proudfit and Jacobs retains no trace of Scots dialect.

Appendix III

THE *DVERGATAL* (THE DWARF NAMES)

As Tolkien himself noted, 'The dwarf-names, and the wizard's, are from the Elder Edda' (see page 859). In fact, they come from a list known as the *Dvergatal* ('dwarf-tally'). This list appears both in the *Völuspá* [c.1000 AD], the first poem in the collection variously known as the *Elder Edda* or *Poetic Edda*, in what is generally considered to be an interpolation to the original poem,[1] as well as in the *Gylfaginning* ('The Deluding of Gylfi') in Snorri Sturluson's *Prose Edda* (also sometimes known as the *Younger Edda* [1223]). We have it on Tolkien's own authority that he took the dwarf-names from the *Elder Edda* rather than the *Prose Edda*, but close comparison of the two reveals that in fact he consulted both. Accordingly, I give here both versions, starting with the relevant passage from the former. The Old Norse text I have taken from Finnur Jónsson's famous edition (*Sæmundar-Edda* [1905], pages 3–5), which seems to have been considered the definitive standard at the time Tolkien was writing *The Hobbit*. The translation comes from Ursula Dronke's edition (Volume II, pages 9–11) which, while still in progress,[2] sets the modern standard with its exhaustive editorial apparatus and insightful and informative commentary. In the following presentation of the *Völuspá*'s version of the *Dvergatal*, I italicize names of significance for *The Hobbit*; readers of *The Lord of the Rings* will recognize several more names used in the sequel (e.g., Nar), but for the most part I pass over these for our present purpose. I have not attempted to standardize the names, since Tolkien himself sometimes chose a variant from one source, sometimes from another, and deliberately altered some of the names he took (e.g. *Dvalin* > *Dwalin* and probably also *Blain* > *Balin*).

9. Þá gengu regin öll	9. Then the powers all strode
á rökstóla,	to their thrones of fate,
ginnheilög god,	sacrosanct gods,
ok gættusk of þat,	and gave thought to this:
hvárt skyldi dverga	whether they should create
dróttir skepja	companies of dwarfs
ór Brimis blódi	from Brimer's Blood
ok ór *Bláins* leggjum.	and from *Bláinn's* limbs.

10. Þar vas Módsognir
mæztr of ordinn
dverga allra,
en *Durinn* annarr;
Þeir manlíkun
mörg of gerdu,
dverga í jördu,
sem *Durinn* sagdi.

10. There did Mootsucker [Mótsognir]
become most esteemed
of all dwarfs,
and Doorward [*Durinn*] next.
They fashioned many
figurines,
these dwarfs, out of earth,
as Doorward [*Durinn*] told:

11. Nyi ok Nidi,
Nordri, Sudri,
Austri, Vestri,
Alþjófr, *Dvalinn*,
Bívurr, *Bávurr*,
Bömburr, *Nori*,
Ánn ok Ánarr,
Ái, Mjödvitnir.

11. 'New Moon [Nyi] and No Moon [Nidi],
North [Nordri] and South [Sudri],
East [Austri] and West [Vestri],
All-thief [Althiófr], Dawdler [*Dvalinn*],
<Nær, *Nain*, Nipingr, *Dain*>[3]
Trembler [*Bivorr*], Trumbler [*Bávorr*],
Tubby [*Bomburr*], Shipper [*Nóri*],
Friend [Án] and Fighter [Ánarr],
Old Father [*Ái*], Mead Wolf [Miodvitnir],

12. Veigr ok *Gandalfr*,
Vindalfr, *Þráinn*,
Þekkr ok *Þorinn*,
Þrór, Vitr ok Litr,
Nár ok Nyrádr,
nú hefk dverga,
Reginn ok Rádsvidr,
rétt of talda.

12. Potion [Veigr] and Sprite Elf [*Gandálfr*],
Wind Elf [Vindálfr], Yearner [*þrainn*],
Docile [þekkr] and Darer [*þorinn*],
Thrive [*þrór*], Clever [Vitr], and Colour [Litr],
Corpse [Nár] and New Counsellor [Nyrádr] –
now I have the dwarfs
– Power [Reginn] and Plan-wise [Rádsvidr] –
correctly counted.

13. *Fili*, *Kíli*,
Fundinn, Náli,
Heptifili,
Hannarr, Svíurr,
Frár, Hornbori,

13. Trunky [*Fili*], Creeky [*Kili*]
Found [*Fundinn*], Needly [Náli]
Handle [Hepti], Drudge [Vili][4]
Craftsman [Hannarr], Dwindler [Svíorr],
<Billingr, Bruni, Billdr, Buri/Burin/Buin>[5]
Brilliant [Frár], Horn Borer [Hornbori],

Frægr ok Lóni,
Aurvangr, Jari,
Eikinskjaldi.

Famous [Frægr] and Lagooner [Lóni],
Loam Lea [Aurvangr], Earthy [Iari],
Oakenshield [Eikinskialdi].

14. Mál es dverga
í *Dvalins* lidi
ljóna kindum
til Lofars telja,
þeir es sóttu
frá Salarsteini
Aurvanga sjöt
til Jöruvalla.

14. It is time to trace the dwarfs in
Dawdler's [*Dvalins*] troop,
for men's progeny,
back to Praiser [Lofars] –
those dwarfs who sought,
from Mansion's Stone [Salarsteini]
the homes of Loam Leas [Aurvanga]
at Earth Plains [Iorovalla].

15. Þar vas Draupnir
ok DolgÞrasir,
Hár, Haugspori,
Hlévangr, *Glóinn*,
Skirfir, Virfir,
Skáfidr, Ái,

15. There was Dripper [Draupnir]
And Strife Eager [DólgÞrasir],
High [Hár], Grave Treader [Haugspori],
Shelter Field [Hlévangr], Gleamer [*Glói*],
<Dori, Ori, Dvfr, Andvari>[6]
Joiner [Skirvir], Groiner [Virvir]
Crooked Finn [Skáfidr], Old Father [Ái],

16. Alfr ok Yngvi,
Eikinskjaldi,
Fjalarr ok Frosti,
Finnr ok Ginnarr;
Þat mun æ uppi
medan öld lifir,
langnidja-tal
til Lofars hafat.

16. Elf [Álfr] and Yngvi [Yngvi],
Oakenshield [Eikinskialdi],
Hider [Fialarr] and Frosty [Frosti],
Finn [Finnr] and Potent [Ginnarr].
Uplifted in memory
as long as the world lives
will be this list
of Praiser's [Lofars] lineage.'

It will be seen that not all of the names Tolkien took for Thorin & Company come from the *Dvergatal* as it appears in the *Elder Edda*, within the *Völuspá*. Neither Dori nor Ori occurs therein, nor Dain and Nain. Tolkien also prefers the variant *Oin* (given in two manuscripts of the *Prose Edda*) to the *Poetic Edda*'s *Ai*. It is therefore certain that he also consulted the other major source that preserved a somewhat variant text of the *Dvergatal*, Snorri's *Prose Edda*. That Snorri prized the dwarf-list is evident, since he only incorporates roughly half of *Völuspa's* stanzas within his *Gylfaginning* (twenty-eight out of sixty-two) but takes pains to include all those telling of the creation of the dwarves and listing their names.

Snorri gives the passage as follows; I have taken Jean I. Young's translation (*The Prose Edda* [1954], pages 41–42) as my source. As before, I italicize those names used by Tolkien within *The Hobbit*.

All the gods sought then
their judgment-seats,
powers that are supreme
decided how dwarfs
should be brought into being
from bloody surf
and the legs of *Bláin*.

There many dwarfs
resembling men
they made in earth
as *Durin* said.

And the sibyl gives these as their names:

Nyi, Nidi,
Nordri [North], Sudri [South],
Austri [East], Vestri [West],
Althjóf, *Dvalin* [One-lying-in-a-trace],
Nár [Corpse], *Náin*,
Niping, *Dáin*,
Bifur, *Báfur*,
Bömbör, *Nori*,
Óri [Raging One], Ónar,
Óin, Mjödvitnir [Mead-wolf],
Vig and *Ganndálf* [Sorcered-elf],
Vinndálf [Wind-clf], *Thorin*[Bold One],
Fili, *Kili*,
Fundin [Found One], Vali,
Thrór, *Thróin*,
Thekk [Pleasant One], Lit, Vit,
Nyr [New One], Nyrád,
Rekk, Rádsvid [Wise-in-advice].

And these too are dwarfs and they live in rocks, but the above-mentioned live in the earth:

Draupnir, Dólgthvari [Battle-stock],
Haur, Hugstari,
Hledjólf, *Glóin*,
Dóri, *Óri*,
Dúf, Andvari,
Heptifili,
Hár [Tall One], Svíar.

The following, however, came from Svarin's grave-mound to Aurvangar in Jöruvellir, and from these have sprung Lovar; their names are

Skirvir, Virvir,
Skafid, Ái,
Álf, Ingi,
Eikinskjaldi [With-oak-shield],
Fal, Frosti,
Fid, Ginnar [Enticer].

—Snorri Sturluson, *Gylfaginning* ('The Deluding of Gylfi'), *The Prose Edda*, tr. Jean Young [1954], pages 41–42.

It will be seen that despite a few variations in spelling (e.g., 'Báfur' instead of Bofur and 'Thróin' instead of Thrain), all the dwarf-names appearing in *The Hobbit* appear in some form within Snorri's list.[7] Furthermore, Tolkien uses some names (Dori, Ori; Dain, Nain) and forms (Oin) that only appear in Snorri's version of the *Dvergatal*. Accordingly, we can be certain that Tolkien consulted both versions of this 'asterisk text', and continued to draw on it even after he'd completed *The Hobbit*.

NOTES

1 Cf., for example, Vigfusson & Powell's *Corpus Poeticvm Boreale* [1883] Vol. I pages 192 ('The Mnemonic Verses . . . relating to the Dwarves . . . have been removed as most certainly extraneous, though they had crept even into Snorri's text') and 79, and Dronke *The Poetic Edda, Volume II: Mythological Poems* [1997] pages 38, 92, 122, and especially 67.

2 The three volumes published so far of Dronke's edition – *Volume I: Heroic Poems* [1969], *Volume II: Mythological Poems* [1997], and Volume III: Mythological Poems II [2011] – cover only thirteen out of the collection's twenty-nine component poems. The remaining volumes are to cover the Helgi lays and the Sigurd cycle† and the remaining mythological and miscellaneous pieces.

†That is, the portions rewritten by Tolkien as *Volsungakvida En Nyja*; cf. *Letters* p. 452.

3 These four dwarf-names are missing in the Codex Regius [circa 1270], the best manuscript of the *Völuspá*, but they are present in most other manuscripts of the *Dvergatal*, including the Hauksbók [circa 1302–1310, though this material was added circa 1330–1350]; see Dronke, textual notes, page 90, and her notes on the manuscripts, page 61.

4 Dronke reads these as two names, as per the Codex Regius (Hepti, Vili) and Hauksbók (Hefti, Fili); all other manuscripts of the *Dvergatal* give them as a single name (Heptifili); see Dronke, textual notes, page 91.

5 These four names, absent from the Codex Regius, appear in the Hauksbók; see Dronke, textual notes, page 91. *Burin*, a variant of the

fourth name given in one manuscript of Snorri's version (as 'Bvrin'), would later appear in early drafts of *The Lord of the Rings* as the son of Balin, who comes to Rivendell searching for news of his father and thus attends the Council of Elrond; he was later replaced by Gimli son of Gloin (HME VI.395, 397, 400) as the dwarven member of the Fellowship.

6 These four names appear in neither the Codex Regius nor the Hauksbók versions of the *Völuspá*, but only in manuscripts of Snorri's version of the *Dvergatal* (from *Gylfaginning*). In one important manuscript of that work, *Ori* does not appear here but higher up in the list, immediately following Bömburr and Nori in stanza 11, where it replaces the name *Án*. Similarly, in two manuscripts of Snorri's version *Ái* (cf. the last line of stanza 11) is replaced by *Oin*. See Dronke, textual notes, pages 92 and 90.

7 With the possible exception of Balin, unless we accept this as Tolkien's own variant, unattested in the manuscript tradition, of *Blain*, as I have suggested on page 24.

Appendix IV

TOLKIEN'S CORRESPONDENCE WITH ARTHUR RANSOME

The following brief exchange of letters between Tolkien and fellow children's author Arthur Ransome is of interest because it marks one of the few times when Tolkien – whom C. S. Lewis claimed, not quite truthfully, nobody could influence[1] – accepted unsolicited advice on changes he might wish to make to one of his books.

At the time he wrote the letter which initiated the exchange, Ransome was already an established author, having written a book on Poe [1910] and another, controversial at the time, on Wilde [1912] and served as a foreign correspondent to Russia throughout the eventful period before, during, and after the 1917 revolution(s), and had even published a collection of Russian folktales (*Old Peter's Russian Tales* [1916]). He was also, although Tolkien probably did not know this, a childhood friend of E. R. Eddison, an author Tolkien greatly admired and one of his major precursors in the field of modem fantasy.[2] More importantly, in the 1930s Ransome was establishing himself as a popular children's author in England through his 'Swallows and Amazons' series;[3] that same year he had won the first Carnegie medal for the outstanding children's book of the previous year for *Pigeon Post*, the sixth book in the series.[4]

The contact point between Tolkien and Ransome was Stanley Unwin, Tolkien's publisher, who had published at least four of Ransome's many books in the early days of George Allen & Unwin: *Six Weeks in Russia* [1919], *The Crisis in Russia* [1921], *Racundra's First Cruise* [1923], and *The Chinese Puzzle* [1927], as well as Ransome's translation of Iury Libedinsky's *A Week* [1923]. Unwin had shown considerable courage in publishing the 1919 book, which opposed the joint British-French-American invasion of Russia launched in that year in an attempt to topple the new Soviet regime and reinstate a Czarist government,[5] and even though Ransome was now being published by the firm of Jonathan Cape they had apparently remained on good terms. Accordingly, Unwin sent Ransome a copy of the newly published *Hobbit* in the fall of 1937, and soon had the following excerpt of a letter from Ransome to pass along to Tolkien:

Letter #1

I sent a copy of THE HOBBIT to Arthur Ransome, who is temporarily laid up at a nursing home in Norwich, and he writes –

> 'THE HOBBIT is my delight; great fun. Thank you
> for sending him. Do the author's new coloured
> pictures include a portrait of Bilbo Baggins?
> Or does he refrain?'

—Stanley Unwin to JRRT, letter of 15th December 1937,
quoting Arthur Ransome's letter to Unwin,
(unpublished; A&U Archive).

The 'coloured pictures' to which Ransome refers are the four colour plates added to the second printing of the Allen & Unwin edition, which according to Hammond's *Descriptive Bibliography* (page 15) was ready for release on 19th December, although the official release date was a month later (25th January 1938). Clearly, Unwin had sent Ransome a copy of the first printing, which lacked any colour illustrations (other than the dust jacket).

As a result of Unwin's sending the book, Ransome also wrote to Tolkien himself (on 13th December 1937), although it is not known whether Ransome sent the following letter to Tolkien directly (e.g., having looked up his address in *Who's Who*) or as an enclosure accompanying the preceding letter to Unwin.

Letter #2

Sir as a humble hobbit fancier (and one certain that your book will be many times reprinted) may I complain that on page 27 when Gandalf calls Bilbo an excitable hobbit the scribe (human no doubt) has written man by mistake? On page 112 Gandalf calls the goblins little boys, but he means it as an insult so that is no doubt all right. But on page 294 Thorin surely is misrepresented. Why his concern for men? Didn't he say more of us, thinking of dwarves elves goblins and dragons and not of a species which to him must have been very unimportant. The error if it is an error is a natural one due again to the humanity of the scribe to whom we must all be grateful for this chronicle. I am sir yours respectfully

Arthur Ransome[6]

Aside from the complement inherent in receiving such a 'fan letter' from an established fellow author, Tolkien was clearly pleased not just by Ransome's close attention to detail but by his entering into the spirit of the book and maintaining the fiction of Bilbo's authorship and Tolkien's pose as merely the translator of the ancient text (explicitly established in the runes bordering the dust jacket), as his response in kind on 15th December shows.[7]

Letter #3

Dear Mr. Ransome.

I'm sure Mr. Baggins would agree in words such as he used to Thorin – to have been fancied by you, that is more than any hobbit could expect. The scribe too is delighted to be honoured by a note in your own hand, and by criticisms showing so close an acquaintance with the text. My reputation will go up with my children – the eldest are now rather to be classed as men, but on their shelves, winnowed of the chaff left behind in the nursery I notice that their 'Ransomes' remain.[8]

You tempt me grievously to a mythological essay; but I restrain myself, since your criticisms are good even though the offending words may be defensible. For the history of the hobbit must come before many who have not before them the exact history of the world into which Mr. Baggins strayed; and it is unwise to raise issues of such import.

I will replace <u>man</u> on p. 27 by the <u>fellow</u> of an earlier recension. On p. 112[9] I agree in feeling that Gandalf's insult was rather silly and not quite up to form – though of course he would regard the undeveloped males of all two legged species as <u>boys</u>. I'm afraid the blemish can hardly be got over by vocabulary, unless <u>oaves</u> would be an improvement? On p.294 I accept <u>of us</u> as a great improvement: <u>men</u> is there just a loose[10] rendering of Thorin's word for 'people' – the language of those days, unlike modern English, had a word that included the Two Kindreds (Elves and Men) and their likenesses and mockeries. 'Of us' exactly represents this: for Thorin certainly included 'humans' in his comment, for Elves and Dwarves were mightily concerned with them, and well aware that it was their fate to usurp the world; but he was not at that moment thinking chiefly of *Men* (with a capital). The ancient English, of course, would have felt no hesitation in using 'man' of elf, dwarf, goblin, troll, wizard or what not, since they were inclined to make Adam the father of them all . . .

I must apologize for writing at such length. I hope you are

well enough to endure it or forgive it, trusting that your address does not indicate a serious illness. I hope the enclosed list of other minor errors will serve to correct your copy – but, *if* there is a reprint (sales are not very great) I hope you will allow me to send you a corrected copy.

Yours very respectfully . . .

Ransome replied at once, making clear that whatever mythological premise underlay the word-choice it was for him a matter of decorum, what Tolkien himself would have called a slight flaw in the subcreation that sparked a momentary loss of secondary belief, that had motivated him to voice the objection.

Letter #4

To J. R. R. Tolkien

Dec. 17 1937 Norwich

Dear Professor Tolkien,

Thank you for your most interesting letter.

BUT: I did not intend any criticism whatever of the 'boys' of p. 112. I mentioned it only to illustrate (by contrast) my slight discomfort due to 'man' on p. 27. And that discomfort had no relation to mythology. I had very much admired the delicate skill with which you had made Mr. Baggins so Hobbitty (forgive the word) and the word 'man' on p. 27 seemed a leak or a tear in the veil, undoing just a little of what you had done. That was all. I thought the word had slipped from the scribe's pen by accident. The Hobbitness of Mr. Baggins seems to me one of the most difficult and triumphant achievements of the book . . . And so valuable that, regardless of mythology, it seemed worth while to complain about the one word which in one place, just for a moment, raised a faint doubt.

I have copied your corrections into the book. Thank you for letting me have them.

I had an operation nearly a month ago[11] and hope to get out quite soon now. *The Hobbit* has done a great deal to turn these weeks into a pleasure. And as for new editions . . . there will be dozens of them: of that I have no doubt whatever.

Yours sincerely,

Arthur Ransome

—*Signalling from Mars*, page 251.

With that, the brief correspondence between the two men seems to have ceased – not, however, without having left its mark upon *The Hobbit*. The points Ransome had raised Tolkien at once passed along to Allen & Unwin, along with his proposed solutions:

Letter #5

P.S. . . . Mr Arthur Ransome objects to *man* on p. 27 (line 7 from end). Read *fellow* as in earlier recension? He also objects to *more men* on p. 294 l[ine] 11. Read *more of us*? *Men* with a capital is, I think, used in text when 'human kind' are specifically intended; and *man, men* with a minuscule are occasionally and loosely used as 'adult male' and 'people'. But perhaps, although this can be mythologically defended (and is according to Anglo-Saxon usage!), it may be as well to avoid raising mythological issues outside the story. Mr Ransome also seems not to like Gandalf's use of *boys* on p. 112 (lines 11, 13). But, though I agree that his insult was rather silly and not quite up to form, I do not think anything can be done about it now. Unless *oaves* would do? JRRT.

—JRRT to A & U, 19th December 1937; *Letters* p. 28.

Of the three specific 'cruxes' raised by Ransome, it is interesting to note that Tolkien responded differently to each. The first, 'excitable little man', was indeed changed, not to Ransome's proposed 'excitable little *hobbit*', but rather to 'excitable little *fellow*' (DAA.47–48). That is, he agrees with Ransome's criticism that the phrasing of the text needs changing but comes up with his own solution; the 'earlier recension' is of course a fiction referring to the framing device and Tolkien's pose as translator, as comparison to the actual manuscript text (pp. 8 & 39) of this passage shows. The second, 'naughty little boys' (DAA.151–152), was ultimately allowed to stand, since neither Ransome nor Tolkien could find a satisfactory replacement. Tolkien's proposed change of 'boys' to *oaves* (i.e., the plural of *oaf*) would have been extremely problematic, as he would have discovered when he investigated the etymology of the word, because *oaves* (more usually spelled *oafs*; earlier *ouphes, aufs*) in fact derives from *elves* and ties in with the old belief that a physically or mentally disabled child (e.g., one with Down's Syndrome) was a changeling or 'elf' (oaf). Finally, for the third 'crux', the suggested replacement of 'If more men . . . it would be a merrier world' with 'If more *of us* . . .', Tolkien adopted Ransome's correction directly (DAA.348), noting that it was 'a great improvement'.

Beyond these specific corrections, Ransome's objection seems to have led Tolkien to refine his subsequent usage. Even though he had explained some of the concepts underlying his use of the generic *men* (more or less human-shaped creature) as opposed to the specific *Men* (human), Ransome had remained dubious, and Tolkien clearly came to agree with him and henceforth tended to avoid that generic usage, especially in the new book he was just starting, *The Lord of the Rings*. It is interesting to note that in his letter to Ransome, written just days before he began writing *The Lord of the Rings*, Tolkien already lists wizards as a separate race distinct from human men. As for the 'ancient English' belief that all such beings were descendents of Adam, one of his primary sources here was no doubt the *Beowulf*-poet, who describes Grendel as a descendent of Cain (line 107a). Finally, the term 'the Two Kindreds' for the elder and younger children of Ilúvatar, Elves and Men, seems to have arisen in a revision to the 1930 *Quenta* (see HME IV.154 & 156); it was soon adopted into 'the (Earliest) Annals of Beleriand' (HME IV.306), 'The Fall of Númenor' (HME V.18), and the 1937 *Quenta Silmarillion* (e.g. HME V.302). Its presence here, in the context of *The Hobbit*, shows that already in the months immediately following the latter's publication he was explicating details from it in terms of his legendarium and was concerned to show that they were in harmony, a process that reached its culmination with *The Lord of the Rings*.

Finally, the list of 'other minor errors' Tolkien sent Ransome was probably the same ones he submitted to Allen & Unwin the following day (16th December 1937), too late for inclusion in the second printing; cf. Hammond's *Descriptive Bibliography* pages 4, 7, & 15. However, researcher Lyn Mellone has discovered that Ransome's copy of *The Hobbit*, now in the Ransome Room of the Museum of Lakeland Life in Kendal, Cumbria in the northwest corner of England, does indeed have the corrections he received from Tolkien carefully marked in the appropriate places in ink, with those proposed by Ransome (e.g. 'excitable little hobbit') in pencil.[12] Some of these typographical corrections were fixed in the third and fourth printings (*Descriptive Bibliography*, page 16), but most had to wait until the fifth printing (the second edition) of 1951. Although Ransome was still alive (and in fact did not die until 1967, at the age of eighty-two), by this time Tolkien's promise to send him 'a corrected copy' seems to have been forgotten. However, in their entry on Ransome in *The J.R.R. Tolkien Companion and Guide* (Vol. II, pages 813–814), Scull & Hammond note that Tolkien did arrange to have Ransome sent an advance copy of *The Lord of the Rings* and that the recipient 'read it enthusiastically'.

NOTES

1 'No one ever influenced Tolkien – you might as well try to influence a bandersnatch' (CSL to Charles Moorman, 15th May 1959; *Letters of C. S. Lewis*, ed. Walter Hooper [1988], page 481). However, not only did Tolkien change the wording in *The Lord of the Rings* at one point when Rhona Beare questioned the implications of one phrase (see *Letters* pp. 277 & 279), but Lewis himself had a significant impact on 'The Lay of Leithian' (see HME III.315–329). Perhaps significantly, Tolkien tended not to adopt Lewis's suggestions but instead recast passages that Lewis had criticized. It seems fair to conclude, therefore, that he gladly corrected errors brought to his attention but often changed things in his own way rather than directly accepting others' suggestions.

2 For more on Ransome and 'Ric' (Eric Rucker) Eddison, see Ransome's autobiography (*The Autobiography of Arthur Ransome*, ed. Rupert Hart-Davis [1976], pages 37–40) and also the biography by Hugh Brogan† (*The Life of Arthur Ransome* [1984], pages 10–11). Tolkien admired Eddison's *The Worm Ouroboros* [1922] (except for the nomenclature, which is markedly eccentric), but strongly objected to the philosophy behind Eddison's later 'Zimiamvian' books (*Mistress of Mistresses* [1935], *A Fish Dinner in Memison* [1941], and the unfinished *The Mezentian Gate* [1958]) – cf. JRRT to Caroline Whitman Everett, letter of 24th June 1957; *Letters* p. 258. Tolkien and Eddison actually met at least twice when ERE attended Inklings meetings at Lewis's invitation in 1943 and 1944, at which he read from his later works.

† Brogan himself was a correspondent of JRRT when young; see *Letters* pp. 129, 131, 132, 185–186, 224, 225–226, & 230.

3 The books in the 'Swallows and Amazons' series are as follows: #1. *Swallows and Amazons* [1930], #2. *Swallowdale* [1931], #3. *Peter Duck* [1932], #4. *Winter Holiday* [1933], #5. *Coot Club* [1934], #6. *Pigeon Post* [1936], #7. *We Didn't Mean to Go to Sea* [1937], #8. *Secret Water* [1939], #9. *The Big Sic* [1940], #10. *Missee Lee* [1941], #11. *The Picts and the Martyrs* [1943], #12. *Great Northern?* [1947], #13. *Coots in the North* [unfinished; posthumously publ. 1988].

4 Subsequent Carnegie medal winners include such famous books as Mary Norton's *The Borrowers* [1952], C. S. Lewis's *The Last Battle* [1956], Richard Adams' *Watership Down* [1972], and Philip Pullman's *His Dark Materials*, Book I: *Northern Lights* [1995].†

† This last is better known in the United States as *The Golden Compass*.

5 See Ransome's autobiography, pages 268–269, and also Unwin's autobiography, *The Truth About a Publisher* [1960], pages 165–166, for the two men's perspectives.

6 I have taken the text of this letter from a tengwar inscription Tolkien made [Ad.Ms.H.6]. In addition to being very lightly punctuated, the tengwar copy differs in some details from the text published in Ransome's collected letters (*Signalling from Mars: The Letters of Arthur Ransome*, ed. Hugh Brogan [1997], pp. 249–250). For example, Brogan prints 'excit-

able hobbit', 'no doubt right', 'Thorin is surely misinterpreted', and 'the chronicle'. I am grateful to Arden Smith for his aid in translating Tolkien's beautiful tengwar calligraphy back into English letters.

7 The following text is a composite: the first half of Tolkien's letter I have taken from another tengwar transcription by Tolkien himself [Ad. Ms.H.7], while the second half comes from Ransome's collected letters; see Note 10 below. Once again I am grateful to Arden Smith for his timely aid.

8 Men rather than children: John Tolkien was now twenty years old, and Michael seventeen. Confirmation of Tolkien's statement that the 'Swallows and Amazons' books were popular in the Tolkien household and that his sons retained their Ransomes even after they were grown was discovered by researcher Lyn Mellone in the summer of 2006. According to her posting on TarBoard, the online Arthur Ransome discussion board (http://www.tarboard.net/tarboard/messages/23986.htm), Adam Tolkien, Christopher's younger son, responded to her queries by affirming the popularity of the books among Tolkien's children, stating that not only did 'Christopher [recall] specifically *Swallows and Amazons* and *Missee Lee*' – which, as Mellone notes, was published four years after *The Hobbit* and thus testifies to continued interest on their part – but that he had in turn passed them along to his own son, Adam, who had enjoyed them very much in his turn.

9 Here Tolkien accidentally wrote '212' in his tengwar transcription, but the passage in question actually occurs on p. 112 of the first edition; Brogan gives the citation correctly (*Signalling from Mars* p. 250).

10 At this point, Tolkien's tengwar transcription ends, at the bottom of a page [Ad.Ms.H.7], the verso of which [Ad.Ms.H.6] is covered by his transcription of Ransome's letter to him (see above). If Tolkien continued his transcription, it was on a separate sheet of paper which has since become lost. Accordingly, from this point onwards I take the text from Brogan's edition of Ransome's letters, *Signalling from Mars* pp. 250–251.

As before, the tengwar text differs slightly from that published in Ransome's collected letters – e.g., 'could expect' there becomes 'could have expected', 'so close an acquaintance with' becomes 'so close a scrutiny of', and 'will go up' becomes 'would go up'. More importantly, the transcription includes a passage omitted from the published text (the line 'You tempt me grievously' through 'of such import'), in which Tolkien briefly places 'the history of the hobbit' into context with that of 'the world into which Mr. Baggins strayed' – i.e., that of the Silmarillion texts.

11 Ransome's operation: he had undergone surgery for a hernia (Brogan, *Signalling from Mars*, page 249). The 'nursing home' in which he was staying, by the way, was not a euphemism for an old folks' home but rather a convalescent home for those recovering from long-term illness or major surgery.

12 See Mellone's account, detailing each annotation, at the online Ransome discussion list TarBoard, specifically 'http://www.tarboard.net/tarboard/messages/23986.htm. I am also grateful to her for reading and critiquing this Appendix.'

Appendix V

AUTHOR'S COPIES LIST

Like most authors, Tolkien received a number of author's copies of his book when it was published, which he distributed to friends and family. By luck, a listing that represents his working out of who to give copies to survives, written in the flyleaf of the page proofs of the book (Marq. 1/2/3). While we cannot be certain that this list represents his final decisions, having been written at the time the text was finalized (February–March 1937) rather than at the time of the book's release (21st September), we can confirm it on some points, since copies inscribed by Tolkien to some of these recipients have shown up at auctions in recent years. The Bodleian also holds a file of letters Tolkien received regarding *The Hobbit* (MS. Tolkien 21) which includes letters of thanks from many of those listed below, gratefully acknowledging the book's arrival.

Below I give the list (or more properly list*s*) as they appear on the flyleaf, complete with cancellations, and Tolkien's notes to himself (e.g., 'have', indicating that the person in question already has a copy and so need not be sent a presentation copy from Tolkien's limited stock), followed by a section in which I briefly identify the recipients, insofar as this is possible after the lapse of seventy-five years. In addition to the file of letters in the Bodleian, the following draws heavily on such sources as Tolkien's letters (including unpublished letters in the Allen & Unwin archive), the *Tolkien Family Album* by John & Priscilla Tolkien [1992] (hereafter *Family Album*), Scull & Hammond's *J.R.R. Tolkien Companion & Guide*, a list of identifications drawn up by Taum Santoski after a discussion of the topic with Christopher Tolkien, and some details provided to me by Priscilla Tolkien, to whom my thanks; I am grateful to Doug Anderson for providing some dates and correcting me on several points.

The Hobbit

Revise

	✓	~~Self (2)~~
+	1	EVG
		~~C.S.L.~~ ✓ *have*
+	1	Griffiths
+	1	Kilbride
	1	<Marjorie>
	1	Mary
	1	~~Chambers~~ ✓ 1
(+ +)	2	Jennings 2
+	1	A. Mabel
	1	A. Florence
	1	Wrenn
+	1	D'Ardenne
+	1	Helen B
	1	A. Jane
	1	Rattenbury
		Livesleys ✓ *have*
	1	A H Smith
+	1	<?Aunt> J. Grove
+	1	S. Mills
+	1	~~WR Child~~ *have*

~~CSL~~ ~~Ox Mag~~ ✓ *have*
~~<Book> Soc~~ ✓ *have*
~~GSG~~ ✓ *have*

• EVG	1
• A. Grove	1
• D'Ardenne	1
• Griffiths	1
• Helen B.	1
• S Mills	1
Jennings	2
Jennings	•
~~S Mills~~	
• Kilbride	1
~~<illegible>~~	
• A. Florence	1
10	
• Hilary	
• A. Jane	
12	

EVG: E. V. (Eric Valentine) Gordon, 1896–1938. A Canadian Rhodes Scholar, successively Tolkien's student, colleague, and collaborator. Co-editor with Tolkien of *Sir Gawain & the Green Knight* [1925] and several unfinished projects, including editions of *Pearl*, 'The Wanderer', and 'The Seafarer'. Contributor to *Songs for the Philologists*, and author, editor, or translator in his own right of *An Introduction to Old Norse* [1927], *The Battle of Maldon* [1937], and *Scandinavian Archaeology* [1937]. He succeeded Tolkien as Professor of English Language at Leeds and in 1930 became Smith Professor of English Language and Germanic Philology at Manchester in central England. Knighted by the King of Denmark for his contributions to Icelandic studies. His letter thanking Tolkien for this presentation copy, dated 23rd September 1937, is now in the Bodleian (MS. Tolkien 21, folio 57). For more on Gordon, see Douglas A. Anderson's 'An Industrious Little Devil: E. V. Gordon as Friend and Collaborator with Tolkien' in *Tolkien the Medievalist*, ed. Jane Chance [2003], pages 15–25; his photograph can be seen in the *Family Album*, page 47.

C.S.L.: C. S. ('Jack') Lewis, 1898–1963. Co-founder with Tolkien of the Inklings, a tutor at Magdalen College Oxford, and at the time perhaps Tolkien's closest friend. At the time of *The Hobbit*'s publication he had just published his first scholarly book, *The Allegory of Love* [1936], and would shortly publish his first work of fiction, *Out of the Silent Planet* [1938], which had originated in a bargain with Tolkien for them to each write a space-travel or time travel story (for more on this bargain, see my essay '*The Lost Road, The Dark Tower*, and *The Notion Club Papers*' in *Tolkien's Legendarium*, ed. Flieger & Hostetter [1996], pages 199–218). The first outside Tolkien's immediate family to read *The Hobbit*, and contributor of one of the cover blurbs, he ultimately didn't get a presentation copy because A&U sent him a review copy instead (hence his name's cancellation in the list above); cf. Charles Furth's letter to JRRT on 1st June 1937 promising to send Lewis an advance copy (A&U archive). His enthusiastic review ('Prediction is dangerous, but *The Hobbit* may well prove a classic') appeared in *The Times Literary Supplement* on 2nd October 1937 (reprinted in *On Stories* [1982], 81–2), followed by another in the *Times* itself on 8th October. The classic study of the ups and eventual downs of his friendship with Tolkien can be found in Humphrey Carpenter's *The Inklings* [1978].

Griffiths: Elaine Griffiths, 1909–1996. Student of JRRT's, to whom had been entrusted the task of updating John R. Clark Hall's translation of *Beowulf* for Allen & Unwin, with Tolkien to provide a new critical foreword on Old English prosody. Ultimately Griffiths failed to complete the project, which passed instead to Tolkien's colleague C. L. Wrenn (see below). Griffiths however remained a longtime family friend; see *Family Album* page 69 for a brief but warm account, plus a photo. For more on Griffiths and *The Hobbit*, see pages xxxvi, xxxviii, 693–4, & 702 of this book; for an amusing audio account in her own voice of her role in bringing *The Hobbit* to the attention of a publisher, see *J. R. R. Tolkien: An Audio Portrait.*

Kilbride: K. M. (Katharine Mary) Kilbride, 1900–1966, a student of Tolkien's at Leeds to whom he sent both *The Hobbit* and his essay 'Beowulf: The Monsters & the Critics' together. Her letter of thanks, reminiscing about the 'real artistic talent' in the English House at Leeds in the old days ('what fun you must have had drawing out the maps'), is in the Bodleian (MS. Tolkien 21, folio 66). Her inscribed copy, which included a passage in verse from *The Lost Road* (cf. HME V.44), was sold at auction by Sotheby's in December 2002.

Marjorie: Marjorie Incledon, 1891–1973. JRRT's cousin, the elder daughter of his mother Mabel's older sister, May Suffield Incledon. The creator, with her sister Mary, of 'Animalic', the first invented language to which Tolkien was exposed.

Mary: Mary Incledon, 1895–1940. JRRT's cousin, the younger daughter of his mother Mabel's older sister, May Suffield Incledon. Co-creator, with her sister Marjorie, of 'Animalic' and collaborator with Tolkien in the creation of his first invented language, Nevbosh. Godmother of JRRT's oldest son, Fr. John Tolkien.

Chambers: R. W. (Raymond Wilson) Chambers, 1874–1942. Quain Professor of English Language and Literature at University College London, who in 1925 had refused the Rawlinson & Bosworth chair of Anglo Saxon at Oxford, thus opening the way for JRRT's election to that post. A colleague of A. E. Housman and W. P. Ker, he was considered by Tolkien 'the greatest of living Anglo-Saxon scholars' (*Beowulf & the Critics*, ed. Michael Drout [2002], page 32). Among his major publications are *Widsith: A Study in Old English Heroic Legend* [1912], *Beowulf: An Introduction to the Study of the Poem* [1921, rev. ed. 1932], 'Beowulf and the Heroic Age' [1925; called by Tolkien 'the most significant single essay on the poem that I know'], and a biography of Sir Thomas More [1935] which is said to have aided the cause of More's canonization. As documented by Douglas A. Anderson ('R. W. Chambers and *The Hobbit*', in *Tolkien Studies* Vol. III, pages 137–147), Tolkien and Chambers regularly exchanged publications; Chambers is one of the three people to whom Tolkien is known to have shown his alliterative Arthurian poem 'The Fall of Arthur' (the others being E. V. Gordon and C. S. Lewis), and Tolkien also presented Chambers with a fine calligraphic copy of his still-unpublished poem 'Doworst'.

Tolkien's letter to Chambers of 8th February 1937 promising to send him the book is now in the Special Collections of University College London (Chambers Papers 101); his letter to Allen & Unwin requesting Chambers be sent a copy (JRRT to Ch. Furth, 13th August 1937) with an enclosed note that seems not to have survived, and Allen & Unwin's response (Furth to JRRT, 16th August 1937), are in the Allen & Unwin archives. Chambers' two brief notes of thanks upon the book's actual arrival, the first of which Tolkien forwarded to Allen & Unwin (see *Letters*, page 20), are in the Bodleian (MS. Tolkien 21, folios 45 [undated] & 46 [postmarked 7 Sep 1937]).

Jennings: Aileen Jennings (born circa 1924) & Elizabeth Jennings (1926–2001). The two daughters of Dr. H. C. (Henry Cecil) & Madge Jennings, family friends of the Tolkiens who attended the same church. Born in Boston (Lincolnshire, not Massachusetts), the Jennings sisters moved to Oxford with their parents in December 1932/January 1933 when their father became Medical Officer of Health and School Medicine for the County of Oxford, a post which he held for many years. Aileen Jennings, the older sister, may possibly be the 'girl of 12–13' to whom Tolkien referred as having read *The Hobbit* before its submission to Allen & Unwin (*Letters*, page 21).

While Aileen's interests lay in medicine and science, Elizabeth, the younger sister, became a librarian and also a fairly well-known poet who published more than two dozen collections of her poetry. She was associated with 'The Movement', a loose group of poets contemporary with, and sharing some of the same members as, the 'Angry Young Men' of the early 1950s (e.g., Kingsley Amis and Inkling John Wain); they are remembered today primarily for including among their number the poet Philip Larkin. After her death, she was commemorated in her hometown by having a street named after her in north Oxford, 'Elizabeth Jennings Way' in Summertown (not far from Wolvercote Cemetery, where Tolkien is buried).

Aunt Mabel: Mabel Tolkien Mitton, circa 1858–1937, sister of Tolkien's father Arthur. According to Scull & Hammond, the Mittons remained in the Moseley area outside Birmingham (*Companion & Guide* Vol II, page 1009). It is not clear whether Mabel Mitton died before being sent her copy of the book; her sister Florence (see below) complains in her letter to JRRT early the next year that Mabel's death delayed her learning of the book's existence ('I . . . felt if Aunt Mabel had been alive she would have sent it to me'—MS. Tolkien 21, folio 120).

Aunt Florence: Florence Tolkien Hadley, circa 1863–?? [death date unknown], sister of Tolkien's father Arthur. Having immigrated to Canada, she did not learn of the book's existence until early the next year; her letter from Victoria, British Columbia, dated 13th February 1938 and thanking Tolkien and Edith on behalf of herself and her daughter Midge, is now in the Bodleian (MS. Tolkien 21, folio 120).

Note that although she is not included in either list, Tolkien also seems to have sent a copy to his third surviving Tolkien aunt, Grace Tolkien Mountain (born circa 1861, death date unknown); her postcard from Newcastle-on-Tyne is also in the Bodleian (MS. Tolkien 21, folio 88); furthermore, in her letter (folio 120) Florence Hadley mentions 'writ[ing to] Aunt Grace for particulars' about the book after she had heard about its existence from a friend.

Wrenn: C. L. (Charles Leslie) Wrenn, 1895–1969. Fellow Inkling and colleague of Tolkien's in teaching medieval language and literature at Oxford. Previously a lecturer at Leeds (1928–1930), though after Tolkien's time there, at the time of *The Hobbit*'s writing and publication he was University Lecturer in English Language at Oxford (1930–1939). Ultimately, after several years at the University of London, he returned to Oxford, where he succeeded to Tolkien's chair as Rawlinson and Bosworth Professor of Anglo-Saxon in 1946. The Wrenns (Charles, Agnes, and their daughter Carola) and Tolkien family were close enough to vacation together at Lamorna Cove near Land's End in Cornwall in the summer of 1932, an occasion from which the character 'Gaffer Gamgee' entered the family's private mythology, having a cameo in *Mr. Bliss* not long after; a photograph from this vacation appears in the *Family Album*, page 62. When Elaine Griffiths proved unable to complete the revision of the Clark Hall *Beowulf* [circa 1938], Tolkien recommended Wrenn for the project, which he completed in short order; it was published in 1940 with Tolkien's 'Prefatory Remarks', which Wrenn praised as 'the most permanently valuable part of the book' (1950 edition, page vi). In the early to mid-1950s Wrenn is said to have described Tolkien as 'the one man of genius then teaching in the English School' (Scull & Hammond, *Companion & Guide* Vol. II, page 1124), and despite Tolkien's giving Wrenn as an example in 1956 of those fellow academics who disapproved of his writing *The Lord of the Rings* instead of devoting all his time to scholarly work (*Letters of JRRT*, page 238) Wrenn was ultimately co-editor of Tolkien's festschrift, *English and Medieval Studies: Presented to J. R. R. Tolkien on the Occasion of his Seventieth Birthday* [1962]. The Clark Hall collaboration with Tolkien seems to have been his first book; other major works include an edition of *Beowulf* [1953], *An Old English Grammar* (with Randolph Quirk) [1957], and *A Study of Old English Literature* [1967]. For more on Wrenn, see David Bratman's Appendix ('The Inklings: Their Lives and Works') to Diana Pavlac Glyer's *The Company They Keep* [2007], pages 247–8, and the entry in Scull & Hammond's *Companion & Guide* (Vol. II, pages 1123–25).

D'Ardenne: Simone d'Ardenne, 1899–1986; student, family friend, and collaborator of Tolkien's, first on an edition of *The Life and Passion of St. Juliene* [1936], which at Tolkien's insistence appeared only under her name (in order to boost her career), and on an unfinished edition of *Seinte Katerine*, which they proposed to the Early English Text Society in 1936 and later expanded to include *Sawles Warde* as well but ultimately abandoned because of the war and Tolkien's absorption in his fiction (e.g., *The Lord of the Rings*). They did publish several minor articles arising out of the latter project ('"Iþþlen" in *Sawles Warde*' [1947], 'MS. Bodley 34: A Re-Collation of a Collation' [1947–8]). A native Belgian who became Professor of Comparative Grammar at Liège in 1938, d'Ardenne lived with the Tolkien family at Northmoor Road for a year starting in October 1932; she would thus have been a member of the household at the time Tolkien completed *The Hobbit*. In addition to translating Tolkien's *Farmer Giles of Ham* into French [tr. 1937, published 1975], d'Ardenne wrote a warm memoir of Tolkien, 'The Man and the Scholar', that appears in the memorial festschrift *J. R. R. Tolkien: Scholar and Storyteller: Essays in Memoriam*, ed. Mary Salu & Robert T. Farrell [1979], pages 33–7. A photo appears in the *Family Album* (page 68); for more on d'Ardenne, see the account in Scull & Hammond's *Companion & Guide*, Vol. II, pages 202–204.

Helen B: Helen Buckhurst, 1894–1963, a resident student, English language tutor, and Icelandic scholar who had been a Fellow and Tutor at St. Hugh's College, Oxford (1926–1930). Tolkien had been appointed to supervise Buckhurst's thesis, *The Historical Grammar of Old Icelandic*, in December 1927 (Scull & Hammond, *Companion & Guide* Vol. I, page 143), and like so many of his students she became a family friend; she was also a friend of the American medievalist Kemp Malone and his family. An adult convert to Catholicism, in June 1929 she became Priscilla Tolkien's godmother. At the time of *The Hobbit*'s publication she was teaching at Loreto College in St. Albans, Hertfordshire, a Catholic girls' school founded in 1922; her letter of thanks to 'Dear Ronald', dated 23rd September [1937], praises *The Hobbit* as 'delightful . . . my only complaint is that there are not more illustrations. I only hope it is the first of many such books' (MS. Tolkien 21, folio 117). See page 110 and *The Annotated Hobbit* for a discussion of her paper on 'Icelandic Folklore' and the belief that trolls turn to stone in daylight (DAA.80–82).

Aunt Jane: Jane Suffield Neave, 1872–1963, the younger sister of Tolkien's mother Mabel, whose farm in Worcestershire provided the name 'Bag-End' for Bilbo's home (Carpenter, *Tolkien: A Biography*, page 106). As a teacher who was both college-educated, receiving a Bachelor of Science in 1895, and at one point warden of a women's college in St. Andrews Scotland (circa 1911), she not only helped tutor him as a child (*Letters*, page 377) but might have helped inspire his lifelong interest in women's education; he wrote of her in 1961: 'The professional aunt is a fairly recent development, perhaps; but I was fortunate in having an early example: one of the first women to take a science degree. She is now ninety, but only a few years ago went botanizing in Switzerland' (*Letters*, page 308). Jane Neave was among the party of eight who had toured Switzerland with Tolkien in the summer of 1911, the trip which inspired some incidents and scenery in both *The Hobbit* and *The Lord of the Rings*. During the War years and afterwards she lived (sometimes with Tolkien's brother Hilary) on farms in Nottinghamshire (circa 1914) and Worcestershire (circa 1923); in later life she lived near Evesham (outside Birmingham) and in Wales. In 1961 Tolkien prepared the poetry collection *The Adventures of Tom Bombadil* [1962] in response to her request that he 'get out a small book . . . that we old 'uns can afford to buy for Christmas presents' (Carpenter, *Tolkien: A Biography*, page 244). At the time of *The Hobbit*'s publication she was still living on the farm in Worcestershire, but because of her having changed its name she did not receive her copy until early October, after Tolkien had obtained her current address from Hilary. Her letter of 1st October [1937] asking about the book and her letter-card of 9th October 1937 expressing her delight in it ('It is marvellous. I had to stop reading it in the bus this morning because I laughed so much I feared I might be seized as an inebriate or needing other asylum. The origin of Golf finished me.') and calling it 'a great joy' are now in the Bodleian (MS. Tolkien 21, folios 125 & 126). For more on Jane Neave, see Scull & Hammond, *Companion & Guide*, Vol. II, pages 637–8, and Andrew H. Morton's two little books, *Tolkien's Gedling–1914* [2008, with John Hayes] and *Tolkien's Bag End* [2009].

Rattenbury: a colleague of Tolkien's, probably R. M. (Robert Mantle) Rattenbury, 1901–1970, a noted classical scholar who was for many years Lecturer in Classics at the University of Cambridge and later Senior Tutor at Trinity College, Cambridge. Longtime editor of the *Classical Review*, in addition to having contributed a chapter on 'Romance: Traces of Lost Greek Novels' to *New Chapters in the History of Greek Literature*, Third Series, ed. J. U. Powell [1933], he is best known for having published, with T. W. Lumb, what was for many years the standard edition of the *Aethiopica* of Heliodorus, a third- or fourth-century Greek romance [three volumes: 1935, 1938, & 1943]. Aside from his appearance on this list, his only known connections with Tolkien are having been an Assistant Lecturer in Classics at the University of Leeds from 1924 to 1927, thus overlapping with Tolkien's final two years there, and also being a friend of E. V. Gordon.

Livesleys or Livesey: friends of the Tolkien family, probably the Mr. & Mrs. Livesey who, along with their son Edgar, then a teenager, ran a guest house called 'Aurora' in Sidmouth on the Devonshire coast, where the Tolkien family stayed during their summer holiday each year between 1934 and 1937 (it is not clear if they also stayed at the Liveseys' during their 1938 visit). See the *Family Album* (pages 64–5) for a description of these family vacations. Some of the Allen & Unwin correspondence is actually sent from or to 'Aurora', such as Tolkien's letter to Furth on 13th August 1937, in which he notes 'I shall be at above address until Sat. Aug 21', and Furth's reply of 16th August 1937 (Allen & Unwin archives).

A H Smith: A. H. (Hugh) Smith, 1903–1967, a student of Tolkien's at Leeds who married another of Tolkien's Leeds students, Helen Tomlinson. After teaching in Birmingham and Upsalla, in 1930 he joined the English faculty at University College, London, first as Reader and later Lecturer in English, ultimately (after a hiatus of several years doing intelligence work during the War, for which he was decorated) succeeding R. W. Chambers as the Quain Professor in English (in 1949). A specialist in the study of place-name origins from the time of his Ph.D. thesis at Leeds (1926, published in 1928 as *The Place-names of the North Riding* [Yorkshire], with an acknowledgment to Tolkien for his encouragement and philological help), he published many more volumes on the subject covering Yorkshire's East Riding and York itself [1937], Yorkshire's West Riding [1961–63], Gloucestershire [1964–65], and Westmorland [1967], as well as *English Place-Name Elements* [1955], ultimately becoming Director of the English Place-Name Society [1951]. Other significant publications include assisting in the English translation of Erling Monsen's edition of Snorri Sturluson's *Heimskringla: The Lives of the Norse Kings* [1932], an edition of the earliest surviving manuscript of the Anglo-Saxon Chronicle (*The Parker Chronicle* [1935]), and helping to launch Methuen's Old English Library [1933ff]. Smith's interest in printing led him to build an Elizabethan-style hand press which he used to teach students how books like Shakespeare's quartos were made; each seminar created its own little booklet as a class project. The second book thus printed was Tolkien's *Songs for the Philologists* [1936], for which Smith apparently rewrote several of Tolkien's Leeds-era originals.

J. Grove: 'Aunt' Jennie Grove, 1864–1938, a cousin of Tolkien's wife Edith. Jennie Grove lived with Edith Bratt and her mother Francis until the latter's death in 1903, when Edith was sent to a boarding school. She and Edith resumed living together upon Edith's engagement to Tolkien in 1913 and she continued to live with Edith, JRRT, and later young John Tolkien as well until the family's move to Leeds in 1921. She often returned at Christmastime in later years, having become 'a substitute mother to Edith and the nearest thing her four children had to a grandmother' (*Family Album*, page 36; her photograph appears on the same page). Her letter of thanks, dated 23-9-37 (i.e., 23rd September), expressing how 'I am more than delighted with your lovely book . . . you clever old thing, I don't know how you do it', is now in the Bodleian (MS. Tolkien 21, folios 122–4).

S. Mills: Stella M. Mills, 1903–1989, a research student who became a friend of the family. Another of Tolkien's students from his Leeds days, like Tolkien she worked at one time on the *OED* (*Oxford English Dictionary*) under C. T.

Onions, who completed the original edition of the *OED* in 1933. Her major academic work was a translation of *The Saga of Hrolf Kraki* [1933] – the same work which probably inspired the figure of Beorn Medwed; see the commentary on Chapter VII – which appeared with an introduction by E. V. Gordon (who supervised the work); Mills dedicated the volume to JRRT, EVG, and Onions. According to Scull & Hammond's *Companion & Guide*, she later joined the staff of St Joseph's Catholic Primary School in Oxford (*C&G*, Vol. II, page 590). Mills' copy of *The Hobbit* recently surfaced in a rare book dealer's catalogue; although extravagantly rebound, it still includes Tolkien's inscription: 'Stella Mills/from her old friend/J. R. R. Tolkien'.

WR Childe: W. R. (Wilfred Roland) Childe, 1890–1952, a colleague of Tolkien's at Leeds from 1922 onwards as Lecturer on the 'Lit' (literature) side of the English School (as opposed to Tolkien's own 'Lang' or language side). Godfather to Tolkien's youngest son, Christopher. He was best known as a poet, one of the Georgian Poets – indeed, the compiler of the online index to the *Oxford Poetry* series describes him as 'almost too Georgian to be true' (http://www.gnelson.demon.co.uk/oxpoetry/index/ic.html).

Among his books of poetry are *The Little City* [1911], *The Happy Garden* [n.d.], *The Gothic Rose* [1922], *The Hills of Morning* [1923], *Ivory Palaces* [1925], and *Selected Poems* [1936]; he was also either a contributor or co-editor of *Oxford Poetry* for all the volumes between 1910 and 1919, except for 1914 and 1915 (the volume in which Tolkien's own 'Goblin Feet' appeared), contributing pieces such as 'The Fairy Land of Shipscar', 'The Lost Abbot of Gloucester', and 'Sea Fairy'. Tolkien noted in his request for Childe to be sent a copy of *The Hobbit* that Childe 'is an old personal friend. He is specially interested in elves and related creatures. He was (once at any rate) a fairly well-known poet, and is still a good one' (JRRT to A&U, 7th September 1937; A&U archive). In the same letter, Tolkien also notes that Childe 'saw the MS and is well disposed' – i.e., that he read the manuscript of *The Hobbit* before its publication. This is confirmed by Childe's letter of thanks on 27th September 1937, in which he notes 'It is a great pleasure to have it and I shall certainly read it again . . . I wish it all possible success, – which it fully deserves.' (MS. Tolkien 21, folio 41). He follows this up with a postcard (dated 9-10-1937; i.e., 9th October) congratulating Tolkien on the reviews in the *Times* and *Times Literary Supplement* (ibid.).

Second Column

Ox Mag: *The Oxford Magazine*, a local university-focused journal which published Tolkien's article 'The Oxford English School' in 1930 and no less than seven of his poems in the following years: 'Progress in Bimble Town' [1931], 'Errantry' [1933], 'Looney' (= 'The Sea Bell') and 'The Adventures of Tom Bombadil' [both 1934], and 'The Dragon's Visit', 'Knocking at the Door' (= 'The Mewlips'), and 'Iumonna Gold Galdre Bewunden' (= 'The Hoard') [on 4th February, 18th February, & 4th March 1937, respectively]. On 28th May 1937 in a letter to Charles Furth regarding publicity and the release date for the forthcoming book, Tolkien writes of getting 'my friend the editor of the O.U. Magazine, who has been giving it a good dose of my dragon-lore recently, to . . . get a review at the beginning of the autumn term'. On 1st June, Furth writes that they are sending advance copies to both C. S. Lewis (see above) and 'the Editor of "The Oxford University Magazine"'; on 8th July he elaborates that these are 'unbound advance copies for their convenience . . . They will of course both receive proper review copies as well in due course'. In his reply, Tolkien provided the editor's name (R[ussell] Meiggs) and address (Keble College), and an annotation in the margin on this letter by someone at Allen & Unwin indicates that Meigg's copy was 'Sent 14/7' (i.e., 14th July). Meiggs' undated letter in response, so enthusiastic that Tolkien passed it along to Furth (cf. *Letters*, page 20), was a self-described 'uninvited testimonial', declaring that the book should be 'pushed to save children from the sentimental saccharine that is so often foisted on them' and declaring that 'it solves the Christmas problem for a large number of god-children and it will increase my prestige with my sister's youngest, who is a discriminating . . . public.' (MS. Tolkien 21, folio 24).

Russell Meiggs, 1902–1989, was a Classicist; a 'Greats' tutor apparently at Keble at the time of *The Hobbit*'s publication, who in 1939 became Fellow and Tutor in Ancient History at Balliol (1939–1970), adding to this the post of Prefect of Holywell Manor (a residence hall at Balliol) from 1945 to 1969. He is mainly known for his work on the ancient port of Rome, Ostia, at the mouth of the Tiber (*Roman Ostia* [1960]), though he also published on *The Athenian Empire* [1972], *Trees and Timber in the Ancient Mediterranean* [1982], and updated J. B. Bury's *A History of Greece to the Death of Alexander the Great* [1900; rev. ed. 1978].

Book Soc.: possibly the group more formally known as the Society of Bookmen, a club founded by the novelist Hugh Walpole in 1921 (and still thriving today), drawing its membership from literary and publishing folk. Its stated purpose was to encourage 'authors, printers, publishers, binders, or salesmen to get together in the interests of their trade'. Membership is by personal invitation, for life, and was originally limited to seventy-five. It has been said that 'nearly every important book trade issue in the last half century had its first airing at a meeting of the Society' (*The Society of Bookmen: An Informal History, 1921–1984*); Stanley Unwin called it 'a small but representative body whose one and only object is the advancement of the knowledge and appreciation of good literature' (*The Truth About Publishing* [6th edition, 1950], page 260).

Tolkien wrote to Charles Furth on 13th August 1937 that 'The Book Society enquiry was due to the kindness of George Gordon (P[resident] of Magdalen), who acted with great promptness' and asked that they send Gordon a personal copy, since Tolkien's own spare copy he had loaned to Gordon 'has been carried off by some member of the party'; this suggests that Gordon had been championing *The Hobbit* at the group's most recent meeting. Furth replied on 16th August 1937 that they were not only replacing Tolkien's lost copy but sending Dr. Gordon an advance copy as well and not counting either against Tolkien's author's copies (A&U archive). Hence Tolkien's cancellation of both this and the next entry on the list, and his reminder to himself: 'have'.

GSG: George S. Gordon, 1881–1942, who as head of the English School at Leeds had been instrumental in getting Tolkien his appointment there in 1920. In 1922 he became Merton Professor of English Literature at Oxford, from which post he played a decisive role in getting JRRT elected to the Rawlinson and Bosworth professorship at Oxford in 1925. In 1928 he was elected President of Magdalen College, and at the time of *The Hobbit*'s publication had added to this the Professorship of Poetry (a five-year appointment, from 1933–38); after this (1938) he became Vice-Chancellor of the University as well. More a 'man of letters' in the mode of earlier figures, like Leslie Stephen and Edmund Gosse, than a scholar in the modern academic sense, Gordon's essays (collected into such volumes as *Companionable Books* [1925] and *The Discipline of Letters* [1946]) cover a wide range of topics, from Pepys to Sterne to Shelley to 'The Trojans in Britain' ([1924], a paean to invented mythic history). His greatest gifts, however, lay in administration: in his memoir of Gordon (*Letters*, pages 56–8) Tolkien called him '*the very master of men*' and stated that 'my. . . first thoughts of him are always of personal gratitude, of a friend rather than of an academic figure' who always showed kindness and thoughtfulness towards his subordinates. Gordon was a member of the Kolbítars ('Coal-biters'), a group Tolkien founded in 1926 to read all the major sagas in the original Old Icelandic; he also collaborated with Tolkien on an unfinished edition of Chaucer (*Selections from Chaucer's Poetry and Prose*, a.k.a. 'the Clarendon Chaucer'; cf. Scull & Hammond, *Companion & Guide* Vol. II, pages 153–6). His enthusiasm for *The Hobbit* was well known: cf. Tolkien's letter to Charles Furth on 31st August 1937, where Tolkien notes that 'Professor Gordon has actually read the book (supposed to be a rare event); and assures me that he will recommend it generally and to the Book Society' (*Letters*, page 20).

Hilary: Hilary Tolkien, 1894–1976, Tolkien's brother. Unlike his academically-minded older brother, Hilary was a fruit farmer, with 'a small orchard and market garden' (*Companion & Guide*, Vol. II, page 1017) near Evesham (home, incidently, of a famous Green Dragon pub), about forty miles northwest of Oxford, roughly mid-way between Gloucester and Stratford-upon-Avon. His letter of thanks to 'Dear R', dated 24th September 1937, is now in the Bodleian; in it he invites his brother's family for a visit and thanks JRRT for 'the most delightful present of the Hobbit. . . I should have written before but I have been simply devouring your book. . . my great sorrow is that there seems no picture of Bilbo Baggins or the Gollum. . . when the fame of your Hobbit has spread I feel sure others will want to see what he was like . . . I wish your book every success . . . as soon as I have read it all I shall read it to Gabriel [Hilary's oldest son, then aged six] who is always to be found peeping into it in the early morning' (MS. Tolkien 21, folios 127–8). For more on Hilary, see Carpenter's *Tolkien: A Biography*, the *Family Album*, Scull & Hammond's *Companion & Guide*, Vol. II, pages 1016–1017, Andrew H. Morton's *Tolkien's Gedling–1914*, and the brief biography in the back of *Black & White Ogre Country*, ed. Angela Gardner [2009].

From the surviving evidence we can say that Tolkien presented the book to colleagues, former students, and collaborators (three categories with considerable overlap in his case), as well as relatives and family friends. This of course is not a complete listing of everyone to whom Tolkien gave copies of *The Hobbit* – for example, he sent a copy to Mrs. Ruth Smith (*Companion & Guide* Vol. II, page 942), the mother of Tolkien's childhood friend and fellow TCBS member G. B. Smith [died 1916], whose poems Tolkien had edited as *A Spring Harvest* [1918], although so far as we know he did not do so to his former headmaster R. C. Gilson [died 1939], father of Rob Gilson [died 1916], Tolkien's other close friend and fellow TCBS member killed in the War; nor to Christopher Wiseman, the sole other survivor with Tolkien of the TCBS; nor to his former teacher R. W. 'Dickie' Reynolds [died 1948], for whom Tolkien had written 'The Sketch of the Mythology' in 1926. Father Francis would undoubtedly have been included had he not died about a year and a half before, in 1935. Nor, aside from Lewis and Wrenn (both fellow medievalists), did any other member of the Inklings make the list, although we know *The Hobbit* was read to the group (probably upon completion of the typescript in the early autumn of 1936) and they would figure prominently in the creation of its sequel.

We should also note that this listing does not include those who were given copies of the Houghton Mifflin edition when it came out early the following year, which seem to have gone mainly to fellow academics and medievalists in America and Canada such as Francis Magoun of Harvard and Kemp Malone of Johns Hopkins. Magoun's letter of thanks, dated 6th June 1938, is now in the Bodleian (MS. Tolkien 21, folios 83–4); in it he mentions having seen the illustrations in Oxford the summer of the year before, suggesting that Tolkien showed them to him during a visit. After praising the book as a mix of Kipling and Carroll, he goes on to say 'I hope you will do another or others before the children get too old or not old enough. The youngest daughter is just a year, so you have time!'

Addendum

THE SEVENTH PHASE

The following material, found by Christopher Tolkien tucked into one of his father's copies of the second edition of *The Hobbit* (the sixth printing of 1954), was discovered too late to be incorporated into the original edition of this book. But because of its great interest in demonstrating how vividly Tolkien visualized each scene, because it provides details nowhere else available, and because most of it seems to belong to a 'Seventh Phase' and thus represents Tolkien's last bout of work on the book, I have added it here.

The material in question consists of eighteen pages, written at various times but mostly dating from circa 1965–66, to which I have given the designator Ad.Ms.H.S.xx—that is, **Ad**ditional **M**anuscripts **H**obbit **S**upplemental, page xx. The bulk of this material is concerned with the runes used in *The Hobbit*: Tolkien provides several charts that would enable readers to decipher the various writing systems found on the book's maps and in the illustration of Smaug on his hoard ('Conversation with Smaug'; see Plate XI), as well as several more drafts of Bilbo's Contract in different styles and notes on dwarven modes of writing, punctuation, the representation of numbers in tengwar, and so forth. Only some of this material is included below, since its full presentation and analysis belongs rather to a study of the evolution of Tolkien's writing systems such as that being carried out by Arden Smith in the ongoing periodic journal *Parma Eldalamberon*. Also included in these miscellaneous draftings, and presented in full below, are a timeline of events from the opening of the Secret Door to Thorin and Bard's parley, a detailed description of the terrain immediately outside the Lonely Mountain's Front Gate, Tolkien's responses to two queries regarding proposed changes to the text, and a descriptive list of all the dwarves with their characteristic colours. Taken all together, these represent Tolkien's final sustained work on the book.

(i)
Timeline of Events

This timeline fills the bottom half, top margin, and long left margin of a single page [Ad.Ms.H.S.8]. Immediately following upon Tolkien's detailed description of the area around the Lonely Mountain's Front Gate (see Part ii: Notes on a Parley, below), it gives a day-by-day account of the events during the busy fortnight following Thorin & Company's discovery of the Secret Door.

As before, doubtful words are indicated by french brackets < > while illegible passages are represented by open elipses (. . .).

Day **Event**[TN1]

1 Discovery of door,[TN2] day 1. sunset. B's [*added*: first] converse[TN3] with Smaug [> steals cup] evening/night. Smaug comes out. Company take refuge inside tunnel. S. hunts ponies.

2 Noon. Bilbo visits Smaug, returns late afternoon. Evening <company> . . . <the> tunnel.[TN4] Night S. smashes the door and goes off to Lake Town.

2 night. Smaug destroys Lake Town, but is slain by Bard. Night spent in tunnel.

3 Bard sends messages to Elvenking. [*cancelled*: But he has already <been informed> of D's death and Bard's <?men> find him already moving an army towards the L. Mountain <5th> day[TN5]] Dwarves explore Smaug's Hall.

4 Dwarves come out Front Gate near noon. The[y] proceed towards Ravenhill "5 hrs march" p. 254[TN6] They sleep in guardsroom on Ravenhill. They see gathering of birds.[TN7]

5 Bard's messengers meet the Elvenking already on the move with his host towards the L. Mountain. The EK. turns <?south> towards Lake-town. Dwarves <see> even more birds. Roac son of Carc tells them the news (Smaug's death 3 nights ago at moon-rise). Roâc [is sent >] is bidden to send messages to Dain. Dwarves return to the Mt.

6

7 Elfhost reaches Lake Town.

8 ?Fili & Kili sent out to bring back stores.

9

10

11 <head> of the <allied> host reaches the 'rock gates'[TN8] where the river flowed into north end of Long Lake. F & K return and report approach of allies.

[Note: The entries for the following days are written in the left margin.]

[12]

[13] "Then came a night"[TN9] pm day 13 when the Dwarves saw the lights of the host away <South> [> East] in Dale.

14 <the allies> move camp <nearer> and crossed old road. Scouts of Men & elves approach Gate . . . <spread> on either side of <M>.[TN10]

15 Bard and Thorin parley. . . .[TN11]

This brief timeline is self-explanatory; in it, Tolkien details the events of the fifteen days between the discovery of the Secret Door and the beginning of the Siege of the Mountain. Had Tolkien continued it, it would no doubt have extended to include the Battle of Five Armies, the death of Thorin, Bilbo's departure, and perhaps even some highlights from his return journey. Combined with the 1960 Hobbit material given in 'Timelines and Itinerary', especially parts ii, iii, and iv, we see how, although in fragmentary form and never finalized, a reasonably complete timeline of Bilbo's journey could be constructed. For how this timeline relates to those previous efforts, see in particular Text Note 3 on page 828, which if accepted would equate 'Day 1' above with 19th October.

Text Notes

TN1. I have provided these headers for the sake of clarity.

TN2. The word 'door' here is underlined, and written above it is a D-rune ᛞ, as on Thror's map.

TN3. The word appears to be 'converse' (i.e., 'Bilbo converse with Smaug'), but may be intended for 'conversa[tion]' instead (i.e., 'Bilbo's first conversation with Smaug').

TN4. Of the two illegible words represented here by the ellipses, the first ends in '-ts' and the second might be either 'open' or 'again'.

TN5. This cancelled sentence was recast into the entry for the fifth day; see below. The '5' seems to have been written over another letter, which cannot now be read.

TN6. The reference is to Balin's comment near the end of Chapter XIII: 'Not at Home' in the second edition, where he mentions

'. . . the old look-out post at the South-West corner of the Mountain.'

'How far is that?' asked the hobbit.

'Five hours march, I should think. It will be rough going . . .'

—second edition, page 254; cf. DAA.299

TN7. The sequence of these last two sentences is reversed, so as to read 'They see gathering of birds. They sleep in guardsroom on Ravenhill', which more accurately represents the sequence of events in the story.

TN8. The allusion is to the last line of Chapter XIV: 'Fire and Water' in the published book: 'It was thus that in eleven days from the ruin of the town the head of their host passed the rock-gates at the end of the lake and came into the desolate lands.' See DAA.313.

TN9. The reference is to a passage in the middle of Chapter XV: 'The Gathering of Clouds':

"There came a night when suddenly there were many lights as of fires and torches away south in Dale before them.

" 'They have come!' called Balin. 'And their camp is very great . . .' " (DAA.320).

TN10. The illegible passage here consists of roughly three words, the last of which has been replaced by an equally illegible word. In any case, the allusion is to the human and elven host taking up siege quarters in the valley outside the Front Gate. In the original published book the relevant passage read 'That day the camp was moved and was brought right between the arms of the Mountain'; in the 1966 Longmans/Unwin edition – the edition with which this 'Seventh Phase' is associated – that line was changed to read 'That day the camp was moved *to the east side of the river*, right between the arms of the Mountain' (DAA.320; emphasis mine).

TN11. The second half of this entry, consisting of four or five words, is unfortunately illegible to me. The second word is perhaps *days*, and the final word seems to begin with *st-* and ends in an ascender followed by a descender, but I cannot make out the sense of the passage. The relevant section of the text is the account of Thorin's parley with Bard at the end of Chapter XV: 'The Gathering of Clouds', ending in his total rejection of Bard's terms and the beginning of the Siege; cf. DAA.322–4.

(ii)
Notes on a Parley

The following account [Ad.Ms.H.S.6–8], to which I have given the name 'Notes on a Parley', provides an example of Tolkien's endless creativity, his ability to expand upon practically any point in his legendarium—in this case, turning his attention to the exact lay-out of the area immediately below the siege-wall Thorin & Company constructed blocking the Front Gate.

At the top of the first of these three pages (numbered '1', '2', '3' by Tolkien in the margin of each page) Tolkien has scrawled

<u>Hobbit</u>

Arrangement at the Lonely Mt. dwarfroads
and <approachments>   Time-table of Events
from discovery of secret ᛞ door

Immediately below this come two lines of runes:

which, when transliterated, read

This school edition is published
by Longmans Green and company

This shows that this material clearly dates from the period (June–September & November–December 1965) when Tolkien was working on the 1966 Longmans School Edition/Unwin Books (trade paperback) edition of *The Hobbit*, since that edition did indeed include some changes to the descriptions of areas in the vale of Dale; cf. Hammond *Descriptive Bibliography* page 37; DAA.300, 319, & 320. It seems likely that Tolkien wrote out the account which follows to clarify the lay-out of the area in his own mind, rather than for possible inclusion in the book.

According to my visualization of the scene (which was and remains clear) the parleys between the allies and the dwarves took place on a ledge at about the level [*added*: and to the right] of the top of the new defence-wall across the gate, where Bilbo and the Dwarves stood. The picture (+214)[TN1] was meant to fit that, but the later [*added*: defence] works were not shown, since <it> was a picture of what the [scouts saw as >] dwarf-scouts saw as they first approached the Front Gate from outside. ((There is <thus> nothing in the picture to show how Bilbo, when evicted and 'swung down' reached Gandalf and the other emissaries. I think there was a narrow ledge outside the wall above the culvert made for the issue of the stream; at its right (West) it ran towards the new path upon the bottom 'ledge' shown in the picture 214 but left a gap bridge[d] temporarily by a wooden gangway.))[TN2]

The old road had run on the other left (east) side, where in the picture there is a slope of boulders projecting into the stream. The course for some distance from the Gate had been destroyed, and left a slope of boulders, by the Dragon. It had gone on (and still did so further on) down into the valley along the east-bank of the river, and so on away from the Mountain, eastwards towards the Iron Hills. To reach the old town of Dale (of which now only a few ruins remained) a road branched off westward to a place where at [a] <stony> shallow at the beginning of the great eastward bend of the stream there was [> had been] a bridge. At the western end of the bridge a road went east <to> Dale west towards Ravenhill, and south <to the> river[,] along the bank (left) of which it turned[,] passed under the feet of Ravenhill[,] and went away South again towards Long Lake. ((The bridge should be marked \\ as in my . . . copy))[TN3] The "allies"[TN4] moved up along both sides of the river (p. 272), but before long [*written above this*: next day] their camp and main force (272) was made east of the river to command the old outward road—[*cancelled*: <the other>] approach from the east at any <?other> point needed to cross the river. But the Ford by the ruined bridge was also guarded by Elves (see p. 280).[TN5]

The Dwarves did not 'remake' or reopen the ruined stretch of the old road, because they had not time; and what they for the moment needed was a way out for [*cancelled*: themselves >] <any> of their own number sent [*cancelled*: out] on an errand or scouting. They thus cleared and levelled a space at the end of the lower shelf on the west cliff (to their right), which was at about the height of the top of their new wall across the mouth of the Gate. (They expected parleys to take place) From that they had <hurriedly> cleared away some of the obstuctions along the ledge so that a dwarf (or hobbit) on foot could proceed along it. How far? Evidently not all the way to Ravenhill and then down the steps and path from it into the valley:[TN6] <For> Bilbo had only 5 hours in all, and in the dark he could not have got to the camp even in that time. There must have been some way down from the ledge into the valley (see p 280),[TN7] allowing B. <room> to get back to the stream, and so come to the Ford—which [he] would <now> have to cross <the> <?other> way—eastward to go [> get] to the camp. It is probable that the ledge was <partly> artificial made <in> the old days, where people could walk. And guards be posted <?surveying> the valley: and no doubt between the Gate and Ravenhill there were several ways down from the ledge to the valley (though narrow and easily defended). This fits description of battle in which Elves were evidently posted along the ledge as well as on the tops of the ridge of the 'Southern Spur' (eg the one ending in Ravenhill.) but were all to get down to attack enemies in the valley.

Dain naturally approached the Mountain by the old road from the east. It was a weak point in the dwarves' plan that, for outside help to reach them, Dain would have to force the pass between the river and east cliff, and then cross the river by the Ford and so come to the gate along the narrow ledge, where his 500 would be strung out in a line. But the plan was made by Thorin, while he still hoped that Dain would arrive before the 'allies' arrived or had occupied Dale. (He probably also did not suppose that in any case anyone would try to stop Dain, or attack himself. He was very conscious of his rights [> dignity] as lawful 'K. under the Mountain', and convinced of the justice of his position and his 'right' to deal out his treasure at his own free will and <estimate>.

Note: The expedition to Ravenhill [made bef[ore] >] was made on the day of the Dwarves' emergence from the F. Gate. <?took>. . . 5 hours.[TN8] <it went> by old road.

> The text ends here, in the middle of the third page [Ad.Ms.H.S.8], with the Timeline given above crowded onto the rest of this page. In keeping with his preferred role as chronicler of feigned history, it is notable how Tolkien carefully combs through the existing text for clues about the geographical feature he is describing, even citing specific page references, rather than simply re-writing the passage to reflect his new visualization of the scene.

Text Notes

TN1. This is the picture 'The Front Gate' (DAA.256; H-S#130), which appeared on page 214 of the second edition *Hobbit*, near the beginning of Chapter XI.

TN2. These two sentences, which I have enclosed in double parentheses, are bracketed by Tolkien. A final cancelled word, 'which', originally followed 'gangway'.

TN3. This sentence is enclosed in brackets. The single illegible word before 'copy' might be 'control'; in any case, Tolkien is referring to a master copy or check copy of *The Hobbit* in which he has entered all the changes and corrections he has made to the second edition text.

TN4. We might also note in passing that 'allies', the designator he applies several times to the forces opposed to Thorin & Company, is a loaded term for any veteran of the Great War and survivor of the Second World War, wherein the Allies (England, France, the US, etc.) fought the Central Powers and the Axis, respectively.

TN5. This is an allusion to Bilbo's encountering, and being captured by, elven look-outs when crossing the stream on his self-appointed emissary to Bard and the Elvenking (DAA.328).

TN6. Written in the left margin opposite this line is the notation 'Sc. 255'. This is a reference to the description of this terrain on page 255 of the second edition (corresponding to DAA.300).

TN7. This is another allusion to the passage already referred to in Text Note 5, specifically, 'It was very dark, and the road after a while, when *he left the newly made path and climbed down* towards the lower course of the stream, was strange to him. At last he came to the bend where he had to cross the water . . . The bed of the stream was there shallow but already broad, and fording it in the dark was not easy for the little hobbit. He was nearly across when he missed his footing on a round stone and fell into the cold water with a splash . . .' (DAA.328; italics mine). For an account of the construction of this new path, see DAA.319.

TN8. I cannot read the cancelled word or phrase preceding '5 hours'.

(iii)
Responses to Queries

These two brief pieces were apparently written in response to queries on specific points by a typesetter or proofreader at the printer. Both are found on the same sheet [Ms.Ad.H.S.9] and, Christopher Tolkien notes, 'typed on the back of a page from an engagement calendar for 16–22 August 1964'.

For the first query, the passage in question comes from the last sentence of the fourth paragraph of Chapter V: 'Riddles in the Dark'. Groping around for matches, Bilbo's hand 'came on the hilt of his little sword – the little dagger that he got from the trolls, and that he had quite forgotten; *nor do the goblins seem to have noticed it*, as he wore it inside his breeches.' (1st ed., page 81; italics mine). Christopher Tolkien also notes that, in the copy of *The Hobbit* in which these notes were discovered, the relevant passage is changed to 'nor fortunately had the goblins noticed it', the reading which appears in the Unwin

Books edition (page 64) and subsequent editions (cf. DAA.116). The following reponse shows Tolkien's rationale for the change, and reveals how carefully considered his revisions could be.

Queries, p. 64 (former [page] 81)
[*added in pencil*: p. 80 in 3rd ed.]

(a) seem. where the estimate of probability is made by the narrator with reference to a past event seem remains in the present followed by a past infinitive, as in text. Did seem would transfer the estimate to Bilbo.[TN1] I do not think he had time for anything more than relief at feeling the hilt.

Do seem was evidently intended as a remark 'narrator to audience', a tiresome trick of which the author was too fond; I have got rid of some of the cases. For that reason (and not for idiom) I propose the emendation:

nor fortunately had the goblins noticed it.

This should fit the available space.

This second query relates to the sixth paragraph of the same chapter, and Bilbo's discovery that his little sword is an elvish blade: 'somehow he was comforted. It was rather splendid to be wearing a blade made in Gondolin for the goblin-wars *of which so many songs had sung*' (1st ed. page 81; Unwin Books page 64; 3rd ed. page 80; DAA.116; italics mine).

(b) songs had sung. I do not understand the point of this query. The text, besides sounding better, is, I think, perfectly correct English.

If the reader would add to my obligation to him for his attentive reading by stating the nature of his doubt, I should be much interested.

Our sweetest songs are those that tell of saddest thought. If Shelley had written sing for tell, the most cavilling critic could have found fault only in the excessive alliteration. Probably it was to avoid this that the poet used tell instead of the obvious and equally correct sing.

As we see, in this second case, Tolkien rejected the suggested emendation and kept the passage as it was. His reasons for doing so, however, are interesting, as is his rather unexpected citation, apparently from memory, of a line from Percy Bysshe Shelley's 'To a Skylark' [1820] in support for his usage. Tolkien's supposed lack of familiarity with postmedieval literature has sometimes been exaggerated to the point of parody, and evidence to the contrary is abundant. For example, in his draft for 'A Secret Vice', his essay about invented languages (available in *The Monsters & the Critics and Other Essays*, pages 198–223), he briefly discusses James Joyce and Gertrude Stein (MS. Tolkien 24, folio 44), while in an unpublished essay on translating alliterative verse he at one point compares the Old English poem 'The Wanderer' to Wordsworth's 'Resolution and Independence' [1807; better known as 'The Leech Gatherer') before comparing the latter in turn to Lewis

Carroll's parody of it, 'Father William' [1865], which he much prefers (Ms. Tolkien A30/1, folio 119). In fact, he was of course familiar with the full range of English literature up to about 1830 (thus including the Romantics), the point at which 'English studies' terminated when he was a student, and had at least a nodding acquaintance with Victorian and, to a lesser extent, contemporary literature.

Text Note

TN1. Presumably the proofreader had suggested that 'nor do the goblins seem' be changed to 'nor *did* the goblins seem', which Tolkien rejects for the reasons stated.

(iv)
Personae

This single page [Ad.Ms.H.S.10], written in Tolkien's neatest calligraphy, holds a list of all the members of Thorin's expedition other than Bilbo himself. Its tone would suggest that this was compiled for the Longmans' 'school edition' in 1965/66, but Tolkien paleographer Arden Smith argues that the handwriting has 'the very distinct look of manuscripts from the 1930s' (personal communication, April 2011). Although almost all the details given here can be gleaned from the text (and most of them from the first chapter), there are a few details that are new, such as the fact that Dori and Nori are brothers and Ori their cousin, the ages of Fili and Kili ('about 50'), and the respective girths of Bifur, Bofur, and Bombur.

Dwarves

Thorin Oakenshield, son of Thror son of Thrain [> son of Thrain son of Thror],[TN1] King under the Mountain. At the time of the story he was at least 200 [> 195] years old. He had a white beard, a sky-blue hood with a silver tassel, a belt of gold and jewels, and a golden chain round his neck.

Fili and Kili, young dwarves (about 50 years old[TN2]), nephews of Thorin. They had yellow beards; their belts were of silver and their hoods were blue.

Balin, oldest of Thorin's companions, who had escaped with him from the Mountain long ago. His beard was white, and his hood red. He was the look-out man.

Dori and Nori, had purple hoods and silver belts. They were brothers.

Ori, was their cousin. He had a grey hood, and a silver belt.

Oin and Gloin were brothers and the fire-makers. Oin wore a brown hood and Gloin a white hood. Both had golden belts. [*added in pencil*: Glóin was father of Gimli of the L.R.[TN3]]

Dwalin was Balin's brother. He had a blue beard, a dark-green hood and golden belt.

Bifur was a large dwarf with a yellow hood.

Bofur his cousin [> brother[TN4]] was even larger. He also had a yellow hood.

Bombur (brother of Bofur) [*added in pencil*: cousin of <Bifur>[TN5]] was the broadest and fattest of the dwarves. He had a pale green hood.

Gandalf the Wizard had a long white beard; he wore a tall blue hat, a grey cloak, and a long silver scarf; he had large black boots.

At some later point,[TN6] Tolkien underlined the word tall in pencil and added a brief (pencilled) note at the bottom of the page about Gandalf's hat:

> a pity, because in fact I never imagined his hat as being 'tall' —only it had a 'crown' rather <?point> with a wide brim.

Two sketchy attempts to depict the hat follow, each with a wide brim and low crown – in fact, very like the hat worn by the *berg-geist* ('mountain-spirit') in Joseph Madlener's postcard (reproduced in *The Annnotated Hobbit* on the bottom of Plate V), except that Madlener's kindly old mountain-spirit's hat has a flat crown while both of the sketches here for Gandalf's hat have pointed crowns. Contrast this with the two pictures Tolkien drew circa 1936–37 showing Gandalf either approaching or standing at the doorway of Bag-End (Plate III), both of which show a tall, pointy hat with a relatively modest brim; the same hat with a somewhat broader brim can be seen in 'The Three Trolls are turned to Stone' (Plate V [top]).

Text Notes

TN1. Here Tolkien originally wrote *son of Thror son of Thrain*, then encircled 'Thrain' in pencil and marked it to be placed where 'Thror' stood in the line. It is remarkable that even at this late date Tolkien either could not remember or still remained undecided about which was the father and which the grandfather, Thror or Thrain. This strongly supports the assumption that the earlier back-and-forth between the names was the result of inattention, not indecision; it seems as if his instinct was to make Thror the father, yet he kept changing this back to Thrain as the father in deference to the 'historicity' of the established genealogy.

TN2. While this seems in keeping with how the youngest members of Thorin & Company are portrayed in *The Hobbit*, it contradicts the information in the genealogical chart in Appendix A of *The Lord of the Rings*, which gives Fili's age as eighty-two and Kili's as seventy-seven. See Text Note 3 on page 477 for more on what constitutes a 'young dwarf'.

TN3. L.R.; i.e., *The Lord of the Rings.*

TN4. The word 'brother' is faintly pencilled above 'cousin'; see Text Note 34 on pages 322–3 for the shifting relationships between Bifur, Bofur, and Bombur throughout the writing of *The Hobbit.* Interestingly enough, the original reading of 'cousin' here is correct, according to the published text, while making Bofur Bifur's brother reverts to an earlier conception which is more in keeping with the tradition of rhyming brother's names (Fili/Kili, Balin/Dwalin, &c.).

TN5. The very faint words 'cousin of <?Bifur>' are pencilled above 'brother of Bofur'; the last word is nearly illegible but can hardly be anything but 'Bifur' in the context; in any case, 'brother of Bofur' seems not to have been cancelled. Unlike the contemplated change recorded in Text Note 4 above, this addition would not have contradicted the published book, which agrees that Bombur and Bofur are brothers and that Bifur is their cousin. See Text Note 34 on pages 322–3 for more on these relationships.

TN6. Arden Smith suggests that this pencilled addition was much later ('clearly decades later' —op cit); I suspect it dates from the Longmans/Unwin period, whatever the date of the list itself.

(v)
Runic Charts

By far the largest proportion of this 'Seventh Phase' material (thirteen pages out of a total of eighteen [Ad.Ms.H.S.1–5 & 11–18]) concerns runes and scripts. In it Tolkien gives multiple drafts of the various rune-systems, followed by two tables of tengwar letters, one arranged in a dwarven mode and the other adapted for use with Modern English.

The first of these charts exists in three variant states [Ad.Ms.H.S.4, Ad.Ms.H.S.3, and Ad.Ms.H.S.1], one of which is labelled

. Futhorc .
A Runic Alphabet.

The 'futhorc' is the name generally given to the Old English runes; like the modern word 'alphabet' (*alpha*, 'a' + *beta*, 'b'), the name is composed of the letters symbolized by the first few runes: f+u+th+o+r+c. Unlike our modern English letters, which derive from Latin, each rune not only stood for a letter but (as Tolkien notes below) had a name which began with that letter; i.e., the name of the ᚦ rune, which stood for 'th', was *thorn.*

[Table I: Dwarven Runes]
[Ad.Ms.H.S.4]

Runes used by Thorin & Co.

First row:	*f*	*u*	*th*	*o*	*r*	*c*	*g*	*w*
	fire	urn	thorn	ox	road	care	gift	wine.
Second row:	*h*	*n*	*i*	*sh*	*x*	*p*	*z*	*s*
	hail	need	ice	shield	axle	pine	zinc	sun.
Third row:	t	b	e	m	l	ng	ee	d
	tongue	birch	elm	man	land	anger	eel	day
Fourth row:	*y*	*ea*	*oo*	*k*	*ch*	*gh*	*oa*	*a* [TN1]
	yew	ear	ooze	kin	child	ghost	oak	ash.

There is no Q. For qu cw is used.[TN2] The letters represented in English by two letters as ea, oa &c. can also be written with two, as for . But are always used for th, ng, ee, oo. In Runes the same letter is rarely written twice running: either once or the letter is dotted. Thus or for 'letter'. is used for i and j and for u and v. The special shapes [added: *joy*] for j and for v[TN3] can be used but are not counted in the alphabet. A letter sometimes used is or = eo, io as in = George. It is counted as a combination of I + O and called 'ice-ox'. The uprights of runes are sometimes joined: as = ME. The spelling of words by Thorin & Co is often phonetic: thus (dor) for door.

Each rune has a name – a word of one syllable, beginning with the sound represented; except in case of where the name has 2 syllables and the sound comes in the middle. Many of these names are trees: thorn, pine, birch, elm, yew, oak, ash.

The text continues onto the verso of the same sheet [Ad.Ms.H.S.5], which presents a second, complementary runic chart.

These runes are very like, but not the same as the Anglo-Saxon Runes. The Anglo-Saxon runes vary a good deal, but were generally like this:

[Table II: The Futhorc]
[Ad.Ms.H.S.5]

f	*u*	*th (þ)*	*o*	*r*	*ċ*	*ġ*	*w*
feoh	úr	þorn	ós	rád	cén	gifu	wyn
h	*n*	*i*	*eo*	*p*	*x*	*s*	*t*
hægl	nied	ís	éoh	peorð	eolhsand	sigel	tír
b	*e*	*m*	*l*	*ng*	*ē*	*d*	*a*
beorc	eh[TN4]	mann	lagu	ing	éþel	dæg	ác
æ	*y*	*io*	*ea*	*c, k*	*st*	*g*	
æsc	ýr	ioh	éar	= c	stán	gar	

The dwarfs[TN5] only used Runes for special purposes. For writing they used the Elvish alphabet — a bit of which may be seen on one of the pots of gold in picture of dragon.[TN6] It is more complicated but looks better. Here is a bit.

The rest of this page is devoted to a tengwar text of Bilbo's Contract; compare this neat copy with the freehand style of that of the Frontispiece.

'Copy of the original of the letter ([translated>] transcribed on p. 39).'[TN7]

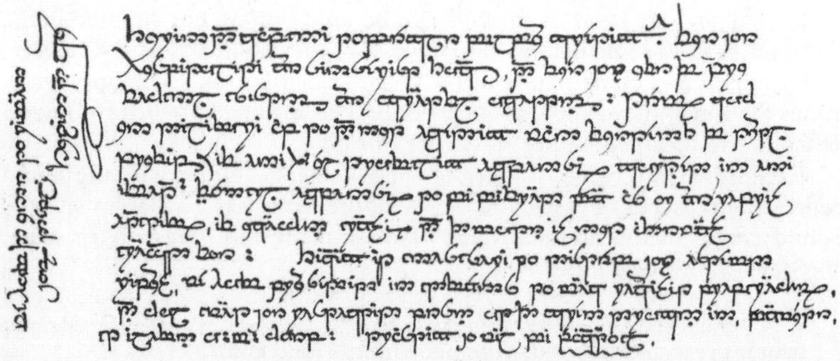

Text Notes

TN1. The last two runes in this line, *oak* and *ash*, are circled in pencil by Tolkien and marked to be moved to the front of this row (the extreme left), which would change the sequence of the Fourth row to *oak*, *ash*, *yew*, *ear*, &c.

TN2. Added above the line in pencil here: 'or quill'.

TN3. At this point Tolkien pencilled a 'v' above the letter but did not complete the word; on one draft of this chart [Ad.Ms.H.S.1] this rune had been identified as 'v. vane'.

TN4. Originally Tolkien wrote two words here, *eoh* and *eh*, as well as two letters above, *eo* and *e*, but in each case he cancelled the first entry (which is already represented by the rune ᛇ in the row above), leaving only *eh* for the rune's name and *e* for its equivalence. As Arden Smith points out (personal communication, April 2011), these are dialectic variants on the same word, with *eh* being the Mercian and *eoh* the West Saxon words for 'horse' (as in the names *Eo*mer and *Eo*wyn). In the two other versions of this chart [Ad. Ms.H.S. 1 & 3], this rune instead represents the word 'elm'. I am grateful to Arden Smith for helping me recover the obliterated readings.

TN5. The usage of aberrant form 'dwarfs' instead of the usual 'dwarves' is Tolkien's.

TN6. Note that this picture was not included in either the Longmans' School Edition nor the Unwin Books trade paperback edition, which would have made this reference rather murky to that audience.

TN7. The transcription appeared on page 39 of the first and second editions, and page 38 of the third edition; in the 1966 Unwin Books edition it was on page 27.

Arden Smith informs me (personal communication, April 2011) that Tolkien's use of the tengwar here in this version of Thorin's Letter bears strong affinities to his usage in the Ransome letters (see Appendix IV); hence it's reasonable to assume that it dates from the same time (December 1937).

(vi)
Fëanorian Letters

Continuing his account of dwarven writing systems, and directly following upon the runic material, Tolkien gives the following account of the dwarven use of elven letters. According to Christopher Tolkien, the first half of what follows [Ad.Ms.H.S.11–14 sequence] is written in blue ink; the second half [Ad.Ms.H.S.15–18], which focuses on using these letters to write modern English, is in black ink.

For books or documents or anything written with pens the better kind of Dwarves (as most other folk of the period) used the running form of the 'Fëanorian' (or Second Elvish) Alphabet.[TN1] As this is a little complicated it was transcribed into our ordinary letters in 'The Hobbit' (though there is a glimpse of it painted on one of the jars in the coloured picture of Smaug's lair).

Here is a copy of the original letter (in Thorin's rather free and bold style) that is transcribed on p. 39.[TN2]

In a more careful way (as in making a book) it would have looked more like this.

The 'book style' tengwar version of Thorin's letter fills rest of this page [Ad.Ms.H.S.11].

Fig 4

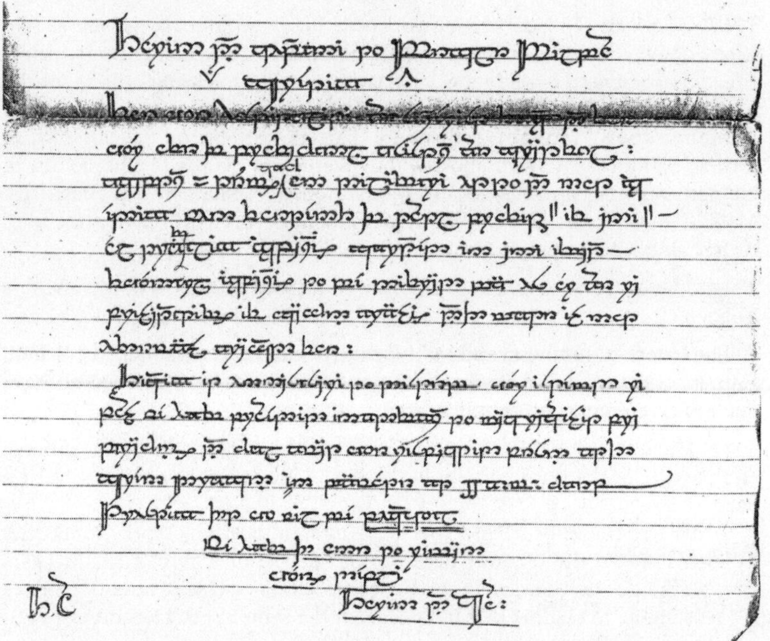

The following chart and its accompanying text takes up the whole of Ad.Ms.H.S.12.

[Table III: The Tengwar (Dwarven Mode)]

[Ad.Ms.H.S.12]

Adaptation of the Feanorian Alphabet as used by Dwarves (and others) for the common or ordinary language: ——

	1.	2.	3.	4.
p-row	*p*	*t*	*ch*	*k*[TN3]
	5	6	7	8
b-row	*b*	*d*	*j*	*g*
f-row	*f*	*th (thin)*	*sh*	*[x]*

v-row	*v*	*th (this)*	*zh (French j)*	*[<yogh>]*
m-row	*m*	*n*	*ñ (ny)*	*ng*
w-row	*w*	*r*	*y*	/
odd-row	*h*	*l*	*r*	*s*
		z.		

The letters 'x' (f-row 4) and '' (v-row 4) which had represented guttural sounds no longer heard in the Common Language, were no longer used. The Dwarves occasionally used for 'h'.

There were originally no vowel-letters[,] the vowels being shown where needed by various marks over or under the consonants: as , , 'tin, tan, bull'. But in writing the common language new letters for vowels were made — but there was a great deal of variation and disagreement about how to use them.

Here is the system used by Thorin (and others).
The letter , being no longer used for a consonant, was used for the vowel a.

= a = o ((before letters of column 4 (etc)))[TN4]
= e = u
= i

The Dwarves, however, as a rule used this alphabet to spell what they said phonetically or (more or less) how they pronounced it. They need not be imitated! But they needed a few more letters.

or for a in 'back'; = a in 'father'.
for u in 'butter'; = u in 'bull'
or a dot underneath for a vague or murmured vowel.
Length of vowel could be marked ´: so = father.
The little r they used when it was not pronounced (so : 'farther'), but when it was: so : merry. This they used like a vowel for er, ir, ur as in fern, third, burst, butter.

There were various other tricks and abbreviations. S was often written or as = ks, x; = 'bats'; and s, z often at the end of a word, as = 'sums'. n or m were usually written ~ above a consonant if one followed:[TN5] as = camp. u or w could similarly be written and i or y as , but in this case they were put over the letter that preceded. As = ai, ay, = au, aw; = kw = qu.

Some common words were shortened (like our &):

so = and; = of; = of the; = the.

To mark Capitals either was written underneath, or the downstroke was doubled: so = I; = D.

For punctuation marks (when any were used) you will find:
as a comma; as a full stop; or as colons (or semicolons).
Exclamations can be marked by before or after or both.
Questions can be marked by before or after or both.
For brackets are used (if anything).

There were no numerals, and if any were required the letters of the alphabet with a dot were used in order except that (which had no other use) = 9, and = 0.

dwarven numerals (Fëanorian)

But the numerals of the older or First Elvish Alphabet were sometimes used

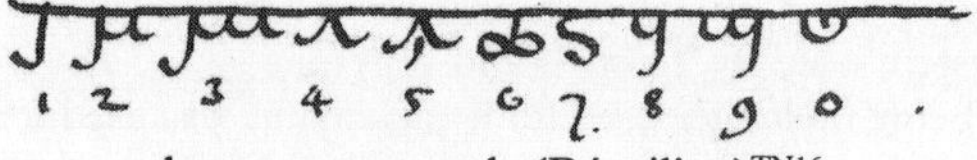

dwarven numerals (Rúmilian)[TN16]

Thorin's letter is very abbreviated and "phonetic" and actually goes like this.

Thorin đ̣ kʌp̄əni tu Bŕglr Bilbow gríting!
Foṛ yuṛ hospitȧliti awr sis̄írist thȧk̄s đ̣ foṛ yúr
ofr v profeshənḷ asistṣ̄ awr grëtful akseptṣ̄. Tŕmz cȧsh on dilivəri
ʌp tu đ̣ not iksíding wʌn foṛtínth v towtḷ profits (if eni) —

and so on. But Bilbo was used to that sort of spelling.

The rest of this page, almost half of Ad.Ms.H.S.14, is left blank.

As noted above, the second half of this material on the use of Elven letters [Ad.Ms.H.S.15–18] is written in black ink. Unlike the preceding material, instead of looking at dwarven usage it focuses on using Fëanorian script for modern English.

[Table IV:] Feanorian applied to English.[TN7]

[Ad.Ms.H.S.15]

p.	*t.*	*tʃ (ch).*	*k.*
b.	*d.*	*dž (j).*	*g.*
f.	*þ(th).*	*ʃ (sh).*	*χ (ch, gh)*
v.	*ð(th).*	*ž (s, z)*	[ ] ʒ
m.	*n.*	*ñ (ni, ny)*	*ŋ (ng)*
w.	*r*	*j (y)*	*ʼ used as vowel: see below.*

Additional Consonantal Signs:

h. l. r. s. z.

is only used where pronunciation is consonantal.

is used where [r] has become vocalic murmur or been absorbed. ar̥ is thus used for [ā] in part. better is spelt . [ə̄] spelt er, ur, ir in E.[nglish] is represented by : as = first.

is [*cancelled*: only] used when followed by w, j [*added*: or prec. by n] as in = swing; [*added*: = dance] [;] = suit; and occasionally when otherwise convenient, esp. finally when an inflexion. In such cases [s] is often reduced to a mere hook , and [z] to . Thus or = once; = dance; but = hats; = roses. is rarely used for . ks = , ps = [,] ts = [.]

A homorganic nasal is usually represented by ‾ above the following consonant = ns, = nt, = nch, = mp, = nk, &c. The sound [j, i̯] is represented usually by above the preceding sound: thus = assume; = tune; = oi̯, = ai̯, = ei̯, &c. The sound [w, u̯] similarly is represented by : as = quick; = au̯ (ou̯), = ou &c. But initially, between vowels, and at the beginning of distinct elements in compounds the full signs [j] and [w] are used. They can be used in all positions.

When n, m, l are vocalic as in button, bottom, bottle they are under-dotted: as , , . The same under-dot or 'vocalic sign' is used occasionally when the vowel in other cases is reduced to a very slight murmur. Thus in quick 'colloquial' writing the reduced atonic pronunciation of such words as at [æt]; of [ov], and [ænd] > ə̣t, ə̣v, n̥d is represented thus:

Note where the nasal over-line is used an under-dot refers to this:

thus: torrent [torṇt] is written

The underdot is also used to mark = [o] as a vowel, when it precedes and sometimes before other letters of this series. Thus = [woʃ] wash, not [wž].

Special abbreviations are = the (for or). = of for . = of the. In colloquial writing the unstressed indefinite article a, an is often written as part of the next word by underdot : thus = a man, an ostrich. Unstressed and is written = ṇd. This in quick writing is often reduced to .

Other rarer abbrev. 'equals' = 'therefore, and so' 'then, next'

Punctuation. Capitals are seldom used. When large initials are required underlining, encircling, or larger writing is used. = John. or or . Brackets ‖ ‖ or . The latter are also often used as quotation marks, when no query or exclamation is involved

Full stop —

Comma not much used; when required

= Tom, the piper[TN8]

Colon

Semicolon

Exclamation } often also placed before in forms

Question } in which case no quotation marks are used.

The vowels.

The old sign originally consonantal is used as [a]

The other vowels are denoted by special signs outside the series, except for vowels developed from [r] which are denoted : see above. is used = [a] in [ai̯] = diphthong in wine; [au̯] = diphthong in town; before ṛ as in [pāt, paṛt] = part; when long as in = father. The sound [æ] is properly denoted (with i-dot), but since this sound is normally defined by position & absence of length the dot is not used much in colloquial writing — esp. not in cases where pronunciation varies between [ā] and [æ] as in [*added above the tengwar in neat ink*: glass]: here neither dot nor length-sign are usual.

The mark of vocalic length is as [kām] calm.

Other vowel signs.

[i]		[ə]	or underdot or
[e]		[ʌ]	
[a]		[y]	
[æ]		[œ]	
[o]			
[u]			

The following is crowded in along the right-hand side of the chart:

<ɜ̄> which in E.[nglish] is always product of er, ir, ur is written .
ɔ̄ is treated a pure long [o] & written as in = all; but or is written as in = port.

A second vowel chart, denoting superscripts (diacriticals) to indicate vowels, is added below the first, in pencil:

i	a	œ
e	ʌ	y
o	ɔ	
u	æ	

In the end, none of these charts and tables made it into the Longmans or Unwin Books edition, although Tolkien did write a note for that edition explaining the runes used in *The Hobbit*. This prefatory note appears in *The Annotated Hobbit* (DAA.27) and has become a standard feature of later editions – e.g., the third edition *Hobbit* (page [8]), the Fiftieth Anniversary *Hobbit* (pages 9–10), and the Seventieth Anniversary *Hobbit* (pages 1–2). Perhaps Tolkien did not complete the material in time for it to be included in the book, and another appropriate opportunity did not come – a pity, given how eagerly so much information on Tolkien's invented scripts would have been welcomed in the mid-sixties by students of his invented languages. Or perhaps it was felt disproportionate to include a lengthy essay devoted to a writing system that did not actually appear in that edition, since the picture of Smaug with Thror's cup – the only place where tengwar is used within *The Hobbit* – did not appear in either the Longmans or Unwin editions.

TEXT NOTES

TN1. So called to distinguish it from Tolkien's older script, the Alphabet of Rúmil, which he had created as early as 1919 and developed during his years at Leeds. For a history of this writing system and several texts in Rúmilic, which looks more like a Dravidian or southeast Asian script than anything in the European tradition,† see *The Alphabet of Rúmil*, ed. Arden R. Smith, *Parma Eldalamberon* XIII, pages 3–90.

†for example, Rúmilic tends to be written in columns from top to bottom, rather than in rows like most European scripts.

TN2. This seems to be a reference to the version given as plate two of the frontispiece, since the description 'in Thorin's rather free and bold style' fits that document much better than it does the careful 'book style' of Ad.Ms.H.S.11 (page 960) or the inscription style of Ad.Ms.H.S.5 (page 904).

TN3. Tolkien originally wrote 'g' here, but cancelled it and replaced it with 'k'.

TN4. Although Tolkien writes 'letters of column 4', the *tengwa* he gives is in fact the top letter in column 3, and the latter seems to reflect his intent.

TN5. "In that case [illegible] [illegible] are used for s, z." [Marginal note by Tolkien, marked for insertion at this point].

TN6. Tolkien has pencilled a third Elvish numeration system in the top margin of Ad.Ms.H.S page 17, but unfortunately it is too faint for me to reproduce with any confidence. Enough of it can be made out, however, to show that it uses the tengwar letters, as in the first numeration system shown here, but it does not assign the same numerical value to the same letters.

TN7. The usual diacritical in 'Fëanorian' is missing here in Tolkien's original.

TN8. This is an allusion to 'Tom, Tom, the piper's son; stole a pig and away he run', an old nursery rhyme (Baring-Gould #126; see *The Annotated Mother Goose*, pages 104–5).

INDEX

This index does not attempt to list every appearance of every name – something which would extend it to interminable length – but rather to enable readers to find specific passages within this work, supplementing the many cross-references within the text itself. An asterisk by a name indicates a member of Thorin & Company.